I0784956

H. Beam Piper

Terro-Human Future History
(Complete SF Omnibus)

OK Publishing 2021

H. Beam Piper

Terro-Human Future History (Complete SF Omnibus)

Uller Uprising, Four-Day Planet, The Cosmic Computer, Space Viking, The Return, Little Fuzzy…

Published by
MUSAICUM
Books

- Advanced Digital Solutions & High-Quality book Formatting -

musaicumbooks@okpublishing.info

2021 OK Publishing

ISBN 978-80-272-7823-7

Contents

The Federation Series

Uller Uprising

H. Beam Piper

Prologue

On Satan's Footstool

The big armor-tender vibrated, gently and not unpleasantly, as the contragravity field alternated on and off, occasionally varying its normal rate of five hundred to the second when some thermal updraft lifted the vehicle and the automatic radar-altimeter control acted to alter the frequency and lower it again. Sometimes it rocked slightly, like a boat on the water, and, in the big screen which served in lieu of a window at the front of the control cabin, the dingy-yellow landscape would seem to tilt a little. If unshielded human eyes could have endured the rays of Nu Puppis, Niflheim's primary, the whole scene would have appeared a vivid Saint Patrick's Day green, the effect of the blue-predominant light on the yellow atmosphere. The outside 'visor-pickup, however, was fitted with filters which blocked out the gamma-rays and X-rays and most of the ultra-violet-rays, and added the longer light-waves of red and orange which were absent, so that things looked much as they would have under the light of a G0-type star like Sol. The air was faintly yellow, the sky was yellow with a greenish cast, and the clouds were green-gray.

A thousand feet below, the local equivalent of a forest grew, the trees, topped with huge ragged leaves, looking like hundred-foot stalks of celery. There would be animal life down there, too-little round things, four inches across, like eight-legged crabs, gnawing at the vegetation, and bigger things, two feet long, with articulated shell-armor and sixteen legs, which fed on the smaller herbivores. Beyond, in the middleground, was open grassland, if one could so call a mat of wormlike colorless or pastel-tinted sprouts, and a river meandered through it. On the skyline, fifty miles away, was a range of low dunes and hills, none more than a thousand feet high.

No human had ever set foot on the surface, or breathed the air, of Niflheim. To have done so would have been instant death; the air was a mixture of free fluorine and fluoride gasses, the soil was metallic fluorides, damp with acid rains, and the river was pure hydrofluoric acid. Even the ordinary spacesuit would have been no protection; the glass and rubber and plastic would have disintegrated in a matter of minutes. People came to Niflheim, and worked the mines and uranium refineries and chemical plants, but they did so inside power-driven and contragravity-lifted armor, and they lived on artificial satellites two thousand miles off-planet. This vehicle, for instance, was built and protected as no spaceship ever had to be, completely insulated and entered only through a triple airlock-an outer lock, which would be evacuated outward after it was closed, a middle lock kept evacuated at all times, and an inner lock, evacuated into the interior of the vehicle before the middle lock could be opened. Niflheim was worse than airless, much worse.

The chief engineer sat at his controls, making the minor lateral adjustments in the vehicle's position which were not possible to the automatic controls. One of the radiomen was receiving from the orbital base; the other was saying, over and over, in an exasperatedly patient voice: "Dr. Murillo. Dr. Murillo. Please come in, Dr. Murillo." At his own panel of instruments, a small man with grizzled black hair around a bald crown, and a grizzled beard, chewed nervously at the stump of a dead cigar and listened intently to what was-or for what wasn't —coming in to his headset receiver. A couple of assistants checked dials and refreshed their memories from notebooks and peered anxiously into the big screen. A large, plump-faced, young man in soiled khaki shirt and shorts, with extremely hairy legs, was doodling on his notepad and eating candy out of a bag. And a black-haired girl in a suit of coveralls three sizes too big for her, and, apparently, not much of anything else, lounged with one knee hooked over her chair-arm, staring into the screen at the distant horizon.

"Dr. Murillo. Dr. Mur—" The radioman broke off in mid-syllable and listened for a moment. "I hear you, doctor, go ahead." Then, a moment later "What's your position, now, doctor?"

"I can see them," the girl said, lifting a hand in front of her. "At two o'clock, about one of my hand's-breadths above the horizon."

The man with the grizzled beard put his face into the fur around the eyepiece of the telescopic-'visor and twisted a dial. "You have good eyes, Miss Quinton," he complimented. "Only four personal armors; Ahmed, ask him where the fifth is."

"We only see four of your personal-armors," the radioman said. "Who's missing, and why?" He waited for a moment, then lowered the hand-phone and turned. "The fifth one's inside the handling-machine. One of the Ullerans. Gorkrink."

The larger of the specks that had appeared on the horizon resolved itself into a handling-machine, a thing like an oversized contragravity-tank, with a bulldozer-blade, a stubby derrick-boom instead of a gun, and jointed, claw-tipped arms to the sides. The smaller dots grew into personal armor-egg-shaped things that sprouted arms and grab-hooks and pushers in all directions. The man with the grizzled beard began talking rapidly into his hand-phone, then hung it up. There was a series of bumps, and the armor-tender, weightless on contragravity, shook as the handling-machine came aboard.

"You ever see any nuclear bombing, Miss Quinton?" the young man with the hairy legs asked, offering her his candy bag.

"Only by telecast, back Sol-side," she replied, helping herself. "Test-shots at the Federation Navy proving-ground on Mars. I never even heard of nuclear bombs being used for mining till I came here, though."

"Well, if this turns out as well as the other job, three months ago, it'll be something to see," he promised. "These volcanoes have been dormant for, oh, maybe as long as a thousand years; there ought to be a pretty good head of gas down there. And the magma'll be thick, viscous stuff, like basalt on Terra. Of course, this won't be anything like basalt in composition-it'll be intensely compressed metallic fluorides, with a very high metal-content. The volcanoes we shot three months ago yielded a fine flow of lava with all sorts of metals-nickel, beryllium, vanadium, chromium, indium, as well as copper and iron."

"What sort of gas were you speaking about?" she asked.

"Hydrogen. That's what's going to make the fireworks; it combines explosively with fluorine. The hydrogen-fluorine combination is what passes for combustion here; the result is hydrofluoric acid, the local equivalent of water. See, the metallic core of this planet is covered, much less thickly than that of Terra, with fluoride rock-fluorspar, and that sort of thing. There's nothing like granite here, for instance. That's why those big dunes, out there, are the best Niflheim has in the way of mountains. The subsurface hydrogen is produced when the acid filters down through the rock, combines with pure metals underneath."

"Dr. Murillo's inside, now," the radioman said. "Just came out of the inner airlock. He'll be up as soon as he gets out of his pressure-suit."

"As soon as he gets here, I'll touch it off," the bearded man said. "Everything set, de Jong?"

"Everything ready, Dr. Gomes," one of his assistants assured him.

The door at the rear of the control-cabin opened, and Juan Murillo, the seismologist, entered, followed by an assistant. Murillo was a big man, copper-skinned, barrel-chested; he looked like a third-or fourth-generation Martian, of Andes Indian ancestry. He came forward and stood behind Gomes' chair, looking down at the instruments. His assistant stopped at the door. This assistant was not human. He was a biped, vaguely humanoid, but he had four arms and a face like a lizard's, and, except for some equipment on a belt, he was entirely naked.

He spoke rapidly to Murillo, in a squeaking jabber. Murillo turned.

"Yes, if you wish, Gorkrink," he said, in the English-Spanish-Afrikaans-Portuguese mixture that was Sixth Century, A.E., Lingua Terra. Then he turned back to Gomes as the Ulleran sat down in a chair by the door.

"Well, she's all yours, Lourenço, shoot the works."

Gomes stabbed the radio-detonator button in front of him. A voice came out of the PA-speaker overhead: "In sixty seconds, the bombs will be detonated ... thirty seconds ... fifteen seconds ... ten seconds ... five seconds, four seconds, three seconds, two seconds, one second...."

Out on the rolling skyline, fifty miles away, a lancelike ray of blue-white light shot up into the gathering dusk —a clump of five rays, really, from five deep shafts in an irregular pentagon half a mile across, blended into one by the distance. An instant later, there was a blinding flash, like sheet-lightning, and a huge ball of varicolored fire belched upward, leaving a series of smoke-rings to float more slowly after it. That fireball flattened, then spread to form the mushroom-head of a column of incandescent gas that mounted to overtake it, engorging the smoke-rings as it rose, twisting, writhing, changing shape, turning to dark smoke in one moment and belching flame and crackling with lightning the next. The armor-tender began to pitch and roll; it was all the engineer and one of the assistants could do, together, to keep it level.

"In about half an hour," the large young man told the girl, "the real fireworks should be starting. What's coming up now is just small debris from the nuclear blast. When the shockwaves get down far enough to crack things open, the gas'll come up, and then steam and ash, and then the magma. This one ought to be twice as good as the one we shot three months ago; it ought to be every bit as good as Krakatoa, on Terra, in 59 Pre-Atomic."

"Well, even this much was worth staying over for," the girl said, watching the screen.

"You going on to Uller on the *City of Canberra?*" Lourenço Gomes asked. "I wish I were; I have to stay over and make another shot, in a month or so, and I've had about all of Niflheim I can take, now. The sooner I get onto a planet where they don't ration the air, the better I'll like it."

"Well, what do you know!" the large young man with the hairy legs mock-marveled. "He doesn't like our nice planet!"

"Nice planet!" Gomes muttered something. "They call Terra God's Footstool; well, I'll give you one guess who uses this thing to prop his cloven hoofs on."

"When are you going to Terra?" the girl asked him.

"Terra? I don't know, a year, two years. But I'm going to Uller on the next ship-the *City of Pretoria* —if we get the next blast off in time. They want me to design some improvements on a couple of power-reactors, so I'll probably see you when I get there."

"Here she comes!" the chief engineer called. "Watch the base of the column!"

The pillar of fiery smoke and dust, still boiling up from where the bombs had gone off far underground, was being violently agitated at the bottom. A series of new flashes broke out, lifting and spreading the incandescent radioactive gasses, and then a great gush of flame rose. A column of pure hydrogen must have rushed up into the vacuum created by the explosion; the next blast of flame, in a lateral sheet, came at nearly ten thousand feet above the ground, and great rags of fire, changing from red to violet and back through the spectrum to red again, went soaring away to dissipate in the upper atmosphere. Then geysers of hot ash and molten rock spouted upward; some of the white-hot debris landed almost at the acid river, half-way to the armor-tender.

"We've started a first-class earthquake, too," the Hispano-Indian Martian Murillo said, looking at the instruments. "About six big cracks opening in the rock-structure. You know, when this quiets down and cools off, we'll have more ore on the surface than we can handle in ten years, and more than we could have mined by ordinary means in fifty."

About four miles from the original blast, another eruption began with a terrific gas-explosion.

"Well, that finishes our work," the large young man said, going to a kitbag in the corner of the cabin and getting out a bottle. "Get some of those plastic cups, over there, somebody; this one calls for a drink."

"That's right," Gomes said. "You do something once, it may be an accident; you repeat the performance, and it's a success." He began pushing papers aside on his desk, and the girl in the too-ample coveralls brought drinking cups.

The Ulleran, in the background, rose quickly and squeaked apologetically. Murillo nodded. "Yes, of course, Gorkrink. No need for you to stay here." The Ulleran went out, closing the door behind him.

"That taboo against Ullerans and Terrans watching each other eat and drink," Murillo said. "What is that, part of their religion?"

"No, it's their version of modesty," the girl replied. "Like some of our sex-inhibitions, which they can't even begin to understand....But you were speaking to him in Lingua Terra; I didn't know any of them understood it."

"Gorkrink does," Murillo said, uncorking the bottle and pouring into the plastic cups. "None of them can speak it, of course, because of the structure of their vocal organs, any more than we can speak their languages without artificial aids. But I can talk to him in Lingua Terra without having to put one of those damn gags in my mouth, and he can pass my instructions on to the others. He's been a big help; I'll be sorry to lose him."

"Lose him?"

"Yes, his year's up; he's going back to Uller on the *Canberra*. You know, it's impossible to keep some trace of fluorine from the air in the handling-machines, or even out on the orbiters, and it plays the devil with their lungs. He wanted to stay on another three months, to help with the next shot, but the medics wouldn't hear of it....He's from Keegark, wherever on Uller that is; claims to be a prince, or something. I know all the other geeks kowtow to him. But he's a damn good worker. Very smart; picks things up the first time you tell him. I'll recommend him unqualifiedly for any kind of work with contragravity or mechanized equipment."

They all had drinks, now, except the chief engineer, who wanted a rain-check on his.

"Well, here's to us," Murillo said. "The first A-bomb miners in history...."

I

Commander-in-Chief Front and Center

General Carlos von Schlichten threw his cigarette away, flexed his hands in his gloves, and set his monocle more firmly in his eye, stepping forward as the footsteps on the stairway behind him ceased and the other officers emerged from the squat flint keep-Captain Cazabielle, the post CO; big, chocolate-brown Brigadier-General Themistocles M'zangwe; little Colonel Hideyoshi O'Leary. Far in front of him, to the left, the horizon was lost in the cloudbank over Takkad Sea; directly in front, and to the right, the brown and gray and black flint mountains sawed into the sky until they vanished in the distance. Unseen below, the old caravan-trail climbed one side of the pass and slid down the other, a sheer five hundred feet below the parapet and the two corner catapult-platforms which now mounted 90-mm guns. On the little hundred-foot-square parade ground in front of the keep, his aircar was parked, and the soldiers were assembled.

Ten or twelve of them were Terrans —a couple of lieutenants, sergeants, gunners, technicians, the sergeant-driver and corporal-gunner of his own car. The other fifty-odd were Ulleran natives. They stood erect on stumpy legs and broad, six-toed feet. They had four arms apiece, one pair from true shoulders and the other connected to a pseudo-pelvis midway down the torso. Their skins were slate-gray and rubbery, speckled with pinhead-sized bits of quartz that had been formed from perspiration, for their body-tissues were silicone instead of carbon-hydrogen. Their narrow heads were unpleasantly saurian; they had small, double-lidded red eyes, and slit-like nostrils, and wide mouths filled with opalescent teeth. Except for their belts and equipment, they were completely naked; the uniform consisted of the emblem of the Chartered Uller Company stencil-painted on chests and backs. Clothing, to them, was unnecessary, either for warmth or modesty. As to the former, they were cold-blooded and could stand a temperature-range of from a hundred and twenty to minus one hundred Centigrade. Von Schlichten had seen them sleeping in the open with their bodies covered with frost or freezing rain; he had also seen them wade through boiling water. As to the second, they had practically no sex-inhibitions; they were all of the same gender, true, functional, hermaphrodites. Any individual among them could bear young, or fertilize the ova of any other individual. Fifteen years ago, when he had come to Uller as a former Terran Federation captain newly commissioned colonel in the army of the Uller Company, it had taken some time before he had become accustomed to the detailing of a non-com and a couple of privates out of each platoon for baby-sitting duty. At least, though, they didn't have the squaw-trouble around army posts on Uller that they had on Thor, where he had last been stationed.

An airjeep, coming in out of the sun, circled the crag-top fort and let down onto the terrace next to von Schlichten's command-car. It carried a bristle of 15-mm machine-guns, and two of the eight 50-mm rocket-tubes on either side were empty and freshly smoke-stained. The duraglass canopy slid back, and the two-man crew-lieutenant-driver and sergeant-gunner—jumped out. Von Schlichten knew them both.

"Lieutenant Kendall; Sergeant Garcia," he greeted. "Good afternoon, gentlemen."

Both saluted, in the informal, hell-with-rank-we're-all-human manner of Terran soldiers on extraterrestrial duty, and returned the greeting.

"How's the Jeel situation?" he asked, then nodded toward the fired rocket-tubes. "I see you had some shooting."

"Yes, sir," the lieutenant said. "Two bands of them. We sighted the first coming up the eastern side of the mountain about two miles this side of the Blue Springs. We got about half of them with MG-fire, and the rest dived into a big rock-crevice. We had to use two rockets on them, and then had to let down and pot a few of them with our pistols. We caught the second band in that little punchbowl place about a mile this side of Zortolk's Old Fort. There were only six of them; they were bunched together, feeding. Off one of their own gang, I'd say; the way we've been keeping them up in the high rocks, they've been eating inside the family quite a bit, lately. We let them have two rockets. No survivors. Not many very big pieces, in fact. We let down at Zortolk's for a beer, after that, and Captain Martinelli told us that one of his jeeps caught what he thinks was the same band that was down off the mountain night-before-last and ate those peasants on Prince Neeldink's estate."

"By God, I'm glad to hear that!" There'd been a perfect hell of a flap about that business. Before the Terrans came to Uller, it was a good year when not more than five hundred farm-folk would be killed and eaten by Jeel cannibals. The incident of two nights ago had been the first of its kind in almost six months, but the nobleman whose serfs had been eaten was practically accusing the Company of responsibility for the crime. "I'll see that Neeldink is informed. The more you do for these damned geeks, the more they expect from you.... When you get your vehicle re-ammoed, lieutenant, suppose you buzz back to where you machine-gunned that first gang. If there are any more around, they'll have moved in for the free meal by now." This breakdown of the Jeels' taboo against eating fellow-tribesmen was one of the best things he'd heard from the cannibal-extermination project for some time.

He turned to Themistocles M'zangwe. "In about two weeks, get a little task-force together. Say ten combat-cars, about twenty airjeeps, and a battalion of Kragan Rifles in troop-carriers. Oh, yes, and this good-for-nothing Konkrook Fencibles outfit of Prince Jaizerd's; they can be used for beaters, and to block escape routes." He turned back to Lieutenant Kendall and Sergeant Garcia. "Good work, boys. And if the synchro-photos show that any of that first bunch got away, don't feel too badly about it. These Jeels can hide on the top of a pool-table."

He climbed into the command-car, followed by Themistocles M'zangwe and Hideyoshi O'Leary. Sergeant Harry Quong and Corporal Hassan Bogdanoff took their places on the front seat; the car lifted, turned to nose into the wind, and rose in a slow spiral. Below, the fort grew smaller, a flat-topped rectangle of masonry overlooking the pass, a gun covering each approach, and two more on the square keep to cover the rocky hogback on which the fort had been built, with the flagpole between them. Once that pole had lifted a banner of ragged black marsh-flopper skin bearing the device of the Kragan riever-chieftain whose family had built the castle; now it carried a neat rectangle of blue bunting emblazoned with the wreathed globe of the Terran Federation and, below that, the blue-gray pennant which bore the vermilion trademark of the Chartered Uller Company.

"Where now, sir?" Harry Quong asked.

He looked at his watch. Seventeen-hundred; there wasn't time for a visit to Zortolk's Old Fort, ten miles to the north at the next pass.

"Back to Konkrook, to the island."

The nose of the car swung east by south; the cold-jet rotors began humming and then the hot-jets were cut in. The car turned from the fort and the mountains and shot away over the foothills toward the coastal plain. Below were forests, yellow-green with new foliage of the second growing season of the equatorial year, veined with narrow dirt roads and spotted with occasional clearings. Farther east, the dirty gray woodsmoke of Uller marked the progress of the charcoal-burnings. It took forty years to burn the forests clear back to the flint cliffs; by the time the burners reached the mountains, the new trees at the seaward edge would be ready to cut. Off to the south, he could see the dark green squares, where the hemlocks and Norway spruce had been planted by the Company. With a little chemical fertilizer, they were doing well, and they made better charcoal than the silicate-heavy native wood. That was the only natural fuel on Uller; there was no coal, of course, since fallen timber and even standing dead trees petrified in a matter of a couple of years. There was too much silica on Uller, and not enough of anything else; what would be coal-seams on Terra were strata of silicified wood. And, of course, there was no petroleum. There was less charcoal being burned now than formerly; the Uller Company had been bringing in great quantities of synthetic thermoconcentrate-fuel, and had been setting up nuclear furnaces and nuclear-electric power-plants, wherever they gained a foothold on the planet.

Beyond the forests came the farmlands. Around the older estates, thick walls of flint and petrified wood had been built, and wide moats dug, to keep out the shellosaurs. But now the moats were dry, and the walls falling into disrepair. Some of the newer farms, land devoted to agriculture with the declining demand for charcoal, had neither moats nor walls. That was the Company, too; the huge shell-armored beasts had become virtually extinct in the Konk Isthmus now, since the introduction of bazookas and recoilless rifles. There seemed to be quite a bit of power-equipment working in the fields, and big contragravity lorries were drifting back and forth, scattering fertilizer, mainly nitrates from Mimir or Yggdrasill. There were still a good number of animal-drawn plows and harrows in use, however.

As planets went, Uller was no bargain, he thought sourly. At times, he wished he had never followed the lure of rapid promotion and fantastically high pay and left the Federation regulars for the army of the Uller Company. If he hadn't, he'd probably be a colonel, at five thousand sols a year, but maybe it would be better to be a middle-aged colonel on a decent planet-Odin, with its two moons, Hugin and Munin, and its wide grasslands and its evergreen forests that looked and even smelled like the pinewoods of Terra, or Baldur, with snow-capped mountains, and clear, cold lakes, and rocky rivers dashing under great vine-hung trees, or Freya, where the people were human to the last degree and the women were so breathtakingly beautiful-than a Company army general at twenty-five thousand on this combination icebox, furnace, wind-tunnel and stonepile, where the water tasted like soapsuds and left a crackly film when it dried; where the temperature ranged, from pole to pole, between two hundred and fifty and minus a hundred and fifty Fahrenheit and the Beaufort-scale ran up to thirty; where nothing that ran or swam or grew was fit for a human to eat, and where the people....

Of course, there were worse planets than Uller. There was Nidhog, cold and foggy, its equatorial zone a gloomy marsh and the rest of the planet locked in eternal ice. There was Bifrost, which always kept the same face turned to its primary; one side blazingly hot and the other close to absolute zero, with a narrow and barely habitable twilight zone between. There was Mimir, swarming with a race of semi-intelligent quasi-rodents, murderous, treacherous, utterly vicious. Or Niflheim. The Uller Company had the franchise for Niflheim, too; they'd had to take that and agree to exploit the planet's resources in order to get the franchise for Uller, which furnished a good quick measure of the comparative merits of the two.

Ahead, the city of Konkrook sprawled along the delta of the Konk river and extended itself inland. The river was dry, now. Except in spring, when it was a red-brown torrent, it never ran more than a trickle, and not at all this late in the northern summer. The aircar lost altitude, and the hot-jet stopped firing. They came gliding in over the suburbs and the yellow-green parks, over the low one-story dwellings and shops, the lofty temples and palaces, the fantastically twisted towers, following a street that became increasingly mean and squalid as it neared the industrial district along the waterfront.

Von Schlichten, on the right, glanced idly down, puffing slowly on his cigarette. Then he stiffened, the muscles around his right eye clamping tighter on the monocle. Leaning forward, he punched Harry Quong lightly on the shoulder.

"Circle back, sergeant; let's have a look at that street again," he directed. "Something going on, down there; looks like a riot."

"Yes, sir; I saw it," the Chinese-Australian driver replied. "Terrans in trouble; bein' mobbed by geeks. Aircar parked right in the bloody middle of it."

The car made a twisting, banking loop and came back, more slowly. Colonel Hideyoshi O'Leary was using the binoculars.

"That's right," he said. "Terrans being mobbed. Two of them, backed up against a house. I saw one of them firing a pistol."

Von Schlichten had the handset of the car's radio, and was punching out the combination of the Company guardhouse on Gongonk Island; he held down the signal button until he got an answer.

"Von Schlichten, in car over Konkrook. Riot on Fourth Avenue, just off Seventy-second Street." No Terran could possibly remember the names of Konkrook's streets; even native troops recruited from outside found the numbers easier to learn and remember. "Geeks mobbing a couple of Terrans. I'm going down, now, to do what I can to help; send troops in a hurry. Kragan Rifles. And stand by; my driver'll give it to you as it happens."

The voice of somebody at the guardhouse, bawling orders, came out of the receiver as he tossed the phone forward over Harry Quong's shoulder; Quong caught it and began speaking rapidly and urgently into it while he steered with the other hand. Von Schlichten took one of the five-pound spiked riot-maces out of the rack in front of him. Themistocles M'zangwe had already drawn his pistol; he shifted it to his left hand and took a mace in his right. The Nipponese-Irish colonel, looking like a homicidally infuriated pixie, had an automatic in one hand and a long dagger in the other.

Harry Quong and Hassan Bogdanoff were old Uller hands; they'd done this sort of work before. Bogdanoff rose into the ball-turret and swung the twin 15-mm's around, cutting loose. Quong brought the car in fast, at about shoulder-height on the mob. Between them, they left a swath of mangled, killed, wounded, and stunned natives. Then, spinning the car around, Quong set it down hard on a clump of rioters as close as possible to the struggling group around the two Terrans. Von Schlichten threw back the canopy and jumped out of the car, O'Leary and M'zangwe behind him.

There was another aircar, a dark maroon civilian job, at the curb; its native driver was slumped forward over the controls, a short crossbow-bolt sticking out of his neck. Backed against the closed door of a house, a Terran with white hair and a small beard was clubbing futilely with an empty pistol. He was wounded, and blood was streaming over his face. His companion, a young woman in a long fur coat, was laying about her with a native bolo-knife.

Von Schlichten's mace had a spiked ball-head, and a four-inch spike in front of that. He smashed the ball down on the back of one Ulleran's head, and jabbed another in the rump with the spike.

"*Zak! Zak!*" he yelled, in pidgin-Ulleran. "*Jik-jik*, you lizard-faced Creator's blunder!"

The Ulleran whirled, swinging a blade somewhere between a big butcherknife and a small machete. His mouth was open, and there was froth on his lips.

"*Znidd suddabit!*" he screamed.

Von Schlichten parried the cut on the steel shaft of his mace. "*Suddabit* yourself, you geek bastard!" he shouted back, ramming the spike-end into the opal-filled mouth. "And *znidd* you, too," he added, recovering and slamming the ball-head down on the narrow saurian skull. The Ulleran went down, spurting a yellow fluid about the consistency of gun-oil. Then, without wasting words, he maced another of the things.

Ahead, one of the natives had caught the wounded Terran with both lower hands, and was raising a dagger with his upper right. The girl in the fur coat swung wildly, slashing the knife-arm, then chopped down on the creature's neck. To one side, a native somewhat better dressed than the others, to the extent of a couple of belts with gold ornaments, drew a Terran automatic. Von Schlichten hurled his mace and drew his pistol, thumbing off the safety as he swung it up, but before he could fire, Hassan Bogdanoff had seen and swung his guns around; the double burst caught the native in the chest and fairly tore him apart.

Another of them closed with the girl, grabbing her right arm with all four hands and biting at her; she screamed and kicked her attacker in the groin, where an Ulleran is, if anything, even more vulnerable than a Terran. The native howled hideously, and von Schlichten, jumping over a couple of corpses, shoved the muzzle of his pistol into the creature's open mouth and pulled the trigger, blowing its head apart like a rotten pumpkin and splashing both himself and the girl with yellow blood and rancid-looking gray-green brains.

Hideyoshi O'Leary, jumping forward after von Schlichten, stuck his dagger into the neck of a rioter and left it there, then caught the girl around the waist with his free arm. Themistocles M'zangwe dropped his mace and swung the frail-looking man onto his back. Together, they struggled back to the command-car, von Schlichten covering the retreat with his pistol. Another rioter —a Zirk nomad from the North, he guessed-was aiming one of the long-barreled native air-rifles, holding the ten-inch globe of the air-chamber in both lower hands. Von Schlichten shot him, and the Zirk literally blew to pieces.

For an instant, he wondered how the small bursting-charge of a 10-mm explosive pistol-bullet could accomplish such havoc, and assumed that the native had been carrying a bomb in his belt. Then another explosion tossed fragmentary corpses nearby, and another and another. Glancing quickly over his shoulder, he saw four combat-cars coming in, firing with 40-mm auto-cannon and 15-mm machine-guns. They swept between the hovels on one side and the warehouses on the other, strafing the mob, darted up to a thousand feet, looped, and came swooping back, and this time there were three long blue-gray troop-carriers behind them.

These landed in the hastily cleared street and began disgorging native Company soldiers-Kragan mercenaries, he noted with satisfaction. They carried a modified version of the regular Terran Federation infantry rifle, stocked and sighted to conform to their physical peculiarities, with long, thorn-like, triangular bayonets. One platoon ran forward, dropped to one knee, and began firing rapidly into what was left of the mob. Four-handed soldiers can deliver a simply astonishing volume of fire, particularly when armed with auto-rifles having twenty-shot drop-out magazines which can be changed with the lower hands without lowering the weapon.

There was a clatter of shod hoofs, and a company of the King of Konkrook's cavalry came trotting up on their six-legged, lizard-headed, quartz-speckled mounts. Some of these charged into side alleys, joyfully lancing and cutting down fleeing rioters, while others dismounted, three tossing their reins to a fourth, and went to work with their crossbows. Von Schlichten, who ordinarily entertained a dim opinion of the King of Konkrook's soldiery, admitted, grudgingly, that it was smart work; four hands were a big help in using a crossbow, too.

A Terran captain of native infantry came over, saluting.

"Are you and your people all right, general?" he asked.

Von Schlichten glanced at the front seat of his car, where Harry Quong, a pistol in his right hand, was still talking into the radio-phone, and Hassan Bogdanoff was putting fresh belts into his guns. Then he saw that the Graeco-African brigadier and the Irish-Japanese colonel had gotten the wounded man into the car. The girl, having dropped her bolo, was leaning against the side of the car, one foot heedlessly in what was left of an Ulleran who had gotten smashed under it, weak with nervous reaction.

"We seem to be, Captain Pedolsky. Very smart work; you must have those vehicles of yours on hyperspace-drive.... How is he, colonel?"

"We'd better get him to the hospital, right away," O'Leary replied. "I think he has a concussion."

"Harry, call the hospital. Tell them what the score is, and tell them we're bringing the casualty in to their top landing stage.... Why, we'll make out very nicely, captain. You'd better stay around with your Kragans and make sure that these geeks of King Jaikark's don't let the riot flare up again and get away from them. And don't let them get the impression that they can maintain order around here without our help; the Company would like to see that attitude discouraged."

"Yes, sir, I understand." Captain Pedolsky opened the pouch on his belt and took out the false palate and tongue-clicker without which no Terran could do more than mouth a crude and barely comprehensible pidgin-Ulleran. Stuffing the gadget into his mouth, he turned and began jabbering orders.

Von Schlichten helped the girl into the car, placing her on his right. The wounded civilian was propped up in the left corner of the seat, and Colonel O'Leary and Brigadier-General M'zangwe took the jump-seats. The driver put on the contragravity-field, and the car lifted up.

"Them, see if there's a flask and a drinking-cup in the door pocket next to you," he said. "I think Miss Quinton could use a drink."

The girl turned. Even in her present disheveled condition, she was beautiful—a trifle on the petite side, with black hair and black eyes that quirked up oddly at the outer corners. Her nails were black-lacquered and spotted with little gold stars, evidently a new feminine fad from Terra.

"I certainly could, general.... How did you know my name?"

"You've been on Uller for the last three months; ever since the *City of Canberra* got in from Niflheim. On Uller, there aren't enough of us that everybody doesn't know all about everybody else. You're Dr. Paula Quinton; you're an extraterrestrial sociographer, and you're a field-agent for the Extraterrestrials' Rights Association, like Mohammed Ferriera, here." He took the cup and flask from Themistocles M'zangwe and poured her a drink. "Take this easy, now; Baldur honey-rum, a hundred and fifty proof."

He watched her sip the stuff cautiously, cough over the first mouthful, and then get the rest of it down.

"More?" When she shook her head, he stoppered the flask and relieved her of the cup. "What were you doing in that district, anyhow?" he wanted to know. "I'd have thought Mohammed Ferriera would have had more sense than to take you there, or go there, himself, for that matter."

"We went to visit a friend of his, a native named Keeluk, who seems to be a sort of combination clergyman and labor leader," she replied. "I'm going to observe labor conditions at the North Pole mines in a short while, and Mr. Keeluk was going to give me letters of introduction to friends of his at Skilk."

With the aid of his monocle, von Schlichten managed to keep a straight face. Neither M'zangwe nor O'Leary had any such aid; the African rolled his eyes and the Japanese-Irishman grimaced.

"We talked with Mr. Keeluk for a while," the girl said, "and when we came out, we found that our driver had been killed and a mob had gathered. Of course, we were carrying pistols; they're part of this survival-kit you make everybody carry, along with the emergency-rations and the water-desilicator. Mr. Ferriera's wasn't loaded, but mine was. When they rushed us, I shot a couple of them, and then picked up that big knife...."

"That's why you're still alive," von Schlichten commented.

"We wouldn't be if you hadn't come along," she told him. "I never in my life saw anything as beautiful as you coming through that mob swinging that war-club!"

"Well, I never saw anything much more beautiful than those 40-mm's beginning to land in the mob," von Schlichten replied.

The aircar swung out over Konkrook Channel and headed toward the blue-gray Company buildings on Gongonk Island, and the Company airport, swarming with lorries and airboats, where the ten thousand-ton *Oom Paul Kruger* had just come in from Keegark, and the Company's one real warship, the cruiser *Procyon*, was lifting out for Grank, in the North. Down at the southern tip of the island, the three-thousand-foot globe of the spaceship *City of Pretoria*, from Niflheim, was loading with cargo for Terra.

"Just what happened, while you and Mr. Ferriera were in Keeluk's house. Miss Quinton?" Hideyoshi O'Leary asked, trying not to sound official. "Was Keeluk with you all the time? Or did he go out for a while, say fifteen or twenty minutes before you left?"

"Why, yes, he did." Paula Quinton looked surprised. "How did you guess it? You see, a dog started barking, behind the house, and he excused himself and...."

"A dog?" von Schlichten almost shouted. The other officers echoed him, and on the front seat, Harry Quong said, "Coo-bli'me!"

"Why, yes...." Paula Quinton's eyes widened. "But there are no dogs on Uller, except a few owned by Terrans. And wasn't there something about...?"

Von Schlichten had the radio-phone and was calling the command car at the scene of the riot. The sergeant-driver answered.

"Von Schlichten here; my compliments to Captain Pedolsky, and tell him he's to make immediate and thorough search of the house in front of which the incident occurred, and adjoining houses. For his information, that's Keeluk's house. Tell him to look for traces of Governor-General Harrington's collie, or any of the other terrestrial animals that have been disappearing-that goat, for instance, or those rabbits. And I want Keeluk brought in, alive and in condition to be interrogated. I'll send more troops, or Constabulary, to help you." He handed the phone to M'zangwe. "You take care of that end of it, Them; you know who can be spared."

"But, what ...?" the girl began.

"That's why you were attacked," he told her. "Keeluk was afraid to let you get away from there alive to report hearing that dog, so he went out and had a gang of thugs rounded up to kill you."

"But he was only gone five minutes."

"In five minutes, I can put all the troops in Konkrook into action. Keeluk doesn't have radio or TV-we hope-but he has his forces concentrated, and he has a pretty good staff."

"But Mr. Keeluk's a friend of ours. He knows what our Association is trying to do for his people...."

"So he shows his appreciation by setting that mob on you. Look, he has a lot of influence in that section. When you were attacked, why wasn't he out trying to quiet the mob?"

"When they jumped you, you tried to get back into the house," M'zangwe put in. "And you found the door barred against you."

"Yes, but...." The girl looked troubled; M'zangwe had guessed right. "But what's all the excitement about the dog? What is it, the sacred totem-animal of the Uller Company?"

"It's just a big brown collie, named Stalin, like half the dogs on Terra. Somebody stole it, and Keeluk was keeping it, and we want to know why. We don't like geek mysteries; not when they lead to murderous attacks on Terrans, at least."

The aircar let down on the hospital landing stage. A stretcher was waiting, with a Terran interne and two Ulleran orderlies. They got the still-unconscious Mohammed Ferriera out of the car.

"You'd better go with them, yourself, Miss Quinton," von Schlichten advised. "You have a couple of nasty-looking bruises and bumps. A couple of abrasions, too, where those geeks grabbed you; they have hides like sandpaper. And better have that coat cleaned, before that goo on it hardens, or it'll be ruined."

"Yes. You have a lot of it on your uniform, too."

He glanced down at the blue-gray jacket. "So I have. And another thing. Those letters Keeluk was going to give you, the ones to his friends in Skilk. Did you get them?"

She felt in the pocket of her coat. "Yes. I still have them."

"I wish you'd let Colonel O'Leary have a look at them. There may be more to them than you think....Hid, will you go with Miss Quinton?"

II

Rakkeed, Stalin, and the Rev. Keeluk

Von Schlichten, in a fresh uniform, sat at the end of the table in Sidney Harrington's office; Harrington and Eric Blount, the Lieutenant-Governor, faced each other across it, over the three-foot disc of an Ulleran chess-board. Harrington had the white, or center, position. Blount, sandy-haired and considerably younger, was playing black, and his pieces were closing in relentlessly from the outer rim.

"Well, then what?" Harrington asked.

Von Schlichten dropped ash from his cigarette into the tray that served all three of them.

"Nothing much," he replied. "Keeluk bugged out as soon as he saw my car let down. We picked up a few of his ragtag-and-bobtail, and they're being questioned now, but I doubt if they'll tell us anything we don't know already. The dog had been kept in a lean-to back of the house; it had been removed, probably as soon as Keeluk called in his goon-gang. At least one of the rabbits had been kept on the premises, too, some time ago. No trace of the goat."

He watched Blount move one of his pieces and nodded approvingly. "The riot's been put down," he continued, "but we're keeping two companies of Kragans in the city, and about a dozen airjeeps patrolling the section from Eightieth down to Sixty-fourth, and from the waterfront back to Eighth Avenue. There is also the equivalent of a regiment of King Jaikark's infantry-spearmen, crossbowmen, and a few riflemen-and two of those outsize cavalry companies of his, helping hold the lid down. They're making mass arrests, indiscriminately. More slaves for Jaikark's court favorite, of course."

"Or else Gurgurk wants them to use for patronage," Blount added. "He's been building quite a political organization, lately. Getting ready to shove Jaikark off the throne, I'd say."

Harrington pushed one of his pieces out along a radial line toward the rim. Blount promptly took a pawn, which, under Ulleran rules, entitled him to a second move. He shifted another piece, a sort of combination knight and bishop, to threaten the piece Harrington had moved.

"Oh, Gurgurk wouldn't dare try anything like that," the Governor-General said. "He knows we wouldn't let him get away with it. We have too much of an investment in King Jaikark."

"Then why's Gurgurk been supporting this damned Rakkeed?" Blount wanted to know, hastily interposing a piece. "Gurgurk can follow one of two lines of policy. He can undertake to heave Jaikark off the throne and seize power, or he has to support Jaikark on the throne. We're subsidizing Jaikark. Rakkeed has been preaching this crusade against the Terrans, and against Jaikark, whom we control. Gurgurk has been subsidizing Rakkeed...."

"You haven't any proof of that," Harrington protested.

"My Intelligence Section has," von Schlichten put in. "We can give sums of money, and dates, and the names of the intermediaries through whom they were paid to Rakkeed. Eric is absolutely correct in making that statement."

"Personally, I think Gurgurk's plan is something like this: Rakkeed will stir up anti-Terran sentiment here in Konkrook, and direct it against our puppet, Jaikark, as well as against us," Blount said. "When the outbreak comes, Jaikark will be killed, and then Gurgurk will step in, seize the Palace, and use the Royal army to put down the revolt that he's incited in the first place. That will put him in the position of the friend of the Company, and most of his dupes will be rounded up and sold as slaves, and King Gurgurk'll pocket the proceeds. The only question is, will Rakkeed let himself be used that way? I think Rakkeed's bigger than Gurgurk ever can be. And more of a threat to the Company. Everywhere we turn, Rakkeed's at the bottom of whatever happens to be wrong. This business, for instance; Keeluk's one of Rakkeed's followers."

"Eric, you have Rakkeed on the brain!" Harrington exclaimed impatiently, then moved the threatened piece counterclockwise on the circle where he had placed it. "He's just a barbarian caravan-driver."

Eric Blount moved the piece that had taken Harrington's pawn.

"Your king's in danger," he warned. "And Hitler was just a paper-hanger."

"Rakkeed has no following, except among the rabble." Harrington puffed furiously at his pipe, trying to figure the best protection for his king.

"You just think he hasn't," Blount retorted. "Here in Konkrook, he's always entertained by one or another of the big ship-owning nobles. They probably deprecate his table-manners, but they just love his politics. And the same thing at Keegark, and at the Free Cities along the Eastern Shore."

"The last time Rakkeed was in Konkrook, he was the guest of the Keegarkan Ambassador," von Schlichten stated. "Intelligence got that from a spy we'd planted among the embassy servants."

"You sure this spy wasn't just romancing?" Harrington asked. "You get so confounded many wild stories about Rakkeed. Three days after he was reported here at Konkrook, he was reported at Skilk, five thousand miles away, said to be having an audience with King Firkked."

"No mystery to that," von Schlichten said. "He travels on our ships, in disguise, coolie-class, on the geek-deck."

"Be a good idea if he could be caught at it, some time," Blount said, making another move. "One of the lower-deck loading ports could be left unlocked, by carelessness, and he could blunder overboard at about five thousand feet." He watched Harrington make a deceptively pointless-looking move. "Sid, this damn dog business worries me."

"Worries me, too. I'm fond of that mutt, and God only knows what sort of stuff he's been getting to eat. And I hate to think of why those geeks stole him, too."

"Well, at risk of seeming heartless, I'm not so much worried for Stalin as I am about why Keeluk was hiding him, and why he was willing to murder the only two Terrans in Konkrook who trust him, to prevent our finding out that he had him."

"A Mr. Keeluk, a clergyman," von Schlichten quoted. He chain-lit another cigarette and stubbed out the old one. "Maybe the Rev. Keeluk wanted Stalin for sacramental purposes."

Blount looked up sharply. "Ritual killing?" he asked. "Or sympathetic magic?"

Von Schlichten shrugged. "Take your choice. Maybe Rakkeed wanted the dog, to kill before a congregation of his followers, killing us by proxy, or in effigy. Or maybe they think we worship Stalin, and getting control of him would give them power over us. I wish we knew a little more about Ulleran psychology."

That wasn't the first time he'd made that wish. Even if sex weren't the paramount psychological factor the ancient Freudians believed, it was an extremely important one, and on Uller most of the fundamental terms of Terran psychology were meaningless. At the same time, the average

Ulleran probably had complexes and neuroses that would have had Freud talking to himself, and they certainly indulged in practices that would have even stood Krafft-Ebing's hair on end.

"One thing," Blount said. "It doesn't take any Ulleran psychologist to know that about eighty percent of them hate us poisonously."

"Oh, rubbish!" Harrington blew the exclamation out around his pipe-stem with a gush of smoke. "A few fanatics hate us, and a few merchants who lost money when we replaced this primitive barter economy of theirs, but nine-tenths of them have benefited enormously from us, and continue to benefit...."

"And hate us more deeply with each new benefit," Blount added. "They resent everything we've done for them."

"Yes, this spaceport proposition of King Orgzild of Keegark looks like it, now doesn't it?" Harrington retorted. "He hates and resents us so much that he's offered us a spaceport at his city...."

"What's it going to cost him?" Blount asked. "He furnishes the land-sequestered from the estate of some noble he executed for treason-and the labor-all forced. We furnish the structural steel, the machine-equipment, the engineering. We get a spaceport we don't really need, and he gets all the business it'll bring to Keegark. Considering the fact that Rakkeed is a welcome guest at his embassy here, and at the Royal Palace at Keegark, I'm beginning to wonder if he isn't fomenting trouble for us here at Konkrook to make us willing to move our main base to his city."

He made a move. Instantly, Harrington slashed out from the middle of the board with one of his heavy-duty, all-purpose pieces and took a piece, then moved again.

"Now look whose king's threatened!" he crowed.

"Yes, I see." Blount brought a piece clockwise around the board and took the threatening piece, then moved again. "I hope you see whose king's threatened, now."

Harrington swore, reached out to move a piece, and then jerked his hand back as though the piece were radioactive. For a while, he sat puffing his pipe and staring at the board.

"In fact, Orgzild's so sure that we're going to accept his offer that he's started building two new power-reactors, to handle the additional power-demand that'll result from the increased business," Blount continued.

"Where's he getting the plutonium?" von Schlichten asked.

"Where can he get it?" Harrington replied. "He just bought four tons of it from us, off the *City of Pretoria*."

"That's a hell of a lot of plutonium," Blount said. "I wonder if he mightn't have some idea of what else plutonium can be used for, beside generating power."

"Oh, God, I hope not!" Harrington exclaimed. "You're going to get me started seeing burglars under the bed, next...."

"Maybe there are burglars," Blount said, pointing with his cigarette-holder to Harrington's threatened king. "Can't you do something about that, Sid?" Then he turned to von Schlichten. "Before we get off the subject, how about those letters the Rev. Keeluk gave to the Quinton girl?"

"All addressed to Skilkans known to be Rakkeed disciples and rabidly anti-Terran," von Schlichten replied. "We radioed the list to Skilk; Colonel Cheng-Li, our intelligence man there, teleprinted us back a lot of material on them that looks like the Newgate Calendar. We turned the letters themselves over to Doc Petrie, the Ulleran philology sharp, who is a pretty fair cryptanalyst. He couldn't find any indications of cipher, but there was a lot of gossip about Keeluk's friends and parishioners which might have arbitrary code-meanings. I'm going to explain the situation to Miss Quinton, and advise her to have nothing to do with any of the people Keeluk gave her letters to."

Harrington had gotten his king temporarily out of danger, losing a piece doing it.

"Think she'll listen to you?" he asked. "These Extraterrestrials' Rights Association people are a lot of blasted fanatics, themselves. We're a gang of bloody-handed, flint-hearted, imperialistic sons of bitches in their book, and anything we say's sure to be a Hitler-sized lie."

"Oh, they're not as bad as all that. I never met the girl before today, but old Mohammed Ferriera's a decent bloke. And their association's really done a lot of good. For one thing, they put an end to the peonage system on Yggdrasill, and I know what conditions were like, there, before they did."

A calculating look came into Harrington's eye. He puffed slowly at his pipe and slid a piece from the center toward the sector of the board nearest him. Blount whistled softly and made a quick re-arrangement.

"Carlos, did you say she told you she was going to Skilk, in the near future?" Harrington asked. "Well, look here; you're going up that way, yourself, with that battalion of Kragans, on the *Aldebaran*. Why don't you invite her to make the trip with you? You can be quite attractive to young ladies, when you try, and she'll be grateful for that rescue this afternoon, which is always a good foundation. Maybe you can plant a couple of ideas where they'll do the most good. She's only been here for three months-since the *Canberra* got in from Niflheim. You know and I know and we all know that there are a lot of things up there at the polar mines that would look like hell to anybody who didn't understand local conditions...."

"Well, Miss Quinton's company won't be any particularly heavy cross for me to bear," von Schlichten replied. "I won't guarantee anything, of course...."

The intercom-speaker on the table whistled several times. Harrington swore, laid down his pipe, and got up, brushing ashes from the front of his coat. He flipped a switch and spoke into the box.

"Governor," a voice replied out of it, "there's a geek procession just landed from a water-barge in front, and is coming up the roadway to Company House. A platoon of Jaikark's Household Guards, with rifles; the Spear of State; a royal litter; about thirty geek nobles, on foot; a gift-litter; another platoon of riflemen, if you say the last syllable quick enough."

"That'll be Gurgurk, coming to tell us how unhappy his Sodden and Inebriated Geekship is about that fracas on Seventy-second Street," Harrington said. "The gift-litter will contain the customary indemnity, at the current market quotation. Have Gurgurk and party admitted, all but the rifle-platoons; give him an honor guard of our Kragans, and keep his own gun-toters outside. Take them to the Reception Hall, and hold them there till I signal from the Audience Hall, and then herd them in."

He came back and made a move. Immediately, Blount took one of his pieces, moved again, took another, and made the third move to which he was entitled.

"I'll mate you in four moves," he predicted. "Want to play it out, before we go down?"

"Sure; what's time to a geek? Gurgurk'd think we were worried about something if we didn't keep him waiting....Good Lord! You do have me over a barrel, Eric!"

III

Four-and-Twenty Geek Heads

Governor-General Sidney Harrington sat on the comfortably upholstered bench on the dais of the Audience Hall, flanked by von Schlichten and Eric Blount. He didn't look particularly regal, even on that high seat-with his ruddy outdoorsman's face and his ragged gray mustache and his old tweed coat spotted with pipe-ashes, he might have been any of the dozen-odd country-gentleman neighbors of von Schlichten's boyhood in the Argentine. But then, to a Terran, any of the kings of Uller would have looked like a freak birth in a lizard-house at a zoo; it was hard to guess what impression Harrington would make on an Ulleran.

He took the false palate and tongue-clicker, officially designated as an "enunciator, Ulleran" and, colloquially, as a geek-speaker, out of his coat pocket and shoved it into his mouth. Von

Schlichten and Blount put in theirs, and Harrington pressed the floor-button with his toe. After a brief interval, the wide doors at the other end of the hall slid open, and the Konkrookan notables, attended by a dozen Company native-officers and a guard of Kragan Rifles, entered. The honor-guard advanced in two columns; between them marched an unclad and heavily armed native carrying an ornate spear with a three-foot blade upright in front of him with all four hands. It was the Konkrookan Spear of State; it represented the proxy-presence of King Jaikark. Behind it stalked Gurgurk, the Konkrookan equivalent of Prime Minister or Grand Vizier; he wore a gold helmet and a thing like a string-vest made of gold wire, and carried a long sword with a two-hand grip, a pair of Terran automatics built for a hand with six four-knuckled fingers, and a pair of matched daggers. He was considerably past the Ulleran prime of life-seventy or eighty, to judge from the worn appearance of his opal teeth, the color of his skin, and the predominantly reddish tint of his quartz-speckles. An immature Ulleran would be a very light gray, white under the arms, and his quartz-specks would run from white to pale yellow. The retinue of nobles behind Gurgurk ran through the whole spectrum, from a princeling who was almost oyster-gray to old Ghroghrank, the Keegarkan Ambassador, who was even blacker and more red-speckled than Gurgurk. All of them carried about as much ironmongery as the Prime Minister-the pistols were all Terran, and the swords and daggers were mostly made either on Terra or at the Terran-operated steel-works on Volund.

Four slaves brought up the rear carrying an ornately inlaid box on poles. When the spear-bearer reached the exact middle of the hall, he halted and grounded his regalia-weapon with a thump. Gurgurk came up and halted a couple of paces behind and to the left of the spear, and all the other nobles drew up in two curved lines some ten paces to the rear, with considerable pushing and jostling and a *sotto voce* argument, with overtones of weapon-fingering, about precedence. All, that is, but Ghroghrank and another noble, who came up and planted themselves beside Gurgurk. Von Schlichten regarded the assemblage sourly through his monocle. Maybe Sid Harrington *did* look regal, after all.

The Governor-General rose slowly and descended from the dais, advancing to within ten paces of the Spear, von Schlichten and Blount accompanying him. Out of the corner of his eye, von Schlichten watched a couple of Kragan mercenaries with fifty-shot machine-rifles move unobtrusively to positions from whence they could, if necessary, spray the visitors with bullets without endangering the Terrans.

"Welcome, Gurgurk," Harrington gibbered through his false palate. "The Company is honored by this visit."

"I come in the name of my royal master, His Sublime and Ineffable Majesty, Jaikark the Seventeenth, King of Konkrook and of all the lands of the Konk Isthmus," Gurgurk squeaked and clicked. "I have the honor to bring with me the Lord Ghroghrank, Ambassador of King Orgzild of Keegark to the court of my royal master."

"And I," Ghroghrank said, after being suitably welcomed, "am honored to be accompanied by Prince Gorkrink, special envoy from my master, his Royal and Imperial Majesty King Orgzild, who is in your city to receive the shipment of power-metal my royal master has been honored to be permitted to purchase from the Company."

More protocol about welcoming Gorkrink. Then Gurgurk cleared his throat with a series of barking sounds.

"My royal master, His Sublime and Ineffable Majesty, is prostrated with grief," he stated solemnly. "Were his sorrow not so overwhelming, he would have come in His Own Sacred Person to express the pain and shame which he feels that people of the Company should be set upon and endangered in the streets of the royal city."

If he weren't doped to the ears, von Schlichten substituted mentally. There was a native drug which had, on its users, the combined effects of hashish, heroin and yohimbine; Jaikark and all his court circle were addicts. He probably hadn't even heard of the riot.

"The soldiers of His Sublime and Ineffable Majesty came most promptly to the aid of the troops of the Company, did they not, General von Schlichten?" Harrington asked.

"Within minutes, Your Excellency," von Schlichten replied gravely. "Their promptness, valor, and efficiency were most exemplary."

Gurgurk spoke at length, expressing himself as delighted, on behalf of his royal master, at hearing such high praise from so distinguished a soldier. Eric Blount then contributed a short speech, beseeching the gods that the deep and beautiful friendship existing between the Chartered Uller Company and His Sublime etcetera would continue unimpaired, and that His Sublime etcetera would enjoy long life and peaceful reign, managing, by a trick of Konkrookan grammar, to imply that the second would be conditional upon the first. The Keegarkan Ambassador then spoke his piece, expressing on behalf of King Orgzild the deepest regret that the people of the Company should be so molested, and managing to hint that things like that simply didn't happen at Keegark.

The Prince Gorkrink then spoke briefly, in sympathy for the great and good friend of all Ulleran peoples, Mohammed Ferriera, who had been injured, and hoping that he would soon enjoy full health again. He also managed to convey King Orgild's pleasure at having obtained the plutonium. Von Schlichten noticed that a few of his more recent quartz-specks were slightly greenish in tinge, a sure sign that he had, not long ago, been exposed to the fluorine-tainted air which men and geeks alike breathed on Niflheim. When a geek prince hired out as a laborer for a year on Niflheim, he did so for only one purpose-to learn Terran technologies.

Gurgurk then announced that so enormous a crime against the friends of His Sublime etcetera had not been allowed to go unpunished, signaling behind him with one of his lower hands for the box to be brought forward. The slaves carried it to the front, set it down, and opened it, taking from it a rug which they spread on the floor. On this, from the box, they placed twenty-four newly severed opal-grinning heads, in four neat rows. They had all been freshly scrubbed and polished, but they still smelled like crushed cockroaches.

The three Terrans looked at them gravely. A double-dozen heads was standard payment for an attack in which no Terran had been killed. Ostensibly, they were the heads of the ringleaders: in practice, they were usually lopped from the first two-dozen prisoners or over-age slaves at hand, without regard for whether the victims had even heard of the crime which they were expiating. If the Extraterrestrial's Rights Association were really serious about the rights of these geeks, they'd advocate booting out all these native princes and turning the whole planet over to the Company. That had been the Terran Federation's idea, from the beginning; why else give the Company's chief representative the title of Governor-General?

There was another long speech from Gurgurk, with the nobles behind him murmuring antiphonal agreement-standard procedure, for which there was a standard pun, geek chorus-and a speech of response from Sid Harrington. Standing stiffly through the whole rigamarole, von Schlichten waited for it to end, as finally it did.

They walked back from the door, whence they had escorted the delegation, and stood looking down at the saurian heads on the rug. Harrington raised his voice and called to a Kragan sergeant whose chevrons were painted on all four arms.

"Take this carrion out and stuff it in the incinerator," he ordered. "If any of you think you can clean up this rug and this box, you're welcome to them."

"Wait a moment," von Schlichten told the sergeant. Then he disgorged and pouched his geek-speaker. "See that head, there?" he asked, rolling it over with his toe. "I killed that geek, myself, with my pistol, while Them and Hid were getting Ferriera into the car. Miss Quinton killed that one with the bolo; see where she chopped him on the back of the neck? The cut that took off the head was a little low, and missed it. And Hid O'Leary stuck a knife in that one." He walked around the rug, turning heads over with his foot. "This was cut-rate head-payment; they just slashed off two-dozen heads at the scene of the riot. I don't like this butchery of worn-out slaves and petty thieves any better than anybody else, but this I don't like either. Six months ago, Gurgurk wouldn't have tried to pull anything like this. Now he's laughing up his non-existent sleeve at us."

"That's what I've been preaching, all along," Eric Blount took up after him. "These geeks need having the fear of Terra thrown into them."

"Oh, nonsense, Eric; you're just as bad as Carlos, here!" Harrington tut-tutted. "Next, you'll be saying that we ought to depose Jaikark and take control ourselves."

"Well, what's wrong with that, for an idea?" von Schlichten demanded. "Don't you think we could? Our Kragans could go through that army of Jaikark's like fast neutrons through toilet-paper."

"My God!" Harrington exploded. "Don't let me hear that kind of talk again! We're not *conquistadores*; we're employees of a business concern, here to make money honestly, by exchanging goods and services with these people...."

He turned and walked away, out of the Audience Hall, leaving von Schlichten and Blount to watch the removal of the geek-heads.

"You know, I went a little too far," von Schlichten confessed. "Or too fast, rather. He's got to be conditioned to accept that idea."

"We can't go too slowly, either," Blount replied. "If we wait for him to change his mind, it'll be the same as waiting for him to retire. And that'll be waiting too long."

Von Schlichten nodded seriously. "Did you notice the green specks in the hide of that Prince Gorkrink?" he asked. "He's just come back from Niflheim. Not on the *Pretoria*, I don't think. Probably on the *Canberra*, three months ago."

"And he's here to get that plutonium, and ship it to Keegark on the *Oom Paul Kruger*," Blount considered. "I wonder just what he learned, on Niflheim."

"I wonder just what's going on at Keegark," von Schlichten said. "Orgzild's pulled down a regular First-Century-model iron curtain. You know, four of our best native Intelligence operatives have been murdered in Keegark in the last three months, and six more have just vanished there."

"Well, I'm going there in a few days, myself, to talk to Orgzild about this spaceport deal," Blount said. "I'll have a talk with Hendrik Lemoyne and MacKinnon. And I'll see what I can find out for myself."

"Well, let's go have a drink," von Schlichten suggested, consulting his watch. "About time for a cocktail."

IV
If You Read It in Stanley-Browne

Von Schlichten and Blount entered the bar together-the Broadway Room, decorated in gleaming plastics and chromium in enthusiastic if slightly inaccurate imitation of a First Century New York nightclub. There were no native servants to spoil the illusion, such as it was: the service was fully automatic. Going to a bartending machine, von Schlichten dialed the cocktail they had decided upon and inserted his key to charge the drinks to his account, filling a four-portion jug.

As they turned away, they almost collided with Hideyoshi O'Leary and Paula Quinton. The girl wore a long-sleeved gown to conceal a bandage on her right wrist, and her face was rather heavily powdered in spots; otherwise she looked none the worse for recent experiences.

"Well, you seem to have gotten yourself repaired, Miss Quinton," he greeted her. "Feel better, now?...Miss Quinton, this is Lieutenant-Governor Blount. Eric, Miss Paula Quinton."

"Delighted, Miss Quinton," Blount said. "Carlos tells us he found you standing over poor Mohammed Ferriera, fighting like a commando. How is Mohammed, by the way? No danger, I hope; we all like him."

Mohammed Ferriera was still unconscious, the girl reported; he had a minor concussion, but the medics were not greatly disturbed, and expected him to be fully recovered in a few weeks. Von Schlichten invited her and her escort to join him and Blount. Colonel O'Leary was carrying a cocktail jug and a couple of glasses; finding a table out of the worst of the noise, they all sat down together.

"I suppose you think it's a joke, our being nearly murdered by the people we came to help," Paula began, a trifle defensively.

"Not a very funny joke," von Schlichten told her. "It's been played on us till it's lost its humor."

"Yes, geek ingratitude's an old story to all of us," Blount agreed. "You stay on this planet very long and you'll see what I mean."

"You call them that, too?" she asked, as though disappointed in him. "Maybe if you stopped calling them geeks, they wouldn't resent you the way they do. You know, that's a nasty name; in the First Century Pre-Atomic, it designated a degraded person who performed some sort of revolting public exhibition...."

"Biting off live chickens' heads, in a sideshow wild-man act," Hideyoshi O'Leary supplied. "When you get up north, watch how the peasants kill these little things like six-legged iguanas that they raise for food."

"That isn't the reason, though," von Schlichten said. "As we use it, the word's pure ono-matopoeia. You've learned some of the languages; you know what they sound like. *Geek-geek-geek.*"

"As far as that goes, you know what the geek name for a Terran is?" Blount asked. "*Suddabit.*"

She looked puzzled for a moment, then slipped in her enunciator. Even in the absence of any native, she used her handkerchief to mask the act.

"Suddabit," she said, distinctly. "Sud-da-a-bit." Taking out the geek-speaker, she put it away. "Why, that's exactly how they'd pronounce it!"

"And don't tell me you haven't heard it before," O'Leary said. "The geeks were screaming it at you, over on Seventy-second Street, this afternoon. *Znidd suddabit*; kill the Terrans. That's Rakkeed the Prophet's whole gospel."

"So you see," Eric Blount rammed home the moral, "this is just another case of nobody with any right to call anybody else's kettle black.... Cigarette?"

"Thank you." She leaned toward the lighter-flame O'Leary had snapped into being. "I suspect that of being a principle you'd like me to bear in mind at the polar mines, when I see, let's say, some laborer being beaten by a couple of overseers with three foot lengths of three-quarter-inch steel cable."

"Well, you could also remember that a native's skin is about half an inch thick, and a good deal tougher than a human's," von Schlichten told her. "And it wouldn't hurt any if you found out how these laborers are treated at home. Mostly they're serfs hired from the big landowners; it's a fact you can easily verify that permission to join the labor-companies at the polar mines is regarded as a privilege, granted as a reward or denied as a punishment. And most of the geek landowners are bitterly critical of the way we treat our labor at the mines; they claim we make them dissatisfied with the treatment they get at home."

"Of course, they're always glad to have the peasants taken off their hands during a slack agricultural season," Blount added, "and we train workers to handle contragravity power-equipment. I won't deny that there's a lot of unnecessary brutality on the part of the native foremen and overseers, which we're trying, gradually, to eliminate. You'll have to remember, though, that we're dealing with a naturally brutal race."

"Of course, mistreatment of native labor is always blamed on other natives, never on the gentle and kindly Terrans," she replied. "That's been SOP on every planet our Association's had any experience with."

"Now look; you just came here from Niflheim," von Schlichten objected. "The Company employs quite a few geeks there; how much brutality did you run into there?"

"Well, I must admit, the Ullerans who work there are very well treated. Except that I don't think it's right to employ any people with silicone body-tissues where they're going to breathe fluorine-tainted air."

"Nobody ought to be employed on that planet!" Hideyoshi O'Leary declared. "I did a two-year hitch there, when I was first commissioned in the Company service."

"I put in two years there, too," Blount supported him. "And I might add that that's a year longer than any Ulleran native is ever allowed to spend on Niflheim. You know what the setup is, there, don't you? The Terran Federation Space Navy discovered and explored both Uller and Niflheim, which made both planets public domain. The Company was originally formed to exploit Uller alone, but the Federation insisted that both planets would have to be franchised to the same company. They wanted Niflheim exploited, mainly because of the uranium-deposits there. As it turned out, the Company's making as much money out of Niflheim as we are out of Uller."

"What you miss is this," von Schlichten pointed out. "On Niflheim, there are about a thousand Terrans, and not more than five hundred geeks, all employed on construction-work and in the mines, on the planet itself, working directly under Terran supervision. We use them because they have four hands, and in the power-driven contragravity armor that's necessary there, they can manipulate more controls and do more things at once than we can. Here on Uller, at the polar mines, there are about ten thousand geeks working under five hundred Terrans, and most of the latter are engineers or technicians who don't do supervisory work. So we have to use native foremen, and they're guilty of what mistreatment the workers suffer."

"And remember, too," O'Leary added, "work at the polar mines can only go on for about two months out of the year-mid-September to mid-November at the Arctic, and mid-March to mid-May at the Antarctic. Naturally, things have to be done in a hurry and under pressure."

"Well, why do you work mines at the poles? Aren't there mineral deposits in places where you can work all year 'round?"

"Not as rich, or as accessible," Blount said. "You know what the seasons are like, at the poles of this planet. The temperature will range from about two-fifty Fahrenheit in mid-summer to a hundred and fifty below in winter. There's the most intense sort of thermal erosion you can imagine-the ice-cap melts in the spring to a sea, which boils away completely by the middle of the summer. There will be violent circular storms of hot wind, blowing away the light sand and dust and leaving the heavier particles of metallic ores and metals behind. Then, when the winds fall, we move in for a couple of months. It isn't really mining, or even quarrying; we just scoop up ore from the surface, load it onto ore-boats, and fly it down to Skilk and Krink and Grank, where it's smelted through the winter. The natives run the smelters; use the heat to thaw frozen food for themselves and their livestock while they're melting the ore. In the north, metallurgy and food-preparation have always been combined that way."

"Yes, if you think the natives who work at the mines feel themselves ill-treated, you might propose closing them down entirely and see what the native reaction would be," von Schlichten told her. "Independently hired free workers can make themselves rich, by native standards, in a couple of seasons; many of the serfs pick up enough money from us in incentive-pay to buy their freedom after one season."

"Well, if the Company's doing so much good on this planet, how is it that this native, Rakkeed, the one you call the Mad Prophet, is able to find such a following?" Paula demanded. "There must be something wrong somewhere."

"That's a fair question," Blount replied, inverting a cocktail jug over his glass to extract the last few drops. "When we came to Uller, we found a culture roughly like that of Europe during the Seventh Century Pre-Atomic, or, more closely, like that of Japan before the beginning of the First Century P. A. We initiated a technological and economic revolution here, and such revolutions have their casualties, too. A number of classes and groups got squeezed pretty badly, like the horse-breeders and harness-manufacturers on Terra by the invention of the automobile, or the coal and hydroelectric interests when direct conversion of nuclear energy to electric current was developed, or the railroads and steamship lines at the time of the discovery of the contragravity-field. Naturally, there's a lot of ill-feeling on the part of merchants and artisans who weren't able or willing to adapt themselves to changing conditions; they're all backing

Rakkeed and yelling *'Znidd suddabit!'* now. You know, it's a shame that geek messiah isn't a smart crook, instead of an honest fanatic; he could take in the equivalent of a couple of million sols a year off the North Uller merchants and the Equatorial Zone shipowners. But it is a fact, which not even Rakkeed can successfully deny, that we've raised the general living standard of this planet by about two hundred percent."

"Rakkeed is a Zirk," von Schlichten said. "They're the nomads who hire out to the northern merchants as caravan-drivers, and also prey, or used to prey, on the caravans as brigands. Since our air-freighters got into operation, neither caravan-driving nor caravan-raiding has been a paying business, and our air-patrols have made caravan-raiding suicidal as well. So the Zirks don't like us. The only thing they know or are willing to learn is handling these six-legged riding-and pack-animals we call hipposaurs. We employ a few of them as cavalry, and a few more of them work as the local equivalent of *gauchos*, and the rest just sit around and listen to Rakkeed's sermons."

Both jugs were empty. Colonel O'Leary, as befitted his junior rank, picked them up; after a good-natured wrangle with von Schlichten, Blount handed the colonel his credit-key.

"The merchants in the north don't like us; beside spoiling the caravan-trade, we're spoiling their local business, because the land-owning barons, who used to deal with them, are now dealing directly with us. At Skilk, King Firkked's afraid his feudal nobility is going to try to force a Runnymede on him, so he's been currying favor with the urban merchants; that makes him as pro-Rakkeed and as anti-Terran as they are. At Krink, King Jonkvank has the support of his barons, but he's afraid of his urban bourgeoisie, and we pay him a handsome subsidy, so he's pro-Terran and anti-Rakkeed. At Skilk, Rakkeed comes and goes openly; at Krink he has a price on his head."

"Jonkvank is not one of the assets we boast about too loudly," Hideyoshi O'Leary said, pausing on his way from the table. "He's as bloody-minded an old murderer as you'd care not to meet in a dark alley anywhere."

"We can turn our backs on him and not expect a knife between our shoulders, anyhow," von Schlichten said. "And we can believe, oh, up to eighty percent of what he tells us, and that's sixty percent better than any of the other native princes, except King Kankad, of course. The Kragans are the only real friends we have on this planet." He thought for a moment. "Miss Quinton, are you doing sociographic research-work here, in addition to your Ex-Rights work?" he asked. "Well, let me advise you to pay some attention to the Kragans. You'll only find them treated at any length at all in that compendium of misinformation, Willard Stanley-Browne's *Short Sociographic History of Beta Hydrae II*, and ninety percent of what Stanley-Browne says about them is completely erroneous."

"Oh, but they're just a parasite-race on the Terrans," Dr. Paula Quinton objected. "You find races like that all through the explored galaxy-pathetic cultural mongrels."

Both men laughed heartily. Colonel O'Leary, returning with the jugs, wanted to know what he'd missed. Blount told him.

"Ha! She's been reading that thing of Stanley-Browne's," he said.

"What's the matter with Stanley-Browne?" Paula demanded.

"Stanley-Browne is one author you can depend on," O'Leary assured her. "If you read it in Stanley-Browne, it's wrong. You know, I don't think she's run into many Kragans. We ought to take her over and introduce her to King Kankad."

Von Schlichten allowed himself to be smitten by an idea. "By Allah, so we had!" he exclaimed. "Look, you're going to Skilk, in the next week, aren't you? Well, do you think you could get all your end-jobs cleared up here and be ready to leave by 0800 Tuesday? That's four days from today."

"I'm sure I could. Why?"

"Well, I'm going to Skilk, myself, with the armed troopship *Aldebaran*. We're stopping at King Kankad's Town to pick up a battalion of Kragan Rifles for duty at the polar mines, where you're going. Suppose we leave here in my command-car, go to Kankad's Town, and wait there till the *Aldebaran* gets in. That would give us about two to three hours. If you think the Kragans are 'pathetic cultural mongrels,' what you'll see there will open your eyes. And I might add that the nearest Stanley-Browne ever came to seeing Kankad's Town was from the air, once, at a distance of four miles."

"Well, they live entirely by serving as mercenary soldiers for the Uller Company, don't they?"

"More or less. You see, when we came to Uller, they were barbarian brigands; had a string of forts along caravan-roads and at fords and mountain-passes, and levied tolls. They raided into Konkrook and Keegark territory, too. Well, we had to break that up. We fought a little war with them, beat them rather badly in a couple of skirmishes, and then made a deal with them. That was before my time, when old Jerry Kirke was Governor-General. He negotiated a treaty with their King, bought their rievers'-forts outright, and paid them a subsidy to compensate for loss of tolls and raid-spoil, and agreed to employ the whole tribe as soldiers. We've taught them a lot-you'll see how much when you visit their town-but they aren't cultural mongrels. You'll like them."

"Well, general, I'll take you up," she said. "But I warn you; if this is some scheme to indoctrinate me with the Uller Company's side of the case and blind me to unjust exploitation of the natives here, I don't propagandize very easily."

"Fair enough, as long as you don't let fear of being propagandized blind you to the good we're doing here, or impair your ability to observe and draw accurate conclusions. Just stay scientific about it and I'll be satisfied. Now, let's take time out for lubrication," he said, filling her glass and passing the jug.

Two hours and five cocktails later, they were still at the table, and they had taught Paula Quinton some twenty verses of *The Heathen Geeks, They Wear No Breeks*, including the four printable ones.

V
You Can Depend on It It's Wrong

Gongonk Island, with its blue-gray Company buildings, and the Terran green of the farms, and the spaceport with its ring of mooring-pylons empty since the *City of Pretoria* had lifted out, two days before, for Terra, was dropping away behind. Von Schlichten held his lighter for Paula Quinton, then lit his own cigarette.

"I was rather horrified, Friday afternoon, at the way you and Colonel O'Leary and Mr. Blount were blaspheming against Stanley-Browne," she said. "His book is practically the sociographers' Koran for this planet. But I've been checking up, since, and I find that everybody who's been here any length of time seems to deride it, and it's full of the most surprising misstatements. I'm either going to make myself famous or get burned at the stake by the Extraterrestrial Sociographic Society after I get back to Terra. In the last three months, I've been really too busy with Ex-Rights work to do much research, but I'm beginning to think there's a great deal in Stanley-Browne's book that will have to be reconsidered."

"How'd you get into this, Miss Quinton?" he asked.

"You mean sociography, or Ex-Rights? Well, my father and my grandfather were both extraterrestrial sociographers-anthropologists whose subjects aren't anthropomorphic-and I majored in sociography at the University of Montevideo. And I've always been in sympathy with extraterrestrial races; one of my great-grandmothers was a Freyan."

"The deuce; I'd never have guessed that, as small and dark as you are."

"Well, another of my great-grandmothers was Japanese," she replied. "The family name's French. I'm also part Spanish, part Russian, part Italian, part English ...the usual modern Argentine mixture."

"I'm an Argentino, too. From La Rioja, over along the Sierra de Velasco. My family lived there for the past five centuries. They came to the Argentine in the Year Three, Atomic Era."

"On account of the Hitler bust-up?"

"Yes. I believe the first one, also a General von Schlichten, was what was then known as a war-criminal."

"That makes us partners in crime, then," she laughed. "The Quintons had to leave France about the same time; they were what was known as collaborationists."

"That's probably why the Southern Hemisphere managed to stay out of the Third and Fourth World Wars," he considered. "It was full of the descendants of people who'd gotten the short end of the Second."

"Do you speak the Kragan language, general?" she asked. "I understand it's entirely different from the other Equatorial Ulleran languages."

"Yes. That's what gives the Kragans an entirely different semantic orientation. For instance, they have nothing like a subject-predicate sentence structure. That's why, Stanley-Browne to the contrary notwithstanding, they are entirely non-religious. Their language hasn't instilled in them a predisposition to think of everything as the result of an action performed by an agent. And they have no definite parts of speech; any word can be used as any part of speech, depending on context. Tense is applied to words used as nouns, not words used as verbs; there are four tenses-spatial-temporal present, things here-and-now; spatial present and temporal remote, things which were here at some other time; spatial remote and temporal present, things existing now somewhere else, and spatial-temporal remote, things somewhere else some other time."

"Why, it's a wonder they haven't developed a Theory of Relativity!"

"They have. It resembles ours about the way the Wright Brothers' airplane resembles this aircar, but I was explaining the Keene-Gonzales-Dillingham Theory and the older Einstein Theory to King Kankad once, and it was beautiful to watch how he picked it up. Half the time, he was a jump ahead of me."

The aircar began losing altitude and speed as they came in over Kraggork Swamp; the treetops below blended into a level plain of yellow-green, pierced by glints of stagnant water underneath and broken by an occasional low hillock, sometimes topped by a stockaded village.

"Those are the swamp-savages' homes," he told her. "Most of what you find in Stanley-Browne about them is fairly accurate. He spent a lot of time among them. He never seems to have realized, though, that they are living now as they have ever since the first appearance of intelligent life on this planet."

"You mean, they're the real aboriginal people of Uller?"

"They and the Jeel cannibals, whom we are doing our best to exterminate," he replied. "You see, at one time, the dominant type of mobile land-life was the thing we call a shellosaur, a big thing, running from five to fifteen tons, plated all over with silicate shell, till it looked like a six-legged pine-cone. Some were herbivores and some were carnivores. There are a few left, in remote places-quite a few in the Southern Hemisphere, which we haven't explored very much. They were a satisfied life-form. Outside of a volcano or an earthquake or an avalanche, nothing could hurt a shellosaur but a bigger shellosaur.

"Finally, of course, they grew beyond their sustenance-limit, but in the meantime, some of them began specializing on mobility instead of armor and began excreting waste-matter instead of turning it to shell. Some of these new species got rid of their shell entirely. *Parahomo sapiens Ulleris* is descended from one of these.

"The shellosaurs were still a serious menace, though. The ancestors of the present Ulleran, the proto-geeks, when they were at about the Java Ape-Man stage of development, took two divergent courses to escape the shellosaurs. Some of them took to the swamps, where the shellosaurs would sink if they tried to follow. Those savages, down there, are still living in the same manner; they never progressed. Others encountered problems of survival which had to be overcome by invention. They progressed to barbarism, like the people of the fishing-villages, and some of them progressed to civilization, like the Konkrookans and the Keegarkans.

"Then, there were others who took to the high rocks, where the shellosaurs couldn't climb. The Jeels are the primitive, original example of that. Most of the North Uller civilizations developed from mountaineer-savages, and so did the Zirks and the other northern plains nomads."

"Well, how about the Kragans?" Paula asked. "Which were they?"

Von Schlichten was scanning the horizon ahead. He pulled over a pair of fifty-power binoculars on a swinging arm and put them where she could use them.

"Right ahead, there; just a little to the left. See that brown-gray spot on the landward edge of the swamp? That's King Kankad's Town. It's been there for thousands of years, and it's always been Kankad's Town. You might say, even the same Kankad. The Kragan kings have always provided their own heirs, by self-fertilization. That's a complicated process, involving simultaneous male and female masturbation, but the offspring is an exact duplicate of the single parent. The present Kankad speaks of his heir as 'Little Me,' which is a fairly accurate way of putting it."

He knew what she was seeing through the glasses —a massive butte of flint, jutting out into the swamp on the end of a sharp ridge, with a city on top of it. All the buildings were multi-storied, some piling upward from the top and some clinging to the sides. The high watchtower at the front now carried a telecast-director, aimed at an automatic relay-station on an unmanned orbiter two thousand miles off-planet.

"They're either swamp-people who moved up onto that rock, or they're mountaineers who came out that far along the ridge and stopped," she said. "Which?"

"Nobody's ever tried to find out. Maybe if you stay on Uller long enough, you can. That ought to be good for about eight to ten honorary doctorates. And maybe a hundred sols a year in book royalties."

"Maybe I'll just do that, general.... What's that, on the little island over there?" she asked, shifting the glasses. "A clump of flat-roofed buildings. Under a red-and-yellow danger-flag."

"That's Dynamite Island; the Kragans have an explosives-plant there. They make nitroglycerine, like all the thalassic peoples; they also make TNT and catastrophite, and propellants. Learned that from us, of course. They also manufacture most of their own firearms, some of them pretty extreme-up to 25-mm for shoulder rifles. Don't ever fire one; it'd break every bone in your body."

"Are they that much stronger than us?"

He shook his head. "Just denser, heavier. They're about equal to us in weight-lifting. They can't run, or jump, as well as we can. We often come out here for games with the Kragans, where the geeks can't watch us. And that reminds me-you're right about that being a term of derogation, because I don't believe I've ever knowingly spoken of a Kragan as a geek, and in fact they've picked up the word from us and apply it to all non-Kragans. But as I was saying, our baseball team has to give theirs a handicap, but their football team can beat the daylights out of ours. In a tug-of-war, we have to put two men on our end for every one of theirs. But they don't even try to play tennis with us."

"Don't the other natives make their own firearms?"

"No, and we're not going to teach them how. The thalassic peoples here in the Equatorial Zone are fairly good empirical, teaspoon-measure, chemists. Well, no, alchemists. They found out how to make nitroglycerine, and use it for blasting and for bombs and mines, and they screw little capsules of it on the ends of their arrows. Most of their chemistry, such as it is, was learned in trying to prevent organic materials, like wood, from petrifying. Up in the north, where it gets cold, they learned a lot about metallurgy and ceramics, and about forced-draft pneumatics, from having to keep fires going all winter to thaw frozen food. They make air-rifles, to shoot metal darts."

The aircar came in, circling slowly over the town on the big rock, and let down on the roof of the castle-like building from which the watchtower rose. There were a dozen or so individuals waiting for them-the five Terrans, three men and two women, from the telecast station, and the rest Kragans. One of these, dark-skinned but with speckles no darker than light amber, armed only with a heavy dagger, came over and clapped von Schlichten on the shoulder, grinning opalescently.

"Greetings, Von!" he squawked in Kragan, then, seeing Paula, switched over to the customary language of the Takkad Sea country. "It makes happiness to see you. How long will you stay with us?"

"Till the *Aldebaran* gets in from Konkrook, to pick up the rifles," von Schlichten replied, in Lingua Terra. He looked at his watch. "Two hours and a half...Kankad, this is Paula Quinton; Paula, King Kankad."

He took out his geek-speaker and crammed it into his mouth. Before any other race on Uller, that would have been the most shocking sort of bad manners, without the token-concealment of the handkerchief. Kankad took it as a matter of course. At some length, von Schlichten explained the nature of Paula's sociographic work, her connection with the Extraterrestrials' Rights Association, and her intention of going to the Arctic mines. Kankad nodded.

"You were right," he said. "I wouldn't have understood all that in your language. If I had read it, maybe, but not if I heard it." He put his upper right hand on Paula's shoulder and uttered a clicking approximation of her name. "I make you one of us," he told her. "You must come back, after the work stops at the mines; if you want to learn about my people, I'll show you what you want to see, and tell you what you want to know. But why not stay here? Why bother about those geeks at the mines; the Company treats them much better than they deserve. Stay here with us; we will make you happy to be with us."

Paula replied slowly: "I thank Kankad, but I must go. Those on Terra who sent me here want me to learn for myself how the workers at the mines are treated. But I will come back-in a hundred, a hundred and fifty days."

Kankad's opal-jeweled grin widened. "Good! We'll be waiting for you." He turned and introduced another Kragan, about his own age, who wore the equipment and insignia of a Company native-major and was freshly painted with the Company emblem. "This is Kormork. He and I have borne young to each other. Kormork, you watch over Paula Quinton." He managed, on the second try, to make it more or less recognizable. "Bring her back safe. Or else find yourself a good place to hide."

Kankad introduced the rest of his people, and von Schlichten introduced the Terrans from the telecast-station. Then Kankad looked at the watch he was wearing on his lower left wrist.

"We will have plenty of time, before the ship comes, to show Paula the town," he suggested. "Von, you know better than I do what she would like to see."

He led the way past a pair of long 90-mm guns to a stone stairway. Von Schlichten explained, as they went down, that the guns of King Kankad's Town were the only artillery above 75-mm on Uller in non-Terran hands. They climbed into an open machine-gun carrier and strapped themselves to their seats, and for two hours King Kankad showed her the sights of the town. They visited the school, where young Kragans were being taught to read Lingua Terra and studied from textbooks printed in Johannesburg and Sydney and Buenos Aires. Kankad showed her the repair-shops, where two-score descendants of Kragan riever-chieftains were working on contragravity equipment, under the supervision of a Scottish-Afrikaner and his Malay-Portuguese wife; the small-arms factory, where very respectable copies of Terran rifles and pistols and auto-weapons were being turned out; the machine-shop; the physics and chemistry labs; the hospital; the ammunition-loading plant; the battery of 155-mm Long Toms, built in Kankad's own shops, which covered the road up the sloping rock-spine behind the city; the printing-shop and book-bindery; the observatory, with a big telescope and an ingenious orrery of the Beta Hydrae system; the nuclear-power plant, part of the original price for giving up brigandage.

Half an hour before the ship from Konkrook was due, they had arrived at the airport, where a gang of Kragans were clearing a berth for the *Aldebaran*. From somewhere, Kankad produced two cold bottles of Cape Town beer for Paula and von Schlichten, and a bowl of some boiling-hot black liquid for himself. Von Schlichten and Paula lit cigarettes; between sips of his bubbling hell-brew, Kankad gnawed on the stalk of some swamp-plant. Paula seemed as much surprised at Kankad's disregard for the eating taboo as she had been at von Schlichten's open flouting of the convention of concealment when he had put in his geek-speaker.

"This is the only place on Uller where this happens," von Schlichten told her. "Here, or in the field when Terran and Kragan soldiers are together. There aren't any taboos between us and the Kragans."

"No," Kankad said. "We cannot eat each others' food, and because our bodies are different, we cannot be the fathers of each others' young. But we have been battle-comrades, and worksharers, and we have learned from each other, my people more from yours than yours from mine. Before you came, my people were like children, shooting arrows at little animals on the beach, and climbing among the rocks at dare-me-and-I-do, and playing war with toy weapons. But we are growing up, and it will not be long before we will stand beside you, as the grown son stands beside his parent, and when that day comes, you will not be ashamed of us."

It was easy to forget that Kankad had four arms and a rubbery, quartz-speckled skin, and a face like a lizard.

"I have always wished that some of your people could come to Terra, to study," von Schlichten said. "I was talking about it with Sid Harrington, only a short while ago. He thinks it would be a good thing, for your people and for mine."

"Yes. I want Little Me, when he's old enough to travel, to visit your world," Kankad said. "And some of the other young ones. And when Little Me is old enough to take over the rule of our people, I would like to go to Terra, myself."

"Some day, I am going to return to Terra; I would like to have you make the trip with me," von Schlichten said.

"That would be wonderful, Von!" Kankad exclaimed. "I want to see your world, before I die. It must be a wonderful place. A world is what its people make it, and your people must be able to make anything of your world that you would want."

"We almost made a lifeless desert, like the poles of Uller, out of our world, once," von Schlichten told him. "Four hundred and more years ago, we fought great wars among ourselves, with weapons such as I hope will never even be thought of on Uller. Our whole Northern Hemisphere, where our greatest nations were, was devastated; much of it is wasteland to this day. But we put an end to that folly in time; we made one nation out of all our people, and swore never to commit such crimes again, and then we built the ships that took us out to the stars. But I want you to see our world, and some of the other worlds that we have visited, I think you would like it."

"I know I would. And with you to tell me what the things I would see meant...." Kankad was silent for a moment. Then he spoke again, changing the subject abruptly.

"I hope Paula will pardon me, but isn't Paula the kind of Terran that bears young?"

"That's right, Kankad. I never bore any, yet, but that's the kind of Terran I am."

"I like Paula," Kankad said. "She has come all the way from Terra to help us, and to learn about us. Of course, the Kragans don't need that kind of help, and the geeks, who would stick a knife in her as soon as she turned her back on them, don't deserve it. But she wants to learn about us, just as I want to learn about Terra. Von, why don't you and Paula have young?" he asked. "I think that would be fine. Then, Little Paula-Von and Little Me could be friends, long after the three of us are dead and gone."

VI

The Bad News Came After the Coffee

The last clatter of silverware and dishes ceased as the native servants finished clearing the table. There was a remaining clatter of cups and saucers; liqueur-glasses tinkled, and an occasional cigarette-lighter clicked. At the head table, the voices seemed louder.

"...don't like it a millisol's worth," Brigadier-General Barney Mordkovitz, the Skilk military CO, was saying to the lady on his right. "They're too confounded meek. Nowadays, nobody yells *'Znidd suddabit!'* at you. Nobody sticks all four thumbs in his mouth and waves his fingers. Nobody commits nuisance on the sidewalk in front of you. They just stand and look at you like a farmer looking at a turkey the week before Christmas, and that I don't like!"

"Oh, bosh!" Jules Keaveney, the Skilk Resident-Agent, at the head of the table, exclaimed. "You soldiers are all alike-begging your pardon, General von Schlichten," he nodded in the direction of the guest of honor. "If they don't bow and scrape to you and get off the sidewalk to let you pass, you say they're insolent and need a lesson. If they do, you say they're plotting insurrection."

"What I said," Mordkovitz repeated, "was that I expect a certain amount of disorder, and a certain minimum show of hostility toward us from some of these geeks, to conform to what I know to be our unpopularity with many of them. When I don't find it, I want to know why."

"I'm inclined," von Schlichten came to his subordinate's support, "to agree. This sudden absence of overt hostility is disquieting. Colonel Cheng-Li," he called on the local Intelligence officer and Constabulary chief. "This fellow Rakkeed was here, about a month ago. Was there any noticeable disorder at that time? Anti-Terran demonstrations, attacks on Company property or personnel, shooting at aircars, that sort of thing?"

"No more than usual, general. In fact, it was when Rakkeed came here that the condition General Mordkovitz was speaking of began to become conspicuous. We did catch some of Rakkeed's disciples trying to get in among the enlisted men of the Tenth N.U.N.I. and the Fifth Zirk Cavalry and promote disaffection. That was reported at the time, sir."

"And acted upon, as far as the civil administration would permit," von Schlichten replied. "And I might say that Lieutenant-Governor Blount has reported from Keegark, where he is now, that the same unnatural absence of hostility exists there."

"Well, of course, general," Keaveney said patronizingly. "King Orgzild has things under pretty tight control at Keegark. He'd not allow a few fanatics to do anything to prejudice these space-port negotiations."

"I wonder if the idea back of that spaceport proposition isn't to get us concentrated at Keegark, where Orgzild could wipe us all out in one surprise blow," somebody down the table suggested.

"Oh, Orgzild wouldn't be crazy enough to try anything like that," Commander Dirk Prinsloo, of the *Aldebaran*, declared. "He'd get away with it for just twelve months-the time it would take to get the news to Terra and for a Federation Space Navy task-force to get here. And then, there'd be little bits of radioactive geek floating around this system as far out as the orbit of Beta Hydrae VII."

"That's quite true," von Schlichten agreed. "The point is, does Orgzild know it? I doubt if he even believes there is a Terra."

"Then where in Space does he think we come from?" Keaveney demanded.

"I believe he thinks Niflheim is our home world," von Schlichten replied. "Or, rather, the string of orbiters and artificial satellites around Niflheim. Where he thinks Niflheim is, I wouldn't even try to guess."

"Well, it takes six months for a ship to go between here and Nif," Prinsloo considered. "Because of the hyperdrive effects, the experienced time of the voyage, inside the ship, is of the order of three weeks. Taking that as the figure, he'd estimate the distance at about a quarter-million miles, assuming the velocity as being the speed of one of our contragravity-ships here on Uller. I'm assuming he doesn't even know there is a hyperdrive."

"Yes. After he'd wiped us out, he might even consider the idea of an invasion of Niflheim with captured contragravity ships," Hideyoshi O'Leary chuckled. "That would be a big laugh-if any of us were alive, then, to do any laughing."

"You don't really believe that, general?" Keaveney asked. His tone was still derisive, but under the derision was uncertainty. After all, von Schlichten had been on Uller for fifteen years, to his two.

"Any question of geek psychology is wide open as far as I'm concerned; the longer I stay here, the less I understand it." Von Schlichten finished his brandy and got out cigarette-case and lighter. "I have an idea of the sort of garbled reports these spies of his who spend a year on Niflheim as laborers bring back."

"You know the line Rakkeed's been taking, of course," Colonel Cheng-Li put in. "He as much as says that Niflheim's our home, and that the farms where we raise food here, and those evergreen plantings on Konk Isthmus and between here and Grank are the beginning of an attempt to drive all native life from this planet and make it over for ourselves."

"And that savage didn't think an idea like that up for himself; he got it from somebody like Orgzild," the black-bearded brigadier-general added. "You know, the main base off Niflheim is practically self-supporting, with hydroponic-gardens and animal-tissue culture vats. And it's enough bigger than one of the *City* ships to pass for a little world. Yes, somebody like Orgzild, or King Firkked here, could easily pick up the idea that that's our home planet."

"But King Kankad was talking about...." Paula Quinton began.

"We were speaking of geeks, not Kragans." Von Schlichten lit his cigarette and held his lighter for hers. "You saw that big Beta Hydrae orrery at Kankad's observatory. Well, there's quite a little story about that. You know, it's generally realized by the natives here that Uller is a globe. The North Zirks have ridden all the way around it, on hipposaur-back, in the high latitudes, and the thalassic peoples at the Equator have sailed all the five equatorial seas and portaged all the isthmuses between. But, of course, Uller is the center of the universe; the sun travels around it, on a rather complicated double-spiral track. As a theory, it explains most of what they're able to observe, and any minor effects that don't conform to it are just ignored. They have a model, a most ingenious affair run by clockwork, at the University of Konkrook, to show the apparent movement and position of Beta Hydrae in the sky; it does so fairly accurately.

"Well, some of our astronomers constructed this orrery, and exhibited it to a gathering of the leading native scholars, who are also the high-priests of the local religion. Sort of combined Academy of Arts and Sciences and College of Cardinals. They almost were massacred. As soon as the assembled pundits saw this thing and grasped its meaning, they began geeking and skreeking and yorking and squawking and brandishing knives-it was blasphemous, and sacrilegious, and undermined the Faith, and invalidated the whole logic-system.

"I was brigadier-general, in command of Konkrook military district, then-the post Them M'zangwe has now. When I got a riot-call from the University, I hustled around with a company of Kragans, and we cleared the hall with the bayonet and ran the reverend professors out onto the campus, and after we got things in hand, the Kragans crowded around the orrery, trying to set it up to show the existing position of the planet relative to the primary and figure out the theory back of it. They were very much interested; some of them must have sent word home about it, because Kankad came in on the next ship, wanting to see it. He was so much taken with it that Sid Harrington gave it to him. It's one of his most cherished possessions, but the Konkrook pundits bite all four thumbs and wave their fingers every time they think of it." He warmed his coffee from a controlled-temperature pot. "You can't use Kragan thinking on any subject as a criterion of what somebody like Orgzild's opinions will be."

"I never could understand the admiration some of you military people have for those cut-throats," Keaveney declared. "Oh, yes, I can. You like them because they do your dirty work for you."

"He reads Stanley-Browne, too, I'll bet," Hideyoshi O'Leary said. "Miss Quinton, how did you like your visit to Kankad's Town? Still think the Kragans are cultural mongrels?"

"Why, they're wonderful! I never expected anything like it. They just seem to have picked up everything they could from us, and then gone on from there to develop a culture of their own with our techniques. For instance, those big guns, the ones they call the Ridge Battery, that they built for themselves. They aren't copies of Terran guns. They don't look like our work, or give you the feel our work would. And that telescope at the observatory," she continued. "Did they build that, too?"

"Yes, all we furnished was a couple of textbooks on lens-grinding and telescope-design, and a book on optics. You see, when we made that deal with them, they realized that we weren't any better fighters than they were; we just had better weapons. To have the same kind of weapons, they'd have to learn to make them, and once they began studying technology, they found that they had to study science. Weapon-making was the entering-wedge; after that, they found that they could use the same skills to make anything else they wanted. Give them another century or so and they'll be one of the great races of the galaxy."

"Yes, and it's a good thing they're our friends, too," Mordkovitz added. "I'm only sorry there are so few of them, and so many of the geeks."

"Yes, the Company ought to let us stockpile nuclear weapons here, just to be on the safe side," another officer, farther down the table, said.

"Well, I'm not exactly in favor of that," von Schlichten replied. "It's the same principle as not allowing guards who have to go in among the convicts to carry firearms. If somebody like Orgzild got hold of a nuclear bomb, even a little old First-Century H-bomb, he could use it for a model and construct a hundred like it, with all the plutonium we've been handing out for power reactors. And there are too few of us, and we're concentrated in too few places, to last long if that happened. What this planet needs, though, is a visit by a fifty-odd-ship task-force of the Space Navy, just to show the geeks what we have back of us. After a show like that, there'd be a lot less *znidd suddabit* around here."

"General, I deplore that sort of talk," Keaveney said. "I hear too much of this mailed-fist-and-rattling-saber stuff from some of the junior officers here, without your giving countenance and encouragement to it. We're here to earn dividends for the stockholders of the Uller Company, and we can only do that by gaining the friendship, respect and confidence of the natives...."

"Mr. Keaveney," Paula Quinton spoke up. "I doubt if even you would seriously accuse the Extraterrestrials' Rights Association of favoring what you call a mailed-fist-and-rattling-saber policy. We've done everything in our power to help these people, and if anybody should have their friendship, we should. Well, only five days ago, in Konkrook, Mr. Mohammed Ferriera and I were attacked by a mob, our native aircar driver was murdered, and if it hadn't been for General von Schlichten and his soldiers, we'd have lost our own lives. Mr. Ferriera is still hospitalized as a result of injuries he received. It seems that General von Schlichten and his Kragans aren't trying to get friendship and confidence; they're willing to settle for respect, in the only way they can get it-by hitting harder and quicker than the geeks can."

Somebody down the table-one of the military, of course-said, "Hear, hear!" Von Schlichten came as close as a man wearing a monocle can to winking at Paula. Good girl, he thought; she's started playing on the Army team!

"Well, of course...." Keaveney began. Then he stopped, as a Terran sergeant came up to the table and bent over Barney Mordkovitz' shoulder, whispering urgently. The black-bearded brigadier rose immediately, taking his belt from the back of his chair and putting it on. Motioning the sergeant to accompany him, he spoke briefly to Keaveney and then came around the table to where von Schlichten sat, the Resident-Agent accompanying him.

"Message just came in from Konkrook, general," he said softly. "Sid Harrington's dead."

It took von Schlichten all of a second to grasp what had been said. "Good God! When? How?"

"Here's all we know, sir," the sergeant said, giving him a radioprint slip. "Came in ten minutes ago."

It was an all-station priority telecast. Governor-General Harrington had died suddenly, in his room, at 2210; there were no details. He glanced at his watch; it was 2243. Konkrook and Skilk were in the same time-zone; that was fast work. He handed the slip to Mordkovitz, who gave it to Keaveney.

"You from the telecast station, sergeant?" he asked. "All right, let's go."

"Wait a minute, general." Keaveney put out a hand to detain him as he took his belt and put it on. "How about this?" He gestured nervously with the radioprint slip.

"Get up and make an announcement, now," von Schlichten told him, fastening the buckle and hitching his pistol and survival-kit into place. "It'll be out all over the planet in half an hour. Never hold news out unnecessarily." He stubbed out his cigarette. "Come on, sergeant."

As he hurried from the banquet-room, he could hear Keaveney tapping on his wine-glass.

"Everybody, please! Let me have your attention! There has just come in a piece of the most tragic news...."

VII
Bismillah! How Dumb Can We Get?

The lights had come on inside the semicircular and now open storm-porch of Company House, but it was still daylight outside. The sky above the mountain to the west was fading from crimson to burnt-orange, and a couple of the brighter stars were winking into visibility. Von Schlichten and the sergeant hurried a hundred yards down the street between low, thick-walled office buildings to the telecast station, next to the Administration Building.

A woman captain met him just inside the door of the big soundproofed room.

"We have a wavelength open to Konkrook, general," she said. "In booth three."

He nodded. "Thank you, captain.... We've all lost a true friend, haven't we?"

Another girl, a tech-sergeant, was in the booth; on the screen was the image of a third young woman, a lieutenant, at Konkrook station. The sergeant rose and started to leave the booth.

"Stick around, sergeant," von Schlichten told her. "I'll want you to take over when I'm through." He sat down in front of the combination visiscreen and pickup. "Now, lieutenant, just what happened?" he asked. "How did he die?"

"We think it was poison, general. General M'zangwe has ordered autopsy and chemical analysis. If you can wait about ten minutes, he'll be able to talk to you, himself."

"Call him. In the meantime, give me everything you know."

"Well, the governor decided to go to bed early; he was going hunting in the morning. I suppose you know his usual routine?"

Von Schlichten nodded. Harrington would have taken a shower, put on his dressing-gown, and then sat down at his desk, lighted his pipe, poured a drink of Terran bourbon, and begun to write his diary.

"Well, at 2210, give or take a couple of minutes, the Kragan guard-sergeant on that floor heard ten pistol-shots, as fast as they could be fired semi-auto, in the governor's room. The door was locked, but he shot it off with his own pistol and went in. He found Governor Harrington on the floor, wearing only his gown, holding an empty pistol. He was in convulsions, frothing at the mouth, in horrible pain. Evidently he'd fired his pistol, which he kept on his desk, to call help; all the bullets had gone into the ceiling. The sergeant punched the emergency button, beside the bed, and reported, then tried to help the governor, but it was too late. One of the medics got there in five minutes, just as he was dying. He'd written his diary up to noon of today, and broken off in the middle of a word. There was a bottle and an overturned glass on his desk. The Constabulary got there a few minutes later, and then Brigadier-General M'zangwe took charge. A white rat, given fifteen drops from the whiskey-bottle, died with the same symptoms in about ninety seconds."

"Who had access to the whiskey-bottle?"

"A geek servant, who takes care of the room. He was caught, an hour earlier, trying to slip off the island without a pass; they were holding him at the guardhouse when Governor Harrington died. He's now being questioned by the Kragans." The girl's face was bleakly remorseless. "I hope they do plenty to him!"

"I hope they don't kill him before he talks."

"Wait a moment, general; we have General M'zangwe, now," the girl said. "I'll switch you over."

The screen broke into a kaleidoscopic jumble of color, then cleared; the chocolate-brown face of Themistocles M'zangwe was looking out of it.

"I heard what happened, how they found him, and about that geek chamber-valet being arrested," von Schlichten said. "Did you get anything out of him?"

"He's admitted putting poison in the bottle, but he claims it was his own idea. But he's one of Father Keeluk's parishioners, so...."

"Keeluk! God damn, so that was it!" von Schlichten almost shouted. "Now I know what he wanted with Stalin, and that goat, and those rabbits!"

Five thousand miles away, in Konkrook, Themistocles M'zangwe whistled.

"*Bismillah*! How dumb can we get?" he cried. "Of course they'd need terrestrial animals, to find out what would poison a Terran! Wait a minute; I'll make a note of that, to spring on this geek, if the Kragans haven't finished him by now." Von Schlichten watched M'zangwe pick up a stenophone and whisper into it for a moment. "All right, Carlos, what else?"

"Has Eric been notified?"

"We called Keegark, but he's in audience with King Orgzild, and we can't reach him."

"Well, who's in charge at Konkrook, now?"

"Not much of anybody. Laviola, the Fiscal Secretary, and Hans Meyerstein, the Banking Cartel's lawyer, and Howlett, the Personnel Chief, and Buhrmann, the Commercial Secretary, have made up a sort of quadrumvirate and are trying to run things. I don't know what would happen if anything came up suddenly...." A blue-gray uniformed arm, with a major's cuff-braid, came into the screen, handing a slip of paper to M'zangwe; he took it, glanced at it, and swore. Von Schlichten waited until he had read it through.

"Well, something has, all right," the African said. "We just got a call from Jaikark's Palace — a revolt's broken out, presumably headed by Gurgurk; Household Guards either mutinied or wiped out by the mutineers, all but those twenty Kragan Rifles we loaned Jaikark. They, and about a dozen of Jaikark's courtiers and their personal retainers, are holding the approaches to the King's apartments. The native-lieutenant in charge of the Kragans just radioed in; says the situation is desperate."

"When a Kragan says that, he means damn near hopeless. Is this being recorded?" When M'zangwe nodded, he continued: "All right. Use the recording for your authority and take charge. I'm declaring martial rule at Konkrook, as of now, 2253. Tell Eric Blount what's happened, and what you've done, as soon as you can get in touch with him. I'm leaving for Konkrook at once; I ought to get in by 0800.

"Now, as to the trouble at the Palace. Don't commit more than one company of Kragans and ten airjeeps and four combat-cars, and tell them to evacuate Jaikark and his followers and our Kragans to Gongonk Island. And alert your whole force. These geek palace revolutions are always synchronized with street-rioting, and this thing seems to have been synchronized with Sid Harrington's death, too. Get our Kragans out if you can't save anybody else from the Palace, but sacrificing thirty or forty men to save twenty is no kind of business. And keep sending reports; I can pick them up on my car radio as I come down." He turned to the girl sergeant. "Keep on this; there'll be more coming in."

He rose and left the booth. If we can pull Jaikark's bacon off the fire, he was thinking, the Company can dictate its own terms to him afterward; if Jaikark's killed, we'll have Gurgurk's head off for it, and then take over Konkrook. In either case, it'll be a long step toward getting rid of all these geek despots. And with Eric Blount as Governor-General....

The girl captain in charge of the station met him as he came out.

"Poison," he told her. "A geek servant did the job, on orders from Gurgurk and possibly Rakkeed. Gurgurk's started a putsch against King Jaikark; I'm going to Konkrook at once. Call the military airport and have my command-car brought to Company House."

Harry Quong and Hassan Bogdanoff had been at the banquet, too; on a world of lizard-faced silicate-eaters, the social difference between a human general and a human aircar-driver was almost infinitesimal. He'd have to talk to Barney Mordkovitz, too; when word of events at Konkrook got out among the local geeks, as it probably had already....

The inner door of the soundproofed telecast-room burst open, three men hurried inside, and it slammed shut behind them. In the brief interval, there had been firing audible from outside. One of the men had a pistol in his right hand, and with his left arm he supported a companion, whose shoulder was mangled and dripped blood. The third man had a burp-gun in his hands. All were in civilian dress-shorts and light jackets. The man with the pistol holstered it and helped his injured companion into a chair. The burp-gunner advanced into the room, looked around, saw von Schlichten, and addressed him.

"General! The geeks turned on us!" he cried. "The Tenth North Uller's mutinied; they're running wild all over the place. They've taken their barracks and supply-buildings, and the lorry-hangars and the maintenance-yard; they're headed this way in a mob. Some of the Zirk Cavalry's joined them."

"How about the Kragans?"

"The Eighteenth Rifles? They're with us. I saw a party of them firing into the mob; I saw some of the Tenth N.U.N.I. tossing a dead Kragan on their bayonets...."

"Have any ammo left for that burp-gun? Come on, then; let's see what it's like at Company House," von Schlichten said. "Captain Malavez, you know what to do about defending this station. Get busy doing it. And have that girl in booth three tell Konkrook what's happened here, and say that I won't be coming down, as planned, just yet."

He opened the door, and the rattle of shots outside became audible again. The civilian with the burp-gun knew better than to let a general go out first; elbowing von Schlichten out of the way, he crouched over his weapon and dashed outside. Drawing his pistol, von Schlichten followed, pulling the door shut after him.

Darkness had fallen, while he had been inside; now the whole Company Reservation was ablaze with electric lights. Somebody at the power-plant —either the regular staff, if they were still holding, or the mutineers, if they had taken it-had thrown on the emergency lights. There was a confused mass of gray-skinned figures in front of Company House, reflected light twinkling on steel over them; from the direction of the native-troops barracks more natives were coming on the run. On the roof of a building across the street, two machine-guns were already firing into the mob. A group of Terrans came running out of a roadway between two buildings, from the direction of the repair-shops; several of them paused to fire behind them with pistols. They started toward Company House, saw what was going on there, and veered, darting into the door of the building from which the auto-weapons were firing. From up the street, a hundred-odd saurian-faced native soldiers were coming at the double, bayonets fixed and rifles at high port; with them ran several Terrans. Motioning his companion to follow, von Schlichten ran to meet them, falling in beside a Terran captain who ran in front.

"What's the score, captain?" he asked.

"Tenth North Uller and the Fifth Cavalry have mutinied; so have these rag-tag Auxiliaries. That mob down there's part of them." He was puffing under the double effort of running and talking. "Whole thing blew up in seconds; no chance to communicate with anybody...."

A Terran woman, in black slacks and an orange sweater, ran across the street in front of them, pursued by a group of enlisted "men" of the Tenth North Uller Native Infantry, all shrieking *"Znidd suddabit!"* The fugitive ran into a doorway across the street; before her pursuers were aware of their danger, the Kragans had swept over them. There was no shooting; the slim, cruel-bladed bayonets did the work. From behind him, as he ran, von Schlichten could hear Kragan voices in a new cry: *"Znidd geek! Znidd geek!"*

The mob were swarming up onto the steps and into the semi-rotunda of the storm-porch. There was shooting, which told him that some of the humans who had been at the banquet were still alive. He wondered, half-sick, how many, and whether they could hold out till he could clear the doorway, and, most of all, he found himself thinking of Paula Quinton. Skidding to a stop within fifty yards of the mob, he flung out his arms crucifix-wise to halt the Kragans. Behind, he could hear the Terrans and native-officers shouting commands to form front.

"Give them one clip, reload, and then give them the bayonet!" he ordered. "Shove them off the steps and then clear the porch!"

"One clip, fire, and reload, at will!" somebody passed it on in Kragan.

The hundred rifles let go all at once, and for five seconds they poured a deafening two thousand rounds into the mutineers. There was some fire in reply; a Zirk corporal narrowly missed him with a pistol, he saw the captain's head fly apart when an explosive rifle-bullet hit him, and half a dozen Kragans went down.

"Reload! Set your safeties!" von Schlichten bellowed. "Charge!"

Under human officers, the North Uller Native Infantry would have stood firm. Even under their native-officers and sergeants, they should not have broken as they did, but the best of these had paid for their loyalty to the Company with their lives, and the rest had destroyed their authority by revolting against the source from which it was derived. At that, the Skilkan peasantry who made up the Tenth Infantry and the Zirk cavalrymen tried briefly to fight as individuals, shrieking *"Znidd suddabit!"* until the Kragans were upon them, stabbing and shooting. They drove the rioters from the steps or killed them there, they wiped out those who had gotten into the semicircle of the storm-porch. The inside doors, von Schlichten saw, were open, but beyond them were Terrans and a dozen or so Kragans. Hideyoshi O'Leary and Barney Mordkovitz seemed to be in command of these.

"We had about thirty seconds' warning," Mordkovitz reported, "and the Kragans in the hall bought us another sixty seconds. Of course, we all had our pistols...."

"Hey! These storm-doors are wedged!" somebody discovered. "Those goddam geek servants...!"

"Yeah, kill any of them you catch," somebody else advised. "If we could have gotten these doors closed...."

The mob, driven from the steps, was trying to reform and renew the attack. From up the street, the machine-guns, silent during the bayonet-fight, began hammering again. The mob surged forward to get out of their fire, and were met by a rifle-blast and a hedge of bayonets at the steps; they surged back, and the machine-guns flailed them again. They started to rush the building from whence the automatic-fire came, and there was a fusillade and a shriek of *"Znidd geek!"* from up the street. They turned and fled in the direction from whence they had come, bullets scourging them from three directions at once.

For a moment, von Schlichten and the three Terrans and eighty-odd Kragans who had survived the fight stood on the steps, weapons poised, seeking more enemies. The machine-guns up the street stuttered a few short bursts and were silent. From behind, the beleaguered Terrans and their Kragan guards were emerging. He saw Jules Keaveney and his wife, Commander Prinsloo of the *Aldebaran*, Harry Quong and Bogdanoff. Ah, there she was! He heaved a breath of relief and waved to her.

The Kragans were already setting about their after-battle chores. About twenty of them spread out on guard; the others, by fours, went into the street, one covering with his rifle while the other three checked on their own casualties, used the short, leaf-shaped swords they carried to slash off the heads of enemy wounded, and collected weapons and ammunition. A couple of hundred more Kragans, led by Native-Major Kormork, the co-parent of young with King Kankad, came up at the double and stopped in front of Company House.

"We were in quarters, aboard the *Aldebaran* and in the guesthouse at the airport," Kormork reported. "We were attacked, fifteen minutes ago, by a mob. We took ten minutes beating them off, and five more getting here. I sent Native-Captain Zeerjeek and the rest of the force to retake the supply-depot and the shops and lorry hangars, which had been taken, and relieve the military airport, which is under attack."

There was still firing from the commercial airport and the smaller military airfield. Once there was a string of heavy explosions that sounded like 80-mm rockets.

"Good enough. I hope you didn't spread yourself out too thin. What's the situation at the commercial airport?"

"The two ships, the *Aldebaran* and the freighter *Northern Star*, are both safe," Kormork replied. "I saw them go on contragravity and rise to about a hundred feet."

"Whose crowd is that you have?" he asked the Terran lieutenant who had taken over command of the first force of Kragans.

"Company 6, Eighteenth Rifles, sir. We were on duty at the guardhouse; fighting broke out in the direction of the native barracks. A couple of runners from Captain Retief of Company 4 came in with word that he was being attacked by mutineers from the Tenth N.U.N.I. but that he was holding them back. So Captain Charbonneau, who was killed a few minutes ago, left a Terran lieutenant and a Kragan native-lieutenant and a couple of native-sergeants and thirty Kragans to hold the guardhouse, and brought the rest of us here."

Von Schlichten nodded. "You'd pass the military airport and the power-plant, wouldn't you?" he asked.

"Yes, sir. The military airport's holding out, and I saw the red-and-yellow danger-lights on the fence around the power-plant."

That meant the power-plant was, for the time, safe; somebody'd turned twenty thousand volts into the fence.

"All right. I'm setting up my command post at the telecast station, where the communication equipment is." He turned to the crowd that had come out onto the porch from inside. "Where's Colonel Cheng-Li?"

"Here, general." The Intelligence and Constabulary officer pushed through the crowd. "I was on the phone, talking to the military airport, the commercial airport, ordnance depot, spaceport, ship-docks and power-plant. All answer. I'm afraid Pop Goode, at the city power-plant, is done for; nobody answers there, but the TV-pickup is still on in the load-dispatcher's room, and the place is full of geeks. Colonel Jarman's coming here with a lorry to get combat-car crews; he's short-handed. Port-Captain Leavitt has all the native labor at the airport and spaceport herded into a repair dock; he's keeping them covered with the forward 90-mm gun of the *Northern Star*. Lorry-hangars, repair-shops and maintenance-yards don't answer."

"That's what I was going to ask you. Good enough. Harry Quong, Hassan Bogdanoff!"

His command-car crew front-and-centered.

"I want you to take Colonel O'Leary up, as soon as my car's brought here.... Hid, you go up and see what's going on. Drop flares where there isn't any light. And take a look at the native-labor camp and the equipment-park, south of the reservation.... Kormork, you take all your gang, and half these soldiers from the Eighteenth, here, and help clear the native-troops barracks. And don't bother taking any prisoners; we can't spare personnel to guard them."

Kormork grinned. The taking of prisoners had always been one of those irrational Terran customs which no Ulleran regarded with favor, or even comprehension.

VIII
Authority of Governor-General von Schlichten

There was fresh intelligence from Konkrook, by the time he returned to the telecast station. Mutiny had broken out there among the laborers and native troops, who outnumbered the Terrans and their Kragan mercenaries on Gongonk Island by five thousand to five hundred and fifteen hundred respectively. The attempt to relieve Jaikark's palace had been called off before the relief-force could be sent; there was heavy and confused fighting all over the island, and most of the combat contragravity and about half the Kragan Rifles had had to be committed to defend the Company farms across the Channel, on the mainland, south of the city. There had also been an urgent call for help from Colonel Rodolfo MacKinnon, in command of Company troops at the Keegark Residency, and another from the Residency at Kwurk, one of the Free Cities on the eastern shore of Takkad Sea.

He called Keegark; a girl, apparently one of the civilian telecast technicians, answered.

"We must have help, General von Schlichten," she told him. "The native troops, all but two hundred Kragans, have mutinied. They have everything here except Company House-docks, airport, everything. We're trying to hold out, but there are thousands of them. Our Takkad Native Infantry, soldiers of King Orgzild's army, and townspeople. They all seem to have firearms...."

"What happened to Eric Blount and your Resident-Agent, Mr. Lemoyne?"

"We don't know. They were at the Palace, talking to King Orgzild. We've tried to call the Palace, but we can't get through, general, we must have help...."

A call came in, a few minutes later, from Krink, five hundred miles to the northeast across the mountains; the Resident-Agent there, one Francis Xavier Shapiro, reported rioting in the city and an attempted palace-revolution against King Jonkvank, and that the Residency was under attack. By way of variety, it was the army of King Jonkvank that had mutinied; the Sixth North Uller Native Infantry and the two companies of Zirk cavalry at Krink were still loyal, along with the Kragans.

There was a pattern to all this. Von Schlichten stood staring at the big map, on the wall, showing the Takkad Sea area at the Equatorial Zone, and the country north of it to the pole, the area of Uller occupied by the Company. He was almost beginning to discern the underlying logic of the past half-hour's events when Keaveney, the Skilk Resident, blundered into him in a half-daze.

"Sorry, general, didn't see you." His face was ashen, and his jowls sagged. Von Schlichten wondered if there could be another spectacle so woe-begone as a back-slapping extrovert with the bottom knocked out of him. "My God, it's happening all over Uller! Not just here at Skilk; everywhere where we have a residency or a trading-station. Why, it's the end of all of us!"

"It's not quite that bad, Mr. Keaveney." He looked at his watch. It was now nearly an hour since the native troops here at Skilk had mutinied. Insurrections like this usually succeeded or failed in the first hour. It was a little early to be certain, but he was beginning to suspect that this one hadn't succeeded. "If we all do our part, we'll come out of it all right," he told Keaveney, more cheerfully than he felt, then turned to ask Brigadier-General Mordkovitz how the fighting was going at the native-troops barracks.

"Not badly, general. Colonel Jarman's got some contragravity up and working. They blew out all four of the Tenth N.U.N.I.'s barracks; the Tenth and the Zirks are trying to defend the cavalry barracks. Some of our Kragans managed to slip around behind the cavalry stables. They're leading out hipposaurs, and sniping at the rear of the cavalry barracks."

"That'll give us some cavalry of our own; a lot of these Kragans are good riders....How about the repair-shops and maintenance-yard and lorry-hangars? I don't want these geeks getting hold of that equipment and using it against us."

"Kormork's outfit are trying to take back the lorry-hangars. Jarman's got a couple of airjeeps and a combat-car helping them."

"...won't be one of us left by this time tomorrow," Keaveney was wailing, to Paula Quinton and another woman. "And the Company is finished!"

"We'd better get him a drink, or a cup of coffee, general," Mordkovitz suggested. "With a knockout-drop in it."

Colonel Cheng-Li, the Intelligence officer, seemed to have somewhat the same idea. He approached Keaveney and tried to quiet him. At the same time, a woman in black slacks and an orange sweater-the one whose pursuers had been overrun by the Kragans at the beginning of the fighting-approached von Schlichten.

"General, King Kankad's calling," she said. "He's on the screen in booth four."

"Right." To avoid any possibility of misunderstanding, he slipped his geek-speaker into his mouth before entering the booth. Kankad's face was looking out of the screen at him, with Phil Yamazaki, the telecast operator at Kankad's Town, standing behind him.

"Von!" The Kragan spoke almost as though in physical pain. "What can I do to help? I have twenty thousand of my people here who are capable of bearing arms, all with firearms, but I have transport for only five hundred. Where shall I send them?"

Von Schlichten thought quickly. Keegark was finished; the Residency stood in the middle of the city, surrounded by two hundred thousand of King Orgzild's troops and subjects. Since Ullerans were bisexual, the total population, less the senile, crippled, and very young, was the military potential. Sending Kankad's five hundred warriors and his meager contragravity there would be the same as shoveling them into a furnace. The people at Keegark would have to be written off, like the twenty Kragans at Jaikark's palace.

"Send them to Konkrook," he decided. "Them M'zangwe's in command, there; he'll need help to hold the Company farms. Maybe he can find additional transport for you. I'll call him."

"I'll send off what force I can, at once," Kankad promised. "How does it go with you at Skilk?"

"We're holding, so far," he replied. "Paula is with me, here; she sends her friendship."

Captain Inez Malavez, the woman officer in charge of the station, put her head into the booth.

"General! Immediate-urgency message from Colonel O'Leary," she said. "Native laborers from the mine-labor camp are pouring into the mine-equipment park. Colonel O'Leary's used all his rockets and MG-ammunition trying to stop them."

"Call you back, later," von Schlichten told Kankad. "I'll see what Them M'zangwe can do about transport; get what force you can started for Konkrook at once."

He left the booth, removing his geek-speaker. "Barney!" he called. "General Mordkovitz! Who's the ranking officer in direct contact with the Eighteenth Rifles? Major Falkenberg?"

"That's right."

"Well, tell him to get as many of his Kragans as he can spare down to the equipment-park." He turned to Inez Malavez. "You call Jarman; tell him what O'Leary reported, and tell him to get cracking on it. Tell him not to let those geeks get any of that equipment onto contragravity; knock it down as fast as they try to lift out with it. And tell him to see what he can do in the way of troop-carriers or lorries, to get Falkenberg's Rifles to the equipment-park.... How's business at the lorry-hangars and maintenance-yard?"

"Kormork's still working on that," the girl captain told him. "Nothing definite, yet."

In one corner of the big room, somebody had thumbtacked a ten-foot-square map of the Company area to the floor. Paula Quinton and Mrs. Jules Keaveney were on their knees beside it, pushing out handfuls of little pink and white pills that somebody had brought in two bottles from the dispensary across the road, each using a billiard-bridge. The girl in the orange sweater had a handful of scribbled notes, and was telling them where to push the pills. There were other objects on the map, too-pistol-cartridges, and cigarettes, and foil-wrapped food-concentrate wafers. Paula, seeing him, straightened.

"The pink are ours, general," she said. "The white are the geeks." Von Schlichten suppressed a grin; that was the second time he'd heard her use that word, this evening. "The cigarettes are airjeeps, the cartridges are combat-cars, and the wafers are lorries or troop-carriers."

"Not exactly regulation map-markers, but I've seen stranger things used.... Captain Malavez!"

"Yes, sir?" The girl captain, rushing past, her hands full of teleprint-sheets, stopped in mid-stride.

"What we need," he told her, "is a big TV-screen, and a pickup mounted on some sort of a contragravity vehicle at about two to five thousand feet directly overhead, to give us an image of the whole area. Can do?"

"Can try, sir. We have an eight-foot circular screen that ought to do all right for two thousand feet. I'll implement that at once."

Going into a temporarily idle telecast booth, he called Konkrook. First he spoke to a civilian who chewed a dead cigar, and then he got Themistocles M'zangwe on the screen.

"How is it, now?" he asked.

"Getting a little better," the Graeco-African replied. "Half an hour ago, we were shooting geeks out the windows, here; now we have them contained between the spaceport and the native-troops and labor barracks, and down the east side of the island to the farms. We have the wire around the farms on the island electrified, and we're using almost all our combat contragravity to keep the farms on the mainland clear." He hesitated for a moment. "Did you hear about Eric and Lemoyne?"

Von Schlichten shook his head.

"We just got a call from Rodolfo MacKinnon. He took a couple of prisoners and made them talk. The whole party that were at Orgzild's palace were massacred. Some of them were lucky enough to get killed fighting. The geeks took Eric and Hendrik alive; rolled them in a puddle of thermoconcentrate fuel and set fire to them. When we can spare the contragravity, we're going to drop something on the Kee-geek embassy, over in town."

"Well, that was what I wanted to call you about-contragravity." He told M'zangwe about King Kankad's offer. "His crowd ought to be coming in in a couple of hours. What can you scrape up to send to Kankad's Town to airlift Kragans in?"

"Well, we have three hundred-and-fifty-foot gun-cutters, one 90-mm gun apiece. The *El-moran*, the *Gaucho*, and the *Bushranger*. But they're not much as transports, and we need them here pretty badly. Then, we have five fertilizer and charcoal scows, and a lot of heavy transport lorries, and two one-eighty-foot pickup boats."

"How about the *Piet Joubert*?" von Schlichten asked. "She was due in Konkrook from the east about 1300 today, wasn't she?"

M'zangwe swore. "She got in, all right. But the geeks boarded her at the dock, within twenty minutes after things started. They tried to lift out with her, and the Channel Battery shot her down into Konkrook Channel, off the Fifty Sixth Street docks."

"Well, you couldn't let the geeks have her, to use against us. What do you hear from the other ships?"

"*Procyon*'s at Grank; we haven't had any reports of any kind from there, which doesn't look so good. The *Northern Lights* is at Grank, too. The *Oom Paul Kruger* should have been at Bwork, in the east, when the gun went off. And the *Jan Smuts* and the *Christiaan De Wett* were both at Keegark; we can assume Orgzild has both of them."

"All right. I'm sending *Aldebaran* to Kankad's, to pick up more reenforcements for you."

"We can use them! And with *Aldebaran*, we ought to be able to take the offensive against the city by this time tomorrow. Anything else?"

"Not at the moment. I'll see about getting *Aldebaran* sent off, now."

Leaving the booth, he heard, above the clatter of communications-machines and hubbub of voices, Jules Keaveney arguing contentiously. Evidently Colonel Cheng-Li's efforts to drag the Resident out of his despondency had been an excessive success.

"But it's crazy! Not just here; everywhere on Uller!" Keaveney was saying. "How did they do it? They have no telecast equipment."

"You have me stopped, Jules," Mordkovitz was replying. "I know a lot of rich geeks have receiving sets, but no sending sets."

The pattern that had been tantalizing von Schlichten took visible shape in his mind. For a moment, he shelved the matter of the *Aldebaran*.

"They didn't need sending equipment, Barney," he said. "They used ours."

"What do you mean?" Keaveney challenged.

"Look what happened. Sid Harrington was poisoned in Konkrook. The news, of course, was sent out at once, as the geeks knew it would be, to every residency and trading-station on Uller, and that was the signal they'd agreed upon, probably months in advance. All they had to do was have that geek servant put poison in Harrington's whiskey, and we did the rest."

"Well, what was our intelligence doing-sleeping?" Keaveney demanded angrily.

"No, they were writing reports for your civil administration blokes to stuff in the wastebasket, and being called mailed-fist-and-rattling-saber alarmists for their pains." He turned away from Keaveney. "Barney, where's Dirk Prinsloo?"

"Aboard his ship. He hitched a ride to the airport with Jarman, when he was here picking up air-crews."

"Call him. Tell him to take the *Aldebaran* to Kankad's Town, at once; as soon as he arrives there, which ought to be about 1100, he's to pick up all the Kragans he can pack aboard and take them to Konkrook. From then on, he'll be under Them M'zangwe's orders."

"To Konkrook?" Keaveney fairly howled. "Are you nuts? Don't you think we need reenforcements here, too?"

"Yes, I do. I'm going to try to get them," von Schlichten told him. "Now pipe down and get out of people's way."

He crossed the room, to where two Kragans, a male sergeant, and the ubiquitous girl in the orange sweater were struggling to get a big circular TV-screen up, then turned to look at the situation-map. A girl tech-sergeant was keeping Paula Quinton and Mrs. Jules Keaveney informed.

"Start pushing geeks out of the Fifth Zirk Cavalry barracks," the sergeant was saying. "The one at the north end, and the one next to it; they're both on fire, now." She tossed a slip into the wastebasket beside her and glanced at the next slip. "And more pink pills back of the barracks and stables, and move them a little to the northwest; Kragans as skirmishers, to intercept geeks trying to slip away from the cavalry barracks."

"Though why we want to do that, I don't know," Mrs. Keaveney said, pushing out a handful of pink pills with her billiard-bridge. "Let them go, and good riddance!"

"I never did like this bridge-of-silver-for-a-fleeing-enemy idea," Paula Quinton said, evicting token-mutineers from the two northern barracks. "There's usually two-way traffic on bridges. Kill them here and we won't have to worry about keeping them out."

Of course, it was easy to be bloodthirsty about pink pills and white pills. Once, on a three-months' reaction-drive voyage from Yggdrasill to Loki, he had taught a couple of professors of extraterrestrial zoology to play *kriegspiel*, and before the end of the trip, he was being horrified by the callous disregard they showed for casualties. But little Paula had the right idea; dead enemies don't hit back.

A young Kragan with his lower left arm in a sling and a daub of antiseptic plaster over the back of his head came up and gave him a radioprint slip. Guido Karamessinis, the Resident-Agent at Grank, had reported, at last. The city, he said, was quiet, but King Yoorkerk's troops had seized the Company airport and docks, taken the *Procyon* and the *Northern Lights* and put guards aboard them, and were surrounding the Residency. He wanted to know what to do.

Von Schlichten managed to get him on the screen, after a while.

"It looks as though Yoorkerk's trying to play both sides at once," he told the Grank Resident. "If the rebellion's put down, he'll come forward as your friend and protector; if we're wiped out elsewhere, he'll yell '*Znidd suddabit!*' and swamp you. Don't antagonize him; we can't afford to fight this war on any more fronts than we are now. We'll try to do something to get you unfrozen, before long."

He called Krink again. A girl with red-gold hair and a dusting of freckles across her nose answered.

"How are you making out?" he asked.

"So far, fine, general. We're in complete control of the Company area, and all our native troops, not just the Kragans, are with us. Jonkvank's pushed the mutineers out of his palace, and we're keeping open a couple of streets between there and here. We air-lifted all our Kragans and half the Sixth N.U.N.I. to the Palace, and we have the Zirks patrolling the streets on 'saurback. Now, we have our lorries and troop-carriers out picking up elements of Jonkvank's loyal troops outside town."

"Who's doing the rioting, then?"

She named three of Jonkvank's regiments. "And the city hoodlums, and priests from the temples of one sect that followed Rakkeed, and Skilkan fifth columnists. Mr. Shapiro can give you the details. Shall I call him?"

"Never mind. He's probably busy, he's not as easy on the eyes as you are, and you're doing all right....How long do you think it'd take, with the equipment you have, to airlift all of Jonkvank's loyal troops into the city?"

"Not before this time tomorrow."

"All right. Are you in radio communication with Jonkvank now?"

"Full telecast, audio-visual," the girl replied. "Just a minute, general."

He put in his geek-speaker. The screen exploded into multi-colored light, then cleared. Within a few minutes, a saurian Ulleran face was looking out of it at him —a harsh-lined, elderly face, with an old scar, quartz-crusted, along one side.

"Your Majesty," von Schlichten greeted him.

Jonkvank pronounced something intended to correspond to von Schlichten's name. "We have image-met under sad circumstances, general," he said.

"Sad for both of us, King Jonkvank; we must help one another. I am told that your soldiers in Krink have risen against you, and that your loyal troops are far from the city."

"Yes. That was the work of my War Minister, Hurkkurk, who was in the pay of King Firkked of Skilk, may Jeels devour him alive! I have Hurkkurk's head here somewhere, if you want to see it, but that will not bring my loyal soldiers to Krink any sooner."

"Dead traitors' heads do not interest me, King Jonkvank," von Schlichten replied, in what he estimated that the Krinkan king would interpret as a tone of cold-blooded cruelty. "There are too many traitors' heads still on traitors' shoulders....What regiments are loyal to you, and where are they now?"

Jonkvank began naming regiments and locating them, all at minor provincial towns at least a hundred miles from Krink.

"Hurkkurk did his work well; I'm afraid you killed him too mercifully," von Schlichten said. "Well, I'm sending the *Northern Star* to Krink. She can only bring in one regiment at a trip, the way they're scattered; which one do you want first?"

Jonkvank's mouth, until now compressed grimly, parted in a gleaming smile. He made an exclamation of pleasure which sounded rather like a boy running along a picket fence with a stick.

"Good, general! Good!" he cried. "The first should be the regiment Murderers, at Furnk; they all have rifles like your soldiers. Have them brought to the Great Square, at the Palace here. And then, the regiment Fear-Makers, at Jeelznidd, and the regiment Corpse-Reapers, at...."

"Let that go until the Murderers are in," von Schlichten advised. "They're at Furnk, you say? I'll send the *Northern Star* there, directly."

"Oh, good, general! I will not soon forget this! And as soon as the work is finished here, I will send soldiers to help you at Skilk. There shall be a great pile of the heads of those who had part in this wickedness, both here and there!"

"Good. Now, if you will pardon me, I'll go to give the necessary orders...."

As he left the booth, he saw Hideyoshi O'Leary in front of the situation-map, and hailed him.

"Harry and Hassan are getting the car re-ammoed; they dropped me off here. Want to come up with us and see the show?"

"No, I want you to go to Krink, as soon as Harry brings the car here again." He told O'Leary what he intended doing. "You'll probably have to go around ahead of the *Star* and alert these regiments. And as soon as things stabilize at Krink, prod Jonkvank into airlifting troops here. You're authorized, in my name, to promise Jonkvank that he can assume political control at Skilk, after we've stuffed Firkked's head in the dustbin."

Jules Keaveney, who always seemed to be where he wasn't wanted, heard that and fairly screamed.

"General von Schlichten! That is a political decision! You have no authority to make promises like that; that is a matter for the Governor-General, at least!"

"Well, as of now, and until a successor to Sid Harrington can be sent here from Terra, I'm Governor-General," von Schlichten told him, mentally thanking Keaveney for reminding him of the necessity for such a step. "Captain Malavez! You will send out an all-station telecast, immediately: Military Commander-in-Chief Carlos von Schlichten, being informed of the deaths of both Governor-General Harrington and Lieutenant-Governor Blount, assumes the duties of Governor-General, as of 0001 today." He turned to Keaveney. "Does that satisfy you?" he asked.

"No, it doesn't. You have no authority to assume a civil position of any sort, let alone the very highest position...."

Von Schlichten unbuttoned his holster and took out his authority, letting Keaveney look into the muzzle of it.

"Here it is," he said. "If you're wise, don't make me appeal to it."

Keaveney shrugged. "I can't argue with that," he said. "But I don't fancy the Uller Company is going to be impressed by it."

"The Uller Company," von Schlichten replied, "is six and a half parsecs away. It takes a ship six months to get from here to Terra, and another six months to get back. A radio message takes a little over twenty-one years, each way." He holstered the pistol again. "You were bitching about how we needed reenforcements, a while ago. Well, here's where we have to reverse Clausewitz and use politics as an extension by other means of war."

"That brings up another question, general," one of Keaveney's subordinates said. "Can we hold out long enough for help to get here from Terra?"

"By the time help could reach us from Terra," von Schlichten replied, "we'll either have this revolt crushed, or there won't be a live Terran left on Uller." He felt a brief sadistic pleasure as he watched Keaveney's face sag in horror. "What do you think we'll live on, for a year?" he asked. "On this planet, there's not more than a three months' supply of any sort of food a human can eat. And the ships that'll be coming in until word of our plight can get to Terra won't bring enough to keep us going. We need the farms and livestock and the animal-tissue culture plant at Konkrook, and the farms at Krink and on the plateau back of Skilk, and we need peace and native labor to work them."

Nobody seemed to have anything to say after that, for a while. Then Keaveney suggested that the next ship was due in from Niflheim in three months, and that it could be used to evacuate all the Terrans on Uller.

"And I'll personally shoot any able-bodied Terran who tries to board that ship," von Schlichten promised. "Get this through your heads, all of you. We are going to break this rebellion, and we are going to hold Uller for the Company and the Terran Federation." He looked around him. "Now, get back to work, all of you," he told the group that had formed around him and Keaveney. "Miss Quinton, you just heard me order my adjutant, Colonel O'Leary, on detached duty to Krink. I want you to take over for him. You'll have rank and authority as colonel for the duration of this war."

She was thunderstruck. "But I know absolutely nothing about military matters. There must be a hundred people here who are better qualified than I am...."

"There are, and they all have jobs, and I'd have to find replacements for them, and replacements for the replacements. You won't leave any vacancy to be filled. And you'll learn, fast enough." He went over to the situation-map again, and looked at the arrangement of pink and white pills. "First of all, I want you to call Jarman, at the military airport, and have an airjeep and driver sent around here for me. I'm going up and have a look around. Barney, keep the show going while I'm out, and tell Colonel Quinton what it's all about."

IX

Don't Push Them Anywhere Put Them Back in the Bottle

He looked at his watch, and stood for a moment, pumping the stale air and tobacco-smoke of the telecast station out of his lungs, as the light airjeep let down into the street. Oh-one-fifteen —two hours and a half since the mutiny at the native-troops barracks had broken out. The Company reservation was still ablaze with lights, and over the roof of the hospital and dispensary and test-lab he could see the glare of the burning barracks. There was more fire-glare to the south, in the direction of the mine-equipment park and the mine-labor camp, and from that direction the bulk of the firing was to be heard.

The driver, a young lieutenant who seemed to be of predominantly Malayan and Polynesian blood, slid back the duraglass canopy for him to climb in, then snapped it into place when he had strapped himself into his seat.

"Can you handle the armament, sir?" he asked.

Von Schlichten nodded approvingly. Not a very flattering question, but the boy was right to make sure, before they started out.

"I've done it, once or twice," he understated. "Let's go; I want a look at what's going on down at the equipment-park and the labor-camp, first."

They lifted up, the driver turning the nose of the airjeep in the direction of the flames and explosions and magnesium-lights to the south and tapping his booster-button gently. The vehicle shot forward and came floating in over the scene of the fighting. The situation-map at the improvised headquarters had shown a mixture of pink and white pills in the mine-equipment park; something was going to have to be done about the lag in correcting it, for the area was entirely in the hands of loyal Company troops, and the mob of laborers and mutinous soldiers had been pushed back into the temporary camp where the workers had been gathered to await transportation to the Arctic. As he feared, the rioting workers, many of whom were trained to handle contragravity equipment, had managed to lift up a number of dump-trucks and power-shovels and bulldozers, intending to use them as improvised airtanks, but Jarman's combat-cars had gotten on the job promptly and all of these had been shot down and were lying in wreckage, mostly among the rows of parked mining-equipment.

From the labor-camp, a surprising volume of fire was being directed against the attack which had already started from the retaken equipment-park. This was just another evidence of the failure of Intelligence and the Constabulary-and consequently of himself-to anticipate the brewing storm. There was, of course, practically no chance of keeping Ullerans from having native weapons, swords, knives, even bows and air-rifles, and a certain number of Volund-made trade-quality automatic pistols could be expected, but most of the fire was coming from military rifles, and now and then he could see the furnace-like backflash of a recoilless rifle or a bazooka, or the steady flicker of a machine-gun. Even if a few of these weapons had been brought from the barracks by retreating Tenth Infantry or Fifth Cavalry mutineers, there were still too many.

Hovering above the fighting, aloof from it, he saw six long troop-carriers land and disgorge Kragan Rifles who had been released by the liquidation of resistance at the native-troops barracks. A little later, two airtanks floated in, and then two more, going off contragravity and lumbering on treads to fire their 90-mm rifles. At the same time, combat-cars swooped in, banging away with their lighter auto-cannon and launching rockets. The titanium prefab-huts, set up to house the laborers and intended to be taken north with them for their stay on the polar desert, were simply wiped away. Among the wreckage, resistance was being blown out like the lights of a candelabrum. Push the white pills out, girls, he thought. Don't push them anywhere; put them back in the bottle. This year, there wouldn't be any mining done at the North Pole; next year, the stockholders'll be bitching about their dividend-checks. And a lot of new machine operators are going to have to be trained for next year's mining. If there is any mining, next year.

He took up the hand-phone and called HQ.

"Von Schlichten, what's the wavelength of the officer in command at the equipment-park?"

A voice at the telecast station furnished it; he punched it out.

"Von Schlichten, right overhead. That you, Major Falkenberg? Nice going, major, how are your casualties?"

"Not too bad. Twenty or thirty Kragans and loyal Skilkans, and eight Terrans killed, about as many wounded."

"Pretty good, considering what you're running into. Get many of your Kragans mounted on those hipposaurs?"

"About a hundred, a lot of 'saurs got shot, while we were leading them out from the stables."

"Well, I can see geeks streaming away from the labor-camp, out the south end, going in the direction of the river. Use what cavalry you have on them, and what contragravity you can spare. I'll drop a few flares to show their position and direction."

Anticipating him, the driver turned the airjeep and started toward the dry Hoork River. Von Schlichten nodded approval and told him to release flares when over the fugitives.

"Right," Falkenberg replied. "I'll get on it at once, general."

"And start moving that mine-equipment up into the Company area. Some of it we can put into the air; the rest we can use to build barricades. None of it do we want the geeks getting hold of, and the equipment-park's outside our practical perimeter. I'll send people to help you move it."

"No need to do that, sir; I have about a hundred and fifty loyal North Ullerans-foremen, technicians, overseers-who can handle it."

"All right. Use your own judgment. Put the stuff back of the native-troops barracks, and between the power-plant and the Company office-buildings, and anywhere else you can." The lieutenant nudged him and pushed a couple of buttons on the dashboard.

"Here go the flares, now."

Immediately, a couple of airjeeps pounced in, to strafe the fleeing enemy. Somebody must have already been issuing orders on another wavelength; a number of Kragans, riding hipposaurs, were galloping into the light of the flares.

"Now, let's have a look at the native barracks and the maintenance-yards," he said. "And then, we'll make a circuit around the Reservation, about two or three miles out. I'm not happy about where Firkked's army is."

The driver looked at him. "I've been worrying about that, too, sir," he said. "I can't understand why he hasn't jumped us, already. I know it takes time to get one of these geek armies on the road, but...."

"He's hoping our native troops and the mine laborers will be able to wipe us out, themselves," von Schlichten said. "For the timidity and stupidity of our enemies, Allah make us truly thankful, amen. It's something no commander should depend on, but be glad when it happens. If Firkked had had a couple of regiments on hand outside the reservation to jump us as soon as the Tenth and the Zirks mutinied, he could have swamped us in twenty minutes and we'll all have had our throats cut by now."

There was nothing going on in the area between the native barracks and the mountains except some sporadic firing as small patrols of Kragans clashed with clumps of fleeing mutineers. All the barracks, even those of the Rifles, were burning; the red-and-yellow danger-lights around the power-plant and the water-works and the explosives magazines were still on. Most of the floodlights were still on, and there was still some fighting around the maintenance-yard. It looked as though the survivors of the Tenth N.U.N.I. were in a few small pockets which were being squeezed out.

There was nothing at all going on north of the Reservation; the countryside, by day a checkerboard of walled fields and small villages, was dark, except for a dim light, here and there, where the occupants of some farmhouse had been awakened by the noise of battle. The airjeep dropped lower, and the driver slid open the window beside him; von Schlichten could hear the grunts and snorts and squawks of farm-animals, similarly aroused.

Then, two miles east of the Reservation, he caught a new sound-the flowing, riverlike, murmur of something vast on the move.

"Hear that, lieutenant?" he asked. "Head for it, at about a thousand feet. When we're directly above it, let go some flares."

"Yes, sir." The younger man had lowered his voice to a whisper. "That's geek, headed for the Reservation."

"Maybe Firkked's army," von Schlichten thought aloud. "Or maybe a city mob."

"Not quite noisy enough for a mob, is it, sir?"

"A tired mob," von Schlichten told him. "They'd start out on a run, yelling '*Znidd Suddabit!*' By the time they got across the bridges to this side of the river, they'd be winded. They'd stop for a blow, and then they'd settle down to steady slogging to save their wind. Sometimes a mob like that's worse than a fresh mob. They get stubborn; they act more deliberately."

The noises were growing clearer, louder. He picked up the phone and punched the wavelength of the military airport.

"Von Schlichten, my compliments to Colonel Jarman. Tell him there's a geek mob, or possibly Firkked's regulars, on the main highway from Skilk, two miles east of the Reservation. Get some combat contragravity over here, at once. We'll light them up for you. And tell Colonel Jarman to start flying patrols up and down along the Hoork River; this may not be the only gang that's coming out to see us."

The sounds were directly below, now-the scuffing of horny-soled feet on the dirt road, the clink and rattle of slung weapons, the clicking and squeeking of Ulleran voices.

The lieutenant said, "Here go the flares, sir."

Von Schlichten shut his eyes, then opened them slowly. The driver, upon releasing the flares, had nosed up, banked, turned, and was coming in again, down the road toward the advancing column. Von Schlichten peered into his all-armament sight, his foot on the machine-gun pedal and his fingers on the rocket buttons. The highway below was jammed with geeks, and they were all stopped dead and staring upward, as though hypnotized by the lights. A second later, they had recovered and were shooting-not at the airjeep, but at the four globes of blazing magnesium. Then he had the close-packed mass of non-humanity in his sights; he tramped the pedal and began punching buttons. He still had four rockets left by the time the mob was behind him.

"All right, let's take another pass at them. Same direction."

The driver put the airjeep into a quick loop and came out of it in front of the mob, who now had their backs turned and were staring in the direction in which they had last seen the vehicle. Again, von Schlichten plowed them with rockets and harrowed them with his guns. Some of the Skilkans were trying to get over the high fences on either side of the road-really stockades of petrified tree-trunks. Others were firing, and this time they were shooting at the airjeep. It took one hit from a heavy shellosaur-rifle, and, immediately, the driver banked and turned away from the road.

"Dammit, why did you do that?" von Schlichten demanded, lifting his foot from the gunpedal. "Are you afraid of the kind of popguns those geeks are using?"

"I am not afraid to risk my vehicle, or myself, sir," the lieutenant replied, with the extreme formality of a very junior officer chewing out a very senior one. "I am, however, afraid to risk my passenger. Generals are not expendable, sir; neither are they issued for use as clay pigeons."

He was right, of course. Von Schlichten admitted it. "I'm too old to play cowboy, like this," he said. "Back to the Reservation, telecast station."

Looking back over his shoulder, he saw eight or ten more flares alight, and the ground-flashes of exploding shells and rockets; the air above the road was sparkling with gun-flames. Jarman must have had some contragravity ready to be sent off on the instant.

While he had been out, somebody had gotten a TV-pickup mounted on a contragravity-lifter and run up to two thousand feet, on the end of a steel-tough tensilon mooring-line. The big circular screen was lit, showing the whole Company Reservation, with the surrounding country-side foreshortened by perspective to the distant lights of Skilk. The map had been taken up from the floor, and a big terrain-board had been brought in from the Chief Engineer's office and set up in its place. In front of the screen, Paula Quinton, Barney Mordkovitz, Colonel Cheng-Li, and, conspicuously silent, Jules Keaveney sat drinking coffee and munching sandwiches. Half a dozen Terrans, of both sexes, were working furiously to get the markers which replaced the pink and white pills placed on the board, and one of Captain Inez Malavez's non-coms, with a headset, was getting combat reports directly from the switchboard. Everything was clicking like well-oiled machinery.

On the TV-screen, the Residency area was ablaze with light, and so were the ship-docks, the airport and spaceport, the shops, and the maintenance-yard. On the terrain-board, the latter was now marked as completely in Company hands. The ruins of the native-troops barracks were still burning, and there was a twinkle of orange-red here and there among the ruins of the labor-camp. Much of the equipment for the polar mines had already been shifted into defensible ground. The rest of the circle was dark, except for the distant lights of Skilk, where the nuclear power plant was apparently still functioning in native hands.

Then, without warning, a spot of white light blazed into being southeast of the Company area and southwest of Skilk, followed by another and another. Instantly, von Schlichten glanced up at the row of smaller screens, and on one of them saw the view as picked up by a patrolling airjeep.

The army of King Firkked of Skilk had finally put in its appearance, coming in two columns, one southward from Skilk and the other northward along the west bank of the dry river. The former had crossed over and joined the latter, about three miles south of the Reservation. The scene in the screen was similar to the one he had, himself, witnessed through his armament-sight. The Skilkan regulars had been marching in formation, some on the road and some along parallel lanes and paths. They had the look of trained and disciplined troops, but they had made the same mistake as the rabble that had been shot up on the north side of the Reservation. Unused to attack from the air, they had all halted in place and were gaping open-mouthed, their opal teeth gleaming in the white flare-light. However, before the aircar had passed over them, the lead company of one regiment, armed with Terran rifles, had begun firing.

In the big screen, it could be seen that Colonel Jarman had thrown most of his available contragravity at them, including the combat-cars, that had already started to form the second wave of the attack on the mob to the north. Other flares bloomed in the darkness, and the fiery trails of rockets curved downward to end in yellow flashes on the ground.

The airjeep with the pickup circled back; the troops on the road and in the adjoining fields had broken. The former were caught between the fences which made Ulleran roads such death-traps when under air-attack. The latter had dispersed, and were running away, individually and by squads; at first, it looked like a panic, but he could see officers signaling to the larger groups of fugitives to open out, apparently directing the flight. By this time, there were ten or twelve combat-cars and about twenty airjeeps at work. In the moving view from the pickup-jeep, he saw what looked like a 90-mm rocket land in the middle of a company that was still trying to defend itself with small-arms fire on the road, wiping out about half of them.

"Make the most of it, boys," Barney Mordkovitz, his mouth full of sandwich, was saying. "Heave it to them; you won't get another chance like that at those buggers."

"Why not?" Colonel Paula Quinton wanted to know. Her military education was progressing, but it still had a few gaps to fill in.

"The next time they're air-struck, they won't stay bunched," Mordkovitz replied. "A lot of them didn't stay bunched this time, if you noticed. And they'll keep out from between the fences."

In the large screen, a quick succession of gun-flashes leaped up from the direction of the Hoork River and shells began bursting over the scene of the attack. The screen tuned to the pickup on the airjeep went dead; in the big screen, there was a twinkling of falling fire. Almost at once, thirty or forty rocket-trails converged on the gun-position, and, for a moment, explosions burned like a bonfire.

"They had a 75-mm at the rear of the column," somebody called from the big switchboard. "Lieutenant Kalanang's jeep was hit; Lieutenant Vermaas is cutting in his pickup on the same wavelength."

The small screen lighted again. In the big screen, a cluster of magnesium-lights appeared above where the Skilkan gun had been; in the small screen, there was a stubbled grain-field, pocked with craters, and the bodies of fifteen or twenty natives, all rather badly mangled. An overturned and apparently destroyed 75-mm gun lay on its side.

Five or six fairly large fires had broken out, by this time, around the point of attack. Von Schlichten nodded approvingly.

"I was wondering how long it'd take somebody to think of that," he said. "Granaries and forage-stacks on some of these farms. They'll burn for half an hour, at least." He looked at his watch. "And by that time, it'll be daylight."

"As far as we know, that was the only 75-mm gun Firkked had," Colonel Cheng-Li said. "He has at least six, possibly ten, 40-mm's. It's a wonder we haven't seen anything of them."

"Well, there's no way of being sure," Jules Keaveney said, "but I have an idea they're all at or around the Palace. Firkked knows about how much contragravity we have. He's probably wondering why we aren't bombing him, now."

"He doesn't know we've sold the Palace to King Jonkvank for an army," von Schlichten said. "And that reminds me-how much contragravity could Firkked scrape together, for an attack on us? I've been expecting a geek *Luftwaffe* over here, at any moment."

Colonel Cheng-Li studied the smoking tip of his cigarette for a moment. "Well, Firkked owns, personally, three ten-passenger aircars, a thing like a troop-carrier that he transports some of his courtiers around in, four airjeeps armed with a pair of 15-mm machine-guns apiece, and two big lorries. There are possibly two hundred vehicles of all types in Skilk and the country around, but some of them are in the hands of natives friendly to us and or hostile to Firkked. I can get the exact figures from the Constabulary office at Company House."

"That's close enough," von Schlichten told him. "And there'll be oodles of thermoconcentrate-fuel, and blasting explosives. Colonel Quinton, suppose you call Ed Wallingsby, the Chief Engineer, right away; have him commissioned colonel. Tell him to get to work making this place secure against air attack; tell him to consult with Colonel Jarman. Tell him to get those geeks Leavitt has penned in the repair-dock at the airport and use them to dig slit-trenches and fill sandbags and so on. He can use Kragan limited-duty wounded to guard them....Mr. Keaveney, you'll begin setting up something in the way of an ARP-organization. You'll have to get along on what nobody else wants. You will also consult with Colonel Jarman, and with Colonel Wallingsby. Better get started on it now. Just think of everything around here that could go wrong in case of an air attack, and try to do something about it in advance."

X

The Geek Luftwaffe and the Kragan Airlift

At 0245, an attack developed on the northwestern corner of the Reservation, in the direction of the explosives magazines. It turned out to be relatively trivial. Remnants of the mob that had been broken up by air attack on the road had gotten together and were making rushes in small bands, keeping well spread out. Beating them off took considerable ammunition, but it was accomplished with negligible casualties to the defenders. They finally stopped coming around daylight.

In the meantime, Themistocles M'zangwe called from Konkrook, appearing in the screen with his left arm in a freshly white sling.

"What the hell have you been doing to yourself?" von Schlichten wanted to know.

"Crossbow-bolt, about half an hour ago. A couple of inches lower and acting Brigadier-General Colbert'd have been talking to you, now, instead of me."

"Lucky it didn't have a nitro-capsule on the end. How are you making out? Have Kankad's people started coming in, yet?"

"Oh, yes, about six hundred of them have gotten in already, in the damnedest collection of vehicles you ever saw. Kankad must be using every scrap of contragravity he has; it's a regular airborne Dunkirk-in-reverse. Kankad sent word that he's coming here in person, as soon as he has things organized at his place. And the geeks here have scraped together an air-force of their own-farm-lorries, aircars, that sort of thing-and they're using them to bomb us here and at the mainland farm, mostly with nitroglycerine. We've shot down about twenty of them, but they're still coming. They tried a boat-attack across the Channel; that's how I got this. We've been doing some bombing, ourselves; we made a down payment for Eric Blount and Hendrik Lemoyne. Took a fifty-ton tank off a fuel-lorry, fitted it with a detonator, filled it with thermoconcentrate, and ferried it over on the *Elmoran* and dumped it on the Keegarkan Embassy. It must have landed in the middle of the central court; in about fifteen seconds, flames were coming out every window in the place." His face became less jovial. "We had something pretty bad happen here, too," he said. "That Konkrook Fencibles rabble of Prince Jaizerd's mutinied, along with the others; they got into the hospital and butchered everybody in the place, patients and staff. The Kragans got there too late to save anybody, but they wiped out the Fencibles. Jaizerd himself was the only one they took alive, and he didn't stay that way very long."

"How are you making out with your Civil Administration crowd?"

M'zangwe grimaced. "I haven't had to put any of them under actual arrest, so far, but we've had to keep Buhrmann away from the communications equipment by force. He wanted to call you up and chew you out for not evacuating everybody in the north to Konkrook."

"Is he crazy?"

"No, just scared. He says you're going to get everybody on Uller massacred by detail, when you could save Konkrook by bringing them all here."

"You tell him I'm going to hold this planet, not just one city. Tell him I have a sense of my duty to the Company and its stockholders, if he hasn't; put it in those terms and he may understand you."

"Yes, I'll try that out on Meyerstein, too. He's in a hell of a state about the losses the Banking Cartel are taking on this deal.... Well, I'll call you when there's anything new."

By 0330, it was daylight; the attacks against the northwest corner of the perimeter stopped entirely. Wallingsby had the three-hundred-odd Skilkan laborers at work; he had gathered up all the tarpaulin he could find, and had the two sewing-machines in the tentmaker's shop running on sandbags. Jules Keaveney, to von Schlichten's agreeable surprise, had taken hold of his ARP assignment, and was doing an efficient job in organizing for fire-fighting, damage-control and first aid. Colonel Jarman had his airjeeps and combat-cars working in ever-widening circles over the countryside, shooting up everything in sight that even looked like contragravity equipment. Some of these patrols had to be recalled, around 1030, when sporadic nuisance-sniping began from the side of the mountain to the west. And, along with everything else, Paula Quinton managed, along with her other work, to get a complete digest prepared of the situation elsewhere in the Terran-occupied parts of the planet.

The situation at Konkrook was brightening steadily. The second wave of Kankad's improvised airlift, reenforced by contragravity from Konkrook, had come in; there were now close to two thousand fresh Kragans on Gongonk Island and the mainland farms, Kankad himself with them. The *Aldebaran* had reached Kankad's Town, and was loading another thousand Kragans.... There was nothing more from Keegark. A message from Colonel MacKinnon had come in at dawn, to the effect that the geeks had penetrated his last defenses and that he was about to blow up the Residency; thereafter Keegark went off the air.... By 0730, the *Northern Star* had landed the regiment Murderers, armed with first-quality Terran infantry-rifles and a few machine-guns and bazookas, at the Palace at Krink, and by 0845 she had returned with another regiment, the Jeel-Feeders. The three-lane street connecting the Palace and the Residency had been widened to six, and then to eight....Guido Karamessinis, at Grank, was still at uneasy peace with King Yoorkerk, who was still undecided whether the rebels or the Company were going to be the eventual victors, and afraid to take any irrevocable step in either direction....Eight men and four women, the survivors of a trading-station on the eastern shore of Takkad Sea, reached Konkrook in a lorry; another trading station, on the south shore, reported by telecast that the natives there had refused to rise against them, and had crucified five of Rakkeed's disciples who had come among them preaching *znidd suddabit.*

At 1100, Paula Quinton and Barney Mordkovitz virtually ordered him to get some sleep. He went to his quarters at Company House, downed a spaceship-captain's-size drink of honey-rum, and slept until 1600. As he dressed and shaved, he could hear, through the open window, the slow sputter of small-arms' fire, punctuated by the occasional *whump-whump-whump* of 40-mm auto-cannon or the hammering of a machine-gun.

Returning to his command-post at the telecast station, the terrain-board showed that the perimeter of defense had been pushed out in a bulge at the northwest corner; the TV-screen pictured a crude breast-work of petrified tree-trunks, sandbags, mining machinery, packing-cases and odds-and-ends, upon which Wallingsby's native laborers were working under guard while a skirmish-line of Kragans had been thrown out another four or five hundred yards and were exchanging pot-shots with Skilkans on the gullied hillside.

"Where's Colonel Quinton?" he asked. "She ought to be taking a turn in the sack, now."

"She's taking one," Major Falkenberg, who had commanded the action at the native-troops barracks and the labor-camp, the night before, told him. "General Mordkovitz chased her off to bed a couple of hours ago, called me in to take her place, and then went out to replace me. Colonel Guilliford's in the hospital; got hit about thirteen hundred. They're afraid he's going to lose a leg."

"That's a bloody shame!" He pointed to the northwest corner of the perimeter on the screen. "Whose idea was that?" he asked. "It's a good one; I ought to have thought of it, myself."

"Your new adjutant," Falkenberg grinned. "She asked somebody what those big domes, up there, were. When they told her there were ten thousand tons of thermoconcentrate, five thousand tons of blasting-explosives, and five tons of plutonium, under them, she damned near fainted, and then she ordered that, right away."

More reports came in. The entire garrison of the small Residency at Kwurk, the most northern of the eastern shore Free Cities, had arrived at Kankad's Town in two hundred-foot contragravity scows and five aircars. Two of the aircars arrived half an hour behind the rest of the refugee flotilla, having turned off at Keegark to pay their respects to King Orgzild. They reported the Keegark Residency in ruins, its central buildings vanished in a huge crater; the *Jan Smuts* and the *Christiaan De Wett* were still in the Company docks, both apparently damaged by the blast which had destroyed the Residency. One of the aircars had rocketed and machine-gunned some Keegarkans who appeared to be trying to repair them; the other blew up King Orgzild's nitroglycerine plant. Von Schlichten called Konkrook and ordered a bombing-mission against Keegark organized, to make sure the two ships stayed out of service.

The *Northern Star* was still bringing loyal troops into Krink. King Jonkvank, whom von Schlichten called, was highly elated.

"We are killing traitors wherever we find them!" he exulted. "The city is yellow with their blood; their heads are piled everywhere! How is it with you at Skilk?"

"We have killed many, also," von Schlichten boasted. "And tonight, we will kill more; we are preparing bombs of great destruction, which we will rain down upon Skilk until there is not one stone left upon another, or one infant of a day's age left alive!"

Jonkvank reacted as he was intended to. "Oh, no, general, don't do all that!" he exclaimed. "You promised me that I should have Skilk, on the word of a Terran. Are you going to give me a city of ruins and corpses? Ruins are no good to anybody, and I am not a Jeel, to eat corpses."

Von Schlichten shrugged. "When you are strong, you can flog your enemies with a whip; when you are weak, all you can do is kill them. If I had five thousand more troops, here...."

"Oh, I will send troops, as soon as I can," Jonkvank hastened to promise. "All my best regiments: the Murderers, the Jeel-Feeders, the Corpse-Reapers, the Devastators, the Fear-Makers. But, now that we have stopped this sinful rebellion, here, I can't take chances that it will break out again as soon as I strip the city of troops."

Von Schlichten nodded. Jonkvank's argument made sense; he would have taken a similar position, himself.

"Well, get as many as you can over here, as soon as possible," he said. "We'll try to do as little damage to Skilk as we can, but..."

At 1830, Paula joined him for her breakfast, while he sat in front of the big screen, eating his dinner. There had been light ground-action along the southern end of the perimeter-King Firkked's regulars, reenforced by Zirk tribesmen and levies of townspeople, all of whom seemed to have firearms, were filtering in through the ruins of the labor-camp and the wreckage of the equipment-park —and there was renewed sniping from the mountainside. The long afternoon of the northern autumn dragged on; finally, at 2200, the sun set, and it was not fully dark for another hour. For some time, there was an ominous quiet, and then, at 0030, the enemy began attacking in force, driving herds of livestock-lumbering six-legged brutes bred by the North Ullerans for food-to test the defenses for electrified wire and land-mines. Most of these were shot down or blown up, but a few got as far as the wire, which, by now, had been strung and electrified completely around the perimeter.

Behind them came parties of Skilkan regulars with long-handled insulated cutters; a couple of cuts were made in the wire, and a section of it went dead. The line, at this point, had been rather thinly held; the defenders immediately called for air-support, and Jarman ordered fifteen of his remaining twenty airjeeps and five combat-cars into the fight. No sooner were they committed than the radar on the commercial airport control-tower picked up air vehicles approaching from the north, and the air-raid sirens began howling and the searchlights went on.

As a protection from the sudden fury of the summer and winter gales, the buildings were all low, thick-walled, and provided with steel doors and window-shutters which were electrically operated and centrally controlled. These slammed shut in every occupied building. The contra-gravity which had been sent to support the ground-defense at the south side of the Reservation turned to meet this new threat, and everything else available, including the four heavy airtanks, lifted up. Meanwhile, guns began firing from the ground and from rooftops.

There had been four aircars, ordinary passenger vehicles equipped with machine-guns on improvised mounts, and ten big lorries converted into bombers, in the attack. All the lorries, and all but one of the makeshift fighter-escort, were shot down, but not before explosive and thermoconcentrate bombs were dumped all over the place. One lorry emptied its load of ther-moconcentrate-bombs on the control-building at the airport, starting a raging fire and putting the radar out of commission. A repair-shop at the ordnance-depot was set on fire, and a quan-tity of small-arms and machine-gun ammunition piled outside for transportation to the outer defenses blew up. An explosive bomb landed on the roof of the building between Company House and the telecast station, blowing a hole in the roof and demolishing the upper floor. And another load of thermoconcentrate, missing the power-plant, set fire to the dry grass between it and the ruins of the native-troops barracks.

Before the air-attack had been broken up, the soldiers of King Firkked and their irregular supporters were swarming through the dead section of wire. They had four or five big farm-trac-tors, nuclear-powered but unequipped with contragravity-generators, which they were using like ground-tanks of the First Century. This attack penetrated to the middle of the Reservation before it was stopped and the attackers either killed or driven out; for the first time since daybreak, the red-and-yellow lights came on around the power-plant.

As soon as the combined air and ground attack was beaten off, von Schlichten ordered all his available contragravity up, flying patrols around the Reservation and retaliatory bombing missions against Skilk, and began bombarding the city with his 90-mm guns. A number of fires broke out, and at about 0200 a huge expanding globe of orange-red flame soared up from the city.

"There goes Firkked's thermoconcentrate stock," he said to Paula, who was standing beside him in front of the screen.

Half an hour later, he discovered that he had been overly optimistic. Much of the enemy's supply of Terran thermoconcentrate had been destroyed, but enough remained to pelt the Reservation and the Company buildings with incendiaries, when a second and more severe air-attack developed, consisting of forty or fifty makeshift lorry-bombers and fifteen aircars. The previous attack von Schlichten had viewed in the screen at the telecast station; it was his questionable good fortune to observe the second one directly, having been out inspecting the defenses around the ordnance-depot at the time.

Like the first, the second air-attack was beaten off, or, more exactly, down. Most of the enemy contragravity was destroyed; at least two dozen vehicles crashed inside the Reservation. As in the first instance, there was a simultaneous ground attack from the southern side, with a demonstration-attack at the north end. For a while, von Schlichten found himself fighting hand-to-hand, first with his pistol and then, when his ammunition was gone, with a picked-up rifle and bayonet. It was full daylight before the last of the attackers was either killed or driven out.

Five minutes later, while he was reloading his pistol-clips with salvaged cartridges, the *Northern Star* came bulking over the mountains from the west.

XI
Of Princedoms Which Have Been Won by Conquest

Holstering his pistol, he raced for the telecast station, to receive a call from a Colonel Khalid ib'n Talal, a Zanzibar Arab, aboard the approaching ship.

"I've one of Jonkvank's regiments, the Jeel-Feeders, armed with Terran 9-mm rifles and a few bazookas; I have a company of our Zirks, with their mounts, and a battalion of the Sixth N.U.N.I.; I also have four 90-mm guns, Terran-manned," he reported. "What's the situation, general, and where do you want me to land?"

Von Schlichten described the situation succinctly, in an ancient and unprintable military cliche. "Try landing south of the Reservation, a little west of the ruins of the labor-camp," he advised. "The bulk of Firkked's army is in that section, and I want them run out as soon as possible. We'll give you all the contragravity and fire support we can."

The *Northern Star* let down slowly, firing her guns and dropping bombs; as she descended, rifle-fire spurted from all her lower-deck portholes. There was cheering, human and Ulleran, from inside the battered defense-perimeter; combat-cars, airjeeps, and improvised bombers lifted out to strafe the Skilkans on the ground, and the four airtanks moved out to take position and open fire with their 90-mm's, helping to flush King Firkked's regulars and auxiliaries out of the gullies and ruins and drive them south along the mountain, away from where the ship would land and also away from the city of Skilk. The *Northern Star* set down quickly, and troops and artillery began to be unloaded, joining in the fighting.

It was five hundred miles to Krink; three hours after lifting out, the *Northern Star* was back again, with two more of King Jonkvank's infantry regiments, and by 1300, when the fourth load arrived from Krink, the fighting was entirely on the eastern bank of the dry Hoork River.

This last contingent of reenforcements was landed in the eastern suburbs of Skilk and began fighting their way into the city from the rear.

It was evident, however, that the pacification of Skilk would not be accomplished as rapidly as von Schlichten wished-street fighting, against a determined enemy, is notoriously slow work-and he decided to risk the *Northern Star* in an attack against the Palace itself, and, over the objections of Paula Quinton, Jules Keaveney, and Barney Mordkovitz, to lead the attack in person.

Inside the city, he found that the Zirk cavalry from Krink had thrust up one of the broader streets to within a thousand yards of the Palace, and, supported by infantry, contragravity, and a couple of airtanks, were pounding and hacking at a mass of Skilkans whose uniform lack of costume prevented distinguishing between soldiery and townsfolk. Very few of these, he observed, seemed to be using firearms; with his glasses, he could see them shooting with long northern air-rifles and a few Takkad Sea crossbows. Either weapon would shoot clear through a Terran or half-way through an Ulleran at fifty yards, but at over two hundred they were almost harmless. There were a few fires still burning from the bombardment of the night before-Ulleran, and particularly North Ulleran, cities did not burn well-and the blaze which had consumed the bulk of Firkked's stock of thermoconcentrate fuel had long ago burned out, leaving an area of six or eight blocks blackened and lifeless.

The ship let down, while the six combat-cars which had accompanied her buzzed the Palace roof, strafing it to keep it clear, and the Kragans aboard fired with their rifles. She came to rest on seven-eighths weight reduction, and even before the gangplanks were run out, the Kragans were dropping to the flat roof, running to stairhead penthouses and tossing grenades into them.

The taking of the Palace was a gruesome business. Knowing exactly how much mercy they would have shown had they been storming the Residency, Firkked's soldiers and courtiers fought desperately and had to be exterminated, floor by floor, room by room, hallway by hallway. There was some attempt at escape from the ground floor as von Schlichten and his Kragans fought their way down from above, but the *Northern Star* and her escort of combat-cars and airjeeps bombed and machine-gunned and rocketed the fugitives from above, and the loyal Zirk cavalry, bursting through the mob, came up shooting and lancing. By this time, an aircar fitted with a sound-amplifier was circling overhead, while a loyal native-officer of the Sixth N.U.N.I. shouted offers of quarter and orders to the troops to spare any who surrendered.

Driving down from above, von Schlichten and his Kragans slithered over floors increasingly greasy with yellow Ulleran blood. He had picked up a broadsword at the foot of the first stairway down; a little later, he tossed it aside in favor of another, better balanced and with a better guard. There was a furious battle at the doorways of the throne room; finally, climbing over the bodies of their own dead and the enemy's, they were inside.

Here there was no question of quarter whatever, at least as long as Firkked lived; North Ulleran nobles did not surrender under the eyes of their king, and North Ulleran kings did not surrender their thrones alive. There was also a tradition, of which von Schlichten was mindful, that a king must only be killed by his conqueror, in personal combat, with steel.

With a wedge of Kragan bayonets around him and the picked-up broadsword in his hand, he fought his way to the throne, where Firkked waited, a sword in one of his upper hands, his Spear of State in the other, and a dagger in each lower hand. With his left hand, von Schlichten detached the bayonet from the rifle of one of his followers and went forward, trying not to think of the absurdity of a man of the Sixth Century A.E., the representative of a civilized Chartered Company, dueling to the death with swords with a barbarian king for a throne he had promised to another barbarian, or of what could happen on Uller if he allowed this four-armed monstrosity to kill him.

It was not as bad as it looked, however. The ornate Spear of State, in spite of its long, cruel-looking blade, was not an especially good combat-weapon, at least for one hand, and Firkked seemed confused by the very abundance of his armament. After a few slashes and jabs, von Schlichten knocked the unwieldy thing from his opponent's hand. This raised a fearful ululation from the Skilkan nobility, who had stopped fighting to watch the duel; evidently it was the very worst sort of a bad omen. Firkked, seemingly relieved to be disencumbered of the thing, caught his sword in both hands and aimed a roundhouse swing at von Schlichten's head; von Schlichten dodged, crippled one of Firkked's lower hands with a quick slash, and lunged at the royal belly. Firkked used his remaining dagger to parry, backed a step closer to his throne, and took another swing with his sword, which von Schlichten parried on the bayonet in his left hand. Then, backing, he slashed at the inside of Firkked's leg with the thousand-year-old *coup-de-Jarnac*. Firkked, unable to support the weight of his dense-tissued body on one leg, stumbled; von Schlichten ran him neatly through the breast with his sword and through the throat with the bayonet.

There was silence in the throne room for an instant, and then, with a horrible collective shriek, the Skilkans threw down their weapons. One of von Schlichten's Kragans slung his rifle and picked up the Spear of State with all four hands, taking his post ceremoniously behind the victor. A couple of others dragged the body of Firkked to the edge of the dais, and one of them drew his leaf-shaped short-sword and beheaded it.

At mid-afternoon, von Schlichten was on the roof of the Palace, holding the Spear of State, with Firkked's head impaled on the point, while a Terran technician aimed an audio-visual recorder.

"This," he said, with the geek-speaker in his mouth, "is King Firkked's Spear of State, and here, upon it, is King Firkked's head. Two days ago, Firkked was at peace with the Company, and Firkked was King in Skilk. If he had not dared raise his feeble hand against the might of the Uller Company, he would still be alive, and his Spear would still be borne behind him. So must all those who rise against the Company perish.... Cut."

The camera stopped. A Kragan came forward and took the Spear of State, with its grisly burden, carrying it to a nearby wall and leaning it up, like a piece of stage property no longer required for this scene but needed for the next. Von Schlichten took out his geek-speaker, wiped and pouched it, and took his cigarette case from his pocket.

"Well, this is the limit!" Paula Quinton, who had come up during the filming of the scene, exploded. "I thought you had to kill him yourself in order to encourage your soldiers; I didn't think you wanted to make a movie of it to show your friends. I'm through; you can find yourself a new adjutant!"

Von Schlichten tapped the cigarette on the gold-and-platinum case and stared at her through his monocle.

"You can't resign," he told her. "Resignations of officers are not being accepted until the end of hostilities. In any case, I shouldn't care to have you go; you're the best adjutant, Hideyoshi O'Leary not excepted, I ever had. Sit down, colonel." He lit the cigarette. "Your politico-military education still needs a little filling in.

"At Grank, we have two ships. One is the *Northern Lights*, sister ship of the *Northern Star*. The other is the cruiser *Procyon*, the only real warship on Uller, with a main battery of four 200-mm guns. How King Yoorkerk was able to get control of those ships I don't know, but there will be a board of inquiry and maybe a couple of courts-martial, when things get stabilized to a point where we can afford such luxuries. As it is, we need those ships desperately, and as soon as he gets in, I'm sending Hideyoshi O'Leary to Grank with the *Northern Star* and a load of Kragan Rifles, to pry them loose. The audio-visual of which this is the last scene is going to be one of the crowbars he's going to use."

"Oh! I get it!" Her eyes widened with pleasure at having finally caught on; she accepted the cigarette and the light von Schlichten offered. "Good old *nervenkrieg*!"

"Yes. A little idea I adapted from my Nazi ancestors of four hundred and fifty years ago. Hideyoshi's going to treat King Yoorkerk to a movie-show. Want to bet he won't loosen up and release *Procyon* and *Northern Lights* and unblockade the Grank Residency after he sees that shot of Firkked's head leering at him off the point of that overgrown asagai? As I said, that's only the last scene, too. I've been having scenes shot all through this fight; some of them are really horrifying."

"But why did you have to fight Firkked yourself?" she asked. "You took an awful chance, with two hands to his four."

"Not so awful, remember what I told you about the physical limitations of Ullerans. But I had to kill him myself, with a sword; according to local custom that makes me King of Skilk."

"Why, your Majesty!" She rose and curtsied mockingly. "But I thought you were going to make Jonkvank King of Skilk."

He shook his head. "Just Viceroy," he corrected. "I'm handing the Spear of State down to him, not up to him; he'll reign as my vassal, and, consequently, as vassal of the Company, and before long, he won't be much more at Krink either. That'll take a little longer-there'll have to be military missions, and economic missions, and trade-agreements, and all the rest of it, first-but he's on the way to becoming a puppet-prince."

Half an hour later, a large and excessively ornate air-launch, specially built at the Konkrook shipyards for King Jonkvank, was sighted coming over the mountain from the east. An escort of combat-cars was sent to meet it, and a battalion of Kragans and the survivors of Firkked's court were drawn up on the Palace roof.

"His Majesty, Jonkvank, King of Krink!" the former herald of King Firkked's court, now herald to King Carlos von Schlichten, shouted, banging on a brass shield with the flat of his sword, as Jonkvank descended from his launch, attended by a group of his nobles and his Spear of State, with Hideyoshi O'Leary and Francis N. Shapiro shepherding them. As the guests advanced across the roof, the herald banged again on his shield.

"His Majesty, Carlos von Schlichten," —which came out more or less as Karlok vonk Zlik-denk —"King, by right of combat, of Skilk!"

Von Schlichten advanced to meet his fellow-monarch, his own Spear of State, with Firkked's head still grinning from it, two paces behind him.

Jonkvank stopped, his face contorted with saurian rage.

"What is this?" he demanded. "You told me that I could be King of Skilk; is this how a Terran keeps his word?"

"A Terran's word is always good, Jonkvank," von Schlichten replied, omitting the titles, as was proper in one sovereign addressing another. "My word was that you should reign in Skilk, and my word stands. But these things must be done decently, according to custom and law. I killed Firkked in single combat. Had I not done so, the Spear of Skilk would have been left lying, for any of the young of Firkked to pick up. Is that not the law?"

Jonkvank nodded grudgingly. "It is the law," he admitted.

"Good. Now, since I killed Firkked in lawful manner, his Spear is mine, and what is mine I can give as I please. I now give you the Spear of Skilk, to carry in my name, as I promised."

The Kragan who was carrying the ceremonial weapon tossed the head of Firkked from the point; another Kragan kicked it aside and advanced to wipe the spear-blade with a rag. Von Schlichten took the Spear and gave it to Jonkvank.

"This is not good!" one of the Skilkan nobles protested. He had a better right than any of the others to protest; he had, a few hours before, ridden in at the head of a company of his retainers to swear loyalty to the Company. "That you should rule over us, yes. You killed Firkked in single combat, and you are the soldier of the Company, which is mighty, as all here have seen. But that this foreigner be given the Spear of Skilk, that is not good!"

Some of the others, emboldened by his example, were jabbering agreement.

"Listen, all of you!" von Schlichten shouted. "Here is no question of Krink ruling over Skilk. Does it matter who holds the Spear of Skilk, when he does so in my name? And King Jonkvank will be no foreigner. He will come and live among you, and later he will travel back and forth between Krink and Skilk, and he will leave the Spear of Krink in Krink, and the Spear of Skilk in Skilk, and in Skilk he will be a Skilkan."

That seemed to satisfy everybody except Jonkvank, and he had wit enough not to make an issue of it. He even had the Spear of Krink carried back aboard his launch, out of sight, and when he accompanied von Schlichten, an hour later, to see Hideyoshi O'Leary off for Grank, he had the Spear of Skilk carried behind him. When he was alone with von Schlichten, in the room that had been King Firkked's bedchamber, however, he exploded: "What is all this foolishness which you promised these people in my name and which I must now carry out? That I am to leave the Spear of Skilk in Skilk and the Spear of Krink in Krink, and come here to live...."

"You wish to hold Skilk?" von Schlichten asked.

"I intend to hold Skilk. To begin with, there shall be a great killing here. A very great killing: of all those who advised that fool of a Firkked to start this business; of those who gave shelter to the false prophet, Rakkeed, when he was here; of the faithless priests who gave ear to his abominable heresies and allowed him to spew out his blasphemies in the temples; of those who sent spies to Krink, to corrupt and pervert my soldiers and nobles; of those who...."

"All that is as it should be," von Schlichten agreed. "Except that it must be done quickly and all at once, before the memories of these crimes fade from the minds of the people. And great care must be taken to kill only those who can be proven to be guilty of something; thus it will be said that the justice of King Jonkvank is terrible to evildoers but a protection and a shield to those who keep the peace and obey the laws. Thus you will gain the name of being a wise and just king. And when the priests are to be killed it should be done under the direction of those other priests who were faithful to the gods and whom King Firkked drove out of their temples, and it must be done in the name of the gods. Thus will you be esteemed a pious, and not an impious, king. As to why you must be a Skilkan in Skilk, you heard the words of Flurknurk, and how the others agreed with him. It must not be allowed to seem that the city has come under foreign rule. And you must not change the laws, unless the people petition you to do so, nor must you increase the taxes, and you must not confiscate the estates of those who are put to death, for the death of parents is always forgiven before the loss of patrimonies. And you should select certain Skilkan nobles, and become the father of their young, and above all, you must leave none of the young of Firkked alive, to raise rebellion against you later."

Jonkvank nodded, deeply impressed. "By the gods, Karlok vonk Zlikdenk, this is wisdom! Now it is to be seen why the likes of Firkked cannot prevail against you, or against the Company as long as you are the Company's upper sword-arm!"

Honesty tempted von Schlichten, for a moment, to disclaim originality for the principles he had just enunciated, even at the price of trying to pronounce the name of Niccolo Machiavelli with a geek-speaker. On second thought, however, considerations of policy restrained him. If Jonkvank ever heard of *The Prince*, nothing would satisfy him short of an Ulleran translation, and von Schlichten would have been just about as happy over an Ulleran translation of a complete set of Bethe-cycle bomb specifications.

XII
The Shadow of Niflheim

The sun slid lower and lower toward the horizon behind them as the aircar bulleted south along the broad valley and dry bed of the Hoork River, nearing the zone of equal day and night. Hassan Bogdanoff drove while Harry Quong finished his lunch, then changed places to begin his own. Von Schlichten got two bottles of beer from the refrigerated section of the lunch-hamper and opened one for Paula Quinton and one for himself.

"What are we going to do with these geeks," —she was using the nasty and derogatory word unconsciously and by custom, now —"after this is all over? We can't just tell them, 'Jolly well played, nice game, wasn't it?' and go back to where we were Wednesday evening."

"No, we can't. There's going to have to be a Terran seizure of political power in every part of this planet that we occupy, and as soon as we're consolidated around and north of Takkad Sea, we're going to have to move in elsewhere," he replied. "Keegark, Konkrook, and the Free Cities, of course, will be relatively easy. They're in arms against us now, and we can take them over by force. We had to make that deal with Jonkvank, or, rather, I did, so that will be a slower process, but we'll get it done in time. If I know that pair as well as I think I do, Jonkvank and Yoorkerk will give us plenty of pretexts, before long. Then, we can start giving them government by law instead of by royal decree, and real courts of justice; put an end to the head-payment system, and to these arbitrary mass arrests and tax-delinquency imprisonments that are nothing but slave-raids by the geek princes on their own people. And, gradually, abolish serfdom. In a couple of centuries, this planet will be fit to admit to the Federation, like Odin and Freya."

"Well, won't that depend a lot on whom the Company sends here to take Harrington's place?"

"Unless I'm much mistaken, the Company will confirm me," he replied. "Administration on Uller is going to be a military matter for a long time to come, and even the Banking Cartel and the mercantile interests in the Company are going to realize that, and see the necessity for taking political control. The Federation Government owns a bigger interest in the Company than the public realizes, too; they've always favored it. And just to make sure, I'm sending Hid O'Leary to Terra on the next ship, to make a full report on the situation."

"You think it'll be cleared up by then? The *City of Montevideo* is due in from Niflheim in a little under three months."

"It'll have to be cleared up by then. We can't keep this war going more than a month, at the present rate. Police-action, and mopping-up, yes, full-scale war, no."

"Ammunition?" she asked.

He looked at her in pleased surprise. "Your education has been progressing, at that," he said. "You know, a lot of professional officers, even up to field rank in the combat branches, seem to think that ammo comes down miraculously from Heaven, in contragravity lorries, every time they pray into a radio for it. It doesn't; it has to be produced as fast as it's expended, and we haven't been doing that. So we'll have to lick these geeks before it runs out, because we can't lick them with gunbutts and bayonets."

"Well, how about nuclear weapons?" Paula asked. "I hate to suggest it—I know what they did on Mimir, and Fenris, and Midgard, and what they did on Terra, during the First Century. But it may be our only chance."

He finished his beer and shoved the bottle into the waste-receiver, then got out his cigarettes.

"I'd hate to have to make a decision like that, Paula," he told her. "The military use of nuclear energy is the last-well, the next-to-last—thing I'd want to see on Uller. Fortunately, or unfortunately, it's a decision I won't have to make. There isn't a single nuclear bomb on the planet. The Company's always refused to allow them to be manufactured or stockpiled here."

"I don't think there'd be any criticism of your making them, now, general. And there's certainly plenty of plutonium. You could make A-bombs, at least."

"There isn't anybody here who even knows how to make one. Most of our nuclear engineers could work one up, in about three months, when we'd either not need one or not be alive."

"Dr. Gomes, who came in on the *Pretoria*, two weeks ago, can make them," she contradicted. "He built at least a dozen of them on Niflheim, to use in activating volcanoes and bringing ore-bearing lava to the surface."

Von Schlichten's hand, bringing his lighter to the tip of his cigarette, paused for a second. Then he completed the operation, snapped it shut, and put it away.

"When did all this happen?"

She took time out for mental arithmetic; even a spaceship officer had to do that, when a question of interstellar time-relations arose.

"About three-fifty days ago, Galactic Standard. They'd put off the first shot, six bombs, before I got in from Terra. I saw the second shot a day or so before I left Niflheim on the *Canberra*. Dr. Gomes had to stay over till the *Pretoria* to put off the third shot. Why?"

"Did you run into a geek named Gorkrink, while you were on Nif?" he asked her. "And what sort of work was he doing?"

"Gorkrink? I don't seem to remember....Oh, yes! He was helping Dr. Murillo, the seismologist. His year was up after the second shot; he came to Uller on the *Canberra*. Dr. Murillo was sorry to lose him. He understood Lingua Terra perfectly; Dr. Murillo could talk to him, the way you do with Kankad, without using a geek-speaker."

"Well, but what sort of work...?"

"Helping set and fire the A-bombs.... *Oh! Good Lord!*"

"You can say that again, and deal in Allah, Shiva, and Kali," von Schlichten told her. "Especially Kali....Harry! See if you can get some more speed out of this can. I want to get to Konkrook while it's still there!"

It was full dark when Konkrook came in view beyond the East Konk Mountains, a lurid smear on the underside of the clouds, and, at Gongonk Island and at the Company farms to the south, a couple of bunches of searchlights fingering about in the sky. When von Schlichten turned on the outside sound-pickup, he could hear the distant tom-tomming of heavy guns, and the crash of shells and bombs. Keeping the car high enough to be above the trajectories of incoming shells, Harry Quong circled over the city while Hassan Bogdanoff talked to Gongonk Island on the radio.

The city was in a bad way. There were seventy-five to a hundred big fires going, and a new one started in a rising ball of thermoconcentrate flame while they watched. The three gun-cutters, *Elmoran*, *Gaucho*, and *Bushranger*, and about fifty big freight lorries converted to bombers, were shuttling back and forth between the island and the city. The Royal Palace was on fire from end to end, and the entire waterfront and industrial district were in flames. Combat-cars and airjeeps were diving in to shell and rocket and machine-gun streets and buildings. He saw six big bomber-lorries move in dignified procession to unload, one after the other, on a row of buildings along what the Terrans called South Tenth Street, and on the roofs of buildings a block away, red and blue flares were burning, and he could see figures, both human and Ulleran, setting up mortars and machine-guns.

Landing on the top stage of Company House, on the island, they were met by a Terran whom von Schlichten had seen, a few days ago, bossing native-labor at the spaceport, but who was now wearing a major's insignia. He greeted von Schlichten with a salute which he must have learned from some movie about the ancient French Foreign Legion. Von Schlichten seriously returned it in kind.

"Everybody's down in the Governor-General's office, sir," he said. "Your office, that is. King Kankad's here with us, too."

He accompanied them to the elevator, then turned to a telephone; when von Schlichten and Paula reached the office, everybody was crowded at the door to greet them: Themistocles M'zangwe, his arm in a sling; Hans Meyerstein, the Johannesburg lawyer, who seemed to have even more Bantu blood than the brigadier-general; Morton Buhrmann, the Commercial Superintendent; Laviola, the Fiscal Secretary; a dozen or so other officers and civil administrators. There was a hubbub of greetings, and he was pleased to detect as much real warmth from the civil administration crowd as from the officers.

"Well, I'm glad to be back with you," he replied, generally. "And let me present Colonel Paula Quinton, my new adjutant; Hid O'Leary's on duty in the north....Them, this was a perfectly splendid piece of work here; you can take this not only as a personal congratulation, but as a sort of unit citation for the whole crowd. You've all behaved simply above praise." He turned to King Kankad, who was wearing a pair of automatics in shoulder-holsters for his upper hands and another pair in cross-body belt holsters for his lower. "And what I've said for anybody else goes double for you, Kankad," he added, clapping the Kragan on the shoulder.

"All he did was save the lot of us!" M'zangwe said. "We were hanging on by our fingernails here till his people started coming in. And then, after you sent the *Aldebaran*...."

"Where is the *Aldebaran*, by the way? I didn't see her when I came in."

"Based on Kankad's, flying bombardment against Keegark, and keeping an eye out for those ships. Prinsloo caught the *De Wett* in the docks there and smashed her, but the *Jan Smuts* got away, and we haven't been able to locate the *Oom Paul Kruger*, either. They're probably both on the Eastern Shore, gathering up reenforcements for Orgzild," M'zangwe said.

"Our ability to move troops rapidly is what's kept us on top this long, and Orgzild's had plenty of time to realize it," von Schlichten said. "When we get *Procyon* down here, I'm going to send her out, with a screen of light scout-vehicles, to find those ships and get rid of them.... How's Hid been making out, at Grank, by the way? I didn't have my car-radio on, coming down."

That touched off another hubbub: "Haven't you heard, general?" ... "Oh, my God, this is simply out of this continuum!" ... "Well, tell him, somebody!" ... "No, get Hid on the screen; it's his story!"

Somebody busied himself at the switchboard. The rest of them sat down at the long conference-table. Laviola and Meyerstein and Buhrmann were especially obsequious in seating von Schlichten in Sid Harrington's old chair, and in getting a chair for Paula Quinton. After a while, the jumbled colors on the big screen resolved themselves into an image of Hideyoshi O'Leary, grinning like a pussy-cat beside an empty goldfish-bowl.

"Well, what happened?" von Schlichten asked, after they had exchanged greetings. "How did Yoorkerk like the movies? And did you get the *Procyon* and the *Northern Lights* loose?"

"Yoorkerk was deeply impressed," O'Leary replied. "His story is that he is and always was the true and ever-loving friend of the Company; he acted to prevent quote certain disloyal elements unquote from harming the people and property of the Company. *Procyon's* on the way to Konkrook. I'm holding *Northern Lights* here and *Northern Star* at Skilk; where do you want them sent?"

"Leave *Northern Star* at Skilk, for the time being. Tell the Company's great and good friend King Yoorkerk that the Company expects him to contribute some soldiers for the campaign here and against Keegark, when that starts; be sure you get the best-armed and best-trained regiments he has, and get them down here as soon as possible. Don't send any of your Kragans or Karamessinis' troops here, though; hold them in Grank till we make sure of the quality of Yoorkerk's friendship."

"Well, general, I think we can be pretty sure, now. You see, he turned Rakkeed the Prophet over to me...."

"*What?*" Von Schlichten felt his monocle starting to slip and took a firmer grip on it. "Who?"

"Pay me, Them; he didn't drop it," Hideyoshi O'Leary said. "Why, Rakkeed the Prophet. Yoorkerk was holding our ships and our people in case we lost; he was also holding Rakkeed at the Palace in case we won. Of course, Rakkeed thought he was an honored guest, right up till Yoorkerk's guards dragged him in and turned him over to us...."

"That geek," von Schlichten said, "is too smart for his own good. Some of these days he's going to play both ends against the middle and both ends'll fold in on him and smash him." A suspicion occurred to him. "You sure this is Rakkeed? It would be just like Yoorkerk to try to sell us a ringer."

O'Leary shook his head solemnly. "I thought of that, right away. This is the real article; Karamessinis' Constabulary and Intelligence officers certified him for me. What do you want me to do, send him down to Konkrook?"

Von Schlichten shook his head. "Get the priests of the locally venerated gods to put him on trial for blasphemy, heresy, impersonating a prophet, practicing witchcraft without a license, or any other ecclesiastical crimes you or they can think of. Then, after he's been given a scrupulously fair trial, have the soldiers of King Yoorkerk behead him, and stick his head up over a big sign, in all native languages, 'Rakkeed the False Prophet.' And have audio-visuals made of the whole business, trial and execution, and be sure that the priests and Yoorkerk's officers are in the foreground and our people stay out of the pictures."

"Soap and towels, for General Pontius von Pilate!" Paula Quinton called out.

"That's an idea; I was wondering what to give Yoorkerk as a testimonial present," Hideyoshi O'Leary said. "A nice thirty-piece silver set!"

"Quite appropriate," von Schlichten approved. "Well, you did a first-class job. I want you back with us as soon as possible-incidentally, you're now a brigadier-general —but not till the situation at Grank-Krink-Skilk is stabilized. And, eventually, you'll probably have to set up permanent headquarters in the north."

After Hideyoshi O'Leary had thanked him and signed off, and the screen was dark again, he turned to the others.

"Well, gentlemen, I don't think we need worry too much about the north, for the next few days. How long do you estimate this operation against Konkrook's going to take, to complete pacification, Them?"

"How complete is complete pacification, general?" Themistocles M'zangwe wanted to know. "If you mean to the end of organized resistance by larger than squad-size groups, I'd say three days, give or take twelve hours. Of course, there'll be small groups holding out for a couple of weeks, particularly in the farming country and back in the forest...."

"We can forget them; that's minor-tactics stuff. We'll need to keep some kind of an occupation force here for some time; they can deal with that. We'll have to get to work on Keegark, as soon as possible; after we've reduced Keegark, we'll be able to reorganize for a campaign against the Free Cities on the Eastern Shore."

"Begging your pardon, general, but reduce is a mild word for what we ought to do to Keegark," Hans Meyerstein said. "We ought to raze that city as flat as a football field, and then play football on it with King Orgzild's head."

"Any special reason?" von Schlichten asked. "In addition to the Blount-Lemoyne massacre, that is?"

"I should say so, general!" Themistocles M'zangwe backed Meyerstein up. "Bob, you tell him."

Colonel Robert Grinell, the Intelligence officer, got up and took the cigar out of his mouth. He was short and round-bodied and bald-headed, but he was old Terran Federation Regular Army.

"Well, general, we've been finding out quite a bit about the genesis of this business, lately," he said. "From up north, it probably looked like an all-Rakkeed show; that's how it was supposed to look. But the whole thing was hatched at Keegark, by King Orgzild. We've managed to capture a few prominent Konkrookans" —he named half a dozen —"who've been made to talk, and a number of others have come in voluntarily and furnished information. Orgzild conceived the scheme in the beginning; Rakkeed was just the messenger-boy. My face gets the color of the Company trademark every time I think that the whole thing was planned for over a year, right under our noses, even to the signal that was to touch the whole thing off...."

"The poisoning of Sid Harrington, and our announcement of his death?" von Schlichten asked.

"You figured that out yourself, sir? Well, that was it." Grinell went on to elaborate, while von Schlichten tried to keep the impatience out of his face. Beside him, Paula Quinton was fidgeting, too; she was thinking, as he was, of what King Orgzild and Prince Gorkrink were doing now. "And I know positively that the order for the poisoning of Sid Harrington came from the Keegarkan Embassy here, and was passed down through Gurgurk and Keeluk to this geek here who actually put the poison in the whiskey."

"Yes. I agree that Keegark should be wiped out, and I'd like to have an immediate estimate on the time it'll take to build a nuclear bomb to do the job. One of the old-fashioned plutonium fission A-bombs will do quite well."

Everybody turned quickly. There was a momentary silence, and then Colonel Evan Colbert, of the Fourth Kragan Rifles, the senior officer under Themistocles M'zangwe, found his voice.

"If that's an order, general, we'll get it done. But I'd like to remind you, first, of the Company policy on nuclear weapons on this planet."

"I'm aware of that policy. I'm also aware of the reason for it. We've been compelled, because of the lack of natural fuel on Uller, to set up nuclear power reactors and furnish large quantities of plutonium to the geeks to fuel them. The Company doesn't want the natives here learning of the possibility of using nuclear energy for destructive purposes. Well, gentlemen, that's a dead issue. They've learned it, thanks to our people on Niflheim, and unless my estimate is entirely wrong, King Orgzild already has at least one First-Century Nagasaki-type plutonium bomb. I am inclined to believe that he had at least one such bomb, probably more, at the time when orders were sent to his embassy here, for the poisoning of Governor-General Harrington."

With that, he selected a cigarette from his case, offered it to Paula, and snapped his lighter. She had hers lit, and he was puffing on his own, when the others finally realized what he had told them.

"That's impossible!" somebody down the table shouted, as though that would make it so. Another-one of the civil administration crowd-almost exactly repeated Jules Keaveney's words at Skilk: "What the hell was Intelligence doing, sleeping?"

"General von Schlichten," Colonel Grinell took oblique cognizance of the question, "you've just made, by implication, a most grave charge against my department. If you're not mistaken in what you've just said, I deserve to be court-martialed."

"I couldn't bring charges against you, colonel; if it were a court-martial matter, I'd belong in the dock with you," von Schlichten told him. "It seems, though, that a piece of vital information was possessed by those who were unable to evaluate it, and until this afternoon, I was ignorant of its existence. Colonel Quinton, suppose you repeat what you told me, on the way down from Skilk."

"Well, general, don't you think we ought to have Dr. Gomes do that?" Paula asked. "After all, he constructed those bombs on Niflheim, and it'll be he who'll have to build ours."

"That's right." He looked around. "Where's Dr. Lourenço Gomes, the nuclear engineer who came in on the *Pretoria*, two weeks ago? Send out for him, and get him in here at once."

There was another awkward silence. Then Kent Pickering, the chief of the Gongonk Island power-plant, cleared his throat.

"Why, general, didn't you know? Dr. Gomes is dead. He was killed during the first half hour of the uprising."

XIII
A Bag of Tricks We Don't Have

He flinched inwardly, and tightened his eye-muscles on the edge of the monocle to keep from flinching physically as well, trying to freeze out of his face the consternation he felt.

"That's bad, Kent," he said. "Very bad. I'd been counting heavily on Dr. Gomes to design a bomb of our own."

"Well, general, if you please." That was Air-Commodore Leslie Hargreaves. "You say you suspect that King Orgzild has developed a nuclear bomb. If that's true, it's a horrible danger to all of us. But I find it hard to believe that the Keegarkans could have done so, with their resources and at their technological level. Now, if it had been the Kragans, that would have been different, but...."

"Paula, you'd better carry on and explain what you told me, and add anything else you can think of that might be relevant....Is that sound-recorder turned on? Then turn it on, somebody; we want this taped."

Paula rose and began talking: "I suppose you all understand what conditions are on Niflheim, and how these Ulleran native workers are employed; however, I'd better begin by explaining the purpose for which these nuclear bombs were designed and used...."

He smiled; she realized that he needed time to think, and she was stalling to provide it. He drew a pencil and pad toward him and began doodling in a bored manner, deliberately closing his mind to what she was saying. There were two assumptions, he considered: first, that King Orgzild already possessed a nuclear bomb which he could use when he chose, and, second, that in the absence of Dr. Gomes, such a bomb could only be produced on Gongonk Island after lengthy experimental work. If both of these assumptions were true, he had just heard the death-sentence of every Terran on Uller. The first he did not for a moment doubt. The reasons for making it were too good. He dismissed it from further consideration and concentrated on the second.

"...what's known as a Nagasaki-type bomb, the first type of plutonium-bomb developed," Paula was saying. "Really, it's a technological antique, but it was good enough for the purpose, and Dr. Gomes could build it with locally available materials...."

That was the crux of it. The plutonium bomb, from a military standpoint, was as obsolete as the flintlock musket had been at the time of the Second World War. He reviewed, quickly, the history of weapons-development since the beginning of the Atomic Era. The emphasis, since the end of the Second World War, had all been on nuclear weapons and rocket-missiles. There had been the H-bomb, itself obsolescent, and the Bethe-cyle bomb, and the subneutron bomb, and the omega-ray bomb, and the nega-matter bomb, and then the end of civilization in the Northern Hemisphere and the rise of the new civilization in South America and South Africa and Australia. Today, the small-arms and artillery his troops were using were merely slight refinements on the weapons of the First Century, and all the modern nuclear weapons used by the Terran Federation were produced at the Space Navy base on Mars, by a small force of experts whose skills were almost as closed to the general scientific and technical world as the secrets of a medieval guild. The old A-bomb was an historical curiosity, and there was nobody on Uller who had more than a layman's knowledge of the intricate technology of modern nuclear weapons. There were plenty of good nuclear-power engineers on Gongonk Island, but how long would it take them to design and build a plutonium bomb?

"...also has a good understanding of Lingua Terra," Paula was saying. "He and Dr. Murillo conversed bilingually, just as I've heard General von Schlichten and King Kankad talking to one another. I haven't any idea whether or not Gorkrink could read Lingua Terra, or, if so, what papers or plans he might have seen."

"Just a minute, Paula," he said. "Colonel Grinell, what does your branch have on this Gorkrink?"

"He's the son of King Orgzild, and the daughter of Prince Jurnkonk," Grinell said. "We knew he'd signed on for Nif, two years ago, but the story we got was that he'd fallen out of favor at court and had been exiled. I can see, now, that that was planted to mislead us. As to whether or not he can read Lingua Terra, my belief is that he can. We know that he can understand it when spoken. He could have learned to read at one of those schools Mohammed Ferriera set up, ten or fifteen years ago."

"And Dr. Gomes and Dr. Murillo and Dr. Livesey left papers and plans lying around all over the place," Paula added. "If he went to Niflheim as a spy, he could have copied almost anything."

"Well, there you have it," von Schlichten said. "When Gorkrink found out that plutonium can be used for bombs, he began gathering all the information he could. And as soon as he got home, he turned it all over to Pappy Orgzild."

"That still doesn't mean that the Kee-geeks were able to do anything with it," Air-Commodore Hargreaves argued.

"I think it does," von Schlichten differed. "As soon as Orgzild would hear about the possibility of making a plutonium bomb, he'd set up an A-bomb project, and don't think of it in terms of the old First Century Manhattan Project. There would be no problem of producing fissionables-we've been scattering refined plutonium over this planet like confetti."

"Well, an A-bomb's a pretty complicated piece of mechanism, even if you have the plans for it," Kent Pickering said. "As I recall, there have to be several subcritical masses of plutonium, or U-235, or whatever, blown together by shaped charges of explosive, all of which have to be fired simultaneously. That would mean a lot of electrical fittings that I can't see these geeks making by hand."

"I can," Paula said. "Have you ever seen the work these native jewelers do? And didn't you tell me about a clockwork thing they have at the university here, to show the apparent movements of the sun...."

"That's right," von Schlichten said. "And what they couldn't make, they could have bought from us; we've sold them a lot of electrical equipment."

"All right, they could have built an A-bomb," Buhrmann said. "But did they?"

"We assume they tried to. Gorkrink got back from Nif on the Canberra, three months ago," von Schlichten said. "If Orgzild decided to build an A-bomb, he wouldn't give the signal for this uprising until he either had one or knew he couldn't make one, and he wouldn't give up trying in only three months. Therefore, I think we can assume that he succeeded, and had succeeded at the time he sent Gorkrink here to get that four tons of plutonium we let him have, and, incidentally, to tell Ghroghrank to pass the word to have Sid Harrington poisoned according to plan."

"Then why didn't he just use it on us at the start of the uprising?" Meyerstein wanted to know.

"Why should he? Getting rid of us is only the first step in Orgzild's plan," Grinell said. "Back as far as geek history goes, the Kings of Keegark have been trying to conquer Konkrook and the Free Cities and make themselves masters of the whole Takkad Sea area. Let Konkrook wipe us out, and then he can move in his troops and take Konkrook. Or, if we beat off the geeks here, as we seem to be doing, he can bomb us out and then move in on Konkrook. I think that as long as we're fighting here, he'll wait. The more damage we do to Konkrook, the easier it'll be for him."

"Then we'd better start dragging our feet on the Konkrook front," Laviola said. "And get busy trying to build a bomb of our own."

Von Schlichten looked up at the big screen, on which the battle of Konkrook was being projected from an overhead pickup.

"I'll agree on the second half of it," von Schlichten said. "And we'll also have to set up some kind of security-patrol system against bombers from Keegark. And as soon as *Procyon* gets here, we'll have to send her out to hunt down and destroy those two Boer-class freighters, the *Jan Smuts* and the *Kruger*. And we'll have to arrange for protection of Kankad's Town; that's sure to be another of Orgzild's high-priority targets. As to the action against Konkrook, I'll rely on your advice, Them. Can we delay the fall of the city for any length of time?"

M'zangwe shook his head. "When we divert contragravity to security-patrol work, the ground action'll slow up a little, of course. But the geeks are about knocked out, now."

"The hell with it, then. I doubt if we'd be able to buy much time from Orgzild by delaying victory in the city, and we'll probably need the troops as workers over here." He turned to Pickering. "Dr. Pickering, what sort of a crew can you scrape together to design a bomb for us?" he asked.

"Well, there's Martirano, and Sternberg, and Howard Fu-Chung, and Piet van Reenen, and...." He nodded to himself. "I can get six or eight of them in here in about twenty minutes; I'll have a project set up and working in a couple of hours. There has to be somebody qualified on duty at the plant, all the time, of course, but...."

"All right, call them in. I want the bomb finished by yesterday afternoon. And everybody with you, and you, yourself, had better revert to civilian status. This isn't something you can do by the numbers, and I don't want anybody who doesn't know what it's all about pulling rank on your outfit. Go ahead, call in your gang, and let me know what you'll be able to do, as soon as possible."

He turned to Hargreaves. "Les, you'll have charge of flying the security patrols, and doing anything else you can to keep Orgzild from bombing us before we can bomb him. You'll have priority on everything second only to Pickering."

Hargreaves nodded. "As you say, general, we'll have to protect Kankad's, as well as this place. It's about five hundred miles from here to Kankad's, and eight-fifty miles from Kankad's to Keegark...."

He stopped talking to von Schlichten, and began muttering to himself, running over the names of ships, and the speeds and pay-load capacities of airboats, and distances. In about five minutes, he would have a programme worked out; in the meantime, von Schlichten could only be patient and contain himself. He looked along the table, and caught sight of a thin-faced, saturnine-looking man in a green shirt, with a colonel's three concentric circles marked on the shoulders in silver-paint. Emmett Pearson, the communications chief.

"Emmett," he said, "those orbiters you have strung around this planet, two thousand miles out, for telecast rebroadcast stations. How much of a crew could be put on one of them?"

Pearson laughed. "Crew of what, general? White mice, or trained cockroaches? There isn't room inside one of those things for anything bigger to move around."

"Well, I know they're automatic, but how do you service them?"

"From the outside. They're only ten feet through, by about twenty in length, with a fifteen-foot ball at either end, and everything's in sections, which can be taken out. Our maintenance-gang goes up in a thing like a small spaceship, and either works on the outside in spacesuits, or puts in a new section and brings the unserviceable one down here to the shops."

"Ah, and what sort of a thing is this small spaceship, now?"

"A thing like a pair of fifty-ton lorries, with airlocks between, and connected at the middle; airtight, of course, and pressurized and insulated like a spaceship. One side's living quarters for a six-man crew-sometimes the gang's out for as long as a week at a time-and the other side's a workshop."

That sounded interesting. With contragravity, of course, terms like "escape-velocity" and "mass-ratio" were of purely antiquarian interest.

"How long," he asked Pearson, "would it take to fit that vehicle with a full set of detection instruments-radar, infrared and ultra-violet vision, electron-telescope, heat and radiation detectors, the whole works-and spot it about a hundred to a hundred and fifty miles above Keegark?"

"That I couldn't say, general," Emmett Pearson replied. "It'd have to be a shipyard job, and a lot of that stuff's clear outside my department. Ask Air-Commodore Hargreaves."

"Les!" he called out. "Wake up, Les!"

"Just a second, general." Hargreaves scribbled frantically on his pad. "Now," he said, raising his head. "What is it, sir?"

"Emmett, here, has a junior-grade spaceship that he uses to service those orbital telecast-relay stations of his. He'll tell you what it's like. I want it fitted with every sort of detection device that can be crammed into or onto it, and spotted above Keegark. It should, of course, be high enough to cover not only the Keegark area, but Konkrook, Kankad's, and the lower Hoork and Konk river-valleys."

"Yes, I get it." Hargreaves snatched up a phone, punched out a combination, and began talking rapidly into it in a low voice. After a while, he hung up. "All right, Mr. Pearson-Colonel Pearson, I mean. Have your space-buggy sent around to the shipyard. My boys'll fix it up." He made a note on another piece of paper. "If we live through this, I'm going to have a couple of supra-atmosphere ships in service on this planet.... Now, general, I have a tentative setup. We're going to need the *Elmoran* for patrol work south and east of Konkrook, and the *Gaucho* and *Bushranger* to the north and northeast, based on Kankad's. We'll keep the *Aldebaran* at Kankad's, and use her for emergencies. And we'll have patrols of light contragravity like this." He handed a map, with red-pencil and blue-pencil markings, along to von Schlichten. "Red are Kankad-based; blue are Konkrook-based."

"That looks all right," von Schlichten said. "There's another thing, though. We want scout-vehicles to cover the Keegark area with radiation-detectors. These geeks are quite well aware of radiation-danger from fissionables, but they're accustomed to the ordinary industrial-power reactors, which are either very lightly shielded or unshielded on top. We want to find out where Orgzild's bomb-plant is."

"Yes, general, as soon as we can get radiation detectors sent out to Kankad's, we'll have a couple of fast aircars fitted with them for that job."

"We have detectors, at our laboratory and reaction-plant," Kankad said. "And my people can make more, as soon as you want them." He thought for a moment. "Perhaps I should go to the town, now. I could be of more use there than here."

Kent Pickering, who had been talking with his experts at a table apart, returned.

"We've set up a programme, general," he said. "It's going to be a lot harder than I'd anticipated. None of us seem to know exactly what we have to do in building one of those things. You see, the uranium or plutonium fission-bomb's been obsolete for over four hundred years. It was a classified-secret matter long after its obsolescence, because it hadn't been rendered any the less deadly by being superseded-there was that A-bomb that the Christian Anarchist Party put together at Buenos Aires in 378 A.E., for instance. And then, after it was declassified, it had been so far superseded that it was of only antiquarian interest; the textbooks dealt with it only in general terms. The principles, of course, are part of basic nuclear science; the "secret of the A-bomb" was just a bag of engineering tricks that we don't have, and which we will have to rediscover. Design of tampers, design of the chemical-explosive charges to bring subcritical masses together, case-design, detonating mechanism, things like that."

"The complete data on even the old Hiroshima and Nagasaki types is still in existence, of course. You can get it at places like the University of Montevideo Library, or Jan Smuts Memorial Library at Cape Town. But we don't have it here. We're detailing a couple of junior technicians to make a search of the library here on Gongonk Island, but we're not optimistic. We just can't afford to pass up any chance, even when it approaches zero-probability."

Von Schlichten nodded. "That's about what I'd expected," he said. "I suppose Gomes got his data out of one of the dustier storage-stacks at Jan Smuts or Montevideo, in the first place.... Well, I still want that bomb finished by yesterday afternoon, but since that's impractical, you'll have to take a little-but as little as possible-longer."

"What are we going to do about publicity on this?" Howlett, the personnel man, asked. "We don't want this getting out in garbled form-though how it could be made worse by garbling I couldn't guess-and having the troops watching the sky over their shoulders and going into a panic as soon as they saw something they didn't understand."

"No, we don't. I've seen a couple of troop-panics," von Schlichten said. "There can't be anything much worse than a panic."

"I think the Terrans ought to be told the worst," Hargreaves said. "And told that our only hope is to get a bomb of our own built and dropped first. As to the Kragans.... What do you think, King Kankad?"

"Tell them that we are building a bomb to destroy Keegark; that we are running short of ammunition, and that it is our only hope of finishing the war before the ammunition is gone," Kankad said. "Tell them something of what sort of a bomb it is. But do not tell them that King Orgzild already has such a bomb. Old Kankad, who made me out of himself, told me about how our people fled in panic from the weapons of the Terrans, when your people and mine were still enemies. This thing is to the weapons they faced then as those weapons were to the old Kragans' spears and bows.... And when the geeks from Grank come here, tell them that we are winning and that if they fight well, they can share the loot of Konkrook and Keegark."

Von Schlichten looked up at the big screen. Already, Themistocles M'zangwe had ordered the Channel Battery to reduce fire; the big guns were firing singly, in thirty-second-interval salvos. There was less bombing, too; contragravity was being drawn out of the battle.

"Well, we all have things to do," he said, "and I think we've discussed everything there is to discuss. Anybody think of anything we've forgotten?... Then we're adjourned."

He and Paula Quinton took the elevator to the roof, and sat side by side, silently watching the conflagration that was raging across the channel and the nearer flashes of the big guns along the island's city side.

"Wednesday night, I thought we were all cooked," Paula told him. "Cleaning up the north in two days seemed like an impossibility, too. Maybe you'll do it again."

"If I pull this one out of the fire, I won't be a general; I'll be a magician," he said. "Pickering'll be a magician, I mean; he's the boy who'll save our bacon, if it's saveable." He looked somberly across the flame-reflecting water. "Let's not kid ourselves; we're just kicking and biting at the guards on the way up the gallows-steps."

"Well, why stop till the trap's sprung?" she asked. "What'll happen to these people on this planet, after we're atomized?"

"That I don't want to think about. Kankad's Town will get the second bomb; Orgzild won't dare leave the Kragans after he's wiped us out. Yoorkerk and Jonkvank, in the north, will turn on Keaveney and Shapiro and Karamessinis and Hid O'Leary and wipe them out. And when the next ship gets in here and they find out what happened, they'll send the Federation Space Navy, and this planet'll get it worse than Fenris did. They'll blast anything that has four arms and a face like a lizard...."

Half a dozen aircars lifted suddenly from the airport and streaked away to the northeast. As they went past, in the light of the burning city, he could see that at least three of them had multiple rocket-launchers on top. In a matter of seconds, a gun-cutter raced after them, and a second, which had been over Konkrook, jettisoned a bomb and turned away to follow.

"Maybe that's it," Paula said.

"Well, if it is, we won't be any better off anywhere else than here," he told her. "Let's stay and watch."

After what seemed like a long time, however, a twinkle of lights showed over the East Konk Mountains. They weren't the flashes of explosions; some were magnesium flares, and some were the lights of a ship.

"That's *Procyon*, from Grank," he said. "Everybody gets a good mark for this-detection stations, interceptors, gun-cutters. If that had been it, there'd have been a good chance of stopping it." He felt better than he had since Pickering had told him that Lourenço Gomes was dead. "It's a good thing Gorkrink didn't pick up any dope on guided missiles, while he was at it. As long as they have to deliver it with contragravity, we have a chance."

They rose from the balustrade where they had been sitting, and, for the first time, he discovered that he had had his left arm over her shoulder and that she had had her right hand resting on the point of his right hip, just above his pistol. He picked up the folder of papers she had been carrying, and put her into the elevator ahead of him, and it was only when they parted on the living-quarters level that he recalled having followed the older protocol of gallantry rather than the precedence of military rank.

XIV
The Reviewers Panned Hell Out of It

He woke with a guilty start and looked up at the clock on the ceiling; it was 0945. Kicking himself free of the covers, he slid his feet to the floor and sprinted for the bathroom. While he was fussing to get the shower adjusted to the right temperature, he bludgeoned his conscience by telling himself that a wide-awake general is more good than a half-asleep general, that there was nothing he could do but hope that Hargreaves's patrols would keep the bomb away from Konkrook until Pickering's brain-trust came up with one of their own, and that the fact that the commander-in-chief was making sack-time would be much better for morale than the spectacle of him running around in circles. He shaved carefully; a stubble of beard on his chin might betray the fact that he was worried. Then he dressed, put his monocle in his eye, and called the headquarters that had been set up in Sid Harrington's —now his-office. A girl at the switchboard appeared on his screen, and gave place to Paula Quinton, who had been up for the past two hours.

"The *Northern Lights* got in about three hours ago, general," she told him. "She had four of King Yoorkerk's infantry regiments aboard-the Seventh, Glorious-and-Terrible, the Fourth, Firm-in-Adversity, the Second, Strength-of-the-Throne, and the Twelfth, Forever-Admirable. They're the sorriest-looking rabble I ever saw, but Hideyoshi says they're the best Yoorkerk has, and they all have Terran-style rifles. General M'zangwe broke them into battalions, and put a battalion in with each of the Kragan regiments. I think they're more afraid of the Kragans than they are of the rebels."

He nodded. That was probably the best way to employ them, within the existing situation. The trouble was, Them M'zangwe was incurably tactical-minded. Put those geeks of Yoorkerk's in with the Kragans and they'd be most useful in conquering Konkrook, but the trouble was that, after associating with Kragans, they might develop into reasonably good troops themselves, to the undesired improvement of King Yoorkerk's army. On the other hand maybe not. Keep them in Company service long enough, and they might want to forget about Yoorkerk and stay there.

"How's the situation over in town?" he asked.

"Well, it's slowing up, since we began pulling contragravity out," she told him, "but the geeks are breaking up rapidly....Oh, there was something funny about that hassle, last evening, when the *Procyon* came in. Two contragravity vehicles, an aircar and an air-lorry, that went out to meet the ship, are unaccounted for."

"You mean two of our vehicles are missing?"

She shook her head, frowning in perplexity. "Well, no. All the vehicles that answered that unidentified-aircraft alert returned, but there were these two that went out that we haven't any record of. Colonel Grinell is investigating, but he can't find out anything...."

"Tell him not to waste any more time," he said. "Those two were probably geeks from Konkrook. You know, that's how the von Schlichten family got out of Germany, in the Year Three-flew a bomber to Spain. The Konkrook war-criminals are getting out before the Army of Occupation moves in."

"Well, the posts at the old Kragan castles report some contragravity, and parties riding 'saurs, moving west from the city," she told him. "There are a lot of refugees on the roads. And combat reports from Konkrook agree that resistance is getting weaker every hour....And the supra-atmosphere observation-craft —they're beginning to call her the *Sky-Spy* —is up a hundred and fifty miles over Keegark. We have radar and vision screens and telemetered radiation and other detectors here, tuned to her. They're installing a similar set on the *Northern Lights* at the shipyard. By the way, Air-Commodore Hargreaves wants to know if he can take a pair of 155-mm rifles from the Channel Battery and mount them on the *Lights*."

"Yes, of course, he can have anything he wants, as long as it isn't urgently needed for the bomb project."

"*Sky-Spy* reports normal contragravity traffic between Keegark and the farming-villages around-aircars, lorries, a few scows-but nothing suspicious. No trace of either of the Boer-class ships. Kankad's people are building receiving sets to install on the *Procyon* and the *Aldebaran*, and another set for Kankad's Town. Pickering and his people are still working, but they all look pretty frustrated. They have Major Thornton, at the ammunition plant, doing experimental work on chemical-explosive charges to bring the subcritical masses together and hold them together till an explosion can be produced; they're using most of the skilled electrical and electronics people to work up a detonating device. That's why Kankad's people are doing most of the detection-device work. Hargreaves is fitting a lot of small craft — combat-cars and civilian aircars-with radar sets, to use for patrolling."

"That sounds good," von Schlichten said. "I'll be around and see how things are, after I've had some breakfast."

He had breakfast at the main cafeteria, four floors down; there wasn't as much laughing and talking as usual, but the crowd there seemed in good spirits. He spent some time at headquarters, watching Keegark by TV and radar. So far, nothing had been done about direct reconnaissance over Keegark with radiation-detectors, but Hargreaves reported that a couple of privately owned aircars were being fitted for the job.

He made a flying inspection trip around the island, and visited the farms south of the city, on the mainland, and, finally, made a sweep in the command-car over the city itself. Reconnaissance in person was an archaic and unprogressive procedure, and it was a good way to get generals killed, but one could see a lot of things that would be missed on TV. He let down several times in areas that had already been taken, and talked to company and platoon officers. For one thing, King Yoorkerk's flamboyantly named regiments weren't quite as bad as Paula had thought. She'd been spoiled by the Kragans in her appreciation of other native troops. They had good, standard-quality, Volund-made arms; they were brave and capable; and they had been just enough insulted by being integrated into Kragan regiments to try to make a good showing.

By noon, resistance in the city was beginning to cave in. Surrender flags were appearing on one after another of the Konkrookan rebel strong-points, and at 1430, after he had returned to the Island, a delegation, headed by the Konkrookan equivalent of Lord Mayor and composed largely of prominent merchants, came across the channel under a flag of truce to surrender the city's Spear of State, with abject apologies for not having Gurgurk's head on the point of it. Gurgurk, they reported, had fled to Keegark by air the night before, which explained the incident of the unaccountable aircar and lorry. The Channel Battery stopped firing, and, with the exception of an occasional spatter of small-arms fire, the city fell silent.

At 1600, von Schlichten visited the headquarters Pickering had set up in the office building at the power-plant. As he stepped off the lift on the third floor, a girl, running down the hall with her arms full of papers in folders, collided with him; the load of papers flew in all directions. He stooped to help her pick them up.

"Oh, general! Isn't it wonderful?" she cried. "I just can't believe it!"

"Isn't what wonderful?" he asked.

"Oh, don't you know? They've got it!"

"Huh? They have?" He gathered up the last of the big envelopes and gave them to her. "When?"

"Just half an hour ago. And to think, those books were around here all the time, and....Oh, I've got to run!" She disappeared into the lift.

Inside the office, one of Pickering's engineers was sitting on the middle of his spinal column, a stenograph-phone in one hand and a book in the other. Once in a while, he would say something into the mouthpiece of the phone. Two other nuclear engineers had similar books spread out on a desk in front of them; they were making notes and looking up references in the *Nuclear Engineers' Handbook*, and making calculations with their sliderules. There was a huddle around the drafting-boards, where two more such books were in use.

"Well, what's happened?" he demanded, catching Pickering by the arm as he rushed from one group to another.

"Ha! We have it!" Pickering cried. "Everything we need! Look!"

He had another of the books under his arm. He held it out to von Schlichten, and von Schlichten suddenly felt sicker than he had ever felt since, at the age of fourteen, he had gotten drunk for the first time. He had seen men crack up under intolerable strain before, but this was the first time he had seen a whole roomful of men blow their tops in the same manner.

The book was a novel—a jumbo-size historical novel, of some seven or eight hundred pages. Its dust-jacket bore a slightly-more-than-bust-length picture of a young lady with crimson hair and green eyes and jade earrings and a plunging-not to say power-diving—neckline that left her affiliation with the class of Mammalia in no doubt whatever. In the background, a mushroom-topped smoke-column rose, and away from it something intended to be a four-motor propeller-driven bomber of the First Century was racing madly. The title, he saw, was *Dire Dawn*, and the author was one Hildegarde Hernandez.

"Well, it has a picture of an A-bomb explosion on it," he agreed.

"It has more than that; it has the whole business. Case specifications, tampers, charge design, detonating device, everything. Why, the end-papers even have diagrams, copies of the original Nagasaki-bomb drawings. Look."

Von Schlichten looked. He had no more than the average intelligent layman's knowledge of nuclear physics-enough to recharge or repair a conversion-unit —but the drawings looked authentic enough. They seemed to be copies of ancient blueprints, lettered in First Century English, with Lingua Terra translations added, and marked TOP SECRET and U.S. ARMY CORPS OF ENGINEERS and MANHATTAN ENGINEERING DISTRICT.

"And look at this!" Pickering opened at a marked page and showed it to him. "And this!" He opened where another slip of paper had been inserted. "Everything we want to know, practically."

"I don't get this." He wasn't sick, anymore, just bewildered. "I read some reviews of this thing. All the reviewers panned hell out of it —'World War II Through a Bedroom Keyhole'; 'Henty in Black Lace Panties' —that sort of thing."

"Yeh, yeh, sure," Pickering agreed. "But this Hernandez had illusions of being a great serious historical novelist, see. She won't try to write a book till she's put in years of research-actually, about six months' research by a herd of librarians and college-juniors and other such literary coolies-and she boasts that she never yet has been caught in an error of historical background detail.

"Well, this opus is about the old Manhattan Project. The heroine is a sort of super-Mata-Hari, who is, alternately and sometimes simultaneously, in the pay of the Nazis, the Soviets, the Vatican, Chiang Kai-Shek, the Japanese Emperor, and the Jewish International Bankers, and she sleeps with everybody but Joe Stalin and Mao Tse-tung, and of course, she is in on every step of the A-bomb project. She even manages to stow away on the *Enola Gay*, with the help of a general she's spent fifty incandescent pages seducing.

"In order to tool up for this production-job, La Hernandez did her researching just where Lourenço Gomes probably did his-University of Montevideo Library. She even had access to the photostats of the old U.S. data that General Lanningham brought to South America after the debacle in the United States in A.E. 114. Those end-papers are part of the Lanningham stuff. As far as we've been able to check mathematically, everything is strictly authentic and practical. We'll have to run a few more tests on the chemical-explosive charges-we don't have any data on the exact strength of the explosives they used then-and the tampers and detonating device will need to be tested a little. But in about half an hour, we ought to be able to start drawing plans for the case, and as soon as they're finished, we'll rush them to the shipyard foundries for casting."

Von Schlichten handed the book back to Pickering, and sighed deeply. "And I thought everybody here had gone off his rocker," he said. "We will erect, on the ruins of Keegark, a hundred-foot statue of Señorita Hildegarde Hernandez....How did you get onto this?"

Pickering pointed to a young man with dull brick colored hair, who was punching out some kind of a problem on a small computing machine.

"Piet van Reenen, over there, he has a girl-friend whose taste runs to this sort of literary bubble-gum. She told him it was all in a book she'd just read, and showed him. We descended in force on the bookshop and grabbed every copy in stock. We are now running a sort of gaseous-diffusion process, to separate the nuclear physics from the pornography. I must say, Hildegarde has her biological data very well in hand, too."

"I'll bet she'd have fun writing a novel about these geeks," von Schlichten said. "Well, how soon do you think you can have a bomb ready for us?"

"Casting the cases is going to slow us down the most," Pickering said. "But, even with that, we ought to have one ready in three days, at the most. By two weeks, we'll be turning them out on an assembly-line."

"I hope we don't need more than one. But you'd better produce at least half a dozen. And have some practice-bombs made up, out of concrete or anything, as long as they're the right weight and airfoil and have some way of releasing smoke. Get them done as soon as you have your case designed. We want to be able to make a couple of practice drops."

There was no use, he thought, of raising hopes which might prove premature. He told Paula Quinton, of course, and Themistocles M'zangwe, and, by telecast on sealed beam, King Kankad and Air-Commodore Hargreaves. Beyond that, there was nothing to do but wait, and hope that Hargreaves could keep Orgzild's bombers away from Gongonk Island and Kankad's Town and that Hildegarde Hernandez had been playing fair with her public. He visited the city, where a few pockets of diehard resistance were being liquidated, and where everybody who had not been too deeply and publicly involved in the *znidd suddabit* conspiracy was now coming forward and claiming to have been a lifelong friend of the Terrans and the Company. Von Schlichten returned to Gongonk Island, debating with himself whether to declare a general amnesty or to set up a dozen guillotines in the city and run them around the clock for a week. There were cogent arguments for and against either procedure.

By 2100, the last organized resistance had been wiped out, and curfew had been imposed, and peace of a sort restored. There was still the threat from Keegark, but it was looking less ominous now than it had the evening before. Von Schlichten and Paula were having dinner in the Broadway Room, confident that there was nothing left to do that they could do anything about, when the extension phone that had been plugged in at their table rang.

"Colonel Quinton here," Paula identified herself into it, and listened for a moment. "There has? When?...Well, where did it come from?...I see. And the direction?...Anything else?"

Apparently there was nothing else. She hung up, and turned to von Schlichten.

"The *Sky-Spy* just detected a ship lifting out from Keegark, presumed one of the Boer-class freighters, either the *Jan Smuts* or the *Oom Paul Kruger*. It was first picked up on contragravity at about a hundred feet, rising vertically from near the Palace. The supposition is the geeks had her camouflaged since the time Commander Prinsloo first bombarded Keegark with the *Aldebaran*. That was about twenty minutes ago; at last report, she's fifty miles north of Keegark, headed up the Hoork River."

Von Schlichten started thinking aloud: "That could be a feint, to draw our ships north after her, and leave the approach to Konkrook or Kankad's open, but that would be presuming that they know about the *Sky-Spy*, and I doubt that, though not enough to take chances on. They know we have ground and ship-radar, and they may think they can slip down the Konk Valley either undetected or mistaken for one of our ships from North Uller."

He picked up the phone. "Get me through on telecast to Air-Commodore Hargreaves, aboard the *Procyon*," he said. "I'll take it in the office; I'll be up directly." He rose. "Finish your dinner, and have the rest of mine sent up," he told Paula.

Leaving the elevator, he rushed into the big headquarters room just as contact was established with the *Procyon*, on station over the northwestern corner of Takkad Sea, between Kankad's Town and Keegark. The *Aldebaran*, he knew, was west of Keegark; the *Northern Lights*, now fitted with a pair of 155-mm guns, in addition to her 90's, had just arrived at Kankad's. He had the *Aldebaran* sent north along the crest of the mountain-range between the Hoork and Konk river-valleys, where she could cover both with her own radar and other detection-devices and exchange information with the *Sky-Spy*, and the *Gaucho* sent in what looked like the right course to intercept the Boer-class freighter from Keegark. The *Northern Lights*, also with screens tuned to the *Sky-Spy*, was sent to take over the *Aldebaran's* regular station. Finally, he called Skilk and had the *Northern Star* sent south down the Hoork Valley.

After that, there was nothing to do but wait, and watch the screens. Paula Quinton put in an appearance shortly after he had finished calling Skilk, pushing a cocktail-wagon on which their interrupted dinners had been placed. They finished eating, and drank coffee, and smoked. Most of the rest of his staff who were not busy on the bomb-project or at the shipyards or with the occupation of Konkrook drifted in; they all sat and stared from one to another of the screens, which told, in radar-patterns and direct vision and telescopic vision and heat and radiation detection, the story of what was going on to the northeast of them.

Keegark was dark, on the vision-screen; evidently King Orgzild had invented the blackout, too. Not that it did him any good; the radar-screen showed the city clearly, and it was just as clear on the radiation and heat-screens. The Keegarkan ship was completely blacked out, but the radiations from her engines and the distinctive radiation-pattern of her contragravity-field showed clearly, and there was a speck that marked her position on the radar-screen. The same position was marked with a pin-point of light on the vision-screen —some device on the *Sky-Spy*, synchronized with the detectors, kept it focused there. The Company ships and contragravity vehicles all were carrying topside lights, visible only from above, which flashed alternate red and blue to identify them.

Time crawled slowly around the clock-face on the wall, the sixty-five-second minutes of Uller dragging like hours. The spots that marked the enemy ship and her hunters crawled, too; seen from the hundred-and-fifty-mile altitude of the *Sky-Spy*, even the six-hundred-mile speed of the *Gaucho* was barely visible. They drank coffee till the stuff revolted them; they smoked until their throats and mouths were dry, they watched the screens until they thought that they would see them in their dreams forever. Then the *Gaucho* reported radar-contact with the Keegarkan ship, which had begun to turn in a hairpin-shaped course and was coming south down the Konk Valley.

After that, the *Gaucho* began reporting directly, and her topside identification-light went out.

"...doused our lights; we're down in the valley, altitude about a thousand feet. We're trying to get a glimpse of her against the sky," a voice came in. "We're cutting in our forward TV-pickup." The voice repeated, several times, the wavelength, and somebody got an auxiliary screen tuned in. There was nothing visible on it but the darkness of the valley, the star-jeweled sky, and the loom of the East Konk Mountains. "We still can't see her, but we ought to, any moment; radar shows her well above the mountains. Ah, there she is; she just obscured Beta Hydrae V; she's moving toward that big constellation to the east of it, the one they call Finnegan's Goat. Now she'll be right in the center of the screen; we're going straight for her. We're going to try to slow her down till the *Aldebaran* can get here...."

The enemy ship was vaguely visible, now, becoming clearer in the starlight. She was a Boer-class freighter, all right. Probably the *Jan Smuts*; the *Oom Paul Kruger* had last been reported at Bwork, and there was little chance that she had slipped into Keegark since the uprising had started. For all anybody knew, she could have been destroyed in the fighting before the Bwork Residency fell.

"All right, we have her spotted; we're going to open up on her," the voice from the *Gaucho* announced. "She has two 90's to our one; we'll try to disable them, first." The vision-screen lit with the indirect glare of the gun-flash, and the image in it jiggled violently as the ship shook to the recoil, then steadied again, with the enemy ship visible in the middle of it, growing larger and larger as the *Gaucho* rushed toward her. The gun fired again and again, flooding the screen with momentary yellow light and disturbing the image as the recoil shook the gun-cutter. The enemy ship began firing in reply, the shots were all wide misses. Apparently the geek guncrew didn't know how to synchronize the radar sights, and were ignorant of the correct setting for the proximity-fuses. The *Gaucho*'s searchlights came on, bathing her quarry in light. It was the *Jan Smuts*; the name and the figurehead-bust of the old soldier-philosopher were plainly visible. Her forward gun had been knocked out, and she was trying to swing about to get a field of fire for her stern-gun.

"We're going to give her a rocket-salvo," the voice said. "Watch this, now!"

The rockets leaped forward, from the topside racks, four and four and four and four, at half-second intervals. The first four hit the *Smuts* amidships and low, exploding with a flare that grew before it could die away as the second four landed. Nobody ever saw the third and fourth four land. The *Jan Smuts* vanished in a blaze of light that blinded everybody in the room; when they could see again, after some thirty seconds, the screen was dark.

In the direct-vision screen from the *Sky-Spy*, the whole countryside of the Konk Valley, five hundred miles north of Konkrook, was lighted. The heat and radiation detectors were going insane. And in the shifting confusion on the radar-screen, there was no trace either of the *Jan Smuts* or the *Gaucho*.

"Well, the geeks did have an A-bomb," Themistocles M'zangwe said, at length. "I'd been trying to kid myself that we were just preparing against a million-to-one chance. I wonder how many more they have."

"Paula, find out who was in command of the *Gaucho*; he'd be a junior-grade lieutenant. Fix up orders promoting him to navy captain, as of now. It's probably the only thing we can do for him, anymore. And promotions of the same order for everybody else aboard that cutter. Authority Carlos von Schlichten, acting Governor-General." He picked up a phone. "Get me Commander Prinsloo, on *Aldebaran*...."

He ordered Prinsloo to launch airboats and make a search; cautioned him to be careful of radiation, but to take no chances on any of the *Gaucho*'s complement being still alive and in need of help. While that was going on, the *Sky-Spy* reported another ship coming over her horizon to the east, from the direction of Bwork. That would be the *Oom Paul Kruger*. Hargreaves had already learned of the advent of the second freighter. He was unwilling to take the *Procyon* off her station until the *Aldebaran* returned from the Konk Valley. In this, von Schlichten concurred.

Somebody suggested that a drink would be in order. They had just watched the all-but-certain death of three Terran officers, fifteen Terran airmen, and ten Kragans, but they had all been living in too close companionship with death in the past three days-or was it three centuries-to be too deeply affected. And they had also watched, at least for a day or so, the removal of the threat that had hung over their heads. And they had seen proof that they had a defense against King Orgzild's bombs.

They were still mixing cocktails when Pickering phoned in.

"Some good news, general, from Operation 'Hildegarde.' We ought to have at least one bomb ready to drop by 1500 tomorrow, four or five more by next midnight," he said. "We don't need to have cases cast. We got our dimensions decided, and we find that there are a lot of big empty liquid-oxygen flasks, or tanks, rather, at the spaceport, that'll accommodate everything-fissionables, explosive-charges, tampers, detonator, and all."

"Well, go ahead with it. Make up a few of them; as many as you can between now and 2400 Sunday." He thought for a moment. "Don't waste time on those practice bombs I mentioned. We'll make a practice drop with a live bomb. And don't throw away the design for the cast case. We may need that, later on."

XV

A Place in my Heart for Hildegarde

The company fleet hung off Keegark, at fifteen thousand feet, in a belt of calm air just below the seesawing currents from the warming Antarctic and the cooling deserts of the Arctic. There was the *Procyon*, from the bridge of which von Schlichten watched the movements of the other ships and airboats and the distant horizon. The *Aldebaran* was ten miles off, to the west, her metal sheathing glinting in the red light of the evening sun. There was the *Northern Star*, down from Skilk, a smaller and more distant twinkle of reflected light to the north of *Aldebaran*. The *Northern Lights* was off to the east, and between her and *Procyon* was a fifth ship; turning the arm-mounted binoculars around, he could just make out, on her bow, the figurehead bust of a man in an ancient tophat and a fringe of chin-beard. She was the *Oom Paul Kruger*, captured by the *Procyon* after a chase across the mountains northeast of Keegark the day before. And, remote from the other ships, to the south, a tiny speck of blue-gray, almost invisible against the sky, and a smaller twinkle of reflected sunlight —a garbage-scow, unflatteringly but somewhat aptly rechristened *Hildegarde Hernandez*, which had been altered as a bomb-carrier, and the gun-cutter *Elmoran*. With the glasses, he could see a bulky cylinder being handled off the scow and loaded onto the improvised bomb-catapult on the *Elmoran*'s stern. Shortly thereafter, the gun-cutter broke loose from the tender and began to approach the fleet.

"General, I must protest against your doing this," Air-Commodore Hargreaves said. "There's simply no sense in it. That bomb can be dropped without your personal supervision aboard, sir, and you're endangering yourself unnecessarily. That infernal machine hasn't been tested or anything; it might even let go on the catapult when you try to drop it. And we simply can't afford to lose you, now."

"No, what would become of us, if you go out there and blow yourself up with that contraption?" Buhrmann supported him. "My God, I thought Don Quixote was a Spaniard, instead of a German!"

"Argentino," von Schlichten corrected. "And don't try to sell me that Irreplaceable Man line, either. Them M'zangwe can replace me, Hid O'Leary can replace him, Barney Mordkovitz can replace him, and so on down to where you make a second lieutenant out of some sergeant. We've been all over this last evening. Admitted we can't take time for a long string of test-shots, and admitted we have to use an untested weapon; I'm not sending men out under those circumstances and staying here on this ship and watch them blow themselves up. If that bomb's our only hope, it's got to be dropped right, and I'm not going to take a chance on having it dropped by a crew who think they've been sent out on a suicide mission. What happened to the *Gaucho* when she blew the *Smuts* up is too fresh in everybody's mind. But if I, who ordered the mission, accompany it, they'll know I have some confidence that they'll come back alive."

"Well I'm coming along, too, general," Kent Pickering spoke up. "I made the damned thing, and I ought to be along when it's dropped, on the principle that a restaurant-proprietor ought to be seen eating his own food once in a while."

"I still don't see why we couldn't have made at least one test shot, first," Hans Meyerstein, the Banking Cartel man, objected.

"Well, I'll tell you why," Paula Quinton spoke up. "There's a good chance that the geeks don't know we have a bomb of our own. They may believe that it was something invented on Niflheim for mining purposes, and that we haven't realized its military application. There's more than a good chance that the loss of the *Jan Smuts* has temporarily demoralized them. Personally, I believe that both King Orgzild and Prince Gorkrink were aboard her when she blew up. That's something we'll never know, positively, of course. That ship and everything and everybody in her were simply vaporized, and the particles are registering on our geigers now. But I'm as sure as I am of anything about these geeks that one or both of them accompanied her."

"Paula knows what she's talking about," King Kankad jabbered in the Takkad Sea language which they all understood. "Just like Von saying that he has to go on our cutter, to encourage the crew. They always insist that their kings and generals go into battle, particularly if something important is to be done. They think the gods get angry if they don't."

"And we have to hit them now," von Schlichten said. "They still have a couple of bombs left. We haven't been able to locate them with detectors, but those geeks Kankad's men caught on that commando-raid, last night, say that there were at least three of them made. We can't take a chance that some fanatic may load one into an aircar and make a kamikaze-raid on Gongonk Island."

The *Elmoran* ran alongside, with her Masai-warrior figurehead and the black cylinder on her catapult aft. Somebody had painted, on the bomb: DIRE DAWN *by Hildegarde Hernandez. Compliments of the author to H.M. King Orgzild of Keegark.* A canvas-entubed gangway was run out to connect the ship with the cutter. Von Schlichten and Kent Pickering went down the ladder from the bridge, the others accompanying them. As he stepped into the gangway, Paula Quinton fell in behind him.

"Where do you think you're going?" he demanded.

"Along with you," she replied. "I'm your adjutant, I believe."

"You definitely are not going along. Personally, I don't believe there's any danger, but I'm not having you run any unnecessary risks...."

"Von, I don't know much about the way Terrans think, except about fighting and about making things," Kankad told him. "And I don't know anything at all about the kind of Terrans who have young. But I believe this is something important to Paula. Let her go with you, because if you go alone and don't come back, I don't think she will ever be happy again."

He looked at Kankad curiously, wondering, as he had so often before, just what went on inside that lizard-skull. Then he looked at Paula, and, after a moment, he nodded.

"All right, colonel, objection withdrawn," he said.

Aboard the *Elmoran*, they gave the bomb a last-minute inspection and checked the catapult and the bomb-sight, and then went up on the bridge.

"Ready for the bombing mission, sir?" the skipper, a Lieutenant (j.g.) Morrison, asked.

"Ready if you are, lieutenant. Carry on; we're just passengers."

"Thank you, sir. We'd thought of going in over the city at about five thousand for a target-check, turning when we're half-way back to the mountains, and coming back for our bombing-run at fifteen thousand. Is that all right, sir?"

Von Schlichten nodded. "You're the skipper, lieutenant. You'd better make sure, though, that as soon as the bomb-off signal is flashed, your engineer hits his auxiliary rocket-propulsion button. We want to be about fifteen miles from where that thing goes off."

The lieutenant (j.g.) muttered something that sounded unmilitarily like, "You ain't foolin', brother!"

"No, I'm not," von Schlichten agreed. "I saw the *Jan Smuts* on the TV-screen."

The *Elmoran* pointed her bow, and the long blade of the figurehead warrior's spear, toward Keegark. The city grew out of the ground-mist, a particolored blur at the delta of the dry Hoork River, and then a color-splashed triangle between the river and the bay and the hills on the landward side, and then it took shape, cross-ruled with streets and granulated with buildings. As they came in, von Schlichten, who had approached it from the air many times before, could distinguish the landmarks-the site of King Orgzild's nitroglycerin plant, now a crater surrounded by a quarter-mile radius of ruins; the Residency, another crater since Rodolfo MacKinnon had blown it up under him; the smashed *Christiaan De Wett* at the Company docks; King Orgzild's Palace, fire-stained and with a hole blown in one corner by the *Aldebaran's* bombs.... Then they were past the city and over open country.

"I wish we had some idea where the rest of those bombs are stored, sir," Lieutenant Morrison said. "We don't seem to have gotten anything significant when we flew reconnaissance with the radiation detectors."

"No, about all that was picked up was the main power-plant, and the radiation-escape from there was normal," Pickering agreed. "The bombs themselves wouldn't be detectable, except to the extent that, say, a nuclear-conversion engine for an airboat would be. They probably have them underground, somewhere, well shielded."

"Those prisoners Kankad's commandos dragged in only knew that they were in the city somewhere," von Schlichten considered. "How about midway between the Palace and the Residency for our ground-zero, lieutenant? That looks like the center of the city."

The cutter turned and started back, having risen another ten thousand feet. Morrison passed the word to the bombardier. The city, with the sea beyond it now, came rushing at them, and von Schlichten, standing at the front of the bridge, discovered that he had his arm around Paula's waist and was holding her a little more closely than was military. He made no attempt to release her, however.

"There's nothing to worry about, really," he was assuring her. "Pickering's boys built this thing according to the best principles of engineering, and the stuff they got out of that big-economy-size shilling-shocker all checked mathematically...."

The red light on the bridge flashed, and the intercom shouted, *"Bomb off!"* He forced Paula down on the bridge deck and crouched beside her.

"Cover your eyes," he warned. "You remember what the flash was like in the screen when the *Jan Smuts* blew up. And we didn't get the worst of it; the pickup on the *Gaucho* was knocked out too soon."

He kept on lecturing her about gamma-rays and ultra-violet rays and X-rays and cosmic rays, trying to keep making some sort of intelligent sounds while they clung together and waited, and, with the other half of his mind, trying not to think of everything that could go wrong with that jerry-built improvisation they had just dumped onto Keegark. If it didn't blow, and the geeks found it, they'd know that another one would be along shortly, and....

An invisible hand caught the gun-cutter and hurled her end-over-end, sending von Schlichten and Paula sprawling at full length on the deck, still clinging to one another. There was a blast of almost palpable sound, and a sensation of heat that penetrated even the airtight superstructure of the *Elmoran*. An instant later, there was another, and another, similar shock. Two more bombs had gone off behind them, in Keegark; that meant that they had found King Orgzild's remaining nuclear armament. There were shattering sounds of breaking glass, and heavy thumps that told of structural damage to the cutter, and hoarse shouts, and lurid cursing as Morrison and his airmen struggled with the controls. The cutter began losing altitude, but she was back on a reasonably even keel. Von Schlichten rose, helping Paula to her feet, and found that they had been kissing one another passionately. They were still in each other's arms when the pitching and rolling of the cutter ceased and somebody tapped him on the shoulder.

He came out of the embrace and looked around. It was Lieutenant (j.g.) Morrison.

"What the devil, lieutenant?" he demanded.

"Sorry to interrupt, sir, but we're starting back to *Procyon*. And here, you'll want this, I suppose." He held out a glass disc. "I never expected to see it, but at that it took three A-bombs to blow you loose from your monocle."

"Oh, that?" Von Schlichten took his trademark and set it in his eye. "I didn't lose it," he lied. "I just jettisoned it. Don't you know, lieutenant, that no gentleman ever wears a monocle while he's kissing a lady?"

He looked around. They were at about eight hundred to a thousand feet above the water, with a stiff following wind away from the explosion area. The 90-mm gun, forward, must have been knocked loose and carried away; it was gone, and so was the TV-pickup and the radar. Something, probably the gun, had slammed against the front of the bridge-the metal skeleton was bent in, and the armor-glass had been knocked out. The cutter was vibrating properly, so the contragravity-field had not been disturbed, and her jets were firing.

"It was the second and third bombs that did the damage, sir," Morrison was saying. "We'd have gone through the effects of our own bomb with nothing more than a bad shaking-of course, on contragravity, we're weightless relative to the air-mass, but she was built to stand the winds in the high latitudes. But the two geek bombs caught us off balance...."

"You don't need to apologize, lieutenant. You and your crew behaved splendidly, lieutenant-commander, best traditions, and all that sort of thing. It was a pleasure, commander, hope to be aboard with you again, captain."

They found Kent Pickering at the rear of the bridge, and joined him looking astern. Even von Schlichten, who had seen H-bombs and Bethe-cycle bombs, was impressed. Keegark was completely obliterated under an outward-rolling cloud of smoke and dust that spread out for five miles at the bottom of the towering column.

There had been a hundred and fifty thousand people in that city, even if their faces were the faces of lizards and they had four arms and quartz-speckled skins. What fraction of them were now alive, he could not guess. He had to remind himself that they were the people who had burned Eric Blount and Hendrik Lemoyne alive; that two of the three bombs that had contributed to that column of boiling smoke had been made in Keegark, by Keegarkans, and that, with a few causal factors altered, he was seeing what would have happened to Konkrook. Perhaps every Terran felt a superstitious dread of nuclear energy turned to the purposes of war; small wonder, after what they had done on their own world.

For one thing, he thought grimly, the next geek who picks up the idea of soaking a Terran in thermoconcentrate and setting fire to him will drop it again like a hot potato. And the next geek potentate who tries to organize an anti-Terran conspiracy, or the next crazy caravan-driver who preached *znidd suddabit*, will be lynched on the spot. But this must be the last nuclear bomb used on Uller....

Drunkard's morning-after resolution! he told himself contemptuously. The next time, it will come easier, and easier still the time after that. After you drop the first bomb, there is no turning back, any more than there had been after Hiroshima, four-hundred-and-fifty-odd years ago. Why, he had even been considering just where, against the mountains back of Bwork, he would drop a demonstration bomb as a prelude to a surrender demand.

You either went on to the inevitable catastrophe, or you realized, in time, that nuclear armament and nationalism cannot exist together on the same planet, and it is easier to banish a habit of thought than a piece of knowledge. Uller was not ready for membership in the Terran Federation; then its people must bow to the Terran Pax. The Kragans would help-as proconsuls, administrators, now, instead of mercenaries. And there must be manned orbital stations, and the Residencies must be moved outside the cities, away from possible blast-areas. And Sid Harrington's idea of encouraging the natives to own their own contragravity-ships must be shelved, for a long time to come. Maybe, in a century or so....

Kankad had a good idea, at that, a most meritorious idea. He was sold on it, already, and he doubted if it would take much salesmanship with Paula, either. Already, she was clinging to his arm with obvious possessiveness. Maybe their grandchildren, and the Kankad of that time, would see Uller a civilized member of the Federation....

They paused, as the gun-cutter nuzzled up to the *Procyon* and the canvas-entubed gangway was run out and made fast, looking back at the fearful thing that had sprouted from where Keegark had been.

"You know," Paula was saying, echoing his earlier thought, "but for that female pornographer, that would have been Konkrook."

He nodded. "Yes. I hope you won't mind, but there will always be a place in my heart for Hildegarde."

Then they turned their backs upon the abomination of Keegark's desolation and went up the gangway together, looking very little like a general and his adjutant.

With a broadsword in his hand, von Schlichten fought his way toward the throne. There Firkked waited, a sword in one of his upper hands, his Spear of State in the other, and a dagger in each lower hand. Von Schlichten fought on, trying not to think of the absurdity of a man of the Sixth Century A.E., the representative of a civilized Chartered Company, dueling to the death with a barbarian king for a throne he had promised to another barbarian ...or of what could happen on Uller if he allowed this four-armed monstrosity to kill him!

Four-Day Planet

by H. Beam Piper

Dedication

1
The Ship from Terra

I went through the gateway, towing my equipment in a contragravity hamper over my head. As usual, I was wondering what it would take, short of a revolution, to get the city of Port Sandor as clean and tidy and well lighted as the spaceport area. I knew Dad's editorials and my sarcastic news stories wouldn't do it. We'd been trying long enough.

The two girls in bikinis in front of me pushed on, still gabbling about the fight one of them had had with her boy friend, and I closed up behind the half dozen monster-hunters in long trousers, ankle boots and short boat-jackets, with big knives on their belts. They must have all been from the same crew, because they weren't arguing about whose ship was fastest, had the toughest skipper, and made the most money. They were talking about the price of tallow-wax, and they seemed to have picked up a rumor that it was going to be cut another ten centisols a pound. I eavesdropped shamelessly, but it was the same rumor I'd picked up, myself, a little earlier.

"Hi, Walt," somebody behind me called out. "Looking for some news that's fit to print?"

I turned my head. It was a man of about thirty-five with curly brown hair and a wide grin. Adolf Lautier, the entertainment promoter. He and Dad each owned a share in the Port Sandor telecast station, and split their time between his music and drama-films and Dad's newscasts.

"All the news is fit to print, and if it's news the *Times* prints it," I told him. "Think you're going to get some good thrillers this time?"

He shrugged. I'd just asked that to make conversation; he never had any way of knowing what sort of films would come in. The ones the *Peenemünde* was bringing should be fairly new, because she was outbound from Terra. He'd go over what was aboard, and trade one for one for the old films he'd shown already.

"They tell me there's a real Old-Terran-style Western been showing on Völund that ought to be coming our way this time," he said. "It was filmed in South America, with real horses."

That would go over big here. Almost everybody thought horses were as extinct as dinosaurs. I've seen so-called Westerns with the cowboys riding Freyan *oukry*. I mentioned that, and then added:

"They'll think the old cattle towns like Dodge and Abilene were awful sissy places, though."

"I suppose they were, compared to Port Sandor," Lautier said. "Are you going aboard to interview the distinguished visitor?"

"Which one?" I asked. "Glenn Murell or Leo Belsher?"

Lautier called Leo Belsher something you won't find in the dictionary but which nobody needs to look up. The hunters, ahead of us, heard him and laughed. They couldn't possibly have agreed more. He was going to continue with the fascinating subject of Mr. Leo Belsher's ancestry and personal characteristics, and then bit it off short. I followed his eyes, and saw old Professor Hartzenbosch, the principal of the school, approaching.

"Ah, here you are, Mr. Lautier," he greeted. "I trust that I did not keep you waiting." Then he saw me. "Why, it's Walter Boyd. How is your father, Walter?"

I assured him as to Dad's health and inquired about his own, and then asked him how things were going at school. As well as could be expected, he told me, and I gathered that he kept his point of expectation safely low. Then he wanted to know if I were going aboard to interview Mr. Murell.

"Really, Walter, it is a wonderful thing that a famous author like Mr. Murell should come here to write a book about our planet," he told me, very seriously, and added, as an afterthought: "Have you any idea where he intends staying while he is among us?"

"Why, yes," I admitted. "After the *Peenemünde* radioed us their passenger list, Dad talked to him by screen, and invited him to stay with us. Mr. Murell accepted, at least until he can find quarters of his own."

There are a lot of good poker players in Port Sandor, but Professor Jan Hartzenbosch is not one of them. The look of disappointment would have been comical if it hadn't been so utterly pathetic. He'd been hoping to lasso Murell himself.

"I wonder if Mr. Murell could spare time to come to the school and speak to the students," he said, after a moment.

"I'm sure he could. I'll mention it to him, Professor," I promised.

Professor Hartzenbosch bridled at that. The great author ought to be coming to his school out of respect for him, not because a seventeen-year-old cub reporter sent him. But then, Professor Hartzenbosch always took the attitude that he was conferring a favor on the *Times* when he had anything he wanted publicity on.

The elevator door opened, and Lautier and the professor joined in the push to get into it. I hung back, deciding to wait for the next one so that I could get in first and get back to the rear, where my hamper wouldn't be in people's way. After a while, it came back empty and I got on, and when the crowd pushed off on the top level, I put my hamper back on contragravity and towed it out into the outdoor air, which by this time had gotten almost as cool as a bake-oven.

I looked up at the sky, where everybody else was looking. The *Peenemünde* wasn't visible; it was still a few thousand miles off-planet. Big ragged clouds were still blowing in from the west, very high, and the sunset was even brighter and redder than when I had seen it last, ten hours before. It was now about 1630.

Now, before anybody starts asking just who's crazy, let me point out that this is not on Terra, nor on Baldur nor Thor nor Odin nor Freya, nor any other rational planet. This is Fenris, and on Fenris the sunsets, like many other things, are somewhat peculiar.

Fenris is the second planet of a G_4 star, six hundred and fifty light-years to the Galactic southwest of the Sol System. Everything else equal, it should have been pretty much Terra type; closer to a cooler primary and getting about the same amount of radiation. At least, that's what the book says. I was born on Fenris, and have never been off it in the seventeen years since.

Everything else, however, is not equal. The Fenris year is a trifle shorter than the Terran year we use for Atomic Era dating, eight thousand and a few odd Galactic Standard hours. In that time, Fenris makes almost exactly four axial rotations. This means that on one side the sun is continuously in the sky for a thousand hours, pouring down unceasing heat, while the other side is in shadow. You sleep eight hours, and when you get up and go outside-in an insulated vehicle, or an extreme-environment suit-you find that the shadows have moved only an inch or so, and it's that much hotter. Finally, the sun crawls down to the horizon and hangs there for a few days-periods of twenty-four G.S. hours-and then slides slowly out of sight. Then, for about a hundred hours, there is a beautiful unfading sunset, and it's really pleasant outdoors. Then it gets darker and colder until, just before sunrise, it gets almost cold enough to freeze CO_2. Then the sun comes up, and we begin all over again.

You are picking up the impression, I trust, that as planets go, Fenris is nobody's bargain. It isn't a real hell-planet, and spacemen haven't made a swear word out of its name, as they have with the name of fluorine-atmosphere Nifflheim, but even the Reverend Hiram Zilker, the Orthodox-Monophysite preacher, admits that it's one of those planets the Creator must have gotten a trifle absent-minded with.

The chartered company that colonized it, back at the end of the Fourth Century A.E., went bankrupt in ten years, and it wouldn't have taken that long if communication between Terra and Fenris hadn't been a matter of six months each way. When the smash finally came, two hundred and fifty thousand colonists were left stranded. They lost everything they'd put into the company, which, for most of them, was all they had. Not a few lost their lives before the Federation Space Navy could get ships here to evacuate them.

But about a thousand, who were too poor to make a fresh start elsewhere and too tough for Fenris to kill, refused evacuation, took over all the equipment and installations the Fenris Company had abandoned, and tried to make a living out of the planet. At least, they stayed alive. There are now twenty-odd thousand of us, and while we are still very poor, we are very tough, and we brag about it.

There were about two thousand people-ten per cent of the planetary population-on the wide concrete promenade around the spaceport landing pit. I came out among them and set down the hamper with my telecast cameras and recorders, wishing, as usual, that I could find some ten or twelve-year-old kid weak-minded enough to want to be a reporter when he grew up, so that I could have an apprentice to help me with my junk.

As the star-and only-reporter of the greatest-and only-paper on the planet, I was always on hand when either of the two ships on the Terra-Odin milk run, the *Peenemünde* and the *Cape Canaveral*, landed. Of course, we always talk to them by screen as soon as they come out of hyperspace and into radio range, and get the passenger list, and a speed-recording of any news they are carrying, from the latest native uprising on Thor to the latest political scandal on Venus. Sometime the natives of Thor won't be fighting anybody at all, or the Federation Member Republic of Venus will have some nonscandalous politics, and either will be the man-bites-dog story to end man-bites-dog stories. All the news is at least six months old, some more than a year. A spaceship can log a light-year in sixty-odd hours, but radio waves still crawl along at the same old 186,000 mps.

I still have to meet the ships. There's always something that has to be picked up personally, usually an interview with some VIP traveling through. This time, though, the big story coming in on the *Peenemünde* was a local item. Paradox? Dad says there is no such thing. He says a paradox is either a verbal contradiction, and you get rid of it by restating it correctly, or it's a structural contradiction, and you just call it an impossibility and let it go at that. In this case, what was coming in was a real live author, who was going to write a travel book about Fenris, the planet with the four-day year. Glenn Murell, which sounded suspiciously like a nom de plume, and nobody here had ever heard of him.

That was odd, too. One thing we can really be proud of here, besides the toughness of our citizens, is our public library. When people have to stay underground most of the time to avoid being fried and/or frozen to death, they have a lot of time to kill, and reading is one of the cheaper and more harmless and profitable ways of doing it. And travel books are a special favorite here. I suppose because everybody is hoping to read about a worse place than Fenris. I had checked on Glenn Murell at the library. None of the librarians had ever heard of him, and there wasn't a single mention of him in any of the big catalogues of publications.

The first and obvious conclusion would be that Mr. Glenn Murell was some swindler posing as an author. The only objection to that was that I couldn't quite see why any swindler would come to Fenris, or what he'd expect to swindle the Fenrisians out of. Of course, he could be on the lam from somewhere, but in that case why bother with all the cover story? Some of our better-known citizens came here dodging warrants on other planets.

I was still wondering about Murell when somebody behind me greeted me, and I turned around. It was Tom Kivelson.

Tom and I are buddies, when he's in port. He's just a shade older than I am; he was eighteen around noon, and my eighteenth birthday won't come till midnight, Fenris Standard Sundial Time. His father is Joe Kivelson, the skipper of the *Javelin*; Tom is sort of junior engineer, second gunner, and about third harpooner. We went to school together, which is to say a couple of years at Professor Hartzenbosch's, learning to read and write and put figures together. That is all the schooling anybody on Fenris gets, although Joe Kivelson sent Tom's older sister, Linda, to school on Terra. Anybody who stays here has to dig out education for himself. Tom and I were still digging for ours.

Each of us envied the other, when we weren't thinking seriously about it. I imagined that sea-monster hunting was wonderfully thrilling and romantic, and Tom had the idea that being a newsman was real hot stuff. When we actually stopped to think about it, though, we realized that neither of us would trade jobs and take anything at all for boot. Tom couldn't string three sentences-no, one sentence-together to save his life, and I'm just a town boy who likes to live in something that isn't pitching end-for-end every minute.

Tom is about three inches taller than I am, and about thirty pounds heavier. Like all monster-hunters, he's trying to grow a beard, though at present it's just a blond chin-fuzz. I was surprised to see him dressed as I was, in shorts and sandals and a white shirt and a light jacket. Ordinarily, even in town, he wears boat-clothes. I looked around behind him, and saw the brass tip of a scabbard under the jacket. Any time a hunter-ship man doesn't have his knife on, he isn't wearing anything else. I wondered about his being in port now. I knew Joe Kivelson wouldn't bring his ship in just to meet the *Peenemünde*, with only a couple of hundred hours' hunting left till the storms and the cold.

"I thought you were down in the South Ocean," I said.

"There's going to be a special meeting of the Co-op," he said. "We only heard about it last evening," by which he meant after 1800 of the previous Galactic Standard day. He named another hunter-ship captain who had called the *Javelin* by screen. "We screened everybody else we could."

That was the way they ran things in the Hunters' Co-operative. Steve Ravick would wait till everybody had their ships down on the coast of Hermann Reuch's Land, and then he would call a meeting and pack it with his stooges and hooligans, and get anything he wanted voted through. I had always wondered how long the real hunters were going to stand for that. They'd been standing for it ever since I could remember anything outside my own playpen, which, of course, hadn't been too long.

I was about to say something to that effect, and then somebody yelled, "There she is!" I took a quick look at the radar bowls to see which way they were pointed and followed them up to the sky, and caught a tiny twinkle through a cloud rift. After a moment's mental arithmetic to figure how high she'd have to be to catch the sunlight, I relaxed. Even with the telephoto, I'd only get a picture the size of a pinhead, so I fixed the position in my mind and then looked around at the crowd.

Among them were two men, both well dressed. One was tall and slender, with small hands and feet; the other was short and stout, with a scrubby gray-brown mustache. The slender one had a bulge under his left arm, and the short-and-stout job bulged over the right hip. The former was Steve Ravick, the boss of the Hunters' Co-operative, and his companion was the Honorable Morton Hallstock, mayor of Port Sandor and consequently the planetary government of Fenris.

They had held their respective positions for as long as I could remember anything at all. I could never remember an election in Port Sandor, or an election of officers in the Co-op. Ravick had a bunch of goons and triggermen —I could see a couple of them loitering in the background-who kept down opposition for him. So did Hallstock, only his wore badges and called themselves police.

Once in a while, Dad would write a blistering editorial about one or the other or both of them. Whenever he did, I would put my gun on, and so would Julio Kubanoff, the one-legged compositor who is the third member of the Times staff, and we would take turns making sure nobody got behind Dad's back. Nothing ever happened, though, and that always rather hurt me. Those two racketeers were in so tight they didn't need to care what the Times printed or 'cast about them.

Hallstock glanced over in my direction and said something to Ravick. Ravick gave a sneering laugh, and then he crushed out the cigarette he was smoking on the palm of his left hand. That was a regular trick of his. Showing how tough he was. Dad says that when you see somebody showing off, ask yourself whether he's trying to impress other people, or himself. I wondered which was the case with Steve Ravick.

Then I looked up again. The *Peenemünde* was coming down as fast as she could without over-heating from atmosphere friction. She was almost buckshot size to the naked eye, and a couple of tugs were getting ready to go up and meet her. I got the telephoto camera out of the hamper, checked it, and aimed it. It has a shoulder stock and handgrips and a trigger like a submachine gun. I caught the ship in the finder and squeezed the trigger for a couple of seconds. It would be about five minutes till the tugs got to her and anything else happened, so I put down the camera and looked around.

Coming through the crowd, walking as though the concrete under him was pitching and rolling like a ship's deck on contragravity in a storm, was Bish Ware. He caught sight of us, waved, overbalanced himself and recovered, and then changed course to starboard and bore down on us. He was carrying about his usual cargo, and as usual the manifest would read, *Baldur honey-rum, from Harry Wong's bar.*

Bish wasn't his real name. Neither, I suspected, was Ware. When he'd first landed on Fenris, some five years ago, somebody had nicknamed him the Bishop, and before long that had gotten cut to one syllable. He looked like a bishop, or at least like what anybody who's never seen a bishop outside a screen-play would think a bishop looked like. He was a big man, not fat, but tall and portly; he had a ruddy face that always wore an expression of benevolent wisdom, and the more cargo he took on the wiser and more benevolent he looked.

He had iron-gray hair, but he wasn't old. You could tell that by the backs of his hands; they weren't wrinkled or crepy and the veins didn't protrude. And drunk or sober-though I never remembered seeing him in the latter condition-he had the fastest reflexes of anybody I knew. I saw him, once, standing at the bar in Harry Wong's, knock over an open bottle with his left elbow. He spun half around, grabbed it by the neck and set it up, all in one motion, without spilling a drop, and he went on talking as though nothing had happened. He was quoting Homer, I remembered, and you could tell that he was thinking in the original ancient Greek and translating to Lingua Terra as he went.

He was always dressed as he was now, in a conservative black suit, the jacket a trifle longer than usual, and a black neckcloth with an Uller organic-opal pin. He didn't work at anything, but quarterly-once every planetary day —a draft on the Banking Cartel would come in for him, and he'd deposit it with the Port Sandor Fidelity & Trust. If anybody was unmannerly enough to ask him about it, he always said he had a rich uncle on Terra.

When I was a kid-well, more of a kid than I am now —I used to believe he really was a bishop-unfrocked, of course, or ungaitered, or whatever they call it when they give a bishop the heave-ho. A lot of people who weren't kids still believed that, and they blamed him on every denomination from Anglicans to Zen Buddhists, not even missing the Satanists, and there were all sorts of theories about what he'd done to get excommunicated, the mildest of which was that somewhere there was a cathedral standing unfinished because he'd hypered out with the building fund. It was generally agreed that his ecclesiastical organization was paying him to stay out there in the boondocks where he wouldn't cause them further embarrassment.

I was pretty sure, myself, that he was being paid by somebody, probably his family, to stay out of sight. The colonial planets are full of that sort of remittance men.

Bish and I were pretty good friends. There were certain old ladies, of both sexes and all ages, of whom Professor Hartzenbosch was an example, who took Dad to task occasionally for letting me associate with him. Dad simply ignored them. As long as I was going to be a reporter, I'd have to have news sources, and Bish was a dandy. He knew all the disreputable characters in town, which saved me having to associate with all of them, and it is sad but true that you get very few news stories in Sunday school. Far from fearing that Bish would be a bad influence on me, he rather hoped I'd be a good one on Bish.

I had that in mind, too, if I could think of any way of managing it. Bish had been a good man, once. He still was, except for one thing. You could tell that before he'd started drinking, he'd really been somebody, somewhere. Then something pretty bad must have happened to him, and now he was here on Fenris, trying to hide from it behind a bottle. Something ought to be done to give him a shove up on his feet again. I hate waste, and a man of the sort he must have been turning himself into the rumpot he was now was waste of the worst kind.

It would take a lot of doing, though, and careful tactical planning. Preaching at him would be worse than useless, and so would simply trying to get him to stop drinking. That would be what Doc Rojansky, at the hospital, would call treating the symptoms. The thing to do was make him want to stop drinking, and I didn't know how I was going to manage that. I'd thought, a couple of times, of getting him to work on the Times, but we barely made enough money out of it for ourselves, and with his remittance he didn't need to work. I had a lot of other ideas, now and then, but every time I took a second look at one, it got sick and died.

2
Reporter Working

Bish came over and greeted us solemnly.

"Good afternoon, gentlemen. Captain Ahab, I believe," he said, bowing to Tom, who seemed slightly puzzled; the education Tom had been digging out for himself was technical rather than literary. "And Mr. Pulitzer. Or is it Horace Greeley?"

"Lord Beaverbrook, your Grace," I replied. "Have you any little news items for us from your diocese?"

Bish teetered slightly, getting out a cigar and inspecting it carefully before lighting it.

"We-el," he said carefully, "my diocese is full to the hatch covers with sinners, but that's scarcely news." He turned to Tom. "One of your hands on the *Javelin* got into a fight in Martian Joe's, a while ago. Lumped the other man up pretty badly." He named the Javelin crewman, and the man who had been pounded. The latter was one of Steve Ravick's goons. "But not fatally, I regret to say," Bish added. "The local Gestapo are looking for your man, but he made it aboard Nip Spazoni's *Bulldog*, and by this time he's halfway to Hermann Reuch's Land."

"Isn't Nip going to the meeting, tonight?" Tom asked.

Bish shook his head. "Nip is a peace-loving man. He has a well-founded suspicion that peace is going to be in short supply around Hunters' Hall this evening. You know, of course, that Leo Belsher's coming in on the *Peenemünde* and will be there to announce another price cut. The new price, I understand, will be thirty-five centisols a pound."

Seven hundred sols a ton, I thought; why, that would barely pay ship expenses.

"Where did you get that?" Tom asked, a trifle sharply.

"Oh, I have my spies and informers," Bish said. "And even if I hadn't, it would figure. The only reason Leo Belsher ever comes to this Eden among planets is to negotiate a new contract, and who ever heard of a new contract at a higher price?"

That had all happened before, a number of times. When Steve Ravick had gotten control of the Hunters' Co-operative, the price of tallow-wax, on the loading floor at Port Sandor spaceport, had been fifteen hundred sols a ton. As far as Dad and I could find out, it was still bringing the same price on Terra as it always had. It looked to us as if Ravick and Leo

Belsher, who was the Co-op representative on Terra, and Mort Hallstock were simply pocketing the difference. I was just as sore about what was happening as anybody who went out in the hunter-ships. Tallow-wax is our only export. All our imports are paid for with credit from the sale of wax.

It isn't really wax, and it isn't tallow. It's a growth on the Jarvis's sea-monster; there's a layer of it under the skin, and around organs that need padding. An average-sized monster, say a hundred and fifty feet long, will yield twelve to fifteen tons of it, and a good hunter kills about ten monsters a year. Well, at the price Belsher and Ravick were going to cut from, that would run a little short of a hundred and fifty thousand sols for a year. If you say it quick enough and don't think, that sounds like big money, but the upkeep and supplies for a hunter-ship are big money, too, and what's left after that's paid off is divided, on a graduated scale, among ten to fifteen men, from the captain down. A hunter-boat captain, even a good one like Joe Kivelson, won't make much more in a year than Dad and I make out of the *Times*.

Chemically, tallow-wax isn't like anything else in the known Galaxy. The molecules are huge; they can be seen with an ordinary optical microscope, and a microscopically visible molecule is a curious-looking object, to say the least. They use the stuff to treat fabric for protective garments. It isn't anything like collapsium, of course, but a suit of waxed coveralls weighing only a couple of pounds will stop as much radiation as half an inch of lead.

Back when they were getting fifteen hundred a ton, the hunters had been making good money, but that was before Steve Ravick's time.

It was slightly before mine, too. Steve Ravick had showed up on Fenris about twelve years ago. He'd had some money, and he'd bought shares in a couple of hunter-ships and staked a few captains who'd had bad luck and got them in debt to him. He also got in with Morton Hallstock, who controlled what some people were credulous enough to take for a government here. Before long, he was secretary of the Hunters' Co-operative. Old Simon MacGregor, who had been president then, was a good hunter, but he was no businessman. He came to depend very heavily on Ravick, up till his ship, the *Claymore*, was lost with all hands down in Fitzwilliam Straits. I think that was a time bomb in the magazine, but I have a low and suspicious mind. Professor Hartzenbosch has told me so repeatedly. After that, Steve Ravick was president of the Co-op. He immediately began a drive to increase the membership. Most of the new members had never been out in a hunter-ship in their lives, but they could all be depended on to vote the way he wanted them to.

First, he jacked the price of wax up, which made everybody but the wax buyers happy. Everybody who wasn't already in the Co-op hurried up and joined. Then he negotiated an exclusive contract with Kapstaad Chemical Products, Ltd., in South Africa, by which they agreed to take the entire output for the Co-op. That ended competitive wax buying, and when there was nobody to buy the wax but Kapstaad, you had to sell it through the Co-operative or you didn't sell it at all. After that, the price started going down. The Co-operative, for which read Steve Ravick, had a sales representative on Terra, Leo Belsher. He wrote all the contracts, collected all the money, and split with Ravick. What was going on was pretty generally understood, even if it couldn't be proven, but what could anybody do about it?

Maybe somebody would try to do something about it at the meeting this evening. I would be there to cover it. I was beginning to wish I owned a bullet-proof vest.

Bish and Tom were exchanging views on the subject, some of them almost printable. I had my eyes to my binoculars, watching the tugs go up to meet the *Peenemünde*.

"What we need for Ravick, Hallstock and Belsher," Tom was saying, "is about four fathoms of harpoon line apiece, and something to haul up to."

That kind of talk would have shocked Dad. He is very strong for law and order, even when there is no order and the law itself is illegal. I'd always thought there was a lot of merit in what Tom was suggesting. Bish Ware seemed to have his doubts, though.

"Mmm, no; there ought to be some better way of doing it than that."

"Can you think of one?" Tom challenged.

I didn't hear Bish's reply. By that time, the tugs were almost to the ship. I grabbed up the telephoto camera and aimed it. It has its own power unit, and transmits directly. In theory, I could tune it to the telecast station and put what I was getting right on the air, and what I was doing was transmitting to the *Times*, to be recorded and 'cast later. Because it's not a hundred per cent reliable, though, it makes its own audiovisual record, so if any of what I was sending didn't get through, it could be spliced in after I got back.

I got some footage of the tugs grappling the ship, which was now completely weightless, and pulling her down. Through the finder, I could see that she had her landing legs extended; she looked like a big overfed spider being hauled in by a couple of gnats. I kept the butt of the camera to my shoulder, and whenever anything interesting happened, I'd squeeze the trigger. The first time I ever used a real submachine gun had been to kill a blue slasher that had gotten into one of the ship pools at the waterfront. I used three one-second bursts, and threw bits of slasher all over the place, and everybody wondered how I'd gotten the practice.

A couple more boats, pushers, went up to help hold the ship against the wind, and by that time she was down to a thousand feet, which was half her diameter. I switched from the shoulder-stock telephoto to the big tripod job, because this was the best part of it. The ship was weightless, of course, but she had mass and an awful lot of it. If anybody goofed getting her down, she'd take the side of the landing pit out, and about ten per cent of the population of Fenris, including the ace reporter for the Times, along with it.

At the same time, some workmen and a couple of spaceport cops had appeared, taken out a section of railing and put in a gate. The *Peenemünde* settled down, turned slowly to get her port in line with the gate, and lurched off contragravity and began running out a bridge to the promenade. I got some shots of that, and then began packing my stuff back in the hamper.

"You going aboard?" Tom asked. "Can I come along? I can carry some of your stuff and let on I'm your helper."

Glory be, I thought; I finally got that apprentice.

"Why, sure," I said. "You tow the hamper; I'll carry this." I got out what looked like a big camera case and slung it over my shoulder. "But you'll have to take me out on the *Javelin*, sometime, and let me shoot a monster."

He said it was a deal, and we shook on it. Then I had another idea.

"Bish, suppose you come with us, too," I said. "After all, Tom and I are just a couple of kids. If you're with us, it'll look a lot more big-paperish."

That didn't seem to please Tom too much. Bish shook his head, though, and Tom brightened.

"I'm dreadfully sorry, Walt," Bish said. "But I'm going aboard, myself, to see a friend who is en route through to Odin. A Dr. Watson; I have not seen him for years."

I'd caught that name, too, when we'd gotten the passenger list. Dr. John Watson. Now, I know that all sorts of people call themselves Doctor, and Watson and John aren't too improbable a combination, but I'd read *Sherlock Holmes* long ago, and the name had caught my attention. And this was the first, to my knowledge, that Bish Ware had ever admitted to any off-planet connections.

We started over to the gate. Hallstock and Ravick were ahead of us. So was Sigurd Ngozori, the president of the Fidelity & Trust, carrying a heavy briefcase and accompanied by a character with a submachine gun, and Adolf Lautier and Professor Hartzenbosch. There were a couple of spaceport cops at the gate, in olive-green uniforms that looked as though they had been sprayed on, and steel helmets. I wished we had a city police force like that. They were Odin Dock & Shipyard Company men, all former Federation Regular Army or Colonial Constabulary. The spaceport wasn't part of Port Sandor, or even Fenris; the Odin Dock & Shipyard Company was the government there, and it was run honestly and efficiently.

They knew me, and when they saw Tom towing my hamper they cracked a few jokes about the new *Times* cub reporter and waved us through. I thought they might give Bish an argument, but they just nodded and let him pass, too. We all went out onto the bridge, and across the pit to the equator of the two-thousand-foot globular ship.

We went into the main lounge, and the captain introduced us to Mr. Glenn Murell. He was fairly tall, with light gray hair, prematurely so, I thought, and a pleasant, noncommittal face. I'd have pegged him for a businessman. Well, I suppose authoring is a business, if that was his business. He shook hands with us, and said:

"Aren't you rather young to be a newsman?"

I started to burn on that. I get it all the time, and it burns me all the time, but worst of all on the job. Maybe I am only going-on-eighteen, but I'm doing a man's work, and I'm doing it competently.

"Well, they grow up young on Fenris, Mr. Murell," Captain Marshak earned my gratitude by putting in. "Either that or they don't live to grow up."

Murell unhooked his memophone and repeated the captain's remark into it. Opening line for one of his chapters. Then he wanted to know if I'd been born on Fenris. I saw I was going to have to get firm with Mr. Murell, right away. The time to stop that sort of thing is as soon as it starts.

"Who," I wanted to know, "is interviewing whom? You'll have at least five hundred hours till the next possible ship out of here; I only have two and a half to my next deadline. You want coverage, don't you? The more publicity you get, the easier your own job's going to be."

Then I introduced Tom, carefully giving the impression that while I handled all ordinary assignments, I needed help to give him the full VIP treatment. We went over to a quiet corner and sat down, and the interview started.

The camera case I was carrying was a snare and a deceit. Everybody knows that reporters use recorders in interviews, but it never pays to be too obtrusive about them, or the subject gets recorder-conscious and stiffens up. What I had was better than a recorder; it was a recording radio. Like the audiovisuals, it not only transmitted in to the *Times*, but made a recording as insurance against transmission failure. I reached into a slit on the side and snapped on the switch while I was fumbling with a pencil and notebook with the other hand, and started by asking him what had decided him to do a book about Fenris.

After that, I fed a question every now and then to keep him running, and only listened to every third word. The radio was doing a better job than I possibly could have. At the same time, I was watching Steve Ravick, Morton Hallstock and Leo Belsher at one side of the room, and Bish Ware at the other. Bish was within ear-straining range. Out of the corner of my eye, I saw another man, younger in appearance and looking like an Army officer in civvies, approach him.

"My dear Bishop!" this man said in greeting.

As far as I knew, that nickname had originated on Fenris. I made a mental note of that.

"How are you?" Bish replied, grasping the other's hand. "You have been in Afghanistan, I perceive."

That did it. I told you I was an old *Sherlock Holmes* reader; I recognized that line. This meeting was prearranged, neither of them had ever met before, and they needed a recognition code. Then I returned to Murell, and decided to wonder about Bish Ware and "Dr. Watson" later.

It wasn't long before I was noticing a few odd things about Murell, too, which confirmed my original suspicions of him. He didn't have the firm name of his alleged publishers right, he didn't know what a literary agent was and, after claiming to have been a newsman, he consistently used the expression "news service." I know, everybody says that-everybody but newsmen. They always call a news service a "paper," especially when talking to other newsmen.

Of course, there isn't any paper connected with it, except the pad the editor doodles on. What gets to the public is photoprint, out of a teleprinter. As small as our circulation is, we have four or five hundred of them in Port Sandor and around among the small settlements in the archipelago, and even on the mainland. Most of them are in bars and cafes and cigar stores and places like that, operated by a coin in a slot and leased by the proprietor, and some of the big hunter-ships like Joe Kivelson's *Javelin* and Nip Spazoni's *Bulldog* have them.

But long ago, back in the First Centuries, Pre-Atomic and Atomic Era, they were actually printed on paper, and the copies distributed and sold. They used printing presses as heavy as a spaceship's engines. That's why we still call ourselves the Press. Some of the old papers on Terra, like *La Prensa* in Buenos Aires, and the Melbourne *Times*, which used to be the London *Times* when there was still a London, were printed that way originally.

Finally I got through with my interview, and then shot about fifteen minutes of audiovisual, which would be cut to five for the 'cast. By this time Bish and "Dr. Watson" had disappeared, I supposed to the ship's bar, and Ravick and his accomplices had gotten through with their conspiracy to defraud the hunters. I turned Murell over to Tom, and went over to where they were standing together. I'd put away my pencil and pad long ago with Murell; now I got them out ostentatiously as I approached.

"Good day, gentlemen," I greeted them. "I'm representing the Port Sandor *Times*."

"Oh, run along, sonny; we haven't time to bother with you," Hallstock said.

"But I want to get a story from Mr. Belsher," I began.

"Well, come back in five or six years, when you're dry behind the ears, and you can get it," Ravick told me.

"Our readers aren't interested in the condition of my ears," I said sweetly. "They want to read about the price of tallow-wax. What's this about another price cut? To thirty-five centisols a pound, I understand."

"Oh, Steve, the young man's from the news service, and his father will publish whatever he brings home," Belsher argued. "We'd better give him something." He turned to me. "I don't know how this got out, but it's quite true," he said. He had a long face, like a horse's. At least, he looked like pictures of horses I'd seen. As he spoke, he pulled it even longer and became as doleful as an undertaker at a ten-thousand-sol funeral.

"The price has gone down, again. Somebody has developed a synthetic substitute. Of course, it isn't anywhere near as good as real Fenris tallow-wax, but try and tell the public that. So Kapstaad Chemical is being undersold, and the only way they can stay in business is cut the price they have to pay for wax...."

It went on like that, and this time I had real trouble keeping my anger down. In the first place, I was pretty sure there was no substitute for Fenris tallow-wax, good, bad or indifferent. In the second place, it isn't sold to the gullible public, it's sold to equipment manufacturers who have their own test engineers and who have to keep their products up to legal safety standards. He didn't know this balderdash of his was going straight to the *Times* as fast as he spouted it; he thought I was taking it down in shorthand. I knew exactly what Dad would do with it. He'd put it on telecast in Belsher's own voice.

Maybe the monster-hunters would start looking around for a rope, then.

When I got through listening to him, I went over and got a short audiovisual of Captain Marshak of the *Peenemünde* for the 'cast, and then I rejoined Tom and Murell.

"Mr. Murell says he's staying with you at the *Times*," Tom said. He seemed almost as disappointed as Professor Hartzenbosch. I wondered, for an incredulous moment, if Tom had been trying to kidnap Murell away from me. "He wants to go out on the *Javelin* with us for a monster-hunt."

"Well, that's swell!" I said. "You can pay off on that promise to take me monster-hunting, too. Right now, Mr. Murell is my big story." I reached into the front pocket of my "camera" case for the handphone, to shift to two-way. "I'll call the *Times* and have somebody come up with a car to get us and Mr. Murell's luggage."

"Oh, I have a car. Jeep, that is," Tom said. "It's down on the Bottom Level. We can use that."

Funny place to leave a car. And I was sure that he and Murell had come to some kind of an understanding, while I was being lied to by Belsher. I didn't get it. There was just too much going on around me that I didn't get, and me, I'm supposed to be the razor-sharp newshawk who gets everything.

3
Bottom Level

It didn't take long to get Murell's luggage assembled. There was surprisingly little of it, and nothing that looked like photographic or recording equipment. When he returned from a final gathering-up in his stateroom, I noticed that he was bulging under his jacket, too, on the left side at the waist. About enough for an 8.5-mm pocket automatic. Evidently he had been briefed on the law-and-order situation in Port Sandor.

Normally, we'd have gone off onto the Main City Level, but Tom's jeep was down on the Bottom Level, and he made no suggestion that we go off and wait for him to bring it up. I didn't suggest it, either. After all, it was his jeep, and he wasn't our hired pilot. Besides, I was beginning to get curious. An abnormally large bump of curiosity is part of every newsman's basic equipment.

We borrowed a small handling-lifter and one of the spaceport roustabouts to tow it for us, loaded Murell's luggage and my things onto it, and started down to the bottomside cargo hatches, from which the ship was discharging. There was no cargo at all to go aboard, except mail and things like Adolf Lautier's old film and music tapes. Our only export is tallow-wax, and it all goes to Terra. It would be picked up by the Cape *Canaveral* when she got in from Odin five hundred hours from now. But except for a few luxury items from Odin, everything we import comes from Terra, and the *Peenemünde* had started discharging that already. We rode down on a contragravity skid loaded with ammunition. I saw Murell looking curiously at the square cases, marked TERRAN FEDERATION ARMED FORCES, and 50-MM, MK. 608, ANTIVEHICLE AND ANTIPERSONNEL, 25 ROUNDS, and OVERAGE. PRACTICE ONLY. NOT TO BE ISSUED FOR SERVICE, and INSPECTED AND CONDEMNED. The hunters bought that stuff through the Co-op. It cost half as much as new ammo, but that didn't help them any. The difference stopped with Steve Ravick. Murell didn't comment, and neither did Tom or I.

We got off at the bottom of the pit, a thousand feet below the promenade from which I had come aboard, and stopped for a moment. Murell was looking about the great amphitheater in amazement.

"I knew this spaceport would be big when I found out that the ship landed directly on the planet," he said, "but I never expected anything like this. And this serves a population of twenty thousand?"

"Twenty-four thousand, seven hundred and eight, if the man who got pounded in a barroom fight around 1330 hasn't died yet," I said. "But you have to remember that this place was built close to a hundred years ago, when the population was ten times that much." I'd gotten my story from him; now it was his turn to interview me. "You know something about the history of Fenris, I suppose?"

"Yes. There are ample sources for it on Terra, up to the collapse of the Fenris Company," he said. "Too much isn't known about what's been happening here since, which is why I decided to do this book."

"Well, there were several cities built, over on the mainland," I told him. "They're all abandoned now. The first one was a conventional city, the buildings all on the surface. After one day-and-night cycle, they found that it was uninhabitable. It was left unfinished. Then they started digging in. The Chartered Fenris Company shipped in huge quantities of mining and earth-moving equipment-that put the company in the red more than anything else-and they began making burrow-cities, like the ones built in the Northern Hemisphere of Terra during the Third and Fourth World Wars, or like the cities on Luna and Mercury Twilight Zone and

Titan. There are a lot of valuable mineral deposits over on the mainland; maybe in another century our grandchildren will start working them again.

"But about six years before the Fenris Company went to pieces, they decided to concentrate in one city, here in the archipelago. The sea water stays cooler in the daytime and doesn't lose heat so rapidly in the nighttime. So they built Port Sandor, here on Oakleaf Island."

"And for convenience in monster-hunting?"

I shook my head. "No. The Jarvis's sea-monster wasn't discovered until after the city was built, and it was years after the company had gone bankrupt before anybody found out about what tallow-wax was good for."

I started telling him about the native life-forms of Fenris. Because of the surface temperature extremes, the marine life is the most highly developed. The land animals are active during the periods after sunset and after sunrise; when it begins getting colder or hotter, they burrow, or crawl into caves and crevices among the rocks, and go into suspended animation. I found that he'd read up on that, and not too much of his information was incorrect.

He seemed to think, though, that Port Sandor had also been mined out below the surface. I set him right on that.

"You saw what it looked like when you were coming down," I said. "Just a flat plateau, with a few shaft-head domes here and there, and the landing pit of the spaceport. Well, originally it was a valley, between two low hills. The city was built in the valley, level by level, and then the tops of the hills were dug off and bulldozed down on top of it. We have a lot of film at the public library of the construction of the city, step by step. As far as I know, there are no copies anywhere off-planet."

He should have gotten excited about that, and wanted to see them. Instead, he was watching the cargo come off-food-stuffs, now-and wanted to know if we had to import everything we needed.

"Oh, no. We're going in on the Bottom Level, which is mainly storage, but we have hydroponic farms for our vegetables and carniculture plants for meat on the Second and Third Levels. That's counting down from the Main City Level. We make our own lumber, out of reeds harvested in the swamps after sunrise and converted to pulpwood, and we get some good hardwood from the native trees which only grow in four periods of two hundred hours a year. We only use that for furniture, gunstocks, that sort of thing. And there are a couple of mining camps and smelters on the mainland; they employ about a thousand of our people. But every millisol that's spent on this planet is gotten from the sale of tallow-wax, at second or third hand if not directly."

That seemed to interest him more. Maybe his book, if he was really writing one, was going to be an economic study of Fenris. Or maybe his racket, whatever it was, would be based on something connected with our local production. I went on telling him about our hydroponic farms, and the carniculture plant where any kind of animal tissue we wanted was grown-Terran pork and beef and poultry, Freyan *zhoumy* meat, Zarathustran veldtbeest....He knew, already, that none of the native life-forms, animal or vegetable, were edible by Terrans.

"You can get all the *paté de foie gras* you want here," I said. "We have a chunk of goose liver about fifty feet in diameter growing in one of our vats."

By this time, we'd gotten across the bottom of the pit, Murell's luggage and my equipment being towed after us, and had entered the Bottom Level. It was cool and pleasant here, lighted from the ceiling fifty feet overhead, among the great column bases, two hundred feet square and two hundred yards apart, that supported the upper city and the thick roof of rock and earth that insulated it. The area we were entering was stacked with tallow-wax waiting to be loaded onto the *Cape Canaveral* when she came in; it was vacuum-packed in plastic skins, like big half-ton Bologna sausages, each one painted with the blue and white emblem of the Hunters' Co-operative. He was quite interested in that, and was figuring, mentally, how much wax there was here and how much it was worth.

"Who does this belong to?" he wanted to know. "The Hunters' Co-operative?"

Tom had been letting me do the talking up to now, but he answered that question, very emphatically.

"No, it doesn't. It belongs to the hunters," he said. "Each ship crew owns the wax they bring in in common, and it's sold for them by the Co-op. When the captain gets paid for the wax he's turned over to the Co-op, he divides the money among the crew. But every scrap of this belongs to the ships that took it, up till it's bought and paid for by Kapstaad Chemical."

"Well, if a captain wants his wax back, after it's been turned over for sale to the Co-op, can he get it?" Murell asked.

"Absolutely!"

Murell nodded, and we went on. The roustabout who had been following us with the lifter had stopped to chat with a couple of his fellows. We went on slowly, and now and then a vehicle, usually a lorry, would pass above us. Then I saw Bish Ware, ahead, sitting on a sausage of wax, talking to one of the Spaceport Police. They were both smoking, but that was all right. Tallow-wax will burn, and a wax fire is something to get really excited about, but the ignition point is 750° C., and that's a lot hotter than the end of anybody's cigar. He must have come out the same way we did, and I added that to the "wonder-why" file. Pretty soon, I'd have so many questions to wonder about that they'd start answering each other. He saw us and waved to us, and then suddenly the spaceport cop's face got as white as my shirt and he grabbed Bish by the arm. Bish didn't change color; he just shook off the cop's hand, got to his feet, dropped his cigar, and took a side skip out into the aisle.

"Murell!" he yelled. "Freeze! On your life; don't move a muscle!"

Then there was a gun going off in his hand. I didn't see him reach for it, or where he drew it from. It was just in his hand, firing, and the empty brass flew up and came down on the concrete with a jingle on the heels of the report. We had all stopped short, and the roustabout who was towing the lifter came hurrying up. Murell simply stood gaping at Bish.

"All right," Bish said, slipping his gun back into a shoulder holster under his coat. "Step carefully to your left. Don't move right at all."

Murell, still in a sort of trance, obeyed. As he did I looked past his right shin and saw what Bish had been shooting at. It was an irregular gray oval, about sixteen inches by four at its widest and tapering up in front to a cone about six inches high, into which a rodlike member, darker gray, was slowly collapsing and dribbling oily yellow stuff. The bullet had gone clear through and made a mess of dirty gray and black and green body fluids on the concrete.

It was what we call a tread-snail, because it moves on a double row of pads like stumpy feet and leaves a trail like a tractor. The fishpole-aerial thing it had erected out of its head was its stinger, and the yellow stuff was venom. A tenth of a milligram of it in your blood and it's "Get the Gate open, St. Peter; here I come."

Tom saw it as soon as I did. His face got the same color as the cop's. I don't suppose mine looked any better. When Murell saw what had been buddying up to him, I will swear, on a warehouse full of Bibles, Korans, Torah scrolls, Satanist grimoires, Buddhist prayer wheels and Thoran Grandfather-God images, that his hair literally stood on end. I've heard that expression all my life; well, this time I really saw it happen. I mentioned that he seemed to have been reading up on the local fauna.

I looked down at his right leg. He hadn't been stung-if he had, he wouldn't be breathing now-but he had been squirted, and there were a couple of yellow stains on the cloth of his trouser leg. I told him to hold still, used my left hand to pull the cloth away from his leg, and got out my knife and flipped it open with the other hand, cutting away the poisoned cloth and dropping it on the dead snail.

Murell started making an outcry about cutting up his trousers, and said he could have had them cleaned. Bish Ware, coming up, told him to stop talking like an imbecile.

"No cleaner would touch them, and even if they were cleaned, some of the poison would remain in the fabric. Then, the next time you were caught in the rain with a scratch on your leg, Walt, here, would write you one of his very nicest obituaries."

Then he turned to the cop, who was gabbling into his belt radio, and said: "Get an ambulance, quick. Possible case of tread-snail skin poisoning." A moment later, looking at Murell's leg, he added, "Omit 'possible.'"

There were a couple of little spots on Murell's skin that were beginning to turn raw-liver color. The raw poison hadn't gotten into his blood, but some of it, with impurities, had filtered through the cloth, and he'd absorbed enough of it through his skin to make him seriously ill. The cop jabbered some more into the radio, and the laborer with the lifter brought it and let it down, and Murell sat down on his luggage. Tom lit a cigarette and gave it to him, and told him to remain perfectly still. In a couple of minutes, an ambulance was coming, its siren howling.

The pilot and his helper were both jackleg medics, at least as far as first aid. They gave him a drink out of a flask, smeared a lot of gunk on the spots and slapped plasters over them, and helped him into the ambulance, after I told him we'd take his things to the *Times* building.

By this time, between the shot and the siren, quite a crowd had gathered, and everybody was having a nice little recrimination party. The labor foreman was chewing the cop out. The warehouse superintendent was chewing him out. And somebody from the general superintendent's office was chewing out everybody indiscriminately, and at the same time mentioning to me that Mr. Fieschi, the superintendent, would be very much pleased if the *Times* didn't mention the incident at all. I told him that was editorial policy, and to talk to Dad about it. Nobody had any idea how the thing had gotten in, but that wasn't much of a mystery. The Bottom Level is full of things like that; they can stay active all the time because the temperature is constant. I supposed that eventually they'd pick the dumbest day laborer in the place and make him the patsy.

Tom stood watching the ambulance whisk Murell off, dithering in indecision. The poisoning of Murell seemed like an unexpected blow to him. That fitted what I'd begun to think. Finally, he motioned the laborer to pick up the lifter, and we started off toward where he had parked his jeep, outside the spaceport area.

Bish walked along with us, drawing his pistol and replacing the fired round in the magazine. I noticed that it was a 10-mm Colt-Argentine Federation Service, commercial type. There aren't many of those on Fenris. A lot of 10-mm's, but mostly South African Sterbergs or Vickers-Bothas, or Mars-Consolidated Police Specials. Mine, which I wasn't carrying at the moment, was a Sterberg 7.7-mm Olympic Match.

"You know," he said, sliding the gun back under his coat, "I would be just as well pleased as Mr. Fieschi if this didn't get any publicity. If you do publish anything about it, I wish you'd minimize my own part in it. As you have noticed, I have some slight proficiency with lethal hardware. This I would prefer not to advertise. I can usually avoid trouble, but when I can't, I would like to retain the advantage of surprise."

We all got into the jeep. Tom, not too graciously, offered to drop Bish wherever he was going. Bish said he was going to the *Times*, so Tom lifted the jeep and cut in the horizontal drive. We got into a busy one-way aisle, crowded with lorries hauling food-stuffs to the refrigeration area. He followed that for a short distance, and then turned off into a dimly lighted, disused area.

Before long, I began noticing stacks of tallow-wax, put up in the regular outside sausage skins but without the Co-op markings. They just had the names of hunter-ships —*Javelin, Bulldog, Helldiver, Slasher,* and so on.

"What's that stuff doing in here?" I asked. "It's a long way from the docks, and a long way from the spaceport."

"Oh, just temporary storage," Tom said. "It hasn't been checked in with the Co-op yet."

That wasn't any answer-or maybe it was. I let it go at that. Then we came to an open space about fifty feet square. There was a jeep, with a 7-mm machine gun mounted on it, and half a dozen men in boat-clothes were playing cards at a table made out of empty ammunition boxes. I noticed they were all wearing pistols, and when a couple of them saw us, they got up and grabbed rifles. Tom let down and got out of the jeep, going over and talking with them for a few minutes. What he had to tell them didn't seem to bring any noticeable amount of sunlight into their lives. After a while he came back, climbed in at the controls, and lifted the jeep again.

4
Main City Level

The ceiling on Main City Level is two hundred feet high; in order to permit free circulation of air and avoid traffic jams, nothing is built higher than a hundred and fifty feet except the square buildings, two hundred yards apart, which rest on foundations on the Bottom Level and extend up to support the roof. The *Times* has one of these pillar-buildings, and we have the whole thing to ourselves. In a city built for a quarter of a million, twenty thousand people don't have to crowd very closely on one another. Naturally, we don't have a top landing stage, but except for the buttresses at the corners and solid central column, the whole street floor is open.

Tom hadn't said anything after we left the stacks of wax and the men guarding them. We came up a vehicle shaft a few blocks up Broadway, and he brought the jeep down and floated it in through one of the archways. As usual, the place was cluttered with equipment we hadn't gotten around to repairing or installing, merchandise we'd taken in exchange for advertising, and vehicles, our own and everybody else's. A couple of mechanics were tinkering on one of them. I decided, for the oomptieth time, to do something about cleaning it up. Say in another two or three hundred hours, when the ships would all be in port and work would be slack, and I could hire a couple of good men to help.

We got Murell's stuff off the jeep, and I hunted around till I found a hand-lifter.

"Want to stay and have dinner with us, Tom?" I asked.

"Uh?" It took him a second or so to realize what I'd said. "Why, no, thanks, Walt. I have to get back to the ship. Father wants to see me before the meeting."

"How about you, Bish? Want to take potluck with us?"

"I shall be delighted," he assured me.

Tom told us good-by absent-mindedly, lifted the jeep, and floated it out into the street. Bish and I watched him go; Bish looked as though he had wanted to say something and then thought better of it. We floated Murell's stuff and mine over to the elevator beside the central column, and I ran it up to the editorial offices on the top floor.

We came out in a big room, half the area of the floor, full of worktables and radios and screens and photoprinting machines. Dad, as usual, was in a gray knee-length smock, with a pipe jutting out under his ragged mustache, and, as usual, he was stopping every minute or so to relight it. He was putting together the stuff I'd transmitted in for the audiovisual newscast. Over across the room, the rest of the *Times* staff, Julio Kubanoff, was sitting at the composing machine, his peg leg propped up and an earphone on, his fingers punching rapidly at the key-board as he burned letters onto the white plastic sheet with ultraviolet rays for photographing. Julio was an old hunter-ship man who had lost a leg in an accident and taught himself his new trade. He still wore the beard, now white, that was practically the monster-hunters' uniform.

"The stuff come in all right?" I asked Dad, letting down the lifter.

"Yes. What do you think of that fellow Belsher?" he asked. "Did you ever hear such an impudent string of lies in your life?" Then, out of the corner of his eye, he saw the lifter full of luggage, and saw somebody with me. "Mr. Murell? Please excuse me for a moment, till I get this blasted thing together straight." Then he got the film spliced and the sound record matched, and looked up. "Why, Bish? Where's Mr. Murell, Walt?"

"Mr. Murell has had his initiation to Fenris," I said. "He got squirted by a tread-snail almost as soon as he got off the ship. They have him at the spaceport hospital; it'll be 2400 before they get all the poison sweated out of him."

I went on to tell him what had happened. Dad's eyes widened slightly, and he took the pipe out of his mouth and looked at Bish with something very reasonably like respect.

"That was mighty sharp work," he said. "If you'd been a second slower, we'd be all out of visiting authors. That would have been a nice business; story would have gotten back to Terra, and been most unfortunate publicity for Fenris. And, of course," he afterthoughted, "most unfortunate for Mr. Murell, too."

"Well, if you give this any publicity, I would rather you passed my own trifling exploit over in silence," Bish said. "I gather the spaceport people wouldn't be too happy about giving the public the impression that their area is teeming with tread-snails, either. They have enough trouble hiring shipping-floor help as it is."

"But don't you want people to know what you did?" Dad demanded, incredulously. Everybody wanted their names in print or on 'cast; that was one of his basic articles of faith. "If the public learned about this —" he went on, and then saw where he was heading and pulled up short. It wouldn't be tactful to say something like, "Maybe they wouldn't think you were just a worthless old soak."

Bish saw where Dad was heading, too, but he just smiled, as though he were about to confer his episcopal blessing.

"Ah, but that would be a step out of character for me," he said. "I must not confuse my public. Just as a favor to me, Ralph, say nothing about it."

"Well, if you'd rather I didn't....Are you going to cover this meeting at Hunters' Hall, tonight, Walt?" he asked me.

"Would I miss it?"

He frowned. "I could handle that myself," he said. "I'm afraid this meeting's going to get a little rough."

I shook my head. "Let's face it, Dad," I said. "I'm a little short of eighteen, but you're sixty. I can see things coming better than you can, and dodge them quicker."

Dad gave a rueful little laugh and looked at Bish.

"See how it goes?" he asked. "We spend our lives shielding our young and then, all of a sudden, we find they're shielding us." His pipe had gone out again and he relit it. "Too bad you didn't get an audiovisual of Belsher making that idiotic statement."

"He didn't even know I was getting a voice-only. All the time he was talking, I was doodling in a pad with a pencil."

"Synthetic substitutes!" Dad snorted. "Putting a synthetic tallow-wax molecule together would be like trying to build a spaceship with a jackknife and a tack hammer." He puffed hard on his pipe, and then excused himself and went back to his work.

Editing an audiovisual telecast is pretty much a one-man job. Bish wanted to know if he could be of assistance, but there was nothing either of us could do, except sit by and watch and listen. Dad handled the Belsher thing by making a film of himself playing off the recording, and interjecting sarcastic comments from time to time. When it went on the air, I thought, Ravick wasn't going to like it. I would have to start wearing my pistol again. Then he made a tape on the landing of the *Peenemünde* and the arrival of Murell, who he said had met with a slight accident after leaving the ship. I took that over to Julio when Dad was finished, along with a tape on the announced tallow-wax price cut. Julio only grunted and pushed them aside. He was setting up the story of the fight in Martian Joe's —a "local bar," of course; nobody ever gets shot or stabbed or slashed or slugged in anything else. All the news *is* fit to print, sure, but you can't give your advertisers and teleprinter customers any worse name than they have already. A paper has to use some judgment.

Then Dad and Bish and I went down to dinner. Julio would have his a little later, not because we're too good to eat with the help but because, around 1830, the help is too busy setting up the next paper to eat with us. The dining room, which is also the library, living room, and general congregating and loafing place, is as big as the editorial room above. Originally, it was an office, at a time when a lot of Fenris Company office work was being done here. Some of the furniture is original, and some was made for us by local cabinetmakers out of native hardwood. The dining table, big enough for two ships' crews to eat at, is an example of the latter. Then, of course, there are screens and microbook cabinets and things like that, and a refrigerator to save going a couple of hundred feet to the pantry in case anybody wants a snack.

I went to that and opened it, and got out a bulb of concentrated fruit juice and a bottle of carbonated water. Dad, who seldom drinks, keeps a few bottles around for guests. Seems most of our "guests" part with information easier if they have something like the locally made hydroponic potato schnapps inside them for courage.

"You drink Baldur honey-rum, don't you, Bish?" he said, pawing among the bottles in the liquor cabinet next to the refrigerator. "I'm sure I have a bottle of it. Now wait a minute; it's here somewhere."

When Dad passes on and some medium claims to have produced a spirit communication from him, I will not accept it as genuine without the expression: "Now wait a minute; it's here somewhere."

Bish wanted to know what I was fixing for myself, and I told him.

"Never mind the rum, Ralph. I believe," he said, "that I shall join Walt in a fruit fizz."

Well, whattaya know! Maybe my stealthy temperance campaign was having results. Dad looked positively startled, and then replaced the bottle he was holding.

"I believe I'll make it unanimous," he said. "Fix me up a fruit fizz, too, Walt."

I mixed two more fruit fizzes, and we carried them over to the table. Bish sipped at his critically.

"Palatable," he pronounced it. "Just a trifle on the mild side, but definitely palatable."

Dad looked at him as though he still couldn't believe the whole thing. Dinner was slow coming. We finished our fizzes, and Bish and I both wanted repeats, and Dad felt that he had to go along. So I made three more. We were finishing them when Mrs. Laden started bringing in the dinner. Mrs. Laden is a widow; she has been with us since my mother died, the year after I was born. She is violently anti-liquor. Reluctantly, she condones Dad taking a snort now and then, but as soon as she saw Bish Ware, her face started to stiffen.

She put the soup on the table and took off for the kitchen. She always has her own dinner with Julio. That way, while they're eating he can tell her all the news that's fit to print, and all the gossip that isn't.

For the moment, the odd things I'd been noticing about our distinguished and temporarily incapacitated visitor came under the latter head. I told Dad and Bish about my observations, beginning with the deafening silence about Glenn Murell at the library. Dad began popping immediately.

"Why, he must be an impostor!" he exclaimed. "What kind of a racket do you think he's up to?"

"Mmm-mm; I wouldn't say that, not right away," Bish said. "In the first place, Murell may be his true name and he may publish under a nom de plume. I admit, some of the other items are a little suspicious, but even if he isn't an author, he may have some legitimate business here and, having heard a few stories about this planetary Elysium, he may be exercising a little caution. Walt, tell your father about that tallow-wax we saw, down in Bottom Level Fourth Ward."

I did, and while I was talking Dad sat with his soup spoon poised halfway to his mouth for at least a minute before he remembered he was holding it.

"Now, that is funny," he said when I was through. "Why do you suppose...?"

"Somebody," Bish said, "some group of ship captains, is holding wax out from the Co-operative. There's no other outlet for it, so my guess is that they're holding it for a rise in price. There's only one way that could happen, and that, literally, would be over Steve Ravick's dead body. It could be that they expect Steve's dead body to be around for a price rise to come in over."

I was expecting Dad to begin spouting law-and-order. Instead, he hit the table with his fist; not, fortunately, the one that was holding the soup spoon.

"Well, I hope so! And if they do it before the *Cape Canaveral* gets in, they may fix Leo Belsher, too, and then, in the general excitement, somebody might clobber Mort Hallstock, and that'd be grand slam. After the triple funeral, we could go to work on setting up an honest co-operative and an honest government."

"Well, I never expected to hear you advocating lynch law, Dad," I said.

He looked at me for a few seconds.

"Tell the truth, Walt, neither did I," he admitted. "Lynch law is a horrible thing; don't make any mistake about that. But there's one thing more horrible, and that's no law at all. And that is the present situation in Port Sandor.

"You know what the trouble is, here? We have no government. No legal government, anyhow; no government under Federation law. We don't even have a Federation Resident-Agent. Before the Fenris Company went broke, it was the government here; when the Space Navy evacuated the colonists, they evacuated the government along with them. The thousand who remained were all too busy keeping alive to worry about that. They didn't even care when Fenris was reclassified from Class III, uninhabited but inhabitable, to Class II, inhabitable only in artificial environment, like Mercury or Titan. And when Mort Hallstock got hold of the town-meeting pseudo government they put together fifty years ago and turned it into a dictatorship, nobody realized what had happened till it was too late. Lynch law's the only recourse we have."

"Ralph," Bish told him, "if anything like that starts, Belsher and Hallstock and Ravick won't be the only casualties. Between Ravick's goons and Hallstock's police, they have close to a hundred men. I won't deny that they could be cleaned out, but it wouldn't be a lynching. It would be a civil war."

"Well, that's swell!" Dad said. "The Federation Government has never paid us any attention; the Federation planets are scattered over too many million cubic light-years of space for the Government to run around to all of them wiping everybody's noses. As long as things are quiet here, they'll continue to do nothing for us. But let a story hit the big papers on Terra, *Revolution Breaks Out on Fenris* —and that'll be the story I'll send to Interworld News-and watch what happens."

"I will tell you what will happen," Bish Ware said. "A lot of people will get killed. That isn't important, in itself. People are getting killed all the time, in a lot worse causes. But these people will all have friends and relatives who will take it up for them. Start killing people here in a faction fight, and somebody will be shooting somebody in the back out of a dark passage a hundred years from now over it. You want this planet poisoned with blood feuds for the next century?"

Dad and I looked at one another. That was something that hadn't occurred to either of us, and it should have. There were feuds, even now. Half the little settlements on the other islands and on the mainland had started when some group or family moved out of Port Sandor because of the enmity of some larger and more powerful group or family, and half our shootings and knife fights grew out of old grudges between families or hunting crews.

"We don't want it poisoned for the next century with the sort of thing Mort Hallstock and Steve Ravick started here, either," Dad said.

"Granted." Bish nodded. "If a civil war's the only possible way to get rid of them, that's what you'll have to have, I suppose. Only make sure you don't leave a single one of them alive when it's over. But if you can get the Federation Government in here to clean the mess up, that would be better. Nobody starts a vendetta with the Terran Federation."

"But how?" Dad asked. "I've sent story after story off about crime and corruption on Fenris. They all get the file-and-forget treatment."

Mrs. Laden had taken away the soup plates and brought us our main course. Bish sat toying with his fork for a moment.

"I don't know what you can do," he said slowly. "If you can stall off the blowup till the *Cape Canaveral* gets in, and you can send somebody to Terra...."

All of a sudden, it hit me. Here was something that would give Bish a purpose; something to make him want to stay sober.

"Well, don't say, 'If *you* can,'" I said. "Say, 'If *we* can.' You live on Fenris, too, don't you?"

5
Meeting Out of Order

Dad called the spaceport hospital, after dinner, and talked to Doc Rojansky. Murell was asleep, and in no danger whatever. They'd given him a couple of injections and a sedative, and his system was throwing off the poison satisfactorily. He'd be all right, but they thought he ought to be allowed to rest at the hospital for a while.

By then, it was time for me to leave for Hunters' Hall. Julio and Mrs. Laden were having their dinner, and Dad and Bish went up to the editorial office. I didn't take a car. Hunters' Hall was only a half dozen blocks south of the Times, toward the waterfront. I carried my radio-under-false-pretense slung from my shoulder, and started downtown on foot.

The business district was pretty well lighted, both from the ceiling and by the stores and restaurants. Most of the latter were in the open, with small kitchen and storage buildings. At a table at one of them I saw two petty officers from the *Peenemünde* with a couple of girls, so I knew the ship wasn't leaving immediately. Going past the Municipal Building, I saw some activity, and an unusually large number of police gathered around the vehicle port. Ravick must have his doubts about how the price cut was going to be received, and Mort Hallstock was mobilizing his storm troopers to give him support in case he needed it. I called in about that, and Dad told me fretfully to be sure to stay out of trouble.

Hunters' Hall was a four-story building, fairly substantial as buildings that don't have to support the roof go, with a landing stage on top and a vehicle park underneath. As I came up, I saw a lot of cars and jeeps and ships' boats grounded in and around it, and a crowd of men, almost all of them in boat-clothes and wearing whiskers, including quite a few characters who had never been out in a hunter-ship in their lives but were members in the best of good standing of the Co-operative. I also saw a few of Hallstock's uniformed thugs standing around with their thumbs in their gun belts or twirling their truncheons.

I took an escalator up to the second floor, which was one big room, with the escalators and elevators in the rear. It was the social room, decorated with photos and models and so-lidigraphs of hunter-ships, photos of record-sized monsters lashed alongside ships before cut-ting-up, group pictures of ships's crews, monster tusks, dried slashers and halberd fish, and a whole monster head, its tusked mouth open. There was a big crowd there, too, at the bar, at the game machines, or just standing around in groups talking.

I saw Tom Kivelson and his father and Oscar Fujisawa, and went over to join them. Joe Kivelson is just an outsize edition of his son, with a blond beard that's had thirty-five years' more growth. Oscar is skipper of the *Pequod* —he wouldn't have looked baffled if Bish Ware called him Captain Ahab-and while his family name is Old Terran Japanese, he had blue eyes and red hair and beard. He was almost as big as Joe Kivelson.

"Hello, Walt," Joe greeted me. "What's this Tom's been telling me about Bish Ware shooting a tread-snail that was going to sting Mr. Murell?"

"Just about that," I said. "That snail must have crawled out from between two stacks of wax as we came up. We never saw it till it was all over. It was right beside Murell and had its stinger up when Bish shot it."

"He took an awful chance," Kivelson said. "He might of shot Mr. Murell."

I suppose it would look that way to Joe. He is the planet's worst pistol shot, so according to him nobody can hit anything with a pistol.

"He wouldn't have taken any chance not shooting," I said. "If he hadn't, we'd have been running the Murell story with black borders."

Another man came up, skinny, red hair, sharp-pointed nose. His name was Al Devis, and he was Joe Kivelson's engineer's helper. He wanted to know about the tread-snail shooting, so

I had to go over it again. I hadn't anything to add to what Tom had told them already, but I was the *Times*, and if the *Times* says so it's true.

"Well, I wouldn't want any drunk like Bish Ware shooting around me with a pistol," Joe Kivelson said.

That's relative, too. Joe doesn't drink.

"Don't kid yourself, Joe," Oscar told him. "I saw Bish shoot a knife out of a man's hand, one time, in One Eye Swanson's. Didn't scratch the guy; hit the blade. One Eye has the knife, with the bullet mark on it, over his back bar, now."

"Well, was he drunk then?" Joe asked.

"Well, he had to hang onto the bar with one hand while he fired with the other." Then he turned to me. "How is Murell, now?" he asked.

I told him what the hospital had given us. Everybody seemed much relieved. I wouldn't have thought that a celebrated author of whom nobody had ever heard before would be the center of so much interest in monster-hunting circles. I kept looking at my watch while we were talking. After a while, the Times newscast came on the big screen across the room, and everybody moved over toward it.

They watched the *Peenemünde* being towed down and berthed, and the audiovisual interview with Murell. Then Dad came on the screen with a record player in front of them, and gave them a play-off of my interview with Leo Belsher.

Ordinary bad language I do not mind. I'm afraid I use a little myself, while struggling with some of the worn-out equipment we have at the paper. But when Belsher began explaining about how the price of wax had to be cut again, to thirty-five centisols a pound, the language those hunters used positively smelled. I noticed, though, that a lot of the crowd weren't saying anything at all. They would be Ravick's boys, and they would have orders not to start anything before the meeting.

"Wonder if he's going to try to give us that stuff about substitutes?" Oscar said.

"Well, what are you going to do?" I asked.

"I'll tell you what we're not going to do," Joe Kivelson said. "We're not going to take his price cut. If he won't pay our price, he can use his substitutes."

"You can't sell wax anywhere else, can you?"

"Is that so, we can't?" Joe started.

Before he could say anything else, Oscar was interrupting:

"We can eat for a while, even if we don't sell wax. Sigurd Ngozori'll carry us for a while and make loans on wax. But if the wax stops coming in, Kapstaad Chemical's going to start wondering why...."

By this time, other *Javelin* men came drifting over-Ramón Llewellyn, the mate, and Abdullah Monnahan, the engineer, and Abe Clifford, the navigator, and some others. I talked with some of them, and then drifted off in the direction of the bar, where I found another hunter captain, Mohandas Gandhi Feinberg, whom everybody simply called the Mahatma. He didn't resemble his namesake. He had a curly black beard with a twisted black cigar sticking out of it, and nobody, after one look at him, would have mistaken him for any apostle of nonviolence.

He had a proposition he was enlisting support for. He wanted balloting at meetings to be limited to captains of active hunter-ships, the captains to vote according to expressed wishes of a majority of their crews. It was a good scheme, though it would have sounded better if the man who was advocating it hadn't been a captain himself. At least, it would have disenfranchised all Ravick's permanently unemployed "unemployed hunters." The only trouble was, there was no conceivable way of getting it passed. It was too much like trying to curtail the powers of Parliament by act of Parliament.

The gang from the street level started coming up, and scattered in twos and threes around the hall, ready for trouble. I'd put on my radio when I'd joined the Kivelsons and Oscar, and I kept it on, circulating around and letting it listen to the conversations. The Ravick people were either saying nothing or arguing that Belsher was doing the best he could, and if Kapstaad wouldn't pay more than thirty-five centisols, it wasn't his fault. Finally, the call bell for the meeting began clanging, and the crowd began sliding over toward the elevators and escalators.

The meeting room was on the floor above, at the front of the building, beyond a narrow hall and a door at which a couple of Ravick henchmen wearing guns and sergeant-at-arms brassards were making everybody check their knives and pistols. They passed me by without getting my arsenal, which consisted of a sleep-gas projector camouflaged as a jumbo-sized lighter and twenty sols in two rolls of forty quarter sols each. One of these inside a fist can make a big difference.

Ravick and Belsher and the secretary of the Co-op, who was a little scrawny henpecked-husband type who never had an opinion of his own in his life, were all sitting back of a big desk on a dais in front. After as many of the crowd who could had found seats and the rest, including the Press, were standing in the rear, Ravick pounded with the chunk of monster tusk he used for a gavel and called the meeting to order.

"There's a bunch of old business," he said, "but I'm going to rule that aside for the moment. We have with us this evening our representative on Terra, Mr. Leo Belsher, whom I wish to present. Mr. Belsher."

Belsher got up. Ravick started clapping his hands to indicate that applause was in order. A few of his zombies clapped their hands; everybody else was quiet. Belsher held up a hand.

"Please don't applaud," he begged. "What I have to tell you isn't anything to applaud about."

"You're tootin' well right it isn't!" somebody directly in front of me said, very distinctly.

"I'm very sorry to have to bring this news to you, but the fact is that Kapstaad Chemical Products, Ltd., is no longer able to pay forty-five centisols a pound. This price is being scaled down to thirty-five centisols. I want you to understand that Kapstaad Chemical wants to give you every cent they can, but business conditions no longer permit them to pay the old price. Thirty-five is the absolute maximum they can pay and still meet competition—"

"Aaah, knock it off, Belsher!" somebody shouted. "We heard all that rot on the screen."

"How about our contract?" somebody else asked. "We do have a contract with Kapstaad, don't we?"

"Well, the contract will have to be re-negotiated. They'll pay thirty-five centisols or they'll pay nothing."

"They can try getting along without wax. Or try buying it somewhere else!"

"Yes; those wonderful synthetic substitutes!"

"Mr. Chairman," Oscar Fujisawa called out. "I move that this organization reject the price of thirty-five centisols a pound for tallow-wax, as offered by, or through, Leo Belsher at this meeting."

Ravick began clamoring that Oscar was out of order, that Leo Belsher had the floor.

"I second Captain Fujisawa's motion," Mohandas Feinberg said.

"And Leo Belsher doesn't have the floor; he's not a member of the Co-operative," Tom Kivelson declared. "He's our hired employee, and as soon as this present motion is dealt with, I intend moving that we fire him and hire somebody else."

"I move to amend Captain Fujisawa's motion," Joe Kivelson said. "I move that the motion, as amended, read, '—and stipulate a price of seventy-five centisols a pound.'"

"You're crazy!" Belsher almost screamed.

Seventy-five was the old price, from which he and Ravick had been reducing until they'd gotten down to forty-five.

Just at that moment, my radio began making a small fuss. I unhooked the handphone and brought it to my face.

"Yeah?"

It was Bish Ware's voice: "Walt, get hold of the Kivelsons and get them out of Hunters' Hall as fast as you can," he said. "I just got a tip from one of my … my parishioners. Ravick's going to stage a riot to give Hallstock's cops an excuse to raid the meeting. They want the Kivelsons."

"Roger." I hung up, and as I did I could hear Joe Kivelson shouting:

"You think we don't get any news on this planet? Tallow-wax has been selling for the same price on Terra that it did eight years ago, when you two crooks started cutting the price. Why, the very ship Belsher came here on brought the quotations on the commodity market —"

I edged through the crowd till I was beside Oscar Fujisawa. I decided the truth would need a little editing; I didn't want to use Bish Ware as my source.

"Oscar, Dad just called me," I told him. "A tip came in to the Times that Ravick's boys are going to fake a riot and Hallstock's cops are going to raid the meeting. They want Joe and Tom. You know what they'll do if they get hold of them."

"Shot while resisting arrest. You sure this is a good tip, though?"

Across the room, somebody jumped to his feet, kicking over a chair.

"That's a double two-em-dashed lie, you etaoin shrdlu so-and-so!" somebody yelled.

"Who are you calling a so-and-so, you thus-and-so-ing such-and-such?" somebody else yelled back, and a couple more chairs got smashed and a swirl of fighting started.

"Yes, it is," Oscar decided. "Let's go."

We started plowing through the crowd toward where the Kivelsons and a couple more of the *Javelin* crew were clumped. I got one of the rolls of quarter sols into my right fist and let Oscar go ahead. He has more mass than I have.

It was a good thing I did, because before we had gone ten feet, some character got between us, dragged a two-foot length of inch-and-a-half high-pressure hose out of his pant leg, and started to swing at the back of Oscar's head. I promptly clipped him behind the ear with a fist full of money, and down he went. Oscar, who must have eyes in the back of his head, turned and grabbed the hose out of his hand before he dropped it, using it to clout somebody in front of him. Somebody else came pushing toward us, and I was about to clip him, too, when he yelled, "Watch it, Walt; I'm with it!" It was Cesário Vieira, another *Javelin* man; he's engaged to Linda Kivelson, Joe's daughter and Tom's sister, the one going to school on Terra.

Then we had reached Tom and Joe Kivelson. Oscar grabbed Joe by the arm.

"Come on, Joe; let's get moving," he said. "Hallstock's Gestapo are on the way. They have orders to get you dead or alive."

"Like blazes!" Joe told him. "I never chickened out on a fight yet, and —"

That's what I'd been afraid of. Joe is like a Zarathustra veldtbeest; the only tactics he knows is a headlong attack.

"You want to get your crew and your son killed, and yourself along with them?" Oscar asked him. "That's what'll happen if the cops catch you. Now are you coming, or will I have to knock you senseless and drag you out?"

Fortunately, at that moment somebody took a swing at Joe and grazed his cheek. It was a good thing that was all he did; he was wearing brass knuckles. Joe went down a couple of feet, bending at the knees, and caught this fellow around the hips with both hands, straightening and lifting him over his head. Then he threw him over the heads of the people in front of him. There were yells where the human missile landed.

"That's the stuff, Joe!" Oscar shouted. "Come on, we got them on the run!"

That, of course, converted a strategic retreat into an attack. We got Joe aimed toward the doors and before he knew it, we were out in the hall by the elevators. There were a couple of Ravick's men, with sergeant-at-arms arm bands, and two city cops. One of the latter got in Joe's way. Joe punched him in the face and knocked him back about ten feet in a sliding stagger before he dropped. The other cop grabbed me by the left arm.

I slugged him under the jaw with my ten-sol right and knocked him out, and I felt the wrapping on the coin roll break and the quarters come loose in my hand. Before I could drop them into my jacket pocket and get out the other roll, one of the sergeants at arms drew a gun. I just hurled the handful of coins at him. He dropped the pistol and put both hands to his face, howling in pain.

I gave a small mental howl myself when I thought of all the nice things I could have bought for ten sols. One of Joe Kivelson's followers stooped and scooped up the fallen pistol, firing a couple of times with it. Then we all rushed Joe into one of the elevators and crowded in behind him, and as I turned to start it down I could hear police sirens from the street and also from the landing stage above. In the hall outside the meeting room, four or five of Ravick's free-drink mercenaries were down on all fours scrabbling for coins, and the rest of the pursuers from the meeting room were stumbling and tripping over them. I wished I'd brought a camera along, too. The public would have loved a shot of that. I lifted the radio and spoke into it:

"This is Walter Boyd, returning you now to the regular entertainment program."

A second later, the thing whistled at me. As the car started down and the doors closed I lifted the handphone. It was Bish Ware again.

"We're going down in the elevator to Second Level Down," I said. "I have Joe and Tom and Oscar Fujisawa and a few of the *Javelin* crew with me. The place is crawling with cops now."

"Go to Third Level Down and get up on the catwalk on the right," Bish said. "I'll be along to pick you up."

"Roger. We'll be looking for you."

The car stopped at Second Level Down. I punched a button and sent it down another level. Joe Kivelson, who was dabbing at his cheek with a piece of handkerchief tissue, wanted to know what was up.

"We're getting a pickup," I told him. "Vehicle from the *Times*."

I thought it would save arguments if I didn't mention who was bringing it.

6

Elementary, My Dear Kivelson

Before we left the lighted elevator car, we took a quick nose count. Besides the Kivelsons, there were five *Javelin* men-Ramón Llewellyn, Abdullah Monnahan, Abe Clifford, Cesário Vieira, and a whitebeard named Piet Dumont. Al Devis had been with us when we crashed the door out of the meeting room, but he'd fallen by the way. We had a couple of flashlights, so, after sending the car down to Bottom Level, we picked our way up the zigzag iron stairs to the catwalk, under the seventy-foot ceiling, and sat down in the dark.

Joe Kivelson was fretting about what would happen to the rest of his men.

"Fine captain I am, running out and leaving them!"

"If they couldn't keep up, that's their tough luck," Oscar Fujisawa told him. "You brought out all you could. If you'd waited any longer, none of us would have gotten out."

"They won't bother with them," I added. "You and Tom and Oscar, here, are the ones they want."

Joe was still letting himself be argued into thinking he had done the right thing when we saw the lights of a lorry coming from uptown at ceiling level. A moment later, it backed to the catwalk, and Bish Ware stuck his head out from the pilot's seat.

"Where do you gentlemen wish to go?" he asked.

"To the *Javelin*," Joe said instantly.

"Huh-uh," Oscar disagreed. "That's the first place they'll look. That'll be all right for Ramón and the others, but if they catch you and Tom, they'll shoot you and call it self-defense, or take you in and beat both of you to a jelly. This'll blow over in fifteen or twenty hours, but I'm not going anywhere near my ship, now."

"Drop us off on Second Level Down, about Eighth Street and a couple of blocks from the docks," the mate, Llewellyn, said. "We'll borrow some weapons from Patel the Pawnbroker and then circulate around and see what's going on. But you and Joe and Oscar had better go underground for a while."

"The *Times*," I said. "We have a whole pillar-building to ourselves; we could hide half the population."

That was decided upon. We all piled into the lorry, and Bish took it to an inconspicuous place on the Second Level and let down. Ramón Llewellyn and the others got out. Then we went up to Main City Level. We passed within a few blocks of Hunters' Hall. There was a lot of noise, but no shooting.

Joe Kivelson didn't have anything to say, on the trip, but he kept looking at the pilot's seat in perplexity and apprehension. I think he expected Bish to try to ram the lorry through every building we passed by or over.

We found Dad in the editorial department on the top floor, feeding voice-tape to Julio while the latter made master sheets for teleprinting. I gave him a quick rundown on what had happened that he hadn't gotten from my radio. Dad cluck-clucked in disapproval, either at my getting into a fight, assaulting an officer, or, literally, throwing money away.

Bish Ware seemed a little troubled. "I think," he said, "that I shall make a circuit of my diocese, and see what can be learned from my devoted flock. Should I turn up anything significant, I will call it in."

With that, he went tottering over to the elevator, stumbling on the way and making an unepiscopal remark. I watched him, and then turned to Dad.

"Did he have anything to drink after I left?" I asked.

"Nothing but about five cups of coffee."

I mentally marked that: *Add oddities, Bish Ware.* He'd been at least four hours without liquor, and he was walking as unsteadily as when I'd first seen him at the spaceport. I didn't know any kind of liquor that would persist like that.

Julio had at least an hour's tape to transcribe, so Dad and Joe and Tom and Oscar and I went to the living room on the floor below. Joe was still being bewildered about Bish Ware.

"How'd he manage to come for us?" he wanted to know.

"Why, he was here with me all evening," Dad said. "He came from the spaceport with Walt and Tom, and had dinner with us. He called a few people from here, and found out about the fake riot and police raid Ravick had cooked up. You'd be surprised at how much information he can pick up around town."

Joe looked at his son, alarmed.

"Hey! You let him see —" he began.

"The wax on Bottom Level, in the Fourth Ward?" I asked. "He won't blab about that. He doesn't blab things where they oughtn't be blabbed."

"That's right," Dad backed me up. He was beginning to think of Bish as one of the *Times* staff, now. "We got a lot of tips from him, but nothing we give him gets out." He got his pipe lit again. "What about that wax, Joe?" he asked. "Were you serious when you made that motion about a price of seventy-five centisols?"

"I sure was!" Joe declared. "That's the real price, and always has been, and that's what we get or Kapstaad doesn't get any more wax."

"If Murell can top it, maybe Kapstaad won't get any more wax, period," I said. "Who's he with-Interstellar Import-Export?"

Anybody would have thought a barbwire worm had crawled onto Joe Kivelson's chair seat under him.

"Where'd you hear that?" he demanded, which is the Galaxy's silliest question to ask any newsman. "Tom, if you've been talking —"

"He hasn't," I said. "He didn't need to. It sticks out a parsec in all directions." I mentioned some of the things I'd noticed while interviewing Murell, and his behavior after leaving the ship. "Even before I'd talked to him, I wondered why Tom was so anxious to get aboard with me. He didn't know we'd arranged to put Murell up here; he was going to take him to see that wax, and then take him to the *Javelin*. You were going to produce him at the meeting and have him bid against Belsher, only that tread-snail fouled your lines for you. So then you thought you had to stall off a new contract till he got out of the hospital."

The two Kivelsons and Oscar Fujisawa were looking at one another; Joe and Tom in consternation, and Oscar in derision of both of them. I was feeling pretty good. Brother, I thought, Sherlock Holmes never did better, himself.

That, all of a sudden, reminded me of Dr. John Watson, whom Bish perceived to have been in Afghanistan. That was one thing Sherlock H. Boyd hadn't deduced any answers for. Well, give me a little more time. And more data.

"You got it all figured out, haven't you?" Joe was asking sarcastically. The sarcasm was as hollow as an empty oil drum.

"The *Times*," Dad was saying, trying not to sound too proud, "has a very sharp reportorial staff, Joe."

"It isn't Interstellar," Oscar told me, grinning. "It's Argentine Exotic Organics. You know, everybody thought Joe, here, was getting pretty high-toned, sending his daughter to school on Terra. School wasn't the only thing she went for. We got a letter from her, the last time the Cape Canaveral was in, saying that she'd contacted Argentine Organics and that a man was coming out on the *Peenemünde*, posing as a travel-book author. Well, he's here, now."

"You'd better keep an eye on him," I advised. "If Steve Ravick gets to him, he won't be much use to you."

"You think Ravick would really harm Murell?" Dad asked.

He thought so, too. He was just trying to comfort himself by pretending he didn't.

"What do you think, Ralph?" Oscar asked him. "If we get competitive wax buying, again, seventy-five a pound will be the starting price. I'm not spending the money till I get it, but I wouldn't be surprised to see wax go to a sol a pound on the loading floor here. And you know what that would mean."

"Thirty for Steve Ravick," Dad said. That puzzled Oscar, till I explained that "thirty" is newsese for "the end." "I guess Walt's right. Ravick would do anything to prevent that." He thought for a moment. "Joe, you were using the wrong strategy. You should have let Ravick get that thirty-five centisol price established for the Co-operative, and then had Murell offer seventy-five or something like that."

"You crazy?" Joe demanded. "Why, then the Co-op would have been stuck with it."

"That's right. And as soon as Murell's price was announced, everybody would drop out of the Co-operative and reclaim their wax, even the captains who owe Ravick money. He'd have nobody left but a handful of thugs and barflies."

"But that would smash the Co-operative," Joe Kivelson objected. "Listen, Ralph; I've been in the Co-operative all my life, since before Steve Ravick was heard of on this planet. I've worked hard for the Co-operative, and —"

You didn't work hard enough, I thought. You let Steve Ravick take it away from you. Dad told Joe pretty much the same thing:

"You don't have a Co-operative, Joe. Steve Ravick has a racket. The only thing you can do with this organization is smash it, and then rebuild it with Ravick and his gang left out."

Joe puzzled over that silently. He'd been thinking that it was the same Co-operative his father and Simon MacGregor and the other old hunters had organized, and that getting rid of Ravick was simply a matter of voting him out. He was beginning to see, now, that parliamentary procedure wasn't any weapon against Ravick's force and fraud and intimidation.

"I think Walt has something," Oscar Fujisawa said. "As long as Murell's in the hospital at the spaceport, he's safe, but as soon as he gets out of Odin Dock & Shipyard territory, he's going to be a clay pigeon."

Tom hadn't been saying anything. Now he cleared his throat.

"On the *Peenemünde*, I was talking about taking Mr. Murell for a trip in the *Javelin*," he said. "That was while we were still pretending he'd come here to write a book. Maybe that would be a good idea, anyhow."

"It's a cinch we can't let him get killed on us," his father said. "I doubt if Exotic Organics would send anybody else out, if he was."

"Here," Dad said. "We'll run the story we have on him in the morning edition, and then correct it and apologize to the public for misleading them and explain in the evening edition. And before he goes, we can have him make an audiovisual for the 'cast, telling everybody who he is and announcing the price he's offering. We'll put that on the air. Get enough publicity, and Steve Ravick won't dare do anything to him."

Publicity, I thought, is the only weapon Dad knows how to use. He thinks it's invincible. Me, I wouldn't bet on what Steve Ravick wouldn't dare do if you gave me a hundred to one. Ravick had been in power too long, and he was drunker on it than Bish Ware ever got on Baldur honey-rum. As an intoxicant, rum is practically a soft drink beside power.

"Well, do you think Ravick's gotten onto Murell yet?" Oscar said. "We kept that a pretty close secret. Joe and I knew about him, and so did the Mahatma and Nip Spazoni and Corkscrew Finnegan, and that was all."

"I didn't even tell Tom, here, till the *Peenemünde* got into radio range," Joe Kivelson said. "Then I only told him and Ramón and Abdullah and Abe and Hans Cronje."

"And Al Devis," Tom added. "He came into the conning tower while you were telling the rest of us."

The communication screen began buzzing, and I went and put it on. It was Bish Ware, calling from a pay booth somewhere.

"I have some early returns," he said. "The cops cleared everybody out of Hunters' Hall except the Ravick gang. Then Ravick reconvened the meeting, with nobody but his gang. They were very careful to make sure they had enough for a legal quorum under the bylaws, and then they voted to accept the new price of thirty-five centisols a pound."

"That's what I was afraid of," Joe Kivelson said. "Did they arrest any of my crew?"

"Not that I know of," Bish said. "They made a few arrests, but turned everybody loose later. They're still looking for you and your son. As far as I know, they aren't interested in anybody else." He glanced hastily over his shoulder, as though to make sure the door of the booth was secure. "I'm with some people, now. I'll call you back later."

"Well, that's that, Joe," Oscar said, after Bish blanked the screen. "The Ravick Co-op's stuck with the price cut. The only thing left to do is get everybody out of it we can, and organize a new one."

"I guess that's so," Joe agreed. "I wonder, though if Ravick has really got wise to Murell."

"Walt figured it out since the ship got in," Oscar said. "Belsher's been on the ship with Murell for six months. Well, call it three; everything speeds up about double in hyperspace. But in three months he ought to see as much as Walt saw in a couple of hours."

"Well, maybe Belsher doesn't know what's suspicious, the way Walt does," Tom said.

"I'm sure he doesn't," I said. "But he and Murell are both in the wax business. I'll bet he noticed dozens of things I never even saw."

"Then we'd better take awfully good care of Mr. Murell," Tom said. "Get him aboard as fast as we can, and get out of here with him. Walt, you're coming along, aren't you?"

That was what we'd agreed, while Glenn Murell was still the famous travel-book author. I wanted to get out of it, now. There wouldn't be anything happening aboard the *Javelin*, and a lot happening here in Port Sandor. Dad had the same idea, only he was one hundred per cent for my going with Murell. I think he wanted me out of Port Sandor, where I wouldn't get in the way of any small high-velocity particles of lead that might be whizzing around.

7

Aboard the *Javelin*

We heard nothing more from Bish Ware that evening. Joe and Tom Kivelson and Oscar Fujisawa slept at the *Times* Building, and after breakfast Dad called the spaceport hospital about Murell. He had passed a good night and seemed to have thrown off all the poison he had absorbed through his skin. Dad talked to him, and advised him not to leave until somebody came for him. Tom and I took a car-and a pistol apiece and a submachine gun-and went to get him. Remembering, at the last moment, what I had done to his trousers, I unpacked his luggage and got another suit for him.

He was grateful for that, and he didn't lift an eyebrow when he saw the artillery we had with us. He knew, already, what the score was, and the rules, or absence thereof, of the game, and accepted us as members of his team. We dropped to the Bottom Level and went, avoiding traffic, to where the wax was stored. There were close to a dozen guards there now, all heavily armed.

We got out of the car, I carrying the chopper, and one of the gang there produced a probe rod and microscope and a testing kit and a microray scanner. Murell took his time going over the wax, jabbing the probe rod in and pulling samples out of the big plastic-skinned sausages at random, making chemical tests, examining them under the microscope, and scanning other cylinders to make sure there was no foreign matter in them. He might not know what a literary agent was, but he knew tallow-wax.

I found out from the guards that there hadn't been any really serious trouble after we left Hunter's Hall. The city police had beaten a few men up, natch, and run out all the anti-Ravick hunters, and then Ravick had reconvened the meeting and acceptance of the thirty-five centisol price had been voted unanimously. The police were still looking for the Kivelsons. Ravick seemed to have gotten the idea that Joe Kivelson was the mastermind of the hunters' cabal against him. I know if I'd found that Joe Kivelson and Oscar Fujisawa were in any kind of a conspiracy together, I wouldn't pick Joe for the mastermind. It was just possible, I thought, that Oscar had been fostering this himself, in case anything went wrong. After all, self-preservation is the first law, and Oscar is a self-preserving type.

After Murell had finished his inspection and we'd gotten back in the car and were lifting, I asked him what he was going to offer, just as though I were the skipper of the biggest ship out of Port Sandor. Well, it meant as much to us as it did to the hunters. The more wax sold for, the more advertising we'd sell to the merchants, and the more people would rent teleprinters from us.

"Eighty centisols a pound," he said. Nice and definite; quite a difference from the way he stumbled around over listing his previous publications. "Seventy-five's the Kapstaad price, re-gardless of what you people here have been getting from that crook of a Belsher. We'll have to go far enough beyond that to make him have to run like blazes to catch up. You can put it in the *Times* that the day of monopolistic marketing on Fenris is over."

When we got back to the *Times*, I asked Dad if he'd heard anything more from Bish.

"Yes," he said unhappily. "He didn't call in, this morning, so I called his apartment and didn't get an answer. Then I called Harry Wong's. Harry said Bish had been in there till after midnight, with some other people." He named three disreputables, two female and one male. "They were drinking quite a lot. Harry said Bish was plastered to the ears. They finally went out, around 0130. He said the police were in and out checking the crowd, but they didn't make any trouble."

I nodded, feeling very badly. Four and a half hours had been his limit. Well, sometimes a ninety per cent failure is really a triumph; after all, it's a ten per cent success. Bish had gone four and a half hours without taking a drink. Maybe the percentage would be a little better the next time. I was surely old enough to stop expecting miracles.

The mate of the *Pequod* called in, around noon, and said it was safe for Oscar to come back to the ship. The mate of the *Javelin*, Ramón Llewellyn, called in with the same report, that along the waterfront, at least, the heat was off. However, he had started an ambitious-looking overhaul operation, which looked as though it was good for a hundred hours but which could be dropped on a minute's notice, and under cover of this he had been taking on supplies and ammunition.

We made a long audiovisual of Murell announcing his price of eighty centisols a pound for wax on behalf of Argentine Exotic Organics, Ltd. As soon as that was finished, we loaded the boat-clothes we'd picked up for him and his travel kit and mine into a car, with Julio Kubanoff to bring it back to the *Times*, and went to the waterfront. When we arrived, Ramón Llewellyn had gotten things cleared up, and the *Javelin* was ready to move as soon as we came aboard.

On the Main City Level, the waterfront is a hundred feet above the ship pools; the ships load from and discharge onto the First Level Down. The city roof curves down all along the south side of the city into the water and about fifty feet below it. That way, even in the post-sunset and post-dawn storms, ships can come in submerged around the outer breakwater and under the roof, and we don't get any wind or heavy seas along the docks.

Murell was interested in everything he saw, in the brief time while we were going down along the docks to where the *Javelin* was berthed. I knew he'd never actually seen it before, but he must have been studying pictures of it, because from some of the remarks he made, I could tell that he was familiar with it.

Most of the ships had lifted out of the water and were resting on the wide concrete docks, but the *Javelin* was afloat in the pool, her contragravity on at specific-gravity weight reduction. She was a typical hunter-ship, a hundred feet long by thirty abeam, with a squat conning tower amidships, and turrets for 50-mm guns and launchers for harpoon rockets fore and aft. The only thing open about her was the air-and-water lock under the conning tower. Julio, who was piloting the car, set it down on the top of the aft gun turret. A couple of the crewmen who were on deck grabbed our bags and hurried them inside. We followed, and as soon as Julio lifted away, the lock was sealed.

Immediately, as the contragravity field dropped below the specific gravity of the ship, she began submerging. I got up into the conning tower in time to see the water of the boat pool come up over the armor-glass windows and the outside lights come on. For a few minutes, the *Javelin* swung slowly and moved forward, feeling her way with fingers of radar out of the pool and down the channel behind the breakwater and under the overhang of the city roof. Then the water line went slowly down across the windows as she surfaced. A moment later she was on full contragravity, and the ship which had been a submarine was now an aircraft.

Murell, who was accustomed to the relatively drab sunsets of Terra, simply couldn't take his eyes from the spectacle that covered the whole western half of the sky-high clouds streaming away from the daylight zone to the west and lighted from below by the sun. There were more clouds coming in at a lower level from the east. By the time the *Javelin* returned to Port Sandor, it would be full dark and rain, which would soon turn to snow, would be falling. Then we'd be in for it again for another thousand hours.

Ramón Llewellyn was saying to Joe Kivelson: "We're one man short; Devis, Abdullah's helper. Hospital."

"Get hurt in the fight, last night? He was right with us till we got out to the elevators, and then I missed him."

"No. He made it back to the ship about the same time we did, and he was all right then. Didn't even have a scratch. Strained his back at work, this morning, trying to lift a power-unit cartridge by hand."

I could believe that. Those things weighed a couple of hundred pounds. Joe Kivelson swore.

"What's he think this is, the First Century Pre-Atomic? Aren't there any lifters on the ship?"

Llewellyn shrugged. "Probably didn't want to bother taking a couple of steps to get one. The doctor told him to take treatment and observation for a day or so."

"That's Al Devis?" I asked. "What hospital?" Al Devis's strained back would be good for a two-line item; he'd feel hurt if we didn't mention it.

"Co-op hospital."

That was all right. They always sent in their patient lists to the *Times*. Tom was griping because he'd have to do Devis's work and his own.

"You know anything about engines, Walt?" he asked me.

"I know they generate a magnetic current and convert rotary magnetic current into one-directional repulsion fields, and violate the daylights out of all the old Newtonian laws of motion and attraction," I said. "I read that in a book. That was as far as I got. The math got a little complicated after that, and I started reading another book."

"You'd be a big help. Think you could hit anything with a 50-mm?" Tom asked. "I know you're pretty sharp with a pistol or a chopper, but a cannon's different."

"I could try. If you want to heave over an empty packing case or something, I could waste a few rounds seeing if I could come anywhere close to it."

"We'll do that," he said. "Ordinarily, I handle the after gun when we sight a monster, but somebody'll have to help Abdullah with the engines."

He spoke to his father about it. Joe Kivelson nodded.

"Walt's made some awful lucky shots with that target pistol of his, I know that," he said, "and I saw him make hamburger out of a slasher, once, with a chopper. Have somebody blow a couple of wax skins full of air for targets, and when we get a little farther southeast, we'll go down to the surface and have some shooting."

I convinced Murell that the sunset would still be there in a couple of hours, and we took our luggage down and found the cubbyhole he and I would share with Tom for sleeping quarters. A hunter-ship looks big on the outside, but there's very little room for the crew. The engines are much bigger than would be needed on an ordinary contragravity craft, because a hunter-ship operates under water as well as in the air. Then, there's a lot of cargo space for the wax, and the boat berth aft for the scout boat, so they're not exactly built for comfort. They don't really need to be; a ship's rarely out more than a hundred and fifty hours on any cruise.

Murell had done a lot of reading about every phase of the wax business, and he wanted to learn everything he could by actual observation. He said that Argentine Exotic Organics was going to keep him here on Fenris as a resident buyer and his job was going to be to deal with the hunters, either individually or through their co-operative organization, if they could get rid of Ravick and set up something he could do business with, and he wanted to be able to talk the hunters' language and understand their problems.

So I took him around over the boat, showing him everything and conscripting any crew members I came across to explain what I couldn't. I showed him the scout boat in its berth, and we climbed into it and looked around. I showed him the machine that packed the wax into skins, and the cargo holds, and the electrolytic gills that extracted oxygen from sea water while we were submerged, and the ship's armament. Finally, we got to the engine room, forward. He whistled when he saw the engines.

"Why, those things are big enough for a five-thousand-ton freighter," he said.

"They have to be," I said. "Running submerged isn't the same as running in atmosphere. You ever done any swimming?"

He shook his head. "I was born in Antarctica, on Terra. The water's a little too cold to do much swimming there. And I've spent most of my time since then in central Argentine, in the pampas country. The sports there are horseback riding and polo and things like that."

Well, whattaya know! Here was a man who had not only seen a horse, but actually ridden one. That in itself was worth a story in the *Times*.

Tom and Abdullah, who were fussing around the engines, heard that. They knocked off what they were doing and began asking him questions —I suppose he thought they were awfully silly, but he answered all of them patiently-about horses and riding. I was looking at a couple of spare power-unit cartridges, like the one Al Devis had strained his back on, clamped to the deck out of the way.

They were only as big as a one-liter jar, rounded at one end and flat at the other where the power cable was connected, but they weighed close to two hundred pounds apiece. Most of the weight was on the outside; a dazzlingly bright plating of collapsium-collapsed matter, the electron shell collapsed onto the nucleus and the atoms in actual physical contact-and absolutely nothing but nothing could get through it. Inside was about a kilogram of strontium-90; it would keep on emitting electrons for twenty-five years, normally, but there was a miniature plutonium reactor, itself shielded with collapsium, which, among other things, speeded that process up considerably. A cartridge was good for about five years; two of them kept the engines in operation.

The engines themselves converted the electric current from the power cartridges into magnetic current, and lifted the ship and propelled it. Abdullah was explaining that to Murell and Murell seemed to be getting it satisfactorily.

Finally, we left them; Murell wanted to see the sunset some more and went up to the conning tower where Joe and Ramón were, and I decided to take a nap while I had a chance.

8
Practice, 50-MM Gun

It seemed as though I had barely fallen asleep before I was wakened by the ship changing direction and losing altitude. I knew there were clouds coming in from the east, now, on the lower air currents, and I supposed that Joe was taking the *Javelin* below them to have a look at the surface of the sea. So I ran up to the conning tower, and when I got there I found that the lower clouds were solid over us, it was growing dark, and another hunter-ship was approaching with her lights on.

"Who is she?" I asked.

"*Bulldog*, Nip Spazoni," Joe told me. "Nip's bringing my saloon fighter aboard, and he wants to meet Mr. Murell."

I remembered that the man who had roughed up the Ravick goon in Martian Joe's had made his getaway from town in the *Bulldog*. As I watched, the other ship's boat dropped out from her stern, went end-over-end for an instant, and then straightened out and came circling around astern of us, matching our speed and ejecting a magnetic grapple.

Nip Spazoni and another man climbed out with life lines fast to their belts and crawled along our upper deck, catching life lines that were thrown out to them and snapping onto them before casting loose the ones from their boat. Somebody at the lock under the conning tower hauled them in.

Nip Spazoni's name was Old Terran Italian, but he had slanted Mongoloid eyes and a sparse little chin-beard, which accounted for his nickname. The amount of intermarriage that's gone on since the First Century, any resemblance between people's names and their appearances is purely coincidental. Oscar Fujisawa, who looks as though his name ought to be Lief Ericsson, for example.

"Here's your prodigal, Joe," he was saying, peeling out of his parka as he came up the ladder. "I owe him a second gunner's share on a monster, fifteen tons of wax."

"Hey, that was a good one. You heading home, now?" Then he turned to the other man, who had followed Nip up the ladder. "You didn't do a very good job, Bill," he said. "The so-and-so's out of the hospital by now."

"Well, you know who takes care of his own," the crewman said. "Give me something for effort; I tried hard enough."

"No, I'm not going home yet," Nip was answering. "I have hold-room for the wax of another one, if he isn't bigger than ordinary. I'm going to go down on the bottom when the winds start and sit it out, and then try to get a second one." Then he saw me. "Well, hey, Walt; when did you turn into a monster-hunter?"

Then he was introduced to Murell, and he and Joe and the man from Argentine Exotic Organics sat down at the chart table and Joe yelled for a pot of coffee, and they started talking prices and quantities of wax. I sat in, listening. This was part of what was going to be the big story of the year. Finally they got that talked out, and Joe asked Nip how the monsters were running.

"Why, good; you oughtn't to have any trouble finding one," Nip said. "There must have been a Nifflheim of a big storm off to the east, beyond the Lava Islands. I got mine north of Cape Terror. There's huge patches of sea-spaghetti drifting west, all along the coast of Hermann Reuch's Land. Here." He pulled out a map. "You'll find it all along here."

Murell asked me if sea-spaghetti was something the monsters ate. His reading-up still had a few gaps, here and there.

"No, it's seaweed; the name describes it. Screwfish eat it; big schools of them follow it. Gulpers and funnelmouths and bag-bellies eat screwfish, and monsters eat them. So wherever you find spaghetti, you can count on finding a monster or two."

"How's the weather?" Joe was asking.

"Good enough, now. It was almost full dark when we finished the cutting-up. It was raining; in fifty or sixty hours it ought to be getting pretty bad." Spazoni pointed on the map. "Here's about where I think you ought to try, Joe."

<hr>

I screened the Times, after Nip went back to his own ship. Dad said that Bish Ware had called in, with nothing to report but a vague suspicion that something nasty was cooking. Steve Ravick and Leo Belsher were taking things, even the announcement of the Argentine Exotic Organics price, too calmly.

"I think so, myself," he added. "That gang has some kind of a knife up their sleeve. Bish is trying to find out just what it is."

"Is he drinking much?" I asked.

"Well, he isn't on the wagon, I can tell you that," Dad said. "I'm beginning to think that he isn't really sober till he's half plastered."

There might be something to that, I thought. There are all kinds of weird individualities about human metabolism; for all I knew, alcohol might actually be a food for Bish. Or he might have built up some kind of immunity, with antibodies that were themselves harmful if he didn't have alcohol to neutralize them.

The fugitive from what I couldn't bring myself to call justice proved to know just a little, but not much, more about engines than I did. That meant that Tom would still have to take Al Devis's place, and I'd have to take his with the after 50-mm. So the ship went down to almost sea surface, and Tom and I went to the stern turret.

The gun I was to handle was an old-model Terran Federation Army infantry-platoon accompanying gun. The mount, however, was power-driven, like the mount for a 90-mm contragravity tank gun. Reconciling the firing mechanism of the former with the elevating and traversing gear of the latter had produced one of the craziest pieces of machinery that ever gave an ordnance engineer nightmares. It was a local job, of course. An ordnance engineer in Port Sandor doesn't really have to be a raving maniac, but it's a help.

Externally, the firing mechanism consisted of a pistol grip and trigger, which looked all right to me. The sight was a standard binocular light-gun sight, with a spongeplastic mask to save the gunner from a pair of black eyes every time he fired it. The elevating and traversing gear was combined in one lever on a ball-and-socket joint. You could move the gun diagonally in any direction in one motion, but you had to push or pull the opposite way. Something would go plonk when the trigger was pulled on an empty chamber, so I did some dry practice at the crests of waves.

"Now, mind," Tom was telling me, "this is a lot different from a pistol."

"So I notice," I replied. I had also noticed that every time I got the cross hairs on anything and squeezed the trigger, they were on something else when the trigger went plonk. "All this gun needs is another lever, to control the motion of the ship."

"Oh, that only makes it more fun," Tom told me.

Then he loaded in a clip of five rounds, big expensive-looking cartridges a foot long, with bottle-neck cases and pointed shells.

The targets were regular tallow-wax skins, blown up and weighted at one end so that they would float upright. He yelled into the intercom, and one was chucked overboard ahead. A moment later, I saw it bobbing away astern of us. I put my face into the sight-mask, caught it, centered the cross hairs, and squeezed. The gun gave a thunderclap and recoiled past me, and when I pulled my face out of the mask, I saw a column of water and spray about fifty feet left and a hundred yards over.

"You won't put any wax in the hold with that kind of shooting," Tom told me.

I fired again. This time, there was no effect at all that I could see. The shell must have gone away over and hit the water a couple of miles astern. Before Tom could make any comment on that shot, I let off another, and this time I hit the water directly in front of the bobbing wax skin. Good line shot, but away short.

"Well, you scared him, anyhow," Tom said, in mock commendation.

I remembered some of the comments I'd made when I'd been trying to teach him to hit something smaller than the target frame with a pistol, and humbled myself. The next two shots were reasonably close, but neither would have done any damage if the rapidly vanishing skin had really been a monster. Tom clucked sadly and slapped in another clip.

"Heave over another one," he called. "That monster got away."

The trouble was, there were a lot of tricky air currents along the surface of the water. The engines were running on lift to match exactly the weight of the ship, which meant that she had no weight at all, and a lot of wind resistance. The drive was supposed to match the wind speed, and the ship was supposed to be kept nosed into the wind. A lot of that is automatic, but it can't be made fully so, which means that the pilot has to do considerable manual correcting, and no human alive can do that perfectly. Joe Kivelson or Ramón Llewellyn or whoever was at the controls was doing a masterly job, but that fell away short of giving me a stable gun platform.

I caught the second target as soon as it bobbed into sight and slammed a shell at it. The explosion was half a mile away, but the shell hadn't missed the target by more than a few yards. Heartened, I fired again, and that shot was simply dreadful.

"I know what you're doing wrong," Tom said. "You're squeezing the trigger."

"Huh?"

I pulled my face out of the sight-mask and looked at him to see if he were exhibiting any other signs of idiocy. That was like criticizing somebody for using a fork instead of eating with his fingers.

"You're not shooting a pistol," he continued. "You don't have to hold the gun on the target with the hand you shoot with. The mount control, in your other hand, does that. As soon as the cross hairs touch the target, just grab the trigger as though it was a million sols getting away from you. Well, sixteen thousand; that's what a monster's worth now, Murell prices. Jerking won't have the least effect on your hold whatever."

So that was why I'd had so much trouble making a pistol shot out of Tom, and why it would take a special act of God to make one out of his father. And that was why monster-hunters caused so few casualties in barroom shootings around Port Sandor, outside of bystanders and back-bar mirrors. I felt like Newton after he'd figured out why the apple bopped him on the head.

"You mean like this?" I asked innocently, as soon as I had the hairs on the target again, violating everything I held most sacredly true about shooting.

The shell must have passed within inches of the target; it bobbed over flat and the weight pulled it up again into the backwave from the shell and it bobbed like crazy.

"That would have been a dead monster," Tom said. "Let's see you do it again."

I didn't; the next shot was terrible. Overconfidence. I had one more shot, and I didn't want to use up another clip of the *Javelin's* ammo. They cost like crazy, even if they were Army rejects. The sea current was taking the target farther away every second, but I took my time on the next one, bringing the horizontal hair level with the bottom of the inflated target and traversing quickly, grabbing the trigger as soon as the vertical hair touched it. There was a water-spout, and the target shot straight up for fifty feet; the shell must have exploded directly under it. There was a sound of cheering from the intercom. Tom asked if I wanted to fire another clip. I told him I thought I had the hang of it now, and screwed a swab onto the ramrod and opened the breech to clean the gun.

Joe Kivelson grinned at me when I went up to the conning tower.

"That wasn't bad, Walt," he said. "You never manned a 50-mm before, did you?"

"No, and it's all backward from anything I ever learned about shooting," I said. "Now, suppose I get a shot at a monster; where do I try to hit him?"

"Here, I'll show you." He got a block of lucite, a foot square on the end by two and a half feet long, out of a closet under the chart table. In it was a little figure of a Jarvis's sea-monster; long body tapering to a three-fluked tail, wide horizontal flippers like the wings of an old pre-contragravity aircraft, and a long neck with a little head and a wide tusked mouth.

"Always get him from in front," he said. "Aim right here, where his chest makes a kind of V at the base of the neck. A 50-mm will go six or eight feet into him before it explodes, and it'll explode among his heart and lungs and things. If it goes straight along his body, it'll open him up and make the cutting-up easier, and it won't spoil much wax. That's where I always shoot."

"Suppose I get a broadside shot?"

"Why, then put your shell right under the flukes at the end of the tail. That'll turn him and position him for a second shot from in front. But mostly, you'll get a shot from in front, if the ship's down near the surface. Monsters will usually try to attack the ship. They attack anything around their own size that they see," he told me. "But don't ever make a body shot broadside-to. You'll kill the monster, but you'll blow about five thousand sols' worth of wax to Nifflheim doing it."

It had been getting dusky while I had been shooting; it was almost full dark now, and the *Javelin's* lights were on. We were making close to Mach 3, headed east now, and running away from the remaining daylight.

We began running into squalls of rain, and then rain mixed with wet snow. The underside lights came on, and the lookout below began reporting patches of sea-spaghetti. Finally, the boat was dropped out and went circling away ahead, swinging its light back and forth over the water, and radioing back reports. Spaghetti. Spaghetti with a big school of screwfish working on it. Funnel-mouths working on the screwfish. Finally the speaker gave a shrill whistle.

"*Monster ho!*" the voice yelled. "About ten points off your port bow. We're circling over it now."

"Monster ho!" Kivelson yelled into the intercom, in case anybody hadn't heard. "All hands to killing stations." Then he saw me standing there, wondering what was going to happen next. "Well, mister, didn't you hear me?" he bellowed. "Get to your gun!"

Gee! I thought. I'm one of the crew, now.

"Yes sir!" I grabbed the handrail of the ladder and slid down, then raced aft to the gun turret.

9
Monster Killing

There was a man in the turret, waiting to help me. He had a clip of five rounds in the gun, the searchlight on, and the viewscreen tuned to the forward pickup. After checking the gun and loading the chamber, I looked in that, and in the distance, lighted by the boat above and the searchlight of the *Javelin*, I saw a long neck with a little head on the end of it weaving about. We were making straight for it, losing altitude and speed as we went.

Then the neck dipped under the water and a little later reappeared, coming straight for the advancing light. The forward gun went off, shaking the ship with its recoil, and the head ducked under again. There was a spout from the shell behind it.

I took my eyes from the forward screen and looked out the rear window, ready to shove my face into the sight-mask. An instant later, the head and neck reappeared astern of us. I fired, without too much hope of hitting anything, and then the ship was rising and circling.

As soon as I'd fired, the monster had sounded, headfirst. I fired a second shot at his tail, in hope of crippling his steering gear, but that was a clean miss, too, and then the ship was up to about five thousand feet. My helper pulled out the partly empty clip and replaced it with a full one, giving me five and one in the chamber.

If I'd been that monster, I thought, I'd have kept on going till I was a couple of hundred miles away from this place; but evidently that wasn't the way monsters thought, if thinking is what goes on inside a brain cavity the size of a quart bottle in a head the size of two oil drums on a body as big as the ship that was hunting him. He'd found a lot of gulpers and funnelmouths, and he wasn't going to be chased away from his dinner by somebody shooting at him.

I wondered why they didn't eat screwfish, instead of the things that preyed on them. Maybe they did and we didn't know it. Or maybe they just didn't like screwfish. There were a lot of things we didn't know about sea-monsters.

For that matter, I wondered why we didn't grow tallow-wax by carniculture. We could grow any other animal matter we wanted. I'd often thought of that.

The monster wasn't showing any inclination to come to the surface again, and finally Joe Kivelson's voice came out of the intercom:

"Run in the guns and seal ports. Secure for submersion. We're going down and chase him up."

My helper threw the switch that retracted the gun and sealed the gun port. I checked that and reported, "After gun secure." Hans Cronje's voice, a moment later, said, "Forward gun secure," and then Ramón Llewellyn said, "Ship secure; ready to submerge."

Then the *Javelin* began to settle, and the water came up over the window. I didn't know what the radar was picking up. All I could see was the screen and the window; water lighted for about fifty feet in front and behind. I saw a cloud of screwfish pass over and around us, spinning rapidly as they swam as though on lengthwise axis-they always spin counterclockwise, never clockwise. A couple of funnelmouths were swimming after them, overtaking and engulfing them.

Then the captain yelled, "Get set for torpedo," and my helper and I each grabbed a stanchion. A couple of seconds later it seemed as though King Neptune himself had given the ship a poke in the nose; my hands were almost jerked loose from their hold. Then she swung slowly, nosing up and down, and finally Joe Kivelson spoke again:

"We're going to surface. Get set to run the guns out and start shooting as soon as we're out of the water."

"What happened?" I asked my helper.

"Must have put the torp right under him and lifted him," he said. "He could be dead or stunned. Or he could be live and active and spoiling for a fight."

That last could be trouble. The *Times* had run quite a few stories, some with black borders, about ships that had gotten into trouble with monsters. A hunter-ship is heavy and it is well-armored —install hyperdrive engines in one, and you could take her from here to Terra-but a monster is a tough brute, and he has armor of his own, scales an inch or so thick and tougher than sole leather. A lot of chair seats around Port Sandor are made of single monster scales. A monster strikes with its head, like a snake. They can smash a ship's boat, and they've been known to punch armor-glass windows out of their frames. I didn't want the window in front of me coming in at me with a monster head the size of a couple of oil drums and full of big tusks following it.

The *Javelin* came up fast, but not as fast as the monster, which seemed to have been injured only in his disposition. He was on the surface already, about fifty yards astern of us, threshing with his forty-foot wing-fins, his neck arched back to strike. I started to swing my gun for the chest shot Joe Kivelson had recommended as soon as it was run out, and then the ship was swung around and tilted up forward by a sudden gust of wind. While I was struggling to get the sights back on the monster, the ship gave another lurch and the cross hairs were right on its neck, about six feet below the head. I grabbed the trigger, and as soon as the shot was off, took my eyes from the sights. I was just a second too late to see the burst, but not too late to see the monster's neck jerk one way out of the smoke puff and its head fly another. A second later, the window in front of me was splashed with blood as the headless neck came down on our fantail.

Immediately, two rockets jumped from the launcher over the gun turret, planting a couple of harpoons, and the boat, which had been circling around since we had submerged, dived into the water and passed under the monster, coming up on the other side dragging another harpoon line. The monster was still threshing its wings and flogging with its headless neck. It takes a monster quite a few minutes to tumble to the fact that it's been killed. My helper was pounding my back black and blue with one hand and trying to pump mine off with the other, and I was getting an ovation from all over the ship. At the same time, a couple more harpoons went into the thing from the ship, and the boat put another one in from behind.

I gathered that shooting monsters' heads off wasn't at all usual, and hastened to pass it off as pure luck, so that everybody would hurry up and deny it before they got the same idea themselves.

We hadn't much time for ovations, though. We had a very slowly dying monster, and before he finally discovered that he was dead, a couple of harpoons got pulled out and had to be replaced. Finally, however, he quieted down, and the boat swung him around, bringing the tail past our bow, and the ship cut contragravity to specific-gravity level and settled to float on top of the water. The boat dived again, and payed out a line that it brought up and around and up again, lashing the monster fast alongside.

"All right," Kivelson was saying, out of the intercom. "Shooting's over. All hands for cutting-up."

I pulled on a parka and zipped it up and went out onto the deck. Everybody who wasn't needed at engines or controls was there, and equipment was coming up from below-power saws and sonocutters and even a solenoid jackhammer. There were half a dozen floodlights, on small contragravity lifters; they were run up on lines fifty feet above the ship's deck. By this time it was completely dark and fine snow was blowing. I could see that Joe Kivelson was anxious to get the cutting-up finished before the wind got any worse.

"Walt, can you use a machine gun?" he asked me.

I told him I could. I was sure of it; a machine gun is fired in a rational and decent manner.

"Well, all right. Suppose you cover for us from the boat," he said. "Mr. Murell can pilot for you. You never worked at cutting-up before, and neither did he. You'd be more of a hindrance than a help and so would he. But we do need a good machine gunner. As soon as we start throwing out waste, we'll have all the slashers and halberd fish for miles around. You just shoot them as fast as you see them."

He was courteous enough not to add: "And don't shoot any of the crew."

The boat came in and passed out the lines of its harpoons, and Murell and I took the places of Cesário Vieira and the other man. We went up to the nose, and Murell took his place at the controls, and I got back of the 7-mm machine gun and made sure that there were plenty of extra belts of ammo. Then, as we rose, I pulled the goggles down from my hood, swung the gun away from the ship, and hammered off a one-second burst to make sure it was working, after which I settled down, glad I had a comfortable seat and wasn't climbing around on that monster.

They began knocking scales loose with the jackhammer and cutting into the leathery skin underneath with sonocutters. The sea was getting heavy, and the ship and the attached monster had begun to roll.

"That's pretty dangerous work," Murell said. "If a man using one of those cutters slipped...."

"It's happened," I told him. "You met our peg-legged compositor, Julio. That was how he lost his leg."

"I don't blame them for wanting all they can get for tallow-wax."

They had the monster opened down the belly, and were beginning to cut loose big chunks of the yellow tallow-wax and throw them into cargo nets and swing them aboard with lifters, to be chucked down the cargo hatches. I was only able to watch that for a minute or so and tell Murell what was going on, and then the first halberd fish, with a spearlike nose and sharp ridges of the nearest thing to bone you find on Fenris, came swimming up. I swung the gun on the leader and gave him a second of fire, and then a two-second burst on the ones behind. Then I waited for a few seconds until the survivors converged on their dead and injured companions and gave them another burst, which wiped out the lot of them.

It was only a couple of seconds after that that the first slasher came in, shiny as heat-blued steel and waving four clawed tentacles that grew around its neck. It took me a second or so to get the sights on him. He stopped slashing immediately. Slashers are smart; you kill them and they find it out right away.

Before long, the water around the ship and the monster was polluted with things like that. I had to keep them away from the men, now working up to their knees in water, and at the same time avoid massacring the crew I was trying to protect, and Murell had to keep the boat in position, in spite of a steadily rising wind, and every time I had to change belts, there'd be a new rush of things that had to be shot in a hurry. The ammunition bill for covering a cutting-up operation is one of the things that runs up expenses for a hunter-ship. The ocean bottom around here must be carpeted with machine-gun brass.

Finally, they got the job done, and everybody went below and sealed ship. We sealed the boat and went down after her. The last I saw, the remains of the monster, now stripped of wax, had been cast off, and the water around it was rioting with slashers and clawbeaks and halberd fish and similar marine unpleasantnesses.

10
Mayday, Mayday

Getting a ship's boat berthed inside the ship in the air is tricky work under the best of conditions; the way the wind was blowing by now, it would have been like trying to thread a needle inside a concrete mixer. We submerged after the ship and went in underwater. Then we had to wait in the boat until the ship rose above the surface and emptied the water out of the boat berth. When that was done and the boat berth was sealed again, the ship went down seventy fathoms and came to rest on the bottom, and we unsealed the boat and got out.

There was still the job of packing the wax into skins, but that could wait. Everybody was tired and dirty and hungry. We took turns washing up, three at a time, in the little ship's latrine which, for some reason going back to sailing-ship days on Terra, was called the "head." Finally the whole sixteen of us gathered in the relatively comfortable wardroom under the after gun turret.

Comfortable, that is, to the extent that everybody could find a place to sit down, or could move about without tripping over somebody else. There was a big pot of coffee, and everybody had a plate or bowl of hot food. There's always plenty of hot food to hand on a hunter-ship; no regular meal-times, and everybody eats, as he sleeps, when he has time. This is the only time when a whole hunter crew gets together, after a monster has been killed and cut up and the ship is resting on the bottom and nobody has to stand watch.

Everybody was talking about the killing, of course, and the wax we had in the hold, and counting the money they were going to get for it, at the new eighty-centisol price.

"Well, I make it about fourteen tons," Ramón Llewellyn, who had been checking the wax as it went into the hold, said. He figured mentally for a moment, and added, "Call it twenty-two thousand sols." Then he had to fall back on a pencil and paper to figure shares.

I was surprised to find that he was reckoning shares for both Murell and myself.

"Hey, do we want to let them do that?" I whispered to Murell. "We just came along for the ride."

"I don't want the money," he said. "These people need every cent they can get."

So did I, for that matter, and I didn't have salary and expense account from a big company on Terra. However, I hadn't come along in the expectation of making anything out of it, and a newsman has to be careful about the outside money he picks up. It wouldn't do any harm in the present instance, but as a practice it can lead to all kinds of things, like playing favorites, coloring news, killing stories that shouldn't be killed. We do enough of that as it is, like playing down the tread-snail business for Bish Ware and the spaceport people, and never killing anybody except in a "local bar." It's hard to draw a line on that sort of thing.

"We're just guests," I said. "We don't work here."

"The dickens you are," Joe Kivelson contradicted. "Maybe you came aboard as guests, but you're both part of the crew now. I never saw a prettier shot on a monster than Walt made-took that thing's head off like a chicken on a chopping block-and he did a swell job of covering for the cutting-up. And he couldn't have done that if Murell hadn't handled the boat the way he did, and that was no easy job."

"Well, let's talk about that when we get to port," I said. "Are we going right back, or are we going to try for another monster?"

"I don't know," Joe said. "We could stow the wax, if we didn't get too much, but if we stay out, we'll have to wait out the wind and by then it'll be pretty cold."

"The longer we stay out, the more the cruise'll cost," Abdullah Monnahan, the engineer, said, "and the expenses'll cut into the shares."

"Tell the truth, I'm sort of antsy to get back," Joe Kivelson said. "I want to see what's going on in Port Sandor."

"So am I," Murell said. "I want to get some kind of office opened, and get into business. What time will the *Cape Canaveral* be getting in? I want a big cargo, for the first time."

"Oh, not for four hundred hours, at the least," I said. "The spaceships always try to miss the early-dark and early-daylight storms. It's hard to get a big ship down in a high wind."

"That'll be plenty of time, I suppose," Murell said. "There's all that wax you have stored, and what I can get out of the Co-operative stores from crews that reclaim it. But I'm going to have a lot to do."

"Yes," I agreed. "Dodging bullets, for one."

"Oh, I don't expect any trouble," Murell said. "This fellow Ravick's shot his round."

He was going to say something else, but before he could say it there was a terrific roar forward. The whole ship bucked like a recoiling gun, throwing everybody into a heap, and heeled over to starboard. There were a lot of yells, particularly from those who had been splashed with hot coffee, and somebody was shouting something about the magazines.

"The magazines are aft, you dunderhead," Joe Kivelson told him, shoving himself to his feet. "Stay put, everybody; I'll see what it is."

He pulled open the door forward. An instant later, he had slammed it shut and was dogging it fast.

"Hull must be ruptured forward; we're making water. It's spouting up the hatch from the engine room like a geyser," he said. "Ramón, go see what it's like in the boat berth. The rest of you, follow him, and grab all the food and warm clothing you can. We're going to have to abandon."

He stood by the doorway aft, shoving people through and keeping them from jamming up, saying: "Take it easy, now; don't crowd. We'll all get out." There wasn't any panic. A couple of men were in the doorway of the little galley when I came past, handing out cases of food. As nothing was coming out at the instant, I kept on, and on the way back to the boat-berth hatch, I pulled down as many parkas and pairs of overpants as I could carry, squeezing past Tom, who was collecting fleece-lined hip boots. Each pair was buckled together at the tops; a hunter always does that, even at home ashore.

Ramón had the hatch open, and had opened the top hatch of the boat, below. I threw my double armload of clothing down through it and slid down after, getting out of the way of the load of boots Tom dumped ahead of him. Joe Kivelson came down last, carrying the ship's log and some other stuff. A little water was trickling over the edge of the hatch above.

"It's squirting up from below in a dozen places," he said, after he'd sealed the boat. "The whole front of the ship must be blown out."

"Well, now we know what happened to Simon MacGregor's *Claymore*," I said, more to myself than to anybody else.

Joe and Hans Cronje, the gunner, were getting a rocket out of the locker, detaching the harpoon and fitting on an explosive warhead. He stopped, while he and Cronje were loading it into the after launcher, and nodded at me.

"That's what I think, too," he said. "Everybody grab onto something; we're getting the door open."

I knew what was coming and started hugging a stanchion as though it were a long-lost sweetheart, and Murell, who didn't but knew enough to imitate those who did, hugged it from the other side. The rocket whooshed out of the launcher and went off with a deafening bang outside. For an instant, nothing happened, and I told Murell not to let go. Then the lock burst in and the water, at seventy fathoms' pressure, hit the boat. Abdullah had gotten the engines on and was backing against it. After a little, the pressure equalized and we went out the broken lock stern first.

We circled and passed over the *Javelin*, and then came back. She was lying in the ooze, a quarter over on her side, and her whole bow was blown out to port. Joe Kivelson got the square box he had brought down from the ship along with the log, fussed a little with it, and then launched it out the disposal port. It was a radio locator. Sometimes a lucky ship will get more wax than the holds' capacity; they pack it in skins and anchor it on the bottom, and drop one of those gadgets with it. It would keep on sending a directional signal and the name of the ship for a couple of years.

"Do you really think it was sabotage?" Murell was asking me. Blowing up a ship with sixteen men aboard must have seemed sort of extreme to him. Maybe that wasn't according to Terran business ethics. "Mightn't it have been a power unit?"

"No. Power units don't blow, and if one did, it would vaporize the whole ship and a quarter of a cubic mile of water around her. No, that was old fashioned country-style chemical explosive. Cataclysmite, probably."

"Ravick?" he asked, rather unnecessarily.

"You know how well he can get along without you and Joe Kivelson, and here's a chance to get along without both of you together." Everybody in the boat was listening, so I continued: "How much do you know about this fellow Devis, who strained his back at the last moment?"

"Engine room's where he could have planted something," Joe Kivelson said.

"He was in there by himself for a while, the morning after the meeting," Abdullah Monnahan added.

"And he disappeared between the meeting room and the elevator, during the fight," Tom mentioned. "And when he showed up, he hadn't been marked up any. I'd have thought he'd have been pretty badly beaten-unless they knew he was one of their own gang."

"We're going to look Devis up when we get back," somebody said pleasantly.

"If we get back," Ramón Llewellyn told him. "That's going to take some doing."

"We have the boat," Hans Cronje said. "It's a little crowded, but we can make it back to Port Sandor."

"I hope we can," Abe Clifford, the navigator, said. "Shall we take her up, Joe?"

"Yes, see what it's like on top," the skipper replied.

Going up, we passed a monster at about thirty fathoms. It stuck its neck out and started for us. Monnahan tilted the boat almost vertical and put on everything the engines had, lift and drive parallel. An instant later, we broke the surface and shot into the air.

The wind hit the boat as though it had been a ping-pong ball, and it was several seconds, and bad seconds at that, before Monnahan regained even a semblance of control. There was considerable bad language, and several of the crew had bloody noses. Monnahan tried to get the boat turned into the wind. A circuit breaker popped, and red lights blazed all over the instrument panel. He eased off and let the wind take over, and for a while we were flying in front of it like a rifle bullet. Gradually, he nosed down and submerged.

"Well, that's that." Joe Kivelson said, when we were back in the underwater calm again. "We'll have to stay under till the wind's over. Don't anybody move around or breathe any deeper than you have to. We'll have to conserve oxygen."

"Isn't the boat equipped with electrolytic gills?" Murell asked.

"Sure, to supply oxygen for a maximum of six men. We have sixteen in here."

"How long will our air last, for sixteen of us?" I asked.

"About eight hours."

It would take us fifty to get to Port Sandor, running submerged. The wind wouldn't even begin to fall in less than twenty.

"We can go south, to the coast of Hermann Reuch's Land," Abe Clifford, the navigator, said. "Let me figure something out."

He dug out a slide rule and a pencil and pad and sat down with his back to the back of the pilot's seat, under the light. Everybody watched him in a silence which Joe Kivelson broke suddenly by bellowing:

"Dumont! You light that pipe and I'll feed it to you!"

Old Piet Dumont grabbed the pipe out of his mouth with one hand and pocketed his lighter with the other.

"Gosh, Joe; I guess I just wasn't thinking..." he began.

"Well, give me that pipe." Joe put it in the drawer under the charts. "Now you won't have it handy the next time you don't think."

After a while, Abe Clifford looked up. "Ship's position I don't have exactly; somewhere around East 25 Longitude, South 20 Latitude. I can't work out our present position at all, except that we're somewhere around South 30 Latitude. The locator signal is almost exactly north-by-northeast of us. If we keep it dead astern, we'll come out in Sancerre Bay, on Hermann Reuch's Land. If we make that, we're all right. We'll be in the lee of the Hacksaw Mountains, and we can surface from time to time to change air, and as soon as the wind falls we can start for home."

Then he and Abdullah and Joe went into a huddle, arguing about cruising speed submerged. The results weren't so heartening.

"It looks like a ten-hour trip, submerged," Joe said. "That's two hours too long, and there's no way of getting more oxygen out of the gills than we're getting now. We'll just have to use less. Everybody lie down and breathe as shallowly as possible, and don't do anything to use energy. I'm going to get on the radio and see what I can raise."

Big chance, I thought. These boat radios were only used for communicating with the ship while scouting; they had a strain-everything range of about three hundred miles. Hunter-ships don't crowd that close together when they're working. Still, there was a chance that somebody else might be sitting it out on the bottom within hearing. So Abe took the controls and kept the signal from the wreck of the *Javelin* dead astern, and Joe Kivelson began speaking into the radio:

"Mayday, Mayday, Mayday, Mayday. Captain Kivelson, *Javelin*, calling. My ship was wrecked by an explosion; all hands now in scout boat, proceeding toward Sancerre Bay, on course south-by-southwest from the wreck. Locator signal is being broadcast from the *Javelin*. Other than that, we do not know our position. Calling all craft, calling Mayday."

He stopped talking. The radio was silent except for an occasional frying-fat crackle of static. Then he began over again.

I curled up, trying to keep my feet out of anybody's face and my face clear of anybody else's feet. Somebody began praying, and somebody else told him to belay it, he was wasting oxygen.

I tried to go to sleep, which was the only practical thing to do. I must have succeeded. When I woke again, Joe Kivelson was saying, exasperatedly:

"Mayday, Mayday, Mayday, Mayday..."

11

Darkness and Cold

The next time I woke, Tom Kivelson was reciting the Mayday, Mayday incantation into the radio, and his father was asleep. The man who had been praying had started again, and nobody seemed to care whether he wasted oxygen or not. It was a Theosophist prayer to the Spirit Guides, and I remembered that Cesário Vieira was a Theosophist. Well, maybe there really were Spirit Guides. If there were, we'd all be finding out before long. I found that I didn't care one hoot which way, and I set that down to oxygen deficiency.

Then Glenn Murell broke in on the monotone call for help and the prayer.

"We're done for if we stay down here another hour," he said. "Any argument on that?"

There wasn't any. Joe Kivelson opened his eyes and looked around.

"We haven't raised anything at all on the radio," Murell went on. "That means nobody's within an hour of reaching us. Am I right?"

"I guess that's about the size of it," Joe Kivelson conceded.

"How close to land are we?"

"The radar isn't getting anything but open water and schools of fish," Abe Clifford said. "For all I know, we could be inside Sancerre Bay now."

"Well, then, why don't we surface?" Murell continued. "It's a thousand to one against us, but if we stay here our chances are precisely one hundred per cent negative."

"What do you think?" Joe asked generally. "I think Mr. Murell's stated it correctly."

"There is no death," Cesário said. "Death is only a change, and then more of life. I don't care what you do."

"What have we got to lose?" somebody else asked. "We're broke and gambling on credit now."

"All right; we surface," the skipper said. "Everybody grab onto something. We'll take the Nifflheim of a slamming around as soon as we're out of the water."

We woke up everybody who was sleeping, except the three men who had completely lost consciousness. Those we wrapped up in blankets and tarpaulins, like mummies, and lashed them down. We gathered everything that was loose and made it fast, and checked the fastenings of everything else. Then Abdullah Monnahan pointed the nose of the boat straight up and gave her everything the engines could put out. Just as we were starting upward, I heard Cesário saying:

"If anybody wants to see me in the next reincarnation, I can tell you one thing; I won't reincarnate again on Fenris!"

The headlights only penetrated fifty or sixty feet ahead of us. I could see slashers and claw-beaks and funnelmouths and gulpers and things like that getting out of our way in a hurry. Then we were out of the water and shooting straight up in the air.

It was the other time all over again, doubled in spades, only this time Abdullah didn't try to fight it; he just kept the boat rising. Then it went end-over-end, again and again. I think most of us blacked out; I'm sure I did, for a while. Finally, more by good luck than good management, he got us turned around with the wind behind us. That lasted for a while, and then we started keyholing again. I could see the instrument panel from where I'd lashed myself fast; it was going completely bughouse. Once, out the window in front, I could see jagged mountains ahead. I just shut my eyes and waited for the Spirit Guides to come and pick up the pieces.

When they weren't along, after a few seconds that seemed like half an hour, I opened my eyes again. There were more mountains ahead, and mountains to the right. This'll do it, I thought, and I wondered how long it would take Dad to find out what had happened to us. Cesário had started praying again, and so had Abdullah Monnahan, who had just remembered that he had been brought up a Moslem. I hoped he wasn't trying to pray in the direction of Mecca, even allowing that he knew which way Mecca was from Fenris generally. That made me laugh, and then I thought, This is a fine time to be laughing at anything. Then I realized that things were so bad that anything more that happened was funny.

I was still laughing when I discovered that the boat had slowed to a crawl and we were backing in between two high cliffs. Evidently Abdullah, who had now stopped praying, had gotten enough control of the boat to keep her into the wind and was keeping enough speed forward to yield to it gradually. That would be all right, I thought, if the force of the wind stayed constant, and as soon as I thought of that, it happened. We got into a relative calm, the boat went forward again, and then was tossed up and spun around. Then I saw a mountain slope directly behind us, out the rear window.

A moment later, I saw rocks and boulders sticking out of it in apparent defiance of gravitation, and then I realized that it was level ground and we were coming down at it backward. That lasted a few seconds, and then we hit stern-on, bounced and hit again. I was conscious up to the third time we hit.

The next thing I knew, I was hanging from my lashings from the side of the boat, which had become the top, and the headlights and the lights on the control panel were out, and Joe Kivelson was holding a flashlight while Abe Clifford and Glenn Murell were trying to get me untied and lower me. I also noticed that the air was fresh, and very cold.

"Hey, we're down!" I said, as though I were telling anybody anything they didn't know. "How many are still alive?"

"As far as I know, all of us," Joe said. "I think I have a broken arm." I noticed, then, that he was holding his left arm stiffly at his side. Murell had a big gash on top of his head, and he was mopping blood from his face with his sleeve while he worked.

When they got me down, I looked around. Somebody else was playing a flashlight around at the stern, which was completely smashed. It was a miracle the rocket locker hadn't blown up, but the main miracle was that all, or even any, of us were still alive.

We found a couple of lights that could be put on, and we got all of us picked up and the unconscious revived. One man, Dominic Silverstein, had a broken leg. Joe Kivelson's arm was, as he suspected, broken, another man had a fractured wrist, and Abdullah Monnahan thought a couple of ribs were broken. The rest of us were in one piece, but all of us were cut and bruised. I felt sore all over. We also found a nuclear-electric heater that would work, and got it on. Tom and I rigged some tarpaulins to screen off the ruptured stern and keep out the worst of the cold wind. After they got through setting and splinting the broken bones and taping up Abdullah's ribs, Cesário and Murell got some water out of one of the butts and started boiling it for coffee. I noticed that Piet Dumont had recovered his pipe and was smoking it, and Joe Kivelson had his lit.

"Well, where are we?" somebody was asking Abe Clifford.

The navigator shook his head. "The radio's smashed, so's the receiver for the locator, and so's the radio navigational equipment. I can state positively, however, that we are on the north coast of Hermann Reuch's Land."

Everybody laughed at that except Murell. I had to explain to him that Hermann Reuch's Land was the antarctic continent of Fenris, and hasn't any other coast.

"I'd say we're a good deal west of Sancerre Bay," Cesário Vieira hazarded. "We can't be east of it, the way we got blown west. I think we must be at least five hundred miles east of it."

"Don't fool yourself, Cesário," Joe Kivelson told him. "We could have gotten into a turbulent updraft and been carried to the upper, eastward winds. The altimeter was trying to keep up with the boat and just couldn't, half the time. We don't know where we went. I'll take Abe's estimate and let it go at that."

"Well, we're up some kind of a fjord," Tom said. "I think it branches like a Y, and we're up the left branch, but I won't make a point of that."

"I can't find anything like that on this map," Abe Clifford said, after a while.

Joe Kivelson swore. "You ought to know better than that, Abe; you know how thoroughly this coast hasn't been mapped."

"How much good will it do us to know where we are, right now?" I asked. "If the radio's smashed, we can't give anybody our position."

"We might be able to fix up the engines and get the boat in the air again, after the wind drops." Monnahan said. "I'll take a look at them and see how badly they've been banged up."

"With the whole stern open?" Hans Cronje asked. "We'd freeze stiffer than a gun barrel before we went a hundred miles."

"Then we can pack the stern full of wet snow and let it freeze, instead of us," I suggested. "There'll be plenty of snow before the wind goes down."

Joe Kivelson looked at me for a moment. "That would work," he said. "How soon can you get started on the engines, Abdullah?"

"Right away. I'll need somebody to help me, though. I can't do much the way you have me bandaged up."

"I think we'd better send a couple of parties out," Ramón Llewellyn said. "We'll have to find a better place to stay than this boat. We don't all have parkas or lined boots, and we have a couple of injured men. This heater won't be enough; in about seventy hours we'd all freeze to death sitting around it."

Somebody mentioned the possibility of finding a cave.

"I doubt it," Llewellyn said. "I was on an exploring expedition down here, once. This is all igneous rock, mostly granite. There aren't many caves. But there may be some sort of natural shelter, or something we can make into a shelter, not too far away. We have two half-ton lifters; we could use them to pile up rocks and build something. Let's make up two parties. I'll take one; Abe, you take the other. One of us can go up and the other can go down."

We picked parties, trying to get men who had enough clothing and hadn't been too badly banged around in the landing. Tom wanted to go along, but Abdullah insisted that he stay and help with the inspection of the boat's engines. Finally six of us-Llewellyn, myself, Glenn Murell, Abe Clifford, old Piet Dumont, and another man-went out through the broken stern of the boat. We had two portable floodlights —a scout boat carries a lot of equipment-and Llewellyn took the one and Clifford the other. It had begun to snow already, and the wind was coming straight up the narrow ravine into which we had landed, driving it at us. There was a stream between the two walls of rock, swollen by the rains that had come just before the darkness, and the rocks in and beside it were coated with ice. We took one look at it and shook our heads. Any exploring we did would be done without trying to cross that. We stood for a few minutes trying to see through the driving snow, and then we separated, Abe Clifford, Dumont and the other man going up the stream and Ramón Llewellyn, Glenn Murell and I going down.

A few hundred yards below the boat, the stream went over a fifty-foot waterfall. We climbed down beside it, and found the ravine widening. It was a level beach, now, or what had been a beach thousands of years ago. The whole coast of Hermann Reuch's land is sinking in the Eastern Hemisphere and rising in the Western. We turned away from the stream and found that the wind was increasing in strength and coming at us from the left instead of in front. The next thing we knew, we were at the point of the mountain on our right and we could hear the sea roaring ahead and on both sides of us. Tom had been right about that V-shaped fjord, I thought.

We began running into scattered trees now, and when we got around the point of the mountain we entered another valley.

Trees, like everything else on Fenris, are considerably different from anything analogous on normal planets. They aren't tall, the biggest not more than fifteen feet high, but they are from six to eight feet thick, with all the branches at the top, sprouting out in all directions and reminding me of pictures of Medusa. The outside bark is a hard shell, which grows during the beginning of our four hot seasons a year. Under that will be more bark, soft and spongy, and this gets more and more dense toward the middle; and then comes the hardwood core, which may be as much as two feet thick.

"One thing, we have firewood," Murell said, looking at them.

"What'll we cut it with; our knives?" I wanted to know.

"Oh, we have a sonocutter on the boat," Ramón Llewellyn said. "We can chop these things into thousand-pound chunks and float them to camp with the lifters. We could soak the spongy stuff on the outside with water and let it freeze, and build a hut out of it, too." He looked around, as far as the light penetrated the driving snow. "This wouldn't be a bad place to camp."

Not if we're going to try to work on the boat, I thought. And packing Dominic, with his broken leg, down over that waterfall was something I didn't want to try, either. I didn't say anything. Wait till we got back to the boat. It was too cold and windy here to argue, and besides, we didn't know what Abe and his party might have found upstream.

12
Castaways Working

We had been away from the boat for about two hours; when we got back, I saw that Abdullah and his helpers had gotten the deck plates off the engine well and used them to build a more substantial barricade at the ruptured stern. The heater was going and the boat was warm inside, not just relatively to the outside, but actually comfortable. It was even more crowded, however, because there was a ton of collapsium shielding, in four sections, and the generator and power unit, piled in the middle. Abdullah and Tom and Hans Cronje were looking at the converters, which to my not very knowing eye seemed to be in a hopeless mess.

There was some more work going on up at the front. Cesário Vieira had found a small portable radio that wasn't in too bad condition, and had it apart. I thought he was doing about the most effective work of anybody, and waded over the pile of engine parts to see what he was doing. It wasn't much of a radio. A hundred miles was the absolute limit of its range, at least for sending.

"Is this all we have?" I asked, looking at it. It was the same type as the one I carried on the job, camouflaged in a camera case, except that it wouldn't record.

"There's the regular boat radio, but it's smashed up pretty badly. I was thinking we could do something about cannibalizing one radio out of parts from both of them."

We use a lot of radio equipment on the *Times*, and I do a good bit of work on it. I started taking the big set apart and then remembered the receiver for the locator and got at that, too. The trouble was that most of the stuff in all the sets had been miniaturized to a point where watchmaker's tools would have been pretty large for working on them, and all we had was a general-repair kit that was just about fine enough for gunsmithing.

While we were fooling around with the radios, Ramón Llewellyn was telling the others what we found up the other branch of the fjord. Joe Kivelson shook his head over it.

"That's too far from the boat. We can't trudge back and forth to work on the engines. We could cut firewood down there and float it up with the lifters, and I think that's a good idea about using slabs of the soft wood to build a hut. But let's build the hut right here."

"Well, suppose I take a party down now and start cutting?" the mate asked.

"Not yet. Wait till Abe gets back and we see what he found upstream. There may be something better up there."

Tom, who had been poking around in the converters, said:

"I think we can forget about the engines. This is a machine-shop job. We need parts, and we haven't anything to make them out of or with."

That was about what I'd thought. Tom knew more about lift-and-drive engines than I'd ever learn, and I was willing to take his opinion as confirmation of my own.

"Tom, take a look at this mess," I said. "See if you can help us with it."

He came over, looked at what we were working on, and said, "You need a magnifier for this. Wait till I see something." Then he went over to one of the lockers, rummaged in it, and found a pair of binoculars. He came over to us again, sat down, and began to take them apart. As soon as he had the two big objective lenses out, we had two fairly good magnifying glasses.

That was a big help, but being able to see what had to be done was one thing, and having tools to do it was another. So he found a sewing kit and a piece of emery stone, and started making little screwdrivers out of needles.

After a while, Abe Clifford and Piet Dumont and the other man returned and made a beeline for the heater and the coffeepot. After Abe was warmed a little, he said:

"There's a little waterfall about half a mile up. It isn't too hard to get up over it, and above, the ground levels off into a big bowl-shaped depression that looks as if it had been a lake bottom, once. The wind isn't so bad up there, and this whole lake bottom or whatever it is is grown up with trees. It would be a good place to make a camp, if it wasn't so far from the boat."

"How hard would it be to cut wood up there and bring it down?" Joe asked, going on to explain what he had in mind.

"Why, easy. I don't think it would be nearly as hard as the place Ramón found."

"Neither do I," the mate agreed. "Climbing up that waterfall down the stream with a half tree trunk would be a lot harder than dropping one over beside the one above." He began zipping up his parka. "Let's get the cutter and the lifters and go up now."

"Wait till I warm up a little, and I'll go with you," Abe said.

Then he came over to where Cesário and Tom and I were working, to see what we were doing. He chuckled appreciatively at the midget screwdrivers and things Tom was making.

"I'll take that back, Ramón," he said. "I can do a lot more good right here. Have you taken any of the radio navigational equipment apart, yet?" he asked us.

We hadn't. We didn't know anything about it.

"Well, I think we can get some stuff out of the astrocompass that can be used. Let me in here, will you?"

I got up. "You take over for me," I said. "I'll go on the wood-chopping detail."

Tom wanted to go, too; Abe told him to keep on with his toolmaking. Piet Dumont said he'd guide us, and Glenn Murell said he'd go along. There was some swapping around of clothes and we gathered up the two lifters and the sonocutter and a floodlight and started upstream.

The waterfall above the boat was higher than the one below, but not quite so hard to climb, especially as we had the two lifters to help us. The worst difficulty, and the worst danger, was from the wind.

Once we were at the top, though, it wasn't so bad. We went a couple of hundred yards through a narrow gorge, and then we came out onto the old lake bottom Abe had spoken about. As far as our lights would shine in the snow, we could see stubby trees with snaky branches growing out of the tops.

We just started on the first one we came to, slicing the down-hanging branches away to get at the trunk and then going to work on that. We took turns using the sonocutter, and the rest of us stamped around to keep warm. The first trunk must have weighed a ton and a half, even after the branches were all off; we could barely lift one end of it with both lifters. The spongy stuff, which changed from bark to wood as it went in to the middle, was two feet thick. We cut that off in slabs, to use for building the hut. The hardwood core, once we could get it lit, would make a fine hot fire. We could cut that into burnable pieces after we got it to camp. We didn't bother with the slashings; just threw them out of the way. There was so much big stuff here that the branches weren't worth taking in.

We had eight trees down and cut into slabs and billets before we decided to knock off. We didn't realize until then how tired and cold we were. A couple of us had taken the wood to the waterfall and heaved it over at the side as fast as the others got the trees down and cut up. If we only had another cutter and a couple more lifters, I thought. If we only had an airworthy boat....

When we got back to camp, everybody who wasn't crippled and had enough clothes to get away from the heater came out and helped. First, we got a fire started-there was a small arc torch, and we needed that to get the dense hardwood burning-and then we began building a hut against the boat. Everybody worked on that but Dominic Silverstein. Even Abe and Cesário knocked off work on the radio, and Joe Kivelson and the man with the broken wrist gave us a little one-handed help. By this time, the wind had fallen and the snow was coming down thicker. We made snow shovels out of the hard outer bark, although they broke in use pretty often, and banked snow up against the hut. I lost track of how long we worked, but finally we had a place we could all get into, with a fireplace, and it was as warm and comfortable as the inside of the boat.

We had to keep cutting wood, though. Before long it would be too cold to work up in the woods, or even go back and forth between the woods and the camp. The snow finally stopped, and then the sky began to clear and we could see stars. That didn't make us happy at all. As long as the sky was clouded and the snow was falling, some of the heat that had been stored during the long day was being conserved. Now it was all radiating away into space.

The stream froze completely, even the waterfall. In a way, that was a help; we could slide wood down over it, and some of the billets would slide a couple of hundred yards downstream. But the cold was getting to us. We only had a few men working at woodcutting-Cesário, and old Piet Dumont, and Abe Clifford and I, because we were the smallest and could wear bigger men's parkas and overpants over our own. But as long as any of us could pile on enough clothing and waddle out of the hut, we didn't dare stop. If the firewood ran out, we'd all freeze stiff in no time at all.

Abe Clifford got the radio working, at last. It was a peculiar job as ever was, but he thought it would have a range of about five hundred miles. Somebody kept at it all the time, calling Mayday. I think it was Bish Ware who told me that Mayday didn't have anything to do with the day after the last of April; it was Old Terran French, *m'aidez*, meaning "help me." I wondered how Bish was getting along, and I wasn't too optimistic about him.

Cesário and Abe and I were up at the waterfall, picking up loads of firewood-we weren't bothering, now, with anything but the hard and slow-burning cores-and had just gotten two of them hooked onto the lifters. I straightened for a moment and looked around. There wasn't a cloud in the sky, and two of Fenris's three moons were making everything as bright as day. The glisten of the snow and the frozen waterfall in the double moonlight was beautiful.

I turned to Cesário. "See what all you'll miss, if you take your next reincarnation off Fenris," I said. "This, and the long sunsets and sunrises, and —"

Before I could list any more sights unique to our planet, the 7-mm machine gun, down at the boat, began hammering; a short burst, and then another, and another and another.

13

The Beacon Light

We all said, "Shooting!" and, "The machine gun!" as though we had to tell each other what it was.

"Something's attacking them," Cesário guessed.

"Oh, there isn't anything to attack them now," Abe said. "All the critters are dug in for the winter. I'll bet they're just using it to chop wood with."

That could be; a few short bursts would knock off all the soft wood from one of those big billets and expose the hard core. Only why didn't they use the cutter? It was at the boat now.

"We better go see what it is," Cesário insisted. "It might be trouble."

None of us was armed; we'd never thought we'd need weapons. There are quite a few Fenrisian land animals, all creepers or crawlers, that are dangerous, but they spend the extreme hot and cold periods in burrows, in almost cataleptic sleep. It occurred to me that something might have burrowed among the rocks near the camp and been roused by the heat of the fire.

We hadn't carried a floodlight with us-there was no need for one in the moonlight. Of the two at camp, one was pointed up the ravine toward us, and the other into the air. We began yelling as soon as we caught sight of them, not wanting to be dusted over lightly with 7-mm's before anybody recognized us. As soon as the men at the camp heard us, the shooting stopped and they started shouting to us. Then we could distinguish words.

"Come on in! We made contact!"

We pushed into the hut, where everybody was crowded around the underhatch of the boat, which was now the side door. Abe shoved through, and I shoved in after him. Newsman's conditioned reflex; get to where the story is. I even caught myself saying, "Press," as I shoved past Abdullah Monnahan.

"What happened?" I asked, as soon as I was inside. I saw Joe Kivelson getting up from the radio and making place for Abe. "Who did you contact?"

"The Mahatma; *Helldiver*," he said. "Signal's faint, but plain; they're trying to make a directional fix on us. There are about a dozen ships out looking for us: *Helldiver*, *Pequod*, *Bulldog*, *Dirty Gertie*..." He went on naming them.

"How did they find out?" I wanted to know. "Somebody pick up our Mayday while we were cruising submerged?"

Abe Clifford was swearing into the radio. "No, of course not. We don't know where in Nifflheim we are. All the instruments in the boat were smashed."

"Well, can't you shoot the stars, Abe?" The voice —I thought it was Feinberg's —was almost as inaudible as a cat's sneeze.

"Sure we can. If you're in range of this makeshift set, the position we'd get would be practically the same as yours," Abe told him. "Look, there's a floodlight pointed straight up. Can you see that?"

"In all this moonlight? We could be half a mile away and not see it."

"We've been firing with a 7-mm," the navigator said.

"I know; I heard it. On the radio. Have you got any rockets? Maybe if you shot one of them up we could see it."

"Hey, that's an idea! Hans, have we another rocket with an explosive head?"

Cronje said we had, and he and another man got it out and carried it from the boat. I repeated my question to Joe Kivelson.

"No. Your Dad tried to call the *Javelin* by screen; that must have been after we abandoned ship. He didn't get an answer, and put out a general call. Nip Spazoni was nearest, and he cruised around and picked up the locator signal and found the wreck, with the boat berth blown open and the boat gone. Then everybody started looking for us."

Feinberg was saying that he'd call the other ships and alert them. If the *Helldiver* was the only ship we could contact by radio, the odds were that if they couldn't see the rocket from Feinberg's ship, nobody else could. The same idea must have occurred to Abe Clifford.

"You say you're all along the coast. Are the other ships west or east of you?"

"West, as far as I know."

"Then we must be way east of you. Where are you now?"

"About five hundred miles east of Sancerre Bay."

That meant we must be at least a thousand miles east of the bay. I could see how that happened. Both times the boat had surfaced, it had gone straight up, lift and drive operating together. There is a constant wind away from the sunlight zone at high level, heated air that has been lifted, and there is a wind at a lower level out of the dark zone, coming in to replace it. We'd gotten completely above the latter and into the former.

There was some yelling outside, and then I could hear Hans Cronje:

"Rocket's ready for vertical launching. Ten seconds, nine, eight, seven, six, five, four, three, two, one; rocket off!"

There was a whoosh outside. Clifford, at the radio, repeated: "Rocket off!" Then it banged, high overhead. "Did you see it? he asked.

"Didn't see a thing," Feinberg told him.

"Hey, I know what they would see!" Tom Kivelson burst out. "Say we go up and set the woods on fire?"

"Hey, that's an idea. Listen, Mahatma; we have a big forest of flowerpot trees up on a plateau above us. Say we set that on fire. Think you could see it?"

"I don't see why not, even in this moonlight. Wait a minute, till I call the other ships."

Tom was getting into warm outer garments. Cesário got out the arc torch, and he and Tom and I raced out through the hut and outdoors. We hastened up the path that had been tramped and dragged to the waterfall, got the lifters off the logs, and used them to help ourselves up over the rocks beside the waterfall.

We hadn't bothered doing anything with the slashings, except to get them out of our way, while we were working. Now we gathered them into piles among the trees, placing them to take advantage of what little wind was still blowing, and touched them off with the arc torch. Soon we had the branches of the trees burning, and then the soft outer wood of the trunks. It actually began to get uncomfortably hot, although the temperature was now down around minus 90° Fahrenheit.

Cesário was using the torch. After he got all the slashings on fire, he started setting fire to the trees themselves, going all around them and getting the soft outer wood burning. As soon as he had one tree lit, he would run on to another.

"This guy's a real pyromaniac," Tom said to me, wiping his face on the sleeve of his father's parka which he was wearing over his own.

"Sure I am," Cesário took time out to reply. "You know who I was about fifty reincarnations ago? Nero, burning Rome." Theosophists never hesitated to make fun of their religion, that way. The way they see it, a thing isn't much good if it can't stand being made fun of. "And look at the job I did on Moscow, a little later."

"Sure; I remember that. I was Napoleon then. What I'd have done to you if I'd caught you, too."

"Yes, and I know what he was in another reincarnation," Tom added. "Mrs. O'Leary's cow!"

Whether or not Cesário really had had any past astral experience, he made a good job of firebugging on this forest. We waited around for a while, far enough back for the heat to be just comfortable and pleasant, until we were sure that it was burning well on both sides of the frozen stream. It even made the double moonlight dim, and it was sending up huge clouds of fire-reddened smoke, and where the fire didn't light the smoke, it was black in the moonlight. There wouldn't be any excuse for anybody not seeing that. Finally, we started back to camp.

As soon as we got within earshot, we could hear the excitement. Everybody was jumping and yelling. "They see it! They see it!"

The boat was full of voices, too, from the radio:

"*Pequod* to *Dirty Gertie*, we see it, too, just off our port bow...Yes, *Bulldog*, we see your running lights; we're right behind you...*Slasher* to *Pequod*: we can't see you at all. Fire a flare, please..."

I pushed in to the radio. "This is Walter Boyd, *Times* representative with the *Javelin* castaways," I said. "Has anybody a portable audiovisual pickup that I can use to get some pictures in to my paper with?"

That started general laughter among the operators on the ships that were coming in.

"We have one, Walt," Oscar Fujisawa's voice told me. "I'm coming in ahead in the *Pequod* scout boat; I'll bring it with me."

"Thanks, Oscar," I said. Then I asked him: "Did you see Bish Ware before you left port?"

"I should say I did!" Oscar told me. "You can thank Bish Ware that we're out looking for you now. Tell you about it as soon as we get in."

14
The Rescue

The scout boat from the *Pequod* came in about thirty minutes later, from up the ravine where the forest fire was sending up flame and smoke. It passed over the boat and the hut beside it and the crowd of us outside, and I could see Oscar in the machine gunner's seat aiming a portable audiovisual telecast camera. After he got a view of us, cheering and waving our arms, the boat came back and let down. We ran to it, all of us except the man with the broken leg and a couple who didn't have enough clothes to leave the fire, and as the boat opened I could hear Oscar saying:

"Now I am turning you over to Walter Boyd, the *Times* correspondent with the *Javelin* castaways."

He gave me the camera when he got out, followed by his gunner, and I got a view of them, and of the boat lifting and starting west to guide the ships in. Then I shut it off and said to him:

"What's this about Bish Ware? You said he was the one who started the search."

"That's right," Oscar said. "About thirty hours after you left port, he picked up some things that made him think the *Javelin* had been sabotaged. He went to your father, and he contacted me-Mohandas Feinberg and I still had our ships in port-and started calling the *Javelin* by screen. When he couldn't get response, your father put out a general call to all hunter-ships. Nip Spazoni reported boarding the *Javelin*, and then went searching the area where he thought you'd been hunting, picked up your locator signal, and found the *Javelin* on the bottom with her bow blown out and the boat berth open and the boat gone. We all figured you'd head south with the boat, and that's where we went to look."

"Well, Bish Ware; he was dead drunk, last I heard of him," Joe Kivelson said.

"Aah, just an act," Oscar said. "That was to fool the city cops, and anybody else who needed fooling. It worked so well that he was able to crash a party Steve Ravick was throwing at Hunters' Hall, after the meeting. That was where he picked up some hints that Ravick had a spy in the *Javelin* crew. He spent the next twenty or so hours following that up, and heard about your man Devis straining his back. He found out what Devis did on the *Javelin*, and that gave him the idea that whatever the sabotage was, it would be something to the engines. What did happen, by the way?"

A couple of us told him, interrupting one another. He nodded.

"That was what Nip Spazoni thought when he looked at the ship. Well, after that he talked to your father and to me, and then your father began calling and we heard from Nip."

You could see that it absolutely hurt Joe Kivelson to have to owe his life to Bish Ware.

"Well, it's lucky anybody listened to him," he grudged. "I wouldn't have."

"No, I guess maybe you wouldn't," Oscar told him, not very cordially. "I think he did a mighty sharp piece of detective work, myself."

I nodded, and then, all of a sudden, another idea, under *Bish Ware, Reformation of,* hit me. Detective work; that was it. We could use a good private detective agency in Port Sandor. Maybe I could talk him into opening one. He could make a go of it. He had all kinds of contacts, he was handy with a gun, and if he recruited a couple of tough but honest citizens who were also handy with guns and built up a protective and investigative organization, it would fill a long-felt need and at the same time give him something beside Baldur honey-rum to take his mind off whatever he was drinking to keep from thinking about. If he only stayed sober half the time, that would be a fifty per cent success.

Ramón Llewellyn was wanting to know whether anybody'd done anything about Al Devis.

"We didn't have time to bother with any Al Devises," Oscar said. "As soon as Bish figured out what had happened aboard the *Javelin*, we knew you'd need help and need it fast. He's keeping an eye on Al for us till we get back."

"That's if he doesn't get any drunker and forget," Joe said.

Everybody, even Tom, looked at him in angry reproach.

"We better find out what he drinks and buy you a jug of it, Joe," Oscar's gunner told him.

The *Helldiver*, which had been closest to us when our signal had been picked up, was the first ship in. She let down into the ravine, after some maneuvering around, and Mohandas Feinberg and half a dozen of his crew got off with an improvised stretcher on a lifter and a lot of blankets. We got our broken-leg case aboard, and Abdullah Monnahan, and the man with the broken wrist. There were more ships coming, so the rest of us waited. Joe Kivelson should have gone on the *Helldiver*, to have his broken arm looked at, but a captain's always the last man off, so he stayed.

Oscar said he'd take Tom and Joe, and Glenn Murell and me, on the *Pequod*. I was glad of that. Oscar and his mate and his navigator are all bachelors, and they use the *Pequod* to throw parties on when they're not hunting, so it is more comfortably fitted than the usual hunter-ship. Joe decided not to try to take anything away from the boat. He was going to do something about raising the *Javelin*, and the salvage ship could stop here and pick everything up.

"Well, one thing," Oscar told him. "Bring that machine gun, and what small arms you have. I think things are going to get sort of rough in Port Sandor, in the next twenty or so hours."

I was beginning to think so, myself. The men who had gotten off the *Helldiver*, and the ones who got off Corkscrew Finnegan's *Dirty Gertie* and Nip Spazoni's *Bulldog* were all talking about what was going to have to be done about Steve Ravick. Bombing *Javelin* would have been a good move for Ravick, if it had worked. It hadn't, though, and now it was likely to be the thing that would finish him for good.

It wasn't going to be any picnic, either. He had his gang of hoodlums, and he could count on Morton Hallstock's twenty or thirty city police; they'd put up a fight, and a hard one. And they were all together, and the hunter fleet was coming in one ship at a time. I wondered if the Ravick-Hallstock gang would try to stop them at the water front, or concentrate at Hunters' Hall or the Municipal Building to stand siege. I knew one thing, though. However things turned out, there was going to be an awful lot of shooting in Port Sandor before it was over.

Finally, everybody had been gotten onto one ship or another but Oscar and his gunner and the Kivelsons and Murell and myself. Then the *Pequod*, which had been circling around at five thousand feet, let down and we went aboard. The conning tower was twice as long as usual on a hunter-ship, and furnished with a lot of easy chairs and a couple of couches. There was a big combination view and communication screen, and I hurried to that and called the *Times*.

Dad came on, as soon as I finished punching the wave-length combination. He was in his shirt sleeves, and he was wearing a gun. I guess we made kind of a show of ourselves, but, after all, he'd come within an ace of being all out of family, and I'd come within an ace of being all out, period. After we got through with the happy reunion, I asked him what was the situation in Port Sandor. He shook his head.

"Not good, Walt. The word's gotten around that there was a bomb planted aboard the *Javelin*, and everybody's taking just one guess who did it. We haven't expressed any opinions one way or another, yet. We've been waiting for confirmation."

"Set for recording," I said. "I'll give you the story as far as we know it."

He nodded, reached one hand forward out of the picture, and then nodded again. I began with our killing the monster and going down to the bottom after the cutting-up, and the explosion. I told him what we had seen after leaving the ship and circling around it in the boat.

"The condition of the hull looked very much like the effect of a charge of high explosive exploding in the engine room," I finished.

"We got some views of it, transmitted in by Captain Spazoni, of the *Bulldog*," he said. "Captain Courtland, of the Spaceport Police, has expressed the opinion that it could hardly be anything but a small demolition bomb. Would you say accident can be ruled out?"

"I would. There was nobody in the engine room at the time; we were resting on the bottom, and all hands were in the wardroom."

"That's good enough," Dad said. "We'll run it as 'very convincing and almost conclusive' evidence of sabotage." He'd shut off the recorder for that. "Can I get the story of how you abandoned ship and landed, now?"

His hand moved forward, and the recorder went on again. I gave a brief account of our experiences in the boat, the landing and wreck, and our camp, and the firewood cutting, and how we had repaired the radio. Joe Kivelson talked for a while, and so did Tom and Glenn Murell. I was going to say something when they finished, and I sat down on one of the couches. I distinctly remember leaning back and relaxing.

The next thing I knew, Oscar Fujisawa's mate was shaking me awake.

"We're in sight of Port Sandor," he was telling me.

I mumbled something, and then sat up and found that I had been lying down and that somebody had thrown a blanket over me. Tom Kivelson was still asleep under a blanket on the other couch, across from me. The clock over the instrument panel had moved eight G.S. hours. Joe Kivelson wasn't in sight, but Glenn Murell and Oscar were drinking coffee. I went to the front window, and there was a scarlet glow on the horizon ahead of me.

That's another sight Cesário Vieria will miss, if he takes his next reincarnation off Fenris. Really, it's nothing but damp, warm air, blown up from the exhaust of the city's main ventilation plant, condensing and freezing as it hits the cold air outside, and floodlighted from below. I looked at it for a while, and then got myself a cup of coffee and when I had finished it I went to the screen.

It was still tuned to the *Times*, and Mohandas Feinberg was sitting in front of it, smoking one of his twisted black cigars. He had a big 10-mm Sterberg stuffed into the waistband of his trousers.

"You guys poked along," he said. "I always thought the *Pequod* was fast. We got in three hours ago."

"Who else is in?"

"Corkscrew and some of his gang are here at the *Times*, now. *Bulldog* and *Slasher* just got in a while ago. Some of the ships that were farthest west and didn't go to your camp have been in quite a while. We're having a meeting here. We are organizing the Port Sandor Vigilance Committee and Renegade Hunters' Co-operative."

15

Vigilantes

When the *Pequod* surfaced under the city roof, I saw what was cooking. There were twenty or more ships, either on the concrete docks or afloat in the pools. The waterfront was crowded with men in boat clothes, forming little knots and breaking up to join other groups, all milling about talking excitedly. Most of them were armed; not just knives and pistols, which is normal costume, but heavy rifles or submachine guns. Down to the left, there was a commotion and people were getting out of the way as a dozen men come pushing through, towing a contra-gravity skid with a 50-mm ship's gun on it. I began not liking the looks of things, and Glenn Murell, who had come up from his nap below, was liking it even less. He'd come to Fenris to buy tallow-wax, not to fight a civil war. I didn't want any of that stuff, either. Getting rid of Ravick, Hallstock and Belsher would come under the head of civic improvements, but towns are rarely improved by having battles fought in them.

Maybe I should have played dumb and waited till I'd talked to Dad face to face, before making any statements about what had happened on the *Javelin*, I thought. Then I shrugged that off. From the minute the *Javelin* had failed to respond to Dad's screen-call and the general call had gone out to the hunter-fleet, everybody had been positive of what had happened. It was too much like the loss of the *Claymore*, which had made Ravick president of the Co-op.

Port Sandor had just gotten all of Steve Ravick that anybody could take. They weren't going to have any more of him, and that was all there was to it.

Joe Kivelson was grumbling about his broken arm; that meant that when a fight started, he could only go in swinging with one fist, and that would cut the fun in half. Another reason why Joe is a wretched shot is that he doesn't like pistols. They're a little too impersonal to suit him. They weren't for Oscar Fujisawa; he had gotten a Mars-Consolidated Police Special out of the chart-table drawer and put it on, and he was loading cartridges into a couple of spare clips. Down on the main deck, the gunner was serving out small arms, and there was an acrimonious argument because everybody wanted a chopper and there weren't enough choppers to go around. Oscar went over to the ladder head and shouted down at them.

"Knock off the argument, down there; you people are all going to stay on the ship. I'm going up to the *Times*; as soon as I'm off, float her out into the inner channel and keep her afloat, and don't let anybody aboard you're not sure of."

"That where we're going?" Joe Kivelson asked.

"Sure. That's the safest place in town for Mr. Murell and I want to find out exactly what's going on here."

"Well, here; you don't need to put me in storage," Murell protested. "I can take care of myself."

Add, Famous Last Words, I thought.

"I'm sure of it, but we can't take any chances," Oscar told him. "Right now, you are Fenris's Indispensable Man. If you're not around to buy tallow-wax, Ravick's won the war."

Oscar and Murell and Joe and Tom Kivelson and I went down into the boat; somebody opened the port and we floated out and lifted onto the Second Level Down. There was a fringe of bars and cafes and dance halls and outfitters and ship chandlers for a couple of blocks back, and then we ran into the warehouse district. Oscar ran up town to a vehicle shaft above the Times Building, careful to avoid the neighborhood of Hunters' Hall or the Municipal Building.

There was a big crowd around the *Times*, mostly business district people and quite a few women. They were mostly out on the street and inside the street-floor vehicle port. Not a disorderly crowd, but I noticed quite a few rifles and submachine guns. As we slipped into the vehicle port, they recognized the *Pequod's* boat, and there was a rush after it. We had trouble getting down without setting it on anybody, and more trouble getting out of it. They were all friendly-too friendly for comfort. They began cheering us as soon as they saw us.

Oscar got Joe Kivelson, with his arm in a sling, out in front where he could be seen, and began shouting: "Please make way; this man's been injured. Please don't crowd; we have an injured man here." The crowd began shoving back, and in the rear I could hear them taking it up: "Joe Kivelson; he's been hurt. They're carrying Joe Kivelson off." That made Joe curse a blue streak, and somebody said, "Oh, he's been hurt real bad; just listen to him!"

When we got up to the editorial floor, Dad and Bish Ware and a few others were waiting at the elevator for us. Bish was dressed as he always was, in his conservative black suit, with the organic opal glowing in his neckcloth. Dad had put a coat on over his gun. Julio was wearing two pistols and a knife a foot long. There was a big crowd in the editorial office-ships' officers, merchants, professional people. I noticed Sigurd Ngozori, the banker, and Professor Hartzenbosch-he was wearing a pistol, too, rather self-consciously —and the Zen Buddhist priest, who evidently had something under his kimono. They all greeted us enthusiastically and shook hands with us. I noticed that Joe Kivelson was something less than comfortable about shaking hands with Bish Ware. The fact that Bish had started the search for the *Javelin* that had saved our lives didn't alter the opinion Joe had formed long ago that Bish was just a worthless old souse. Joe's opinions are all collapsium-plated and impervious to outside influence.

I got Bish off to one side as we were going into the editorial room.

"How did you get onto it?" I asked.

He chuckled deprecatingly. "No trick at all," he said. "I just circulated and bought drinks for people. The trouble with Ravick's gang, it's an army of mercenaries. They'll do anything for the price of a drink, and as long as my rich uncle stays solvent, I always have the price of a drink. In the five years I've spent in this Garden Spot of the Galaxy, I've learned some pretty surprising things about Steve Ravick's operations."

"Well, surely, nobody was going around places like Martian Joe's or One Eye Swanson's boasting that they'd put a time bomb aboard the *Javelin*," I said.

"It came to pretty nearly that," Bish said. "You'd be amazed at how careless people who've had their own way for a long time can get. For instance, I've known for some time that Ravick has spies among the crews of a lot of hunter-ships. I tried, a few times, to warn some of these captains, but except for Oscar Fujisawa and Corkscrew Finnegan, none of them would listen to me. It wasn't that they had any doubt that Ravick would do that; they just wouldn't believe that any of their crew were traitors.

"I've suspected this Devis for a long time, and I've spoken to Ramón Llewellyn about him, but he just let it go in one ear and out the other. For one thing, Devis always has more money to spend than his share of the *Javelin* take would justify. He's the showoff type; always buying drinks for everybody and playing the big shot. Claims to win it gambling, but all the times I've ever seen him gambling, he's been losing.

"I knew about this hoard of wax we saw the day Murell came in for some time. I always thought it was being held out to squeeze a better price out of Belsher and Ravick. Then this friend of mine with whom I was talking aboard the *Peenemünde* mentioned that Murell seemed to know more about the tallow-wax business than about literary matters, and after what happened at the meeting and afterward, I began putting two and two together. When I crashed that party at Hunters' Hall, I heard a few things, and they all added up.

"And then, about thirty hours after the Javelin left port, I was in the Happy Haven, and who should I see, buying drinks for the house, but Al Devis. I let him buy me one, and he told me he'd strained his back hand-lifting a power-unit cartridge. A square dance got started a little later, and he got into it. His back didn't look very strained to me. And then I heard a couple of characters in One Eye Swanson's betting that the *Javelin* would never make port again."

I knew what had happened from then on. If it hadn't been for Bish Ware, we'd still be squatting around a fire down on the coast of Hermann Reuch's Land till it got too cold to cut wood, and then we'd freeze. I mentioned that, but Bish just shrugged it off and suggested we go on in and see what was happening inside.

"Where is Al Devis?" I asked. "A lot of people want to talk to him."

"I know they do. I want to get to him first, while he's still in condition to do some talking of his own. But he just dropped out of sight, about the time your father started calling the *Javelin*."

"Ah!" I drew a finger across under my chin, and mentioned the class of people who tell no tales. Bish shook his head slowly.

"I doubt it," he said. "Not unless it was absolutely necessary. That sort of thing would have a discouraging effect the next time Ravick wanted a special job done. I'm pretty sure he isn't at Hunters' Hall, but he's hiding somewhere."

Joe Kivelson had finished telling what had happened aboard the *Javelin* when we joined the main crowd, and everybody was talking about what ought to be done with Steve Ravick. Oddly enough, the most bloodthirsty were the banker and the professor. Well, maybe it wasn't so odd. They were smart enough to know what Steve Ravick was really doing to Port Sandor, and it hurt them as much as it did the hunters. Dad and Bish seemed to be the only ones present who weren't in favor of going down to Hunters' Hall right away and massacring everybody in it, and then doing the same at the Municipal Building.

"That's what I say!" Joe Kivelson was shouting. "Let's go clean out both rats' nests. Why, there must be a thousand hunter-ship men at the waterfront, and look how many people in town who want to help. We got enough men to eat Hunters' Hall whole."

"You'll find it slightly inedible, Joe," Bish told him. "Ravick has about thirty men of his own and fifteen to twenty city police. He has at least four 50-mm's on the landing stage above, and he has half a dozen heavy machine guns and twice that many light 7-mm's."

"Bish is right," somebody else said. "They have the vehicle port on the street level barricaded, and they have the two floors on the level below sealed off. We got men all around it and nobody can get out, but if we try to blast our way in, it's going to cost us like Nifflheim."

"You mean you're just going to sit here and talk about it and not do anything?" Joe demanded.

"We're going to do something, Joe," Dad told him. "But we've got to talk about what we're going to do, and how we're going to do it, or it'll be us who'll get wiped out."

"Well, we'll have to decide on what it'll be, pretty quick," Mohandas Gandhi Feinberg said.

"What are things like at the Municipal Building?" Oscar Fujisawa asked. "You say Ravick has fifteen to twenty city cops at Hunters' Hall. Where are the rest of them? That would only be five to ten."

"At the Municipal Building," Bish said. "Hallstock's holed up there, trying to pretend that nothing out of the ordinary is happening."

"Good. Let's go to the Municipal Building, first," Oscar said. "Take a couple of hundred men, make a lot of noise, shoot out a few windows and all yell, 'Hang Mort Hallstock!' loud enough, and he'll recall the cops he has at Hunters' Hall to save his own neck. Then the rest of us can make a quick rush and take Hunters' Hall."

"We'll have to keep our main force around Hunters' Hall while we're demonstrating at the Municipal Building," Corkscrew Finnegan said. "We can't take a chance on Ravick's getting away."

"I couldn't care less whether he gets away or not," Oscar said. "I don't want Steve Ravick's blood. I just want him out of the Co-operative, and if he runs out from it now, he'll never get back in."

"You want him, and you want him alive," Bish Ware said. "Ravick has close to four million sols banked on Terra. Every millisol of that's money he's stolen from the monster-hunters of this planet, through the Co-operative. If you just take him out and string him up, you'll have the Nifflheim of a time getting hold of any of it."

That made sense to all the ship captains, even Joe Kivelson, after Dad reminded him of how much the salvage job on the *Javelin* was going to cost. It took Sigurd Ngozori a couple of minutes to see the point, but then, hanging Steve Ravick wasn't going to cost the Fidelity & Trust Company anything.

"Well, this isn't my party," Glenn Murell said, "but I'm too much of a businessman to see how watching somebody kick on the end of a rope is worth four million sols."

"Four million sols," Bish said, "and wondering, the rest of your lives, whether it was justice or just murder."

The Buddhist priest looked at him, a trifle startled. After all, he was the only clergyman in the crowd; he ought to have thought of that, instead of this outrageous mock-bishop.

"I think it's a good scheme," Dad said. "Don't mass any more men around Hunters' Hall than necessary. You don't want the police to be afraid to leave when Hallstock calls them in to help him at Municipal Building."

Bish Ware rose. "I think I'll see what I can do at Hunters' Hall, in the meantime," he said. "I'm going to see if there's some way in from the First or Second Level Down. Walt, do you still have that sleep-gas gadget of yours?"

I nodded. It was, ostensibly, nothing but an oversized pocket lighter, just the sort of a thing a gadget-happy kid would carry around. It worked perfectly as a lighter, too, till you pushed in on a little gismo on the side. Then, instead of producing a flame, it squirted out a small jet of sleep gas. It would knock out a man; it would almost knock out a Zarathustra veldtbeest.

I'd bought it from a spaceman on the *Cape Canaveral*. I'd always suspected that he'd stolen it on Terra, because it was an expensive little piece of work, but was I going to ride a bicycle six hundred and fifty light-years to find out who it belonged to? One of the chemists' shops at Port Sandor made me up some fills for it, and while I had never had to use it, it was a handy thing to have in some of the places I had to follow stories into, and it wouldn't do anybody any permanent damage, the way a gun would.

"Yes; it's down in my room. I'll get it for you," I said.

"Be careful, Bish," Dad said. "That gang would kill you sooner than look at you."

"Who, me?" Bish staggered into a table and caught hold of it. "Who'd wanna hurt me? I'm just good ol' Bish Ware. *Good* ol' Bish! nobody hurt him; he'sh everybody's friend." He let go of the table and staggered into a chair, upsetting it. Then he began to sing:

> *"Come all ye hardy spacemen, and harken while I tell*
> *Of fluorine-tainted Nifflheim, the Planetary Hell."*

Involuntarily, I began clapping my hands. It was a superb piece of acting-Bish Ware sober playing Bish Ware drunk, and that's not an easy role for anybody to play. Then he picked up the chair and sat down on it.

"Who do you have around Hunters' Hall, and how do I get past them?" he asked. "I don't want a clipful from somebody on my own side."

Nip Spazoni got a pencil and a pad of paper and began drawing a plan.

"This is Second Level Down," he said. "We have a car here, with a couple of men in it. It's watching this approach here. And we have a ship's boat, over here, with three men in it, and a 7-mm machine gun. And another car-no, a jeep, here. Now, up on the First Level Down, we have two ships' boats, one here, and one here. The password is 'Exotic,' and the countersign is 'Organics.'" He grinned at Murell. "Compliment to your company."

"Good enough. I'll want a bottle of liquor. My breath needs a little touching up, and I may want to offer somebody a drink. If I could get inside that place, there's no telling what I might be able to do. If one man can get in and put a couple of guards to sleep, an army can get in after him."

Brother, I thought, if he pulls this one off, he's in. Nobody around Port Sandor will ever look down on Bish Ware again, not even Joe Kivelson. I began thinking about the detective agency idea again, and wondered if he'd want a junior partner. Ware & Boyd, Planetwide Detective Agency.

I went down to the floor below with him and got him my lighter gas-projector and a couple of spare fills for it, and found the bottle of Baldur honey-rum that Dad had been sure was around somewhere. I was kind of doubtful about that, and he noticed my hesitation in giving it to him and laughed.

"Don't worry, Walt," he said. "This is strictly for protective coloration-and odoration. I shall be quite sparing with it, I assure you."

I shook hands with him, trying not to be too solemn about it, and he went down in the elevator and I went up the stairs to the floor above. By this time, the Port Sandor Vigilance Committee had gotten itself sorted out. The rank-and-file Vigilantes were standing around yacking at one another, and a smaller group-Dad and Sigurd Ngozori and the Reverend Sugitsuma and Oscar and Joe and Corkscrew and Nip and the Mahatma-were in a huddle around Dad's editorial table, discussing strategy and tactics.

"Well, we'd better get back to the docks before it starts," Corkscrew was saying. "No hunter crew will follow anybody but their own ships' officers."

"We'll have to have somebody the uptown people will follow," Oscar said. "These people won't take orders from a woolly-pants hunter captain. How about you, Sigurd?"

The banker shook his head. "Ralph Boyd's the man for that," he said.

"Ralph's needed right here; this is G.H.Q.," Oscar said. "This is a job that's going to have to be run from one central command. We've got to make sure the demonstration against Hallstock and the operation against Hunters' Hall are synchronized."

"I have about a hundred and fifty workmen, and they all have or can get something to shoot with," another man said. I looked around, and saw that it was Casmir Oughourlian, of Rodriguez & Oughourlian Shipyards. "They'll follow me, but I'm not too well known uptown."

"Hey, Professor Hartzenbosch," Mohandas Feinberg said. "You're a respectable-looking duck; you ever have any experience leading a lynch mob?"

Everybody laughed. So, to his credit, did the professor.

"I've had a lot of experience with children," the professor said. "Children are all savages. So are lynch mobs. Things that are equal to the same thing are equal to one another. Yes, I'd say so."

"All right," Dad said. "Say I'm Chief of Staff, or something. Oscar, you and Joe and Corkscrew and the rest of you decide who's going to take over-all command of the hunters. Casmir, you'll command your workmen, and anybody else from the shipyards and engine works and repair shops and so on. Sigurd, you and the Reverend, here, and Professor Hartzenbosch gather up all the uptown people you can. Now, we'll have to decide on how much force we need to scare Mort Hallstock, and how we're going to place the main force that will attack Hunters' Hall."

"I think we ought to wait till we see what Bish Ware can do," Oscar said. "Get our gangs together, and find out where we're going to put who, but hold off the attack for a while. If he can get inside Hunters' Hall, we may not even need this demonstration at the Municipal Building."

Joe Kivelson started to say something. The rest of his fellow ship captains looked at him severely, and he shut up. Dad kept on jotting down figures of men and 50-mm guns and vehicles and auto weapons we had available.

He was still doing it when the fire alarm started.

16
Civil War Postponed

The moaner went on for thirty seconds, like a banshee mourning its nearest and dearest. It was everywhere, Main City Level and the four levels below. What we have in Port Sandor is a volunteer fire organization-or disorganization, rather-of six independent companies, each of which cherishes enmity for all the rest. It's the best we can do, though; if we depended on the city government, we'd have no fire protection at all. They do have a central alarm system, though, and the *Times* is connected with that.

Then the moaner stopped, and there were four deep whistle blasts for Fourth Ward, and four more shrill ones for Bottom Level. There was an instant's silence, and then a bedlam of shouts from the hunter-boat captains. That was where the tallow-wax that was being held out from the Co-operative was stored.

"Shut up!" Dad roared, the loudest I'd ever heard him speak. "Shut up and listen!"

"Fourth Ward, Bottom Level," a voice from the fire-alarm speaker said. "This is a tallow-wax fire. It is not the Co-op wax; it is wax stored in an otherwise disused area. It is dangerously close to stored 50-mm cannon ammunition, and it is directly under the pulpwood lumber plant, on the Third Level Down, and if the fire spreads up to that, it will endanger some of the growing vats at the carniculture plant on the Second Level Down. I repeat, this is a tallow-wax fire. Do not use water or chemical extinguishers."

About half of the Vigilantes, businessmen who belonged to one or another of the volunteer companies had bugged out for their fire stations already. The Buddhist priest and a couple of doctors were also leaving. The rest, mostly hunter-ship men, were standing around looking at one another.

Oscar Fujisawa gave a sour laugh. "That diversion idea of mine was all right," he said. "The only trouble was that Steve Ravick thought of it first."

"You think he started the fire?" Dad began, and then gave a sourer laugh than Oscar's. "Am I dumb enough to ask that?"

I had started assembling equipment as soon as the feint on the Municipal Building and the attack on Hunters' Hall had gotten into the discussion stage. I would use a jeep that had a heavy-duty audiovisual recording and transmitting outfit on it, and for situations where I'd have to leave the jeep and go on foot, I had a lighter outfit like the one Oscar had brought with him in the Pequod's boat. Then I had my radio for two-way conversation with the office. And, because this wasn't likely to be the sort of war in which the rights of noncombatants like war correspondents would be taken very seriously, I had gotten out my Sterberg 7.7-mm.

Dad saw me buckling it on, and seemed rather distressed.

"Better leave that, Walt," he said. "You don't want to get into any shooting."

Logical, I thought. If you aren't prepared for something, it just won't happen. There's an awful lot of that sort of thinking going on. As I remember my Old Terran history, it was even indulged in by governments, at one time. None of them exists now.

"You know what all crawls into the Bottom Level," I reminded him. "If you don't, ask Mr. Murell, here. One sent him to the hospital."

Dad nodded; I had a point there. The abandoned sections of Bottom Level are full of tread-snails and other assorted little nasties, and the heat of the fire would stir them all up and start them moving around. Even aside from the possibility that, having started the fire, Steve Ravick's gang would try to take steps to keep it from being put out too soon, a gun was going to be a comforting companion, down there.

"Well, stay out of any fighting. Your job's to get the news, not play hero in gun fights. I'm no hero; that's why I'm sixty years old. I never knew many heroes that got that old."

It was my turn to nod. On that, Dad had a point. I said something about getting the news, not making it, and checked the chamber and magazine of the Sterberg, and then slung my radio and picked up the audiovisual outfit.

Tom and Joe Kivelson had left already, to round up the scattered Javelin crew for fire fighting. The attack on the Municipal Building and on Hunters' Hall had been postponed, but it wasn't going to be abandoned. Oscar and Professor Hartzenbosch and Dad and a couple of others were planning some sort of an observation force of a few men for each place, until the fire had been gotten out or under control. Glenn Murell decided he'd go out with me, at least as far as the fire, so we went down to the vehicle port and got the jeep out. Main City Level Broadway was almost deserted; everybody had gone down below where the excitement was. We started down the nearest vehicle shaft and immediately got into a jam, above a lot of stuff that was going into the shaft from the First Level Down, mostly manipulators and that sort of thing. There were no police around, natch, and a lot of volunteers were trying to direct traffic and getting in each other's way. I got some views with the jeep camera, just to remind any of the public who needed reminding what our city administration wasn't doing in an emergency. A couple of pieces of apparatus, a chemical tank and a pumper marked SALAMANDER VOLUNTEER FIRE COMPANY NO. 3 came along, veered out of the jam, and continued uptown.

"If they know another way down, maybe we'd better follow them," Murell suggested.

"They're not going down. They're going to the lumber plant, in case the fire spreads upward," I said. "They wouldn't be taking that sort of equipment to a wax fire."

"Why not?"

I looked at him. "I thought you were in the wax business," I said.

"I am, but I'm no chemist. I don't know anything about how wax burns. All I know is what it's used for, roughly, and who's in the market for it."

"Well, you know about those jumbo molecules, don't you?" I asked. "They have everything but the kitchen sink in them, including enough oxygen to sustain combustion even under water or in a vacuum. Not enough oxygen to make wax explode, like powder, but enough to keep it burning. Chemical extinguishers are all smothering agents, and you just can't smother a wax fire. And water's worse than useless."

He wanted to know why.

"Burning wax is a liquid. The melting point is around 250 degrees Centigrade. Wax ignites at 750. It has no boiling point, unless that's the burning point. Throw water on a wax fire and you get a steam explosion, just as you would if you threw it on molten metal, and that throws the fire around and spreads it."

"If it melts that far below the ignition point, wouldn't it run away before it caught fire?"

"Normally, it would. That's why I'm sure this fire was a touch-off. I think somebody planted a thermoconcentrate bomb. A thermoconcentrate flame is around 850 Centigrade; the wax would start melting and burning almost instantaneously. In any case, the fire will be at the bottom of the stacks. If it started there, melted wax would run down from above and keep the fire going, and if it started at the top, burning wax would run down and ignite what's below."

"Well, how in blazes do you put a wax fire out?" he wanted to know.

"You don't. You just pull away all the wax that hasn't caught fire yet, and then try to scatter the fire and let it burn itself out.... Here's our chance!"

All this conversation we had been screaming into each other's ears, in the midst of a pandemonium of yelling, cursing, siren howling and bell clanging; just then I saw a hole in the vertical traffic jam and edged the jeep into it, at the same time remembering that the jeep carried, and I was entitled to use, a fire siren. I added its howls to the general uproar and dropped down one level. Here a string of big manipulators were trying to get in from below, sprouting claw hooks and grapples and pusher arms in all directions. I made my siren imitate a tail-tramped tomcat a couple of times, and got in among them.

Bottom Level Broadway was a frightful mess, and I realized that we had come down right between two units of the city power plant, big mass-energy converters. The street was narrower than above, and ran for a thousand yards between ceiling-high walls, and everything was bottlenecked together. I took the jeep up till we were almost scraping the ceiling, and Murell, who had seen how the audiovisual was used, took over with it while I concentrated on inching forward. The noise was even worse down here than it had been above; we didn't attempt to talk.

Finally, by impudence and plain foolhardiness, I got the jeep forward a few hundred yards, and found myself looking down on a big derrick with a fifty-foot steel boom tipped with a four-clawed grapple, shielded in front with sheet steel like a gun shield. It was painted with the emblem of the Hunters' Co-operative, but the three men on it looked like shipyard workers. I didn't get that, at all. The thing had been built to handle burning wax, and was one of three kept on the Second Level Down under Hunters' Hall. I wondered if Bish Ware had found a way for a gang to get in at the bottom of Hunters' Hall. I simply couldn't see Steve Ravick releasing equipment to fight the fire his goons had started for him in the first place.

I let down a few feet, gave a polite little scream with my siren, and then yelled down to the men on it:

"Where'd that thing come from?"

"Hunters' Hall; Steve Ravick sent it. The other two are up at the fire already, and if this mess ahead doesn't get straightened out...." From there on, his remarks were not suitable for publication in a family journal like the *Times*.

I looked up ahead, rising to the ceiling again, and saw what was the matter. It was one of the dredgers from the waterfront, really a submarine scoop shovel, that they used to keep the pools and the inner channel from sanding up. I wasn't surprised it was jammed; I couldn't see how they'd gotten this far uptown with it. I got a few shots of that, and then unhooked the handphone of my radio. Julio Kubanoff answered.

"You getting everything I'm sending in?" I asked.

"Yes. What's that two-em-dashed thing up ahead, one of the harbor dredgers?"

"That's right. Hey, look at this, once." I turned the audiovisual down on the claw derrick. "The men on it look like Rodriguez & Oughourlian's people, but they say Steve Ravick sent it. What do you know about it?"

"Hey, Ralph! What's this Walt's picked up about Ravick sending equipment to fight the fire?" he yelled.

Dad came over, and nodded. "It wasn't Ravick, it was Mort Hallstock. He commandeered the Co-op equipment and sent it up," he said. "He called me and wanted to know whom to send for it that Ravick's gang wouldn't start shooting at right away. Casmir Oughourlian sent some of his men."

Up front, something seemed to have given way. The dredger went lurching forward, and everything moved off after it.

"I get it," I said. "Hallstock's getting ready to dump Ravick out the airlock. He sees, now, that Ravick's a dead turkey; he doesn't want to go into the oven along with him."

"Walt, can't you ever give anybody credit with trying to do something decent, once in a while?" Dad asked.

"Sure I can. Decent people. There are a lot of them around, but Mort Hallstock isn't one of them. There was an Old Terran politician named Al Smith, once. He had a little saying he used in that kind of case: 'Let's look at the record.'"

"Well, Mort's record isn't very impressive, I'll give you that," Dad admitted. "I understand Mort's up at the fire now. Don't spit in his eye if you run into him."

"I won't," I promised. "I'm kind of particular where I spit."

Things must be looking pretty rough around Municipal Building, I thought. Maybe Mort's afraid the people will start running Fenris again, after this. He might even be afraid there'd be an election.

By this time, I'd gotten the jeep around the dredger-we'd come to the end of the nuclear-power plant buildings-and cut off into open country. That is to say, nothing but pillar-buildings two hundred yards apart and piles of bagged mineral nutrients for the hydroponic farms. We could see a blaze of electric lights ahead where the fire must be, and after a while we began to run into lorries and lifter-skids hauling ammunition away from the area. Then I could see a big mushroom of greasy black smoke spreading out close to the ceiling. The electric lights were brighter ahead, and there was a confused roar of voices and sirens and machines.

And there was a stink.

There are a lot of stinks around Port Sandor, though the ventilation system carries most of them off before they can spread out of their own areas. The plant that reprocesses sewage to get organic nutrients for the hydroponic farms, and the plant that digests hydroponic vegetation to make nutrients for the carniculture vats. The carniculture vats themselves aren't any flower gardens. And the pulp plant where our synthetic lumber is made. But the worst stink there is on Fenris is a tallow-wax fire. Fortunately, they don't happen often.

17
Tallow-Wax Fire

Now that we were out of the traffic jam, I could poke along and use the camera myself. The wax was stacked in piles twenty feet high, which gave thirty feet of clear space above them, but the section where they had been piled was badly cut up by walls and full of small extra columns to support the weight of the pulp plant above and the carniculture vats on the level over that. However, the piles themselves weren't separated by any walls, and the fire could spread to the whole stock of wax. There were more men and vehicles on the job than room for them to work. I passed over the heads of the crowd around the edges and got onto a comparatively unobstructed side where I could watch and get views of the fire fighters pulling down the big skins of wax and loading them onto contragravity skids to be hauled away. It still wasn't too hot to work unshielded, and they weren't anywhere near the burning stacks, but the fire seemed to be spreading rapidly. The dredger and the three shielded derricks hadn't gotten into action yet.

I circled around clockwise, dodging over, under and around the skids and lorries hauling wax out of danger. They were taking them into the section through which I had brought the jeep a few minutes before, and just dumping them on top of the piles of mineral nutrients.

The operation seemed to be directed from an improvised headquarters in the area that had been cleared of ammunition. There were a couple of view screens and a radio, operated by women. I saw one of the teachers I'd gone to school to a few years ago, and Joe Kivelson's wife, and Oscar Fujisawa's current girl friend, and Sigurd Ngozori's secretary, and farther off there was an equally improvised coffee-and-sandwich stand. I grounded the jeep, and Murell and I got out and went over to the headquarters. Joe Kivelson seemed to be in charge.

I have, I believe, indicated here and there that Joe isn't one of our mightier intellects. There are a lot of better heads, but Joe can be relied upon to keep his, no matter what is happening or how bad it gets. He was sitting on an empty box, his arm in a now-filthy sling, and one of Mohandas Feinberg's crooked black cigars in his mouth. Usually, Joe smokes a pipe, but a cigar's less bother for a temporarily one-armed man. Standing in front of him, like a schoolboy in front of the teacher, was Mayor Morton Hallstock.

"But, Joe, they simply won't!" His Honor was wailing. "I did talk to Mr. Fieschi; he says he knows this is an emergency, but there's a strict company directive against using the spaceport area for storage of anything but cargo that has either just come in or is being shipped out on the next ship."

"What's this all about?" Murell asked.

"Fieschi, at the spaceport, won't let us store this wax in the spaceport area," Joe said. "We got to get it stored somewhere; we need a lot of floor space to spread this fire out on, once we get into it. We have to knock the burning wax cylinders apart, and get them separated enough so that burning wax won't run from one to another."

"Well, why can't we store it in the spaceport area?" Murell wanted to know. "It is going out on the next ship. I'm consigning it to Exotic Organics, in Buenos Aires." He turned to Joe. "Are those skins all marked to indicate who owns them?"

"That's right. And any we gather up loose, from busted skins, we can figure some way of settling how much anybody's entitled to from them."

"All right. Get me a car and run me to the spaceport. Call them and tell them I'm on the way. I'll talk to Fieschi myself."

"Martha!" Joe yelled to his wife. "Car and driver, quick. And then call the spaceport for me; get Mr. Fieschi or Mr. Mansour on screen."

Inside two minutes, a car came in and picked Murell up. By that time, Joe was talking to somebody at the spaceport. I called the paper, and told Dad that Murell was buying the wax for his company as fast as it was being pulled off the fire, at eighty centisols a pound. He said that would go out as a special bulletin right away. Then I talked to Morton Hallstock, and this time he wasn't giving me any of the run-along-sonny routine. I told him, rather hypocritically, what a fine thing he'd done, getting that equipment from Hunters' Hall. I suspect I sounded as though I were mayor of Port Sandor and Hallstock, just seventeen years old, had done something the grownups thought was real smart for a kid. If so, he didn't seem to notice. Somebody connected with the press was being nice to him. I asked him where Steve Ravick was.

"Mr. Ravick is at Hunters' Hall," he said. "He thought it would be unwise to make a public appearance just now." Oh, brother, what an understatement! "There seems to be a lot of public feeling against him, due to some misconception that he was responsible for what happened to Captain Kivelson's ship. Of course, that is absolutely false. Mr. Ravick had absolutely nothing to do with that. He wasn't anywhere near the *Javelin*."

"Where's Al Devis?" I asked.

"Who? I don't believe I know him."

After Hallstock got into his big black air-limousine and took off, Joe Kivelson gave a short laugh.

"I could have told him where Al Devis is," he said. "No, I couldn't, either," he corrected himself. "That's a religious question, and I don't discuss religion."

I shut off my radio in a hurry. "Who got him?" I asked.

Joe named a couple of men from one of the hunter-ships.

"Here's what happened. There were six men on guard here; they had a jeep with a 7-mm machine gun. About an hour ago, a lorry pulled in, with two men in boat-clothes on it. They said that Pierre Karolyi's *Corinne* had just come in with a hold full of wax, and they were bringing it up from the docks, and where should they put it? Well, the men on guard believed that; Pierre'd gone off into the twilight zone after the *Helldiver* contacted us, and he could have gotten a monster in the meantime.

"Well, they told these fellows that there was more room over on the other side of the stacks, and the lorry went up above the stacks and started across, and when they were about the middle, one of the men in it threw out a thermoconcentrate bomb. The lorry took off, right away. The only thing was that there were two men in the jeep, and one of them was at the machine gun. They'd lifted to follow the lorry over and show them where to put this wax, and as soon as the bomb went off, the man at the gun grabbed it and caught the lorry in his sights and let go. This fellow hadn't been covering for cutting-up work for years for nothing. He got one burst right in the control cabin, and the lorry slammed into the next column foundation. After they called in an alarm on the fire the bomb had started, a couple of them went to see who'd been in the lorry. The two men in it were both dead, and one of them was Al Devis."

"Pity," I said. "I'd been looking forward to putting a recording of his confession on the air. Where is this lorry now?"

Joe pointed toward the burning wax piles. "Almost directly on the other side. We have a couple of men guarding it. The bodies are still in it. We don't want any tampering with it till it can be properly examined; we want to have the facts straight, in case Hallstock tries to make trouble for the men who did the shooting."

I didn't know how he could. Under any kind of Federation law at all, a man killed committing a felony-and bombing and arson ought to qualify for that-is simply bought and paid for; his blood is on nobody's head but his own. Of course, a small matter like legality was always the least of Mort Hallstock's worries.

"I'll go get some shots of it," I said, and then I snapped on my radio and called the story in.

Dad had already gotten it, from fire-alarm center, but he hadn't heard that Devis was one of the deceased arsonists. Like me, he was very sorry to hear about it. Devis as Devis was no loss, but alive and talking he'd have helped us pin both the wax fire and the bombing of the *Javelin* on Steve Ravick. Then I went back and got in the jeep.

They were beginning to get in closer to the middle of the stacks where the fire had been started. There was no chance of getting over the top of it, and on the right there were at least five hundred men and a hundred vehicles, all working like crazy to pull out unburned wax. Big manipulators were coming up and grabbing as many of the half-ton sausages as they could, and lurching away to dump them onto skids or into lorries or just drop them on top of the bags of nutrient stacked beyond. Jeeps and cars would dart in, throw grapnels on the end of lines, and then pull away all the wax they could and return to throw their grapnels again. As fast as they pulled the big skins down, men with hand-lifters like the ones we had used at our camp to handle firewood would pick them up and float them away.

That seemed to be where the major effort was being made, at present, and I could see lifter-skids coming in with big blower fans on them. I knew what the strategy was, now; they were going to pull the wax away to where it was burning on one side, and then set up the blowers and blow the heat and smoke away on that side. That way, on the other side more men could work closer to the fire, and in the long run they'd save more wax.

I started around the wax piles to the left, clockwise, to avoid the activity on the other side, and before long I realized that I'd have done better not to have. There was a long wall, ceiling-high, that stretched off uptown in the direction of the spaceport, part of the support for the weight of the pulpwood plant on the level above, and piled against it was a lot of junk machinery of different kinds that had been hauled in here and dumped long ago and then forgotten. The wax was piled almost against this, and the heat and smoke forced me down.

I looked at the junk pile and decided that I could get through it on foot. I had been keeping up a running narration into my radio, and I commented on all this salvageable metal lying in here forgotten, with our perennial metal shortages. Then I started picking my way through it, my portable audiovisual camera slung over my shoulder and a flashlight in my hand. My left hand, of course; it's never smart to carry a light in your right, unless you're left-handed.

The going wasn't too bad. Most of the time, I could get between things without climbing over them. I was going between a broken-down press from the lumber plant and a leaky 500-gallon pressure cooker from the carniculture nutrient plant when I heard something moving behind me, and I was suddenly very glad that I hadn't let myself be talked into leaving my pistol behind.

It was a thing the size of a ten-gallon keg, with a thick tail and flippers on which it crawled, and six tentacles like small elephants' trunks around a circular mouth filled with jagged teeth halfway down the throat. There are a dozen or so names for it, but mostly it is called a meat-grinder.

The things are always hungry and try to eat anything that moves. The mere fact that I would be as poisonous to it as any of the local flora or fauna would be to me made no difference; this meat-grinder was no biochemist. It was coming straight for me, all its tentacles writhing.

I had had my Sterberg out as soon as I'd heard the noise. I also remembered that my radio was on, and that I was supposed to comment on anything of interest that took place around me.

"Here's a meat-grinder, coming right for me," I commented in a voice not altogether steady, and slammed three shots down its tooth-studded gullet. Then I scored my target, at the same time keeping out of the way of the tentacles. He began twitching a little. I fired again. The meat-grinder jerked slightly, and that was all.

"Now I'm going out and take a look at that lorry." I was certain now that the voice was shaky.

The lorry-and Al Devis and his companion-had come to an end against one of the two-hundred-foot masonry and concrete foundations the columns rest on. It had hit about halfway up and folded almost like an accordion, sliding down to the floor. With one thing and another, there is a lot of violent death around Port Sandor. I don't like to look at the results. It's part of the job, however, and this time it wasn't a pleasant job at all.

The two men who were guarding the wreck and contents were sitting on a couple of boxes, smoking and watching the fire-fighting operation.

I took the partly empty clip out of my pistol and put in a full one on the way back, and kept my flashlight moving its circle of light ahead and on both sides of me. That was foolish, or at least unnecessary. If there'd been one meat-grinder in that junk pile, it was a safe bet there wasn't anything else. Meat-grinders aren't popular neighbors, even for tread-snails. As I approached the carcass of the grinder I had shot I found a ten-foot length of steel rod and poked it a few times. When it didn't even twitch, I felt safe in walking past it.

I got back in the jeep and returned to where Joe Kivelson was keeping track of what was going on in five screens, including one from a pickup on a lifter at the ceiling, and shouting orders that were being reshouted out of loudspeakers all over the place. The Odin Dock & Shipyard equipment had begun coming out; lorries picking up the wax that had been dumped back from the fire and wax that was being pulled off the piles, and material-handling equipment. They had a lot of small fork-lifters that were helping close to the fire.

A lot of the wax was getting so soft that it was hard to handle, and quite a few of the plastic skins had begun to split from the heat. Here and there I saw that outside piles had begun to burn at the bottom, from burning wax that had run out underneath. I had moved around to the right and was getting views of the big claw-derricks at work picking the big sausages off the tops of piles, and while I was swinging the camera back and forth, I was trying to figure just how much wax there had been to start with, and how much was being saved. Each of those plastic-covered cylinders was a thousand pounds; one of the claw-derricks was picking up two or three of them at a grab....

I was still figuring when shouts of alarm on my right drew my head around. There was an uprush of flame, and somebody began screaming, and I could see an ambulance moving toward the center of excitement and firemen in asbestos suits converging on a run. One of the piles must have collapsed and somebody must have been splashed. I gave an involuntary shudder. Burning wax was hotter than melted lead, and it stuck to anything it touched, worse than napalm. I saw a man being dragged out of further danger, his clothes on fire, and asbestos-suited firemen crowding around to tear the burning garments from him. Before I could get to where it had happened, though, they had him in the ambulance and were taking him away. I hoped they'd get him to the hospital before he died.

Then more shouting started around at the right as a couple more piles began collapsing. I was able to get all of that-the wax sausages sliding forward, the men who had been working on foot running out of danger, the flames shooting up, and the gush of liquid fire from below. All three derricks moved in at once and began grabbing wax cylinders away on either side of it.

Then I saw Guido Fieschi, the Odin Dock & Shipyard's superintendent, and caught him in my camera, moving the jeep toward him.

"Mr. Fieschi!" I called. "Give me a few seconds and say something."

He saw me and grinned.

"I just came out to see how much more could be saved," he said. "We have close to a thousand tons on the shipping floor or out of danger here and on the way in, and it looks as though you'll be able to save that much more. That'll be a million and a half sols we can be sure of, and a possible three million, at the new price. And I want to take this occasion, on behalf of my company and of Terra-Odin Spacelines, to welcome a new freight shipper."

"Well, that's wonderful news for everybody on Fenris," I said, and added mentally, "with a few exceptions." Then I asked if he'd heard who had gotten splashed.

"No. I know it happened; I passed the ambulance on the way out. I certainly hope they get to work on him in time."

Then more wax started sliding off the piles, and more fire came running out at the bottom. Joe Kivelson's voice, out of the loudspeakers all around, was yelling:

"Everybody away from the front! Get the blowers in; start in on the other side!"

18
The Treason of Bish Ware

I wanted to find out who had been splashed, but Joe Kivelson was too busy directing the new phase of the fight to hand out casualty reports to the press, and besides, there were too many things happening all at once that I had to get. I went around to the other side where the incendiaries had met their end, moving slowly as close to the face of the fire as I could get and shooting the burning wax flowing out from it. A lot of equipment, including two of the three claw-derricks and a dredger-they'd brought a second one up from the waterfront-were moving to that side. By the time I had gotten around, the blowers had been maneuvered into place and were ready to start. There was a lot of back-and-forth yelling to make sure that everybody was out from in front, and then the blowers started.

It looked like a horizontal volcanic eruption; burning wax blowing away from the fire for close to a hundred feet into the clear space beyond. The derricks and manipulators and the cars and jeeps with grapnels went in on both sides, snatching and dragging wax away. Because they had the wind from the blowers behind them, the men could work a lot closer, and the fire wasn't spreading as rapidly. They were saving a lot of wax; each one of those big sausages that the lifters picked up and floated away weighed a thousand pounds, and was worth, at the new price, eight hundred sols.

Finally, they got everything away that they could, and then the blowers were shut down and the two dredge shovels moved in, scooping up the burning sludge and carrying it away, scattering it on the concrete. I would have judged that there had been six or seven million sols' worth of wax in the piles to start with, and that a little more than half of it had been saved before they pulled the last cylinder away.

The work slacked off; finally, there was nothing but the two dredges doing anything, and then they backed away and let down, and it was all over but standing around and watching the scattered fire burn itself out. I looked at my watch. It was two hours since the first alarm had come in. I took a last swing around, got the spaceport people gathering up wax and hauling it away, and the broken lake of fire that extended downtown from where the stacks had been, and then I floated my jeep over to the sandwich-and-coffee stand and let down, getting out. Maybe, I thought, I could make some kind of deal with somebody like Interworld News on this. It would make a nice thrilling feature-program item. Just a little slice of life from Fenris, the Garden Spot of the Galaxy.

I got myself a big zhoumy-loin sandwich with hot sauce and a cup of coffee, made sure that my portable radio was on, and circulated among the fire fighters, getting comments. Everybody had been a hero, natch, and they were all very unbashful about admitting it. There was a great deal of wisecracking about Al Devis buying himself a ringside seat for the fire he'd started. Then I saw Cesário Vieira and joined him.

"Have all the fire you want, for a while?" I asked him.

"Brother, and how! We could have used a little of this over on Hermann Reuch's Land, though. Have you seen Tom around anywhere?"

"No. Have you?"

"I saw him over there, about an hour ago. I guess he stayed on this side. After they started blowing it, I was over on Al Devis's side." He whistled softly. "Was that a mess!"

There was still a crowd at the fire, but they seemed all to be townspeople. The hunters had gathered where Joe Kivelson had been directing operations. We finished our sandwiches and went over to join them. As soon as we got within earshot, I found that they were all in a very ugly mood.

"Don't fool around," one man was saying as we came up. "Don't even bother looking for a rope. Just shoot them as soon as you see them."

Well, I thought, a couple of million sols' worth of tallow-wax, in which they all owned shares, was something to get mean about. I said something like that.

"It's not that," another man said. "It's Tom Kivelson."

"What about him?" I asked, alarmed.

"Didn't you hear? He got splashed with burning wax," the hunter said. "His whole back was on fire; I don't know whether he's alive now or not."

So that was who I'd seen screaming in agony while the firemen tore his burning clothes away. I pushed through, with Cesário behind me, and found Joe Kivelson and Mohandas Feinberg and Corkscrew Finnegan and Oscar Fujisawa and a dozen other captains and ships' officers in a huddle.

"Joe," I said, "I just heard about Tom. Do you know anything yet?"

Joe turned. "Oh, Walt. Why, as far as we know, he's alive. He was alive when they got him to the hospital."

"That's at the spaceport?" I unhooked my handphone and got Dad. He'd heard about a man being splashed, but didn't know who it was. He said he'd call the hospital at once. A few minutes later, he was calling me back.

"He's been badly burned, all over the back. They're preparing to do a deep graft on him. They said his condition was serious, but he was alive five minutes ago."

I thanked him and hung up, relaying the information to the others. They all looked worried. When the screen girl at a hospital tells you somebody's serious, instead of giving you the well-as-can-be-expected routine, you know it is serious. Anybody who makes it alive to a hospital, these days, has an excellent chance, but injury cases do die, now and then, after they've been brought in. They are the "serious" cases.

"Well, I don't suppose there's anything we can do," Joe said heavily.

"We can clean up on the gang that started this fire," Oscar Fujisawa said. "Do it now; then if Tom doesn't make it, he's paid for in advance."

Oscar, I recalled, was the one who had been the most impressed with Bish Ware's argument that lynching Steve Ravick would cost the hunters the four million sols they might otherwise be able to recover, after a few years' interstellar litigation, from his bank account on Terra. That reminded me that I hadn't even thought of Bish since I'd left the *Times*. I called back. Dad hadn't heard a word from him.

"What's the situation at Hunters' Hall?" I asked.

"Everything's quiet there. The police left when Hallstock commandeered that fire-fighting equipment. They helped the shipyard men get it out, and then they all went to the Municipal Building. As far as I know, both Ravick and Belsher are still in Hunters' Hall. I'm in contact with the vehicles on guard at the approaches; I'll call them now."

I relayed that. The others nodded.

"Nip Spazoni and a few others are bringing men and guns up from the docks and putting a cordon around the place on the Main City Level," Oscar said. "Your father will probably be hearing that they're moving into position now."

He had. He also said that he had called all the vehicles on the First and Second Levels Down; they all reported no activity in Hunters' Hall except one jeep on Second Level Down, which did not report at all.

Everybody was puzzled about that.

"That's the jeep that reported Bish Ware going in on the bottom," Mohandas Feinberg said. "I wonder if somebody inside mightn't have gotten both the man on the jeep and Bish."

"He could have left the jeep," Joe said. "Maybe he went inside after Bish."

"Funny he didn't call in and say so," somebody said.

"No, it isn't," I contradicted. "Manufacturers' claims to the contrary, there is no such thing as a tap-proof radio. Maybe he wasn't supposed to leave his post, but if he did, he used his head not advertising it."

"That makes sense," Oscar agreed. "Well, whatever happened, we're not doing anything standing around up here. Let's get it started."

He walked away, raising his voice and calling, "*Pequod*! *Pequod*! All hands on deck!"

The others broke away from the group, shouting the names of their ships to rally their crews. I hurried over to the jeep and checked my equipment. There wasn't too much film left in the big audiovisual, so I replaced it with a fresh sound-and-vision reel, good for another couple of hours, and then lifted to the ceiling. Worrying about Tom wouldn't help Tom, and worrying about Bish wouldn't help Bish, and I had a job to do.

What I was getting now, and I was glad I was starting a fresh reel for it, was the beginning of the First Fenris Civil War. A long time from now, when Fenris was an important planet in the Federation, maybe they'd make today a holiday, like Bastille Day or the Fourth of July or Federation Day. Maybe historians, a couple of centuries from now, would call me an important primary source, and if Cesário's religion was right, maybe I'd be one of them, saying, "Well, after all, is Boyd such a reliable source? He was only seventeen years old at the time."

Finally, after a lot of yelling and confusion, the Rebel Army got moving. We all went up to Main City Level and went down Broadway, spreading out side streets when we began running into the cordon that had been thrown around Hunters' Hall. They were mostly men from the waterfront who hadn't gotten to the wax fire, and they must have stripped the guns off half the ships in the harbor and mounted them on lorries or cargo skids.

Nobody, not even Joe Kivelson, wanted to begin with any massed frontal attack on Hunters' Hall.

"We'll have to bombard the place," he was saying. "We try to rush it and we'll lose half our gang before we get in. One man with good cover and a machine gun's good for a couple of hundred in the open."

"Bish may be inside," I mentioned.

"Yes," Oscar said, "and even aside from that, that building was built with our money. Let's don't burn the house down to get rid of the cockroaches."

"Well, how are you going to do it, then?" Joe wanted to know. Rule out frontal attack and Joe's at the end of his tactics.

"You stay up here. Keep them amused with a little smallarms fire at the windows and so on. I'll take about a dozen men and go down to Second Level. If we can't do anything else, we can bring a couple of skins of tallow-wax down and set fire to it and smoke them out."

That sounded like a pretty expensive sort of smudge, but seeing how much wax Ravick had burned uptown, it was only fair to let him in on some of the smoke. I mentioned that if we got into the building and up to Main City Level, we'd need some way of signaling to avoid being shot by our own gang, and got the wave-length combination of the Pequod scout boat, which Joe and Oscar were using for a command car. Oscar picked ten or twelve men, and they got into a lorry and went uptown and down a vehicle shaft to Second Level. I followed in my jeep, even after Oscar and his crowd let down and got out, and hovered behind them as they advanced on foot to Hunters' Hall.

The Second Level Down was the vehicle storage, where the derricks and other equipment had been kept. It was empty now except for a workbench, a hand forge and some other things like that, a few drums of lubricant, and several piles of sheet metal. Oscar and his men got inside and I followed, going up to the ceiling. I was the one who saw the man lying back of a pile of sheet metal, and called their attention.

He wore boat-clothes and had black whiskers, and he had a knife and a pistol on his belt. At first I thought he was dead. A couple of Oscar's followers, dragging him out, said:

"He's been sleep-gassed."

Somebody else recognized him. He was the lone man who had been on guard in the jeep. The jeep was nowhere in sight.

I began to be really worried. My lighter gadget could have been what had gassed him. It probably was; there weren't many sleep-gas weapons on Fenris. I had to get fills made up specially for mine. So it looked to me as though somebody had gotten mine off Bish, and then used it to knock out our guard. Taken it off his body I guessed. That crowd wasn't any more interested in taking prisoners alive than we were.

We laid the man on a workbench and put a rolled-up sack under his head for a pillow. Then we started up the enclosed stairway. I didn't think we were going to run into any trouble, though I kept my hand close to my gun. If they'd knocked out the guard, they had a way out, and none of them wanted to stay in that building any longer than they had to.

The First Level Down was mostly storerooms, with nobody in any of them. As we went up the stairway to the Main City Level, we could hear firing outside. Nobody inside was shooting back. I unhooked my handphone.

"We're in," I said when Joe Kivelson answered. "Stop the shooting; we're coming up to the vehicle port."

"Might as well. Nobody's paying any attention to it," he said.

The firing slacked off as the word was passed around the perimeter, and finally it stopped entirely. We went up into the open arched vehicle port. It was barricaded all around, and there were half a dozen machine guns set up, but not a living thing.

"We're going up," I said. "They've all lammed out. The place is empty."

"You don't know that," Oscar chided. "It might be bulging with Ravick's thugs, waiting for us to come walking up and be mowed down."

Possible. Highly improbable, though, I thought. The escalators weren't running, and we weren't going to alert any hypothetical ambush by starting them. We tiptoed up, and I even drew my pistol to show that I wasn't being foolhardy. The big social room was empty. A couple of us went over and looked behind the bar, which was the only hiding place in it. Then we went back to the rear and tiptoed to the third floor.

The meeting room was empty. So were the offices behind it. I looked in all of them, expecting to find Bish Ware's body. Maybe a couple of other bodies, too. I'd seen him shoot the tread-snail, and I didn't think he'd die unpaid for. In Steve Ravick's office, the safe was open and a lot of papers had been thrown out. I pointed that out to Oscar, and he nodded. After seeing that, he seemed to relax, as though he wasn't expecting to find anybody any more. We went to the third floor. Ravick's living quarters were there, and they were magnificently luxurious. The hunters, whose money had paid for all that magnificence and luxury, cursed.

There were no bodies there, either, or on the landing stage above. I unhooked the radio again.

"You can come in, now," I said. "The place is empty. Nobody here but us Vigilantes."

"Huh?" Joe couldn't believe that. "How'd they get out?"

"They got out on the Second Level Down." I told him about the sleep-gassed guard.

"Did you bring him to? What did he say?"

"Nothing; we didn't. We can't. You get sleep-gassed, you sleep till you wake up. That ought to be two to four hours for this fellow."

"Well, hold everything; we're coming in."

We were all in the social room; a couple of the men had poured drinks or drawn themselves beers at the bar and rung up no sale on the cash register. Somebody else had a box of cigars he'd picked up in Ravick's quarters on the fourth floor and was passing them around. Joe and about two or three hundred other hunters came crowding up the escalator, which they had turned on below.

"You didn't find Bish Ware, either, I'll bet," Joe was saying.

"I'm afraid they took him along for a hostage," Oscar said. "The guard was knocked out with Walt's gas gadget, that Bish was carrying."

"Ha!" Joe cried. "Bet you it was the other way round; Bish took them out."

That started an argument. While it was going on, I went to the communication screen and got the *Times*, and told Dad what had happened.

"Yes," he said. "That was what I was afraid you'd find. Glenn Murell called in from the spaceport a few minutes ago. He says Mort Hallstock came in with his car, and he heard from some of the workmen that Bish Ware, Steve Ravick and Leo Belsher came in on the Main City Level in a jeep. They claimed protection from a mob, and Captain Courtland's police are protecting them."

19
Masks Off

There was dead silence for two or three seconds. If a kitten had sneezed, everybody would have heard it. Then it started, first an inarticulate roar, and then a babel of unprintabilities. I thought I'd heard some bad language from these same men in this room when Leo Belsher's announcement of the price cut had been telecast, but that was prayer meeting to this. Dad was still talking. At least, I saw his lips move in the screen.

"Say that again, Ralph," Oscar Fujisawa shouted.

Dad must have heard him. At least, his lips moved again, but I wasn't a lip reader and neither was Oscar. Oscar turned to the mob-by now, it was that, pure and simple-and roared, in a voice like a foghorn, *"Shut up and listen!"* A few of those closest to him heard him. The rest kept on shouting curses. Oscar waited a second, and then pointed his submachine gun at the ceiling and hammered off the whole clip.

"Shut up, a couple of hundred of you, and listen!" he commanded, on the heels of the blast. Then he turned to the screen again. "Now, Ralph; what was it you were saying?"

"Hallstock got to the spaceport about half an hour ago," Dad said. "He bought a ticket to Terra. Sigurd Ngozori's here; he called the bank and one of the clerks there told him that Hallstock had checked out his whole account, around three hundred thousand sols. Took some of it in cash and the rest in Banking Cartel drafts. Murell says that his information is that Bish Ware, Steve Ravick and Leo Belsher arrived earlier, about an hour ago. He didn't see them himself, but he talked with spaceport workmen who did."

The men who had crowded up to the screen seemed to have run out of oaths and obscenities now. Oscar was fitting another clip into his submachine gun.

"Well, we'll have to go to the spaceport and get them," he said. "And take four ropes instead of three."

"You'll have to fight your way in," Dad told him. "Odin Dock & Shipyard won't let you take people out of their spaceport without a fight. They've all bought tickets by now, and Fieschi will have to protect them."

"Then we'll kick the blankety-blank spaceport apart," somebody shouted.

That started it up again. Oscar wondered if getting silence was worth another clip of cartridges, and decided it wasn't. He managed to make himself heard without it.

"We'll do nothing of the kind. We need that spaceport to stay alive. But we will take Ravick and Belsher and Hallstock —"

"And that etaoin shrdlu traitor of a Ware!" Joe Kivelson added.

"And Bish Ware," Oscar agreed. "They only have fifty police; we have three or four thousand men."

Three or four thousand undisciplined hunters, against fifty trained, disciplined and organized soldiers, because that was what the spaceport police were. I knew their captain, and the lieutenants. They were old Regular Army, and they ran the police force like a military unit.

"I'll bet Ware was working for Ravick all along," Joe was saying.

That wasn't good thinking even for Joe Kivelson. I said:

"If he was working for Ravick all along, why did he tip Dad and Oscar and the Mahatma on the bomb aboard the *Javelin*? That wasn't any help to Ravick."

"I get it," Oscar said. "He never was working for anybody but Bish Ware. When Ravick got into a jam, he saw a way to make something for himself by getting Ravick out of it. I'll bet, ever since he came here, he was planning to cut in on Ravick somehow. You notice, he knew just how much money Ravick had stashed away on Terra? When he saw the spot Ravick was in, Bish just thought he had a chance to develop himself another rich uncle."

I'd been worse stunned than anybody by Dad's news. The worst of it was that Oscar could be right. I hadn't thought of that before. I'd just thought that Ravick and Belsher had gotten Bish drunk and found out about the way the men were posted around Hunters' Hall and the lone man in the jeep on Second Level Down.

Then it occurred to me that Bish might have seen a way of getting Fenris rid of Ravick and at the same time save everybody the guilt of lynching him. Maybe he'd turned traitor to save the rest of us from ourselves.

I turned to Oscar. "Why get excited about it?" I asked. "You have what you wanted. You said yourself that you couldn't care less whether Ravick got away or not, as long as you got him out of the Co-op. Well, he's out for good now."

"That was before the fire," Oscar said. "We didn't have a couple of million sols' worth of wax burned. And Tom Kivelson wasn't in the hospital with half the skin burned off his back, and a coin toss whether he lives or not."

"Yes. I thought you were Tom's friend," Joe Kivelson reproached me.

I wondered how much skin hanging Steve Ravick would grow on Tom's back. I didn't see much percentage in asking him, though. I did turn to Oscar Fujisawa with a quotation I remembered from *Moby Dick*, the book he'd named his ship from.

"How many barrels will thy vengeance yield thee, even if thou gettest it, Captain Ahab?" I asked. *"It will not fetch thee much in our Nantucket market."*

He looked at me angrily and started to say something. Then he shrugged.

"I know, Walt," he said. "But you can't measure everything in barrels of whale oil. Or skins of tallow-wax."

Which was one of those perfectly true statements which are also perfectly meaningless. I gave up. My job's to get the news, not to make it. I wondered if that meant anything, either.

They finally got the mob sorted out, after a lot of time wasted in pillaging Ravick's living quarters on the fourth floor. *However, the troops stopped to loot the enemy's camp.* I'd come across that line fifty to a hundred times in history books. Usually, it had been expensive looting; if the enemy didn't counterattack, they managed, at least, to escape. More to the point, they gathered up all the cannon and machine guns around the place and got them onto contragravity in the street. There must have been close to five thousand men, by now, and those who couldn't crowd onto vehicles marched on foot, and the whole mass, looking a little more like an army than a mob, started up Broadway.

Since it is not proper for reporters to loot on the job, I had gotten outside in my jeep early and was going ahead, swinging my camera back to get the parade behind me. Might furnish a still-shot illustration for somebody's History of Fenris in a century or so.

Broadway was empty until we came to the gateway to the spaceport area. There was a single medium combat car there, on contragravity halfway to the ceiling, with a pair of 50-mm guns and a rocket launcher pointed at us, and under it, on the roadway, a solitary man in an olive-green uniform stood.

I knew him; Lieutenant Ranjit Singh, Captain Courtland's second-in-command. He was a Sikh. Instead of a steel helmet, he wore a striped turban, and he had a black beard that made Joe Kivelson's blond one look like Tom Kivelson's chin-fuzz. On his belt, along with his pistol, he wore the little kirpan, the dagger all Sikhs carry. He also carried a belt radio, and as we approached he lifted the phone to his mouth and a loudspeaker on the combat car threw his voice at us:

"All right, that's far enough, now. The first vehicle that comes within a hundred yards of this gate will be shot down."

One man, and one combat car, against five thousand, with twenty-odd guns and close to a hundred machine guns. He'd last about as long as a pint of trade gin at a Sheshan funeral. The only thing was, before he and the crew of the combat car were killed, they'd wipe out about ten or fifteen of our vehicles and a couple of hundred men, and they would be the men and vehicles in the lead.

Mobs are a little different from soldiers, and our Rebel Army was still a mob. Mobs don't like to advance into certain death, and they don't like to advance over the bodies and wreckage of their own forward elements. Neither do soldiers, but soldiers will do it. Soldiers realize, when they put on the uniform, that some day they may face death in battle, and if this is it, this is it.

I got the combat car and the lone soldier in the turban-that would look good in anybody's history book-and moved forward, taking care that he saw the *Times* lettering on the jeep and taking care to stay well short of the deadline. I let down to the street and got out, taking off my gun belt and hanging it on the control handle of the jeep. Then I walked forward.

"Lieutenant Ranjit," I said, "I'm representing the *Times*. I have business inside the spaceport. I want to get the facts about this. It may be that when I get this story, these people will be satisfied."

"We will, like Nifflheim!" I heard Joe Kivelson bawling, above and behind me. "We want the men who started the fire my son got burned in."

"Is that the Kivelson boy's father?" the Sikh asked me, and when I nodded, he lifted the phone to his lips again. "Captain Kivelson," the loudspeaker said, "your son is alive and under skin-grafting treatment here at the spaceport hospital. His life is not, repeat not, in danger. The men you are after are here, under guard. If any of them are guilty of any crimes, and if you can show any better authority than an armed mob to deal with them, they may, may, I said, be turned over for trial. But they will not be taken from this spaceport by force, as long as I or one of my men remains alive."

"That's easy. We'll get them afterward," Joe Kivelson shouted.

"Somebody may. You won't," Ranjit Singh told him. "Van Steen, hit that ship's boat first, and hit it at the first hostile move anybody in this mob makes."

"Yes, sir. With pleasure," another voice replied.

Nobody in the Rebel Army, if that was what it still was, had any comment to make on that. Lieutenant Ranjit turned to me.

"Mr. Boyd," he said. None of this sonny-boy stuff; Ranjit Singh was a man of dignity, and he respected the dignity of others. "If I admit you to the spaceport, will you give these people the facts exactly as you learn them?"

"That's what the *Times* always does, Lieutenant." Well, almost all the facts almost always.

"Will you people accept what this *Times* reporter tells you he has learned?"

"Yes, of course." That was Oscar Fujisawa.

"I won't!" That was Joe Kivelson. "He's always taking the part of that old rumpot of a Bish Ware."

"Lieutenant, that remark was a slur on my paper, as well as myself," I said. "Will you permit Captain Kivelson to come in along with me? And somebody else," I couldn't resist adding, "so that people will believe him?"

Ranjit Singh considered that briefly. He wasn't afraid to die—I believe he was honestly puzzled when he heard people talking about fear-but his job was to protect some fugitives from a mob, not to die a useless hero's death. If letting in a small delegation would prevent an attack on the spaceport without loss of life and ammunition-or maybe he reversed the order of importance-he was obliged to try it.

"Yes. You may choose five men to accompany Mr. Boyd," he said. "They may not bring weapons in with them. Sidearms," he added, "will not count as weapons."

After all, a kirpan was a sidearm, and his religion required him to carry that. The decision didn't make me particularly happy. Respect for the dignity of others is a fine thing in an officer, but like journalistic respect for facts, it can be carried past the point of being a virtue. I thought he was over-estimating Joe Kivelson's self-control.

Vehicles in front began grounding, and men got out and bunched together on the street. Finally, they picked their delegation: Joe Kivelson, Oscar Fujisawa, Casmir Oughourlian the shipyard man, one of the engineers at the nutrient plant, and the Reverend Hiram Zilker, the Orthodox-Monophysite preacher. They all had pistols, even the Reverend Zilker, so I went back to the jeep and put mine on. Ranjit Singh had switched his radio off the speaker and was talking to somebody else. After a while, an olive-green limousine piloted by a policeman in uniform and helmet floated in and grounded. The six of us got into it, and it lifted again.

The car let down in a vehicle hall in the administrative area, and the police second lieutenant, Chris Xantos, was waiting alone, armed only with the pistol that was part of his uniform and wearing a beret instead of a helmet. He spoke to us, and ushered us down a hallway toward Guido Fieschi's office.

I get into the spaceport administrative area about once in twenty or so hours. Oughourlian is a somewhat less frequent visitor. The others had never been there, and they were visibly awed by all the gleaming glass and brightwork, and the soft lights and the thick carpets. All Port Sandor ought to look like this, I thought. It could, and maybe now it might, after a while.

There were six chairs in a semicircle facing Guido Fieschi's desk, and three men sitting behind it. Fieschi, who had changed clothes and washed since the last time I saw him, sat on the extreme right. Captain Courtland, with his tight mouth under a gray mustache and the quadruple row of medal ribbons on his breast, was on the left. In the middle, the seat of honor, was Bish Ware, looking as though he were presiding over a church council to try some rural curate for heresy.

As soon as Joe Kivelson saw him, he roared angrily:

"There's the dirty traitor who sold us out! He's the worst of the lot; I wouldn't be surprised if—"

Bish looked at him like a bishop who has just been contradicted on a point of doctrine by a choirboy.

"Be quiet!" he ordered. "I did not follow this man you call Ravick here to this … this running-hot-and-cold Paradise planet, and I did not spend five years fraternizing with its unwashed citizenry and creating for myself the role of town drunkard of Port Sandor, to have him taken from me and lynched after I have arrested him. People do not lynch my prisoners."

"And who in blazes are you?" Joe demanded.

Bish took cognizance of the question, if not the questioner.

"Tell them, if you please, Mr. Fieschi," he said.

"Well, Mr. Ware is a Terran Federation Executive Special Agent," Fieschi said. "Captain Courtland and I have known that for the past five years. As far as I know, nobody else was informed of Mr. Ware's position."

After that, you could have heard a gnat sneeze.

Everybody knows about Executive Special Agents. There are all kinds of secret agents operating in the Federation-Army and Navy Intelligence, police of different sorts, Colonial Office agents, private detectives, Chartered Company agents. But there are fewer Executive Specials than there are inhabited planets in the Federation. They rank, ex officio, as Army generals and Space Navy admirals; they have the privilege of the floor in Parliament, they take orders from nobody but the President of the Federation. But very few people have ever seen one, or talked to anybody who has.

And Bish Ware —*good ol' Bish; he'sh everybodysh frien'* —was one of them. And I had been trying to make a man of him and reform him. I'd even thought, if he stopped drinking, he might make a success as a private detective-at Port Sandor, on Fenris! I wondered what color my face had gotten now, and I started looking around for a crack in the floor, to trickle gently and unobtrusively into.

And it should have been obvious to me, maybe not that he was an Executive Special, but that he was certainly no drunken barfly. The way he'd gone four hours without a drink, and seemed to be just as drunk as ever. That was right-just as drunk as he'd ever been; which was to say, cold sober. There was the time I'd seen him catch that falling bottle and set it up. No drunken man could have done that; a man's reflexes are the first thing to be affected by alcohol. And the way he shot that tread-snail. I've seen men who could shoot well on liquor, but not quick-draw stuff. That calls for perfect co-ordination. And the way he went into his tipsy act at the *Times* —veteran actor slipping into a well-learned role.

He drank, sure. He did a lot of drinking. But there are men whose systems resist the effects of alcohol better than others, and he must have been an exceptional example of the type, or he'd never have adopted the sort of cover personality he did. It would have been fairly easy for him. Space his drinks widely, and never take a drink unless he *had* to, to maintain the act. When he was at the Times with just Dad and me, what did he have? A fruit fizz.

Well, at least I could see it after I had my nose rubbed in it. Joe Kivelson was simply gaping at him. The Reverend Zilker seemed to be having trouble adjusting, too. The shipyard man and the chemical engineer weren't saying anything, but it had kicked them for a loss, too. Oscar Fujisawa was making a noble effort to be completely unsurprised. Oscar is one of our better poker players.

"I thought it might be something like that," he lied brazenly. "But, Bish … Excuse me, I mean, Mr. Ware…"

"Bish, if you please, Oscar."

"Bish, what I'd like to know is what you wanted with Ravick," he said. "They didn't send any Executive Special Agent here for five years to investigate this tallow-wax racket of his."

"No. We have been looking for him for a long time. Fifteen years, and I've been working on it that long. You might say, I have made a career of him. Steve Ravick is really Anton Gerrit."

Maybe he was expecting us to leap from our chairs and cry out, "Aha! The infamous Anton Gerrit! Brought to book at last!" We didn't. We just looked at one another, trying to connect some meaning to the name. It was Joe Kivelson, of all people, who caught the first gleam.

"I know that name," he said. "Something on Loki, wasn't it?"

Yes; that was it. Now that my nose was rubbed in it again, I got it.

"The Loki enslavements. Was that it?" I asked. "I read about it, but I never seem to have heard of Gerrit."

"He was the mastermind. The ones who were caught, fifteen years ago, were the underlings, but Ravick was the real Number One. He was responsible for the enslavement of from twenty to thirty thousand Lokian natives, gentle, harmless, friendly people, most of whom were worked to death in the mines."

No wonder an Executive Special would put in fifteen years looking for him. You murder your grandmother, or rob a bank, or burn down an orphanage with the orphans all in bed upstairs, or something trivial like that, and if you make an off-planet getaway, you're reasonably safe. Of course there's such a thing as extradition, but who bothers? Distances are too great, and communication is too slow, and the Federation depends on every planet to do its own policing.

But enslavement's something different. The Terran Federation is a government of and for-if occasionally not by-all sapient peoples of all races. The Federation Constitution guarantees equal rights to all. Making slaves of people, human or otherwise, is a direct blow at everything the Federation stands for. No wonder they kept hunting fifteen years for the man responsible for the Loki enslavements.

"Gerrit got away, with a month's start. By the time we had traced him to Baldur, he had a year's start on us. He was five years ahead of us when we found out that he'd gone from Baldur to Odin. Six years ago, nine years after we'd started hunting for him, we decided, from the best information we could get, that he had left Odin on one of the local-stop ships for Terra, and dropped off along the way. There are six planets at which those Terra-Odin ships stop. We sent a man to each of them. I drew this prize out of the hat.

"When I landed here, I contacted Mr. Fieschi, and we found that a man answering to Gerrit's description had come in on the *Peenemünde* from Odin seven years before, about the time Gerrit had left Odin. The man who called himself Steve Ravick. Of course, he didn't look anything like the pictures of Gerrit, but facial surgery was something we'd taken for granted he'd have done. I finally managed to get his fingerprints."

Special Agent Ware took out a cigar, inspected it with the drunken oversolemnity he'd been drilling himself into for five years, and lit it. Then he saw what he was using and rose, holding it out, and I went to the desk and took back my lighter-weapon.

"Thank you, Walt. I wouldn't have been able to do this if I hadn't had that. Where was I? Oh, yes. I got Gerrit-alias-Ravick's fingerprints, which did not match the ones we had on file for Gerrit, and sent them in. It was eighteen months later that I got a reply on them. According to his fingerprints, Steve Ravick was really a woman named Ernestine Coyón, who had died of acute alcoholism in the free public ward of a hospital at Paris-on-Baldur fourteen years ago."

"Why, that's incredible!" the Reverend Zilker burst out, and Joe Kivelson was saying: "Steve Ravick isn't any woman...."

"Least of all one who died fourteen years ago," Bish agreed. "But the fingerprints were hers. A pauper, dying in a public ward of a big hospital. And a man who has to change his identity, and who has small, woman-sized hands. And a crooked hospital staff surgeon. You get the picture now?"

"They're doing the same thing on Tom's back, right here," I told Joe. "Only you can't grow fingerprints by carniculture, the way you can human tissue for grafting. They had to have palm and finger surfaces from a pair of real human hands. A pauper, dying in a free-treatment ward, her body shoved into a mass-energy converter." Then I thought of something else. "That showoff trick of his, crushing out cigarettes in his palm," I said.

Bish nodded commendingly. "Exactly. He'd have about as much sensation in his palms as I'd have wearing thick leather gloves. I'd noticed that.

"Well, six months going, and a couple of months waiting on reports from other planets, and six months coming, and so on, it wasn't until the *Peenemünde* got in from Terra, the last time, that I got final confirmation. Dr. Watson, you'll recall."

"Who, you perceived, had been in Afghanistan," I mentioned, trying to salvage something. Showing off. The one I was trying to impress was Walt Boyd.

"You caught that? Careless of me," Bish chided himself. "What he gave me was a report that they had finally located a man who had been a staff surgeon at this hospital on Baldur at the time. He's now doing a stretch for another piece of malpractice he was unlucky enough to get caught at later. We will not admit making deals with any criminals, in jail or out, but he is willing to testify, and is on his way to Terra now. He can identify pictures of Anton Gerrit as those of the man he operated on fourteen years ago, and his testimony and Ernestine Coyón's fingerprints will identify Ravick as that man. With all the Colonial Constabulary and Army Intelligence people got on Gerrit on Loki, simple identification will be enough. Gerrit was proven guilty long ago, and it won't be any trouble, now, to prove that Ravick is Gerrit."

"Why didn't you arrest him as soon as you got the word from your friend from Afghanistan?" I wanted to know.

"Good question; I've been asking myself that," Bish said, a trifle wryly. "If I had, the *Javelin* wouldn't have been bombed, that wax wouldn't have been burned, and Tom Kivelson wouldn't have been injured. What I did was send my friend, who is a Colonial Constabulary detective, to Gimli, the next planet out. There's a Navy base there, and always at least a couple of destroyers available. He's coming back with one of them to pick Gerrit up and take him to Terra. They ought to be in in about two hundred and fifty hours. I thought it would be safer all around to let Gerrit run loose till then. There's no place he could go.

"What I didn't realize, at the time, was what a human H-bomb this man Murell would turn into. Then everything blew up at once. Finally, I was left with the choice of helping Gerrit escape from Hunters' Hall or having him lynched before I could arrest him." He turned to Kivelson. "In the light of what you knew, I don't blame you for calling me a dirty traitor."

"But how did I know..." Kivelson began.

"That's right. You weren't supposed to. That was before you found out. You ought to have heard what Gerrit and Belsher-as far as I know, that is his real name-called me after they found out, when they got out of that jeep and Captain Courtland's men snapped the handcuffs on them. It even shocked a hardened sinner like me."

There was a lot more of it. Bish had managed to get into Hunters' Hall just about the time Al Devis and his companion were starting the fire Ravick-Gerrit-had ordered for a diversion. The whole gang was going to crash out as soon as the fire had attracted everybody away. Bish led them out onto the Second Level Down, sleep-gassed the lone man in the jeep, and took them to the spaceport, where the police were waiting for them.

As soon as I'd gotten everything, I called the *Times*. I'd had my radio on all the time, and it had been coming in perfectly. Dad, I was happy to observe, was every bit as flabbergasted as I had been at who and what Bish Ware was. He might throw my campaign to reform Bish up at me later on, but at the moment he wasn't disposed to, and I was praising Allah silently that I hadn't had a chance to mention the detective agency idea to him. That would have been a little too much.

"What are they doing about Belsher and Hallstock?" he asked.

"Belsher goes back to Terra with Ravick. Gerrit, I mean. That's where he collected his cut on the tallow-wax, so that is where he'd have to be tried. Bish is convinced that somebody in Kapstaad Chemical must have been involved, too. Hallstock is strictly a local matter."

"That's about what I thought. With all this interstellar back-and-forth, it'll be a long time before we'll be able to write thirty under the story."

"Well, we can put thirty under the Steve Ravick story," I said.

Then it hit me. The Steve Ravick story was finished; that is, the local story of racketeer rule in the Hunters' Co-operative. But the Anton Gerrit story was something else. That was Federation-wide news; the end of a fifteen-year manhunt for the most wanted criminal in the known Galaxy. And who had that story, right in his hot little hand? Walter Boyd, the ace-and only-reporter for the mighty Port Sandor *Times*.

"Yes," I continued. "The Ravick story's finished. But we still have the Anton Gerrit story, and I'm going to work on it right now."

20
Finale

They had Tom Kivelson in a private room at the hospital; he was sitting up in a chair, with a lot of pneumatic cushions around him, and a lunch tray on his lap. He looked white and thin. He could move one arm completely, but the bandages they had loaded him with seemed to have left the other free only at the elbow. He was concentrating on his lunch, and must have thought I was one of the nurses, or a doctor, or something of the sort.

"Are you going to let me have a cigarette and a cup of coffee, when I'm through with this?" he asked.

"Well, I don't have any coffee, but you can have one of my cigarettes," I said.

Then he looked up and gave a whoop. "Walt! How'd you get in here? I thought they weren't going to let anybody in to see me till this afternoon."

"Power of the press," I told him. "Bluff, blarney, and blackmail. How are they treating you?"

"Awful. Look what they gave me for lunch. I thought we were on short rations down on Hermann Reuch's Land. How's Father?"

"He's all right. They took the splint off, but he still has to carry his arm in a sling."

"Lucky guy; he can get around on his feet, and I'll bet he isn't starving, either. You know, speaking about food, I'm going to feel like a cannibal eating carniculture meat, now. My whole back's carniculture." He filled his mouth with whatever it was they were feeding him and asked, through it: "Did I miss Steve Ravick's hanging?"

I was horrified. "Haven't these people told you anything?" I demanded.

"Nah; they wouldn't even tell me the right time. Afraid it would excite me."

So I told him; first who Bish Ware really was, and then who Ravick really was. He gaped for a moment, and then shoveled in more food.

"Go on; what happened?"

I told him how Bish had smuggled Gerrit and Leo Belsher out on Second Level Down and gotten them to the spaceport, where Courtland's men had been waiting for them.

"Gerrit's going to Terra, and from there to Loki. They want the natives to see what happens to a Terran who breaks Terran law; teach them that our law isn't just to protect us. Belsher's going to Terra, too. There was a big ship captains' meeting; they voted to reclaim their wax and sell it individually to Murell, but to retain membership in the Co-op. They think they'll have to stay in the Co-op to get anything that's gettable out of Gerrit's and Belsher's money. Oscar Fujisawa and Cesário Vieira are going to Terra on the *Cape Canaveral* to start suit to recover anything they can, and also to petition for reclassification of Fenris. Oscar's coming back on the next ship, but Cesário's going to stay on as the Co-op representative. I suppose he and Linda will be getting married."

"Natch. They'll both stay on Terra, I suppose. Hey, whattaya know! Cesário's getting off Fenris without having to die and reincarnate."

He finished his lunch, such as it was and what there was of it, and I relieved him of the tray and set it on the floor beyond his chair. I found an ashtray and lit a cigarette for him and one for myself, using the big lighter. Tom looked at it dubiously, predicting that sometime I'd push the wrong thing and send myself bye-byes for a couple of hours. I told him how Bish had used it.

"Bet a lot of people wanted to hang him, too, before they found out who he was and what he'd really done. What's my father think of Bish, now?"

"Bish Ware is a great and good man, and the savior of Fenris," I said. "And he was real smart, to keep an act like that up for five years. Your father modestly admits that it even fooled him."

"Bet Oscar Fujisawa knew it all along."

"Well, Oscar modestly admits that he suspected something of the sort, but he didn't feel it was his place to say anything."

Tom laughed, and then wanted to know if they were going to hang Mort Hallstock. "I hope they wait till I can get out of here."

"No, Odin Dock & Shipyard claim he's a political refugee and they won't give him up. They did loan us a couple of accountants to go over the city books, to see if we could find any real evidence of misappropriation, and whattaya know, there were no city books. The city of Port Sandor didn't keep books. We can't even take that three hundred thousand sols away from him; for all we can prove, he saved them out of his five-thousand-sol-a-year salary. He's shipping out on the *Cape Canaveral*, too."

"Then we don't have any government at all!"

"Are you fooling yourself we ever had one?"

"No, but —"

"Well, we have one now. A temporary dictatorship; Bish Ware is dictator. Fieschi loaned him Ranjit Singh and some of his men. The first thing he did was gather up the city treasurer and the chief of police and march them to the spaceport; Fieschi made Hallstock buy them tickets, too. But there aren't going to be any unofficial hangings. This is a law-abiding planet, now."

A nurse came in, and disapproved of Tom smoking and of me being in the room at all.

"Haven't you had your lunch yet?" she asked Tom.

He looked at her guilelessly and said, "No; I was waiting for it."

"Well, I'll get it," she said. "I thought the other nurse had brought it." She started out, and then she came back and had to fuss with his cushions, and then she saw the tray on the floor.

"You did so have your lunch!" she accused.

Tom looked at her as innocently as ever. "Oh, you mean these samples? Why, they were good; I'll take all of them. And a big slab of roast beef, and brown gravy, and mashed potatoes. And how about some ice cream?"

It was a good try; too bad it didn't work.

"Don't worry, Tom," I told him. "I'll get my lawyer to spring you out of this jug, and then we'll take you to my place and fill you up on Mrs. Laden's cooking."

The nurse sniffed. She suspected, quite correctly, that whoever Mrs. Laden was, she didn't know anything about scientific dietetics.

When I got back to the *Times*, Dad and Julio had had their lunch and were going over the teleprint edition. Julio was printing corrections on blank sheets of plastic and Dad was cutting them out and cementing them over things that needed correcting on the master sheets. I gave Julio a short item to the effect that Tom Kivelson, son of Captain and Mrs. Joe Kivelson, one of the *Javelin* survivors who had been burned in the tallow-wax fire, was now out of all danger, and recovering. Dad was able to scrounge that onto the first page.

There was a lot of other news. The T.F.N. destroyer *Simón Bolivar*, en route from Gimli to pick up the notorious Anton Gerrit, alias Steve Ravick, had come out of hyperspace and into radio range. Dad had talked to the skipper by screen and gotten interviews, which would be telecast, both with him and Detective-Major MacBride of the Colonial Constabulary. The

Simón Bolivar would not make landing, but go into orbit and send down a boat. Detective-Major MacBride (alias Dr. John Watson) would remain on Fenris to take over local police activities.

More evidence had been unearthed at Hunters' Hall on the frauds practiced by Leo Belsher and Gerrit-alias-Ravick; it looked as though a substantial sum of money might be recovered, eventually, from the bank accounts and other holdings of both men on Terra. Acting Resident-Agent Gonzalo Ware-Ware, it seemed, really was his right name, but look what he had in front of it-had promulgated more regulations and edicts, and a crackdown on the worst waterfront dives was in progress. I'll bet the devoted flock was horrified at what their beloved bishop had turned into. Bish would leave his diocese in a lot healthier condition than he'd found it, that was one thing for sure. And most of the gang of thugs and plug-uglies who had been used to intimidate and control the Hunters' Co-operative had been gathered up and jailed on vagrancy charges; prisoners were being put to work cleaning up the city.

And there was a lot about plans for a registration of voters, and organization of election boards, and a local electronics-engineering firm had been awarded a contract for voting machines. I didn't think there had ever been a voting machine on Fenris before.

"The commander of the *Bolivar* says he'll take your story to Terra with him, and see that it gets to Interworld News," Dad told me as we were sorting the corrected master sheets and loading them into the photoprint machine, to be sent out on the air. "The *Bolivar*'ll make Terra at least two hundred hours ahead of the *Cape Canaveral*. Interworld will be glad to have it. It isn't often they get a story like that with the first news of anything, and this'll be a big story."

"You shouldn't have given me the exclusive by-line," I said. "You did as much work on it as I did."

"No, I didn't, either," he contradicted, "and I knew what I was doing."

With the work done, I remembered that I hadn't had anything to eat since breakfast, and I went down to take inventory of the refrigerator. Dad went along with me, and after I had assembled a lunch and sat down to it, he decided that his pipe needed refilling, lit it, poured a cup of coffee and sat down with me.

"You know, Walt, I've been thinking, lately," he began.

Oh-oh, I thought. When Dad makes that remark, in just that tone, it's all hands to secure ship for diving.

"We've all had to do a lot of thinking, lately," I agreed.

"Yes. You know, they want me to be mayor of Port Sandor."

I nodded and waited till I got my mouth empty. I could see a lot of sense in that. Dad is honest and scrupulous and public-spirited; too much so, sometimes, for his own good. There wasn't any question of his ability, and while there had always been antagonism between the hunter-ship crews and waterfront people and the uptown business crowd, Dad was well liked and trusted by both parties.

"Are you going to take it?" I asked.

"I suppose I'll have to, if they really want me. Be a sort of obligation."

That would throw a lot more work on me. Dad could give some attention to the paper as mayor, but not as much as now.

"What do you want me to try to handle for you?" I asked.

"Well, Walt, that's what I've been thinking about," he said. "I've been thinking about it for a long time, and particularly since things got changed around here. I think you ought to go to school some more."

That made me laugh. "What, back to Hartzenbosch?" I asked. "I could teach him more than he could teach me, now."

"I doubt that, Walt. Professor Hartzenbosch may be an old maid in trousers, but he's really a very sound scholar. But I wasn't thinking about that. I was thinking about your going to Terra to school."

"Huh?" I forgot to eat, for a moment. "Let's stop kidding."

"I didn't start kidding; I meant it."

"Well, think again, Dad. It costs money to go to school on Terra. It even costs money to go to Terra."

"We have a little money, Walt. Maybe more than you think we do. And with things getting better, we'll lease more teleprinters and get more advertising. You're likely to get better than the price of your passage out of that story we're sending off on the *Bolivar*, and that won't be the end of it, either. Fenris is going to be in the news for a while. You may make some more money writing. That's why I was careful to give you the by-line on that Gerrit story." His pipe had gone out again; he took time out to relight it, and then added: "Anything I spend on this is an investment. The *Times* will get it back."

"Yes, that's another thing; the paper," I said. "If you're going to be mayor, you won't be able to do everything you're doing on the paper now, and then do all my work too."

"Well, shocking as the idea may be, I think we can find somebody to replace you."

"Name one," I challenged.

"Well, Lillian Arnaz, at the Library, has always been interested in newspaper work," he began.

"A girl!" I hooted. "You have any idea of some of the places I have to go to get stories?"

"Yes. I have always deplored the necessity. But a great many of them have been closed lately, and the rest are being run in a much more seemly manner. And she wouldn't be the only reporter. I hesitate to give you any better opinion of yourself than you have already, but it would take at least three people to do the work you've been doing. When you get back from Terra, you'll find the *Times* will have a very respectable reportorial staff."

"What'll I be, then?" I wondered.

"Editor," Dad told me. "I'll retire and go into politics full time. And if Fenris is going to develop the way I believe it will, the editor of the *Times* will need a much better education than I have."

I kept on eating, to give myself an excuse for silence. He was right, I knew that. But college on Terra; why, that would be at least four years, maybe five, and then a year for the round trip....

"Walt, this doesn't have to be settled right away," Dad said. "You won't be going on the *Simón Bolivar*, along with Ravick and Belsher. And that reminds me. Have you talked to Bish lately? He'd be hurt if you didn't see him before he left."

The truth was, I'd been avoiding Bish, and not just because I knew how busy he was. My face felt like a tallow-wax fire every time I thought of how I'd been trying to reform him, and I didn't quite know what I'd be able to say to him if I met him again. And he seemed to me to be an entirely different person, as though the old Bish Ware, whom I had liked in spite of what I'd thought he was, had died, and some total stranger had taken his place.

But I went down to the Municipal Building. It didn't look like the same place. The walls had been scrubbed; the floors were free from litter. All the drove of loafers and hangers-on had been run out, or maybe jailed and put to work. I looked into a couple of offices; everybody in them was busy. A few of the old police force were still there, but their uniforms had been cleaned and pressed, they had all shaved recently, and one or two looked as though they liked being able to respect themselves, for a change.

The girl at the desk in the mayor's outside office told me Bish had a delegation of uptown merchants, who seemed to think that reform was all right in its place but it oughtn't to be carried more than a few blocks above the waterfront. They were protesting the new sanitary regulations. Then she buzzed Bish on the handphone, and told me he'd see me in a few minutes. After a while, I heard the delegation going down the hall from the private office door. One of them was saying:

"Well, this is what we've always been screaming our heads off for. Now we've got it good and hard; we'll just have to get used to it."

When I went in, Bish rose from his desk and came to meet me, shaking my hand. He looked and was dressed like the old Bish Ware I'd always known.

"Glad you dropped in, Walt. Find a seat. How are things on the *Times?*"

"You ought to know. You're making things busy for us."

"Yes. There's so much to do, and so little time to do it. Seems as though I've heard somebody say that before."

"Are you going back to Terra on the *Simón Bolivar?*"

"Oh, Allah forbid! I made a trip on a destroyer, once, and once is enough for a lifetime. I won't even be able to go on the *Cape Canaveral*; I'll take the *Peenemünde* when she gets in. I'm glad MacBride-Dr. Watson-is going to stop off. He'll be a big help. Don't know what I'd have done without Ranjit Singh."

"That won't be till after the *Cape Canaveral* gets back from Terra."

"No. That's why I'm waiting. Don't publish this, Walt, I don't want to start any premature rumors that might end in disappointments, but I've recommended immediate reclassification to Class III, and there may be a Colonial Office man on the *Cape Canaveral* when she gets in. Resident-Agent, permanent. I hope so; he'll need a little breaking in."

"I saw Tom Kivelson this morning," I said. "He seems to be getting along pretty well."

"Didn't anybody at the hospital tell you about him?" Bish asked.

I shook my head. He cursed all hospital staffs.

"I wish military security was half as good. Why, Tom's permanently injured. He won't be crippled, or anything like that, but there was considerable unrepairable damage to his back muscles. He'll be able to get around, but I doubt it he'll ever be able to work on a huntership again."

I was really horrified. Monster-hunting was Tom's whole life. I said something like that.

"He'll just have to make a new life for himself. Joe says he's going to send him to school on Terra. He thinks that was his own idea, but I suggested it to him."

"Dad wants me to go to school on Terra."

"Well, that's a fine idea. Tom's going on the *Peenemünde*, along with me. Why don't you come with us?"

"That would be great, Bish. I'd like it. But I just can't."

"Why not?"

"Well, they want Dad to be mayor, and if he runs, they'll all vote for him. He can't handle this and the paper both alone."

"He can get help on both jobs."

"Yes, but ... Why, it would be years till I got back. I can't sacrifice the time. Not now."

"I'd say six years. You can spend your voyage time from here cramming for entrance qualifications. Schools don't bother about academic credits any more; they're only interested in how much you know. You take four years' regular college, and a year postgrading, and you'll have all the formal education you'll need."

"But, Bish, I can get that here, at the Library," I said. "We have every book on film that's been published since the Year Zero."

"Yes. And you'd die of old age before you got a quarter through the first film bank, and you still wouldn't have an education. Do you know which books to study, and which ones not to bother with? Or which ones to read first, so that what you read in the others will be comprehensible to you? That's what they'll give you on Terra. The tools, which you don't have now, for educating yourself."

I thought that over. It made sense. I'd had a lot of the very sort of trouble he'd spoken of, trying to get information for myself in proper order, and I'd read a lot of books that duplicated other books I'd read, and books I had trouble understanding because I hadn't read some other book first. Bish had something there. I was sure he had. But six years!

I said that aloud, and added: "I can't take the time. I have to be doing things."

"You'll do things. You'll do them a lot better for waiting those six years. You aren't eighteen yet. Six years is a whole third of your past life. No wonder it seems long to you. But you're thinking the wrong way; you're relating those six years to what has passed. Relate them to what's ahead of you, and see how little time they are. You take ordinary care of yourself and keep out of any more civil wars, and you have sixty more years, at least. Your six years at school are only one-tenth of that. I was fifty when I came here to this Creator's blunder of a planet. Say I had only twenty more years; I spent a quarter of them playing town drunk here. I'm the one who ought to be in a rush and howling about lost time, not you. I ought to be in such a hurry I'd take the *Simón Bolivar* to Terra and let this place go to-to anywhere you might imagine to be worse."

"You know, I don't think you like Fenris."

"I don't. If I were a drinking man, this planet would have made a drunkard of me. Now, you forget about these six years chopped out of your busy life. When you get back here, with an education, you'll be a kid of twenty-four, with a big long life ahead of you and your mind stocked with things you don't have now that will help you make something-and more important, something enjoyable-out of it."

There was a huge crowd at the spaceport to see us off, Tom and Bish Ware and me. Mostly, it was for Bish. If I don't find a monument to him when I get back, I'll know there is no such thing as gratitude. There had been a big banquet for us the evening before, and I think Bish actually got a little tipsy. Nobody can be sure, though; it might have been just the old actor back in his role. Now they were all crowding around us, as many as could jam in, in the main lounge of the *Peenemünde*. Joe Kivelson and his wife. Dad and Julio and Mrs. Laden, who was actually being cordial to Bish, and who had a bundle for us that we weren't to open till we were in hyperspace. Lillian Arnaz, the girl who was to take my place as star reporter. We were going to send each other audiovisuals; advice from me on the job, and news from the *Times* from her. Glenn Murell, who had his office open by now and was grumbling that there had been a man from Interstellar Import-Export out on the *Cape Canaveral*, and if the competition got any stiffer the price of tallow-wax would be forced up on him to a sol a pound. And all the *Javelin* hands who had been wrecked with us on Hermann Reuch's Land, and the veterans of the Civil War, all but Oscar and Cesário, who will be at the dock to meet us when we get to Terra.

I wonder what it'll be like, on a world where you go to bed every time it gets dark and get up when it gets light, and can go outdoors all the time. I wonder how I'll like college, and meeting people from all over the Federation, and swapping tall stories about our home planets.

And I wonder what I'll learn. The long years ahead, I can't imagine them now, will be spent on the *Times*, and I ought to learn things to fit me for that. But I can't get rid of the idea about carniculture growth of tallow-wax. We'll have to do something like that. The demand for the stuff is growing, and we don't know how long it'll be before the monsters are hunted out. We know how fast we're killing them, but we don't know how many there are or how fast they breed. I'll talk to Tom about that; maybe between us we can hit on something, or at least lay a foundation for somebody else who will.

The crowd pushed out and off the ship, and the three of us were alone, here in the lounge of the *Peenemünde*, where the story started and where it ends. Bish says no story ends, ever. He's wrong. Stories die, and nothing in the world is deader than a dead news story. But before they do, they hatch a flock of little ones, and some of them grow into bigger stories still. What happens after the ship lifts into the darkness, with the pre-dawn glow in the east, will be another, a new, story.

But to the story of how the hunters got an honest co-operative and Fenris got an honest government, and Bish Ware got Anton Gerrit the slaver, I can write

The End.

The Cosmic Computer

Junkyard Planet

by

H. Beam Piper

I

Thirty minutes to Litchfield.

Conn Maxwell, at the armor-glass front of the observation deck, watched the landscape rush out of the horizon and vanish beneath the ship, ten thousand feet down. He thought he knew how an hourglass must feel with the sand slowly draining out.

It had been six months to Litchfield when the *Mizar* lifted out of La Plata Spaceport and he watched Terra dwindle away. It had been two months to Litchfield when he boarded the *City of Asgard* at the port of the same name on Odin. It had been two hours to Litchfield when the *Countess Dorothy* rose from the airship dock at Storisende. He had had all that time, and now it was gone, and he was still unprepared for what he must face at home.

Thirty minutes to Litchfield.

The words echoed in his mind as though he had spoken them aloud, and then, realizing that he never addressed himself as sir, he turned. It was the first mate.

He had a clipboard in his hand, and he was wearing a Terran Federation Space Navy uniform of forty years, or about a dozen regulation-changes, ago. Once Conn had taken that sort of thing for granted. Now it was obtruding upon him everywhere.

"Thirty minutes to Litchfield, sir," the first officer repeated, and gave him the clipboard to check the luggage list. Valises, two; trunks, two; microbook case, one. The last item fanned a small flicker of anger, not at any person, not even at himself, but at the whole infernal situation. He nodded.

"That's everything. Not many passengers left aboard, are there?"

"You're the only one, first class, sir. About forty farm laborers on the lower deck." He dismissed them as mere cargo. "Litchfield's the end of the run."

"I know. I was born there."

The mate looked again at his name on the list and grinned.

"Sure; you're Rodney Maxwell's son. Your father's been giving us a lot of freight lately. I guess I don't have to tell you about Litchfield."

"Maybe you do. I've been away for six years. Tell me, are they having labor trouble now?"

"Labor trouble?" The mate was surprised. "You mean with the farm-tramps? Ten of them for every job, if you call that trouble."

"Well, I noticed you have steel gratings over the gangway heads to the lower deck, and all your crewmen are armed. Not just pistols, either."

"Oh. That's on account of pirates."

"Pirates?" Conn echoed.

"Well, I guess you'd call them that. A gang'll come aboard, dressed like farm-tramps; they'll have tommy guns and sawed-off shotguns in their bindles. When the ship's airborne and out of reach of help, they'll break out their guns and take her. Usually kill all the crew and passengers.

They don't like to leave live witnesses," the mate said. "You heard about the *Harriet Barne*, didn't you?"

She was Transcontinent & Overseas, the biggest contragravity ship on the planet.

"They didn't pirate her, did they?"

The mate nodded. "Six months ago; Blackie Perales' gang. There was just a tag end of a radio call, that ended in a shot. Time the Air Patrol got to her estimated position it was too late. Nobody's ever seen ship, officers, crew or passengers since."

"Well, great Ghu; isn't the Government doing anything about it?"

"Sure. They offered a big reward for the pirates, dead or alive. And there hasn't been a single case of piracy inside the city limits of Storisende," he added solemnly.

The Calder Range had grown to a sharp blue line on the horizon ahead, and he could see the late afternoon sun on granite peaks. Below, the fields were bare and brown, and the woods were autumn-tinted. They had been green with new foliage when he had last seen them, and the wine-melon fields had been in pink blossom. Must have gotten the crop in early, on this side of the mountains. Maybe they were still harvesting, over in the Gordon Valley. Or maybe this gang below was going to the wine-pressing. Now that he thought of it, he'd seen a lot of cask staves going aboard at Storisende.

Yet there seemed to be less land under cultivation now than six years ago. He could see squares of bracken and low brush that had been melon fields recently, among the new forests that had grown up in the past forty years. The few stands of original timber towered above the second growth like hills; those trees had been there when the planet had been colonized.

That had been two hundred years ago, at the beginning of the Seventh Century, Atomic Era. The name "Poictesme" told that-Surromanticist Movement, when they were rediscovering James Branch Cabell. Old Genji Gartner, the scholarly and half-piratical space-rover whose ship had been the first to enter the Trisystem, had been devoted to the romantic writers of the Pre-Atomic Era. He had named all the planets of the Alpha System from the books of Cabell, and those of Beta from Spenser's *Faerie Queene*, and those of Gamma from Rabelais. Of course, the camp village at his first landing site on this one had been called Storisende.

Thirty years later, Genji Gartner had died there, after seeing Storisende grow to a metropolis and Poictesme become a Member Republic in the Terran Federation. The other planets were uninhabitable except in airtight dome cities, but they were rich in minerals. Companies had been formed to exploit them. No food could be produced on any of them except by carniculture and hydroponic farming, and it had been cheaper to produce it naturally on Poictesme. So Poictesme had concentrated on agriculture and had prospered. At least, for about a century.

Other colonial planets were developing their own industries; the manufactured goods the Gartner Trisystem produced could no longer find a profitable market. The mines and factories on Jurgen and Koshchei, on Britomart and Calidore, on Panurge and the moons of Pantagruel closed, and the factory workers went away. On Poictesme, the offices emptied, the farms contracted, forests reclaimed fields, and the wild game came back.

Coming toward the ship out of the east, now, was a vast desert of crumbling concrete-landing fields and parade grounds, empty barracks and toppling sheds, airship docks, stripped gun emplacements and missile-launching sites. These were more recent, and dated from Poictesme's second hectic prosperity, when the Gartner Trisystem had been the advance base for the Third Fleet-Army Force, during the System States War.

It had lasted twelve years. Millions of troops were stationed on or routed through Poictesme. The mines and factories reopened for war production. The Federation spent trillions on trillions of sols, piled up mountains of supplies and equipment, left the face of the world cluttered with installations. Then, without warning, the System States Alliance collapsed, the rebellion ended, and the scourge of peace fell on Poictesme.

The Federation armies departed. They took the clothes they stood in, their personal weapons, and a few souvenirs. Everything else was abandoned. Even the most expensive equipment had been worth less than the cost of removal.

The people who had grown richest out of the War had followed, taking their riches with them. For the next forty years, those who remained had been living on leavings. On Terra, Conn had told his friends that his father was a prospector, leaving them to interpret that as one who searched, say, for uranium. Rodney Maxwell found quite a bit of uranium, but he got it by taking apart the warheads of missiles.

Now he was looking down on the granite spines of the Calder Range; ahead the misty Gordon Valley sloped and widened to the north. Twenty minutes to Litchfield, now. He still didn't know what he was going to tell the people who would be waiting for him. No; he knew that; he just didn't know how. The ship swept on, ten miles a minute, tearing through thin puffs of cloud. Ten minutes. The Big Bend was glistening redly in the sunlit haze, but Litchfield was still hidden inside its curve. Six. Four. The *Countess Dorothy* was losing speed and altitude. Now he could see it, first a blur and then distinctly. The Airlines Building, so thick as to look squat for all its height. The yellow block of the distilleries under their plume of steam. High Garden Terrace; the Mall.

Moment by moment, the stigmata of decay became more evident. Terraces empty or littered with rubbish; gardens untended and choked with wild growth; blank-staring windows, walls splotched with lichens. At first, he was horrified at what had happened to Litchfield in six years. Then he realized that the change had been in himself. He was seeing it with new eyes, as it really was.

The ship came in five hundred feet above the Mall, and he could see cracked pavements sprouting grass, statues askew on their pedestals, waterless fountains. At first he thought one of them was playing, but what he had taken for spray was dust blowing from the empty basin. There was a thing about dusty fountains, some poem he'd read at the University.

The fountains are dusty in the Graveyard of Dreams;

The hinges are rusty, they swing with tiny screams.

Was Poictesme a Graveyard of Dreams? No; Junkyard of Empire. The Terran Federation had impoverished a hundred planets, devastated a score, actually depopulated at least three, to keep the System States Alliance from seceding. It hadn't been a victory. It had only been a lesser defeat.

There was a crowd, almost a mob, on the dock; nearly everybody in topside Litchfield. He spotted old Colonel Zareff, with his white hair and plum-brown skin, and Tom Brangwyn, the town marshal, red-faced and bulking above everybody else. Kurt Fawzi, the mayor, well to the front. Then he saw his father and mother, and his sister Flora, and waved to them. They waved back, and then everybody was waving. The gangway-port opened, and the Academy band struck up, enthusiastically if inexpertly, as he descended to the dock.

His father was wearing a black suit with a long coat, cut to the same pattern as the one he had worn six years ago. Blackout curtain cloth. It was fairly new, but the coat had begun to acquire a permanent wrinkle across the right hip, over the pistol butt. His mother's dress was new, and so was Flora's, made for the occasion. He couldn't be sure just which of the Federation Armed Forces had provided the material, but his father's shirt was Med Service sterilon.

Ashamed to be noticing things like that, he clasped his father's hand, kissed his mother, embraced his sister. There were a few, but very few, gray threads in his father's mustache; a few more squint-wrinkles around the eyes. His mother's hair was all gray, now, and she was heavier. She seemed shorter, but that would be because he'd grown a few inches in the last six years. For a moment, he was surprised that Flora actually looked younger. Then he realized that to seventeen, twenty-three is practically middle age, but to twenty-three, twenty-nine is almost contemporary. He noticed the glint on her left hand and caught it to look at the ring.

"Hey! Zarathustra sunstone! Nice," he said. "Where is he, Sis?"

He'd never met her fiancé; Wade Lucas hadn't come to Litchfield to practice medicine until the year after he'd gone to Terra.

"Oh, emergency," Flora said. "Obstetrical case; that won't wait on anything. In Tramptown, of course. But he'll be at the party....Oops, I shouldn't have said that; that's supposed to be a surprise."

"Don't worry; I'll be surprised," he promised.

Then Kurt Fawzi was pushing forward, holding out his hand. Thinner, and grayer, but just as effusive as ever.

"Welcome home, Conn. Judge, shake hands with him and tell him how glad we all are to see him back....Now, Franz, put away the recorder; save the interview for the *Chronicle* till later. Ah, Professor Kellton; one pupil Litchfield Academy can be proud of!"

He shook hands with them: Judge Ledue, Franz Veltrin, old Professor Dolf Kellton. They were all happy; how much, he wondered, because he was Conn Maxwell, Rodney Maxwell's son, home from Terra, and how much because of what they hoped he'd tell them. Kurt Fawzi, edging him aside, was the first to speak of it.

"Conn, what did you find out?" he whispered. "Do you know where it is?"

He stammered, then saw Tom Brangwyn and Colonel Klem Zareff approaching, the older man tottering on a silver-headed cane and the younger keeping pace with him. Neither of them had been born on Poictesme. Tom Brangwyn had always been reticent about where he came from, but Hathor was a good guess. There had been political trouble on Hathor twenty years ago; the losers had had to get off-planet in a hurry to dodge firing squads. Klem Zareff never was reticent about his past. He came from Ashmodai, one of the System States planets, and he had commanded a regiment, and finally a division that had been blasted down to less than regimental strength, in the Alliance Army. He always wore a little rosette of System States black and green on his coat.

"Hello, boy," he croaked, extending a hand. "Good to see you again."

"It sure is, Conn," the town marshal agreed, then lowered his voice. "Find out anything definite?"

"We didn't have much time, Conn," Kurt Fawzi said, "but we've arranged a little celebration for you. We'll start it with a dinner at Senta's."

"You couldn't have done anything I'd have liked better, Mr. Fawzi. I'd have to have a meal at Senta's before I'd really feel at home."

"Well, it'll be a couple of hours. Suppose we all go up to my office, in the meantime. Give the ladies a chance to fix up for the party, and have a little drink and a talk together."

"You want to do that, Conn?" his father asked. There was an odd undernote of anxiety, or reluctance, in his voice.

"Yes, of course. I'd like that."

His father turned to speak to his mother and Flora. Kurt Fawzi was speaking to his wife, interrupting himself to shout instructions to some laborers who were bringing up a contragravity skid. Conn turned to Colonel Zareff.

"Good melon crop this year?" he asked.

The old Rebel cursed. "Gehenna of a big crop; we're up to our necks in melons. This time next year we'll be washing our feet in brandy."

"Hold onto it and age it; you ought to see what they charge for a drink of Poictesme brandy on Terra."

"This isn't Terra, and we aren't selling it by the drink," Colonel Zareff said. "We're selling it at Storisende Spaceport, for what the freighter captains pay us. You've been away too long, Conn. You've forgotten what it's like to live in a poor-house."

The cargo was coming off, now. Cask staves, and more cask staves. Zareff swore bitterly at the sight, and then they started toward the wide doors of the shipping floor, inside the Airlines Building. Outgoing cargo was beginning to come out; casks of brandy, of course, and a lot of boxes and crates, painted light blue and bearing the yellow trefoil of the Third Fleet-Army

Force and the eight-pointed red star of Ordnance. Cases of rifles; square boxes of ammunition; crated auto-cannon. Conn turned to his father.

"This our stuff?" he asked. "Where did you dig it?"

Rodney Maxwell laughed. "You know the old Tenth Army Headquarters, over back of Snagtooth, in the Calders? Everybody knows that was cleaned out years ago. Well, always take a second look at these things everybody knows. Ten to one they're not so. It always bothered me that nobody found any underground attack-shelters. I took a second look, and sure enough, I found them, right underneath, mined out of the solid rock. Conn, you'd be surprised at what I found there."

"Where are you going to sell that stuff?" he asked, pointing at a passing skid. "There's enough combat equipment around now to outfit a private army for every man, woman and child in Poictesme."

"Storisende Spaceport. The freighter captains buy it, and sell it on some of the planets that were colonized right before the War and haven't gotten industrialized yet. I'm clearing about two hundred sols a ton on it."

The skid at which he had pointed was loaded with cases of M504 submachine guns. Even used, one was worth fifty sols. Allowing for packing weight, his father was selling those tommy guns for less than a good café on Terra got for one drink of Poictesme brandy.

II

He had been in Kurt Fawzi's office before, once or twice, with his father; he remembered it as a dim, quiet place of genteel conviviality and rambling conversation. None of the lights were bright, and the walls were almost invisible in the shadows. As they entered, Tom Brangwyn went to the long table and took off his belt and holster, laying it down. One by one, the others unbuckled their weapons and added them to the pile. Klem Zareff's cane went on the table with his pistol; there was a sword inside it.

That was something else he was seeing with new eyes. He hadn't started carrying a gun when he had left for Terra, and he was wondering, now, why any of them bothered to. Why, there wouldn't be a shooting a year in Litchfield, if you didn't count the Tramptowners, and they stayed south of the docks and off the top level.

Or perhaps that was just it. Litchfield was peaceful because everybody was prepared to keep it that way. It certainly wasn't because of anything the Planetary Government did to maintain order.

Now Brangwyn was setting out glasses, filling a pitcher from a keg in the corner of the room. The last time Conn had been here, they'd given him a glass of wine, and he'd felt very grown-up because they didn't water it for him.

"Well, gentlemen," Kurt Fawzi was saying, "let's have a toast to our returned friend and new associate. Conn, we're all anxious to hear what you've found out, but even if you didn't learn anything, we're still happy to have you back with us. Gentlemen; to our friend and neighbor. Welcome home, Conn!"

"Well, it's wonderful to be back, Mr. Fawzi," he began.

"Here, none of this mister foolishness; you're one of us, now, Conn. And drink up, everybody. We have plenty of brandy, if we don't have anything else."

"You can say that again, Kurt." That was one of the distillery people; he'd remember the name in a moment. "When this new crop gets pressed and fermented...."

"I don't know where in Gehenna I'm going to vat mine till it ferments," Klem Zareff said.

"Or why," another planter added. "Lorenzo, what are you going to be paying for wine?"

Lorenzo Menardes; that was the name. The distiller said he was worrying about what he'd be able to get for brandy.

"Oh, please," Fawzi interrupted. "Not today; not when our boy's home and is going to tell us how we can solve all our problems."

"Yes, Conn." That was Morgan Gatworth, the lawyer. "You did find out where Merlin is, didn't you?"

That set them all off. He was still holding his drink; he downed it in one gulp, barely tasting it, and handed the glass to Tom Brangwyn for a refill, and caught a frown on his father's face. One did not gulp drinks in Kurt Fawzi's office.

Well, neither did one blast everybody's hopes with half a dozen words, and that was what he was trying to force himself to do. He wanted to blurt out the one quick sentence and get it over with, but the words wouldn't come out of his throat. He lowered the second drink by half; the brandy was beginning to warm him and dissolve the cold lump in his stomach. Have to go easy, though. He wasn't used to this kind of drinking, and he wanted to stay sober enough to talk sense until he'd told them what he had to.

"I hope," he said, "that you don't expect me to show you the cross on the map, where the computer is buried."

All the eyes around him began to look troubled. Most of them had been expecting precisely that. His father was watching him anxiously.

"But it's still here on Poictesme, isn't it?" one of the melon planters asked. "They didn't take it away with them?"

"Most of you gentlemen," he said, "contributed to sending me to school on Terra, to study cybernetics and computer theory. It wouldn't do us any good to find Merlin if none of us could operate it. Well, I've done that. I can use any known type of computer, and train assistants. After I graduated, I was offered a junior instructorship to computer physics at the University."

"You didn't mention that, son," his father said.

"The letter would have come on the same ship I did. Besides, I didn't think it was very important."

"I think it is." There was a catch in old Dolf Kellton's voice. "One of my boys from the Academy offered a place on the faculty of the University of Montevideo, on Terra!" He finished his drink and held out his glass for more, something he almost never did.

"Conn means," Kurt Fawzi explained, "that it had nothing to do with Merlin."

All right; now tell them the truth.

"I was also to find out anything I could about a secret giant computer used during the War by the Third Fleet-Army Force, code-named Merlin. I went over all the records available to the public; I used your letter, Professor, and the head of our Modern History department secured me access to non-public material, some of it still classified. For one thing, I have locations and maps and plans of every Federation installation built here between 842 and 854, the whole period of the War." He turned to his father. "There are incredible things still undiscovered; most of the important installations were built in duplicate, sometimes triplicate, as a precaution against space attack. I know where all of them are."

"Space attack!" Klem Zareff was indignant. "There never was a time we could have attacked Poictesme. Even if we'd had the ships, we were fighting a purely defensive war. Aggression was no part of our policy —"

He interrupted: "Excuse me, Colonel. The point I was trying to make is that, with all I was able to learn, I could find nothing, not one single word, about any giant strategic planning computer called Merlin, or any Merlin Project."

There! He'd gotten that out. Now go on and tell them about the old man in the dome-house on Luna. The room was silent, except for the small insectile hum of the electric clock. Then somebody set a glass on the table, and it sounded like a hammer blow.

"Nothing, Conn?"

Kurt Fawzi was incredulous. Judge Ledue's hand shook as though palsied as he tried to relight his cigar. Dolf Kellton was looking at the drink in his hand as though he had no idea what it was. The others found their voices, one by one.

"Of course, it was the most closely guarded secret..."

"But after forty years..."

"Hah, don't tell me about security!" Colonel Zareff barked. "You should have seen the lengths our staff went to. I remember, once, on Mephistopheles..."

"But there *was* a computer code-named Merlin," Judge Ledue was insisting, to convince himself more than anybody else. "Its memory-bank contained all human knowledge. It was capable of scanning all its data instantaneously, and combining, and forming associations, and reasoning with absolute accuracy, and extrapolating to produce new facts, and predicting future events, and..."

And if you'd asked such a computer, "Is there a God?" it would have simply answered, "Present."

"We'd have won the War, except for Merlin," Zareff was declaring.

"Conn, from what you've learned of computers generally, how big would Merlin have to be?" old Professor Kellton asked.

"Well, the astrophysics computer at the University occupied a volume of a hundred thousand cubic feet. For all Merlin was supposed to do, I'd say something of the order of three million to five million.

"Well, it's a cinch they didn't haul that away with them," Lester Dawes, the banker, said.

"Oh, lots of places on Poictesme where they could have hid a thing like that," Tom Brangwyn said. "You know, a planet's a mighty big place."

"It doesn't have to be on Poictesme, even," Morgan Gatworth pointed out. "It could be anywhere in the Trisystem."

"You know where I'd have put it?" Lorenzo Menardes asked. "On one of the moons of Pantagruel."

"But that's in the Gamma System, three light years away," Kurt Fawzi objected. "There isn't a hypership on this planet, and it would take half a lifetime to get there on normal-space drive."

Conn was lifting his glass to his lips. He set it down again and rose to his feet.

"Then," he said, "we will build a hypership. On Koshchei there are shipyards and hyperdrive engines and everything we will need. We only need one normal-space interplanetary ship to get out there, and we're in business."

"Well, I don't know we need one," Judge Ledue said. "That was only an idea of Lorenzo's. I think Merlin's right here on Poictesme."

"We don't know it is," Conn replied. "And we don't know we won't need a ship. Merlin may be on Koshchei; that's where the components would be fabricated, and the Armed Forces weren't hauling anything any farther than they had to. Koshchei's only two and a half minutes away by radio; that's practically in the next room. Look; here's how they could have done it."

He went on talking, about remote controls and radio transmission and positronic brains and neutrino-circuits. They believed it all, even the little they understood. They would believe anything he told them about Merlin-except the truth.

"But this will take money," Lester Dawes said. "And after that infernal deluge of unsecured paper currency thirty years ago..."

"I have no doubt," Judge Ledue began, "that the Planetary Government at Storisende would give assistance. I have some slight influence with President Vyckhoven..."

"Huh-*uh*!" That was one of Klem Zareff's fellow planters. "We don't want Jake Vyckhoven or any of this First-Families-of-Storisende oligarchy in this at all. That's the gang that bankrupted the Government with doles and work relief, and everybody else with worthless printing-press money after the War, and they've been squatting in a circle deploring things ever since. Some of these days Blackie Perales and his pirates'll sack Storisende, for all they'd be able to do to stop him."

"We get a ship out to Koshchei, and the next thing you know we'll be the Planetary Government," Tom Brangwyn said.

Rodney Maxwell finished the brandy in his glass and set it on the table, then went to the pile of belts and holsters and began rummaging for his own. Kurt Fawzi looked up in surprise.

"Rod, you're not leaving are you?" he asked.

"Yes. It's only half an hour till time for dinner, and I think Conn and I ought to have a little fresh air. Besides, you know, we haven't seen each other for six years." He buckled on the heavy automatic and settled the belt over his hips. "You didn't have a gun, did you, Conn?" he asked. "Well, let's go."

III

It wasn't until they were down to the main level and outside in the little plaza to the east of the Airlines Building that his father broke the silence.

"That was quite a talk you gave them, Conn. They believed every word of it. I even caught myself starting to believe it once or twice."

Conn stopped short; his father halted beside him. "Why didn't you tell them the truth, son?" Rodney Maxwell asked.

The question, which he had been throwing at himself, angered him. "Why didn't I just grab a couple of pistols and shoot the lot of them?" he retorted. "It wouldn't have killed them any deader, and it wouldn't have hurt as much."

"There is no Merlin. Is that it?"

He realized, suddenly, that his father had known, or suspected that all along. He started to say something, then checked himself and began again:

"There never was one. I was going to tell them, but you saw them. I couldn't."

"You're sure of it?"

"The whole thing's a myth. I'm quoting the one man in the Galaxy who ought to know. The man who commanded the Third Force here during the War."

"Foxx Travis!" His father's voice was soft with wonder. "I saw him once, when I was eight years old. I thought he'd died long ago. Why, he must be over a hundred."

"A hundred and twelve. He's living on Luna; low gravity's all that keeps him alive."

"And you talked to him?"

"Yes."

There'd been a girl in his third-year biophysics class; he'd found out that she was a great-granddaughter of Force General Travis. It had taken him until his senior midterm vacation to wangle an invitation to the dome-house on Luna. After that, it had been easy. As soon as Foxx Travis had learned that one of his great-granddaughter's guests was from Poictesme, he had insisted on talking to him.

"What did he tell you?"

The old man had been incredibly thin and frail. Under normal gravitation, his life would have gone out like a blown match. Even at one-sixth G, it had cost him effort to rise and greet the guest. There had been a younger man, a mere stripling of seventy-odd; he had been worried, and excused himself at once. Travis had laughed after he had gone out.

"Mike Shanlee; my aide-de-camp on Poictesme. Now he thinks he's my keeper. He'll have a squad of doctors and a platoon of nurses in here as soon as you're gone, so take your time. Now, tell me how things are on Poictesme...."

"Just about that," he told his father. "I finally mentioned Merlin, as an old legend people still talked about. I was ashamed to admit anybody really believed in it. He laughed, and said, 'Great Ghu, is that thing still around? Well, I suppose so; it was all through the Third Force during the War. Lord only knows how these rumors start among troops. We never contradicted it; it was good for morale.'"

They had started walking again, and were out on the Mall; the sky was flaming red and orange from high cirrus clouds in the sunset light. They stopped by a dry fountain, perhaps the one from which he had seen the dust blowing. Rodney Maxwell sat down on the edge of the basin and got out two cigars, handing one to Conn, who produced his lighter.

"Conn, they wouldn't have believed you *and* Foxx Travis," he said. "Merlin's a religion with those people. Merlin's a robot god, something they can shove all their problems onto. As soon as they find Merlin, everybody will be rich and happy, the Government bonds will be redeemed at face value plus interest, the paper money'll be worth a hundred Federation centisols to the sol, and the leaves and wastepaper will be raked off the Mall, all by magic." He muttered an unprintability and laughed bitterly.

"I didn't know you were the village atheist, Father."

"In a religious community, the village atheist keeps his doubts to himself. I have to do business with these Merlinolators. It's all I can do to keep Flora from antagonizing them at school."

Flora was a teacher; now she was assistant principal of the grade schools. Professor Kellton was also school superintendent. He could see how that would be.

"Flora's not a True Believer, then?"

Rodney Maxwell shook his head. "That's largely Wade Lucas's influence, I'd say. You know about him."

Just from letters. Wade Lucas was from Baldur; he'd gone off-planet as soon as he'd gotten his M.D. Evidently the professional situation there was the same as on Terra; plenty of opportunities, and fifty competitors for each one. On Poictesme, there were few opportunities, but nobody competed for anything, not even to find Merlin.

"He'd never heard of Merlin till he came here, and when he did, he just couldn't believe in it. I don't blame him. I've heard about it all my life, and I can't."

"Why not?"

"To begin with, I suppose, because it's just another of these things everybody believes. Then, I've had to do some studying on the Third Force occupation of Poictesme to know where to go and dig, and I never found any official, or even reliably unofficial, mention of anything of the sort. Forty years is a long time to keep a secret, you know. And I can't see why they didn't come back for it after the pressure to get the troops home was off, or why they didn't build a dozen Merlins. This isn't the only planet that has problems they can't solve for themselves."

"What's Mother's attitude on Merlin?"

"She's against it. She thinks it isn't right to make machines that are smarter than people."

"I'll agree. It's scientifically impossible."

"That's what I've been trying to tell her. Conn, I noticed that after Kurt Fawzi started talking about how long it would take to get to the Gamma System, you jumped right into it and began talking up a ship. Did you think that if you got them started on that it would take their minds off Merlin?"

"That gang up in Fawzi's office? Nifflheim, no! They'll go on hunting Merlin till they die. But I was serious about the ship. An idea hit me. You gave it to me; you and Klem Zareff."

"Why, I didn't say a word..."

"Down on the shipping floor, before we went up. You were talking about selling arms and ammunition at a profit of two hundred sols a ton, and Klem was talking as though a bumper crop was worse than a Green Death epidemic. If we had a hypership, look what we could do. How much do you think a settler on Hoth or Malebolge or Irminsul would pay for a good rifle and a thousand rounds? How much would he pay for his life? —that's what it would come to. And do you know what a fifteen-cc liqueur glass of Poictesme brandy sells for on Terra? One sol; Federation money. I'll admit it costs like Nifflheim to run a hypership, but look at the difference between what these tramp freighter captains pay at Storisende and what they get."

"I've been looking at it for a long time. Maybe if we had a few ships of our own, these planters would be breaking new ground instead of cutting their plantings, and maybe we'd get some money on this planet that was worth something. You have a good idea there, son. But maybe there's an angle to it you haven't thought of."

Conn puffed slowly at the cigar. Why couldn't they grow tobacco like this on Terra? Soil chemicals, he supposed; that wasn't his subject.

"You can't put this scheme over on its own merits. This gang wouldn't lift a finger to build a hypership. They've completely lost hope in everything but Merlin."

"Well, can do. I'll even convince them that Merlin's a space-station, in orbit off Koshchei. I think I could do that."

"You know what it'll cost? If you go ahead with it, I'm in it with you, make no mistake about that. But you and I will be the only two people on Poictesme who can be trusted with the truth. We'll have to lie to everybody else, with every word we speak. We'll have to lie to Flora, and we'll have to lie to your mother. Your mother most of all. She believes in absolutes. Lying is absolutely wrong, no matter whom it helps; telling the truth is absolutely right, no matter how much damage it does or how many hearts it breaks. You think this is going to be worth a price like that?"

"Don't you?" he demanded, and then pointed along the crumbling and littered Mall. "Look at that. Pretend you never saw it before and are looking at it for the first time. And then tell me whether it'll be worth it or not."

His father took a cigar from his mouth. For a moment, he sat staring silently.

"Great Ghu!" Rodney Maxwell turned. "I wonder how that sneaked up on me; I honestly never realized.... Yes, Conn. This is a cause worth lying for." He looked at his watch. "We ought to be starting for Senta's, but let's take a few minutes and talk this over. How are you going to get it started?"

"Well, convince them that I can find Merlin and that they can't find it without me. I think I've done that already. Then convince them that we'll have to have a ship to get to Koshchei, and —"

"Won't do. That'll take money, and money's something none of this gang has."

"You heard me talk about the stuff I found out on Terra? Father, you have no idea what all there is. You remember the old Force Command Headquarters, the one the Planetary Government took over? I know where there's a duplicate of that, completely underground. It has everything the other one had, and a lot more, because it'll be cram-full of supplies to be used in case of a general blitz that would knock out everything on the planet. And a chain of hospitals. And a spaceport, over on Barathrum, that was built inside the crater of an extinct volcano. There won't be any hyperships there of course, but there'll be equipment and material. We might be able to build a ship there. And supply depots, all over the planet; none of them has ever been opened since the War. Don't worry about financing; we have that."

His father, he could see, appreciated what he had brought home from Terra. He was nodding, with quick head jerks, at each item.

"That'll do it, all right. Now, listen; what we want to do is get a company organized, a regular limited-liability company, with a charter. We'll contribute the information you brought back from Terra, and we'll get the rest of this gang to put all the money we can twist out of them into it, so we'll be sure they won't say, 'Aw, Nifflheim with it!' and walk out on us as soon as the going gets a little tough." Rodney Maxwell got to his feet, hitching his gun-belt. "I'll pass the word to Kurt to get a meeting set up for tomorrow afternoon."

"What'll we call this company? Merlin Rediscovery, Ltd?"

"No! We keep Merlin out of it. As far as the public is supposed to know, this is just a war-material prospecting company. I'll impress on them that Merlin is to be kept a secret. That way, we'll have to engage in regular prospecting and salvage work as a front. I'll see to it that the front is also the main objective." He nodded down the Mall, toward the sunset, which was blazing even higher and redder. "Well, let's go. You don't want to be late for your own welcome-home party."

They walked slowly, still talking, until they came to the end of the Mall. The escalators to the level below weren't working. Now that he thought of it, they hadn't been when he had gone away, six years ago, but he could remember riding up and down on them as a small child. For a moment they stood in the sunset light, looking down on the lower terrace as they finished their cigars.

Senta's was mostly outdoors, the tables under the open sky. The people gathered below were looking at the sunset, too; Litchfielders loved to watch sunsets, maybe because a sunset was one of the few things economic conditions couldn't affect. There was Kurt Fawzi, the center of a group to whom he was declaiming earnestly; there was his mother, and Flora, and Flora's fiancé, who was the uncomfortable lone man in an excited feminine flock. And there was Senta herself, short and dumpy, in one of her preposterous red and purple dresses, bubbling happily one moment and screaming invective at some laggard waiter the next.

They threw away their cigars and started down the long, motionless escalator. Conn Maxwell, Hero of the Hour, marching to Destiny. He seemed to hear trumpets sounding before him.

And an occasional muted Bronx cheer.

IV

The alarm chimed softly beside his bed; he reached out and silenced it, and lay looking at the early sunlight in the windows, and found that he was wishing himself back in his dorm room at the University. No, back in this room, ten years ago, before any of this had started. For a while, he imagined himself thirteen years old and knowing everything he knew now, and he began mapping a campaign to establish himself as Litchfield's Juvenile Delinquent Number One, to the end that Kurt Fawzi and Dolf Kellton and the rest of them would never dream of sending him to school on Terra to find out where Merlin was.

But he couldn't even go back to yesterday afternoon in Kurt Fawzi's office and tell them the truth. All he could do was go ahead. It had seemed so easy, when he and his father had been talking on the Mall; just get a ship built, and get out to Koshchei, and open some of the shipyards and engine works there, and build a hypership. Sure; easy-once he got started.

He climbed out of bed, knuckled the sleep-sand out of his eyes, threw his robe around him, and started across the room to the bath cubicle.

They had decided to have breakfast together his first morning home. The party had broken up late, and then there had been the excitement of opening the presents he had brought back from Terra. Nobody had had a chance to talk about Merlin, or about what he was going to do, now that he was home. That, and his career of mendacity, would start at breakfast. He wanted to let his father get to the table first, to run interference for him; he took his time with his toilet and dressed carefully and slowly. Finally, he zipped up the short waist-length jacket and went out.

His father and mother and Flora were at the table, and the serving-robot was floating around a few inches off the floor, steam trailing from its coffee urn and its tray lid up to offer food. He greeted everybody and sat down at his place, and the robot came around to him. His mother had selected all the things he'd been most fond of six years ago: shovel-snout bacon, hotcakes, starberry jam, things he hadn't tasted since he had gone away. He filled his plate and poured a cup of coffee.

"You don't want to bother coming out to the dig with me this morning, do you?" his father was saying. "I'll be back here for lunch, and we'll go to the meeting in the afternoon."

"Meeting?" Flora asked. "What meeting?"

"Oh, we didn't have time to tell you," Rodney Maxwell said. "You know, Conn brought back a lot of information on locations of supply depots and things like that. An amazing list of things that haven't been discovered yet. It's going to be too much for us to handle alone; we're organizing a company to do it. We'll need a lot of labor, for one thing; jobs for some of these Tramptowners."

"That's going to be something awfully big," his mother said dubiously. "You never did anything like that before."

"I never had the kind of a partner I have now. It's Maxwell & Son, from now on."

"Who's going to be in this company?" Flora wanted to know.

"Oh, everybody around town; Kurt and the Judge and Klem, and Lester Dawes. All that crowd."

"The Fawzis' Office Gang," Flora said disparagingly. "I suppose they'll want Conn to take them right to where Merlin is, the first thing."

"Well, not the first thing," Conn said. "Merlin was one thing I couldn't find out anything about on Terra."

"I'll bet you couldn't!"

"The people at Armed Forces Records would let me look at everything else, and make microcopies and all, but not one word about computers. Forty years, and they still have the security lid welded shut on that."

Flora looked at him in shocked surprise. "You don't mean to tell me you believe in that thing?"

"Sure. How do you think they fought a war around a perimeter of close to a thousand light-years? They couldn't do all that out of their heads. They'd have to have computers, and the one they'd use to correlate everything and work out grand-strategy plans would have to be a dilly. Why, I'd give anything just to look at the operating panels for that thing."

"But that's just a silly story; there never was anything like Merlin. No wonder you couldn't find out about it. You were looking for something that doesn't exist, just like all these old cranks that sit around drinking brandy and mooning about what Merlin's going to do for them, and never doing anything for themselves."

"Oh, they're going to do something, now, Flora," his father told her. "When we get this company organized —"

"You'll dig up a lot of stuff you won't be able to sell, like that stuff you've been bringing in from Tenth Army, and then you'll go looping off chasing Merlin, like the rest of them. Well, maybe that'll be a little better than just sitting in Kurt Fawzi's office talking about it, but not much."

It kept on like that. Conn and his father tried several times to change the subject; each time Flora ignored the effort and returned to her diatribe. Finally, she put her plate and cup on the robot's tray and got to her feet.

"I have to go," she said. "Maybe I can do something to keep some of these children from growing up to be Merlin-worshipers like their parents."

She flung out of the room angrily. Mrs. Maxwell looked after her in distress.

"And I thought it was going to be so nice, having breakfast together again," she lamented.

Somehow the breakfast wasn't quite as good as he'd thought it was at first. He wondered how many more breakfasts like that he was going to have to sit through. He and his father finished quickly and got up, while his mother started the robot to clearing the table.

"Conn," she said, after his father had gone out, "you shouldn't have gotten Flora started like that."

"I didn't get Flora started; she's equipped with a self-starter. If she doesn't believe in Merlin, that's her business. A lot of these people do, and I'm going to help them hunt for it. That's why they all chipped in to send me to school on Terra; remember?"

"Yes, I know." Her voice was heavy with distress. "Conn, do you really believe there is a ... that thing?" she asked.

"Why, of course." He was mildly surprised at how sincerely and straightforwardly he said it. "I don't know where it is, but it's somewhere on Poictesme, or in the Alpha System."

"Well, do you think it would be a good thing to find it?"

That surprised him. Everybody knew it would be, and his mother didn't share his father's attitude about things everybody knew. She hadn't any business questioning a fundamental postulate like that.

"It frightens me," she continued. "I don't even like to think about it. A soulless intelligence; it seems evil to me."

"Well, of course it's soulless. It's a machine, isn't it? An aircar's soulless, but you're not afraid to ride in one."

"But this is different. A machine that can think. Conn, people weren't meant to make machines like that, wiser than they are."

"Now wait a minute, Mother. You're talking to a computerman now." Professional authority was something his mother oughtn't to question. "A computer like Merlin isn't intelligent, or wise, or anything of the sort. It doesn't think; the people who make computers and use them do the thinking. A computer's a tool, like a screwdriver; it has to have a man to use it."

"Well, but...."

"And please, don't talk about what people are *meant* to do. People aren't *meant* to do things; they *mean* to do things, and nine times out of ten, they end by doing them. It may take a hundred thousand years from a Stone Age savage in a cave to the captain of a hyperspace ship, but sooner or later they get there."

His mother was silent. The soulless machine that had been clearing the table floated out of the room, the dishwasher in its rectangular belly gurgling. Maybe what he had told her was logical, but women aren't impressed by logic. She knew better-for the good old feminine reason, *Because.*

"Wade Lucas wanted me to drop in on him for a checkup," he mentioned. "That's rubbish; I had one for my landing pratique on the ship. He just wants to size up his future brother-in-law."

"Well, you ought to go see him."

"How did Flora come to meet him, anyhow?"

"Well, you know, he came from Baldur. He was in Storisende, looking for an opening to start a practice, and he heard about some medical equipment your father had found somewhere and came out to see if he could buy it. Your father and Judge Ledue and Mr. Fawzi talked him into opening his office here. Then he and Flora got acquainted...." She asked, anxiously: "What did you think of him, Conn?"

"Seems like a regular guy. I think I'll like him." A husband like Wade Lucas might be a good thing for Flora. "I'll drop in on him, sometime this morning."

His mother went toward the rear of the house-more soulless machines, like the housecleaning-robot, and the laundry-robot, to look after. He went into his father's office and found the cigar humidor, just where it had been when he'd stolen cigars out of it six years ago and thought his father never suspected what he was doing.

Now, why didn't they export this tobacco? It was better than anything they grew on Terra; well, at least it was different, just as Poictesme brandy was different from Terran bourbon or Baldur honey-rum. That was the sort of thing that could be sold in interstellar trade anytime and anywhere; the luxury goods that were unique. Staple foodstuffs, utility textiles, metal products, could be produced anywhere, and sooner or later they were. That was the reason for the original, pre-War depression: the customers were all producing for themselves. He'd talk that over with his father. He wished he'd had time to take some economics at the University.

He found the file his father kept up-to-date on salvage sites found and registered with the Claims Office in Storisende. Some of the locations he had brought back data for had been discovered, but, to his relief, not the underground duplicate Force Command Headquarters, and not the spaceport on the island continent of Barathrum, to the east. That was all right.

He went to the house-defense arms closet and found a 10-mm Navy pistol, and a belt and spare clips. Making sure that the pistol and magazines were loaded, he buckled it on. He debated getting a vehicle out of the hangar on the landing stage, decided against it, and started downtown on foot.

One of the first people he met was Len Yeniguchi, the tailor. He would be at the meeting that afternoon. He managed, while talking, to comment on the cut of Conn's suit, and finger the material.

"Ah, nice," he complimented. "Made on Terra? We don't see cloth like that here very often." He meant it wasn't Armed Forces salvage.

"Father ought to be around to see you with a bolt of material, to have a suit made," he said. "For Ghu's sake, either talk him into having a short jacket like this, or get him to buy himself a shoulder holster. He's ruined every coat he ever owned, carrying a gun on his hip."

A little farther on, he came to a combat car grounded in the middle of the street. It was green, with black trimmings, and lettered in black, GORDON VALLEY HOME GUARD. Tom Brangwyn was standing beside it, talking to a young man in a green uniform.

"Hello, Conn." The town marshal looked at his hip and grinned. "See you got all your clothes on this morning. You were just plain indecent, yesterday.... You know Fred Karski, don't you?"

Yes, now that Tom mentioned it, he did. He and Fred had gone to school together at the Litchfield Academy. But the six years since they'd seen each other last had made a lot of difference in both of them. He was beginning to think that the only strangers in Litchfield were his own contemporaries. They shook hands, and Conn looked at the combat car and Fred Karski's uniform.

"What's going on?" he asked. "The System States Alliance to business again?"

Karski laughed. "Oh, that's the Colonel's idea. Green and black were his colors in the War, and he's in command of the regiment."

"Regiment? You need a whole regiment?" Conn asked.

"Well, it's two companies, each about the size of a regular army platoon, but we have to call it a regiment so he can keep his old Rebel Army rank."

"We could use a regiment, Conn," Tom Brangwyn said seriously. "You have no idea how bad things have gotten. Over on the east coast, the outlaws are looting whole towns. About four months ago, they sacked Waterville; burned the whole town and killed close to a hundred people. That was Blackie Perales' gang."

"Who is this Blackie Perales? I heard the name mentioned in connection with the *Harriet Barne*."

"Blackie Perales is anybody the Planetary Government can't catch, which means practically any outlaw," Fred Karski said.

"No, Fred; there is a Blackie Perales," Tom Brangwyn said. "He used to be a planter, down in the south. The banks foreclosed on him when he couldn't pay his notes, and he turned outlaw. That's the way it's going, all around. Every time a planter loses his plantation or a farmer loses his farm, or a mechanic loses his job, he turns outlaw. Take Tramptown, here. We used to plant nothing but melons. Then, when the sale for wine and brandy dropped, the melon-planters began cutting their melon crops and raising produce, instead of buying it from up north, and turning land into pasture for cattle. The people we used to buy foodstuffs from couldn't sell all they raised, and that threw a lot of farmhands out of work. So they got the idea there was work here, and they came flocking in, and when they couldn't get jobs, they just stayed in Tramptown, stealing anything they could. We don't even try to police Tramptown any more; we just see to it they don't come up here."

"Well, where do these outlaws and pirates who are looting whole towns come from?"

"Down in the Badlands, mostly. None of them have been bothering us, since we organized the Home Guard. They tried to, a couple of times, at first. There may have been a few survivors; they spread it around that Gordon Valley wasn't any outlaws' health resort."

"Why don't you join us, Conn?" Fred Karski asked. "All our old gang belong."

"I'd like to, but I'm afraid I'm going to be kind of busy."

Brangwyn nodded. "Yes. You will be, at that," he agreed.

"So I hear," Fred Karski said. "Do you really know where it is, Conn?"

"Well, no." He went into the routine about Merlin being still classified triple-top secret. "But we'll find it. It may take time, but we will."

They talked for a while. He asked more questions about the Home Guard. His father, it seemed, had donated all the equipment. They had a hundred and seventy men on the active list, but they had a reserve of over eight hundred, and combat vehicles and weapons on all the plantations and in all the towns along the river. The reserve had only been turned out twice; both times, outlaw attacks had been stopped dead-literally. The Home Guard, it appeared, was not given to making arrests or taking prisoners. Finally, he parted from them, strolling on along the row of stores and business places, many vacant, under the south edge of the Mall, until he saw a fluorolite sign, WADE LUCAS, M. D. He entered.

Lucas wasn't busy. They went into his consultation office, and Conn took off his gun-belt and hung it up; Lucas offered cigarettes, and they lighted and sat down.

"I see you've started carrying one," he said, nodding to the pistol Conn had laid aside.

"Civic obligation. I'm going to be too busy for Home Guard duty, but if I can protect myself, it'll save somebody else the job of protecting me."

"Maybe if there weren't so many guns around, there wouldn't be so much trouble."

He felt his good opinion of Wade Lucas start to slip. The Liberals on Terra had been full of that kind of talk, which was why only four out of ten of last year's graduating class at Armed Forces Academy had been able to get active commissions. The last war had been a disaster, so don't prepare for another one; when it comes, let it be a worse disaster.

"Guns don't make trouble; people make trouble. If the troublemakers are armed, you have to be armed too. When did you last see an Air Patrol boat around here, or even a Constabulary trooper? All we have here is the Home Guard and Tom Brangwyn and three deputies, and his pay and theirs is always six months in arrears."

Lucas nodded. "A bankrupt government, an unemployment rate that rises every year, currency that buys less every month. And do-it-yourself justice." The doctor blew a smoke ring and watched it float toward the ventilator-intake. "You said you're going to be busy. This company your father's talking about organizing?"

"That's right. You're going to be at the meeting at the Academy this afternoon, aren't you?"

"Yes. Just what are you going to do, after you get it organized?"

"Well, I brought back information on a great deal of undiscovered equipment and stores that the Third Force left behind...." He talked on for some time, keeping to safe generalities. "It's too big for my father and me to handle alone, even if we didn't feel morally obligated to take in the people who contributed toward sending me to school on Terra. You ought to be interested in it. I know of six fully supplied hospitals, intended to take care of the casualties in case of a System States space-attack. You can imagine, better than I can, what would be in them."

"Yes. Medical supplies of all sorts are getting hard to find. But look here; you're not going to let these people waste time looking for this alleged computer, this thing they call Merlin, are you?"

"We're looking for any valuable war material. I don't know the location of Merlin, but —"

"I'll bet you don't!" Lucas said vehemently. That was the same thing Flora had said.

" —but Merlin is undoubtedly the most valuable item of abandoned TF equipment on this planet. In the long run, I'd say, more valuable than everything else together. We certainly aren't going to ignore it."

"Good heavens, Conn! You aren't like these people here; you were educated at the University of Montevideo."

"So I was. I studied computer theory and practice. I have some doubts about Merlin being able to do some of the things these laymen like Kellton and Fawzi and Judge Ledue think it could. Those sorts of misconceptions and exaggerations have to be allowed for. But I have no doubt whatever that the master computer with which they did their strategic planning is probably the greatest mechanism of its sort ever built, and I have no doubt whatever that it still exists somewhere in the Alpha System."

He almost convinced himself of it. He did not, however, convince Wade Lucas, who was now regarding him with narrow-eyed suspicion.

"You mean you categorically state that that computer actually exists?"

"That, I think, was the general idea. Yes. I certainly do believe that Merlin exists."

Maybe he was telling the truth. Merlin existed in the beliefs and hopes of people like Dolf Kellton and Klem Zareff and Judge Ledue and Kurt Fawzi. Merlin was a god to them. Well, take Ghu, the Thoran Grandfather-God. Ghu was as preposterous, theologically, as Merlin was technologically; Ghu, except to Thorans, was a Federation-wide joke. But he'd known a couple of Thorans at the University, funny little fellows, with faces like terriers, their bodies covered with matted black hair. They believed in Ghu the way he believed in the Second Law of Thermodynamics. Ghu was with them every moment of their lives. Take away their belief in Ghu, and they would have been lost and wretched.

As lost and wretched as Kurt Fawzi or Judge Ledue, if they lost their belief in Merlin. He started to say something like that, and then thought better of it.

Yes, Virginia, there *is* a Santa Claus.

V

The meeting was at the Academy; when Conn and his father arrived, they found the central hall under the topside landing stage crowded. Kurt Fawzi and Professor Kellton had constituted themselves a reception committee. Franz Veltrin was in evidence with his audiovisual recorder, and Colonel Zareff was leaning on his silver-headed sword cane. Tom Brangwyn, in an unaccustomed best-suit. Wade Lucas, among a group of merchants, arguing heatedly. Lorenzo Menardes, the distiller, and Lester Dawes, the banker, and Morgan Gatworth, the lawyer, talking to Judge Ledue. About four times as many as had been in Fawzi's office the afternoon before.

Finally, everybody was shepherded into a faculty conference room; there was a long table, and a shorter one T-wise at one end. Fawzi and Kellton conducted them to this. Both of them were trying to preside, Kellton because it was his Academy, and Fawzi ex officio as mayor and professional leading citizen, and because he had come to regard Merlin as his own private project. After everybody else was seated, the two rival chairmen-presumptive remained on their feet. Fawzi was saying, "Let's come to order; we must conduct this meeting regularly," and Kellton was saying, "Gentlemen, please; let me have your attention."

If either of them took the chair, the other would resent it. Conn got to his feet again.

"Somebody will have to preside," he said, loudly enough to cut through the babble at the long table. "Would you take the chair, Judge Ledue?"

That stopped it. Neither of them wanted to contest the honor with the president-judge of the Gordon Valley court.

"Excellent suggestion, Conn. Judge, will you preside?" Professor Kellton, who had seen himself losing out to Fawzi, asked. Fawzi threw one quick look around, estimated the situation, and got with it. "Of course, Judge. You're the logical chairman. Here, will you sit here?"

Judge Ledue took the chair, looked around for something to use as a gavel, and rapped sharply with a paperweight.

"Young Mr. Conn Maxwell, who has just returned from Terra, needs no introduction to any of you," he began. Then, having established that, he took the next ten minutes to introduce Conn. When people began fidgeting, he wound up with: "Now, only about a dozen of us were at the informal meeting in Mr. Fawzi's office, yesterday. Conn, would you please repeat what you told us? Elaborate as you see fit."

Conn rose. He talked briefly about his studies on Terra to qualify himself as an expert. Then he began describing the wealth of abandoned and still undiscovered Federation war material and the many installations of which he had learned, careful to avoid giving clues to exact locations.

The spaceport; the underground duplicate Force Command Headquarters; the vast underground arsenals and shops and supply depots. Everybody was awed, even his father; he hadn't had time to tell him more than a fraction of it.

Finally, somebody from the long table interrupted:

"Well, Conn; how about Merlin? That's what we're interested in."

Wade Lucas snorted indignantly.

"He's telling you about real things, things worth millions of sols, and you want him to talk about that idiotic fantasy!"

There was an angry outcry. Nobody actually shouted *To the stake with the blasphemer!* but that was the general idea. Judge Ledue was rapping loudly for order.

"I don't know the exact location of Merlin." Conn strove to make himself heard. "The whole subject's classified top secret. But I am certain that Merlin exists, if not on Poictesme then somewhere in the Alpha System, and I am equally certain that we can find it."

Cheers. He waited for the hubbub to subside. Lucas was trying to yell above it.

"You admit you couldn't learn anything about this so-called Merlin, but you're still certain it exists?"

"Why are you certain it doesn't?"

"Why, the whole thing's absurdly fantastic!"

"Maybe it is, to a layman like you. I studied computers, and it isn't to me."

"Well, take all these elaborate preparations against space attack you were telling us about. I think Colonel Zareff, here, who served in the Alliance Army, will bear me out that such an attack was plainly impossible."

Zareff started to agree, then realized that he was aiding and comforting the enemy. "Intelligence lag," he said. "What do you expect, with General Headquarters thirty parsecs from the fighting?"

"Yes. A computer can only process the data that's been taped into it," Conn said. That was a point he wanted to ram home, as forcibly and as often as possible. "I suppose Merlin classified an Alliance attack on Poictesme as a low-order probability, but war is the province of chance; Clausewitz said that a thousand years ago. Foxx Travis wasn't the sort of commander to let himself get caught, even by a very low-order probability."

"Well how do you explain the absence, after forty years, of any mention, in any history of the War, of Merlin? How do you get around that?"

"I don't have to. How do you get around it?"

"Huh?" Lucas was startled.

"Yes. Stories about Merlin were all over Poictesme, all through the Third Force, even to the enemy. Say the stories were unfounded; say Merlin never existed. Yet the belief in Merlin was an important historical fact, and no history of the War gives it so much as a footnote." He paused for effect, then continued: "That can mean only one thing. Systematic suppression, backed by the whole force of the Terran Federation. A gigantic conspiracy of silence!"

Brother! If they swallow that, I have it made; they'll swallow anything!

They did, all but Lucas. He banged his fist on the table.

"Now I've heard everything!" he shouted in disgust.

"Not quite everything, Doctor," Morgan Gatworth said. "You will hear, one of these days, that we have found Merlin."

"Yes, that'll be the day!" Lucas sprang to his feet, his chair toppling behind him. He shoved it aside with his foot. "I'm not going to argue with you. Conn Maxwell gave you a thousand-year-old quotation; I'll give you another, from Thomas Paine: 'To argue with those who have renounced the use and authority of reason is as futile as to administer medicine to the dead.' I'll add this. Conn Maxwell knows better than this balderdash he's been spouting to you. I don't know what his racket is, and I'm not staying to find out. You will, though-to your regret."

He turned and strode from the room. There was a moment's silence, after the door slammed behind him. Too bad, Conn thought. He would have made a good friend. Now he was going to make a very nasty enemy.

"Well, let's get to business," his father said. "We don't have to argue about the existence of Merlin; we know that. Let's discuss the question of finding it."

"I still think it's somewhere off-planet," Lorenzo Menardes said. "The moons of Pantagruel...."

Evidently he'd read something, or seen an old film, about the moons of Pantagruel.

"No, that's too far; they'd keep it where they could use it."

"The old GHQ," Lester Dawes suggested. "Suppose it's down under that, like the place Rodney found under Tenth Army."

"I hope not," Gathworth said. "The Planetary Government took that over."

"Well, wherever it is, finding it is going to be expensive," Rodney Maxwell said. "Now, to finance the search, I propose we use this information my son brought back from Terra. Doctor Lucas was right about one thing; that's worth millions of sols. Well, I propose, also, that we set up a company and get it chartered; a prospecting company, to operate under the Abandoned Property Act of 867. My son and I will contribute this information as our share in the capitalization of the company. The work of opening these Federation installations can go on concurrently with the search for Merlin, and the profits can finance it."

Silence for a moment, then a bedlam of cheering.

"Well, let's get organized," Gatworth said. "What will we call this company?"

A number of voices shouted suggestions. Rodney Maxwell managed to get recognition and partial silence.

"It is of the first importance," he said, "that we keep our real objective-Merlin-as close a secret as possible. The Planetary Government would like to get hold of it-and I leave you to ask yourselves how far Jake Vyckhoven and his cronies are to be trusted with anything like that-and I have no doubt the Federation might try to take it away from us."

"Couldn't do it, Rodney," Judge Ledue objected. "Everything the Federation abandoned in the Trisystem is public domain now. We have a Federation Supreme Court ruling —"

"What's legality to the Federation?" Klem Zareff demanded. "They fought a criminally illegal war of aggression against my people."

Down the table, somebody started singing "Rally Round the Banner, the Banner Black and Green."

"Well, I think it's a good idea to keep quiet about it, myself," Kurt Fawzi said.

"All right," Rodney Maxwell said. "Then we don't want this company to sound like anything but another salvage company. I suggest we call it Litchfield Exploration & Salvage."

"Good name, Rodney," Dawes approved. "That a motion? I second it."

Unanimously carried. They had a name, now, anyhow. Everybody began suggesting other topics for consideration-capitalization, application for charter, election of officers, stock issues. Conn paid less and less attention. Industrial finance and organization wasn't his subject, either. His father was plunging happily into it as though he had been promoting companies all his life. Conn sat and doodled with his six-color pen, mostly spherical hyperspace ships.

"We can't get all this cleared up now," Lester Dawes was protesting. "Your Honor, I mean, Mr. Chairman; I suggest that committees be appointed...."

More hassling; everybody wanted to be on all the committees. Finally, they appointed enough committees to include everybody.

"Well, that seems to be cleared up," Judge Ledue said, "I suggest a meeting day after tomorrow evening; the committees should have everything set up, and we should be able to organize ourselves and elect permanent officers. Is there anything else to discuss, or do I hear a motion to adjourn?"

Somebody thought they ought to have some idea of what the first operation would be.

"You heard me mention a spaceport," Conn said. "I can tell you, now, that it's over on Barathrum, inside the crater of an extinct volcano. I think we ought to have a look at that, first of all."

"I know you seemed to think yesterday that Merlin is off-planet," Fawzi said, "I'm inclined to disagree, Conn. I think it's right here on Poictesme."

"We ought to nail that spaceport down first," Conn argued.

"Conn, you mentioned an underground duplicate of Travis's general headquarters," Zareff said. "They thought we'd possibly send a fleet here to blitz Poictesme, or they wouldn't have built that. And this underground headquarters would be the safest place on the planet; they'd make sure of that. Staff brass don't like to get caught out in the rain, not when it's raining hellburners and planetbusters. Merlin would be too big to take there along with them, so they'd put it there in the first place."

That made sense. If he'd been Foxx Travis, and if there had been a Merlin, that was exactly where he'd have put it himself. But there was no Merlin, and he wanted a ship. He argued mulishly for a little, then saw that it was hopeless and gave in.

"I want to find Merlin as much as any of you," he said. "More. Merlin was the only thing I was trained for. We'll look there first."

Somebody asked where, approximately, this underground Force Command headquarters was.

"Why, it's in the Badlands, over between the Blaubergs and the east coast."

"Great Ghu! We'll need an army to go in there!" Tom Brangwyn said. "That's where all these outlaws have been coming from, Blackie Perales and all."

"Then we'll get an army together," Klem Zareff said happily. "Might make a little of that reward money that's been offered."

"We'll need more than that. Well need excavation equipment, and labor. Lots of labor," Conn said. "It's a couple of hundred feet below the surface; from the plans, I'd say they just dug a big pit, built the headquarters in it, and filled it in. There are two entrances, a vertical shaft and a horizontal tunnel."

"When they pulled out, they probably filled the shaft and vitrified the rock at the outer ends," his father added. "That was what they did at Tenth Army."

Another idea hit him. "Mr. Mayor, do you think you could set up some kind of a public-works program here in Litchfield? We can't start this till after the wine-pressing's over, and we'll need a lot of labor, as I pointed out. Now, it's important that we keep all our projects a secret until we can get our claims filed. If we start this municipal fix-up-and-clean-up program, we can give work to a lot of these drifters who haven't been able to get jobs on the plantations, get them organized into gangs, and keep them together till we're ready for the Force Command job."

Lorenzo Menardes supported the idea. "And while they were boondoggling around in Litchfield, we could pick out the best workers, get rid of the incompetents, and train a few supervisors. That's going to be one of our worst headaches; getting capable supervisors."

"You telling me?" Rodney Maxwell asked. "That was what I was wondering about: where we'd get gang-bosses. And another thing; this municipal housecleaning would mask our real preparations."

"Well, we need something like that," Fawzi said. "We've needed it for a long time. I guess it took Conn, coming home from Terra, to see how badly we've let the town get run down. Franz, suppose you and Tom Brangwyn and Lorenzo form a committee on that. Look around, see what needs fixing up worst, and set up a project. Who's city engineer now?"

"Abe O'Leary; he died six years ago," Dawes said. "You never appointed his successor."

"Well, I guess I never got around to that," the mayor of Litchfield admitted.

When the meeting finally adjourned, they went up and got in the car; his father lifted it straight up to thirty thousand feet and started circling. An aircar was one place where they could talk safely.

"Conn, I was kind of worried, down there. You were being a little too positive. You know, you're only twenty-three. As long as you agree with those people, you're a brilliant young man;

you start getting ideas of your own, and you're just a half-baked kid. You let the older and wiser heads run things. You can't begin to hope to foul things up the way they can. Look at all the experience they've had."

"But we've got to have a ship. Everything depends on that."

"I know it does. We'll get a ship. Let Kurt Fawzi and Klem Zareff and the rest of them have this duplicate Force Command thing first, though. Keep them happy. As soon as we have that opened, you can take a gang and run over to Barathrum and grab your spaceport. Wait till they find out that Merlin isn't at Force Command Duplicate. Then you can convince them it's really on Koshchei."

VI

The car Rodney Maxwell got out of the hangar the next morning wasn't the one he and Conn had gone to the meeting in; it was the one he had flown in from Tenth Army HQ at noon of the previous day. An Army reconnaissance job, slim and needlelike, completely enclosed, looking more like a missile than a vehicle, and armored in dazzling, iridescent collapsium. There was something to living on Poictesme, at that; only a millionaire on Terra could have owned a car like that.

"Nice," Conn said. "Where did you dig it?"

"Where we're going, Tenth Army."

"I'll bet she'll do Mach Three."

"Better than that. I've never had her above 2.5, but the airspeed gauge is marked up to four. And she has everything: all kinds of detection instruments, cameras, audiovisual pickups, armament. And the armor; you can take her through any kind of radiation."

The armor was only a couple of micromicrons thick, but it would stop anything. It was collapsed matter, the electron shells of the atoms collapsed upon the nuclei, the atoms in actual contact. That plating made eighth-inch sheet steel as heavy as twelve-inch armor plate, and in texture and shielding properties, lead was like sponge by comparison.

They climbed in, and Rodney Maxwell snapped on the screens that served as windows. Conn leaned back and looked at the underside view in a screen on the roof of the car, as his father started the lift-engine.

"Still think it's worth the price, son?" his father asked.

The price had begun to rise; even so, he was afraid that what they had paid so far was only the down payment. Dinner last evening. Flora, who had evidently been talking to Wade Lucas, shouting accusations at them; his mother fleeing from the table in tears. As the car rose, he reached out and turned on and adjusted the telescreen for the under-view.

"Keep your eye on that, Father," he said. "That's what we're paying to get rid of."

A distillery, bigger than the Menardes plant, long closed and now half roofless and crumbling. Rows of warehouses, empty after the War until taken over by homeless vagrants. Jerry-built shanties with rattletrap aircars grounded around them. Tramptown, a festering sore on the south side of Litchfield.

"If we put this over," he continued, "all those tramps will have steady work and good homes. We can have a park there, with fountains that'll work. Maybe even Flora and Mother will think we've done something worth doing."

"It'll be kind of hard to take in the meantime, though, but if you can take it, I can." Rodney Maxwell turned off the underside teleview screen and put on the forward one. "See that little pink spot over there? Sunrise on the east side of Snagtooth; Tenth Army's just behind us. Now, let's see if this airspeed gauge is telling the truth or just bragging."

Sudden acceleration pushed them back in their seats. The calibrations on the gauge rose swiftly; the pink-lighted peak grew swiftly in the teleview screen. The gauge hadn't been bragging, it had been understating; the car had more speed than the instrument could register.

Two and a half minutes from Litchfield, they were decelerating and swinging slowly around Snagtooth, looking down on a tilted plateau that ended on the western side in a sheer drop of almost a thousand feet.

There were ruinous buildings on it: barracks and storehouses and offices, an airship dock and an air-traffic control tower from which all the glass had long ago vanished, a great steel telecast tower that had fallen, crushing a couple of buildings. Young trees had already grown among the wreckage.

"Look over there, on the slope below it; there's one entrance to the shelters." There was a clearing among the evergreens, half a mile from the buildings, and raw earth, and a couple of big scows grounded near. "They bulldozed rock and earth over the end of the tunnel. Then, there's another one down on that bench, a couple of hundred feet below the edge of the plateau. They blasted rock down over that. The main entrance is a vertical shaft under that pre-stressed concrete dome. That was chapel, auditorium, or something. They just covered it with sheet metal and poured a foot of concrete on top."

They floated down above the broken roofs and crumbling walls, and grounded in the area between the main administration building and the offices, back of the ship docks. Once, he supposed, it had been a lawn. Then it had been a jungle. Now it was a scuffed, littered, bare-trodden work-yard. Men were straggling out of the administration building, lighting pipes and cigarettes; they all wore new but work-soiled infantry battle dress. All of them waved and shouted greetings; one, about Conn's own age, approached. As he got out, Conn saw the resemblance to Lester Dawes, the banker, before he recognized Anse Dawes, who had been one of his closest friends six years ago. They shook hands and pounded each other on the back.

"Hey, you're looking great, Conn!" They all told him that; he'd begin to believe it pretty soon. "Sorry I couldn't make the party, but somebody had to sit on the lid here, and Jerry Rivas and I cut cards for it and Jerry won."

"You didn't tell me Anse was with you," he reproached his father. Rodney Maxwell said he'd been saving that for a surprise.

When Conn asked Anse what was the matter with the bank, he said: "For the birds; I'd as soon count sheets of toilet paper as this stuff we're using for money. Sooner. Toilet paper can be used for something, and this paper money's too stiff. Maybe some of this stuff we're digging here isn't worth much, but at least it's real."

That was something else the Maxwell Plan would have to take care of. Gresham's Law was running hog-wild on Poictesme. A Planetary Government sol was worth about ten centisols, Federation, and aside from deposit boxes, woolen socks under the mattress, and tin cans buried in the corner of the cellar, Federation currency was nonexistent.

"Had breakfast yet?" Rodney Maxwell asked.

"Oh, hours ago. I was out and shot another spikenose; it's hanging up back of the kitchen, waiting for the cook to skin it and cut it up." He grinned at Conn. "You don't get this kind of hunting in a bank, either."

"Jerry still inside? I want to see him. Suppose you take Conn around and show him the sights. And don't worry about him bumping you out of a job. Worry about the six or eight extra jobs you'll have to do besides your own, from now on."

Conn and Anse crossed the yard and entered one of the office buildings, through a big breach in the wall. Anse said: "I did that myself; 90-mm tank gun. When we want a wall out of the way, we get it out of the way." Inside were a lot of lifters and skids and power shovels and things; laborers were assembling for work assignments. Most of them had been with his father six years ago and he knew them. They hadn't done any growing up in the meantime. They climbed into an airjeep and floated out over the edge of the plateau, letting down past the sheer cliff to where the lower lateral shaft had been opened. A great deal of rock had been shoveled and bulldozed away to expose it; it was twenty feet high and forty wide. Anse simply steered the jeep inside and up the tunnel.

There were occasional lights on at the ceiling. Anse said they were all powered from their own nuclear-electric conversion units. "We don't have the central power on here; there's a big mass-energy converter, but we're tearing it down to ship out."

That was something they could get a good price for. Maybe even one-tenth of what it was worth. At least they wouldn't have to sell it by the ton.

The tunnel ended in an enormous room a couple of hundred feet square and fifty high. There was a wide aisle up the middle; on either side, contragravity equipment was massed. Tanks with long 90-mm guns. Combat cars. Small airboats. Rank on rank of air-cavalry single-mounts, egg-shaped things just big enough for a man to sit in, with quadruple machine guns in front and flame-jets behind. Ambulances armored against radiation; decontamination units; mobile workshops; mobile kitchens. Troop carriers, jeeps, staff cars; power shovels, manipulators, lifters. All waiting, for forty years, to swarm out as soon as the bombs that never came stopped falling.

They floated the jeep along hallways beyond, and got down to look into rooms. Work was already going on in the power plant; a gang under a slim young man whom Anse introduced as Mohammed Matsui were using repair-robots to get canisters of live plutonium out of a reactor. Workshops. Laundries. Storerooms. Kitchens, some stripped and a few still intact. A hospital. Guardhouse and lockup.

More storerooms on the level above, reached by returning to the vehicle hangar and lifting to an upper entrance. By this time, gangs were at work there, too, moving contragravity skids in empty and out loaded.

"The CO here must have had squirrel blood," Anse said. "I think when the evacuation orders came through he just gathered up everything there was topside and crammed it down here, any old way. Honest to Ghu, this place was packed solid when we found it. Nobody'd believe it."

"Wait till you see the next one."

"You mean there's another place like this?"

"You can say so. You can say a twenty-megaton thermonuclear is like a hand grenade, too."

Anse Dawes simply didn't believe that.

When they got back to the Administration Building on top, they found Rodney Maxwell, Jerry Rivas, the general foremen, and half a dozen gang foremen, in consultation.

"We're getting a hundred and fifty more men and ten farm scows from Litchfield," his father said. "Dave McCade's coming out from our yard, and Tom Brangwyn's sending one of his deputies to help boss them. Well have to keep an eye on this crowd; they're all Tramptown hoodlums, but that's the best we can get. We're going to have to get this place cleaned out in a hurry. We only have about two weeks till the wine-pressing's over, and then we want to start the next operation. Conn, did you see all that engineering equipment, down on the bottom level?"

"Yes. I think we ought to leave a lot of that here-the shovels and bulldozers and manipulators and so on. We can move it direct to Force Command. How are we fixed for blasting explosives?"

"Name it and we have it. Cataclysmite, FJ-7, anything you want."

"We'll need a lot of it."

"We're going to have to get a ship. I mean a contragravity ship, a freighter; first, to move this stuff out of here, and then to move the stuff out of Force Command. And we want it mounted with heavy armament, too. We not only want a freighter, we want a fighting ship."

"You think so?"

"I'm sure of it," Rodney Maxwell said. "Where we're going is full of outlaws; there must be hundreds of them holing up over there. That's where all the trouble on the east coast comes from. Now, outlaws are sure-thing players. They want to be alive to spend their loot, and they won't tackle anything that's too tough for them. A lot of guards and combat equipment may look like a loss on the books, but the books won't show how much of a loss you might take if you didn't have them. I want this operation armed till it'll be too much for all the outlaws on the planet to tackle."

That made sense. It also made sense out of the billions of sols the Federation had spent preparing for an invasion that never came. If it had come and found them unprepared, the loss might have been the war itself.

The scows and the newly hired workers began arriving a little after noon. The scows had been borrowed from plantations where the crop had been gotten in; there were melon leaves and bits of vine in the bottoms. The workers were a bleary-eyed and unsavory lot; Conn had a suspicion, which Brangwyn's deputy confirmed, that they had been collected by mass vagrancy arrests in Tramptown. As soon as they started arriving, Jerry Rivas hurried down to the old provost-marshal's headquarters and came back with a lot of rubber billy-clubs, which he issued to his gang-bosses, regular and temporary. A few times they had to be used. By evening, however, the insubordinate and troublesome had been quieted. They would all steal anything they could put in their pockets, but that was to be expected. By evening, too, the contents of the underground treasure trove was moving out in a steady stream, and scows were shuttling to and from Litchfield.

Rodney Maxwell was going back to town after lunch the next day. Conn wanted to know if he should go along.

"No, you stay here; help keep things moving. Remember what I told you about the older and wiser heads? Let me handle them. I've been around them, heaven pity me, longer than you have. Just give me an audiovisual of your proxy and I'll vote your stock."

"How much stock do I have, by the way?"

"The same as I have-ten thousand five hundred shares of common, at twenty centisols a share. But watch where it goes after we open Force Command."

His father was back, two days later, to report:

"We're organized. Kurt Fawzi's president, of course, and does he love it. That'll keep him out of mischief. Dolf Kellton's secretary; he has an office force at the Academy and can conscript students to help. He's organizing a research team from his seniors and post-grad students to work in the Planetary Library at Storisende. There are a lot of old Third Force records there; he may find something useful. Of course, Lester Dawes is treasurer."

"What are you?"

"Vice-president in charge of operations. That's what I spent all yesterday log-rolling, baby-kissing and cigar-passing to get."

"And what am I, if it's a fair question?"

"You have a very distinguished position; you are a non-office-holding stockholder. The only other one is Judge Ledue; as a member of the judiciary, he did not feel it proper to accept official position in a private corporation. Tom Brangwyn's Chief of Company Police; Klem Fawzi is Commander of the Company Guards. And we have a law firm in Storisende lined up to handle our charter application. Sterber, Flynn & Chen-Wong. Sterber's married to Jake Vyckhoven's sister, Flynn's son is married to the daughter of the Secretary of the Treasury, and Chen-Wong is a nephew of the Chief Justice. All of them are directly descended from members of Genji Gartner's original crew."

"You don't anticipate any trouble about getting the charter?"

"Not exactly. And Lester Dawes is in Storisende now, trying to find us a contragravity ship. There are about a dozen in the hands of receivers for bankrupt shipping companies; he might find one that's still airworthy. Oh; you remember how I insisted on absolute secrecy about our Merlin objective? That's working out better than my fondest expectations. It's leaking like a machine-gunned water tank, and everybody it leaks to is positive that we know exactly where Merlin is or we wouldn't be trying to keep it a secret."

Three days later, Conn hitched a ride on a freight-scow to Litchfield. From the air, he could see a haze of bonfire smoke over High Garden Terrace, and a gang of men at work. There were more men at work on the Mall and along the streets on either side. He went up from the yard below the house, where the scow was being unloaded, and found his mother in the living room watching a screen play with one eye and keeping the other on a soulless machine like a miniature contragravity tank, which was going over the carpet with a vacuum cleaner and taking swipes at the furniture with a rotary dustmop. She was glad to see him, and then became troubled.

"Conn, when Flora comes home, you won't argue with her, will you?"

"Only in self-defense." That was the wrong thing to say. He changed it to, "No; I won't argue with her at all," and then quoted Wade Lucas quoting Thomas Paine. Then he had to assure his mother a couple of times that there really was a Merlin, and then assure her that it wouldn't get loose and hurt anybody if he did find it.

In the middle of his assurances about the harmlessness of Merlin, the housecleaning-robot began knocking things off the top of a table.

"Oscar! You stop that!" his mother yelled.

Oscar, deaf as the adder, kept on. Conn yelled at his mother to use her control; she remembered that she had one, a thing like an old-fashioned pocket watch, around her neck on a chain, and got the robot stopped.

No wonder she was afraid of Merlin.

He took advantage of the interruption to get to his room and change clothes, then went up to the hangar and got out an air-cavalry mount. About fifty men were working on High Garden Terrace, pruning and trimming and leveling the lawns. There was a big vitrifier on the Mall-even at five hundred feet he could feel the heat from it-chuffing and clanking and pouring lavalike molten rock for a new pavement. And all the nymphs and satyrs and dryads and fauns and centaurs had had their pedestals rebuilt and were sand-blasted clean.

He landed on the top of the Airlines Building and rode a lift down to the office where Kurt Fawzi neglected the affairs of his shipline agency, his brokerage business, and the city of Litchfield. The afternoon habitués had begun to gather-Raymond Fitch, the used-vehicles dealer, Lorenzo Menardes, Judge Ledue, Tom Brangwyn, Klem Zareff. Fawzi was on the screen, talking to somebody with sandy hair and a suit that didn't seem to be made of any sort of Federation Armed Forces material, about warehouse facilities. The addresses they were mentioning were in Storisende.

"No, Leo, I don't know when," Fawzi was saying, "but don't you worry. You just have space for it, and we'll fill it up. And don't ask me what sort of stuff. You know what a salvage operation's like; you just haul out the stuff as you come to it."

Tom Brangwyn, lounging in one of the deep chairs, looked up.

"Hello, Conn. We're having a time. Another two hundred tramps came in on the *Countess* this morning, and Ghu only knows how many in their own vehicles, and they all seem to think if there's work for some there ought to be work for all, and some of them are getting nasty."

"We can use some more out at the dig. The ones you sent out Thursday are doing all right, once they found out we weren't taking any foolishness."

Fawzi turned away from the screen. "Well, Conn, we're in," he said. "The charter was granted this morning; now we're Litchfield Exploration & Salvage, Ltd. And Lester Dawes has found us a contragravity ship."

"How much will it cost us?"

Fawzi began to laugh. "Conn, this'll slay you! She isn't costing us a centisol. You know those old ships on Mothball Row, back of the old West End ship docks at Storisende?"

Conn nodded. He'd seen them before he had gone away, and from the *City of Asgard* coming in —a lot of old Army Transport craft, covered with muslin and sprayed with protectoplast. The Planetary Government had taken them over after the War and forgotten them.

"Well, Lester's getting one of them for us under the old 878 Commercial Enterprise Encouragement Act. She's an Army combat freighter, regimental ammunition ship. Of course, she still has armament; we'll have to pay to get that off."

"Why?"

Fawzi looked at him in surprise. "It would only be in the way and add weight. We want her for a cargo ship, don't we?"

"That's what she was built for. What kind of armament?"

Fawzi didn't know. Klem Zareff did.

"Four 115-mm rifles, two fore and two aft. A pair of lift-and-drive missile launchers amidships. And a secondary gun battery of 70-mm's and 50-mm auto-cannon. I know the class; we captured a few of them. Good ships."

Fawzi was horrified. "Why, that's more firepower than the whole Air Patrol. Look, the Government won't like our having anything like that."

"They're giving her to us, aren't they?" Menardes asked.

"Gehenna with what the Government likes!" the old Rebel swore. "If they'd put a few of those ships into commission, they could wipe out these outlaws and a private company wouldn't need an armed ship."

"May I use your screen, Kurt?" Conn asked.

When Fawzi nodded, he punched out the combination of the operating office at Tenth Army, and finally got his father on. He told him about the ship.

"There's talk about tearing the armament out," he added.

"Is that so, now? Well, I'll call Lester Dawes before he can get started on it. I think I'll go in to Storisende tomorrow and see the ship for myself. See what I can do about ammunition for those guns, too."

"But, Rod," Fawzi protested, joining the conversation, "we don't want to start a war."

"No. We want to stay out of one. You don't do that by disarming. We're taking that ship down into the Badlands. Remember?" Rodney Maxwell said. "Ever hear the name Blackie Perales?"

Fawzi had. He stopped arguing about armament. Instead, he began worrying about how much the civic clean-up campaign was costing Litchfield.

"You think we really need that, Rod?"

"Of course we do. You'd be surprised how much labor we're going to need, and how hard up we're going to be for capable supervisors. This thing's a training program, Kurt, and we'll need every man we train on it."

"But it's costing like Niflheim, Rod. We're going to bankrupt the city."

"Worse than it is now, you mean? Oh, don't worry, Kurt. As soon as we find Merlin, everything'll be all right."

Franz Veltrin came in, shortly after Rodney Maxwell was off the screen. He dropped his audiovisual camera and sound recorder on the table, laid his pistol-belt on top of them and took a drink of brandy, downing it with the audible satisfaction of a thirsty horse at a trough. Then he looked around accusingly.

"Somebody's been talking!" he declared. "I've had all the news services on the planet on my screen today; they all want the story about what's happening here. They've heard we know where Merlin is; that Conn Maxwell found out on Terra."

"They just put two and two together and threw seven," Conn said. "A *Herald-Guardian* ship-news reporter interviewed me when I got in, and found out I'd been studying cybernetics and computer theory on Terra. What did you tell them?"

"Complete denial. We don't know a thing about Merlin. Naturally, they didn't believe me. A bunch of them are coming out here tomorrow. What are we going to tell them? We'll all have to have the same story."

"I," said Judge Ledue, "am not going to be interviewed, I am leaving town till they're gone."

"Why don't you steer them onto Wade Lucas?" Conn asked. "If you want anything denied, he'll do it for you."

Everybody thought that was a wonderful idea, except Klem Zareff, and he waited until Conn was ready to go and rode up to the landing stage with him.

"Conn, I know this Lucas is going to marry your sister," he began, "but how much do you know about him?"

"Not much. He seems like a nice chap. I don't hold what he said at the meeting against him. I suppose if I'd come from off-planet, I wouldn't believe in Merlin either."

"Hah! But doesn't he believe in Merlin?"

"He makes noises like it."

"You know what I think?" Klem Zareff lowered his voice to a whisper. "I think he's a Federation spy! I think the Federation's lost Merlin. That's why they haven't come back to get it long ago."

"Pretty big thing to mislay."

"It could happen. There'd only be a few scientists and some high staff officers who'd know where it was. Well, say they all went back to Terra on the same ship, and the ship was lost at space. Sabotage, one of our commerce raiders that hadn't heard the War was over, maybe just an ordinary accident. But the ship's lost, and the location of Merlin's lost with her."

"That could happen," Conn agreed seriously.

"All right. So ever since, they've had people here, listening, watching, spying. This Lucas; he showed up here about a year after you went to Terra. And who does he get engaged to? Your sister. And what does he do here? Goes around arguing that there is no Merlin, getting people to argue with him, getting them mad, so they'll blurt out anything they know. I'm an old field officer; I know all the prisoner-interrogation tricks in the book, and that's always been one of the best."

"Then why did he act the way he did at the meeting? All he did there was cut himself off from learning anything more from any of us. In his place, would you have done that? No; you'd have tried to take the lead in hunting for Merlin yourself. Now wouldn't you?"

Zareff was silent, first puzzled, and then hurt. Now he would have to tear the whole idea down and build it over.

Flora was quite friendly when she came home from school. She'd found out, somewhere, that Conn had been the originator of the municipal face-lifting project. He was tempted, briefly, to tell her a little, if not all, of the truth about the Maxwell Plan, then decided against it. The way to keep a secret was to confide it to nobody; every time you did, you doubled, maybe even squared, the chances of exposure.

He told his father, when Rodney Maxwell came in from the dig, about his talk with Klem Zareff.

"How long's he been like that, anyhow?" he asked.

"As long as I've known him. When it comes to melons and wine and bossing tramp labor and taking care of his money and coming in out of the rain, Klem Zareff's as sane as I am. But on the subject of the Terran Federation, he's crazy as a bedbug. What is a bedbug, anyhow?"

"They have them on Terra, in places like Tramptown. They have places like Tramptown on Terra, too."

"Uhuh. I suppose, in Klem's boots, I'd be just as crazy as he is," Rodney Maxwell said. "One minute, he had a wife and two children in Kindelburg, on Ashmodai, and the next minute Kindelburg was a puddle of radioactive slag."

"That was in '51, wasn't it? I read about it," Conn said. "It was a famous victory."

That was from a poem, too.

Rodney Maxwell flew to Storisende early the next morning. Conn rode back to Tenth Army on an empty scow and pitched into the job of getting the stores and equipment out of the underground shelters. More farm-tramps arrived, and had to be pounded into obedience and taught the work. At the same time, Litchfield was getting a steady influx of job-seekers, and a secondary swarm of thugs, grifters and gangsters who followed them. Klem Zareff, having gotten all his melons pressed, came out to Tenth Army, where he selected fifty of the best men from the work-gangs and began drilling them as soldiers to guard the next operation. The manual of arms, drill and salute he taught them was, of course, System States Alliance.

A week later, the ship arrived from Storisende; a hundred and sixty feet, three thousand tons, small enough to be berthed inside a hyperspace transport, and fast enough to get a load of ammunition to troops at the front, unload, and get out again before the enemy could zero in on her, and armed to fight off any Army Air Force combat craft. The delay had been in recruiting officers and crew. The captain and chief engineer were out-of-work shipline officers, the gunner was a former Federation artillery officer, and the crew looked more like pirates than most pirates did.

They christened her the *Lester Dawes*, because Dawes had secured her and because the name began with the initials of Litchfield Exploration & Salvage. From then on, it was a race to see whether the Tenth Army attack-shelters would be emptied before the wine was all pressed, or vice versa.

VII

Fifty-two years before, they had come to the mesa in the Badlands and dug a pit on top of it, a thousand feet in diameter and more than five hundred deep, and in it they built a duplicate of the headquarters for Third Fleet-Army Force Command. They built a shaft a hundred feet in diameter like a chimney at one side, and they ran a tunnel out through solid rock to the head of a canyon half a mile away. Then they buried the whole thing. Twelve years later, when the War was over, they sealed both entrances and went away and left it.

For a month each winter, cold rains from the east lashed the desert; for the rest of the year, it was swept by windblown sand. Wiregrass sprouted, and thornbush grew; Nature, the master-camoufleur, completed the work of hiding the forgotten headquarters. Little things not unlike rabbits scampered over it, and bigger things, vaguely foxlike, hunted them. Hunted men came, too, their aircars skimming low. None of them had the least idea what was underneath.

The mesa-top came suddenly to life, just as the sun edged up out of the east. Conn and his father and Anse Dawes came in first, in the recon-car with which they had scouted and photographed the site a few days before. They circled at a thousand feet, fired a smoke bomb, and then let down near where Conn's map showed the head of the vertical shaft. The rest followed, first a couple of combat cars that circled slowly, scanning the ground, and then the *Lester Dawes* with her big guns and her load of equipment, and behind a queue of boats and scows and heavy engineering equipment on contragravity and troop carriers full of workmen and guards, flanked by air cavalry, which circled above while everything else landed, then scattered out over a fifty-mile radius. Occasionally there was a hammering of machine guns, either because somebody saw something on the ground that might need shooting at or simply because it was a beautiful morning to make a noise.

The ship settled quickly and daintily, while Conn and Anse and Rodney Maxwell sat in the car and watched. Immediately, she began opening like a beetle bursting from its shell, large sections of armor swinging outward. Except for the bridge and the gun turrets, almost the whole ship could be opened; she had been designed to land in the middle of a battle and deliver ammunition when seconds could mean the difference between life and death. Jeeps and lifters and manipulators and things floated out of her. Scows began landing and unloading prefab-hut elements. A water tank landed, and the cook-shed began going up beside it; a lorry came in with scanning and probing equipment, and a couple of men jumped off and huddled over a photoprint copy of one of Conn's maps.

Conn lifted the car again and coasted it half a mile to where the cleft in the mesa started. There were half a dozen claw-armed manipulators already there, and two giant power shovels. Jerry Rivas and one of the engineers Kurt Fawzi had hired had gotten out of a jeep and were looking at another photoprint of the map. Rivas pointed to the head of the canyon, where a mass of rock had slid down.

"That's it; you can still see where they put off the shots."

The canyon was long enough and wide enough for the *Lester Dawes* to land in it; she could be loaded directly from the tunnel. The manipulators began moving in, wrestling with the larger chunks of rock and dragging or carrying them away. Power shovels began grunting and clanking and rumbling; dust rose in a thick column. Toward midmorning, the troop carriers which served as school buses in Litchfield arrived, loaded with more workmen. A lorry lettered Storisende Herald-Guardian came in, hovered over the canyon, and began transmitting audiovisuals. More news-folk put in an appearance.

The earth and rock at the top of the tunnel entrance fell away, revealing the vitrified stone lintel; everybody cheered and dug harder. More aircars arrived, getting in each other's and everybody else's way. Raymond Fitch, Lester Dawes, Lorenzo Menardes and Morgan Gatworth. Dolf Kellton, playing hookey from school. Kurt Fawzi; he landed in the canyon and watched every shovelful of rock lifted, as though trying to help with mental force. Tom Brangwyn, with a score of the Home Guard to reinforce the Company Police. Klem Zareff called in his air cavalry to help control the sightseers. Nobody was making trouble; they were just getting in the way.

At eleven, Rodney Maxwell went aboard the *Lester Dawes* to use the radio and telescreen equipment. By then, two time zones west in Storisende, the Claims Office was opening; he filed preliminary claim to an underground installation with at least two entrances in uninhabited country, and claimed a ten-mile radius around it. By that time, the gang working on top had uncovered a vitrified slab over the hundred-foot circle of the vertical shaft and were cracking it with explosives. According to the scanners, it was full of loose rubble for a hundred feet down. Below that, the microrays hit something impenetrable.

Toward midafternoon, the tunnel in the canyon was cleared. It had been vitrified solid; the scanners reported that it was plugged for ten feet. A contragravity tank let down in front of it, with a solenoid jackhammer mounted where the gun should have been, and began pounding, running a hole in for a blast shot. There were more explosions topside; when Conn took a jeep up to observe progress there, he found the vitrified rock blown completely off the vertical shaft, exposing the rubble that had been dumped into it. The gang on the mesa-top had discovered something else; a grid of auro-copper bussbars buried four feet underground. Ten to one, radio and telescreen signals would be transmitted to that from below, and then probably picked up and rebroadcast from a relay station on one or another of the high buttes in the neighborhood. Time enough to look for that later. He returned to the canyon, where the lateral tunnel was now almost completely open.

When it was clear, they sent a snooper in first. It was a robot, looking slightly like a short-tailed tadpole, six feet long by three feet at the thickest. It transmitted a view of the tunnel as it went slowly in; the air, it found, was breathable, and there were no harmful radiations or other dangers. According to the plans, there should be a big room at the other end, slightly curved, a hundred feet wide by a hundred on either side of the tunnel entrance. The robot entered this, and in its headlight they could see reconnaissance-cars, and contragravity tanks with 90-mm guns. It swerved slightly to the left, and then the screen stopped receiving, the telemetered instruments went dead and the robot's signal stopped.

"Tom," Rodney Maxwell said, "you keep the crowd back. Klem, stay with the screens; I'll transmit to you. I'm going in to see what's wrong."

He started to give Conn an argument when he wanted to accompany him.

"No," Conn said. "I'm going along. What do you think I went to Terra to study robotics for?"

His father snapped on the screen and pickup of the jeep that was standing nearby. "You getting it, Klem?" he asked. "Okay, Conn. Let's go."

Half a mile ahead, at the other end of the tunnel, they could see a flicker of light that grew brighter as they advanced. The snooper still had its light on and was moving about. Once they caught a momentary signal from it. As Rodney Maxwell piloted the jeep, Conn kept talking to Klem Zareff, outside. Then they were at the end of the tunnel and entering the room ahead; it was full of vehicles, like the one on the bottom level at Tenth Army HQ. As soon as they were inside, Klem Zareff's voice in the radio stopped, as though the set had been shot out.

"Klem! What's wrong? We aren't getting you," his father was saying.

The snooper was drifting aimlessly about, avoiding the parked vehicles. Conn used the manual control to set it down and deactivate it, then got out and went to examine it.

"Take the jeep over to the tunnel entrance," he told his father. "Move out into the tunnel a few feet; relay from me to Klem."

The jeep moved over. A moment later his father cried, "He's getting me; I'm getting him. What's the matter with the radio in here? The snooper's all right, isn't it?"

It was. Conn reactivated it and put it up above the tops of the vehicles.

"Sure. We just can't transmit out."

"But only half a mile of rock; that set's good for more than that. It'll transmit clear through Snagtooth."

"It won't transmit through collapsium."

His father swore disgustedly, repeating it to Zareff outside. Conn could hear the old soldier, in the radio, make a similar remark. They should have all expected that, in the first place. If the Third Force High Command was expecting to sit out a nuclear bombardment in this place, they'd armor it against anything.

"Bring the gang in; it's safe as far as we've gotten," his father said. "We'll just have to string wires out."

Conn used his flashlight and found the power unit for the room lights; all the overhead lights were wired to one unit, if wired were the word for gold-leaf circuits cemented to the walls and covered with insulating paint. For the heavy stuff, like the ventilator fans, they'd have to find the central power plant. He looked around the big room, poking into some of the closets that lined it. Radiation-proof clothing. Tools. Arms and ammunition. First-aid kits. Emergency rations. All the vehicles were plated in shimmering collapsium.

The crowd started coming in: the work-gangs selected for the first exploration work, most of them old hands of Rodney Maxwell's; the engineers they had recruited; Mohammed Matsui-he had a gang of his own, the same one he had been using in tearing down the converter at Tenth Army; the stockholders and officials; the press. And everybody else Tom Brangwyn's police hadn't been able to keep out.

The power plant was at the extreme bottom; Matsui began looking it over at once. Above it they found the service facilities-air-and-water plant; pumps for the artesian well; sewage disposal. Then repair ships, and a laboratory, and laundries and kitchens above that.

"Where do you suppose it is?" Kurt Fawzi was asking. "Up at the very top, I suppose. Let's go up and work down; I can't wait till we've found it."

Like a kid on Christmas Eve, Conn thought. And there was no Santa Claus, and Christmas had been abolished.

The place was built in concentric circles, level above level. Combat equipment nearest the tunnel exit and nearest the vertical shaft, and ambulances and decontamination units and equipment for relief and rebuilding next. Storerooms, mile on circular mile of them. Not the hasty packrat cramming he'd seen at Tenth Army; everything had been brought in in order, carefully piled or racked, and then left. More stores for the next three levels up; then living quarters. Enlisted men's and women's quarters, no signs of occupancy. Enlisted kitchens and mess halls, untouched.

Most of the officers' quarters were similarly unused, but here and there some had been occupied. A sloppily made bed. A used cake of soap in the bathroom. An empty bottle in a closet. Officers' commissary stores had been used from and replaced; the officers' mess hall and kitchen had been in constant use, and the officers' club had a comfortably scuffed and lived-in look. There had been a few people there all the time of the War.

"Men and women, all officers or civilians," Klem Zareff said. "Didn't even have enlisted men to cook for them. And we haven't found a scrap of paper with writing on it, or an inch of recorded sound-tape or audiovisual film. Remember those big wire baskets, down at the mass-energy converters? Before they left, they disintegrated every scrap of writing or recording. This is where Merlin is; they were the people who worked with it."

And above, offices. General Staff. War Planning, with an incredibly complex star-map of the theater of war. Judge Advocate General. Inspector General. Service of Supply. They were full of computers, each one firing the hopes of people like Fawzi and Dolf Kellton and Judge Ledue, but they were only special-purpose machines, the sort to be found in any big business office. The Storisende Stock Exchange probably had much bigger ones.

Then they found big ones, rank on rank of cabinets, long consoles studded with lights and buttons, programming machines.

"It's Merlin!" Fawzi almost screamed. "We've found it!"

One of the reporters who had followed them in snatched his radio handphone from his belt and jabbered, then, realizing that the collapsium shielding kept him from getting out with it, he replaced it and bolted away.

"Hold it!" Conn yelled at the others, who were also becoming hysterical. "Wait till I take a look at this thing."

They managed to calm themselves. After all, he should know what it was; wasn't that why he'd gone to school on Terra? They followed him from machine to machine, first hopefully and then fearfully. Finally he turned, shaking his head and feeling like the doctor in a film show, telling the family that there's no hope for Grandpa.

"This is not Merlin. This is the personnel-file machine. It's taped for the records and data of every man and woman in the Third Force for the whole War. It's like the student-record machine at the University."

"Might have known it; this section in here's marked G-1 all over everything; that's personnel. Wouldn't have Merlin in here," Klem Zareff was saying.

"Well, we'll just keep on hunting for it till we do find it," Kurt Fawzi said. "It's here some-where. It has to be."

The next level up was much smaller. Here were the offices of the top echelons of the Force Command Staff. They, unlike the ones below, had been used; from them, too, every scrap of writing or film or record-tape had vanished.

Finally, they entered the private office of Force-General Foxx Travis. It had not only been used, it was in disorder. Ashtrays full, many of the forty-year-old cigarette ends lipstick tinted. Chairs shoved around at random. Three bottles on the desk, with Terran bourbon labels; two empty and one with about an inch of whisky left in it. But no glasses.

That bothered Conn. Somehow, he couldn't quite picture the commander and staff of the Third Fleet-Army Force passing bottles around and drinking from the neck. Then he noticed that the wall across the room was strangely scarred and scratched. Dropping his eye to the floor under it, he caught the twinkle of broken glass. They had gathered here, and talked for a long time. Then they had risen, for a final toast, and when it was drunk, they had hurled their glasses against the wall and smashed them.

Then they had gone out, leaving the broken glass and the empty bottles; knowing that they would never return.

VIII

Before they returned to the lower level into which the lateral tunnel entered, Matsui and his gang had the power plant going; the ventilator fans were humming softly, and whenever they pressed a starting button, the escalators began to move. They got the pumps going, and the oxygen-generators, and the sewage disposal system. Until the communication center could be checked and the relay station found, they ran a cable out to the *Lester Dawes*, landed in the canyon, and used her screen-and-radio equipment. Before the Claims Office in Storisende closed, Rodney Maxwell had transmitted in recorded views of the interior, and enough of a description for a final claim. They also received teleprint copies of the Storisende papers. The first story, in an extra edition of the *Herald-Guardian*, was headlined, MERLIN FOUND! That would have been the reporter who bolted off prematurely when they first saw the personnel record machines. Conn wondered if he still had a job. A later edition corrected this, but was full of extravagant accounts of what had been discovered. Merlin or no Merlin, Force Command Duplicate was the biggest abandoned-property discovery since the Third Force left the Trisystem.

The camp they had set up on top of the mesa was used, that night, only by Klem Zareff's guards. Everybody else was inside, eating cold rations when hungry and, when they could keep awake no longer, bedding down on piles of blankets or going up to the barracks rooms above.

The next day they found the relay station which rebroadcast signals from the buried aerial-or wouldn't one say, sub-terrial? —on top of the mesa. As Conn had expected, it was on top of a high butte three and a half miles to the south; it had been so skillfully camouflaged that none of the outlaw bands who roamed the Badlands had found it. After that, Force Command Duplicate was in communication with the rest of Poictesme.

They moved into the staff headquarters at the top; Foxx Travis's office, tidied up, became the headquarters for the company officials and chief supervisors. The workmen quartered themselves in the enlisted barracks, helping themselves liberally to anything they found. The crowds of sightseers kept swarming in, giving Tom Brangwyn's police plenty to do. Tom himself turned the marshal's office in Litchfield over to his chief deputy. Klem Zareff insisted on more men for his guard force. A dozen gunboats, eighty-foot craft mounting one 90-mm gun, several smaller auto-cannon and one missile-launcher, had been found; he took them over immediately, naming them for capital ships of the old System States Navy. It took some argument to dissuade him from repainting all of them black and green. He kept them all in the air, with a swarm of smaller airboats and combat-cars, circling the underground headquarters at a radius of a hundred miles. These patrols reported a general exodus from the region. At least a dozen outlaw bands, all with fast contragravity, had been camped inside the zone. Some fled at once; the rest needed only a few warning shots to send them away. Other bands, looking like legitimate prospecting parties, began to filter into the Badlands. Zareff came to Rodney Maxwell-instead of Kurt Fawzi, the titular head of the company, which was significant-to find out what policy regarding them would be.

"Well, we have no right to keep them out, as long as they stay outside our ten-mile radius," Conn's father said. "And as we're the only thing that even looks like law around here, I'd say we have an obligation to give them protection. Have your boats investigate them; if they're legitimate, tell them they can call on us for help if they need it."

Conn protested, privately.

"There's a lot of stuff around here, in small caches," he said. "Equipment for guerrilla companies, in event of invasion. When work slacks off here, we could pick that stuff up."

"Conn, there's an old stock-market maxim: 'A bear can make money sometimes, and a bull can make money sometimes, but in the long run, a hog always loses.' Let the other people find some of this; it'll all help the Plan. Fact is, I've been thinking of leaking some information, if I can do it without Fawzi and that gang finding out. Do you know a good supply depot or something like that, say over on Acaire, or on the west coast? Big enough to be important, and to start a second prospectors' rush away from us."

"How about one of those hospitals?"

"No; not a hospital. We might use them to talk Wade Lucas into joining us. A lot of medical stores would be a good bait for him. I'm afraid he's going to make trouble if we don't do something about him."

"Well, how about engineering and construction equipment? I know where there's a lot of that, down to the southwest."

"That's farming country; that stuff'll be useful down there. I'll do that."

The next morning, Rodney Maxwell scorched the stratosphere to Storisende in his recon-car. The day after he got back, there was a big discovery of engineering equipment to the southwest and, as he had anticipated, a second rush of prospectors. They had the vertical shaft clear now, and the *Lester Dawes* was shuttling back and forth between Force Command Duplicate and Storisende. Other ships were coming in, now, mostly privately owned freighting ships. They bought almost anything, as fast as it came out.

The stock market had been paralyzed for a couple of days after the discovery of Force Command; nobody seemed to know what to sell and what to hold. Now it was going perfectly insane. Twenty or thirty new companies were being formed; unlike Litchfield Exploration & Salvage, they were all offering their stock to the public. A week after the opening of Force Command, the Stock Exchange reported the first half-million-share day since the War. A week after that, there were two million-share days in succession.

Some of the L. E. & S. stockholders who had come out on the first day began drifting back to Litchfield. Lester Dawes was the first to defect; there was nothing he could do at Force Command, and a great deal that needed his personal attention at the bank. Morgan Gatworth and Lorenzo Menardes and one or two others followed. Kurt Fawzi, however, refused to leave. Merlin was somewhere here at Force Command, he was sure of it, and he wasn't leaving till it was found. Neither were Franz Veltrin or Dolf Kellton or Judge Ledue. Tom Brangwyn resigned as town marshal; Klem Zareff was too busy even to think of Merlin; he had almost as many men under his command, and twice as much contragravity, as he had had when the System States Alliance Army had surrendered.

Conn flew to Litchfield, and found that the public works project had come to a stop at noon of the day when Force Command was entered, and that nothing had been done on it since. The cold vitrifier was still standing in the middle of the Mall, and topside Litchfield was littered in a dozen places with forsaken equipment and half-completed paving. There was no one in Kurt Fawzi's office in the Airlines Building, and the employment office was jammed with migratory workers vainly seeking jobs.

He hunted up Morgan Gatworth, the lawyer.

"Can't some of you get things started again?" he wanted to know. "This place is worse than it was before they started cleaning up."

"Yes, I know." Gatworth walked to an open window and looked down on the littered Mall. "But everybody just dropped everything as soon as you opened Force Command. Kurt Fawzi's not been back here since."

"Well, you're here. Lester Dawes and Lorenzo Menardes are here. Why don't you just take over. Kurt Fawzi couldn't care less what you do; he's forgotten he is mayor of Litchfield. He's forgotten there is a Litchfield."

"Well, I don't like to just move into the mayor's office and take over...."

From somewhere below, a submachine gun hammered. There were yells, pistol shots, and the submachine gun hammered again, a couple of short bursts.

"Some of the farm-tramps who can't get jobs, trying to steal something to eat, I suppose," Conn commented. Gatworth was frowning thoughtfully. He'd only need one more, very slight, push. "Why don't you talk to Wade Lucas. He's got brains, and he's honest-nobody but an honest man would have made himself as unpopular as Lucas has. If you pretend to be disillusioned with this Merlin business it might help convince him."

"He was blaming you and your father for what's been going on here in the last two weeks. Yes. He'd help get things straightened out."

At home, he found his mother simply dazed. She was happy to see him, and solicitous about his and his father's health. It seemed at times, though, as if he were somebody she had never met before. Events had gotten so far beyond her that she wasn't even trying to catch up.

Flora, returning from school, stopped short when she saw him.

"Well! I hope you like what you've done!" she greeted him.

"For a start, yes."

"For a start! You know what you've done?"

"Yes. I don't know what you think I've done, though. Tell me."

"You've turned everything into a madhouse; you've sent this whole world Merlin-crazy. Look at the stock market...."

"You look at it. All I can see is a pack of lunatics playing Russian roulette with five chambers loaded out of six. Some of this so-called stock that's being peddled around isn't worth five millisols a share-Seekers for Merlin, Ltd., closed today at a hundred and seventy. You notice, there isn't any L. E. & S. being traded. If you don't believe me, talk to Lester Dawes; he'll tell you what we think of this market."

"Well, it's your fault!"

"In part it's my fault that any of these quarter-wits have any money to play the market with. They wouldn't have money enough to play a five-centisol slot machine if we hadn't gotten a little business started."

There was just a little truth to that, too. A few woolen socks were coming out from under mattresses, and a few tin cans were being exhumed in cellars, since the new flood of Federation equipment and supplies had gotten on the market. He'd seen a freshly lettered sign on Len Yeniguchi's tailor shop: QUARTER PRICE IN FEDERATION CURRENCY.

That night, however, he had one of the nightmares he used to have as a child—a dream of climbing up onto a huge machine and getting it started, and then clinging, helpless and terrified, unable to stop it as it went faster and faster toward destruction.

Klem Zareff's patrols were encountering larger outlaw bands, the result of gang mergers. They were fighting with prospecting parties, and prospecting parties were fighting one another. Much of this was making the newscasts. One battle, between two regularly chartered prospecting companies, lasted three days, with an impressive casualty list.

Public demands were growing that the Planetary Government do something about the situation; the Government was wondering what to do, or how. There were indignant questions in Parliament. Finally, the Government dragged a couple of armed ships off Mothball Row—a combat freighter like the *Lester Dawes*, and a big assault transport-and began trying to get them into commission.

And, of course, the market boom was still on. The newscasts were full of that, too. He had started worrying about *if* a bust came; now he was worrying about what would happen *when* it did. Another good reason for wanting to get to Koshchei and getting a hypership built; when the bust came, he and his father would want one, very badly.

In any case, it was time to begin getting an expedition ready for Barathrum Spaceport. Quite a few of the new companies had large contragravity craft, and the nascent Planetary Air Navy was approaching a state of being. He wanted to get out there before anybody else did.

Maybe if they got the hypership built soon enough, it would start a second, sound boom that would cushion the crash of the present speculative market when it came, as come it must.

He talked to Klem Zareff about borrowing a couple of the eighty-foot gunboats. Zareff's attitude was automatically negative.

"We mustn't weaken our defense-perimeter; we'd be inviting disaster. Why, this whole country in here is simply swarming with outlaws. They fired on one of our gunboats, the *Werewolf*, yesterday."

He'd heard about that; somebody had launched a missile from the ground, and the *Werewolf* had detonated it with a counter-missile. It had probably been some legitimate prospecting company who'd taken the L. E. & S. craft for a pirate.

"And there was a battle down in the Devil's Pigpen day before yesterday."

That had been outlaws; they had been annihilated by something calling itself Seekers for Merlin, Ltd., whose stock was still skyrocketing on the Exchange. He mentioned that.

"These other prospecting companies are doing a lot of our outlaw-fighting for us, and as long as the country's full of small independent parties, the outlaws go after them and leave us alone."

"Yes, and I have my doubts about a lot of these prospecting companies, and a lot of the outlaws, too," Zareff said. "I think a lot of both are Federation agents; they're waiting till we find Merlin, and then they'll all jump us."

"Well," Conn adjusted his argument to the old Rebel's obsession, "I'll admit that, as a possibility. If so, we'll need heavier weapons than we have. This spaceport on Barathrum might be just the place to get them."

"Yes. It might. Defense armament, and stored ships' weapons. Say, if we grab that place and move all the heavy guns and missiles here, we could stand off anybody." The thought of a fight with minions of the Terran Federation seemed to have shaved ten years off his age in a twinkling. "You take the *Lester Dawes*, and, let's say, three of these gunboats. Let me see. *Goblin*, Fred Karski. And *Vampire*, Charley Gatworth. And *Dragon*, Stefan Jorisson. They're all good men. Home Guard; trained them myself."

"Aren't you coming, Colonel?"

"Oh, I'd like to, Conn, but I can't. I don't want to be away from here; no telling what might happen. But you keep in constant screen-contact; if you get into any trouble, I'll come with everything I can put into the air."

IX

Barathrum was a grim land, naked black and gray. Spines and crags of bare rock jutted up, lava-flows like black glaciers twisting among them. It was split by faults and fissures, pimpled with ash-cones. Except for the seabirds that nested among the cliffs and the few thin patches of green where seeds windblown from the mainland had taken root, it was as lifeless as when some ancient convulsion had thrust it up from the sea, Barathrum was a dead Inferno, untenanted even by the damned; by comparison, the Badlands seemed lushly fertile.

The four craft crossed above the line of white breakers that marked the division of sea and land; the gunboat *Goblin* in the lead, her sisters, *Vampire* and *Dragon* to right and left and a little behind, and the *Lester Dawes* a few miles in the rear. Fred Karski was at the *Goblin's* controls; Conn, beside him, was peering ahead into the teleview screen and shifting his eyes from it to the map and back again.

Somebody behind him was saying that it would be a nice place to be air-wrecked. Somebody else was telling him not to joke about it. From the radio, his father was asking: "Can you see it, yet?"

"Not yet. We're on the right map-and-compass direction; we should before long."

"We're picking up radiation," Fred Karski said. "Way above normal count. I hope the place isn't hot."

"We're getting that, too," Rodney Maxwell said. "Looks like power radiation; something must be on there."

After forty years, that didn't seem likely. He leaned over to look at the omnigeiger, then whistled. If that was normal leakage from inactive power units, there must be enough of them to power ten towns the size of Litchfield.

"Something's operating there," he said, and then realized what that meant. Somebody had beaten them to the spaceport. That would be one of the new companies formed after the opening of Force Command. He was wishing, now, that he hadn't let himself be talked out of coming here first. Older and wiser heads indeed!

Fred Karski whistled shrilly into his radio phone. "Attention everybody! General alert. Prepare for combat; prepare to take immediate evasive action. We must assume that the spaceport is occupied, and that the occupants are hostile. Captain Poole, will you please make ready aboard your ship? Reduce both speed and altitude, and ready your guns and missiles at once."

"Well, now, wait a minute, young fellow," Poole began to argue. "You don't know —"

"No. I don't. And I want all of us alive after we find out, too," Karski replied.

Rodney Maxwell's voice, in the background, said something indistinguishable. Poole said ungraciously, "Well, all right, if you think so...."

The *Lester Dawes* began dropping to the rear and going down toward the ground. Conn returned to the teleview screen in time to see the truncated cone of the extinct volcano rise on the horizon, dwarfing everything around it. Fred Karski was talking to Colonel Zareff, back at Force Command, giving him the radiation count.

"That's occupied," the old soldier replied. "Mass-energy converter going. Now, Fred, don't start any shooting unless you have to, but don't get yourself blown to MC waiting on them to fire the first shot."

The dark cone bulked higher and higher in the screen. It must be seven miles around the crater, and a mile deep; when that thing blew out, ten or fifteen thousand years ago, it must have been something to see, preferably from a ship a thousand miles off-planet. It was so huge that it was hard to realize that the jumbled foothills around it were themselves respectably lofty mountains.

When they were within five miles of it, something twinkled slightly near the summit. An instant later, the missileman, in his turret overhead, shouted:

"Missile coming up; counter-missile off!"

"Grab onto something, everybody!" Karski yelled, bracing himself in his seat.

Conn, on his feet, flung his arms around an upright stanchion and hung on. Fred's hand gave a twisting jerk on the steering handle; the *Goblin* went corkscrewing upward. In the rearview screen, Conn saw a pink fireball blossom far below. The sound and the shock-wave never reached them; the *Goblin* outran them. *Dragon* and *Vampire* were spiraling away in opposite directions. The radio was loud with voices, and a few of the words were almost printable. A gong began clanging from the command post on top of the mesa on the mainland.

"Be quiet, all of you!" Klem Zareff was bellowing. "And get back from there. Back three or four miles; close enough so they won't dare use thermonuclears. Take cover behind one of those ridges, where they can't detect you. Then we can start figuring what the Gehenna to do next."

That made sense. And get it settled who's in command of this Donnybrook, while we're at it, Conn thought. He looked into the rear and sideview screens, and taking cover immediately made even more sense. Two more fireballs blossomed, one dangerously close to the *Dragon*. Guns were firing from the mountaintop, too, big ones, and shells were bursting close to them. He saw a shell land on and another beside one of the enemy gun positions —115-mm's from the *Lester Dawes*, he supposed. He continued to cling to the stanchion, and the *Goblin* shot straight up, and he was expecting to see the sky blacken and the stars come out when the gunboat leveled and started circling down again. The mountainside, he saw, was sending up a lightning-crackling tower of smoke and dust that swelled into a mushroom top.

Klem Zareff, on the radio, was demanding to know who'd launched that.

"We did, sir; *Dragon*," Stefan Jorisson was replying. "We had to get rid of it. We took a hit. Gun turret's smashed, Milt Hennant's dead, and Abe Samuels probably will be before I'm done talking, and if we get this crate down in one piece, it'll do for a miracle till a real one happens."

"Well, be careful how you shoot those things off," his father implored, from the *Lester Dawes*. "Get one inside the crater and we won't have any spaceport."

The *Lester Dawes* vanished behind a mountain range a few miles from the volcano. The *Dragon*, still airborne but in obvious difficulties, was limping after her, and the *Vampire* was covering the withdrawal, firing rapidly but with doubtful effect with her single 90-mm and tossing out counter-missiles. There was another fireball between her and the mountain. Then, when the *Dragon* had followed the *Lester Dawes* to safety, she turned tail and bolted, the *Goblin* following. As they approached the mountains, something the shape of a recon-car and about half the size passed them going in the opposite direction. As they dropped into the chasm on the other side, another nuclear went off at the volcano.

When Conn and Fred left the *Goblin* and boarded the ship, they found Rodney Maxwell, Captain Poole, and a couple of others on the bridge. Charley Gatworth, the skipper of the *Vampire*, Morgan Gatworth's son, was with them, and, imaged in a screen, so was Klem Zareff. One of the other screens, from a pickup on the *Vampire*, showed the *Dragon* lying on her side, her turret crushed and her gun, with the muzzle-brake gone, bent upward. A couple of lorries from the *Lester Dawes* were alongside; as Conn watched, a blanket-wrapped body, and then another, were lowered from the disabled gunboat.

"Fred, how are you and Charley fixed for counter-missiles?" Zareff was asking. "Get loaded up with them off the ship, as many as you can carry. Charley, you go up on top of this ridge above, and take cover where you can watch the mountain. Transmit what you see back to the ship. Fred, you take a position about a quarter way around from where you are now. Don't let them send anything over, but don't start anything yourselves. I'm coming out with everything I can gather up here; I'll be along myself in a couple of hours, and the rest will be stringing in after me. In the meantime, Rodney, you're in command."

Well, that settled that. There was one other point, though.

"Colonel," Conn said, "I assume that this spaceport is occupied by one of these new prospecting companies. We have no right to take it away from them, have we?"

"They fired on us without warning," Karski said. "They killed Milt, and it's ten to one Abe won't live either. We owe them something for that."

"We do, and we'll pay off. Conn, you assume wrong. This gang's been at the spaceport long enough to get the detection system working and put the defense batteries on ready. They didn't do that since this morning, and up to last evening they neglected to file claim. I'll assume they're on the wrong side of the law. They're outlaws, Conn. All the raids along the east coast; everybody's blamed them on the Badlands gangs. I'll admit they're responsible for some of it, but I'll bet this gang at the spaceport is doing most of it."

That was reasonable. Barathrum was closer to the scene of the worst outlaw depredations than the Badlands, not more than an hour at Mach Two. And nobody ever thought of Barathrum as an outlaw hangout. People rarely thought of Barathrum at all. He liked the idea. The only thing against it was that he wanted so badly to believe it.

They brought the body of Milt Hennant aboard, and Abe Samuels, swathed in bandages and immobilized by narcotic injections. A few more of the *Dragon*'s six-man crew had been injured. Jorrisson, the skipper, had one trouser leg slit to the belt and his right thigh splinted and bandaged; he took over the *Lester Dawes'* missile controls, which he could manage sitting in one place. Fred Karski and Charley Gatworth went aboard their craft and lifted out.

For a long time, nothing happened. Conn got out the plans of the volcano spaceport and the photomaps of the surrounding area. The principal entrance, the front door of the spaceport, was the crater of the extinct volcano itself. It was ringed, outside, with launching-sites and gun positions, and according to the data he had, some of the guns were as big as 250-mm. How many outlaws there were to man them was a question a lot of people could get killed trying to answer. The ship docks and shops were down on the level of the crater floor, in caverns, both natural and excavated, that extended far back into the mountain. There were two galleries, one above the other, extending entirely around the inside of the crater near the top; passages from them gave access to the outside gun and missile positions.

With a dozen ships the size of the *Lester Dawes*, about five thousand men, and a CO who wasn't concerned with trivialities like casualties, they could have taken the place in half an hour. With what they had, trying to fight their way in at the top was out of the question.

There was another way in. He had known about it from the beginning, and he was trying desperately to think of a way not to utilize it. It was a tunnel two miles long, running into some of the bottom workshops and storerooms back of the ship berths from a big blowhole or small crater at the foot of the mountain. According to the fifty-year-old plans, it was big enough to take a gunboat in, and on paper it looked like a royal highway straight to the heart of the enemy's stronghold.

To Conn, it looked like a wonderful place to commit suicide. He'd only had a short introductory course, in one semester, in military and protective robotics, just enough to give him a foundation if he wanted to go into that branch of the subject later. It was also enough to give him an idea of the sort of booby-traps that tunnel could be filled with. He knew what he'd have put into it if he'd been defending that place.

Colonel Zareff had sent one last message from Force Command when he lifted off with a flight of recon-cars. After that, he maintained a communication blackout. It was an hour and a half before he got close enough to be detected from the outlaw stronghold. Immediately, the volcano began spewing out missiles. Poole hastily took the *Lester Dawes* ten miles down the rift-valley in sixty seconds, while Stefan Jorisson put out a nuclear-warhead missile and left it circling about where the ship had been. From their respective positions, Fred Karski and Charley Gatworth filled the airspace midway to the volcano with counter-missiles, each loaded with four rockets. There were explosions, fireballs in the air and rising cumulus clouds of varicolored smoke and dust. Only about half the enemy missiles reached the *Lester Dawes'* former position.

When their controllers, back at the volcano, couldn't see the ship in their screens, the missiles bunched together. Immediately, Jorisson sent his missile up to join them and detonated it. Including his own, eight nuclear weapons went off together in a single blast that shook the ground like an earthquake and churned the air like a hurricane. Klem Zareff came on-screen at once.

"Now what did you do?" he demanded. "Blew the whole place up, didn't you?"

Rodney Maxwell told him. Zareff laughed. "They might just think they got the ship; all the pickups would be smashed before they could see what really happened. You're about ten miles south of that? Be with you in a few minutes."

They got a screen on for his rearview pickup. Zareff had with him a dozen recon-cars, some of them under robo-control; six gunboats followed, and behind them, to the horizon, other craft were strung out-airboats, troop carriers, and freight-scows. They could see enemy missiles approaching in Zareff's front screen; counter-missiles got most of them, and a couple of pilotless recon-cars were sacrificed. The *Lester Dawes* blasted more missiles as they crossed the top of the mountain range. Then Zareff's car was circling in and entering at one of the ship's open cargo-ports. Zareff and Anse Dawes got out.

"Gunboats are only half an hour behind," Zareff said. "Get some screens on to them, Anse; you know the combinations. Now let's see what kind of a mess we're in here."

It was almost a miracle, the way the tottering old man Conn had seen on the dock at Litchfield when he had arrived from Terra had been rejuvenated.

The rest of the reinforcements arrived slowly, sending missiles and counter-missiles out ahead of them. Zareff began worrying about the supply; the enemy didn't seem to be running short. By 1300 —Conn noted the time incredulously; the battle seemed to have been going on forever, instead of just four hours-the *Lester Dawes* had moved halfway around the volcano and was almost due west of it, and the eight gunboats were spaced all around the perimeter. Then one stopped transmitting; in the other screens, there was a rising fireball where she had been. The radio was loud with verbal reports.

"*Poltergeist,*" Zareff said, naming half a dozen names. One or two of them had been schoolmates of Conn's at the Academy; he knew how he'd feel about it later, but now it simply didn't register.

"They're launching missiles faster than we can shoot them down," he said.

"That's usually the beginning of the end," Zareff said. "I saw it happen too often during the War. We've got to get inside that place. It's a lot of harmless fun to send contragravity robots out to smash each other, but it doesn't win battles. Battles are won by men, standing with their feet on the ground, using personal weapons."

"We'll have to win this one pretty soon," Rodney Maxwell said. "The amount of nuclear energy we've been releasing will be detectable anywhere on the planet by now. The Government has a ship like the *Lester Dawes* in commission; if this keeps on, she'll be coming out for a look."

"Then we'll have help," Captain Poole said.

"We need Government help like we need the polka-dot fever," Rodney Maxwell said. "If they get in it, they'll claim the spaceport themselves, and we'll have fought a battle for nothing."

Well, that was it, then. The spaceport was essential to the Maxwell Plan. He'd gotten seven men killed-eight, if the recon-car that was taking Abe Samuels to the hospital in Litchfield didn't make it in time-and it was up to him to see that they hadn't died for nothing. He spread the photo-map and the spaceport plans on the chart table.

"Look at this," he said.

Klem Zareff looked at it. He didn't like it any better than Conn had. He studied the plan for a moment, chewing his cigar.

"You know, it's possible they don't know that thing exists," he said, without too much conviction. "You'll be betting the lives of at least twenty men; fewer than that couldn't accomplish anything."

"I'll be putting mine on the table along with them," Conn said. "I'll lead them in."

He was wishing he hadn't had to say that. He did, though. It was the only thing he could say.

"You better pick the men to go with me, Colonel," he continued. "You know them better than I do. We'll need working equipment, too; I have no idea what we may have to take out of the way, inside."

"I won't call for volunteers," Zareff said. "I'll pick Home Guards; they did their volunteering when they joined."

"Let me pick one man, Colonel," Anse Dawes said. "I'll pick me."

X

They sent a snooper in first; it picked up faint radiation leakage from inactive power units of overhead lights, and nothing else. The tunnel stretched ahead of it, empty, and dark beyond its infrared vision. After it had gone a mile without triggering anything, the jeep followed, Anse Dawes piloting and Conn at the snooper controls watching what it transmitted back. The two lorries followed, loaded with men and equipment, and another jeep brought up the rear. They had cut screen-and-radio communication with the outside; they weren't even using inter-vehicle communication.

At length, the snooper emerged into a big cavern, swinging slowly to scan it. The walls and ceiling were rough and irregular; it was natural instead of excavated. Only the floor had been leveled smooth. There were a lot of things in it, machinery and vehicles, all battered and in poor condition, dusty and cobwebbed: the spaceport junkheap. A passage, still large enough for one of the gunboats, led deeper into the mountain toward the crater. They sent the snooper in and, after a while, followed.

They came to other rectangular, excavated caverns. On the plans, they were marked as storerooms. Cases and crates, indeterminate shrouded objects; some had never been disturbed, but here and there they found evidence of recent investigation.

Beyond was another passage, almost as wide as the Mall in Litchfield; even the *Lester Dawes* could have negotiated it. According to the plans, it ran straight out to the ship docks and the open crater beyond. Anse turned the jeep into a side passage, and Conn recalled the snooper and sent it ahead. On the plan, it led to another natural cavern, half its width shown as level with the entrance. The other half was a pit, marked as sixty feet deep; above this and just under the ceiling, several passages branched out in different directions.

The snooper reported visible light ahead; fluoroelectric light from one of the upper passages, and firelight from the pit. The air-analyzer reported woodsmoke and a faint odor of burning oil. He sent the snooper ahead, tilting it to look down into the pit.

A small fire was burning in the center; around it, in a circle, some hundred and fifty people, including a few women and children, sat, squatted or reclined. A low hum of voices came out of the soundbox.

"Who the blazes are they?" Anse whispered. "I can't see any way they could have gotten down there."

They were in rags, and they weren't armed; there wasn't so much as a knife or a pistol among them. Conn motioned the lorries and the other jeep forward.

"Prisoners," he said. "I think they were hauled down here on a scow, shoved off, and left when the fighting started. Cover me," he told the men in the lorries. "I'm going down and talk to them."

Somebody below must have heard something. As Anse took the jeep over and started floating it down, the circle around the fire began moving, the women and children being pushed to the rear and the men gathering up clubs and other chance weapons. By the time the jeep grounded, the men in the pit were standing defensively in front of the women and children.

They were all dirty and ragged; the men were unshaven. There was a tall man with a grizzled beard, in greasy coveralls; another man with a black beard and an old Space Navy uniform, his head bandaged with a dirty and blood-caked rag; another in the same uniform, wearing a cap on which the Terran Federation insignia had been replaced by the emblem of Transcontinent & Overseas Shiplines and the words CHIEF ENGINEER. And beside the tall man with the gray beard, was a girl in baggy trousers and a torn smock. Like the others, she was dirty, but in spite of the rags and filth, Conn saw that she was beautiful. Black hair, dark eyes, an impudently tilted nose.

They all looked at him in hostility that gradually changed to perplexity and then hope.

"Who are you?" the tall man with the gray beard asked. "You're none of this gang here."

"Litchfield Exploration & Salvage; I'm Conn Maxwell."

That meant nothing; none of them had been near a news-screen lately.

"What's going on topside?" the man with the bandaged head and the four stripes on his sleeve asked. "There was firing, artillery and nuclears, and they herded us down here. Have you cleaned the bloody murderers out?"

"We're working on it," Conn said. "I take it they aren't friends of yours?"

Foolish Question of the Year; they all made that evident.

"They took my ship; they murdered my first officer and half my crew and passengers...."

"They burned our home and killed our servants," the girl said. "They kidnapped my father and me...."

"They've been keeping us here as slaves."

"It's the Blackie Perales gang," the tall man with the gray beard said. "They've been making us work for them, converting a blasted tub of a contragravity ship into a spacecraft. I beg your pardon, Captain Nichols; she was a fine ship-for her intended purpose."

"You're Captain Nichols?" Anse Dawes exclaimed. "Of the *Harriet Barne*?"

"That's right. The *Harriet Barne's* here; they've been making us work on her, to convert her to an interplanetary craft, of all idiotic things."

"My name's Yves Jacquemont," the man with the gray beard said. "I'm a retired hyperspace maintenance engineer; I had a little business at Waterville, buying, selling and rebuilding agricultural machinery. This gang found out about me; they raided and burned our village and carried me and my daughter, Sylvie, away. We've been working for them for the last four months, tearing Captain Nichols' ship down and armoring her with collapsium."

"How many pirates are there here?"

That started an argument. Nobody was quite sure; two hundred and fifty seemed to be the highest estimate, which Conn decided to play safe by accepting.

"You get us out of here," Yves Jacquemont was saying. "All we want is a chance at them."

"How about arms? You can't do much with clubs and fists."

"Don't worry about that; we know where to get arms. The treasure house, where they store their loot. There's plenty of arms and ammunition, and anything else you can think of. They've used us to help stow the stuff; we know where it is."

"Anse, you remember those scows we saw, in the big room before we came to the broad passage? Take four men in the jeep; have them lift two of them and bring them here. Then, you get out to the end of the tunnel and call the *Lester Dawes*. Tell them what's happened, tell them they can get gunboats all the way in, and wait to guide them when they arrive."

When Anse turned and climbed into the jeep, he asked Yves Jacquemont: "Why does this Perales want an interplanetary ship?"

"He's crazy!" Jacquemont swore. "Paranoid; megalomaniac. He talks of organizing all the pirates and outlaws on the planet into one band and making himself king. He's heard that there are Space Navy superweapons on Koshchei —I suppose there are, at that-and he wants to get a lot of planetbusters and hellburners and annihilators." He lowered his voice. "Captain Nichols and I were going to fix up something that'd blow the *Harriet Barne* up as soon as he got her out of atmosphere."

He talked for a while to Jacquemont and his daughter Sylvie, and to Nichols and the chief engineer, whose name was Vibart. There was evidently nothing else at the spaceport of which a spaceship could be built, but there were foundries and rolling-mills and a collapsed-matter producer. The *Harriet Barne* was gutted, half torn down, and half armored with new collapsium-plated sheet steel. It might be possible to continue the work on her and take her to space.

Then the two scows floated over the top of the pit and began letting down. They got the prisoners into them, the combat-effective men in one and the women and children in the other. At the top, he took over the remaining jeep, getting Jacquemont, his daughter, and the two contragravityship officers in with him.

"Up to the top," Jacquemont said. "Take the middle passage, and turn right at the next intersection."

As they approached the section where the pirates stored their loot, the sound of guns and explosions grew louder, and they began picking up radio and screen signals, all of which were scrambled and incomprehensible. The pirates, in different positions, talking among themselves. With all that, it ought to be safe to use their own communication equipment; nobody would notice it.

The treasure room looked like a giant pack rat's nest. Cases and crates of merchandise, bales, boxes, barrels. Machinery. Household and industrial robots. The prisoners piled out of the two scows and began rummaging. Somebody found a case of cigarettes and smashed it open; in a moment, cartons were being tossed around and opened, and everybody was smoking. The pirates evidently hadn't issued any tobacco rations to their prisoners.

And they found arms and ammunition, began ripping open cases, handing out rifles, pistols, submachine guns. The prisoners grabbed them even more hungrily than the cigarettes. Sylvie Jacquemont took charge of the ammunition; she had three men opening boxes for her, while she passed out boxes of cartridges and made sure that everybody had ammunition to fit their weapons. A ragged man who might have been a farm-tramp or a rich planter before his capture had gotten a bale of cloth open and was tossing rags around while the chief engineer inspected weapons and showed people how to clean out the cosmoline and fill their spare magazines.

Conn collected a few of his own party.

"Let's look these robots over," he said. "Find about half a dozen we can load with blasting explosive and send ahead of us on contragravity."

They found several-an electric-light servicer, a couple of wall-and-window washers, a serving-robot that looked as if it had come from a restaurant, and an all-purpose robo-janitor. In the passage outside, they began loading the lorries with bricks of ionite and packages of cataclysmite, packing all the scrap-iron and other junk around the explosives that they could. As soon as they had weapons, the prisoners came swarming out, making more noise than was necessary and a good deal more than was safe. Sylvie Jacquemont, with a submachine gun slung from one shoulder and a canvas bag of spare magazines from the other, came over to see what he was doing.

"Well, look what you're doing to him!" she mock-reproached. "That's a dirty trick to play on a little robot!"

He grinned at her. "You and my mother would get along. She always treats robots like people."

"Well, they are, sort of. They aren't alive-at least, I don't think they are-but they do what you tell them, and they learn tricks, and they have personalities."

That was true. He didn't think robots were alive, either, though biophysics professors tended to become glibly evasive when pinned down to defining life. Robots could learn, if you used the term loosely enough. And any robot with more than five hundred hours service picked up a definite and often exasperating personality.

"I've been working with them, and tearing them down and fixing them, ever since I was in pigtails," she added.

The half-dozen natural leaders among the prisoners-Jacquemont and his daughter, the two *Harriet Barne* officers, and a couple of others-bent over the photoprinted plans Conn had, located their position, and told him as much as they could about what lay ahead. Sylvie Jacquemont could handle robots; she would ride in the front seat of the jeep while he piloted. Vibart, the chief engineer, and Yves Jacquemont would ride behind. Nichols would ride in the scow with the fighting men. One lorry of his own party would follow the jeep; the other would bring up the rear.

He snapped on the screen and punched the ship combination. Stefan Jorisson appeared in it.

"Hi, Conn! You all right?" He raised his voice. "Conn's on-screen!"

His father appeared at Jorisson's shoulder and, a moment later, Klem Zareff.

"Well, we're in, all right," he said. "We just picked up an army, too." He swung the jeep to get the crowd in the pickup, explaining who they were. "Did you hear from Anse?"

"Yes, he just screened in," Rodney Maxwell said. "He said a gunboat can get in."

"That's right; clear into the crater."

"Well, we're going to put three of them inside," Zareff told him. "*Werewolf*, *Zombi*, and *Dero*. And a troop carrier with fifty men; flamethrowers, portable machine guns, bomb-launchers; regular special-weapons section. What can you do where you are?"

"Here? Nothing. We're going to work around to the other side of the crater, and then find a vertical shaft and go up topside and make as much disturbance as we can."

"That's it!" Zareff approved. "Pull them off balance; as soon as we get in, we'll go straight to the top. Look for us in about an hour; it's going to take time getting to the tunnel-mouth without being spotted from above."

He lifted the jeep and started off; the lorry, and the scows and the other lorry, followed; the snooper and the bomb-robots went ahead like a pack of hunting dogs. They went through great chambers, dark and silent and bulking with dusty machines. Jacquemont explained that the prisoners had never gotten into this section; the *Harriet Barne* was a mile or so to their right. Conn turned left, when the noise of firing from outside became plainer. A foundry. A machine-shop which seemed to have been abandoned in the middle of some rush job that hadn't really been necessary. They came to a place even the snooper couldn't enter, choked to the ceiling with dead vegetation, hydroponic seed-plants that had been left untended to grow wild and die. They emerged into outside light, in vast caves a mile high and open onto the crater, and looked across the floor that had been leveled and vitrified to the other side, three and a half miles away.

He didn't know whether to be more awed by the original eruption that had formed the crater or by the engineering feat of carving these docks and ship-berths, big enough for the hugest hyperspaceship, into it.

At first, he had been afraid of getting into position too soon before the task force from outside could profit by the diversion. Then he began to worry about the time it was taking to get halfway around the crater. He could hear artillery thundering continuously above. Except at the very beginning of the battle, there had been little gunfire. He wondered if both sides were running out of lift-and-drive missiles, or if the fighting had gotten too close for anybody to risk using nuclear weapons.

He was also worrying about the women and children among the released prisoners.

"Why did the pirates bother with them?" he asked Sylvie.

"They used the women and some of the old men to do housekeeping chores for them," she said. "Mostly, though, they were hostages; if the men didn't work, Perales threatened to punish the women and children. I wasn't doing any housework; I'm too good a mechanic. I was helping on the ship."

"Well, what'll I do with them when the fighting starts? I can't take them into battle."

"You'll have to; it'll be the safest place for them. You can't leave them anywhere and risk having them recaptured."

"That means we'll have to detach some men to cover them, and that'll cut our striking force down." He whistled at the sound-pickup of his screen and told his father about it. "What do I do with these people, anyhow?"

"You're the officer in command, Conn," his father told him. "Your decision. How soon can you attack? We're almost through to the crater."

"There's a vertical shaft right above us, and a lot of noise at the top. We'll send up a couple of bomb-robots to clear things at the shaft-head and follow with everything we have."

"Noncombatants and all?"

He nodded. "Only thing we can do." An old quotation occurred to him. "'If you want to make an omelet, you have to break eggs.'"

He wondered who'd said that in the first place. One of the old Pre-Atomic conquerors; maybe Hitler. No, Hitler would have said, "If you want to make sauerkraut, you have to chop cabbage." Maybe it was Caesar.

"We'd better send Gumshoe Gus up, first," Sylvie suggested.

"You handle him. Take a quick look around, and then pull him back. We'll need him later." It was the first time he'd ever caught himself calling a robot "him," instead of "it." He thought for a second, and added: "Give your father and Mr. Vibart the controls for the two window-washers; you handle the snooper."

He gave more instructions: Yves Jacquemont to turn his bomb-robot right, Vibart to turn his left; the two lorries to follow the jeep up the shaft, the scows to follow. Then he leaned back and looked at the screens that had been rigged under the top of the jeep. A circle of light appeared in one, growing larger and brighter as the snooper approached the top of the shaft; two more came on as the bomb-robots followed.

"All right; follow me," he said into the inter-vehicle radio, and started the jeep slowly up the shaft.

The snooper popped out of the shaft, onto a gallery that had been cut into the solid rock, fifty feet high and a hundred and fifty across, with a low parapet on the outside and the mile-deep crater beyond. There were a few grounded aircars and lorries in sight, and a medium airboat rested a hundred or so feet on the right of the shaft-opening. Fifteen or twenty men were clustered around it, with a lifter loaded with ammunition. They looked like any crowd of farm-tramps. Suddenly, one of them saw the snooper, gave a yell, and fired at it with a rifle. Sylvie pulled it back into the shaft; her father and the chief engineer sent the two bomb-robots up onto the gallery. The right-hand robot sped at the airboat; the last thing Conn saw in its screen was a face, bearded and villainous and contorted with fright, looking out the pilot's window of the airboat. Then it went dead, and there was a roar from above. On the other side, several men were firing straight at the pickup of the other robot; it went dead, too, and there was a second explosion.

In the communication screen, somebody was yelling, "Give them another one for Milt Hennant!" and his father was urging him to get in fast, before they recovered.

In peace or war, screen communication was a wonderful thing. The only trouble was that it let in too many kibitzers.

The gallery, when the jeep emerged onto it, was empty except for casualties, a few still alive. The side of the airboat was caved in; the lifter-load of ammunition had gone up with the bomb. He moved the jeep to the right of the shaft and waited for the vehicles behind him, suffering a brief indecision.

Never divide your force in the presence of the enemy.

There had been generals who had done that and gotten away with it, but they'd had names like Foxx Travis and Robert E. Lee and Napoleon-Napoleon; that was who'd made that crack about omelets! They'd known what they were doing. He was playing this battle by ear.

There was a lot of shouting ahead to the right. That meant live pirates, a deplorable situation which ought to be corrected at once. The communication screen was noisy, now; his father had gotten to the top gallery with the three gun cutters, and was meeting resistance. He formed his column, his jeep and one of the lorries in front, the scows next, and the second lorry behind, and started around the gallery counterclockwise, the snoopers and the three remaining bomb-robots ahead. They began running into resistance almost at once.

Bullets spatted on the armor glass in front of him, spalling it and blotching it with metal until he found that he could steer better by the show-back of his view-pickup. He used that until the pickup was shot out. Then his father began wanting to know, from the communication screen, what was going on and where he was. A bomb or something went off directly under the jeep, bouncing it almost to the ceiling; he found that it was impossible to lift it again after it settled to the floor of the gallery, and they all piled out to fight on foot. Sommers and his gang from the number one lorry were also afoot; their vehicle had been disabled. He saw them lifting wounded into one of the scows.

They blew up the light-service robot to clear a nest of pirates who had taken cover ahead of them. They sent the robo-janitor up a side passage and exploded it in a missile-launching position on the outside of the mountain; that produced a tremendous explosion. They began running out of cartridges, and had to stop and glean more from enemy casualties. They expended their last bomb-robot, the restaurant server, to break up another pirate resistance point.

At length he found himself, with Sylvie and her father and one of the Home Guardsmen from Sommers' lorry, lying behind an aircar somebody had knocked out with a bazooka, with two dead pirates for company and a dozen distressingly live ones ahead behind an improvised barricade. Behind, there was frantic firing; the rear-guard seemed to have run into trouble, probably from some gang that had come down from the upper level. He wondered what his father was doing with the gunboats; since abandoning the jeep, he had lost his only means of contact.

Suddenly, the men in front jumped up from their barricade and came running toward him. Been reinforced, now they're counterattacking. His rifle was empty; he drew his pistol and shot one of them, and then he saw that they were throwing up their hands and yelling for quarter. This was something new.

He looked around quickly, to make sure none of the liberated prisoners except Jacquemont and his daughter were around, and then called to a couple of his own men to come up and help him. While they were relieving the pirates of their pistol belts and cartridge bandoliers, more came up, their hands over their heads, herded by a combat car from which Tom Brangwyn covered them with a pair of 12-mm machine guns. Tom hadn't put in an appearance before he had taken his commando force into the tunnel; he hadn't even known the chief of Company Police was on Barathrum.

"Well, nice seeing you," he greeted. "How did you get in?"

"Over the top," Brangwyn told him. "Everything's caved in on the other side. We have a quarter of the top gallery, and half of this one. Your father's cleaning up above. Klem's got some men working along the outside."

Sylvie was tugging at his arm. "Hey, look! Look at that!" she was clamoring. "Who's she belong to?"

He looked; the *Lester Dawes* was coming over the edge of the crater.

"She's ours," he said. "It's all over but the mopping up. And counting the egg breakage."

XI

The shooting died down to occasional rattles of small arms, usually followed by yells for quarter. An explosion thundered from across the crater. The *Lester Dawes* fired her big guns a few times. A machine gun stuttered. A pistol banged, far away. It took two hours before all the pirates had been hunted out of hiding and captured, or killed if found by their former captives, who were accepting no surrender whatever.

Blackie Perales had been one of the latter; he had been found, his clothes in rags and covered with dirt and grease, hiding under a machine in one of the shops back of the dock in which the *Harriet Barne* was being rebuilt. He had tried to claim that he was one of the pirates' prisoners who had eluded the roundup at the beginning of the battle and had been hiding there since. As soon as the real prisoners saw and recognized him, they had fallen upon him and clubbed, kicked and stamped him out of any resemblance to humanity. At that, what he got was probably only a fraction of what he deserved.

The egg breakage had been heavy, and not at all confined to the bad eggs. A third gunboat, the *Banshee*, had been destroyed with all hands during the final attack from outside; in addition, a dozen men had been killed during the fighting in the galleries. Everybody was shocked, except Klem Zareff, who had been in battles before. He was surprised that the casualties had been so light.

At first glance, the spaceport looked like a handsome prize of victory. The docks and workshops were all in good condition; at worst, they only needed cleaning up. There was a collapsium plant, with its own mass-energy converter. There were foundries and machine-shops and forging-shops and a rolling-mill, almost completely robotic. At first, Conn thought that it might be possible to build a hyperdrive ship here, without having to go to Koshchei at all.

Closer examination disabused him of this hope. There was nothing of which the framework of a ship could be built, and no way of producing heavy structural steel. The rolling-mill was good enough to turn out eighth-inch sheet material which when plated with a few micromicrons of collapsium would be as good as a hundred feet of lead against space-radiations, but that was the ship's skin. A ship needed a skeleton, too. The only thing to do was go on with the *Harriet Barne*.

It was sunset before he finished his tour of inspection and let his jeep down in a vehicle hall off the lower gallery outside what had originally been the spaceport officers' club. It was crowded, and a victory celebration seemed to be getting under way. He saw his father with Yves Jacquemont, Sylvie, Tom Brangwyn, and Captain Nichols. Nichols had gotten clean clothes from the pirates' store of loot, and had bathed and shaved. So had Jacquemont, though he had contented himself with trimming his beard. It took him a second or so to recognize the young lady in feminine garb as his erstwhile battle comrade, Sylvie.

"Well, our pay goes on from the day we were captured," Nichols was saying. "My instructions are to resume command of the ship. Tomorrow, they're sending a party out to go over her."

Conn stopped short. "What's this about the ship?"

"Captain Nichols was in screen contact with his company's office in Storisende," Rodney Maxwell said. "They're continuing him in command of her."

"But ...but we took that ship! We lost three gunboats and about twenty-five men...."

"She still belongs to Transcontinent & Overseas," his father said. "That's been the law on stolen property as long as there's been any law."

Of course; he should have known that. Did know it; just didn't think.

"We broke an awful lot of eggs for no omelet; fought a battle for nothing."

"Well, of course, I'm prejudiced," Sylvie said, "but I don't think getting us out of the hands of that bloodthirsty maniac and his cutthroats was nothing."

"Wiping out the Perales gang wasn't nothing, Conn," Tom Brangwyn said. "You got no idea at all how bad things were, the last couple of years."

"I know. I'm sorry." He was ashamed of himself. "But I needed a ship, and now we have no ship at all."

"A ship means something to you?" Yves Jacquemont asked.

"Yes." He told him why. "If we could get to Koshchei, we could build a hypership of our own, and get our brandy and things to markets where we could get a decent price for them."

"I know. I was in and out of Storisende on these owner-captain tramps for a couple of years before I decided to retire and settle here," Jacquemont said. "The profit on a cargo of Poictesme brandy on Terra or Baldur is over a thousand percent."

"Well, don't give up too soon," Nichols advised. "You can't keep the *Harriet Barne*, of course, but you're entitled to prize-money on her, and that ought to buy you something you could build a spaceship out of."

"That's right," Jacquemont said. "Everything else besides the frame can be made here. Look, these pirates burned me out; except for the money I have in the bank, I lost everything, home, business and all. As soon as I can find a place for Sylvie to stay, I'll come back and go to work for your company building a spaceship. And a lot of the men who were working here are farm-tramps and drifters, one job's as good as another as long as they get paid for it. And I know a few good men in Storisende-engineers-who'd be glad for a job, too."

"You think it would be all right with Mother and Flora if Sylvie stayed with us?" Conn asked.

"Of course it would; they'd be glad to have her." Rodney Maxwell turned to Yves Jacquemont. "Let's consider that fixed up. Now, suppose you and I go into Storisende, and...."

The Transcontinent & Overseas people arrived at Barathrum Spaceport the next morning; a rear-rank vice-president, a front-rank legal-eagle, and three engineers. They were horrified at what they saw. The *Harriet Barne* had been gutted. Bulkheads and decks had been ripped out and relocated incomprehensibly; the bridge and the control room under it were gone; she had been stripped to her framework, and the whole underside was sheathed in shimmering collapsium.

"Great Ghu!" the vice-president almost howled. "That isn't *our* ship!"

"That's the *Harriet Barne*," her captain said. "She looks a little ragged now, but —"

"You helped these pirates do this to her?"

"If I hadn't, they'd have cut my throat and gotten somebody else to help them. My throat's more valuable to me than the ship is to you; I can't get anybody to build me a new one."

"Well, understand," one of the engineers said, "they were converting her into an interplanetary ship. It wouldn't cost much to finish the job."

"We need an interplanetary ship like we need a hole in the head!" The vice-president turned to Rodney Maxwell. "Just how much prize-money do you think you're entitled to for this wreck?"

"I wouldn't know; that's up to Sterber, Flynn & Chen-Wong. Up to the court, if we can settle it any other way."

"You mean you'd litigate about this?" the lawyer demanded, and began to laugh.

"If we have to. Look, if you people don't want her, sign her over to Litchfield Exploration & Salvage. But if you do want her, you'll have to pay for her."

"We'll give you twenty thousand sols," the lawyer said. "We don't want to be tightfisted. After all, you fought a gang of pirates and lost some men and a couple of boats; we have some moral obligation to you. But you'll have to realize that this ship, in her present state, is practically valueless."

"The collapsium on her is worth twice that, and the engines are worth even more," Jacquemont said. "I worked on them."

The discussion ended there. By midafternoon, Luther Chen-Wong, the junior partner of the law firm, arrived from Storisende with a couple of engineers of his own. Reporters began arriving; both sides were anxious to keep them away from the ship. Conn took care of them, assisted by Sylvie, who had rummaged an even more attractive costume out of what she called the loot-cellar. The reporters all used up a lot of film footage on her. And the Fawzis' Office Gang arrived from Force Command, bitterly critical of the value of the spaceport against its cost in lives and equipment. Brangwyn and Zareff returned to Force Command with them. A Planetary Air Patrol ship arrived and removed the captured pirates. The liberated prisoners were airlifted to Litchfield.

The third day after the battle, Conn and his father and Sylvie and her father flew to Litchfield. To Conn's surprise, Flora greeted him cordially, and Wade Lucas, rather stiffly, congratulated him. Maybe it was as Tom Brangwyn had said; he hadn't been on Poictesme in the last four or five years and didn't know how bad things had gotten. His mother seemed to think he had won the Battle of Barathrum single-handed.

He was even more surprised and gratified that Flora made friends with Sylvie immediately. His mother, however, regarded the engineer's daughter with badly concealed hostility, and seemed to doubt that Sylvie was the kind of girl she wanted her son getting involved with. Outwardly, of course, she was quite gracious.

Rodney Maxwell and Yves Jacquemont flew to Storisende the next morning, both more optimistic about finding a ship than Conn thought the circumstances warranted. Conn stayed at home for the next few days, luxuriating in idleness. He and Sylvie tore down his mother's household robots and built sound-sensors into them, keying them to respond to their names and to a few simple commands, and including recorded-voice responses in a thick Sheshan accent. All the smart people on Terra, he explained, had Sheshan humanoid servants.

His mother was delighted. Robots that would answer when she spoke to them were a lot more companionable. She didn't seem to think, however, that Sylvie's mechanical skills were ladylike accomplishments. Nice girls, Litchfield model, weren't quite so handy with a spot-welder. That was what Conn liked about Sylvie; she was like the girls he'd known at the University.

They were strolling after dinner, down the Mall. The air was sharp and warned that autumn had definitely arrived; the many brilliant stars, almost as bright as the moon of Terra, were coming out in the dusk.

"Conn, this thing about Merlin," she began. "Do you really believe in it? Ever since Dad and I came to Poictesme, I've been hearing about it, but it's just a story, isn't it?"

He was tempted to tell her the truth, and sternly put the temptation behind him.

"Of course there's a Merlin, Sylvie, and it's going to do wonderful things when we find it."

He looked down the starlit Mall ahead of him. Somebody, maybe Lester Dawes and Morgan Gatworth and Lorenzo Menardes, had gotten things finished and cleaned up. The pavement was smooth and unbroken; the litter had vanished.

"It's done wonderful things already, just because people started looking for it," he said. "Some of these days, they're going to realize that they had Merlin all along and didn't know it."

There was a faint humming from somewhere ahead, and he was wondering what it was. Then they came to the long escalators, and he saw that they were running.

"Why, look! They got them fixed! They're running!"

Sylvie grinned at him and squeezed his arm.

"I get you, chum," she said. "Of course there's a Merlin."

Maybe he didn't have to tell her the truth.

When they returned to the house, his mother greeted him:

"Conn, your father's been trying to get you ever since you went out. Call him, right away; Ritz-Gartner Hotel, in Storisende. It's something about a ship."

It look a little time to get his father on-screen. He was excited and happy.

"Hi, Conn; we have one," he said.

"What kind of a ship?"

"You know her. The *Harriet Barne*."

That he hadn't expected. Something off Mothball Row that would have to be flown to Barathrum and torn down and completely rebuilt, but not the one that was there already, partly finished.

"How the dickens did you wangle that?"

"Oh, it was Yves' idea, to start with. He knew about her; the T. & O.'s been losing money on her for years. He said if they had to pay prize-money on her and then either restore her to original condition or finish the job and build a spaceship they didn't want, it would almost bankrupt the company. They got up as high as fifty thousand sols for prize-money and we just laughed at them. So we made a proposition of our own.

"We proposed organizing a new company, subsidiary to both L. E. & S. and T. & O., to engage in interplanetary shipping; both companies to assign their equity in the *Harriet Barne* to the new company, the work of completing her to be done at our spaceport and the labor cost to be shared. This would give us our spaceship, and get T. & O. off the hook all around. Everybody was for it except the president of T. & O. Know anything about him?"

Conn shook his head. His father continued:

"Name's Jethro Sastraman. He could play Scrooge in *Christmas Carol* without any makeup at all. He hasn't had a new idea since he got out of college, and that was while the War was still going on. 'Preposterous; utterly visionary and impractical,'" his father mimicked. "Fortunately, a majority of the big stockholders didn't agree; they finally bullied him into agreeing. We're calling the new company Alpha-Interplanetary, we have an application for charter in, and that'll go through almost automatically."

"Who's going to be the president of this new company?"

"You know him. Character named Rodney Maxwell. Yves is going to be vice-president in charge of operations; he's flying to Barathrum tomorrow or the next day with a gang of technicians we're recruiting. T. & O. are giving us Clyde Nichols and Mack Vibart, and a lot of men from their shipyard. I'm staying here in Storisende; we're opening an office here. By this time next week, we're all going to wish we'd been born quintuplets."

"And Conn Maxwell, I suppose, will be an influential non-office-holding stockholder?"

"That's right. Just like in L. E. & S."

XII

He found Jerry Rivas and Anse Dawes and a score of workmen making a survey and inventory of the spaceport. Captain Nichols and four of the original crew of the *Harriet Barne*, who had shared his captivity among the pirates, had stayed to take care of the ship. And Fred Karski, with one gun-cutter and a couple of light airboats, was keeping up a routine guard. All of them had heard about the formation of Alpha-Interplanetary when Conn arrived.

The next day, Yves Jacquemont arrived, accompanied by Mack Vibart, a gang from the T. & O. shipyard, and a dozen engineers and construction men whom he had recruited around Storisende. More workers arrived in the next few days, including a number who had already worked on the ship as slaves of the Perales gang.

It didn't take Conn long to appreciate the problems involved in the conversion. Built to operate only inside planetary atmosphere and gravitation, the *Harriet Barne* was long and narrow, like an old ocean ship; more than anything else, she had originally resembled a huge submarine. Spaceships, either interplanetary or interstellar, were always spherical with a pseudogravity system at the center. This, of course, the *Harriet Barne* lacked.

"Well, are we going to make the whole trip in free fall?" he wanted to know.

"No, we'll use our acceleration for pseudograv halfway, and deceleration the other half," Jacquemont told him. "We'll be in free fall about ten or fifteen hours. What we're going to have to do will be to lift off from Poictesme in the horizontal position the ship was designed for, and then make a ninety-degree turn after we're off-planet, with our lift and our drive working together, just like one of the old rocket ships before the Abbott Drive was developed."

That meant, of course, that the after bulkheads would become decks, and explained a lot of the oddities he had noticed about the conversion job. It meant that everything would have to be mounted on gimbals, everything stowed so as to be secure in either position, and nothing placed where it would be out of reach in either.

Jacquemont and Nichols took charge of the work on the ship herself. Chief Engineer Vibart, with a gang of half-taught, self-taught and untaught helpers, went back to working the engines over, tearing out all the safety devices that were intended to keep the ship inside planetary atmosphere, and arranging the lift engines so that they could be swung into line with the drive engines. There was a lot of cybernetic and robotic equipment, and astrogational equipment, that had to be made from scratch. Conn picked a couple of helpers and went to work on that.

From time to time, he was able to snatch a few minutes to read teleprint papers or listen to audiovisual newscasts from Storisende. He was always disappointed. There was much excitement about the new interplanetary company, but the emphasis was all wrong. People weren't interested in getting hyperships built, or opening the mines and factories on Koshchei, or talking about all the things now in short supply that could be produced there. They were talking about Merlin, and they were all positive, now, that something found at Force Command Duplicate had convinced Litchfield Exploration & Salvage that the giant computer was somewhere off-planet.

Rodney Maxwell flew in from Storisende; he was accompanied by Wade Lucas, who shook hands cordially with Conn.

"Can you spare us Jerry Rivas for a while?" Rodney Maxwell asked.

"Well, ask Yves Jacquemont; he's vice-president in charge of operations. As an influential non-office-holding stockholder, I'd think so. He's only running around helping out here and there."

"We want him to take charge of opening those hospitals you were telling us about. Wade and I are forming a new company, Mainland Medical Materials, Ltd. Going to act as broker for L. E. & S. in getting rid of medical stores. Nobody in the company knows where to sell that stuff or what we ought to get for it."

Wade Lucas began to talk about how desperately some types of drug and some varieties of diagnostic equipment were needed. Conn had it on the tip of his tongue to ask Lucas whether he thought that was a racket, too. Lucas must have read his mind.

"I really didn't understand how much good this would do," he said. "I wouldn't have spoken so forcefully against it if I had. I thought it was nothing but this Merlin thing —"

"Aaagh! Don't talk to me about Merlin!" Conn interrupted. "I have to talk to Kurt Fawzi and that crowd about Merlin till I'm sick of the whole subject."

His father shot him a warning glance; Lucas was looking at him in surprise. He hastened to change the subject:

"I see Len made you a suit out of that material," he said to his father. "And I see you're not bulging the coat out behind with a hip-holster."

"Oh, I stopped carrying a gun; I'm a city man, now. Nobody carries one in Storisende. Won't even be necessary in Litchfield before long. Our new marshal had a regular reign of terror in Tramptown for a few days, and you wouldn't know the place. Wade, here, is acting mayor now."

They went back to talking about the new company. "You're going to have so many companies you won't be able to to keep track of them before long," Conn said.

"Well, I'm doing something about that. A holding company; Trisystem Investments, Ltd.; you're a non-office-holding stockholder in that, too."

Merlin was now a political issue. A bill had been introduced in Parliament to amend the Abandoned Property Act of 867 and nationalize Merlin, when and if discovered and regardless by whom. The support seemed to come from an extremist minority; everybody else, including the Administration, was opposed to it. There was considerable acrimony, however, on the propositions: 1) that Merlin was too important to the prosperity of Poictesme to become a private monopoly; and 2) that Merlin was too important, etc., to become a political football and patronage plum.

It was discovered, after they were half assembled, that the controls for the *Harriet Barne* would only work while she was in a horizontal position. The whole thing had to be torn out and rebuilt. There was also trouble with the air-and-water recycling system. The *City of Nefertiti* came in from Aton for Odin; Rodney Maxwell was almost frantic because they hadn't gotten together a cargo of medical stores from the first hospital to be opened.

"There's all sorts of stuff," he was fuming, by screen. "Stuff that's in short supply anywhere and that we could get good prices for off-planet. Get Federation sols for it, too."

"The *City of Asgard* will be along in six months," Conn said. "You can have a real cargo assembled by then. You can make arrangements in advance to dispose of it on Terra or Baldur or Marduk."

"There are a couple of other companies interested in interplanetary ships now," his father added. "One of them had gotten four old freighters off Mothball Row, and they're tearing them down and cannibalizing them into one spaceship. That work's being done here at Storisende Spaceport. And another company has gotten title to a couple of old office buildings and has a gang at work dismantling them for the structural steel. I think they're going to build a real spaceship."

That wasn't anything to worry about either. The *Harriet Barne* was better than half finished. There was a collapsium plant at Storisende Spaceport, but Yves Jacquemont said it was only half the size of the one at Barathrum; it would be three months before it could produce armor for one, let alone both, ships.

The crackpots were getting into the act, now, too. A spirit medium on the continent of Acaire, to the north, had produced a communication purporting to originate with a deceased Third Force Staff officer, now in the Spirit World. There was considerable detail, all ludicrous to Conn's professional ear. And a fanatic in one of the small towns on the west coast was quoting the Bible, the Koran, and the Bhagavadgita to prove that if Merlin were ever found, Divine vengeance in a spectacular form would fall not only on Poictesme but on the entire Galaxy.

The spaceship that was building at Storisende got into the news; on-screen, it appeared that the work was progressing rapidly. So was the work of demolishing a block of empty buildings to get girders for the second ship, on which work had not yet been started. The one under construction seemed to be of cruciform design, like an old-fashioned pre-contragravity winged airplane. The design puzzled everybody at Barathrum. Yves Jacquemont thought that perhaps there would be decks in the cross-arm which would be used when the ship was running on combined lift and drive.

"Well, till we can get a shipyard going on Koshchei and build some real spaceships, there are going to be some rare-looking objects traveling around the Alpha System. I wonder what the next one's going to look like —a flying sky-scraper?" Conn said.

"What I wonder," Yves Jacquemont replied, "is where all the old interplanetary ships got to. There must have been hundreds of them running back and forth from here to Janicot and Koshchei and Jurgen and Horvendile during the War. They must have gone somewhere."

"Couldn't they all have been fitted with Dillingham hyperdrive engines and used in the evacuation?"

"Possible. But the average interplanetary ship isn't very big; five hundred to seven-fifty feet in diameter. One of those things couldn't carry more than a couple of hundred people, after you put in all the supplies and the hydroponic tanks and carniculture vats and so on for a four- to six-month voyage. I can't see the economy of altering anything that small for interstellar work. Why, the smallest of these tramp freighters that come in here will run about fifteen hundred feet."

They didn't just disintegrate when peace broke out, that was for sure. And there certainly weren't any of them left on Poictesme. He puzzled over it briefly, then shoved it aside. He had more important things to think about.

In his spare time he was studying, along with his other work, everything he could find on Koshchei, with an intensity he had not given to anything since cramming for examinations at the University. There was a lot of it.

The fourth planet of Alpha Gartner was older than Poictesme; geologists claimed that it was the oldest thing, the sun excepted, in the system, and astrophysicists were far from convinced that it hadn't been captured from either Beta or Gamma when the three stars had been much closer together. It had certainly been formed at a much higher temperature than Janicot or Poictesme or Jurgen or Horvendile. For better than a billion years, it had been molten-hot, and it had lost most of its lighter elements in gaseous form along with its primary atmosphere, leaving little to form a light-rock crust. All that had remained had been a core of almost pure iron and a mantle that was mostly high-grade iron ore.

The same process had gone on, as it cooled, as on any Terra-size planet. After the surface had started to congeal, gases, mostly carbon dioxide and water vapor, had come up to form a secondary atmosphere, the water vapor forming a cloud envelope, condensing, and sending down rain that returned immediately as steam. Solar radiations and electric discharges broke some of that into oxygen and hydrogen; most of the hydrogen escaped into space. Finally, the surface cooled further and the rain no longer steamed off.

The whole planet started to rust. It had been rusting, slowly, for the billion or so years that had followed, and almost all the free oxygen had become locked in iron oxide. The air was almost pure carbon dioxide. It would have been different if life had ever appeared on Koshchei, but apparently the right amino acids never assembled. Some attempts had been made to introduce vegetation after the colonization of Poictesme, but they had all failed.

Men went to Koshchei; they worked out of doors in oxygen helmets, and lived in airtight domes and generated their own oxygen. There had been mines, and smelters, and blast furnaces and steel mills. And there had been shipyards, where hyperships up to three thousand feet had been built. They had all been abandoned when the War had ended; they were waiting there, on an empty, lifeless planet. Some of them had been built by the Third Fleet-Army Force during the War; most of them dated back almost a century before that, to the original industrial boom. All of them could be claimed under the Abandoned Property Act of 867, since all had been taken over by the Federation, and the original owners, or their heirs, compensated.

And there was the matter of selecting a crew. As an influential non-office-holding stockholder in all the companies involved, Conn Maxwell, of course, would represent them. He would also serve as astrogator. Clyde Nichols would command the ship in atmosphere, and act as first mate in space. Mack Vibart would be chief engineer at all times. Yves Jacquemont would be first officer under Nichols, and captain outside atmosphere. They had three real space crewmen, named Roddell, Youtsko and O'Keefe, who had been in Storisende jail as a result of a riotous binge when their ship had lifted out, six months before. The rest of the company-Jerry

Rivas, Anse Dawes, Charley Gatworth, Mohammed Matsui, and four other engineers, Ludvyckson, Gomez, Karanja and Retief-rated as ordinary spacemen for the trip, and would do most of the exploration work after landing.

They got the controls put up; they would work in either position. The engines were lifted in and placed. Conn finished the robo-pilot and the astrogational computers and saw them installed. The air-and-water recycling system went in. The collapsium armor went on. In the news-screen, they saw the spaceship at Storisende still far from half finished, with swarms of heavy-duty lifters and contragravity machiners around it, and a set of landing-stands, on which the second ship was to be built, in the process of construction.

A tramp hyperspace freighter landed at Storisende, the *Andromeda*, five months from Terra, with a cargo of general merchandise. Rodney Maxwell and Wade Lucas had assembled a cargo of medicines and hospital equipment which they thought could be sold profitably. They began dickering with the owner-captain of the hypership.

A farm-tramp down in the tobacco country to the south, evidently ignorant that the former commander of the Third Force was still alive, had proclaimed himself to be the reincarnation of Foxx Travis and was forbidding everybody, on pain of court-martial and firing squad, from meddling with Merlin. And an evangelist in the west was declaring that Merlin was really Satan in mechanical shape.

The *Harriet Barne* was finished. The first test, lifting her to three hundred miles, turning her bow-up, and taking her another thousand miles, had been a success. They brought her back and set her down in the middle of the crater, and began getting the supplies aboard. Kurt Fawzi, Klem Zareff, Judge Ledue, Franz Veltrin and the others flew over from Force Command. Sylvie Jacquemont came from Litchfield, and so did Wade Lucas, Morgan Gatworth, Lester Dawes, Lorenzo Menardes and a number of others. Neither Conn's mother nor sister came.

"I don't know what's the matter with those two," Sylvie told him. "They always seem to be scrapping with each other now, and the only thing they can agree on is that you and your father ought to stop whatever you're doing, right away. Your mother can't adjust to your father being a big Storisende businessman, and she says he'll lose every centisol he has and both of you will probably go to jail, and then she's afraid you will find Merlin, and Flora's sure you and your father are swindling everybody on the planet."

"Sylvie, I had no idea things would be like that," he told her contritely. "I wish I hadn't suggested that you stay there, now."

"Oh, it isn't so bad, so far. Your mother and I get along all right when Flora isn't there, and Flora and I get along when your mother isn't around. Mealtimes aren't much fun, though."

His father came out from Storisende, looked the ship over, and seemed relieved.

"I'm glad you're ready to get off," he said. "You know this hyperspace freighter, the *Andromeda*? Some private group in Storisende has chartered her. She's loading supplies now. I have a private detective agency, Barton-Massarra, trying to find out where's she's going. I think you'd better get this ship off, right away."

"We have everything aboard, all the supplies and everything," Jacquemont told him. "We can lift off tonight."

XIII

The ship lurched slightly. In the outside screens, the lights around, the crowd that was waving good-bye, and the floor of the crater began receding. The sound pickups were full of cheering, and the boom of a big gun at one of the top batteries, and the recorded and amplified music of a band playing the traditional "Spacemen's Hymn."

"It's been a long time since I heard that played in earnest," Jacquemont said. "Well, we're off to see the Wizard."

The lights dwindled and merged into a tiny circle in the darkness of the crater. The music died away; the cannon shots became a faint throbbing. Finally, there was silence, and only the stars above and the dark land and the starlit sea below. After a long while a sunset glow, six hours past on Barathrum, appeared in the west, behind the now appreciable curvature of the planet.

"Stand by for shift to vertical," Captain Nichols called, his voice echoing from PA-outlets through the ship.

"Ready for shift, Captain Nichols," Jacquemont reported from the duplicate-control panel.

Conn went to the after bulkhead, leaning his back against it. "Ready here, Captain," he said. Other voices took it up. Lights winked on the control panels.

"Shifting over," Nichols said. "Your ship now, Captain Jacquemont."

"Thank you, Mr. Nichols."

The deck began to tilt, and then he was lying on his back, his feet against the side of the control room, which had altered its shape and dimensions. There was a jar as the drive went on in line with the new direction of the lift and the ship began accelerating. He got to his feet, and he and Charley Gatworth went to the astrogational computer and began checking the data and setting the course for the point in space at which Koshchei would be in a hundred and sixty hours.

"Course set, Captain," he reported to Jacquemont, after a while.

A couple of lights winked on the control panel. There was nothing more to do but watch Poictesme dwindle behind, and listen to the newscasts, and take turns talking to friends on the planet.

They approached the halfway point; the acceleration rate decreased, and the gravity indicator dropped, little by little. Everybody was enjoying the new sense of lightness, romping and sky-larking like newly landed tourists on Luna. It was fun, as long as they landed on their feet at each jump, and the food and liquids stayed on plates and in glasses and cups. Yves Jacquemont began posting signs in conspicuous places:

WEIGHT IS WHAT YOU LIFT, MASS IS WHAT HURTS
WHEN IT HITS YOU.
WEIGHT DEPENDS ON GRAVITY; MASS IS ALWAYS CONSTANT.

His father came on-screen from his office in Storisende. By then, there was a 30-second time lag in communication between the ship and Poictesme.

"My private detectives found out about the *Andromeda*," he said. "She's going to Panurge, in the Gamma System. They have a couple of computermen with them, one they hired from the Stock Exchange, and one they practically shanghaied away from the Government. And some of the people who chartered the ship are members of a family that were interested in a positronic-equipment plant on Panurge at the time of the War."

"That's all right, then; we don't need to worry about that any more. They're just hunting for Merlin."

Some of his companions were looking at him curiously. A little later, Piet Ludvyckson, the electromagnetics engineer, said: "I thought you were looking for Merlin, Conn."

"Not on Koschchei. We're looking for something to build a hypership out of. If I had Merlin in my hip pocket right now, I'd trade it for one good ship like the *City of Asgard* or the *City of Nefertiti*, and give a keg of brandy and a box of cigars to boot. If we had a ship of our own, we'd be selling lots of both, and not for Storisende Spaceport prices, either."

"But don't you think Merlin's important?" Charley Gatworth, who had overheard him, asked.

"Sure. If we find Merlin, we can run it for President. It would make a better one than Jake Vyckhoven."

He let it go at that. Plenty of opportunities later to expand the theme.

The gravitation gauge dropped to zero. Now they were in free fall, and it lasted twice as long as Yves Jacquemont had predicted. There were a few misadventures, none serious and most of them comic-For example, when Jerry Rivas opened a bottle of beer, everybody was chasing the amber globules and catching them in cups, and those who were splashed were glad it hadn't been hot coffee.

They made their second, 180-degree turnover while weightless. Then they began decelerating and approached Koshchei stern-on, and the gravity gauge began climbing slowly up again, and things began staying put, and they were walking instead of floating. Koshchei grew larger and larger ahead; the polar icecaps, and the faint dappling of clouds, and the dark wiggling lines on the otherwise uniform red-brown surface which were mountain ranges became visible. Finally they began to see, first with the telescopic screens and then without magnification, the little dots and specks that were cities and industrial centers.

Then they were in atmosphere, and Jacquemont made the final shift, to horizontal position, and turned the ship over to Nichols.

For a moment, the scout-boat tumbled away from the ship and Conn was back in free fall. Then he got on the lift-and-drive and steadied it, and pressed the trigger button, firing a green smoke bomb. Beside him, Yves Jacquemont put on the radio and the screen pickups. He could see the ship circling far above, and the manipulator-boat, with its claw-arms and grapples, breaking away from it. Then he looked down on the endless desert of iron oxide that stretched in all directions to the horizon, until he saw a spot, optically the size of a five-centisol piece, that was the shipbuilding city of Port Carpenter. He turned the boat toward it, firing four more green smokes at three-second intervals. The manipulator-boat started to follow, and the *Harriet Barne*, now a distant speck in the sky, began coming closer.

Below, as he cut speed and altitude, he could see the pock-marks of open-pit mines and the glint of sunlight on bright metal and armor-glass roofs, the blunt conical stacks of nuclear furnaces and the twisted slag-flows, like the ancient lava-flows of Barathrum. And, he reflected, he was an influential non-office-holding stockholder in every bit of it, as soon as they could screen Storisende and get claims filed.

A high tower rose out of the middle of Port Carpenter, with a glass-domed mushroom top. That would be the telecast station; the administrative buildings were directly below it and around its base. He came in slowly over the city, above a spaceport with its empty landing pits in a double circle around a traffic-control building, and airship docks and warehouses beyond. More steel mills. Factories, either hemispherical domes or long buildings with rounded tops. Ship-construction yards and docks; for the most part, these were empty, but on some of them the landing-stands of spaceships, like eight-and ten-legged spiders, waiting for forty years for hulls to be built on them. A few spherical skeletons of ships, a few with some of the outer skin on. It wasn't until he was passing close to them that he realized how huge they were. And stacks of material-sheet steel, deckplate, girders-and contragravity lifters and construction machines, all left on jobs that were never finished, the bright rustless metal dulled by forty years of rain and windblown red dust. They must have been working here to the very last, and then, when the evacuation elsewhere was completed, they had dropped whatever they were doing, piled into such ships as were completed, and lifted away.

The mushroom-topped tower rose from the middle of a circular building piled level on level, almost half a mile across. He circled over it, saw an airship dock, and called the *Harriet Barne* while Jacquemont talked to Jerry Rivas, piloting the manipulator-boat. Rivas came in and joined them in the air; they hovered over the dock and helped the ship down when she came in, nudging her into place.

By the time Conn and Jacquemont and Rivas and Anse Dawes and Roddell and Youtsko and Karanja were out on the dock in oxygen helmets, the ship's airlock was opening and Nichols and Vibart and the others were coming out, towing a couple of small lifters loaded with equipment.

The airlocked door into the building, at the end of the dock, was closed; when somebody pulled the handle, it refused to open. That meant it was powered from the central power plant, wherever that was. There was a plug socket beside it, with the required voltage marked over it. They used an extension line from a power unit on one of the lifters to get it open, and did the same with the inner door; when it was open, they passed into a dim room that stretched away ahead of them and on either side.

It looked like a freight-shipping room; there were a few piles of boxes and cases here and there, and a litter of packing material everywhere. A long counter-desk, and a bank of robo-clerks behind it. According to the air-analyzer, the oxygen content inside was safely high. They all pulled off their fishbowl helmets and slung them.

"Well, we can bunk inside here tonight," somebody said. "It won't be so crowded here."

"We'll bunk here after we find the power plant and get the ventilator fans going," Jacque-mont said.

Anse Dawes held up the cigarette he had lighted; that was all the air-analyzer he needed.

"That looks like enough oxygen," he said.

"Yes, it makes its own ventilation; convection," Jacquemont said. "But you go to sleep in here, and you'll smother in a big puddle of your own exhaled CO_2. Just watch what the smoke from that cigarette's doing."

The smoke was hanging motionless a few inches from the hot ash on the end of the cigarette.

"We'll have to find the power plant, then," Matsui, the power-engineer said. "Down at the bottom and in the middle, I suppose, and anybody's guess how deep this place goes."

"We'll find plans of the building," Jerry Rivas said. "Any big dig I've ever been on, you could always find plans. The troubleshooters always had them; security officer, and maintenance engineer."

There were inside-use vehicles in the big room; they loaded what they had with them onto a couple of freight-skids and piled on, starting down a passage toward the center of the building. The passageways were well marked with direction-signs, and they found the administrative area at the top and center, around the base of the telecast-tower. The security offices, from which police, military guard, fire protection and other emergency services were handled, had a fine set of plans and maps, not only for the building itself but for everything else in Port Carpenter. The power plant, as Matsui had surmised, was at the very bottom, directly below.

The only trouble, after they found it, was that it was completely dead. The reactors wouldn't react, the converters wouldn't convert, and no matter how many switches they shoved in, there was no power output. The inside telemetered equipment, of course, was self-powered. Some of them were dead, too, but from those which still worked Mohammed Matsui got a uniformly disheartening story.

"You know what happened?" he said. "When this gang bugged out, back in 854, they left the power on. Now the conversion mass is all gone, and the plutonium's all spent. We'll have to find more plutonium, and tear this whole thing down and refuel it, and repack the mass-conversion chambers-provided nothing's eaten holes in itself after the mass inside was all converted."

"How long will it take?" Conn asked.

"If we can find plutonium, and if we can find robots to do the work inside, and if there's been no structural damage, and if we keep at it —a couple of days."

"All right; let's get at it. I don't know where we'll find shipyards like these anywhere else, and if we do, things'll probably be as bad there. We came here to fix things up and start them, didn't we?"

It didn't take as long as Mohammed Matsui expected. They found the fissionables magazine, and in it plenty of plutonium, each subcritical slug in a five-hundred-pound collapsium canister. There were repair-robots, and they only had to replace the cartridges in the power units of three of them. They sent them inside the collapsium-shielded death-to-people area-transmitter robots, to relay what the others picked up through receptors wire-connected with the outside; foremen-robots, globes a yard in diameter covered with horns and spikes like old-fashioned ocean-navy mines; worker-robots, in a variety of shapes, but mostly looking like many-clawed crabs.

Neither the converter nor the reactor had sustained any damage while the fissionables were burning out. So the robots began tearing out reactor-elements, and removing plutonium slugs no longer capable of sustaining chain reaction but still dangerously radioactive. Nuclear reactors had become simpler and easier to service since the First Day of the Year Zero, when Enrico Fermi put the first one into operation, but the principles remained the same. Work was less back-breaking and muscle-straining, but it called for intense concentration on screens and meters and buttons that was no less exhausting.

The air around them began to grow foul. Finally, the air-analyzer squawked and flashed red lights to signal that the oxygen had dropped below the safety margin. They had no mobile fan equipment, or time to hunt any; they put on their fishbowl helmets and went back to work. After twelve hours, with a few short breaks, they had the reactors going. Jerry Rivas and a couple of others took a heavy-duty lifter and went looking for conversion mass; they brought back a couple of tons of scrap-iron and fed it to the converters. A few seconds after it was in, the pilot lights began coming on all over the panels. They took two more hours to get the oxygen-separator and the ventilator fans going, and for good measure they started the water pumps and the heating system. Then they all went outside to the ship to sleep. The sun was just coming up.

It was sunset when they rose and returned to the building. The airlocks opened at a touch on the operating handles. Inside, the air was fresh and sweet, the temperature was a pleasantly uniform 75 degrees Fahrenheit, the fans were humming softly, and there was running hot and cold water everywhere.

Jerry Rivas, Anse Dawes, and the three tramp freighter fo'c'sle hands took lifters and equipment and went off foraging. The rest of them went to the communications center to get the telecast station, the radio beacon, and the inside-screen system into operation. There were a good many things that had to be turned on manually, and more things that had been left on, forty years ago, and now had to be repowered or replaced. They worked at it most of the night; before morning, almost everything was working, and they were sending a signal across twenty-eight million miles to Storisende, on Poictesme.

It was late evening, Storisende time, but Rodney Maxwell, who must have been camping beside his own screen, came on at once, which is to say five and a half minutes later.

"Well, I see you got in somewhere. Where are you, and how is everything?"

Then he picked up a cigar out of an ashtray in front of him and lit it, waiting.

"Port Carpenter; we're in the main administration building," Conn told him. He talked for a while about what they had found and done since their arrival. "Have you an extra viewscreen, fitted for recording?" he asked.

Five and a half minutes later, his father nodded. "Yes, right here." He leaned forward and away from the communication screen in front of him. "I have it on." He gave the wave-length combination. "Ready to receive."

"This is about all we have, now. Views we took coming in, from the ship and a scout-boat." He started transmitting them. "We haven't sent in any claims yet. I wasn't sure whether I should make them for Alpha-Interplanetary, or Litchfield Exploration & Salvage."

"Don't bother sending in anything to the Claims Office," his father said. "Send anything you want to claim in here to me, and I'll have Sterber, Flynn & Chen-Wong file them. They'll be made for a new company we're organizing."

"What? Another one?"

His father nodded, grinning. "Koshchei Exploitation & Development; we've made application already. We can't claim exclusive rights to the whole planet, like the old interstellar exploration companies did before the War, but since you're the only people on the planet, we can come pretty close to it by detail." He was looking to one side, at the other screen. "Great Ghu, Conn! This place of yours all together beats everything I ever dug, Force Command and Barathrum Spaceport included. How big would you say it is? More than ten miles in radius?"

"About five or six. Ten or twelve miles across."

"That's all right, then. We'll just claim the building you're in, now, and the usual ten-mile radius, the same as at Force Command. We'll claim the place as soon as the company's chartered; in the meantime, send in everything else you can get views of."

They set up a regular radio-and-screen watch after that. Charley Gatworth and Piet Ludvyckson, both of whom were studying astrogation in hopes of qualifying as space officers after they had a real spaceship, elected themselves to that duty; it gave them plenty of time for study. Jerry Rivas and Anse Dawes, with whomever they could find to help them, were making a systematic search. They looked first of all for foodstuffs, and found enough in the storerooms of three restaurants on the executive level to feed their own party in gourmet style for a year, and enough in the main storerooms to provision an army. They even found refrigerators and freeze-bins full of meat and vegetables fresh after forty years. That surprised everybody, for the power units had gone dead long ago. Then it was noticed that they were covered with collapsium. Anything that would stop cosmic rays was a hundred percent efficient as a heat insulator.

Coming in, the first day, Conn had seen an almost completed hypership bulking above the domes and roofs of Port Carpenter in the distance. He saw it again on screen from a pickup atop the central tower. As soon as the party was comfortably settled in the executive apartments on the upper levels, he and Yves Jacquemont and Mack Vibart and Schalk Retief, the construction engineer, found an aircar in one of the hangars and went to have a closer look at her.

She had all her collapsium on, except for a hundred-foot circle at the top and a number of rectangular openings around the sides. Yves Jacquemont said that would be where the airlocks would go.

"They always put them on last. But don't be surprised at anything you find or don't find inside. As soon as the skeleton's up they put the armor on, and then build the rest of the ship out from the middle. It might be slower getting material in through the airlock openings, but it holds things together while they're working."

They put on the car's lights, lifted to the top, and let down through the upper opening. It was like entering a huge globular spider's web, globe within globe of interlaced girders and struts and braces, extending from the center to the outer shell. Even the spider was home —a three-hundred-foot ball of collapsium, looking tiny at the very middle.

"Why, this isn't a ship!" Vibart cried in disgust. "This is just the outside of a ship. They haven't done a thing inside."

"Oh, yes, they have," Jacquemont contradicted, aiming a spotlight toward the shimmering ball in the middle. "They have all the engines in-Abbott lift-and-drive, Dillingham hyperdrives, pseudograv, power reactors, converters, everything. They wouldn't have put on the shielding if they hadn't. They did that as soon as they had the outside armor on."

"Wonder why they didn't finish her, if they got that far," Retief said.

"They didn't need her. They'd had it; they wanted to go home."

"Well, we're not going to finish her, not with any fifteen men," Retief said. "One man has only two hands, two feet and one brain; he can only handle so much robo-equipment at a time."

"I never expected we'd build a ship ourselves," Conn said. "We came to look the place over and get a few claims staked. When we've done that, we'll go back and get a real gang together."

"I don't know where you'll find them," Jacquemont commented. "We'll need a couple of hundred, and they ought all to be graduate engineers. We can't do this job with farm-tramps."

"You made some good shipyard men out of farm-tramps on Barathrum."

"And what'll you do for supervisors?"

"You're one. General superintendent. Mack, you and Schalk are a couple of others. You just keep a day ahead of your men in learning the job, you'll do all right."

Vibart turned to Jacquemont. "You know, Yves, he'll do it," he said. "He doesn't know how impossible this is, and when we try to tell him, he won't believe us. You can't stop a guy like that. All right, Conn; deal me in."

"I won't let anybody be any crazier than I am," Jacquemont declared, and then looked around the vastness of the empty ship with its lacework of steel. "All you need is about ten million square feet of decks and bulkheads, an air-and-water system, hydroponic tanks and carniculture vats, astrogation and robo-pilot equipment, about which I know very little, a hyperspace pilot system, about which I know nothing at all....Conn, why don't you just build a new Merlin? It would be simpler."

"I don't want a new Merlin. I'm not even interested in the original Merlin. This is what I want, right here."

He told his father, by screen, about the ship. "I believe we can finish her, but not with the gang that's here. We'll need a couple of hundred men. Now, with the supplies we've found, we can stay here indefinitely. Should we do more exploring and claim some more of these places, or should we come home right away and start recruiting, and then come back with a large party, start work on the ship, and explore and make further claims as we have time?" he asked.

"Better come back as soon as possible. Just explore Port Carpenter, find out what's going to be needed to finish the ship and what facilities you have to produce it, and get things cleaned up a little so that you can start work as soon as you have people to do it. I'm organizing an-other company-don't laugh, now; I've only started promotioneering-which I think we will call Trisystem & Interstellar Spacelines. Get me all the views you can of the ship herself and of the steel mills and that sort of thing that will produce material for finishing her; I want to use them in promotion. By the way, has she a name?"

"Only a shipyard construction number."

"Then suppose you call her *Ouroboros*, after Genji Gartner's old ship, the one that discovered the Trisystem."

"*Ouroboros II*; that's fine. Will do."

"Good. I'll have Sterber, Flynn & Chen-Wong make application for a charter right away. We'll have to make Alpha-Interplanetary one of the stockholding companies, and also Koschchei Exploitation & Development, and, of course, Litchfield Exploration & Salvage...."

It was a pity there really wasn't a Merlin. If this kept on nothing else would be able to figure out who owned how much stock in what.

They found the on-the-job engineering office for the ship in a small dome half a mile from the construction dock. Yves Jacquemont and Mack Vibart and Schalk Retief moved in and buried themselves to the ears in specifications and blueprints. The others formed into parties of three or four, and began looking about production facilities for material. There was a steel mill a mile from the construction site; it was almost fully robotic. Iron ore went in at one end, and finished sheet steel and girders and deck plates came out at the other, and a dozen men could handle the whole thing. There was a collapsium plant; there were machine-shops and forging-shops. Every time they finished inspecting one, Yves Jacquemont would have a list of half a dozen more plants that he wanted found and examined yesterday morning at the latest.

Some of them were in a frightful mess; work had been suspended and everybody had gone away leaving everything as it was. Some were in perfect order, ready to go into operation again as soon as power was put on. It had depended, apparently, upon the personal character of whoever had been in charge in the end. The nuclear-electric power unit plant was in the latter class. The man in charge of it evidently hadn't believed in leaving messes behind, even if he didn't expect to come back.

It was built in the shape of a T. One side of the cross-stroke contained the cartridge-case plant, where presses formed sheet-steel cylinders, some as small as a round of pistol ammunition and some the size of ten-gallon kegs. They moved toward the center on a production line, finally reaching a matter-collapser where they were plated with collapsium. From the other side, radioactive isotopes, mostly reactor-waste, came in through evacuated and collapsium-shielded chambers, were sorted, and finally, where the cross-arm of the T joined the downstroke, packed in the collapsium cases. The production line continued at right angles down the long building in which the apparatus which converted nuclear energy to electric current was assembled and packed; at the end, the finished power cartridges came off, big ones for heavy machines and tiny ones for things like hand tools and pocket lighters and razors. There were stacks of them, in all sizes, loaded on skids and ready to move out. Except for the minute and unavoidable leakage of current, they were as good as the day they were assembled, and would be for another century.

Like almost everything else, the power-cartridge plant was airtight and had its own oxygen-generator. The air-analyzer reported the oxygen insufficient to support life. That was understandable; there were a lot of furnaces which had evidently been hot when the power was cut off; they had burned up the oxygen before cooling. They put on their oxygen equipment when they got out of the car.

"I'll go back and have a look at the power plant," Matsui said. "If it's like the rest of this place, it'll be ready to go as soon as the reactors are started. I wish everybody here had left things like this."

"Well, we'll have to check everything to make sure nothing was left on when the main power was cut," Conn said. "Don't do anything back there till we give you the go-ahead."

Matsui nodded and set off on foot along the broad aisle in the middle. Conn looked around in the dim light that filtered through the dusty glass overhead. On either side of the central aisle were two production lines; between each pair, at intervals, stood massive machines which evidently fabricated parts for the power cartridges. Over them, and over the machines directly involved in production, were receptor aerials, all oriented toward a stubby tower, twenty feet thick and fifty in height, topped by a hemispherical dome.

"That'll be the control tower for all the machinery in here," he decided. "Anse, suppose you and I go take a look at it."

"We'll take a look at the machines," Rivas said. "Clyde, you and I can work back on the right and then come down on the other side. You know anything about this stuff?"

"Me? Nifflheim, no," Nichols said. "I know a robo-control when I see one, and I know whether it's set to receive or not."

There was a self-powered lift inside the control tower. Conn and Anse rode it to the top and got out, Anse snapping on his flashlight. It was dark in the dome at the top; instead of windows there were viewscreens all around it. Five men had worked here; at least, there were four chairs at four intricate control panels, one for each of the four production lines, and a fifth chair in front of a number of communication screens. There was a heavy-duty power unit, turned off. Conn threw the switch. Lights came on inside, and the outside viewscreens lit.

They were examining the control-panels when Conn's belt radio buzzed. He plugged it in on his helmet. It was Mohammed Matsui.

"There's one big power plant back here," the engineer said. "Right in the middle. It only powers what's in front of it. There must be another one in either wing, for the isotope plant and the cartridge-case plant. I'll go look at them. But the power's been cut off from the machines in the main building. There's four big switches, one for each production line —"

He was interrupted by a shout, almost a shriek, from somewhere. It sounded like Jerry Rivas. A moment later, Rivas was clamoring:

"Conn! What did you turn on? Turn it off, right away!"

Anse jumped to the switch, pulling it with one hand and getting on his flashlight with the other. The lights went out and the screens went dark.

"It's off."

"The dickens it is!" Rivas disputed. "There are a couple of big supervisor-robots circling around, and a flock of workers...."

At the same time, Clyde Nichols began cursing. Or maybe he was praying; it was hard to be certain.

"But we pulled the switch. It was only the lights and viewscreens in here, anyhow."

"It didn't do any good. Pull another one."

Matsui, back at the power plant, was wanting to know what was wrong. Captain Nichols stopped cursing-or praying? —and said, "Mutiny, that's what! The robots have turned on us!"

He knew what had happened, or was almost sure he did. A radio impulse had gone out, somehow, from the control tower. Something they hadn't checked, that had been left on. There was just enough current-leakage from the units in the robots to keep the receptors active for forty years. The supervisor-robots had gone active, and they had activated the rest. Once on, cutting the current from the control tower wouldn't turn them off again.

"Put the switch in again, Anse; the damage is done and you won't make it any worse."

When the screens came on, he looked around from one to another. The two supervisors, big ovoid things like the small round ones they had used in repairing the power reactors the first day, were circling aimlessly near the roof, one clockwise and the other counterclockwise, dodging obstructions and getting politely out of each other's way. At lower altitude, a dozen assorted worker-robots were moving about, and more were emerging from cells at the end of the building. Sweepers, with rotary brooms and rakes, crablike all-purpose handling robots, a couple of vacuum-cleaning robots, each with a flexible funnel-tipped proboscis and a bulging dust-sack. One tiling, a sort of special job designed to get into otherwise inaccessible places, had a twenty-foot, many-jointed, claw-tipped arm in front. It passed by and slightly over the tower, saw Clyde Nichols, and swooped toward him. With a howl, Nichols dived under one of the large machines between two production lines. A pistol went off a couple of times. That would be Jerry Rivas. Nobody else bothered with a gun on Koshchei, but he carried one as some people carry umbrellas, whether he expected to need it or not and because he would feel lost without it.

That he took in at one glance. Then he was looking at the control panels. The switches and buttons were all marked for machine-control in different steps of power-unit production. That was all for the big stuff, powered centrally. There weren't any controls for lifters or conveyers or other mobile equipment. Evidently they were handled out in the shop, from mobile control-vehicles. He did find, on the communication-screen panel, a lot of things that had been left on. He snapped them off, one after another, snapping them on when a screen went dark. There were fifteen or twenty robots, some rather large, in the air or moving on the floor by now.

"We can't do anything here," he told Anse. "These are the shop-cleaning robots. They were the last things used here when the place closed down, and the two supervisors were probably controlled from a vehicle, and it's anybody's guess where that is now. When you threw that switch, it sent out an impulse that activated them. They're running their instruction-tapes, and putting the others through all their tricks."

Three more shots went off. Jerry Rivas was shouting: "Hey, whattaya know! I killed one of the buggers!"

There were any number of ways in which a work-robot could be shot out of commission with a pistol. All of them would be by the purest of pure luck. The next time we go into a place like this, Conn thought, we take a couple of bazookas along.

"Turn everything off and let's go. See what we can do outside."

Anse put on his flashlight and pulled the switch. They got into the lift and rode down, going outside. As soon as they emerged, they saw a rectangular object fifteen feet long settle over their aircar, let down half a dozen clawed arms, and pick it up, flying away with it. It had taped instructions to remove anything that didn't belong in the aisleway; it probably asked the supervisor about the aircar, and the supervisor didn't return an inhibitory signal, so it went ahead. Conn and Anse both shouted at it, knowing perfectly well that shouting was futile. Then they were running for their lives with one of the crablike all-purpose jobs after them. They dived under the slightly raised bed of a long belt-conveyer and crawled. Jerry Rivas fired another shot, somewhere.

The robots themselves were having troubles. They had done all the work they were supposed to do; now the supervisors were insisting that they do it over again. Uncomplainingly, they swept and raked and vacuum-cleaned where they had vacuum-cleaned and raked and swept forty years ago. The scrap-pickers, having picked all the scrap, were going over the same places and finding nothing, and then getting deflected and gathering a lot of things not definable as scrap, and then circling around, darting away from one another in obedience to their radar-operated evasion-systems, and trying to get to the outside scrap pile, and finding that the doors wouldn't open because the door openers weren't turned on, and finally dumping what they were carrying when the supervisors gave them no instructions.

One of them seemed to have dumped something close to where Clyde Nichols was hiding; if his language had been a little stronger, it would have burned out Conn's radio. Their own immediate vicinity being for the moment clear of flying robots, Conn and Anse rolled from under the conveyer and legged it between the two production lines. Immediately, three of the crablike all-purpose handling-robots saw them, if that was the word for it, and came dashing for them, followed by a thing that was mostly dump-lifter; it was banging its bin-lid up and down angrily. About fifty yards ahead, Jerry Rivas stepped from behind a machine and fired; one of the handling-robots flashed green from underneath, went off contragravity, and came down with a crash. Immediately, like wolves on a wounded companion, the other two pounced upon it, dragging and pulling against each other. That was a hunk of junk; their orders were to remove it.

The mobile trash-bin went zooming up to the ceiling, reversed within twenty feet of it and came circling back to the ground, to go zooming up again. It had gone crazy, literally. It had been getting too many contradictory orders from its supervisor, and its circuits were over-loaded and its relays jammed. Rats in mazes and human-type people in financial difficulties go psychotic in very much the same way.

The two surviving all-purpose robots were also headed for a padded repair shop. They had come close enough to each other to activate their anticollision safeties. Immediately, they flew apart. Then their order to pick up that big piece of junk took over, and they started forward again, to be bounced apart as soon as they were within five feet of one another. If left alone, their power units would run down in a year or so; until then, they would keep on trying.

Soulless intelligences, indeed! Then it occurred to him that for the past however-long-it-had-been he hadn't heard from Mohammed Matsui. He jiggled his radio.

"Ham, where are you? Are you still alive?"

"I'm back at the power plant," Matsui said exasperatedly. "There's a big thing circling around here; every time I stick my head out, he makes a dive at me. I didn't know robots would attack people."

"They don't. He just thinks you're some more trash he's been told to gather up."

Matsui was indignant. Conn laughed.

"On the level, Ham. He has photoelectric vision, and a picture of what that aisle is supposed to look like. When you get out in it, he knows you don't belong there and tries to grab you."

"Hey, there's a lot of junk in here in a couple of baskets at the converter. Say I chuck one out to him; what would he do?"

"Grab it and take it away, like he's taped to do."

"Okay; wait a minute."

They couldn't see the archway to the power plant, or even the robot that had Matsui penned up, but after a few minutes they saw it soaring away, clutching a big wire basket full of broken boxes and other rubbish. It headed for the mutually repelling swarm of robots around the door that wouldn't open for them. Conn and Anse and Jerry ran toward the rear, joined by Clyde Nichols, who popped up from behind a pile of spools of electric wire. They made it just before the coffin-shaped thing that had carried off the aircar came over to investigate.

"You want to be careful back there," Matsui told them, as they started toward the temporary safety of the power plant. "All the reactor-repair robots are there; don't get *them* on the warpath next."

Of course! There were always repair-robots at a power plant, to go into places no human could enter and live. Behind the collapsium shielding, they wouldn't have been activated.

"Let's have a look at them. What kind?"

"Standard reactor-servicers; the same we used at the administration center."

Matsui opened the door, and they went into the power plant. Conn and Matsui put on the service-power and activated the two supervisors; they, in turn, activated their workers. It was tricky work getting them all outside the collapsium-walled power-plant area; each worker had to be passed through by the supervisor inside, under Matsui's control. Because of the close quarters at which they worked inside the reactor and the converter, they weren't fitted with anticollision repulsors, and, working under close human supervision, they all had audiovisual pickups. It took some time to get adequate screens set up outside the collapsium.

Finally, they were ready. Their two supervisors went up to the ceiling, one controlled by Conn and the other by Matsui. The larger, egg-shaped shop-labor supervisors were still moving in irregular orbits; those of the workers still able to receive commands were trying to obey them, and the rest were jammed in a swarm at the other end.

First one, and then the other of the labor-boss robots were captured. They were by now at the end of what might, loosely, be called their wits. They weren't used to operating without orders, and had been sending out commands largely at random. Now they came to a stop, and then began moving in tight, guided circles; one by one, the worker robots still able to heed them were brought to ground and turned off. That left the swarm at the door. The worker-robots under direct control of the power-plant supervisors went after them, grappling them and hauling them down to where Anse and Jerry Rivas and Captain Nichols could turn them off manually.

The aircar was a hopeless wreck, but its radio was still functioning. Conn called Charley Gatworth, who called a gang under Gomez, working not far away; they came with another car.

It took all the next day for a gang of six of them to get the place straightened up. Neither Conn nor Gomez, who was a roboticist himself, would trust any of the workers or the two supervisors; their experiences out of control had rendered them unreliable. They took out their power units and left them to be torn down and repaired later. Other robots were brought in to replace them. When they were through, the power-unit cartridge plant was ready for operation.

Jerry Rivas wanted to start production immediately.

"We'll have to go back to Poictesme pretty soon," he said. "We don't want to go back empty. Well, I know that no matter what we dug up, and what we could sell or couldn't sell, there's always a market for power-unit cartridges. Electric-light units, household-appliance units, aircar and airboat units, any size at all. We run that plant at full capacity for a few days and we can load the *Harriett Barne* full, and I'll bet the whole cargo will be sold in a week after we get in."

XV

The *Harriet Barne* settled comfortably at the dock, the bunting-swathed tugs lifting away from her. They had the outside sound pickups turned as low as possible, and still the noise was deafening. The spaceport was jammed, people on the ground and contragravity vehicles swarming above, with police cars vainly trying to keep them in order. All the bands in Storisende seemed to have been combined; they were blaring the "Planetary Hymn";

When they opened the airlock, there was a hastily improvised ceremonial barge, actually a farm-scow completely draped in red and white, the Planetary colors. They all stopped, briefly, as they came out, to enjoy the novelty of outdoor air which could actually be breathed. Conn saw his father in the scow, and beside him Sylvie Jacquemont, trying, almost successfully, to keep from jumping up and down in excitement. Morgan Gatworth to meet his son, and Lester Dawes to meet his. Kurt Fawzi, Dolf Kellton, Colonel Zareff, Tom Brangwyn. He didn't see his mother, or his sister. Flora he had hardly counted on, but he was disappointed that his mother wasn't there to meet him.

Sylvie was embracing her father as he shook hands with his; then she threw her arms around his neck.

"Oh, Conn, I'm so happy! I was watching everything I could on-screen, everything you saw, and all the places you were, and everything you were doing...."

The scow-pardon, ceremonial barge-gave a slight lurch, throwing them together. Over her shoulder, he saw his father and Yves Jacquemont exchanging grins. Then they had to break it up while he shook hands with Fawzi and Judge Ledue and the others, and by the time that was over, the barge was letting down in front of the stand at the end of the dock, and the band was still deafening Heaven with "Genji Gartner's Body," and they all started up the stairs to be greeted by Planetary President Vyckhoven; he looked like an elderly bear who has been too well fed for too long in a zoo. And by Minister-General Murchison, who represented the Terran Federation on Poictesme. He was thin and balding, and he looked as though he had just mistaken the vinegar cruet for the wine decanter. Genji Gartner's soul stopped marching on, but the speeches started, and that was worse. And after the speeches, there was the parade, everybody riding in transparent-bodied aircars, and the *Lester Dawes* and the two ships of the new Planetary Air Navy and a swarm of gunboats in column five hundred feet above, all firing salutes.

In spite of what wasn't, but might just as well have been, a concerted conspiracy to keep them apart, he managed to get a few words privately with Sylvie.

"My mother; she didn't get here. Is anything wrong?"

"Is anything anything else? I've been in the middle of it ever since you went away. Your mother's still moaning about all these companies your father's promoting-he never used to do anything like that, and it's all too big, and it's going to end in a big smash. And then she gets onto Merlin. You know, she won't say Merlin, she always calls it, 'that thing.'"

"I've noticed that."

"Then she begins talking about all the horrible things that'll happen when it's found, and that sets Flora off. Flora says Merlin's a big fake, and you and your father are using it to rob thousands of widows and orphans of their life savings, and that sets your mother off again. Self-sustaining cyclic reaction, like the Bethe solar-phoenix. And every time I try to pour a little oil on the troubled waters, I find I've gotten it on the fire instead. And then, Flora had this fight with Wade Lucas, and of course, she blames you for that."

"Good heavens, why?"

"Well, she couldn't blame it on herself, could she? Oh, you mean why the fight? Lucas is in business with your father now, and she can't convince him that you and your father are a pair of quadruple-dyed villains, I suppose. Anyhow, the engagement is *phttt*! Conn, is my father going back to Koshchei?"

"As soon as we can round up some people to help us on the ship."

"Then I'm going along. I've had it, Conn. I'm a combat-fatigue case."

"But, Sylvie; that isn't any place for a girl."

"Oh, poo! This is Sylvie. We're old war buddies. We soldiered together on Barathrum; remember?"

"Well, you'd be the only girl, and...."

"That's what you think. If you expect to get any kind of a gang together, at least a third of them will be girls. A lot of technicians are girls, and when work gets slack, they're always the first ones to get shoved out of jobs. I'll bet there are a thousand girl technicians out of work here-any line of work you want to name. I know what I'll do; I'll make a telecast appearance. I still have some news value, from the Barathrum business. Want to bet that I won't be the working girl's Joan of Arc by this time next week?"

That cheered him. A girl can punch any kind of a button a man can, and a lot of them knew what buttons to punch, and why. Say she could find fifty girls....

He had a slightly better chance to talk to his father before the banquet at the Executive Palace that evening. They shared the same suite at the Ritz-Gartner, and even welcoming committees seldom chase their victims from bedroom to bath.

"Yes, I know all about it," Rodney Maxwell said bitterly. "I was home, a couple of weeks ago. Flora simply will not speak to me, and your mother begged me, in tears, to quit everything we're doing here. I tried to give her some idea of what would happen if I dropped this, even supposing I could; she wouldn't listen to me." He finished putting the studs in his shirt. "You still think this is worth what it's costing us?"

"You saw the views we sent back. There's work on Koshchei for a million people, at least. Why, even these two makeshift ships they're putting together here at Storisende are giving work, one way or another, to almost a thousand. Think what things will be like a year from now, if this keeps on."

Rodney Maxwell gave a wry laugh. "Didn't know I had a real Simon-pure altruist for a son."

"Pardner, when you call me that, smile."

"I am smiling. With some slight difficulty."

He didn't think well of the banquet. Back in Litchfield, Senta would have fired half her human help and taken a sledgehammer to her robo-chef for a meal like that. Even his father's camp cook would have been ashamed of it. And there were more speeches.

President Vyckhoven managed to get hold of him and Yves Jacquemont afterward, and steered them into his private study.

"Have you any real reason for thinking that Merlin might be on Koshchei?" the Planetary President asked.

"Great Ghu, no! We weren't looking for Merlin, Mr. President. We were looking for a hypership. We have one, too. Calling her *Ouroboros II*. Twenty-five-hundred-footer. We expect to have her to space in a few months. I surely don't need to tell you what that will do toward restoring planetary prosperity."

"No, of course not; a hypership of our own. But...." He looked from one to the other of them. "But I understood.... That is, Mr. Kurt Fawzi was saying...."

"Mr. Fawzi is looking for Merlin here on Poictesme. If anybody finds it, that's where it'll be found. I'm interested in getting business started again. If Merlin is found, it would help, of course." He shrugged.

"Don't look at me," Jacquemont said. "Mr. Maxwell-both of them, father and son-want some spaceships. They hired me to help build them. That's all I have in it." Then he relit the cigar the President had given him and leaned back in his chair, staring at the stuffed alcesoid head with the seven-foot hornspread above the fireplace.

Conn described the interview to his father after they were back at the hotel.

"I hope you convinced him. You know, he's afraid of Merlin. A lot of people have been saying that if Merlin's found, it should be used to determine Government policy. A few extremists are beginning to say that Merlin ought to *be* the Government, and Jake Vyckhoven and his cronies ought to be dumped. Into the handiest mass-energy converter, preferably. You know, if anybody found Merlin and started it auditing the Planetary Treasury, Jake Vyckhoven'd be the one who'd be wanting a hypership."

Tom Brangwyn ran him down the next morning in the dining room.

"Conn, I wish you'd come along with me," he said. "Some of us are up in Kurt's suite; we'd all like to talk to you."

Somehow, he was acting as though he were making an arrest. That might have been nothing but professional habit. Conn went up to Fawzi's suite, and found Fawzi and Judge Ledue and Dolf Kellton and close to a dozen others there.

"I'm glad you could come, Conn," the Judge greeted him. Now that the defendant had arrived, the trial could begin. "I wish your father could have gotten here. I asked him to come, but he had a prior engagement. A meeting with some of the financial people here, about some company he's interested in."

"That's right; Trisystem & Interstellar Spacelines."

"Interstellar!" Kurt Fawzi almost howled. "Great Ghu! Now it isn't enough to go out to Koshchei; he wants to go clear out of the Trisystem. That's what we wanted to talk about; all this nonsense you and your father are in. Merlin's right here on Poictesme. It's right at Force Command, and if your father hadn't robbed us of all our best men, like Jerry Rivas and Anse Dawes, we'd have found it by now. I don't think you and your father care a hoot if we ever find Merlin or not!"

"Kurt, that's a dreadful thing to say," Dolf Kellton objected in a shocked voice.

"It's a dreadful thing to have to say," Fawzi replied, "but you tell me what Conn Maxwell or Rodney Maxwell are doing to help find it."

"Who showed you where Force Command was?" Klem Zareff asked.

Nobody could think of any good quick comeback to that.

Conn took advantage of the pause to ask, "Why do you want to find Merlin?"

"Why do we ..." Fawzi spluttered indignantly. "If you don't know...."

"I know why I do. I want to see if you do. Do you?"

"Merlin would answer so many questions," Dolf Kellton told him gently. "Questions I can't answer for myself."

"With Merlin, we could set up a legal code and a system of jurisprudence that would give everybody absolute justice," Judge Ledue said.

As if absolute justice wasn't the last thing anybody in his right senses would want; a robot-judge would have the whole planet in jail inside a month.

"We have a man who joined us after you went off to Koshchei, Conn," Franz Veltrin said. "A Mr. Carl Leibert. He's some kind of a clergyman, from over Morven way. He says that Merlin could formulate an entirely new religion, which would regenerate humanity."

"Well, I don't have any such lofty ideas," Fawzi said. "I just want Merlin to show us how to get some prosperity here; bring things back to what they were before Poictesme went broke."

"And that's what Father and I are trying to do. You're going into the woods with a book on how to chop down a tree, and no ax." Fawzi looked at him in surprise, started to say something, and thought better of it. "If we want prosperity, we need tools. Our problem is loss of markets. If we find Merlin, and tape it with everything that's happened in the forty years since it was shut down, Merlin will tell us where to find new markets. But the markets won't come to us. We'll have to do our own exporting, and we'll need ships. Now, you men have been studying about Merlin, and hunting for Merlin, all your lives. I can't add anything to what you know, and neither can my father. You find Merlin, and we'll have the ships ready when you do find it."

"Kurt, I think he has a point," somebody said.

"You're blasted well right he has," Klem Zareff put in. "If it wasn't for Conn Maxwell, you know where we'd be? Back in Litchfield, sitting around in Kurt's office, talking about how wonderful things'll be when we find Merlin, and doing nothing to find it."

"Kurt, I believe Conn is entitled to an apology," Judge Ledue ruled. "How close we are to finding Merlin I don't know, but it is due to him that we have any hope of finding it at all."

"Conn, I'm sorry," Fawzi said. "I oughtn't to have said some of the things I did. But we're all on edge; we've been having so much trouble....Conn, it's right there at Force Command; I know it is. We've been all over the place. We have shafts sunk at each of the corners; we've used scanners, and put off echo shots. Nothing. We looked for additional passages out of the headquarters; there aren't any. But it has to be somewhere around. It just *has* to be!"

"Maybe if I go out to Force Command with you, I might see something you've overlooked. And if I can't, I'll try to scrape up some stuff on Koshchei for you. Deep-vein scanners, that sort of thing, from the mines."

They took the *Lester Dawes* out at a little past noon and turned south and east. Everybody aboard was happy-except Conn Maxwell. He was thinking of the years and years ahead of these trusting, hopeful old men, each year the grave of another expectation. Two hundred miles from Force Command, the *Goblin* met them, her sides still spalled and dented from the hits she had taken in Barathrum Spaceport. When they came in sight of it, the mesa-top was deserted. Fawzi began wondering where in Nifflheim all the drilling rigs, and the seismo-trucks, were. Somebody with a pair of binoculars called attention to activity on the side of the high butte on top of which the relay station was located. Fawzi began swearing exasperatedly.

"Might be something Mr. Leibert thought of," Franz Veltrin suggested.

"Then why in blazes didn't he screen us about it?"

"Who is this Leibert?" Conn asked. "Somebody mentioned him this morning, I think."

"He joined us after you left, Conn," Dolf Kellton said. "He's a clergyman from Morven. No regular denomination; he has a sect of his own."

"Yah, he would!" Klem Zareff rumbled. "Pious fraud!"

"He's really a good man, Conn; Klem's prejudiced. He says we ought to use Merlin to show us the true nature of God, and how to live in accordance with the Divine Will. He says Merlin can teach us a new religion."

A new religion, based on Merlin; that would be good. And then the fanatics who thought Merlin was the Devil would start a holy war to wipe out the servants of Satan, and with all the combat equipment that was lying around on this planet.... For the first time since this business started, he began to feel really frightened.

An aircar came bulleting away from the butte and landed on the mesa as the *Lester Dawes* set down. The man who met them at the head of the vertical shaft wore Federation fatigues-baggy trousers, ankle boots and long smock, dyed black. He was bareheaded, and his white hair was almost shoulder-long. He had a white beard.

"Welcome, Brothers," he greeted, a hand raised in benediction. "And who is this with you?"

His voice was high and quavery; not a good pulpit voice, Conn thought.

Kurt Fawzi introduced Conn, and Leibert grasped his hand with a grip that was considerably stronger than his voice.

"Bless you, young man! It is to you alone that we owe our thanks that we are about to find the Great Computer. Every sapient being in the Galaxy will honor your name for a thousand years."

"Well, I hadn't counted on quite that much, Mr. Leibert. If it'll only help a few of these people to make a decent living I'll be satisfied."

Leibert shook his head sadly. "You think entirely in material terms, young man," he reproved. "Forget these things; acquire the higher spiritual values. The Great Computer must not be degraded to such uses; we should let it show us how to lift ourselves to a high spiritual plane...."

It went on like that, after they went down to Foxx Travis's —now Fawzi's —office, where there were silver-stoppered decanters instead of the old green-glass pitcher, and gold-plated ashtrays, and thick carpets on the floor. The man was a lunatic; he made Fawzi's office gang look frigidly sane. Furthermore, he was an ignoramus. He had no idea what a computer could or couldn't do. Anybody who could build a computer of the sort he thought Merlin was wouldn't need it, he *would* be God.

As he talked, Conn began to be nagged by an odd sense of recognition. He'd seen this Carl Leibert before, somewhere, and somehow he was sure that the long white hair and the untrimmed beard weren't part of the picture. That puzzled him. He doubted if he'd have remembered Leibert from six years ago, almost seven, now, though a lot of itinerant evangelists showed up in Litchfield. That might have been it.

"I tell you, the Great Computer is there, in the heart of the butte," Leibert was insisting, now. "It has been revealed to me in a dream. It is completely buried. After it was made, no human touched it. The men who were here and used it in the War communicated with it only by radio."

That could be so. There were fully robotic computers, intended for use in places where no human could go and live. There was a big one on Nifflheim, armored against the fluorine atmosphere and the hydrofluoric-acid rains. But there was no point in that here, the things were enormously complicated, and military engineering of any sort emphasized simplicity — *Aaaagh!* Was he beginning to believe this balderdash himself?

Klem Zareff fell in with him as they were going to dinner. "Revealed in a dream!" the old Rebel snorted. "One thing you can always get away with lying about is what you dream."

"You think he's lying? I think he's just crazy."

"That's what he wants you to think. Look, Conn, he knows Merlin is here; he's trying to keep us from it. That's why he shifted all that equipment over on the butte. He's working for Sam Murchison."

"I thought your theory was that the Federation had lost Merlin."

"It was, at first. It doesn't look that way to me now. It's right here at Force Command, somewhere. They don't want it found, and they're going to do everything they can to stop us. I oughtn't to have left this fellow Leibert here alone; well, I won't do that again. Get Tom Brangwyn to help me."

XVI

The voyage back to Koshchei had been a week-long nightmare. When she had been the pride and budget-wrecker of Transcontinent & Overseas Airline, the *Harriet Barne* had accommodated two hundred first-class and five hundred lower-deck passengers, but the conversion to a spaceship had drastically reduced her capacity. The three hundred men and women who had been recruited for the Koshchei colony had been crammed into her with brutal disregard for comfort, privacy or anything else except the ability of the air-recyclers to keep them breathing. When Captain Nichols set her down at the administration building at Port Carpenter, a few had had to be carried off, but they were all alive, which made the trip an unqualified success.

The dozen leaders of the expedition were congratulating themselves on that in one of the executive offices after the first dinner at Port Carpenter. Rodney Maxwell, in Storisende, had joined them in screen-image; he was mostly listening, and sometimes contributing a remark apropos of something the rest of them had said five minutes ago.

"Our hypership," Conn was saying, "is going to have to be item two on the agenda. The first thing we need is a ship for the Poictesme-Koshchei run. By this time next year, we ought to have a thousand to fifteen hundred people here at the least. We can't haul them all on that flying sardine can."

"We'll need supplies, too. What was left here won't last forever," Nichols added.

"And you're going to have to run this at a profit," Luther Chen-Wong, who had come along for first hand experience and to help with administrative work, added. "You have a big payroll to meet, and you'll have to keep the stockholders happy. People like Jethro Sastraman and some of these Storisende bankers aren't going to be satisfied with promises and long-term prospects; they'll want dividends."

"We'll have to get claims staked on something besides Port Carpenter, too. Those ships that are building at Storisende will be finished before long," Jerry Rivas said. "If we don't get some more things claimed, the first thing you know, we'll own Port Carpenter and nothing else."

"Well, let's see what we can find in the way of a big airboat, or a small ship," Conn said. "Jerry, you can pick a party for exploring. Just zigzag around the planet and transmit in locations and views of whatever you find, and we'll send it on to Storisende."

"And don't pick anybody for your exploring party that can't be spared from anything here," Jacquemont added. "We don't want to have to chase you halfway around the world to bring back the only specialist in something yesterday at the latest."

"Are you going to come along, Conn?" Rivas asked.

"Oh, Lord, no! I'm going to be doing fifteen things at once here."

All the computer work. Finding materials to make astrogational equipment and robo-pilots. Studying hyperspace theory-fortunately, there was an excellent library here-and setting up classes, and teaching school. And keeping in touch with his father, on Poictesme. It was making him nervous not to know what sort of foolishness the older and wiser heads might be getting into.

The next morning, they began organizing work-gangs and setting up committees. Three men, two girls and about twenty robots got an open-pit iron mine started; as soon as the steel mill was ready, ore started coming in. Anse Dawes had a gang looking for something they could build a 350-foot interplanetary ship out of; Jacquemont and Mack Vibart were getting plans and specifications and making lists of needed materials. Conn gathered a dozen men and women and started classes in computer theory and practice; at the same time, he and Charley Gatworth were teaching themselves and each other hyperspatial astrogation, which was the art of tossing a ship into some everythingless noplace outside normal space-time, and then pulling her out again by her bootstraps at some other place in the normal continuum, light-years away.

Roughly, it compared to shooting hummingbirds on the wing, blindfolded, with a not particularly accurate pistol, from a mile-a-minute merry-go-round.

That was something you could only do with a computer. A human, with a slide rule, a pencil and pad, could figure it out, of course-if he had fifty-odd thousand years to do it. A good computer did it in thirty seconds. That was one difference between people and computers. The other difference was that the desirability of making a hyperspace jump would never occur to a computer, unless somebody pushed a button and taped in instructions.

They found a three-hundred-foot globular skeleton, probably the nucleus of a big hyperspace ship, and decided that was big enough for what they wanted. The entire colony got to work on it. Photoprinted plans and specifications poured out as Jacquemont and a couple of draftsmen got them up. Steel came out of the steel mill at one end while ore came in at the other. A swarm of big contragravity machines, some robotic and some human-operated, clustered around the skeletal hull like hornets building a nest.

Trisystem & Interstellar Spacelines was chartered; the lawyers reported having to overcome a little more resistance than usual from the Government about that. And the bill to nationalize Merlin, which had died in committee, was resuscitated and was being debated hotly on the floor of Parliament. The Administration was now supporting it.

"Are they completely crazy?" Conn wanted to know, when he heard about that. "They pass that bill and nobody's going to look for Merlin if they know the Government will snatch it as soon as they find it."

"That is precisely Jake Vyckhoven's idea," his father replied. "I told you he was afraid of Merlin. He's getting more afraid of it every day."

He had reason to. There was a growing sentiment in favor of turning the entire Government over to the computer as soon as it was found. To his horror, Conn heard himself named as chairman of a committee that should be set up to operate it. The moderates, who had merely wanted Merlin used in an advisory capacity, were dropping out; the agitation was coming from extremists who wanted Merlin to be the whole Government, and now the extremists were developing an extreme wing of their own, who called themselves Cybernarchists and started wearing colored-shirt uniforms and greeting each other with an archaic stiff-arm salute, and the words, "Hail Merlin!"

And the followers of the gospel-shouter on the west coast were now cropping up all over the mainland, and on the continent of Acaire to the north, and another cult, non-religious, was convinced that Merlin was a living machine, with conscious intelligence of its own and awesome psi-powers, a sort of super-Golem, which, if found and awakened, would enslave the whole Galaxy. Fortunately, these two hated each other as venomously as both did the Cybernarchists, and spent most of their energies attacking each other's meetings. The news-services were beginning to publish casualty lists, some heavy enough for outpost fighting between a couple of regular armies.

One thing, it helped the employment situation. Everybody was hiring mercenaries.

"But what," Conn asked, "are the sane people doing?"

"You ought to know," his father told him. "I suspect that you have all of them on Koshchei now."

The sane people, if that was what they were, were being busy. They were putting a set of Abbott lift-and-drive engines together, and Conn's computer class was estimating the mass of the finished ship and the amount of energy needed to overcome gravitation and give it constant acceleration from Koshchei to Poictesme. They were learning, by trial and error, largely error, how to build a set of pseudograv engines. And they were putting together a hundred and one other things, all of which was good training for the time they'd be ready to start work on *Ouroboros II*.

Jerry Rivas had found a contragravity craft which seemed to have been used by some top official for business and inspection trips, had gathered a crew of non-specialists who weren't urgently needed at Port Carpenter, and set out to circumnavigate the planet. It worked just the reverse of expectation. He found a big uranium mine, with an isotope-separation plant and a battery of plutonium-breeders; that meant that Mohammed Matsui and half a dozen other nuclear-power people had to get into another boat and speed after him to see what he had really found. As soon as they landed, Rivas took off again to discover a copper mine and a complex of smelters and processing plants. That took a few more experts, or reasonable facsimiles, away from Port Carpenter. And then he found a whole city that manufactured nothing but computers and robo-controls and things like that.

Conn loaded his whole computer-theory class onto a freight-scow and took them there. By the time he landed, his father was screening him from Storisende.

"When are you going to get the ship finished?" he was asking. "Kurt Fawzi's pestering the daylights out of me. He wants that equipment you promised him."

"We're working on it. What's happened, has Carl Leibert had another revelation?"

"I don't know about that. Kurt's sure Merlin is directly under Force Command. And speaking about Leibert, Klem Zareff's been after me about him. You know I've contracted for the full-time and exclusive services of this Barton-Massarra detective agency. Well, Klem wants me to put them to work investigating Leibert."

"Yes, I know; Leibert's a Terran Federation spy. Why do you need the full-time services of the biggest private detective agency on Poictesme?"

"There have been some odd things happening. People have been trying to bribe and intimidate some of my office help. I have found microphones and screen-pickups planted around. I caught one of our clerks trying to make copies of voice-tapes. I think it's some of these other Merlin-chasing companies, trying to find out how close we are to it. Klem Zareff is recruiting more guards. But how soon are you going to get that ship built?"

"We're working on it. That's all I know, now."

He went back to work getting a classroom ready for his students. If he'd accepted that instructorship at Montevideo, he wouldn't be a full professor now, but none of the rest of this would be happening, either.

That night, he had the dream about starting the big machine and not being able to stop it again.

There was street-fighting in Storisende between the Cybernarchists and Government troops. There was a pitched battle in the west between the Armageddonists (Merlin-is-Satan) and the Human Supremacy League (Merlin-is-the-Golem), with heavy losses and claims of victory on both sides. President Vyckhoven proclaimed planet-wide martial law, and then discovered that he had nothing to enforce it with.

Luther Chen-Wong screened him from Port Carpenter. His voice was almost inaudibly low at first.

"Conn, I just had a call from Jerry and Clyde. I think we can knock off work on that ship we're building now. We won't need it."

"Have they found a ship?" If they had, it would be the first one anybody had found. "Where?"

"They haven't found *a* ship, Conn; they've found all of them. All the ships in the Alpha System except the *Harriet Barne* and the two they're building at Storisende. The place is marked on the map as Sickle Mountain Naval Observatory. It's just a bitty little dot, but the map was made before the evacuation started. It's where most of the troops in the system were embarked on hyperships, I think. Wait till I show you the views."

Conn put on another screen; the first view was from an altitude of five miles. He didn't need Luther's voice to identify Sickle Mountain; a long curve, with a spur at right angles to one end, the name must have suggested itself to whoever saw it first. The observatory had been built where the handle of the sickle joined the blade; as the ship from which the view had been taken had approached, the details grew plainer. At the same time, it became evident that the plain inside the curve of the sickle was powdered with tiny sparkles, like tinsel dust on red-brown velvet.

"Great Ghu, are those all ships?"

"That's right. Look at this one, now."

The view changed. The aircraft was down, now, below the crest of the mountain, circling slowly above the plain. Hundreds, no, over a thousand, of them; two- and three-and five-hundred-footers, and here and there a thousand-footer that could have been converted into a hypership if anybody had wanted to take the trouble. The view changed again; this time from an aircar dropped from the ship, he supposed; it was down almost to the tops of the ships, and he could read names and home ports: *Pixie*, Chloris; *Helen O'Loy*, Anaïtis. They were from Jurgen. *Sky-Rover*, Port Saunders; she was from Horvendile. Ships from Storisende, and Yellowmarsh on Janicot, and....

"Now we know where they all went."

It was logical, of course. Most of the hyperships used in the evacuation had been built here. It had been less trouble to lead the troops and the civilian workers from Poictesme and the other planets onto small normal-space ships and bring them here than to take the big ships away on short interplanetary runs to the other planets.

"Have you screened my father yet?"

"Yes. This is going to knock the bottom out of the companies that are building those ships at Storisende, I'm afraid."

"Their tough luck."

"It could be everybody's tough luck. Both those companies have been issuing stock, and there's been a lot of speculation in it. This market's so inflated now that a puncture at one place might blow the whole thing out."

He knew that. He shrugged. "Father will have to think of something. Tell him I'll screen him from Sickle Mountain."

Then he went back to his classroom.

"All right, class dismissed," he said. "You have twenty minutes to get your bags packed. We're going to work for real, now."

Airboats and airships flocked to Sickle Mountain; some of them hastened back to Port Carpenter for loads of food, for there was none in the storehouses at the embarkation camp. They inspected ship after ship, and chose two three-hundred-footers. They sent airships and freight-scows to the dozen-odd cities and industrial centers that had been already explored, to gather cargo, as far as possible the items in shortest supply on Poictesme.

"Don't worry about a market smash," his father told him. "We have that taken care of. Trisystem Investments has just bought up a lot of stock in both of those companies, and we've set up agreements with them-informally, of course; we'll have to get them voted on by our own companies-to sell them ships from Koshchei. In return, the company that's building the ship out of four air-freighters will go to Janicot, and the company that's building a ship out of the old Leitzenring Building will go to Jurgen, and they'll both stay off Koshchei. Sterber, Flynn & Chen-Wong will probably be defending antitrust suits till the end of time. The Planetary Government has stopped liking us, you know."

"Then we'll have to get one that will like us. There'll be an election about this time next year, won't there?"

His father nodded. "To use one of your expressions, we're working on it. How soon can you get your ships in?"

"We'll be loaded and ready to lift off in a week. Another week for the trip."

"Well, don't forget that equipment you promised Kurt Fawzi."

"We'll have that on. Jerry Rivas is gathering it up now."

"How are you fixed for arms on Koshchei?"

"Arms? Why, there are some. There was a pretty big force of Space Marines on duty here, and they left everything they couldn't carry in their hands. Why? The Armageddonists and the Cybernarchists and Human Supremacy bought all you had on hand?"

"They're buying, but I wasn't thinking of that. I was thinking that your crews might need something to argue their way off the ships at Storisende with. Things are getting just slightly rugged here, now."

XVII

There were no bands or speeches when they came in this time. A lot of contragravity vehicles circled widely around the spaceport, but except for a few news-service cars, the police were keeping them back of a two-mile radius around the landing-pits. A couple of gunboats were making tight circles above, and on the dock were more vehicles and a horde of police and guards.

When Rodney Maxwell came across the bridge from the dock after they opened the airlocks, he was followed by a dozen Barton-Massarra private police, as villainous-looking a collection of ruffians as Conn had ever seen. He was wearing a new suit, with a waist-length jacket instead of the long coat he usually wore, and there was a holstered automatic on each hip. In Litchfield, he never carried more than one pistol, and Storisende was supposed to be an orderly place where nobody needed to go armed. More than anything else, that told Conn approximately what had been going on while he had been on Koshchei.

"Ship-guard," his father told Yves Jacquemont. "All your crew can come off; they'll take care of things. Get your people in that troop carrier over there. Everybody will stay at Interplanetary

Building. None of the hotels are safe, not even the Ritz-Gartner. And be sure everybody's well armed when they come off the ship."

Jacquemont nodded. "I know the drill; I've been in Port Oberth on Venus and Skorvann on Loki. Any law we want, we make for ourselves."

"That's about it. I'll see you there. Conn, I wish you'd come with me. Somebody here wants to talk to you."

He wondered if his mother, or Flora, had come to Storisende. When he asked his father as they crossed onto the dock, there was a brief twinge of pain in Rodney Maxwell's face.

"No, they're not having anything to do —*Duck; quick!*"

Then his father was diving under a lifter-truck that stood empty on the dock. The private police were scattering for cover, and an auto-cannon began pom-pomming. Conn took one quick look in the direction in which it was firing, saw an aircar that had broken through the police line and was rushing toward them, and dived under the lifter after his father. As he did, he saw a missile flash out from one of the gunboats like a thrown knife. Then he huddled beside his father and put his arms over his head.

He felt the heat and shock of the explosion and, an instant later, heard the roar. When nothing immediately disastrous happened after he had counted fifteen seconds, he stuck his head out and looked up. The gunboat was struggling to regain her equilibrium, and the aircar had vanished in a fireball. They both emerged, straightening. His father was brushing himself with his hands and saying something about always having to duck under something when he had a new suit on.

"Robot control, probably; could have been launched from anywhere in town. Why, no; your mother and Flora aren't speaking to either of us, any more. Pity, of course, but I'm glad they're in Litchfield. It's a little healthier there."

They walked to the slim recon-car and climbed in, pulling the door shut after them. Wade Lucas was waiting for them at the controls.

"There, you see!" he began, as soon as he had the car lifting. "What I've been telling you. We'll have to stop this."

"Conn, meet our new partner. I told him everything you told me, out on the Mall, the day you came home. I had to," his father hastened to add. "He'd figured most of it out for himself. The only thing to do was admit him to the lodge and give him the oath."

"I didn't know about General Travis; I didn't even know he was still alive," Lucas said. "But the rest of it was pretty obvious, once I stopped jumping to conclusions and did a little thinking. You know, ever since I came here I've been preaching to these people to stop looking for Merlin and do something to help themselves. You're smarter than I am, Conn; instead of opposing them, you're guiding them."

"Did you tell Flora?"

Lucas shook his head. "I tried to explain what you're trying to do, but she wouldn't listen. She just told me I'd gotten to be as big a crook as you two." He had the car up to fifty thousand; putting it into a wide circle around the city, he locked the controls and got out his cigarettes. "Rod, we've got to stop this. You were just lucky this time. Some of these days your luck's going to run out."

"How can we stop?" Conn demanded. "Tell them the truth? They'd lynch us, and then go on hunting for Merlin."

"Worse than that; it'd be a smash worse than the one when the War ended. I was only ten then, but I can remember that very plainly. We can't stop it, and we wouldn't dare stop it if we could."

"What's been going on here in the last month?" Conn asked. "I've been too busy to keep in touch. I know there's been rioting, and these crackpot sects, but...."

"I think this is personal to us. There have been some ugly things happening. There were four attempts to burglarize our offices. I told you about some of the other stuff, the microphones we found, and so on. The worst thing was Lucy Nocero, my secretary. She just vanished, a couple of weeks ago. Three days later, the police found her wandering in a park, a complete imbecile. Somebody who either didn't know how to use one or didn't care what happened had used a mind-probe on her. It's twenty to one she'll never recover."

"It's this Storisende financial crowd," Wade Lucas said. "They had things all their own way till Alpha-Interplanetary was organized. Now they're getting shoved into the background, and they don't like it."

"They're making more money than they ever did, and they just love it," Rodney Maxwell said. "I'd think it was either Jake Vyckhoven or Sam Murchison."

"Murchison!" Lucas hooted. "Why, he's nobody! Federation Minister-General; all the authority of the Terran Federation, and nothing to enforce it with. He doesn't have a position, here; he has a disease. Sleeping sickness."

"He certainly doesn't believe there is a Merlin, does he?" Conn asked.

"I don't know what he believes, but he's getting to be Klem Zareff's opposite number. He thinks this whole thing's a plot against the Federation. It's a good thing Klem didn't get around to repainting his combat vehicles black and green, the way he did the Home Guard stuff at Litchfield."

"I'd be more likely to think it was Vyckhoven."

"Could be. Or it could be the Armageddonists, or Human Supremacy; I am ashamed to say that this heil-Merlin Cybernarchist gang are friendly to us. Or it could be some of the banking crowd, or some of these rival space-companies. Barton-Massarra is trying to find out. Well, we have some of Wade's pet suspects at Interplanetary Building now. There's been a meeting going for the last week to partition the Alpha Gartner System."

The Interplanetary Building had been a medium-class residence hotel at the time of the War. Junior staff officers and civilian technicians and their families had lived there. It had been vacant ever since the disastrous outbreak of peace. Now it had a big new fluorolite sign, and housed the offices of all the Maxwell companies. There was a truculent display of anti-vehicle weapons on the top landing stage, and more Barton-Massarra private police. They looked even more villainous then the ones at the spaceport. Conn recalled having heard that most of the Blackie Perales gang had been discharged for lack of evidence; he wondered how many of them had hired with Barton-Massarra.

The meeting was in a big conference room six floors down; it had been going on uninterrupted for days, with all the interested companies' representatives standing watch-and-watch around the clock. Lester Dawes and Morgan Gatworth and Lorenzo Menardes were there for L. E. & S.; Transcontinent & Overseas was represented; there were people from Alpha-Interplanetary, and bankers and financiers, and people from the companies building the two ships at the spaceport. And J. Fitzwilliam Sterber, the lawyer.

And reporters, phoning stories in and getting audiovisual interviews of anybody who would hold still long enough. They converged in a rush as Conn and his father and Lucas came in.

"No statement, gentlemen!" Rodney Maxwell shouted, above the babble of their questions. "When we have anything to release, it will be released to all of you."

Jacquemont and Nichols had already arrived; Lucas went to them and began talking about stevedores and lifters to get off the cargoes from the ships. Conn hastened to join them.

"The scanning and mining equipment aboard the *Helen O'Loy,*" he said. "That shouldn't be unloaded here; we'll take the ship out to Force Command and unload it there."

Out of the corner of his eye, he saw, a lurking reporter snatch the handphone off his radio and begin talking; it would be stated authoritatively that Merlin was at Force Command and would be uncovered as soon as special equipment from Koshchei arrived.

Everybody at the long table was shouting at everybody else. The Jurgen and Janicot Companies wanted to buy ships from Koshchei Exploitation & Development. The Alpha-Interplanetary director, who was also a vice-president of Transcontinent & Overseas, opposed that;

another director of A-I, who was also board chairman of Koshchei Exploitation & Development, wanted to sell ships to anybody who had the price, the Transcontinent & Overseas man was calling him a traitor to the company, and one of the stockbrokers, who was also a vice-president of Trisystem Investments and a director of Trisystem & Interstellar Spacelines, was wanting to know which company. And a banker who was stockholder in all the companies was shouting that they were all a gang of crooks, and J. Fitzwilliam Sterber was declaring that anybody who called him a crook could continue the discussion through seconds.

Conn suddenly realized that dueling had never been illegal on Poictesme. He wondered how many duels this meeting was going to hatch.

The next afternoon the *Helen O'Loy* was unloaded, all but the mining equipment; Conn and Yves Jacquemont and Charley Gatworth and a few others took her out to Force Command. They were met by Klem Zareff's armed airboats two hundred and fifty miles from the mesa, and they found the place in more of a state of siege than when the Badlands had been full of outlaws. A lot of heavy armament seemed to have been moved in from Barathrum Spaceport, and Zareff had more men and firepower than he had ever commanded during the System States War. If Minister-General Murchison was convinced that the Merlin excitement was a cover for some seditious plot against the Federation, this ought to give him food for thought.

There was still work, mostly boring lateral shafts for echo shots, going on at the butte, under the relay station. That was Leibert, who was still insisting that that was where Merlin was buried. There was also some work on top of the mesa, by those who were convinced that that was where Merlin was to be found. Kurt Fawzi was taking the lead in that. Franz Veltrin and Dolf Kellton sided with Leibert, and Fawzi's office clique had split into two factions. Judge Ledue was maintaining strict impartiality, as befitted his judicial position.

"Why hasn't your father gotten those detectives of his to work on this fake preacher?" Zareff wanted to know, when he and Tom Brangwyn were able to talk to Conn alone.

"Well, they've been busy," Conn said. "Trying to keep him alive, for one thing. You heard about the robo-bomb somebody launched at us the day we brought the ships in, didn't you?"

"Yes, and we heard about the Nocero girl, too," Brangwyn said. "But hasn't it ever occurred to you or your dad that this fellow that calls himself Leibert might be mixed up with the gang that did that?"

"You suspect him, too?"

Brangwyn nodded. "I took a few audiovisuals of him, when he didn't know it; I sent them to some different law-enforcement people over in Morven, where he says he comes from. They never saw him before, and couldn't find anybody who did."

"Well? He just doesn't have a police record, then."

"He says he's a preacher. Preachers don't go off in the woods by themselves to preach; they get up in pulpits, in front of a lot of people. Those towns over in Morven are small enough for everybody to have known something about him. He's a fake, I tell you."

"Let me have copies of those audiovisuals, Tom. I'll see what can be found out about him. I'm beginning to wonder about him myself. I'm sure I've seen him, somewhere...."

When he got back to Storisende, he found that the marathon conference on the sixth floor down at the Interplanetary Building had finally come to an end. Everybody seemed satisfied, and apparently nobody was going to have pistols and coffee with anybody else about it.

"We have things fixed up," his father told him. "The gang who are building the ship out of four air-freighters are chartered as Janicot Industries, Ltd.; they're going to specialize in chemical products. The other company has a charter now, too. They're going to operate on Jurgen and Horvendile. We'll sell them ships, and Alpha-Interplanetary will put on scheduled trips to all three planets and also Koshchei. We're getting along very nicely with them, except that everybody's competing for technicians and skilled labor. We have two hundred more people signed up for Koshchei. What you want to do is train as many of them as you can for ship-operation. Alpha-Interplanetary is going to start a training program here at Storisende; you'd better leave one of your ships for them to work on, and send back as many ships as you can find officers and crews for."

"We're getting things really started."

"Yes. The only trouble is...." His father frowned. "I don't understand these people, Conn. Everybody ought to be making millions out of this by this time next year, but all any of them, even these Storisende bankers, can talk about is how soon we're going to find Merlin."

"I wish we could stop that, somehow. Listen; I have it. Merlin never was on Poictesme; Merlin was a space-station a few thousand miles off-planet; there was a crew of operators aboard, and they communicated with Force Command by radio. When the War ended, they took it outside the system and shot off a planetbuster inside her. No more Merlin. How would that be?"

His father shook his head. "Wouldn't do. If anybody believed it, which I doubt, they'd just quit. The market would collapse, everybody would be broke, it would just be the end of the War all over again. Conn, we can't let it stop now. We're going too fast to stop; if we tried it, we'd smash up and break our necks."

XVIII

Jerry Rivas, Mack Vibart and Luther Chen-Wong had been keeping things running on Koshchei. Work on the interplanetary ship at Port Carpenter had stopped when the Sickle Mountain ships had been found; it had never been resumed. When Conn returned, he found work started on the *Ouroboros II*. Some of the two hundred newcomers who came in on the *Helen O'Loy* had special skills needed on the hypership; most of them went with Clyde Nichols and Charley Gatworth to Sickle Mountain to train as normal-space officers and crewmen. Some of them, it was hoped, would later qualify for hyperspace work. Sylvie, who had been one of the star pupils in the computer class, was now helping him with the long lists of needed materials, some of which had to be brought from other places as much as a thousand miles away. Jerry Rivas went back to exploring; Nichols had to drop his space-training work temporarily to organize a fleet of air-freighters; usually, the men best able to operate them were urgently needed on some job at the construction dock.

Ships lifted out almost daily from Sickle Mountain. They tried to get some kind of salable cargo for each one, without depriving themselves of what they needed for themselves. Some of the ships came back loaded with provisions and bringing new recruits-for instance, the teaching of physics and mathematics almost stopped at Storisende College because the professors had been virtually shanghaied.

Conn found himself losing touch with affairs on Poictesme. Ships had landed on both Janicot and Horvendile and were sending back claims to abandoned factories. By that time they had all the decks into the *Ouroboros II*, and he was working aboard, getting the astrogational and hyperspace instruments put in place. The hypership *Andromeda* was back from the Gamma System; there was close secrecy about what the expedition had found, but the newscasts were full of conjectures about Merlin, and the market went into another dizzy upward spiral. Litchfield Exploration & Salvage opened a huge munitions depot, and combat equipment, once almost unsalable, was selling as fast as it came out. The Government was buying some, but by no means all of it.

"Conn, can you come back here to Poictesme for a while?" his father asked. "Things have turned serious. I don't like to talk about it by screen-too many people know our scrambler combinations. But I wish you were here."

He started to object; there were millions, well, a couple of hundred, things he had to attend to. The look on his father's face stopped him.

"Ship leaving Sickle Mountain tomorrow morning," he said. "I'll be aboard."

The voyage back to Poictesme was a needed rest. He felt refreshed when he got off at Storisende Spaceport and was met by his father and Wade Lucas in one of the slim recon-cars. They greeted him briefly and took the car up and away from the city, where it was safe to talk.

"Conn, I'm scared," his father said. "I'm beginning to think there really is a Merlin, after all."

"Oh, come off it! I know it's contagious, but I thought you'd been vaccinated."

"I'm beginning to think so, too," Lucas said. "I don't like it at all."

"You know what that gang who took the *Andromeda* to Panurge found?"

"They were looking for the plant that fabricated the elements for Merlin, weren't they?"

"Yes. They found it. My Barton-Massarra operatives got to some of the crew. This place had been turning out material for a computer of absolutely unconventional design; the two computermen they had with them couldn't make head or tail of half of it. And every blueprint, every diagram, every scrap of writing or recording, had been destroyed. But they found one thing, a big empty fiber folder that had fallen under something and been overlooked. It was marked: TOP SECRET. PROJECT MERLIN."

"Project Merlin could have been anything," Conn started to say. No. Project Merlin was something they made computer parts for.

"Dolf Kellton's research crew, at the Library here, came across some references to Project Merlin, too. For instance, there was a routine division court-martial, a couple of second lieutenants, on a very trivial charge. Force Command ordered the court-martial stopped, and the two officers simply dropped out of the Third Force records, it was stated that they were engaged in work connected with Project Merlin. That's an example; there were half a dozen things like that."

"Tell him what Kurt Fawzi and his crew found," Wade Lucas said.

"Yes. They have a fifty-foot shaft down from the top of the mesa almost to the top of the underground headquarters. They found something on top of the headquarters; a disc-shaped mass, fifty feet thick and a hundred across, armored in collapsium. It's directly over what used to be Foxx Travis's office."

"That's not a tenth big enough for anything that could even resemble Merlin."

"Well, it's something. I was out there day before yesterday. They're down to the collapsium on top of this thing; I rode down the shaft in a jeep and looked at it. Look, Conn, we don't know what this Project Merlin was; all this lore about Merlin that's grown up since the War is pure supposition."

"But Foxx Travis told me, categorically, that there was no Merlin Project," Conn said. "The War's been over forty years; it's not a military secret any longer. Why would he lie to me?"

"Why did you lie to Kurt Fawzi and the others and tell them there was a Merlin? You lied because telling the truth would hurt them. Maybe Travis had the same reason for lying to you. Maybe Merlin's too dangerous for anybody to be allowed to find."

"Great Ghu, are you beginning to think Merlin is the Devil, or Frankenstein's Monster?"

"It might be something just as bad. Maybe worse. I don't think a man like Foxx Travis would lie if he didn't have some overriding moral obligation to."

"And we know who's been making most of the trouble for us, too," Lucas added.

"Yes," Rodney Maxwell said, "we do. And sometime I'm going to invite Klem Zareff to kick my pants-seat. Sam Murchison, the Terran Federation Minister-General."

"How'd you get that?"

"Barton-Massarra got some of it; they have an operative planted in Murchison's office. And some of our banking friends got the rest. This Human Supremacy League is being financed by somebody. Every so often, their treasurer makes a big deposit at one of the banks here, all Federation currency, big denomination notes. When I asked them to, they started keeping a record of the serial numbers and checking withdrawals. The money was paid out, at the First Planetary Bank, to Mr. Samuel S. Murchison, in person. The Armegeddonists are getting money, too, but they're too foxy to put theirs through the banks. I believe they're the ones who mind-probed Lucy Nocero. Barton-Massarra believe, but they can't prove, that Human Supremacy launched that robo-bomb at us, that time at the spaceport."

"Have you done anything with those audiovisuals of Leibert?"

"Gave them to Barton-Massarra. They haven't gotten anything, yet."

"So we have to admit that Klem wasn't crazy after all. What do you want me to do?"

"Go out to Force Command and take charge. We have to assume that there may be a Merlin, we have to assume that it may be dangerous, and we have to assume that Kurt Fawzi and his covey of Merlinolators are just before digging it up. Your job is to see that whatever it is doesn't get loose."

The trouble was, if he started giving orders around Force Command he'd stop being a brilliant young man and become a half-baked kid, and one word from him and the older and wiser heads would do just what they pleased. He wondered if the pro-Leibert and anti-Leibert factions were still squabbling; maybe if he went out of his way to antagonize one side, he'd make allies of the other. He took the precaution of screening in, first; Kurt Fawzi, with whom he talked, was almost incoherent with excitement. At least, he was reasonably sure that none of Klem Zareff's trigger-happy mercenaries would shoot him down coming in.

The well, fifty feet in diameter, went straight down from the top of the mesa; as the head-quarters had been buried under loose rubble, they'd had to vitrify the sides going down. He let down into the hole in a jeep, and stood on the collapsium roof of whatever it was they had found. It wasn't the top of the headquarters itself; the microray scannings showed that. It was a drum-shaped superstructure, a sort of underground penthouse. And there they were stopped. You didn't cut collapsium with a cold chisel, or even an atomic torch. He began to see how he was going to be able to take charge here.

"You haven't found any passage leading into it?" he asked, when they were gathered in Fawzi's —formerly Foxx Travis's —office.

"Nifflheim, no! If we had, we'd be inside now." Tom Brangwyn swore. "And we've been all over the ceiling in here, and we can't find anything but vitrified rock and then the collapsium shielding."

"Sure. There are collapsium-cutters, at Port Carpenter, on Koshchei. They do it with cosmic rays."

"But collapsium will stop cosmic rays," Zareff objected.

"Stop them from penetrating, yes. A collapsium-cutter doesn't penetrate; it abrades. Throws out a rotary beam and works like a grinding-wheel, or a buzz-saw."

"Well, could you get one down that hole?" Judge Ledue asked.

He laughed. "No. The thing is rather too large. In the first place, there's a full-sized power-reactor, and a mass-energy converter. With them, you produce negamatter-atoms with negatively charged protons and positive electrons, positrons. Then, you have to bring them into contact with normal positive-matter —That's done in a chamber the size of a fifty-gallon barrel, made of collapsium and weighing about a hundred tons. Then you have to have a pseudograv field to impart rotary motion to your cosmic-ray beam, and the generator door that would lift ten ships the size of the *Lester Dawes*. Then you need another fifty to a hundred tons of collapsium to shield your cutting-head. The cutting-head alone weighs three tons. The rotary beam that does the cutting," he mentioned as an afterthought, "is about the size of a silver five-centisol piece."

Nobody said anything for a few seconds. Carl Leibert stated that Divine Power would aid them. Nobody paid much attention; Leibert's stock seemed to have gone bearish since he had found nothing in the butte and Fawzi had found that whatever-it-was on top of Force Command.

"Means we're going to dig the whole blasted top off, clear down to where that thing is," Zareff said. "That'll take a year."

"Oh, no. Maybe a couple of weeks, after we get started," Conn told them. "It'll take longer to get the stuff loaded on a ship and hauled here than it will to get that thing uncovered and opened."

He told them about the machines they used in the iron mines on Koshchei, and as he talked, he stopped worrying about how he was going to take charge here. He had just been unanimously elected Indispensable Man.

"Bless you, young man!" Carl Leibert cried. "At last, the Great Computer! Those who come after will reckon this the Year Zero of the Age of Regeneration. I will go to my chamber and return thanks in prayer."

"He's been doing a lot of praying lately," Tom Brangwyn remarked, after Leibert had gone out. "He's moved into the chaplain's quarters, back of the pandenominational chapel on the fourth level down. Always keeps his door locked, too."

"Well, if he wants privacy for his devotions, that's his business. Maybe we could all do with a little prayer," Veltrin said.

"Probably praying to Sam Murchison by radio," Klem Zareff retorted. "I'd like to see inside those rooms of his."

He called Yves Jacquemont at Port Carpenter after dinner. When he told Jacquemont what he wanted and why, the engineer remarked that it was a pity screens couldn't be fitted with olfactory sensors, so that he could smell Conn's breath.

"I am not drunk. I am not crazy. And I am not exercising my sense of humor. I don't know what Fawzi and his gang have here, but if it isn't Merlin it's something just as hot. We want at it, soonest, and we'll have to dig a couple of hundred feet of rock off it and open a collapsium can."

"How are we going to get that stuff on a ship?"

"Anything been done to that normal-space job we started since I saw it last? Can you find engines for it? And is there anything about those mining machines or the cutter that would be damaged by space-radiation or re-entry heat?"

Yves Jacquemont was silent for a good deal longer than the interplanetary time-lag warranted. Finally he nodded.

"I get it, Conn. We won't put the things in a ship; we'll build a ship around them. No; that stuff can all be hauled open to space. They use things like that at space stations and on asteroids and all sorts of places. We'll have to stop work on *Ouroboros*, though."

"Let *Ouroboros* wait. We are going to dig up Merlin, and then everybody is going to be rich and happy, and live happily forever after."

Jacquemont looked at him, silent again for longer than the usual five and a half minutes.

"You almost said that with a straight face." After all, Jacquemont hadn't been cleared yet for the Awful Truth About Merlin, but, like his daughter, he'd been doing some guessing. "I wish I knew how much of this Merlin stuff you believe."

"So do I, Yves. Maybe after we get this thing open, I'll know."

To give himself a margin of safety, Jacquemont had estimated the arrival of the equipment at three weeks. A week later, he was on-screen to report that the skeleton ship-they had christened her *The Thing*, and when Conn saw screen views of her he understood why-was finished and the collapsium-cutter and two big mining machines were aboard. Evidently nobody on Koshchei had done a stroke of work on anything else.

"Sylvie's coming along with her; so are Jerry Rivas and Anse Dawes and Ham Matsui and Gomez and Karanja and four or five others. They'll be ready to go to work as soon as she lands and unloads," Jacquemont added.

That was good; they were all his own people, unconnected with any of the Merlin-hunting factions at Force Command. In case trouble started, he could rely on them.

"Well, dig out some shootin'-irons for them," he advised. "They may need them here."

Depending, of course, on what they found when they opened that collapsium can on top of Force Command, and how the people there reacted to it.

The Thing took a hundred and seventy hours to make the trip; conditions in the small shielded living quarters and control cabin were apparently worse than on the *Harriet Barne* on her second trip to Koschchei. Everybody at Force Command was anxious and excited. Carl Leibert kept to his quarters most of the time, as though he had to pray the ship across space.

At the same time, reports of the near completion of *Ouroboros II* were monopolizing the newscasts, to distract public attention from what was happening at Force Command. Cargo was being collected for her; instead of washing their feet in brandy, next year people would be drinking water. Lorenzo Menardes had emptied his warehouses of everything over a year old; so had most of the other distillers up and down the Gordon Valley. Melon and tobacco planters were talking about breaking new ground and increasing their cultivated acreage for the next year. Agricultural machinery was in demand and bringing high prices. So were stills, and tobacco-factory machinery. It began to look as though the Maxwell Plan was really getting started.

It was decided to send the hypership to Baldur on her first voyage; that was Wade Lucas's suggestion. He was going with her himself, to recruit scientific and technical graduates from his alma mater, the University of Paris-on-Baldur, and from the other schools there. Conn was enthusiastic about that, remembering the so-called engineers on Koshchei, running around with a monkey-wrench in one hand and a textbook in the other, trying to find out what they were supposed to do while they were doing it. Poictesme had been living for too long on the leavings of wartime production; too few people had bothered learning how to produce anything.

The Thing finally settled onto the mesa-top. It looked like something from an old picture of the construction work on one of the Terran space-stations in the First Century. Immediately, every piece of contragravity equipment in the place converged on her; men dangled on safety lines hundreds of feet above the ground, cutting away beams and braces with torches. The two giant mining machines, one after the other, floated free on their own contragravity and settled into place. *The Thing* lifted, still carrying the collapsium-cutting equipment, and came to rest on the brush-grown flat beyond, out of the way.

If Yves Jacquemont had overestimated the time required to get the equipment loaded and lifted off from Koshchei, Conn had been overoptimistic about the speed with which the top of the mesa could be stripped off. Digging away the rubble with which the pit had been filled, and even the solid rock around it, was easier than getting the stuff out of the way. Farm-scows came in from all over, as fast as they and pilots for them could be found; the rush to get brandy and tobacco to Storisende had caused an acute shortage of vehicles.

One by one, the members of the old Fawzi's Office gang came drifting in-Lorenzo Menardes, Morgan Gatworth, Lester Dawes. None of them had any skills to contribute, but they brought plenty of enthusiasm. Rodney Maxwell came whizzing out from Storisende now and then to watch the progress of the work. Of all the crowd, he and Conn watched the two steel giants strip away the tableland with apprehension instead of hope. No, there was a third. Carl Leibert had stopped secluding himself in his quarters; he still talked rapturously about the miracles Merlin would work, but now and then Conn saw him when he thought he was unobserved. His face was the face of a condemned man.

The *Ouroboros II* was finished. The whole planet saw, by screen, the ship lift out; watched from the ship the dwindling away of Koshchei and saw Poictesme grow ahead of her. Twelve hours before she landed, work at Force Command stopped. Everybody was going to Storisende-Sylvie, whose father would command her on her voyage to Baldur, Morgan Gatworth, whose son would be first officer and astrogator, everybody. Except Carl Leibert.

"Then I'm not going either," Klem Zareff decided. "Somebody's got to stay here and keep an eye on that snake."

"No, nor me," Tom Brangwyn said. "And if he starts praying again, I'm going to go and pray along with him."

Conn stayed, too, and so did Jerry Rivas and Anse Dawes. They watched the newscast of the lift-out, a week later. It was peaceful and harmonious; everybody, regardless of their attitudes on Merlin, seemed agreed that this was the beginning of a new prosperity for the planet. There were speeches. The bands played "Genji Gartner's Body," and the "Spaceman's Hymn."

And, at the last, when the officers and crew were going aboard, Conn saw his sister Flora clinging to Wade Lucas's arm. She was one of the small party who went aboard for a final farewell. When she came off, along with Sylvie, she was wiping her eyes, and Sylvie was comforting her. Seeing that made Conn feel better even than watching the ship itself lift away from Storisende.

XIX

When Sylvie returned from Storisende, she had Flora with her. Conn's sister greeted him embarrassedly; Sylvie led both of them out of the crowd and over to the edge of the excavation.

"Go ahead, Flora," she urged. "Make up with Conn. It won't be any harder than making up with Wade was."

"How did that happen, by the way?" Conn asked.

"Your girlfriend," Flora said. "She came to the house and practically forced me into a car and flew me into Storisende, and then made me keep quiet and listen while Wade told me the truth."

"I wasn't completely sure what the truth was myself till Wade opened up," Sylvie admitted. "I had a pretty good idea, though."

"I always hated that Merlin thing," Flora burst out. "All those old men in Fawzi's office, dreaming about the wonderful things Merlin was going to do, with everything crumbling around them and everybody getting poorer every year, and doing nothing, nothing! And when you were coming home, I was expecting you to tell them there was no Merlin and to go to work and do something for themselves. But you didn't, and I couldn't see what you were trying to do. And then when Wade joined you and Father, I thought he was either helping you put over some kind of a swindle or else he'd started believing in Merlin himself. I should have seen what you were trying to do from the beginning. At least, from when you talked them into cleaning the town up and fixing the escalators and getting the fountains going again."

So the fountains weren't dusty any more.

"How's Mother taking things now?"

Flora looked distressed. "She goes around wringing her hands. Honestly. I never saw anybody doing that outside a soap opera. Half the time she thinks you and Father are a pair of unprincipled scoundrels, and the other half she thinks you're going to let Merlin destroy the world."

"I'm beginning to be afraid of something like that myself."

"Huh? But Merlin's just a big fake, isn't it? You're using it to make these people do something they wouldn't do for themselves, aren't you?"

"It started that way. What do you think all this is about?" he asked, gesturing toward the excavation and the two giant mining machines digging and blasting and pounding away at the rock.

"Well, to keep Kurt Fawzi and that crowd happy, I suppose. It seems like an awful waste of time, though."

"I'm afraid it isn't. I'm afraid Merlin, or something just as bad, is down there. That's why I'm here, instead of on Koshchei. I want to keep people like Fawzi from doing anything foolish with it when they find it."

"But there *can't* be a Merlin!"

"I'm afraid there is. Not the sort of a Merlin Fawzi expects to find; that thing's too small for that. But there's something down there...."

The question of size bothered him. That drum-shaped superstructure couldn't even hold the personnel-record machine they had found here, or the computers at the Storisende Stock Exchange. It could have been an intelligence-evaluator, or an enemy-intentions predictor, but it seemed small even for that. It would be something *like* a computer; that was as far as he was able to go. And it could be something completely outside the reach of his imagination.

At the back of his mind, the suspicion grew that Carl Leibert knew exactly what it was. And he became more and more convinced that he had seen the self-styled preacher before.

Finally, the whole top of the hundred-foot collapsium-covered structure was uncovered, and the excavation had been leveled out wide enough to accommodate all the massive paraphernalia of the collapsium-cutter. They put *The Thing* onto contragravity again, and brought her down in place; the work of lifting off the reactor and the converter and the rest of it, piece by piece, began. Finally, everything was set up.

A dozen and a half of them were gathered in the room that had become their meeting-place, after dinner. They were all too tired to start the cutting that night, and at the same time excited and anxious. They talked in disconnected snatches, and then somebody put on one of the telecast screens. A music program was just ending; there was a brief silence, and then a commentator appeared, identifying his news-service. He spoke rapidly and breathlessly, his professional gravity cracking all over.

"The hypership *City of Asgard*, from Aton, has just come into telecast range," he began. "We have received an exclusive Interworld News Service story, recently brought to Aton on the Pan-Federation Spacelines ship *Magellanic*, from Terra.

"News of revived interest in the Third Force computer, Merlin, having reached Terra by way of Odin, representatives of Interworld News, to which this service subscribes, interviewed retired Force-General Foxx Travis, now living, at the advanced age of a hundred and fourteen, on Luna. General Travis, who commanded the Third Fleet-Army Force here during the War, categorically denied that there had ever existed any super-computer of the sort.

"We bring you, now, a recorded interview with General Travis, made on Luna...."

For an instant, Conn felt the room around him whirling dizzily, and then he caught hold of himself. Everybody else was shouting in sudden consternation, and then everybody was hushing everybody else and making twice as much noise. The screen flickered; the commentator vanished, and instead, seated in the deep-cushioned chair, was the thin and frail old man with whom Conn had talked two years before, and through an open segment of the dome-roof behind him the full Earth shone, the continents of the Western Hemisphere plainly distinguishable. A young woman in starchy nurse's white bent forward solicitously from beside the chair, handing him a small beaker from which he sipped some stimulant. He looked much as he had when Conn had talked to him. But there was something missing....

Oh, yes. The comparative youngster of seventy-some —"Mike Shanlee ... my *aide-de-camp* on Poictesme ... now he thinks he's my keeper...." He wasn't in evidence, and he should be. Then Conn knew where and when he had seen the man who claimed to be a preacher named Carl Leibert.

"There is absolutely no truth in it, gentlemen," Travis was saying. "There never was any such computer. I only wish there had been; it would have shortened the War by years. We did, of course, use computers of all sorts, but they were all the conventional types used by business organizations...."

The rest was lost in a new outburst of shouting: General Travis, in the screen, continued in dumb-show. The only thing Conn could distinguish was Leibert's —Shanlee's —voice, screaming: "Can it be a lie? Is there no Great Computer?" Then Kurt Fawzi was pounding on the top of the desk and bellowing, "Shut up! Listen!"

"Frankly, I'm surprised," Travis was continuing. "Young Maxwell talked to me, here in this room, a couple of years ago; I told him then that nothing of the sort existed. If he's back on Poictesme telling people there is, he's lying to them and taking advantage of their credulity. There never was anything called Project Merlin...."

"Hah, who's a liar now?" Klem Zareff shouted. "Dolf, what did your people find in the Library?"

"Why, that's right!" Professor Kellton exclaimed. "My students did find a dozen references to Project Merlin. He couldn't be ignorant of anything like that."

"This youth has been lying to us all along!" the old man with the beard cried, pointing an accusing finger at Conn. "He has created false hopes; he has given us faith in a delusion. Why, he is the wickedest monster in human history!"

"Well, thank you, General Travis," another voice, from the screen-speaker, was saying. The only calm voice in the room. "That was a most excellent statement, sir. It should...."

"Conn, you didn't tell us you'd talked to General Travis," Morgan Gatworth was saying. "Why didn't you?"

"Because I never believed anything he told me. You were in Kurt Fawzi's office the day I came home; you know how shocked everybody was when I told you I hadn't been able to learn anything positive. Why should I repeat his lies and discourage everybody that much more? Why, he'd deny there was a Merlin if he was sitting on top of it," Conn declared. "He wants the credit for winning the War, not for letting Merlin win it for him."

"I don't blame Conn," Klem Zareff said. "If he'd told us that then, some of us might have believed it."

"And look what we found," Kurt Fawzi added, pointing at the ceiling. "Is that Merlin up there, or isn't it?"

"That little thing!" Shanlee cried scornfully. "How could that be Merlin? I am going to my chamber, to pray for forgiveness for this wretch."

He turned and started for the door.

"Stop him, Tom!" Conn said, and Tom Brangwyn put himself in front of the older man, gripping his right arm. Shanlee tried, briefly, to resist.

"Seems to me you lost faith in Merlin awfully quick," the former town marshal of Litchfield said. "You knew there was a Merlin all along, and you never wanted us to find it."

Franz Veltrin, who had been "Leibert's" most enthusiastic adherent, had also lost faith suddenly; he was shouting vituperation at the Prophet of Merlin.

"Knock it off, Franz; he was only doing his duty," Conn said. "Weren't you, General Shanlee?"

It took almost a minute before they stopped yelling for an explanation and allowed him to make one. He caught Klem Zareff's comment: "Must be pretty hot, if they have to send a general to handle it."

"I talked to Travis, yes. He gave me the same story he just repeated on that interview," Conn said, picking his way carefully between fact and fiction. "After I went back to Montevideo, he and this aide of his must have been afraid I didn't believe it, which I didn't. When I was ready to graduate, I got this offer of an instructorship; that was a bribe to keep me on Terra and off Poictesme. When I turned it down and took the *Mizar* home, Travis sent Shanlee after me. He must have grown that beard and that pageboy bob on the way out. I suppose he contacted Murchison as soon as he landed. Wait a minute."

He went to the communication screen and punched out a combination. A girl appeared and singsonged: "Barton-Massarra, Investigation and Protection."

"Conn Maxwell here. We gave you some audiovisuals of a man with a white beard, alias Carl Leibert," he began.

"Just a sec, Mr. Maxwell." She spoke quickly into a handphone. The screen flickered, and she was replaced by a hard-faced young man in dark clothes.

"Hello, Mr. Maxwell; Joe Massarra. We haven't anything on Leibert yet."

"Are any of the officers of the *Andromeda* where you can contact them? Let them see those audiovisual. I'll bet that beard was grown aboard ship coming out from Terra."

Bedlam broke out suddenly. Shanlee, who had been standing passively, his right arm loosely grasped by Tom Brangwyn, came down on Brangwyn's instep with the heel of his left foot and hit Brangwyn under the chin with the heel of his left palm. Wrenching his arm free, he started for the door. Sylvie Jacquemont snatched a chair and threw it along the floor; it hit the fleeing man's ankles and brought him down. Half a dozen men piled on top of him, and Brangwyn was yelling to them not to choke him to death till he could answer some questions.

"Hey, what's going on?" the detective-agency man in the screen was asking. "Need help? We'll start a car right away."

"Everything's under control, thank you."

Massarra hesitated for a moment. "What's the dope on this statement that was on telecast a few minutes ago?" he asked.

"Travis doesn't want us to find Merlin. What you just heard was one of his people, planted here at Force Command. We're going to question him when we have time. But there isn't a word of truth in that statement you just heard on the *Herald-Guardian* newscast. Merlin exists, and we've found it. We'll have it opened inside of thirty hours at most."

That was the line he was going to take with everybody. As soon as he had Massarra off the screen, he was punching the combination of his father's private screen at Interplanetary Building. It took five interminable minutes before Rodney Maxwell came on. He could hear Klem Zareff shouting orders into one of the inside communication screens-general turnout, everything on combat-ready; guards to come at once to the office.

"How close are you to digging that thing out?" his father asked as soon as he appeared.

"We're down to it; we can start cutting the collapsium any time now."

"Start cutting it ten minutes ago," his father told him. "And don't leave Force Command till you have it open. How many men and vehicles does Klem have for defense? You'll need all of them in a couple of hours. Everybody here is stunned, now; they'll come out of it inside an hour, and they'll come out fighting."

"You'd better come out here." He turned, saw Jerry Rivas helping hold Shanlee in a chair, and shouted to him: "Jerry! Turn out the workmen. Start cutting the can open right away." He turned back to his father. "Klem's just ordered all his force out. Are you coming here?"

"I can't. In about an hour, everything's going up with a bang. I have to be here to grab a few of the pieces."

"You'll do a lot of good in jail, or on the end of a rope."

"Chance I have to take," his father replied. "I think I'll have a couple of hours. If anybody from the press calls you, what are you going to tell them?"

Conn repeated the line he had taken already. His father nodded.

"All right. I'll call you later. If I can. Just keep things going at your end."

A dozen of Klem Zareff's men were crowding into the room.

"This man's under close arrest," the old soldier was telling them. "He is very important and very dangerous. Take him out somewhere, search him to the skin, take his clothes away from him and give him a robe. He's to be watched every second; make sure he hasn't poison or other suicide means. He's to be questioned later."

As soon as Rodney Maxwell was off the screen, there was a call-signal. It was one of the news-services, wanting a statement.

"I'll take it," Gatworth said, and then began talking:

"This statement of General Travis's is completely false. There is a Merlin, and we've found it...."

They found something that might be good-enough Merlin for the next thirty hours. That superstructure was just big enough for the manually operated parts of a computer like Merlin; the input and output, and the programming machines.

XX

Klem Zareff's guardsmen were mercenaries. A little over a year ago they had, at best, been homeless drifters, and not a few had been outlaws. Now they were soldiers, well fed, clothed, quartered and equipped, and well and regularly paid. They had a good thing; they were willing to fight to keep it, Merlin or no Merlin. Conn left them to their commander. He did gather the workmen for a short harangue, but that wasn't really necessary. They had a good thing, too, and most of them realized that they were working toward a better thing. They could be depended upon, too.

They came crowding out and manned lifters; they got the heavy collapsium-cutter maneuvered into place and the shielding down around the cutting-head. After that, there were only four men who could work, each in his own heavily shielded cabin. In spite of the shielding that covered the actual work, there was an awesome display of multicolored light; it was like being in the middle of an aurora borealis. What was going on where that tiny rotating beam of cosmic rays was grinding at the collapsium simply couldn't have been imagined.

Conn would have liked to stay outside; he could not. Too many things were happening in too many places, and it was all coming in by screen. Rioting had broken out in Storisende and in a dozen other places. He saw, on a news-screen, a mob raging in front of the Executive Palace; yellow-shirted Cybernarchists were battling with city police and Planetary troops, Armageddonists and Human Supremacy Leaguers were fighting both and one another. Above all the confused noise of shouting and shooting, an amplifier was braying: *"It's a lie! It's a lie! Merlin has been found!"* Newsmen began arriving-Zareff's men had orders to pass them through the cordon that had been put up around Force Command-and they took up his time. It was worth it, though. They could tell him what was going on.

J. Fitzwilliam Sterber called. Rodney Maxwell had been arrested, on a farrago of fraud charges —"I don't know who he's supposed to have defrauded; the Planetary Government is the sole complainant" —and bail was being illegally denied. Sterber's lawyerly soul was outraged, but he was grimly elated. "You wait till things quiet down a little. We're going to start a false-arrest suit —"

"If you're alive to." Apparently Sterber hadn't thought of that. "What do you think's going to happen when the Stock Exchange opens?"

"It's going to be bad. But don't worry; your father must have foreseen something like this. He gave me instructions, and instructed a few more people." He named some of the Trisystem Investments people and some of the bankers. "We're going to try to brace the market as long as we can. Nobody who keeps his head is going to lose anything in the long run."

Luther Chen-Wong called from Port Carpenter, on Koshchei. He and Clyde Nichols and a young mathematics professor named Simon Macquarte had been running the colony, in Conn's absence and since Yves Jacquemont had gone to space in the *Ouroboros II.*

"Well, they caught up with you," he said. Evidently he had figured out what the search for Merlin was all about, too. "What do we do about it?"

"Well, we are just before finding Merlin, here. I hope we find it before things get too bad." He told Luther the situation of the moment. "Have you people started on another hypership yet?"

"We're getting organized to. I don't suppose it's advisable to send any more ships in to Storisende for a while? And are you sure this thing you've found is Merlin?"

"I don't know what it is. It's only big enough for the apparatus they'd need to operate a thing like Merlin-Yes, Luther. I am sure we have found Merlin."

Chen-Wong looked at him curiously. "I hope so. I can't think of anything else that can stop this business."

Tom Brangwyn was in the room when he turned from the screen.

"We searched Leibert's—Shanlee's—rooms," he said. "We found a bomb."

"What kind of a bomb?"

"Vest-pocket thermonuclear. He seems to have gotten the fissionables by taking apart a couple of light tactical missiles; the whole thing's packed inside a hundred-pound power-cartridge case. It was in a traveling-bag under his bed. And you know how it was to be fired? With a regular 40-mm flare-pistol, welded into the end of the bomb. The flare-powder had been taken out of the cartridge, and it had been reloaded with a big charge of rifle-powder. I suppose it would blow one subcritical mass into another. But the only way he could have fired the bomb would have been by pulling the trigger."

And blowing himself up along with it. He must have wanted Merlin destroyed pretty badly.

"Have you questioned him yet?"

"Not yet. I wanted to tell you about it first."

He looked at his watch. Only four hours had passed since the newscast; why, that seemed like months, ago, now.

"All right, Tom; we'll go talk to him. Where's the Colonel?"

Zareff was surrounded by a dozen screens, keeping in touch with the *Lester Dawes* and the gunboats and combat cars, and the gun positions with which he had ringed Force Command. It was only a little army, maybe, but he was a busy commander-in-chief.

"You take care of it. Tell me what you get from him. I can't leave now. There's a report of a number of aircraft approaching from the west now...."

They found Judge Ledue, and Kurt Fawzi and Dolf Kellton, who were just sitting around wishing there was something to do to help. They gave Franz Veltrin and Sylvie Jacquemont the job of keeping the representatives of the press amused. Then they went down to the room in which General Mike Shanlee was held under guard.

Shanlee, wearing a bathrobe and nothing else, was lying on a cot, sleeping peacefully; three of Zareff's men were sitting on chairs, watching him narrowly.

"All right; you can go," Conn told them. "We'll take care of him."

Shanlee woke instantly; he sat up and swung his legs over the edge of the cot.

"You have my name and rank," he said, and his voice no longer quavered. "My serial number is—" He recited a string of figures. "And that's all you're getting out of me."

"We'll get anything we want out of you," Conn told him. "You know what a mind-probe is? You should; your accomplices used one on my father's secretary. She's a hopeless imbecile now. You'll be, too, when we're through with you. But before then, you'll have given us everything you know."

Kellton began to protest. "Conn, you can't do a thing like that!"

"A mind-probe is utterly illegal; why, it's a capital offense!" Ledue exclaimed. "Conn I forbid you...."

"Judge, don't make me call those guards and have you removed," Conn said.

"You can stop bluffing," Shanlee told him. "Where would you get a mind-probe?"

"Out of the Chief of Intelligence's office, here in his headquarters. I should imagine it was to be used in interrogating Alliance prisoners, during the War. I think Colonel Zareff would enjoy helping to use it on you. He used to be an Alliance officer."

Shanlee was silent. Conn sat down in one of the chairs, at the small table.

"General Shanlee, would you describe General Foxx Travis as a man of honor and integrity? And would you so describe yourself?" Shanlee said nothing. "Yet both of you have lied, deliberately and repeatedly, to conceal the existence of Merlin. And we found that bomb in your room. You were willing to blow up this headquarters and everybody, yourself included, in it, to keep us from getting at Merlin. Well, you know that we can make you tell us the truth, maybe when it's too late, and you know that we are going to get Merlin. We're cutting the collapsium off that thing above now."

Shanlee laughed. "You're supposed to be a computerman. You think that little thing could be Merlin?"

"The controls and programming machine for Merlin." He turned to Kurt Fawzi. "You always claimed that Merlin was here in Force Command. You had it backward. Force Command is inside Merlin."

"What do you mean, Conn?"

"The walls; the fifty-foot walls, shielded inside and out. Merlin-the circuitry, the memory-bank, the relays, everything-was installed inside them. What's up above is only what was needed to operate the computer. Isn't that true, General?"

Shanlee had stopped his derisive laughter. He sat on the edge of the cot, tensing as though for a leap at Conn's throat.

"That won't help, either. If you try it, we won't shoot you. We'll just overpower you and start mind-probing right away. Now; you feel that suppressing Merlin was worth any sacrifice. We're not unreasonable. If you can convince us that Merlin ought not to be brought to light.... Well, you can't do any harm by talking, and you may do some good. You may even accomplish your mission."

"He can't talk us out of it," Kurt Fawzi seemed determined to spoil things by saying. "Conn, I'm coming around to Klem's way of thinking. They just don't want anybody else to have it."

"No, we don't," Shanlee said. "We don't want the whole Federation breaking up into bloody anarchy, and that's what'll happen if you dig that thing up and put it into operation."

Nobody said anything except Fawzi, who began an indignant contradiction and then subsided. Tom Brangwyn lit a cigarette.

"Would you mind letting me have one of those?" Shanlee said. "I haven't had a smoke since I came here. It wouldn't have been in character."

Brangwyn took one out of the pack, lit it at the tip of his own, and gave it to Shanlee with his left hand, his right ready to strike. Shanlee laughed in real amusement.

"Oh, Brother!" he reproved, in his former pious tones. "You distrust your fellow man; that is a sin."

He rose slowly, the bathrobe flapping at his bare shins, and sat down across the table from Conn.

"All right," he said. "I'll tell you about it. I'll tell you the truth, which will be something of a novelty all around."

Shanlee puffed for a moment at the cigarette; it must really have tasted good after his long abstinence.

"You know, we were really caught off balance when the War ended. It even caught Merlin short; information lag, of course. The whole Alliance caved in all at once. Well, we fed Merlin all the data available, and analyzed the situation. Then we did something we really weren't called upon to do, because that was policy-planning and wasn't our province, but we were going to move an occupation army into System States planets, and we didn't want to do anything that would embarrass the Federation Government later. We fed Merlin every scrap of available information on political and economic conditions everywhere in the Federation, and set up a long-term computation of the general effects of the War.

"The extrapolation was supposed to run five hundred years in the future. It didn't. It stopped, at a point a trifle over two hundred years from now, with a statement that no computation could be made further because at that point the Terran Federation would no longer exist."

The others, who had taken chairs facing him, looked at him blankly.

"No more Federation?" Judge Ledue asked incredulously. "Why, the Federation, the Federation...."

The Federation would last forever. Anybody knew that. There just couldn't be no more Federation.

"That's right," Shanlee said. "We had trouble believing it, too. Remember, we were Federation officers. The Federation was our religion. Just like patriotism used to be, back in the days of nationalism. We checked for error. We made detail analyses. We ran it all over again. It was no use.

"In two hundred years, there won't be any Terran Federation. The Government will collapse, slowly. The Space Navy will disintegrate. Planets and systems will lose touch with Terra and with one another. You know what it was like here, just before the War? It will be like that on every planet, even on Terra. Just a slow crumbling, till everything is gone; then every planet will start sliding back, in isolation, into barbarism."

"Merlin predicted that?" Kurt Fawzi asked, shocked.

If Merlin said so, it had to be true.

Shanlee nodded. "So we ran another computation; we added the data of publication of this prognosis. You know, Merlin can't predict what you or I would do under given circumstances, but Merlin can handle large-group behavior with absolute accuracy. If we made public Merlin's prognosis, the end would come, not in two centuries but in less than one, and it wouldn't be a slow, peaceful decay; it would be a bomb-type reaction. Rebellions. Overthrow of Federation authority, and then revolt and counterrevolt against planetary authority. Division along sectional or class lines on individual planets. Interplanetary wars; what we fought the Alliance to prevent. Left in ignorance of the future, people would go on trying to make do with what they had. But if they found out that the Federation was doomed, everybody would be trying to snatch what they could, and end by smashing everything. Left in ignorance, there might be a planet here and there that would keep enough of the old civilization to serve, in five or so centuries, as a nucleus for a new one. Informed in advance of the doom of the Federation, they would all go down together in the same bloody shambles, and there would be a Galactic night of barbarism for no one knows how many thousand years."

"We don't want anything like that to happen!" Tom Brangwyn said, in a frightened voice.

"Then pull everybody out of here and blow the place up, Merlin along with it," Shanlee said.

"No! We'll not do that!" Fawzi shouted. "I'll shoot the man dead who tries it!"

"Why didn't you people blow Merlin up?" Conn asked.

"We'd built it; we'd worked with it. It was part of us, and we were part of it. We couldn't. Besides, there was a chance that it might survive the Federation; when a new civilization arose, it would be useful. We just sealed it. There were fewer than a hundred of us who knew about it. We all took an oath of secrecy. We spent the rest of our lives trying to suppress any mention of Merlin or the Merlin Project. You have no idea how shocked both General Travis and I were when you told us that the story was still current here on Poictesme. And when we found that you'd been getting into the records of the Third Force, I took the next ship I could, a miserable little freighter, and when I landed and found out what was happening, I contacted Murchison and scared the life out of him with stories about a secessionist conspiracy. All this Armageddonist, Human Supremacy, Merlin-is-the-Devil, stuff that's been going on was started by Murchison. And he succeeded in scaring Vyckhoven with the Cybernarchists, too."

"This computation on the future of the Federation is still in the back-work file?" Conn asked.

Shanlee nodded. "We were criminally reckless; I can see that, now. Let me beg, again, that you destroy the whole thing."

"We'll have to talk it over among ourselves," Judge Ledue said. "The five of us, here, cannot presume to speak for everybody. We will, of course, have to keep you confined; I hope you will understand that we cannot accept your parole."

"Is there anything you want in the meantime?" Conn asked.

"I would like something to smoke, and some clothes," General Shanlee said. "And a shave and a haircut."

XXI

All through the night, a shifting blaze of many-colored light rose and dimmed the stars above the mesa. They stared in awe, marveling at the energy that was pouring out of the converters into a tiny spot that inched its way around the collapsium shielding. It must have been visible for hundreds of miles; it was, for there was a new flood of rumors circulating in Storisende and repeated and denied by the newscasts, now running continuously. Merlin had been found. Merlin had been blown up by Government troops. Merlin was being transported to Storisende to be installed as arbiter of the Government. Merlin the Monster was destroying the planet. Merlin the Devil was unchained.

Conn and Kurt Fawzi and Dolf Kellton and Judge Ledue and Tom Brangwyn clustered together, talking in whispers. They had told nobody, yet, of the interview with Shanlee.

"You think it would make all that trouble?" Kellton was asking anxiously, hoping that the others would convince him that it wouldn't.

"Maybe we had better destroy it," Judge Ledue faltered. "You see what it's done already; the whole planet's in anarchy. If we let this go on...."

"We can't decide anything like that, just the five of us," Brangwyn was insisting. "We'll have to get the others together and see what they think. We have no right to make any decision like this for them."

"They're no more able to make the decision than we are," Conn said.

"But we've got to; they have a right to know...."

"If you decide to destroy Merlin, you'll have to decide to kill me, first," Kurt Fawzi said, his voice deadly calm. "You won't do it while I'm alive."

"But, Kurt," Ledue expostulated. "You know why these people here at Storisende are rioting? It's because they've lost hope, because they're afraid and desperate. The Terran Federation is something everybody feels they have to have, for peace and order and welfare. If people thought it was breaking up, they'd be desperate, too. They'd do the same insane things these people here on this planet are doing. General Shanlee was right. Don't destroy the hope that keeps them sane."

"We don't need to do that," Kurt Fawzi argued. "We can use Merlin to solve our own problems; we don't need to tell the whole Federation what's going to happen in two hundred years."

"It would get out; it couldn't help getting out," Ledue said.

"Let's not try to decide it ourselves," Conn said. "Let's get Merlin into operation, and run a computation on it."

"You mean, ask Merlin to tell us whether it ought to be destroyed or not?" Ledue asked incredulously. "Let Merlin put itself on trial, and sentence itself to destruction?"

"Merlin is a computer; computers deal only in facts. Computers are machines; they have no sense of self-preservation. If Merlin ought to be destroyed, Merlin will tell us so."

"You willing to leave it up to Merlin, Kurt?" Tom Brangwyn asked.

Fawzi gulped. "Yes. If Merlin says we ought to, we'll have to do it."

Toward noon, a telecast went out from Koshchei, on a dozen different wave-lengths. Conn, half asleep in a chair in the commander-in-chief's office, saw Simon Macquarte, the young mathematics professor from Storisende College who had become one of the leaders of the colony, appear in the screen. The next moment, he was fully awake, shocked by Macquarte's words:

"This is not a threat; this is a solemn, even a prayerful, warning. We do not want to use genocidal weapons of mass destruction against the world of our birth. But whether we do or not rests solely with you.

"We came here with a dream of a better world, a world of happiness and plenty for all. We have been working, on Koshchei, to build such a world on Poictesme. Now you are smashing that dream. When it is gone, we will have nothing to live for-except revenge. And we will take that revenge, make no mistake.

"We have the weapons with which to take it. Remember, this was a Federation naval base and naval arsenal during the War. Here the Federation Navy built their super-missiles, the missiles which devastated Ashmodai, and Belphegor, and Baphomet, and hundreds of these weapons are here. We have them, ready for launching. Once they are launched, with the robo-pilots set for targets on Poictesme, you will have a hundred and sixty hours, at the most, to live.

"We will launch them immediately if there is another attack made upon Force Command Duplicate HQ, or upon Interplanetary Building in Storisende, or if Rodney Maxwell is killed, no matter by whom or under what circumstances.

"We beg you, earnestly and prayerfully, not to force us to do this dreadful thing. We speak to each one of you, for each one of you holds the fate of the planet in his own hands."

The image faded from the screen. As it did, Conn was looking from one to another of the people in the room with him. All were dumbfounded, most of them frightened.

"They wouldn't do it, would they?" Lorenzo Menardes was asking. "Conn, you know those people. They wouldn't really?"

"Don't depend on it, Lorenzo," Klem Zareff said. "It's hard for a lot of people to shoot somebody ten feet away with a pistol. But just sending off a missile; that's nothing but setting a lot of dials and then pushing a button."

"I'm not worrying about whether they'd do it or not," Conn said. "What I'm worrying about is how many people will believe they will."

Apparently a good many people did. Zareff's combat vehicles began reporting a cessation of fighting. The newscasts, repeating the ultimatum from Koshchei, told of fewer and fewer disorders in the city or elsewhere; by midafternoon, the rioting had stopped.

By that time, too, Rodney Maxwell was on-screen. He was, Conn noticed, wearing his pistols again.

"What happened?" he asked. "They let you out on bail?"

Maxwell shook his head. "Charges dismissed; they didn't have anything to charge me with in the first place. But they haven't let me out yet."

"You're wearing your guns."

"Yes, but they still have me penned up here at the Executive Palace; they're practically keeping me in the safe. I wish our people on Koshchei hadn't mentioned me in their ultimatum; Jake Vyckhoven's afraid to let me run around loose for fear some lunatic shoots me and starts the planetbusters coming in. Jake did one good thing, though. He ordered the Stock Exchange closed, and declared a five-day bank holiday. By that time, you ought to have Merlin opened and working, and then the market'll be safe."

Conn simply replied, "I hope so." There was no telling what kind of taps there might be on the screen his father was using; he couldn't risk telling him about Shanlee, or about the last computation which Merlin had made. "If we send the *Lester Dawes* in, do you think you might talk them into letting you come out here?"

"I can try."

Flora arrived at Force Command that afternoon.

"I would have come sooner," she said, "but Mother's had a complete collapse. It happened last evening; she's in the hospital. I was with her until just an hour and a half ago. She's still unconscious."

"You mean she's in danger?"

"I don't know. They think she's all right, except for the shock. It was the Travis statement that did it."

"Think I ought to go to her?"

Flora shook her head. "Just keep on with what you're doing here. There isn't anything you can do for her now."

"The best thing you can do for her, Conn, is prove that you weren't lying about Merlin," Sylvie told him.

The *Lester Dawes* didn't make it from Force Command to Storisende and back until after dark, and the green and white and red and orange lights were rising in folds and waves. Rodney Maxwell had heard about his wife's condition; it was the first thing he spoke of when Conn and Flora and Sylvie met him as he got off the ship.

"There isn't anything we can do, Father," Flora said. "They'll call us when there's any change."

He said the same thing Sylvie had said. "The only thing we can do is get that infernal thing uncovered. Once we do this, everything'll be all right. We'll show your mother that it isn't a fake and it isn't anything dangerous; we'll put a stop to all these horror-stories about mechanical devils and living machines...."

Conn drew his father off where the girls couldn't overhear.

"This is something worse," he said. "This is a bomb that could blow up the whole Federation."

"Are you going nuts, too?" his father demanded.

Conn told him about Shanlee; he repeated, almost word for word, the story Shanlee had told.

"Do you believe that?" his father asked.

"Don't you? You were in Storisende when the Travis statement came out; you saw how people acted. If this story gets out, people will be acting the same way on every planet in the Federation. Not just places like Poictesme; planets like Terra and Baldur and Marduk and Odin and Osiris. It would be the end of everything civilized, everywhere."

"Why didn't they use Merlin to save the Federation?"

"It's past saving. It's been past saving since before the War. The War was what gave it the final shove. If they could have used Merlin to reverse the process, they wouldn't have sealed it away."

"But you know, Conn, we can't destroy Merlin. If we did, the same people who went crazy over the Travis statement would go crazy all over again, worse than ever. We'd be destroying everything we planned for, and we'd be destroying ourselves. That bluff young Macquarte and Luther Chen-Wong and Bill Nichols made wouldn't work twice. And if they weren't bluffing...."

His father shuddered.

"And if we don't, how long do you think civilization will last here, if it blows up all over the rest of the Federation?"

The big machine cut on, a little spot of raw energy grinding away the collapsium, inch by inch; the undulating curtains of colored light illuminated the Badlands for miles around. Then, when the first hint of dawn came into the east, they went out. The steady roar of the generators that had battered every ear for over twenty-four hours stopped. There was unbelieving silence, and then shouts.

The workmen swarmed out to man lifters. Slowly the heavy apparatus-the reactor and the converters, the cutting machine, and the shielding around it-was lifted away. Finally, a lone lifter came in and men in radiation-suits went down to hook on grapples, and it lifted away, carrying with it a ten-foot-square sheet of thin steel that weighed almost thirty tons.

When they had battered a hole in the vitrified rock underneath, guards brought up General Shanlee. Somebody almost up to professional standards had given him a haircut; the beard was gone, too. A Federation Army officer's uniform had been found reasonably close to his size, and somebody had even provided him with the four stars of his retirement rank. He was, again, the man Conn had seen in the dome-house on Luna.

"Well, you got it open," he said, climbing down from the airjeep that had brought him. "Now, what are you going to do with it?"

"We can't make up our minds," Conn said. "We're going to let the computer tell us what to do with it."

Shanlee looked at him, startled. "You mean, you're going to have Merlin judge itself and decide its own fate?" he asked. "You'll get the same result we did."

They let a ladder down the hole and descended-Conn and his father, Kurt Fawzi, Jerry Rivas, then Shanlee and his two guards, then others-until a score of them were crowded in the room at the bottom, their flashlights illuminating the circular chamber, revealing ceiling-high metal cabinets, banks of button- and dial-studded control panels, big keyboards. It was Shanlee who found the lights and put them on.

"Powered from the central plant, down below," he said. "The main cables are disguised as the grounding-outlet. If this thing had been on when you put on the power, you'd have had an awful lot of power going nowhere, apparently."

Rodney Maxwell was disappointed. "I know this stuff looks awfully complex, but I'd have expected there to be more of it."

"Oh, I didn't get a chance to tell you about that. This is only the operating end," Conn said, and then asked Shanlee if there were inspection-screens. When Shanlee indicated them, he began putting them on. "This is the real computer."

They all gave the same view, with minor differences-long corridors, ten feet wide, between solid banks of steel cabinets on either side. Conn explained where they were, and added:

"Kurt and the rest of them were sitting here, all this time, wondering where Merlin was; it was all around them."

"Well, how did you get up here?" Fawzi asked. "We couldn't find anything from below."

"No, you couldn't." Shanlee was amused. "Watch this."

It was so simple that nobody had ever guessed it. Below, back of the Commander-in-chief's office, there was a closet, fifteen feet by twenty. They had found it empty except for some bits of discarded office-gear, and had used it as a catch-all for everything they wanted out of the way. Shanlee went to where four thick steel columns rose from floor to ceiling in a rectangle around a heavy-duty lifter, pressing a button on a control-box on one of them. The lifter, and the floor under it, rose, with a thick mass of vitrified rock underneath. The closet, full of the junk that had been thrown into it, followed.

"That's it," he said. "We just tore out the controls inside that and patched it up a little. There's a sheet of collapsium-plate under the floor. Your scanners simply couldn't detect any-thing from below."

Confident that Merlin would decree its own destruction, Shanlee gave his parole; the others accepted it. The newsmen were admitted to the circular operating room and encouraged to send out views and descriptions of everything. Then the lift controls were reinstalled, the lid was put back on top, and the only access to the room was through the office below. The entrance to this was always guarded by Zarel's soldiers or Brangwyn's police.

There were only a score of them who could be let in on the actual facts. For the most part, they were the same men who had been in Fawzi's office on the afternoon of Conn's return, a year and a half ago. A few others-Anse Dawes, Jerry Rivas, and five computermen Conn had trained on Koshchei-had to be trusted. Conn insisted on letting Sylvie Jacquemont in on the revised Awful Truth About Merlin. They spent a lot of their time together, in Travis's office, for the most part sunk in dejection.

They had finally found Merlin; now they must lose it. They were trying to reconcile them-selves and take comfort from the achievement, empty as it was. They could see no way out. If Merlin said that Merlin had to be destroyed, that was it. Merlin was infallible. Conn hated the thought of destroying that machine with his whole being, not because it was an infallible oracle, but because it was the climactic masterpiece of the science he had spent years studying. To destroy it was an even worse sacrilege to him than it was to the Merlinolators. And Rodney

Maxwell was thinking of the public effects. What the Travis statement had started would be nothing by comparison.

"You know, we can keep the destruction of Merlin a secret," Conn said. "It'll take some work down at the power plant, but we can overload all the circuits and burn everything out at once." He turned to Shanlee. "I don't know why you people didn't think of that."

Shanlee looked at him in surprise. "Why, now that you mention it, neither do I," he admitted. "We just didn't."

"Then," Conn continued, "we can tinker up something in the operating room that'll turn out what will look like computation results. As far as anybody outside ourselves will know, Merlin will still be solving everybody's problems. We'll do like any fortuneteller; tell the customer what he wants to believe and keep him happy."

More lies; lies without end. And now he'd have a machine to do his lying for him, a dummy computer that wouldn't compute anything. And all he'd wanted, to begin with, had been a ship to haul some brandy to where they could get a fair price for it.

Peace had returned. At first, it had been a frightened and uneasy peace. The bluff-he hoped that was what it had been-by the Koshchei colonists had shocked everybody into momentary inaction. In the twenty-four hours that had followed, the forces of sanity and order had gotten control again. Merlin existed and had been found. As for Travis's statement, the old general had been bound by a wartime oath of secrecy to deny Merlin's existence. The majority relaxed, ashamed of their hysterical reaction. As for the Cybernarchists and Armageddonists and Human Supremacy Leaguers, government and private police, vastly augmented by volunteers, speedily rounded up the leaders; their followers dispersed, realizing that Merlin was nothing but a lot of dials and buttons, and interestedly watching the broadcast views of it.

The banks were still closed, but discreet back-door withdrawals were permitted to keep business going; so was the Stock Exchange, but word was going around the brokerage offices that Trisystem Investments was in the market for a long list of securities. Nobody was willing to do anything that might upset the precarious balance; everybody was talking about the bright future, when Merlin would guide Poictesme to ever greater and more splendid prosperity.

Conn's father and sister flew to Litchfield; Flora stayed with her mother, and Rodney Maxwell returned to Force Command, shaking his head gravely.

"She's still unconscious, Conn," he said. "She just lies there, barely breathing. The doctors don't know....I wish Wade hadn't gone on the ship."

The price of what he had wanted to do was becoming unendurably high for Conn.

They ran off the computations Merlin had made forty years before, and rechecked them. There had been no error. The Terran Federation, overextended, had been cracking for a century before the War; the strain of that conflict had started an irreversible breakup. Two centuries for the Federation as such; at most, another century of irregular trade and occasional war between independent planets, Galaxy full of human-populated planets as poor as Poictesme at its worst. Or, aware of the future, sudden outbursts of desperate violence, then anarchy and barbarism.

It took a long time to set up the new computation. Forty years of history for almost five hundred planets had to be abstracted and summarized and translated from verbal symbols to the electro-mathematical language of computers and fed in. Conn and Sylvie and General Shanlee and the three men and two women Conn had taught on Koshchei worked and rested briefly and worked again. Finally, it was finished.

"General; you're the oldest Merlin hand," Conn said, gesturing to the red button at the main control panel, "You do it."

"You do it, Conn. None of us would be here except for you."

"Thank you, General."

He pressed the button. They all stood silently watching the output slot.

Even a positronic computer does not work instantaneously. Nothing does. Conn took his eyes from the slot from which the tape would come, and watched the second-hand of the clock above it. The wait didn't seem like hours to him; it only seemed like seventy-five seconds, that way. Then the bell rang, and the tape began coming out.

It took another hour and a half of button-punching; the Braille-like symbols on the tape had to be retranslated, and even Merlin couldn't do that for itself. Merlin didn't think in human terms.

It was the same as before. In ignorance, the peoples of the Federation worlds would go on, striving to keep things running until they wore out, and then sinking into apathetic acceptance. Deprived of hope, they would turn to frantic violence and smash everything they most wanted to preserve. Conn pushed another button.

The second information-request went in: *What is the best course to be followed under these conditions by the people of Poictesme?* It had taken some time to phrase that in symbols a computer would find comprehensible; the answer, at great length, emerged in two minutes eight seconds. Retranslating it took five hours.

In the beginning and for the first ten years, it was, almost item for item, the Maxwell Plan. Export trade, specialized in luxury goods. Brandies and wines, tobacco; a long list of other exportable commodities, and optimum markets. Reopening of industrial plants; establishment of new industries. Attainment of economic self-sufficiency. Cultural self-sufficiency; establishment of universities, institutes of technology, research laboratories. Then the Maxwell Plan became the Merlin Plan; the breakup of the Federation was a fact that entered into the computation. Build-up of military strength to resist aggression by other planetary governments. Defense of the Gartner Trisystem. Lists of possible aggressor planets. Revival of interstellar communications and trade; expeditions, conquest and re-education of natives....

"We can't begin to handle this without Merlin," Conn said. "If that means blowing up the Federation, let it blow. We'll start a new one here."

"No; if there's a general, violent collapse of the Federation, it'll spread to Poictesme," Shanlee told him. "Let's ask Merlin the big question."

Merlin took a good five minutes to work that one out. The question had to include a full description of Merlin, and a statement of the information which must be kept secret. The answer was even more lengthy, but it was summed up in the first word: *Falsification.*

"So Merlin's got to be a liar, too, along with the rest of us!" Sylvie cried. "Conn, you've corrupted his morals!"

The rest of it was false data which must be taped in, and lists of corrections which must be made in evaluating any computation into which such data might enter. There was also a statement that, after fifty years, suppression of the truth and circulation of falsely optimistic statements about the Federation would no longer have any importance.

"Well, that's it," Conn said. "Merlin thought himself out of a death sentence."

They crowded into the lift and went down to the office below. Everybody who knew what had been going on upstairs was there. Most of them were nursing drinks; almost everybody was smoking. All of them were silent, until Judge Ledue took his cigar from his mouth.

"Has the jury reached a verdict?" he asked, clinging with courtroom formality to his self-control.

"Yes, your Honor. We find the defendant, Merlin, not guilty as charged."

In the uproar his words released, Rodney Maxwell got to his feet and came quickly to Conn.

"Flora called just a while ago. Your mother is conscious; she's asking for us. Flora says she seems perfectly normal."

"We'll go right away; take a recon-car. General, will you explain things till I get back? Sylvie, do you want to come with us?"

XXII

It was autumn again, the second autumn since he had landed from the *City of Asgard* at Storisende and taken the *Countess Dorothy* home to Litchfield. Again the fields were bare and brown; all up and down the Gordon Valley the melons were harvested, and the wine-pressing was ready to start.

The house was crowded today. All top-level Litchfield seemed to have turned out, and there were guests from Storisende, and even a few who had made the trip from Koshchei to be there, Simon Macquarte, the president of Koshchei Tech; Conn would always remember him in the screen threatening a whole planet with devastation. Luther Chen-Wong, the chief executive of Koshchei Colony. Clyde Nichols, the president of Koshchei Airlines.

He almost bumped into Yves Jacquemont, coming in from the hall. Jacquemont's beard had been trimmed down to a small imperial, and he was wearing the uniform of Trisystem & Interstellar Spacelines, nothing at all like a Federation Space Navy uniform. He was laughing about something; he threw an arm over Conn's shoulder, and they went into the front parlor together.

"Oh, Gehenna of a big crop!" he heard Klem Zareff's voice, chuckling happily, above the babble in the room. "You wouldn't believe it. Why, we had to build six new vats...."

The thin-faced, white-haired man in the chair beside him said something. Mike Shanlee and Klem Zareff, old enemies, were now fast friends. Shanlee had come in from Force Command with Conn that morning. He had stayed on Poictesme as nominal head of Project Merlin, and intended to remain there for the rest of his life.

"Oh, there aren't any more farm-tramps," Zareff replied. "Everybody's getting factory jobs off-planet. I have an awful time getting help, and what I can get won't work for less than ten sols a day. Why, they're even organizing a union...."

There were feminine shrieks from across the room, and a stampede. The housecleaning-robot had come in, running its vacuum-cleaning hose around and brandishing its mops. He saw his mother break away from a group of older ladies and shout:

"*Oscar!*"

The robot stopped dead. "Yash'm?" a voice came out of it, Sheshan-accented.

"Go out!" his mother commanded. "Go to kitchen. Stay there."

"Yash'm." The robot floated out the door to the hall.

His mother rejoined her friends. Probably telling them, for the thousandth time, that her boy Conn fixed up the sound receptors and voice for Oscar. Or harping on how Conn had been telling everybody the truth, all along, and people wouldn't believe him.

Sylvie came up to him and caught his arm. "Come on, Conn; they're going to start the rehearsal," she said.

"They've been going to start it for an hour," her father told her.

"Well, they're really going to start it now."

"All right. You two run along," Yves Jacquemont said. "And you'd better start rehearsing for your own wedding before long. The *Genji* will be ready to hyper out in another month, and I don't want to be at space when my only daughter gets married."

They pushed through the crowd, dragging Conn's mother with them toward the big living room beyond. On the way, Mrs. Maxwell stopped to try to drag Judge Ledue out of a chair.

"Judge, the rehearsal is starting; they can't do it without you."

Ledue clung to his chair. "They daren't do it with me, Mrs. Maxwell. If I get into it, it won't be a rehearsal; they'll be really married, and then there won't be any point in having a wedding tomorrow."

"Oh, Morgan!" Conn called across the room to Gatworth. "You've just been appointed temporary judge for the wedding rehearsal!"

There was a big crowd around Wade Lucas, in the next room; he was telling them about the voyage to Baldur, from which he had returned, and the one to Irminsul, with a cargo of arms, machine tools and contragravity vehicles, on which he and his bride would go for their honeymoon. There was another crowd around Flora; she was telling them about the new fashions on Baldur, which had been brought back on the *Ouroboros II*.

"Where's your father?" his mother was asking him. "He has to rehearse giving the bride away."

"Probably in his office. I'll go get him."

"You'll get into an argument with somebody and forget to come back," his mother said. "Sylvie, you go with him, and bring both of them back."

"When'll we have our wedding, Sylvie?" he asked as they went off together.

"Well, before Dad goes to Aditya with the *Genji*. That'll have to be in a month."

"Two weeks? That ought to be plenty of time to get ready, and let people recover from this one."

"Everybody's here now. Let's make it a double wedding tomorrow," she suggested.

He hadn't been prepared for that. "Well, I hadn't expected....Sure! Good idea!" he agreed.

There was a crowd in Rodney Maxwell's little office-Fawzi and some others, and some Storisende people. One of the latter was vociferating:

"Jake Vyckhoven's no good, and he never was any good!"

"Well, you have to admit, if he hadn't ordered the banks and the Stock Exchange closed that time, we'd have had a horrible panic —"

"Admit nothing of the kind! Jethro, you were there, you'll bear me out. About a dozen of us were at Executive Palace for hours, bullying him into that. Why, we almost had to twist one of his arms while he was signing the order with the other. And now he has the gall to run for re-election on the strength of his heroic actions at the time of the Travis Hoax!"

"I know who we want for President!" another Storisende man exclaimed. "He's right here in this room!"

"Yes!" Rodney Maxwell almost bellowed, before the other man could say anything else. "Here he is!" He grabbed Kurt Fawzi by the arm and yanked him to his feet. "Here's the man most responsible for finding Merlin; the man who first suggested sending my son Conn to Terra to school, the man who, more than anyone else, devoted his life to the search for Merlin, the man whose inextinguishable faith and indomitable courage kept that search alive through its darkest hours. Everybody, get a drink; a toast to our next President, Kurt Fawzi!"

Conn was sure he heard his father add: "Ghu, what a narrow escape!"

Then he and Sylvie began chanting, in unison, *"We want Fawzi! We want Fawzi!"*

Space Viking

Vengeance is a strange human motivation —
it can drive a man to do things
which he neither would nor could achieve without it...
and because of that it lies behind some of the
greatest sagas of human literature!

by H. Beam Piper

I

They stood together at the parapet, their arms about each other's waists, her head against his cheek. Behind, the broad leaved shrubbery gossiped softly with the wind, and from the lower main terrace came music and laughing voices. The city of Wardshaven spread in front of them, white buildings rising from the wide spaces of green treetops, under a shimmer of sun-reflecting aircars above. Far away, the mountains were violet in the afternoon haze, and the huge red sun hung in a sky as yellow as a ripe peach.

His eye caught a twinkle ten miles to the southwest, and for an instant he was puzzled. Then he frowned. The sunlight on the two thousand-foot globe of Duke Angus' new ship, the *Enterprise*, back at the Gorram shipyards after her final trial cruise. He didn't want to think about that, now.

Instead, he pressed the girl closer and whispered her name, "Elaine," and then, caressing every syllable, "Lady Elaine Trask of Traskon."

"Oh, no, Lucas!" Her protest was half joking and half apprehensive. "It's bad luck to be called by your married name before the wedding."

"I've been calling you that in my mind since the night of the Duke's ball, when you were just home from school on Excalibur."

She looked up from the corner of her eye.

"That was when I started calling me that, too," she confessed.

"There's a terrace to the west at Traskon New House," he told her. "Tomorrow, we'll have our dinner there, and watch the sunset together."

"I know. I thought that was to be our sunset-watching place."

"You have been peeking," he accused. "Traskon New House was to be your surprise."

"I always was a present-peeker, New Year's and my birthdays. But I only saw it from the air. I'll be very surprised at everything inside," she promised. "And very delighted."

And when she'd seen everything and Traskon New House wasn't a surprise any more, they'd take a long space trip. He hadn't mentioned that to her, yet. To some of the other Sword-Worlds —Excalibur, of course, and Morglay and Flamberge and Durendal. No, not Durendal; the war had started there again. But they'd have so much fun. And she would see clear blue skies again, and stars at night. The cloud-veil hid the stars from Gram, and Elaine had missed them, since coming home from Excalibur.

The shadow of an aircar fell briefly upon them and they looked up and turned their heads, in time to see it sink with graceful dignity toward the landing-stage of Karval House, and he glimpsed its blazonry-sword and atom-symbol, the badge of the ducal house of Ward. He wondered if it were Duke Angus himself, or just some of his people come ahead of him. They should get back to their guests, he supposed. Then he took her in his arms and kissed her, and she responded ardently. It must have been all of five minutes since they'd done that before.

A slight cough behind them brought them apart and their heads around. It was Sesar Karvall, gray-haired and portly, the breast of his blue coat gleaming with orders and decorations and the sapphire in the pommel of his dress-dagger twinkling.

"I thought I'd find you two here," Elaine's father smiled. "You'll have tomorrow and tomorrow and tomorrow together, but need I remind you that today we have guests, and more coming every minute."

"Who came in the Ward car?" Elaine asked.

"Rovard Grauffis. And Otto Harkaman; you never met him, did you, Lucas?"

"No; not by introduction. I'd like to, before he spaces out." He had nothing against Harkaman personally; only against what he represented. "Is the Duke coming?"

"Oh, surely. Lionel of Newhaven and the Lord of Northport are coming with him. They're at the Palace now." Karvall hesitated. "His nephew's back in town."

Elaine was distressed; she started to say: "Oh, dear! I hope he doesn't —"

"Has Dunnan been bothering Elaine again?"

"Nothing to take notice of. He was here, yesterday, demanding to speak with her. We got him to leave without too much unpleasantness."

"It'll be something for me to take notice of, if he keeps it up after tomorrow."

For his seconds and Andray Dunnan's, that was; he hoped it wouldn't come to that. He didn't want to have to shoot a kinsman to the house of Ward, and a crazy man to boot.

"I'm terribly sorry for him," Elaine was saying. "Father, you should have let me talk to him. I might have made him understand."

Sesar Karvall was shocked. "Child, you couldn't have subjected yourself to that! The man is insane!" Then he saw her bare shoulders, and was even more shocked. "Elaine, your shawl!"

Her hands went up and couldn't find it; she looked about in confused embarrassment. Amused, Lucas picked it from the shrub onto which she had tossed it and draped it over her shoulders, his hands lingering briefly. Then he gestured to the older man to precede them, and they entered the arbored walk. At the other end, in an open circle, a fountain played; white marble girls and boys bathing in the jade-green basin. Another piece of loot from one of the Old Federation planets; that was something he'd tried to avoid in furnishing Traskon New House. There'd be a lot of that coming to Gram, after Otto Harkaman took the *Enterprise* to space.

"I'll have to come back, some time, and visit them," Elaine whispered to him. "They'll miss me."

"You'll find a lot of new friends at your new home," he whispered back. "You wait till tomorrow."

"I'm going to put a word in the Duke's ear about that fellow," Sesar Karvall, still thinking of Dunnan, was saying. "If he speaks to him, maybe it'll do some good."

"I doubt it. I don't think Duke Angus has any influence over him at all."

Dunnan's mother had been the Duke's younger sister; from his father he had inherited what had originally been a prosperous barony. Now it was mortgaged to the top of the manor-house aerial-mast. The Duke had once assumed Dunnan's debts, and refused to do so again. Dunnan had gone to space a few times, as a junior officer on trade-and-raid voyages into the Old Federation. He was supposed to be a fair astrogator. He had expected his uncle to give him command of the *Enterprise*, which had been ridiculous. Disappointed in that, he had recruited a mercenary company and was seeking military employment: It was suspected that he was in correspondence with his uncle's worst enemy, Duke Omfray of Glaspyth.

And he was obsessively in love with Elaine Karvall, a passion which seemed to nourish itself on its own hopelessness. Maybe it would be a good idea to take that space trip right away. There ought to be a ship leaving Bigglersport for one of the other Sword-Worlds, before long.

They paused at the head of the escalators; the garden below was thronged with guests, the bright shawls of the ladies and the coats of the men making shifting color-patterns among the flower-beds and on the lawns and under the trees. Serving-robots, flame-yellow and black in the Karvall colors, floated about playing soft music and offering refreshments. There was a continuous spiral of changing costume-color around the circular robo-table. Voices babbled happily like a mountain river.

As they stood looking down, another aircar circled low; green and gold, lettered PANPLANET NEWS SERVICE. Sesar Karvall swore in irritation.

"Didn't there use to be something they called privacy?" he asked.

"It's a big story, Sesar."

It was; more than the marriage of two people who happened to be in love with each other. It was the marriage of the farming and ranching barony of Traskon and the Karvall steel mills. More, it was public announcement that the wealth and fighting-men of both baronies were now aligned behind Duke Angus of Wardshaven. So it was a general holiday. Every industry had closed down at noon today, and would be closed until morning-after-next, and there would be dancing in every park and feasting in every tavern. To Sword-Worlders, any excuse for a holiday was better than none.

"They're our people, Sesar; they have a right to have a good time with us. I know everybody at Traskon is watching this by screen."

He raised his hand and waved to the news car, and when it swung its pickup around, he waved again. Then they went down the long escalator.

Lady Lavina Karvall was the center of a cluster of matrons and dowagers, around which tomorrow's bridesmaids fluttered like many-colored butterflies. She took possession of her daughter and dragged her into the feminine circle. He saw Rovard Grauffis, small and saturnine, Duke Angus' henchman, and Burt Sandrasan, Lady Lavina's brother. They spoke, and then an upper-servant, his tabard blazoned with the yellow flame and black hammer of Karvall mills, approached his master with some tale of domestic crisis, and the two went away together.

"You haven't met Captain Harkaman, Lucas," Rovard Grauffis said. "I wish you'd come over and say hello and have a drink with him. I know your attitude, but he's a good sort. Personally, I wish we had a few like him around here."

That was his main objection. There were fewer and fewer men of that sort on any of the Sword-Worlds.

II

A dozen men clustered around the bartending robot-his cousin and family lawyer, Nikkolay Trask; Lothar Ffayle, the banker; Alex Gorram, the shipbuilder, and his son Basil; Baron Rathmore; more of the Wardshaven nobles whom he knew only distantly. And Otto Harkaman.

Harkaman was a Space Viking. That would have set him apart, even if he hadn't topped the tallest of them by a head. He wore a short black jacket, heavily gold-braided, and black trousers inside ankle-boots; the dagger on his belt was no mere dress-ornament. His tousled red-brown hair was long enough to furnish extra padding in a combat-helmet, and his beard was cut square at the bottom.

He had been fighting on Durendal, for one of the branches of the royal house contesting fratricidally for the throne. The wrong one; he had lost his ship, and most of his men and, almost, his own life. He had been a penniless refugee on Flamberge, owning only the clothes he stood in and his personal weapons and the loyalty of half a dozen adventurers as penniless as himself, when Duke Angus had invited him to Gram to command the *Enterprise.*

"A pleasure, Lord Trask. I've met your lovely bride-to-be, and now that I meet you, let me congratulate both." Then, as they were having a drink together, he put his foot in it by asking: "You're not an investor in the Tanith Adventure, are you?"

He said he wasn't, and would have let it go at that. Young Basil Gorram had to get his foot in, too.

"Lord Trask does not approve of the Tanith Adventure," he said scornfully. "He thinks we should stay home and produce wealth, instead of exporting robbery and murder to the Old Federation for it."

The smile remained on Otto Harkaman's face; only the friendliness was gone. He unobtrusively shifted his drink to his left hand.

"Well, our operations are definable as robbery and murder," he agreed. "Space Vikings are professional robbers and murderers. And you object? Perhaps you find me personally objectionable?"

"I wouldn't have shaken your hand or had a drink with you if I did. I don't care how many planets you raid or cities you sack, or how many innocents, if that's what they are, you massacre in the Old Federation. You couldn't possibly do anything worse than those people have been doing to one another for the past ten centuries. What I object to is the way you're raiding the Sword-Worlds."

"You're crazy!" Basil Gorram exploded.

"Young man," Harkaman reproved, "the conversation was between Lord Trask and myself. And when somebody makes a statement you don't understand, don't tell him he's crazy. Ask him what he means. What *do* you mean, Lord Trask?"

"You should know; you've just raided Gram for eight hundred of our best men. You raided me for close to forty vaqueros, farm-workers, lumbermen, machine-operators, and I doubt I'll be able to replace them with as good." He turned to the elder Gorram. "Alex, how many have you lost to Captain Harkaman?"

Gorram tried to make it a dozen; pressed, he admitted to a score and a half. Roboticians, machine-supervisors, programmers, a couple of engineers, a foreman. There was grudging agreement from the others. Burt Sandrasan's engine-works had lost almost as many, of the same kind. Even Lothar Ffayle admitted to losing a computerman and a guard-sergeant.

And after they were gone, the farms and ranches and factories would go on, almost but not quite as before. Nothing on Gram, nothing on any of the Sword-Worlds, was done as efficiently as three centuries ago The whole level of Sword-World life was sinking, like the east coastline of this continent, so slowly as to be evident only from the records and monuments of the past. He said as much, and added:

"And the genetic loss. The best Sword-World genes are literally escaping to space, like the atmosphere of a low-gravity planet, each generation begotten by fathers slightly inferior to the last. It wasn't so bad when the Space Vikings raided directly from the Sword-Worlds; they got home once in a while. Now they're conquering planets in the Old Federation for bases, and staying there."

Everybody had begun to relax; this wouldn't be a quarrel. Harkaman, who had shifted his drink back to his right hand, chuckled.

"That's right. I've fathered my share of brats in the Old Federation, and I know Space Vikings whose fathers were born on Old Federation planets." He turned to Basil Gorram. "You see, the gentleman isn't crazy, at all. That's what happened to the Terran Federation, by the way. The good men all left to colonize, and the stuffed shirts and yes-men and herd-followers and safety-firsters stayed on Terra and tried to govern the galaxy."

"Well, maybe this is all new to you, captain," Rovard Grauffis said sourly, "but Lucas Trask's dirge for the Decline and Fall of the Sword-Worlds is an old song to the rest of us. I have too much to do to stay here and argue."

Lothar Ffayle evidently did intend to stay and argue.

"All you're saying, Lucas, is that we're expanding. You want us to sit here and build up population pressure like Terra in the First Century?"

"With three and a half billion people spread out on twelve planets? They had that many on Terra alone. And it took us eight centuries to reach that."

That had been since the Ninth Century, Atomic Era, at the end of the Big War. Ten thousand men and women on Abigor, refusing to surrender, had taken the remnant of the System States Alliance navy to space, seeking a world the Federation had never heard of and wouldn't find for a long time. That had been the world they had called Excalibur. From it, their grandchildren had colonized Joyeuse and Durendal and Flamberge; Haulteclere had been colonized in the next generation from Joyeuse, and Gram from Haulteclere.

"We're not expanding, Lothar; we're contracting. We stopped expanding three hundred and fifty years ago, when that ship came back to Morglay from the Old Federation and reported what had been happening out there since the Big War. Before that, we were discovering new planets and colonizing them. Since then, we've been picking the bones of the dead Terran Federation."

Something was going on by the escalators to the landing stage. People were moving excitedly in that direction, and the news cars were circling like vultures over a sick cow. Harkaman wondered, hopefully, if it mightn't be a fight.

"Some drunk being bounced." Nikkolay, Lucas' cousin, commented. "Sesar's let all Wardshaven in here, today. But, Lucas, this Tanith adventure; we're not making any hit-and-run raid. We're taking over a whole planet; it'll be another Sword-World in forty or fifty years."

"Inside another century, we'll conquer the whole Federation," Baron Rathmore declared. He was a politician and never let exaggeration worry him.

"What I don't understand," Harkaman said, "is why you support Duke Angus, Lord Trask, if you think the Tanith adventure is doing Gram so much harm."

"If Angus didn't do it, somebody else would. But Angus is going to make himself King of Gram, and I don't think anybody else could do that. This planet needs a single sovereignty. I don't know how much you've seen of it outside this duchy, but don't take Wardshaven as typical. Some of these duchies, like Glaspyth or Didreksburg, are literal snake pits. All the major barons are at each other's throats, and they can't even keep their own knights and petty-barons in order.

Why, there's a miserable little war down in Southmain Continent that's been going on for over two centuries."

"That's probably where Dunnan's going to take that army of his," a robot-manufacturing baron said. "I hope it gets wiped out, and Dunnan with it."

"You don't have to go to Southmain; just go to Glaspyth," somebody else said.

"Well, if we don't get a planetary monarchy to keep order, this planet will decivilize like anything in the Old Federation."

"Oh, *come*, Lucas!" Alex Gorram protested. "That's pulling it out too far."

"Yes, for one thing, we don't have the Neobarbarians," somebody said. "And if they ever came out here, we'd blow them to Em-See-Square in nothing flat. Might be a good thing if they did, too; it would stop us squabbling among ourselves."

Harkaman looked at him in surprise. "Just who do you think the Neobarbarians are, anyhow?" he asked. "Some race of invading nomads; Attila's Huns in spaceships?"

"Well, isn't that who they are?" Gorram asked.

"Nifflheim, no! There aren't a dozen and a half planets in the Old Federation that still have hyperdrive, and they're all civilized. That's if 'civilized' is what Gilgamesh is," he added. "These are homemade barbarians. Workers and peasants who revolted to seize and divide the wealth and then found they'd smashed the means of production and killed off all the technical brains.

Survivors on planets hit during the Interstellar Wars, from the Eleventh to the Thirteenth Centuries, who lost the machinery of civilization. Followers of political leaders on local-dictatorship planets. Companies of mercenaries thrown out of employment and living by pillage. Religious fanatics following self-anointed prophets."

"You think we don't have plenty of Neobarbarian material here on Gram?" Trask demanded. "If you do, take a look around."

Glaspyth, somebody said.

"That collection of over-ripe gallows-fruit Andray Dunnan's recruited," Rathmore mentioned.

Alex Gorram was grumbling that his shipyard was full of them; agitators stirring up trouble, trying to organize a strike to get rid of the robots.

"Yes," Harkaman pounced on that last. "I know of at least forty instances, on a dozen and a half planets, in the last eight centuries, of anti-technological movements. They had them on Terra, back as far as the Second Century Pre-Atomic. And after Venus seceded from the First Federation, before the Second Federation was organized."

"You're interested in history?" Rathmore asked.

"A hobby. All spacemen have hobbies. There's very little work aboard ship in hyperspace; boredom is the worst enemy. My guns-and-missiles officer, Vann Larch, is a painter. Most of his work was lost with the *Corisande* on Durendal, but he kept us from starving a few times on Flamberge by painting pictures and selling them. My hyperspatial astrogator, Guatt Kirbey, composes music; he tries to express the mathematics of hyperspatial theory in musical terms. I don't care much for it, myself," he admitted. "I study history. You know, it's odd; practically everything that's happened on any of the inhabited planets happened on Terra before the first spaceship."

The garden immediately around them was quiet, now; everybody was over by the landing-stage escalators. Harkaman would have said more, but at that moment he saw half a dozen of Sesar Karvall's uniformed guardsmen run past. They were helmeted and in bullet-proofs; one of them had an auto-rifle, and the rest carried knobbed plastic truncheons. The Space Viking set down his drink.

"Let's go," he said. "Our host is calling up his troops; I think the guests ought to find battle-stations, too."

III

The gaily-dressed crowd formed a semicircle facing the landing-stage escalators; everybody was staring in embarrassed curiosity, those behind craning over the shoulders of those in front. The ladies had drawn up their shawls in frigid formality; many had even covered their heads. There were four news-service cars hovering above; whatever was going on was getting a planetwide screen showing. The Karvall guardsmen were trying to get through; their sergeant was saying, over and over, "Please, ladies and gentlemen; your pardon, noble sir," and getting nowhere.

Otto Harkaman swore disgustedly and shoved the sergeant aside. "Make way, here!" he bellowed. "Let these guards pass." With that, he almost hurled a gaily-dressed gentleman aside on either hand; they both turned to glare angrily, then got hastily out of his way. Meditating briefly on the uses of bad manners in an emergency, Trask followed, with the others; the big Space Viking plowed to the front, where Sesar Karvall and Rovard Grauffis and several others were standing.

Facing them, four men in black cloaks stood with their backs to the escalators. Two were commonfolk retainers; hired gunmen, to be precise. They were at pains to keep their hands plainly in sight, and seemed to be wishing themselves elsewhere. The man in front wore a diamond sunburst jewel on his beret, and his cloak was lined with pale blue silk. His thin, pointed face was deeply lined about the mouth and penciled with a thin black mustache. His eyes showed white all around the irises, and now and then his mouth would twitch in an involuntary grimace. Andray Dunnan; Trask wondered briefly how soon he would have to look at him from twenty-five meters over the sights of a pistol. The face of the slightly taller man who stood at his shoulder was paper-white, expressionless, with a black beard. His name was Nevil Ormm, nobody was quite sure whence he had come, and he was Dunnan's henchman and constant companion.

"You lie!" Dunnan was shouting. "You lie damnably, in your stinking teeth, all of you! You've intercepted every message she's tried to send me."

"My daughter has sent you no messages, Lord Dunnan," Sesar Karvall said, with forced patience. "None but the one I just gave you, that she wants nothing whatever to do with you."

"You think I believe that? You're holding her a prisoner; Satan only knows how you've been torturing her to force her into this abominable marriage —"

There was a stir among the bystanders; that was more than well-mannered restraint could stand. Out of the murmur of incredulous voices, one woman's was quite audible:

"Well, really! He actually *is* crazy!"

Dunnan, like everybody else, heard it. "Crazy, am I?" he blazed. "Because I can see through this hypocritical sham? Here's Lucas Trask, he wants an interest in Karvall mills, and here's Sesar Karvall, he wants access to iron deposits on Traskon land. And my loving uncle, he wants the help of both of them in stealing Omfray of Glaspyth's duchy. And here's this loan-shark of a Ffayle, trying to claw my lands away from me, and Rovard Grauffis, the fetchdog of my uncle who won't lift a finger to save his kinsman from ruin, and this foreigner Harkaman who's swindled me out of command of the *Enterprise*. You're all plotting against me —"

"Sir Nevil," Grauffis said, "you can see that Lord Dunnan's not himself. If you're a good friend to him, you'll get him out of here before Duke Angus arrives."

Ormm leaned forward and spoke urgently in Dunnan's ear. Dunnan pushed him angrily away.

"Great Satan, are you against me, too?" he demanded.

Ormm caught his arm. "You fool, do you want to ruin everything, now —" He lowered his voice; the rest was inaudible.

"No, curse you, I won't go till I've spoken to her, face to face —"

There was another stir among the spectators; the crowd was parting, and Elaine was coming through, followed by her mother and Lady Sandrasan and five or six other matrons. They all had their shawls over their heads, right ends over left shoulders; they all stopped except Elaine, who took a few steps forward and confronted Andray Dunnan. He had never seen her look more beautiful, but it was the icy beauty of a honed dagger.

"Lord Dunnan, what do you wish to say to me?" she asked. "Say it quickly and then go; you are not welcome here."

"Elaine!" Dunnan cried, taking a step forward. "Why do you cover your head; why do you speak to me as a stranger? I am Andray, who loves you. Why are you letting them force you into this wicked marriage?"

"No one is forcing me; I am marrying Lord Trask willingly and happily, because I love him. Now, please, go and make no more trouble at my wedding."

"That's a lie! They're making you say that! You don't have to marry him; they can't make you. Come with me now. They won't dare stop you. I'll take you away from all these cruel, greedy people. You love me, you've always loved me. You've told me you loved me, again and again —"

Yes, in his own private dream-world, a world of fantasy that had now become Andray Dunnan's reality, in which an Elaine Karvall whom his imagination had created existed only to love him. Confronted by the real Elaine, he simply rejected the reality.

"I never loved you, Lord Dunnan, and I never told you so. I never hated you, either, but you are making it very hard for me not to. Now go, and never let me see you again."

With that, she turned and started back through the crowd, which parted in front of her. Her mother and her aunt and the other ladies followed.

"You lied to me!" Dunnan shrieked after her. "You lied all the time. You're as bad as the rest of them, all scheming and plotting against me, betraying me. I know what it's about; you all want to cheat me of my rights, and keep my usurping uncle on the ducal throne. And you, you false-hearted harlot, you're the worst of them all!"

Sir Nevil Ormm caught his shoulder and spun him around, propelling him toward the escalators. Dunnan struggled, screaming inarticulately like a wounded wolf. Ormm was cursing furiously.

"You two!" he shouted. "Help me, here. Get hold of him."

Dunnan was still howling as they forced him onto the escalator, the backs of the two retainers' cloaks, badged with the Dunnan crescent, light blue on black, hiding him. After a little, an aircar with the blue crescent blazonry lifted and sped away.

"Lucas, he's crazy," Sesar Karvall was insisting. "Elaine hasn't spoken fifty words to him since he came back from his last voyage —"

He laughed and put a hand on Karvall's shoulder. "I know that, Sesar. You don't think, do you, that I need assurance of it?"

"Crazy, I'll say he's crazy," Rovard Grauffis put in. "Did you hear what he said about his rights? Wait till his Grace hears about that."

"Does he lay claim to the ducal throne, Sir Rovard?" Otto Harkaman asked, sharply and seriously.

"Oh, he claims that his mother was born a year and a half before Duke Angus and the true date of her birth falsified to give Angus the succession. Why, his present Grace was three years old when she was born. I was old Duke Fergus' esquire; I carried Angus on my shoulder when Andray Dunnan's mother was presented to the lords and barons the day after she was born."

"Of course he's crazy," Alex Gorram agreed. "I don't know why the Duke doesn't have him put under psychiatric treatment."

"I'd put him under treatment," Harkaman said, drawing a finger across under his beard. "Crazy men who pretend to thrones are bombs that ought to be deactivated, before they blow things up."

"We couldn't do that," Grauffis said. "After all, he's Duke Angus' nephew —"

"I could do it," Harkaman said. "He only has three hundred men in this company of his. Why you people ever let him recruit them Satan only knows," he parenthesized. "I have eight hundred; five hundred ground-fighters. I'd like to see how they shape up in combat, before we space out. I can have them ready for action in two hours, and it'd be all over before midnight."

"No, Captain Harkaman; his Grace would never permit it," Grauffis vetoed. "You have no idea of the political harm that would do among the independent lords on whom we're counting for support. You weren't here on Gram when Duke Ridgerd of Didreksburg had his sister Sancia's second husband poisoned —"

IV

They halted under the colonnade; beyond, the lower main terrace was crowded, and a medley of old love songs was wafting from the sound outlets, for the sixth or eighth time around. He looked at his watch; it was ninety seconds later than the last time he had done so. Give it fifteen more minutes to get started, and another fifteen to get away after the marriage toasts and the felicitations. And no marriage, however pompous, lasted more than half an hour. An hour, then, till he and Elaine would be in the aircar, bulleting toward Traskon.

The love songs stopped abruptly; after a momentary silence, a trumpet, considerably amplified, blared; the "Ducal Salute." The crowd stopped shifting, the buzz of voices ceased. At the head of the landing-stage escalators there was a glow of color and the ducal party began moving down. A platoon of guards in red and yellow, with gilded helmets and tasseled halberds. An esquire bearing the Sword of State. Duke Angus, with his council, Otto Harkaman among them; the Duchess Flavia and her companion-ladies. The household gentlemen, and their ladies. More guardsmen. There was a great burst of cheering; the news-service aircars got into position above the procession. Cousin Nikkolay and a few others stepped out from between the pillars into the sunlight; there was a similar movement at the other side of the terrace. The ducal party reached the end of the central walkway, halted and deployed.

"All right; let's shove off," Cousin Nikkolay said, stepping forward.

Ten minutes since they had come outside; another five to get into position. Fifty minutes, now, till he and Elaine-Lady Elaine Trask of Traskon, for real and for always-would be going home.

"Sure the car's ready?" he asked, for the hundredth time.

His cousin assured him that it was. Figures in Karvall black and flame-yellow appeared across the terrace. The music began again, this time the stately "Nobles' Wedding March," arrogant and at the same time tender. Sesar Karvall's gentleman-secretary, and the Karvall lawyer; executives of the steel mills, the Karvall guard-captain. Sesar himself, with Elaine on his arm; she was wearing a shawl of black and yellow. He looked around in sudden fright; "For the love of Satan, where's our shawl?" he demanded, and then relaxed when one of his gentlemen exhibited it, green and tawny in Traskon colors. The bridesmaids, led by Lady Lavina Karvall. Finally they halted, ten yards apart, in front of the Duke.

"Who approaches us?" Duke Angus asked of his guard-captain.

He had a thin, pointed face, almost femininely sensitive, and a small pointed beard. He was bareheaded except for the narrow golden circlet which he spent most of his waking time scheming to convert into a royal crown. The guard-captain repeated the question.

"I am Sir Nikkolay Trask; I bring my cousin and liege-lord, Lucas, Lord Trask, Baron of Traskon. He comes to receive the Lady-Demoiselle Elaine, daughter of Lord Sesar Karvall, Baron of Karvall mills, and the sanction of your Grace to the marriage between them."

Sir Maxamon Zhorgay, Sesar Karvall's henchman, named himself and his lord; they brought the Lady-Demoiselle Elaine to be wed to Lord Trask of Traskon. The Duke, satisfied that these were persons whom he could address directly, asked if the terms of the marriage-agreement had been reached; both parties affirmed this. Sir Maxamon passed a scroll to the Duke; Duke Angus began to read the stiff and precise legal phraseology. Marriages between noble houses were not matters to be left open to dispute; a great deal of spilled blood and burned powder had resulted from ambiguity on some point of succession or inheritance or dower rights. Lucas bore it patiently; he didn't want his great-grandchildren and Elaine's shooting it out over a matter of a misplaced comma.

"And these persons here before us do enter into this marriage freely?" the Duke asked, when the reading had ended. He stepped forward as he spoke, and his esquire gave him the two-hand Sword of State, heavy enough to behead a bisonoid. Trask stepped forward; Sesar Karvall brought Elaine up. The lawyers and henchmen obliqued off to the sides. "How say you, Lord Trask?" he asked, almost conversationally.

"With all my heart, your Grace."

"And you, Lady-Demoiselle Elaine?"

"It is my dearest wish, your Grace."

The Duke took the sword by the blade and extended it; they laid their hands on the jeweled pommel.

"And do you, and your houses, avow us, Angus, Duke of Wardshaven, to be your sovereign prince, and pledge fealty to us and to our legitimate and lawful successors?"

"We do." Not only he and Elaine, but all around them, and all the throng in the gardens, answered, the spectators in shouts. Very clearly, above it all, somebody, with more enthusiasm than discretion, was bawling: *"Long live Angus the First of Gram!"*

"And we, Angus, do confer upon you two, and your houses, the right to wear our badge as you see fit, and pledge ourself to maintain your rights against any and all who may presume to invade them. And we declare that this marriage between you two, and this agreement between your respective houses, does please us, and we avow you two, Lucas and Elaine, to be lawfully wed, and who so questions this marriage challenges us, in our teeth and to our despite."

That wasn't exactly the wording used by a ducal lord on Gram. It was the formula employed by a planetary king, like Napolyon of Flamberge or Rodolf of Excalibur. And, now that he thought of it, Angus had consistently used the royal first-person plural. Maybe that fellow who had shouted about Angus the First of Gram had only been doing what he'd been paid to do. This was being telecast, and Omfray of Glaspyth and Ridgerd of Didreksburg would both be listening; as of now, they'd start hiring mercenaries. Maybe that would get rid of Dunnan for him.

The Duke gave the two-hand sword back to his esquire. The young knight who was carrying the green and tawny shawl handed it to him, and Elaine dropped the black and yellow one from her shoulders, the only time a respectable woman ever did that in public, and her mother caught and folded it. He stepped forward and draped the Trask colors over her shoulders, and then took her in his arms. The cheering broke out again, and some of Sesar Karvall's guardsmen began firing a pom-pom somewhere.

<hr>

It took a little longer than he had expected to finish with the toasts and shake hands with those who crowded around. Finally, the exit march started, down the long walkway to the landing stage, and the Duke and his party moved away to the rear to prepare for the wedding feast at which everybody but the bride and groom would celebrate. One of the bridesmaids gave Elaine a huge sheaf of flowers, which she was to toss back from the escalator; she held it in the crook of one arm and clung to his with the other.

"Darling; we really made it!" she was whispering, as though it were too wonderful to believe. Well, wasn't it?

One of the news cars-orange and blue, that was Westlands Telecast & Teleprint-had floated just ahead of them and was letting down toward the landing stage. For a moment, he was angry; that went beyond the outer-orbit limits of journalistic propriety, even for Westlands T & T. Then he laughed; today he was too happy for anger about anything. At the foot of the escalator, Elaine kicked off her gilded slippers-there was another pair in the car; he'd seen to that personally-and they stepped onto the escalator and turned about. The bridesmaids rushed forward, and began struggling for the slippers, to the damage and disarray of their gowns, and when they were half way up, Elaine heaved the bouquet and it burst apart among them like a bomb of colored fragrance, and the girls below snatched at the flowers, shrieking deliriously. Elaine stood, blowing kisses to everybody, and he was shaking his clasped hands over his head, until they were at the top.

When they turned and stepped off, the orange and blue aircar had let down directly in front of them, blocking their way. Now he was really furious, and started forward with a curse. Then he saw who was in the car.

Andray Dunnan, his thin face contorted and the narrow mustache writhing on his upper lip; he had a slit beside the window open and was tilting the barrel of a submachine gun up and out of it.

He shouted, and at the same time tripped Elaine and flung her down. He was throwing himself forward to cover her when there was a blasting multiple report. Something sledged him in the chest; his right leg crumpled under him. He fell —

He fell and fell and fell, endlessly, through darkness, out of consciousness.

V

He was crucified, and crowned with a crown of thorns. Who had they done that to? Somebody long ago, on Terra. His arms were drawn out stiffly, and hurt; his feet and legs hurt, too, and he couldn't move them, and there was this prickling at his brow. And he was blind.

No; his eyes were just closed. He opened them, and there was a white wall in front of him, patterned with a blue snow-crystal design, and he realized that it was a ceiling and that he was lying on his back. He couldn't move his head, but by shifting his eyes he saw that he was completely naked and surrounded by a tangle of tubes and wires, which puzzled him briefly. Then he knew that he was not on a bed, but on a robomedic, and the tubes would be for medication and wound drainage and intravenous feeding, and the wires would be to electrodes imbedded in his body for diagnosis, and the crown-of-thorns thing would be more electrodes for an encephalograph. He'd been on one of those robomedics before, when he had been gored by a bisonoid on the cattle range.

That was what it was; he was still under treatment. But that seemed so long ago; so many things-he must have dreamed them-seemed to have happened.

Then he remembered, and struggled futilely to rise.

"Elaine!" he called. "Elaine, where are you?"

There was a stir and somebody came into his limited view; his cousin, Nikkolay Trask.

"Nikkolay; Andray Dunnan," he said. "What happened to Elaine?"

Nikkolay winced, as though something he had expected to hurt had hurt worse than he had expected.

"Lucas." He swallowed. "Elaine ... Elaine is dead."

Elaine is dead. That didn't make sense.

"She was killed instantly, Lucas. Hit six times; I don't think she even felt the first one. She didn't suffer at all."

Somebody moaned, and then he realized that it had been himself.

"You were hit twice," Nikkolay was telling him. "One in the leg; smashed the femur. And one in the chest. That one missed your heart by an inch."

"Pity it did." He was beginning to remember clearly, now. "I threw her down, and tried to cover her. I must have thrown her straight into the burst and only caught the last of it myself." There was something else; oh, yes. "Dunnan. Did they get him?"

Nikkolay shook his head. "He got away. Stole the *Enterprise* and took her off-planet."

"I want to get him myself."

He started to rise again; Nikkolay nodded to someone out of sight. A cool hand touched his chin, and he smelled a woman's perfume, nothing at all like Elaine's. Something like a small insect bit him on the neck. The room grew dark.

Elaine was dead. There was no more Elaine, nowhere at all. Why, that must mean there was no more world. So that was why it had gotten so dark.

He woke again, fitfully, and it would be daylight and he could see the yellow sky through an open window or it would be night and the wall-lights would be on. There would always be somebody with him. Nikkolay's wife, Dame Cecelia; Rovard Grauffis; Lady Lavina Karvall-he must have slept a long time, for she was so much older than he remembered-and her brother, Burt Sandrasan. And a woman with dark hair, in a white smock with a gold caduceus on her breast.

Once, Duchess Flavia, and once Duke Angus himself. He asked where he was, not much caring. They told him, at the Ducal Palace.

He wished they'd all go away, and let him go wherever Elaine was.

Then it would be dark, and he would be trying to find her, because there was something he wanted desperately to show her. Stars in the sky at night, that was it. But there were no stars, there was no Elaine, there was no anything, and he wished that there was no Lucas Trask, either.

But there was an Andray Dunnan. He could see him standing black-cloaked on the terrace, the diamonds in his beret-jewel glittering evilly; he could see the mad face peering at him over the rising barrel of the submachine gun. And then he would hunt for him without finding him, through the cold darkness of space.

The waking periods grew longer, and during them his mind was clear. They relieved him of his crown of electronic thorns. The feeding tubes came out, and they gave him cups of broth and fruit juice. He wanted to know why he had been brought to the Palace.

"About the only thing we could do," Rovard Grauffis told him. "They had too much trouble at Karvall House as it was. You know, Sesar got shot, too."

"No." So that was why Sesar hadn't come to see him. "Was he killed?"

"Wounded; he's in worse shape than you are. When the shooting started, he went charging up the escalator. Didn't have anything but his dress-dagger. Dunnan gave him a quick burst; I think that was why he didn't have time to finish you off. By that time, the guards who'd been shooting blanks from that rapid-fire gun got in a clip of live rounds and fired at him. He got out of there as fast as he could. They have Sesar on a robomedic like yours. He isn't in any danger."

The drainage tubes and medication tubes came out; the tangle of wires around him was removed, and the electrodes with them. They bandaged his wounds and dressed him in a loose robe and lifted him from the robomedic to a couch, where he could sit up when he wished; they began giving him solid food, and wine to drink, and allowed him to smoke. The woman doctor told him he'd had a bad time, as though he didn't know that. He wondered if she expected him to thank her for keeping him alive.

"You'll be up and around in a few weeks," his cousin added. "I've seen to it that everything at Traskon New House will be ready for you by then."

"I'll never enter that house as long as I live, and I wish that wouldn't be more than the next minute. That was to be Elaine's house. I won't go to it alone."

The dreams troubled his sleep less and less as he grew stronger. Visitors came often, bringing amusing little gifts, and he found that he enjoyed their company. He wanted to know what had really happened, and how Dunnan had gotten away.

"He pirated the *Enterprise*," Rovard Grauffis told him. "He had that company of mercenaries of his, and he'd bribed some of the people at the Gorram shipyards. I thought Alex would kill his chief of security when he found out what had happened. We can't prove anything-we're trying hard enough to-but we're sure Omfray of Glaspyth furnished the money. He's been denying it just a shade too emphatically."

"Then the whole thing was planned in advance."

"Taking the ship was; he must have been planning that for months; before he started recruiting that company. I think he meant to do it the night before the wedding. Then he tried to persuade the Lady-Demoiselle Elaine to elope with him-he seems to have actually thought that was possible-and when she humiliated him, he decided to kill both of you first." He turned to Otto Harkaman, who had accompanied him. "As long as I live, I'll regret not taking you at your word and accepting your offer, then."

"How did he get hold of that Westlands Telecast and Teleprint car?"

"Oh. The morning of the wedding, he screened Westlands editorial office and told them he had the inside story on the marriage and why the Duke was sponsoring it. Made it sound as though there was some scandal; insisted that a reporter come to Dunnan House for a face-to-face interview. They sent a man, and that was the last they saw him alive; our people found his body at Dunnan House when we were searching the place afterward. We found the car at the shipyard; it had taken a couple of hits from the guns at Karvall House, but you know what these press cars are built to stand. He went directly to the shipyard, where his men already had the *Enterprise*; as soon as he arrived, she lifted out."

He stared at the cigarette between his fingers. It was almost short enough to burn him. With an effort, he leaned forward to crush it out.

"Rovard, how soon will that second ship be finished?"

Grauffis laughed bitterly. "Building the *Enterprise* took everything we had. The duchy's on the edge of bankruptcy now. We stopped work on the second ship six months ago because we didn't have enough money to keep on with her and still get the *Enterprise* finished. We were expecting the *Enterprise* to make enough in the Old Federation to finish the second one. Then, with two ships and a base on Tanith, the money would begin coming in instead of going out. But now —"

"It leaves me where I was on Flamberge," Harkaman added. "Worse. King Napolyon was going to help the Elmersans, and I'd have gotten a command in that. It's too late for that now."

He picked up his cane and used it to push himself to his feet. The broken leg had mended, but he was still weak. He took a few tottering steps, paused to lean on the cane, and then forced himself on to the open window and stood for a moment staring out. Then he turned.

"Captain Harkaman, it might be that you could still get a command, here on Gram. That's if you don't mind commanding under me as owner-aboard. I am going hunting for Andray Dunnan."

They both looked at him. After a moment, Harkaman said:

"I'd count it an honor, Lord Trask. But where will you get a ship?"

"She's half finished now. You already have a crew for her. Duke Angus can finish her for me, and pay for it by pledging his new barony of Traskon."

He had known Rovard Grauffis all his life; until this moment, he had never seen Duke Angus' henchman show surprise.

"You mean, you'll trade Traskon for that ship?" he demanded.

"Finished, equipped and ready for space, yes."

"The Duke will agree to that," Grauffis said promptly. "But, Lucas; Traskon is all you own."

"If I have a ship, I won't need them. I am turning Space Viking."

That brought Harkaman to his feet with a roar of approval. Grauffis looked at him, his mouth slightly open.

"Lucas Trask-Space Viking," he said. "Now I've heard everything."

Well, why not? He had deplored the effects of Viking raiding on the Sword-Worlds, because Gram was a Sword-World, and Traskon was on Gram, and Traskon was to have been the home where he and Elaine would live and where their children and children's children would be born and live. Now the little point on which all of it had rested was gone.

"That was another Lucas Trask, Rovard. He's dead, now."

VI

Grauffis excused himself to make a screen call and then returned to excuse himself again. Evidently Duke Angus had dropped whatever he was doing as soon as he heard what his henchman had to tell him. Harkaman was silent until after he was out of the room, then said:

"Lord Trask, this is a wonderful thing for me. It's not been pleasant to be a shipless captain living on strangers' bounty. I'd hate, though, to have you think, some time, that I'd advanced my own fortunes at the expense of yours."

"Don't worry about that. If anybody's being taken advantage of, you are. I need a space-captain, and your misfortune is my own good luck."

Harkaman started to pack tobacco into his pipe. "Have you ever been off Gram, at all?" he asked.

"A few years at the University of Camelot, on Excalibur. Otherwise, no."

"Well, have you any conception of the sort of thing you're setting yourself to?" The Space Viking snapped his lighter and puffed. "You know, of course, how big the Old Federation is.

You know the figures, that is, but do they mean anything to you? I know they don't to a good many spacemen, even. We talk glibly about ten to the hundredth power, but emotionally we still count, 'One, Two, Three, Many.' A ship in hyperspace logs about a light-year an hour. You can go from here to Excalibur in thirty hours. But you could send a radio message announcing the birth of a son, and he'd be a father before it was received. The Old Federation, where you're going to hunt Dunnan, occupies a space-volume of two hundred billion cubic light-years. And you're hunting for one ship and one man in that. How are you going to do it, Lord Trask?"

"I haven't started thinking about how; all I know is that I have to do it. There are planets in the Old Federation where Space Vikings come and go; raid-and-trade bases, like the one Duke Angus planned to establish on Tanith. At one or another of them, I'll pick up word of Dunnan, sooner or later."

"We'll hear where he was a year ago, and by the time we get there, he'll be gone for a year and a half to two years. We've been raiding the Old Federation for over three hundred years, Lord Trask. At present, I'd say there are at least two hundred Space Viking ships in operation. Why haven't we raided it bare long ago? Well, that's the answer: distance and voyage-time. You know, Dunnan could die of old age-which is not a usual cause of death among Space Vikings-before you caught up with him. And your youngest ship's-boy could die of old age before he found out about it."

"Well, I can go on hunting for him till I die, then. There's nothing else that means anything to me."

"I thought it was something like that. I won't be with you, all your life. I want a ship of my own, like the *Corisande*, that I lost on Durendal. Some day, I'll have one. But till you can command your own ship, I'll command her for you. That's a promise."

Some note of ceremony seemed indicated. Summoning a robot, he had it pour wine for them, and they pledged each other.

Rovard Grauffis had recovered his aplomb by the time he returned accompanied by the Duke. If Angus had ever lost his, he gave no indication of it. The effect on everybody else was literally seismic. The generally accepted view was that Lord Trask's reason had been unhinged by his tragic loss; there might, he conceded, be more than a crumb of truth in that. At first, his cousin Nikkolay raged at him for alienating the barony from the family, and then he learned that Duke Angus was appointing him vicar-baron and giving him Traskon New House for his residence. Immediately he began acting like one at the death-bed of a rich grandmother. The Wardshaven financial and industrial barons, whom he had known only distantly, on the other hand, came flocking around him, offering assistance and hailing him as the savior of the duchy. Duke Angus' credit, almost obliterated by the loss of the *Enterprise*, was firmly re-established, and theirs with it.

There were conferences at which lawyers and bankers argued interminably; he attended a few at first, found himself completely uninterested, and told everybody so. All he wanted was a ship; the best ship possible, as soon as possible. Alex Gorram had been the first to be notified; he had commenced work on the unfinished sister-ship of the *Enterprise* immediately. Until he was strong enough to go to the shipyard himself, he watched the work on the two-thousand-foot globular skeleton by screen, and conferred either in person or by screen with engineers and shipyard executives. His rooms at the ducal palace were converted, almost overnight, from sickrooms to offices. The doctors, who had recently been urging him to find new interests and activities, were now warning of the dangers of overexertion. Harkaman finally added his voice to theirs.

"You take it easy, Lucas." They had dropped formality and were on a first-name basis now. "You got hulled pretty badly; you let damage-control work on you, and don't strain the machinery till it's fixed. We have plenty of time. We're not going to get anywhere chasing Dunnan. The only way we can catch him is by interception. The longer he moves around in the Old

Federation before he hears we're after him, the more of a trail he'll leave. Once we can establish a predictable pattern, we'll have a chance. Then, some time, he'll come out of hyperspace somewhere and find us waiting for him."

"Do you think he went to Tanith?"

Harkaman heaved himself out of his chair and prowled about the room for a few minutes, then came back and sat down again.

"No. That was Duke Angus' idea, not his. He couldn't put in a base on Tanith, anyhow. You know the kind of a crew he has."

There had been an extensive inquiry into Dunnan's associates and accomplices; Duke Angus was still hoping for positive proof to implicate Omfray of Glaspyth in the piracy. Dunnan had with him a dozen and a half employees of the Gorram shipyards whom he had corrupted. There was some technical ability among them, but for the most part they were agitators and trouble-makers and incompetent workmen. Even under the circumstances, Alex Gorram was glad to see the last of them. As for Dunnan's own mercenary company, there were about a score of former spacemen among them; the rest graded down from bandits through thugs and sneak-thieves to barroom bums. Dunnan himself was an astrogator, not an engineer.

"That gang aren't even good enough for routine raiding," Harkaman said. "They'd never under any circumstances be able to put in a base on Tanith. Unless Dunnan's completely crazy, which I doubt, he's gone to some regular Viking base planet, like Hoth or Nergal or Dagon or Xochitl, to recruit officers and engineers and able spacemen."

"All that machinery and robotic equipment and so on that was going to Tanith-was that aboard when he took the ship?"

"Yes, and that's another reason why he'd go to some planet like Hoth or Nergal or Xochitl. On a Viking-occupied planet in the Old Federation, that stuff's almost worth its weight in gold."

"What's Tanith like?"

"Almost completely Terra-type, third of a Class-G sun. Very much like Haulteclere or Flamberge. It was one of the last planets the Federation colonized before the Big War. Nobody knows what happened, exactly. There wasn't any interstellar war; at least, you don't find any big slag-puddles where cities used to be. They probably did a lot of fighting among themselves, after they got out of the Federation. There's still some traces of combat-damage around. Then they started to decivilize, down to the pre-mechanical level-wind and water power and animal power. They have draft-animals that look like introduced Terran carabaos, and a few small sailboats and big canoes and bateaux on the rivers. They have gunpowder, which seems to be the last thing any people lose.

"I was there, five years ago. I liked Tanith for a base. There's one moon, almost solid nickel iron, and fissionable-ore deposits. Then, like a fool, I hired out to the Elmersans on Durendal and lost my ship. When I came here, your Duke was thinking about Xipototec. I convinced him that Tanith was a better planet for his purpose."

"Dunnan might go there, at that. He might think he was scoring one on Duke Angus. After all, he has all that equipment."

"And nobody to use it. If I were Dunnan, I'd go to Nergal, or Xochitl. There are always a couple of thousand Space Vikings on either, spending their loot and taking it easy between raids. He could sign on a full crew on either. I suggest we go to Xochitl, first. We might pick up news of him, if nothing else."

All right, they'd try Xochitl first. Harkaman knew the planet, and was friendly with the Haulteclere noble who ruled it.

The work went on at the Gorram shipyard; it had taken a year to build the *Enterprise*, but the steel-mills and engine-works were over the preparatory work of tooling up, and material and equipment was flowing in a steady stream. Lucas let them persuade him to take more rest, and day by day grew stronger. Soon he was spending most of his time at the shipyard, watching the engines go in-Abbot lift-and-drive for normal space, Dillingham hyperdrive, power-converters, pseudograv, all at the center of the globular ship. Living quarters and workshops went in next, all armored in collapsium-plated steel. Then the ship lifted out to an orbit a thousand miles off-planet, followed by swarms of armored work-craft and cargo-lighters; the rest of the work was more easily done in space. At the same time, the four two-hundred-foot pinnaces that would be carried aboard were being finished. Each of them had its own hyperdrive engines, and could travel as far and as fast as the ship herself.

Otto Harkaman was beginning to be distressed because the ship still lacked a name. He didn't like having to speak of her as "her," or "the ship," and there were many things soon to go on that should be name-marked. *Elaine*, Trask thought, at once, and almost at once rejected it. He didn't want her name associated with the things that ship would do in the Old Federation. *Revenge, Avenger, Retribution, Vendetta*; none appealed to him. A news-commentator, turgidly eloquent about the nemesis which the criminal Dunnan had invoked against himself, supplied it, *Nemesis* it was.

Now he was studying his new profession of interstellar robbery and murder against which he had once inveighed. Otto Harkaman's handful of followers became his teachers. Vann Larch, guns-and-missiles, who was also a painter; Guatt Kirbey, sour and pessimistic, the hyperspatial astrogator who tried to express his science in music; Sharll Renner, the normal-space astrogator. Alvyn Karffard, the exec, who had been with Harkaman longest of all. And Sir Paytrik Morland, a local recruit, formerly guard-captain to Count Lionel of Newhaven, who commanded the ground-fighters and the combat contragravity. They were using the farms and villages of Traskon for drill and practice, and he noticed that while the *Nemesis* would carry only five hundred ground and air fighters, over a thousand were being trained.

He commented to Rovard Grauffis.

"Yes. Don't mention it outside," the Duke's henchman said. "You and Sir Paytrik and Captain Harkaman will pick the five hundred best. The Duke will take the rest into his service. Some of these days, Omfray of Glaspyth will find out what a Space Viking raid is really like."

And Duke Angus would tax his new subjects of Glaspyth to redeem the pledges on his new barony of Traskon. Some old Pre-Atomic writer Harkaman was fond of quoting had said, "Gold will not always get you good soldiers, but good soldiers can get you gold."

The *Nemesis* came back to the Gorram yards and settled onto her curved landing legs like a monstrous spider. The *Enterprise* had borne the Ward sword and atom-symbol; the *Nemesis* should bear his own badge, but the bisonoid head, tawny on green, of Traskon, was no longer his. He chose a skull impaled on an upright sword, and it was blazoned on the ship when he and Harkaman took her out for her shakedown cruise.

When they landed again at the Gorram yards, two hundred hours later, they learned that a tramp freighter from Morglay had come into Bigglersport in their absence with news of Andray Dunnan. Her captain had come to Wardshaven at Duke Angus' urgent invitation and was waiting for them at the Ducal Palace.

They sat, a dozen of them, around a table in the Duke's private apartments. The freighter captain, a small, precise man with a graying beard, alternately puffed at a cigarette and sipped from a beaker of brandy.

"I spaced out from Morglay two hundred hours ago," he was saying. "I'd been there twelve local days, three hundred Galactic Standard hours, and the run from Curtana was three hundred and twenty. This ship, the *Enterprise*, spaced out from there several days before I did. I'd say she's twelve hundred hours out of Windsor, on Curtana, now."

The room was still. The breeze fluttered curtains at the open windows; from the garden below, winged night-things twittered.

"I never expected it," Harkaman said. "I thought he'd take the ship out to the Old Federation at once." He poured wine for himself. "Of course, Dunnan's crazy. A crazy man has an advantage, sometimes, like a left-handed knife-fighter. He does unexpected things."

"That wasn't such a crazy move," Rovard Grauffis said. "We have very little direct trade with Curtana. It's only an accident we heard about this when we did."

The freighter captain's beaker was half empty. He filled it to the brim from the decanter.

"She was the first Gram ship there for years," he agreed. "That attracted notice, of course. And his having the blazonry changed, from the sword and atom-symbol to the blue crescent. And the ill-feeling on the part of other captains and planet-side employers about the men he'd lured away from them."

"How many men and what kind?"

The man with the gray beard shrugged. "I was too busy getting a cargo together for Morglay, to pay much attention. Almost a full spaceship complement, officers and spacemen of every kind. And a lot of industrial engineers and technicians."

"Then he is going to use that equipment that was aboard, and put in a base somewhere," somebody said.

"If he left Curtana twelve hundred hours ago, he's still in hyperspace," Guatt Kirbey said. "It's over two thousand from Curtana to the nearest Old Federation planet."

"How far to Tanith?" Duke Angus asked. "I'm sure that's where he's gone. He'd expect me to finish the other ship and equip her like the *Enterprise* and send her out; he'd want to get there first."

"I'd thought that Tanith would be the last place he'd go," Harkaman said, "but this changes the whole outlook. He could have gone to Tanith."

"He's crazy, and you're trying to apply sane logic to him," Guatt Kirbey said. "You're figuring what you'd do, and you aren't crazy. Of course, I've had my doubts, at times, but —"

"Yes, he's crazy, and Captain Harkaman's allowing for that," Rovard Grauffis said. "Dunnan hates all of us. He hates his Grace, here. He hates Lord Lucas, and Sesar Karvall; of course, he may think he killed both of them. He hates Captain Harkaman. So how could he score all of us off at once? By taking Tanith."

"You say he was buying supplies and ammunition?"

"That's right. Gun ammunition, ship's missiles, and a lot of ground-defense missiles."

"What was he buying them with? Trading machinery?"

"No. Gold."

"Yes. Lothar Ffayle found out that a lot of gold was transferred to Dunnan from banks in Glaspyth and Didreksburg," Grauffis said. "He got that aboard when he took the ship, evidently."

"All right," Trask said. "We can't be sure of anything, but we have some reasons for thinking he went to Tanith, and that's more than we have for any other planet in the Old Federation. I won't try to estimate the odds against our finding him there, but they're a good deal bigger anywhere else. We'll go there, first."

VII

The outside viewscreen, which had been vacantly gray for over three thousand hours, was now a vertiginous swirl of color, the indescribable color of a collapsing hyperspatial field. No two observers ever saw it alike, and no imagination could vision the actuality. Trask found that he was holding his breath. So, he noticed, was Otto Harkaman, beside him. It was something, evidently, that nobody got used to. Even Guatt Kirbey, the astrogator, was sitting with his pipe clenched in his mouth, staring at the screen.

Then, in an instant, the stars, which had literally not been there before, filled the screen with a blaze of splendor against the black velvet backdrop of normal space. Dead in the center, brighter than all the rest, Ertado's Star, the sun of Tanith, burned yellowly. The light from it was ten hours old.

"Pretty good, Guatt," Harkaman said, picking up his cup.

"Good, Gehenna; it was perfect," somebody else said.

Kirbey was relighting his pipe. "Oh, I suppose it'll have to do," he grudged, around the stem. He had gray hair and an untidy mustache, and nothing was ever quite good enough to satisfy him. "I could have made it a little closer. Need three microjumps, now, and I'll have to cut the last one pretty fine. Now don't bother me." He began punching buttons for data and fiddling with setscrews and verniers.

For a moment, in the screen, Trask could see the face of Andray Dunnan. He blinked it away and reached for his cigarettes, and put one in his mouth wrong-end-to. When he reversed it and snapped his lighter, he saw that his hand was trembling. Otto Harkaman must have seen that, too.

"Take it easy, Lucas," he whispered. "Keep your optimism under control. We only think he might be here."

"I'm sure he is. He has to be."

No; that was the way Dunnan, himself, thought. Let's be sane about this.

"We have to assume he is. If we do, and he isn't it's a disappointment. If we don't, and he is, it's a disaster."

Others, it seemed, thought the same way. The battle-stations board was a solid blaze of red light for full combat readiness.

"All right," Kirbey said. "Jumping."

Then he twisted the red handle to the right and shoved it in viciously. Again the screen boiled with colored turbulence; again dark and mighty forces stalked through the ship like demons in a sorcerer's tower. The screen turned featureless gray as the pickups stared blindly into some dimensionless noplace. Then it convulsed with color again, and this time Ertado's Star, still in the center, was a coin-sized disk, with the little sparks of its seven planets scattered around it. Tanith was the third-the inhabitable planet of a G-class system usually was. It had a single moon, barely visible in the telescopic screen, five hundred miles in diameter and fifty thousand off-planet.

"You know," Kirbey said, as though he was afraid to admit it, "that wasn't too bad. I think we can make it in one more microjump."

Some time, Trask supposed, he'd be able to use the expression "micro-" about a distance of fifty-five million miles, too.

"What do you think about it?" Harkaman asked him, as deferentially as though seeking expert guidance instead of examining his apprentice. "Where should Guatt put us?"

"As close as possible, of course." That would be a light-second at the least; if the *Nemesis* came out of hyperspace any closer to anything the size of Tanith, the collapsing field itself would kick her back. "We have to assume Dunnan's been there at least nine hundred hours. By that time, he could have put in a detection-station, and maybe missile-launchers, on the moon. The *Enterprise* carries four pinnaces, the same as the *Nemesis*; in his place, I'd have at least two of them on off-planet patrol. So let's accept it that we'll be detected as soon as we come out of the last jump, and come out with the moon directly between us and the planet. If it's occupied, we can knock it off on the way in."

"A lot of captains would try to come out with the moon masked off by the planet," Harkaman said.

"Would you?"

The big man shook his tousled head. "No. If they have launchers on the moon, they could launch at us in a curve around the planet, by data relayed from the other side, and we'd be at a disadvantage replying. Just go straight in. You hearing this, Guatt?"

"Yeah. It makes sense. Sort of. Now, stop pestering me. Sharll, look here a minute."

The normal-space astrogator conferred with him; Alvyn Karffard, the executive officer, joined them. Finally Kirbey pulled out the big red handle, twisted it, and said, "All right, jumping." He shoved it in. "I suppose I cut it too fine; now we'll get kicked back half a million miles."

The screen convulsed again; when it cleared the third planet was directly in the center; its small moon, looking almost as large, was a little above and to the right, sunlit on one side and planetlit on the other. Kirbey locked the red handle, gathered up his tobacco and lighter and things from the ledge, and pulled down the cover of the instrument-console, locking it.

"All yours, Sharll," he told Renner.

"Eight hours to atmosphere," Renner said. "That's if we don't have to waste a lot of time shooting up Junior, there."

Vann Larch was looking at the moon in the six hundred power screen.

"I don't see anything to shoot. Five hundred miles; one planetbuster, or four or five thermonuclears," he said.

It wasn't right, Trask thought indignantly. Minutes ago, Tanith had been six and a half billion miles away. Seconds ago, fifty-odd million. And now, a quarter of a million, and looking close enough to touch in the screen, it would take them eight hours to reach it. Why, on hyperdrive you could go forty-eight trillion miles in that time.

Well, it took a man just as long to walk across a room today as it had taken Pharaoh the First, or Homo Sap.

In the telescopic screen Tanith looked like any picture of any Terra-type planet from space, with cloud-blurred contours of seas and continents and a vague mottling of gray and brown and green, topped at the pole by an icecap. None of the surface features, not even the major mountain ranges or rivers, were yet distinguishable, but Harkaman and Sharll Renner and Alvyn Karffard and the other old hands seemed to recognize it. Karffard was talking by phone to Paul Koreff, the signals-and-detection officer, who could detect nothing from the moon and nothing that was getting through the Van Allen belt from the planet.

Maybe they'd guessed wrong, at that. Maybe Dunnan hadn't gone to Tanith at all.

Harkaman, who had the knack of putting himself to sleep at will, with some sixth or n-th sense posted as a sentry, leaned back in his chair and closed his eyes. Trask wished he could, too. It would be hours before anything happened, and until then he needed all the rest he could get. He drank more coffee, chain-smoked cigarettes; he rose and prowled about the command room, looking at screens. Signals-and-detection was getting a lot of routine stuff-Van Allen count, micrometeor count, surface temperature, gravitation-field strength, radar and scanner echoes. He went back to his chair and sat down, staring at the screen-image. The planet didn't seem to be getting any closer at all, and it ought to; they were approaching it at better than escape velocity. He sat and stared at it.

He woke with a start. The screen-image was much larger, now. River courses and the shadow lines of mountains were clearly visible. It must be early autumn in the northern hemisphere; there was snow down to the sixtieth parallel and a belt of brown was pushing south against the green. Harkaman was sitting up, eating lunch. By the clock, it was four hours later.

"Have a good nap?" he asked. "We're picking up some stuff, now. Radio and screen signals. Not much, but some. The locals wouldn't have learned enough for that in the five years since I was here. We didn't stay long enough, for one thing."

On decivilized planets that were visited by Space Vikings, the locals picked up bits and scraps of technology very quickly. In the four months of idleness and long conversations while they were in hyperspace he had heard many stories confirming that. But from the level to which Tanith had sunk, radio and screen communication in five years was a little too much of a jump.

"You didn't lose any men, did you?"

That happened frequently-men who took up with local women, men who had made themselves unpopular with their shipmates, men who just liked the planet and wanted to stay. They were always welcomed by the locals for what they could do and teach.

"No, we weren't there long enough for that. Only three hundred and fifty hours. This we're getting is outside stuff; somebody's there beside the locals."

Dunnan. He looked again at the battle-stations board; it was still uniformly red-lighted. Everything was on full combat ready. He summoned a mess-robot, selected a couple of dishes, and began to eat. After the first mouthful, he called to Alvyn Karffard:

"Is Paul getting anything new?" he asked.

Karffard checked. A little contragravity-field distortion effect. It was still too far to be sure. He went back to his lunch. He had finished it and was lighting a cigarette over his coffee when a red light flashed and a voice from one of the speakers shouted.

"Detection! Detection from planet! Radar, and microray!"

Karffard began talking rapidly into a hand-phone; Harkaman unhooked one beside him and listened.

"Coming from a definite point, about twenty-fifth north parallel," he said, aside. "Could be from a ship hiding against the planet. There's nothing at all on the moon."

They seemed to be approaching the planet more and more rapidly. Actually, they weren't, the ship was decelerating to get into an orbit, but the decreasing distance created the illusion of increasing speed. The red lights flashed once more.

"*Ship detected!* Just outside atmosphere, coming around the planet from the west."

"Is she the *Enterprise?*"

"Can't tell, yet," Karffard said, and then cried: "There she is, in the screen! That spark, about thirty degrees north, just off the west side."

Aboard her, too, voices from speakers would be shouting, "Ship detected!" and the battle station board would be blazing red. And Andray Dunnan, at the command-desk—

"She's calling us." That was Paul Koreff's voice, out of the squawk-box on the desk. "Standard Sword-World impulse-code. Interrogative: What ship are you? Informative: her screen combination. Request: Please communicate."

"All right," Harkaman said. "Let's be polite and communicate. What's her screen-combination?"

Koreff's voice gave it, and Harkaman punched it out. The communication screen in front of them lit at once; Trask shoved over his chair beside Harkaman's, his hands tightening on the arms. Would it be Dunnan himself, and what would his face show when he saw who confronted him out of his own screen?

It took him an instant to realize that the other ship was not the *Enterprise* at all. The *Enterprise* was the *Nemesis'* twin; her command room was identical with his own. This one was different in arrangements and fittings. The *Enterprise* was a new ship; this one was old, and had suffered for years at the hands of a slack captain and a slovenly crew.

And the man who sat facing him in the screen was not Andray Dunnan, or any man he had ever seen before. A dark-faced man, with an old scar that ran down one cheek from a little below the eye; he had curly black hair, on his head and on a V of chest exposed by an open shirt. There was an ashtray in front of him, and a thin curl of smoke rose from a cigar in it, and coffee steamed in an ornate but battered silver cup beside it. He was grinning gleefully.

"Well! Captain Harkaman, of the *Enterprise*, I believe! Welcome to Tanith. Who's the gentleman with you? He isn't the Duke of Wardshaven, is he?"

VIII

He glanced quickly at the showback over the screen, to assure himself that his face was not betraying him. Beside him, Otto Harkaman was laughing.

"Why, Captain Valkanhayn; this is an unexpected pleasure. That's the *Space Scourge* you're in, I take it? What are you doing here on Tanith?"

A voice from one of the speakers shouted that a second ship had been detected coming over the north pole. The dark-faced man in the screen smirked quite complacently.

"That's Garvan Spasso, in the *Lamia*," he said. "And what we're doing here, we've taken this planet over. We intend keeping it, too."

"Well! So you and Garvan have teamed up. You two were just made for one another. And you have a little planet, all your very own. I'm so happy for both of you. What are you getting out of it-beside poultry?"

The other's self-assurance started to slip. He slapped it back into place.

"Don't kid me; we know why you're here. Well, we got here first. Tanith is our planet. You think you can take it away from us?"

"I know we could, and so do you," Harkaman told him. "We outgun you and Spasso together; why, a couple of our pinnaces could knock the *Lamia* apart. The only question is, do we want to bother?"

By now, he had recovered from his surprise, but not from his disappointment. If this fellow thought the *Nemesis* was the *Enterprise* —Before he could check himself, he had finished the thought aloud.

"Then the *Enterprise* didn't come here at all!"

The man in the screen started. "Isn't that the *Enterprise* you're in?"

"Oh, no. Pardon my remissness, Captain Valkanhayn," Harkaman apologized. "This is the *Nemesis*. The gentleman with me, Lord Lucas Trask, is owner-aboard, for whom I am commanding. Lord Trask, Captain Boake Valkanhayn, of the *Space Scourge*. Captain Valkanhayn is a Space Viking." He said that as though expecting it to be disputed. "So, I am told, is his associate, Captain Spasso, whose ship is approaching. You mean to tell me that the *Enterprise* hasn't been here?"

Valkanhayn was puzzled, slightly apprehensive.

"You mean the Duke of Wardshaven has two ships?"

"As far as I know, the Duke of Wardshaven hasn't any ships," Harkaman replied. "This ship is the property and private adventure of Lord Trask. The *Enterprise*, for which we are looking, is owned and commanded by one Andray Dunnan."

The man with the scarred face and hairy chest had picked up his cigar and was puffing on it mechanically. Now he took it out of his mouth as though he wondered how it had gotten there in the first place.

"But isn't the Duke of Wardshaven sending a ship here to establish a base? That was what we'd heard. We heard you'd gone from Flamberge to Gram to command for him."

"Where did you hear this? And when?"

"On Hoth. That'd be about two thousand hours ago; a Gilgamesher brought the news from Xochitl."

"Well, considering it was fifth or sixth hand, your information was good enough, when it was fresh. It was a year and a half old when you got it, though. How long have you been here on Tanith?"

"About a thousand hours." Harkaman clucked sadly at that.

"Pity you wasted all that time. Well, it was nice talking to you, Boake. Say hello to Garvan for me when he comes up."

"You mean you're not staying?" Valkanhayn was horrified, an odd reaction for a man who had just been expecting a bitter battle to drive them away. "You're just spacing right out again?"

Harkaman shrugged. "Do we want to waste time here, Lord Trask? The *Enterprise* has obviously gone somewhere else. She was still in hyperspace when Captain Valkanhayn and his accomplice arrived here."

"Is there anything worth staying for?" That seemed to be the reply Harkaman was expecting. "Beside poultry, that is?"

Harkaman shook his head. "This is Captain Valkanhayn's planet; his and Captain Spasso's. Let them be stuck with it."

"But, look; this is a good planet. There's a big local city, maybe ten or twenty thousand people; temples and palaces and everything. Then, there are a couple of old Federation cities. The one we're at is in good shape, and there's a big spaceport. We've been doing a lot of work on it. And the locals won't give you any trouble. All they have is spears and a few crossbows and matchlocks —"

"I know. I've been here."

"Well, couldn't we make some kind of a deal?" Valkanhayn asked. A mendicant whine was beginning to creep into his voice. "I can get Garvan on screen and switch him over to your ship —"

"Well, we have a lot of Sword-World merchandise aboard," Harkaman said. "We could make you good prices on some of it. How are you fixed for robotic equipment?"

"But aren't you going to stay here?" Valkanhayn was almost in a panic. "Listen, suppose I talk to Garvan, and we all get together on this. Just excuse me for a minute —"

As soon as he had blanked out, Harkaman threw back his head and guffawed as though he had just heard the funniest and bawdiest joke in the galaxy. Trask, himself, didn't feel like laughing.

"The humor escapes me," he admitted. "We came here on a fools' errand."

"I'm sorry, Lucas." Harkaman was still shaking with mirth. "I know it's a letdown, but that pair of chiseling chicken thieves! I could almost pity them, if it weren't so funny." He laughed again. "You know what their idea was?"

Trask shook his head. "Who are they?"

"What I called them, a couple of chicken thieves. They raid planets like Set and Hertha and Melkarth, where the locals haven't anything to fight with-or anything worth fighting for. I didn't know they'd teamed up, but that figures. Nobody else would team up with either of them. What must have happened, this story of Duke Angus' Tanith adventure must have filtered out to them, and they thought that if they got here first, I'd think it was cheaper to take them in than run them out. I probably would have, too. They do have ships, of a sort, and they do raid, after a fashion. But now, there isn't going to be any Tanith base, and they have a no-good planet and they're stuck with it."

"Can't they make anything out of it themselves?"

"Like what?" Harkaman hooted. "They have no equipment, and they have no men. Not for a job like that. The only thing they can do is space out and forget it."

"We could sell them equipment."

"We could if they had anything to use for money. They haven't. One thing, we do want to let down and give the men a chance to walk on ground and look at a sky for a while. The girls here aren't too bad, either," Harkaman said. "As I remember, some of them even take a bath, now and then."

"That's the kind of news of Dunnan we're going to get. By the time we'd get to where he's been reported, he'd be a couple of thousand light-years away," he said disgustedly. "I agree; we ought to give the men a chance to get off the ship, here. We can stall this pair along for a while and we won't have any trouble with them."

The three ships were slowly converging toward a point fifteen thousand miles off-planet and over the sunset line. The *Space Scourge* bore the device of a mailed fist clutching a comet by the head; it looked more like a whisk broom than a scourge. The *Lamia* bore a coiled snake with the head, arms and bust of a woman. Valkanhayn and Spasso were taking their time about screening back, and he began to wonder if they weren't maneuvering the *Nemesis* into a cross-fire position. He mentioned this to Harkaman and Alvyn Karffard; they both laughed.

"Just holding ship's meetings," Karffard said. "They'll be yakking back and forth for a couple of hours, yet."

"Yes; Valkanhayn and Spasso don't own their ships," Harkaman explained. "They've gone in debt to their crews for supplies and maintenance till everybody owns everything in common. The ships look like it, too. They don't even command, really; they just preside over elected command-councils."

Finally, they had both of the more or less commanders on screen. Valkanhayn had zipped up his shirt and put on a jacket. Garvan Spasso was a small man, partly bald. His eyes were a shade too close together, and his thin mouth had a bitterly crafty twist. He began speaking at once:

"Captain, Boake tells me you say you're not here in the service of the Duke of Wardshaven at all." He said it aggrievedly.

"That's correct," Harkaman said. "We came here because Lord Trask thought another Gram ship, the *Enterprise*, would be here. Since she isn't, there's no point in our being here. We do hope, though, that you won't make any difficulty about our letting down and giving our men a couple of hundred hours' liberty. They've been in hyperspace for three thousand hours."

"See!" Spasso clamored. "He wants to trick us into letting him land —"

"Captain Spasso," Trask cut in. "Will you please stop insulting everybody's intelligence, your own included." Spasso glared at him, belligerently but hopefully. "I understand what you thought you were going to do here. You expected Captain Harkaman here to establish a base for the Duke of Wardshaven, and you thought, if you were here ahead of him and in a posture of defense, that he'd take you into the Duke's service rather than waste ammunition and risk damage and casualties wiping you out. Well, I'm very sorry, gentlemen. Captain Harkaman is in my service, and I'm not in the least interested in establishing a base on Tanith."

Valkanhayn and Spasso looked at each other. At least, in the two side-by-side screens, their eyes shifted, each to the other's screen on his own ship.

"I get it!" Spasso cried suddenly. "There's two ships, the *Enterprise* and this one. The Duke of Wardshaven fitted out the *Enterprise*, and somebody else fitted out this one. They both want to put in a base here!"

That opened a glorious vista. Instead of merely capitalizing on their nuisance-value, they might find themselves holding the balance of power in a struggle for the planet. All sorts of profitable perfidies were possible.

"Why, sure you can land, Otto," Valkanhayn said. "I know what it's like to be three thousand hours in hyper, myself."

"You're at this old city with the two tall tower-buildings, aren't you?" Harkaman asked. He looked up at the viewscreen. "Ought to be about midnight there now. How's the spaceport? When I was here, it was pretty bad."

"Oh, we've been fixing it up. We got a big gang of locals working for us —"

The city was familiar, from Otto Harkaman's descriptions and from the pictures Vann Larch had painted during the long jump from Gram. As they came in, it looked impressive, spreading for miles around the twin buildings that spired almost three thousand feet above it, with a great spaceport like an eight-pointed star at one side. Whoever had built it, in the sunset splendor of the old Terran Federation, must have done so confident that it would become the metropolis of a populous and prospering world. Then the sun of the Federation had gone down. Nobody knew what had happened on Tanith after that, but evidently none of it had been good.

At first, the two towers seemed as sound as when they had been built; gradually it became apparent that one was broken at the top. For the most part, the smaller buildings scattered widely around them were standing, though here and there mounds of brush-grown rubble showed where some had fallen in. The spaceport looked good —a central octagon mass of buildings, the landing-berths, and, beyond, the triangular areas of airship docks and warehouses. The central building was outwardly intact, and the ship-berths seemed clear of wreckage and rubble.

By the time the *Nemesis* was following the *Space Scourge* and the *Lamia* down, towed by her own pinnaces, the illusion that they were approaching a living city had vanished. The interspaces between the buildings were choked with forest-growth, broken by a few small fields and garden-plots. At one time, there had been three of the high buildings, literally vertical cities in themselves. Where the third had stood was a glazed crater, with a ridge of fallen rubble lying away from it. Somebody must have landed a medium missile, about twenty kilotons, against its base. Something of the same sort had scored on the far edge of the spaceport, and one of the eight arrowheads of docks and warehouses was an indistinguishable slag-pile.

The rest of the city seemed to have died of neglect rather than violence. It certainly hadn't been bombed out. Harkaman thought most of the fighting had been done with subneutron bombs or Omega-ray bombs, that killed the people without damaging the real estate. Or bio-weapons; a man-made plague that had gotten out of control and all but depopulated the planet.

"It takes an awful lot of people, working together at an awful lot of jobs, to keep a civilization running. Smash the installations and kill the top technicians and scientists, and the masses don't know how to rebuild and go back to stone hatchets. Kill off enough of the masses and even if the planet and the know-how is left, there's nobody to do the work. I've seen planets that decivilized both ways. Tanith, I think, is one of the latter."

That had been during one of the long after-dinner bull sessions on the way out from Gram. Somebody, one of the noble gentlemen-adventurers who had joined the company after the piracy of the *Enterprise* and the murder, had asked:

"But some of them survived. Don't they know what happened?"

"'*In the old times, there were sorcerers. They built the old buildings by wizard arts. Then the sorcerers fought among themselves and went away,*'" Harkaman said. "That's all they know about it."

You could make any kind of an explanation out of that.

As the pinnaces pulled and nudged the *Nemesis* down to her berth, he could see people, far down on the spaceport floor, at work. Either Valkanhayn and Spasso had more men than the size of their ships indicated, or they had gotten a lot of locals to work for them. More than the population of the moribund city, at least as Harkaman remembered it.

There had been about five hundred in all; they lived by mining the old buildings for metal, and trading metalwork for food and textiles and powder and other things made elsewhere. It was accessible only by oxcarts traveling a hundred miles across the plains; it had been built by a contragravity-using people with utter disregard for natural travel and transportation routes.

. "I don't envy the poor buggers," Harkaman said, looking down at the antlike figures on the spaceport floor. "Boake Valkanhayn and Garvan Spasso have probably made slaves of the lot of them. If I was really going to put in a base here, I wouldn't thank that pair for the kind of public-relations work they've been doing among the locals."

IX

That was just about the situation. Spasso and Valkanhayn and some of their officers met them on the landing stage of the big building in the middle of the spaceport, where they had established quarters. Entering and going down a long hallway, they passed a dozen men and women gathering up rubbish from the floor with shovels and with their hands and putting it into a lifter-skid. Both sexes wore shapeless garments of coarse cloth, like ponchos, and flat-soled sandals. Watching them was another local in a kilt, buskins and a leather jerkin; he wore a short sword on his belt and carried a wickedly thonged whip. He also wore a Space Viking combat helmet, painted with the device of Spasso's *Lamia*. He bowed as they approached, putting a hand to his forehead. After they had passed, they could hear him shouting at the others, and the sound of whip-blows.

You make slaves out of people, and some will always be slave-drivers; they will bow to you, and then take it out on the others. Harkaman's nose was twitching as though he had a bit of rotten fish caught in his mustache.

"We have about eight hundred of them. There were only three hundred that were any good for work here; we gathered the rest up at villages along the big river," Spasso was saying.

"How do you get food for them?" Harkaman asked. "Or don't you bother?"

"Oh, we gather that up all over," Valkanhayn told him. "We send parties out with landing craft. They'll let down on a village, run the locals out, gather up what's around and bring it here. Once in a while they put up a fight, but the best they have is a few crossbows and some muzzle-loading muskets. When they do, we burn the village and machine-gun everybody we see."

"That's the stuff," Harkaman approved. "If the cow doesn't want to be milked, just shoot her. Of course, you don't get much milk out of her again, but —"

The room to which their hosts guided them was at the far end of the hall. It had probably been a conference room or something of the sort, and originally it had been paneled, but the paneling had long ago vanished. Holes had been dug here and there in the walls, and he remembered having noticed that the door was gone and the metal groove in which it had slid had been pried out.

There was a big table in the middle, and chairs and couches covered with colored spreads. All the furniture was handmade, cunningly pegged together and highly polished. On the walls hung trophies of weapons-thrusting-spears and throwing-spears, crossbows and quarrels, and a number of heavy guns, crude things, but carefully made.

"Pick all this stuff up off the locals?" Harkaman asked.

"Yes, we got most of it at a big town down at the forks of the river," Valkanhayn said. "We shook it down a couple of times. That's where we recruited the fellows we're using to boss the workers."

Then he picked up a stick with a leather-covered knob and beat on a gong, bawling for wine. A voice, somewhere, replied, "Yes, master; I come!" and in a few moments a woman entered carrying a jug in either hand. She was wearing a blue bathrobe several sizes too large for her, instead of the poncho things the slaves in the hallway wore. She had dark brown hair and gray eyes; if she had not been so obviously frightened she would have been beautiful. She set the jugs on the table and brought silver cups from a chest against the wall: when Spasso dismissed her, she went out hastily.

"I suppose it's silly to ask if you're paying these people anything for the work they do or for the things you take from them," Harkaman said. From the way the *Space Scourge* and *Lamia* people laughed, it evidently was. Harkaman shrugged. "Well, it's your planet. Make any kind of a mess out of it you want to."

"You think we *ought* to pay them?" Spasso was incredulous. "Damn bunch of savages!"

"They aren't as savage as the Xochitl locals were when Haulteclere took it over. You've been there; you've seen what Prince Viktor does with them now."

"We haven't got the men or equipment they have on Xochitl," Valkanhayn said. "We can't afford to coddle the locals."

"You can't afford not to," Harkaman told him. "You have two ships, here. You can only use one for raiding; the other will have to stay here to hold the planet. If you take them both away, the locals, whom you have been studiously antagonizing, will swamp whoever you leave behind. And if you don't leave anybody behind, what's the use of having a planetary base?"

"Well, why don't you join us," Spasso finally came out with it. "With our three ships we could have a real thing, here."

Harkaman looked at him inquiringly. "The gentlemen," Trask said, "are putting this wrongly. They mean, why don't we let them join us?"

"Well, if you want to put it like that," Valkanhayn conceded. "We'll admit, your *Nemesis* would be the big end of it. But why not? Three ships, we could have a real base here. Nikky Gratham's father only had two when he started on Jagannath, and look what the Grathams got there now."

"Are we interested?" Harkaman asked.

"Not very, I'm afraid. Of course, we've just landed; Tanith may have great possibilities. Suppose we reserve decision for a while and look around a little."

There were stars in the sky, and, for good measure, a sliver of moon on the western horizon. It was only a small moon, but it was close. He walked to the edge of the landing stage, and

Elaine was walking with him. The noise from inside, where the *Nemesis* crew were feasting with those of the *Lamia* and *Space Scourge*, grew fainter. To the south, a star moved; one of the pinnaces they had left on off-planet watch. There was firelight far below, and he could hear singing. Suddenly he realized that it was the poor devils of locals whom Valkanhayn and Spasso had enslaved. Elaine went away quickly.

"Have your fill of Space Viking glamour, Lucas?"

He turned. It was Baron Rathmore, who had come along to serve for a year or so and then hitch a ride home from some base planet and cash in politically on having been with Lucas Trask.

"For the moment. I'm told that this lot aren't typical."

"I hope not. They're a pack of sadistic brutes, and piggish along with it."

"Well, brutality and bad manners I can condone, but Spasso and Valkanhayn are a pair of ignominious little crooks, and stupid along with it. If Andray Dunnan had gotten here ahead of us, he might have done one good thing in his wretched life. I can't understand why he didn't come here."

"I think he still will," Rathmore said. "I knew him and I knew Nevil Ormm. Ormm's ambitious, and Dunnan is insanely vindictive —" He broke off with a sour laugh. "I'm telling *you* that!"

"Why didn't he come here directly, then?"

"Maybe he doesn't want a base on Tanith. That would be something constructive; Dunnan's a destroyer. I think he took that cargo of equipment somewhere and sold it. I think he'll wait till he's fairly sure the other ship is finished. Then he'll come in and shoot the place up, the way —" He bit that off abruptly.

"The way he did my wedding; I think of it all the time."

The next morning, he and Harkaman took an aircar and went to look at the city at the forks of the river. It was completely new, in the sense that it had been built since the collapse of Federation civilization and the loss of civilized technologies. It was huddled on a long, irregularly triangular mound, evidently to raise it above flood-level. Generations of labor must have gone into it. To the eyes of a civilization using contragravity and powered equipment it wasn't at all impressive. Fifty to a hundred men with adequate equipment could have gotten the thing up in a summer. It was only by forcing himself to think in terms of spadeful after spadeful of earth, cartload after cartload creaking behind straining beasts, timber after timber cut with axes and dressed with adzes, stone after stone and brick after brick, that he could appreciate it. They even had it walled, with a palisade of tree-trunks behind which earth and rocks had been banked, and along the river were docks, at which boats were moored. The locals simply called it Tradetown.

As they approached, a big gong began booming, and a white puff of smoke was followed by the thud of a signal-gun. The boats, long canoe-like craft and round-bowed, many-oared barges, put out hastily into the river; through binoculars they could see people scattering from the surrounding fields, driving cattle ahead of them. By the time they were over the city, nobody was in sight. They seemed to have developed a pretty fair air-raid warning system in the nine-hundred-odd hours in which they had been exposed to the figurative mercies of Boake Valkanhayn and Garvan Spasso. It hadn't saved them entirely; a section of the city had been burned, and there were evidences of shelling. Light chemical-explosive stuff; this city was too good a cow for even those two to kill before the milking was over.

They circled slowly over it at a thousand feet. When they turned away, black smoke began rising from what might have been pottery works or brick-kilns on the outskirts; something resinous had evidently been fed to the fires. Other columns of black smoke began rising across the countryside on both sides of the river.

"You know, these people are civilized, if you don't limit the term to contragravity and nuclear energy," Harkaman said. "They have gunpowder, for one thing, and I can think of some rather impressive Old Terran civilizations that didn't have that much. They have an organized society, and anybody who has that is starting toward civilization."

"I hate to think of what'll happen to this planet if Spasso and Valkanhayn stay here long."

"Might be a good thing, in the long run. Good things in the long run are often tough while they're happening. I know what'll happen to Spasso and Valkanhayn, though. They'll start decivilizing, themselves. They'll stay here for a while, and when they need something they can't take from the locals they'll go chicken-stealing after it, but most of the time they'll stay here lording it over their slaves, and finally their ships will wear out and they won't be able to fix them. Then, some time, the locals'll jump them when they aren't watching and wipe them out. But in the meantime, the locals'll learn a lot from them."

They turned the aircar west again along the river. They looked at a few villages. One or two dated from the Federation period; they had been plantations before whatever it was had happened. More had been built within the past five centuries. A couple had recently been destroyed, in punishment for the crime of self-defense.

"You know," he said, at length, "I'm going to do everybody a favor. I'm going to let Spasso and Valkanhayn persuade me to take this planet away from them."

Harkaman, who was piloting, turned sharply. "You crazy or something?"

"'When somebody makes a statement you don't understand, don't tell him he's crazy. Ask him what he means.' Who said that?"

"On target," Harkaman grinned. "What *do* you mean, Lord Trask?'"

"I can't catch Dunnan by pursuit; I'll have to get him by interception. You know the source of that quotation, too. This looks to me like a good place to intercept him. When he learns I have a base here, he'll hit it, sooner or later. And even if he doesn't, we can pick up more information on him, when ships start coming in here, than we would batting around all over the Old Federation."

Harkaman considered for a moment, then nodded. "Yes, if we could set up a base like Nergal or Xochitl," he agreed. "There'll be four or five ships, Space Vikings, traders, Gilgameshers and so on, on either of those planets all the time. If we had the cargo Dunnan took to space in the *Enterprise*, we could start a base like that. But we haven't anything near what we need, and you know what Spasso and Valkanhayn have."

"We can get it from Gram. As it stands, the investors in the Tanith Adventure, from Duke Angus down, lost everything they put into it. If they're willing to throw some good money after bad, they can get it back, and a handsome profit to boot. And there ought to be planets above the rowboat and ox-cart level not too far away that could be raided for a lot of things we'd need."

"That's right; I know of half a dozen within five hundred light-years. They won't be the kind Spasso and Valkanhayn are in the habit of raiding, though. And besides machinery, we can get gold, and valuable merchandise that could be sold on Gram. And if we could make a go of it, you'd go farther hunting Dunnan by sitting here on Tanith than by going looking for him. That was the way we used to hunt marsh pigs on Colada, when I was a kid; just find a good place and sit down and wait."

They had Valkanhayn and Spasso aboard the *Nemesis* for dinner; it didn't take much guiding to keep the conversation on the subject of Tanith and its resources, advantages and possibilities. Finally, when they had reached brandy and coffee, Trask said idly:

"I believe, together, we could really make something out of this planet."

"That's what we've been telling you, all along," Spasso broke in eagerly. "This is a wonderful planet —"

"It could be. All it has now is possibilities. We'd need a spaceport, for one thing."

"Well, what's this, here?" Valkanhayn wanted to know.

"It was a spaceport," Harkaman told him. "It could be one again. And we'd need a shipyard, capable of any kind of heavy repair work. Capable of building a complete ship, in fact. I never saw a ship come into a Viking base planet with any kind of a cargo worth dickering over that hadn't taken some damage getting it. Prince Viktor of Xochitl makes a good half of his money on ship repairs, and so do Nikky Gratham on Jagannath and the Everrards on Hoth."

"And engine works, hyperdrive, normal space and pseudograv," Trask added. "And a steel mill, and a collapsed-matter plant. And robotic-equipment works, and —"

"Oh, that's out of all reason!" Valkanhayn cried. "It would take twenty trips with a ship the size of this one to get all that stuff here, and how'd we ever be able to pay for it?"

"That's the sort of base Duke Angus of Wardshaven planned. The *Enterprise*, practically a duplicate of the *Nemesis*, carried everything that would be needed to get it started, when she was pirated."

"When she was —?"

"Now you're going to have to tell the gentlemen the truth," Harkaman chuckled.

"I intend to." He laid his cigar down, sipped some of his brandy, and explained about Duke Angus' Tanith adventure. "It was part of a larger plan; Angus wanted to gain economic supremacy for Wardshaven to forward his political ambitions. It was, however, an entirely practical business proposition. I was opposed to it, because I thought it would be too good a proposition for Tanith and work to the disadvantage of the home planet in the end." He told them about the *Enterprise*, and the cargo of industrial and construction equipment she carried, and then told them how Andray Dunnan had pirated her.

"That wouldn't have annoyed me at all; I had no money invested in the project. What did annoy me, to put it mildly, was that just before he took the ship out, Dunnan shot up my wedding, wounded me and my father-in-law, and killed the lady to whom I had been married for less than half an hour. I fitted out this ship at my own expense, took on Captain Harkaman, who had been left without a command when the *Enterprise* was pirated, and came out here to hunt Dunnan down and kill him. I believe that I can do that best by establishing a base on Tanith myself. The base will have to be operated at a profit, or it can't be operated at all." He picked up the cigar again and puffed slowly. "I am inviting you gentlemen to join me as partners."

"Well, you still haven't told us how we're going to get the money to finance it," Spasso insisted.

"The Duke of Wardshaven, and the others who invested in the original Tanith adventure will put it up. It's the only way they can recover what they lost on the *Enterprise*."

"But then, this Duke of Wardshaven will be running it, not us," Valkanhayn objected.

"The Duke of Wardshaven," Harkaman reminded him, "is on Gram. We are here on Tanith. There are three thousand light-years between."

That seemed a satisfactory answer. Spasso, however, wanted to know who would run things here on Tanith.

"We'll have to hold a meeting of all three crews," he began.

"We will do nothing of the kind," Trask told him. "I will be running things here on Tanith. You people may allow your orders to be debated and voted on, but I don't. You will inform your respective crews to that effect. Any orders you give them in my name will be obeyed without argument."

"I don't know how the men'll take that," Valkanhayn said.

"I know how they'll take it if they're smart," Harkaman told him. "And I know what'll happen if they aren't. I know how you've been running your ships, or how your ships' crews have been running you. Well, we don't do it that way. Lucas Trask is owner, and I'm captain. I obey his orders on what's to be done, and everybody else obeys mine on how to do it."

Spasso looked at Valkanhayn, then shrugged. "That's how the man wants it, Boake. You want to give him an argument? I don't."

"The first order," Trask said, "is that these people you have working here are to be paid. They are not to be beaten by these plug-uglies you have guarding them. If any of them want to leave, they may do so; they will be given presents and furnished transportation home. Those who wish to stay will be issued rations, furnished with clothing and bedding and so on as they need it, and paid wages. We'll work out some kind of a pay-token system and set up a commissary where they can buy things."

Disks of plastic or titanium or something, stamped and uncounterfeitable. Get Alvyn Karffard to see about that. Organize work-gangs, and promote the best and most intelligent to foremen. And those guards could be taken in hand by some ground-fighter sergeant and given Sword-World weapons and tactical training; use them to train others; they'd need a sepoy army of some sort. Even the best of good will is no substitute for armed force, conspicuously displayed and unhesitatingly used when necessary.

"And there'll be no more of this raiding villages for food or anything else. We will pay for anything we get from any of the locals."

"We'll have trouble about that," Valkanhayn predicted. "Our men think anything a local has belongs to anybody who can take it."

"So do I," Harkaman said. "On a planet I'm raiding. This is our planet, and our locals. We don't raid our own planet or our own people. You'll just have to teach them that."

X

It took Valkanhayn and Spasso more time and argument to convince their crews than Trask thought necessary. Harkaman seemed satisfied, and so was Baron Rathmore, the Wardshaven politician.

"It's like talking a lot of uncommitted small landholders into taking somebody's livery-and-maintenance," the latter said. "You can't use too much pressure; make them think it's their own idea."

There were meetings of both crews, with heated arguments; Baron Rathmore made frequent speeches, while Lord Trask of Tanith and Admiral Harkaman-the titles were Rathmore's suggestion-remained loftily aloof. On both ships, everybody owned everything in common, which meant that nobody owned anything. They had taken over Tanith on the same basis of diffused ownership, and nobody in either crew was quite stupid enough to think that they could do anything with the planet by themselves. By joining the *Nemesis*, it appeared that they were getting something for nothing. In the end, they voted to place themselves under the authority of Lord Trask and Admiral Harkaman. After all, Tanith would be a feudal lordship, and the three ships together a fleet.

Admiral Harkaman's first act of authority was to order a general inspection of fleet units. He wasn't shocked by the condition of the two ships, but that was only because he had expected much worse. They were spaceworthy; after all, they had gotten here from Hoth under their own power. They were only combat-worthy if the combat weren't too severe. His original estimate that the *Nemesis* could have knocked both of them to pieces was, if anything, over-conservative. The engines were only in fair shape, and the armament was bad.

"We aren't going to spend our time sitting here on Tanith," he told the two captains. "This planet is a raiding base, and 'raiding' is the operative word. And we are not going to raid easy planets. A planet that can be raided with impunity isn't worth the time it takes getting to it. We are going to have to fight on every planet we hit, and I am not going to jeopardize the lives of the men under me, which includes your crews as well as mine, because of under-powered and under-armed ships."

Spasso tried to argue. "We've been getting along."

Harkaman cursed. "Yes. I know how you've been getting along; chicken-stealing on planets like Set and Xipototec and Melkarth. Not making enough to cover maintenance expenses; that's why your ship's in the shape she is. Well, those days are over. Both ships ought to have a full overhaul, but we'll have to skip that till we have a shipyard of our own. But I will insist, at least, that your guns and launchers are in order. And your detection equipment; you didn't get a fix on the *Nemesis* till we were less than twenty thousand miles off-planet."

"We had better get the *Lamia* in condition first," Trask said. "We can put her on off-planet watch, instead of that pair of pinnaces."

Work on the *Lamia* started the next day, and considerable friction-heat was generated between her officers and the engineers sent over from the *Nemesis*. Baron Rathmore went aboard, and came back laughing.

"You know how that ship's run?" he asked. "There's a sort of soviet of officers; chief engineer, exec, guns-and-missiles, astrogator and so on. Spasso's just an animated ventriloquist's dummy. I talked to all of them. None of them can pin me down to anything, but they think we're going to heave Spasso out of command and appoint one of them, and each one thinks he'll be it. I don't know how long that'll last, it's a string-and-tape job like the one we're having to do on the ship. It'll hold till we get something better."

"We'll have to get rid of Spasso," Harkaman agreed. "I think we'll put one of our own people in his place. Valkanhayn can stay in command of the *Space Scourge*; he's a spaceman. But Spasso's no good for anything."

The local problem was complicated, too. The locals spoke Lingua Terra of a sort, like every descendant of the race that had gone out from the Sol system in the Third Century, but it was a barely comprehensible sort. On civilized planets, the language had been frozen unalterably in microbooks and voice tapes. But microbooks can only be read and sound tapes heard with the aid of electricity, and Tanith had lost that long ago.

Most of the people Spasso and Valkanhayn had kidnaped and enslaved came from villages within a radius of five hundred miles. About half of them wanted to be repatriated; they were given gifts of knives, tools, blankets, and bits of metal which seemed to be the chief standard of value and medium of exchange, and shipped home. Finding their proper villages was not easy. At each such village, the news was spread that the Space Vikings would hereafter pay for what they received.

The *Lamia* was overhauled as rapidly as possible. She was still far from being a good ship, but she was much closer to being one than before. She was fitted with the best detection equipment that could be assembled, and put on orbit; Alvyn Karffard took command of her, with some of Spasso's officers, some of Valkanhayn's, and a few from the *Nemesis*. Harkaman was intending to use her for retraining of all the *Lamia* and *Space Scourge* officers, and rotated them back and forth.

The labor guards, a score in number, were relieved of their duties, issued Sword-World firearms, and given intensive training. The trade tokens, stamps of colored plastic, were introduced, and a store was set up where they could be exchanged for Sword-World items. After a while, it dawned on the locals that the tokens could also be used for trading among themselves; money seemed to have been one of the adjuncts of civilization that had been lost along Tanith's downward path. A few of them were able to use contragravity hand-lifters and hand-towed lifter-skids; several were even learning to operate things like bulldozers, at least to the extent of knowing which lever or button did what. Give them a little time, Trask thought, watching a gang at work down on the spaceport floor. It won't be many years before half of them will be piloting aircars.

As soon as the *Lamia* was on orbital watch, the *Space Scourge* was set down at the spaceport and work started on her. It was decided that Valkanhayn would take her to Gram; enough *Nemesis* people would go along to insure good faith on his part, and to talk to Duke Angus and the Tanith investors. Baron Rathmore, and Paytrik Morland, and several other Wardshaven gentlemen-adventurers for the latter function; Alvyn Karffard to act as Valkanhayn's exec, with private orders to supersede him in command if necessary, and Guatt Kirbey to do the astrogating.

"We'll have to take the *Nemesis* and the *Space Scourge* out, first, and make a big raid," Harkaman said. "We can't send the *Space Scourge* back to Gram empty. When Baron Rathmore and Lord Valpry and the rest of them talk to Duke Angus and the Tanith investors, they'll have to have a lot more than some travel films of Tanith. They'll have to be able to show that Tanith is producing. We ought to have a little money of our own to invest, too."

"But, Otto; both ships?" That worried Trask. "Suppose Dunnan comes and finds nobody here but Spasso and the *Lamia*?"

"Chance we'll have to take. Personally, I think we have a year to a year and a half before Dunnan shows up here. I know, we were fooled trying to guess what he'd do before. But the sort of raid I have in mind, we'll need two ships, and in any case, I don't want to leave both those ships here while we're gone, even if you do."

"When it comes to that, I don't think I do, either. But we can't trust Spasso here alone, can we?"

"We'll leave enough of our people to make sure. We'll leave Alvyn-that'll mean a lot of work for me that he'd otherwise do, on the ship. And Baron Rathmore, and young Valpry, and the men who've been training our sepoys. We can shuffle things around and leave some of Valkanhayn's men in place of some of Spasso's. We might even talk Spasso into going along. That'll mean having to endure him at our table, but it would be wise."

"Have you picked a place to raid?"

"Three of them. First, Khepera. That's only thirty light-years from here. That won't amount to much; just chicken-stealing. It'll give our green hands some relatively safe combat-training, and it'll give us some idea of how Spasso's and Valkanhayn's people behave, and give them confidence for the next job."

"And then?"

"Amaterasu. My information about Amaterasu is about twenty years old. A lot of things can happen in twenty years. All I know of it —I was never there myself-is it's fairly civilized-about like Terra just before the beginning of the Atomic Era. No nuclear energy, they lost that, and of course nothing beyond it, but they have hydroelectric and solarelectric power, and nonnuclear jet aircraft, and some very good chemical-explosive weapons, which they use very freely on each other. It was last known to have been raided by a ship from Excalibur twenty years ago."

"That sounds promising. And the third planet?"

"Beowulf. We won't take enough damage on Amaterasu to make any difference there, but if we saved Amaterasu for last, we might be needing too many repairs."

"It's like that?"

"Yes. They have nuclear energy. I don't think it would be wise to mention Beowulf to Captains Spasso and Valkanhayn. Wait till we've hit Khepera and Amaterasu. They may be feeling like heroes, then."

XI

Khepera left a bad taste in Trask's mouth. He was still tasting it when the colored turbulence died out of the screen and left the gray nothingness of hyperspace. Garvan Spasso-they had had no trouble in inducing him to come along-was staring avidly at the screen as though he could still see the ravished planet they had left.

"That was a good one; that was a good one!" he was crowing. He'd said that a dozen times since they had lifted out. "Three cities in five days, and all the stuff we gathered up around them. We took over two million stellars."

And did ten times as much damage getting it, and there was no scale of values by which to compute the death and suffering.

"Knock it off, Spasso. You said that before."

There was a time when he wouldn't have spoken to the fellow, or anybody else, like that. Gresham's law, extended: Bad manners drive out good manners. Spasso turned on him indignantly.

"Who do you think you are —?"

"He thinks he's Lord Trask of Tanith," Harkaman said. "He's right, too; he is." He looked searchingly at Trask for a moment, then turned back to Spasso. "I'm just as tired as he is of hearing you pop your mouth about a lousy two million stellars. Nearer a million and a half, but two million's nothing to pop about. Maybe it would be for the *Lamia*, but we have a three-ship fleet and a planetary base to meet expenses on. Out of this raid, a ground-fighter or an able spaceman will get a hundred and fifty stellars. We'll get about a thousand, ourselves. How long do you think we can stay in business doing this kind of chicken-stealing."

"You call this chicken-stealing?"

"I call it chicken-stealing, and so'll you before we get back to Tanith. If you live that long."

For a moment, Spasso was still affronted. Then, temporarily, his vulpine face showed avaricious hope, and then apprehension. Evidently he knew Otto Harkaman's reputation, and some of the things Harkaman had done weren't his idea of an easy way to make money.

Khepera had been easy; the locals hadn't had anything to fight with. Small arms, and light cannon which hadn't been able to fire more than a few rounds. Wherever they had attempted resistance, the combat cars had swooped in, dropping bombs and firing machine guns and auto-cannon. Yet they had fought, bitterly and hopelessly-just as he would have, defending Traskon.

Trask busied himself getting coffee and a cigarette from one of the robots. When he looked up, Spasso had gone away, and Harkaman was sitting on the edge of the desk, loading his short pipe.

"Well, you saw the elephant, Lucas," Harkaman said. "You don't seem to have liked it."

"Elephant?"

"Old Terran expression I read somewhere. All I know is that an elephant was an animal about the size of one of your Gram megatheres. The expression means, experiencing something for the first time which makes a great impression. Elephants must have been something to see. This was your first Viking raid. You've seen it, now."

He'd been in combat before; he'd led the fighting-men of Traskon during the boundary dispute with Baron Manniwel, and there were always bandits and cattle rustlers. He'd thought it would be like that. He remembered, five days, or was it five ages, ago, his excited anticipation as the city grew and spread in the screen and the *Nemesis* came dropping down toward it. The pinnaces, his four and the two from the *Space Scourge*, had gone spiraling out a hundred miles beyond the city; the *Space Scourge* had gone into a tighter circle twenty miles from its center; the *Nemesis* had continued her relentless descent until she was ten miles from the ground, before she began spewing out landing craft, and combat cars, and the little egg-shaped one-man air-cavalry mounts. It had been thrilling. Everything had gone perfectly; not even Valkanhayn's gang had goofed.

Then the screenviews had begun coming in. The brief and hopeless fight in the city. He could still see that silly little field gun, it must have been around seventy or eighty millimeter, on a high-wheeled carriage, drawn by six shaggy, bandy-legged beasts. They had gotten it un-limbered and were trying to get it on a target when a rocket from an aircar landed directly under the muzzle. Gun, caisson, crew, even the draft team fifty yards behind, had simply vanished.

Or the little company, some of them women, trying to defend the top of a tall and half-ru-inous building with rifles and pistols. One air-cavalryman wiped them all out with his machine guns.

"They don't have a chance," he'd said, half-sick. "But they keep on fighting."

"Yes; stupid of them, isn't it?" Harkaman, beside him, had said.

"What would you do in their place?"

"Fight. Try to kill as many Space Vikings as I could before they got me. Terro-humans are all stupid like that. That's why we're human."

If the taking of the city had been a massacre, the sack that had followed had been a man-made Hell. He had gone down, along with Harkaman, while the fighting, if it could be so called, was still going on. Harkaman had suggested that the men ought to see him moving about among them; for his own part, he had felt a compulsion to share their guilt.

He and Sir Paytrik Morland had been on foot together in one of the big hollow buildings that had stood since Khepera had been a Member Republic of the Terran Federation. The air was acrid with smoke, powder smoke and the smoke of burning. It was surprising, how much would burn, in this city of concrete and vitrified stone. It was surprising, too, how well-kept everything was, at least on the ground level. These people had taken pride in their city.

They found themselves alone, in a great empty hallway; the noise and horror of the sack had moved away from them, or they from it, and then, when they entered a side hall, they saw a man, one of the locals, squatting on the floor with the body of a woman cradled on his lap. She was dead, half her head had been blown off, but he was clasping her tightly, her blood staining his shirt, and sobbing heartbrokenly. A carbine lay forgotten on the floor beside him.

"Poor devil," Morland said, and started forward.

"No."

Trask stopped him with his left hand. With his right, he drew his pistol and shot the man dead. Morland was horrified.

"Great Satan, Lucas! Why did you do that?"

"I wish Andray Dunnan had done that for me." He thumbed the safety on and holstered the pistol. "None of this would be happening if he had. How many more happinesses do you think we've smashed here today? And we don't even have Dunnan's excuse of madness."

The next morning, with everything of value collected and sent aboard, they had started cross-country for five hundred miles to another city, the first hundred over a countryside asmoke from burning villages Valkanhayn's men had pillaged the night before. There was no warning; Khepera had lost electricity and radio and telegraph, and the spread of news was at the speed of one of the beasts the locals insisted on calling horses. By midafternoon, they had finished with that city. It had been as bad as the first one.

One thing, it was the center of a considerable cattle country. The cattle were native to the planet, heavy-bodied unicorns the size of a Gram bisonoid or one of the slightly mutated Terran carabaos on Tanith, with long hair like a Terran yak. He had detailed a dozen of the *Nemesis* ground-fighters who had been vaqueros on his Traskon ranches to collect a score of cows and four likely bulls, with enough fodder to last them on the voyage. The odds were strongly against any of them living to acclimate themselves to Tanith, but if they did, they might prove to be one of the most valuable pieces of loot from Khepera.

The third city was at the forks of a river, like Tradetown on Tanith. Unlike it, this was a real metropolis. They should have gone there first of all. They spent two days systematically pillaging it. The Kheperans carried on considerable river-traffic, with stern-wheel steamboats, and the waterfront was lined with warehouses crammed with every sort of merchandise. Even better, the Kheperans had money, and for the most part it was gold specie, and the bank vaults were full of it.

Unfortunately, the city had been built since the fall of the Federation and the climb up from the barbarism that had followed, and a great deal of it was of wood. Fires started almost at once, and it was almost completely on fire by the end of the second day. It had been visible in the telescopic screen even after they were out of atmosphere, a black smear until the turning planet carried it into darkness and then a lurid glow.

"It was a filthy business."

Harkaman nodded. "Robbery and murder always are. You don't have to ask me who said that Space Vikings are professional robbers and murderers, but who was it said that he didn't care how many planets were raided and how many innocents massacred in the Old Federation?"

"A dead man. Lucas Trask of Traskon."

"You wish, now, that you'd kept Traskon and stayed on Gram?"

"No. If I had, I'd have spent every hour wishing I was doing what I'm doing now. I can get used to this, I suppose."

"I think you will. At least, you kept your rations down. I didn't on my first raid, and had bad dreams about it for a year." He gave his coffee cup back to the robot and got to his feet. "Get a little rest, for a couple of hours. Then draw some alcodote-vitamin pills from the medic. As soon as things are secured, there'll be parties all over the ship, and we'll be expected to look in on every one of them, have a drink, and say 'Well done, boys.'"

Elaine came to him, while he was resting. She looked at him in horror, and he tried to hide his face from her, and then realized that he was trying to hide it from himself.

XII

They came straight down on Eglonsby, on Amaterasu, the *Nemesis* and the *Space Scourge* side by side. The radar had picked them up at point-five light-seconds; by this time the whole planet knew they were coming, and nobody was wondering why. Paul Koreff was monitoring at least twenty radio stations, assigning somebody to each one as it was identified. What was coming in was uniformly excited, some panicky, and all in fairly standard Lingua Terra.

Garvan Spasso was perturbed. So, in the communication screen from the *Space Scourge*, was Boake Valkanhayn.

"They got radio, and they got radar," he clamored.

"Well, so what?" Harkaman asked. "They had radio and radar twenty years ago, when Rock Morgan was here in the *Coalsack*. But they don't have nuclear energy, do they?"

"Well, no. I'm picking up a lot of industrial electrical discharge, but nothing nuclear."

"All right. A man with a club can lick a man with his fists. A man with a gun can lick half a dozen with clubs. And two ships with nuclear weapons can lick a whole planet without them. Think it's time, Lucas?"

He nodded. "Paul, can you cut in on that Eglonsby station yet?"

"What are you going to do?" Valkanhayn wanted to know, against it in advance.

"Summon them to surrender. If they don't, we will drop a hellburner, and then we will pick out another city and summon it to surrender. I don't think the second one will refuse. If we are going to be murderers, we'll do it right, this time."

Valkanhayn was aghast, probably at the idea of burning an unlooted city. Spasso was sputtering something about, "...Teach the dirty Neobarbs a lesson —" Koreff told him he was switched on. He picked up a hand-phone.

"Space Vikings *Nemesis* and *Space Scourge*, calling the city of Eglonsby. Space Vikings...."

He repeated it for over a minute; there was no reply.

"Vann," he called Guns-and-Missiles. "A subcrit display job, about four miles over the city."

He laid the phone down and looked to the underside viewscreen. A little later, a silvery shape dropped away from the ship's south pole. The telescopic screen went off, and the unmagnified screen darkened as the filters went on. Valkanhayn, aboard the other ship, was shouting a warning about his own screens. The only unfiltered screen aboard the *Nemesis* was the one tuned to the falling missile. The city of Eglonsby rushed upward in it, and then it went suddenly dark. There was an orange-yellow blaze in the other screens. After a while, the filters went off and the telescopic screen went on again. He picked up the phone.

"Space Vikings calling Eglonsby; this is your last warning. Communicate at once."

Less than a minute later, a voice came out of one of the speakers:

"Eglonsby calling Space Vikings. Your bomb has done great damage. Will you hold your fire until somebody in authority can communicate with you? This is the chief operator at the central State telecast station; I have no authority to say anything to you, or discuss anything."

"Oh, good, that sounds like a dictatorship," Harkaman was saying. "Grab the dictator and shove a pistol in his face and you have everything."

"There is nothing to discuss. Get somebody who has authority to surrender the city to us. If this is not done within the hour, the city and everybody in it will be obliterated."

Only minutes later, a new voice said:

"This is Gunsalis Jan, secretary to Pedrosan Pedro, President of the Council of Syndics. We will switch President Pedrosan over as soon as he can speak directly to the personage in supreme command of your ships."

"That is myself; switch him to me at once."

After a delay of less than fifteen seconds they had President Pedrosan Pedro.

"We are prepared to resist, but we realize what this would cost in lives and destruction of property," he began.

"You don't begin to. Do you know anything about nuclear weapons?"

"From history; we have no nuclear power of any sort. We can find no fissionables on this planet."

"The cost, as you put it, would be everything and everybody in Eglonsby and for a radius of almost a hundred miles. Are you still prepared to resist?"

The President of the Council of Syndics wasn't and said so. Trask asked him how much authority his position gave him.

"I have all powers in any emergency. I think," the voice added tonelessly, "that this is an emergency. The council will automatically ratify any decision I make."

Harkaman depressed a button in front of him. "What I said; dictatorship, with parliamentary false front."

"If he isn't a false-front dictator for some oligarchy." He motioned to Harkaman to take his thumb off the button. "How large is this Council?"

"Sixteen, elected by the Syndicates they represent. There is the Syndicate of Labor, the Syndicate of Manufacturers, the Syndicate of Small Businesses, the...."

"Corporate State, First Century Pre-Atomic on Terra. Benny the Moose," Harkaman said. "Let's all go down and talk to them."

When they were sure that the public had been warned to make no resistance, the *Nemesis* went down to two miles, bulking over the center of the city. The buildings were low by the standards of a contragravity-using people, the highest barely a thousand feet and few over five hundred, and they were more closely set than Sword-Worlders were accustomed to, with broad roadways between. In several places there were queer arrangements of crossed roadways, apparently leading nowhere. Harkaman laughed when he saw them.

"Airstrips. I've seen them on other planets where they've lost contragravity. For winged aircraft powered by chemical fuel. I hope we have time for me to look around, here. I'll bet they even have railroads here."

The "great damage" caused by the bomb was about equal to the effect of a medium hurricane; he had seen worse from high winds at Traskon. Mostly it had been moral, which had been the kind intended.

They met President Pedrosan and the council of Syndics in a spacious and well-furnished chamber near the top of one of the medium-high buildings. Valkanhayn was surprised; in a loud aside he considered that these people must be almost civilized. They were introduced. Amaterasuan surnames preceded personal names, which hinted at a culture and a political organization making much use of registration by alphabetical list. They all wore garments which had the indefinable but unmistakable appearance of uniforms. When they had all seated themselves at a large oval table, Harkaman drew his pistol and used the butt for a gavel.

"Lord Trask, will you deal with these people directly?" he asked, stiffly formal.

"Certainly, Admiral." He spoke to the President, ignoring the others. "We want it understood that we control this city, and we expect complete submission. As long as you remain submissive to us, we will do no damage beyond removal of the things we wish to take from it, and there will be no violence to any of your people, or any indiscriminate vandalism. This visit we are paying you will cost you heavily, make no mistake about that, but whatever the cost, it will be a cheap price for avoiding what we might otherwise do."

The President and the Syndics exchanged relieved glances. Let the taxpayers worry about the cost; they'd come out of it with whole skins.

"You understand, we want maximum value and minimum bulk," he continued. "Jewels, objects of art, furs, the better grades of luxury goods of all kinds. Rare-element metals. And monetary metals, gold and platinum. You have a metallic-based currency, I suppose?"

"Oh, no!" President Pedrosan was slightly scandalized. "Our currency is based on services to society. Our monetary unit is simply called a credit."

Harkaman snorted impolitely. Evidently he'd seen economic systems like that before. Trask wanted to know if they used gold or platinum at all.

"Gold, to some extent, for jewelry." Evidently they weren't complete economic puritans. "And platinum in industry, of course."

"If they want gold, they should have raided Stolgoland," one of the Syndics said. "They have a gold-standard currency." From the way he said it, he might have been accusing them of eating with their fingers, and possibly of eating their own young.

"I know, the maps we're using for this planet are a few centuries old; Stolgoland doesn't seem to appear on them."

"I wish it didn't appear on ours, either." That was General Dagró Ector, Syndic for State Protection.

"It would have been a good thing for this whole planet if you'd decided to raid them instead of us," somebody else said.

"It isn't too late for these gentlemen to make that decision," Pedrosan said. "I gather that gold is a monetary metal among your people?" When Trask nodded, he continued: "It is also the basis of the Stolgonian currency. The actual currency is paper, theoretically redeemable in gold. In actuality, the circulation of gold has been prohibited, and the entire gold wealth of the nation is concentrated in vaults at three depositories. We know exactly where they are."

"You begin to interest me, President Pedrosan."

"I do? Well, you have two large spaceships and six smaller craft. You have nuclear weapons, something nobody on this planet has. You have contragravity, something that is hardly more than a legend here. On the other hand, we have a million and a half ground-troops, jet aircraft, armored ground-vehicles, and chemical weapons. If you will undertake to attack Stolgoland, we will place this entire force at your disposal; General Dagró will command them as you direct. All that we ask is that, when you have loaded the gold hoards of Stolgoland aboard your ships, you will leave our troops in possession of the country."

That was all there was to that meeting. There was a second one; only Trask, Harkaman and Sir Paytrik Morland represented the Space Vikings, and the Eglonsby government was represented by President Pedrosan and General Dagró. They met more intimately, in a smaller and more luxurious room in the same building.

"If you're going to declare war on Stolgoland, you'd better get along with it," Morland advised.

"What?" Pedrosan seemed to have only the vaguest idea of what he was talking about. "You mean, warn them? Certainly not. We will attack them by surprise. It will be nothing but plain self-defense," he added righteously. "The oligarchic capitalists of Stolgoland have been plotting to attack us for years."

"Yes. If you had carried out your original intention of looting Eglonsby, they would have invaded us the moment your ships lifted out. It's exactly what I'd do in their place."

"But you maintain nominally friendly relations with them?"

"Of course. We are civilized. The peace-loving government and people of Eglonsby...."

"Yes, Mr. President; I understand. And they have an embassy here?"

"They call it that!" cried Dagró. "It is a nest of vipers, a plague-spot of espionage and subversion...!"

"We'll grab that ourselves, right away," Harkaman said. "You won't be able to round up all their agents outside it, and if we tried to, it would cause suspicion. We'll have to put up a front to deceive them."

"Yes. You will go on the air at once, calling on the people to collaborate with us, and you will specifically order your troops mobilized to assist us in collecting the tribute we are levying on Eglonsby," Trask said. "In that way, if any Stolgonian spies see your troops concentrated around our landing craft, they'll think it's to help us load our loot."

"And we'll announce that a large part of the tribute will consist of military equipment," Dagró added. "That will explain why our guns and tanks are being loaded on your contragravity vehicles."

When the Stolgonian embassy was seized by the Space Vikings, the ambassador asked to be taken at once to their leader. He had a proposition: If the Space Vikings would completely disable the army of Eglonsby and admit Stolgonian troops when they were ready to leave, the invaders would bring with them ten thousand kilos of gold. Trask affected to be very hospitable to the offer.

Stolgoland lay across a narrow and shallow sea from the State of Eglonsby; it was dotted with islands, and every one of them was, in turn, dotted with oil wells. Petroleum was what kept the aircraft and ground-vehicles of Amaterasu in operation; oil, rather than ideology, was at the root of the enmity between the two nations. Apparently the Stolgonian espionage in Eglonsby was completely deceived, and the reports Trask allowed the captive ambassador to make confirmed the deception. Hourly the Eglonsby radio stations poured out exhortations to the people to co-operate with the Space Vikings, with an occasional lamentation about the masses of war materials being taken. Eglonsby espionage in Stolgoland was similarly active. The Stolgonian armies were being massed at four seaports on the coast facing Eglonsby, and there was a frantic gathering of every sort of ship available. By this time, any sympathy that Trask might have felt for either party had evaporated.

The invasion of Stolgoland started the fifth morning after their arrival over Eglonsby. Before dawn, the six pinnaces went in, making a wide sweep around the curvature of the planet and coming in from the north, two to each of the three gold-troves. They were detected by radar, eventually but too late for any effective resistance to be organized. Two were even taken without a shot; by mid-morning all three had been blown open and the ingots and specie were being removed.

The four seaports from whence the Stolgonian invasion of Eglonsby was to have been launched were neutralized by nuclear bombing. Neutralized was a nice word, Trask thought; there was no echo in it of the screams of the still-living, maimed and burned and blinded, around the fringes of ground-zero. The *Nemesis* and the *Space Scourge*, from landing craft and from the ships themselves, landed Eglonsby troops on Stolgonopolis. While they were sacking the city, with all the usual atrocities, the Space Vikings were loading the gold, and anything else that was of more than ordinary value, aboard the ships.

They were still at it the next morning when President Pedrosan arrived at the newly conquered capital, announcing his intention of putting the Stolgonian chief of state and his cabinet
on trial as war criminals. Before sunset, they were back over Eglonsby. The loot might run
as high as a half-billion Excalibur stellars. Boake Valkanhayn and Garvan Spasso were simply
beyond astonishment and beyond words.

The looting of Eglonsby then began.

They gathered up machinery, and stocks of steel and light-metal alloys. The city was full of
warehouses, and the warehouses were crammed with valuables. In spite of the socialistic and
egalitarian verbiage behind which the government operated, there seemed to be a numerous
elite class and if gold were not a monetary metal it was not despised for purposes of ostentation.
There were several large art museums. Vann Larch, their nearest approach to an art specialist,
took charge of culling the best from them.

And there was a vast public library. Into this Otto Harkaman vanished, with half a dozen
men and a contragravity scow. Its historical section would be much poorer in the future.

President Pedrosan Pedro was on the radio from Stolgonopolis that night.

"Is this how you Space Vikings keep faith?" he demanded indignantly. "You've abandoned me
and my army here in Stolgoland, and you're sacking Eglonsby. You promised to leave Eglonsby
alone if I helped you get the gold of Stolgoland."

"I promised nothing of the kind. I promised to help you take Stolgoland. You've taken it,"
Trask told him. "I promised to avoid unnecessary damage or violence. I've already hanged a
dozen of my own men for rape, murder and wanton vandalism. Now, we expect to be out of
here in twenty-four hours. You'd better be back here before then. Your own people are starting
to loot. We did not promise to control them for you."

That was true. What few troops had been left behind, and the police, were unable to cope
with the mobs that were pillaging in the wake of the Space Vikings. Everybody seemed to be
trying to grab what he could and let the Vikings be blamed for it. He had been able to keep
his own people in order. There had been at least a dozen cases of rape and wanton murder, and
the offenders had been promptly hanged. None of their shipmates, not even the *Space Scourge*
company, seemed resentful. They felt the culprits had deserved what they'd gotten; not for
what they'd done to the locals, but for disobeying orders.

A few troops had been flown in from Stolgoland by the time they had gotten their vehicles
stowed and were lifting out. They didn't seem to be making much headway. Harkaman, who
had gotten his load of microbooks stowed and was at the command desk, laughed heartily.

"I don't know what Pedrosan'll do. Gehenna, I don't even know what I'd do, if I'd gotten
myself into a mess like that. He'll probably bring half his army back, leave the other half in
Stolgoland, and lose both. Suppose we drop in, in about three or four years, just out of curiosity.
If we make twenty per cent of what we did this time, the trip would pay for itself."

After they went into hyperspace and had the ship secured, the parties lasted three Galactic
standard days, and nobody was at all sober. Harkaman was drooling over the mass of historical
material he had found. Spasso was jubilant. Nobody could call this chicken-stealing. He kept
repeating that as long as he was able to say anything. Khepera, he conceded, had been. Lousy
two or three million stellars; poo!

XIII

Beowulf was bad.

Valkanhayn and Spasso had both been opposed to the raid. Nobody raided Beowulf; Beowulf
was too tough. Beowulf had nuclear energy and nuclear weapons and contragravity and normal-
space craft, they even had colonies on a couple of other planets of their system. They had

everything but hyperdrive. Beowulf was a civilized planet, and you didn't raid civilized planets, not and get away with it.

And beside, hadn't they gotten enough loot on Amaterasu?

"No, we did not," Trask told them. "If we're going to make anything out of Tanith, we're going to need power, and I don't mean windmills and waterwheels. As you've remarked, Beowulf has nuclear energy. That's where we get our plutonium and our power units."

So they went to Beowulf. They came out of hyperspace eight light-hours from the F-7 star of which Beowulf was the fourth planet, and twenty light-minutes apart. Guatt Kirbey made a microjump that brought the ships within practical communicating distance, and they began making plans in an intership screen conference.

"There are, or were, three chief sources of fissionable ores," Harkaman said. "The last ship to raid here and get away was Stefan Kintour's *Princess of Lyonesse*, sixty years ago. He hit one on the Antarctic continent; according to his account, everything there was fairly new. He didn't mess things up too badly, and it ought to be still operating. We'll go in from the south pole, and we'll have to go in fast."

They shifted personnel and equipment. They would go in bunched, the pinnaces ahead; they and the *Space Scourge* would go down to the ground, while the better-armed *Nemesis* would hover above to fight off local contragravity, shoot down missiles, and generally provide overhead cover. Trask transferred to the *Space Scourge*, taking with him Morland and two hundred of the *Nemesis* ground-fighters. Most of the single-mounts, landing craft and manipulators and heavy-duty lifters went with him, jamming the decks around the vehicle ports of Valkanhayn's ship.

They jumped in to six light-minutes, and while Valkanhayn's astrogator was still fiddling with his controls they began sensing radar and microray detection. When they came out again, they were two light-seconds off the south pole, and half a dozen ships were either in orbit or coming up from the planet. All normal-space craft, of course, but some were almost as big as the *Nemesis*.

From there on, it was a nightmare.

Ships pounded at them with guns, and they pounded back. Missiles went out, and counter-missiles stopped them in rapidly expanding and quickly vanishing globes of light. Red lights flashed on the damage board, and sirens howled and klaxons squawked. In the outside-view screens, they saw the *Nemesis* vanish in a blaze of radiance, and then, while their hearts were still in their throats, come out of it again. Red lights went off on the board as damage-control crews and their robots sealed the breaches in the hull and pumped air back into evacuated areas, and then more red lights came on.

Occasionally, he would glance toward Boake Valkanhayn, who sat motionless in his chair, chewing a cigar that had gone out long ago. He wasn't enjoying it, but he wasn't showing fear. Once a Beowulfer vanished in a supernova flash, and when the ball of incandescence widened to nothing the ship was gone. All Valkanhayn said was: "Hope one of our boys did that."

They fought their way in and down, toward the atmosphere. Another Beowulf ship blew up, a craft about the size of Spasso's *Lamia*. A moment later, another; Valkanhayn was pounding the desk in front of him with his fist and yelling: "That was one of ours! Find out who launched it; get his name!"

Missiles were coming up from the planet, now. Valkanhayn's detection officer was trying to locate the source. While he was trying, a big melon-shaped thing fell away from the *Nemesis*, and in the jiggling, radiation-distorted intership screen Harkaman's image was laughing.

"Hellburner just went off; target about 50° south, 25° east of the sunrise line. That's where those missiles are coming from."

Counter-missiles sped toward the big metal melon; defense missiles, robot-launched, met them. The hellburner's track was marked first by expanding red and orange globes in airless space and then by fire-puffs after it entered atmosphere. It vanished into the darkness beyond the sunset, and then made sunlight of its own. It *was* sunlight; a Bethe solar-phoenix reaction, and it would sustain itself for hours. He hoped it hadn't landed within a thousand miles of their objective.

The ground operation was a nightmare of a different sort. He went down in a command car, with Paytrik Morland and a couple of others. There were missiles and gun batteries. There were darting patterns of flights of combat vehicles, blazing gunfire, and single vehicles that shot past or blew up in front of them. Robots on contragravity-military robots, with missiles to launch, and working robots with only their own mass to hurl, flung themselves mindlessly at them. Screens that went crazy from radiation; speakers that jabbered contradictory orders. Finally, the battle, which had raged in the air over two thousand square miles of mines and refineries and reaction plants, became two distinct and concentrated battles, one at the packing plant and storage vaults and one at the power-unit cartridge factory.

Three pinnaces came down to form a triangle over each; the *Space Scourge* hung midway between, poured out a swarm of vehicles and big claw-armed manipulators; armored lighters and landing craft shuttled back and forth. The command car looped and dodged from one target to the other; at one, keg-like canisters of plutonium, collapsium-plated and weighing tons apiece, were coming out of the vaults, and at the other lifters were bringing out loads of nuclear-electric power-unit cartridges, some as big as a ten liter jar, to power a spaceship engine, and some small as a round of pistol ammunition, for things like flashlights.

Every hour or so, he looked at his watch, and it would be three or four minutes later.

At last, when he was completely convinced that he had really been killed, and was damned and would spend all eternity in this fire-riven chaos, the *Nemesis* began firing red flares and the speakers in all the vehicles were signaling recall. He got aboard the *Space Scourge* somehow, after assuring himself that nobody who was alive was left behind.

There were twenty-odd who weren't, and the sick bay was full of wounded who had gone up with cargo, and more were being helped off the vehicles as they were berthed. The car in which he had been riding had been hit several times, and one of the gunners was bleeding under his helmet and didn't seem aware of it. When he got to the command room, he found Boake Valkanhayn, his face drawn and weary, getting coffee from a robot and lacing it with brandy.

"That's it," he said, blowing on the steaming cup. It was the battered silver one that had been in front of him when he had first appeared in the *Nemesis'* screen. He nodded toward the damage screen; everything had been patched up, or the outer decks around breached portions of the hull sealed. "Ship secure." He set down the silver mug and lit a cigar. "To quote Garvan Spasso, 'Nobody can call that chicken-stealing.'"

"No. Not even if you count Tizona giraffe-birds as chickens. That Gram gum-pear brandy you're putting in that coffee? I'll have the same. Just leave out the coffee."

XIV

The *Lamia's* detection picked them up as soon as they were out of the last microjump; Trask's gnawing fear that Dunnan might attack in their absence had been groundless. Incredibly, he realized, they had been gone only thirty-odd Galactic Standard days, and in that time Alvyn Karffard had done an incredible amount of work.

He had gotten the spaceport completely cleared of rubble and debris, and he had the woods cleared away from around it and the two tall buildings. The locals called the city Rivvin; a few inscriptions found here and there in it indicated that the original name had been Rivington. He had done considerable mapping, in some detail of the continent on which it was located and, in general, of the rest of the planet. And he had established friendly relations with the people of Tradetown and made friends with their king.

Nobody, not even those who had collected it, quite believed their eyes when the loot was unloaded. The little herd of long haired unicorns-the Khepera locals had called them kreggs, probably a corruption of the name of some naturalist who had first studied them-had come through the voyage and even the Battle of Beowulf in good shape. Trask and a few of his former cattlemen from Traskon watched them anxiously, and the ship's doctor, acting veterinarian, made elaborate tests of vegetation they would be likely to eat. Three of the cows proved to be with calf; these were isolated and watched over with especial solicitude.

The locals were inclined to take a poor view of the kreggs, at first. Cattle ought to have two horns, one on either side, curved back. It wasn't right for cattle to have only one horn, in the middle, slanting forward.

Both ships had taken heavy damage. The *Nemesis* had one pinnace berth knocked open, and everybody was glad the Beowulfers hadn't noticed that and gotten a missile inside. The *Space Scourge* had taken a hit directly on her south pole while lifting out from the planet, and a good deal of the southern part of the ship was sealed off when she came in. The *Nemesis* was repaired as far as possible and put on off-planet patrol, then they went to work on the *Space Scourge*, transferring much of her armament to ground defense, clearing out all the available cargo space, and repairing her hull as far as possible. To repair her completely was a job for a regular shipyard, like Alex Gorram's on Gram. And that was where the work would be done.

Boake Valkanhayn would command her on the voyage to and from Gram. Since Beowulf, Trask had not only ceased to dislike the man, but was beginning to admire him. He had been a good man once, before ill fortune which had been only partly of his own making had overtaken him. He'd just let himself go and stopped caring. Now he had taken hold of himself again. It had started showing after they had landed on Amaterasu. He had begun to dress more neatly and speak more grammatically; to look and act more like a spaceman and less like a barfly. His men had begun to jump to obey when he gave an order. He had opposed the raid on Beowulf, but that had been the dying struggle of the chicken-thief he had been. He had been scared, going in; well, who hadn't been, except a few greenhorns brave with the valor of ignorance. But he had gone in, and fought his ship well, and had held his station over the fissionables plant in a hell of bombs and missile, and he had made sure everybody who had gone down and who was still alive was aboard before he lifted out.

He was a Space Viking again.

Garvan Spasso wasn't, and never would be. He was outraged when he heard that Valkanhayn would take his ship, loaded with much of the loot of the three planets, to Gram. He came to Trask, fairly spluttering about it.

"You know what'll happen?" he demanded. "He'll space out with that cargo, and that'll be the last any of us'll hear of him again. He'll probably take it to Joyeuse or Excalibur and buy himself a lordship with it."

"Oh, I doubt that, Garvan. A number of our people are going along-Guatt Kirbey will be the astrogator; you'd trust him, wouldn't you? And Sir Paytrik Morland, and Baron Rathmore, and Lord Valpry, and Rolve Hemmerding...." He was silent for a moment, struck by an idea. "Would you be willing to make the trip in the *Space Scourge*, too?"

Spasso would, very decidedly. Trask nodded.

"Good. Then we'll be sure nothing crooked is pulled," he said seriously.

After Spasso was gone, he got in touch with Baron Rathmore.

"See to it that he gets as much money that's due him as possible, when you get to Gram. And ask Duke Angus, as a favor to give him some meaningless position with a suitably impressive title, Lord Chamberlain of the Ducal Washroom, or something. Then he can prime him with misinformation and give him an opportunity to sell it to Omfray of Glaspyth. Then, of course, he could be contacted to sell Omfray out to Angus. A couple of times around and somebody'll stick a knife in him, and then we'll be rid of him for good."

They loaded the *Space Scourge* with gold from Stolgoland, and paintings and statues from the art museums and fabrics and furs and jewels and porcelains and plate from the markets of Eglonsby. They loaded sacks and kegs of specie from Khepera. Most of the Khepera loot wasn't worth hauling to Gram, but it was far enough in advance of their own technologies to be priceless to the Tanith locals.

Some of these were learning simple machine operations, and a few were able to handle contragravity vehicles that had been fitted with adequate safety devices. The former slave guards had all become sergeants and lieutenants in an infantry regiment that had been formed, and the King of Tradetown borrowed some to train his own army. Some genius in the machine shop altered a matchlock musket to flintlock and showed the local gunsmiths how to do it.

The kreggs continued to thrive, after the *Space Scourge* departed. Several calves were born, and seemed to be doing well; the biochemistry of Tanith and Khepera were safely alike. Trask had hopes for them. Every Viking ship had its own carniculture vats, but men tired of carniculture meat, and fresh meat was always in demand. Some day, he hoped, kregg-beef would be an item of sale to ships putting in on Tanith, and the long-haired hides might even find a market in the Sword-Worlds. They had contragravity scows plying between Rivington and Tradetown regularly, now, and air-lorries were linking the villages. The boatmen of Tradetown rioted occasionally against this unfair competition. And in Rivington itself, bulldozers and power shovels and manipulators labored, and there was always a rising cloud of dust over the city.

There was so much to do, and only a trifle under twenty-five Galactic Standard hours in a day to do it. There were whole days in which he never thought once of Andray Dunnan.

A hundred and twenty-five days to Gram, and a hundred and twenty-five days back. They had long ago passed. Of course, there would be the work of repairing the *Space Scourge*, the conferences with the investors in the original Tanith Adventure, the business of gathering the needed equipment for the new base. Even so, he was beginning to worry a little. Worry about something as far out of his control as the *Space Scourge* was useless, he knew. He couldn't help it, though. Even Harkaman, usually imperturbable, began to be fretful, after two hundred and seventy days had passed.

They were relaxing in the living quarters they had fitted out at the top of the spaceport building before retiring, both sprawled wearily in chairs that had come from one of the better hotels of Eglonsby, their drinks between them on a low table, the top of which was inlaid with something that looked like ivory but wasn't. On the floor beside it lay the plans for a reaction-plant and mass-energy converter they would build as soon as the *Space Scourge* returned with equipment for producing collapsium-plated shielding.

"Of course, we could go ahead with it, now," Harkaman said. "We could tear enough armor off the *Lamia* to shield any kind of a reaction plant."

That was the first time either of them had gotten close to the possibility that the ship mightn't return. Trask laid his cigar in the ashtray-it had come from President Pedrosan Pedro's private office-and splashed a little more brandy into his glass.

"She'll be coming before long. We have enough of our people aboard to make sure nobody else tries to take the ship. And I really believe, now, that Valkanhayn can be trusted."

"I do, too. I'm not worried about what might happen on the ship. But we don't know what's been happening on Gram. Glaspyth and Didreksburg could have teamed up and jumped Wardshaven before Duke Angus was ready to invade Glaspyth. Boake might be landing the ship in a trap at Wardshaven."

"Be a sorry looking trap after it closed on him. That would be the first time in history that a Sword-World was raided by Space Vikings." Harkaman looked at his half-empty glass, then filled it to the top. It was the same drink he had started with, just as a regiment that has been decimated and recruited up to strength a few times is still the same regiment.

The buzz of the communication screen-one of the few things in the room that hadn't been looted somewhere-interrupted him. They both rose; Harkaman, still carrying his drink, went to put it on. It was a man on duty in the control room, overhead, reporting that two emergences had just been detected at twenty light-minutes due north of the planet. Harkaman gulped his drink and set down the empty glass.

"All right. You put out a general alert? Switch anything that comes in over to this screen." He got out his pipe and was packing tobacco into it mechanically. "They'll be out of the last microjump and about two light-seconds away in a few minutes."

Trask sat down again, saw that his cigarette had burned almost to the tip, and lit a fresh one from it, wishing he could be as calm about it as Harkaman. Three minutes later, the control tower picked up two emergences at a light-second and a half, a thousand or so miles apart. Then the screen flickered, and Boake Valkanhayn was looking out of it, from the desk in the newly refurbished command room of the *Space Scourge*.

He was a newly refurbished Boake Valkanhayn, too. His heavily braided captain's jacket looked like the work of one of the better tailors on Gram, and on the breast was a large and ornate knight's star, of unfamiliar design, bearing, among other things, the sword and atom-symbol of the house of Ward.

"Prince Trask; Count Harkaman," he greeted. "*Space Scourge*, Tanith; thirty-two hundred hours out of Wardshaven on Gram, Baron Valkanhayn commanding, accompanied by chartered freighter *Rozinante*, Durendal, Captain Morbes. Requesting permission and instructions to orbit in."

"Baron Valkanhayn?" Harkaman asked.

"That's right," Valkanhayn grinned. "And I have a vellum scroll the size of a blanket to prove it. I have a whole cargo of scrolls. One says you're Otto, Count Harkaman, and another says you're Admiral of the Royal Navy of Gram."

"He did it!" Trask cried. "He made himself King of Gram!"

"That's right. And you're his trusty and well-loved Lucas, Prince Trask, and Viceroy of his Majesty's Realm of Tanith."

Harkaman bristled at that. "The Gehenna you say. This is *our* Realm of Tanith."

"Is his Majesty making it worth while to accept his sovereignty?" Trask asked. "That is, beside vellum scrolls?"

Valkanhayn was still grinning. "Wait till we start sending cargo down. And wait till you see what's crammed into the other ship."

"Did Spasso come back with you?" Harkaman asked.

"Oh, no. Sir Garvan Spasso entered the service of his Majesty, King Angus. He is Chief of Police at Glaspyth, now, and nobody can call what he's doing there chicken-stealing, either. Any chickens he steals, he steals the whole farm to get them."

That didn't sound good. Spasso could make King Angus' name stink all over Glaspyth. Or maybe he'd allow Spasso to crush the adherents of Omfray, and then hang him for his oppression of the people. He'd read about somebody who'd done something like that, in one of Harkaman's Old Terran history books.

Baron Rathmore had stayed on Gram; so had Rolve Hemmerding. The rest of the gentlemen-adventurers, all with shiny new titles of nobility, had returned. From them, as the two ships were getting into orbit, he learned what had happened on Gram since the *Nemesis* had spaced out.

Duke Angus had announced his intention of carrying on with the Tanith Adventure, and had started construction of a new ship at the Gorram yards. This had served plausibly to explain all the activities of preparation for the invasion of Glaspyth, and had deceived Duke Omfray completely. Omfray had already started a ship of his own; the entire resources of his duchy were thrown into an effort to get her finished and to space ahead of the one Angus was building. Work was going on frantically on her when the Wardshaven invaders hit Glaspyth; she was now nearing completion as a unit of the Royal Navy. Duke Omfray had managed to escape to Didreksburg; when Angus' troops moved in on the latter duchy, he had escaped again, this time off-planet. He was now eating the bitter bread of exile at the court of his wife's uncle, the King of Haulteclere.

The Count of Newhaven, the Duke of Bigglersport, and the Lord of Northport, all of whom had favored the establishment of a planetary monarchy, had immediately acknowledged Angus as their sovereign. So, with a knife at his throat, had the Duke of Didreksburg. Many other feudal magnates had refused to surrender their sovereignty. That might mean fighting, but Paytrik, now Baron, Morland, doubted it.

"The *Space Scourge* stopped that," he said. "When they heard about the base here, and saw what we'd shipped to Gram, they started changing their minds. Only subjects of King Angus will be allowed to invest in the Tanith Adventure."

As for accepting King Angus' annexation of Tanith and accepting his sovereignty, that would also be advisable. They would need a Sword World outlet for the loot they took or obtained by barter from other Space Vikings, and until they had adequate industries of their own, they would be dependent on Gram for many things which could not be gotten by raiding.

"I suppose the King knows I'm not out here for my health, or his profit?" he asked Lord Valpry, during one of the screen conversations as the *Space Scourge* was getting into orbit. "My business out here is Andray Dunnan."

"Oh, yes," the Wardshaven noble replied. "In fact, he told me, in so many words, that he would be most happy if you sent him his nephew's head in a block of lucite. What Dunnan did touched his honor, too. Sovereign princes never see any humor in things like that."

"I suppose he knows that sooner or later Dunnan will try to attack Tanith?"

"If he doesn't, it isn't because I didn't tell him often enough. When you see the defense armament we're bringing, you'll think he does."

It was impressive, but nothing to the engineering and industrial equipment. Mining robots for use on the iron Moon of Tanith, and normal-space transports for the fifty thousand mile run between planet and satellite. A collapsed-matter producer; now they could collapsium-plate their own shielding. A small, fully robotic, steel mill that could be set up and operated on the satellite. Industrial robots, and machinery to make machinery. And, best of all, two hundred engineers and highly skilled technicians.

Quite a few industrial baronies on Gram would realize, before long, what they had lost in those men. He wondered what Lord Trask of Traskon would have thought about that.

The Prince of Tanith was no longer interested in what happened to Gram. Maybe, if things prospered for the next century or so, his successors would be ruling Gram by viceroy from Tanith.

XV

As soon as the *Space Scourge* was unloaded, she was put on off-planet watch; Harkaman immediately spaced out in the *Nemesis*, while Trask remained behind. They began unloading the *Rozinante*, after setting her down at Rivington Spaceport. After that was done, her officers and crew took a holiday which lasted a month, until the *Nemesis* returned. Harkaman must have made quick raids on half a dozen planets. None of the cargo he brought back was spectacularly valuable, and he dismissed the whole thing as chicken-stealing, but he had lost some men and the ship showed a few fresh scars. A good deal of what was transshipped to the *Rozinante* was manufactured goods which would compete with merchandise produced on Gram.

"That load will be a come-down, after what the *Space Scourge* took back, but we didn't want to send the *Rozinante* back empty," he said. "One thing, I had time to do a little reading, between stops."

"The books from the Eglonsby library?"

"Yes. I learned a curious thing about Amaterasu. Do you know why that planet was so extensively colonized by the Federation, when there don't seem to be any fissionable ores? The planet produced gadolinium."

Gadolinium was essential to hyperdrive engines; the engines of a ship the size of the *Nemesis* required fifty pounds of it. On the Sword-Worlds, it was worth several times its weight in gold. If they still mined it, Amaterasu would repay a second visit.

When he mentioned it, Harkaman shrugged. "Why should they mine it? There's only one thing it's good for, and you can't run a spaceship on Diesel oil. I suppose the mines could be reopened, and new refineries built, but...."

"We could trade plutonium for gadolinium. They have none of their own. We could charge our own prices for it, and we wouldn't need to tell them what gadolinium sells for on the Sword-Worlds."

"We could, if we could do business with anybody there, after what we did to Eglonsby and Stolgoland. Where would we get plutonium?"

"Why do you think the Beowulfers don't have hyperships, when they have everything else?"

Harkaman snapped his fingers. "By Satan, that's it!" Then he looked at Trask in alarm. "Hey, you're not thinking of selling Amaterasu plutonium and Beowulf gadolinium, are you?"

"Why not? We could make a big profit on both ends of the deal."

"You know what would happen next, don't you? There'd be ships from both planets all over the place in a few years. We want that like we want a hole in the head."

He couldn't see the objection. Tanith and Amaterasu and Beowulf could work up a very good triangular trade; all three would profit. It wouldn't cost men and ship-damage and ammunition, either. Maybe a mutual defense alliance, too. Think about it later; there was too much to do here on Tanith at present.

There had been mines on the Moon of Tanith before the collapse of the Federation; they had been stripped of their equipment afterward, while Tanith was still fighting a rearguard battle against barbarism, but the underground chambers and man-made caverns could still be used, and in time the mines were reopened and the steel mill put in, and eventually ingots of finished steel were coming down by shuttle-craft. In the meantime, the shipyard had been laid out and was taking shape.

The Gram ship *Queen Flavia* —she had been the one found unfinished at Glaspyth-came in three months after the *Rozinante* started back; she must have been finished while Valkanhayn was still in hyperspace. She carried considerable cargo, some of it superfluous but all of it useful; everybody was investing in the Tanith Adventure now, and the money had to be spent for something. Better, she brought close to a thousand men and women; the leakage of brains and ability from the Sword-Worlds was turning into a flood. Among them was Basil Gorram. Trask remembered him as an insufferable young twerp, but he seemed to be a good shipyard man. He very frankly predicted that in a few years his father's yards at Wardshaven would be idle and all the Tanith ships would be Tanith-built. A junior partner of Lothar Ffayle's also came out, to establish a branch of the Bank of Wardshaven at Rivington.

As soon as the *Queen Flavia* had discharged her cargo and passengers, she took on five hundred ground-fighters from the *Lamia*, *Nemesis* and *Space Scourge* companies and spaced out on a raiding voyage. While she was gone, the second ship, the one Duke Angus had started at Wardshaven and King Angus had finished, the *Black Star*, came in.

Trask was slightly incredulous at realizing that she had spaced out from Gram almost exactly two years after the *Nemesis* had departed. He still hadn't any idea where Andray Dunnan was, or what he was doing, or how to find him.

The news of the Gram base on Tanith spread slowly, first by the scheduled liners and tramp freighters that linked the Sword-Worlds, and then by trading ships and outbound Space Vikings to the Old Federation. Two years and six months after the *Nemesis* had come out of hyperspace to find Boake Valkanhayn and Garvan Spasso on Tanith, the first independent Space Viking came in, to sell a cargo and get repairs. They bought his loot-he had been raiding some planet rather above the level of Khepera and below that of Amaterasu-and healed the wounds his ship had taken getting it. He had been dealing with the Everrard family on Hoth, and professed himself much more satisfied with the bargains he had gotten on Tanith and swore to return.

He had never even heard of Andray Dunnan or the *Enterprise*.

It was a Gilgamesher that brought the first news.

He had first heard of Gilgameshers-the word was used indiscriminately for a native of or a ship from Gilgamesh-on Gram, from Harkaman and Karffard and Vann Larch and the others. Since coming to Tanith, he had heard about them from every Space Viking, never in complimentary and rarely in printable terms.

Gilgamesh was rated, with reservations, as a civilized planet though not on a level with Odin or Isis or Baldur or Marduk or Aton or any of the other worlds which had maintained the culture of the Terran Federation uninterruptedly. Perhaps Gilgamesh deserved more credit; its people had undergone two centuries of darkness and pulled themselves out of it by their bootstraps. They had recovered all the old techniques, up to and including the hyperdrive.

They didn't raid; they traded. They had religious objections to violence, though they kept these within sensible limits, and were able and willing to fight with fanatical ferocity in defense of their home planet. About a century before, there had been a five-ship Viking raid on Gilgamesh; one ship had returned and had been sold for scrap after reaching a friendly base. Their ships went everywhere to trade, and wherever they traded a few of them usually settled, and where they settled they made money, sending most of it home. Their society seemed to be a loose theo-socialism, and their religion an absurd potpourri of most of the major monotheisms of the Federation period, plus doctrinal and ritualistic innovations of their own. Aside from their propensity for sharp trading, their bigoted refusal to regard anybody not of their creed as more than half human, and the maze of dietary and other taboos in which they hid from social contact with others, made them generally disliked.

After their ship had gotten into orbit, three of them came down to do business. The captain and his exec wore long coats, almost knee-length, buttoned to the throat, and small white caps like forage caps; the third, one of their priests, wore a robe with a cowl, and the symbol of their religion, a blue triangle in a white circle, on his breast. They all wore beards that hung down from their cheeks, with their chins and upper lips shaved. They all had the same righteous, disapproving faces, they all refused refreshments of any sort, and they sat uneasily as though fearing contamination from the heathens who had sat in their chairs before them. They had a mixed cargo of general merchandise picked up here and there on subcivilized planets, in which nobody on Tanith was interested. They also had some good stuff-vegetable-amber and flame-bird plumes from Irminsul; ivory or something very like it from somewhere else; diamonds and Uller organic opals and Zarathustra sunstones. They also had some platinum. They wanted machinery, especially contragravity engines and robots.

The trouble was, they wanted to haggle. Haggling, it seemed, was the Gilgamesh planetary sport.

"Have you ever heard of a Space Viking ship named the *Enterprise?*" he asked them, at the seventh or eighth impasse in the bargaining. "She bears a crescent, light blue on black. Her captain's name is Andray Dunnan."

"A ship so named, with such a device, raided Chermosh more than a year ago," the priest-supercargo said. "Some of our people tarry on Chermosh to trade. This ship sacked the city in which they were; some of them lost heavily in world's goods."

"That's a pity."

The Gilgamesh priest shrugged. "It is as Yah the Almighty wills," he said, then brightened slightly. "The Chermoshers are heathens and worshipers of false gods. The Space Vikings looted their temple and destroyed it utterly; they carried away the graven images and abominations. Our people bore witness that there was much wailing and lamentation among the idolators."

So that was the first entry on the Big Board. It covered, optimistically, the whole of one wall in his office, and for some time that one chalked note about the raid on Chermosh, and the date, as nearly as it could be approximated, looked very lonely on it. The captain of the *Black Star* brought back material for a couple more. He had put in on several planets known to be temporarily occupied by Space Vikings, to barter loot, give his men some time off-ship, and make inquiries, and he had names for a couple of planets raided by the blue crescent ship. One was only six months old.

The way news filtered about in the Old Federation, that was practically hot off the stove.

The owner-captain of the *Alborak* had something to add, when he brought his ship in six months later. He sipped his drink slowly, as though he had limited himself to one and wanted to make it last as long as possible.

"Almost two years ago, on Jagannath," he said. "The *Enterprise* was on orbit there, getting some light repairs. I met the man a few times. Looks just like those pictures, but he's wearing a small pointed beard, now. He'd sold a lot of loot. General merchandise, precious and semi-precious stones, a lot of carved and inlaid furniture that looked as though it had come from some Neobarb king's palace, and some temple stuff. Buddhist; there were a couple of big gold Dai-Butsus. His crew were standing drinks for all comers. Some of them were pretty dark above the collar, as though they'd been on a hot-star planet not too long before. And he had a lot of Imhotep furs to sell, simply fabulous stuff."

"What kind of repairs? Combat damage?"

"That was my impression. He spaced out a little over a hundred hours after I came in, in company with another ship. The *Starhopper*, Captain Teodor Vaghn. The talk was that they were making a two-ship raid somewhere." The captain of the *Alborak* thought for a moment. "One other thing. He was buying ammunition, everything from pistol cartridges to hellburners. And he was buying all the air-and-water recycling equipment, and all the carniculture and hydroponic equipment, he could get."

That was something to know. He thanked the Space Viking, and then asked:

"Did he know, at the time, that I'm out here hunting for him?"

"If he did, nobody else on Jagannath did. I didn't hear about it, myself, till six months afterward."

That evening, he played off the recording he had made of the conversation for Harkaman and Valkanhayn and Karffard and some of the others. Somebody instantly said:

"That temple stuff came from Chermosh. They're Buddhists, there. That checks with the Gilgamesher's story."

"He got the furs on Imhotep; he traded for them," Harkaman said. "Nobody gets anything off Imhotep by raiding. The planet's in the middle of a glaciation, the land surface down to the fiftieth parallel is iced over solid. There is one city, ten or fifteen thousand, and the rest of the population is scattered around in settlements of a couple of hundred all along the face of the glaciers. They're all hunters and trappers. They have some contragravity, and when a ship comes in, they spread the news by radio and everybody brings his furs to town. They use telescope sights, and everybody over ten years old can hit a man in the head at five hundred yards. And big weapons are no good; they're too well dispersed. So the only way to get anything out of them is to trade for it."

"I think I know where he was," Alvyn Karffard said. "On Imhotep, silver is a monetary metal. On Agni, they use silver for sewer-pipe. Agni is a hot-star planet, class B-3 sun. And on Agni they are tough, and they have good weapons. That could be where the *Enterprise* took that combat damage."

That started an argument as to whether he'd gone to Chermosh first. It was sure that he had gone to Agni and then Imhotep. Guatt Kirbey tried to figure both courses.

"It doesn't tell us anything, either way," he said at length. "Chermosh is away off to the side from Agni and Imhotep in either case."

"Well, he does have a base, somewhere, and it's not on any Terra-type planet," Valkanhayn said. "Otherwise, what would he want with all that air-and-water and hydroponic and carni-culture stuff?"

The Old Federation area was full of non-Terra-type planets, and why should anybody bother going to any of them? Any planet that wasn't oxygen-atmosphere, six to eight thousand miles in diameter, and within a narrow surface-temperature range, wasn't worth wasting time on. But a planet like that, if one had the survival equipment, would make a wonderful hideout.

"What sort of a captain is this Teodor Vaghn?" he asked.

"A good one," Harkaman said promptly. "He has a nasty streak-sadistic-but he knows his business and he has a good ship and a well-trained crew. You think he and Dunnan have teamed up?"

"Don't you? I think, now that he has a base, Dunnan is getting a fleet together."

"He'll know we're after him by now," Vann Larch said. "And he knows where we are, and that puts him one up on us."

XVI

So Andray Dunnan was haunting him again. Tiny bits of information came in-Dunnan's ship had been on Hoth, on Nergal, selling loot. Now he sold for gold or platinum, and bought little, usually arms and ammunition. Apparently his base, wherever it was, was fully self-sufficient. It was certain, too, that Dunnan knew he was being hunted. One Space Viking who had talked with him quoted him as saying: "I don't want any trouble with Trask, and if he's smart he won't look for any with me." This made him all the more positive that somewhere Dunnan was building strength for an attack on Tanith. He made it a rule that there should always be at least two ships in orbit off Tanith in addition to the *Lamia*, which was on permanent patrol, and he installed more missile-launching stations both on the moon and on the planet.

There were three ships bearing the Ward swords and atom-symbol, and a fourth building on Gram. Count Lionel of Newhaven was building one of his own, and three big freighters shuttled across the three thousand light-years between Tanith and Gram. Sesar Karvall, who had never recovered from his wounds, had died; Lady Lavina had turned the barony and the business over to her brother, Burt Sandrasan, and gone to live on Excalibur. The shipyard at Rivington was finished, and now they had built the landing-legs of Harkaman's *Corisande II*, and were putting up the skeleton.

And they were trading with Amaterasu, now. Pedrosan Pedro had been overthrown and put to death by General Dagró Ector during the disorders following the looting of Eglonsby; the troops left behind in Stolgoland had mutinied and made common cause with their late enemies. The two nations were in an uneasy alliance, with several other nations combining against them, when the *Nemesis* and the *Space Scourge* returned and declared peace against the whole planet. There was no fighting; everybody knew what had happened to Stolgoland and Eglonsby. In the end, all the governments of Amaterasu joined in a loose agreement to get the mines reopened and resume production of gadolinium, and to share in the fissionables being imported in exchange.

It had been harder, and had taken a year longer, to do business with Beowulf. The Beowulfers had a single planetary government, and they were inclined to shoot first and negotiate afterward, a natural enough attitude in view of experiences of the past. However, they had enough old Federation-period textbooks still in microprint to know what could be done with gadolinium. They decided to write off the past as fair fight and no bad blood, and start over again.

It would be some years before either planet had hyperships of their own. In the meantime, both were good customers, and rapidly becoming good friends. A number of young Amatera-suans and Beowulfers had come to Tanith to study various technologies.

The Tanith locals were studying, too. In the first year, Trask had gathered the more intelligent boys of ten to twelve from each community and begun teaching them. In the past year, he had sent the most intelligent of them off to Gram to school. In another five years, they'd be coming home to teach; in the meantime, he was bringing teachers to Tanith from Gram. There was a school at Tradetown, and others in some of the larger villages, and at Rivington there was something that could almost be called a college. In another ten years or so, Tanith would be able to pretend to the status of civilization.

If only Andray Dunnan and his ships didn't come too soon. They would be beaten off, he was confident of that; but the damage Tanith would take, in the defense, would set back his work for years. He knew all too well what Space Viking ships could do to a planet. He'd have to find Dunnan's base, smash it, destroy his ships, kill the man himself, first. Not to avenge that murder six years ago on Gram; that was long ago and far away, and Elaine was vanished, and so was the Lucas Trask who had loved and lost her. What mattered now was planting and nurturing civilization on Tanith.

But where would he find Dunnan, in two hundred billion cubic light-years? Dunnan had no such problem. He knew where his enemy was.

And Dunnan was gathering strength. The *Yo-Yo*, Captain Vann Humfort; she had been reported twice, once in company with the *Starhopper*, and once with the *Enterprise*. She bore a blazon of a feminine hand dangling a planet by a string from one finger; a good ship, and an able, ruthless captain. The *Bolide*; she and the *Enterprise* had made a raid on Ithunn. The Gilgameshers had settled there and one of their ships had brought that story in.

And he recruited two ships at once on Melkarth, and there was a good deal of mirth about that among the Tanith Space Vikings.

Melkarth was strictly a poultry planet. Its people had sunk to the village-peasant level; they had no wealth worth taking or carrying away. It was, however, a place where a ship could be set down, and there were women, and the locals had not lost the art of distillation, and made potent liquors. A crew could have fun there, much less expensively than on a regular Viking base planet, and for the last eight years a Captain Nial Burrik, of the *Fortuna*, had been occupying it, taking his ship out for occasional quick raids and spending most of the time living from day to day almost on the local level. Once in a while, a Gilgamesher would come in to see if he had anything to trade. It was a Gilgamesher who brought the story to Tanith, and it was almost two years old when he told it.

"We heard it from the people of the planet, the ones who live where Burrik had his base. First, there was a trading ship came in. You may have heard of her; she is the one called the *Honest Horris*."

Trask laughed at that. Her captain, Horris Sasstroff, called himself "Honest Horris," a misnomer which he had also bestowed on his ship. He was a trader of sorts. Even the Gilgameshers despised him, and not even a Gilgamesher would have taken a wretched craft like the *Honest Horris* to space.

"He had been to Melkarth before," the Gilgamesher said. "He and Burrik are friends." He pronounced that like a final and damning judgment of both of them. "The story the locals told our brethren of the *Fairdealer* was that the *Honest Horris* was landed beside Burrik's ship for ten days, when two other ships came in. They said one had the blue crescent badge, and the other bore a green monster leaping from one star to another."

The *Enterprise* and the *Starhopper*. He wondered why they'd gone to a planet like Melkarth. Maybe they knew in advance whom they'd find there.

"The locals thought there would be fighting, but there was not. There was a great feast, of all four crews. Then everything of value was loaded aboard the *Fortuna*, and all four ships lifted and spaced out together. They said Burrik left nothing of any worth whatever behind; they were much disappointed at that."

"Have any of them been back since?"

All three Gilgameshers, captain, exec, and priest, shook their heads.

"Captain Gurrash of the *Fairdealer* said it had been over a year before his ship put in there. He could still see where the landing legs of the ships had pressed into the ground, but the locals said they had not been back."

That made two more ships about which inquiries must be made. He wondered, for a moment, why in Gehenna Dunnan would want ships like that; they must make the *Space Scourge* and the *Lamia* as he had first seen them look like units of the Royal Navy of Excalibur. Then he became frightened, with an irrational retrospective fright at what might have happened. It could have, too, at any time in the last year and a half; either or both of those ships could have come in on Tanith completely unsuspected. It was only by the sheerest accident that he had found out, even now, about them.

Everybody else thought it was a huge joke. They thought it would be a bigger joke if Dunnan sent those ships to Tanith now, when they were warned and ready for them.

There were other things to worry about. One was the altering attitude of his Majesty Angus I. When the *Space Scourge* returned, the newly-titled Baron Valkanhayn brought with him, along with the princely title and the commission as Viceroy of Tanith, a most cordial personal audiovisual greeting, warm and friendly. Angus had made it seated at his desk, bare headed and smoking a cigarette. The one which had come on the next ship out was just as cordial, but the King was not smoking and wore a small gold-circled cap-of-maintenance. By the time they had three ships in service on scheduled three-month arrivals, a year and a half later, he was speaking from his throne, wearing his crown and employing the first person plural for himself and finally the third person singular for Trask. By the end of the fourth year, there was no audiovisual message from him in person, and a stiff complaint from Rovard Grauffis to the effect that His Majesty felt it unseemly for a subject to address his sovereign while seated, even by audiovisual. This was accompanied by a rather apologetic personal message from Grauffis-now Prime Minister-to the effect that His Majesty felt compelled to stand on his royal dignity at all times, and that, after all, there was a difference between the position and dignity of the Duke of Wardshaven and that of the Planetary King of Gram.

Prince Trask of Tanith couldn't quite see it. The King was simply the first nobleman of the planet. Even kings like Rodolf of Excalibur or Napolyon of Flamberge didn't try to be anything more. Thereafter, he addressed his greetings and reports to the Prime Minister, always with a personal message, to which Grauffis replied in kind.

Not only the form but also the content of the messages from Gram underwent change. His Majesty was most dissatisfied. His Majesty was deeply disappointed. His Majesty felt that His Majesty's colonial realm of Tanith was not contributing sufficiently to the Royal Exchequer. And his Majesty felt that Prince Trask was placing entirely too much emphasis upon trade and not enough upon raiding; after all, why barter with barbarians when it was possible to take what you wanted from them by force?

And there was the matter of the *Blue Comet*, Count Lionel of Newhaven's ship. His Majesty was most displeased that the Count of Newhaven was trading with Tanith from his own space-port. All goods from Tanith should pass through the Wardshaven spaceport.

"Look, Rovard," he told the audiovisual camera which was recording his reply to Grauffis. "You saw the *Space Scourge* when she came in, didn't you? That's what happens to a ship that raids a planet where there's anything worth taking. Beowulf is lousy with fissionables; they'll give us all the plutonium we can load, in exchange for gadolinium, which we sell them at about twice Sword-World prices. We trade plutonium on Amaterasu for gadolinium, and get it for about half Sword-World prices." He pressed the stop-button, until he could remember the ancient formula. "You may quote me as saying that whoever has advised His Majesty that that isn't good business is no friend to His Majesty or to the Realm.

"As for the complaint about the *Blue Comet*; as long as she is owned and operated by the Count of Newhaven, who is a stockholder in the Tanith Adventure, she has every right to trade here."

He wondered why His Majesty didn't stop Lionel of Newhaven from sending the *Blue Comet* out from Gram. He found out from her skipper, the next time she came in.

"He doesn't dare, that's why. He's King as long as the great lords like Count Lionel and Joris of Bigglersport and Alan of Northport want him to be. Count Lionel has more men and more guns and contragravity than he has, now, and that's without the help he'd get from everybody else. Everything's quiet on Gram now, even the war on Southmain Continent's stopped. Everybody wants to keep it that way. Even King Angus isn't crazy enough to do anything to start a war. Not yet, anyhow."

"Not *yet?*"

The captain of the *Blue Comet*, who was one of Count Lionel's vassal barons, was silent for a moment.

"You ought to know, Prince Trask," he said. "Andray Dunnan's grandmother was the King's mother. Her father was old Baron Zarvas of Blackcliffe. He was what was called an invalid, the last twenty years of his life. He was always attended by two male nurses about the size of Otto Harkaman. He was also said to be slightly eccentric."

The unfortunate grandfather of Duke Angus had always been a subject nice people avoided. The unfortunate grandfather of King Angus was probably a subject everybody who valued their necks avoided.

Lothar Ffayle had also come out on the *Blue Comet*. He was just as outspoken.

"I'm not going back. I'm transferring most of the funds of the Bank of Wardshaven out here; from now on, it'll be a branch of the Bank of Tanith. This is where the business is being done. It's getting impossible to do business at all in Wardshaven. What little business there is to do."

"Just what's been happening?"

"Well, taxation, first. It seems the more money came in from here, the higher taxes got on Gram. Discriminatory taxes, too; pinched the small landholding and industrial barons and favored a few big ones. Baron Spasso and his crowd."

"Baron Spasso, now?"

Ffayle nodded. "Of about half of Glaspyth. A lot of the Glaspyth barons lost their baronies-some of them their heads-after Duke Omfray was run out. It seems there was a plot against the life of His Majesty. It was exposed by the zeal and vigilance of Sir Garvan Spasso, who was elevated to the peerage and rewarded with the lands of the conspirators."

"You said business was bad, as business?"

Ffayle nodded again. "The big Tanith boom has busted. It got oversold; everybody wanted in on it. And they should never have built those two last ships, the *Speedwell* and the *Goodhope*; the return on them didn't justify it. Then, you're creating your own industries and building your own equipment and armament here; that's caused a slump in industry on Gram. I'm glad Lavina Karvall has enough money invested to live on. And finally, the consumers' goods market is getting flooded with stuff that's coming in from here and competing with Gram industry."

Well, that was understandable. One of the ships that made the shuttle-trip to Gram would carry enough in her strong rooms, in gold and jewels and the like, to pay a handsome profit on the voyage. The bulk-goods that went into the cargo holds was practically taking a free ride, so anything on hand, stuff that nobody would ordinarily think of shipping in interstellar trade, went aboard. A two thousand foot freighter had a great deal of cargo space.

Baron Trask of Traskon hadn't even begun to realise what Tanith base was going to cost Gram.

XVII

As might be expected, the Beowulfers finished their hypership first. They had started with everything but a little know-how which had been quickly learned. Amaterasu had had to begin by creating the industry they needed to create the industry they needed to build a ship. The Beowulf ship-she was named *Viking's Gift* —came in on Tanith five and a half years after the *Nemesis* and the *Space Scourge* had raided Beowulf; her skipper had fought a normal-drive ship in that battle. Beside plutonium and radioactive isotopes, she carried a general cargo of the sort of luxury-goods unique to Beowulf which could always find a market in interstellar trade.

After selling the cargo and depositing the money in the Bank of Tanith, the skipper of the *Viking's Gift* wanted to know where he could find a good planet to raid. They gave him a list, none too tough but all slightly above the chicken-stealing level, and another list of planets he was *not* to raid; planets with which Tanith was trading.

Six months later they learned that he had showed up on Khepera, with which they were now trading, and had flooded the market there with plundered textiles, hardware, ceramics and plastics. He had bought kregg-meat and hides.

"You see what you did, now?" Harkaman clamored. "You thought you were making a customer; what you made was a competitor."

"What I made was an ally. If we ever do find Dunnan's planet, we'll need a fleet to take it. A couple of Beowulf ships would help. You know them; you fought them, too."

Harkaman had other worries. While cruising in *Corisande II*, he had come in on Vitharr, one of the planets where Tanith ships traded, to find it being raided by a Space Viking ship based on Xochitl. He had fought a short but furious ship-action, battering the invader until he was glad to hyper out. Then he had gone directly to Xochitl, arriving on the heels of the ship he had beaten, and had had it out both with the captain and Prince Viktor, serving them with an ultimatum to leave Tanith trade-planets alone in the future.

"How did they take it?" Trask asked, when he returned to report.

"Just about the way you would have. Viktor said his people were Space Vikings, not Gilgameshers. I told him we weren't Gilgameshers, either, as he'd find out on Xochitl the next time one of his ships raided one of our planets. Are you going to back me up? Of course, you can always send Prince Viktor my head, and an apology —"

"If I have to send him anything, I'll send him a sky full of ships and a planet full of hellburners. You did perfectly right, Otto; exactly what I'd have done in your place."

There the matter rested. There were no more raids by Xochitl ships on any of their trade-planets. No mention of the incident was made in any of the reports sent back to Gram. The Gram situation was deteriorating rapidly enough. Finally, there was an audiovisual message from Angus himself; he was seated on his throne, wearing his crown, and he began speaking from the screen abruptly:

"We, Angus, King of Gram and Tanith, are highly displeased with our subject, Lucas, Prince and Viceroy of Tanith; we consider ourselves very badly served by Prince Trask. We therefore command him to return to Gram, and render to us account of his administration of our colony and realm of Tanith."

After some hasty preparations, Trask recorded a reply. He was sitting on a throne, himself, and he wore a crown just as ornate as King Angus', and robes of white and black Imhotep furs.

"We, Lucas, Prince of Tanith," he began, "are quite willing to acknowledge the suzerainty of the King of Gram, formerly Duke of Wardshaven. It is our earnest desire, if possible, to remain at peace and friendship with the King of Gram, and to carry on trade relations with him and with his subjects.

"We must, however, reject absolutely any efforts on his part to dictate the internal policies of our realm of Tanith. It is our earnest hope," —dammit, he'd said "earnest," he should have thought of some other word —"that no act on the part of his Majesty the King of Gram will create any breach in the friendship existing between his realm and ours."

Three months later, the next ship, which had left Gram while King Angus' summons was still in hyperspace, brought Baron Rathmore. Shaking hands with him as he left the landing craft, Trask wanted to know if he'd been sent out as the new Viceroy. Rathmore started to laugh and ended by cursing vilely.

"No. I've come out to offer my sword to the King of Tanith," he said.

"Prince of Tanith, for the time being," Trask corrected. "The sword, however, is most acceptable. I take it you've had all of our blessed sovereign you can stomach?"

"Lucas, you have enough ships and men here to take Gram," Rathmore said. "Proclaim yourself King of Tanith and then lay claim to the throne of Gram and the whole planet would rise for you."

Rathmore had lowered his voice, but even so the open landing stage was no place for this sort of talk. He said so, ordered a couple of the locals to collect Rathmore's luggage, and got him into a hall-car, taking him down to his living quarters. After they were in private, Rathmore began again:

"It's more than anybody can stand! There isn't one of the old great nobility he hasn't alienated, or one of the minor barons, the landholders and industrialists, the people who were always the backbone of Gram. And it goes from them down to the commonfolk. Assessments on the lords, taxes on the people, inflation to meet the taxes, high prices, debased coinage. Everybody's being beggared except this rabble of new lords he has around him, and that slut of a wife and her greedy kinfolk...."

Trask stiffened. "You're not speaking of Queen Flavia, are you?" he asked softly.

Rathmore's mouth opened slightly. "Great Satan, don't you know? No, of course not; the news would have come on the same ship I did. Why, Angus divorced Flavia. He claimed that she was incapable of giving him an heir to the throne. He remarried immediately."

The girl's name meant nothing to Trask; he did know of her father, a Baron Valdiva. He was lord of a small estate south of the Ward lands and west of Newhaven. Most of his people were out-and-out bandits and cattle-rustlers, and he was as close to being one himself as he could get.

"Nice family he's married into. A credit to the dignity of the throne."

"Yes. You wouldn't know this Lady-Demoiselle Evita; she was only seventeen when you left Gram, and hadn't begun to acquire a reputation outside her father's lands. She's made up for lost time since, though. And she has enough uncles and aunts and cousins and ex-lovers and what-not to fill out an infantry regiment, and every one of them's at court with both hands out to grab everything they can."

"How does Duke Joris like this?" The Duke of Bigglersport was Queen Flavia's brother. "I daresay he's less than delighted."

"He's hiring mercenaries, is what he's doing, and buying combat contragravity. Lucas, why don't you come back? You have no idea what a reputation you have on Gram, now. Everybody would rally to you."

He shook his head, "I have a throne, here on Tanith. On Gram I want nothing. I'm sorry for the way Angus turned out, I thought he'd make a good King. But since he's made an intolerable King, the lords and people of Gram will have to get rid of him for themselves. I have my own tasks, here."

Rathmore shrugged. "I was afraid that would be it," he said. "Well, I offered my sword; I won't take it back. I can help you in what you're doing on Tanith."

The captain of the free Space Viking *Damnthing* was named Roger-fan-Morvill Esthersan, which meant that he was some Sword-Worlder's acknowledged bastard by a woman of one of the Old Federation planets. His mother's people could have been Nergalers; he had coarse black hair, a mahogany-brown skin, and red-brown, almost maroon, eyes. He tasted the wine the robot poured for him and expressed appreciation, then began unwrapping the parcel he had brought in.

"Something I found while raiding on Tetragrammaton," he said. "I thought you might like to have it. It was made on Gram."

It was an automatic pistol, with a belt and holster. The leather was bisonoid-hide; the buckle of the belt was an oval enameled with a crescent, pale blue on black. The pistol was a plain 10-mm military model with grooved plastic grips; on the receiver it bore the stamp of the House of Hoylbar, the firearms manufacturers of Glaspyth. Evidently it was one of the arms Duke Omfray had provided for Andray Dunnan's original mercenary company.

"Tetragrammaton?" He glanced over to the Big Board; there was no previous report from that planet. "How long ago?"

"I'd say about three hundred hours. I came from there directly, less than two hundred and fifty hours. Dunnan's ships had left the planet three days before I got there."

That was practically sizzling hot. Well, something like that had to happen, sooner or later. The Space Viking was asking him if he knew what sort of a place Tetragrammaton was.

Neobarbarian, trying to recivilize in a crude way. Small population, concentrated on one continent; farming and fisheries. A little heavy industry, in a small way, at a couple of towns. They had some nuclear power, introduced a century or so ago by traders from Marduk, one of the really civilized planets. They still depended on Marduk for fissionables; their export product was an abominably-smelling vegetable oil which furnished the base for delicate perfumes, and which nobody was ever able to synthesize properly.

"I heard they had steel mills in operation, now," the half-breed Space Viking said. "It seems that somebody on Rimmon has just re-invented the railroad, and they need more steel than they can produce for themselves. I thought I'd raid Tetragrammaton for steel and trade it on Rimmon for a load of heaven-tea. When I got there, though, the whole planet was in a mess; not raiding, but plain wanton destruction. The locals were just digging themselves out of it when I landed. Some of them, who didn't think they had anything at all left to lose, gave me a fight. I captured a few of them, to find out what had happened. One of them had that pistol; he said he'd taken it off a Space Viking he'd killed. The ships that raided them were the *Enterprise* and the *Yo-Yo*. I knew you'd want to hear about it. I got some of the locals' stories on tape."

"Well, thank you. I'll want to hear those tapes. Now, you say you want steel?"

"Well, I haven't any money. That's why I was going to raid Tetragrammaton."

"Nifflheim with the money; your cargo's paid for already. This," he said, touching the pistol, "and whatever's on the tapes."

They played off the tapes that evening. They weren't particularly informative. The locals who had been interrogated hadn't been in actual contact with Dunnan's people except in combat. The man who had been carrying the 10-mm Hoylbar was the best witness of the lot, and he knew little. He had caught one of them alone, shot him from behind with a shotgun, taken his pistol, and then gotten away as quickly as he could. They had sent down landing craft, it seemed, and said they wanted to trade; then something must have happened, nobody knew what, and they had begun a massacre and sacked the town. After returning to their ships, they had opened fire with nuclear missiles.

"Sounds like Dunnan," Hugh Rathmore said in disgust. "He just went kill-crazy. The bad blood of Blackcliffe."

"There are funny things about this," Boake Valkanhayn said. "I'd say it was a terror-raid, but who in Gehenna was he trying to terrorize?"

"I wondered about that, too." Harkaman frowned. "This town where he landed seems, such as it was, to have been the planetary capital. They just landed, pretending friendship, which I can't see why they needed to pretend, and then began looting and massacring. There wasn't anything of real value there; all they took was what the men could carry themselves or stuff into their landing craft, and they did that because they have what amounts to a religious taboo against landing anywhere and leaving without stealing something. The real loot was at these two other towns; a steel mill and big stocks of steel at one, and all that skunk-apple oil at the other. So what did they do? They dropped a five-megaton bomb on each one, and blew both of them to Em-See-Square. That was a terror-raid pure and simple, but as Boake inquires, just who were they terrorizing? If there were big cities somewhere else on the planet, it would figure. But there aren't. They blew out the two biggest cities, and all the loot in them."

"Then they wanted to terrorize somebody off the planet."

"But nobody'd hear about it off-planet," somebody protested.

"The Mardukans would; they trade with Tetragrammaton," the acknowledged bastard of somebody named Morvill said. "They have a couple of ships a year there."

"That's right," Trask agreed. "Marduk."

"You mean, you think Dunnan's trying to terrorize *Marduk*?" Valkanhayn demanded. "Great Satan, even he isn't crazy enough for that!"

Baron Rathmore started to say something about what Andray Dunnan was crazy enough to do, and what his uncle was crazy enough to do. It was just one of the cracks he had been making since he'd come to Tanith and didn't have to look over his shoulder while he was making them.

"I think he is, too," Trask said. "I think that is exactly what he is doing. Don't ask me why; as Otto is fond of remarking, he's crazy and we aren't, and that gives him an advantage. But what have we gotten, since those Gilgameshers told us about his picking up Burrik's ship and the *Honest Horris*? Until today, we've heard nothing from any other Space Viking. What we have gotten was stories from Gilgameshers about raids on planets where they trade, and every one of them is also a planet where Marduk ships trade. And in every case, there has been little or nothing reported about valuable loot taken. The stories are all about wanton and murderous bombings. I think Andray Dunnan is making war on Marduk."

"Then he's crazier than his grandfather and his uncle both!" Rathmore cried.

"You mean, he's making a string of terror-raids on their trade-planets, hoping to pull the Mardukan space-navy away from the home planet?" Harkaman had stopped being incredulous. "And when he gets them all lured away, he'll make a fast raid?"

"That's what I think. Remember our fundamental postulate: Dunnan is crazy. Remember how he convinced himself that he was the rightful heir to the ducal crown of Wardshaven?" And remember his insane passion for Elaine; he pushed that thought hastily from him. "Now, he's convinced that he's the greatest Space Viking in history. He has to do something worthy of that distinction. When was the last time anybody attacked a civilized planet? I don't mean Gilgamesh, I mean a planet like Marduk."

"A hundred and twenty years ago; Prince Havilgar of Haulteclere, six ships, against Aton. Two ships got back. He didn't. Nobody's tried it since," Harkaman said.

"So Dunnan the Great will do it. I hope he tries," he surprised himself by adding. "That's provided I find out what happened. Then I could stop thinking about him."

There was a time when he had dreaded the possibility that somebody else might kill Dunnan before he could.

XVIII

Seshat, Obidicut, Lugaluru, Audhumla.

The young man elevated by his father's death in the Dunnan raid to the post of hereditary President of the democratic Republic of Tetragrammaton had been sure that the Marduk ships which came to his planet traded also on those. There had been some difficulty about making contact, and the first face-to-face meeting had begun in an atmosphere of bitter distrust on his part. They had met out of doors; around them, spread wrecked and burned buildings, and hastily constructed huts and shelters, and wide spaces of charred and slagged rubble.

"They blew up the steel mill here, and the oil-refinery at Jannsboro. They bombed and strafed the little farm-towns and villages. They scattered radioactives that killed as many as the bombing. And after they had gone away, this other ship came."

"The *Damnthing*? She bore the head of a beast with three very big horns?"

"That's the one. They did a little damage, at first. When the captain found out what had happened to us, he left some food and medicines for us." Roger-fan-Morvill Esthersan hadn't mentioned that.

"Well, we'd like to help you, if we can. Do you have nuclear power? We can give you a little equipment. Just remember it of us, when you're back on your feet; we'll be back to trade later. But don't think you owe us anything. The man who did this to you is my enemy. Now, I want to talk to every one of your people who can tell me anything at all...."

Seshat was the closest; they went there first. They were too late. Seshat had had it already, and on the evidence of the radioactivity counters, not too long ago. Four hundred hours at most. There had been two hellburners; the cities on which they had fallen were still-smoking pits literally burned into the ground and the bedrock below, at the center of five hundred mile radii of slag and lava and scorched earth and burned forests. There had been a planetbuster; it had started a major earthquake. And half a dozen thermonuclears. There were probably quite a few survivors —a human planetary population is extremely hard to exterminate completely-but within a century they'd be back to the loincloth and the stone hatchet.

"We don't even know Dunnan did it, personally," Paytrik Morland said. "For all we know, he's down in an air-tight cave city on some planet nobody ever heard of, sitting on a golden throne, surrounded by a harem."

He had begun to suspect that Dunnan was doing something of just the sort. The Greatest Space Viking of History would naturally found a Space Viking empire.

"An emperor goes out to look his empire over, now and then; I don't spend all my time on Tanith. Say we try Audhumla next. It's the farthest away. We might get there while he's still shooting up Obidicut and Lugaluru. Guatt, figure us a jump for it."

When the colored turbulence washed away and the screen cleared, Audhumla looked like Tanith or Khepera or Amaterasu or any other Terra-type planet, a big disk brilliant with reflected sunlight and glowing with starlit and moonlit atmosphere on the other. There was a single rather large moon, and, in the telescopic screen, the usual markings of seas and continents and rivers and mountain-ranges. But there was nothing to show....

Oh, yes; lights on the darkened side, and from the size they must be vast cities. All the available data for Audhumla was long out of date; a considerable civilization must have developed in the last half dozen centuries.

Another light appeared, a hard blue-white spark that spread into a larger, less brilliant yellow light. At the same time, all the alarm-devices in the command-room went into a pandemonium of jangling and flashing and squawking and howling and shouting. Radiation. Energy-release. Contragravity distortion effects. Infra-red output. A welter of indecipherable radio and com-munication-screen signals. Radar and scanner-ray beams from the planet.

Trask's fist began hurting; he found that he had been pounding the desk in front of him with it. He stopped it.

"We caught him, we caught him!" he was yelling hoarsely. "Full speed in, continuous ac-celeration, as much as we can stand. We'll worry about decelerating when we're in shooting distance."

The planet grew steadily larger; Karffard was taking him at his word about continuous accel-eration. There'd be a Gehenna of a bill to pay when they started decelerating. On the planet, more bombs were going off just outside atmosphere beyond the sunset line.

"Ship observed. Altitude about a hundred to five hundred miles-hundreds, not thousands —
35° North Latitude, 15° west of the sunset line. Ship is under fire, bomb explosions near her,"
a voice whooped.

Somebody else was yelling that the city lights were really burning cities, or burning forests.
The first voice, having stopped, broke in again:

"Ship is visible in telescopic screen, just at the sunset line. And there's another ship detected
but not visible, somewhere around the equator, and a third one somewhere out of sight, we
can just get the fringe of her contragravity field around the planet."

That meant there were two sides, and a fight. Unless Dunnan had picked up a third ship,
somewhere. The telescopic view shifted; for a moment the planet was completely off-screen,
and then its curvature came into the screen against a star-scattered background. They were
almost in to two thousand miles now; Karffard was yelling to stop acceleration and trying to
put the ship into a spiral orbit. Suddenly they caught a glimpse of one of the ships.

"She's in trouble." That was Paul Koreff's voice. "She's leaking air and water vapor like crazy."

"Well, is she a good guy or a bad guy?" Morland was yelling back, as though Koreff's spectroscopes could distinguish. Koreff ignored that.

"Another ship making signal," he said. "She's the one coming up over the equator. Sword-
World impulse code; her communication-screen combination, and an identify-yourself."

Karffard punched out the combination as Koreff furnished it. While Trask was desperately
willing his face into immobility, the screen lighted. It wasn't Andray Dunnan; that was a disappointment. It was almost as good, though. His henchman, Sir Nevil Ormm.

"Well, Sir Nevil! A pleasant surprise," he heard himself saying. "We last met on the terrace
at Karvall House, did we not?"

For once, the paper-white face of Andray Dunnan's *âme damnée* showed expression, but
whether it was fear, surprise, shock, hatred, anger, or what combination of them, Trask could
no more than guess.

"Trask! Satan curse you...!"

Then the screen went blank. In the telescopic screen, the other ship came on unfalteringly.
Paul Koreff, who had gotten more data on mass, engine energy-output and dimensions, was
identifying her as the *Enterprise*.

"Well, go for her! Give her everything!"

They didn't need the order; Vann Larch was speaking rapidly into his hand-phone, and Alvyn
Karffard was hurling his voice all over the *Nemesis*, warning of sudden deceleration and direction change, and while he was speaking, things in the command room began sliding. In the
telescopic screen, the other ship was plainly visible; he could see the oval patch of black with
the blue crescent, and in his screen Dunnan would be seeing the sword-impaled skull of the
Nemesis.

If only he could be sure Dunnan was there to see it. If it had only been Dunnan's face,
instead of Ormm's, that he had seen in the screen. As it was, he couldn't be sure, and if one of
the missiles that were already going out made a lucky hit, he might never be sure. He didn't
care who killed Dunnan, or how. All he wanted was to know that Dunnan's death had set him
free from a self-assumed obligation that was now meaningless to him.

The *Enterprise* launched counter-missiles; so did the *Nemesis*. There were momentarily un-
bearable flashes of pure energy and from them globes of incandescence spread and vanished.
Something must have gotten through; red lights flashed on the damage board. It had been
something heavy enough even to jolt the huge mass of the *Nemesis*. At the same time, the
other ship took a hit from something that would have vaporized her had she not been armored
in collapsium. Then, as they passed close together, guns hammered back and forth along with
missiles, and then the *Enterprise* was out of sight around the horizon.

Another ship, the size of Otto Harkaman's *Corisande II*, was approaching; she bore a tapering, red-nailed feminine hand dangling a planet by a string. They rushed toward each other, planting a garden of evanescent fire-flowers between them; they pounded one another with guns, and then they sped apart. At the same time, Paul Koreff was picking up an impulse-code signal from the third, crippled, ship; a screen combination. Trask punched it out as he received it.

A man in space armor was looking out of the screen. That was bad, if they had to suit up in the command room. They still had air; his helmet was off, but it was attached and hinged back. On his breastplate was a device of a dragonlike beast perched with its tail around a planet, and a crown above. He had a thin, high-cheeked face, with a vertical wrinkle between his eyes, and a clipped blond mustache.

"Who are you, stranger. You're fighting my enemies; does that make you a friend."

"I'm a friend of anybody who owns Andray Dunnan his enemy. Sword-World ship *Nemesis*; I'm Prince Lucas Trask of Tanith, commanding."

"Royal Mardukan ship *Victrix*." The thin-faced man gave a wry laugh. "Not been living up to her name so well. I'm Prince Simon Bentrik, commanding."

"Are you still battle-worthy?"

"We can fire about half our guns; we still have a few missiles left. Seventy per cent of the ship's sealed off, and we've been holed in a dozen places. We have power enough for lift and some steering-way. We can't make lateral way except at the expense of lift."

Which made the *Victrix* practically a stationary target. He yelled over his shoulder at Karffard to cut speed all he could without tearing things apart.

"When that cripple comes into view, start circling around her. Get into a tight circle above her." He turned back to the man in the screen. "If we can get ourselves slowed down enough, we'll do all we can to cover you."

"All you can is all you can; thank you, Prince Trask."

"Here comes the *Enterprise*!" Karffard shouted, with obscenely blasphemous embellishments. "She hairpinned on us."

"Well, do something about her!"

Vann Larch was already doing it. The *Enterprise* had taken damage in the last exchange; Koreff's spectroscopes showed her halo-ed with air and water vapor. Her instruments would be getting the same story from the *Nemesis*; wedge-shaped segments extending six to eight decks in were sealed off in several places. Then the only thing that could be seen with certainty was the blaze of mutually destroying missiles between. The short-range gun duel began and ended as they passed.

In the screen, he had seen a fat round-nosed thing come up from the *Victrix*, curving far out ahead of the passing *Enterprise*. She was almost out of sight around the planet when she ran head-on into it, and vanished in an awesome blaze. For a moment, he thought she had been destroyed, then she lurched into sight and went around the curvature of Audhumla.

Trask and the Mardukan were shaking hands with themselves at each other in their screens; everybody in the *Nemesis* command room was screaming: "Well shot, *Victrix*! Well shot!"

Then the *Yo-Yo* was coming around again, and Vann Larch was saying, "Gehenna with this fooling around! I'll fix the expurgated unprintability!"

He yelled orders —a jumble of code letters and numbers-and things began going out. Most of them blew up in space. Then the *Yo-Yo* blew up, very quietly, as things do where there is no air to carry shock-and sound-waves, but very brilliantly. There was brief daylight all over the night side of the planet.

"That was our planetbuster," Larch said. "I don't know what we'll use on Dunnan."

"I didn't know we had one," Trask admitted.

"Otto had a couple built on Beowulf. The Beowulfers are good nuclear weaponeers."

The *Enterprise* came back, hastily, to see what had blown up. Larch put off another entertainment of small stuff, with a fifty megaton thermonuclear, viewscreen-piloted, among them. It had its own arsenal of small missiles, and it got through. In the telescopic screen, a jagged hole was visible just below the equator of the *Enterprise*, the edges curling outward. Something, possibly a heavy missile in an open tube, ready for launching, had gone off inside her. What the inside of the ship was like, or how many of her company were still alive, was hard to guess.

There were some, and her launchers were still spewing out missiles. They were intercepted and blew up. The hull of the *Enterprise* bulked huge in the guidance-screen of the missile and filled it; the jagged crater that had obliterated the bottom of Dunnan's blue crescent blazon spread to fill the whole screen. The screen went milky white as the pickup went off.

All the other screens blazed briefly, until their filters went on. Even afterward, they glared like the cloud-veiled sun of Gram at high noon. Finally, when the light-intensity had dropped and the filters went off, there was nothing left of the *Enterprise* but an orange haze.

Somebody-Paytrik, Baron Morland, he saw-was pounding him on the back and screaming inarticulately in his ear. A dozen space-armored officers with planet-perched dragons on their breasts were crowding beside Prince Bentrik in the screen from the *Victrix*, whooping like drunken bisonoid-herders on payday night.

"I wonder," he said, almost inaudibly, "if I'll ever know if Andray Dunnan was on that ship."

XIX

Prince Trask of Tanith and Prince Simon Bentrik were dining together on an upper terrace of what had originally been the mansion house of a Federation period plantation. It had been a number of other things since; now it was the municipal building of a town that had grown around it, which had, somehow, escaped undamaged from the Dunnan blitz. Normally about five or ten thousand, the place was now jammed with almost fifty thousand homeless refugees from half a dozen other towns that had been destroyed, overflowing the buildings and crowding into a sprawling camp of hastily built huts and shelters, and already permanent buildings were going up to accommodate them. Everybody, locals, Mardukans and Space Vikings, had been busy with the work of relief and reconstruction; this was the first meal the two commanders had been able to share in any leisure at all. Prince Bentrik's enjoyment of it was somewhat impaired by the fact that from where he sat he could see, in the distance, the sphere of his disabled ship.

"I doubt we can get her off-planet again, let alone into hyperspace."

"Well, we'll get you and your crew to Marduk in the *Nemesis*, then." They were both speaking loudly, above the clank and clatter of machinery below. "I hope you didn't think I'd leave you stranded here."

"I don't know how either of us will be received. Space Vikings haven't been exactly popular on Marduk, lately. They may thank you for bringing me back to stand trial," Bentrik said bitterly. "Why, I'd have anybody shot who let his ship get caught as I did mine. Those two were down in atmosphere before I knew they'd come out of hyperspace."

"I think they were down on the planet before your ship arrived."

"Oh, that's ridiculous, Prince Trask!" the Mardukan cried. "You can't hide a ship on a planet. Not from the kind of instruments we have in the Royal Navy."

"We have pretty fair detection ourselves," Trask reminded him. "There's one place where you can do it. At the bottom of an ocean, with a thousand or so feet of water over her. That's where I was going to hide the *Nemesis*, if I got here ahead of Dunnan."

Prince Bentrik's fork stopped half way to his mouth. He lowered it slowly to his plate. That was a theory he'd like to accept, if he could.

"But the locals. They didn't know about it."

"They wouldn't. They have no off-planet detection of their own. Come in directly over the ocean, out of the sun, and nobody'd see the ship."

"Is that a regular Space Viking trick?"

"No. I invented it myself, on the way from Seshat. But if Dunnan wanted to ambush your ship, he'd have thought of it, too. It's the only practical way to do it."

Dunnan, or Nevil Ormm; he wished he knew, and was afraid he would go on wishing all his life.

Bentrik started to pick up his fork again, changed his mind, and sipped from his wineglass instead.

"You may find you're quite welcome on Marduk, at that," he said. "These raids have only been a serious problem in the last four years. I believe, as you do, that this enemy of yours is responsible for all of them. We have half the Royal Navy out now, patrolling our trade-planets. Even if he wasn't aboard the *Enterprise* when you blew her up, you've put a name on him and can tell us a good deal about him." He set down the wineglass. "Why, if it weren't so utterly ridiculous, one might even think he was making war on Marduk."

From Trask's viewpoint, it wasn't ridiculous at all. He merely mentioned that Andray Dunnan was psychotic and let it go at that.

The *Victrix* was not completely unrepairable, although quite beyond the resources at hand. A fully equipped engineer-ship from Marduk could patch her hull and replace her Dillinghams and her Abbot lift-and-drive engines and make her temporarily spaceworthy, until she could be gotten to a shipyard. They concentrated on repairing the *Nemesis*, and in another two weeks she was ready for the voyage.

The six hundred hour trip to Marduk passed pleasantly enough. The Mardukan officers were good company, and found their Space Viking opposite numbers equally so. The two crews had become used to working together on Audhumla, and mingled amicably off watch, interesting themselves in each other's hobbies and listening avidly to tales of each other's home planets. The Space Vikings were surprised and disappointed at the somewhat lower intellectual level of the Mardukans. They couldn't understand that; Marduk was supposed to be a civilized planet, wasn't it? The Mardukans were just as surprised, and inclined to be resentful, that the Space Vikings all acted and talked like officers. Hearing of it, Prince Bentrik was also puzzled. Fo'c'sle hands on a Mardukan ship belonged definitely to the lower orders.

"There's still too much free land and free opportunity on the Sword-Worlds," Trask explained. "Nobody does much bowing and scraping to the class above him; he's too busy trying to shove himself up into it. And the men who ship out as Space Vikings are the least class-conscious of the lot. Think my men may have trouble on Marduk about that? They'll all insist on doing their drinking in the swankiest places in town."

"No. I don't think so. Everybody will be so amazed that Space Vikings aren't twelve feet tall, with three horns like a Zarathustra damnthing and a spiked tail like a Fafnir mantichore that they won't even notice anything less. Might do some good, in the long run. Crown Prince Edvard will like your Space Vikings. He's much opposed to class distinctions and caste prejudices. Says they have to be eliminated before we can make democracy really work."

The Mardukans talked a lot about democracy. They thought well of it; their government was a representative democracy. It was also a hereditary monarchy, if that made any kind of sense. Trask's efforts to explain the political and social structure of the Sword-Worlds met the same incomprehension from Bentrik.

"Why, it sounds like feudalism to me!"

"That's right; that's what it is. A king owes his position to the support of his great nobles; they owe theirs to their barons and landholding knights; they owe theirs to their people. There are limits beyond which none of them can go; after that, their vassals turn on them."

"Well, suppose the people of some barony rebel? Won't the king send troops to support the baron?"

"What troops? Outside a personal guard and enough men to police the royal city and hold the crown lands, the king has no troops. If he wants troops, he has to get them from his great nobles; they have to get them from their vassal barons, who raise them by calling out their people." That was another source of dissatisfaction with King Angus of Gram; he had been augmenting his forces by hiring off-planet mercenaries. "And the people won't help some other baron oppress his people; it might be their turn next."

"You mean, the people are armed?" Prince Bentrik was incredulous.

"Great Satan, aren't yours?" Prince Trask was equally surprised. "Then your democracy's a farce, and the people are only free on sufferance. If their ballots aren't secured by arms, they're worthless. Who has the arms on your planet?"

"Why, the Government."

"You mean the King?"

Prince Bentrik was shocked. Certainly not; horrid idea. That would be ... why, it would be *despotism*! Besides, the King wasn't the Government, at all; the Government ruled in the King's name. There was the Assembly; the Chamber of Representatives, and the Chamber of Delegates. The people elected the Representatives, and the Representatives elected the Delegates, and the Delegates elected the Chancellor. Then, there was the Prime Minister; he was appointed by the King, but the King had to appoint him from the party holding the most seats in the Chamber of Representatives, and he appointed the Ministers, who handled the executive work of the Government, only their subordinates in the different Ministries were career-officials who were selected by competitive examination for the bottom jobs and promoted up the bureaucratic ladder from there.

This left Trask wondering if the Mardukan constitution hadn't been devised by Goldberg, the legendary Old Terran inventor who always did everything the hard way. It also left him wondering just how in Gehenna the Government of Marduk ever got anything done.

Maybe it didn't. Maybe that was what saved Marduk from having a real despotism.

"Well, what prevents the Government from enslaving the people? The people can't; you just told me that they aren't armed, and the Government is."

He continued, pausing now and then for breath, to catalogue every tyranny he had ever heard of, from those practiced by the Terran Federation before the Big War to those practiced at Eglonsby on Amaterasu by Pedrosan Pedro. A few of the very mildest were pushing the nobles and people of Gram to revolt against Angus I.

"And in the end," he finished, "the Government would be the only property owner and the only employer on the planet, and everybody else would be slaves, working at assigned tasks, wearing Government-issued clothing and eating Government food, their children educated as the Government prescribes and trained for jobs selected for them by the Government, never reading a book or seeing a play or thinking a thought that the Government had not approved...."

Most of the Mardukans were laughing, now. Some of them were accusing him of being just too utterly ridiculous.

"Why, the people *are* the Government. The people would not legislate themselves into slavery."

He wished Otto Harkaman were there. All he knew of history was the little he had gotten from reading some of Harkaman's books, and the long, rambling conversations aboard ship in hyperspace or in the evenings at Rivington. But Harkaman, he was sure, could have furnished hundreds of instances, on scores of planets and over ten centuries of time, in which people had done exactly that and hadn't known what they were doing, even after it was too late.

"They have something about like that on Aton," one of the Mardukan officers said.

"Oh, Aton; that's a dictatorship, pure and simple. That Planetary Nationalist gang got into control fifty years ago, during the crisis after the war with Baldur...."

"They were voted into power by the people, weren't they?"

"Yes; they were," Prince Bentrik said gravely. "It was an emergency measure, and they were given emergency powers. Once they were in, they made the emergency permanent."

"That couldn't happen on Marduk!" a young nobleman declared.

"It could if Zaspar Makann's party wins control of the Assembly at the next election," somebody else said.

"Oh, then Marduk's safe! The sun'll go nova first," one of the junior Royal Navy officers said.

After that, they began talking about women, a subject any spaceman will drop any other subject to discuss.

Trask made a mental note of the name of Zaspar Makann, and took occasion to bring it up in conversation with his shipboard guests. Every time he talked about Makann to two or more Mardukans, he heard at least three or more opinions about the man. He was a political demagogue; on that everybody agreed. After that, opinions diverged.

Makann was a raving lunatic, and all the followers he had were a handful of lunatics like him. He might be a lunatic, but he had a dangerously large following. Well, not so large; maybe they'd pick up a seat or so in the Assembly, but that was doubtful-not enough of them in any representative district to elect an Assemblyman. He was just a smart crook, milking a lot of half-witted plebeians for all he could get out of them. Not just plebes, either; a lot of industrialists were secretly financing him, in hope that he would help them break up the labor unions. You're nuts; everybody knew the labor unions were backing him, hoping he'd scare the employers into granting concessions. You're both nuts; he was backed by the mercantile interests; they were hoping he'd run the Gilgameshers off the planet.

Well, that was one thing you had to give him credit for. He wanted to run out the Gilgameshers. Everybody was in favor of that.

Now, Trask could remember something he'd gotten from Harkaman. There had been Hitler, back at the end of the First Century Pre-Atomic; hadn't he gotten into power because everybody was in favor of running out the Christians, or the Moslems, or the Albigensians, or somebody?

XX

Marduk had three moons; a big one, fifteen hundred miles in diameter, and two insignificant twenty-mile chunks of rock. The big one was fortified, and a couple of ships were in orbit around it. The *Nemesis* was challenged as she emerged from her last hyperjump; both ships broke orbit and came out to meet her, and several more were detected lifting away from the planet.

Prince Bentrik took the communication screen, and immediately encountered difficulties. The commandant, even after the situation had been explained twice to him, couldn't understand. A Royal Navy fleet unit knocked out in a battle with Space Vikings was bad enough, but being rescued and brought to Marduk by another Space Viking simply didn't make sense. He then screened the Royal Palace at Malverton, on the planet; first he was icily polite to somebody several echelons below him in the peerage, and then respectfully polite to somebody he addressed as Prince Vandarvant. Finally, after some minutes' wait, a frail, white-haired man in a little black cap-of-maintenance appeared in the screen. Prince Bentrik instantly sprang to his feet. So did all the other Mardukans in the command room.

"Your Majesty! I am most deeply honored!"

"Are you all right, Simon?" the old gentleman asked solicitously. "They haven't done anything to you, have they?"

"Saved my life, and my men's, and treated me like a friend and a comrade, Your Majesty. Have I your permission to present, informally, their commander, Prince Trask of Tanith?"

"Indeed you may, Simon. I owe the gentleman my deepest thanks."

"His Majesty, Mikhyl the Eighth, Planetary King of Marduk," Prince Bentrik said. "His Highness, Lucas, Prince Trask, Planetary Viceroy of Tanith for his Majesty Angus the First of Gram."

The elderly monarch bowed his head slightly; Trask bowed a little more deeply, from the waist.

"I am very happy, Prince Trask, first, I confess, at the safe return of my kinsman Prince Bentrik, and then at the honor of meeting one in the confidence of my fellow sovereign King Angus of Gram. I will never be ungrateful for what you did for my cousin and for his officers and men. You must stay at the Palace while you are on this planet; I am giving orders for your reception, and I wish you to be formally presented to me this evening." He hesitated briefly. "Gram; that is one of the Sword-Worlds, is it not?" Another brief hesitation. "Are you really a Space Viking, Prince Trask?"

Maybe he'd expected Space Vikings to have three horns and a spiked tail and stand twelve feet tall, himself.

It took several hours for the *Nemesis* to get into orbit. Bentrik spent most of them in a screen-booth, and emerged visibly relieved.

"Nobody's going to be sticky about what happened on Audhumla," he told Trask. "There will be a Board of Inquiry. I'm afraid I had to mix you up in that. It's not only about the action on Audhumla; everybody from the Space Minister down wants to hear what you know about this fellow Dunnan. Like yourself, we all hope he went to Em-See-Square along with his flagship, but we can't take it for granted. We have over a dozen trade-planets to protect, and he's hit more than half of them already."

The process of getting into orbit took them around the planet several times, and it was a more impressive spectacle at each circuit. Of course, Marduk had a population of almost two billion, and had been civilized, with no hiatus of Neobarbarism, since it had first been colonized in the Fourth Century. Even so, the Space Vikings were amazed-and stubbornly refusing to show it-at what they saw in the telescopic screens.

"Look at that city!" Paytrik Morland whispered. "We talk about the civilized planets, but I never realized they were anything like this. Why, this makes Excalibur look like Tanith!"

The city was Malverton, the capital; like any city of a contragravity-using people, it lay in a rough circle of buildings towering out of green interspaces, surrounded by the smaller circles of spaceports and industrial suburbs. The difference was that any of these were as large as Camelot on Excalibur or four Wardshavens on Gram, and Malverton itself was almost half the size of the whole barony of Traskon.

"They aren't any more civilized that we are, Paytrik. There are just more of them. If there were two billion people on Gram-which I hope there never will be-Gram would have cities like this, too."

One thing; the government of a planet like Marduk would have to be something more elaborate than the loose feudalism of the Sword-Worlds. Maybe this Goldberg-ocracy of theirs had been forced upon them by the sheer complexity of the population and its problems.

Alvyn Karffard took a quick look around him to make sure none of the Mardukans were in earshot.

"I don't care how many people they have," he said. "Marduk can be had. A wolf never cares how many sheep there are in a flock. With twenty ships, we could take this planet like we took Eglonsby. There'd be losses coming in, sure, but after we were in and down, we'd have it."

"Where would we get twenty ships?"

Tanith, at a pinch, could muster five or six, counting the free Space Vikings who used the base facilities; they would have to leave a couple to hold the planet. Beowulf had one, and another almost completed, and now there was an Amaterasu ship. But to assemble a Space Viking armada of twenty....He shook his head. The real reason why Space Vikings had never raided a civilized planet successfully had always been their inability to combine under one command in sufficient strength.

Besides, he didn't want to raid Marduk. A raid, if successful, would yield immense treasures, but cause a hundred, even a thousand, times as much destruction, and he didn't want to destroy anything civilized.

The landing stages of the palace were crowded when he and Prince Bentrik landed, and, at a discreet distance, swarms of air-vehicles circled, creating a control problem for the police. Parting from Bentrik, he was escorted to the suite prepared for him; it was luxurious in the extreme but scarcely above Sword-World standards. There were a surprising number of human servants, groveling and fawning and getting underfoot and doing work robots could have been doing better. What robots there were were inefficient, and much work and ingenuity had been lavished on efforts to copy human form to the detriment of function.

After getting rid of most of the superfluous servants, he put on a screen and began sampling the newscasts. There were telescopic views of the *Nemesis* from some craft on orbit nearby, and he watched the officers and men of the *Victrix* being disembarked; there were other views of their landing at some naval installation on the ground, and he could see reporters being chevied away by Navy ground-police. And there was a wide range of commentary opinion.

The Government had already denied that, (1) Prince Bentrik had captured the *Nemesis* and brought her in as a prize, and, (2) the Space Vikings had captured Prince Bentrik and were holding him for ransom. Beyond that, the Government was trying to sit on the whole story, and the Opposition was hinting darkly at corrupt deals and sinister plots. Prince Bentrik arrived in the midst of an impassioned tirade against pusillanimous traitors surrounding his Majesty who were betraying Marduk to the Space Vikings.

"Why doesn't your Government publish the facts and put a stop to that nonsense?" Trask asked.

"Oh, let them rave," Bentrik replied. "The longer the Government waits, the more they'll be ridiculed when the facts are published."

Or, the more people will be convinced that the Government had something to hush up, and had to take time to construct a plausible story. He kept the thought to himself. It was their government; how they mismanaged it was their own business. He found that there was no bartending robot; he had to have a human servant bring drinks. He made up his mind to have a few of the *Nemesis* robots sent down to him.

The formal presentation would be in the evening; there would be a dinner first, and because Trask had not yet been formally presented, he couldn't dine with the King, but because he was, or claimed to be, Viceroy of Tanith, he ranked as a chief of state and would dine with the Crown Prince, to whom there would be an informal introduction first.

This took place in a small ante-chamber off the banquet hall; the Crown Prince and Crown Princess and Princess Bentrik were there when they arrived. The Crown Prince was a man of middle age, graying at the temples, with the glassy stare that betrayed contact lenses. The resemblance between him and his father was apparent; both had the same studious and im-practical expression, and might have been professors on the same university faculty. He shook hands with Trask, assuring him of the gratitude of the Court and Royal Family.

"You know, Simon is next in succession, after myself and my little daughter," he said. "That's too close to take chances with him." He turned to Bentrik. "I'm afraid this is your last space adventure, Simon. You'll have to be a spaceport spaceman from now on."

"I shan't be sorry," Princess Bentrik said. "And if anybody owes Prince Trask gratitude, I do." She pressed his hands warmly. "Prince Trask, my son wants to meet you, very badly. He's ten years old, and he thinks Space Vikings are romantic heroes."

"He should be one, for a while."

He should just see a planet Space Vikings had raided.

Most of the people at the upper end of the table were diplomats-ambassadors from Odin and Baldur and Isis and Ishtar and Aton and the other civilized worlds. No doubt they hadn't actually expected horns and a spiked tail, or even tattooing and a nose ring, but after all, Space Vikings were just some sort of Neobarbarians, weren't they? On the other hand, they had all seen views and gotten descriptions of the *Nemesis*, and had heard about the ship-action on Audhumla, and this Prince Trask—a Space Viking prince; that sounded civilized enough-had saved a life with only three other lives, one almost at an end, between it and the throne. And they had heard about the screen conversation with King Mikhyl. So they were courteous through the meal, and tried to get as close as possible to him in the procession to the throne room.

King Mikhyl wore a golden crown topped by the planetary emblem, which must have weighed twice as much as a combat helmet, and fur-edged robes that would weigh more than a suit of space armor. They weren't nearly as ornate, though, as the regalia of King Angus I of Gram. He rose to clasp Prince Bentrik's hand, calling him "dear cousin," and congratulating him on his gallant fight and fortunate escape. That knocks any court-martial talk on the head, Trask thought. He remained standing to shake hands with Trask, calling him "valued friend to me and my house." First person singular; that must be causing some lifted eyebrows.

Then the King sat down, and the rest of the roomful filed up onto the dais to be received, and finally it was over and the king rose and proceeded, followed by his immediate suite between the bowing and curtsying court and out the wide doors. After a decent interval, Crown Prince Edvard escorted him and Prince Bentrik down the same route, the others falling in behind, and across the hall to the ballroom, where there was soft music and refreshments. It wasn't too unlike a court reception on Excalibur, except that the drinks and canapes were being dispensed by human servants.

He was wondering what sort of court functions Angus the First of Gram was holding by now.

After half an hour, a posse of court functionaries approached and informed him that it had pleased his Majesty to command Prince Trask to attend him in his private chambers. There was an audible gasp at this; both Prince Bentrik and the Crown Prince were trying not to grin too broadly. Evidently this didn't happen too often. He followed the functionaries from the ballroom, and the eyes of everybody else followed him.

Old King Mikhyl received him alone, in a small, comfortably shabby room behind vast ones of incredible splendor. He wore fur-lined slippers and a loose robe with a fur collar, and his little black cap-of-maintenance. He was standing when Trask entered; when the guards closed the door and left them alone, he beckoned Trask to a couple of chairs, with a low table, on which were decanters and glasses and cigars, between.

"It's a presumption on royal authority to summon you from the ballroom," he began, after they had seated themselves and filled glasses. "You are quite the cynosure, you know."

"I'm grateful to Your Majesty. It's both comfortable and quiet here, and I can sit down. Your Majesty was the center of attention in the throne room, yet I seemed to detect a look of relief as you left it."

"I try to hide it, as much as possible." The old King took off the little gold-circled cap and hung it on the back of his chair. "Majesty can be rather wearying, you know."

So he could come here and put it off. Trask felt that some gesture should be made on his own part. He unfastened the dress-dagger from his belt and laid it on the table. The King nodded.

"Now, we can be a couple of honest tradesmen, our shops closed for the evening, relaxing over our wine and tobacco," he said. "Eh, Goodman Lucas?"

It seemed like an initiation into a secret society whose ritual he must guess at step by step.

"Right, Goodman Mikhyl."

They lifted their glasses to each other and drank; Goodman Mikhyl offered cigars, and Goodman Lucas held a light for him.

"I hear a few hard things about your trade, Goodman Lucas."

"All true, and mostly understated. We're professional murderers and robbers, as one of my fellow tradesmen says. The worst of it is that robbery and murder become just that: a trade, like servicing robots or selling groceries."

"Yet you fought two other Space Vikings to cover my cousin's crippled *Victrix*. Why?"

So he must tell his tale, so worn and smooth, again. King Mikhyl's cigar went out while he listened.

"And you have been hunting him ever since? And now, you can't be sure whether you killed him or not?"

"I'm afraid I didn't. The man in the screen is the only man Dunnan can really trust. One or the other would stay wherever he has his base all the time."

"And when you do kill him; what then?"

"I'll go on trying to make a civilized planet of Tanith. Sooner or later, I'll have one quarrel too many with King Angus, and then we will be our Majesty Lucas the First of Tanith, and we will sit on a throne and receive our subjects. And I'll be glad when I can get my crown off and talk to a few men who call me 'shipmate,' instead of 'Your Majesty.'"

"Well, it would violate professional ethics for me to advise a subject to renounce his sovereign, of course, but that might be an excellent thing. You met the ambassador from Ithavoll at dinner, did you not? Three centuries ago, Ithavoll was a colony of Marduk-it seems we can't afford colonies, any more-and it seceded from us. Ithavoll was then a planet like your Tanith seems to be. Today, it is a civilized world, and one of Marduk's best friends. You know, sometimes I think a few lights are coming on again, here and there in the Old Federation. If so, you Space Vikings are helping to light them."

"You mean the planets we use as bases, and the things we teach the locals?"

"That, too, of course. Civilization needs civilized technologies. But they have to be used for civilized ends. Do you know anything about a Space Viking raid on Aton, over a century ago?"

"Six ships from Haulteclere; four destroyed, the other two returned damaged and without booty."

The King of Marduk nodded.

"That raid saved civilization on Aton. There were four great nations; the two greatest were at the brink of war, and the others were waiting to pounce on the exhausted victor and then fight each other for the spoils. The Space Vikings forced them to unite. Out of that temporary alliance came the League for Common Defense, and from that the Planetary Republic. The Republic's a dictatorship, now, and just between Goodman Mikhyl and Goodman Lucas it's a nasty one and our Majesty's Government doesn't like it at all. It will be smashed sooner or later, but they'll never go back to divided sovereignty and nationalism again. The Space Vikings frightened them out of that when the dangers inherent in it couldn't. Maybe this man Dunnan will do the same for us on Marduk."

"You have troubles?"

"You've seen decivilized planets. How does it happen?"

"I know how it's happened on a good many: War. Destruction of cities and industries. Survivors among ruins, too busy keeping their own bodies alive to try to keep civilization alive. Then they lose all knowledge of how to be civilized."

"That's catastrophic decivilization. There is also decivilization by erosion, and while it's going on, nobody notices it. Everybody is proud of their civilization, their wealth and culture. But trade is falling off; fewer ships come in each year. So there is boastful talk about planetary self-sufficiency; who needs off-planet trade anyhow? Everybody seems to have money, but the government is always broke. Deficit spending-and always the vital social services for which the government has to spend money. The most vital one, of course, is buying votes to keep the government in power. And it gets harder for the government to get anything done.

"The soldiers are sloppier at drill, and their uniforms and weapons aren't taken care of. The noncoms are insolent. And more and more parts of the city are dangerous at night, and then even in the daytime. And it's been years since a new building went up, and the old ones aren't being repaired any more."

Trask closed his eyes. Again, he could feel the mellow sun of Gram on his back, and hear the laughing voices on the lower terrace, and he was talking to Lothar Ffayle and Rovard Grauffis and Alex Gorram and Cousin Nikkolay and Otto Harkaman. He said:

"And finally, nobody bothers fixing anything up. And the power-reactors stop, and nobody seems to be able to get them started again. It hasn't quite gotten that far on the Sword-Worlds yet."

"It hasn't here, either. Yet." Goodman Mikhyl slipped away; King Mikhyl VIII looked across the low table at his guest. "Prince Trask, have you heard of a man named Zaspar Makann?"

"Occasionally. Nothing good about him."

"He is the most dangerous man on this planet," the King said. "And I can make nobody believe it. Not even my son."

XXI

Prince Bentrik's ten-year-old son, Count Steven of Ravary, wore the uniform of an ensign of the Royal Navy; he was accompanied by his tutor, an elderly Navy captain. They both stopped in the doorway of Trask's suite, and the boy saluted smartly.

"Permission to come aboard, sir?" he asked.

"Welcome aboard, count; captain. Belay the ceremony and find seats; you're just in time for second breakfast."

As they sat down, he aimed his ultraviolet light-pencil at a serving robot. Unlike Mardukan robots, which looked like surrealist conceptions of Pre-Atomic armored knights, it was a smooth ovoid floating a few inches from the floor on its own contragravity; as it approached, its top opened like a bursting beetle shell and hinged trays of food swung out. The boy looked at it in fascination.

"Is that a Sword-World robot, sir, or did you capture it somewhere?"

"It's one of our own." He was pardonably proud; it had been built on Tanith a year before. "Has an ultrasonic dishwasher underneath, and it does some cooking on top, at the back."

The elderly captain was, if anything, even more impressed than his young charge. He knew what went into it, and he had some conception of the society that would develop things like that.

"I take it you don't use many human servants, with robots like that," he said.

"Not many. We're all low-population planets, and nobody wants to be a servant."

"We have too many people on Marduk, and all of them want soft jobs as nobles' servants," the captain said. "Those that want any kind of jobs."

"You need all your people for fighting men, don't you?" the boy count asked.

"Well, we need a good many. The smallest of our ships will carry five hundred men; most of them around eight hundred."

The captain lifted an eyebrow. The complement of the *Victrix* had been three hundred, and she'd been a big ship. Then he nodded.

"Of course. Most of them are ground-fighters."

That started Count Steven off. Questions, about battles and raids and booty and the planets Trask had seen.

"I wish I were a Space Viking!"

"Well, you can't be, Count Ravary. You're an officer of the Royal Navy. You're supposed to fight Space Vikings."

"I won't fight you."

"You'd have to, if the King commanded," the old captain told him.

"No. Prince Trask is my friend. He saved my father's life."

"And I won't fight you, either, count. We'll make a lot of fireworks, and then we'll each go home and claim victory. How would that be?"

"I've heard of things like that," the captain said. "We had a war with Odin, seventy years ago, that was mostly that sort of battles."

"Besides, the King is Prince Trask's friend, too," the boy insisted. "Father and Mummy heard him say so, right on the Throne. Kings don't lie when they're on the Throne, do they?"

"Good Kings don't," Trask told him.

"Ours is a good King," the young Count of Ravary declared proudly. "I would do anything my King commanded. Except fight Prince Trask. My house owes Prince Trask a debt."

Trask nodded approvingly. "That's the way a Sword-World noble would talk, Count Steven," he said.

The Board of Inquiry, that afternoon, was more like a small and very sedate cocktail party. An Admiral Shefter, who seemed to be very high high-brass, presided while carefully avoiding the appearance of doing so. Alvyn Karffard and Vann Larch and Paytrik Morland were there from the *Nemesis*, and Bentrik and several of the officers from the *Victrix*, and there were a couple of Naval Intelligence officers, and somebody from Operational Planning, and from Ship Construction and Research & Development. They chatted pleasantly and in a deceptively random manner for a while. Then Shefter said:

"Well, there's no blame or censure of any sort for the way Commodore Prince Bentrik was surprised. That couldn't have been avoided, at the time." He looked at the Research & Development officer. "It shouldn't be allowed to happen many more times, though."

"Not many more, sir. I'd say it'll take my people a month, and then the time it'll take to get all the ships equipped as they come in."

Ship Construction didn't think that would take too long.

"We'll see to it that you get full information on the new submarine detection system, Prince Trask," the admiral said.

"You gentlemen understand you'll have to keep it under your helmets, though," one of the Intelligence men added. "If it got out that we were informing Space Vikings about our technical secrets...." He felt the back of his neck in a way that made Trask suspect that beheadment was the customary form of execution on Marduk.

"We'll have to find out where the fellow has his base," Operational Planning said. "I take it, Prince Trask, that you're not going to assume that he was on his flagship when you blew it, and just put paid to him and forget him?"

"Oh, no. I'm assuming that he wasn't. I don't believe he and Ormm went anywhere on the same ship, after he came out here and established a base. I think one of them would stay home all the time."

"Well, we'll give you everything we have on them," Shefter promised. "Most of that is classified and you'll have to keep quiet about it, too. I just skimmed over the summary of what you gave us; I daresay we'll both get a lot of new information. Have you any idea at all where he might be based, Prince Trask?"

"Only that we think it's a non-Terra-type planet." He told them about Dunnan's heavy purchases of air-and-water recycling equipment and carniculture and hydroponic material. "That, of course, helps a great deal."

"Yes; there are only about five million planets in the former Federation space-volume that are inhabitable in artificial environment. Including a few completely covered by seas, where you could put in underwater dome cities if you had the time and material."

One of the Intelligence officers had been nursing a glass with a tiny remnant of cocktail in it. He downed it suddenly, filled the glass again, and glowered at it in silence for a while. Then he drank it briskly and refilled it.

"What I should like to know," he said, "is how this double obscenity of a Dunnan knew we'd have a ship on Audhumla just when we did," he said. "Your talking about underwater dome-cities reminded me of it. I don't think he just pulled that planet out of a hat and then went there prepared to sit on the bottom of the ocean for a year and a half waiting for something to turn up. I think he knew the *Victrix* was coming to Audhumla, and just about when."

"I don't like that, commodore," Shefter said.

"You think I do, sir?" the Intelligence officer countered. "There it is, though. We all have to face it."

"We do," Shefter agreed. "Get on it, commodore, and I don't need to caution you to screen everybody you put onto it very carefully." He looked at his own glass; it had a bare thimbleful in the bottom. He replenished it slowly and carefully. "It's been a long time since the Navy's had anything like this to worry about." He turned to Trask. "I suppose I can get in touch with you at the Palace whenever I must?"

"Well, Prince Trask and I have been invited as house-guests at Prince Edvard's, I mean Baron Cragdale's, hunting lodge," Bentrik said. "We'll be going there directly from here."

"Ah." Admiral Shefter smiled slightly. Beside not having three horns and a spiked tail, this Space Viking was definitely *persona grata* with the Royal Family. "Well, we'll keep in contact, Prince Trask."

The hunting lodge where Crown Prince Edvard was simple Baron Cragdale lay at the head of a sharply-sloping mountain valley down which a river tumbled. Mountains rose on either side in high scarps, some topped with perpetual snow, glaciers curling down from them. The lower ranges were forested, as was the valley between, and there was a red-mauve alpenglow on the great peak that rose from the head of the valley. For the first time in over a year, Elaine was with him, silently clinging to him to see the beauty of it through his eyes. He had thought that she had gone from him forever.

The hunting lodge itself was not quite what a Sword-Worlder would expect a hunting lodge to be. At first sight, from the air, it looked like a sundial, a slender tower rising like a gnomen above a circle of low buildings and formal gardens. The boat landed at the foot of it, and he and Prince and Princess Bentrik and the young Count of Ravary and his tutor descended. Immediately, they were beset by a flurry of servants; the second boat, with the Bentrik servants and their luggage, was circling in to land. Elaine, he discovered, wasn't with him any more, and then he was separated from the Bentriks and was being floated up an inside shaft in a lifter-car. More servants installed him in his rooms, unpacked his cases, drew his bath and even tried to help him take it, and fussed over him while he dressed.

There were over a score for dinner. Bentrik had warned him that he'd find some odd types; maybe he meant that they wouldn't all be nobles. Among the commoners there were some professors, mostly social sciences, a labor leader, a couple of Representatives and a member of the Chamber of Delegates, and a couple of social workers, whatever that meant.

His own table companion was a Lady Valerie Alvarath. She was beautiful—black hair, and almost startlingly blue eyes, a combination unusual in the Sword-Worlds —and she was intelligent, or at least cleverly articulate. She was introduced as the lady-companion of the Crown Prince's daughter. When he asked where the daughter was, she laughed.

"She won't be helping entertain visiting Space Vikings for a long time, Prince Trask. She is precisely eight years old; I saw her getting ready for bed before I came down here. I'll look in on her after dinner."

Then the Crown Princess Melanie, on his other hand, asked him some question about Sword-World court etiquette. He stuck to generalities, and what he could remember from a presentation at the court of Excalibur during his student days. These people had a monarchy since before Gram had been colonized; he wasn't going to admit that Gram's had been established since he went off-planet. The table was small enough for everybody to hear what he was saying and to feed questions to him. It lasted all through the meal, and continued when they adjourned for coffee in the library.

"But what about your form of government, your social structure, that sort of thing?" somebody, impatient with the artificialities of the court, wanted to know.

"Well, we don't use the word government very much," he replied. "We talk a lot about authority and sovereignty, and I'm afraid we burn entirely too much powder over it, but government always seems to us like sovereignty interfering in matters that don't concern it. As long as sovereignty maintains a reasonable semblance of good public order and makes the more serious forms of crime fairly hazardous for the criminals, we're satisfied."

"But that's just negative. Doesn't the government do anything positive for the people?"

He tried to explain the Sword-World feudal system to them. It was hard, he found, to explain something you have taken for granted all your life to somebody who is quite unfamiliar with it.

"But the government-the sovereignty, since you don't like the other word-doesn't do anything for the people!" one of the professors objected. "It leaves all the social services to the whim of the individual lord or baron."

"And the people have no voice at all; why, that's tyranny," a professor Assemblyman added.

He tried to explain that the people had a very distinct and commanding voice, and that barons and lords who wanted to stay alive listened attentively to it. The Assemblyman changed his mind; that wasn't tyranny, it was anarchy. And the professor was still insistent about who performed the social services.

"If you mean schools and hospitals and keeping the city clean, the people do that for themselves. The government, if you want to think of it as that, just sees to it that nobody's shooting at them while they're doing it."

"That isn't what Professor Pullwell means, Lucas. He means old-age pensions," Prince Bentrik said. "Like this thing Zaspar Makann's whooping for."

He'd heard about that, on the voyage from Audhumla. Every person on Marduk would be retired on an adequate pension after thirty years regular employment or at the age of sixty. When he had wanted to know where the money would come from, he had been told that there would be a sales tax, and that the pensions must all be spent within thirty days, which would stimulate business, and the increased business would provide tax money to pay the pensions.

"We have a joke about three Gilgameshers space-wrecked on an uninhabited planet," he said. "Ten years later, when they were rescued, all three were immensely wealthy, from trading hats with each other. That's about the way this thing will work."

One of the lady social workers bristled; it wasn't right to make derogatory jokes about racial groups. One of the professors harrumphed; wasn't a parallel at all, the Self-Sustaining Rotary Pension Plan was perfectly feasible. With a shock, Trask recalled that he was a professor of economics.

Alvyn Karffard wouldn't need any twenty ships to loot Marduk. Just infiltrate it with about a hundred smart confidence men and inside a year they'd own everything on it.

That started them all off on Zaspar Makann, though. Some of them thought he had a few good ideas, but was damaging his own case by extremism. One of the wealthier nobles said that he was a reproach to the ruling class; it was their fault that people like Makann could gain a following. One old gentleman said that maybe the Gilgameshers were to blame, themselves, for some of the animosity toward them. He was immediately set upon by all the others and verbally torn to pieces on the spot.

Trask didn't feel it proper to quote Goodman Mikhyl to this crowd. He took the responsibility upon himself for saying:

"From what I've heard of him, I think he's the most serious threat to civilized society on Marduk."

They didn't call him crazy, after all he was a guest, but they didn't ask him what he meant, either. They merely told him that Makann was a crackpot with a contemptible following of half-wits, and just wait till the election and see what happened.

"I'm inclined to agree with Prince Trask," Bentrik said soberly. "And I'm afraid the election results will be a shock to us, not to Makann."

He hadn't talked that way on the ship. Maybe he'd been looking around and doing some thinking, since he got back. He might have been talking to Goodman Mikhyl, too. There was a screen in the room. He nodded toward it.

"He's speaking at a rally of the People's Welfare Party at Drepplin, now," he said. "May I put it on, to show you what I mean?"

When the Crown Prince assented, he snapped on the screen and twiddled at the selector.

A face looked out of it. The features weren't Andray Dunnan's —the mouth was wider, the cheekbones broader, the chin more rounded. But his eyes were Dunnan's, as Trask had seen them on the terrace of Karvall House. Mad eyes. His high-pitched voice screamed:

"Our beloved sovereign is a prisoner! He is surrounded by traitors! The Ministries are full of them! They are all traitors! The bloodthirsty reactionaries of the falsely so-called Crown Loyalist Party! The grasping conspiracy of the interstellar bankers! The dirty Gilgameshers! They are all leagued together in an unholy conspiracy! And now this Space Viking, this bloody-handed monster from the Sword-Worlds...."

"Shut the horrible man off," somebody was yelling, in competition with the hypnotic scream of the speaker.

The trouble was, they couldn't. They could turn off the screen, but Zaspar Makann would go on screaming, and millions all over the planet would still hear him. Bentrik twiddled the selector. The voice stuttered briefly, and then came echoing out of the speaker, but this time the pickup was somewhere several hundred feet above a great open park. It was densely packed with people, most of them wearing clothes a farm tramp on Gram wouldn't be found dead in, but here and there among them were blocks of men in what was almost but not quite military uniform, each with a short and thick swagger-stick with a knobbed head. Across the park, in the distance, the head and shoulders of Zaspar Makann loomed a hundred feet high in a huge screen. Whenever he stopped for breath, a shout would go up, beginning with the blocks of uniformed men:

"Makann! Makann! Makann the Leader! Makann to Power!"

"You even let him have a private army?" he asked the Crown Prince.

"Oh, those silly buffoons and their musical-comedy uniforms," the Crown Prince shrugged. "They aren't armed."

"Not visibly," he granted. "Not yet."

"I don't know where they'd get arms."

"No, Your Highness," Prince Bentrik said. "Neither do I. That's what I'm worried about."

XXII

He succeeded, the next morning, in convincing everybody that he wanted to be alone for a while, and was sitting in a garden, watching the rainbows in the midst of a big waterfall across the valley. Elaine would have liked that, but she wasn't with him, now.

Then he realized that somebody was speaking to him, in a small, bashful voice. He turned, and saw a little girl in shorts and a sleeveless jacket, holding in her arms a long-haired blond puppy with big ears and appealing eyes.

"Hello, both of you," he said.

The puppy wriggled and tried to lick the girl's face.

"Don't, Mopsy. We want to talk to this gentleman," she said. "Are you really and truly the Space Viking?"

"Really and truly. And who are you two?"

"I'm Myrna. And this is Mopsy."

"Hello, Myrna. Hello, Mopsy."

Hearing his name, the puppy wriggled again and dropped from the child's arms; after a brief hesitation, he came over and jumped onto Trask's lap, licking his face. While he petted the dog, the girl came over and sat on the bench beside him.

"Mopsy likes you," she said. After a moment, she added: "I like you, too."

"And I like you," he said. "Would you want to be my girl? You know, a Space Viking has to have a girl on every planet. How would you like to be my girl on Marduk?"

Myrna thought that over carefully. "I'd like to, but I couldn't. You see, I'm going to have to be Queen, some day."

"Oh?"

"Yes. Grandpa is King now, and when he's through being King, Pappa will have to be King, and then when he's through being King, I can't be King because I'm a girl, so I'll have to be Queen. And I can't be anybody's girl, because I'm going to have to marry somebody I don't know, for reasons of state." She thought some more, and lowered her voice. "I'll tell you a secret. I am a Queen now."

"Oh, you are?"

She nodded. "We are Queen, in our own right, of our Royal Bedroom, our Royal Playroom, and our Royal Bathroom. And Mopsy is our faithful subject."

"Is Your Majesty absolute ruler of these domains?"

"No," she said disgustedly. "We must at all times defer to our Royal Ministers, just like Grandpa has to. That means, I have to do just what they tell me to. That's Lady Valerie, and Margot, and Dame Eunice, and Sir Thomas. But Grandpa says they are good and wise ministers. Are you really a Prince? I didn't know Space Vikings were Princes."

"Well, my King says I am. And I am ruler of my planet, and I'll tell you a secret. I don't have to do what anybody tells me."

"Gee! Are you a tyrant? You're awfully big and strong. I'll bet you've slain just hundreds of cruel and wicked enemies."

"Thousands, Your Majesty."

He wished that weren't literally true; he didn't know how many of them had been little girls like Myrna and little dogs like Mopsy. He found that he was holding both of them tightly. The girl was saying: "But you feel bad about it." These children must be telepaths!

"A Space Viking who is also a Prince must do many things he doesn't want to do."

"I know. So does a Queen. I hope Grandpa and Pappa don't get through being King for just years and years." She looked over his shoulder. "Oh! And now I suppose I've got to do something else I don't want to. Lessons, I bet."

He followed her eyes. The girl who had been his dinner companion was approaching; she wore a wide sunshade hat, and a gown that trailed filmy gauze like sunset-colored mist. There was another woman, in the garb of an upper servant, with her.

"Lady Valerie and who else?" he whispered.

"Margot. She's my nurse. She's awful strict, but she's nice."

"Prince Trask, has Her Highness been bothering you?" Lady Valerie asked.

"Oh, far from it." He rose, still holding the funny little dog. "But you should say, Her Majesty. She has informed me that she is sovereign of three princely domains. And of one dear loving subject." He gave the subject back to the sovereign.

"You should not have told Prince Trask that," Lady Valerie chided. "When Your Majesty is outside her domains, Your Majesty must remain incognito. Now, Your Majesty must go with the Minister of the Bedchamber; the Minister of Education awaits an audience."

"Arithmetic, I bet. Well, good-by, Prince Trask. I hope I can see you again. Say good-by, Mopsy."

She went away with her nurse, the little dog looking back over her shoulder.

"I came out to enjoy the gardens alone," he said, "and now I find I'd rather enjoy them in company. If your Ministerial duties do not forbid, could you be the company?"

"But gladly, Prince Trask. Her Majesty will be occupied with serious affairs of state. Square root. Have you seen the grottoes? They're down this way."

That afternoon, one of the gentlemen-attendants caught up with him; Baron Cragdale would be gratified if Prince Trask could find time to talk with him privately. Before they had talked more than a few minutes, however, Baron Cragdale abruptly became Crown Prince Edvard.

"Prince Trask, Admiral Shefter tells me that you and he are having informal discussions about co-operation against this mutual enemy of ours, Dunnan. This is fine; it has my approval, and the approval of Prince Vandarvant, the Prime Minister, and, I might add, that of Goodman Mikhyl. I think it ought to go further, though. A formal treaty between Tanith and Marduk would be greatly to the advantage of both."

"I'd be inclined to think so, Prince Edvard. But aren't you proposing marriage on rather short acquaintance? It's only been fifty hours since the *Nemesis* orbited in here."

"Well, we know a bit about you and your planet beforehand. There's a large Gilgamesher colony here. You have a few on Tanith, haven't you? Well, anything one Gilgamesher knows, they all find out, and ours are co-operative with Naval intelligence."

That would be why Andray Dunnan was having no dealings with Gilgameshers. It would also be what Zaspar Makann meant when he ranted about the Gilgamesh Interstellar Conspiracy.

"I can see where an arrangement like that would be mutually advantageous. I'd be quite in favor of it. Co-operation against Dunnan, of course, and reciprocal trade-rights on each other's trade-planets, and direct trade between Marduk and Tanith. And Beowulf and Amaterasu would come into it, too. Does this also have the approval of the Prime Minister and the King?"

"Goodman Mikhyl's in favor of it; there's a distinction between him and the King, as you'll have noticed. The King can't be in favor of anything till the Assembly or the Chancellor express an opinion. Prince Vandarvant favors it personally; as Prime Minister, he is reserving his opinion. We'll have to get the support of the Crown Loyalist Party before he can take an unequivocal position."

"Well, Baron Cragdale; speaking as Baron Trask of Traskon, suppose we just work out a rough outline of what this treaty ought to be, and then consult, unofficially, with a few people whom you can trust, and see what can be done about presenting it to the proper government officials...."

The Prime Minister came to Cragdale that evening, heavily incognito and accompanied by several leaders of the Crown Loyalist Party. In principle, they all favored a treaty with Tanith. Politically, they had doubts. Not before the election; too controversial a subject. "Controversial," it appeared, was the dirtiest dirty-name anything could be called on Marduk. It would alienate the labor vote; they'd think increased imports would threaten employment in Mardukan industries. Some of the interstellar trading companies would like a chance at the Tanith planets; others would resent Tanith ships being given access to theirs. And Zaspar Makann's party were already shrieking protests about the *Nemesis* being repaired by the Royal Navy.

And a couple of professors who inclined toward Makann had introduced a resolution calling for the court-martial of Prince Bentrik and an investigation of the loyalty of Admiral Shefter. And somebody else, probably a stooge of Makann's, was claiming that Bentrik had sold the *Victrix* to the Space Vikings and that the films of the battle of Audhumla were fakes, photographed in miniature at the Navy Moon Base.

Admiral Shefter, when Trask flew in to see him the next day, was contemptuous about this last.

"Ignore the whole bloody thing; we get something like that before every general election. On this planet, you can always kick the Gilgameshers and the Armed Forces with impunity, neither have votes and neither can kick back. The whole thing'll be forgotten the day after the election. It always is."

"That's if Makann doesn't win the election," Trask qualified.

"That's no matter who wins the election. They can't any of them get along without the Navy, and they bloody well know it."

Trask wanted to know if Intelligence had been getting anything.

"Not on how Dunnan found out the *Victrix* had been ordered to Audhumla, no," Shefter said. "There wasn't any secrecy about it; at least a thousand people, from myself down to the shoeshine boys, could have known about it as soon as the order was taped.

"As for the list of ships you gave me, yes. One of them puts in to this planet regularly; she spaced out from here only yesterday morning. The *Honest Horris*."

"Well, great Satan, haven't you done anything?"

"I don't know if there's anything we can do. Oh, we're investigating, but....You see, this ship first showed up here four years ago, commanded by some kind of a Neobarb, not a Gilgamesher, named Horris Sasstroff. He claimed to be from Skathi; the locals there have a few ships, the Space Vikings had a base on Skathi about a hundred or so years ago. Naturally, the ship had no papers. Tramp trading among the Neobarbs, it might be years before you'd put in on a planet where they'd ever heard of ship's papers.

"The ship seems to have been in bad shape, probably abandoned on Skathi as junk a century ago and tinkered up by the locals. She was in here twice, according to the commercial shipping records, and the second time she was in too bad shape to be moved out, and Sasstroff couldn't pay to have her rebuilt, so she was libeled for spaceport charges and sold. Some one-lung trading company bought her and fixed her up a little; they went bankrupt in a year or so, and she was bought by another small company, Startraders, Ltd., and they've been using her on a milk-run to and from Gimli. They seem to be a legitimate outfit, but we're looking into them. We're looking for Sasstroff, too, but we haven't been able to find him."

"If you have a ship out Gimli way, you might find out if anybody there knows anything about her. You may discover that she hasn't been going there at all."

"We might, at that," Shefter agreed. "We'll just find out."

Everybody at Cragdale knew about the projected treaty with Tanith by the morning after Trask's first conversation with Prince Edvard on the subject. The Queen of the Royal Bedroom, the Royal Playroom and the Royal Bathroom was insisting that her domains should have a treaty with Tanith, too.

It was beginning to look to Trask as though that would be the only treaty he'd sign on Marduk, and he was having his doubts about that.

"Do you think it would be wise?" he asked Lady Valerie Alvarath. The Queen of three rooms and one four-footed subject had already decreed that Lady Valerie should be the Space Viking Prince's girl on the planet of Marduk. "If it got out, these People's Welfare lunatics would pick it up and twist it into evidence of some kind of a sinister plot."

"Oh, I believe Her Majesty could sign a treaty with Prince Trask," Her Majesty's Prime Minister decided. "But it would have to be kept very secret."

"Gee!" Myrna's eyes widened. "A real secret treaty; just like the wicked rulers of the old dictatorship!" She hugged her subject ecstatically. "I'll bet Grandpa doesn't even have any secret treaties!"

In a few days, everybody on Marduk knew that a treaty with Tanith was being discussed. If they didn't, it was no fault of Zaspar Makann's party, who seemed to command a disconcertingly large number of telecast stations, and who drenched the ether with horror stories of Space Viking atrocities and denunciations of carefully unnamed traitors surrounding the King and the Crown Prince who were about to betray Marduk to rapine and plunder. The leak evidently did not come from Cragdale, for it was generally believed that Trask was still at the Royal Palace in Malverton. At least, that was where the Makannists were demonstrating against him.

He watched such a demonstration by screen; the pickup was evidently on one of the landing stages of the palace, overlooking the wide parks surrounding it. They were packed almost solid with people, surging forward toward the thin cordon of police. The front of the mob looked like a checkerboard —a block in civilian dress, then a block in the curiously effeminate-looking uniforms of Zaspar Makann's People's Watchmen, then more in ordinary garb, and more People's Watchmen. Over the heads of the crowds, at intervals, floated small contragravity lifters on which were mounted the amplifiers that were bellowing:

"SPACE VI-KING —GO HOME! SPACE VI-KING —GO HOME!"

The police stood motionless, at parade rest; the mob surged closer. When they were fifty yards away, the blocks of People's Watchmen ran forward, then spread out until they formed a line six deep across the entire front; other blocks, from the rear, pushed the ordinary demonstrators aside and took their place. Hating them more every second, Trask grudged approval of a smart and disciplined maneuver. How long, he wondered, had they been drilling in that sort of tactics? Without stopping, they continued their advance on the police, who had now shifted their stance.

"SPACE VI-KING —GO HOME! SPACE VI-KING —GO HOME!"

"Fire!" he heard himself yelling. "Don't let them get any closer, fire now!"

They had nothing to fire with; they had only truncheons, no better weapons than the knobbed swagger-sticks of the People's Watchmen. They simply disappeared, after a brief flurry of blows, and the Makann storm-troopers continued their advance.

And that was that. The gates of the Palace were shut; the mob, behind a front of Makann People's Watchmen, surged up to them and stopped. The loud-speakers bellowed on, reiterating their four-word chant.

"Those police were murdered," he said. "They were murdered by the man who ordered them out there unarmed."

"That would be Count Naydnayr, the Minister of Security," somebody said.

"Then he's the one you want to hang for it."

"What else would you have done?" Crown Prince Edvard challenged.

"Put up about fifty combat cars. Drawn a deadline, and opened machine-gun fire as soon as the mob crossed it, and kept on firing till the survivors turned tail and ran. Then sent out more cars, and shot everybody wearing a People's Watchmen uniform, all over town. Inside forty-eight hours, there'd be no People's Welfare party, and no Zaspar Makann either."

The Crown Prince's face stiffened. "That may be the way you do things in the Sword-Worlds, Prince Trask. It's not the way we do things here on Marduk. Our government does not propose to be guilty of shedding the blood of its people."

He had it on the tip of his tongue to retort that if they didn't, the people would end by shedding theirs. Instead, he said softly:

"I'm sorry, Prince Edvard. You had a wonderful civilization here on Marduk. You could have made almost anything of it. But it's too late now. You've torn down the gates; the barbarians are in."

XXIII

The colored turbulence faded into the gray of hyperspace; five hundred hours to Tanith. Guatt Kirbey was securing his control-panel, happy to return to his music. And Vann Larch would go back to his paints and brushes, and Alvyn Karffard to the working model of whatever it was he had left unfinished when the *Nemesis* had emerged at the end of the jump from Audhumla.

Trask went to the index of the ship's library and punched for *History, Old Terran*. There was plenty of that, thanks to Otto Harkaman. Then he punched for *Hitler, Adolf*. Harkaman was right; anything that could happen in a human society had already happened, in one form or another, somewhere and at some time. Hitler could help him understand Zaspar Makann.

By the time the ship came out, with the yellow sun of Tanith in the middle of the screen, he knew a great deal about Hitler, occasionally referred to as Schicklgruber, and he understood, with sorrow, how the lights of civilization on Marduk were going out.

Beside the *Lamia*, stripped of her Dillinghams and crammed with heavy armament and detection instruments, the *Space Scourge* and the *Queen Flavia* were on off-planet watch. There were half a dozen other ships on orbit just above atmosphere; a Gilgamesher, one of the Gram-Tanith freighters, a couple of free-lance Space Vikings, and a new and unfamiliar ship. When he asked the moonbase who she was, he was told that she was the *Sun Goddess*, Amaterasu. That was, by almost a year, better than he had expected of them. Otto Harkaman was out in the *Corisande*, raiding and visiting the trade-planets.

He found his cousin, Nikkolay Trask, at Rivington; when he inquired about Traskon, Nikkolay cursed.

"I don't know anything about Traskon; I haven't anything to do with Traskon, any more. Traskon is now the personal property of our well loved-very well loved-Queen Evita. The Trasks don't own enough land on Gram now for a family cemetery. You see what you did?" he added bitterly.

"You needn't rub it in, Nikkolay. If I'd stayed on Gram, I'd have helped put Angus on the throne, and it would have been about the same in the end."

"It could be a lot different," Nikkolay said. "You could bring your ships and men back to Gram and put yourself on the throne."

"No; I'll never go back to Gram. Tanith's my planet, now. But I will renounce my allegiance to Angus. I can trade on Morglay or Joyeuse or Flamberge just as easily."

"You won't have to; you can trade with Newhaven and Bigglersport. Count Lionel and Duke Joris are both defying Angus; they've refused to furnish him men, they've driven out his tax collectors, those they haven't hanged, and they're building ships of their own. Angus is building ships, too. I don't know whether he's going to use them to fight Bigglersport and Newhaven, or attack you, but there's going to be a war before another year's out."

The *Goodhope* and the *Speedwell*, he found, had gone back to Gram. They were commanded by men who had come into favor at the court of King Angus recently. The *Black Star* and the *Queen Flavia* —whose captain had contemptuously ignored an order from Gram to re-christen her *Queen Evita* —had remained. They were his ships, not King Angus'. The captain of the merchantman from Wardshaven now on orbit refused to take a cargo to Newhaven; he had been chartered by King Angus, and would take orders from no one else.

"All right," Trask told him. "This is your last voyage here. You bring that ship back under Angus of Wardshaven's charter and we'll fire on her."

Then he had the regalia he had worn in his last audiovisual to Angus dusted off. At first, he had decided to proclaim himself King of Tanith. Lord Valpry, Baron Rathmore and his cousin all advised against it.

"Just call yourself Prince of Tanith," Valpry said. "The title won't make any difference in your authority here, and if you do lay claim to the throne of Gram, nobody can say you're a foreign king trying to annex the planet."

He had no intention of doing anything of the kind, but Valpry was quite in earnest.

So he sat on his throne, as sovereign Prince of Tanith, and renounced his allegiance to "Angus, Duke of Wardshaven, self-styled King of Gram." They sent it back on the otherwise empty freighter. Another copy went to the Count of Newhaven, along with a cargo in the *Sun Goddess*, the first non-Space-Viking ship into Gram from the Old Federation.

Seven hundred and fifty hours after the return of the *Nemesis*, the *Corisande II* emerged from her last microjump, and immediately Harkaman began hearing of the Battle of Audhumla and the destruction of the *Yo-Yo* and the *Enterprise*. At first, he merely reported a successful raiding voyage, from which he was bringing rich booty. Oddly varigated booty, it was remarked, when he began itemizing it.

"Why, yes," he replied. "Secondhand booty. I raided Dagon for it."

Dagon was a Space Viking base planet, occupied by a character named Fedrig Barragon. A number of ships operated from it, including a couple commanded by Barragon's half-breed sons.

"Barragon's ships were raiding one of our planets," Harkaman said. "Ganpat. They looted a couple of cities, destroyed one, killed a lot of the locals. I found out about it from Captain Ravallo of the *Black Star*, on Indra; he'd just been from Ganpat. Beowulf wasn't too far out of the way, so we put in there, and found the *Grendelsbane* just ready to space out." The *Grendelsbane* was the second of Beowulf's ships, sister to the *Viking's Gift*. "So she joined us, and the three of us went to Dagon. We blew up one of Barragon's ships, and put the other one down out of commission, and then we sacked his base. There was a Gilgamesher colony there; we didn't bother them. They'll tell what we did, and why."

"That should furnish Prince Viktor of Xochitl something to ponder," Trask said. "Where are the other ships, now?"

"The *Grendelsbane* went back to Beowulf; she'll stop at Amaterasu to do a little trading on the way. The *Black Star* went to Xochitl. Just a friendly visit, to say hello to Prince Viktor for you. Ravallo has a lot of audiovisuals we made during the Dagon Operation. Then she's going to Jagannath to visit Nikky Gratham."

Harkaman approved his attitude and actions with regard to King Angus.

"We don't need to do business with the Sword-Worlds at all. We have our own industries, we can produce what we need, and we can trade with Beowulf and Amaterasu, and with Xochitl and Jagannath and Hoth, if we can make any sort of agreement with them; everybody agrees to let everybody else's trade-planets alone. It's too bad you couldn't get some kind of an agreement with Marduk." Harkaman regretted that for a few seconds, and then shrugged. "Our grandchildren, if any, will probably be raiding Marduk."

"You think it'll be like that?"

"Don't you? You were there; you saw what's happening. The barbarians are rising; they have a leader, and they're uniting. Every society rests on a barbarian base. The people who don't understand civilization, and wouldn't like it if they did. The hitchhikers. The people who create nothing, and who don't appreciate what others have created for them, and who think civilization is something that just exists and that all they need to do is enjoy what they can understand of it-luxuries, a high living standard, and easy work for high pay. Responsibilities? Phooey! What do they have a government for?"

Trask nodded. "And now, the hitchhikers think they know more about the car than the people who designed it, so they're going to grab the controls. Zaspar Makann says they can, and he's the Leader." He poured a drink from a decanter that had been looted on Pushan; there was a planet where a republic had been overthrown in favor of a dictatorship four centuries ago, and the planetary dictatorship had fissioned into a dozen regional dictatorships, and now they were down to the peasant-village and handcraft-industry level. "I don't understand it, though.

I was reading about Hitler, on the way home. I wouldn't be surprised if Zaspar Makann had been reading about Hitler, too. He's using all Hitler's tricks. But Hitler came to power in a country which had been impoverished by a military defeat. Marduk hasn't fought a war in almost two generations, and that one was a farce."

"It wasn't the war that put Hitler into power. It was the fact that the ruling class of his nation, the people who kept things running, were discredited. The masses, the homemade barbarians, didn't have anybody to take their responsibilities for them. What they have on Marduk is a ruling class that has been discrediting itself. A ruling class that's ashamed of its privileges and shirks its duties. A ruling class that has begun to believe that the masses are just as good as they are, which they manifestly are not. And a ruling class that won't use force to maintain its position. And they have a democracy, and they are letting the enemies of democracy shelter themselves behind democratic safeguards."

"We don't have any of this democracy in the Sword-Worlds, if that's the word for it," he said. "And our ruling class aren't ashamed of their power, and our people aren't hitchhikers, and as long as they get decent treatment they don't try to run things. And we're not doing so well."

The Morglay dynastic war of a couple of centuries ago, still sputtering and smoking. The Oskarsan-Elmersan War on Durendal, into which Flamberge and now Joyeuse had intruded. And the situation on Gram, fast approaching critical mass. Harkaman nodded agreement.

"You know why? Our rulers are the barbarians among us. There isn't one of them-Napolyon of Flamberge, Rodolf of Excalibur, or Angus of about half of Gram-who is devoted to civilization or anything else outside himself, and that's the mark of the barbarian."

"What are you devoted to, Otto?"

"You. You are my chieftain. That's another mark of the barbarian."

Before he had left Marduk, Admiral Shefter had ordered a ship to Gimli to check on the *Honest Horris*; a few men and a pinnace would be left behind to contact any ship from Tanith. He sent Boake Valkanhayn off in the *Space Scourge*.

Lionel of Newhaven's *Blue Comet* came in from Gram with a cargo of general merchandise. Her captain wanted fissionables and gadolinium; Count Lionel was building more ships. There was a rumor that Omfray of Glaspyth was laying claim to the throne of Gram, in the right of his great-grandmother's sister, who had been married to the great-grandfather of Duke Angus. It was a completely trivial and irrelevant claim, but the story was that it would be supported by King Konrad of Haulteclere.

Immediately, Baron Rathmore, Lord Valpry, Lothar Ffayle and the other Gram people began clamoring that he should go back with a fleet and seize the throne for himself. Harkaman, Valkanhayn, Karffard and the other Space Vikings were as vehement against it. Harkaman had the loss of the other *Corisande* on Durendal to remember, and the others wanted no part in Sword-World squabbles, and there was renewed agitation that he should start calling himself King of Tanith.

He refused to do either, which left both parties dissatisfied. So partisan politics had finally come to Tanith. Maybe that was another milestone of progress.

And there was the Treaty of Khepera, between the Princely State of Tanith, the Commonwealth of Beowulf, and the Planetary League of Amaterasu. The Kheperans agreed to allow bases on their planet, to furnish workers, and to send students to school on all three planets. Tanith, Beowulf and Amaterasu obligated themselves to joint defense of Khepera, to free trade among themselves, and to render one another armed assistance.

That *was* a milestone of progress, and no argument about it.

The *Space Scourge* returned from Gimli, and Valkanhayn reported that nobody on the planet had ever seen or heard of the *Honest Horris*. They had found a Mardukan Navy ship's pinnace there, manned entirely by officers, some of them Navy Intelligence. According to them, the investigation into the activities of that ship had come to an impasse. The ostensible owners claimed, and had papers to prove it, that they had chartered her to a private trader, and he claimed, and had papers to prove it, that he was a citizen of the Planetary Republic of Aton, and as soon as they began questioning him, he was rescued by the Atonian ambassador, who lodged a vehement protest with the Mardukan Foreign Ministry. Immediately, the People's Welfare Party had leaped into the incident and branded the investigation as an unwarranted persecution of a national of a friendly power at the instigation of corrupt tools of the Gilgamesh Interstellar Conspiracy.

"So that's it," Valkanhayn finished. "It seems they're having an election and they're afraid to antagonize anybody who might have a vote. So the Navy had to drop the investigation. Everybody on Marduk's scared of this Makann. You think there might be some tie-up between him and Dunnan?"

"The idea's occurred to me. Have there been any more raids on Marduk trade-planets since the Battle of Audhumla?"

"A couple. The *Bolide* was on Audhumla a while ago. There were a couple of Mardukan ships there, and they had the *Victrix* fixed up enough to do some fighting. They ran the *Bolide* out."

A study of the time between the destruction of the *Enterprise* and *Yo-Yo* and the appearance of the *Bolide* could give them a limiting radius around Audhumla. It did; seven hundred light-years, which also included Tanith.

So he sent Harkaman in the *Corisande* and Ravallo in the *Black Star* to visit the planets Marduk traded with, looking for Dunnan ships and exchanging information and assistance with the Royal Mardukan Navy. Almost at once, he regretted it; the next Gilgamesher into orbit on Tanith brought a story that Prince Viktor was collecting a fleet on Xochitl. He sent warnings off to Amaterasu and Beowulf and Khepera.

A ship came in from Bigglersport, a heavily armed chartered freighter. There was sporadic fighting in a dozen places on Gram, now-resistance to efforts on the part of King Angus to collect taxes, and raids by unidentified persons on estates confiscated from alleged traitors and given to Garvan Spasso, who had now been promoted from Baron to Count. And Rovard Grauffis was dead; poisoned, everybody said, either by Spasso or Queen Evita or both. Even with the threat from Xochitl, some of the former Wardshaven nobles began talking about sending ships to Gram.

Less than a thousand hours after he had left, Ravallo was back in the *Black Star*.

"I went to Gimli, and I wasn't there fifty hours before a Mardukan Navy ship came in. They were glad to see me; it saved them sending off a pinnace for Tanith. They had news for you, and a couple of passengers."

"Passengers?"

"Yes. You'll see who they are when they come down. And don't let anybody with side-whiskers and buttoned-up coats see them," Ravallo said. "What those people know gets all over the place before long."

The visitors were Lucile, Princess Bentrik, and her son, the young Count of Ravary. They dined with Trask; only Captain Ravallo was also present.

"I didn't want to leave my husband, and I didn't want to come here and impose myself and Steven on you, Prince Trask," she began, "but he insisted. We spent the whole voyage to Gimli concealed in the captain's quarters; only a few of the officers knew we were aboard."

"Makann won the election. Is that it?" he asked. "And Prince Bentrik doesn't want to risk you and Steven being used as hostages?"

"That's it," she said. "He didn't really win the election, but he might as well have. Nobody has a majority of seats in the Chamber of Representatives but he's formed a coalition with several of the splinter parties, and I'm ashamed to say that a number of Crown Loyalist members-Crowd of Disloyalists, I call them-are voting with him, now. They've coined some ridiculous phrase about the 'wave of the future,' whatever that means."

"If you can't lick them, join them," Trask said.

"If you can't lick them, lick their boots," the Count of Ravary put in.

"My son is a trifle bitter," Princess Bentrik said. "I must confess to a trace of bitterness, too."

"Well, that's the Representatives," Trask said. "What about the rest of the government?"

"With the splinter-party and Disloyalist support, they got a majority of seats in the Delegates. Most of them would have indignantly denied, a month before, having any connection with Makann, but a hundred out of a hundred and twenty are his supporters. Makann, of course, is Chancellor."

"And who is Prime Minister?" he asked. "Andray Dunnan?"

She looked slightly baffled for an instant then said, "Oh. No. The Prime Minister is Crown Prince Edvard. No; Baron Cragdale. That isn't a royal title, so by some kind of a fiction I can't pretend to understand he is not Prime Minister as a member of the Royal Family."

"If you can't ..." the boy started.

"Steven! I forbid you to say that about ... Baron Cragdale. He believes, very sincerely, that the election was an expression of the will of the people, and that it is his duty to bow to it."

He wished Otto Harkaman were there. He could probably name, without stopping for breath, a hundred great nations that went down into rubble because their rulers believed that they should bow instead of rule, and couldn't bring themselves to shed the blood of their people. Edvard would have been a fine and admirable man, as a little country baron. Where he was, he was a disaster.

He asked if the People's Watchman had dragged their guns out from under the bed and started carrying them in public yet.

"Oh, yes. You were quite right; they were armed, all the time. Not just small arms; combat vehicles and heavy weapons. As soon as the new government was formed, they were given status as a part of the Planetary Armed Forces. They have taken over every police station on the planet."

"And the King?"

"Oh, he carries on, and shrugs and says, 'I just reign here.' What else can he do? We've been whittling down and filching away the powers of the Throne for the last three centuries."

"What is Prince Bentrik doing, and why did he think there was danger that you two would be used as hostages?"

"He's going to fight," she said. "Don't ask me how, or what with. Maybe as a guerrilla in the mountains, I don't know. But if he can't lick them, he won't join them. I wanted to stay with him and help him; he told me I could help him best by placing myself and Steven where he wouldn't worry about us."

"I wanted to stay," the boy said. "I could have fought with him. But he said that I must take care of Mother. And if he were killed, I must be able to avenge him."

"You talk like a Sword-Worlder; I told you that once before." He hesitated, then turned again to Princess Bentrik. "How is little Princess Myrna?" he asked, and then, trying to be casual, added, "and Lady Valerie?"

She seemed so clearly real and present to him, blue eyes and space-black hair, more real than Elaine had been to him for years.

"They're at Cragdale; they'll be safe there. I hope."

XXIV

Attempting to conceal the presence on Tanith of Prince Bentrik's wife and son was pushing caution beyond necessity. Admitted that the news would leak back to Marduk via Gilgamesh, it was over seven hundred light-years to the latter and almost a thousand from there to the former. Better that Princess Lucile should enjoy Rivington society, such as it was, and escape, for a moment now and then, from anxiety about her husband. At ten-no, almost twelve; it had been a year and a half since Trask had left Marduk-the boy Count of Ravary was more easily diverted. At last, he was among real Space Vikings, on a Space Viking planet, and he was trying to be everywhere and see everything at once. No doubt he would be imagining himself a Space Viking, returning to Marduk with a vast armada to rescue his father and the King from Zaspar Makann.

Trask was satisfied with that; as a host he left much to be desired. He had his worries, too, and all of them bore the same name: Prince Viktor of Xochitl. He went over with Manfred Ravallo everything the captain of the *Black Star* could tell him. He had talked once with Viktor; the lord of Xochitl had been coldly polite and noncommittal. His subordinates had been frankly hostile. There had been five ships on orbit or landed at Viktor's spaceport beside the usual Gilgameshers and itinerant traders, two of them Viktor's own, and a big armed freighter had come in from Haulteclere as the *Black Star* was leaving. There was considerable activity at the shipyards and around the spaceport, as though in preparation for something on a large scale.

Xochitl was a thousand light-years from Tanith. He rejected immediately the idea of launching a preventative attack; his ships might reach Xochitl to find it undefended, and then return to find Tanith devastated. Things like that had happened in space-war. The only thing to do was sit tight, defend Tanith when Viktor attacked, and then counterattack if he had any ships left by that time. Prince Viktor was probably reasoning in the same way.

He had no time to think about Andray Dunnan, except, now and then, to wish that Otto Harkaman would stop thinking about him and bring the *Corisande* home. He needed that ship on Tanith, and the wits and courage of her commander.

More news-Gilgamesh sources-came in from Xochitl. There were only two ships, both armed merchantmen, on the planet. Prince Viktor had spaced out with the rest an estimated two thousand hours before the story reached him. That was twice as long as it would take the Xochitl armada to reach Tanith. He hadn't gone to Beowulf; that was only sixty-five hours from Tanith and they would have heard about it long ago. Or Amaterasu, or Khepera. How many ships he had was a question; not fewer than five, and possibly more. He could have slipped into the Tanith system and hidden his ships on one of the outer uninhabitable planets. He sent Valkanhayn and Ravallo microjumping their ships from one to another to check. They returned to report in the negative. At least, Viktor of Xochitl wasn't camped inside their own system, waiting for them to leave Tanith open to attack.

But he was somewhere, and up to nothing even resembling good, and there was no possible way of guessing when his ships would be emerging on Tanith. The only thing to do was wait for him. When he did, Trask was confident that he would emerge from hyperspace into serious trouble. He had the *Nemesis*, the *Space Scourge*, the *Black Star* and *Queen Flavia*, the strongly rebuilt *Lamia*, and several independent Space Viking ships, among them the *Damnthing* of his friend Roger-fan-Morvill Esthersan, who had volunteered to stay and help in the defense. This, of course, was not pure altruism. If Viktor attacked and had his fleet blown to Em-See-Square, Xochitl would lie open and unprotected, and there was enough loot on Xochitl to cram everybody's ships. Everybody's ships who had ships when the Battle of Tanith was over, of course.

He was apologetic to Princess Bentrik:

"I'm very sorry you jumped out of Zaspar Makann's frying pan into Prince Viktor's fire," he began.

She laughed at that. "I'll take my chances on the fire. I seem to see a lot of good firemen around. If there is a battle you will see that Steven's in a safe place, won't you?"

"In a space attack, there are no safe places. I'll keep him with me."

The young Count of Ravary wanted to know which ship he would serve on when the attack came.

"Well, you won't be on any ship, Count. You'll be on my staff."

Two days later, the *Corisande* came out of hyperspace. Harkaman was guardedly noncommittal by screen. Trask took a landing craft and went out to meet the ship.

"Marduk doesn't like us, any more," Harkaman told him. "They have ships on all their trade-planets, and they all have orders to fire on any, repeat any, Space Vikings, including the ships of the self-styled Prince of Tanith. I got this from Captain Garravay of the *Vindex*. After we were through talking, we fought a nice little ship-to-ship action for him to make films of. I don't think anybody could see anything wrong with it."

"This order came from Makann?"

"From the Admiral commanding. He isn't your friend Shefter; Shefter retired on account of quote ill-health unquote. He is now in a quote hospital unquote."

"Where's Prince Bentrik?"

"Nobody knows. Charges of high treason were brought against him, and he just vanished. Gone underground, or secretly arrested and executed; take your choice."

He wondered just what he'd tell Princess Lucile and Count Steven.

"They have ships on all the planets they trade with. Fourteen of them. That isn't to catch Dunnan. That's to disperse the Navy away from Marduk. They don't trust the Navy. Is Prince Edvard still Prime Minister?"

"Yes, as of Garravay's last information. It seems Makann is behaving in a scrupulously legal manner, outside of making his People's Watchmen part of the armed forces. Protesting his devotion to the King every time he opens his mouth."

"When will the fire be, I wonder?"

"Huh? Oh yes, you were reading up on Hitler. That I don't know. Probably happened by now."

He just told Princess Lucile that her husband had gone into hiding; he couldn't be sure whether she was relieved or more worried. The boy was sure that he was doing something highly romantic and heroic.

Some of the volunteers tired of waiting, after another thousand hours, and spaced out. The *Viking's Gift* of Beowulf came in with a cargo, and went on orbit after discharging it to join the watch. A Gilgamesher came in from Amaterasu and reported everything quiet there; as soon as her captain had sold his cargo, with a minimum of haggling, he spaced out again. His behavior convinced everybody that the attack would come in a matter of hours.

It didn't.

Three thousand hours had passed since the first warning had reached Tanith, that made five thousand since Viktor's ships were supposed to have left Xochitl. There were those, Boake Valkanhayn among them, who doubted, now, if he ever had.

"The whole thing's just a big Gilgamesher lie," he was declaring. "Somebody-Nikky Gratham, or the Everrards, or maybe Viktor himself-paid them to tell us that, to pin our ships down here. Or they made it up themselves, so they could make hay on our trade-planets."

"Let's go down to the Ghetto and clean out the whole gang," somebody else took up. "Anything one of them's in, they're all in together."

"Nifflheim with that; let's all space out for Xochitl," Manfred Ravallo proposed. "We have enough ships to lick them on Tanith, we have enough to lick them on their own planet."

He managed to talk them out of both courses of action-what was he, anyhow; sovereign Prince of Tanith, or the non-ruling King of Marduk, or just the chieftain of a disciplineless gang of barbarians? One of the independents spaced out in disgust. The next day, two others came in, loaded with booty from a raid on Braggi, and decided to stay around for a while and see what happened.

And four days after that, a five-hundred-foot hyperspace yacht, bearing the daggers and chevrons of Bigglersport, came in. As soon as she was out of the last microjump, she began calling by screen.

Trask didn't know the man who was screening, but Hugh Rathmore did; Duke Joris' confidential secretary.

"Prince Trask; I must speak to you as soon as possible," he began, almost stuttering. Whatever the urgency of his mission, one would have thought that a three-thousand-hour voyage would have taken some of the edge from it. "It is of the first importance."

"You are speaking to me. This screen is reasonably secure. And if it's of the first importance, the sooner you tell me about it...."

"Prince Trask, you must come to Gram, with every man and every ship you can command. Satan only knows what's happening there now, but three thousand hours ago, when the Duke sent me off, Omfray of Glaspyth was landing on Wardshaven. He has a fleet of eight ships, furnished to him by his wife's kinsman, the King of Haulteclere. They are commanded by King Konrad's Space Viking cousin, the Prince of Xochitl."

Then a look of shocked surprise came into the face of the man in the screen, and Trask wondered why, until he realized that he had leaned back in his chair and was laughing uproariously. Before he could apologize, the man in the screen had found his voice.

"I know, Prince Trask; you have no reason to think kindly of King Angus-the former King Angus, or maybe even the late King Angus, I suppose he is now-but a murderer like Omfray of Glaspyth...."

It took a little time to explain to the confidential secretary of the Duke of Bigglersport the humor of the situation.

There were others at Rivington to whom it was not immediately evident. The professional Space Vikings, men like Valkanhayn and Ravallo and Alvyn Karffard, were disgusted. Here they'd been sitting, on combat alert, all these months, and, if they'd only known, they could have gone to Xochitl and looted it clean long ago. The Gram party were outraged. Angus of Wardshaven had been bad enough, with the hereditary taint of the Mad Baron of Blackcliffe, and Queen Evita and her rapacious family, but even he was preferable to a murderous villain-some even called him a fiend in human shape-like Omfray of Glaspyth.

Both parties, of course, were positive as to where their Prince's duty lay. The former insisted that everything on Tanith that could be put into hyperspace should be dispatched at once to Xochitl, to haul back from it everything except a few absolutely immovable natural features of the planet. The latter clamored, just as loudly and passionately, that everybody on Tanith who could pull a trigger should be embarked at once on a crusade for the deliverance of Gram.

"You don't want to do either, do you?" Harkaman asked him, when they were alone after the second day of acrimony.

"Nifflheim, no! This crowd that wants an attack on Xochitl; you know what would happen if we did that?" Harkaman was silent, waiting for him to continue. "Inside a year, four or five of these small planet-holders like Gratham and the Everrards would combine against us and make a slag-pile out of Tanith."

Harkaman nodded agreement. "Since we warned him the first time, Viktor's kept his ships away from our planets. If we attacked Xochitl now, without provocation, nobody'd know what to expect from us. People like Nikky Gratham and Tobbin of Nergal and the Everrards of Hoth get nervous around unpredictable dangers, and when they get nervous they get trigger-happy." He puffed slowly on his pipe and then said: "Then you'll be going back to Gram."

"That doesn't follow; just because Valkanhayn and Ravallo and that crowd are wrong doesn't make Valpry and Rathmore and Ffayle right. You heard what I was telling those very people at Karvall House, the day I met you. And you've seen what's been happening on Gram since we came out here. Otto, the Sword-Worlds are finished; they're half decivilized now. Civilization is alive and growing here on Tanith. I want to stay here and help it grow."

"Look, Lucas," Harkaman said. "You're Prince of Tanith, and I'm only the Admiral. But I'm telling you; you'll have to do something, or this whole setup of yours will fall apart. As it stands, you can attack Xochitl and the Back-To-Gram party would go along, or you can decide on this crusade against Omfray of Glaspyth and the Raid-Xochitl-Now party would go along. But if you let this go on much longer, you won't have any influence over either party."

"And then I will be finished. And in a few years, Tanith will be finished." He rose and paced across the room and back. "Well, I won't raid Xochitl; I told you why, and you agreed. And I won't spend the men and ships and wealth of Tanith in any Sword-World dynastic squabble. Great Satan, Otto; you were in the Durendal War. This is the same thing, and it'll go on for another half a century."

"Then what will you do?"

"I came out here after Andray Dunnan, didn't I?" he asked.

"I'm afraid Ravallo and Valpry, or even Valkanhayn and Morland, won't be as interested in Dunnan as you are."

"Then I will interest them in him. Remember, I was reading up on Hitler, coming in from Marduk? I will tell them all a big lie. Such a big lie that nobody will dare to disbelieve it."

XXV

"Do you think I was afraid of Viktor of Xochitl?" he demanded. "Half a dozen ships; we could make a new Van Allen belt around Tanith of them, with what we have here. Our real enemy is on Marduk, not Xochitl; his name's Zaspar Makann. Zaspar Makann, and Andray Dunnan, the man I came out from Gram to hunt; they're in alliance, and I believe Dunnan is on Marduk, himself, now."

The delegation who had come out from Gram in the yacht of the Duke of Bigglersport were unimpressed. Marduk was only a name to them, one of the fabulous civilized Old Federation planets no Sword-Worlder had ever seen. Zaspar Makann wasn't even that. And so much had happened on Gram since the murder of Elaine Karvall and the piracy of the *Enterprise* that they had completely forgotten Andray Dunnan. That put them at a disadvantage. All the people whom they were trying to convince, the half-hundred members of the new nobility of Tanith, spoke a language they didn't understand. They didn't even understand the proposition, and couldn't argue against it.

Paytrik Morland, who was Gram-born and had been speaking for a return in force to fight against Omfray of Glaspyth and his supporters, defected from them at once. He had been on Marduk and knew who Zaspar Makann was; he had made friends with the Royal Navy officers, and had been shocked to hear that they were now enemies. Manfred Ravallo and Boake Valkanhayn, among the more articulate of the Raid-Xochitl-Now party, snatched up the idea and seemed convinced that they'd thought of it themselves all along. Valkanhayn had been on Gimli and talked to Mardukan naval officers; Ravallo had brought Princess Bentrik to Tanith and heard her stories on the voyage. They began adducing arguments in support of Trask's thesis. Of course Dunnan and Makann were in collusion. Who tipped Dunnan off that the *Victrix* would be on Audhumla? Makann; his spies in the Navy tipped him. What about the *Honest Horris*; wasn't Makann blocking any investigation about her? Why was Admiral Shefter retired as soon as Makann got into power?

"Well, here; we don't know anything about this Zaspar Makann," the confidential secretary and spokesman of the Duke of Bigglersport began.

"No, you don't," Otto Harkaman told him. "I suggest you keep quiet and listen, till you find out a little about him."

"Why, I wouldn't be surprised if Dunnan was on Marduk all the time we were hunting for him," Valkanhayn said.

Trask began to wonder. What would Hitler have done if he'd told one of his big lies, and then found it turning into the truth? Maybe Makann had been on Marduk....No; he couldn't have hidden half a dozen ships on a civilized planet. Not even at the bottom of an ocean.

"I wouldn't be surprised," Alvyn Karffard was shouting, "if Andray Dunnan *was* Zaspar Makann. I know he doesn't look like Dunnan, we all saw him on screen, but there's such a thing as plastic surgery."

That was making the big lie just a trifle too big. Zaspar Makann was six inches shorter than Dunnan; there are some things no plastic surgery could do. Paytrik Morland, who had known Dunnan and had seen Makann on screen, ought to have known that too, but he either didn't think of it or didn't want to weaken a case he had completely accepted.

"As far as I can find out, nobody even heard of Makann till about five years ago. That would be about the time Dunnan would have arrived on Marduk," he said.

By this time, the big room in which they were meeting had become a babel of voices, everybody trying to convince everybody else that they'd known it all along. Then the Back-To-Gram party received its *coup-de-grace*; Lothar Ffayle, to whom the emissaries of Duke Joris had looked for their strongest support, went over.

"You people want us to abandon a planet we've built up from nothing, and all the time and money we've invested in it, to go back to Gram and pull your chestnuts out of the fire? Gehenna with you! We're staying here and defending our own planet. If you're smart, you'll stay here with us."

The Bigglersport delegation was still on Tanith, trying to recruit mercenaries from the King of Tradetown and dickering with a Gilgamesher to transport them to Gram, when the big lie turned into something like the truth.

The observation post on the Moon of Tanith picked up an emergence at twenty light-minutes due north of the planet. Half an hour later, there was another one at five light-minutes; a very small one, and then a third at two light-seconds, and this was detectable by radar and microray as a ship's pinnace. He wondered if something had happened on Amaterasu or Beowulf; somebody like Gratham or the Everrards might have decided to take advantage of the defensive mobilization on Tanith. Then they switched the call from the pinnace over to his screen, and Prince Simon Bentrik was looking out of it.

"I'm glad to see you! Your wife and son are here, worried about you, but safe and well." He turned to shout to somebody to find young Count Steven of Ravary and tell him to tell his mother. "How are you?"

"I had a broken leg when I left Moonbase, but that's mended on the way," Bentrik said. "I have little Princess Myrna aboard with me. For all I know, she's Queen of Marduk, now." He gulped slightly. "Prince Trask, we've come as beggars. We're begging help for our planet."

"You've come as honored guests, and you'll get all the help we can give you." He blessed the Xochitl invasion scare, and the big lie which was rapidly ceasing to be a lie; Tanith had the ships and men and the will to act. "What happened? Makann deposed the King and took over?"

It came to that, Bentrik told him. It had started even before the election. The People's Watchmen had possessed weapons that had been made openly and legally on Marduk for trade to the Neobarbarian planets and then clandestinely diverted to secret People's Welfare arsenals. Some of the police had gone over to Makann; the rest had been terrorized into inaction. There had been riots fomented in working-class districts of all the cities as pretexts for further terrorization. The election had been a farce of bribery and intimidation. Even so, Makann's party had failed of a complete majority in the Chamber of Representatives, and had been compelled to patch up a shady coalition in order to elect a favorable Chamber of Delegates.

"And, of course, they elected Makann Chancellor; that did it," Bentrik said. "All the opposition leaders in the Chamber of Representatives have been arrested, on all kinds of ridiculous charges-sex-crimes, receiving bribes, being in the pay of foreign powers, nothing too absurd. Then they rammed through a law empowering the Chancellor to fill vacancies in the Chamber of Representatives by appointment."

"Why did the Crown Prince lend himself to a thing like that?"

"He hoped that he could exercise some control. The Royal Family is an almost holy symbol to the people. Even Makann was forced to pretend loyalty to the King and the Crown Prince...."

"It didn't work; he played right into Makann's hands. What happened?"

The Crown Prince had been assassinated. The assassin, an unknown man believed to be a Gilgamesher, had been shot to death by People's Watchmen guarding Prince Edvard at once. Immediately Makann had seized the Royal Palace to protect the King, and immediately there had been massacres by People's Watchmen everywhere. The Mardukan Planetary Army had ceased to exist; Makann's story was that there had been a military plot against the King and the government. Scattered over the planet in small detachments, the army had been wiped out in two nights and a day. Now Makann was recruiting it up again, exclusively from the People's Welfare Party.

"You weren't just sitting on your hands, were you?"

"Oh, no," Bentrik replied. "I was doing something I wouldn't have thought myself capable of, a few years ago. Organizing a mutineering conspiracy in the Royal Mardukan Navy. After Admiral Shefter was forcibly retired and shut up in an insane asylum, I disappeared and turned into a civilian contragravity-lifter operator at the Malverton Navy Yard. Finally, when I was suspected, one of the officers-he was arrested and tortured to death later-managed to smuggle me onto a lighter for the Moonbase. I was an orderly in the hospital there. The day the Crown Prince was murdered, we had a mutiny of our own. We killed everybody we even suspected of being a Makannist. The Moonbase has been under attack from the planet ever since."

There was a stir behind him; turning, he saw Princess Bentrik and the boy enter the room. He rose.

"We'll talk about this later. There are some people here...."

He motioned them forward and turned away, shoo-ing everybody else out of the room.

The news was all over Rivington, and then all over Tanith, while the pinnace was still coming down. There was a crowd at the spaceport, staring as the little craft, with its blazon of the crowned and planet-throned dragon, settled onto its landing legs, and reporters of the Tanith News Service with their screen pickups. He met Prince Bentrik, a little in advance of the others, and managed to whisper to him hastily:

"While you're talking to anybody here, always remember that Andray Dunnan is working with Zaspar Makann, and as soon as Makann consolidates his position he's sending an expedition against Tanith."

"How in blazes did you find that out, here?" Bentrik demanded. "From the Gilgameshers?"

Then Harkaman and Rathmore and Valkanhayn and Lothar Ffayle and the others were crowding up behind, and more people were coming off the pinnace, and Prince Bentrik was trying to embrace both his wife and his son at the same time.

"Prince Trask." He started at the voice, and was looking into deep blue eyes under coal-black hair. His pulse gave a sudden jump, and he said, "Valerie!" and then, "Lady Alvarath; I'm most happy to see you here." Then he saw who was beside her, and squatted on his heels to bring himself down to a convenient size. "And Princess Myrna. Welcome to Tanith, Your Highness!"

The child flung her arms around his neck. "Oh, Prince Lucas! I'm so glad to see you. There's been such awful things happened!"

"There won't be anything awful happen here, Princess Myrna. You are among friends; friends with whom you have a treaty. Remember?"

The child began to cry, bitterly. "That was when I was just a play-Queen. And now I know what they meant when they talked about when Grandpa and Pappa would be through being King. Pappa didn't even get to be King!"

Something big and warm and soft was trying to push between them; a dog with long blond hair and floppy ears. In a year and a half, puppies can grow surprisingly. Mopsy was trying to lick his face. He took the dog by the collar and straightened.

"Lady Valerie, will you come with us?" he asked. "I'm going to find quarters for Princess Myrna."

"Is it Princess Myrna, or is it Queen Myrna?" he asked.

Prince Bentrik shook his head. "We don't know. The King was alive when we left Moonbase, but that was five hundred hours ago. We don't know anything about her mother, either. She was at the Palace when Prince Edvard was murdered; we've heard absolutely nothing about her. The King made a few screen appearances, parroting things Makann wanted him to say. Under hypnosis. That was probably the very least of what they did to him. They've turned him into a zombi."

"Well, how did Myrna get to Moonbase?"

"That was Lady Valerie, as much as anybody else. She and Sir Thomas Kobbly, and Captain Rainer. They armed the servants at Cragdale with hunting rifles and everything else they could scrape up, captured Prince Edvard's space-yacht, and took off in her. Took a couple of hits from ground batteries getting off, and from ships around Moonbase getting in. Ships of the Royal Mardukan Navy!" he added furiously.

The pinnace in which they had made the trip to Tanith had taken a few hits, too, running the blockade. Not many; her captain had thrown her into hyperspace almost at once.

"They sent the yacht off to Gimli," Bentrik said. "From there, they'll try to rally as many of the Royal Navy units as haven't gone over to Makann. They're to assemble on Gimli and await my return. If I don't return in fifteen hundred hours from the time I left Moonbase, they're to use their own judgment. I'd expect that they'd move in on Marduk and attack."

"That's sixty-odd days," Otto Harkaman said. "That's an awfully long time to expect that lunar base to hold out, against a whole planet."

"It's a strong base. It was built four hundred years ago, when Marduk was fighting a combination of six other planets. It held out against continuous attack, once, for almost a year. It's been constantly strengthened ever since."

"And what have they to throw at it?" Harkaman persisted.

"When I left, six ships of the former Royal Navy, that had gone over to Makann. Four fifteen-hundred-footers, same class as the *Victrix*, and two thousand-footers. Then, there were four of Andray Dunnan's ships —"

"You mean, he really is on Marduk?"

"I thought you knew that, and I was wondering how you'd found out. Yes: *Fortuna*, *Bolide*, and two armed merchantmen, a Baldurbuilt ship called the *Reliable*, and your friend *Honest Horris*."

"You didn't really believe Dunnan was on Marduk?" Boake Valkanhayn asked.

"Actually, I didn't. I had to have some kind of a story, to talk those people out of that crusade against Omfray of Glaspyth." He left unmentioned Valkanhayn's own insistence on a plundering expedition against Xochitl. "Now that it turns out to be true, I'm not surprised. We decided, long ago, that Dunnan was planning to raid Marduk. It appears that we underestimated him. Maybe he was reading about Hitler, too. He wasn't planning any raid; he was planning conquest, in the only way a great civilization can be conquered-by subversion."

"Yes," Harkaman put in. "Five years ago, when Dunnan started this programme, who was this Makann, anyhow?"

"Nobody," Bentrik said. "A crackpot agitator in Drepplin; he had a coven of fellow-crackpots, who met in the back room of a saloon and had their office in a cigar box. The next year, he had a suite of offices and was buying time on a couple of telecasts. The year after that, he had three telecast stations of his own, and was holding rallies and meetings of thousands of people. And so on, upward."

"Yes. Dunnan financed him, and moved in behind him, the same way Makann moved in behind the King. And Dunnan will have him shot the way he had Prince Edvard shot, and use the murder as a pretext to liquidate his personal followers."

"And then he'll own Marduk. And we'll have the Mardukan navy coming out of hyperspace on Tanith," Valkanhayn added. "So we go to Marduk and smash him now, while he's still little enough to smash."

There had been a few who had wanted to do that about Hitler, and a great many, later, who had regretted that it hadn't been done.

"The *Nemesis*, the *Corisande*, and the *Space Scourge* for sure?" he asked.

Harkaman and Valkanhayn agreed; Valkanhayn thought the *Viking's Gift* of Beowulf would go along, and Harkaman was almost sure of the *Black Star* and *Queen Flavia*. He turned to Bentrik.

"Start that pinnace off for Gimli at once; within the hour if possible. We don't know how many ships will be gathered there, but we don't want them wasted in detail-attacks. Tell whoever's in command there that ships from Tanith are on the way, and to wait for them."

Fifteen hundred hours, less the five hundred Bentrik was in space from Marduk. He hadn't time to estimate voyage-time to Gimli from the other Mardukan trade-planets, and nobody could estimate how many ships would respond.

"It may take us a little time to get an effective fleet together. Even after we get through arguing about it. Argument," he told Bentrik, "is not exclusively a feature of democracies."

Actually, there was very little argument, and most of that among the Mardukans. Prince Bentrik insisted that Crown Princess Myrna would have to be taken along; King Mikhyl would be either dead or brainwashed into imbecility by now, and they would have to have somebody to take the throne. Lady Valerie Alvarath, Sir Thomas Kobbly, the tutor, and the nurse Margot refused to be separated from her. Prince Bentrik was equally firm, with less success, on leaving his wife and son on Tanith. In the end, it was agreed that the entire Mardukan party would space out on the *Nemesis*.

The leader of the Bigglersport delegation attempted an impassioned tirade about going to the aid of strangers while their own planet was being enslaved. He was booed down by everybody else and informed that Tanith was being defended where a planet ought to be, on somebody else's real estate. When the Bigglersporters emerged from the meeting, they found that their own space-yacht had been commandeered and sent off to Amaterasu and Beowulf for assistance, that the regiment of local infantry they had enlisted from the King of Tradetown had been taken over by the Rivington authorities, and that the Gilgamesh freighter they had chartered to transport them to Gram would now take them to Marduk.

The problem broke into two halves: the purely naval action that would be fought to relieve the Moon of Marduk, if it still held out, and to destroy the Dunnan and Makann ships, and the ground-fighting problem of wiping out Makann's supporters and restoring the Mardukan monarchy. A great many of the people of Marduk would be glad of a chance to turn on Makann, once they had arms and were properly supported. Combat weapons were almost unknown among the people, however, and even sporting arms uncommon. All the small arms and light artillery and auto-weapons available were gathered up.

The *Grendelsbane* came in from Beowulf, and the *Sun Goddess* from Amaterasu. Three independent Space Viking ships were still in orbit on Tanith; they joined the expedition. There would be trouble with them on Marduk; they'd want to loot. Let the Mardukans worry about that. They could charge it off as part of the price for letting Zaspar Makann get into power in the first place.

There were twelve spacecraft in line outside the Moon of Tanith, counting the three independents and the forcibly chartered Gilgamesher troop-transport; that was the biggest fleet Space Vikings had ever assembled in their history. Alvyn Karffard said as much while they were checking the formation by screen.

"It isn't a Space Viking fleet," Prince Bentrik differed. "There are only three Space Vikings in it. The rest are the ships of three civilized planets. Tanith, Beowulf and Amaterasu."

Karffard was surprised. "You mean *we're* civilized planets? Like Marduk, or Baldur or Odin, or...?"

"Well, aren't you?"

Trask smiled. He'd begun to suspect something of the sort a couple of years ago. He hadn't really been sure until now. His most junior staff officer, Count Steven of Ravary, didn't seem to appreciate the compliment.

"We *are* Space Vikings!" he insisted. "And we are going to battle with the Neobarbarians of Zaspar Makann."

"Well, I won't argue the last half of it, Steven," his father told him.

"Are you people done yakking about who's civilized and who isn't?" Guatt Kirbey asked. "Then give the signal. All the other ships are ready to jump."

Trask pressed the button on the desk in front of him. A light went on over Kirbey's control panel as one would on each of the other ships. He said, "Jumping," around the stem of his pipe, and twisted the red handle and shoved it in.

Four hundred and fifty hours, in the private universe that was the *Nemesis*; outside, nothing else existed, and inside there was nothing to do but wait, as each hour carried them six trillion miles nearer to Gimli. At first, the ruthless and terrible Space Viking, Steven, Count of Ravary, was wildly excited, but before long he found that there was nothing exciting going on; it was just a spaceship, and he'd been on ships before. Her Highness the Crown Princess, or maybe her Majesty the Queen of Marduk, stopped being excited about the same time, and she and Steven and Mopsy played together. Of course, Myrna was only a girl, and two years younger than Steven, but she was, or at least might be, his sovereign, and beside, she had been in a space action, if you call what lies between a planet and its satellite space and if you call being shot at without being able to shoot back an action, and Relentless Ravary, the Interstellar Terror, had not. This rather made up for being a girl and a mere baby of going-on-ten.

One thing, there were no lessons. Sir Thomas Kobbly fancied himself as a landscape-painter and spent most of his time arguing techniques with Vann Larch, and Steven's tutor, Captain Rainer was a normal-space astrogator and found a kindred spirit in Sharll Renner. This left Lady Valerie Alvarath at a loose end. There were plenty of volunteers to help her fill in the time, but Rank Hath Its Privileges; Trask undertook to see to it that she did not suffer excessively from shipboard ennui.

Sharll Renner and Captain Rainer approached him, during the cocktail hour before dinner, some hundred hours short of emergence.

"We think we've figured out where Dunnan's base is," Renner said.

"Oh, good!" Everybody else had, on a different planet. "Where's yours?"

"Abaddon," the Count of Ravary's tutor said. When he saw that the name meant nothing to Trask, he added, "The ninth, outer, planet of the Marduk system." He said it disgustedly.

"Yes; remember how you had Boake and Manfred out with their ships, checking our outside planets to see if Prince Viktor might be hiding on one of them? Well, what with the time element, and the way the *Honest Horris* was shuttling back and forth from Marduk to some place that wasn't Gimli, and the way Dunnan was able to bring his ships in as soon as the shooting started on Marduk, we thought he must be on an uninhabited outer planet of the Marduk system."

"I don't know why we never thought of that, ourselves," Rainer put in. "I suppose because nobody ever thinks of Abaddon for any reason. It's only a small planet, about four thousand miles in diameter, and it's three and a half billion miles from primary. It's frozen solid. It would take almost a year to get to it on Abbot drive, and if your ship has Dillinghams, why not take a little longer and go to a good planet? So nobody bothered with Abaddon."

But for Dunnan's purpose, it would be perfect. He called Prince Bentrik and Alvyn Karffard to him; they found the idea instantly convincing. They talked about it through dinner, and held a general discussion afterward. Even Guatt Kirbey, the ship's pessimist, could find no objection to it. Trask and Bentrik began at once making battle plans. Karffard wondered if they hadn't better wait till they got to Gimli and discuss it with the others.

"No," Trask told him. "This is the flagship; here's where the strategy is decided."

"Well, how about the Mardukan Navy?" Captain Rainer asked. "I think Fleet Admiral Bargham's in command at Gimli."

Prince Simon Bentrik was silent for a moment, as though he realized, with reluctance, that the big decision was no longer avoidable.

"He may be, at present, but he won't be when I get there. I will be."

"But ... Your Highness, he's a fleet admiral; you're just a commodore."

"I am not just a commodore. The King is a prisoner, and for all we know dead. The Crown Prince is dead. The Princess Myrna is a child. I am assuming the position of Regent and Prince-Protector of the Realm."

XXVI

There was a little difficulty on Gimli with Fleet Admiral Bargham. Commodores didn't give orders to fleet admirals. Well, maybe regents did, but who gave Prince Bentrik authority to call himself regent? Regents were elected by the Chamber of Delegates, on nomination of the Chancellor.

"That's Zaspar Makann and his stooges you're talking about?" Bentrik laughed.

"Well, the Constitution...." He thought better of that, before somebody asked him what Constitution. "Well, a Regent has to be chosen by election. Even members of the Royal Family can't just make themselves Regent by saying they are."

"I can. I just have. And I don't think there are going to be many more elections, at least for the present. Not till we make sure the people of Marduk can be trusted with the control of the government."

"Well, the pinnace from Moonbase reported that there were six Royal navy battleships and four other craft attacking them," Bargham objected. "I only have four ships here; I sent for the ones on the other trade-planets, but I haven't heard from any of them. We can't go there with only four ships."

"Sixteen ships," Bentrik corrected. "No, fifteen and one Gilgamesher we're using for a troop-ship. I think that's enough. You'll remain here on Gimli, in any case, admiral; as soon as the other ships come in, you'll follow to Marduk with them. I am now holding a meeting aboard the Tanith flagship *Nemesis*. I want your four ship-commanders aboard immediately. I am not including you because you're remaining here to bring up the late comers and as soon as this meeting is over we are spacing out."

Actually, they spaced out sooner; the meeting lasted the whole three hundred and fifty hours to Abaddon. A ship's captain, if he has a good exec, as all of them had, needs only sit at his command-desk and look important while the ship is going into and emerging from a long jump; the rest of the time he can study ancient history or whatever his shipboard hobby is. Rather than waste three hundred and fifty hours of precious time, each captain turned his ship over to his exec and remained aboard the *Nemesis*; even on so spacious a craft the officers' country north of the engine rooms was crowded like a tourist hotel in mid-season. One of the four

Mardukans was the Captain Garravay who had smuggled Bentrik's wife and son off Marduk, and the other three were just as pro-Bentrik, pro-Tanith, and anti-Makann. They were, on general principles, also anti-Bargham. There must be something wrong with any fleet admiral who remained in his command after Zaspar Makann came to power.

So, as soon as they spaced out, there was a party. After that, they settled down to planning the Battle of Abaddon.

There was no Battle of Abaddon.

It was a dead planet, one side in night and the other in dim twilight from the little speck of a sun three and a half billion miles away, jagged mountains rising out of the snow that covered it from pole to pole. The snow on top would be frozen CO_2; according to the thermocouples, the surface temperature was well below minus-100 Centigrade. No ships on orbit circled it; there was a little faint radiation, which could have been from naturally radioactive minerals; there was no electrical discharge detectable.

There was considerable bad language in the command room of the *Nemesis*. The captains of the other ships were screening in, wanting to know what to do.

"Go on in," Trask told them. "Englobe the planet, and go down to within a mile if necessary. They could be hiding somewhere on it."

"Well, they're not hiding at the bottom of any ocean, that's for sure," somebody said. It was one of those feeble jokes at which everybody laughs because nothing else is laughable about the situation.

Finally, they found it, at the north pole, which was no colder than anywhere else on the planet. First radiation leakage, the sort that would come from a closed-down nuclear power plant. Then a modicum of electrical discharge. Finally the telescopic screens picked up the spaceport, a huge oval amphitheater excavated out of a valley between two jagged mountain ranges.

The language in the command room was just as bad, but the tone had changed. It was surprising what a wide range of emotions could be expressed by a few simple blasphemies and obscenities. Everybody who had been deriding Sharll Renner were now acclaiming him.

But it was lifeless. The ships came crowding in; air-locked landing-craft full of space-armored ground-fighters went down. Screens in the command room lit as they transmitted in views. Depressions in the carbon-dioxide snow where the hundred-foot pad-feet of ships' landing-legs had pressed down. Ranks of cargo-lighters that had plied to and from other ships or orbit. And, all around the cliff-walled perimeter, air-locked doors to caverns and tunnels. A great many men, with a great deal of equipment, had been working here in the estimated five or six years since Andray Dunnan-or somebody-had constructed this base.

Andray Dunnan. They found his badge, the crescent, blue on black, on things. They found equipment that Harkaman recognized as having been part of the original cargo stolen with the *Enterprise*. They even found, in his living quarters, a blown-up photoprint picture of Nevil Ormm, draped in black. But what they did not find was a single vehicle small enough to be taken aboard a ship, or a single scrap of combat equipment, not even a pistol or a hand grenade.

Dunnan had gone, but they knew whither, and where to find him. The conquest of Marduk had moved into its final phase.

Marduk was on the other side of the sun from Abaddon with ninety-five million miles-close, but not inconveniently so, Trask thought-to spare. Guatt Kirbey and the Mardukan astrogator who was helping him made it within a light-minute. The Mardukan thought that was fine; Kirbey didn't. The last microjump was aimed at the Moon of Marduk, which was plainly visible in the telescopic screen. They came out within a light-second and a half, which Kirbey admitted was reasonably close. As soon as the screens cleared, they saw that they weren't too late. The Moon of Marduk was under fire and firing back.

They'd have detection, and he knew what they were detecting—a clump of sixteen rending distortions of the fabric of space-time, as sixteen ships came into sudden existence in the normal continuum. Beside him, Bentrik had a screen on; it was still milky-white, and he was speaking into a radio hand-phone.

"Simon Bentrik, Prince-Protector of Marduk, calling Moonbase." Then, slowly, he repeated his screen-combination twice. "Come in, Moonbase; this is Simon Bentrik, Prince-Protector, speaking."

He waited ten seconds, and was about to start again, when the screen flickered. The man who appeared in it wore the insignia of a Mardukan navy commodore. He needed a shave, but he was grinning happily. Bentrik greeted him by name.

"Hello, Simon; glad to see you. Your Highness, I mean; what is this Prince-Protector thing?"

"Somebody had to do it. Is the King still alive?"

The grin slid off the commodore's face, starting with his eyes.

"We don't know. At first, Makann had him speaking by screen-you know what it was like-urging everybody to obey and co-operate with 'our trusted Chancellor.' Makann always appeared on the screen with him."

Bentrik nodded. "I remember."

"Before you left, Makann kept quiet, and let the King make the speech. After a while, the King wasn't able to speak coherently; he'd stammer, and repeat. So then Makann did all the talking; they couldn't even depend on him to parrot what they were giving him with an earplug phone. Then he stopped appearing entirely. I suppose there were physical symptoms they couldn't allow to be seen." Bentrik was cursing horribly under his breath; the officer at Moonbase nodded. "I hope for his sake that he is dead."

Poor Goodman Mikhyl. Bentrik was saying, "So do I." Trask agreed, mentally. The commodore at Moonbase was still talking:

"We got two more renegade RMN ships, within a hundred hours after you left." He named them. "And we got one of the Dunnan ships, the *Fortuna*. We blew out the Malverton Navy Yard. They're still using the Antarctic Naval Base, but we've knocked out a good deal of that. We got the *Honest Horris*. They made two attempts to land on us and lost a couple of ships. Eight hundred hours ago, they were joined by the rest of Dunnan's fleet, five ships. They made a landing on Malverton while it was turned away from us. Makann announced that they were RMN units from the trade-planets that had joined him. I suppose the planet-side public swallowed that. He also announced that their commander, Admiral Dunnan, was in command of the People's Armed Forces."

Dunnan's ground-fighters would be in control of Malverton. By now, the odds were that Makann was as much his prisoner as King Mikhyl VIII had been Makann's.

"So Dunnan has conquered Marduk. All he has to do, now, is make it stick," he said. "I see four ships off Moonbase; how many more have they?"

"These are *Bolide* and *Eclipse*, Dunnan's ships, and former Royal Mardukan Navy ships *Champion* and *Guardian*. There are five orbiting off the planet: Ex-RMNS *Paladin*, and Dunnan ships *Starhopper*, *Banshee*, *Reliable* and *Exporter*. The last two are listed as merchantmen, but they're performing like regulation battlecraft."

The four that had been circling Moonbase broke orbit and started toward the relieving fleet; one took a hit from a Moonbase missile, which staggered her but did no evident damage. Two ships which had been orbiting the planet also changed course and started out. The command room was silent except for a subdued chuckling from a computer which was estimating enemy intentions by observed data and Games Theory. Three more came hurrying out from the planet, and the two in the lead slowed to let them catch up. He wanted to be able to engage the four from off the satellite before the five from the planet joined them, but Karffard's computers said it couldn't be done.

"All right, we have to take all our bad eggs in one basket," he said. "Try to hit them as soon after they join as possible."

The computers began chuckling again. The serving-robots were doing a rush business in hot coffee. Prince Bentrik's son, sitting beside his father, had stopped being Ruthless Ravary the Demon of the Spaceways and was a very young officer going into his first space battle, more scared and at the same time happier than he had ever been in his short life. Captain Garravay of the *Vindex* was making signal to the other ships from Gimli: *"Royal Navy; smash the traitors first!"* He could understand and sympathize, even if he couldn't approve of putting personal ahead of tactical considerations, and made a quick sealed-beam call to Harkaman to be prepared to plug any holes they left in formation if they broke away in search of vengeance. He also ordered the *Black Star* and the *Sun Goddess* to shepherd the lightly armed and troop-crammed Gilgamesh freighter out of danger. The two clumps of Dunnan-Makann ships were converging rapidly, and Alvyn Karffard was screaming into a phone to somebody to get more speed.

At a thousand miles, the missiles started going out, and the two groups of ships, four and five, were equidistant from each other and from the allied fleet, at the points of a triangle that was growing smaller by the second. The first fire-globes of intercepted missiles spread from their seeds of brief white light. A red light flashed on the damage-board. An enemy ship took a hit. The captain of the *Queen Flavia* was on a screen, saying that his ship was heavily damaged. Three ships bearing the Mardukan dragon-and-planet circled madly around each other at what looked, in the screen, like just over pistol-range, two of them firing into the third, which was replying desperately. The third one blew up, and somebody was yelling out of a screenspeaker, "Scratch one traitor!"

Another ship blew up somewhere, and then another. He heard somebody say, "There went one of ours," and wondered which one it was. Not the *Corisande*, he hoped; no, it wasn't, he could see her rushing after two other ships which were, in turn, speeding toward the *Black Star*, the *Sun Goddess* and the Gilgamesh freighter. Then the *Nemesis* and the *Starhopper* were within gun-range, pounding each other savagely.

The battle had tied itself into a ball of gyrating, fire-spitting ships that went rolling toward the planet, which was swinging in and out of the main viewscreen and growing rapidly larger. By the time they were down to the inner edge of the exosphere, the ball had started to unwind, ship after ship dropping out of it and going into orbit, some badly damaged and some going to attack damaged enemies. Some of them were completely around the planet, hidden by it. He saw three ships approaching *Corisande*, *Sun Goddess*, and the Gilgamesher. He got Harkaman on the screen.

"Where's the *Black Star*?" he asked.

"Gone to Em-See-Square," Harkaman replied. "We got the two Dunnan-Makanns. *Bolide* and *Reliable*."

Then young Steven of Ravary, who had been monitoring one of the intership screens, had a call from Captain Gompertz of the *Grendelsbane*, and at the same moment somebody else was yelling, "Here comes the *Starhopper* again!"

"Tell him to wait a moment; we have troubles," he said.

Nemesis and *Starhopper* sledge-hammered each other and parried with counter-missiles, and then, quite unexpectedly, the *Starhopper* went to Em-See-Square.

There was an awful lot of Em being converted to Ee off Marduk, today. Including Manfred Ravallo; that grieved him. Manfred was a good man, and a good friend. He had a girl in Rivington....Nifflheim, there were eight hundred good men aboard the *Black Star*, and most of them had girls who'd wait in vain for them on Tanith. Well, what had Otto Harkaman said, so long ago, on Gram? Something about old age not being a usual cause of death among Space Vikings, wasn't it?

Then he remembered that Gompertz of the *Grendelsbane* was trying to get him. He told young Count Steven to switch him over.

"We just lost one of our Mardukans," Gompertz told him, in his staccato Beowulf accent. "I think she was the *Challenger*. The ship that got her looks like the *Banshee*; I'm turning to engage her."

"Which way; west around the planet? Be right with you, captain."

XXVII

It was like finishing a word puzzle. You sit staring at it, looking for more spaces to print letters into, and suddenly you realize that there are no more, that the puzzle is done. That was how the space-battle of Marduk, the Battle *off* Marduk, ended. Suddenly there were no more colored fire-globes opening and fading, no more missiles coming, no more enemy ships to throw missiles at. Now it was time to take a count of his own ships, and then begin thinking about the Battle *on* Marduk.

The *Black Star* was gone. So was RMNS *Challenger*, and RMNS *Conquistador*. *Space Scourge* was badly hammered; worse than after the Beowulf raid, Boake Valkanhayn said. The *Viking's Gift* was heavily damaged, too, and so was the *Corisande*, and so, from the looks of the damage board, was the *Nemesis*. And three ships were missing-the three independent Space Vikings, *Harpy*, *Curse of Cagn*, and Roger-fan-Morvill Esthersan's *Damnthing*.

Prince Bentrik frowned over that. "I can't think that all three of those ships would have been destroyed, without anybody seeing it happen."

"Neither can I. But I can think that all those ships broke out of the battle together and headed in for the planet. They didn't come here to help liberate Marduk, they came here to fill their cargo holds. I only hope the people they're robbing all voted the Makann ticket in the last election." A crumb of comfort occurred to him, and he passed it on. "The only people who are armed to resist them will be Makann's storm-troops and Dunnan's pirates; they'll be the ones to get killed."

"We don't want any more killing than...." Prince Simon broke off suddenly. "I'm beginning to talk like his late Highness Crown Prince Edvard," he said. "He didn't want bloodshed, either, and look whose blood was shed. If they're doing what you think they are, I'm afraid we'll have to kill a few of your Space Vikings, too."

"They aren't my Space Vikings." He was a little surprised to find that, after almost eight years of bearing the name himself, he was using it as an other-people label. Well, why not? He was the ruler of the civilized planet of Tanith, wasn't he? "But let's not start fighting them till the main war's over. Those three shiploads are no worse than a bad cold; Makann and Dunnan are the plague."

It would still take four hours to get down, in a spiral of deceleration. They started the telecasts which had been filmed and taped on the voyage from Gimli. The Prince-Protector Simon Bentrik spoke: The illegal rule of the traitor Makann was ended. His deluded followers were advised to return to their allegiance to the Crown. The People's Watchmen were ordered to surrender their arms and disband; in localities where they refused, the loyal people were called upon to co-operate with the legitimate armed forces of the Crown in exterminating them, and would be furnished arms as soon as possible.

Little Princess Myrna spoke: "If my grandfather is still alive, he is your King; if he is not, I am your Queen, and until I am old enough to rule in my own right, I accept Prince Simon as Regent and Protector of the Realm, and I call on all of you to obey him as I will."

"You didn't say anything about representative government, or democracy, or the constitution," Trask mentioned. "And I noticed the use of the word 'rule,' instead of 'reign.'"

"That's right," the self-proclaimed Prince-Protector said. "There's something wrong with democracy. If there weren't, it couldn't be overthrown by people like Makann, attacking it from within by democratic procedures. I don't think it's fundamentally unworkable. I think it just has a few of what engineers call bugs. It's not safe to run a defective machine till you learn the defects and remedy them."

"Well, I hope you don't think our Sword-World feudalism doesn't have bugs." He gave examples, and then quoted Otto Harkaman about barbarism spreading downward from the top instead of upward from the bottom.

"It may just be," he added, "that there is something fundamentally unworkable about government itself. As long as *Homo sapiens terra* is a wild animal, which he has always been and always will be until he evolves into something different in a million or so years, maybe a workable system of government is a political science impossibility, just as transmutation of elements was a physical-science impossibility as long as they tried to do it by chemical means."

"Then we'll just have to make it work the best way we can, and when it breaks down, hope the next try will work a little better, for a little longer," Bentrik said.

———————————————————

Malverton grew in the telescopic screens as they came down. The Navy Spaceport, where Trask had landed almost two years before, was in wreckage, sprinkled with damaged ships that had been blasted on the ground, and slagged by thermonuclear fires. There was fighting in the air all over the city proper, on building-tops, on the ground, and in the air. That would be the *Damnthing-Harpy-Curse of Cagn* Space Vikings. The Royal Palace was the center of one of half a dozen swirls of battle that had condensed out of the general skirmishing.

Paytrik Morland started for it with the first wave of ground-fighters from the *Nemesis*. The Gilgamesh freighter, like most of her ilk, had huge cargo ports all around; these began opening and disgorging a swarm of everything from landing-craft and hundred-foot airboats to one man air-cavalry single-mounts. The top landing-stages and terraces of the palace were almost obscured by the flashes of auto-cannon shells and the smoke and dust of projectiles. Then the first vehicles landed, the firing from the air stopped, and men fanned out as skirmishers, occasionally firing with small arms.

Trask and Bentrik were in the armory off the vehicle-bay, putting on combat equipment, when the twelve-year-old Count of Ravary joined them and began rummaging for weapons and a helmet.

"You're not going," his father told him. "I'll have enough to worry about taking care of myself...."

That was the wrong approach. Trask interrupted:

"You're to stay aboard, Count," he said. "As soon as things stabilize, Princess Myrna will have to come down. You'll act as her personal escort. And don't think you're being shoved into the background. She's Crown Princess, and if she isn't Queen now, she will be in a few years. Escorting her now will be the foundation of your naval career. There isn't a young officer in the Royal Navy who wouldn't trade places with you."

"That was the right way to handle him, Lucas," Bentrik approved, after the boy had gone away, proud of his opportunity and his responsibility.

"It'll do just what I said for him." He stopped for a moment, to play with an idea that had just struck him. "You know, the girl will be Queen in a few years, if she isn't now. Queens need Prince Consorts. Your son's a good boy; I liked him the first moment I saw him, and I've liked him better ever since. He'd be a good man on the throne beside Queen Myrna."

"Oh, that's out of the question. Not the matter of consanguinity, they're about a sixteenth cousin. But people would say I was abusing the Protectorship to marry my son onto the Throne."

"Simon, speaking as one sovereign prince to another, you have a lot to learn. You've learned one important lesson already, that a ruler must be willing to use force and shed blood to enforce his rule. You have to learn, too, that a ruler cannot afford to be guided by his fears of what people will say about him. Not even what history will say about him. A ruler's only judge is himself."

Bentrik slid the transpex visor of his helmet up and down experimentally, checked the chambers of his pistol and carbine.

"All that matters to me is the peace and well-being of Marduk. I'll have to talk it over with ...with my only judge. Well, let's go."

The top terraces were secure when their car landed. More vehicles were coming down and discharging men; a swarm of landing craft were sinking past the building toward the ground two thousand feet below. Auto-weapons and small arms and light cannon banged, and bombs and recoilless-rifle shells crashed, on the lower terraces. They put the car down one of the shaftways until they ran into heavy fire from below, at the limit of the advance, and then turned into a broad hallway, floating high enough to clear the heads of the men on foot. It looked like the part of the Palace where he had lodged when he had been a guest there but it probably wasn't.

They came to hastily constructed barricades of furniture and statuary and furnishings, behind which Makann's People's Watchmen and Andray Dunnan's Space Vikings were making resistance. They entered rooms dusty with powdered plaster and acrid with powder fumes, littered with corpses. They passed lifter-skids being towed out with wounded. They went through rooms crowded with their own men —*"Keep your fingers off things; this isn't a looting expedition!"* *"You stupid cretin, how did you know there wasn't a man hiding behind that?"* In one huge room, ballroom or concert room or something, there were prisoners herded, and men from the *Nemesis* were setting up polyencephalographic veridicators, sturdy chairs with wires and adjustable helmets and translucent globes mounted over them. A couple of Morland's men were hustling a People's Watchman to one and strapping him into a chair.

"You know what this is, don't you?" one of them was saying. "This is a veridicator. That globe'll light blue; the moment you try to lie to us, it'll turn red. And the moment it turns red, I'm going to hammer your teeth down your throat with the butt of this pistol."

"Have you found anything out about the King, yet?" Bentrik asked him.

He turned. "No. Nobody we've questioned so far knows anything later than a month ago about him. He just disappeared." He was going to say something else, saw Bentrik's face, and changed his mind.

"He's dead," Bentrik said dully. "They tortured him and brainwashed him and used him as a ventriloquist's dummy on the screen as long as they could; when they couldn't let the people see him any more, they stuffed him into a converter."

They did find Zaspar Makann, hours later. Maybe he could have told them something, if he had been alive, but he and a few of his fanatical followers had barricaded themselves in the Throne room and died trying to defend it. They found Makann on the Throne, the top of his head blown away, a pistol death-gripped in his hand, and the Great Crown lying on the floor, the velvet inner cap bullet-pierced and splattered with blood and brain tissue. Prince Bentrik picked it up and looked at it disgustedly.

"We'll have to have something done about that," he said. "I really didn't think he'd do just this. I thought he wanted to abolish the Throne, not sit on it."

Except for one chandelier smashed and several corpses that had to be dragged out, the Ministerial Council room was intact. They set up headquarters there. Boake Valkanhayn and several other ship-captains joined them. There was fighting going on in several places inside the Palace, and the city was still in a turmoil. Somebody managed to get in touch with the captains of the *Damnthing*, the *Harpy* and the *Curse of Cagn* and bring them to the Palace. Trask attempted to reason with them, to no avail.

"Prince Trask, you're my friend, and you've always dealt fairly with me," Roger-fan-Morvill Esthersan said. "But you know just how far any Space Viking captain can control his crew. These men didn't come here to correct the political mistakes of Marduk. They came here for what they could haul away. I could get myself killed trying to stop them now...."

"I wouldn't even try," the captain of the *Curse of Cagn* put in. "I came here for what I could make out of this planet, myself."

"You can try to stop them," said the captain of the *Harpy*. "You'll find it even harder than what you're doing now."

Trask looked at some of the reports that had come in from elsewhere on the planet. Harkaman had landed on one of the big cities to the east, and the people had risen against Makann's local bosses and were helping wipe out the People's Watchmen with arms they had been furnished. Valkanhayn's exec had landed on a large concentration camp where close to ten thousand of Makann's political enemies had been penned; he had distributed all his available weapons and was calling for more. Gompertz of the *Grendelsbane* was at Drepplin; he reported just the reverse. The people there had risen in support of the Makann regime, and he wanted authorization to use nuclear weapons against them.

"Could you talk your people into going to some other city?" Trask asked. "We have a city for you; big industrial center. It ought to be fine looting. Drepplin."

"The people there are Mardukan subjects, too," Bentrik began. Then he shrugged. "It's not what we'd like to do, it's what we have to. By all means, gentlemen. Take your men to Drepplin, and nobody will object to anything you do."

"And when you have that place looted out, try Abaddon. You were aground there, Captain Esthersan. You know what all Dunnan left there."

A couple of Space Vikings-no, Royal Army of Tanith men-brought in the old woman, dirty, in rags, almost exhausted.

"She wants to talk to Prince Bentrik; won't talk to anybody else. Says she knows where the King is."

Bentrik rose quickly, brought her to a chair, poured a glass of wine for her.

"He's still alive, Your Highness. The Crown Princess Melanie and I ... I'm sorry, Your Highness; Dowager Crown Princess ... have been taking care of him, the best way we could. If you'll only come quickly...."

Mikhyl VIII, Planetary King of Marduk, lay on a pallet of filthy bedding on the floor of a narrow room behind a mass-energy converter which disposed of the rubbish and sewage and generated power for some of the fixed equipment on one of the middle floors of the east wing of the palace. There was a bucket of water, and on a rough wooden bench lay a cloth-wrapped bundle of food. A woman, haggard and disheveled, wearing a suit of greasy mechanic's coveralls and nothing else, squatted beside him. The Crown Princess Melanie, whom Trask remembered as the charming and gracious hostess of Cragdale. She tried to rise, and staggered.

"Prince Bentrik! And it's Prince Trask of Tanith!" she cried. "Just hurry; get him out of here and to where he can be taken care of. Please." Then she sat down again on the floor and fell over, unconscious.

They couldn't get the story. The Princess Melanie had collapsed completely. Her companion, another noblewoman of the court, could only ramble disconnectedly. And the King merely lay, bathed and fed in a clean bed, and looked up at them wonderingly, as though nothing he saw or heard conveyed any meaning to him. The doctors could do nothing.

"He has no mind, no more mind than a new-born baby. We can keep him alive, I don't know how long. That's our professional duty. But it's no kindness to His Majesty."

The little pockets of resistance in the Palace were wiped out, through the next morning and afternoon. All but one, far underground, below the main power plant. They tried sleep-gas; the defenders had blowers and sent it back at them. They tried blasting; there was a limit to what the fabric of the building would stand. And nobody knew how long it would take to starve them out.

On the third day, a man crawled out, pushing a white shirt tied to the barrel of a carbine ahead of him.

"Is Prince Lucas Trask of Tanith here?" he asked. "I won't speak to anybody else."

They brought Trask quickly. All that was visible of the other man was the carbine-barrel and the white shirt. When Trask called to him, he raised his head above the rubble behind which he was hiding.

"Prince Trask, we have Andray Dunnan here; he was leading us, but now we've disarmed him and are holding him. If we turn him over to you, will you let us go?"

"If you all come out unarmed, and bring Dunnan with you, I promise you, the rest of you will be let outside this building and allowed to go away unharmed."

"All right. We'll be coming out in a minute." The man raised his voice. "It's agreed!" he called. "Bring him out."

There were fewer than two score of them. Some wore the uniforms of high officers of the People's Watchmen or of People's Welfare Party functionaries; a few wore the heavily braided short jackets of Space Viking officers. Among them, they propelled a thin-faced man with a pointed beard, and Trask had to look twice at him before he recognized the face of Andray Dunnan. It looked more like the face of Duke Angus of Wardshaven as he last remembered it. Dunnan looked at him in incurious contempt.

"Your dotard king couldn't rule without Zaspar Makann, and Makann couldn't rule without me, and neither can you," he said. "Shoot this gang of turncoats, and I'll rule Marduk for you." He looked at Trask again. "Who are you?" he demanded. "I don't know you."

Trask slipped the pistol from his holster, thumbing off the safety.

"I am Lucas Trask. You've heard that name before," he said. "Stand away from behind him, you people."

"Oh, yes; the poor fool who thought he was going to marry Elaine Karvall. Well, you won't, Lord Trask of Traskon. She loves me, not you. She's waiting for me now, on Gram...."

Trask shot him through the head. Dunnan's eyes widened in momentary incredulity; then his knees gave way, and he fell forward on his face. Trask thumbed on the safety and holstered the pistol, and looked at the body on the concrete.

It hadn't made the least difference. It had been like shooting a snake, or one of the nasty scorpion-things that infested the old buildings in Rivington. Just no more Andray Dunnan.

"Take that carrion and stuff it in a mass-energy converter," he said. "And I don't want anybody to mention the name of Andray Dunnan to me again."

He didn't look at them haul Dunnan's body away on a lifter-skid; he watched the fifty-odd leaders of the overthrown misgovernment of Marduk shamble away to freedom, guarded by Paytrik Morland's riflemen. Now there was something to reproach himself for; he'd committed a separate and distinct crime against Marduk by letting each one of them live. Unless recognized and killed by somebody outside, every one of them would be at some villainy before next sunrise. Well, King Simon I could cope with that.

He started when he realized how he had thought of his friend. Well, why not? Mikhyl's mind was dead; his body would not survive it more than a year. Then a child Queen, and a long regency, and long regencies were dangerous. Better a strong King, in name as well as power. And the succession could be safeguarded by marrying Steven and Myrna. Myrna had accepted, at eight, that she must some day marry for reasons of state; why not her playmate Steven?

And Simon Bentrik would see the necessity. He was neither a fool nor a moral coward; he only needed to take some time to adjust to ideas. The rabble who had bought their lives with their leader's had gone, now. Slowly, he followed them, thinking.

Don't press the idea on Simon too hard; just expose him to it and let him adopt it. And there would be the treaty-Tanith, Marduk, Beowulf, Amaterasu; eventually, treaties with the other civilized planets. Nebulously, the idea of a League of Civilized Worlds began to take shape in his mind.

Be a good idea if he adopted the title of King of Tanith for himself. And cut loose from the Sword-Worlds; especially cut loose from Gram. Let Viktor of Xochitl have it. Or Garvan Spasso. Viktor wouldn't be the last Space Viking to take his ships back against the Sword-Worlds. Sooner or later, civilization in the Old Federation would drive them all home to loot the planets that had sent them out.

Well, if he was going to be a king, shouldn't he have a queen? Kings usually did. He climbed into the little hall-car and started up a long shaft. There was Valerie Alvarath. They'd enjoyed each other's society on the *Nemesis*. He wondered if she would want to make it permanent, even on a throne....

Elaine was with him. He felt her beside him, almost tangibly. Her voice was whispering to him: *She loves you, Lucas. She'll say yes. Be good to her, and she'll make you happy.* Then she was gone, and he knew that she would never return.

Good-by, Elaine.

The Return

by

H. Beam Piper

I

Altamont cast a quick, routine glance at the instrument panels and then looked down through the transparent nose of the helicopter at the yellow-brown river five hundred feet below. Next he scraped the last morsel from his plate and ate it.

"What did you make this out of, Jim?" he asked. "I hope you kept notes while you were concocting it. It's good."

"The two smoked pork chops left over from yesterday evening," Loudons said, "and that bowl of rice that's been taking up space in the refrigerator the last couple of days, together with a little egg powder and some milk. I ground the chops up and mixed them with the rice and other stuff. Then added some bacon, to make grease to fry it in."

Altamont chuckled. That was Loudons, all right: he could take a few left-overs, mess them together, pop them in the skillet, and have a meal that would turn the chef back at the Fort green with envy. He filled his cup and offered the pot.

"Caffchoc?" he asked.

Loudons held his cup out to be filled, blew on it, sipped, and then hunted on the ledge under the desk for the butt of the cigar he had half-smoked the evening before.

"Did you ever drink coffee, Monty?" the socio-psychologist asked, getting the cigar drawing to his taste.

"Coffee? No. I've read about it, of course. We'll have to organize an expedition to Brazil, sometime, to get seeds and try raising some."

Loudons blew a smoke ring toward the rear of the cabin.

"A much overrated beverage," he replied. "We found some, once, when I was on that expedition into Idaho, in what must have been the stockroom of a hotel. Vacuum-packed in moisture-proof containers, and free from radioactivity. It wasn't nearly as good as caffchoc.

"But then, I suppose, a pre-bustup coffee drinker couldn't stomach this stuff we're drinking."

Loudons looked forward, up the river they were following. "Get anything on the radio?" he asked. "I noticed you took us up to about ten thousand, while I was shaving."

Altamont got out his pipe and tobacco pouch, filling the former slowly and carefully.

"Not a whisper. I tried Colony Three, in the Ozarks, and I tried to call in that tribe of workers in Louisiana. I couldn't get either."

"Maybe if we tried to get a little more power on the set...."

That was Loudons, too, Altamont thought. There wasn't a better man at the Fort, when it came to dealing with people. But confront him with a problem about things and he was lost.

That was one of the reasons why he and the stocky, phlegmatic social scientist made such a good team, he thought. As far as he, himself, was concerned, people were just a mysterious, exasperatingly unpredictable order of things which were subject to no known natural laws.

And Loudons thought the same thing about machines: he couldn't psychoanalyze them.

Altamont gestured with his pipe toward the nuclear-electric conversion unit, between the control-cabin and the living quarters in the rear of the boxcar-sized helicopter.

"We have enough power back there to keep this windmill in the air twenty-four hours a day, three hundred and sixty-five days a year, for the next fifteen years," he said. "We just don't have enough radio. If I'd step up the power on this set any more, it'd burn out before I could say, 'Altamont calling Fort Ridgeway.'"

"How far are we from Pittsburgh now?" Loudons wanted to know.

Altamont looked across the cabin at the big map of the United States as they had been, the red and green and blue and yellow patchwork of vanished political divisions. The colors gleamed through the transparent overlay on which this voyage of re-discovery was plotted.

The red line of their journey started at Fort Ridgeway, in what had been Arizona. It angled east by a little north, to Colony Three, in northern Arkansas ... sharply northeast to St. Louis and its lifeless ruins ... then to Chicago and Gary, where little bands of Stone Age reversions stalked and fought and ate each other ... Detroit, where things that had completely forgotten they were human emerged from their burrows only at night ... Cleveland, where a couple of cobalt bombs must have landed in the lake and drenched everything with radioactivity that still lingered after two centuries ... Akron, where vegetation was only beginning to break through the glassy slag ... Cincinnati, where they had last stopped....

"How's the leg this morning, Jim?" he asked.

"Little stiff. Doesn't hurt much, though."

"Why, we're about fifty miles, as we follow that river, and that's relatively straight." He looked down through the transparent nose of the copter at a town, now choked with trees that grew among the tumbled walls. "I think that's Aliquippa."

Loudons looked and shrugged, then looked again and pointed.

"There's a bear. Just ducked into that church or movie theater or whatever. I wonder what he thinks we are."

Altamont puffed slowly at his pipe. "I wonder if we're going to find anything at all in Pittsburgh."

"You mean people, as distinct from those biped beasts we've found so far? I doubt it," Loudons replied, finishing his caffchoc and wiping his mustache with the back of his hand. "I think the whole eastern half of the country is nothing but forest like this, and the highest type of life is just about three cuts below Homo Neanderthalensis, almost impossible to contact, and even more impossible to educate."

"I wasn't thinking about that. I've just about given up hope of finding anybody or even a reasonably high level of barbarism," Altamont said. "I was thinking about that cache of microfilmed books that was buried at the Carnegie Library."

"If it was buried," Loudons qualified. "All we have is that article in that two-century-old copy of Time about how the people at the library had constructed the crypt and were beginning the microfilming. We don't know if they ever had a chance to get it finished, before the rockets started landing."

They passed over a dam of flotsam that had banked up at a wrecked bridge and accumulated enough mass to resist the periodic floods that had kept the river usually clear. Three human figures fled across a sand-flat at one end of it and disappeared into the woods. Two of them carried spears tipped with something that sparkled in the sunlight, probably shards of glass.

"You know, Monty, I get nightmares, sometimes, thinking about what things must be like in Europe," Loudons said.

Five or six wild cows went crashing through the brush below. Altamont nodded when he saw them.

"Maybe tomorrow, we'll let down and shoot a cow," he said. "I was looking in the freeze-locker and the fresh meat's getting a little low. Or a wild pig, if we find a good stand of oak trees. I could enjoy what you'd do with some acorn-fed pork."

He looked across the table. "Finished?" he asked Loudons. "Take over, then. I'll go back and wash the dishes."

They rose, and Loudons, favoring his left leg, moved over to the seat at the controls.

Altamont gathered up the two cups, the stainless-steel dishes, and the knives and the forks and spoons, going up the steps over the shielded converter and ducking his head to avoid the seat in the forward top machine-gun turret. He washed and dried the dishes, noting with satisfaction that the gauge of the water tank was still reasonably high, and glanced out one of the windows. Loudons was taking the big helicopter upstairs, for a better view.

Now and then, among the trees, there would be a glint of glassy slag, usually in a fairly small circle. That was to be expected: beside the three or four H-bombs that had fallen on the Pittsburgh area, mentioned in the transcripts of the last news to reach the Fort from the outside, the whole district had been pelted, more or less at random, with fission bombs.

West of the confluence of the Allegheny and the Monongahela, it would probably be worse than this.

"Can you see Pittsburgh yet, Jim?" he called out.

"Yes, it's a mess! Worse than Gary, worse than Akron even."

"Monty! Come here! I think I have something!"

Picking up the pipe he had laid down, Altamont hurried forward, dodging his six-foot length under the gun turret and swinging down from the walkway over the converter.

"What is it?" he asked.

"Smoke. A lot of smoke, twenty or thirty fires at the very least."

Loudons had shifted from Forward to Hover and was peering through a pair of binoculars. "See that island, the long one? Across the river from it, on the north side, toward this end. Yes, by Einstein! And I can see cleared ground, and what I think are houses, inside a stockade...."

II

Murray Hughes walked around the corner of the cabin into the morning sunlight, lacing his trousers, with his hunting shirt thrown over his bare shoulders. He found, without much surprise, that his father had also slept late. Verner Hughes was just beginning to shave.

Inside the kitchen, his mother and the girls were clattering pots and skillets.

Outside the kitchen door, his younger brother, Hector, was noisily chopping wood.

Going through the door, he filled another of the light-metal basins with hot water, found his razor, and went outside again, setting the basin on the bench.

Most of the ware in the Hughes cabin was of light-metal. Murray and his father had mined it in the dead city up the river, from a place where it had floated to the top of a puddle of slag, back when the city had been blasted, at the end of the hard times.

It had been hard work, but the stuff had been easy to carry down to where they had hidden their boat. And, for once, they'd had no trouble with the Scowrers.

Too bad they couldn't say as much for yesterday's hunting trip!

As he rubbed lather into the stubble on his face, he cursed with irritation. That had been a bad-luck hunt, all around.

They had gone out before dawn, hunting into the hills to the north. They'd spent the day at it, and shot one small wild pig. Lucky it was small, at that. They'd have had to abandon a full-grown one, after the Scowrers had began hunting them. Six of them, as big a band as he'd ever seen together at one time, had managed to cut them off from the stockade. He and his father had been forced to circle miles out of their way.

His father had shot one, and he'd had to leave his hatchet sticking in the skull of another, when his rifle had misfired.

That meant a trip to the gunsmith's, for a new hatchet and to have the mainspring of the rifle replaced. Nobody could afford to have a rifle that couldn't be trusted, least of all a hunter and prospector.

On top of everything else, he had had a few words with Alex Barrett, the gunsmith, the other day.

Well, at least that could be smoothed over. Barrett would be glad to do business with him, once the gunsmith saw that hard tool-steel he had dug out of that place down the river. Hardest steel either he or his father had ever found, and it hadn't been atom-spoiled, either.

He cleaned, wiped and stropped his razor and put it back in the case. He threw out the wash-water on the compost pile and went into the cabin, putting on his shirt and his belt. Then he passed through to the front porch, where his father was already eating at the table.

The people of the Toon like to eat in the open. It was something they'd always done, just as they'd always like to eat together in the evenings.

He sweetened his cup of chicory with a lump of maple sugar and began to sip it before he sat down, standing with one foot on the bench and looking down across the parade ground, past the Aitch-Cue House, toward the river and the wall.

"If you're coming around to Alex's way of thinking-and mine-it won't hurt you to admit it, son," his father said.

Murray turned, looking at his father with the beginning of anger, and then he grinned. The elders were constantly keeping the young men alert with these tests. He checked back over his actions since he had come out onto the porch.

...to the table, sugar in his chicory, one foot on the bench ...which had reminded him again of the absence of the hatchet from his belt and brought an automatic frown ...then the glance toward the gunsmith's shop, and across the parade ground ...the glance including the houses into which so much labor had gone, the wall that had been built from rubble and topped with pointed stakes, the white slabs of marble that marked the graves of the First Tenant and the men of the Old Toon....

He had thought, at that moment, that maybe his father and Alex Barrett and Reader Rawson and Tenant Mycroft Jones and the others were right: there were too many things here that could not be moved along with them, if they decided to move.

It would be false modesty, refusal to see things as they were, not to admit that he was the leader of the younger men, and the boys of the Irregulars. He had been forced to face the responsibilities of that fact since last winter.

Then, the usual theological arguments about the proper order of the Sacred Books and the true nature of the Risen One had been replaced by a violent controversy when Sholto Jiminez and Birdy Edwards had reopened the old question of the advisability of moving the Toon and settling elsewhere.

He had been in favor of the idea himself and found that the other young men had followed his lead. But, for the last month or so, he had begun to doubt the wisdom of it.

It was probably reluctance to admit this to himself that had brought on the strained feelings between himself and his old friend, the gunsmith.

"I'll have to drill the Irregulars, today," he said. "Birdy Edwards has been drilling them while we've been hunting. But I'll go up and see Alex about a new hatchet and fixing my rifle. I'll have a talk with him."

He stepped forward to the edge of the porch, still munching on a honey-dipped piece of cornbread, and glanced up at the sky. That was a queer bird; he had never seen a bird with a wing action like that.

Then he realized that the object was not a bird at all.

His father was staring at it, too.

"Murray! That's ...that's like the old stories from the time of the wars!"

But Murray was already racing across the parade ground toward the Aitch-Cue House, where the big iron ring hung by its chain from a gallows-like post, with a hammer beside it.

III

The stockaded village became larger, details grew plainer, as the helicopter came slanting down and began spiraling around it.

It was a fairly big place, some forty or fifty acres in a rough parallelogram, surrounded by a wall of varicolored stone and brick and concrete rubble from old ruins, topped with a palisade of pointed poles. There was a small jetty projecting into the river, to which six or eight boats of different sorts were tied; a gate opened onto this from the wall.

Inside the stockade, there were close to a hundred buildings, ranging from small cabins to a structure with a belfry. It seemed to have been a church, partly ruined in the war of two centuries ago and later rebuilt.

A stream came down from the woods, across the cultivated land around the fortified village. There was a rough flume which carried the water from a dam close to the edge of the forest and provided a fall to turn a mill wheel.

"Look, strip farming," Loudons pointed. "See the alternate strips of grass and plowed ground. These people understand soil conservation."

"They have horses, too."

As he spoke, three riders left the village at a gallop. They separated, and the people in the fields, who had all started for the village, turned and began hurrying toward the woods. Two of the riders headed for a pasture in which cattle had been grazing and started herding them also into the woods.

For a while, there was a scurrying of little figures in the village below. Then, not a moving thing was in sight.

"There's good organization," Loudons said. "Everybody seems to know what to do, and how to get it done promptly. And look how neat the whole place is. Policed up. I'll bet anything we'll find that they have a military organization, or a military tradition at least."

"We'll have a lot to find out: you can't understand a people until you understand their background and their social organization."

"Humph. Let me have a look at their artifacts: that will tell what kind of people they are," Altamont said, swinging the glasses back and forth over the enclosure. "Water-power mill, water-power sawmill-building on the left side of the water wheel, see the pile of fresh lumber beside it. Blacksmith shop, and from that chimney, I'd say a small foundry, too.

"Wonder what that little building out on the tip of the island is, it has a water wheel too. Undershot wheel, and it looks like it could be raised or lowered. Now, I wonder...."

"Monty, I think we ought to land right in the middle of the enclosure, on that open plaza thing, in front of the building that looks like a reconditioned church. That's probably the Royal Palace, or the Pentagon, or the Kremlin, or whatever."

Altamont started to object, paused, and then nodded. "I think you're right, Jim. From the way they scattered, and got their livestock into the woods, they probably expect us to bomb them. We have to get inside and that's the quickest way to do it." He thought for a moment. "We'd better be armed, when we go out. Pistols, auto-carbines, and a few of those concussion-grenades in case we have to break up a concerted attack. I'll get them."

The plaza, the houses and the cabins around it, the two-hundred-year-old church, all were silent and apparently lifeless as they set the helicopter down. Once Loudons caught a movement inside the door of a house, and saw a metallic glint.

"There's a gun up there," he said. "Looks like a four-pounder. Brass. I knew that smith-shop was also a foundry. See that little curl of smoke? That's the gunner's slow-match.

"I'd thought maybe that thing on the island was a powder mill. That would be where they'd put it. Probably extract their niter from the dung of their horses and cows. Sulfur probably from coal-mine drainage.

"Jim, this is really something!"

"I hope they don't cut loose with that thing," Loudons said, looking apprehensively at the brass-rimmed black muzzle that was covering them from the belfry. "I wonder if we ought to-Oh-oh, here they come!"

Three or four young men stepped out of the wide door of the old church. They wore fringed buckskin trousers and buckskin shirts and odd caps of deerskin with visors to shade the eyes and similar beaks behind to protect the neck. They had powder horns and bullet pouches slung over their shoulders, and long rifles in their hands. They stepped aside as soon as they were out. Carefully avoiding any gesture of menace, they simply stood, watching the helicopter which had landed in their village.

Three other men followed them out. They, too, wore buckskins and the odd double-visored caps. One had a close-cropped white beard, and on the shoulders of his buckskin shirt, he wore the single silver bars of a first lieutenant of the vanished United States Army. He had a pistol on his belt. The pistol had the saw-handle grip of an automatic, but it was a flintlock, as were the rifles of the young men who stood so watchfully on either side of the door.

Two middle-aged men accompanied the bearded man and the trio advanced toward the helicopter.

"All right, come on, Monty."

Loudons opened the door and let down the steps. Picking up an auto-carbine, he slung it and stepped out of the helicopter, Altamont behind him. They advanced to meet the party from the church, halting when they were about twenty feet apart.

"I must apologize, lieutenant, for dropping in on you so unceremoniously."

Loudons stopped, wondering if the man with the white beard understood a word of what he was saying.

"The natural way to come in, when you travel in the air," the old man replied. "At least, you came in openly. I can promise you a better reception than that you got at the city to the west of us a couple of days ago."

"Now how did you know that we had trouble the day-before-yesterday?" Loudons demanded.

The old man's eyes sparkled with child-like pleasure. "That surprises you, my dear sir? In a moment, I daresay you'll be surprised at the simplicity of it.

"You have a nasty rip in the left leg of your trousers, and the cloth around it is stained with blood. Through the rip, I perceive a bandage. Obviously, you have suffered a recent wound. I further observe that the side of your flying machine bears recent scratches, as though from the spears or throwing hatchets of the Scowrers. Evidently, they attacked you as you were landing. It is fortunate that these cannibal devils are too stupid and too anxious for human flesh to exercise patience."

"Well, that explains how you knew that we'd recently been attacked," Loudons told him. "But how did you guess that it had been to the west of here, in a ruined city?"

"I never guess," the oldster with the silver bar and the keystone-shaped red patch on his left shoulder replied. "It is a shocking habit-destructive to the logical faculties. What seems strange to you is only so because you do not follow my train of thought.

"For example, the wheels and their framework under your flying machine are splashed with mud which seems to be predominantly brick-dust, mixed with plaster. Obviously, you landed recently in a dead city, either during or after a rain. There was a rain here yesterday evening, the wind being from the west. Obviously, you followed behind the rain as it came up the river. And now that I look at your boots, I see traces of the same sort of mud, around the soles and in front of the heels.

"But this is heartless of us, keeping you standing here on a wounded leg, sir. Come in, and let our medic take a look at it."

"Well, thank you, lieutenant," Loudons replied. "But don't bother your medic. I've attended to the wound myself, and it wasn't serious to begin with."

"You are a doctor?" the white-haired man asked.

"Of sorts. A sort of general scientist. My name is Loudons. My friend, Mr. Altamont, here, is a scientist, too."

There was an immediate reaction: all three of the elders of the village, and the young riflemen who had accompanied them, exchanged glances of surprise.

Loudons dropped his hand to the grip of his slung auto-carbine and Altamont sidled away from his partner, his hand moving as if by accident toward the butt of his pistol. The same thought was in both men's minds, that these people might feel, as the heritage of the war of two centuries ago, a hostility to science and scientists.

There was no hostility, however, in their manner as the old man came forward with out-stretched hand.

"I am Tenant Mycroft Jones, the Toon Leader here," he said. "This is Stamford Rawson, our Reader, and Verner Hughes, our Toon Sarge. This is his son, Murray Hughes, the Toon Sarge of the Irregulars.

"But come into the Aitch-Cue House, gentlemen. We have much to talk about."

By this time, the villagers had begun to emerge from the log cabins and rubble-walled houses around the plaza and the old church. Some of them, mostly the young men, were carrying rifles, but the majority were unarmed. About half of them were women, in short deerskin skirts or homespun dresses. There were a number of children, the younger ones almost completely naked.

"Sarge," the old man told one of the youths, "post a guard over this flying machine. Don't let anybody meddle with it. And have all the noncoms and techs report here, on the double." He turned and shouted up at the truncated steeple: "Atherton, sound 'All Clear!'"

A horn up in the belfry began blowing, apparently to advise the people who had run from the fields into the forest that there was no danger.

They went through the open doorway of the old stone church and entered the big room inside. The building had evidently once been gutted by fire, two centuries ago, but portions of the wall had been restored. The floor had been replaced by one of rough planks, and there was a plank ceiling at about ten feet.

The room was apparently used as a community center. There were a number of benches and chairs, all very neatly made; and along one wall, out of the way, ten or fifteen long tables had been stacked, the tops in a pile and the trestles on the tops.

The walls were decorated with trophies of weapons—a number of M-12 rifles and M-16 submachine-guns, all in good, clean condition; a light machine rifle; two bazookas. Among them were cruder weapons, stone-and metal-tipped spears and clubs, the work of the wild men of the woods.

A stairway led to the second floor, and it was up this stairway that the man who bore the title of Toon Leader conducted them, to a small room furnished with a long table, a number of chairs, and several big wooden chests bound with iron.

"Sit down, gentlemen," the Toon Leader invited, going to a cupboard and producing a large bottle stoppered with a corncob and a number of small cups.

"It's a little early in the day," he went on, "but this is a very special occasion.

"You smoke a pipe, I take it?" he asked Altamont. "Then try some of this, of our own growth and curing."

He extended a doeskin moccasin, which seemed to be the tobacco container.

Altamont looked at the thing dubiously, then filled his pipe from it.

The oldster drew his pistol, pushed a little wooden plug into the vent, added some tow to the priming, and, aiming at the wall, snapped it. Evidently, at time the formality of plugging the vent had been overlooked: there were a number of holes in the wall there.

This time, however, the pistol didn't go off. The old man shook out the smoldering tow, blew it into flame, and lit a candle from it, offering the light to Altamont.

Loudons got out a cigar and lit it from the candle; the others filled and lighted pipes. The Toon Leader reprimed his pistol, then holstered it, took off his belt and laid it aside, an example the others followed.

They drank ceremoniously, and then seated themselves at the table. As they did, two more men entered the room. They were introduced as Alexander Barrett, the gunsmith and Stanley Markovitch, the distiller.

The Toon Leader began by asking, "You come, then, from the west?"

"Are you from Utah?" the gunsmith interrupted, suspiciously.

"Why, no, we're from Arizona. A place called Fort Ridgeway," Loudons said.

The others nodded, in the manner of people who wish to conceal ignorance. It was obvious that none of them had ever heard of Fort Ridgeway, or Arizona either.

"You say you come from a fort? Then the wars aren't over yet?" Sarge Hughes asked.

"The wars have been over for a long time. You know how terrible they were. You know how few in all the countries were left alive," Loudons said.

"None that we know of, beside ourselves and the Scowrers, until you came," the Toon Leader said.

"We have found only a few small groups, in the whole country, who have managed to save anything of the Old Times. Most of them lived in little villages and cultivated land. A few had horses or cows. None, that we have ever found before, made guns and powder for themselves. But they remembered that they were men, and did not eat one another.

"Whenever we find a group of people like this, we try to persuade them to let us help them."

"Why?" the Toon Leader asked. "Why do you do this for people that you have never met before? What do you want from them-from us-in return for your help?"

He was speaking to Altamont, rather than to Loudons. It seemed obvious that he believed Altamont to be the leader and Loudons the subordinate.

"Because we are trying to bring back the best of the Old Times," Altamont told him. "Look, you have had troubles, here. So have we, many times. Years when the crops didn't ...didn't...." He looked at Loudons, aware that his partner should be talking now, and also suddenly aware that Loudons had recognized the situation and left the leadership up to him....

"...years that the crops failed. Years of storms, or floods. Troubles with those beast-men in the woods.

"And you were alone, as we were, with no one to help.

"We want to put all men who are still men in touch with one another, so that they can help each other in trouble, and work together.

"If this isn't done, everything that makes men different from beasts will soon be no more."

"He's right. One of us, alone, is helpless," the Reader said. "It is only in the Toon that there is strength. He wants to organize a Toon of all Toons."

"That's about it. We are beginning to make helicopters, like the one Loudons and I came in. We'll furnish your community with one or more of them. We can give you a radio, so that you can communicate with other communities. We can give you rifles and machine guns and ammunition, to fight the-the Scowrers, did you call them? And we can give you atomic engines, so that you can build machines for yourselves."

"Some of our people, —Alex Barrett here, the gunsmith, and Stan Markovitch, the distiller, and Harrison Grant, the iron-worker —get their living by making things. How'd they make out, after your machines came in here?" Verner Hughes asked.

"We've thought of that. We had that problem with other groups we've helped," Loudons said. "In some communities, everybody owns everything in common and so we don't have much of a problem. Is that the way you do it, here?"

"Well, no. If a man makes a thing, or digs it out of the ruins, or catches it in the woods, it's his."

"Then we'll work out some way. Give the machines to the people who are already in a trade, or something like that. We'll have to talk it over with you and with the people concerned."

"How is it you took so long finding us?" Alex Barrett asked. "It's been two hundred or so years since the Wars."

"Alex! You see but you do not observe!" The Toon Leader rebuked. "These people have their flying machines, which are highly complicated mechanisms. They would have to make tools and machines to make them, and tools and machines to make those tools and machines. They would have to find materials, often going in search of them. The marvel is not that they took so long, but that they did it so quickly."

"That's right," Altamont said. "Originally, Fort Ridgeway was a military research and development center. As the country became disorganized, the Government set this project up to develop ways of improvising power and transportation and communication methods and extracting raw materials. If they'd had a little more time, they might have saved the country.

"As it was, they were able to keep themselves alive, and keep something like civilization going at the Fort, while the whole country was breaking apart around them.

"Then, when the rockets stopped falling, they started to rebuild. Fortunately, more than half the technicians at the Fort were women, so there was no question of them dying out.

"But it's only been in the last twenty years that we've been able to make nuclear-electric engines, and this is the first time any of us have gotten east of the Mississippi."

"How did your group manage to survive?" Loudons asked. "You call it the Toon. I suppose that's what the word platoon has become, with time. You were, originally, a military platoon?"

"Pla-toon!" the white-bearded man said. "Of all the unpardonable stupidities! Of course that's what it was. And the title, Tenant, was originally lieu-tenant. I know that, though we have dropped all use of the first part of the word. But that should have led me, if I had used my wits, to deduce platoon from toon."

The Tenant shook his head in dismay at his stupidity and Loudons found himself forced to say, "One syllable like that could have come from many words."

IV

The Tenant smiled at Loudons and said, "Your courtesy does not excuse our stupidity. We know our history and we should have identified the word accurately.

"Yes, we were originally a ...a pla-toon of soldiers, two hundred years ago, at the time when the Wars ended. The old Toon, and the First Tenant, were guarding POWs, and there, sir," —to Loudons —"is a word we cannot trace. We have no idea what they were. In any event, the pows were all killed by a big bomb, and the First Tenant, Lieutenant Gilbert Dunbar, took his platoon and started to march to DeeCee, where the government was.

"But there was no government any more.

"They fought with people along the way. When they needed food, or ammunition, or animals to pull their wagons, they took them, and killed those who tried to prevent them. Other people joined the toon, and when they found women they wanted, they took them.

"They did all sorts of things that would have been crimes if there had been any law, but since there was no law, it was obvious that they could be no crime.

"The First Ten-Lieutenant-kept his men together, because he had The Books. Each evening, at the end of each day's march, he read to his men out of them."

Altamont knew without looking at his associate that Loudons would be inconspicuously jotting down notes. The last was an item the sociologist would be sure to record: the white-bearded Tenant had pronounced that reference to a written testament in capital letters.

The story was continuing....

"...finally, they came here. There had been a town here, but it had been burned and destroyed, and there were people camping in the ruins.

"Some of them fought and were killed, others came in and joined the platoon.

"At first, they built shelters around this building and made this their fort. Then they cleared away the ruins, and built new houses. When the cartridges for the rifles began to get scarce, they began to make gunpowder, and new rifles, like these we are using now, to shoot without cartridges.

"Lieutenant Dunbar did this out of his own knowledge because there is nothing in The Books about making gunpowder. The guns in The Books are rifles and shotguns and revolvers and airguns. Except for the airguns, which we haven't been able to make, these all shot cartridges.

"As with your people, we did not die out because we too had women. Neither did we increase greatly-too many died or were killed young. But several times we've had to tear down the wall and rebuild it, to make room inside for more houses. And we've been clearing out a little more land for the fields each year.

"We still read and follow the teachings of The Books: we have made laws for ourselves out of them."

There was a silence during which Altamont felt himself to be the focus of attention; not obtrusively, but, nonetheless, insistently. However, this was Loudon's field and Altamont pre-ferred not to speak.

"And we are waiting for the Slain and Risen One," Tenant Jones added, and there was no doubt that he was looking at Altamont intently. "It is impossible that He will not, sooner or later, deduce the existence of this community, if He has not done so already."

Again the silence and lack of movement, broken by Loudons this time, when he picked up the candle to re-lit his cigar. Mentally, Altamont thanked his partner.

"Well, sir," the Toon Leader changed the subject abruptly, "enough of this talk about the past. If I understand rightly, it is the future in which you gentlemen are interested." He pushed back the cuff of his hunting shirt and looked at an old and worn wrist watch. "Eleven hundred: we'll have lunch shortly.

"This afternoon, you will meet the other people of the Toon, and this evening, at eighteen hundred, we'll have a mess together. Then, when we have everyone together, we can talk over your offer to help us, and decide what it is that you can give us that we can use."

"You spoke, a while ago, of what you could do for us, in return," Altamont said. He knew that now he would have to be the one to stress their original mission: Loudons would probably be so fascinated by this society that the sociologist might never remember the primary reason for coming to Pittsburgh.

"There's one thing you can do, no further away than tomorrow, if you're willing."

He had no time to wonder at the interchange of glances around the table before the Toon Leader said, "And that is —?"

"In Pittsburgh, somewhere, there is an underground crypt, full of books. Not printed and bound books, but spools of microfilm. Do you know what that is?"

The men of the Toon shook their heads. Altamont continued:

"They are spools on which strips of films are wound and on which pictures have been taken of books, page by page. We can make other, larger pictures from them, big enough to be read —"

"Oh, photographs, which you can enlarge. I can understand that. You mean, you can make many copies of them?"

"That's right. And you shall have copies, as soon as we can take the originals back to Fort Ridgeway, where we have the equipment for enlarging them. But while we have information which will help us to find the crypt where the books are, we will need help in getting it open."

"Of course! This is wonderful. Copies of The Books!" the Reader exclaimed. "We thought that we had the only one left in the world!"

"Not just The Books, Stamford, other books," the Toon Leader told him. "The books mentioned in The Books. But of course we will help you. You have a map to show where they are?"

"Not a map, just some information. But we can work out the location of the crypt."

"A ritual," Stamford Rawson said happily. "Of course!"

V

They lunched together at the house of Toon Sarge Hughes with the Toon Leader and the Reader and five or six of the leaders of the community. The food was plentiful, but Altamont found himself wishing that the first book they found in the Carnegie Library crypt would be a cook-book.

In the afternoon, he and Loudons separated.

Loudons attached himself to the Tenant, the Reader and an old woman, Irene Klein, who was almost a hundred years old and was the repository and arbiter of most of the community's oral legends.

Altamont, on the other hand, started with Alex Barrett, the gunsmith, and Mordecai Ricci, the miller, to inspect the gunshop and the grist mill. They were later joined by a half dozen more of the village craftsmen and so also visited the forge and foundry, the sawmill and the wagon shop. Altamont additionally looked at the flume, a rough structure of logs lined with sheet aluminum; and at the nitriary, a shed-roofed pit in which potassium nitrate was extracted from the community's animal refuse.

But he reversed matters when it came to visiting the powder mill on the island: he became the host and took them by helicopter to the island and then for a trip up the river.

The guests were a badly-scared lot, for the first few minutes, as they watched the ground receding under them through the transparent plastic nose. Then, when nothing serious seemed to be happening, exhilaration took the place of fear. By the time they set down on the tip of the island, the eight men were confirmed aviation enthusiasts.

The trip up-river was an even bigger success, the high point coming when Altamont set his controls for Hover, pointed out a snarl of driftwood in the stream, and allowed his passengers to fire one of the machine-guns at it.

The lead balls of their own black-powder rifles would have plunked into the water-logged wood without visible effect. The copper-jacketed machine-gun bullets ripped it to splinters.

They returned for a final visit to the distillery awed by what they had seen.

VI

"Monty, I don't know what the devil to make of this crowd," Loudons said, that evening, after the feast, when they had entered the helicopter and were preparing to retire.

"We've run into some weird communities-that lot down in New Mexico who live in the church and claim that they have a divine mission to redeem the world by prayer, fasting, and flagellation.

"Or those yogis in Los Angeles —"

"Or the Blackout Boys in Detroit!" Altamont interrupted. He had good reason to remember them.

"That's understandable," Loudons said, "after what their ancestors went through in the last war. And so are the others, in their own way.

"But this crowd here!" Loudons put down his cigar and began chewing on his mustache, a sure sign that he was more than puzzled: he was a very worried man.

Altamont respected his partner's abilities in this area. However, he also knew that the best way to get his friend to work any problem was to have him do it in conversation.

"What has you stopped, Jim?"

"Number of things, Monty. They're hard to explain because —" the sociologist shrugged, winced a little as the gesture pushed his leg down on the edge of his bunk —"well, let me just mention them.

"These people are the descendants of an old United States Army platoon, yet they have a fully-developed religion centered on a slain and resurrected god.

"Now, Monty, with all due respect to the old US Army, that just doesn't make sense! Normally, it would take thousands of years for a slain-god religion to develop, and then only in a special situation, from the field-fertility magic of primitive agriculturists.

"Well, you saw those people's fields from the air. Some members of that old platoon were men who knew the latest methods of scientific farming. They didn't need naive fairy tales about the planting and germination of seed."

"Sure this religion isn't just a variant of Christianity?"

"Absolutely not!

"In the first place, these Sacred Books cannot be the Bible-you heard Tenant Jones say that they mentioned firearms that used cartridges. That means they can't be older than 1860 at the earliest.

"And, in the second place, this slain god wasn't crucified, or put to death by any form of execution: he perished, together with his enemy, in combat, and both god and devil were later resurrected."

Loudons picked up his cigar again. "By the way, the Enemy is supposed to be the mastermind back of these cannibal savages in the woods and also in the ruins."

"Did you get a look at these Sacred Books, or find out what they might be?"

Loudons shook his head disgustedly. "Every time I brought up the question, they evaded me. The Tenant sent the Reader out to bring in this old lady, Irene Klein-she was a perfect gold-mine of information about the history and traditions of the platoon, by the way-and then he sent the Reader out on some other errand, undoubtedly to pass the word around not to talk to us about their religion."

"I don't get that," Altamont said. "They showed me everything-their gunshop, their powder mill, their defenses, everything."

He smoked in silence for a moment, then added, in an apologetic tone, "Jim, I'm sure you've thought of this: the slain god couldn't be the original platoon commander, could he?"

"I've thought of it, and he isn't, Monty.

"No, definitely not, though they have the greatest respect for his memory-decorate his grave regularly, drink toasts to him, and so on. But he hasn't been deified. They got the idea for this god of theirs out of the Sacred Books."

Loudons put the cigar down again and returned to chewing his mustache. "Monty, this has me worried like the devil:

"I believe that they suspect that you are the Slain and Risen One!"

Altamont considered the idea, then nodded slowly. "Could be, at that. I know the Tenant came up to me, very respectfully, and said, 'I hope you don't think, sir, that I was presumptuous in trying to display my humble deductive abilities to you.'"

"What did you say?" Loudons demanded rather sharply.

"Told him certainly not, that he'd used a good, quick method of demonstrating that he and his people weren't like those mindless subhumans in the woods."

"That was all right," Loudons approved, but then his worries returned. "I don't know how we're going to handle this —"

"Jim, how about that pows business? Is there something there?"

"Monty!" Loudons voice was drily chiding as he took a pad of paper and scribbled briefly. "Take a look and figure for yourself."

Altamont looked at the paper. Loudons had simply printed the first three letters of the word in capitals and separated each letter with a period. "Ouch! Yes, of course, that's what an infantry platoon would be guarding.

"Go ahead, Jim, this is your end of our business. I'll stay out of it and, especially, I'll keep my mouth shut."

"I don't think you'll be able to," Loudons said soberly. "As things stand now, they only suspect that you are their deity.

"And that means this: we're on trial here!"

"We have been in spots like this before, Jim," Altamont reminded his friend.

"Not like this, Monty, and let me explain.

"I get the impression here that logic, not faith, is the supreme religious virtue. And get this, Monty, because it's something practically unheard of: skepticism is a religious obligation, not a sin!

"I wish I knew...."

VII

Tenant Mycroft Jones, Reader Stamford Rawson, Toon Sarge Verner Hughes, and his son, Murray Hughes, sat around the bare-topped table in the room on the second floor of the Aitch-Cue House. A lighted candle flickered in the cool breeze that came in through the open window, throwing their shadows back and forth on the walls.

"Pass the tantalus, Murray," the Tenant said, and the youngest of the four handed the corncob-corked bottle to the eldest. Tenant Jones filled his cup and then sat staring at it, while Verner Hughes thrust his pipe into the toe of the moccasin and filled it. Finally, the Tenant drank about half the clear, wild-plum brandy.

"Gentlemen, I am baffled," he confessed. "We have three alternate possibilities here and we dare not disregard any of them.

"Either this man who calls himself Altamont is truly He, or his is merely what we are asked to believe, one of a community of men like ours, with more of the old knowledge than we possess."

"You know my views," Verner Hughes said. "I cannot believe that He was more than a man, as we are. A great, a good, a wise man, but a man and mortal."

"Let's not go into that, now." The Reader emptied his cup and took the bottle, filling it again. "You know my views, too. I hold that He is no longer upon earth in the flesh, but lives in the spirit and is only with us in the spirit.

"But you said there were three possibilities, none of which can be eliminated. What was your third possibility, Tenant?"

"That they are creatures of the Enemy, perhaps that one or the other of them is the Enemy."

Reader Rawson, lifting his cup to his lips, almost strangled. The Hugheses, father and son stared at Tenant Jones in horror.

"The Enemy-with such weapons and resources!" Murray Hughes gasped. Then he emptied his cup and refilled it. "No! I can't believe that: he would have struck before this and wiped us all out!"

"Not necessarily, Murray," the Tenant replied. "Until he became convinced that his agents, the Scowrers, could do nothing against us, he would bide his time. He sits motionless, like a spider, at the center of the web; he does little himself; his agents are numerous.

"Or, perhaps, he wishes to recruit us into this hellish organization."

"It is a possibility," the Reader admitted, "and one which we can neither accept or reject safely. And we must learn the truth as soon as possible. If this man is really He, we must not spurn Him on mere suspicion. If he is a man, come to help us, we must accept his help; if he is speaking the truth, the people who sent him could do wonders for us, and the greatest wonder would be to make us again a part of a civilized community.

"And if he is the Enemy...." Rawson left the sentence unfinished, but his face was grim.

"But if he is really He," Murray said, a little diffidently, for he was not yet accustomed to being included in the council of the elders, "I think we are on trial."

"What do you mean, son? Oh, I see. Of course, I don't believe that he is, but that's mere doubt, not negative certainty. However, if I'm wrong, if this man is truly He, we are worthy of him, we will penetrate his disguise."

"A very pretty problem, gentlemen," the Tenant said, smacking his lips over his brandy, "for all that it may be a deadly serious one for us. There is, of course, nothing we can do tonight. But, tomorrow, we have promised to help our visitors, whoever they may be, in searching for this crypt in the city.

"Murray, you were to be in charge of the detail that was to accompany them. Carry on as arranged, and say nothing of our suspicions, but advise your men to keep a sharp watch on the strangers, that they may learn all they can from them.

"Stamford, you and Verner and I will go along. We should, if we have any wits at all, observe something."

VIII

"Listen to this infernal thing!" Altamont raged. "'Wielding a gold-plated spade handled with oak from an original rafter of the Congressional Library, at three-fifteen one afternoon last week—' One afternoon last week!" He cursed luridly. "Why couldn't that blasted magazine say what afternoon? I've gone over a lot of twentieth century copies of that magazine and that expression was a regular cliche with them."

Loudons looked over his shoulder at the photostated magazine page.

"Well, we know it was between June thirteen and nineteen, inclusive," he said. "And there's a picture of the university president, complete with gold-plated spade, breaking ground. Call it Wednesday, the sixteenth. Over there's the tip of the shadow of the old Cathedral of Learning, about a hundred yards away. There are so many inexactitudes, that one'll probably cancel out the other."

"That's so, and it's also pretty futile getting angry at somebody who's been dead two hundred years, but why couldn't they say Wednesday, or Monday, or Saturday, or whatever?"

Monty checked back in the astronomical handbook, and the photostated pages of the old almanac, then looked over his calculations. "All right, here is the angle of the shadow, and the compass-bearing.

"I had a look, yesterday, when I was taking the local citizenry on that junket. The old baseball diamond at Forbes Field is plainly visible, and I located the ruins of the Cathedral of Learning from that.

"Here's the above-sea-level altitude of the top of the tower. After you've landed us, go up to this altitude-use the barometric altimeter, not the radar-and hold position."

Loudons leaned forward from the desk to the contraption Altamont had rigged up in the nose of the helicopter; one of the telescope-sighted hunting rifles clamped in a vise, with a compass and a spirit-level under it.

"Rifle's pointing downward at the correct angle now?" he asked. "Good. Then all I have to do is to hold the helicopter steady, keep it at the right altitude, level and pointed in the right direction, and watch through the sight while you move the flag around, and direct you by radio."

"Simple, if I had been born quintuplets!"

"Mr. Altamont! Doctor Loudons!" a voice outside the helicopter called. "Are you ready for us now?"

Altamont went to the open door and looked out. The old Toon Leader, the Reader, Toon Sarge Hughes, his son and four young men in buckskins with slung rifles were standing outside.

"I have decided," the Tenant said, "that Mr. Rawson and Sarge Hughes and I would be of more help than an equal number of young men. We may not be as active, but we do know the old ruins better, especially the paths and hiding places of the Scowrers. These four young men you probably met last evening, but it will do no harm to introduce them again.

"Birdy Edwards; Sholto Jiminez; Jefferson Burns; Murdo Olsen."

"Very pleased, Tenant, gentlemen. I met all of you young men last evening and I remember you," Altamont said. "Now, if you'll crowd in here, I'll explain what we're going to try to do."

He showed them the old picture. "You see where the shadow of a tall building falls?" he asked. "We know the height and location of this building. Doctor Loudons will hold this helicopter at exactly the position of the top of the building and aim through the sights of the rifle, there. One of you will have this flag in his hand, and will move it back and forth. Doctor Loudons will tell us when the flag is in sight of the rifle."

"He'll need a good pair of lungs to do that," Verner Hughes commented.

"We'll use the radio. A portable set on the ground, and the helicopter's radio set," Altamont said.

To his surprise, he was met with looks of incomprehension. He had not supposed that these people would have lost all memory of radio communication.

"Why, that's wonderful!" the Reader exclaimed, when the explanation was concluded. "You can talk directly. How much better than just sending a telegram!"

"But, finding the crypt by the shadow, that's exactly like the —" Murray Hughes began, then stopped short. Immediately, he began talking about the rifle that was to be used as a surveying transit, comparing it with the ones in the big first-floor room at the Aitch-Cue House.

Locating the point where the shadow of the old Cathedral of Learning had fallen proved easier than either Altamont or Loudons had expected. The towering building was now a tumbled mass of slagged rubble, but it was quite possible to determine its original center, and with the old data from the excellent reference library at Fort Ridgeway, its height above sea level was known. After a little jockeying, the helicopter came to a hovering stop, and the slanting barrel of the rifle in the vise pointed downward along the line of the shadow that had been cast on that afternoon in June, 1993.

The cross-hairs of the scope sight centered almost exactly on the spot Altamont had estimated on the map.

Guiding himself by peering through the rifle-sight, Loudons brought the helicopter slanting down to land on the sheet of fused glass that had once been a grassy campus.

"Well, this is probably it," Altamont said. "We didn't have to bother fussing around with that flag after all. That hump over there looks as though it had been a small building, and there's nothing corresponding to it on the city map. That may be the bunker over the stair-head to the crypt."

They began unloading equipment —a small, portable nuclear-electric conversion unit, a powerful solenoid-hammer, crowbars and intrenching tools, tins of blasting plastic. They took out the two hunting rifles and the auto-carbines, and Altamont showed the young men of Murray Hughes' detail how to use them.

"If you will pardon me, sir," the Tenant said to Altamont, "I think it would be a good idea if your companion went up in the flying machine and circled over us, to keep watch for the Scowrers. There are quite a few of them, particularly farther up the rivers, to the east, where the damage was not so great and they can find cellars and shelters and buildings to live in."

"Good idea. That way, we won't have to put out guards," Altamont said. "From the looks of this, we'll need every body to help dig into that thing. Hand out one of the portable radios, Jim and go up to about a thousand feet. If you see anything suspicious, give us a yell, then spray it with bullets, and find out what it is afterward."

They waited until the helicopter had climbed to position and was circling above, and then turned their attention to the place where the sheet of fused earth and stone bulged upward. It must have been almost ground-zero of one of the hydrogen-bombs: the wreckage of the Cathedral of Learning had fallen predominantly to the north, and the Carnegie Library was tumbled to the east.

"I think the entrance would be on this side, toward the Library," Altamont said. "Let's try it, to begin with."

He used the solenoid-hammer, slowly pounding a hole in the glaze, and placed a small charge of the plastic explosive. Chunks of the lava-like stuff pelted down between the little mound and the huge one of the old library, blowing a hole six feet in diameter and the two and a half feet deep, revealing concrete bonded with crushed steel-mill slag.

"We missed the door," Altamont said. "That means we'll have to tunnel in through who knows how much concrete. Well...."

He used a second and larger charge, after digging a hole a foot deep. When he and his helpers came up to look, they found a large mass of concrete blown out, and solid steel behind it. Altamont cut two more holes, one on either side of the blown-out place, and fired a charge in each of them, bringing down more concrete.

He found he hadn't missed the door after all. It had merely been concreted over.

A few more shots cleared it, and after some work, they got it open. There was a room inside, concrete-floored and entirely empty. Altamont stood in the doorway and inspected the interior with his flashlight; he heard somebody behind him say something about a most peculiar sort of dark-lantern.

Across the small room, on the opposite wall, was a bronze plaque.

The plaque carried quite a lengthy inscription, including the names of all the persons and institutions participating in the microfilm project. The History Department at the Fort would be interested in that, but the only thing that interested Altamont was the statement that the floor had been laid over the trapdoor leading to the vault where the microfilms were stored. He went outside to the radio.

"Hello, Jim. We're inside, but the films were stored in an underground vault, and so we have to tear up a concrete floor," he said. "Go back to the village and gather up all the men you can carry. I don't want to use explosives inside. The interior of the crypt oughtn't to be damaged. Besides, I don't know what a blast in there might do to the film, and I don't want to take any chances."

"No, of course not. How thick do you think the floor is?"

"Haven't the least idea. Plenty thick, I would guess. Those films would have to be well-buried, to shield them from radioactivity. We can expect that it will take some time."

"All right. I'll be back as soon as I can."

The helicopter turned and went windmilling away, over what had been the Golden Triangle, down the Ohio. Altamont went back to the little concrete bunker and sat down, lighting his pipe. Murray Hughes and his four riflemen spread out, one circling around the glazed butte that had been the Cathedral of Learning, another climbing to the top of the old Library, and the others taking positions to the south and east.

Altamont sat in silence, smoking his pipe and trying to form some conception of the wealth under that concrete floor.

It was no use.

Jim Loudons probably understood a little more clearly what those books would mean to the world of today, and what they could do toward shaping the world of the future.

There was a library at Fort Ridgeway, and it was an excellent one ... for its purpose. In 1996, when the rockets had come crashing down, it had contained the cream of the world's technical knowledge-and very little else. There was only a little fiction, a few books of ideas, just enough to give the survivors a tantalizing glimpse of the world of their fathers.

But now....

A rifle banged to the south and east, and banged again. Either Murray Hughes or Birdy Edwards: it was one of the two hunting rifles from the helicopter.

On the heels of the reports, they heard a voice shouting, "Scowrers! A lot of them, coming from up the river!"

A moment later, there was a light whip-crack of one of the muzzleloaders, from the top of the old Carnegie Library, and Altamont could see a wisp of grey-white smoke drifting away from where it had been fired.

Altamont jumped to his feet and raced for the radio, picking it up and bring it to the bunker.

Tenant Jones, old Reader Rawson, and Verner Hughes had caught up their rifles. The Tenant was shouting. "Come on in! Everybody, come on in!"

The boy on top of the library began scrambling down. Another came running from the direction of the half-demolished Cathedral of Learning, a third from the baseball field that had served as Altamont's point of reference the afternoon before.

The fourth, Murray Hughes, was running in from the ruins of the old Carnegie Tech buildings, and Birdy Edwards sped up the main road from Schenley Park. Once, twice, as he ran, Murray Hughes paused, turned, and fired behind him.

Then his pursuers came into sight!

They ran erect, they wore a few rags of skin garments, and they carried spears and hatchets and clubs, so they were probably classifiable as men. But their hair was long and unkempt, and their bodies were almost black with dirt and from the sun. A few of them were yelling, but most of them ran silently. They ran more swiftly than the boy they were pursuing: the distance between them narrowed every moment. There were at least fifty of them.

Verner Hughes' rifle barked, one of them dropped. As cooly as though he were shooting squirrels instead of his son's pursuers, he dropped the butt of the rifle to the ground, poured a charge of powder, patched a ball and rammed it home, replaced the ramrod. Tenant Jones fired then, and Birdy Edwards joined them, beginning to shoot with the telescope-sighted rifle.

The young man who had been north of the Cathedral of Learning had one of the auto-carbines; luckily, Altamont had providently set the control for semi-auto before giving it to him. He dropped to one knee and began to empty the clip, shooting slowly and deliberately, picking off the runners who were in the lead.

The boy who had started to climb down off the Library halted, fired his flintlock, and began reloading it.

Altamont, sitting down and propping his elbows on his knees, took both hands to the automatic which was his only weapon, emptying the magazine and replacing it. The last three savages he shot in the back: they had had enough and were running for their lives.

So far, everybody was safe. The boy in the Library came down through a place where the wall had fallen. Murray Hughes stopped running and came slowly toward the bunker, putting a fresh clip into his rifle. The others came drifting in.

"Altamont, calling Loudons," the scientist from Fort Ridgeway was saying into the radio. "Monty to Jim: can you hear me?"

Silence.

"We'd better get ready for another attack," Birdy Edwards said. "There's another gang coming from down that way. I never saw so many Scowrers!"

"Maybe there's a reason, Birdy," Tenant Jones said. "The Enemy is after big game, this time."

"Jim, where the devil are you?" Altamont fairly yelled into the radio; and as he did, he knew the answer. Loudons was in the village, away from the helicopter, gathering tools and workers.

Nothing to do but keep on trying!

"Here they come!" Reader Rawson warned.

"How far can these rifles be depended on?" Birdy Edwards wanted to know.

Altamont straightened, saw the second band of savages approaching about four hundred yards away.

"Start shooting now," he said. "Aim for the upper part of their bodies."

The two auto-loading rifles began to crack. After the first few shots, the savages took cover. Evidently they understood the capabilities and limitations of the villagers' flintlocks, but this was a terrifying surprise to them.

"Jim!"—Altamont was almost praying into the radio—"Come in, Jim!"

"What is it, Monty? I was outside."

Altamont told him.

"Those fellows you had up with you yesterday, think they could be trusted to handle the guns? A couple of them are here with me," Loudons inquired.

"Take a chance on it! It won't cost anything but my life, and that's not worth much at the present."

"All right, hold on. We'll be there in a few minutes."

"Loudons is bringing the helicopter," Altamont told the others. "All we have to do is to hold on, here, until he comes."

A naked savage raised his head from behind what might, two hundred years ago, have been a cement park-bench and he was only a hundred yards away. Reader Rawson promptly killed him and began reloading.

"I think you're right, Tenant," he said. "The Scowrers have never attacked in bands like this before. They must have a powerful reason and I can think of only one."

"That's what I'm beginning to think, too," Verner Hughes agreed. "At least, we've eliminated the third of your possibilities, Tenant. And I think probably the second, as well."

Altamont wondered what they were double-talking about. There wasn't any particular mystery about the mass attack of the wild men to him.

Debased as they were, they still possessed speech and the ability to transmit experiences. No matter how beclouded in superstition, they still remembered that aircraft dropped bombs, and bombs killed people, and where people had been killed, they would find fresh meat. They had seen the helicopter circling about, and had heard the blasting: everyone in the area had been drawn to the scene as soon as Loudons had gone down the river.

But they seemed to have forgotten that aircraft carried guns, although they did spring to their feet and start to run at the return of the helicopter.

However, most of them did not run far.

IX

Altamont and Loudons shook hands many times in front of the Aitch-Cue House, and listened to many good wishes, and repeated their promise to return. Most of the microfilmed books were to be stored in the old church. They were taking with them only the catalogue and a few of the most important works. Finally, they entered the helicopter. The crowd shouted farewell as they rose.

Altamont, at the controls, waited until they had gained five thousand feet, then turned on a compass-course for Colony Three.

"I can't wait until we're in radio range of the Fort, Jim. This is one report that I really want to make," he said.

"Of all the wonderful luck!" he went on. "And I don't know which is the more important: finding those books, or finding those people. In a few years, when we can get them supplied with modern equipment and instructed in its use —

"What's the matter, Jim? You should be even more excited than I am."

"I'm not very happy about this, Monty," Loudons confessed. "I keep thinking about what's going to happen to them."

"Why, nothing's going to happen to them. They're going to be given the means of producing more food, keeping more of them alive, giving them more leisure to develop themselves in —"

"Monty, I saw the Sacred Books."

"The deuce! What were they?"

"It. One volume. A collection of works. We have it at the Fort and I've read it. How I ever missed all those clues —"

"You see, Monty, what I'm worried about is what's going to happen to those people when they find out that we're not really Sherlock Holmes and Doctor Watson...."

Omnilingual

To translate writings, you need a key to the code-and if the last writer of Martian died forty thousand years before the first writer of Earth was born ... how could the Martian be translated...?

By H. Beam Piper

Martha Dane paused, looking up at the purple-tinged copper sky. The wind had shifted since noon, while she had been inside, and the dust storm that was sweeping the high deserts to the east was now blowing out over Syrtis. The sun, magnified by the haze, was a gorgeous magenta ball, as large as the sun of Terra, at which she could look directly. Tonight, some of that dust would come sifting down from the upper atmosphere to add another film to what had been burying the city for the last fifty thousand years.

The red loess lay over everything, covering the streets and the open spaces of park and plaza, hiding the small houses that had been crushed and pressed flat under it and the rubble that had come down from the tall buildings when roofs had caved in and walls had toppled outward. Here, where she stood, the ancient streets were a hundred to a hundred and fifty feet below the surface; the breach they had made in the wall of the building behind her had opened into the sixth story. She could look down on the cluster of prefabricated huts and sheds, on the brush-grown flat that had been the waterfront when this place had been a seaport on the ocean that was now Syrtis Depression; already, the bright metal was thinly coated with red dust. She thought, again, of what clearing this city would mean, in terms of time and labor, of people and supplies and equipment brought across fifty million miles of space. They'd have to use machinery; there was no other way it could be done. Bulldozers and power shovels and draglines; they were fast, but they were rough and indiscriminate. She remembered the digs around Harappa and Mohenjo-Daro, in the Indus Valley, and the careful, patient native laborers-the painstaking foremen, the pickmen and spademen, the long files of basketmen carrying away the earth. Slow and primitive as the civilization whose ruins they were uncovering, yes, but she could count on the fingers of one hand the times one of her pickmen had damaged a valuable object in the ground. If it hadn't been for the underpaid and uncomplaining native laborer, archaeology would still be back where Wincklemann had found it. But on Mars there was no native labor; the last Martian had died five hundred centuries ago.

Something started banging like a machine gun, four or five hundred yards to her left. A solenoid jack-hammer; Tony Lattimer must have decided which building he wanted to break into next. She became conscious, then, of the awkward weight of her equipment, and began redistributing it, shifting the straps of her oxy-tank pack, slinging the camera from one shoulder and the board and drafting tools from the other, gathering the notebooks and sketchbooks under her left arm. She started walking down the road, over hillocks of buried rubble, around snags of wall jutting up out of the loess, past buildings still standing, some of them already breached and explored, and across the brush-grown flat to the huts.

There were ten people in the main office room of Hut One when she entered. As soon as she had disposed of her oxygen equipment, she lit a cigarette, her first since noon, then looked from one to another of them. Old Selim von Ohlmhorst, the Turco-German, one of her two fellow archaeologists, sitting at the end of the long table against the farther wall, smoking his big curved pipe and going through a looseleaf notebook. The girl ordnance officer, Sachiko

Koremitsu, between two droplights at the other end of the table, her head bent over her work. Colonel Hubert Penrose, the Space Force CO, and Captain Field, the intelligence officer, listening to the report of one of the airdyne pilots, returned from his afternoon survey flight. A couple of girl lieutenants from Signals, going over the script of the evening telecast, to be transmitted to the *Cyrano*, on orbit five thousand miles off planet and relayed from thence to Terra via Lunar. Sid Chamberlain, the Trans-Space News Service man, was with them. Like Selim and herself, he was a civilian; he was advertising the fact with a white shirt and a sleeveless blue sweater. And Major Lindemann, the engineer officer, and one of his assistants, arguing over some plans on a drafting board. She hoped, drawing a pint of hot water to wash her hands and sponge off her face, that they were doing something about the pipeline.

She started to carry the notebooks and sketchbooks over to where Selim von Ohlmhorst was sitting, and then, as she always did, she turned aside and stopped to watch Sachiko. The Japanese girl was restoring what had been a book, fifty thousand years ago; her eyes were masked by a binocular loup, the black headband invisible against her glossy black hair, and she was picking delicately at the crumbled page with a hair-fine wire set in a handle of copper tubing. Finally, loosening a particle as tiny as a snowflake, she grasped it with tweezers, placed it on the sheet of transparent plastic on which she was reconstructing the page, and set it with a mist of fixative from a little spraygun. It was a sheer joy to watch her; every movement was as graceful and precise as though done to music after being rehearsed a hundred times.

"Hello, Martha. It isn't cocktail-time yet, is it?" The girl at the table spoke without raising her head, almost without moving her lips, as though she were afraid that the slightest breath would disturb the flaky stuff in front of her.

"No, it's only fifteen-thirty. I finished my work, over there. I didn't find any more books, if that's good news for you."

Sachiko took off the loup and leaned back in her chair, her palms cupped over her eyes.

"No, I like doing this. I call it micro-jigsaw puzzles. This book, here, really is a mess. Selim found it lying open, with some heavy stuff on top of it; the pages were simply crushed." She hesitated briefly. "If only it would mean something, after I did it."

There could be a faintly critical overtone to that. As she replied, Martha realized that she was being defensive.

"It will, some day. Look how long it took to read Egyptian hieroglyphics, even after they had the Rosetta Stone."

Sachiko smiled. "Yes. I know. But they did have the Rosetta Stone."

"And we don't. There is no Rosetta Stone, not anywhere on Mars. A whole race, a whole species, died while the first Crò-Magnon cave-artist was daubing pictures of reindeer and bison, and across fifty thousand years and fifty million miles there was no bridge of understanding.

"We'll find one. There must be something, somewhere, that will give us the meaning of a few words, and we'll use them to pry meaning out of more words, and so on. We may not live to learn this language, but we'll make a start, and some day somebody will."

Sachiko took her hands from her eyes, being careful not to look toward the unshaded light, and smiled again. This time Martha was sure that it was not the Japanese smile of politeness, but the universally human smile of friendship.

"I hope so, Martha: really I do. It would be wonderful for you to be the first to do it, and it would be wonderful for all of us to be able to read what these people wrote. It would really bring this dead city to life again." The smile faded slowly. "But it seems so hopeless."

"You haven't found any more pictures?"

Sachiko shook her head. Not that it would have meant much if she had. They had found hundreds of pictures with captions; they had never been able to establish a positive relationship between any pictured object and any printed word. Neither of them said anything more, and after a moment Sachiko replaced the loup and bent her head forward over the book.

Selim von Ohlmhorst looked up from his notebook, taking his pipe out of his mouth.

"Everything finished, over there?" he asked, releasing a puff of smoke.

"Such as it was." She laid the notebooks and sketches on the table. "Captain Gicquel's started airsealing the building from the fifth floor down, with an entrance on the sixth; he'll start putting in oxygen generators as soon as that's done. I have everything cleared up where he'll be working."

Colonel Penrose looked up quickly, as though making a mental note to attend to something later. Then he returned his attention to the pilot, who was pointing something out on a map.

Von Ohlmhorst nodded. "There wasn't much to it, at that," he agreed. "Do you know which building Tony has decided to enter next?"

"The tall one with the conical thing like a candle extinguisher on top, I think. I heard him drilling for the blasting shots over that way."

"Well, I hope it turns out to be one that was occupied up to the end."

The last one hadn't. It had been stripped of its contents and fittings, a piece of this and a bit of that, haphazardly, apparently over a long period of time, until it had been almost gutted. For centuries, as it had died, this city had been consuming itself by a process of auto-cannibalism. She said something to that effect.

"Yes. We always find that-except, of course, at places like Pompeii. Have you seen any of the other Roman cities in Italy?" he asked. "Minturnae, for instance? First the inhabitants tore down this to repair that, and then, after they had vacated the city, other people came along and tore down what was left, and burned the stones for lime, or crushed them to mend roads, till there was nothing left but the foundation traces. That's where we are fortunate; this is one of the places where the Martian race perished, and there were no barbarians to come later and destroy what they had left." He puffed slowly at his pipe. "Some of these days, Martha, we are going to break into one of these buildings and find that it was one in which the last of these people died. Then we will learn the story of the end of this civilization."

And if we learn to read their language, we'll learn the whole story, not just the obituary. She hesitated, not putting the thought into words. "We'll find that, sometime, Selim," she said, then looked at her watch. "I'm going to get some more work done on my lists, before dinner."

For an instant, the old man's face stiffened in disapproval; he started to say something, thought better of it, and put his pipe back into his mouth. The brief wrinkling around his mouth and the twitch of his white mustache had been enough, however; she knew what he was thinking. She was wasting time and effort, he believed; time and effort belonging not to herself but to the expedition. He could be right, too, she realized. But he had to be wrong; there had to be a way to do it. She turned from him silently and went to her own packing-case seat, at the middle of the table.

Photographs, and photostats of restored pages of books, and transcripts of inscriptions, were piled in front of her, and the notebooks in which she was compiling her lists. She sat down, lighting a fresh cigarette, and reached over to a stack of unexamined material, taking off the top sheet. It was a photostat of what looked like the title page and contents of some sort of a periodical. She remembered it; she had found it herself, two days before, in a closet in the basement of the building she had just finished examining.

She sat for a moment, looking at it. It was readable, in the sense that she had set up a purely arbitrary but consistently pronounceable system of phonetic values for the letters. The long vertical symbols were vowels. There were only ten of them; not too many, allowing separate characters for long and short sounds. There were twenty of the short horizontal letters, which meant that sounds like -ng or -ch or -sh were single letters. The odds were millions to one against her system being anything like the original sound of the language, but she had listed several thousand Martian words, and she could pronounce all of them.

And that was as far as it went. She could pronounce between three and four thousand Martian words, and she couldn't assign a meaning to one of them. Selim von Ohlmhorst believed that she never would. So did Tony Lattimer, and he was a great deal less reticent about saying so. So, she was sure, did Sachiko Koremitsu. There were times, now and then, when she began to be afraid that they were right.

The letters on the page in front of her began squirming and dancing, slender vowels with fat little consonants. They did that, now, every night in her dreams. And there were other dreams, in which she read them as easily as English; waking, she would try desperately and vainly to remember. She blinked, and looked away from the photostatted page; when she looked back, the letters were behaving themselves again. There were three words at the top of the page, over-and-underlined, which seemed to be the Martian method of capitalization. *Mastharnorvod Tadavas Sornhulva.* She pronounced them mentally, leafing through her notebooks to see if she had encountered them before, and in what contexts. All three were listed. In addition, *masthar* was a fairly common word, and so was *norvod*, and so was *nor*, but *-vod* was a suffix and nothing but a suffix. *Davas*, was a word, too, and *ta-* was a common prefix; *sorn* and *hulva* were both common words. This language, she had long ago decided, must be something like German; when the Martians had needed a new word, they had just pasted a couple of existing words together. It would probably turn out to be a grammatical horror. Well, they had published magazines, and one of them had been called *Mastharnorvod Tadavas Sornhulva.* She wondered if it had been something like the *Quarterly Archaeological Review*, or something more on the order of *Sexy Stories.*

A smaller line, under the title, was plainly the issue number and date; enough things had been found numbered in series to enable her to identify the numerals and determine that a decimal system of numeration had been used. This was the one thousand and seven hundred and fifty-fourth issue, for Doma, 14837; then Doma must be the name of one of the Martian months. The word had turned up several times before. She found herself puffing furiously on her cigarette as she leafed through notebooks and piles of already examined material.

Sachiko was speaking to somebody, and a chair scraped at the end of the table. She raised her head, to see a big man with red hair and a red face, in Space Force green, with the single star of a major on his shoulder, sitting down. Ivan Fitzgerald, the medic. He was lifting weights from a book similar to the one the girl ordnance officer was restoring.

"Haven't had time, lately," he was saying, in reply to Sachiko's question. "The Finchley girl's still down with whatever it is she has, and it's something I haven't been able to diagnose yet. And I've been checking on bacteria cultures, and in what spare time I have, I've been dissecting specimens for Bill Chandler. Bill's finally found a mammal. Looks like a lizard, and it's only four inches long, but it's a real warm-blooded, gamogenetic, placental, viviparous mammal. Burrows, and seems to live on what pass for insects here."

"Is there enough oxygen for anything like that?" Sachiko was asking.

"Seems to be, close to the ground." Fitzgerald got the headband of his loup adjusted, and pulled it down over his eyes. "He found this thing in a ravine down on the sea bottom-Ha, this page seems to be intact; now, if I can get it out all in one piece —"

He went on talking inaudibly to himself, lifting the page a little at a time and sliding one of the transparent plastic sheets under it, working with minute delicacy. Not the delicacy of the Japanese girl's small hands, moving like the paws of a cat washing her face, but like a steam-hammer cracking a peanut. Field archaeology requires a certain delicacy of touch, too, but Martha watched the pair of them with envious admiration. Then she turned back to her own work, finishing the table of contents.

The next page was the beginning of the first article listed; many of the words were unfamiliar. She had the impression that this must be some kind of scientific or technical journal; that could be because such publications made up the bulk of her own periodical reading. She doubted if it were fiction; the paragraphs had a solid, factual look.

At length, Ivan Fitzgerald gave a short, explosive grunt.

"Ha! Got it!"

She looked up. He had detached the page and was cementing another plastic sheet onto it.

"Any pictures?" she asked.

"None on this side. Wait a moment." He turned the sheet. "None on this side, either." He sprayed another sheet of plastic to sandwich the page, then picked up his pipe and relighted it.

"I get fun out of this, and it's good practice for my hands, so don't think I'm complaining," he said, "but, Martha, do you honestly think anybody's ever going to get anything out of this?"

Sachiko held up a scrap of the silicone plastic the Martians had used for paper with her tweezers. It was almost an inch square.

"Look; three whole words on this piece," she crowed. "Ivan, you took the easy book."

Fitzgerald wasn't being sidetracked. "This stuff's absolutely meaningless," he continued. "It had a meaning fifty thousand years ago, when it was written, but it has none at all now."

She shook her head. "Meaning isn't something that evaporates with time," she argued. "It has just as much meaning now as it ever had. We just haven't learned how to decipher it."

"That seems like a pretty pointless distinction," Selim von Ohlmhorst joined the conversation. "There no longer exists a means of deciphering it."

"We'll find one." She was speaking, she realized, more in self-encouragement than in controversy.

"How? From pictures and captions? We've found captioned pictures, and what have they given us? A caption is intended to explain the picture, not the picture to explain the caption. Suppose some alien to our culture found a picture of a man with a white beard and mustache sawing a billet from a log. He would think the caption meant, 'Man Sawing Wood.' How would he know that it was really 'Wilhelm II in Exile at Doorn?'"

Sachiko had taken off her loup and was lighting a cigarette.

"I can think of pictures intended to explain their captions," she said. "These picture language-books, the sort we use in the Service-little line drawings, with a word or phrase under them."

"Well, of course, if we found something like that," von Ohlmhorst began.

"Michael Ventris found something like that, back in the Fifties," Hubert Penrose's voice broke in from directly behind her.

She turned her head. The colonel was standing by the archaeologists' table; Captain Field and the airdyne pilot had gone out.

"He found a lot of Greek inventories of military stores," Penrose continued. "They were in Cretan Linear B script, and at the head of each list was a little picture, a sword or a helmet or a cooking tripod or a chariot wheel. That's what gave him the key to the script."

"Colonel's getting to be quite an archaeologist," Fitzgerald commented. "We're all learning each others' specialties, on this expedition."

"I heard about that long before this expedition was even contemplated." Penrose was tapping a cigarette on his gold case. "I heard about that back before the Thirty Days' War, at Intelligence School, when I was a lieutenant. As a feat of cryptanalysis, not an archaeological discovery."

"Yes, cryptanalysis," von Ohlmhorst pounced. "The reading of a known language in an unknown form of writing. Ventris' lists were in the known language, Greek. Neither he nor anybody else ever read a word of the Cretan language until the finding of the Greek-Cretan bilingual in 1963, because only with a bilingual text, one language already known, can an unknown ancient language be learned. And what hope, I ask you, have we of finding anything like that here? Martha, you've been working on these Martian texts ever since we landed here-for the last six months. Tell me, have you found a single word to which you can positively assign a meaning?"

"Yes, I think I have one." She was trying hard not to sound too exultant. *"Doma.* It's the name of one of the months of the Martian calendar."

"Where did you find that?" von Ohlmhorst asked. "And how did you establish —?"

"Here." She picked up the photostat and handed it along the table to him. "I'd call this the title page of a magazine."

He was silent for a moment, looking at it. "Yes. I would say so, too. Have you any of the rest of it?"

"I'm working on the first page of the first article, listed there. Wait till I see; yes, here's all I found, together, here." She told him where she had gotten it. "I just gathered it up, at the time, and gave it to Geoffrey and Rosita to photostat; this is the first I've really examined it."

The old man got to his feet, brushing tobacco ashes from the front of his jacket, and came to where she was sitting, laying the title page on the table and leafing quickly through the stack of photostats.

"Yes, and here is the second article, on page eight, and here's the next one." He finished the pile of photostats. "A couple of pages missing at the end of the last article. This is remarkable; surprising that a thing like a magazine would have survived so long."

"Well, this silicone stuff the Martians used for paper is pretty durable," Hubert Penrose said. "There doesn't seem to have been any water or any other fluid in it originally, so it wouldn't dry out with time."

"Oh, it's not remarkable that the material would have survived. We've found a good many books and papers in excellent condition. But only a really vital culture, an organized culture, will publish magazines, and this civilization had been dying for hundreds of years before the end. It might have been a thousand years before the time they died out completely that such activities as publishing ended."

"Well, look where I found it; in a closet in a cellar. Tossed in there and forgotten, and then ignored when they were stripping the building. Things like that happen."

Penrose had picked up the title page and was looking at it.

"I don't think there's any doubt about this being a magazine, at all." He looked again at the title, his lips moving silently. *"Mastharnorvod Tadavas Sornhulva.* Wonder what it means. But you're right about the date —*Doma* seems to be the name of a month. Yes, you have a word, Dr. Dane."

Sid Chamberlain, seeing that something unusual was going on, had come over from the table at which he was working. After examining the title page and some of the inside pages, he began whispering into the stenophone he had taken from his belt.

"Don't try to blow this up to anything big, Sid," she cautioned. "All we have is the name of a month, and Lord only knows how long it'll be till we even find out which month it was."

"Well, it's a start, isn't it?" Penrose argued. "Grotefend only had the word for 'king' when he started reading Persian cuneiform."

"But I don't have the word for month; just the name of a month. Everybody knew the names of the Persian kings, long before Grotefend."

"That's not the story," Chamberlain said. "What the public back on Terra will be interested in is finding out that the Martians published magazines, just like we do. Something familiar; make the Martians seem more real. More human."

Three men had come in, and were removing their masks and helmets and oxy-tanks, and peeling out of their quilted coveralls. Two were Space Force lieutenants; the third was a youngish civilian with close-cropped blond hair, in a checked woolen shirt. Tony Lattimer and his helpers.

"Don't tell me Martha finally got something out of that stuff?" he asked, approaching the table. He might have been commenting on the antics of the village half-wit, from his tone.

"Yes; the name of one of the Martian months." Hubert Penrose went on to explain, showing the photostat.

Tony Lattimer took it, glanced at it, and dropped it on the table.

"Sounds plausible, of course, but just an assumption. That word may not be the name of a month, at all-could mean 'published' or 'authorized' or 'copyrighted' or anything like that. Fact is, I don't think it's more than a wild guess that that thing's anything like a periodical." He dismissed the subject and turned to Penrose. "I picked out the next building to enter; that tall one with the conical thing on top. It ought to be in pretty good shape inside; the conical top wouldn't allow dust to accumulate, and from the outside nothing seems to be caved in or crushed. Ground level's higher than the other one, about the seventh floor. I found a good place and drilled for the shots; tomorrow I'll blast a hole in it, and if you can spare some people to help, we can start exploring it right away."

"Yes, of course, Dr. Lattimer. I can spare about a dozen, and I suppose you can find a few civilian volunteers," Penrose told him. "What will you need in the way of equipment?"

"Oh, about six demolition-packets; they can all be shot together. And the usual thing in the way of lights, and breaking and digging tools, and climbing equipment in case we run into broken or doubtful stairways. We'll divide into two parties. Nothing ought to be entered for the first time without a qualified archaeologist along. Three parties, if Martha can tear herself away from this catalogue of systematized incomprehensibilities she's making long enough to do some real work."

She felt her chest tighten and her face become stiff. She was pressing her lips together to lock in a furious retort when Hubert Penrose answered for her.

"Dr. Dane's been doing as much work, and as important work, as you have," he said brusquely. "More important work, I'd be inclined to say."

Von Ohlmhorst was visibly distressed; he glanced once toward Sid Chamberlain, then looked hastily away from him. Afraid of a story of dissension among archaeologists getting out.

"Working out a system of pronunciation by which the Martian language could be transliterated was a most important contribution," he said. "And Martha did that almost unassisted."

"Unassisted by Dr. Lattimer, anyway," Penrose added. "Captain Field and Lieutenant Koremitsu did some work, and I helped out a little, but nine-tenths of it she did herself."

"Purely arbitrary," Lattimer disdained. "Why, we don't even know that the Martians could make the same kind of vocal sounds we do."

"Oh, yes, we do," Ivan Fitzgerald contradicted, safe on his own ground. "I haven't seen any actual Martian skulls-these people seem to have been very tidy about disposing of their dead-but from statues and busts and pictures I've seen. I'd say that their vocal organs were identical with our own."

"Well, grant that. And grant that it's going to be impressive to rattle off the names of Martian notables whose statues we find, and that if we're ever able to attribute any placenames, they'll sound a lot better than this horse-doctors' Latin the old astronomers splashed all over the map of Mars," Lattimer said. "What I object to is her wasting time on this stuff, of which nobody will ever be able to read a word if she fiddles around with those lists till there's another hundred feet of loess on this city, when there's so much real work to be done and we're as shorthanded as we are."

That was the first time that had come out in just so many words. She was glad Lattimer had said it and not Selim von Ohlmhorst.

"What you mean," she retorted, "is that it doesn't have the publicity value that digging up statues has."

For an instant, she could see that the shot had scored. Then Lattimer, with a side glance at Chamberlain, answered:

"What I mean is that you're trying to find something that any archaeologist, yourself included, should know doesn't exist. I don't object to your gambling your professional reputation and making a laughing stock of yourself; what I object to is that the blunders of one archaeologist discredit the whole subject in the eyes of the public."

That seemed to be what worried Lattimer most. She was framing a reply when the communication-outlet whistled shrilly, and then squawked: "Cocktail time! One hour to dinner; cocktails in the library, Hut Four!"

The library, which was also lounge, recreation room, and general gathering-place, was already crowded; most of the crowd was at the long table topped with sheets of glasslike plastic that had been wall panels out of one of the ruined buildings. She poured herself what passed, here, for a martini, and carried it over to where Selim von Ohlmhorst was sitting alone.

For a while, they talked about the building they had just finished exploring, then drifted into reminiscences of their work on Terra-von Ohlmhorst's in Asia Minor, with the Hittite Empire, and hers in Pakistan, excavating the cities of the Harappa Civilization. They finished their drinks-the ingredients were plentiful; alcohol and flavoring extracts synthesized from Martian vegetation-and von Ohlmhorst took the two glasses to the table for refills.

"You know, Martha," he said, when he returned, "Tony was right about one thing. You are gambling your professional standing and reputation. It's against all archaeological experience that a language so completely dead as this one could be deciphered. There was a continuity between all the other ancient languages-by knowing Greek, Champollion learned to read Egyptian; by knowing Egyptian, Hittite was learned. That's why you and your colleagues have never been able to translate the Harappa hieroglyphics; no such continuity exists there. If you insist that this utterly dead language can be read, your reputation will suffer for it."

"I heard Colonel Penrose say, once, that an officer who's afraid to risk his military reputation seldom makes much of a reputation. It's the same with us. If we really want to find things out, we have to risk making mistakes. And I'm a lot more interested in finding things out than I am in my reputation."

She glanced across the room, to where Tony Lattimer was sitting with Gloria Standish, talking earnestly, while Gloria sipped one of the counterfeit martinis and listened. Gloria was the leading contender for the title of Miss Mars, 1996, if you liked big bosomy blondes, but Tony would have been just as attentive to her if she'd looked like the Wicked Witch in "The Wizard of Oz." because Gloria was the Pan-Federation Telecast System commentator with the expedition.

"I know you are," the old Turco-German was saying. "That's why, when they asked me to name another archaeologist for this expedition, I named you."

He hadn't named Tony Lattimer; Lattimer had been pushed onto the expedition by his university. There'd been a lot of high-level string-pulling to that; she wished she knew the whole story. She'd managed to keep clear of universities and university politics; all her digs had been sponsored by non-academic foundations or art museums.

"You have an excellent standing: much better than my own, at your age. That's why it disturbs me to see you jeopardizing it by this insistence that the Martian language can be translated. I can't, really, see how you can hope to succeed."

She shrugged and drank some more of her cocktail, then lit another cigarette. It was getting tiresome to try to verbalize something she only felt.

"Neither do I, now, but I will. Maybe I'll find something like the picture-books Sachiko was talking about. A child's primer, maybe; surely they had things like that. And if I don't. I'll find something else. We've only been here six months. I can wait the rest of my life, if I have to, but I'll do it sometime."

"I can't wait so long," von Ohlmhorst said. "The rest of my life will only be a few years, and when the *Schiaparelli* orbits in, I'll be going back to Terra on the *Cyrano*."

"I wish you wouldn't. This is a whole new world of archaeology. Literally."

"Yes." He finished the cocktail and looked at his pipe as though wondering whether to relight it so soon before dinner, then put it in his pocket. "A whole new world-but I've grown old, and it isn't for me. I've spent my life studying the Hittites. I can speak the Hittite language, though maybe King Muwatallis wouldn't be able to understand my modern Turkish accent. But the things I'd have to learn here-chemistry, physics, engineering, how to run analytic tests on steel girders and beryllo-silver alloys and plastics and silicones. I'm more at home with a civilization that rode in chariots and fought with swords and was just learning how to work iron. Mars is for young people. This expedition is a cadre of leadership-not only the Space Force people, who'll be the commanders of the main expedition, but us scientists, too. And I'm just an old cavalry general who can't learn to command tanks and aircraft. You'll have time to learn about Mars. I won't."

His reputation as the dean of Hittitologists was solid and secure, too, she added mentally. Then she felt ashamed of the thought. He wasn't to be classed with Tony Lattimer.

"All I came for was to get the work started," he was continuing. "The Federation Government felt that an old hand should do that. Well, it's started, now; you and Tony and whoever come out on the *Schiaparelli* must carry it on. You said it, yourself; you have a whole new world. This is only one city, of the last Martian civilization. Behind this, you have the Late Upland Culture, and the Canal Builders, and all the civilizations and races and empires before them, clear back to the Martian Stone Age." He hesitated for a moment. "You have no idea what all you have to learn, Martha. This isn't the time to start specializing too narrowly."

They all got out of the truck and stretched their legs and looked up the road to the tall building with the queer conical cap askew on its top. The four little figures that had been busy against its wall climbed into the jeep and started back slowly, the smallest of them, Sachiko Koremitsu, paying out an electric cable behind. When it pulled up beside the truck, they climbed out; Sachiko attached the free end of the cable to a nuclear-electric battery. At once, dirty gray smoke and orange dust puffed out from the wall of the building, and, a second later, the multiple explosion banged.

She and Tony Lattimer and Major Lindemann climbed onto the truck, leaving the jeep stand by the road. When they reached the building, a satisfyingly wide breach had been blown in the wall. Lattimer had placed his shots between two of the windows; they were both blown out along with the wall between, and lay unbroken on the ground. Martha remembered the first building they had entered. A Space Force officer had picked up a stone and thrown it at one of the windows, thinking that would be all they'd need to do. It had bounced back. He had drawn his pistol-they'd all carried guns, then, on the principle that what they didn't know about Mars might easily hurt them-and fired four shots. The bullets had ricocheted, screaming thinly; there were four coppery smears of jacket-metal on the window, and a little surface spalling. Somebody tried a rifle; the 4000-f.s. bullet had cracked the glasslike pane without penetrating. An oxyacetylene torch had taken an hour to cut the window out; the lab crew, aboard the ship, were still trying to find out just what the stuff was.

Tony Lattimer had gone forward and was sweeping his flashlight back and forth, swearing petulantly, his voice harshened and amplified by his helmet-speaker.

"I thought I was blasting into a hallway; this lets us into a room. Careful; there's about a two-foot drop to the floor, and a lot of rubble from the blast just inside."

He stepped down through the breach; the others began dragging equipment out of the trucks-shovels and picks and crowbars and sledges, portable floodlights, cameras, sketching materials, an extension ladder, even Alpinists' ropes and crampons and pickaxes. Hubert Penrose was shouldering something that looked like a surrealist machine gun but which was really a nuclear-electric jack-hammer. Martha selected one of the spike-shod mountaineer's ice axes, with which she could dig or chop or poke or pry or help herself over rough footing.

The windows, grimed and crusted with fifty millennia of dust, filtered in a dim twilight; even the breach in the wall, in the morning shade, lighted only a small patch of floor. Somebody snapped on a floodlight, aiming it at the ceiling. The big room was empty and bare; dust lay thick on the floor and reddened the once-white walls. It could have been a large office, but there was nothing left in it to indicate its use.

"This one's been stripped up to the seventh floor!" Lattimer exclaimed. "Street level'll be cleaned out, completely."

"Do for living quarters and shops, then," Lindemann said. "Added to the others, this'll take care of everybody on the *Schiaparelli*."

"Seem to have been a lot of electric or electronic apparatus over along this wall," one of the Space Force officers commented. "Ten or twelve electric outlets." He brushed the dusty wall with his glove, then scraped on the floor with his foot. "I can see where things were pried loose."

The door, one of the double sliding things the Martians had used, was closed. Selim von Ohlmhorst tried it, but it was stuck fast. The metal latch-parts had frozen together, molecule bonding itself to molecule, since the door had last been closed. Hubert Penrose came over with the jack-hammer, fitting a spear-point chisel into place. He set the chisel in the joint between the doors, braced the hammer against his hip, and squeezed the trigger-switch. The hammer banged briefly like the weapon it resembled, and the doors popped a few inches apart, then stuck. Enough dust had worked into the recesses into which it was supposed to slide to block it on both sides.

That was old stuff; they ran into that every time they had to force a door, and they were prepared for it. Somebody went outside and brought in a power-jack and finally one of the doors inched back to the door jamb. That was enough to get the lights and equipment through: they all passed from the room to the hallway beyond. About half the other doors were open; each had a number and a single word, *Darfhulva*, over it.

One of the civilian volunteers, a woman professor of natural ecology from Penn State University, was looking up and down the hall.

"You know," she said, "I feel at home here. I think this was a college of some sort, and these were classrooms. That word, up there; that was the subject taught, or the department. And those electronic devices, all where the class would face them; audio-visual teaching aids."

"A twenty-five-story university?" Lattimer scoffed. "Why, a building like this would handle thirty thousand students."

"Maybe there were that many. This was a big city, in its prime," Martha said, moved chiefly by a desire to oppose Lattimer.

"Yes, but think of the snafu in the halls, every time they changed classes. It'd take half an hour to get everybody back and forth from one floor to another." He turned to von Ohlmhorst. "I'm going up above this floor. This place has been looted clean up to here, but there's a chance there may be something above," he said.

"I'll stay on this floor, at present," the Turco-German replied. "There will be much coming and going, and dragging things in and out. We should get this completely examined and recorded first. Then Major Lindemann's people can do their worst, here."

"Well, if nobody else wants it, I'll take the downstairs," Martha said.

"I'll go along with you," Hubert Penrose told her. "If the lower floors have no archaeological value, we'll turn them into living quarters. I like this building: it'll give everybody room to keep out from under everybody else's feet." He looked down the hall. "We ought to find escalators at the middle."

The hallway, too, was thick underfoot with dust. Most of the open rooms were empty, but a few contained furniture, including small seat-desks. The original proponent of the university theory pointed these out as just what might be found in classrooms. There were escalators, up and down, on either side of the hall, and more on the intersecting passage to the right.

"That's how they handled the students, between classes," Martha commented. "And I'll bet there are more ahead, there."

They came to a stop where the hallway ended at a great square central hall. There were elevators, there, on two of the sides, and four escalators, still usable as stairways. But it was the walls, and the paintings on them, that brought them up short and staring.

They were clouded with dirt-she was trying to imagine what they must have looked like originally, and at the same time estimating the labor that would be involved in cleaning them-but they were still distinguishable, as was the word, *Darfhulva*, in golden letters above each of the four sides. It was a moment before she realized, from the murals, that she had at last found a meaningful Martian word. They were a vast historical panorama, clockwise around the room. A group of skin-clad savages squatting around a fire. Hunters with bows and spears, carrying a carcass of an animal slightly like a pig. Nomads riding long-legged, graceful mounts like hornless deer. Peasants sowing and reaping; mud-walled hut villages, and cities; processions of priests and warriors; battles with swords and bows, and with cannon and muskets; galleys, and ships with sails, and ships without visible means of propulsion, and aircraft. Changing costumes and weapons and machines and styles of architecture. A richly fertile landscape, gradually merging into barren deserts and bushlands-the time of the great planet-wide drought. The Canal Builders-men with machines recognizable as steam-shovels and derricks, digging and quarrying and driving across the empty plains with aqueducts. More cities-seaports on the shrinking oceans; dwindling, half-deserted cities; an abandoned city, with four tiny humanoid figures and a thing like a combat-car in the middle of a brush-grown plaza, they and their vehicle dwarfed by the huge lifeless buildings around them. She had not the least doubt; *Darfhulva* was History.

"Wonderful!" von Ohlmhorst was saying. "The entire history of this race. Why, if the painter depicted appropriate costumes and weapons and machines for each period, and got the architecture right, we can break the history of this planet into eras and periods and civilizations."

"You can assume they're authentic. The faculty of this university would insist on authenticity in the *Darfhulva* —History-Department," she said.

"Yes! *Darfhulva* —History! And your magazine was a journal of *Sornhulva*!" Penrose exclaimed. "You have a word, Martha!" It took her an instant to realize that he had called her by her first name, and not Dr. Dane. She wasn't sure if that weren't a bigger triumph than learning a word of the Martian language. Or a more auspicious start. "Alone, I suppose that *hulva* means something like science or knowledge, or study; combined, it would be equivalent to our 'ology. And *darf* would mean something like past, or old times, or human events, or chronicles."

"That gives you three words, Martha!" Sachiko jubilated. "You did it."

"Let's don't go too fast," Lattimer said, for once not derisively. "I'll admit that *darfhulva* is the Martian word for history as a subject of study; I'll admit that *hulva* is the general word and *darf* modifies it and tells us which subject is meant. But as for assigning specific meanings, we can't do that because we don't know just how the Martians thought, scientifically or otherwise."

He stopped short, startled by the blue-white light that blazed as Sid Chamberlain's Kliegettes went on. When the whirring of the camera stopped, it was Chamberlain who was speaking:

"This is the biggest thing yet; the whole history of Mars, stone age to the end, all on four walls. I'm taking this with the fast shutter, but we'll telecast it in slow motion, from the beginning to the end. Tony, I want you to do the voice for it-running commentary, interpretation of each scene as it's shown. Would you do that?"

Would he do that! Martha thought. If he had a tail, he'd be wagging it at the very thought.

"Well, there ought to be more murals on the other floors," she said. "Who wants to come downstairs with us?"

Sachiko did; immediately. Ivan Fitzgerald volunteered. Sid decided to go upstairs with Tony Lattimer, and Gloria Standish decided to go upstairs, too. Most of the party would remain on the seventh floor, to help Selim von Ohlmhorst get it finished. After poking tentatively at the escalator with the spike of her ice axe, Martha led the way downward.

The sixth floor was *Darfhulva*, too; military and technological history, from the character of the murals. They looked around the central hall, and went down to the fifth; it was like the floors above except that the big quadrangle was stacked with dusty furniture and boxes. Ivan Fitzgerald, who was carrying the floodlight, swung it slowly around. Here the murals were of heroic-sized Martians, so human in appearance as to seem members of her own race, each holding some object —a book, or a test tube, or some bit of scientific apparatus, and behind them were scenes of laboratories and factories, flame and smoke, lightning-flashes. The word at the top of each of the four walls was one with which she was already familiar —*Sornhulva*.

"Hey, Martha; there's that word," Ivan Fitzgerald exclaimed. "The one in the title of your magazine." He looked at the paintings. "Chemistry, or physics."

"Both." Hubert Penrose considered. "I don't think the Martians made any sharp distinction between them. See, the old fellow with the scraggly whiskers must be the inventor of the spectroscope; he has one in his hands, and he has a rainbow behind him. And the woman in the blue smock, beside him, worked in organic chemistry; see the diagrams of long-chain molecules behind her. What word would convey the idea of chemistry and physics taken as one subject?"

"*Sornhulva*," Sachiko suggested. "If *hulva's* something like science, "*sorn*" must mean matter, or substance, or physical object. You were right, all along, Martha. A civilization like this would certainly leave something like this, that would be self-explanatory."

"This'll wipe a little more of that superior grin off Tony Lattimer's face," Fitzgerald was saying, as they went down the motionless escalator to the floor below. "Tony wants to be a big shot. When you want to be a big shot, you can't bear the possibility of anybody else being a bigger big shot, and whoever makes a start on reading this language will be the biggest big shot archaeology ever saw."

That was true. She hadn't thought of it, in that way, before, and now she tried not to think about it. She didn't want to be a big shot. She wanted to be able to read the Martian language, and find things out about the Martians.

Two escalators down, they came out on a mezzanine around a wide central hall on the street level, the floor forty feet below them and the ceiling thirty feet above. Their lights picked out object after object below —a huge group of sculptured figures in the middle; some kind of a motor vehicle jacked up on trestles for repairs; things that looked like machine-guns and auto-cannon; long tables, tops littered with a dust-covered miscellany; machinery; boxes and crates and containers.

They made their way down and walked among the clutter, missing a hundred things for every one they saw, until they found an escalator to the basement. There were three basements, one under another, until at last they stood at the bottom of the last escalator, on a bare concrete floor, swinging the portable floodlight over stacks of boxes and barrels and drums, and heaps of powdery dust. The boxes were plastic-nobody had ever found anything made of wood in the city-and the barrels and drums were of metal or glass or some glasslike substance. They were outwardly intact. The powdery heaps might have been anything organic, or anything containing fluid. Down here, where wind and dust could not reach, evaporation had been the only force of destruction after the minute life that caused putrefaction had vanished.

They found refrigeration rooms, too, and using Martha's ice axe and the pistollike vibratool Sachiko carried on her belt, they pounded and pried one open, to find dessicated piles of what had been vegetables, and leathery chunks of meat. Samples of that stuff, rocketed up to the ship, would give a reliable estimate, by radio-carbon dating, of how long ago this building had been occupied. The refrigeration unit, radically different from anything their own culture had produced, had been electrically powered. Sachiko and Penrose, poking into it, found the switches still on; the machine had only ceased to function when the power-source, whatever that had been, had failed.

The middle basement had also been used, at least toward the end, for storage; it was cut in half by a partition pierced by but one door. They took half an hour to force this, and were on the point of sending above for heavy equipment when it yielded enough for them to squeeze through. Fitzgerald, in the lead with the light, stopped short, looked around, and then gave a groan that came through his helmet-speaker like a foghorn.

"Oh, no! *No!*"

"What's the matter, Ivan?" Sachiko, entering behind him, asked anxiously.

He stepped aside. "Look at it, Sachi! Are we going to have to do all that?"

Martha crowded through behind her friend and looked around, then stood motionless, dizzy with excitement. Books. Case on case of books, half an acre of cases, fifteen feet to the ceiling. Fitzgerald, and Penrose, who had pushed in behind her, were talking in rapid excitement; she only heard the sound of their voices, not their words. This must be the main stacks of the university library-the entire literature of the vanished race of Mars. In the center, down an aisle between the cases, she could see the hollow square of the librarians' desk, and stairs and a dumb-waiter to the floor above.

She realized that she was walking forward, with the others, toward this. Sachiko was saying: "I'm the lightest; let me go first." She must be talking about the spidery metal stairs.

"I'd say they were safe," Penrose answered. "The trouble we've had with doors around here shows that the metal hasn't deteriorated."

In the end, the Japanese girl led the way, more catlike than ever in her caution. The stairs were quite sound, in spite of their fragile appearance, and they all followed her. The floor above was a duplicate of the room they had entered, and seemed to contain about as many books. Rather than waste time forcing the door here, they returned to the middle basement and came up by the escalator down which they had originally descended.

The upper basement contained kitchens-electric stoves, some with pots and pans still on them-and a big room that must have been, originally, the students' dining room, though when last used it had been a workshop. As they expected, the library reading room was on the street-level floor, directly above the stacks. It seemed to have been converted into a sort of common living room for the building's last occupants. An adjoining auditorium had been made into a chemical works; there were vats and distillation apparatus, and a metal fractionating tower that extended through a hole knocked in the ceiling seventy feet above. A good deal of plastic furniture of the sort they had been finding everywhere in the city was stacked about, some of it broken up, apparently for reprocessing. The other rooms on the street floor seemed also to have been devoted to manufacturing and repair work; a considerable industry, along a number of lines, must have been carried on here for a long time after the university had ceased to function as such.

On the second floor, they found a museum; many of the exhibits remained, tantalizingly half-visible in grimed glass cases. There had been administrative offices there, too. The doors of most of them were closed, and they did not waste time trying to force them, but those that were open had been turned into living quarters. They made notes, and rough floor plans, to guide them in future more thorough examination; it was almost noon before they had worked their way back to the seventh floor.

Selim von Ohlmhorst was in a room on the north side of the building, sketching the position of things before examining them and collecting them for removal. He had the floor checkerboarded with a grid of chalked lines, each numbered.

"We have everything on this floor photographed," he said. "I have three gangs-all the flood-lights I have-sketching and making measurements. At the rate we're going, with time out for lunch, we'll be finished by the middle of the afternoon."

"You've been working fast. Evidently you aren't being high-church about a 'qualified archaeologist' entering rooms first," Penrose commented.

"Ach, childishness!" the old man exclaimed impatiently. "These officers of yours aren't fools. All of them have been to Intelligence School and Criminal Investigation School. Some of the most careful amateur archaeologists I ever knew were retired soldiers or policemen. But there isn't much work to be done. Most of the rooms are either empty or like this one —a few bits of furniture and broken trash and scraps of paper. Did you find anything down on the lower floors?"

"Well, yes," Penrose said, a hint of mirth in his voice. "What would you say, Martha?"

She started to tell Selim. The others, unable to restrain their excitement, broke in with interruptions. Von Ohlmhorst was staring in incredulous amazement.

"But this floor was looted almost clean, and the buildings we've entered before were all looted from the street level up," he said, at length.

"The people who looted this one lived here," Penrose replied. "They had electric power to the last; we found refrigerators full of food, and stoves with the dinner still on them. They must have used the elevators to haul things down from the upper floor. The whole first floor was converted into workshops and laboratories. I think that this place must have been something like a monastery in the Dark Ages in Europe, or what such a monastery would have been like if the Dark Ages had followed the fall of a highly developed scientific civilization. For one thing, we found a lot of machine guns and light auto-cannon on the street level, and all the doors were barricaded. The people here were trying to keep a civilization running after the rest of the planet had gone back to barbarism; I suppose they'd have to fight off raids by the barbarians now and then."

"You're not going to insist on making this building into expedition quarters, I hope, colonel?" von Ohlmhorst asked anxiously.

"Oh, no! This place is an archaeological treasure-house. More than that; from what I saw, our technicians can learn a lot, here. But you'd better get this floor cleaned up as soon as you can, though. I'll have the subsurface part, from the sixth floor down, airsealed. Then we'll put in oxygen generators and power units, and get a couple of elevators into service. For the floors above, we can use temporary airsealing floor by floor, and portable equipment; when we have things atmosphered and lighted and heated, you and Martha and Tony Lattimer can go to work systematically and in comfort, and I'll give you all the help I can spare from the other work. This is one of the biggest things we've found yet."

Tony Lattimer and his companions came down to the seventh floor a little later.

"I don't get this, at all," he began, as soon as he joined them. "This building wasn't stripped the way the others were. Always, the procedure seems to have been to strip from the bottom up, but they seem to have stripped the top floors first, here. All but the very top. I found out what that conical thing is, by the way. It's a wind-rotor, and under it there's an electric generator. This building generated its own power."

"What sort of condition are the generators in?" Penrose asked.

"Well, everything's full of dust that blew in under the rotor, of course, but it looks to be in pretty good shape. Hey, I'll bet that's it! They had power, so they used the elevators to haul stuff down. That's just what they did. Some of the floors above here don't seem to have been touched, though." He paused momentarily; back of his oxy-mask, he seemed to be grinning. "I don't know that I ought to mention this in front of Martha, but two floors above-we hit a room-it must have been the reference library for one of the departments-that had close to five hundred books in it."

The noise that interrupted him, like the squawking of a Brobdingnagian parrot, was only Ivan Fitzgerald laughing through his helmet-speaker.

Lunch at the huts was a hasty meal, with a gabble of full-mouthed and excited talking. Hubert Penrose and his chief subordinates snatched their food in a huddled consultation at one end of the table; in the afternoon, work was suspended on everything else and the fifty-odd men and women of the expedition concentrated their efforts on the University. By the middle of the afternoon, the seventh floor had been completely examined, photographed and sketched, and the murals in the square central hall covered with protective tarpaulins, and Laurent Gicquel and his airsealing crew had moved in and were at work. It had been decided to seal the central hall at the entrances. It took the French-Canadian engineer most of the afternoon to find all the ventilation-ducts and plug them. An elevator-shaft on the north side was found reaching clear to the twenty-fifth floor; this would give access to the top of the building; another shaft, from the center, would take care of the floors below. Nobody seemed willing to trust the ancient elevators, themselves; it was the next evening before a couple of cars and the necessary machinery could be fabricated in the machine shops aboard the ship and sent down by landing-rocket. By that time, the airsealing was finished, the nuclear-electric energy-converters were in place, and the oxygen generators set up.

Martha was in the lower basement, an hour or so before lunch the day after, when a couple of Space Force officers came out of the elevator, bringing extra lights with them. She was still using oxygen-equipment; it was a moment before she realized that the newcomers had no masks, and that one of them was smoking. She took off her own helmet-speaker, throat-mike and mask and unslung her tank-pack, breathing cautiously. The air was chilly, and musty-acrid with the odor of antiquity-the first Martian odor she had smelled-but when she lit a cigarette, the lighter flamed clear and steady and the tobacco caught and burned evenly.

The archaeologists, many of the other civilian scientists, a few of the Space Force officers and the two news-correspondents, Sid Chamberlain and Gloria Standish, moved in that evening, setting up cots in vacant rooms. They installed electric stoves and a refrigerator in the old Library Reading Room, and put in a bar and lunch counter. For a few days, the place was full of noise and activity, then, gradually, the Space Force people and all but a few of the civilians returned to their own work. There was still the business of airsealing the more habitable of the buildings already explored, and fitting them up in readiness for the arrival, in a year and a half, of the five hundred members of the main expedition. There was work to be done enlarging the landing field for the ship's rocket craft, and building new chemical-fuel tanks.

There was the work of getting the city's ancient reservoirs cleared of silt before the next spring thaw brought more water down the underground aqueducts everybody called canals in mistranslation of Schiaparelli's Italian word, though this was proving considerably easier than anticipated. The ancient Canal-Builders must have anticipated a time when their descendants would no longer be capable of maintenance work, and had prepared against it. By the day after the University had been made completely habitable, the actual work there was being done by Selim, Tony Lattimer and herself, with half a dozen Space Force officers, mostly girls, and four or five civilians, helping.

They worked up from the bottom, dividing the floor-surfaces into numbered squares, measuring and listing and sketching and photographing. They packaged samples of organic matter and sent them up to the ship for Carbon-14 dating and analysis; they opened cans and jars and bottles, and found that everything fluid in them had evaporated, through the porosity of glass and metal and plastic if there were no other way. Wherever they looked, they found evidence of activity suddenly suspended and never resumed. A vise with a bar of metal in it, half cut through and the hacksaw beside it. Pots and pans with hardened remains of food in them; a leathery cut of meat on a table, with the knife ready at hand. Toilet articles on washstands; unmade beds, the bedding ready to crumble at a touch but still retaining the impress of the sleeper's body; papers and writing materials on desks, as though the writer had gotten up, meaning to return and finish in a fifty-thousand-year-ago moment.

It worried her. Irrationally, she began to feel that the Martians had never left this place; that they were still around her, watching disapprovingly every time she picked up something they had laid down. They haunted her dreams, now, instead of their enigmatic writing. At first, everybody who had moved into the University had taken a separate room, happy to escape the crowding and lack of privacy of the huts. After a few nights, she was glad when Gloria Standish moved in with her, and accepted the newswoman's excuse that she felt lonely without somebody to talk to before falling asleep. Sachiko Koremitsu joined them the next evening, and before going to bed, the girl officer cleaned and oiled her pistol, remarking that she was afraid some rust may have gotten into it.

The others felt it, too. Selim von Ohlmhorst developed the habit of turning quickly and looking behind him, as though trying to surprise somebody or something that was stalking him. Tony Lattimer, having a drink at the bar that had been improvised from the librarian's desk in the Reading Room, set down his glass and swore.

"You know what this place is? It's an archaeological *Marie Celeste*!" he declared. "It was occupied right up to the end-we've all seen the shifts these people used to keep a civilization going here-but what was the end? What happened to them? Where did they go?"

"You didn't expect them to be waiting out front, with a red carpet and a big banner, *Welcome Terrans*, did you, Tony?" Gloria Standish asked.

"No, of course not; they've all been dead for fifty thousand years. But if they were the last of the Martians, why haven't we found their bones, at least? Who buried them, after they were dead?" He looked at the glass, a bubble-thin goblet, found, with hundreds of others like it, in a closet above, as though debating with himself whether to have another drink. Then he voted in the affirmative and reached for the cocktail pitcher. "And every door on the old ground level is either barred or barricaded from the inside. How did they get out? And why did they leave?"

The next day, at lunch, Sachiko Koremitsu had the answer to the second question. Four or five electrical engineers had come down by rocket from the ship, and she had been spending the morning with them, in oxy-masks, at the top of the building.

"Tony, I thought you said those generators were in good shape," she began, catching sight of Lattimer. "They aren't. They're in the most unholy mess I ever saw. What happened, up there, was that the supports of the wind-rotor gave way, and weight snapped the main shaft, and smashed everything under it."

"Well, after fifty thousand years, you can expect something like that," Lattimer retorted. "When an archaeologist says something's in good shape, he doesn't necessarily mean it'll start as soon as you shove a switch in."

"You didn't notice that it happened when the power was on, did you," one of the engineers asked, nettled at Lattimer's tone. "Well, it was. Everything's burned out or shorted or fused together; I saw one busbar eight inches across melted clean in two. It's a pity we didn't find things in good shape, even archaeologically speaking. I saw a lot of interesting things, things in advance of what we're using now. But it'll take a couple of years to get everything sorted out and figure what it looked like originally."

"Did it look as though anybody'd made any attempt to fix it?" Martha asked.

Sachiko shook her head. "They must have taken one look at it and given up. I don't believe there would have been any possible way to repair anything."

"Well, that explains why they left. They needed electricity for lighting, and heating, and all their industrial equipment was electrical. They had a good life, here, with power; without it, this place wouldn't have been habitable."

"Then why did they barricade everything from the inside, and how did they get out?" Lattimer wanted to know.

"To keep other people from breaking in and looting. Last man out probably barred the last door and slid down a rope from upstairs," von Ohlmhorst suggested. "This Houdini-trick doesn't worry me too much. We'll find out eventually."

"Yes, about the time Martha starts reading Martian," Lattimer scoffed.

"That may be just when we'll find out," von Ohlmhorst replied seriously. "It wouldn't surprise me if they left something in writing when they evacuated this place."

"Are you really beginning to treat this pipe dream of hers as a serious possibility, Selim?" Lattimer demanded. "I know, it would be a wonderful thing, but wonderful things don't happen just because they're wonderful. Only because they're possible, and this isn't. Let me quote that distinguished Hittitologist, Johannes Friedrich: 'Nothing can be translated out of nothing.' Or that later but not less distinguished Hittitologist, Selim von Ohlmhorst: 'Where are you going to get your bilingual?'"

"Friedrich lived to see the Hittite language deciphered and read," von Ohlmhorst reminded him.

"Yes, when they found Hittite-Assyrian bilinguals." Lattimer measured a spoonful of coffee-powder into his cup and added hot water. "Martha, you ought to know, better than anybody, how little chance you have. You've been working for years in the Indus Valley; how many words of Harappa have you or anybody else ever been able to read?"

"We never found a university, with a half-million-volume library, at Harappa or Mohenjo-Daro."

"And, the first day we entered this building, we established meanings for several words," Selim von Ohlmhorst added.

"And you've never found another meaningful word since," Lattimer added. "And you're only sure of general meaning, not specific meaning of word-elements, and you have a dozen different interpretations for each word."

"We made a start," von Ohlmhorst maintained. "We have Grotefend's word for 'king.' But I'm going to be able to read some of those books, over there, if it takes me the rest of my life here. It probably will, anyhow."

"You mean you've changed your mind about going home on the *Cyrano*?" Martha asked. "You'll stay on here?"

The old man nodded. "I can't leave this. There's too much to discover. The old dog will have to learn a lot of new tricks, but this is where my work will be, from now on."

Lattimer was shocked. "You're nuts!" he cried. "You mean you're going to throw away everything you've accomplished in Hittitology and start all over again here on Mars? Martha, if you've talked him into this crazy decision, you're a criminal!"

"Nobody talked me into anything," von Ohlmhorst said roughly. "And as for throwing away what I've accomplished in Hittitology, I don't know what the devil you're talking about. Everything I know about the Hittite Empire is published and available to anybody. Hittitology's like Egyptology; it's stopped being research and archaeology and become scholarship and history. And I'm not a scholar or a historian; I'm a pick-and-shovel field archaeologist —a highly skilled and specialized grave-robber and junk-picker —and there's more pick-and-shovel work on this planet than I could do in a hundred lifetimes. This is something new; I was a fool to think I could turn my back on it and go back to scribbling footnotes about Hittite kings."

"You could have anything you wanted, in Hittitology. There are a dozen universities that'd sooner have you than a winning football team. But no! You have to be the top man in Martiology, too. You can't leave that for anybody else —" Lattimer shoved his chair back and got to his feet, leaving the table with an oath that was almost a sob of exasperation.

Maybe his feelings were too much for him. Maybe he realized, as Martha did, what he had betrayed. She sat, avoiding the eyes of the others, looking at the ceiling, as embarrassed as though Lattimer had flung something dirty on the table in front of them. Tony Lattimer had, desperately, wanted Selim to go home on the *Cyrano*. Martiology was a new field; if Selim entered it, he would bring with him the reputation he had already built in Hittitology, automatically stepping into the leading role that Lattimer had coveted for himself. Ivan Fitzgerald's words echoed back to her-when you want to be a big shot, you can't bear the possibility of anybody else being a bigger big shot. His derision of her own efforts became comprehensible, too.

It wasn't that he was convinced that she would never learn to read the Martian language. He had been afraid that she would.

———————————

Ivan Fitzgerald finally isolated the germ that had caused the Finchley girl's undiagnosed illness. Shortly afterward, the malady turned into a mild fever, from which she recovered. Nobody else seemed to have caught it. Fitzgerald was still trying to find out how the germ had been transmitted.

They found a globe of Mars, made when the city had been a seaport. They located the city, and learned that its name had been Kukan-or something with a similar vowel-consonant ratio. Immediately, Sid Chamberlain and Gloria Standish began giving their telecasts a Kukan dateline, and Hubert Penrose used the name in his official reports. They also found a Martian calendar; the year had been divided into ten more or less equal months, and one of them had been Doma. Another month was Nor, and that was a part of the name of the scientific journal Martha had found.

Bill Chandler, the zoologist, had been going deeper and deeper into the old sea bottom of Syrtis. Four hundred miles from Kukan, and at fifteen thousand feet lower altitude, he shot a bird. At least, it was a something with wings and what were almost but not quite feathers, though it was more reptilian than avian in general characteristics. He and Ivan Fitzgerald skinned and mounted it, and then dissected the carcass almost tissue by tissue. About seven-eighths of its body capacity was lungs; it certainly breathed air containing at least half enough oxygen to support human life, or five times as much as the air around Kukan.

That took the center of interest away from archaeology, and started a new burst of activity. All the expedition's aircraft-four jetticopters and three wingless airdyne reconnaissance fighters-were thrown into intensified exploration of the lower sea bottoms, and the bio-science boys and girls were wild with excitement and making new discoveries on each flight.

The University was left to Selim and Martha and Tony Lattimer, the latter keeping to himself while she and the old Turco-German worked together. The civilian specialists in other fields, and the Space Force people who had been holding tape lines and making sketches and snapping cameras, were all flying to lower Syrtis to find out how much oxygen there was and what kind of life it supported.

Sometimes Sachiko dropped in; most of the time she was busy helping Ivan Fitzgerald dissect specimens. They had four or five species of what might loosely be called birds, and something that could easily be classed as a reptile, and a carnivorous mammal the size of a cat with birdlike claws, and a herbivore almost identical with the piglike thing in the big *Darfhulva* mural, and another like a gazelle with a single horn in the middle of its forehead.

The high point came when one party, at thirty thousand feet below the level of Kukan, found breathable air. One of them had a mild attack of *sorroche* and had to be flown back for treatment in a hurry, but the others showed no ill effects.

The daily newscasts from Terra showed a corresponding shift in interest at home. The discovery of the University had focused attention on the dead past of Mars; now the public was interested in Mars as a possible home for humanity. It was Tony Lattimer who brought archaeology back into the activities of the expedition and the news at home.

Martha and Selim were working in the museum on the second floor, scrubbing the grime from the glass cases, noting contents, and grease-penciling numbers; Lattimer and a couple of Space Force officers were going through what had been the administrative offices on the other side. It was one of these, a young second lieutenant, who came hurrying in from the mezzanine, almost bursting with excitement.

"Hey, Martha! Dr. von Ohlmhorst!" he was shouting. "Where are you? Tony's found the Martians!"

Selim dropped his rag back in the bucket; she laid her clipboard on top of the case beside her.

"Where?" they asked together.

"Over on the north side." The lieutenant took hold of himself and spoke more deliberately. "Little room, back of one of the old faculty offices-conference room. It was locked from the inside, and we had to burn it down with a torch. That's where they are. Eighteen of them, around a long table —"

Gloria Standish, who had dropped in for lunch, was on the mezzanine, fairly screaming into a radiophone extension:

" ...Dozen and a half of them! Well, of course they're dead. What a question! They look like skeletons covered with leather. No, I do not know what they died of. Well, forget it; I don't care if Bill Chandler's found a three-headed hippopotamus. Sid, don't you get it? We've found the *Martians*!"

She slammed the phone back on its hook, rushing away ahead of them.

Martha remembered the closed door; on the first survey, they hadn't attempted opening it. Now it was burned away at both sides and lay, still hot along the edges, on the floor of the big office room in front. A floodlight was on in the room inside, and Lattimer was going around looking at things while a Space Force officer stood by the door. The center of the room was filled by a long table; in armchairs around it sat the eighteen men and women who had occupied the room for the last fifty millennia. There were bottles and glasses on the table in front of them, and, had she seen them in a dimmer light, she would have thought that they were merely dozing over their drinks. One had a knee hooked over his chair-arm and was curled in foetuslike sleep. Another had fallen forward onto the table, arms extended, the emerald set of a ring twinkling dully on one finger. Skeletons covered with leather, Gloria Standish had called them, and so they were-faces like skulls, arms and legs like sticks, the flesh shrunken onto the bones under it.

"Isn't this something!" Lattimer was exulting. "Mass suicide, that's what it was. Notice what's in the corners?"

Braziers, made of perforated two-gallon-odd metal cans, the white walls smudged with smoke above them. Von Ohlmhorst had noticed them at once, and was poking into one of them with his flashlight.

"Yes; charcoal. I noticed a quantity of it around a couple of hand-forges in the shop on the first floor. That's why you had so much trouble breaking in; they'd sealed the room on the inside." He straightened and went around the room, until he found a ventilator, and peered into it. "Stuffed with rags. They must have been all that were left, here. Their power was gone, and they were old and tired, and all around them their world was dying. So they just came in here and lit the charcoal, and sat drinking together till they all fell asleep. Well, we know what became of them, now, anyhow."

Sid and Gloria made the most of it. The Terran public wanted to hear about Martians, and if live Martians couldn't be found, a room full of dead ones was the next best thing. Maybe an even better thing; it had been only sixty-odd years since the Orson Welles invasion-scare. Tony Lattimer, the discoverer, was beginning to cash in on his attentions to Gloria and his ingratiation with Sid; he was always either making voice-and-image talks for telecast or listening to the news from the home planet. Without question, he had become, overnight, the most widely known archaeologist in history.

"Not that I'm interested in all this, for myself," he disclaimed, after listening to the telecast from Terra two days after his discovery. "But this is going to be a big thing for Martian archaeology. Bring it to the public attention; dramatize it. Selim, can you remember when Lord Carnarvon and Howard Carter found the tomb of Tutankhamen?"

"In 1923? I was two years old, then," von Ohlmhorst chuckled. "I really don't know how much that publicity ever did for Egyptology. Oh, the museums did devote more space to Egyptian exhibits, and after a museum department head gets a few extra showcases, you know how hard it is to make him give them up. And, for a while, it was easier to get financial support for new excavations. But I don't know how much good all this public excitement really does, in the long run."

"Well, I think one of us should go back on the *Cyrano*, when the *Schiaparelli* orbits in," Lattimer said. "I'd hoped it would be you; your voice would carry the most weight. But I think it's important that one of us go back, to present the story of our work, and what we have accomplished and what we hope to accomplish, to the public and to the universities and the learned societies, and to the Federation Government. There will be a great deal of work that will have to be done. We must not allow the other scientific fields and the so-called practical interests to monopolize public and academic support. So, I believe I shall go back at least for a while, and see what I can do —"

Lectures. The organization of a Society of Martian Archaeology, with Anthony Lattimer, Ph.D., the logical candidate for the chair. Degrees, honors; the deference of the learned, and the adulation of the lay public. Positions, with impressive titles and salaries. Sweet are the uses of publicity.

She crushed out her cigarette and got to her feet. "Well, I still have the final lists of what we found in *Halvhulva* —Biology-department to check over. I'm starting on Sornhulva tomorrow, and I want that stuff in shape for expert evaluation."

That was the sort of thing Tony Lattimer wanted to get away from, the detail-work and the drudgery. Let the infantry do the slogging through the mud; the brass-hats got the medals.

She was halfway through the fifth floor, a week later, and was having midday lunch in the reading room on the first floor when Hubert Penrose came over and sat down beside her, asking her what she was doing. She told him.

"I wonder if you could find me a couple of men, for an hour or so," she added. "I'm stopped by a couple of jammed doors at the central hall. Lecture room and library, if the layout of that floor's anything like the ones below it."

"Yes. I'm a pretty fair door-buster, myself." He looked around the room. "There's Jeff Miles; he isn't doing much of anything. And we'll put Sid Chamberlain to work, for a change, too. The four of us ought to get your doors open." He called to Chamberlain, who was carrying his tray over to the dish washer. "Oh, Sid; you doing anything for the next hour or so?"

"I was going up to the fourth floor, to see what Tony's doing."

"Forget it. Tony's bagged his season limit of Martians. I'm going to help Martha bust in a couple of doors; we'll probably find a whole cemetery full of Martians."

Chamberlain shrugged. "Why not. A jammed door can have anything back of it, and I know what Tony's doing-just routine stuff."

Jeff Miles, the Space Force captain, came over, accompanied by one of the lab-crew from the ship who had come down on the rocket the day before.

"This ought to be up your alley, Mort," he was saying to his companion. "Chemistry and physics department. Want to come along?"

The lab man, Mort Tranter, was willing. Seeing the sights was what he'd come down from the ship for. She finished her coffee and cigarette, and they went out into the hall together, gathered equipment and rode the elevator to the fifth floor.

The lecture hall door was the nearest; they attacked it first. With proper equipment and help, it was no problem and in ten minutes they had it open wide enough to squeeze through with the floodlights. The room inside was quite empty, and, like most of the rooms behind closed doors, comparatively free from dust. The students, it appeared, had sat with their backs to the door, facing a low platform, but their seats and the lecturer's table and equipment had been removed. The two side walls bore inscriptions: on the right, a pattern of concentric circles which she recognized as a diagram of atomic structure, and on the left a complicated table of numbers and words, in two columns. Tranter was pointing at the diagram on the right.

"They got as far as the Bohr atom, anyhow," he said. "Well, not quite. They knew about electron shells, but they have the nucleus pictured as a solid mass. No indication of proton-and-neutron structure. I'll bet, when you come to translate their scientific books, you'll find that they taught that the atom was the ultimate and indivisible particle. That explains why you people never found any evidence that the Martians used nuclear energy."

"That's a uranium atom," Captain Miles mentioned.

"It is?" Sid Chamberlain asked, excitedly. "Then they did know about atomic energy. Just because we haven't found any pictures of A-bomb mushrooms doesn't mean —"

She turned to look at the other wall. Sid's signal reactions were getting away from him again; uranium meant nuclear power to him, and the two words were interchangeable. As she studied the arrangement of the numbers and words, she could hear Tranter saying:

"Nuts, Sid. We knew about uranium a long time before anybody found out what could be done with it. Uranium was discovered on Terra in 1789, by Klaproth."

There was something familiar about the table on the left wall. She tried to remember what she had been taught in school about physics, and what she had picked up by accident afterward. The second column was a continuation of the first: there were forty-six items in each, each item numbered consecutively —

"Probably used uranium because it's the largest of the natural atoms," Penrose was saying. "The fact that there's nothing beyond it there shows that they hadn't created any of the transuranics. A student could go to that thing and point out the outer electron of any of the ninety-two elements."

Ninety-two! That was it; there were ninety-two items in the table on the left wall! Hydrogen was Number One, she knew; One, *Sarfaldsorn*. Helium was Two; that was *Tirfaldsorn*. She couldn't remember which element came next, but in Martian it was *Sarfalddavas*. *Sorn* must mean matter, or substance, then. And *davas*; she was trying to think of what it could be. She turned quickly to the others, catching hold of Hubert Penrose's arm with one hand and waving her clipboard with the other.

"Look at this thing, over here," she was clamoring excitedly. "Tell me what you think it is. Could it be a table of the elements?"

They all turned to look. Mort Tranter stared at it for a moment.

"Could be. If I only knew what those squiggles meant —"

That was right; he'd spent his time aboard the ship.

"If you could read the numbers, would that help?" she asked, beginning to set down the Arabic digits and their Martian equivalents. "It's decimal system, the same as we use."

"Sure. If that's a table of elements, all I'd need would be the numbers. Thanks," he added as she tore off the sheet and gave it to him.

Penrose knew the numbers, and was ahead of him. "Ninety-two items, numbered consecutively. The first number would be the atomic number. Then a single word, the name of the element. Then the atomic weight —"

She began reading off the names of the elements. "I know hydrogen and helium; what's *tirfalddavas*, the third one?"

"Lithium," Tranter said. "The atomic weights aren't run out past the decimal point. Hydrogen's one plus, if that double-hook dingus is a plus sign; Helium's four-plus, that's right. And lithium's given as seven, that isn't right. It's six-point nine-four-oh. Or is that thing a Martian minus sign?"

"Of course! Look! A plus sign is a hook, to hang things together; a minus sign is a knife, to cut something off from something-see, the little loop is the handle and the long pointed loop is the blade. Stylized, of course, but that's what it is. And the fourth element, kiradavas; what's that?"

"Beryllium. Atomic weight given as nine-and-a-hook; actually it's nine-point-oh-two."

Sid Chamberlain had been disgruntled because he couldn't get a story about the Martians having developed atomic energy. It took him a few minutes to understand the newest development, but finally it dawned on him.

"Hey! You're reading that!" he cried. "You're reading Martian!"

"That's right," Penrose told him. "Just reading it right off. I don't get the two items after the atomic weight, though. They look like months of the Martian calendar. What ought they to be, Mort?"

Tranter hesitated. "Well, the next information after the atomic weight ought to be the period and group numbers. But those are words."

"What would the numbers be for the first one, hydrogen?"

"Period One, Group One. One electron shell, one electron in the outer shell," Tranter told her. "Helium's period one, too, but it has the outer-only-electron shell full, so it's in the group of inert elements."

"*Trav, Trav. Trav's* the first month of the year. And helium's *Trav, Yenth*; *Yenth* is the eighth month."

"The inert elements could be called Group Eight, yes. And the third element, lithium, is Period Two, Group One. That check?"

"It certainly does. *Sanv, Trav*; *Sanv's* the second month. What's the first element in Period Three?"

"Sodium. Number Eleven."

That's right; it's *Krav, Trav*. Why, the names of the months are simply numbers, one to ten, spelled out.

"*Doma's* the fifth month. That was your first Martian word, Martha," Penrose told her. "The word for five. And if *davas* is the word for metal, and *sornhulva* is chemistry and / or physics, I'll bet Tadavas Sornhulva is literally translated as: Of-Metal Matter-Knowledge. Metallurgy, in other words. I wonder what Mastharnorvod means." It surprised her that, after so long and with so much happening in the meantime, he could remember that. "Something like 'Journal,' or 'Review,' or maybe 'Quarterly.'"

"We'll work that out, too," she said confidently. After this, nothing seemed impossible. "Maybe we can find —" Then she stopped short. "You said 'Quarterly.' I think it was 'Monthly,' instead. It was dated for a specific month, the fifth one. And if *nor* is ten, Mastharnorvod could be 'Year-Tenth.' And I'll bet we'll find that *masthar* is the word for year." She looked at the table on the wall again. "Well, let's get all these words down, with translations for as many as we can."

"Let's take a break for a minute," Penrose suggested, getting out his cigarettes. "And then, let's do this in comfort. Jeff, suppose you and Sid go across the hall and see what you find in the other room in the way of a desk or something like that, and a few chairs. There'll be a lot of work to do on this."

Sid Chamberlain had been squirming as though he were afflicted with ants, trying to contain himself. Now he let go with an excited jabber.

"This is really it! *The* it, not just it-of-the-week, like finding the reservoirs or those statues or this building, or even the animals and the dead Martians! Wait till Selim and Tony see this! Wait till Tony sees it; I want to see his face! And when I get this on telecast, all Terra's going to go nuts about it!" He turned to Captain Miles. "Jeff, suppose you take a look at that other door, while I find somebody to send to tell Selim and Tony. And Gloria; wait till she sees this —"

"Take it easy, Sid," Martha cautioned. "You'd better let me have a look at your script, before you go too far overboard on the telecast. This is just a beginning; it'll take years and years before we're able to read any of those books downstairs."

"It'll go faster than you think, Martha," Hubert Penrose told her. "We'll all work on it, and we'll teleprint material to Terra, and people there will work on it. We'll send them everything we can ...everything we work out, and copies of books, and copies of your word-lists —"

And there would be other tables-astronomical tables, tables in physics and mechanics, for instance-in which words and numbers were equivalent. The library stacks, below, would be full of them. Transliterate them into Roman alphabet spellings and Arabic numerals, and somewhere, somebody would spot each numerical significance, as Hubert Penrose and Mort Tranter and she had done with the table of elements. And pick out all the chemistry textbooks in the Library; new words would take on meaning from contexts in which the names of elements appeared. She'd have to start studying chemistry and physics, herself —

Sachiko Koremitsu peeped in through the door, then stepped inside.

"Is there anything I can do —?" she began. "What's happened? Something important?"

"Important?" Sid Chamberlain exploded. "Look at that, Sachi! We're reading it! Martha's found out how to read Martian!" He grabbed Captain Miles by the arm. "Come on, Jeff; let's go. I want to call the others —" He was still babbling as he hurried from the room.

Sachi looked at the inscription. "Is it true?" she asked, and then, before Martha could more than begin to explain, flung her arms around her. "Oh, it really is! You are reading it! I'm so happy!"

She had to start explaining again when Selim von Ohlmhorst entered. This time, she was able to finish.

"But, Martha, can you be really sure? You know, by now, that learning to read this language is as important to me as it is to you, but how can you be so sure that those words really mean things like hydrogen and helium and boron and oxygen? How do you know that their table of elements was anything like ours?"

Tranter and Penrose and Sachiko all looked at him in amazement.

"That isn't just the Martian table of elements; that's *the* table of elements. It's the only one there is." Mort Tranter almost exploded. "Look, hydrogen has one proton and one electron. If it had more of either, it wouldn't be hydrogen, it'd be something else. And the same with all the rest of the elements. And hydrogen on Mars is the same as hydrogen on Terra, or on Alpha Centauri, or in the next galaxy —"

"You just set up those numbers, in that order, and any first-year chemistry student could tell you what elements they represented." Penrose said. "Could if he expected to make a passing grade, that is."

The old man shook his head slowly, smiling. "I'm afraid I wouldn't make a passing grade. I didn't know, or at least didn't realize, that. One of the things I'm going to place an order for, to be brought on the *Schiaparelli*, will be a set of primers in chemistry and physics, of the sort intended for a bright child of ten or twelve. It seems that a Martiologist has to learn a lot of things the Hittites and the Assyrians never heard about."

Tony Lattimer, coming in, caught the last part of the explanation. He looked quickly at the walls and, having found out just what had happened, advanced and caught Martha by the hand.

"You really did it, Martha! You found your bilingual! I never believed that it would be possible; let me congratulate you!"

He probably expected that to erase all the jibes and sneers of the past. If he did, he could have it that way. His friendship would mean as little to her as his derision-except that his friends had to watch their backs and his knife. But he was going home on the *Cyrano*, to be a big shot. Or had this changed his mind for him again?

"This is something we can show the world, to justify any expenditure of time and money on Martian archaeological work. When I get back to Terra, I'll see that you're given full credit for this achievement —"

On Terra, her back and his knife would be out of her watchfulness.

"We won't need to wait that long," Hubert Penrose told him dryly. "I'm sending off an official report, tomorrow; you can be sure Dr. Dane will be given full credit, not only for this but for her previous work, which made it possible to exploit this discovery."

"And you might add, work done in spite of the doubts and discouragements of her colleagues," Selim von Ohlmhorst said. "To which I am ashamed to have to confess my own share."

"You said we had to find a bilingual," she said. "You were right, too."

"This is better than a bilingual, Martha," Hubert Penrose said. "Physical science expresses universal facts; necessarily it is a universal language. Heretofore archaeologists have dealt only with pre-scientific cultures."

THE END

The Edge of the Knife

By H. Beam Piper

Chalmers stopped talking abruptly, warned by the sudden attentiveness of the class in front of him. They were all staring; even Guellick, in the fourth row, was almost half awake. Then one of them, taking his silence as an invitation to questions found his voice.

"You say Khalid ib'n Hussein's been assassinated?" he asked incredulously. "When did that happen?"

"In 1973, at Basra." There was a touch of impatience in his voice; surely they ought to know that much. "He was shot, while leaving the Parliament Building, by an Egyptian Arab named Mohammed Noureed, with an old U. S. Army M3 submachine-gun. Noureed killed two of Khalid's guards and wounded another before he was overpowered. He was lynched on the spot by the crowd; stoned to death. Ostensibly, he and his accomplices were religious fanatics; however, there can be no doubt whatever that the murder was inspired, at least indirectly, by the Eastern Axis."

The class stirred like a grain-field in the wind. Some looked at him in blank amazement; some were hastily averting faces red with poorly suppressed laughter. For a moment he was puzzled, and then realization hit him like a blow in the stomach-pit. He'd forgotten, again.

"I didn't see anything in the papers about it," one boy was saying.

"The newscast, last evening, said Khalid was in Ankara, talking to the President of Turkey," another offered.

"Professor Chalmers, would you tell us just what effect Khalid's death had upon the Islamic Caliphate and the Middle Eastern situation in general?" a third voice asked with exaggerated solemnity. That was Kendrick, the class humorist; the question was pure baiting.

"Well, Mr. Kendrick, I'm afraid it's a little too early to assess the full results of a thing like that, if they can ever be fully assessed. For instance, who, in 1911, could have predicted all the consequences of the pistol-shot at Sarajevo? Who, even today, can guess what the history of the world would have been had Zangarra not missed Franklin Roosevelt in 1932? There's always that if."

He went on talking safe generalities as he glanced covertly at his watch. Only five minutes to the end of the period; thank heaven he hadn't made that slip at the beginning of the class. "For instance, tomorrow, when we take up the events in India from the First World War to the end of British rule, we will be largely concerned with another victim of the assassin's bullet, Mohandas K. Gandhi. You may ask yourselves, then, by how much that bullet altered the history of the Indian sub-continent. A word of warning, however: The events we will be discussing will be either contemporary with or prior to what was discussed today. I hope that you're all keeping your notes properly dated. It's always easy to become confused in matters of chronology."

He wished, too late, that he hadn't said that. It pointed up the very thing he was trying to play down, and raised a general laugh.

As soon as the room was empty, he hastened to his desk, snatched pencil and notepad. This had been a bad one, the worst yet; he hadn't heard the end of it by any means. He couldn't waste thought on that now, though. This was all new and important; it had welled up suddenly and without warning into his conscious mind, and he must get it down in notes before the "memory" —even mentally, he always put that word into quotes-was lost. He was still scribbling furiously when the instructor who would use the room for the next period entered, followed by a few of his students. Chalmers finished, crammed the notes into his pocket, and went out into the hall.

Most of his own Modern History IV class had left the building and were on their way across the campus for science classes. A few, however, were joining groups for other classes here in Prescott Hall, and in every group, they were the center of interest. Sometimes, when they saw him, they would fall silent until he had passed; sometimes they didn't, and he caught snatches of conversation.

"Oh, brother! Did Chalmers really blow his jets this time!" one voice was saying.

"Bet he won't be around next year."

Another quartet, with their heads together, were talking more seriously.

"Well, I'm not majoring in History, myself, but I think it's an outrage that some people's diplomas are going to depend on grades given by a lunatic!"

"Mine will, and I'm not going to stand for it. My old man's president of the Alumni Association, and...."

That was something he had not thought of, before. It gave him an ugly start. He was still thinking about it as he turned into the side hall to the History Department offices and entered the cubicle he shared with a colleague. The colleague, old Pottgeiter, Medieval History, was emerging in a rush; short, rotund, gray-bearded, his arms full of books and papers, oblivious, as usual, to anything that had happened since the Battle of Bosworth or the Fall of Constantinople. Chalmers stepped quickly out of his way and entered behind him. Marjorie Fenner, the secretary they also shared, was tidying up the old man's desk.

"Good morning, Doctor Chalmers." She looked at him keenly for a moment. "They give you a bad time again in Modern Four?"

Good Lord, did he show it that plainly? In any case, it was no use trying to kid Marjorie. She'd hear the whole story before the end of the day.

"Gave myself a bad time."

Marjorie, still fussing with Pottgeiter's desk, was about to say something in reply. Instead, she exclaimed in exasperation.

"Ohhh! That man! He's forgotten his notes again!" She gathered some papers from Pottgeiter's desk, rushing across the room and out the door with them.

For a while, he sat motionless, the books and notes for General European History II untouched in front of him. This was going to raise hell. It hadn't been the first slip he'd made, either; that thought kept recurring to him. There had been the time when he had alluded to the colonies on Mars and Venus. There had been the time he'd mentioned the secession of Canada from the British Commonwealth, and the time he'd called the U. N. the Terran Federation. And the time he'd tried to get a copy of Franchard's *Rise and Decline of the System States*, which wouldn't be published until the Twenty-eighth Century, out of the college library. None of those had drawn much comment, beyond a few student jokes about the history professor who lived in the future instead of the past. Now, however, they'd all be remembered, raked up, exaggerated, and added to what had happened this morning.

He sighed and sat down at Marjorie's typewriter and began transcribing his notes. Assassination of Khalid ib'n Hussein, the pro-Western leader of the newly formed Islamic Caliphate; period of anarchy in the Middle East; interfactional power-struggles; Turkish intervention. He wondered how long that would last; Khalid's son, Tallal ib'n Khalid, was at school in England when his father was-would be-killed. He would return, and eventually take his father's place, in time to bring the Caliphate into the Terran Federation when the general war came. There were some notes on that already; the war would result from an attempt by the Indian Communists to seize East Pakistan. The trouble was that he so seldom "remembered" an exact date. His "memory" of the year of Khalid's assassination was an exception.

Nineteen seventy-three —why, that was this year. He looked at the calendar. October 16, 1973. At very most, the Arab statesman had two and a half months to live. Would there be any possible way in which he could give a credible warning? He doubted it. Even if there were, he questioned whether he should-for that matter, whether he *could* —interfere....

He always lunched at the Faculty Club; today was no time to call attention to himself by breaking an established routine. As he entered, trying to avoid either a furtive slink or a chip-on-shoulder swagger, the crowd in the lobby stopped talking abruptly, then began again on an obviously changed subject. The word had gotten around, apparently. Handley, the head of the Latin Department, greeted him with a distantly polite nod. Pompous old owl; regarded himself, for some reason, as a sort of unofficial Dean of the Faculty. Probably didn't want to be seen fraternizing with controversial characters. One of the younger men, with a thin face and a mop of unruly hair, advanced to meet him as he came in, as cordial as Handley was remote.

"Oh, hello, Ed!" he greeted, clapping a hand on Chalmers' shoulder. "I was hoping I'd run into you. Can you have dinner with us this evening?" He was sincere.

"Well, thanks, Leonard. I'd like to, but I have a lot of work. Could you give me a rain-check?"

"Oh, surely. My wife was wishing you'd come around, but I know how it is. Some other evening?"

"Yes, indeed." He guided Fitch toward the dining-room door and nodded toward a table. "This doesn't look too crowded; let's sit here."

After lunch, he stopped in at his office. Marjorie Fenner was there, taking dictation from Pottgeiter; she nodded to him as he entered, but she had no summons to the president's office.

The summons was waiting for him, the next morning, when he entered the office after Modern History IV, a few minutes past ten.

"Doctor Whitburn just phoned," Marjorie said. "He'd like to see you, as soon as you have a vacant period."

"Which means right away. I shan't keep him waiting."

She started to say something, swallowed it, and then asked if he needed anything typed up for General European II.

"No, I have everything ready." He pocketed the pipe he had filled on entering, and went out.

The president of Blanley College sat hunched forward at his desk; he had rounded shoulders and round, pudgy fists and a round, bald head. He seemed to be expecting his visitor to stand at attention in front of him. Chalmers got the pipe out of his pocket, sat down in the desk-side chair, and snapped his lighter.

"Good morning, Doctor Whitburn," he said very pleasantly.

Whitburn's scowl deepened. "I hope I don't have to tell you why I wanted to see you," he began.

"I have an idea." Chalmers puffed until the pipe was drawing satisfactorily. "It might help you get started if you did, though."

"I don't suppose, at that, that you realize the full effect of your performance, yesterday morning, in Modern History Four," Whitburn replied. "I don't suppose you know, for instance, that I had to intervene at the last moment and suppress an editorial in the *Black and Green*, derisively critical of you and your teaching methods, and, by implication, of the administration of this college. You didn't hear about that, did you? No, living as you do in the future, you wouldn't."

"If the students who edit the *Black and Green* are dissatisfied with anything here, I'd imagine they ought to say so," Chalmers commented. "Isn't that what they teach in the journalism classes, that the purpose of journalism is to speak for the dissatisfied? Why make exception?"

"I should think you'd be grateful to me for trying to keep your behavior from being made a subject of public ridicule among your students. Why, this editorial which I suppressed actually went so far as to question your sanity!"

"I should suppose it might have sounded a good deal like that, to them. Of course, I have been preoccupied, lately, with an imaginative projection of present trends into the future. I'll quite freely admit that I should have kept my extracurricular work separate from my class and lecture work, but...."

"That's no excuse, even if I were sure it were true! What you did, while engaged in the serious teaching of history, was to indulge in a farrago of nonsense, obvious as such to any child, and damage not only your own standing with your class but the standing of Blanley College as well. Doctor Chalmers, if this were the first incident of the kind it would be bad enough, but it isn't. You've done things like this before, and I've warned you before. I assumed, then, that you were merely showing the effects of overwork, and I offered you a vacation, which you refused to take. Well, this is the limit. I'm compelled to request your immediate resignation."

Chalmers laughed. "A moment ago, you accused me of living in the future. It seems you're living in the past. Evidently you haven't heard about the Higher Education Faculty Tenure Act of 1963, or such things as tenure-contracts. Well, for your information, I have one; you signed it yourself, in case you've forgotten. If you want my resignation, you'll have to show cause, in a court of law, why my contract should be voided, and I don't think a slip of the tongue is a reason for voiding a contract that any court would accept."

Whitburn's face reddened. "You don't, don't you? Well, maybe it isn't, but insanity is. It's a very good reason for voiding a contract voidable on grounds of unfitness or incapacity to teach."

He had been expecting, and mentally shrinking from, just that. Now that it was out, however, he felt relieved. He gave another short laugh.

"You're willing to go into open court, covered by reporters from papers you can't control as you do this student sheet here, and testify that for the past twelve years you've had an insane professor on your faculty?"

"You're.... You're trying to blackmail me?" Whitburn demanded, half rising.

"It isn't blackmail to tell a man that a bomb he's going to throw will blow up in his hand." Chalmers glanced quickly at his watch. "Now, Doctor Whitburn, if you have nothing further to discuss, I have a class in a few minutes. If you'll excuse me...."

He rose. For a moment, he stood facing Whitburn; when the college president said nothing, he inclined his head politely and turned, going out.

Whitburn's secretary gave the impression of having seated herself hastily at her desk the second before he opened the door. She watched him, round-eyed, as he went out into the hall.

He reached his own office ten minutes before time for the next class. Marjorie was typing something for Pottgeiter; he merely nodded to her, and picked up the phone. The call would have to go through the school exchange, and he had a suspicion that Whitburn kept a check on outside calls. That might not hurt any, he thought, dialing a number.

"Attorney Weill's office," the girl who answered said.

"Edward Chalmers. Is Mr. Weill in?"

She'd find out. He was; he answered in a few seconds.

"Hello, Stanly; Ed Chalmers. I think I'm going to need a little help. I'm having some trouble with President Whitburn, here at the college. A matter involving the validity of my tenure-contract. I don't want to go into it over this line. Have you anything on for lunch?"

"No, I haven't. When and where?" the lawyer asked.

He thought for a moment. Nowhere too close the campus, but not too far away.

"How about the Continental; Fontainbleu Room? Say twelve-fifteen."

"That'll be all right. Be seeing you."

Marjorie looked at him curiously as he gathered up the things he needed for the next class.

Stanly Weill had a thin dark-eyed face. He was frowning as he set down his coffee-cup.

"Ed, you ought to know better than to try to kid your lawyer," he said. "You say Whitburn's trying to force you to resign. With your contract, he can't do that, not without good and sufficient cause, and under the Faculty Tenure Law, that means something just an inch short of murder in the first degree. Now, what's Whitburn got on you?"

Beat around the bush and try to build a background, or come out with it at once and fill in the details afterward? He debated mentally for a moment, then decided upon the latter course.

"Well, it happens that I have the ability to prehend future events. I can, by concentrating, bring into my mind the history of the world, at least in general outline, for the next five thousand years. Whitburn thinks I'm crazy, mainly because I get confused at times and forget that something I know about hasn't happened yet."

Weill snatched the cigarette from his mouth to keep from swallowing it. As it was, he choked on a mouthful of smoke and coughed violently, then sat back in the booth-seat, staring speechlessly.

"It started a little over three years ago," Chalmers continued. "Just after New Year's, 1970. I was getting up a series of seminars for some of my postgraduate students on extrapolation of present social and political trends to the middle of the next century, and I began to find that I was getting some very fixed and definite ideas of what the world of 2050 to 2070 would be like. Completely unified world, abolition of all national states under a single world sovereignty, colonies on Mars and Venus, that sort of thing. Some of these ideas didn't seem quite logical; a number of them were complete reversals of present trends, and a lot seemed to depend on arbitrary and unpredictable factors. Mind, this was before the first rocket landed on the Moon, when the whole moon-rocket and lunar-base project was a triple-top secret. But I knew, in the spring of 1970, that the first unmanned rocket would be called the *Kilroy*, and that it would be launched some time in 1971. You remember, when the news was released, it was stated that the rocket hadn't been christened until the day before it was launched, when somebody remembered that old 'Kilroy-was-here' thing from the Second World War. Well, I knew about it over a year in advance."

Weill had been listening in silence. He had a naturally skeptical face; his present expression mightn't really mean that he didn't believe what he was hearing.

"How'd you get all this stuff? In dreams?"

Chalmers shook his head. "It just came to me. I'd be sitting reading, or eating dinner, or talking to one of my classes, and the first thing I'd know, something out of the future would come bubbling up in me. It just kept pushing up into my conscious mind. I wouldn't have an idea of something one minute, and the next it would just be part of my general historical knowledge; I'd know it as positively as I know that Columbus discovered America in. 1492. The only difference is that I can usually remember where I've read something in past history, but my future history I know without knowing how I know it."

"Ah, that's the question!" Weill pounced. "You don't know how you know it. Look, Ed, we've both studied psychology, elementary psychology at least. Anybody who has to work with people, these days, has to know some psychology. What makes you sure that these prophetic impressions of yours aren't manufactured in your own subconscious mind?"

"That's what I thought, at first. I thought my subconscious was just building up this stuff to fill the gaps in what I'd produced from logical extrapolation. I've always been a stickler for detail," he added, parenthetically. "It would be natural for me to supply details for the future. But, as I said, a lot of this stuff is based on unpredictable and arbitrary factors that can't be inferred from anything in the present. That left me with the alternatives of delusion or precognition, and if I ever came near going crazy, it was before the *Kilroy* landed and the news was released. After that, I knew which it was."

"And yet, you can't explain how you can have real knowledge of a thing before it happens. Before it exists," Weill said.

"I really don't need to. I'm satisfied with knowing that I know. But if you want me to furnish a theory, let's say that all these things really do exist, in the past or in the future, and that the present is just a moving knife-edge that separates the two. You can't even indicate the present. By the time you make up your mind to say, 'Now!' and transmit the impulse to your vocal organs, and utter the word, the original present moment is part of the past. The knife-edge has gone over it. Most people think they know only the present; what they know is the past, which they have already experienced, or read about. The difference with me is that I can see what's on both sides of the knife-edge."

Weill put another cigarette in his mouth and bent his head to the flame of his lighter. For a moment, he sat motionless, his thin face rigid.

"What do you want me to do?" he asked. "I'm a lawyer, not a psychiatrist."

"I want a lawyer. This is a legal matter. Whitburn's talking about voiding my tenure contract. You helped draw it; I have a right to expect you to help defend it."

"Ed, have you been talking about this to anybody else?" Weill asked.

"You're the first person I've mentioned it to. It's not the sort of thing you'd bring up casually, in a conversation."

"Then how'd Whitburn get hold of it?"

"He didn't, not the way I've given it to you. But I made a couple of slips, now and then. I made a bad one yesterday morning."

He told Weill about it, and about his session with the president of the college that morning. The lawyer nodded.

"That was a bad one, but you handled Whitburn the right way," Weill said. "What he's most afraid of is publicity, getting the college mixed up in anything controversial, and above all, the reactions of the trustees and people like that. If Dacre or anybody else makes any trouble, he'll do his best to cover for you. Not willingly, of course, but because he'll know that that's the only way he can cover for himself. I don't think you'll have any more trouble with him. If you can keep your own nose clean, that is. Can you do that?"

"I believe so. Yesterday I got careless. I'll not do that again."

"You'd better not." Weill hesitated for a moment. "I said I was a lawyer, not a psychiatrist. I'm going to give you some psychiatrist's advice, though. Forget this whole thing. You say you can bring these impressions into your conscious mind by concentrating?" He waited briefly; Chalmers nodded, and he continued: "Well, stop it. Stop trying to harbor this stuff. It's dangerous, Ed. Stop playing around with it."

"You think I'm crazy, too?"

Weill shook his head impatiently. "I didn't say that. But I'll say, now, that you're losing your grip on reality. You are constructing a system of fantasies, and the first thing you know, they will become your reality, and the world around you will be unreal and illusory. And that's a state of mental incompetence that I can recognize, as a lawyer."

"How about the *Kilroy?*"

Weill looked at him intently. "Ed, are you sure you did have that experience?" he asked. "I'm not trying to imply that you're consciously lying to me about that. I am suggesting that you manufactured a memory of that incident in your subconscious mind, and are deluding yourself into thinking that you knew about it in advance. False memory is a fairly common thing, in cases like this. Even the little psychology I know, I've heard about that. There's been talk about rockets to the Moon for years. You included something about that in your future-history fantasy, and then, after the event, you convinced yourself that you'd known all about it, including the impromptu christening of the rocket, all along."

A hot retort rose to his lips; he swallowed it hastily. Instead, he nodded amicably.

"That's a point worth thinking of. But right now, what I want to know is, will you represent me in case Whitburn does take this to court and does try to void my contract?"

"Oh, yes; as you said, I have an obligation to defend the contracts I draw up. But you'll have to avoid giving him any further reason for trying to void it. Don't make any more of these slips. Watch what you say, in class or out of it. And above all, don't talk about this to anybody. Don't tell anybody that you can foresee the future, or even talk about future probabilities. Your business is with the past; stick to it."

The afternoon passed quietly enough. Word of his defiance of Whitburn had gotten around among the faculty-Whitburn might have his secretary scared witless in his office, but not gossipless outside it-though it hadn't seemed to have leaked down to the students yet. Handley, the Latin professor, managed to waylay him in a hallway, a hallway Handley didn't normally use.

"The tenure-contract system under which we hold our positions here is one of our most valuable safeguards," he said, after exchanging greetings. "It was only won after a struggle, in a time of public animosity toward all intellectuals, and even now, our professional position would be most insecure without it."

"Yes. I found that out today, if I hadn't known it when I took part in the struggle you speak of."

"It should not be jeopardized," Handley declared.

"You think I'm jeopardizing it?"

Handley frowned. He didn't like being pushed out of the safety of generalization into specific cases.

"Well, now that you make that point, yes. I do. If Doctor Whitburn tries to make an issue of ... of what happened yesterday ... and if the court decides against you, you can see the position all of us will be in."

"What do you think I should have done? Given him my resignation when he demanded it? We have our tenure-contracts, and the system was instituted to prevent just the sort of arbitrary action Whitburn tried to take with me today. If he wants to go to court, he'll find that out."

"And if he wins, he'll establish a precedent that will threaten the security of every college and university faculty member in the state. In any state where there's a tenure law."

Leonard Fitch, the psychologist, took an opposite attitude. As Chalmers was leaving the college at the end of the afternoon, Fitch cut across the campus to intercept him.

"I heard about the way you stood up to Whitburn this morning, Ed," he said. "Glad you did it. I only wish I'd done something like that three years ago.... Think he's going to give you any real trouble?"

"I doubt it."

"Well, I'm on your side if he does. I won't be the only one, either."

"Well, thank you, Leonard. It always helps to know that. I don't think there'll be any more trouble, though."

He dined alone at his apartment, and sat over his coffee, outlining his work for the next day. When both were finished, he dallied indecisively, Weill's words echoing through his mind and raising doubts. It was possible that he had been manufacturing the whole thing in his subconscious mind. That was, at least, a more plausible theory than any he had constructed to explain an ability to produce real knowledge of the future. Of course, there was that business about the *Kilroy*. That had been too close on too many points to be dismissed as coincidence. Then, again, Weill's words came back to disquiet him. Had he really gotten that before the event, as he believed, or had he only imagined, later, that he had?

There was one way to settle that. He rose quickly and went to the filing-cabinet where he kept his future-history notes and began pulling out envelopes. There was nothing about the *Kilroy* in the Twentieth Century file, where it should be, although he examined each sheet of notes carefully. The possibility that his notes on that might have been filed out of place by mistake occurred to him; he looked in every other envelope. The notes, as far as they went, were all filed in order, and each one bore, beside the future date of occurrence, the date on which the knowledge-or must he call it delusion? —had come to him. But there was no note on the landing of the first unmanned rocket on Luna.

He put the notes away and went back to his desk, rummaging through the drawers, and finding nothing. He searched everywhere in the apartment where a sheet of paper could have been mislaid, taking all his books, one by one, from the shelves and leafing through them, even books he knew he had not touched for more than three years. In the end, he sat down again at his desk, defeated. The note on the *Kilroy* simply did not exist.

Of course, that didn't settle it, as finding the note would have. He remembered-or believed he remembered-having gotten that item of knowledge-or delusion-in 1970, shortly before the end of the school term. It hadn't been until after the fall opening of school that he had begun making notes. He could have had the knowledge of the robot rocket in his mind then, and neglected putting it on paper.

He undressed, put on his pajamas, poured himself a drink, and went to bed. Three hours later, still awake, he got up, and poured himself another, bigger, drink. Somehow, eventually, he fell asleep.

———————————

The next morning, he searched his desk and book-case in the office at school. He had never kept a diary; now he was wishing that he had. That might have contained something that would be evidence, one way or the other. All day, he vacillated between conviction of the reality of his future knowledge and resolution to have no more to do with it. Once he decided to destroy all the notes he had made, and thought of making a special study of some facet of history, and writing another book, to occupy his mind.

After lunch, he found that more data on the period immediately before the Thirty Days' War was coming into his consciousness. He resolutely suppressed it, knowing as he did that it might never come to him again. That evening, too, he cooked dinner for himself at his apartment, and laid out his class-work for the next day. He'd better not stay in, that evening; too much temptation to settle himself by the living-room fire with his pipe and his notepad and indulge in the vice he had determined to renounce. After a little debate, he decided upon a movie; he put on again the suit he had taken off on coming home, and went out.

———————————

The picture, a random choice among the three shows in the neighborhood, was about Seventeenth Century buccaneers; exciting action and a sound-track loud with shots and cutlass-clashing. He let himself be drawn into it completely, and, until it was finished, he was able to forget both the college and the history of the future. But, as he walked home, he was struck by the parallel between the buccaneers of the West Indies and the space-pirates in the days of the dissolution of the First Galactic Empire, in the Tenth Century of the Interstellar Era. He hadn't been too clear on that period, and he found new data rising in his mind; he hurried his steps, almost running upstairs to his room. It was long after midnight before he had finished the notes he had begun on his return home.

Well, that had been a mistake, but he wouldn't make it again. He determined again to destroy his notes, and began casting about for a subject which would occupy his mind to the exclusion of the future. Not the Spanish Conquistadores; that was too much like the early period of interstellar expansion. He thought for a time of the Sepoy Mutiny, and then rejected it-he could "remember" something much like that on one of the planets of the Beta Hydrae system, in the Fourth Century of the Atomic Era. There were so few things, in the history of the past, which did not have their counter-parts in the future. That evening, too, he stayed at home, preparing for his various classes for the rest of the week and making copious notes on what he would talk about to each. He needed more whiskey to get to sleep that night.

Whitburn gave him no more trouble, and if any of the trustees or influential alumni made any protest about what had happened in Modern History IV, he heard nothing about it. He managed to conduct his classes without further incidents, and spent his evenings trying, not always successfully, to avoid drifting into "memories" of the future....

———————————

He came into his office that morning tired and unrefreshed by the few hours' sleep he had gotten the night before, edgy from the strain, of trying to adjust his mind to the world of Blanley College in mid-April of 1973. Pottgeiter hadn't arrived yet, but Marjorie Fenner was waiting for him; a newspaper in her hand, almost bursting with excitement.

"Here; have you seen it, Doctor Chalmers?" she asked as he entered.

He shook his head. He ought to read the papers more, to keep track of the advancing knife-edge that divided what he might talk about from what he wasn't supposed to know, but each morning he seemed to have less and less time to get ready for work.

"Well, look! Look at that!"

She thrust the paper into his hands, still folded, the big, black headline where he could see it.

KHALID IB'N HUSSEIN ASSASSINATED

He glanced over the leading paragraphs. Leader of Islamic Caliphate shot to death in Basra ... leaving Parliament Building for his palace outside the city ... fanatic, identified as an Egyptian named Mohammed Noureed ... old American submachine-gun ... two guards killed and a third seriously wounded ... seized by infuriated mob and stoned to death on the spot....

For a moment, he felt guilt, until he realized that nothing he could have done could have altered the event. The death of Khalid ib'n Hussein, and all the millions of other deaths that would follow it, were fixed in the matrix of the space-time continuum. Including, maybe, the death of an obscure professor of Modern History named Edward Chalmers.

"At least, this'll be the end of that silly flap about what happened a month ago in Modern Four. This is modern history, now; I can talk about it without a lot of fools yelling their heads off."

She was staring at him wide-eyed. No doubt horrified at his cold-blooded attitude toward what was really a shocking and senseless crime.

"Yes, of course; the man's dead. So's Julius Caesar, but we've gotten over being shocked at his murder."

He would have to talk about it in Modern History IV, he supposed; explain why Khalid's death was necessary to the policies of the Eastern Axis, and what the consequences would be. How it would hasten the complete dissolution of the old U. N., already weakened by the crisis over the Eastern demands for the demilitarization and internationalization of the United States Lunar Base, and necessitate the formation of the Terran Federation, and how it would lead, eventually, to the Thirty Days' War. No, he couldn't talk about that; that was on the wrong side of the knife-edge. Have to be careful about the knife-edge; too easy to cut himself on it.

Nobody in Modern History IV was seated when he entered the room; they were all crowded between the door and his desk. He stood blinking, wondering why they were giving him an ovation, and why Kendrick and Dacre were so abjectly apologetic. Great heavens, did it take the murder of the greatest Moslem since Saladin to convince people that he wasn't crazy?

Before the period was over, Whitburn's secretary entered with a note in the college president's hand and over his signature; requesting Chalmers to come to his office immediately and without delay. Just like that; expected him to walk right out of his class. He was protesting as he entered the president's office. Whitburn cut him off short.

"Doctor Chalmers," —Whitburn had risen behind his desk as the door opened —"I certainly hope that you can realize that there was nothing but the most purely coincidental connection between the event featured in this morning's newspapers and your performance, a month ago, in Modern History Four," he began.

"I realize nothing of the sort. The death of Khalid ib'n Hussein is a fact of history, unalterably set in its proper place in time-sequence. It was a fact of history a month ago no less than today."

"So that's going to be your attitude; that your wild utterances of a month ago have now been vindicated as fulfilled prophesies? And I suppose you intend to exploit this-this coincidence-to the utmost. The involvement of Blanley College in a mess of sensational publicity means nothing to you, I presume."

"I haven't any idea what you're talking about."

"You mean to tell me that you didn't give this story to the local newspaper, the *Valley Times?*" Whitburn demanded.

"I did not. I haven't mentioned the subject to anybody connected with the *Times*, or anybody else, for that matter. Except my attorney, a month ago, when you were threatening to repudiate the contract you signed with me."

"I suppose I'm expected to take your word for that?"

"Yes, you are. Unless you care to call me a liar in so many words." He moved a step closer. Lloyd Whitburn outweighed him by fifty pounds, but most of the difference was fat. Whitburn must have realized that, too.

"No, no; if you say you haven't talked about it to the *Valley Times*, that's enough," he said hastily. "But somebody did. A reporter was here not twenty minutes ago; he refused to say who had given him the story, but he wanted to question me about it."

"What did you tell him?"

"I refused to make any statement whatever. I also called Colonel Tighlman, the owner of the paper, and asked him, very reasonably, to suppress the story. I thought that my own position and the importance of Blanley College to this town entitled me to that much consideration." Whitburn's face became almost purple. "He ... he laughed at me!"

"Newspaper people don't like to be told to kill stories. Not even by college presidents. That's only made things worse. Personally, I don't relish the prospect of having this publicized, any more than you do. I can assure you that I shall be most guarded if any of the *Times* reporters talk to me about it, and if I have time to get back to my class before the end of the period, I shall ask them, as a personal favor, not to discuss the matter outside."

Whitburn didn't take the hint. Instead, he paced back and forth, storming about the reporter, the newspaper owner, whoever had given the story to the paper, and finally Chalmers himself. He was livid with rage.

"You certainly can't imagine that when you made those remarks in class you actually possessed any knowledge of a thing that was still a month in the future," he spluttered. "Why, it's ridiculous! Utterly preposterous!"

"Unusual, I'll admit. But the fact remains that I did. I should, of course, have been more careful, and not confused future with past events. The students didn't understand...."

Whitburn half-turned, stopping short.

"My God, man! You *are* crazy!" he cried, horrified.

The period-bell was ringing as he left Whitburn's office; that meant that the twenty-three students were scattering over the campus, talking like mad. He shrugged. Keeping them quiet about a thing like this wouldn't have been possible in any case. When he entered his office, Stanly Weill was waiting for him. The lawyer drew him out into the hallway quickly.

"For God's sake, have you been talking to the papers?" he demanded. "After what I told you...."

"No, but somebody has." He told about the call to Whitburn's office, and the latter's behavior. Weill cursed the college president bitterly.

"Any time you want to get a story in the *Valley Times*, just order Frank Tighlman not to print it. Well, if you haven't talked, don't."

"Suppose somebody asks me?"

"A reporter, no comment. Anybody else, none of his damn business. And above all, don't let anybody finagle you into making any claims about knowing the future. I thought we had this under control; now that it's out in the open, what that fool Whitburn'll do is anybody's guess."

Leonard Fitch met him as he entered the Faculty Club, sizzling with excitement.

"Ed, this has done it!" he began, jubilantly. "This is one nobody can laugh off. It's direct proof of precognition, and because of the prominence of the event, everybody will hear about it. And it simply can't be dismissed as coincidence...."

"Whitburn's trying to do that."

"Whitburn's a fool if he is," another man said calmly. Turning, he saw that the speaker was Tom Smith, one of the math professors. "I figured the odds against that being chance. There are a lot of variables that might affect it one way or another, but ten to the fifteenth power is what I get for a sort of median figure."

"Did you give that story to the *Valley Times?*" he asked Fitch, suspicion rising and dragging anger up after it.

"Of course, I did," Fitch said. "I'll admit, I had to go behind your back and have some of my postgrads get statements from the boys in your history class, but you wouldn't talk about it yourself...."

Tom Smith was standing beside him. He was twenty years younger than Chalmers, he was an amateur boxer, and he had good reflexes. He caught Chalmers' arm as it was traveling back for an uppercut, and held it.

"Take it easy, Ed; you don't want to start a slugfest in here. This is the Faculty Club; remember?"

"I won't, Tom; it wouldn't prove anything if I did." He turned to Fitch. "I won't talk about sending your students to pump mine, but at least you could have told me before you gave that story out."

"I don't know what you're sore about," Fitch defended himself. "I believed in you when everybody else thought you were crazy, and if I hadn't collected signed and dated statements from your boys, there'd have been no substantiation. It happens that extrasensory perception means as much to me as history does to you. I've believed in it ever since I read about Rhine's work, when I was a kid. I worked in ESP for a long time. Then I had a chance to get a full professorship by coming here, and after I did, I found that I couldn't go on with it, because Whitburn's president here, and he's a stupid old bigot with an air-locked mind...."

"Yes." His anger died down as Fitch spoke. "I'm glad Tom stopped me from making an ass of myself. I can see your side of it." Maybe that was the curse of the professional intellectual, an ability to see everybody's side of everything. He thought for a moment. "What else did you do, beside hand this story to the *Valley Times?* I'd better hear all about it."

"I phoned the secretary of the American Institute of Psionics and Parapsychology, as soon as I saw this morning's paper. With the time-difference to the East Coast, I got him just as he reached his office. He advised me to give the thing the widest possible publicity; he thought that would advance the recognition and study of parapsychology. A case like this can't be ignored; it will demand serious study...."

"Well, you got your publicity, all right. I'm up to my neck in it."

There was an uproar outside. The doorman was saying, firmly:

"This is the Faculty Club, gentlemen; it's for members only. I don't care if you gentlemen are the press, you simply cannot come in here."

"We're all up to our necks in it," Smith said. "Leonard, I don't care what your motives were, you ought to have considered the effect on the rest of us first."

"This place will be a madhouse," Handley complained. "How we're going to get any of these students to keep their minds on their work...."

"I tell you, I don't know a confounded thing about it," Max Pottgeiter's voice rose petulantly at the door. "Are you trying to tell me that Professor Chalmers murdered some Arab? Ridiculous!"

He ate hastily and without enjoyment, and slipped through the kitchen and out the back door, cutting between two frat-houses and circling back to Prescott Hall. On the way, he paused momentarily and chuckled. The reporters, unable to storm the Faculty Club, had gone off in chase of other game and had cornered Lloyd Whitburn in front of Administration Center. They had a jeep with a sound-camera mounted on it, and were trying to get something for telecast. After gesticulating angrily, Whitburn broke away from them and dashed up the steps and into the building. A campus policeman stopped those who tried to follow.

His only afternoon class was American History III. He got through it somehow, though the class wasn't able to concentrate on the Reconstruction and the first election of Grover Cleveland. The halls were free of reporters, at least, and when it was over he hurried to the Library, going to the faculty reading-room in the rear, where he could smoke. There was nobody there but old Max Pottgeiter, smoking a cigar, his head bent over a book. The Medieval History professor looked up.

"Oh, hello, Chalmers. What the deuce is going on around here? Has everybody gone suddenly crazy?" he asked.

"Well, they seem to think I have," he said bitterly.

"They do? Stupid of them. What's all this about some Arab being shot? I didn't know there were any Arabs around here."

"Not here. At Basra." He told Pottgeiter what had happened.

"Well! I'm sorry to hear about that," the old man said. "I have a friend at Southern California, Bellingham, who knew Khalid very well. Was in the Middle East doing some research on the Byzantine Empire; Khalid was most helpful. Bellingham was quite impressed by him; said he was a wonderful man, and a fine scholar. Why would anybody want to kill a man like that?"

He explained in general terms. Pottgeiter nodded understandingly: assassination was a familiar feature of the medieval political landscape, too. Chalmers went on to elaborate. It was a relief to talk to somebody like Pottgeiter, who wasn't bothered by the present moment, but simply boycotted it. Eventually, the period-bell rang. Pottgeiter looked at his watch, as from conditioned reflex, and then rose, saying that he had a class and excusing himself. He would have carried his cigar with him if Chalmers hadn't taken it away from him.

After Pottgeiter had gone Chalmers opened a book-he didn't notice what it was-and sat staring unseeing at the pages. So the moving knife-edge had come down on the end of Khalid ib'n Hussein's life; what were the events in the next segment of time, and the segments to follow? There would be bloody fighting all over the Middle East-with consternation, he remembered that he had been talking about that to Pottgeiter. The Turkish army would move in and try to restore order. There would be more trouble in northern Iran, the Indian Communists would invade Eastern Pakistan, and then the general war, so long dreaded, would come. How far in the future that was he could not "remember," nor how the nuclear-weapons stalemate that had so far prevented it would be broken. He knew that today, and for years before, nobody had dared start an all-out atomic war. Wars, now, were marginal skirmishes, like the one in Indonesia, or the steady underground conflict of subversion and sabotage that had come to be called the Subwar. And with the United States already in possession of a powerful Lunar base.... He wished he could "remember" how events between the murder of Khalid and the Thirty Day's War had been spaced chronologically. Something of that had come to him, after the incident in Modern History IV, and he had driven it from his consciousness.

He didn't dare go home where the reporters would be sure to find him. He simply left the college, at the end of the school-day, and walked without conscious direction until darkness gathered. This morning, when he had seen the paper, he had said, and had actually believed, that the news of the murder in Basra would put an end to the trouble that had started a month ago in the Modern History class. It hadn't: the trouble, it seemed, was only beginning. And with the newspapers, and Whitburn, and Fitch, it could go on forever....

It was fully dark, now; his shadow fell ahead of him on the sidewalk, lengthening as he passed under and beyond a street-light, vanishing as he entered the stronger light of the one ahead.

The windows of a cheap cafe reminded him that he was hungry, and he entered, going to a table and ordering something absently. There was a television screen over the combination bar and lunch-counter. Some kind of a comedy programme, at which an invisible studio-audience was laughing immoderately and without apparent cause. The roughly dressed customers along the counter didn't seem to see any more humor in it than he did. Then his food arrived on the table and he began to eat without really tasting it.

After a while, an alteration in the noises from the television penetrated his consciousness; a news-program had come on, and he raised his head. The screen showed a square in an Eastern city; the voice was saying:

"...Basra, where Khalid ib'n Hussein was assassinated early this morning-early afternoon, local time. This is the scene of the crime; the body of the murderer has been removed, but you can still see the stones with which he was pelted to death by the mob...."

A close-up of the square, still littered with torn-up paving-stones. A Caliphate army officer, displaying the weapon-it was an old M3, all right; Chalmers had used one of those things, himself, thirty years before, and he and his contemporaries had called it a "grease-gun." There were some recent pictures of Khalid, including one taken as he left the plane on his return from Ankara. He watched, absorbed; it was all exactly as he had "remembered" a month ago. It gratified him to see that his future "memories" were reliable in detail as well as generality.

"But the most amazing part of the story comes, not from Basra, but from Blanley College, in California," the commentator was saying, "where, it is revealed, the murder of Khalid was fore-told, with uncanny accuracy, a month ago, by a history professor, Doctor Edward Chalmers...."

There was a picture of himself, in hat and overcoat, perfectly motionless, as though a brief moving glimpse were being prolonged. A glance at the background told him when and where it had been taken —a year and a half ago, at a convention at Harvard. These telecast people must save up every inch of old news-film they ever took. There were views of Blanley campus, and interviews with some of the Modern History IV boys, including Dacre and Kendrick. That was one of the things they'd been doing with that jeep-mounted sound-camera, this afternoon, then. The boys, some brashly, some embarrassedly, were substantiating the fact that he had, a month ago, described yesterday's event in detail. There was an interview with Leonard Fitch; the psychology professor was trying to explain the phenomenon of precognition in layman's terms, and making heavy going of it. And there was the mobbing of Whitburn in front of Administration Center. The college president was shouting denials of every question asked him, and as he turned and fled, the guffaws of the reporters were plainly audible.

An argument broke out along the counter.

"I don't believe it! How could anybody know all that about something before it happened?"

"Well, you heard that-there professor, what was his name. An' you heard all them boys...."

"Ah, college-boys; they'll do anything for a joke!"

"After refusing to be interviewed for telecast, the president of Blanley College finally con-sented to hold a press conference in his office, from which telecast cameras were barred. He denied the whole story categorically and stated that the boys in Professor Chalmers' class had concocted the whole thing as a hoax...."

"There! See what I told you!"

"...stating that Professor Chalmers is mentally unsound, and that he has been trying for years to oust him from his position on the Blanley faculty but has been unable to do so because of the provisions of the Faculty Tenure Act of 1963. Most of his remarks were in the nature of a polemic against this law, generally regarded as the college professors' bill of rights. It is to be stated here that other members of the Blanley faculty have unconditionally confirmed the fact that Doctor Chalmers did make the statements attributed to him a month ago, long before the death of Khalid ib'n Hussein...."

"Yah! How about *that*, now? How'ya gonna get around *that*?"

Beckoning the waitress, he paid his check and hurried out. Before he reached the door, he heard a voice, almost stuttering with excitement:

"Hey! Look! That's *him!*"

He began to run. He was two blocks from the cafe before he slowed to a walk again. That night, he needed three shots of whiskey before he could get to sleep.

A delegation from the American Institute of Psionics and Parapsychology reached Blanley that morning, having taken a strato-plane from the East Coast. They had academic titles and degrees that even Lloyd Whitburn couldn't ignore. They talked with Leonard Fitch, and with the students from Modern History IV, and took statements. It wasn't until after General European History II that they caught up with Chalmers-an elderly man, with white hair and a ruddy face; a young man who looked like a heavy-weight boxer; a middle-aged man in tweeds who smoked a pipe and looked as though he ought to be more interested in grouse-shooting and flower-gardening than in clairvoyance and telepathy. The names of the first two meant nothing to Chalmers. They were important names in their own field, but it was not his field. The name of the third, who listened silently, he did not catch.

"You understand, gentlemen, that I'm having some difficulties with the college administration about this," he told them. "President Whitburn has even gone so far as to challenge my fitness to hold a position here."

"We've talked to him," the elderly man said. "It was not a very satisfactory discussion."

"President Whitburn's fitness to hold his own position could very easily be challenged," the young man added pugnaciously.

"Well, then, you see what my position is. I've consulted my attorney, Mr. Weill and he has advised me to make absolutely no statements of any sort about the matter."

"I understand," the eldest of the trio said. "But we're not the press, or anything like that. We can assure you that anything you tell us will be absolutely confidential." He looked inquiringly at the middle-aged man in tweeds, who nodded silently. "We can understand that the students in your modern history class are telling what is substantially the truth?"

"If you're thinking about that hoax statement of Whitburn's, that's a lot of idiotic drivel!" he said angrily. "I heard some of those boys on the telecast, last night; except for a few details in which they were confused, they all stated exactly what they heard me say in class a month ago."

"And we assume," —again he glanced at the man in tweeds —"that you had no opportunity of knowing anything, at the time, about any actual plot against Khalid's life?"

The man in tweeds broke silence for the first time. "You can assume that. I don't even think this fellow Noureed knew anything about it, then."

"Well, we'd like to know, as nearly as you're able to tell us, just how you became the percipient of this knowledge of the future event of the death of Khalid ib'n Hussein," the young man began. "Was it through a dream, or a waking experience; did you visualize, or have an auditory impression, or did it simply come into your mind...."

"I'm sorry, gentlemen." He looked at his watch. "I have to be going somewhere, at once. In any case, I simply can't discuss the matter with you. I appreciate your position; I know how I'd feel if data of historical importance were being withheld from me. However, I trust that you will appreciate my position and spare me any further questioning."

That was all he allowed them to get out of him. They spent another few minutes being polite to one another; he invited them to lunch at the Faculty Club, and learned that they were lunching there as Fitch's guests. They went away trying to hide their disappointment.

The Psionics and Parapsychology people weren't the only delegation to reach Blanley that day. Enough of the trustees of the college lived in the San Francisco area to muster a quorum for a meeting the evening before; a committee, including James Dacre, the father of the boy in Modern History IV, was appointed to get the facts at first hand; they arrived about noon.

They talked to some of the students, spent some time closeted with Whitburn, and were seen crossing the campus with the Parapsychology people. They didn't talk to Chalmers or Fitch. In the afternoon, Marjorie Fenner told Chalmers that his presence at a meeting, to be held that evening in Whitburn's office, was requested. The request, she said, had come from the trustees' committee, not from Whitburn; she also told him that Fitch would be there. Chalmers promptly phoned Stanly Weill.

"I'll be there along with you," the lawyer said. "If this trustees' committee is running it, they'll realize that this is a matter in which you're entitled to legal advice. I'll stop by your place and pick you up....You haven't been doing any talking, have you?"

He described the interview with the Psionics and Parapsychology people.

"That was all right....Was there a man with a mustache, in a brown tweed suit, with them?"

"Yes. I didn't catch his name...."

"It's Cutler. He's an Army major; Central Intelligence. His crowd's interested in whether you had any real advance information on this. He was in to see me, just a while ago. I have the impression he'd like to see this whole thing played down, so he'll be on our side, more or less and for the time being. I'll be around to your place about eight; in the meantime, don't do any more talking than you have to. I hope we can get this straightened out, this evening. I'll have to go to Reno in a day or so to see a client there...."

<hr>

The meeting in Whitburn's office had been set for eight-thirty; Weill saw to it that they arrived exactly on time. As they got out of his car at Administration Center and crossed to the steps, Chalmers had the feeling of going to a duel, accompanied by his second. The briefcase Weill was carrying may have given him the idea; it was flat and square-cornered, the size and shape of an old case of dueling pistols. He commented on it.

"Sound recorder," Weill said. "Loaded with a four-hour spool. No matter how long this thing lasts, I'll have a record of it, if I want to produce one in court."

Another party was arriving at the same time-the two Psionics and Parapsychology people and the Intelligence major, who seemed to have formed a working partnership. They all entered together, after a brief and guardedly polite exchange of greetings. There were voices raised in argument inside when they came to Whitburn's office. The college president was trying to keep Handley, Tom Smith, and Max Pottgeiter from entering his private room in the rear.

"It certainly is!" Handley was saying. "As faculty members, any controversy involving establishment of standards of fitness to teach under a tenure-contract concerns all of us, because any action taken in this case may establish a precedent which could affect the validity of our own contracts."

A big man with iron-gray hair appeared in the doorway of the private office behind Whitburn; James Dacre.

"These gentlemen have a substantial interest in this, Doctor Whitburn," he said. "If they're here as representatives of the college faculty, they have every right to be present."

Whitburn stood aside. Handley, Smith and Pottgeiter went through the door; the others followed. The other three members of the trustees' committee were already in the room. A few minutes later, Leonard Fitch arrived, also carrying a briefcase.

"Well, everybody seems to be here," Whitburn said, starting toward his chair behind the desk. "We might as well get this started."

"Yes. If you'll excuse me, Doctor." Dacre stepped in front of him and sat down at the desk. "I've been selected as chairman of this committee; I believe I'm presiding here. Start the recorder, somebody."

One of the other trustees went to the sound recorder beside the desk —a larger but probably not more efficient instrument than the one Weill had concealed in his briefcase-and flipped a switch. Then he and his companions dragged up chairs to flank Dacre's, and the rest seated themselves around the room. Old Pottgeiter took a seat next to Chalmers. Weill opened the case on his lap, reached inside, and closed it again.

"What are they trying to do, Ed?" Pottgeiter asked, in a loud whisper. "Throw you off the faculty? They can't do that, can they?"

"I don't know, Max. We'll see...."

"This isn't any formal hearing, and nobody's on trial here," Dacre was saying. "Any action will have to be taken by the board of trustees as a whole, at a regularly scheduled meeting. All we're trying to do is find out just what's happened here, and who, if anybody, is responsible...."

"Well, there's the man who's responsible!" Whitburn cried, pointing at Chalmers. "This whole thing grew out of his behavior in class a month ago, and I'll remind you that at the time I demanded his resignation!"

"I thought it was Doctor Fitch, here, who gave the story to the newspapers," one of the trustees, a man with red hair and a thin, eyeglassed face, objected.

"Doctor Fitch acted as any scientist should, in making public what he believed to be an important scientific discovery," the elder of the two Parapsychology men said. "He believed, and so do we, that he had discovered a significant instance of precognition —a case of real prior knowledge of a future event. He made a careful and systematic record of Professor Chalmers' statements, at least two weeks before the occurrence of the event to which they referred. It is entirely due to him that we know exactly what Professor Chalmers said and when he said it."

"Yes," his younger colleague added, "and in all my experience I've never heard anything more preposterous than this man Whitburn's attempt, yesterday, to deny the fact."

"Well, we're convinced that Doctor Chalmers did in fact say what he's alleged to have said, last month," Dacre began.

"Jim, I think we ought to get that established, for the record," another of the trustees put in. "Doctor Chalmers, is it true that you spoke, in the past tense, about the death of Khalid ib'n Hussein in one of your classes on the sixteenth of last month?"

Chalmers rose. "Yes, it is. And the next day, I was called into this room by Doctor Whitburn, who demanded my resignation from the faculty of this college because of it. Now, what I'd like to know is, why did Doctor Whitburn, in this same room, deny, yesterday, that I'd said anything of the sort, and accuse my students of concocting the story after the event as a hoax."

"One of them being my son," Dacre added. "I'd like to hear an answer to that, myself."

"So would I," Stanly Weill chimed in. "You know, my client has a good case against Doctor Whitburn for libel."

Chalmers looked around the room. Of the thirteen men around him, only Whitburn was an enemy. Some of the others were on his side, for one reason or another, but none of them were friends. Weill was his lawyer, obeying an obligation to a client which, at bottom, was an obligation to his own conscience. Handley was afraid of the possibility that a precedent might be established which would impair his own tenure-contract. Fitch, and the two men from the Institute of Psionics and Parapsychology were interested in him as a source of study-material. Dacre resented a slur upon his son; he and the others were interested in Blanley College as an institution, almost an abstraction. And the major in mufti was probably worrying about the consequences to military security of having a prophet at large. Then a hand gripped his shoulder, and a voice whispered in his ear:

"That's good, Ed; don't let them scare you!"

Old Max Pottgeiter, at least, was a friend.

"Doctor Whitburn, I'm asking you, and I expect an answer, why did you make such statements to the press, when you knew perfectly well that they were false?" Dacre demanded sharply.

"I knew nothing of the kind!" Whitburn blustered, showing, under the bluster, fear. "Yes, I demanded this man's resignation on the morning of October Seventeenth, the day after this incident occurred. It had come to my attention on several occasions that he was making wild and unreasonable assertions in class, and subjecting himself, and with himself the whole faculty of this college, to student ridicule. Why, there was actually an editorial about it written by the student editor of the campus paper, the *Black and Green*. I managed to prevent its publication...." He went on at some length about that. "If I might be permitted access to the drawers of my own desk," he added with elephantine sarcasm, "I could show you the editorial in question."

"You needn't bother; I have a carbon copy," Dacre told him. "We've all read it. If you did, at the time you suppressed it, you should have known what Doctor Chalmers said in class."

"I knew he'd talked a lot of poppycock about a man who was still living having been shot to death," Whitburn retorted. "And if something of the sort actually happened, what of it? Somebody's always taking a shot at one or another of these foreign dictators, and they can't miss all the time."

"You claim this was pure coincidence?" Fitch demanded. "A ten-point coincidence: Event of assassination, year of the event, place, circumstances, name of assassin, nationality of assassin, manner of killing, exact type of weapon used, guards killed and wounded along with Khalid, and fate of the assassin. If that's a simple and plausible coincidence, so's dealing ten royal flushes in succession in a poker game. Tom, you figured that out; what did you say the odds against it were?"

"Was all that actually stated by Doctor Chalmers a month ago?" one of the trustees asked, incredulously.

"It absolutely was. Look here, Mr. Dacre, gentlemen." Fitch came forward, unzipping his briefcase and pulling out papers. "Here are the signed statements of each of Doctor Chalmers' twenty-three Modern History Four students, all made and dated before the assassination. You can refer to them as you please; they're in alphabetical order. And here." He unfolded a sheet of graph paper a yard long and almost as wide. "Here's a tabulated summary of the boys' statements. All agreed on the first point, the fact of the assassination. All agreed that the time was sometime this year. Twenty out of twenty-three agreed on Basra as the place. Why, seven of them even remembered the name of the assassin. That in itself is remarkable; Doctor Chalmers has an extremely intelligent and attentive class."

"They're attentive because they know he's always likely to do something crazy and make a circus out of himself," Whitburn interjected.

"And this isn't the only instance of Doctor Chalmers' precognitive ability," Fitch continued. "There have been a number of other cases...."

Chalmers jumped to his feet; Stanly Weill rose beside him, shoved the cased sound-recorder into his hands, and pushed him back into his seat.

"Gentlemen," the lawyer began, quietly but firmly and clearly. "This is all getting pretty badly out of hand. After all, this isn't an investigation of the actuality of precognition as a psychic phenomenon. What I'd like to hear, and what I haven't heard yet, is Doctor Whitburn's explanation of his contradictory statements that he knew about my client's alleged remarks on the evening after they were supposed to have been made and that, at the same time, the whole thing was a hoax concocted by his students."

"Are you implying that I'm a liar?" Whitburn bristled.

"I'm pointing out that you made a pair of contradictory statements, and I'm asking how you could do that knowingly and honestly," Weill retorted.

"What I meant," Whitburn began, with exaggerated slowness, as though speaking to an idiot, "was that yesterday, when those infernal reporters were badgering me, I really thought that some of Professor Chalmers' students had gotten together and given the *Valley Times* an exaggerated story about his insane maunderings a month ago. I hadn't imagined that a member of the faculty had been so lacking in loyalty to the college...."

"You couldn't imagine anybody with any more intellectual integrity than you have!" Fitch fairly yelled at him.

"You're as crazy as Chalmers!" Whitburn yelled back. He turned to the trustees. "You see the position I'm in, here, with this infernal Higher Education Faculty Tenure Act? I have a madman on my faculty, and can I get rid of him? No! I demand his resignation, and he laughs at me and goes running for his lawyer! And he is a madman! Nobody but a madman would talk the way he does. You think this Khalid ib'n Hussein business is the only time he's done anything like this? Why, I have a list of a dozen occasions when he's done something just as bad, only he didn't have a lucky coincidence to back him up. Trying to get books that don't exist out of the library, and then insisting that they're standard textbooks. Talking about the revolt of the colonies on Mars and Venus. Talking about something he calls the Terran Federation, some kind of a world empire. Or something he calls Operation Triple Cross, that saved the country during some fantastic war he imagined...."

"What did you say?"

The question cracked out like a string of pistol shots. Everybody turned. The quiet man in the brown tweed suit had spoken; now he looked as though he were very much regretting it.

"Is there such a thing as Operation Triple Cross?" Fitch was asking.

"No, no. I never heard anything about that; that wasn't what I meant. It was this Terran Federation thing," the major said, a trifle too quickly and too smoothly. He turned to Chalmers. "You never did any work for PSPB; did you ever talk to anybody who did?" he asked.

"I don't even know what the letters mean," Chalmers replied.

"Politico-Strategic Planning Board. It's all pretty hush-hush, but this term Terran Federation is a tentative name for a proposed organization to take the place of the U. N. if that organization breaks up. It's nothing particularly important, and it only exists on paper."

It won't exist only on paper very long, Chalmers thought. He was wondering what Operation Triple Cross was; he had some notes on it, but he had forgotten what they were.

"Maybe he did pick that up from somebody who'd talked indiscreetly," Whitburn conceded. "But the rest of this tommyrot! Why, he was talking about how the city of Reno had been destroyed by an explosion and fire, literally wiped off the map. There's an example for you!"

He'd forgotten about that, too. It had been a relatively minor incident in the secret struggle of the Subwar; now he remembered having made a note about it. He was sure that it followed closely after the assassination of Khalid ib'n Hussein. He turned quickly to Weill.

"Didn't you say you had to go to Reno in a day or so?" he asked.

Weill hushed him urgently, pointing with his free hand to the recorder. The exchange prevented him from noticing that Max Pottgeiter had risen, until the old man was speaking.

"Are you trying to tell these people that Professor Chalmers is crazy?" he was demanding. "Why, he has one of the best minds on the campus. I was talking to him only yesterday, in the back room at the Library. You know," he went on apologetically, "my subject is Medieval History; I don't pay much attention to what's going on in the contemporary world, and I didn't understand, really, what all this excitement was about. But he explained the whole thing to me, and did it in terms that I could grasp, drawing some excellent parallels with the Byzantine Empire and the Crusades. All about the revolt at Damascus, and the sack of Beirut, and the war between Jordan and Saudi Arabia, and how the Turkish army intervened, and the invasion of Pakistan...."

"When did all this happen?" one of the trustees demanded.

Pottgeiter started to explain; Chalmers realized, sickly, how much of his future history he had poured into the trusting ear of the old medievalist, the day before.

"Good Lord, man; don't you read the papers at all?" another of the trustees asked.

"No! And I don't read inside-dope magazines, or science fiction. I read carefully substantiated facts. And I know when I'm talking to a sane and reasonable man. It isn't a common experience, around here."

Dacre passed a hand over his face. "Doctor Whitburn," he said, "I must admit that I came to this meeting strongly prejudiced against you, and I'll further admit that your own behavior here has done very little to dispel that prejudice. But I'm beginning to get some idea of what you have to contend with, here at Blanley, and I find that I must make a lot of allowances. I had no idea....Simply no idea at all."

"Look, you're getting a completely distorted picture of this, Mr. Dacre," Fitch broke in. "It's precisely as I believed; Doctor Chalmers is an unusually gifted precognitive percipient. You've seen, gentlemen, how his complicated chain of precognitions about the death of Khalid has been proven veridical; I'd stake my life that every one of these precognitions will be similarly verified. And I'll stake my professional reputation that the man is perfectly sane. Of course, abnormal psychology and psychopathology aren't my subjects, but...."

"They're not my subjects, either," Whitburn retorted, "but I know a lunatic by his ravings."

"Doctor Fitch is taking an entirely proper attitude," Pottgeiter said, "in pointing out that abnormal psychology is a specialized branch, outside his own field. I wouldn't dream, myself, of trying to offer a decisive opinion on some point of Roman, or Babylonian, history. Well, if the question of Doctor Chalmers' sanity is at issue here, let's consult somebody who specializes in insanity. I don't believe that anybody here is qualified even to express an opinion on that subject, Doctor Whitburn least of all."

Whitburn turned on him angrily. "Oh, shut up, you doddering old fool!" he shouted. "Look; there's another of them!" he told the trustees. "Another deadhead on the faculty that this Tenure Law keeps me from getting rid of. He's as bad as Chalmers, himself. You just heard that string of nonsense he was spouting. Why, his courses have been noted among the students for years as snap courses in which nobody ever has to do any work...."

Chalmers was on his feet again, thoroughly angry. Abuse of himself he could take; talking that way about gentle, learned, old Pottgeiter was something else.

"I think Doctor Pottgeiter's said the most reasonable thing I've heard since I came in here," he declared. "If my sanity is to be questioned, I insist that it be questioned by somebody qualified to do so."

Weill set his recorder on the floor and jumped up beside him, trying to haul him back into his seat.

"For God's sake, man! Sit down and shut up!" he hissed.

Chalmers shook off his hand. "No, I won't shut up! This is the only way to settle this, once and for all. And when my sanity's been vindicated, I'm going to sue this fellow...."

Whitburn started to make some retort, then stopped short. After a moment, he smiled nastily.

"Do I understand, Doctor Chalmers, that you would be willing to submit to psychiatric examination?" he asked.

"Don't agree; you're putting your foot in a trap!" Weill told him urgently.

"Of course, I agree, as long as the examination is conducted by a properly qualified psychiatrist."

"How about Doctor Hauserman at Northern State Mental Hospital?" Whitburn asked quickly. "Would you agree to an examination by him?"

"Excellent!" Fitch exclaimed. "One of the best men in the field. I'd accept his opinion unreservedly."

Weill started to object again; Chalmers cut him off. "Doctor Hauserman will be quite satisfactory to me. The only question is, would he be available?"

"I think he would," Dacre said, glancing at his watch. "I wonder if he could be reached now." He got to his feet. "Telephone in your outer office, Doctor Whitburn? Fine. If you gentlemen will excuse me...."

It was a good fifteen minutes before he returned, smiling.

"Well, gentlemen, it's all arranged," he said. "Doctor Hauserman is quite willing to examine Doctor Chalmers-with the latter's consent, of course."

"He'll have it. In writing, if he wishes."

"Yes, I assured him on that point. He'll be here about noon tomorrow-it's a hundred and fifty miles from the hospital, but the doctor flies his own plane-and the examination can start at two in the afternoon. He seems familiar with the facilities of the psychology department, here; I assured him that they were at his disposal. Will that be satisfactory to you, Doctor Chalmers?"

"I have a class at that time, but one of the instructors can take it over-if holding classes will be possible around here tomorrow," he said. "Now, if you gentlemen will pardon me, I think I'll go home and get some sleep."

Weill came up to the apartment with him. He mixed a couple of drinks and they went into the living room with them.

"Just in case you don't know what you've gotten yourself into," Weill said, "this Hauserman isn't any ordinary couch-pilot; he's the state psychiatrist. If he gets the idea you aren't sane, he can commit you to a hospital, and I'll bet that's exactly what Whitburn had in mind when he suggested him. And I don't trust this man Dacre. I thought he was on our side, at the start, but that was before your friends got into the act." He frowned into his drink. "And I don't like the way that Intelligence major was acting, toward the last. If he thinks you know something you are not supposed to, a mental hospital may be his idea of a good place to put you away."

"You don't think this man Hauserman would allow himself to be influenced ...? No. You just don't think I'm sane. Do you?"

"I know what Hauserman'll think. He'll think this future history business is a classical case of systematized schizoid delusion. I wish I'd never gotten into this case. I wish I'd never even heard of you! And another thing; in case you get past Hauserman all right, you can forget about that damage-suit bluff of mine. You would not stand a chance with it in court."

"In spite of what happened to Khalid?"

"After tomorrow, I won't stay in the same room with anybody who even mentions that name to me. Well, win or lose, it'll be over tomorrow and then I can leave here."

"Did you tell me you were going to Reno?" Chalmers asked. "Don't do it. You remember Whitburn mentioning how I spoke about an explosion there? It happened just a couple of days after the murder of Khalid. There was-will be —a trainload of high explosives in the railroad yard; it'll be the biggest non-nuclear explosion since the *Mont Blanc* blew up in Halifax harbor in World War One...."

Weill threw his drink into the fire; he must have avoided throwing the glass in with it by a last-second exercise of self-control.

"Well," he said, after a brief struggle to master himself. "One thing about the legal profession; you do hear the damnedest things!... Good night, Professor. And try-please try, for the sake of your poor harried lawyer-to keep your mouth shut about things like that, at least till after you get through with Hauserman. And when you're talking to him, don't, don't, for heaven's sake, *don't*, volunteer anything!"

The room was a pleasant, warmly-colored, place. There was a desk, much like the ones in the classrooms, and six or seven wicker armchairs. A lot of apparatus had been pushed back along the walls; the dust-covers were gay cretonne. There was a couch, with more apparatus, similarly covered, beside it. Hauserman was seated at the desk when Chalmers entered.

He rose, and they shook hands. A man of about his own age, smooth-faced, partially bald. Chalmers tried to guess something of the man's nature from his face, but could read nothing. A face well trained to keep its owner's secrets.

"Something to smoke, Professor," he began, offering his cigarette case.

"My pipe, if you don't mind." He got it out and filled it.

"Any of those chairs," Hauserman said, gesturing toward them.

They were all arranged to face the desk. He sat down, lighting his pipe. Hauserman nodded approvingly; he was behaving calmly, and didn't need being put at ease. They talked at random- at least, Hauserman tried to make it seem so-for some time about his work, his book about the French Revolution, current events. He picked his way carefully through the conversation, alert for traps which the psychiatrist might be laying for him. Finally, Hauserman said:

"Would you mind telling me just why you felt it advisable to request a psychiatric examination, Professor?"

"I didn't request it. But when the suggestion was made, by one of my friends, in reply to some aspersions of my sanity, I agreed to it."

"Good distinction. And why was your sanity questioned? I won't deny that I had heard of this affair, here, before Mr. Dacre called me, last evening, but I'd like to hear your version of it."

He went into that, from the original incident in Modern History IV, choosing every word carefully, trying to concentrate on making a good impression upon Hauserman, and at the same time finding that more "memories" of the future were beginning to seep past the barrier of his consciousness. He tried to dam them back; when he could not, he spoke with greater and greater care lest they leak into his speech.

"I can't recall the exact manner in which I blundered into it. The fact that I did make such a blunder was because I was talking extemporaneously and had wandered ahead of my text. I was trying to show the results of the collapse of the Ottoman Empire after the First World War, and the partition of the Middle East into a loose collection of Arab states, and the passing of British and other European spheres of influence following the Second. You know, when you consider it, the Islamic Caliphate was inevitable; the surprising thing is that it was created by a man like Khalid...."

He was talking to gain time, and he suspected that Hauserman knew it. The "memories" were coming into his mind more and more strongly; it was impossible to suppress them. The period of anarchy following Khalid's death would be much briefer, and much more violent, than he had previously thought. Tallal ib'n Khalid would be flying from England even now; perhaps he had already left the plane to take refuge among the black tents of his father's Bedouins. The revolt at Damascus would break out before the end of the month; before the end of the year, the whole of Syria and Lebanon would be in bloody chaos, and the Turkish army would be on the march.

"Yes. And you allowed yourself to be carried a little beyond the present moment, into the future, without realizing it? Is that it?"

"Something like that," he replied, wide awake to the trap Hauserman had set, and fearful that it might be a blind, to disguise the real trap. "History follows certain patterns. I'm not a Toynbean, by any manner of means, but any historian can see that certain forces generally tend to produce similar effects. For instance, space travel is now a fact; our government has at present a military base on Luna. Within our lifetimes-certainly within the lifetimes of my students-there will be explorations and attempts at colonization on Mars and Venus. You believe that, Doctor?"

"Oh, unreservedly. I'm not supposed to talk about it, but I did some work on the Philadelphia Project, myself. I'd say that every major problem of interplanetary flight had been solved before the first robot rocket was landed on Luna."

"Yes. And when Mars and Venus are colonized, there will be the same historic situations, at least in general shape, as arose when the European powers were colonizing the New World, or, for that matter, when the Greek city-states were throwing out colonies across the Aegean. That's the sort of thing we call projecting the past into the future through the present."

Hauserman nodded. "But how about the details? Things like the assassination of a specific personage. How can you extrapolate to a thing like that?"

"Well...." More "memories" were coming to the surface; he tried to crowd them back. "I do my projecting in what you might call fictionalized form; try to fill in the details from imagination. In the case of Khalid, I was trying to imagine what would happen if his influence were suddenly removed from Near Eastern and Middle Eastern, affairs. I suppose I constructed an imaginary scene of his assassination...."

He went on at length. Mohammed and Noureed were common enough names. The Middle East was full of old U. S. weapons. Stoning was the traditional method of execution; it diffused responsibility so that no individual could be singled out for blood-feud vengeance.

"You have no idea how disturbed I was when the whole thing happened, exactly as I had described it," he continued. "And worst of all, to me, was this Intelligence officer showing up; I thought I was really in for it!"

"Then you've never really believed that you had real knowledge of the future?"

"I'm beginning to, since I've been talking to these Psionics and Parapsychology people," he laughed. It sounded, he hoped, like a natural and unaffected laugh. "They seem to be convinced that I have."

There would be an Eastern-inspired uprising in Azerbaijan by the middle of the next year; before autumn, the Indian Communists would make their fatal attempt to seize East Pakistan. The Thirty Days' War would be the immediate result. By that time, the Lunar Base would be completed and ready; the enemy missiles would be aimed primarily at the rocketports from which it was supplied. Delivered without warning, it should have succeeded-except that every rocketport had its secret duplicate and triplicate. That was Operation Triple Cross; no wonder Major Cutler had been so startled at the words, last evening. The enemy would be utterly overwhelmed under the rain of missiles from across space, but until the moon-rockets began to fall, the United States would suffer grievously.

"Honestly, though, I feel sorry for my friend Fitch," he added. "He's going to be frightfully let down when some more of my alleged prophecies misfire on him. But I really haven't been deliberately deceiving him."

And Blanley College was at the center of one of the areas which would receive the worst of the thermonuclear hell to come. And it would be a little under a year....

"And that's all there is to it!" Hauserman exclaimed, annoyance in his voice. "I'm amazed that this man Whitburn allowed a thing like this to assume the proportions it did. I must say that I seem to have gotten the story about this business in a very garbled form indeed." He laughed shortly. "I came here convinced that you were mentally unbalanced. I hope you won't take that the wrong way, Professor," he hastened to add. "In my profession, anything can be expected. A good psychiatrist can never afford to forget how sharp and fine is the knife-edge."

"The knife-edge!" The words startled him. He had been thinking, at that moment, of the knife-edge, slicing moment after moment relentlessly away from the future, into the past, at each slice coming closer and closer to the moment when the missiles of the Eastern Axis would fall. "I didn't know they still resorted to surgery, in mental cases," he added, trying to cover his break.

"Oh, no; all that sort of thing is as irrevocably discarded as the whips and shackles of Bedlam. I meant another kind of knife-edge; the thin, almost invisible, line which separates sanity from non-sanity. From madness, to use a deplorable lay expression." Hauserman lit another cigarette. "Most minds are a lot closer to it than their owners suspect, too. In fact, Professor, I was so convinced that yours had passed over it that I brought with me a commitment form, made out all but my signature, for you." He took it from his pocket and laid it on the desk. "The modern equivalent of the *lettre-de-cachet*, I suppose the author of a book on the French Revolution would call it. I was all ready to certify you as mentally unsound, and commit you to Northern State Mental Hospital."

Chalmers sat erect in his chair. He knew where that was; on the other side of the mountains, in the one part of the state completely untouched by the H-bombs of the Thirty Days' War. Why, the town outside which the hospital stood had been a military headquarters during the period immediately after the bombings, and the center from which all the rescue work in the state had been directed.

"And you thought you could commit me to Northern State!" he demanded, laughing scornfully, and this time he didn't try to make the laugh sound natural and unaffected. "You-confine *me*, anywhere? Confine a poor old history professor's body, yes, but that isn't me. I'm universal; I exist in all space-time. When this old body I'm wearing now was writing that book on the French Revolution, I was in Paris, watching it happen, from the fall of the Bastile to the Ninth Thermidor. I was in Basra, and saw that crazed tool of the Axis shoot down Khalid ib'n Hussein-and the professor talked about it a month before it happened. I have seen empires rise and stretch from star to star across the Galaxy, and crumble and fall. I have seen...."

Doctor Hauserman had gotten his pen out of his pocket and was signing the commitment form with one hand; with the other, he pressed a button on the desk. A door at the rear opened, and a large young man in a white jacket entered.

"You'll have to go away for a while, Professor," Hauserman was telling him, much later, after he had allowed himself to become calm again. "For how long, I don't know. Maybe a year or so."

"You mean to Northern State Mental?"

"Well....Yes, Professor. You've had a bad crack-up. I don't suppose you realize how bad. You've been working too hard; harder than your nervous system could stand. It's been too much for you."

"You mean, I'm nuts?"

"Please, Professor. I deplore that sort of terminology. You've had a severe psychological breakdown...."

"Will I be able to have books, and papers, and work a little? I couldn't bear the prospect of complete idleness."

"That would be all right, if you didn't work too hard."

"And could I say good-bye to some of my friends?"

Hauserman nodded and asked, "Who?"

"Well, Professor Pottgeiter...."

"He's outside now. He was inquiring about you."

"And Stanly Weill, my attorney. Not business; just to say good-bye."

"Oh, I'm sorry, Professor. He's not in town, now. He left almost immediately after....After...."

"After he found out I was crazy for sure? Where'd he go?"

"To Reno; he took the plane at five o'clock."

Weill wouldn't have believed, anyhow; no use trying to blame himself for that. But he was as sure that he would never see Stanly Weill alive again as he was that the next morning the sun would rise. He nodded impassively.

"Sorry he couldn't stay. Can I see Max Pottgeiter alone?"

"Yes, of course, Professor."

Old Pottgeiter came in, his face anguished. "Ed! It isn't true," he stammered. "I won't believe that it's true."

"What, Max?"

"That you're crazy. Nobody can make me believe that."

He put his hand on the old man's shoulder. "Confidentially, Max, neither do I. But don't tell anybody I'm not. It's a secret."

Pottgeiter looked troubled. For a moment, he seemed to be wondering if he mightn't be wrong and Hauserman and Whitburn and the others right.

"Max, do you believe in me?" he asked. "Do you believe that I knew about Khalid's assassination a month before it happened?"

"It's a horribly hard thing to believe," Pottgeiter admitted. "But, dammit, Ed, you did! I know, medieval history is full of stories about prophecies being fulfilled. I always thought those stories were just legends that grew up after the event. And, of course, he's about a century late for me, but there was Nostradamus. Maybe those old prophecies weren't just *ex post facto* legends, after all. Yes. After Khalid, I'll believe that."

"All right. I'm saying, now, that in a few days there'll be a bad explosion at Reno, Nevada. Watch the papers and the telecast for it. If it happens, that ought to prove it. And you remember what I told you about the Turks annexing Syria and Lebanon?" The old man nodded. "When that happens, get away from Blanley. Come up to the town where Northern State Mental Hospital is, and get yourself a place to live, and stay there. And try to bring Marjorie Fenner along with you. Will you do that, Max?"

"If you say so." His eyes widened. "Something bad's going to happen here?"

"Yes, Max. Something very bad. You promise me you will?"

"Of course, Ed. You know, you're the only friend I have around here. You and Marjorie. I'll come, and bring her along."

"Here's the key to my apartment." He got it from his pocket and gave it to Pottgeiter, with instructions. "Everything in the filing cabinet on the left of my desk. And don't let anybody else see any of it. Keep it safe for me."

The large young man in the white coat entered.

THE END

The Keeper

by H. Beam Piper

> *Evil men had stolen his treasure, and Raud set out with his*
> *deer rifle and his great dog Brave to catch the thieves*
> *before they could reach the Starfolk. That the men had*
> *negatron pistols meant little-Raud was the Keeper....*

When he heard the deer crashing through brush and scuffling the dead leaves, he stopped and stood motionless in the path. He watched them bolt down the slope from the right and cross in front of him, wishing he had the rifle, and when the last white tail vanished in the gray-brown woods he drove the spike of the ice-staff into the stiffening ground and took both hands to shift the weight of the pack. If he'd had the rifle, he could have shot only one of them. As it was, they were unfrightened, and he knew where to find them in the morning.

Ahead, to the west and north, low clouds massed; the white front of the Ice-Father loomed clear and sharp between them and the blue of the distant forests. It would snow, tonight. If it stopped at daybreak, he would have good tracking, and in any case, it would be easier to get the carcasses home over snow. He wrenched loose the ice-staff and started forward again, following the path that wound between and among and over the irregular mounds and hillocks. It was still an hour's walk to Keeper's House, and the daylight was fading rapidly.

Sometimes, when he was not so weary and in so much haste, he would loiter here, wondering about the ancient buildings and the long-vanished people who had raised them. There had been no woods at all, then; nothing but great houses like mountains, piling up toward the sky, and the valley where he meant to hunt tomorrow had been an arm of the sea that was now a three days' foot-journey away. Some said that the cities had been destroyed and the people killed in wars-big wars, not squabbles like the fights between sealing-companies from different villages. He didn't think so, himself. It was more likely that they had all left their homes and gone away in starships when the Ice-Father had been born and started pushing down out of the north. There had been many starships, then. When he had been a boy, the old men had talked about a long-ago time when there had been hundreds of them visible in the sky, every morning and evening. But that had been long ago indeed. Starships came but seldom to this world, now. This world was old and lonely and poor. Like poor lonely old Raud the Keeper.

He felt angry to find himself thinking like that. Never pity yourself, Raud; be proud. That was what his father had always taught him: "Be proud, for you are the Keeper's son, and when I am gone, you will be the Keeper after me. But in your pride, be humble, for what you will keep is the Crown."

The thought of the Crown, never entirely absent from his mind, wakened the anxiety that always slept lightly if at all. He had been away all day, and there were so many things that could happen. The path seemed longer, after that; the landmarks farther apart. Finally, he came out on the edge of the steep bank, and looked down across the brook to the familiar low windowless walls and sharp-ridged roof of Keeper's House; and when he came, at last, to the door, and pulled the latchstring, he heard the dogs inside-the soft, coughing bark of Brave, and the anxious little whimper of Bold-and he knew that there was nothing wrong in Keeper's House.

The room inside was lighted by a fist-sized chunk of lumicon, hung in a net bag of thongs from the rafter over the table. It was old-cast off by some rich Southron as past its best brilliance, it had been old when he had bought it from Yorn Nazvik the Trader, and that had been years ago. Now its light was as dim and yellow as firelight. He'd have to replace it soon, but this trip he had needed new cartridges for the big rifle. A man could live in darkness more easily than he could live without cartridges.

The big black dogs were rising from their bed of deerskins on the stone slab that covered the crypt in the far corner. They did not come to meet him, but stayed in their place of trust, greeting him with anxious, eager little sounds.

"Good boys," he said. "Good dog, Brave; good dog, Bold. Old Keeper's home again. Hungry?"

They recognized that word, and whined. He hung up the ice-staff on the pegs by the door, then squatted and got his arms out of the pack-straps.

"Just a little now; wait a little," he told the dogs. "Keeper'll get something for you."

He unhooked the net bag that held the lumicon and went to the ladder, climbing to the loft between the stone ceiling and the steep snow-shed roof; he cut down two big chunks of smoked wild-ox beef-the dogs liked that better than smoked venison-and climbed down.

He tossed one chunk up against the ceiling, at the same time shouting: "Bold! Catch!" Bold leaped forward, sinking his teeth into the meat as it was still falling, shaking and mauling it. Brave, still on the crypt-slab, was quivering with hunger and eagerness, but he remained in place until the second chunk was tossed and he was ordered to take it. Then he, too, leaped and caught it, savaging it in mimicry of a kill. For a while, he stood watching them growl and snarl and tear their meat, great beasts whose shoulders came above his own waist. While they lived to guard it, the Crown was safe. Then he crossed to the hearth, scraped away the covering ashes, piled on kindling and logs and fanned the fire alight. He lifted the pack to the table and unlaced the deerskin cover.

Cartridges in plastic boxes of twenty, long and thick; shot for the duck-gun, and powder and lead and cartridge-primers; fills for the fire-lighter; salt; needles; a new file. And the deerskin bag of trade-tokens. He emptied them on the table and counted them-tokens, and half-tokens and five-tokens, and even one ten-token. There were always less in the bag, after each trip to the village. The Southrons paid less and less, each year, for furs and skins, and asked more and more for what they had to sell.

He put away the things he had brought from the village, and was considering whether to open the crypt now and replace the bag of tokens, when the dogs stiffened, looking at the door. They got to their feet, neck-hairs bristling, as the knocking began.

He tossed the token-bag onto the mantel and went to the door, the dogs following and standing ready as he opened it.

The snow had started, and now the ground was white except under the evergreens. Three men stood outside the door, and over their shoulders he could see an airboat grounded in the clearing in front of the house.

"You are honored, Raud Keeper," one of them began. "Here are strangers who have come to talk to you. Strangers from the Stars!"

He recognized the speaker, in sealskin boots and deerskin trousers and hooded overshirt like his own-Vahr Farg's son, one of the village people. His father was dead, and his woman was the daughter of Gorth Sledmaker, and he was a house-dweller with his woman's father. A worthless youth, lazy and stupid and said to be a coward. Still, guests were guests, even when brought by the likes of Vahr Farg's son. He looked again at the airboat, and remembered seeing it, that day, made fast to the top-deck of Yorn Nazvik's trading-ship, the Issa.

"Enter and be welcome; the house is yours, and all in it that is mine to give." He turned to the dogs. "Brave, Bold; go watch."

Obediently, they trotted over to the crypt and lay down. He stood aside; Vahr entered, standing aside also, as though he were the host, inviting his companions in. They wore heavy garments of woven cloth and boots of tanned leather with hard heels and stiff soles, and as they came in, each unbuckled and laid aside a belt with a holstered negatron pistol. One was stocky and broad-shouldered, with red hair; the other was slender, dark haired and dark eyed, with a face as smooth as a woman's. Everybody in the village had wondered about them. They were not of Yorn Nazvik's crew, but passengers on the *Issa*.

"These are Empire people, from the Far Stars," Vahr informed him, naming their names. Long names, which meant nothing; certainly they were not names the Southrons from the Warm Seas bore. "And this is Raud the Keeper, with whom your honors wish to speak."

"Keeper's House is honored. I'm sorry that I have not food prepared; if you can excuse me while I make some ready...."

"You think these noblemen from the Stars would eat your swill?" Vahr hooted. "Crazy old fool, these are —"

The slim man pivoted on his heel; his open hand caught Vahr just below the ear and knocked him sprawling. It must have been some kind of trick-blow. That or else the slim stranger was stronger than he looked.

"Hold your miserable tongue!" he told Vahr, who was getting to his feet. "We're guests of Raud the Keeper, and we'll not have him insulted in his own house by a cur like you!"

The man with red hair turned. "I am ashamed. We should not have brought this into your house; we should have left it outside." He spoke the Northland language well, "It will honor us to share your food, Keeper."

"Yes, and see here," the younger man said, "we didn't know you'd be alone. Let us help you. Dranigo's a fine cook, and I'm not bad, myself."

He started to protest, then let them have their way. After all, a guest's women helped the woman of the house, and as there was no woman in Keeper's House, it was not unfitting for them to help him.

"Your friend's name is Dranigo?" he asked. "I'm sorry, but I didn't catch yours."

"I don't wonder; fool mouthed it so badly I couldn't understand it myself. It's Salvadro."

They fell to work with him, laying out eating-tools —there were just enough to go around— and hunting for dishes, of which there were not. Salvadro saved that situation by going out and bringing some in from the airboat. He must have realized that the lumicon over the table was the only light beside the fire in the house, for he was carrying a globe of the luminous plastic with him when he came in, grumbling about how dark it had gotten outside. It was new and brilliant, and the light hurt Raud's eyes, at first.

"Are you truly from the Stars?" he asked, after the food was on the table and they had begun to eat. "Neither I nor any in the village have seen anybody from the Stars before."

The big man with the red hair nodded. "Yes. We are from Dremna."

Why, Dremna was the Great World, at the middle of everything! Dremna was the Empire. People from Dremna came to the cities of Awster and fabulous Antark as Southron traders from the Warm Seas came to the villages of the Northfolk. He stammered something about that.

"Yes. You see, we...." Dranigo began. "I don't know the word for it, in your language, but we're people whose work it is to learn things. Not from other people or from books, but new things, that nobody else knows. We came here to learn about the long-ago times on this world, like the great city that was here and is now mounds of stone and earth. Then, when we go back to Dremna, we will tell other people what we have found out."

Vahr Farg's son, having eaten his fill, was fidgeting on his stool, looking contemptuously at the strangers and their host. He thought they were fools to waste time learning about people who had died long ago. So he thought the Keeper was a fool, to guard a worthless old piece of junk.

Raud hesitated for a moment, then said: "I have a very ancient thing, here in this house. It was worn, long ago, by great kings. Their names, and the name of their people, are lost, but the Crown remains. It was left to me as a trust by my father, who was Keeper before me and to whom it was left by his father, who was Keeper in his time. Have you heard of it?"

Dranigo nodded. "We heard of it, first of all, on Dremna," he said. "The Empire has a Space Navy base, and observatories and relay stations, on this planet. Space Navy officers who had been here brought the story back; they heard it from traders from the Warm Seas, who must have gotten it from people like Yorn Nazvik. Would you show it to us, Keeper? It was to see the Crown that we came here."

Raud got to his feet, and saw, as he unhooked the lumicon, that he was trembling. "Yes, of course. It is an honor. It is an ancient and wonderful thing, but I never thought that it was known on Dremna." He hastened across to the crypt.

The dogs looked up as he approached. They knew that he wanted to lift the cover, but they were comfortable and had to be coaxed to leave it. He laid aside the deerskins. The stone slab was heavy, and he had to strain to tilt it up. He leaned it against the wall, then picked up the lumicon and went down the steps into the little room below, opening the wooden chest and getting out the bundle wrapped in bearskin. He brought it up again and carried it to the table, from which Dranigo and Salvadro were clearing the dishes.

"Here it is," he said, untying the thongs. "I do not know how old it is. It was old even before the Ice-Father was born."

That was too much for Vahr. "See, I told you he's crazy!" he cried. "The Ice-Father has been here forever. Gorth Sledmaker says so," he added, as though that settled it.

"Gorth Sledmaker's a fool. He thinks the world began in the time of his grandfather." He had the thongs untied, and spread the bearskin, revealing the blackened leather box, flat on the bottom and domed at the top. "How long ago do you think it was that the Ice-Father was born?" he asked Salvadro and Dranigo.

"Not more than two thousand years," Dranigo said. "The glaciation hadn't started in the time of the Third Empire. There is no record of this planet during the Fourth, but by the beginning of the Fifth Empire, less than a thousand years ago, things here were very much as they are now."

"There are other worlds which have Ice-Fathers," Salvadro explained. "They are all worlds having one pole or the other in open water, surrounded by land. When the polar sea is warmed by water from the tropics, snow falls on the lands around, and more falls in winter than melts in summer, and so is an Ice-Father formed. Then, when the polar sea is all frozen, no more snow falls, and the Ice-Father melts faster than it grows, and finally vanishes. And then, when warm water comes into the polar sea again, more snow falls, and it starts over again. On a world like this, it takes fifteen or twenty thousand years from one Ice-Father to the next."

"I never heard that there had been another Ice-Father, before this one. But then, I only know the stories told by the old men, when I was a boy. I suppose that was before the first people came in starships to this world."

The two men of Dremna looked at one another oddly, and he wondered, as he unfastened the brass catches on the box, if he had said something foolish, and then he had the box open, and lifted out the Crown. He was glad, now, that Salvadro had brought in the new lumicon, as he put the box aside and set the Crown on the black bearskin. The golden circlet and the four arches of gold above it were clean and bright, and the jewels were splendid in the light. Salvadro and Dranigo were looking at it wide-eyed. Vahr Farg's son was open-mouthed.

"Great Universe! Will you look at that diamond on the top!" Salvadro was saying.

"That's not the work of any Galactic art-period," Dranigo declared. "That thing goes back to the Pre-Interstellar Era." And for a while he talked excitedly to Salvadro.

"Tell me, Keeper," Salvadro said at length, "how much do you know about the Crown? Where did it come from; who made it; who were the first Keepers?"

He shook his head. "I only know what my father told me, when I was a boy. Now I am an old man, and some things I have forgotten. But my father was Runch, Raud's son, who was the son of Yorn, the son of Raud, the son of Runch." He went back six more generations, then faltered and stopped. "Beyond that, the names have been lost. But I do know that for a long time the Crown was in a city to the north of here, and before that it was brought across the sea from another country, and the name of that country was Brinn."

Dranigo frowned, as though he had never heard the name before. "Brinn." Salvadro's eyes widened. "Brinn, Dranigo! Do you think that might be Britain?"

Dranigo straightened, staring, "It might be! Britain was a great nation, once; the last nation to join the Terran Federation, in the Third Century Pre-Interstellar. And they had a king, and a crown with a great diamond...."

"The story of where it was made," Rand offered, "or who made it, has been lost. I suppose the first people brought it to this world when they came in starships."

"It's more wonderful than that, Keeper," Salvadro said. "It was made on this world, before the first starship was built. This world is Terra, the Mother-World; didn't you know that, Keeper? This is the world where Man was born."

He hadn't known that. Of course, there had to be a world like that, but a great world in the middle of everything, like Dremna. Not this old, forgotten world.

"It's true, Keeper," Dranigo told him. He hesitated slightly, then cleared his throat. "Keeper, you're young no longer, and some day you must die, as your father and his father did. Who will care for the Crown then?"

Who, indeed? His woman had died long ago, and she had given him no sons, and the daughters she had given him had gone their own ways with men of their own choosing and he didn't know what had become of any of them. And the village people-they would start picking the Crown apart to sell the jewels, one by one, before the ashes of his pyre stopped smoking.

"Let us have it, Keeper," Salvadro said. "We will take it to Dremna, where armed men will guard it day and night, and it will be a trust upon the Government of the Empire forever."

He recoiled in horror. "Man! You don't know what you're saying!" he cried. "This is the Crown, and I am the Keeper; I cannot part with it as long as there is life in me."

"And when there is not, what? Will it be laid on your pyre, so that it may end with you?" Dranigo asked.

"Do you think we'd throw it away as soon as we got tired looking at it?" Salvadro exclaimed. "To show you how we'll value this, we'll give you ... how much is a thousand imperials in trade-tokens, Dranigo?"

"I'd guess about twenty thousand."

"We'll give you twenty thousand Government trade-tokens," Salvadro said. "If it costs us that much, you'll believe that we'll take care of it, won't you?"

Raud rose stiffly. "It is a wrong thing," he said, "to enter a man's house and eat at his table, and then insult him."

Dranigo rose also, and Salvadro with him. "We had no mind to insult you, Keeper, or offer you a bribe to betray your trust. We only offer to help you fulfill it, so that the Crown will be safe after all of us are dead. Well, we won't talk any more about it, now. We're going in Yorn Nazvik's ship, tomorrow; he's trading in the country to the west, but before he returns to the Warm Seas, he'll stop at Long Valley Town, and we'll fly over to see you. In the meantime, think about this; ask yourself if you would not be doing a better thing for the Crown by selling it to us."

They wanted to leave the dishes and the new lumicon, and he permitted it, to show that he was not offended by their offer to buy the Crown. He knew that it was something very important to them, and he admitted, grudgingly, that they could care for it better than he. At least, they would not keep it in a hole under a hut in the wilderness, guarded only by dogs. But they were not Keepers, and he was. To them, the Crown would be but one of many important things; to him it was everything. He could not imagine life without it.

He lay for a long time among his bed-robes, unable to sleep, thinking of the Crown and the visitors. Finally, to escape those thoughts, he began planning tomorrow morning's hunt.

He would start out as soon as the snow stopped, and go down among the scrub-pines; he would take Brave with him, and leave Bold on guard at home. Brave was more obedient, and a better hunter. Bold would jump for the deer that had been shot, but Brave always tried to catch or turn the ones that were still running.

He needed meat badly, and he needed more deerskins, to make new clothes. He was thinking of the new overshirt he meant to make as he fell asleep....

It was past noon when he and Brave turned back toward Keeper's House. The deer had gone farther than he had expected, but he had found them, and killed four. The carcasses were cleaned and hung from trees, out of reach of the foxes and the wolves, and he would take Brave back to the house and leave him on guard, and return with Bold and the sled to bring in the meat. He was thinking cheerfully of the fresh meat when he came out onto the path from the village, a mile from Keeper's House. Then he stopped short, looking at the tracks.

Three men-no, four-had come from the direction of the village since the snow had stopped. One had been wearing sealskin boots, of the sort worn by all Northfolk. The others had worn Southron boots, with ribbed plastic soles. That puzzled him. None of the village people wore Southron boots, and as he had been leaving in the early morning, he had seen Yorn Nazvik's ship, the *Issa*, lift out from the village and pass overhead, vanishing in the west. Possibly these were deserters. In any case, they were not good people. He slipped the heavy rifle from its snow-cover, checked the chamber, and hung the empty cover around his neck like a scarf. He didn't like the looks of it.

He liked it even less when he saw that the man in sealskin boots had stopped to examine the tracks he and Brave had made on leaving, and had then circled the house and come back, to be joined by his plastic-soled companions. Then they had all put down their packs and their ice-staffs, and advanced toward the door of the house. They had stopped there for a moment, and then they had entered, come out again, gotten their packs and ice-staffs, and gone away, up the slope to the north.

"Wait, Brave," he said. "Watch."

Then he advanced, careful not to step on any of the tracks until he reached the doorstep, where it could not be avoided.

"Bold!" he called loudly. "Bold!"

Silence. No welcoming whimper, no padding of feet, inside. He pulled the latchstring with his left hand and pushed the door open with his foot, the rifle ready. There was no need for that. What welcomed him, within, was a sickening stench of burned flesh and hair.

The new lumicon lighted the room brilliantly; his first glance was enough. The slab that had covered the crypt was thrown aside, along with the pile of deerskins, and between it and the door was a shapeless black heap that, in a dimmer light, would not have been instantly recognizable as the body of Bold. Fighting down an impulse to rush in, he stood in the door, looking about and reading the story of what had happened. The four men had entered, knowing that they would find Bold alone. The one in the lead had had a negatron pistol drawn, and when Bold had leaped at them, he had been blasted. The blast had caught the dog from in front-the chest-cavity was literally exploded, and the neck and head burned and smashed unrecognizably. Even the brass studs on the leather collar had been melted.

That and the ribbed sole-prints outside meant the same thing-Southrons. Every Southron who came into the Northland, even the common crewmen on the trading ships, carried some kind of an energy-weapon. They were good only for fighting-one look at the body of Bold showed what they did to meat and skins.

He entered, then, laying his rifle on the table, and got down the lumicon and went over to the crypt. After a while, he returned, hung up the light again, and dropped onto a stool. He sat staring at the violated crypt and tugging with one hand at a corner of his beard, trying desperately to think.

The thieves had known exactly where the Crown was kept and how it was guarded; after killing Bold, they had gone straight to it, taken it and gone away-three men in plastic-soled Southron boots and one man in soft boots of sealskins, each with a pack and an ice-staff, and two of them with rifles.

Vahr Farg's son, and three deserters from the crew of Yorn Nazvik's ship.

It hadn't been Dranigo and Salvadro. They could have left the ship in their airboat and come back, flying low, while he had been hunting. But they would have grounded near the house, they would not have carried packs, and they would have brought nobody with them.

He thought he knew what had happened. Vahr Farg's son had seen the Crown, and he had heard the two Starfolk offer more trade-tokens for it than everything in the village was worth. But he was a coward; he would never dare to face the Keeper's rifle and the teeth of Brave and Bold alone. So, since none of the village folk would have part in so shameful a crime against the moral code of the Northland, he had talked three of Yorn Nazvik's airmen into deserting and joining him.

And he had heard Dranigo say that the *Issa* would return to Long Valley Town after the trading voyage to the west. Long Valley was on the other side of this tongue of the Ice-Father; it was a good fifteen days' foot-journey around, but by climbing and crossing, they could easily be there in time to meet Yorn Nazvik's ship and the two Starfolk. Well, where Vahr Farg's son could take three Southrons, Raud the Keeper could follow.

Their tracks led up the slope beside the brook, always bearing to the left, in the direction of the Ice-Father. After an hour, he found where they had stopped and unslung their packs, and rested long enough to smoke a cigarette. He read the story they had left in the snow, and then continued, Brave trotting behind him pulling the sled. A few snowflakes began dancing in the air, and he quickened his steps. He knew, generally, where the thieves were going, but he wanted their tracks unobliterated in front of him. The snow fell thicker and thicker, and it was growing dark, and he was tiring. Even Brave was stumbling occasionally before Raud stopped, in a hollow among the pines, to build his tiny fire and eat and feed the dog. They bedded down together, covered by the same sleeping robes.

When he woke, the world was still black and white and gray in the early dawn-light, and the robe that covered him and Brave was powdered with snow, and the pine-branches above him were loaded and sagging.

The snow had completely obliterated the tracks of the four thieves, and it was still falling. When the sled was packed and the dog harnessed to it, they set out, keeping close to the flank of the Ice-Father on their left.

It stopped snowing toward mid-day, and a little after, he heard a shot, far ahead, and then two more, one upon the other. The first shot would be the rifle of Vahr Farg's son; it was a single-loader, like his own. The other two were from one of the light Southron rifles, which fired a dozen shots one after another. They had shot, or shot at, something like a deer, he supposed. That was sensible; it would save their dried meat for the trip across the back of the Ice-Father. And it showed that they still didn't know he was following them. He found their tracks, some hours later.

Toward dusk, he came to a steep building-mound. It had fared better than most of the houses of the ancient people; it rose to twenty times a man's height and on the south-east side it was almost perpendicular. The other side sloped, and he was able to climb to the top, and far away, ahead of him, he saw a tiny spark appear and grow. The fire could not be more than two hours ahead.

He built no fire that evening, but shared a slab of pemmican with Brave, and they huddled together under the bearskin robe. The dog fell asleep at once. For a long time, Raud sat awake, thinking.

At first, he considered resting for a while, and then pressing forward and attacking them as they slept. He had to kill all of them to regain the Crown; that he had taken for granted from the first. He knew what would happen if the Government Police came into this. They would take one Southron's word against the word of ten Northfolk, and the thieves would simply claim the Crown as theirs and accuse him of trying to steal it. And Dranigo and Salvadro-they seemed like good men, but they might see this as the only way to get the Crown for themselves....He would have to settle the affair for himself, before the men reached Long Valley town.

If he could do it here, it would save him and Brave the toil and danger of climbing the Ice-Father. But could he? They had two rifles, one an autoloader, and they had in all likelihood three negatron pistols. After the single shot of the big rifle was fired, he had only a knife and a hatchet and the spiked and pickaxed ice-staff, and Brave. One of the thieves would kill him before he and Brave killed all of them, and then the Crown would be lost. He dropped into sleep, still thinking of what to do.

He climbed the mound of the ancient building again in the morning, and looked long and carefully at the face of the Ice-Father. It would take the thieves the whole day to reach that place where the two tongues of the glacier split apart, the easiest spot to climb. They would not try to climb that evening; Vahr, who knew the most about it, would be the last to advise such a risk. He was sure that by going up at the nearest point he could get to the top of the Ice-Father before dark, and drag Brave up after him. It would be a fearful climb, and he would have most of a day's journey after that to reach the head of the long ravine up which the thieves would come, but when they came up, he could be there waiting for them. He knew what the old rifle could do, to an inch, and there were places where the thieves would be coming up where he could stay out of blaster-range and pick them all off, even with a single-loader.

He knew about negatron pistols, too. They shot little bullets of energy; they were very fast, and did not drop, like a real bullet, so that no judgment of range was needed. But the energy died quickly; the negatrons lived only long enough to go five hundred paces and no more. At eight hundred, he could hit a man easily. He almost felt himself pitying Vahr Farg's son and his companions.

When he reached the tumble of rocks that had been dragged along with and pushed out from the Ice-Father, he stopped and made up a pack-sleeping robes, all his cartridges, as much pemmican as he could carry, and the bag of trade-tokens. If the chase took him to Long Valley Town, he would need money. He also coiled about his waist a long rawhide climbing-rope, and left the sled-harness on Brave, simply detaching the traces.

At first, they walked easily on the sloping ice. Then, as it grew steeper, he fastened the rope to the dog's harness and advanced a little at a time, dragging Brave up after him. Soon he was forced to snub the rope with his ice-staff and chop steps with his hatchet. Toward noon-at least he thought it was noon-it began snowing again, and the valley below was blotted out in a swirl of white.

They came to a narrow ledge, where they could rest, with a wall of ice rising sheerly above them. He would have to climb that alone, and then pull Brave up with the rope. He started working his way up the perpendicular face, clinging by the pick of his ice-staff, chopping footholds with the hatchet; the pack and the slung rifle on his back pulled at him and threatened to drag him down. At length, he dragged himself over the edge and drove the ice-staff in.

"Up, Brave!" he called, tugging on the rope. "Good dog, Brave; come up!"

Brave tried to jump and slipped back. He tried again, and this time Raud snubbed the rope and held him. Below the dog pawed frantically, until he found a paw-hold on one of the chopped-out steps. Raud hauled on the rope, and made another snub.

It seemed like hours. It probably was; his arms were aching, and he had lost all sense of time, or of the cold, or the danger of the narrow ledge; he forgot about the Crown and the men who had stolen it; he even forgot how he had come here, or that he had ever been anywhere else. All that mattered was to get Brave up on the ledge beside him.

Finally Brave came up and got first his fore-paws and then his body over the edge. He lay still, panting proudly, while Raud hugged him and told him, over and over, that he was a good dog. They rested for a long time, and Raud got a slab of pemmican from the pack and divided it with Brave.

It was while they rested in the snow, munching, that he heard the sound for the first time. It was faint and far away, and it sounded like thunder, or like an avalanche beginning, and that puzzled him, for this was not the time of year for either. As he listened, he heard it again, and this time he recognized it-negatron pistols. It frightened him; he wondered if the thieves had met a band of hunters. No; if they were fighting Northfolk, there would be the reports of firearms, too. Or might they be fighting among themselves? Remembering the melted brass studs on Bold's collar, he became more frightened at the thought of what a negatron-blast could do to the Crown.

The noise stopped, then started again, and he got to his feet, calling to Brave. They were on a wide ledge that slanted upward toward the north. It would take him closer to the top, and closer to where Vahr and his companions would come up. Together, they started up, Raud probing cautiously ahead of him with the ice-staff for hidden crevasses. After a while, he came to a wide gap in the ice beside him, slanting toward the top, its upper end lost in swirling snow. So he and Brave began climbing, and after a while he could no longer hear the negatron pistols.

When it was almost too dark to go farther, he suddenly found himself on level snow, and here he made camp, digging a hole and lining it with the sleeping robes.

The sky was clear when he woke, and a pale yellow light was glowing in the east. For a while he lay huddled with the dog, stiff and miserable, and then he forced himself to his feet. He ate, and fed Brave, and then checked his rifle and made his pack.

He was sure, now, that he had a plan that would succeed. He could reach the place where Vahr and the Southrons would come up long before they did, and be waiting for them. In his imagination, he could see them coming up in single file, Vahr Farg's son in the lead, and he could imagine himself hidden behind a mound of snow, the ice-staff upright to brace his left hand and the forestock of the rifle resting on his outthrust thumb and the butt against his shoulder. The first bullet would be for Vahr. He could shoot all of them, one after another, that way....

He stopped, looking in chagrined incredulity at the tracks in front of him-the tracks he knew so well, of one man in sealskin boots and three men with ribbed plastic soles. Why, it couldn't be! They should be no more than half way up the long ravine, between the two tongues of the Ice-Father, ten miles to the north. But here they were, on the back of the Ice-Father and crossing to the west ahead of him. They must have climbed the sheer wall of ice, only a few miles from where he had dragged himself and Brave to the top. Then he remembered the negatron-blasts he had heard. While he had been chopping footholds with a hatchet, they had been smashing tons of ice out of their way.

"Well, Brave," he said mildly. "Old Keeper wasn't so smart, after all, was he? Come on, Brave."

The thieves were making good time. He read that from the tracks —straight, evenly spaced, no weary heel-dragging. Once or twice, he saw where they had stopped for a brief rest. He hoped to see their fire in the evening.

He didn't. They wouldn't have enough fuel to make a big one, or keep it burning long. But in the morning, as he was breaking camp, he saw black smoke ahead.

A few times, he had been in air-boats, and had looked down on the back of the Ice-Father, and it had looked flat. Really, it was not. There were long ridges, sheer on one side and sloping gently on the other, where the ice had overridden hills and low mountains, or had cracked and one side had pushed up over the other. And there were deep gullies where the prevailing winds had scooped away loose snow year after year for centuries, and drifts where it had piled, many of them higher than the building-mounds of the ancient cities. But from a distance, as from above, they all blended into a featureless white monotony.

At last, leaving a tangle of cliffs and ravines, he looked out across a broad stretch of nearly level snow and saw, for the first time, the men he was following. Four tiny dots, so far that they seemed motionless, strung out in single file. Instantly, he crouched behind a swell in the surface and dragged Brave down beside him. One of them, looking back, might see him, as he saw them. When they vanished behind a snow-hill, he rose and hastened forward, to take cover again. He kept at this all day; by alternately resting and running, be found himself gaining on them, and toward evening, he was within rifle-range. The man in the lead was Vahr Farg's son; even at that distance he recognized him easily. The others were Southrons, of course; they wore quilted garments of cloth, and quilted hoods. The man next to Vahr, in blue, carried a rifle, as Vahr did. The man in yellow had only an ice-staff, and the man in green, at the rear, had the Crown on his pack, still in the bearskin bundle.

He waited, at the end of the day, until he saw the light of their fire. Then he and Brave circled widely around their camp, and stopped behind a snow-ridge, on the other side of an open and level stretch a mile wide. He dug the sleeping-hole on the crest of the ridge, making it larger than usual, and piled up a snow breastwork in front of it, with an embrasure through which he could look or fire without being seen.

Before daybreak, he was awake and had his pack made, and when he saw the smoke of the thieves' campfire, he was lying behind his breastwork, the rifle resting on its folded cover, muzzle toward the smoke. He lay for a long time, watching, before he saw the file of tiny dots emerge into the open.

They came forward steadily, in the same order as on the day before, Vahr in the lead and the man with the Crown in the rear. The thieves suspected nothing; they grew larger and larger as they approached, until they were at the range for which he had set his sights. He cuddled the butt of the rifle against his cheek. As the man who carried the Crown walked under the blade of the front sight, he squeezed the trigger.

The rifle belched pink flame and roared and pounded his shoulder. As the muzzle was still rising, he flipped open the breech, and threw out the empty. He inserted a fresh round.

There were only three of them, now. The man with the bearskin bundle was down and motionless. Vahr Farg's son had gotten his rifle unslung and uncovered. The Southron with the other rifle was slower; he was only getting off the cover as Vahr, who must have seen the flash, fired hastily. Too hastily; the bullet kicked up snow twenty feet to the left. The third man had drawn his negatron pistol and was trying to use it; thin hairlines of brilliance were jetting out from his hand, stopping far short of their mark.

Raud closed his sights on the man with the autoloading rifle; as he did, the man with the negatron pistol, realizing the limitations of his weapon, was sweeping it back and forth, aiming at the snow fifty yards in front of him. Raud couldn't see the effect of his second shot-between him and his target, blueish light blazed and twinkled, and dense clouds of steam rose-but he felt sure that he had missed. He reloaded, and watched for movements on the edge of the rising steam.

It cleared, slowly; when it did, there was nothing behind it. Even the body of the dead man was gone. He blinked, bewildered. He'd picked that place carefully; there had been no gully or ravine within running distance. Then he grunted. There hadn't been-but there was now. The negatron pistol again. The thieves were hidden in a pit they had blasted, and they had dragged the body in with them.

He crawled back to reassure Brave, who was guarding the pack, and to shift the pack back for some distance. Then he returned to his embrasure in the snow-fort and resumed his watch. For a long time, nothing happened, and then a head came briefly peeping up out of the pit. A head under a green hood. Raud chuckled mirthlessly into his beard. If he'd been doing that, he'd have traded hoods with the dead man before shoving up his body to draw fire. This kept up, at intervals, for about an hour. He was wondering if they would stay in the pit until dark.

Then Vahr Farg's son leaped out of the pit and began running across the snow. He had his pack, and his rifle; he ran, zig-zag, almost directly toward where Raud was lying. Raud laughed, this time in real amusement. The Southrons had chased Vahr out, as a buck will chase his does in front of him when he thinks there is danger in front. If Vahr wasn't shot, it would be safe for them to come out. If he was, it would be no loss, and the price of the Crown would only have to be divided in two, rather than three, shares. Vahr came to within two hundred yards of Raud's unseen rifle, and then dropped his pack and flung himself down behind it, covering the ridge with his rifle.

Minutes passed, and then the Southron in yellow came out and ran forward. He had the bearskin bundle on his pack; he ran to where Vahr lay, added his pack to Vahr's, and lay down behind it. Raud chewed his underlip in vexation. This wasn't the way he wanted it; that fellow had a negatron pistol, and he was close enough to use it effectively. And he was sheltered behind the Crown; Raud was afraid to shoot. He didn't miss what he shot at-often. But no man alive could say that he never missed.

The other Southron, the one in blue with the autoloading rifle, came out and advanced slowly, his weapon at the ready. Raud tensed himself to jump, aimed carefully, and waited. When the man in blue was a hundred yards from the pit, he shot him dead. The rifle was still lifting from the recoil when he sprang to his feet, turned, and ran. Before he was twenty feet away, the place where he had been exploded; the force of the blast almost knocked him down, and steam blew past and ahead of him. Ignoring his pack and ice-staff, he ran on, calling to Brave to follow. The dog obeyed instantly; more negatron-blasts were thundering and blazing and steaming on the crest of the ridge. He swerved left, ran up another slope, and slid down the declivity beyond into the ravine on the other side.

There he paused to eject the empty, make sure that there was no snow in the rifle bore, and reload. The blasting had stopped by then; after a moment, he heard the voice of Vahr Farg's son, and guessed that the two surviving thieves had advanced to the blasted crest of the other ridge. They'd find the pack, and his tracks and Brave's. He wondered whether they'd come hunting for him, or turn around and go the other way. He knew what he'd do, under the circumstances, but he doubted if Vahr's mind would work that way. The Southron's might; he wouldn't want to be caught between blaster-range and rifle-range of Raud the Keeper again.

"Come, Brave," he whispered, looking quickly around and then starting to run.

Lay a trail down this ravine for them to follow. Then get to the top of the ridge beside it, double back, and wait for them. Let them pass, and shoot the Southron first. By now, Vahr would have a negatron pistol too, taken from the body of the man in blue, but it wasn't a weapon he was accustomed to, and he'd be more than a little afraid of it.

The ravine ended against an upthrust face of ice, at right angles to the ridge he had just crossed; there was a V-shaped notch between them. He turned into this; it would be a good place to get to the top....

He found himself face to face, at fifteen feet, with Vahr Farg's son and the Southron in yellow, coming through from the other side. They had their packs, the Southron had the bearskin bundle, and they had drawn negatron pistols in their hands.

Swinging up the rifle, he shot the Southron in the chest, making sure he hit him low enough to miss the Crown. At the same time, he shouted:

"Catch, Brave!"

Brave never jumped for the deer or wild-ox that had been shot; always for the one still on its feet. He launched himself straight at the throat of Vahr Farg's son-and into the muzzle of Vahr's blaster. He died in a blue-white flash.

Raud had reversed the heavy rifle as Brave leaped; he threw it, butt-on, like a seal-spear, into Vahr's face. As soon as it was out of his fingers, he was jumping forward, snatching out his knife. His left hand found Vahr's right wrist, and he knew that he was driving the knife into Vahr's body, over and over, trying to keep the blaster pointed away from him and away from the body of the dead Southron. At last, the negatron-pistol fell from Vahr's fingers, and the arm that had been trying to fend off his knife relaxed.

He straightened and tried to stand-he had been kneeling on Vahr's body, he found-and reeled giddily. He got to his feet and stumbled to the other body, kneeling beside it. He tried for a long time before he was able to detach the bearskin bundle from the dead man's pack. Then he got the pack open, and found dried venison. He started to divide it, and realized that there was no Brave with whom to share it. He had just sent Brave to his death.

Well, and so? Brave had been the Keeper's dog. He had died for the Crown, and that had been his duty. If he could have saved the Crown by giving his own life, Raud would have died too. But he could not-if Raud died the Crown was lost.

The sky was darkening rapidly, and the snow was whitening the body in green. Moving slowly, he started to make camp for the night.

It was still snowing when he woke. He started to rise, wondering, at first, where Brave was, and then he huddled back among the robes-his own and the dead men's —and tried to go to sleep again. Finally, he got up and ate some of his pemmican, gathered his gear and broke camp. For a moment, and only a moment, he stood looking to the east, in the direction he had come from. Then he turned west and started across the snow toward the edge of the Ice-Father.

The snow stopped before he reached the edge, and the sun was shining when he found a slanting way down into the valley. Then, out of the north, a black dot appeared in the sky and grew larger, until he saw that it was a Government airboat-one of the kind used by the men who measured the growth of the Ice-Father. It came curving in and down toward him, and a window slid open and a man put his head out.

"Want us to lift you down?" he asked. "We're going to Long Valley Town. If that's where you're going, we can take you the whole way."

"Yes. That's where I'm going." He said it as though he were revealing, for the first time, some discovery he had just made. "For your kindness and help, I thank you."

In less time than a man could walk two miles with a pack, they were letting down in front of the Government House in Long Valley Town.

He had never been in the Government House before. The walls were clear glass. The floors were plastic, clean and white. Strips of bright new lumicon ran around every room at the tops of all the walls. There were no fires, but the great rooms were as warm as though it were a midsummer afternoon.

Still carrying his pack and his rifle, Raud went to a desk where a Southron in a white shirt sat. "Has Yorn Nazvik's ship, the *Issa*, been here lately?" he asked.

"About six days ago," the Southron said, without looking up from the papers on his desk. "She's on a trading voyage to the west now, but Nazvik's coming back here before he goes south. Be here in about ten days." He looked up. "You have business with Nazvik?"

Raud shook his head. "Not with Yorn Nazvik, no. My business is with the two Starfolk who are passengers with him. Dranigo and Salvadro."

The Southron looked displeased. "Aren't you getting just a little above yourself, old man, calling the Prince Salsavadran and the Lord Dranigrastan by their familiar names?" he asked.

"I don't know what you're talking about. Those were the names they gave me; I didn't know they had any others."

The Southron started to laugh, then stopped.

"And if I may ask, what is your name, and what business have you with them?" he inquired.

Raud told him his name. "I have something for them. Something they want very badly. If I can find a place to stay here, I will wait until they return —"

The Southron got to his feet. "Wait here for a moment, Keeper," he said. "I'll be back soon."

He left the desk, going into another room. After a while, he came back. This time he was respectful.

"I was talking to the Lord Dranigrastan-whom you know as Dranigo-on the radio. He and the Prince Salsavadran are lifting clear of the *Issa* in their airboat and coming back here to see you. They should be here in about three hours. If, in the meantime, you wish to bathe and rest, I'll find you a room. And I suppose you'll want something to eat, too...."

He was waiting at the front of the office, looking out the glass wall, when the airboat came in and grounded, and Salvadro and Dranigo jumped out and came hurrying up the walk to the doorway.

"Well, here you are, Keeper," Dranigo greeted him, clasping his hand. Then he saw the bearskin bundle under Raud's arm. "You brought it with you? But didn't you believe that we were coming?"

"Are you going to let us have it?" Salvadro was asking.

"Yes; I will sell it to you, for the price you offered. I am not fit to be Keeper any longer. I lost it. It was stolen from me, the day after I saw you, and I have only yesterday gotten it back. Both my dogs were killed, too. I can no longer keep it safe. Better that you take it with you to Dremna, away from this world where it was made. I have thought, before, that this world and I are both old and good for nothing any more."

"This world may be old, Keeper," Dranigo said, "but it is the Mother-World, Terra, the world that sent Man to the Stars. And you-when you lost the Crown, you recovered it again."

"The next time, I won't be able to. Too many people will know that the Crown is worth stealing, and the next time, they'll kill me first."

"Well, we said we'd give you twenty thousand trade-tokens for it," Salvadro said. "We'll have them for you as soon as we can draw them from the Government bank, here. Or give you a check and let you draw them as you want them." Raud didn't understand that, and Salvadro didn't try to explain. "And then we'll fly you home."

He shook his head. "No, I have no home. The place where you saw me is Keeper's House, and I am not the Keeper any more. I will stay here and find a place to live, and pay somebody to take care of me...."

With twenty thousand trade-tokens, he could do that. It would buy a house in which he could live, and he could find some woman who had lost her man, who would do his work for him. But he must be careful of the money. Dig a crypt in the corner of his house for it. He wondered if he could find a pair of good dogs and train them to guard it for him....

Graveyard of Dreams

By H. Beam Piper

> Despite Mr. Shakespeare,
> wealth and name are both dross compared with
> the theft of hope--
> and Maxwell had to rob
> a whole planet of it!

Standing at the armor-glass front of the observation deck and watching the mountains rise and grow on the horizon, Conn Maxwell gripped the metal hand-rail with painful intensity, as though trying to hold back the airship by force. Thirty minutes--twenty-six and a fraction of the Terran minutes he had become accustomed to--until he'd have to face it.

Then, realizing that he never, in his own thoughts, addressed himself as "sir," he turned.

"I beg your pardon?"

It was the first officer, wearing a Terran Federation Space Navy uniform of forty years, or about ten regulation-changes, ago. That was the sort of thing he had taken for granted before he had gone away. Now he was noticing it everywhere.

"Thirty minutes out of Litchfield, sir," the ship's officer repeated. "You'll go off by the midship gangway on the starboard side."

"Yes, I know. Thank you."

The first mate held out the clipboard he was carrying. "Would you mind checking over this, Mr. Maxwell? Your baggage list."

"Certainly." He glanced at the slip of paper. Valises, eighteen and twenty-five kilos, two; trunks, seventy-five and seventy kilos, two; microbook case, one-fifty kilos, one. The last item fanned up a little flicker of anger in him, not at any person, even himself, but at the situation in which he found himself and the futility of the whole thing.

"Yes, that's everything. I have no hand-luggage, just this stuff."

He noticed that this was the only baggage list under the clip; the other papers were all freight and express manifests. "Not many passengers left aboard, are there?"

"You're the only one in first-class, sir," the mate replied. "About forty farm-laborers on the lower deck. Everybody else got off at the other stops. Litchfield's the end of the run. You know anything about the place?"

"I was born there. I've been away at school for the last five years."

"On Baldur?"

"Terra. University of Montevideo." Once Conn would have said it almost boastfully.

The mate gave him a quick look of surprised respect, then grinned and nodded. "Of course; I should have known. You're Rodney Maxwell's son, aren't you? Your father's one of our regular freight shippers. Been sending out a lot of stuff lately." He looked as though he would have liked to continue the conversation, but said: "Sorry, I've got to go. Lot of things to attend to before landing." He touched the visor of his cap and turned away.

The mountains were closer when Conn looked forward again, and he glanced down. Five years and two space voyages ago, seen from the afterdeck of this ship or one of her sisters, the woods had been green with new foliage, and the wine-melon fields had been in pink blossom. He tried to picture the scene sliding away below instead of drawing in toward him, as though to force himself back to a moment of the irretrievable past.

But the moment was gone, and with it the eager excitement and the half-formed anticipations of the things he would learn and accomplish on Terra. The things he would learn--microbook case, one-fifty kilos, one. One of the steel trunks was full of things he had learned and accomplished, too. Maybe they, at least, had some value....

The woods were autumn-tinted now and the fields were bare and brown.

They had gotten the crop in early this year, for the fields had all been harvested. Those workers below must be going out for the wine-pressing. That extra hands were needed for that meant a big crop, and yet it seemed that less land was under cultivation than when he had gone away. He could see squares of low brush among the new forests that had grown up in the last forty years, and the few stands of original timber looked like hills above the second growth. Those trees had been standing when the planet had been colonized.

That had been two hundred years ago, at the middle of the Seventh Century, Atomic Era. The name of the planet--Poictesme--told that: the Surromanticist Movement, when the critics and professors were rediscovering James Branch Cabell.

Funny how much was coming back to him now--things he had picked up from the minimal liberal-arts and general-humanities courses he had taken and then forgotten in his absorption with the science and tech studies.

The first extrasolar planets, as they had been discovered, had been named from Norse mythology--Odin and Baldur and Thor, Uller and Freya, Bifrost and Asgard and Niflheim. When the Norse names ran out, the discoverers had turned to other mythologies, Celtic and Egyptian and Hindu and Assyrian, and by the middle of the Seventh Century they were naming planets for almost anything.

Anything, that is, but actual persons; their names were reserved for stars. Like Alpha Gartner, the sun of Poictesme, and Beta Gartner, a buckshot-sized pink glow in the southeast, and Gamma Gartner, out of sight on the other side of the world, all named for old Genji Gartner, the scholarly and half-piratical adventurer whose ship had been the first to approach the three stars and discover that each of them had planets.

Forty-two planets in all, from a couple of methane-giants on Gamma to airless little things with one-sixth Terran gravity. Alpha II had been the only one in the Trisystem with an oxygen atmosphere and life. So Gartner had landed on it, and named it Poictesme, and the settlement that had grown up around the first landing site had been called Storisende. Thirty years later, Genji Gartner died there, after seeing the camp grow to a metropolis, and was buried under a massive monument.

Some of the other planets had been rich in metals, and mines had been opened, and atmosphere-domed factories and processing plants built. None of them could produce anything but hydroponic and tissue-culture foodstuffs, and natural foods from Poictesme had been less expensive, even on the planets of Gamma and Beta. So Poictesme had concentrated on agriculture and grown wealthy at it.

Then, within fifty years of Genji Gartner's death, the economics of interstellar trade overtook the Trisystem and the mines and factories closed down. It was no longer possible to ship the output to a profitable market, in the face of the growing self-sufficiency of the colonial planets and the irreducibly high cost of space-freighting.

Below, the brown fields and the red and yellow woods were merging into a ten-mile-square desert of crumbling concrete--empty and roofless sheds and warehouses and barracks, brush-choked parade grounds and landing fields, airship docks, and even a spaceport. They were more recent, dating from Poictesme's second brief and hectic prosperity, when the Terran Federation's Third Fleet-Army Force had occupied the Gartner Trisystem during the System States War.

Millions of troops had been stationed on or routed through Poictesme; tens of thousands of spacecraft had been based on the Trisystem; the mines and factories had reopened for war production. The Federation had spent trillions of sols on Poictesme, piled up mountains of stores and arms and equipment, left the face of the planet cluttered with installations.

Then, ten years before anybody had expected it, the rebellious System States Alliance had collapsed and the war had ended. The Federation armies had gone home, taking with them the clothes they stood in, their personal weapons and a few souvenirs. Everything else had been left behind; even the most expensive equipment was worth less than the cost of removal.

Ever since, Poictesme had been living on salvage. The uniform the first officer was wearing was forty years old--and it was barely a month out of the original packing. On Terra, Conn had told his friends that his father was a prospector and let them interpret that as meaning an explorer for, say, uranium deposits. Rodney Maxwell found plenty of uranium, but he got it by taking apart the warheads of missiles.

The old replacement depot or classification center or training area or whatever it had been had vanished under the ship now and it was all forest back to the mountains, with an occasional cluster of deserted buildings. From one or two, threads of blue smoke rose--bands of farm tramps, camping on their way from harvest to wine-pressing. Then the eastern foothills were out of sight and he was looking down on the granite spines of the Calder Range; the valley beyond was sloping away and widening out in the distance, and it was time he began thinking of what to say when he landed. He would have to tell them, of course.

He wondered who would be at the dock to meet him, besides his family. Lynne Fawzi, he hoped. Or did he? Her parents would be with her, and Kurt Fawzi would take the news hardest of any of them, and be the first to blame him because it was bad. The hopes he had built for Lynne and himself would have to be held in abeyance till he saw how her father would regard him now.

But however any of them took it, he would have to tell them the truth.

The ship swept on, tearing through the thin puffs of cloud at ten miles a minute. Six minutes to landing. Five. Four. Then he saw the river bend, glinting redly through the haze in the sunlight; Litchfield was inside it, and he stared waiting for the first glimpse of the city. Three minutes, and the ship began to cut speed and lose altitude. The hot-jets had stopped firing and he could hear the whine of the cold-jet rotors.

Then he could see Litchfield, dominated by the Airport Building, so thick that it looked squat for all its height, like a candle-stump in a puddle of its own grease, the other buildings under their carapace of terraces and landing stages seeming to have flowed away from it. And there was the yellow block of the distilleries, and High Garden Terrace, and the Mall....

At first, in the distance, it looked like a living city. Then, second by second, the stigmata of decay became more and more evident. Terraces empty or littered with rubbish; gardens untended and choked with wild growth; windows staring blindly; walls splotched with lichens and grimy where the rains could not wash them.

For a moment, he was afraid that some disaster, unmentioned in his father's letters, had befallen. Then he realized that the change had not been in Litchfield but in himself. After five years, he was seeing it as it really was. He wondered how his family and his friends would look to him now. Or Lynne.

The ship was coming in over the Mall; he could see the cracked paving sprouting grass, the statues askew on their pedestals, the waterless fountains. He thought for an instant that one of them was playing, and then he saw that what he had taken for spray was dust blowing from the empty basin. There was something about dusty fountains, something he had learned at the University. Oh, yes. One of the Second Century Martian Colonial poets, Eirrarsson, or somebody like that:

There was more to it, but he couldn't remember; something about empty gardens under an empty sky. There must have been colonies inside the Sol System, before the Interstellar Era, that hadn't turned out any better than Poictesme. Then he stopped trying to remember as the ship turned toward the Airport Building and a couple of tugs--Terran Federation contragravity tanks, with derrick-booms behind and push-poles where the guns had been--came up to bring her down.

He walked along the starboard promenade to the gangway, which the first mate and a couple of airmen were getting open.

Most of the population of top-level Litchfield was in the crowd on the dock. He recognized old Colonel Zareff, with his white hair and plum-brown skin, and Tom Brangwyn, the town marshal, red-faced and bulking above the others. It took a few seconds for him to pick out his father and mother, and his sister Flora, and then to realize that the handsome young man beside Flora was his brother Charley. Charley had been thirteen when Conn had gone away. And there was Kurt Fawzi, the mayor of Litchfield, and there was Lynne, beside him, her red-lipped face tilted upward with a cloud of bright hair behind it.

He waved to her, and she waved back, jumping in excitement, and then everybody was waving, and they were pushing his family to the front and making way for them.

The ship touched down lightly and gave a lurch as she went off contragravity, and they got the gangway open and the steps swung out, and he started down toward the people who had gathered to greet him.

His father was wearing the same black best-suit he had worn when they had parted five years ago. It had been new then; now it was shabby and had acquired a permanent wrinkle across the right hip, over the pistol-butt. Charley was carrying a gun, too; the belt and holster looked as though he had made them himself. His mother's dress was new and so was Flora's--probably made for the occasion. He couldn't be sure just which of the Terran Federation services had provided the material, but Charley's shirt was Medical Service sterilon.

Ashamed that he was noticing and thinking of such things at a time like this, he clasped his father's hand and kissed his mother and Flora. Everybody was talking at once, saying things that he heard only as happy sounds. His brother's words were the first that penetrated as words.

"You didn't know me," Charley was accusing. "Don't deny it; I saw you standing there wondering if I was Flora's new boy friend or what."

"Well, how in Niflheim'd you expect me to? You've grown up since the last time I saw you. You're looking great, kid!" He caught the gleam of Lynne's golden hair beyond Charley's shoulder and pushed him gently aside. "Lynne!"

"Conn, you look just wonderful!" Her arms were around his neck and she was kissing him. "Am I still your girl, Conn?"

He crushed her against him and returned her kisses, assuring her that she was. He wasn't going to let it make a bit of difference how her father took the news--if she didn't.

She babbled on: "You didn't get mixed up with any of those girls on Terra, did you? If you did, don't tell me about it. All I care about is that you're back. Oh, Conn, you don't know how much I missed you ... Mother, Dad, doesn't he look just splendid?"

Kurt Fawzi, a little thinner, his face more wrinkled, his hair grayer, shook his hand.

"I'm just as glad to see you as anybody, Conn," he said, "even if I'm not being as demonstrative about it as Lynne. Judge, what do you think of our returned wanderer? Franz, shake hands with him, but save the interview for the *News* for later. Professor, here's one student Litchfield Academy won't need to be ashamed of."

He shook hands with them--old Judge Ledue; Franz Veltrin, the newsman; Professor Kellton; a dozen others, some of whom he had not thought of in five years. They were all cordial and happy--how much, he wondered, because he was their neighbor, Conn Maxwell, Rodney Maxwell's son, home from Terra, and how much because of what they hoped he would tell them? Kurt Fawzi, edging him out of the crowd, was the first to voice that.

"Conn, what did you find out?" he asked breathlessly. "Do you know where it is?"

Conn hesitated, looking about desperately; this was no time to start talking to Kurt Fawzi about it. His father was turning toward him from one side, and from the other Tom Brangwyn and Colonel Zareff were approaching more slowly, the older man leaning on a silver-headed cane.

"Don't bother him about it now, Kurt," Rodney Maxwell scolded the mayor. "He's just gotten off the ship; he hasn't had time to say hello to everybody yet."

"But, Rod, I've been waiting to hear what he's found out ever since he went away," Fawzi protested in a hurt tone.

Brangwyn and Colonel Zareff joined them. They were close friends, probably because neither of them was a native of Poictesme.

The town marshal had always been reticent about his origins, but Conn guessed it was Hathor. Brangwyn's heavy-muscled body, and his ease and grace in handling it, marked him as a man of a high-gravity planet. Besides, Hathor had a permanent cloud-envelope, and Tom Brangwyn's skin had turned boiled-lobster red under the dim orange sunlight of Alpha Gartner.

Old Klem Zareff never hesitated to tell anybody where he came from--he was from Ashmodai, one of the System States planets, and he had commanded a division that had been blasted down to about regimental strength, in the Alliance army.

"Hello, boy," he croaked, extending a trembling hand. "Glad you're home. We all missed you."

"We sure did, Conn," the town marshal agreed, clasping Conn's hand as soon as the old man had released it. "Find out anything definite?"

Kurt Fawzi looked at his watch. "Conn, we've planned a little celebration for you. We only had since day before yesterday, when the spaceship came into radio range, but we're having a dinner party for you at Senta's this evening."

"You couldn't have done anything I'd have liked better, Mr. Fawzi. I'd have to have a meal at Senta's before really feeling that I'd come home."

"Well, here's what I have in mind. It'll be three hours till dinner's ready. Suppose we all go up to my office in the meantime. It'll give the ladies a chance to go home and fix up for the party, and we can have a drink and a talk."

"You want to do that, Conn?" his father asked, a trifle doubtfully. "If you'd rather go home first..."

Something in his father's voice and manner disturbed him vaguely; however, he nodded agreement. After a couple of drinks, he'd be better able to tell them.

"Yes, indeed, Mr. Fawzi," Conn said. "I know you're all anxious, but it's a long story. This'll be a good chance to tell you."

Fawzi turned to his wife and daughter, interrupting himself to shout instructions to a couple of dockhands who were floating the baggage off the ship on a contragravity-lifter. Conn's father had sent Charley off with a message to his mother and Flora.

Conn turned to Colonel Zareff. "I noticed extra workers coming out from the hiring agencies in Storisende, and the crop was all in across the Calders. Big wine-pressing this year?"

"Yes, we're up to our necks in melons," the old planter grumbled. "Gehenna of a big crop. Price'll drop like a brick of collapsium, and this time next year we'll be using brandy to wash our feet in."

"If you can't get good prices, hang onto it and age it. I wish you could see what the bars on Terra charge for a drink of ten-year-old Poictesme."

"This isn't Terra and we aren't selling it by the drink. Only place we can sell brandy is at Storisende spaceport, and we have to take what the trading-ship captains offer. You've been on a rich planet for the last five years, Conn. You've forgotten what it's like to live in a poorhouse. And that's what Poictesme is."

"Things'll be better from now on, Klem," the mayor said, putting one hand on the old man's shoulder and the other on Conn's. "Our boy's home. With what he can tell us, we'll be able to solve all our problems. Come on, let's go up and hear about it."

They entered the wide doorway of the warehouse on the dock-level floor of the Airport Building and crossed to the lift. About a dozen others had joined them, all the important men of Litchfield. Inside, Kurt Fawzi's laborers were floating out cargo for the ship--casks of brandy, of course, and a lot of boxes and crates painted light blue and marked with the wreathed globe of the Terran Federation and the gold triangle of the Third Fleet-Army Force and the eight-pointed red star of Ordnance Service. Long cases of rifles, square boxes of ammunition, machine guns, crated auto-cannon and rockets.

"Where'd that stuff come from?" Conn asked his father. "You dig it up?"

His father chuckled. "That happened since the last time I wrote you. Remember the big underground headquarters complex in the Calders? Everybody thought it had been all cleaned out years ago. You know, it's never a mistake to take a second look at anything that everybody believes. I found a lot of sealed-off sections over there that had never been entered. This stuff's from one of the headquarters defense armories. I have a gang getting the stuff out. Charley and I flew in after lunch, and I'm going back the first thing tomorrow."

"But there's enough combat equipment on hand to outfit a private army for every man, woman and child on Poictesme!" Conn objected. "Where are we going to sell this?"

"Storisende spaceport. The tramp freighters are buying it for newly colonized planets that haven't been industrialized yet. They don't pay much, but it doesn't cost much to get it out, and I've been clearing about three hundred sols a ton on the spaceport docks. That's not bad, you know."

Three hundred sols a ton. A lifter went by stacked with cases of M-504 submachine guns. Unloaded, one of them weighed six pounds, and even a used one was worth a hundred sols. Conn started to say something about that, but then they came to the lift and were crowding onto it.

He had been in Kurt Fawzi's office a few times, always with his father, and he remembered it as a dim, quiet place of genteel conviviality and rambling conversations, with deep, comfortable chairs and many ashtrays. Fawzi's warehouse and brokerage business, and the airline agency, and the government, such as it was, of Litchfield, combined, made few demands on his time and did not prevent the office from being a favored loafing center for the town's elders. The lights were bright only over the big table that served, among other things, as a desk, and the walls were almost invisible in the shadows.

As they came down the hallway from the lift, everybody had begun speaking more softly. Voices were never loud or excited in Kurt Fawzi's office.

Tom Brangwyn went to the table, taking off his belt and holster and laying his pistol aside. The others, crowding into the room, added their weapons to his.

That was something else Conn was seeing with new eyes. It had been five years since he had carried a gun and he was wondering why any of them bothered. A gun was what a boy put on to show that he had reached manhood, and a man carried for the rest of his life out of habit.

Why, there wouldn't be a shooting a year in Litchfield, if you didn't count the farm tramps and drifters, who kept to the lower level or camped in the empty buildings at the edge of town. Or maybe that was it; maybe Litchfield was peaceful because everybody was armed. It certainly wasn't because of anything the Planetary Government at Storisende did to maintain order.

After divesting himself of his gun, Tom Brangwyn took over the bartending, getting out glasses and filling a pitcher of brandy from a keg in the corner.

"Everybody supplied?" Fawzi was asking. "Well, let's drink to our returned emissary. We're all anxious to hear what you found out, Conn. Gentlemen, here's to our friend Conn Maxwell. Welcome home, Conn!"

"Well, it's wonderful to be back, Mr. Fawzi--"

"No, let's not have any of this mister foolishness! You're one of the gang now. And drink up, everybody. We have plenty of brandy, even if we don't have anything else."

"You telling us, Kurt?" somebody demanded. One of the distillery company; the name would come back to Conn in a moment. "When this crop gets pressed and fermented--"

"When I start pressing, I don't know where in Gehenna I'm going to vat the stuff till it ferments," Colonel Zareff said. "Or why. You won't be able to handle all of it."

"Now, now!" Fawzi reproved. "Let's not start moaning about our troubles. Not the day Conn's come home. Not when he's going to tell us how to find the Third Fleet-Army Force Brain."

"You *did* find out where the Brain is, didn't you, Conn?" Brangwyn asked anxiously.

That set half a dozen of them off at once. They had all sat down after the toast; now they were fidgeting in their chairs, leaning forward, looking at Conn fixedly.

"What did you find out, Conn?"

"It's still here on Poictesme, isn't it?"

"Did you find out where it is?"

He wanted to tell them in one quick sentence and get it over with. He couldn't, any more than he could force himself to squeeze the trigger of a pistol he knew would blow up in his hand.

"Wait a minute, gentlemen." He finished the brandy, and held out the glass to Tom Brangwyn, nodding toward the pitcher. Even the first drink had warmed him and he could feel the constriction easing in his throat and the lump at the pit of his stomach dissolving. "I hope none of you expect me to spread out a map and show you the cross on it, where the Brain is. I can't. I can't even give the approximate location of the thing."

Much of the happy eagerness drained out of the faces around him. Some of them were looking troubled; Colonel Zareff was gnawing the bottom of his mustache, and Judge Ledue's hand shook as he tried to relight his cigar. Conn stole a quick side-glance at his father; Rodney Maxwell was watching him curiously, as though wondering what he was going to say next.

"But it is still here on Poictesme?" Fawzi questioned. "They didn't take it away when they evacuated, did they?"

Conn finished his second drink. This time he picked up the pitcher and refilled for himself.

"I'm going to have to do a lot of talking," he said, "and it's going to be thirsty work. I'll have to tell you the whole thing from the beginning, and if you start asking questions at random, you'll get me mixed up and I'll miss the important points."

"By all means!" Judge Ledue told him. "Give it in your own words, in what you think is the proper order."

"Thank you, Judge."

Conn drank some more brandy, hoping he could get his courage up without getting drunk. After all, they had a right to a full report; all of them had contributed something toward sending him to Terra.

"The main purpose in my going to the University was to learn computer theory and practice. It wouldn't do any good for us to find the Brain if none of us are able to use it. Well, I learned enough to be able to operate, program and service any computer in existence, and train assistants. During my last year at the University, I had a part-time paid job programming the big positron-neutrino-photon computer in the astrophysics department. When I graduated, I was offered a position as instructor in positronic computer theory."

"You never mentioned that in your letters, son," his father said.

"It was too late for any letter except one that would come on the same ship I did. Beside, it wasn't very important."

"I think it was." There was a catch in old Professor Kellton's voice. "One of my boys, from the Academy, offered a place on the faculty of the University of Montevideo, on Terra!" He poured himself a second drink, something he almost never did.

"Conn means it wasn't important because it didn't have anything to do with the Brain," Fawzi explained and then looked at Conn expectantly.

All right; now he'd tell them. "I went over all the records of the Third Fleet-Army Force's occupation of Poictesme that are open to the public. On one pretext or another, I got permission to examine the non-classified files that aren't open to public examination. I even got a few peeps at some of the stuff that's still classified secret. I have maps and plans of all the installations that were built on this planet--literally thousands of them, many still undiscovered. Why, we haven't more than scratched the surface of what the Federation left behind here. For instance, all the important installations exist in duplicate, some even in triplicate, as a precaution against Alliance space attack."

"Space attack!" Colonel Zareff was indignant. "There never was a time when the Alliance could have taken the offensive against Poictesme, even if an offensive outside our own space-area had been part of our policy. We just didn't have the ships. It took over a year to move a million and a half troops from Ashmodai to Marduk, and the fleet that was based on Amaterasu was blasted out of existence in the spaceports and in orbit. Hell, at the time of the surrender, we didn't have--"

"They weren't taking chances on that, Colonel. But the point I want to make is that with everything I did find, I never found, in any official record, a single word about the giant computer we call the Third Fleet-Army Force Brain."

For a time, the only sound in the room was the tiny insectile humming of the electric clock on the wall. Then Professor Kellton set his glass on the table, and it sounded like a hammer-blow.

"Nothing, Conn?" Kurt Fawzi was incredulous and, for the first time, frightened. The others were exchanging uneasy glances. "But you must have! A thing like that--"

"Of course it would be one of the closest secrets during the war," somebody else said. "But in forty years, you'd expect *something* to leak out."

"Why, *during* the war, it was all through the Third Force. Even the Alliance knew about it; that's how Klem heard of it."

"Well, Conn couldn't just walk into the secret files and read whatever he wanted to. Just because he couldn't find anything--"

"Don't tell *me* about security!" Klem Zareff snorted. "Certainly they still have it classified; staff-brass'd rather lose an eye than declassify anything. If you'd seen the lengths our staff went to--hell, we lost battles because the staff wouldn't release information the troops in the field needed. I remember once--"

"But there *was* a Brain," Judge Ledue was saying, to reassure himself and draw agreement from the others. "It was capable of combining data, and scanning and evaluating all its positronic memories, and forming association patterns, and reasoning with absolute perfection. It was more than a positronic brain--it was a positronic super-mind."

"We'd have won the war, except for the Brain. We had ninety systems, a hundred and thirty inhabited planets, a hundred billion people--and we were on the defensive in our own space-area! Every move we made was known and anticipated by the Federation. How could they have done that without something like the Brain?"

"Conn, from what you learned of computers, how large a volume of space would you say the Brain would have to occupy?" Professor Kellton asked.

Professor Kellton was the most unworldly of the lot, yet he was asking the most practical question.

"Well, the astrophysics computer I worked with at the University occupies a total of about one million cubic feet," Conn began. This was his chance; they'd take anything he told them about computers as gospel. "It was only designed to handle problems in astrophysics. The Brain, being built for space war, would have to handle any such problem. And if half the stories about the Brain are anywhere near true, it handled any other problem--mathematical, scientific, political, economic, strategic, psychological, even philosophical and ethical. Well, I'd say that a hundred million cubic feet would be the smallest even conceivable."

They all nodded seriously. They were willing to accept that--or anything else, except one thing.

"Lot of places on this planet where a thing that size could be hidden," Tom Brangwyn said, undismayed. "A planet's a mighty big place."

"It could be under water, in one of the seas," Piet Dawes, the banker, suggested. "An underwater dome city wouldn't be any harder to build than a dome city on a poison-atmosphere planet like Tubal-Cain."

"It might even be on Tubal-Cain," a melon-planter said. "Or Hiawatha, or even one of the Beta or Gamma planets. The Third Force was occupying the whole Trisystem, you know." He thought for a moment. "If I'd been in charge, I'd have put it on one of the moons of Pantagruel."

"But that's clear out in the Alpha System," Judge Ledue objected. "We don't have a spaceship on the planet, certainly nothing with a hyperdrive engine. And it would take a lifetime to get out to the Gamma System and back on reaction drive."

Conn put his empty brandy glass on the table and sat erect. A new thought had occurred to him, chasing out of his mind all the worries and fears he had brought with him all the way from Terra.

"Then we'll have to build a ship," he said calmly. "I know, when the Federation evacuated Poictesme, they took every hyperdrive ship with them. But they had plenty of shipyards and spaceports on this planet, and I have maps showing the location of all of them, and barely a third of them have been discovered so far. I'm sure we can find enough hulks, and enough hyperfield generator parts, to assemble a ship or two, and I know we'll find the same or better on some of the other planets.

"And here's another thing," he added. "When we start looking into some of the dome-city plants on Tubal-Cain and Hiawatha and Moruna and Koshchei, we may find the plant or plants where the components for the Brain were fabricated, and if we do, we may find records of where they were shipped, and that'll be it."

"You're right!" Professor Kellton cried, quivering with excitement. "We've been hunting at random for the Brain, so it would only be an accident if we found it. We'll have to do this systematically, and with Conn to help us--Conn, why not build a computer? I don't mean another Brain; I mean a computer to help us find the Brain."

"We can, but we may not even need to build one. When we get out to the industrial planets, we may find one ready except for perhaps some minor alterations."

"But how are we going to finance all this?" Klem Zareff demanded querulously. "We're poorer than snakes, and even one hyperdrive ship's going to cost like Gehenna."

"I've been thinking about that, Klem," Fawzi said. "If we can find material at these shipyards Conn knows about, most of our expense will be labor. Well, haven't we ten workmen competing for every job? They don't really need money, only the things money can buy. We can raise food on the farms and provide whatever else they need out of Federation supplies."

"Sure. As soon as it gets around that we're really trying to do something about this, everybody'll want in on it," Tom Brangwyn predicted.

"And I have no doubt that the Planetary Government at Storisende will give us assistance, once we show that this is a practical and productive enterprise," Judge Ledue put in. "I have some slight influence with the President and--"

"I'm not too sure we want the Government getting into this," Kurt Fawzi replied. "Give them half a chance and that gang at Storisende'll squeeze us right out."

"We can handle this ourselves," Brangwyn agreed. "And when we get some kind of a ship and get out to the other two systems, or even just to Tubal-Cain or Hiawatha, first thing you know, we'll *be* the Planetary Government."

"Well, now, Tom," Fawzi began piously, "the Brain is too big a thing for a few of us to try to monopolize; it'll be for all Poictesme. Of course, it's only proper that we, who are making the effort to locate it, should have the direction of that effort...."

While Fawzi was talking, Rodney Maxwell went to the table, rummaged his pistol out of the pile and buckled it on. The mayor stopped short.

"You leaving us, Rod?"

"Yes, it's getting late. Conn and I are going for a little walk; we'll be at Senta's in half an hour. The fresh air will do both of us good and we have a lot to talk about. After all, we haven't seen each other for over five years."

They were silent, however, until they were away from the Airport Building and walking along High Garden Terrace in the direction of the Mall. Conn was glad; his own thoughts were weighing too heavily within him: I didn't do it. I was going to do it; every minute, I was going to do it, and I didn't, and now it's too late.

"That was quite a talk you gave them, son," his father said. "They believed every word of it. A couple of times, I even caught myself starting to believe it."

Conn stopped short. His father stopped beside him and stood looking at him.

"Why didn't you tell them the truth?" Rodney Maxwell asked.

The question angered Conn. It was what he had been asking himself.

"Why didn't I just grab a couple of pistols off the table and shoot the lot of them?" he retorted. "It would have killed them quicker and wouldn't have hurt as much."

His father took the cigar from his mouth and inspected the tip of it. "The truth must be pretty bad then. There is no Brain. Is that it, son?"

"There never was one. I'm not saying that only because I know it would be impossible to build such a computer. I'm telling you what the one man in the Galaxy who ought to know told me--the man who commanded the Third Force during the War."

"Foxx Travis! I didn't know he was still alive. You actually talked to him?"

"Yes. He's on Luna, keeping himself alive at low gravity. It took me a couple of years, and I was afraid he'd die before I got to him, but I finally managed to see him."

"What did he tell you?"

"That no such thing as the Brain ever existed." They started walking again, more slowly, toward the far edge of the terrace, with the sky red and orange in front of them. "The story was all through the Third Force, but it was just one of those wild tales that get started, nobody knows how, among troops. The High Command never denied or even discouraged it. It helped morale, and letting it leak to the enemy was good psychological warfare."

"Klem Zareff says that everybody in the Alliance army heard of the Brain," his father said. "That was why he came here in the first place." He puffed thoughtfully on his cigar. "You said a computer like the Brain would be an impossibility. Why? Wouldn't it be just another computer, only a lot bigger and a lot smarter?"

"Dad, computermen don't like to hear computers called smart," Conn said. "They aren't. The people who build them are smart; a computer only knows what's fed to it. They can hold more information in their banks than a man can in his memory, they can combine it faster, they don't get tired or absent-minded. But they can't imagine, they can't create, and they can't do anything a human brain can't."

"You know, I'd wondered about just that," said his father. "And none of the histories of the War even as much as mentioned the Brain. And I couldn't see why, after the War, they didn't build dozens of them to handle all these Galactic political and economic problems that nobody seems able to solve. A thing like the Brain wouldn't only be useful for war; the people here aren't trying to find it for war purposes."

"You didn't mention any of these doubts to the others, did you?"

"They were just doubts. You knew for sure, and you couldn't tell them."

"I'd come home intending to--tell them there was no Brain, tell them to stop wasting their time hunting for it and start trying to figure out the answers themselves. But I couldn't. They don't believe in the Brain as a tool, to use; it's a machine god that they can bring all their troubles to. You can't take a thing like that away from people without giving them something better."

"I noticed you suggested building a spaceship and agreed with the professor about building a computer. What was your idea? To take their minds off hunting for the Brain and keep them busy?"

Conn shook his head. "I'm serious about the ship--ships. You and Colonel Zareff gave me that idea."

His father looked at him in surprise. "I never said a word in there, and Klem didn't even once mention--"

"Not in Kurt's office; before we went up from the docks. There was Klem, moaning about a good year for melons as though it were a plague, and you selling arms and ammunition by the ton. Why, on Terra or Baldur or Uller, a glass of our brandy brings more than these freighter-captains give us for a cask, and what do you think a colonist on Agramma, or Sekht, or Hachiman, who has to fight for his life against savages and wild animals, would pay for one of those rifles and a thousand rounds of ammunition?"

His father objected. "We can't base the whole economy of a planet on brandy. Only about ten per cent of the arable land on Poictesme will grow wine-melons. And if we start exporting Federation salvage the way you talk of, we'll be selling pieces instead of job lots. We'll net more, but--"

"That's just to get us started. The ships will be used, after that, to get to Tubal-Cain and Hiawatha and the planets of the Beta and Gamma Systems. What I want to see is the mines and factories reopened, people employed, wealth being produced."

"And where'll we sell what we produce? Remember, the mines closed down because there was no more market."

"No more interstellar market, that's true. But there are a hundred and fifty million people on Poictesme. That's a big enough market and a big enough labor force to exploit the wealth of the Gartner Trisystem. We can have prosperity for everybody on our own resources. Just what do we need that we have to get from outside now?"

His father stopped again and sat down on the edge of a fountain--the same one, possibly, from which Conn had seen dust blowing as the airship had been coming in.

"Conn, that's a dangerous idea. That was what brought on the System States War. The Alliance planets took themselves outside the Federation economic orbit and the Federation crushed them."

Conn swore impatiently. "You've been listening to old Klem Zareff ranting about the Lost Cause and the greedy Terran robber barons holding the Galaxy in economic serfdom while they piled up profits. The Federation didn't fight that war for profits; there weren't any profits to fight for. They fought it because if the System States had won, half of them would be at war among themselves now. Make no mistake about it, politically I'm all for the Federation. But economically, I want to see our people exploiting their own resources for themselves, instead of grieving about lost interstellar trade, and bewailing bumper crops, and searching for a mythical robot god."

"You think, if you can get something like that started, that they'll forget about the Brain?" his father asked skeptically.

"That crowd up in Kurt Fawzi's office? Niflheim, no! They'll go on hunting for the Brain as long as they live, and every day they'll be expecting to find it tomorrow. That'll keep them happy. But they're all old men. The ones I'm interested in are the boys of Charley's age. I'm going to give them too many real things to do--building ships, exploring the rest of the Trisystem, opening mines and factories, producing wealth--for them to get caught in that empty old dream."

He looked down at the dusty fountain on which his father sat. "That ghost-dream haunts this graveyard. I want to give them living dreams that they can make come true."

Conn's father sat in silence for a while, his cigar smoke red in the sunset. "If you can do all that, Conn....You know, I believe you can. I'm with you, as far as I can help, and we'll have a talk with Charley. He's a good boy, Conn, and he has a lot of influence among the other youngsters." He looked at his watch. "We'd better be getting along. You don't want to be late for your own coming-home party."

Rodney Maxwell slid off the edge of the fountain to his feet, hitching at the gunbelt under his coat. Have to dig out his own gun and start wearing it, Conn thought. A man simply didn't go around in public without a gun in Litchfield. It wasn't decent. And he'd be spending a lot of time out in the brush, where he'd really need one.

First thing in the morning, he'd unpack that trunk and go over all those maps. There were half a dozen spaceports and maintenance shops and shipyards within a half-day by airboat, none of which had been looted. He'd look them all over; that would take a couple of weeks. Pick the best shipyard and concentrate on it. Kurt Fawzi'd be the man to recruit labor. Professor Kellton was a scholar, not a scientist. He didn't know beans about hyperdrive engines, but he knew how to do library research.

They came to the edge of High Garden Terrace at the escalator, long motionless, its moving parts rusted fast, that led down to the Mall, and at the bottom of it was Senta's, the tables under the open sky.

A crowd was already gathering. There was Tom Brangwyn, and there was Kurt Fawzi and his wife, and Lynne. And there was Senta herself, fat and dumpy, in one of her preposterous red-and-purple dresses, bustling about, bubbling happily one moment and screaming invective at some laggard waiter the next.

The dinner, Conn knew, would be the best he had eaten in five years, and afterward they would sit in the dim glow of Beta Gartner, sipping coffee and liqueurs, smoking and talking and visiting back and forth from one table to another, as they always did in the evenings at Senta's. Another bit from Eirrarsson's poem came back to him:

> *We sit in the twilight, the shadows among,*
> *And we talk of the happy days when we were brave and young.*

That was for the old ones, for Colonel Zareff and Judge Ledue and Dolf Kellton, maybe even for Tom Brangwyn and Franz Veltrin and for his father. But his brother Charley and the boys of his generation would have a future to talk about. And so would he, and Lynne Fawzi.

Ministry of Disturbance

By H. Beam Piper

Sometimes getting a job is harder than the job after you get it-and sometimes getting out of a job is harder than either!

The symphony was ending, the final triumphant pæan soaring up and up, beyond the limit of audibility. For a moment, after the last notes had gone away, Paul sat motionless, as though some part of him had followed. Then he roused himself and finished his coffee and cigarette, looking out the wide window across the city below-treetops and towers, roofs and domes and arching skyways, busy swarms of aircars glinting in the early sunlight. Not many people cared for João Coelho's music, now, and least of all for the Eighth Symphony. It was the music of another time, a thousand years ago, when the Empire was blazing into being out of the long night and hammering back the Neobarbarians from world after world. Today people found it perturbing.

He smiled faintly at the vacant chair opposite him, and lit another cigarette before putting the breakfast dishes on the serving-robot's tray, and, after a while, realized that the robot was still beside his chair, waiting for dismissal. He gave it an instruction to summon the cleaning robots and sent it away. He could as easily have summoned them himself, or let the guards who would be in checking the room do it for him, but maybe it made a robot feel trusted and important to relay orders to other robots.

Then he smiled again, this time in self-derision. A robot couldn't feel important, or anything else. A robot was nothing but steel and plastic and magnetized tape and photo-micro-positronic circuits, whereas a man-His Imperial Majesty Paul XXII, for instance-was nothing but tissues and cells and colloids and electro-neuronic circuits. There was a difference; anybody knew that. The trouble was that he had never met anybody-which included physicists, biologists, psychologists, psionicists, philosophers and theologians-who could define the difference in satisfactorily exact terms. He watched the robot pivot on its treads and glide away, trailing steam from its coffee pot. It might be silly to treat robots like people, but that wasn't as bad as treating people like robots, an attitude which was becoming entirely too prevalent. If only so many people didn't act like robots!

He crossed to the elevator and stood in front of it until a tiny electroencephalograph inside recognized his distinctive brain-wave pattern. Across the room, another door was popping open in response to the robot's distinctive wave pattern. He stepped inside and flipped a switch-there were still a few things around that had to be manually operated-and the door closed behind him and the elevator gave him an instant's weightlessness as it started to drop forty floors.

When it opened, Captain-General Dorflay of the Household Guard was waiting for him, with a captain and ten privates. General Dorflay was human. The captain and his ten soldiers weren't. They wore helmets, emblazoned with the golden sun and superimposed black cogwheel of the Empire, and red kilts and black ankle boots and weapons belts, and the captain had a narrow gold-laced cape over his shoulders, but for the rest, their bodies were covered with a stiff mat of black hair, and their faces were slightly like terriers'. (For all his humanity, Captain-General Dorflay's face was more like a bulldog's.) They were hillmen from the southern hemisphere of Thor, and as a people they made excellent mercenaries. They were crack shots, brave and crafty fighters, totally uninterested in politics off their own planet, and, because they had grown up in a patriarchial-clan society, they were fanatically loyal to anybody whom they accepted as their chieftain. Paul stepped out and gave them an inclusive nod.

"Good morning, gentlemen."

"Good morning, Your Imperial Majesty," General Dorflay said, bowing the couple of inches consistent with military dignity. The Thoran captain saluted by touching his forehead, his heart, which was on the right side, and the butt of his pistol. Paul complimented him on the smart appearance of his detail, and the captain asked how it could be otherwise, with the example and inspiration of his imperial majesty. Compliment and response could have been a playback from every morning of the ten years of his reign. So could Dorflay's question: "Your Majesty will proceed to his study?"

He wanted to say, "No, to Niffelheim with it; let's get an aircar and fly a million miles somewhere," and watch the look of shocked incomprehension on the captain-general's face. He couldn't do that, though; poor old Harv Dorflay might have a heart attack. He nodded slowly.

"If you please, general."

Dorflay nodded to the Thoran captain, who nodded to his men. Four of them took two paces forward; the rest, unslinging weapons, went scurrying up the corridor, some posting themselves along the way and the rest continuing to the main hallway. The captain and two of his men started forward slowly; after they had gone twenty feet, Paul and General Dorflay fell in behind them, and the other two brought up the rear.

"Your Majesty," Dorflay said, in a low voice, "let me beg you to be most cautious. I have just discovered that there exists a treasonous plot against your life."

Paul nodded. Dorflay was more than due to discover another treasonous plot; it had been ten days since the last one.

"I believe you mentioned it, general. Something about planting loose strontium-90 in the upholstery of the Audience Throne, wasn't it?"

And before that, somebody had been trying to smuggle a fission bomb into the Palace in a wine cask, and before that, it was a booby trap in the elevator, and before that, somebody was planning to build a submachine gun into the viewscreen in the study, and —

"Oh, no, Your Majesty; that was-Well, the persons involved in that plot became alarmed and fled the planet before I could arrest them. This is something different, Your Majesty. I have learned that unauthorized alterations have been made on one of the cooking-robots in your private kitchen, and I am positive that the object is to poison Your Majesty."

They were turning into the main hallway, between the rows of portraits of past emperors, Paul and Rodrik, Paul and Rodrik, alternating over and over on both walls. He felt a smile growing on his face, and banished it.

"The robot for the meat sauces, wasn't it?" he asked.

"Why —! Yes, Your Majesty."

"I'm sorry, general. I should have warned you. Those alterations were made by roboticists from the Ministry of Security; they were installing an adaptation of a device used in the criminalistics-labs, to insure more uniform measurements. They'd done that already for Prince Travann, the Minister, and he'd recommended it to me."

That was a shame, spoiling poor Harv Dorflay's murder plot. It had been such a nice little plot, too; he must have had a lot of fun inventing it. But a line had to be drawn somewhere. Let him turn the Palace upside down hunting for bombs; harass ladies-in-waiting whose lovers he suspected of being hired assassins; hound musicians into whose instruments he imagined firearms had been built; the emperor's private kitchen would have to be off limits.

Dorflay, who should have been looking crestfallen but relieved, stopped short-shocking breach of Court etiquette-and was staring in horror.

"Your Majesty! Prince Travann did that openly and with your consent? But, Your Majesty, I am convinced that it is Prince Travann himself who is the instigator of every one of these diabolical schemes. In the case of the elevator, I became suspicious of a man named Samml Ganner, one of Prince Travann's secret police agents. In the case of the gun in the viewscreen, it was a technician whose sister is a member of the household of Countess Yirzy, Prince Travann's mistress. In the case of the fission bomb——"

The two Thorans and their captain had kept on for some distance before they had discovered that they were no longer being followed, and were returning. He put his hand on General Dorflay's shoulder and urged him forward.

"Have you mentioned this to anybody?"

"Not a word, Your Majesty. This Court is so full of treachery that I can trust no one, and we must never warn the villain that he is suspected —"

"Good. Say nothing to anybody." They had reached the door of the study, now. "I think I'll be here until noon. If I leave earlier, I'll flash you a signal."

He entered the big oval room, lighted from overhead by the great star-map in the ceiling, and crossed to his desk, with the viewscreens and reading screens and communications screens around it, and as he sat down, he cursed angrily, first at Harv Dorflay and then, after a moment's reflection, at himself. He was the one to blame; he'd known Dorflay's paranoid condition for years. Have to do something about it. Any psycho-medic would certify him; be no problem at all to have him put away. But be blasted if he'd do that. That was no way to repay loyalty, even insane loyalty. Well, he'd find a way.

He lit a cigarette and leaned back, looking up at the glowing swirl of billions of billions of tiny lights in the ceiling. At least, there were supposed to be billions of billions of them; he'd never counted them, and neither had any of the seventeen Rodriks and sixteen Pauls before him who had sat under them. His hand moved to a control button on his chair arm, and a red patch, roughly the shape of a pork chop, appeared on the western side.

That was the Empire. Every one of the thousand three hundred and sixty-five inhabited worlds, a trillion and a half intelligent beings, fourteen races-fifteen if you counted the Zarathus-tran Fuzzies, who were almost able to qualify under the talk-and-build-a-fire rule. And that had been the Empire when Rodrik VI had seen the map completed, and when Paul II had built the Palace, and when Stevan IV, the grandfather of Paul I, had proclaimed Odin the Imperial planet and Asgard the capital city. There had been some excuse for staying inside that patch of stars then; a newly won Empire must be consolidated within before it can safely be expanded. But that had been over eight centuries ago.

He looked at the Daily Schedule, beautifully embossed and neatly slipped under his desk glass. Luncheon on the South Upper Terrace, with the Prime Minister and the Bench of Imperial Counselors. Yes, it was time for that again; that happened as inevitably and regularly as Harv Dorflay's murder plots. And in the afternoon, a Plenary Session, Cabinet and Counselors. Was he going to have to endure the Bench of Counselors twice in the same day? Then the vexation was washed out of his face by a spreading grin. Bench of Counselors; that was the answer! Elevate Harv Dorflay to the Bench. That was what the Bench was for, a gold-plated dustbin for the disposal of superannuated dignitaries. He'd do no harm there, and a touch of outright lunacy might enliven and even improve the Bench.

And in the evening, a banquet, and a reception and ball, in honor of His Majesty Ranulf XIV, Planetary King of Durendal, and First Citizen Zhorzh Yaggo, People's Manager-in-Chief of and for the Planetary Commonwealth of Aditya. Bargain day; two planetary chiefs of state in one big combination deal. He wondered what sort of prizes he had drawn this time, and closed his eyes, trying to remember. Durendal, of course, was one of the Sword-Worlds, settled by refugees from the losing side of the System States War in the time of the old Terran Federation, who had reappeared in Galactic history a few centuries later as the Space Vikings. They all had monarchial and rather picturesque governments; Durendal, he seemed to recall, was a sort of quasi-feudalism. About Aditya he was less sure. Something unpleasant, he thought; the titles of the government and its head were suggestive.

He lit another cigarette and snapped on the reading screen to see what they had piled onto him this morning, and then swore when a graph chart, with jiggling red and blue and green lines, appeared. Chart day, too. Everything happens at once.

It was the interstellar trade situation chart from Economics. Red line for production, green line for exports, blue for imports, sectioned vertically for the ten Viceroyalties and sub-sectioned for the Prefectures, and with the magnification and focus controls he could even get data for individual planets. He didn't bother with that, and wondered why he bothered with the charts at all. The stuff was all at least twenty days behind date, and not uniformly so, which accounted for much of the jiggling. It had been transmitted from Planetary Proconsulate to Prefecture, and from Prefecture to Viceroyalty, and from there to Odin, all by ship. A ship on hyperdrive could log light-years an hour, but radio waves still had to travel 186,000 mps. The supplementary chart for the past five centuries told the real story-three perfectly level and perfectly parallel lines.

It was the same on all the other charts. Population fluctuating slightly at the moment, completely static for the past five centuries. A slight decrease in agriculture, matched by an increase in synthetic food production. A slight population movement toward the more urban planets and the more densely populated centers. A trend downward in employment-nonworking population increasing by about .0001 per cent annually. Not that they were building better robots; they were just building them faster than they wore out. They all told the same story —a stable economy, a static population, a peaceful and undisturbed Empire; eight centuries, five at least, of historyless tranquility. Well, that was what everybody wanted, wasn't it?

He flipped through the rest of the charts, and began getting summarized Ministry reports. Economics had denied a request from the Mining Cartel to authorize operations on a couple of uninhabited planets; danger of local market gluts and overstimulation of manufacturing. Permission granted to Robotics Cartel to —— Request from planetary government of Durendal for increase of cereal export quotas under consideration-they wouldn't want to turn that down while King Ranulf was here. Impulsively, he punched out a combination on the communication screen and got Count Duklass, Minister of Economics.

Count Duklass had thinning red hair and a plump, agreeable, extrovert's face. He smiled and waited to be addressed.

"Sorry to bother Your Lordship," Paul greeted him. "What's the story on this export quota request from Durendal? We have their king here, now. Think he's come to lobby for it?"

Count Duklass chuckled. "He's not doing anything about it, himself. Have you met him yet, sir?"

"Not yet. He's to be presented this evening."

"Well, when you see him —I think the masculine pronoun is permissible-you'll see what I mean, sir. It's this Lord Koreff, the Marshal. He came here on business, and had to bring the king along, for fear somebody else would grab him while he was gone. The whole object of Durendalian politics, as I understand, is to get possession of the person of the king. Koreff was on my screen for half an hour; I just got rid of him. Planet's pretty heavily agricultural, they had a couple of very good crop years in a row, and now they have grain running out their ears, and they want to export it and cash in."

"Well?"

"Can't let them do it, Your Majesty. They're not suffering any hardship; they're just not making as much money as they think they ought to. If they start dumping their surplus into interstellar trade, they'll cause all kinds of dislocations on other agricultural planets. At least, that's what our computers all say."

And that, of course, was gospel. He nodded.

"Why don't they turn their surplus into whisky? Age it five or six years and it'd be on the luxury goods schedule and they could sell it anywhere."

Count Duklass' eyes widened. "I never thought of that, Your Majesty. Just a microsec; I want to make a note of that. Pass it down to somebody who could deal with it. That's a wonderful idea, Your Majesty!"

He finally got the conversation to an end, and went back to the reports. Security, as usual, had a few items above the dead level of bureaucratic procedure. The planetary king of Excalibur had been assassinated by his brother and two nephews, all three of whom were now fighting among themselves. As nobody had anything to fight with except small arms and a few light cannon, there would be no intervention. There had been intervention on Behemoth, however, where a whole continent had tried to secede from the planetary republic and the Imperial Navy had been requested to send a task force. That was all right, in both cases. No interference with anything that passed for a planetary government, but only one sovereignty on any planet with nuclear weapons, and only one supreme sovereignty in a galaxy with hyperdrive ships.

And there was rioting on Amaterasu, because of public indignation over a fraudulent election. He looked at that in incredulous delight. Why, here on Odin there hadn't been an election in the past six centuries that hadn't been utterly fraudulent. Nobody voted except the nonworkers, whose votes were bought and sold wholesale, by gangster bosses to pressure groups, and no decent person would be caught within a hundred yards of a polling place on an election day. He called the Minister of Security.

Prince Travann was a man of his own age-they had been classmates at the University-but he looked older. His thin face was lined, and his hair was almost completely white. He was at his desk, with the Sun and Cogwheel of the Empire on the wall behind him, but on the breast of his black tunic he wore the badge of his family, a silver planet with three silver moons. Unlike Count Duklass, he didn't wait to be spoken to.

"Good morning, Your Majesty."

"Good morning, Your Highness; sorry to bother you. I just caught an interesting item in your report. This business on Amaterasu. What sort of a planet is it, politically? I don't seem to recall."

"Why, they have a republican government, sir; a very complicated setup. Really, it's a junk heap. When anything goes badly, they always build something new into the government, but they never abolish anything. They have a president, a premier, and an executive cabinet, and a tricameral legislature, and two complete and distinct judiciaries. The premier is always the presidential candidate getting the next highest number of votes. In the present instance, the president, who controls the planetary militia, is accusing the premier, who controls the police, of fraud in the election of the middle house of the legislature. Each is supported by the judiciary he controls. Practically every citizen belongs either to the militia or the police auxiliaries. I am looking forward to further reports from Amaterasu," he added dryly.

"I daresay they'll be interesting. Send them to me in full, and red-star them, if you please, Prince Travann."

He went back to the reports. The Ministry of Science and Technology had sent up a lengthy one. The only trouble with it was that everything reported was duplication of work that had been done centuries before. Well, no. A Dr. Dandrik, of the physics department of the Imperial University here in Asgard announced that a definite limit of accuracy in measuring the velocity of accelerated subnucleonic particles had been established —16.067543333 —times light-speed. That seemed to be typical; the frontiers of science, now, were all decimal points. The Ministry of Education had a little to offer; historical scholarship was still active, at least. He was reading about a new trove of source-material that had come to light on Uller, from the Sixth Century Atomic Era, when the door screen buzzed and flashed.

He lit it, and his son Rodrik appeared in it, with Snooks, the little red hound, squirming excitedly in the Crown Prince's arms. The dog began barking at once, and the boy called through the phone:

"Good morning, father; are you busy?"

"Oh, not at all." He pressed the release button. "Come on in."

Immediately, the little hound leaped out of the princely arms and came dashing into the study and around the desk, jumping onto his lap. The boy followed more slowly, sitting down in the deskside chair and drawing his foot up under him. Paul greeted Snooks first-people can wait, but for little dogs everything has to be right now-and rummaged in a drawer until he found some wafers, holding one for Snooks to nibble. Then he became aware that his son was wearing leather shorts and tall buskins.

"Going out somewhere?" he asked, a trifle enviously.

"Up in the mountains, for a picnic. Olva's going along."

And his tutor, and his esquire, and Olva's companion-lady, and a dozen Thoran riflemen, of course, and they'd be in continuous screen-contact with the Palace.

"That ought to be a lot of fun. Did you get all your lessons done?"

"Physics and math and galactiography," Rodrik told him. "And Professor Guilsan's going to give me and Olva our history after lunch."

They talked about lessons, and about the picnic. Of course, Snooks was going on the picnic, too. It was evident, though, that Rodrik had something else on his mind. After a while, he came out with it.

"Father, you know I've been a little afraid, lately," he said.

"Well, tell me about it, son. It isn't anything about you and Olva, is it?"

Rod was fourteen; the little Princess Olva thirteen. They would be marriageable in six years. As far as anybody could tell, they were both quite happy about the marriage which had been arranged for them years ago.

"Oh, no; nothing like that. But Olva's sister and a couple others of mother's ladies-in-waiting were to a psi-medium, and the medium told them that there were going to be changes. Great and frightening changes was what she said."

"She didn't specify?"

"No. Just that: great and frightening changes. But the only change of that kind I can think of would be ...well, something happening to you."

Snooks, having eaten three wafers, was trying to lick his ear. He pushed the little dog back into his lap and pummeled him gently with his left hand.

"You mustn't let mediums' gabble worry you, son. These psi-mediums have real powers, but they can't turn them off and on like a water tap. When they don't get anything, they don't like to admit it, and they invent things. Always generalities like that; never anything specific."

"I know all that." The boy seemed offended, as though somebody were explaining that his mother hadn't really found him out in the rose garden. "But they talked about it to some of their friends, and it seems that other mediums are saying the same thing. Father, do you remember when the Haval Valley reactor blew up? All over Odin, the mediums had been talking about a terrible accident, for a month before that happened."

"I remember that." Harv Dorflay believed that somebody had been falsely informed that the emperor would visit the plant that day. "These great and frightening changes will probably turn out to be a new fad in abstract sculpture. Any change frightens most people."

They talked more about mediums, and then about aircars and aircar racing, and about the Emperor's Cup race that was to be flown in a month. The communications screen began flashing and buzzing, and after he had silenced it with the busy-button for the third time, Rodrik said that it was time for him to go, came around to gather up Snooks, and went out, saying that he'd be home in time for the banquet. The screen began to flash again as he went out.

It was Prince Ganzay, the Prime Minister. He looked as though he had a persistent low-level toothache, but that was his ordinary expression.

"Sorry to bother Your Majesty. It's about these chiefs-of-state. Count Gadvan, the Chamberlain, appealed to me, and I feel I should ask your advice. It's the matter of precedence."

"Well, we have a fixed rule on that. Which one arrived first?"

"Why, the Adityan, but it seems King Ranulf insists that he's entitled to precedence, or, rather, his Lord Marshal does. This Lord Koreff insists that his king is not going to yield precedence to a commoner."

"Then he can go home to Durendal!" He felt himself growing angry-all the little angers of the morning were focusing on one spot. He forced the harshness out of his voice. "At a court function, somebody has to go first, and our rule is order of arrival at the Palace. That rule was established to avoid violating the principle of equality to all civilized peoples and all planetary governments. We're not going to set it aside for the King of Durendal, or anybody else."

Prince Ganzay nodded. Some of the toothache expression had gone out of his face, now that he had been relieved of the decision.

"Of course, Your Majesty." He brightened a little. "Do you think we might compromise? Alternate the precedence, I mean?"

"Only if this First Citizen Yaggo consents. If he does, it would be a good idea."

"I'll talk to him, sir." The toothache expression came back. "Another thing, Your Majesty. They've both been invited to attend the Plenary Session, this afternoon."

"Well, no trouble there; they can enter by different doors and sit in visitors' boxes at opposite ends of the hall."

"Well, sir, I wasn't thinking of precedence. But this is to be an Elective Session-new Ministers to replace Prince Havaly, of Defense, deceased, and Count Frask, of Science and Technology, elevated to the Bench. There seems to be some difference of opinion among some of the Ministers and Counselors. It's very possible that the Session may degenerate into an outright controversy."

"Horrible," Paul said seriously. "I think, though, that our distinguished guests will see that the Empire can survive difference of opinion, and even outright controversy. But if you think it might have a bad effect, why not postpone the election?"

"Well-It's been postponed three times, already, sir."

"Postpone it permanently. Advertise for bids on two robot Ministers, Defense, and Science and Technology. If they're a success, we can set up a project to design a robot emperor."

The Prime Minister's face actually twitched and blanched at the blasphemy. "Your Majesty is joking," he said, as though he wanted to be reassured on the point.

"Unfortunately, I am. If my job could be robotized, maybe I could take my wife and my son and our little dog and go fishing for a while."

But, of course, he couldn't. There were only two alternatives: the Empire or Galactic anarchy. The galaxy was too big to hold general elections, and there had to be a supreme ruler, and a positive and automatic-which meant hereditary-means of succession.

"Whose opinion seems to differ from whose, and about what?" he asked.

"Well, Count Duklass and Count Tammsan want to have the Ministry of Science and Technology abolished, and its functions and personnel distributed. Count Duklass means to take over the technological sections under Economics, and Count Tammsan will take over the science part under Education. The proposal is going to be introduced at this Session by Count Guilfred, the Minister of Health and Sanity. He hopes to get some of the bio-and psycho-science sections for his own Ministry."

"That's right. Duklass gets the hide, Tammsan gets the head and horns, and everybody who hunts with them gets a cut of the meat. That's good sound law of the chase. I'm not in favor of it, myself. Prince Ganzay, at this session, I wish you'd get Captain-General Dorflay nominated for the Bench. I feel that it is about time to honor him with elevation."

"General Dorflay? But why, Your Majesty?"

"Great galaxy, do you have to ask? Why, because the man's a raving lunatic. He oughtn't even to be trusted with a sidearm, let alone five companies of armed soldiers. Do you know what he told me this morning?"

"That somebody is training a Nidhog swamp-crawler to crawl up the Octagon Tower and bite you at breakfast, I suppose. But hasn't that been going on for quite a while, sir?"

"It was a gimmick in one of the cooking robots, but that's aside from the question. He's finally named the master mind behind all these nightmares of his, and who do you think it is? Yorn Travann!"

The Prime Minister's face grew graver than usual. Well, it was something to look grave about; some of these days — —

"Your Majesty, I couldn't possibly agree more about the general's mental condition, but I really should say that, crazy or not, he is not alone in his suspicions of Prince Travann. If sharing them makes me a lunatic, too, so be it, but share them I do."

Paul felt his eyebrows lift in surprise. "That's quite too much and too little, Prince Ganzay," he said.

"With your permission, I'll elaborate. Don't think that I suspect Prince Travann of any childish pranks with elevators or viewscreens or cooking-robots," the Prime Minister hastened to disclaim, "but I definitely do suspect him of treasonous ambitions. I suppose Your Majesty knows that he is the first Minister of Security in centuries who has assumed personal control of both the planetary and municipal police, instead of delegating his *ex officio* powers.

"Your Majesty may not know, however, of some of the peculiar uses he has been making of those authorities. Does Your Majesty know that he has recruited the Security Guard up to at least ten times the strength needed to meet any conceivable peace-maintenance problem on this planet, and that he has been piling up huge quantities of heavy combat equipment-guns up to 200-millimeter, heavy contragravity, even gun-cutters and bomb-and-rocket boats? And does Your Majesty know that most of this armament is massed within fifteen minutes' flight-time of this Palace? Or that Prince Travann has at his disposal from two and a half to three times, in men and firepower, the combined strength of the Planetary Militia and the Imperial Army on this planet?"

"I know. It has my approval. He's trying to salvage some of the young nonworkers through exposing them to military discipline. A good many of them, I believe, have gone off-planet on their discharge from the SG and hired as mercenaries, which is a far better profession than vote selling."

"Quite a plausible explanation: Prince Travann is nothing if not plausible," the Prime Minister agreed. "And does Your Majesty know that, because of repeated demands for support from the Ministry of Security, the Imperial Navy has been scattered all over the Empire, and that there is not a naval craft bigger than a scout-boat within fifteen hundred light-years of Odin?"

That was absolutely true. Paul could only nod agreement. Prince Ganzay continued:

"He has been doing some peculiar things as Police Chief of Asgard, too. For instance, there are two powerful nonworkers' voting-bloc bosses, Big Moogie Blisko and Zikko the Nose —I assure Your Majesty that I am not inventing these names; that's what the persons are actually called-who have been enjoying the favor and support of Prince Travann. On a number of occasions, their smaller rivals, leaders of less important gangs, have been arrested, often on trumped-up charges, and held incommunicado until either Moogie or Zikko could move into their territories and annex their nonworker followers. These two bloc-bosses are subsidized, respectively, by the Steel and Shipbuilding Cartels and by the Reaction Products and Chemical Cartels, but actually, they are controlled by Prince Travann. They, in turn, control between them about seventy per cent of the nonworkers in Asgard."

"And you think this adds up to a plot against the Throne?"

"A plot to seize the Throne, Your Majesty."

"Oh, come, Prince Ganzay! You're talking like Dorflay!"

"Hear me out, Your Majesty. His Imperial Highness is fourteen years old; it will be eleven years before he will be legally able to assume the powers of emperor. In the dreadful event of your immediate death, it would mean a regency for that long. Of course, your Ministers and Counselors would be the ones to name the Regent, but I know how they would vote with Security Guard bayonets at their throats. And regency might not be the limit of Prince Travann's ambitions."

"In your own words, quite plausible, Prince Ganzay. It rests, however, on a very questionable foundation. The assumption that Prince Travann is stupid enough to want the Throne."

He had to terminate the conversation himself and blank the screen. Viktor Ganzay was still staring at him in shocked incredulity when his image vanished. Viktor Ganzay could not imagine anybody not wanting the Throne, not even the man who had to sit on it.

He sat, for a while, looking at the darkened screen, a little worried. Viktor Ganzay had a much better intelligence service than he had believed. He wondered how much Ganzay had found out that he hadn't mentioned. Then he went back to the reports. He had gotten down to the Ministry of Fine Arts when the communications screen began calling attention to itself again.

When he flipped the switch, a woman smiled out of it at him. Her blond hair was rumpled, and she wore a dressing gown; her smile brightened as his face appeared in her screen.

"Hi!" she greeted him.

"Hi, yourself. You just get up?"

She raised a hand to cover a yawn. "I'll bet you've been up reigning for hours. Were Rod and Snooks in to see you yet?"

He nodded. "They just left. Rod's going on a picnic with Olva in the mountains." How long had it been since he and Marris had been on a picnic —a real picnic, with less than fifty guards and as many courtiers along? "Do you have much reigning to do, this afternoon?"

She grimaced. "Flower Festivals. I have to make personal tri-di appearances, live, with messages for the loving subjects. Three minutes on, and a two-minute break between. I have forty for this afternoon."

"Ugh! Well, have a good time, sweetheart. All I have is lunch with the Bench, and then this Plenary Session." He told her about Ganzay's fear of outright controversy.

"Oh, fun! Maybe somebody'll pull somebody's whiskers, or something. I'm in on that, too."

The call-indicator in front of him began glowing with the code-symbol of the Minister of Security.

"We can always hope, can't we? Well, Yorn Travann's trying to get me, now."

"Don't keep him waiting. Maybe I can see you before the Session." She made a kissing motion with her lips at him, and blanked the screen.

He flipped the switch again, and Prince Travann was on the screen. The Security Minister didn't waste time being sorry to bother him.

"Your Majesty, a report's just come in that there's a serious riot at the University; between five and ten thousand students are attacking the Administration Center, lobbing stench bombs into it, and threatening to hang Chancellor Khane. They have already overwhelmed and disarmed the campus police, and I've sent two companies of the Gendarme riot brigade, under an officer I can trust to handle things firmly but intelligently. We don't want any indiscriminate stunning or tear-gassing or shooting; all sorts of people can have sons and daughters mixed up in a student riot."

"Yes. I seem to recall student riots in which the sons of his late Highness Prince Travann and his late Majesty Rodrik XXI were involved." He deliberated the point for a moment, and added: "This scarcely sounds like a frat-fight or a panty-raid, though. What seems to have triggered it?"

"The story I got —a rather hysterical call for help from Khane himself-is that they're protesting an action of his in dismissing a faculty member. I have a couple of undercovers at the University, and I'm trying to contact them. I sent more undercovers, who could pass for students, ahead of the Gendarmes to get the student side of it and the names of the ring-leaders." He glanced down at the indicator in front of him, which had begun to glow. "If you'll pardon me, sir, Count Tammsan's trying to get me. He may have particulars. I'll call Your Majesty back when I learn anything more."

There hadn't been anything like that at the University within the memory of the oldest old grad. Chancellor Khane, he knew, was a stupid and arrogant old windbag with a swollen sense of his own importance. He made a small bet with himself that the whole thing was Khane's fault, but he wondered what lay behind it, and what would come out of it. Great plagues from little microbes start. Great and frightening changes — —

The screen got itself into an uproar, and he flipped the switch. It was Viktor Ganzay again. He looked as though his permanent toothache had deserted him for the moment.

"Sorry to bother Your Majesty, but it's all fixed up," he reported. "First Citizen Yaggo agreed to alternate in precedence with King Ranulf, and Lord Koreff has withdrawn all his objections. As far as I can see, at present, there should be no trouble."

"Fine. I suppose you heard about the excitement at the University?"

"Oh, yes, Your Majesty. Disgraceful affair!"

"Simply shocking. What seems to have started it, have you heard?" he asked. "All I know is that the students were protesting the dismissal of a faculty member. He must have been exceptionally popular, or else he got a more than ordinary raw deal from Khane."

"Well, as to that, sir, I can't say. All I learned was that it was the result of some faculty squabble in one of the science departments; the grounds for the dismissal were insubordination and contempt for authority."

"I always thought that when authority began inspiring contempt, it had stopped being authority. Did you say science? This isn't going to help Duklass and Tammsan any."

"I'm afraid not, Your Majesty." Ganzay didn't look particularly regretful. "The News Cartel's gotten hold of it and are using it; it'll be all over the Empire."

He said that as though it meant something. Well, maybe it did; a lot of Ministers and almost all the Counselors spent most of their time worrying about what people on planets like Chermosh and Zarathustra and Deirdre and Quetzalcoatl might think, in ignorance of the fact that interest in Empire politics varied inversely as the square of the distance to Odin and the level of corruption and inefficiency of the local government.

"I notice you'll be at the Bench luncheon. Do you think you could invite our guests, too? We could have an informal presentation before it starts. Can do? Good. I'll be seeing you there."

When the screen was blanked, he returned to the reports, ran them off hastily to make sure that nothing had been red-starred, and called a robot to clear the projector. After a while, Prince Travann called again.

"Sorry to bother Your Majesty, but I have most of the facts on the riot, now. What happened was that Chancellor Khane sacked a professor, physics department, under circumstances which aroused resentment among the science students. Some of them walked out of class and went to the stadium to hold a protest meeting, and the thing snowballed until half the students were in it. Khane lost his head and ordered the campus police to clear the stadium; the students rushed them and swamped them. I hope, for their sakes, that none of my men ever let anything like that happen. The man I sent, a Colonel Handrosan, managed to talk the students into going back to the stadium and continuing the meeting under Gendarme protection."

"Sounds like a good man."

"Very good, Your Majesty. Especially in handling disturbances. I have complete confidence in him. He's also investigating the background of the affair. I'll give Your Majesty what he's learned, to date. It seems that the head of the physics department, a Professor Nelse Dandrik, had been conducting an experiment, assisted by a Professor Klenn Faress, to establish more accurately the velocity of subnucleonic particles, beta micropositos, I believe. Dandrik's story, as relayed to Handrosan by Khane, is that he reached a limit and the apparatus began giving erratic results."

Prince Travann stopped to light a cigarette. "At this point, Professor Dandrik ordered the experiment stopped, and Professor Faress insisted on continuing. When Dandrik ordered the apparatus dismantled, Faress became rather emotional about it-obscenely abusive and threatening, according to Dandrik. Dandrik complained to Khane, Khane ordered Faress to apologize, Faress refused, and Khane dismissed Faress. Immediately, the students went on strike. Faress confirmed the whole story, and he added one small detail that Dandrik hadn't seen fit to mention. According to him, when these micropositos were accelerated beyond sixteen and a fraction times light-speed, they began registering at the target before the source registered the emission."

"Yes, I—*What did you say?*"

Prince Travann repeated it slowly, distinctly and tonelessly.

"That was what I thought you said. Well, I'm going to insist on a complete investigation, including a repetition of the experiment. Under direction of Professor Faress."

"Yes, Your Majesty. And when that happens, I mean to be on hand personally. If somebody is just before discovering time-travel, I think Security has a very substantial interest in it."

The Prime Minister called back to confirm that First Citizen Yaggo and King Ranulf would be at the luncheon. The Chamberlain, Count Gadvan, called with a long and dreary problem about the protocol for the banquet. Finally, at noon, he flashed a signal for General Dorflay, waited five minutes, and then left his desk and went out, to find the mad general and his wirehaired soldiers drawn up in the hall.

There were more Thorans on the South Upper Terrace, and after a flurry of porting and presenting and ordering arms and hand-saluting, the Prime Minister advanced and escorted him to where the Bench of Counselors, all thirty of them, total age close to twenty-eight hundred years, were drawn up in a rough crescent behind the three distinguished guests. The King of Durendal wore a cloth-of-silver leotard and pink tights, and a belt of gold links on which he carried a jeweled dagger only slightly thicker than a knitting needle. He was slender and willowy, and he had large and soulful eyes, and the royal beautician must have worked on him for a couple of hours. Wait till Marris sees this; oh, brother!

Koreff, the Lord Marshal, wore what was probably the standard costume of Durendal, a fairly long jerkin with short sleeves, and knee-boots, and his dress dagger looked as though it had been designed for use. Lord Koreff looked as though he would be quite willing and able to use it; he was fleshy and full-faced, with hard muscles under the flesh.

First Citizen Yaggo, People's Manager-in-Chief of and for the Planetary Commonwealth of Aditya, wore a one-piece white garment like a mechanic's coveralls, with the emblem of his government and the numeral 1 on his breast. He carried no dagger; if he had worn a dress weapon, it would probably have been a slide rule. His head was completely shaven, and he had small, pale eyes and a rat-trap mouth. He was regarding the Durendalians with a distaste that was all too evidently reciprocated.

King Ranulf appeared to have won the toss for first presentation. He squeezed the Imperial hand in both of his and looked up adoringly as he professed his deep honor and pleasure. Yaggo merely clasped both his hands in front of the emblem on his chest and raised them quickly to the level of his chin, saying: "At the service of the Imperial State," and adding, as though it hurt him, "Your Imperial Majesty." Not being a chief of state, Lord Koreff came third; he merely shook hands and said, "A great honor, Your Imperial Majesty, and the thanks, both of myself and my royal master, for a most gracious reception." The attempt to grab first place having failed, he was more than willing to forget the whole subject. There was a chance that finding a way to dispose of the grain surplus might make the difference between his staying in power at home or not.

Fortunately, the three guests had already met the Bench of Counselors. Immediately after the presentation of Lord Koreff, they all started the two hundred yards march to the luncheon pavilion, the King of Durendal clinging to his left arm and First Citizen Yaggo stumping dourly on his right, with Prince Ganzay beyond him and Lord Koreff on Ranulf's left.

"Do you plan to stay long on Odin?" he asked the king.

"Oh. I'd *love* to stay for simply *months*! Everything is so *wonderful*, here in Asgard; it makes our little capital of Roncevaux seem so *utterly* provincial. I'm going to tell Your Imperial Majesty a secret. I'm going to see if I can lure some of your *wonderful* ballet dancers back to Durendal with me. Aren't I *naughty*, raiding Your Imperial Majesty's theaters?"

"In keeping with the traditions of your people," he replied gravely. "You Sword-Worlders used to raid everywhere you went."

"I'm afraid those bad old days are long past, Your Imperial Majesty," Lord Koreff said. "But we Sword-Worlders got around the galaxy, for a while. In fact, I seem to remember reading that some of our brethren from Morglay or Flamberge even occupied Aditya for a couple of centuries. Not that you'd guess it to look at Aditya now."

It was First Citizen Yaggo's turn to take precedence-the seat on the right of the throne chair. Lord Koreff sat on Ranulf's left, and, to balance him, Prince Ganzay sat beyond Yaggo and dutifully began inquiring of the People's Manager-in-Chief about the structure of his government, launching him on a monologue that promised to last at least half the luncheon. That left the King of Durendal to Paul; for a start, he dropped a compliment on the cloth-of-silver leotard.

King Ranulf laughed dulcetly, brushed the garment with his fingertips, and said that it was just a simple thing patterned after the Durendalian peasant costume.

"You have peasants on Durendal?"

"Oh, *dear*, yes! Such quaint, *charming* people. Of course, they're all poor, and they wear such *funny* ragged clothes, and travel about in rackety old aircars, it's a wonder they don't fall apart in the air. But they're so *wonderfully* happy and carefree. I often wish I were one of them, instead of king."

"Nonworking class, Your Imperial Majesty," Lord Koreff explained.

"On Aditya," First Citizen Yaggo declared, "there are no classes, and on Aditya everybody works. 'From each according to his ability; to each according to his need.'"

"On Aditya," an elderly Counselor four places to the right of him said loudly to his neighbor, "they don't call them classes, they call them sociological categories, and they have nineteen of them. And on Aditya, they don't call them nonworkers, they call them occupational reservists, and they have more of them than we do."

"But of course, I was born a king," Ranulf said sadly and nobly. "I have a duty to my people."

"No, they don't vote at all," Lord Koreff was telling the Counselor on his left. "On Durendal, you have to pay taxes before you can vote."

"On Aditya the crime of taxation does not exist," the First Citizen told the Prime Minister.

"On Aditya," the Counselor four places down said to his neighbor, "there's nothing to tax. The state owns all the property, and if the Imperial Constitution and the Space Navy let them, the State would own all the people, too. Don't tell me about Aditya. First big-ship command I had was the old *Invictus*, 374, and she was based on Aditya for four years, and I'd sooner have spent that time in orbit around Niffelheim."

Now Paul remembered who he was; old Admiral-now Prince-Counselor —Gaklar. He and Prince-Counselor Dorflay would get along famously. The Lord Marshal of Durendal was replying to some objection somebody had made:

"No, nothing of the sort. We hold the view that every civil or political right implies a civil or political obligation. The citizen has a right to protection from the Realm, for instance; he therefore has the obligation to defend the Realm. And his right to participate in the government of the Realm includes his obligation to support the Realm financially. Well, we tax only property; if a nonworker acquires taxable property, he has to go to work to earn the taxes. I might add that our nonworkers are very careful to avoid acquiring taxable property."

"But if they don't have votes to sell, what do they live on?" a Counselor asked in bewilderment.

"The nobility supports them; the landowners, the trading barons, the industrial lords. The more nonworking adherents they have, the greater their prestige." And the more rifles they could muster when they quarreled with their fellow nobles, of course. "Beside, if we didn't do that, they'd turn brigand, and it costs less to support them than to have to hunt them out of the brush and hang them."

"On Aditya, brigandage does not exist."

"On Aditya, all the brigands belong to the Secret Police, only on Aditya they don't call them Secret Police, they call them Servants of the People, Ninth Category."

A shadow passed quickly over the pavilion, and then another. He glanced up quickly, to see two long black troop carriers, emblazoned with the Sun and Cogwheel and armored fist of Security, pass back of the Octagon Tower and let down on the north landing stage. A third followed. He rose quickly.

"Please remain seated, gentlemen, and continue with the luncheon. If you will excuse me for a moment, I'll be back directly." I hope, he added mentally.

Captain-General Dorflay, surrounded by a dozen officers, Thoran and human, had arrived on the lower terrace at the base of the Octagon Tower. They had a full Thoran rifle company with them. As he went down to them, Dorflay hurried forward.

"It has come, Your Majesty!" he said, as soon as he could make himself heard without raising his voice. "We are all ready to die with Your Majesty!"

"Oh, I doubt it'll come quite to that, Harv," he said. "But just to be on the safe side, take that company and the gentlemen who are with you and get up to the mountains and join the Crown Prince and his party. Here." He took a notepad from his belt pouch and wrote rapidly, sealing the note and giving it to Dorflay. "Give this to His Highness, and place yourself under his orders. I know; he's just a boy, but he has a good head. Obey him exactly in everything, but under no circumstances return to the Palace or allow him to return until I call you."

"Your Majesty is ordering me away?" The old soldier was aghast.

"An emperor who has a son can be spared. An emperor's son who is too young to marry can't. You know that."

Harv Dorflay was only mad on one subject, and even within the frame of his madness he was intensely logical. He nodded. "Yes, Your Imperial Majesty. We both serve the Empire as best we can. And I will guard the little Princess Olva, too." He grasped Paul's hand, said, "Farewell, Your Majesty!" and dashed away, gathering his staff and the company of Thorans as he went. In an instant, they had vanished down the nearest rampway.

The emperor watched their departure, and, at the same time, saw a big black aircar, bearing the three-mooned planet, argent on sable, of Travann, let down onto the south landing stage, and another troop carrier let down after it. Four men left the aircar-Yorn, Prince Travann, and three officers in the black of the Security Guard. Prince Ganzay had also left the table: he came from one direction as Prince Travann advanced from the other. They converged on the emperor.

"What's happening here, Prince Travann?" Prince Ganzay demanded. "Why are you bringing all these troops to the Palace?"

"Your Majesty," Prince Travann said smoothly, "I trust that you will pardon this disturbance. I'm sure nothing serious will happen, but I didn't dare take chances. The students from the University are marching on the Palace-perfectly peaceful and loyal procession; they're bringing a petition for Your Majesty-but on the way, while passing through a nonworkers' district, they were attacked by a gang of hooligans connected with a voting-bloc boss called Nutchy the Knife. None of the students were hurt, and Colonel Handrosan got the procession out of the district promptly, and then dropped some of his men, who have since been re-enforced, to deal with the hooligans. That's still going on, and these riots are like forest fires; you never know when they'll shift and get out of control. I hope the men I brought won't be needed here. Really, they're a reserve for the riot work; I won't commit them, though, until I'm sure the Palace is safe."

He nodded. "Prince Travann, how soon do you estimate that the student procession will arrive here?" he asked.

"They're coming on foot, Your Majesty. I'd give them an hour, at least."

"Well, Prince Travann, will you have one of your officers see that the public-address screen in front is ready; I'll want to talk to them when they arrive. And meanwhile, I'll want to talk to Chancellor Khane, Professor Dandrik, Professor Faress and Colonel Handrosan, together. And Count Tammsan, too; Prince Ganzay, will you please screen him and invite him here immediately?"

"Now, Your Majesty?" At first, the Prime Minister was trying to suppress a look of incredulity; then he was trying to keep from showing comprehension. "Yes, Your Majesty; at once." He frowned slightly when he saw two of the Security Guard officers salute Prince Travann instead of the emperor before going away. Then he turned and hurried toward the Octagon Tower.

The officer who had gone to the aircar to use the radio returned and reported that Colonel Handrosan was bringing the Chancellor and both professors from the University in his command-car, having anticipated that they would be wanted. Paul nodded in pleasure.

"You have a good man there, Prince," he said. "Keep an eye on him."

"I know it, Your Majesty. To tell the truth, it was he who organized this march. Thought they'd be better employed coming here to petition you than milling around the University getting into further mischief."

The other officer also returned, bringing a portable viewscreen with him on a contragravity-lifter. By this time, the Bench of Counselors and the three off-planet guests had become anxious and left the luncheon pavilion in a body. The Counselors were looking about uneasily, noticing the black uniformed Security Guards who had left the troop carrier and were taking position by squads all around the emperor. First Citizen Yaggo, and King Ranulf and Lord Koreff, also seemed uneasy. They were avoiding the proximity of Paul as though he had the green death.

The viewscreen came on, and in it the city, as seen from an aircar at two thousand feet, spread out with the Palace visible in the distance, the golden pile of the Octagon Tower jutting up from it. The car carrying the pickup was behind the procession, which was moving toward the Palace along one of the broad skyways, with Gendarmes and Security Guards leading, following and flanking. There were a few Imperial and planetary and school flags, but none of the quantity-made banners and placards which always betray a planned demonstration.

Prince Ganzay had been gone for some time, now. When he returned, he drew Paul aside.

"Your Majesty," he whispered softly, "I tried to summon Army troops, but it'll be hours before any can get here. And the Militia can't be mobilized in anything less than a day. There are only five thousand Army Regulars on Odin, now, anyhow."

And half of them officers and noncoms of skeleton regiments. Like the Navy, the Army had been scattered all over the Empire-on Behemoth and Amida and Xipetotec and Astarte and Jotunnheim-in response to calls for support from Security.

"Let's have a look at this rioting, Prince Travann," one of the less decrepit Counselors, a retired general, said. "I want to see how your people are handling it."

The officers who had come with Prince Travann consulted briefly, and then got another pickup on the screen. This must have been a regular public pickup, on the front of a tall building. It was a couple of miles farther away; the Palace was visible only as a tiny glint from the Octagon Tower, on the skyline. Half a dozen Security aircars were darting about, two of them chasing a battered civilian vehicle and firing at it. On rooftops and terraces and skyways, little clumps of Security Guards were skirmishing, dodging from cover to cover, and sometimes individuals or groups in civilian clothes fired back at them. There was a surprising absence of casualties.

"Your Majesty!" the old general hissed in a scandalized whisper. "That's nothing but a big fake! Look, they're all firing blanks! The rifles hardly kick at all, and there's too much smoke for propellant-powder."

"I noticed that." This riot must have been carefully prepared, long in advance. Yet the student riot seemed to have been entirely spontaneous. That puzzled him; he wished he knew just what Yorn Travann was up to. "Just keep quiet about it," he advised.

More aircars were arriving, big and luxurious, emblazoned with the arms of some of the most distinguished families in Asgard. One of the first to let down bore the device of Duklass, and from it the Minister of Economics, the Minister of Education, and a couple of other Ministers, alighted. Count Duklass went at once to Prince Travann, drawing him away from King Ranulf and Lord Koreff and talking to him rapidly and earnestly. Count Tammsan approached at a swift half-run.

"Save Your Majesty!" he greeted, breathlessly. "What's going on, sir? We heard something about some petty brawl at the University, that Prince Ganzay had become alarmed about, but now there seems to be fighting all over the city. I never saw anything like it; on the way here we had to go up to ten thousand feet to get over a battle, and there's a vast crowd on the Avenue of the Arts, and ——" He took in the Security Guards. "Your Majesty, just what *is* going on?"

"Great and frightening changes." Count Tammsan started; he must have been to a psi-medium, too. "But I think the Empire is going to survive them. There may even be a few improvements, before things are done."

A blue-uniformed Gendarme officer approached Prince Travann, drawing him away from Count Duklass and speaking briefly to him. The Minister of Security nodded, then turned back to the Minister of Economics. They talked for a few moments longer, then clasped hands, and Travann left Duklass with his face wreathed in smiles. The Gendarme officer accompanied him as he approached.

"Your Majesty, this is Colonel Handrosan, the officer who handled the affair at the University."

"And a very good piece of work, colonel." He shook hands with him. "Don't be surprised if it's remembered next Honors Day. Did you bring Khane and the two professors?"

"They're down on the lower landing-stage, Your Majesty. We're delaying the students, to give Your Majesty time to talk to them."

"We'll see them now. My study will do." The officer saluted and went away. He turned to Count Tammsan. "That's why I asked Prince Ganzay to invite you here. This thing's become too public to be ignored; some sort of action will have to be taken. I'm going to talk to the students; I want to find out just what happened before I commit myself to anything. Well, gentlemen, let's go to my study."

Count Tammsan looked around, bewildered. "But I don't understand ——" He fell into step with Paul and the Minister of Security; a squad of Security Guards fell in behind them. "I don't understand what's happening," he complained.

An emperor about to have his throne yanked out from under him, and a minister about to stage a *coup d'etat*, taking time out to settle a trifling academic squabble. One thing he did understand, though, was that the Ministry of Education was getting some very bad publicity at a time when it could be least afforded. Prince Travann was telling him about the hooligans' attack on the marching students, and that worried him even more. Nonworking hooligans acted as voting-bloc bosses ordered; voting-bloc bosses acted on orders from the political manipulators of Cartels and pressure-groups, and action downward through the nonworkers was usually accompanied by action upward through influences to which ministers were sensitive.

There were a dozen Security Guards in black tunics, and as many Household Thorans in red kilts, in the hall outside the study, fraternizing amicably. They hurried apart and formed two ranks, and the Thoran officer with them saluted.

Going into the study, he went to his desk; Count Tammsan lit a cigarette and puffed nervously, and sat down as though he were afraid the chair would collapse under him. Prince Travann sank into another chair and relaxed, closing his eyes. There was a bit of wafer on the floor by Paul's chair, dropped by the little dog that morning. He stooped and picked it up, laying it on his desk, and sat looking at it until the door screen flashed and buzzed. Then he pressed the release button.

Colonel Handrosan ushered the three University men in ahead of him-Khane, with a florid, arrogant face that showed worry under the arrogance; Dandrik, gray-haired and stoop-shouldered, looking irritated; Faress, young, with a scrubby red mustache, looking bellicose. He greeted them collectively and invited them to sit, and there was a brief uncomfortable silence which everybody expected him to break.

"Well, gentlemen," he said, "we want to get the facts about this affair in some kind of order. I wish you'd tell me, as briefly and as completely as possible, what you know about it."

"There's the man who started it!" Khane declared, pointing at Faress.

"Professor Faress had nothing to do with it," Colonel Handrosan stated flatly. "He and his wife were in their apartment, packing to move out, when it started. Somebody called him and told him about the fighting at the stadium, and he went there at once to talk his students into dispersing. By that time, the situation was completely out of hand; he could do nothing with the students.

"Well, I think we ought to find out, first of all, why Professor Faress was dismissed," Prince Travann said. "It will take a good deal to convince me that any teacher able to inspire such loyalty in his students is a bad teacher, or deserves dismissal."

"As I understand," Paul said, "the dismissal was the result of a disagreement between Professor Faress and Professor Dandrik about an experiment on which they were working. I believe, an experiment to fix more exactly the velocity of accelerated subnucleonic particles. Beta micropositos, wasn't it, Chancellor Khane?"

Khane looked at him in surprise. "Your Majesty, I know nothing about that. Professor Dandrik is head of the physics department; he came to me, about six months ago, and told me that in his opinion this experiment was desirable. I simply deferred to his judgment and authorized it."

"Your Majesty has just stated the purpose of the experiment," Dandrik said. "For centuries, there have been inaccuracies in mathematical descriptions of subnucleonic events, and this experiment was undertaken in the hope of eliminating these inaccuracies." He went into a lengthy mathematical explanation.

"Yes, I understand that, professor. But just what was the actual experiment, in terms of physical operations?"

Dandrik looked helpless for a moment. Faress, who had been choking back a laugh, interrupted:

"Your Majesty, we were using the big turbo-linear accelerator to project fast micropositos down an evacuated tube one kilometer in length, and clocking them with light, the velocity of which has been established almost absolutely. I will say that with respect to the light, there were no observable inaccuracies at any time, and until the micropositos were accelerated to 16.067543333-1/3 times light-speed, they registered much as expected. Beyond that velocity, however, the target for the micropositos began registering impacts before the source registered emission, although the light target was still registering normally. I notified Professor Dandrik about this, and — —"

"You notified him. Wasn't he present at the time?"

"No, Your Majesty."

"Your Majesty, I am head of the physics department of the University. I have too much administrative work to waste time on the technical aspects of experiments like this," Dandrik interjected.

"I understand. Professor Faress was actually performing the experiment. You told Professor Dandrik what had happened. What then?"

"Why, Your Majesty, he simply declared that the limit of accuracy had been reached, and ordered the experiment dropped. He then reported the highest reading before this anticipation effect was observed as the newly established limit of accuracy in measuring the velocity of accelerated micropositos, and said nothing whatever in his report about the anticipation effect."

"I read a summary of the report. Why, Professor Dandrik, did you omit mentioning this slightly unusual effect?"

"Why, because the whole thing was utterly preposterous, that's why!" Dandrik barked; and then hastily added, "Your Imperial Majesty." He turned and glared at Faress; professors do not glare at galactic emperors. "Your Majesty, the limit of accuracy had been reached. After that, it was only to be expected that the apparatus would give erratic reports."

"It might have been expected that the apparatus would stop registering increased velocity relative to the light-speed standard, or that it would begin registering disproportionately," Faress said. "But, Your Majesty, I'll submit that it was not to be expected that it would register impacts before emissions. And I'll add this. After registering this slight apparent jump into the future, there was no proportionate increase in anticipation with further increase of acceleration. I wanted to find out why. But when Professor Dandrik saw what was happening, he became almost hysterical, and ordered the accelerator shut down as though he were afraid it would blow up in his face."

"I think it has blown up in his face," Prince Travann said quietly. "Professor, have you any theory, or supposition, or even any wild guess, as to how this anticipation effect occurs?"

"Yes, Your Highness. I suspect that the apparent anticipation is simply an observational illusion, similar to the illusion of time-reversal experienced when it was first observed, though not realized, that positrons sometimes exceeded light-speed."

"Why, that's what I've been saying all along!" Dandrik broke in. "The whole thing is an illusion, due — —"

"To having reached the limit of observational accuracy; I understand, Professor Dandrik. Go on, Professor Faress."

"I think that beyond 16.067543333-1/3 times light-speed, the micropositos ceased to have any velocity at all, velocity being defined as rate of motion in four-dimensional space-time. I believe they moved through the three spatial dimensions without moving at all in the fourth, temporal, dimension. They made that kilometer from source to target, literally, in nothing flat. Instantaneity."

That must have been the first time he had actually come out and said it. Dandrik jumped to his feet with a cry that was just short of being a shriek.

"He's crazy! Your Majesty, you mustn't ... that is, well, I mean-Please, Your Majesty, don't listen to him. He doesn't know what he's saying. He's raving!"

"He knows perfectly well what he's saying, and it probably scares him more than it does you. The difference is that he's willing to face it and you aren't."

The difference was that Faress was a scientist and Dandrik was a science teacher. To Faress, a new door had opened, the first new door in eight hundred years. To Dandrik, it threatened invalidation of everything he had taught since the morning he had opened his first class. He could no longer say to his pupils, "You are here to learn from me." He would have to say, more humbly, *We* are here to learn from the Universe."

It had happened so many times before, too. The comfortable and established Universe had fitted all the known facts-and then new facts had been learned that wouldn't fit it. The third planet of the Sol system had once been the center of the Universe, and then Terra, and Sol, and even the galaxy, had been forced to abdicate centricity. The atom had been indivisible-until somebody divided it. There had been intangible substance that had permeated the Universe, because it had been necessary for the transmission of light-until it was demonstrated to be unnecessary and nonexistent. And the speed of light had been the ultimate velocity, once, and could be exceeded no more than the atom could be divided. And light-speed had been constant, regardless of distance from source, and the Universe, to explain certain observed phenomena, had been believed to be expanding simultaneously in all directions. And the things that had happened in psychology, when psi-phenomena had become too obvious to be shrugged away.

"And then, when Dr. Dandrik ordered you to drop this experiment, just when it was becoming interesting, you refused?"

"Your Majesty, I couldn't stop, not then. But Dr. Dandrik ordered the apparatus dismantled and scrapped, and I'm afraid I lost my head. Told him I'd punch his silly old face in, for one thing."

"You admit that?" Chancellor Khane cried.

"I think you showed admirable self-restraint in not doing it. Did you explain to Chancellor Khane the importance of this experiment?"

"I tried to, Your Majesty, but he simply wouldn't listen."

"But, Your Majesty!" Khane expostulated. "Professor Dandrik is head of the department, and one of the foremost physicists of the Empire, and this young man is only one of the junior assistant-professors. Isn't even a full professor, and he got his degree from some school away off-planet. University of Brannerton on Gimli."

"Were you a pupil of Professor Vann Evaratt?" Prince Travann asked sharply.

"Why, yes, sir. I ——"

"Ha, no wonder!" Dandrik crowed. "Your Majesty, that man's an out-and-out charlatan! He was kicked out of the University here ten years ago, and I'm surprised he could even get on the faculty of a school like Brannerton, on a planet like Gimli."

"Why, you stupid old fool!" Faress yelled at him. "You aren't enough of a physicist to oil robots in Vann Evaratt's lab!"

"There, Your Majesty," Khane said. "You see how much respect for authority this hooligan has!"

On Aditya, such would be unthinkable; on Aditya, everybody respects authority. Whether it's respectable or not.

Count Tammsan laughed, and he realized that he must have spoken aloud. Nobody else seemed to have gotten the joke.

"Well, how about the riot, now?" he asked. "Who started that?"

"Colonel Handrosan made an investigation on the spot," Prince Travann said. "May I suggest that we hear his report?"

"Yes indeed. Colonel?"

Handrosan rose and stood with his hands behind his back, looking fixedly at the wall behind the desk.

"Your Majesty, the students of Professor Faress' advanced subnuclear physics class, postgraduate students, all of them, were told of Professor Faress' dismissal by a faculty member who had taken over the class this morning. They all got up and walked out in a body, and gathered outdoors on the campus to discuss the matter. At the next class break, they were joined by other science students, and they went into the stadium, where they were joined, half an hour later, by more students who had learned of the dismissal in the meantime. At no time was the gathering disorderly. The stadium is covered by a viewscreen pickup which is fitted with a recording device; there is a complete audio-visual of the whole thing, including the attack on them by the campus police.

"This attack was ordered by Chancellor Khane, at about 1100; the chief of the campus police was told to clear the stadium, and when he asked if he was to use force, Chancellor Khane told him to use anything he wanted to."

"I did not! I told him to get the students out of the stadium, but ― ―"

"The chief of campus police carries a personal wire recorder," Handrosan said, in his flat monotone. "He has a recording of the order, in Chancellor Khane's own voice. I heard it myself. The police," he continued, "first tried to use gas, but the wind was against them. They then tried to use sono-stunners, but the students rushed them and overwhelmed them. If Your Majesty will permit a personal opinion, while I do not sympathize with their subsequent attack on the Administration Center, they were entirely within their rights in defending themselves in the stadium, and it's hard enough to stop trained and disciplined troops when they are winning. After defeating the police, they simply went on by what might be called the momentum of victory."

"Then you'd say that it's positively established that the students were behaving in a peacable and orderly manner in the stadium when they were attacked, and that Chancellor Khane ordered the attack personally?"

"I would, emphatically, Your Majesty."

"I think we've done enough here, gentlemen." He turned to Count Tammsan. "This is, jointly, the affair of Education and Security. I would suggest that you and Prince Travann join in a formal and public inquiry, and until all the facts have been established and recorded and action decided upon, the dismissal of Professor Faress be reversed and he be restored to his position on the faculty."

"Yes, Your Majesty," Tammsan agreed. "And I think it would be a good idea for Chancellor Khane to take a vacation till then, too."

"I would further suggest that, as this microposito experiment is crucial to the whole question, it should be repeated. Under the personal direction of Professor Faress."

"I agree with that, Your Majesty," Prince Travann said. "If it's as important as I think it is, Professor Dandrik is greatly to be censured for ordering it stopped and for failing to report this anticipation effect."

"We'll consult about the inquiry, including the experiment, tomorrow, Your Highness," Tammsan told Travann.

Paul rose, and everybody rose with him. "That being the case, you gentlemen are all excused. The students' procession ought to be arriving, now, and I want to tell them what's going to be done. Prince Travann, Count Tammsan; do you care to accompany me?"

Going up to the central terrace in front of the Octagon Tower, he turned to Count Tammsan.

"I notice you laughed at that remark of mine about Aditya," he said. "Have you met the First Citizen?"

"Only on screen, sir. He was at me for about an hour, this morning. It seems that they are reforming the educational system on Aditya. On Aditya, everything gets reformed every ten years, whether it needs it or not. He came here to find somebody to take charge of the reformation."

He stopped short, bringing the others to a halt beside him, and laughed heartily.

"Well, we'll send First Citizen Yaggo away happy; we'll make him a present of the most distinguished educator on Odin."

"Khane?" Tammsan asked.

"Khane. Isn't it wonderful; if you have a few problems, you have trouble, but if you have a whole lot of problems, they start solving each other. We get a chance to get rid of Khane and create a vacancy that can be filled by somebody big enough to fill it; the Ministry of Education gets out from under a nasty situation; First Citizen Yaggo gets what he thinks he wants — —"

"And if I know Khane and if I know the People's Commonwealth of Aditya, it won't be a year before Yaggo has Khane shot or stuffs him into jail, and then the Space Navy will have an excuse to visit Aditya, and Aditya'll never be the same afterward," Prince Travann added.

The students massed on the front lawns were still cheering as they went down after addressing them. The Security Guards were conspicuously absent and it was a detail of red-kilted Thoran riflemen who met them as they entered the hall to the Session Chamber. Prince Ganzay approached, attended by two Household Guard officers, a human and a Thoran. Count Tammsan looked from one to the other of his companions, bewildered. The bewildering thing was that everything was as it should be.

"Well, gentlemen," Paul said, "I'm sure that both of you will want to confer for a moment with your colleagues in the Rotunda before the Session. Please don't feel obliged to attend me further."

Prince Ganzay approached as they went down the hall. "Your Majesty, what *is* going on here?" he demanded querulously. "Just who is in control of the Palace-you or Prince Travann? And where is His Imperial Highness, and where is General Dorflay?"

"I sent Dorflay to join Prince Rodrik's picnic party. If you're upset about this, you can imagine what he might have done here."

Prince Ganzay looked at him curiously for a moment. "I thought I understood what was happening," he said. "Now I — — This business about the students, sir; how did it come out?"

Paul told him. They talked for a while, and then the Prime Minister looked at his watch, and suggested that the Session ought to be getting started. Paul nodded, and they went down the hall and into the Rotunda.

The big semicircular lobby was empty, now, except for a platoon of Household Guards, and the Empress Marris and her ladies-in-waiting. She advanced as quickly as her sheath gown would permit, and took his arm; the ladies-in-waiting fell in behind her, and Prince Ganzay went ahead, crying: "My Lords, Your Venerable Highnesses, gentlemen; His Imperial Majesty!"

Marris tightened her grip on his arm as they started forward. "Paul!" she hissed into his ear. "What is this silly story about Yorn Travann trying to seize the Throne?"

"Isn't it? Yorn's been too close the Throne for too long not to know what sort of a seat it is. He'd commit any crime up to and including genocide to keep off it."

She gave a quick skip to get into step with him. "Then why's he filled the Palace with these blackcoats? Is Rod all right?"

"Perfectly all right; he's somewhere out in the mountains, keeping Harv Dorflay out of mischief."

They crossed the Session Hall and took their seats on the double throne; everybody sat down, and the Prime Minister, after some formalities, declared the Plenary Session in being. Almost at once, one of the Prince-Counselors was on his feet begging His Majesty's leave to interrogate the Government.

"I wish to ask His Highness the Minister of Security the meaning of all this unprecedented disturbance, both here in the Palace and in the city," he said.

Prince Travann rose at once. "Your Majesty, in reply to the question of His Venerable Highness," he began, and then launched himself into an account of the student riot, the march to petition the emperor, and the clash with the nonworking class hooligans. "As to the affair at the University, I hesitate to speak on what is really the concern of His Lordship the Minister of Education, but as to the fighting in the city, if it is still going on, I can assure His Venerable Highness that the Gendarmes and Security Guards have it well in hand; the persons responsible are being rounded up, and, if the Minister of Justice concurs, an inquiry will be started tomorrow."

The Minister of Justice assured the Minister of Security that his Ministry would be quite ready to co-operate in the inquiry. Count Tammsan then got up and began talking about the riot at the University.

"What did happen, Paul?" Marris whispered.

"Chancellor Khane sacked a science professor for being too interested in science. The students didn't like it. I think Khane's successor will rectify that. Have a good time at the Flower Festivals?"

She raised her fan to hide a grimace. "I made my schedule," she said. "Tomorrow, I have fifty more booked."

"Your Imperial Majesty!" The Counselor who had risen paused, to make sure that he had the Imperial attention, before continuing: "Inasmuch as this question also seems to involve a scientific experiment, I would suggest that the Ministry of Science and Technology is also interested and since there is at present no Minister holding that portfolio, I would suggest that the discussion be continued after a Minister has been elected."

The Minister of Health and Sanity jumped to his feet.

"Your Imperial Majesty; permit me to concur with the proposal of His Venerable Highness, and to extend it with the subproposal that the Ministry of Science and Technology be abolished, and its functions and personnel divided among the other Ministries, specifically those of Education and of Economics."

The Minister of Fine Arts was up before he was fully seated.

"Your Imperial Majesty; permit me to concur with the proposal of Count Guilfred, and to extend it further with the proposal that the Ministry of Defense, now also vacant, be likewise abolished, and its functions and personnel added to the Ministry of Security under His Highness Prince Travann."

So that was it! Marris, beside him, said, "Well!" He had long ago discovered that she could pack more meaning into that monosyllable than the average counselor could into a half-hour's speech. Prince Ganzay was thunderstruck, and from the Bench of Counselors six or eight voices were babbling loudly at once. Four Ministers were on their feet clamoring for recognition; Count Duklass of Economics was yelling the loudest, so he got it.

"Your Imperial Majesty; it would have been most unseemly in me to have spoken in favor of the proposal of Count Guilfred, being an interested party, but I feel no such hesitation in concurring with the proposal of Baron Garatt, the Minister of Fine Arts. Indeed, I consider it a most excellent proposal ——"

"And I consider it the most diabolically dangerous proposal to be made in this Hall in the last six centuries!" old Admiral Gaklar shouted. "This is a proposal to concentrate all the armed force of the Empire in the hands of one man. Who can say what unscrupulous use might be made of such power?"

"Are you intimating, Prince-Counselor, that Prince Travann is contemplating some tyrannical or subversive use of such power?" Count Tammsan, of all people, demanded.

There was a concerted gasp at that; about half the Plenary Session were absolutely sure that he was. Admiral Geklar backed quickly away from the question.

"Prince Travann will not be the last Minister of Security," he said.

"What I was about to say, Your Majesty, is that as matters stand, Security has a virtual monopoly on armed power on this planet. When these disorders in the city-which Prince Travann's men are now bringing under control-broke out, there was, I am informed, an order sent out to bring Regular Army and Planetary Militia into Asgard. It will be hours before any of the former can arrive, and at least a day before the latter can even be mobilized. By the time any of them get here, there will be nothing for them to do. Is that not correct, Prince Ganzay?"

The Prime Minister looked at him angrily, stung by the realization that somebody else had a personal intelligence service as good as his own, then swallowed his anger and assented.

"Furthermore," Count Duklass continued, "the Ministry of Defense, itself, is an anachronism, which no doubt accounts for the condition in which we now find it. The Empire has no external enemies whatever; all our defense problems are problems of internal security. Let us therefore turn the facilities over to the Ministry responsible for the tasks."

The debate went on and on; he paid less and less attention to it, and it became increasingly obvious that opposition to the proposition was dwindling. Cries of, "Vote! Vote!" began to be heard from its supporters. Prince Ganzay rose from his desk and came to the throne.

"Your Imperial Majesty," he said softly. "I am opposed to this proposition, but I am convinced that enough favor it to pass it, even over Your Majesty's veto. Before the vote is called, does Your Majesty wish my resignation?"

He rose and stepped down beside the Prime Minister, putting an arm over Prince Ganzay's shoulder.

"Far from it, old friend," he said, in a distinctly audible voice. "I will have too much need for you. But, as for the proposal, I don't oppose it. I think it an excellent one; it has my approval." He lowered his voice. "As soon as it's passed, place General Dorflay's name in nomination."

The Prime Minister looked at him sadly for a moment, then nodded, returning to his desk, where he rapped for order and called for the vote.

"Well, if you can't lick them, join them," Marris said as he sat down beside her. "And if they start chasing you, just yell, 'There he goes; follow me!'"

The proposal carried, almost unanimously. Prince Ganzay then presented the name of Captain-General Dorflay for elevation to the Bench of Counselors, and the emperor decreed it. As soon as the Session was adjourned and he could do so, he slipped out the little door behind the throne, into an elevator.

In the room at the top of the Octagon Tower, he laid aside his belt and dress dagger and unfastened his tunic, than sat down in his deep chair and called a serving robot. It was the one which had brought him his breakfast, and he greeted it as a friend; it lit a cigarette for him, and poured a drink of brandy. For a long time he sat, smoking and sipping and looking out the wide window to the west, where the orange sun was firing the clouds behind the mountains, and he realized that he was abominably tired. Well, no wonder; more Empire history had been made today than in the years since he had come to the Throne.

Then something behind him clicked. He turned his head, to see Yorn Travann emerge from the concealed elevator. He grinned and lifted his drink in greeting.

"I thought you'd be a little late," he said. "Everybody trying to climb onto the bandwagon?"

Yorn Travann came forward, unbuckling his belt and laying it with Paul's; he sank into the chair opposite, and the robot poured him a drink.

"Well, do you blame them? What would it have looked like to you, in their place?"

"A *coup d'etat*. For that matter, wasn't that what it was? Why didn't you tell me you were springing it?"

"I didn't spring it; it was sprung on me. I didn't know a thing about it till Max Duklass buttonholed me down by the landing stage. I'd intended fighting this proposal to partition Science and Technology, but this riot blew up and scared Duklass and Tammsan and Guilfred and the rest of them. They weren't too sure of their majority-that's why they had the election postponed a couple of times-but they were sure that the riot would turn some of the undecided Counselors against them. So they offered to back me to take over Defense in exchange for my supporting their proposal. It looked too good to pass up."

"Even at the price of wrecking Science and Technology?"

"It was wrecked, or left to rust into uselessness, long ago. The main function of Technology has been to suppress anything that might threaten this state of economic *rigor mortis* that Duklass calls stability, and the function of Science has been to let muttonheads like Khane and Dandrik dominate the teaching of science. Well, Defense has its own scientific and technical sections, and when we come to carving the bird, Duklass and Tammsan are going to see a lot of slices going onto my plate."

"And when it's all cut up, it will be discovered that there is no provision for original research. So it will please My Majesty to institute an Imperial Office of Scientific Research, independent of any Ministry, and guess who'll be named to head it."

"Faress. And, by the way, we're all set on Khane, too. First Citizen Yaggo is as delighted to have him as we are to get rid of him. Why don't we get Vann Evaratt back, and give him the job?"

"Good. If he takes charge there at the opening of the next academic year, in ten years we'll have a thousand young men, maybe ten times that many, who won't be afraid of new things and new ideas. But the main thing is that now you have Defense, and now the plan can really start firing all jets."

"Yes." Yorn Travann got out his cigarettes and lit one. Paul glanced at the robot, hoping that its feelings hadn't been hurt. "All these native uprisings I've been blowing up out of inter-tribal knife fights, and all these civil wars my people have been manufacturing; there'll be more of them, and I'll start yelling my head off for an adequate Space Navy, and after we get it, these local troubles will all stop, and then what'll we be expected to do? Scrap the ships?"

They both knew what would be done with some of them. It would have to be done stealthily, while nobody was looking, but some of those ships would go far beyond the boundaries of the Empire, and new things would happen. New worlds, new problems. Great and frightening changes.

"Paul, we agreed upon this long ago, when we were still boys at the University. The Empire stopped growing, and when things stop growing, they start dying, the death of petrifaction. And when petrifaction is complete, the cracking and the crumbling starts, and there's no way of stopping it. But if we can get people out onto new planets, the Empire won't die; it'll start growing again."

"You didn't start that thing at the University, this morning, yourself, did you?"

"Not the student riot, no. But the hooligan attack, yes. That was some of my own men. The real hooligans began looting after Handrosan had gotten the students out of the district. We collared all of them, including their boss, Nutchy the Knife, right away, and as soon as we did that, Big Moogie and Zikko the Nose tried to move in. We're cleaning them up now. By tomorrow morning there won't be one of these nonworkers' voting blocks left in Asgard, and by the end of the week they'll be cleaned up all over Odin. I have discovered a plot, and they're all involved in it."

"Wait a moment." Paul got to his feet. "That reminds me; Harv Dorflay's hiding Rod and Olva out in the mountains. I wanted him out of here while things were happening. I'll have to call him and tell him it's safe to come in, now."

"Well, zip up your tunic and put your dagger on; you look as though you'd been arrested, disarmed and searched."

"That's right." He hastily repaired his appearance and went to the screen across the room, punching out the combination of the screen with Rodrik's picnic party.

A young lieutenant of the Household Troops appeared in it, and had to be reassured. He got General Dorflay.

"Your Majesty! You are all right?"

"Perfectly all right, general, and it's quite safe to bring His Imperial Highness in. The conspiracy against the Throne has been crushed."

"Oh, thank the gods! Is Prince Travann a prisoner?"

"Quite the contrary, general. It was our loyal and devoted subject, Prince Travann, who crushed the conspiracy."

"But-But, Your Majesty — —!"

"You aren't to be blamed for suspecting him, general. His agents were working in the very innermost councils of the conspirators. Every one of the people whom you suspected-with excellent reason-was actually working to defeat the plot. Think back, general; the scheme to put the gun in the viewscreen, the scheme to sabotage the elevator, the scheme to introduce assassins into the orchestra with guns built into their trumpets-every one came to your notice because of what seemed to be some indiscretion of the plotters, didn't it?"

"Why ...why, yes, Your Majesty!" By this time tomorrow, he would have a complete set of memories for each one of them. "You mean, the indiscretions were deliberate?"

"Your vigilance and loyalty made it necessary for them to resort to these fantastic expedients, and your vigilance defeated them as fast as they came to your notice. Well, today, Prince Travann and I struck back. I may tell you, in confidence, that every one of the conspirators is dead. Killed in this afternoon's rioting-which was incited for that purpose by Prince Travann."

"Then — — Then there will be no more plots against your life?" There was a note of regret in the old man's voice.

"No more, Your Venerable Highness."

"But — — What did Your Majesty call me?" he asked incredulously.

"I took the honor of being the first to address you by your new title, Prince-Counselor Dorflay."

He left the old man overcome, and blubbering happily on the shoulder of the Crown Prince, who winked at his father out of the screen. Prince Travann had gotten a couple of fresh drinks from the robot and handed one to him when he returned to his chair.

"He'll be finding the Bench of Counselors riddled with treason inside a week," Travann said. "You handled that just right, though. Another case of making problems solve each other."

"You were telling me about a plot you'd discovered."

"Oh, yes: this is one to top Dorflay's best efforts. All the voting-bloc bosses on Odin are in a conspiracy to start a civil war to give them a chance to loot the planet. There isn't a word of truth in it, of course, but it'll do to arrest and hold them for a few days, and by that time some of my undercovers will be in control of every nonworker vote on the planet. After all, the Cartels put an end to competition in every other business; why not a Voting Cartel, too? Then, whenever there's an election, we just advertise for bids."

"Why, that would mean absolute control — —"

"Of the nonworking vote, yes. And I'll guarantee, personally, that in five years the politics of Odin will have become so unbearably corrupt and abusive that the intellectuals, the technicians, the business people, even the nobility, will be flocking to the polls to vote, and if only half of them turn out, they'll snow the nonworkers under. And that'll mean, eventually, an end to vote-selling, and the nonworkers'll have to find work. We'll find it for them."

"Great and frightening changes." Yorn Travann laughed; he recognized the phrase. Probably started it himself. Paul lifted his glass. "To the Minister of Disturbance!"

"Your Majesty!" They drank to each other, and then Yorn Travann said, "We had a lot of wild dreams, when we were boys; it looks as though we're starting to make some of them come true. You know, when we were in the University, the students would never have done what they did today. They didn't even do it ten years ago, when Vann Evaratt was dismissed."

"And Van Evaratt's pupil came back to Odin and touched this whole thing off." He thought for a moment. "I wonder what Faress has, in that anticipation effect."

"I think I can see what can come out of it. If he can propagate a wave that behaves like those micropositos, we may not have to depend on ships for communication. We may be able, some day, to screen Baldur or Vishnu or Aton or Thor as easily as you screened Dorflay, up in the mountains." He thought silently for a moment. "I don't know whether that would be good or bad. But it would be new, and that's what matters. That's the only thing that matters."

"Flower Festivals," Paul said, and, when Yorn Travann wanted to know what he meant, he told him. "When Princess Olva's Empress, she's going to curse the name of Klenn Faress. Flower Festivals, all around the galaxy, without end."

THE END

Oomphel in the Sky

By H. Beam Piper

*Since Logic derives from postulates, it never has, and never will, change a postulate.
And a religious belief is a system of postulates … so how can a man fight a native superstition with logic? Or anything else…?*

Miles Gilbert watched the landscape slide away below him, its quilt of rounded treetops mottled red and orange in the double sunlight and, in shaded places, with the natural yellow of the vegetation of Kwannon. The aircar began a slow swing to the left, and Gettler Alpha came into view, a monstrous smear of red incandescence with an optical diameter of two feet at arm's length, slightly flattened on the bottom by the western horizon. In another couple of hours it would be completely set, but by that time Beta, the planet's G-class primary, would be at its midafternoon hottest. He glanced at his watch. It was 1005, but that was Galactic Standard Time, and had no relevance to anything that was happening in the local sky. It did mean, though, that it was five minutes short of two hours to 'cast-time.

He snapped on the communication screen in front of him, and Harry Walsh, the news editor, looked out of it at him from the office in Bluelake, halfway across the continent. He wanted to know how things were going.

"Just about finished. I'm going to look in at a couple more native villages, and then I'm going to Sanders' plantation to see Gonzales. I hope I'll have a personal statement from him, and the final situation-progress map, in time for the 'cast. I take it Maith's still agreeable to releasing the story at twelve-hundred?"

"Sure; he was always agreeable. The Army wants publicity; it was Government House that wanted to sit on it, and they've given that up now. The story's all over the place here, native city and all."

"What's the situation in town, now?"

"Oh, it's still going on. Some disorders, mostly just unrest. Lot of street meetings that could have turned into frenzies if the police hadn't broken them up in time. A couple of shootings, some sleep-gassing, and a lot of arrests. Nothing to worry about-at least, not immediately."

That was about what he thought. "Maybe it's not bad to have a little trouble in Bluelake," he considered. "What happens out here in the plantation country the Government House crowd can't see, and it doesn't worry them. Well, I'll call you from Sanders'."

He blanked the screen. In the seat in front, the native pilot said: "Some contragravity up ahead, boss." It sounded like two voices speaking in unison, which was just what it was. "I'll have a look."

The pilot's hand, long and thin, like a squirrel's, reached up and pulled down the fifty-power binoculars on their swinging arm. Miles looked at the screen-map and saw a native village just ahead of the dot of light that marked the position of the aircar. He spoke the native name of the village aloud, and added:

"Let down there, Heshto. I'll see what's going on."

The native, still looking through the glasses, said, "Right, boss." Then he turned.

His skin was blue-gray and looked like sponge rubber. He was humanoid, to the extent of being an upright biped, with two arms, a head on top of shoulders, and a torso that housed, among other oddities, four lungs. His face wasn't even vaguely human. He had two eyes in front, close enough for stereoscopic vision, but that was a common characteristic of sapient life forms everywhere. His mouth was strictly for eating; he breathed through separate intakes and outlets, one of each on either side of his neck; he talked through the outlets and had his scent and hearing organs in the intakes. The car was air-conditioned, which was a mercy; an overheated Kwann exhaled through his skin, and surrounded himself with stenches like an organic chemistry lab. But then, Kwanns didn't come any closer to him than they could help when he was hot and sweated, which, lately, had been most of the time.

"A V and a half of air cavalry, circling around," Heshto said. "Making sure nobody got away. And a combat car at a couple of hundred feet and another one just at treetop level."

He rose and went to the seat next to the pilot, pulling down the binoculars that were focused for his own eyes. With them, he could see the air cavalry-egg-shaped things just big enough for a seated man, with jets and contragravity field generators below and a bristle of machine gun muzzles in front. A couple of them jetted up for a look at him and then went slanting down again, having recognized the Kwannon Planetwide News Service car.

The village was typical enough to have been an illustration in a sociography textbook-fields in a belt for a couple of hundred yards around it, dome-thatched mud-and-wattle huts inside a pole stockade with log storehouses built against it, their flat roofs high enough to provide platforms for defending archers, the open oval gathering-place in the middle. There was a big hut at one end of this, the khamdoo, the sanctum of the adult males, off limits for women and children. A small crowd was gathered in front of it; fifteen or twenty Terran air cavalrymen, a couple of enlisted men from the Second Kwannon Native Infantry, a Terran second lieutenant, and half a dozen natives. The rest of the village population, about two hundred, of both sexes and all ages, were lined up on the shadier side of the gathering-place, most of them looking up apprehensively at the two combat cars which were covering them with their guns.

Miles got to his feet as the car lurched off contragravity and the springs of the landing-feet took up the weight. A blast of furnacelike air struck him when he opened the door; he got out quickly and closed it behind him. The second lieutenant had come over to meet him; he extended his hand.

"Good day, Mr. Gilbert. We all owe you our thanks for the warning. This would have been a real baddie if we hadn't caught it when we did."

He didn't even try to make any modest disclaimer; that was nothing more than the exact truth.

"Well, lieutenant, I see you have things in hand here." He glanced at the line-up along the side of the oval plaza, and then at the selected group in front of the khamdoo. The patriarchal village chieftain in a loose slashed shirt; the shoonoo, wearing a multiplicity of amulets and nothing else; four or five of the village elders. "I take it the word of the swarming didn't get this far?"

"No, this crowd still don't know what the flap's about, and I couldn't think of anything to tell them that wouldn't be worse than no explanation at all."

He had noticed hoes and spades flying in the fields, and the cylindrical plastic containers the natives bought from traders, dropped when the troops had surprised the women at work. And the shoonoo didn't have a fire-dance cloak or any other special regalia on. If he'd heard about the swarming, he'd have been dressed to make magic for it.

"What time did you get here, lieutenant?"

"Oh-nine-forty. I just called in and reported the village occupied, and they told me I was the last one in, so the operation's finished."

That had been smart work. He got the lieutenant's name and unit and mentioned it into his memophone. That had been a little under five hours since he had convinced General Maith, in Bluelake, that the mass labor-desertion from the Sanders plantation had been the beginning of a swarming. Some division commanders wouldn't have been able to get a brigade off the ground in that time, let alone landed on objective. He said as much to the young officer.

"The way the Army responded, today, can make the people of the Colony feel a lot more comfortable for the future."

"Why, thank you, Mr. Gilbert." The Army, on Kwannon, was rather more used to obloquy than praise. "How did you spot what was going on so quickly?"

This was the hundredth time, at least, that he had been asked that today.

"Well, Paul Sanders' labor all comes from neighboring villages. If they'd just wanted to go home and spend the end of the world with their families, they'd have been dribbling away in small batches for the last couple of hundred hours. Instead, they all bugged out in a bunch, they took all the food they could carry and nothing else, and they didn't make any trouble before they left. Then, Sanders said they'd been building fires out in the fallow ground and moaning and chanting around them for a couple of days, and idling on the job. Saving their strength for the trek. And he said they had a shoonoo among them. He's probably the lad who started it. Had a dream from the Gone Ones, I suppose."

"You mean, like this fellow here?" the lieutenant asked. "What are they, Mr. Gilbert; priests?"

He looked quickly at the lieutenant's collar-badges. Yellow trefoil for Third Fleet-Army Force, Roman IV for Fourth Army, 907 for his regiment, with C under it for cavalry. That outfit had only been on Kwannon for the last two thousand hours, but somebody should have briefed him better than that.

He shook his head. "No, they're magicians. Everything these Kwanns do involves magic, and the shoonoon are the professionals. When a native runs into something serious, that his own do-it-yourself magic can't cope with, he goes to the shoonoo. And, of course, the shoonoo works all the magic for the community as a whole-rain-magic, protective magic for the village and the fields, that sort of thing."

The lieutenant mopped his face on a bedraggled handkerchief. "They'll have to struggle along somehow for a while; we have orders to round up all the shoonoon and send them in to Bluelake."

"Yes." That hadn't been General Maith's idea; the governor had insisted on that. "I hope it doesn't make more trouble than it prevents."

The lieutenant was still mopping his face and looking across the gathering-place toward Alpha, glaring above the huts.

"How much worse do you think this is going to get?" he asked.

"The heat, or the native troubles?"

"I was thinking about the heat, but both."

"Well, it'll get hotter. Not much hotter, but some. We can expect storms, too, within twelve to fifteen hundred hours. Nobody has any idea how bad they'll be. The last periastron was ninety years ago, and we've only been here for sixty-odd; all we have is verbal accounts from memory from the natives, probably garbled and exaggerated. We had pretty bad storms right after transit a year ago; they'll be much worse this time. Thermal convections; air starts to cool when it gets dark, and then heats up again in double-sun daylight."

It was beginning, even now; starting to blow a little after Alpha-rise.

"How about the natives?" the lieutenant asked. "If they can get any crazier than they are now —"

"They can, and they probably will. They think this is the end of the world. The Last Hot Time." He used the native expression, and then translated it into Lingua Terra. "The Sky Fire-that's Alpha-will burn up the whole world."

"But this happens every ninety years. Mean they always acted this way at periastron?"

He shook his head. "Race would have exterminated itself long ago if they had. No, this is something special. The coming of the Terrans was a sign. The Terrans came and brought oomphel to the world; this a sign that the Last Hot Time is at hand."

"What the devil *is* oomphel?" The lieutenant was mopping the back of his neck with one hand, now, and trying to pull his sticky tunic loose from his body with the other. "I hear that word all the time."

"Well, most Terrans, including the old Kwannon hands, use it to mean trade-goods. To the natives, it means any product of Terran technology, from paper-clips to spaceships. They think it's ...well, not exactly supernatural; extranatural would be closer to expressing their idea. Terrans are natural; they're just a different kind of people. But oomphel isn't; it isn't subject to any of the laws of nature at all. They're all positive that we don't make it. Some of them even think it makes us."

When he got back in the car, the native pilot, Heshto, was lolling in his seat and staring at the crowd of natives along the side of the gathering-place with undisguised disdain. Heshto had been educated at one of the Native Welfare Commission schools, and post-graded with Kwannon Planetwide News. He could speak, read and write Lingua Terra. He was a mathematician as far as long division and decimal fractions. He knew that Kwannon was the second planet of the Gettler Beta system, 23,000 miles in circumference, rotating on its axis once in 22.8 Galactic Standard hours and making an orbital circuit around Gettler Beta once in 372.06 axial days, and that Alpha was an M-class pulsating variable with an average period of four hundred days, and that Beta orbited around it in a long elipse every ninety years. He didn't believe there was going to be a Last Hot Time. He was an intellectual, he was.

He started the contragravity-field generator as soon as Miles was in his seat. "Where now, boss?" he asked.

"Qualpha's Village. We won't let down; just circle low over it. I want some views of the ruins. Then to Sanders' plantation."

"O.K., boss; hold tight."

He had the car up to ten thousand feet. Aiming it in the map direction of Qualpha's Village, he let go with everything he had-hot jets, rocket-booster and all. The forest landscape came hurtling out of the horizon toward them.

Qualpha's was where the trouble had first broken out, after the bug-out from Sanders; the troops hadn't been able to get there in time, and it had been burned. Another village, about the same distance south of the plantation, had also gone up in flames, and at a dozen more they had found the natives working themselves into frenzies and had had to sleep-gas them or stun them with concussion-bombs. Those had been the villages to which the deserters from Sanders' had themselves gone; from every one, runners had gone out to neighboring villages —"The Gone Ones are returning; all the People go to greet them at the Deesha-Phoo. Burn your villages; send on the word. Hasten; the Gone Ones return!"

Saving some of those villages had been touch-and-go, too; the runners, with hours lead-time, had gotten there ahead of the troops, and there had been shooting at a couple of them. Then the Army contragravity began landing at villages that couldn't have been reached in hours by foot messengers. It had been stopped-at least for the time, and in this area. When and where another would break out was anybody's guess.

The car was slowing and losing altitude, and ahead he could see thin smoke rising above the trees. He moved forward beside the pilot and pulled down his glasses; with them he could distinguish the ruins of the village. He called Bluelake, and then put his face to the view-finder and began transmitting in the view.

It had been a village like the one he had just visited, mud-and-wattle huts around an oval gathering-place, stockade, and fields beyond. Heshto brought the car down to a few hundred feet and came coasting in on momentum helped by an occasional spurt of the cold-jets. A few sections of the stockade still stood, and one side of the khamdoo hadn't fallen, but the rest of the structures were flat. There wasn't a soul, human or parahuman, in sight; the only living thing was a small black-and-gray quadruped investigating some bundles that had been dropped in the fields, in hope of finding something tasty. He got a view of that-everybody liked animal pictures on a newscast-and then he was swinging the pickup over the still-burning ruins. In the ashes of every hut he could see the remains of something like a viewscreen or a nuclear-electric stove or a refrigerator or a sewing machine. He knew how dearly the Kwanns cherished such possessions. That they had destroyed them grieved him. But the Last Hot Time was at hand; the whole world would be destroyed by fire, and then the Gone Ones would return.

So there were uprisings on the plantations. Paul Sanders had been lucky; his Kwanns had just picked up and left. But he had always gotten along well with the natives, and his plantation house was literally a castle and he had plenty of armament. There had been other planters who had made the double mistake of incurring the enmity of their native labor and of living in unfortified houses. A lot of them weren't around, any more, and their plantations were gutted ruins.

And there were plantations on which the natives had destroyed the klooba plants and smashed the crystal which lived symbiotically upon them. They thought the Terrans were using the living crystals to make magic. Not too far off, at that; the properties of Kwannon biocrystals had opened a major breakthrough in subnucleonic physics and initiated half a dozen technologies. New kinds of oomphel. And down in the south, where the spongy and resinous trees were drying in the heat, they were starting forest fires and perishing in them in hecatombs. And to the north, they were swarming into the mountains; building great fires there, too, and attacking the Terran radar and radio beacons.

Fire was a factor common to all these frenzies. Nothing could happen without magical assistance; the way to bring on the Last Hot Time was People.

Maybe the ones who died in the frenzies and the swarmings were the lucky ones at that. They wouldn't live to be crushed by disappointment when the Sky Fire receded as Beta went into the long swing toward apastron. The surviving shoonoon wouldn't be the lucky ones, that was for sure. The magician-in-public-practice needs only to make one really bad mistake before he is done to some unpleasantly ingenious death by his clientry, and this was going to turn out to be the biggest magico-prophetic blooper in all the long unrecorded history of Kwannon.

A few minutes after the car turned south from the ruined village, he could see contragravity-vehicles in the air ahead, and then the fields and buildings of the Sanders plantation. A lot more contragravity was grounded in the fallow fields, and there were rows of pneumatic balloon-tents, and field-kitchens, and a whole park of engineering equipment. Work was going on in the klooba-fields, too; about three hundred natives were cutting open the six-foot leafy balls and getting out the biocrystals. Three of the plantation airjeeps, each with a pair of machine guns, were guarding them, but they didn't seem to be having any trouble. He saw Sanders in another jeep, and had Heshto put the car alongside.

"How's it going, Paul?" he asked over his radio. "I see you have some help, now."

"Everybody's from Qualpha's, and from Darshat's," Sanders replied. "The Army had no place to put them, after they burned themselves out." He laughed happily. "Miles, I'm going to save my whole crop! I thought I was wiped out, this morning."

He would have been, if Gonzales hadn't brought those Kwanns in. The klooba was beginning to wither; if left unharvested, the biocrystals would die along with their hosts and crack into worthlessness. Like all the other planters, Sanders had started no new crystals since the hot weather, and would start none until the worst of the heat was over. He'd need every crystal he could sell to tide him over.

"The Welfarers'll make a big forced-labor scandal out of this," he predicted.

"Why, such an idea." Sanders was scandalized. "I'm not forcing them to eat."

"The Welfarers don't think anybody ought to have to work to eat. They think everybody ought to be fed whether they do anything to earn it or not, and if you try to make people earn their food, you're guilty of economic coercion. And if you're in business for yourself and want them to work for you, you're an exploiter and you ought to be eliminated as a class. Haven't you been trying to run a plantation on this planet, under this Colonial Government, long enough to have found that out, Paul?"

Brigadier General Ramón Gonzales had taken over the first-counting down from the landing-stage —floor of the plantation house for his headquarters. His headquarters company had pulled out removable partitions and turned four rooms into one, and moved in enough screens and teleprinters and photoprint machines and computers to have outfitted the main newsroom of *Planetwide News*. The place had the feel of a newsroom —a newsroom after a big story has broken and the 'cast has gone on the air and everybody-in this case about twenty Terran officers and non-coms, half women-standing about watching screens and smoking and thinking about getting a follow-up ready.

Gonzales himself was relaxing in Sanders' business-room, with his belt off and his tunic open. He had black eyes and black hair and mustache, and a slightly equine face that went well with his Old Terran Spanish name. There was another officer with him, considerably younger-Captain Foxx Travis, Major General Maith's aide.

"Well, is there anything we can do for you, Miles?" Gonzales asked, after they had exchanged greetings and sat down.

"Why, could I have your final situation-progress map? And would you be willing to make a statement on audio-visual." He looked at his watch. "We have about twenty minutes before the 'cast."

"You have a map," Gonzales said, as though he were walking tiptoe from one word to another. "It accurately represents the situation as of the moment, but I'm afraid some minor unavoidable inaccuracies may have crept in while marking the positions and times for the earlier phases of the operation. I teleprinted a copy to *Planetwide* along with the one I sent to Division Headquarters."

He understood about that and nodded. Gonzales was zipping up his tunic and putting on his belt and sidearm. That told him, before the brigadier general spoke again, that he was agreeable to the audio-visual appearance and statement. He called the recording studio at *Planetwide* while Gonzales was inspecting himself in the mirror and told them to get set for a recording. It only ran a few minutes; Gonzales, speaking without notes, gave a brief description of the operation.

"At present," he concluded, "we have every native village and every plantation and trading-post within two hundred miles of the Sanders plantation occupied. We feel that this swarming has been definitely stopped, but we will continue the occupation for at least the next hundred to two hundred hours. In the meantime, the natives in the occupied villages are being put to work building shelters for themselves against the anticipated storms."

"I hadn't heard about that," Miles said, as the general returned to his chair and picked up his drink again.

"Yes. They'll need something better than these thatched huts when the storms start, and working on them will keep them out of mischief. Standard megaton-kilometer field shelters, earth and log construction. I think they'll be adequate for anything that happens at periastron."

Anything designed to resist the heat, blast and radiation effects of a megaton thermonuclear bomb at a kilometer ought to stand up under what was coming. At least, the periastron effects; there was another angle to it.

"The Native Welfare Commission isn't going to take kindly to that. That's supposed to be their job."

"Then why the devil haven't they done it?" Gonzales demanded angrily. "I've viewed every native village in this area by screen, and I haven't seen one that's equipped with anything better than those log storage-bins against the stockades."

"There was a project to provide shelters for the periastron storms set up ten years ago. They spent one year arguing about how the natives survived storms prior to the Terrans' arrival here. According to the older natives, they got into those log storage-houses you were mentioning; only about one out of three in any village survived. I could have told them that. Did tell them, repeatedly, on the air. Then, after they decided that shelters were needed, they spent another year hassling over who would be responsible for designing them. Your predecessor here, General Nokami, offered the services of his engineer officers. He was frostily informed that this was a humanitarian and not a military project."

Ramón Gonzales began swearing, then apologized for the interruption. "Then what?" he asked.

"Apology unnecessary. Then they did get a shelter designed, and started teaching some of the students at the native schools how to build them, and then the meteorologists told them it was no good. It was a dugout shelter; the weathermen said there'd be rainfall measured in meters instead of inches and anybody who got caught in one of those dugouts would be drowned like a rat."

"Ha, I thought of that one." Gonzales said. "My shelters are going to be mounded up eight feet above the ground."

"What did they do then?" Foxx Travis wanted to know.

"There the matter rested. As far as I know, nothing has been done on it since."

"And you think, with a disgraceful record of non-accomplishment like that, that they'll protest General Gonzales' action on purely jurisdictional grounds?" Travis demanded.

"Not jurisdictional grounds, Foxx. The general's going at this the wrong way. He actually knows what has to be done and how to do it, and he's going right ahead and doing it, without holding a dozen conferences and round-table discussions and giving everybody a fair and equal chance to foul things up for him. You know as well as I do that that's undemocratic. And what's worse, he's making the natives build them themselves, whether they want to or not, and that's forced labor. That reminds me; has anybody started raising the devil about those Kwanns from Qualpha's and Darshat's you brought here and Paul put to work?"

Gonzales looked at Travis and then said: "Not with me. Not yet, anyhow."

"They've been at General Maith," Travis said shortly. After a moment, he added: "General Maith supports General Gonzales completely; that's for publication. I'm authorized to say so. What else was there to do? They'd burned their villages and all their food stores. They had to be placed somewhere. And why in the name of reason should they sit around in the shade eating Government native-type rations while Paul Sanders has fifty to a hundred thousand sols' worth of crystals dying on him?"

"Yes; that's another thing they'll scream about. Paul's making a profit out of it."

"Of course he's making a profit," Gonzales said. "Why else is he running a plantation? If planters didn't make profits, who'd grow biocrystals?"

"The Colonial Government. The same way they built those storm-shelters. But that would be in the public interest, and if the Kwanns weren't public-spirited enough to do the work, they'd be made to-at about half what planters like Sanders are paying them now. But don't you realize that profit is sordid and dishonest and selfish? Not at all like drawing a salary-cum-expense-account from the Government."

"You're right, it isn't," Gonzales agreed. "People like Paul Sanders have ability. If they don't, they don't stay in business. You have ability and people who don't never forgive you for it. Your very existence is a constant reproach to them."

"That's right. And they can't admit your ability without admitting their own inferiority, so it isn't ability at all. It's just dirty underhanded trickery and selfish ruthlessness." He thought for a moment. "How did Government House find out about these Kwanns here?"

"The Welfare Commission had people out while I was still setting up headquarters," Gonzales said. "That was about oh-seven-hundred."

"This isn't for publication?" Travis asked. "Well, they know, but they can't prove, that our given reason for moving in here in force is false. Of course, we can't change our story now; that's why the situation-progress map that was prepared for publication is incorrect as to the earlier phases. They do not know that it was you who gave us our first warning; they ascribe that to Sanders. And they are claiming that there never was any swarming; according to them, Sanders' natives are striking for better pay and conditions, and Sanders got General Maith to use troops to break the strike. I wish we could give you credit for putting us onto this, but it's too late now."

He nodded. The story was that a battalion of infantry had been sent in to rescue a small detail under attack by natives, and that more troops had been sent in to re-enforce them, until the whole of Gonzales' brigade had been committed.

"That wasted an hour, at the start," Gonzales said. "We lost two native villages burned, and about two dozen casualties, because we couldn't get our full strength in soon enough."

"You'd have lost more than that if Maith had told the governor general the truth and re-quested orders to act. There'd be a hundred villages and a dozen plantations and trading posts burning, now, and Lord knows how many dead, and the governor general would still be arguing about whether he was justified in ordering troop-action." He mentioned several other occasions when something like that had happened. "You can't tell that kind of people the truth. They won't believe it. It doesn't agree with their preconceptions."

Foxx Travis nodded. "I take it we are still talking for nonpublication?" When Miles nodded, he continued: "This whole situation is baffling, Miles. It seems that the government here knew all about the weather conditions they could expect at periastron, and had made plans for them. Some of them excellent plans, too, but all based on the presumption that the natives would co-operate or at least not obstruct. You see what the situation actually is. It should be obvious to everybody that the behavior of these natives is nullifying everything the civil government is trying to do to ensure the survival of the Terran colonists, the production of Terran-type food without which we would all starve, the biocrystal plantations without which the Colony would perish, and even the natives themselves. Yet the Civil Government will not act to stop these native frenzies and swarmings which endanger everything and everybody here, and when the Army attempts to act, we must use every sort of shabby subterfuge and deceit or the Civil Government will prevent us. What ails these people?"

"You have the whole history of the Colony against you, Foxx," he said. "You know, there never was any Chartered Kwannon Company set up to exploit the resources of the planet. At first, nobody realized that there were any resources worth exploiting. This planet was just a scientific curiosity; it was and is still the only planet of a binary system with a native population of sapient beings. The first people who came here were scientists, mostly sociographers and para-anthropologists. And most of them came from the University of Adelaide."

Travis nodded. Adelaide had a Federation-wide reputation for left-wing neo-Marxist "liberalism."

"Well, that established the political and social orientation of the Colonial Government, right at the start, when study of the natives was the only business of the Colony. You know how these ideological cliques form in a government-or any other organization. Subordinates are always chosen for their agreement with the views of their superiors, and the extremists always get to the top and shove the moderates under or out. Well, the Native Affairs Administration became the tail that wagged the Government dog, and the Native Welfare Commission is the big muscle in the tail."

His parents hadn't been of the left-wing Adelaide clique. His mother had been a biochemist; his father a roving news correspondent who had drifted into trading with the natives and made a fortune in keffa-gum before the chemists on Terra had found out how to synthesize hopkinsine.

"When the biocrystals were discovered and the plantations started, the Government attitude was set. Biocrystal culture is just sordid money grubbing. The real business of the Colony is to promote the betterment of the natives, as defined in University of Adelaide terms. That's to say, convert them into ersatz Terrans. You know why General Maith ordered these shoonoon rounded up?"

Travis made a face. "Governor general Kovac insisted on it; General Maith thought that a few minor concessions would help him on his main objective, which was keeping a swarming from starting out here."

"Yes. The Commissioner of Native Welfare wanted that done, mainly at the urging of the Director of Economic, Educational and Technical Assistance. The EETA crowd don't like shoonoon. They have been trying, ever since their agency was set up, to undermine and destroy their influence with the natives. This looked like a good chance to get rid of some of them."

Travis nodded. "Yes. And as soon as the disturbances in Bluelake started, the Constabulary started rounding them up there, too, and at the evacuee cantonments. They got about fifty of them, mostly from the cantonments east of the city-the natives brought in from the flooded tidewater area. They just dumped the lot of them onto us. We have them penned up in a lorry-hangar on the military reservation now." He turned to Gonzales. "How many do you think you'll gather up out here, general?" he asked.

"I'd say about a hundred and fifty, when we have them all."

Travis groaned. "We can't keep all of them in that hangar, and we don't have anywhere else —"

Sometimes a new idea sneaked up on Miles, rubbing against him and purring like a cat. Sometimes one hit him like a sledgehammer. This one just seemed to grow inside him.

"Foxx, you know I have the top three floors of the Suzikami Building; about five hundred hours ago, I leased the fourth and fifth floors, directly below. I haven't done anything with them, yet; they're just as they were when Trans-Space Imports moved out. There are ample water, light, power, air-conditioning and toilet facilities, and they can be sealed off completely from the rest of the building. If General Maith's agreeable, I'll take his shoonoon off his hands."

"What in blazes will you do with them?"

"Try a little experiment in psychological warfare. At minimum, we may get a little better insight into why these natives think the Last Hot Time is coming. At best, we may be able to stop the whole thing and get them quieted down again."

"Even the minimum's worth trying for," Travis said. "What do you have in mind, Miles? I mean, what procedure?"

"Well, I'm not quite sure, yet." That was a lie; he was very sure. He didn't think it was quite time to be specific, though. "I'll have to size up my material a little, before I decide on what to do with it. Whatever happens, it won't hurt the shoonoon, and it won't make any more trouble than arresting them has made already. I'm sure we can learn something from them, at least."

Travis nodded. "General Maith is very much impressed with your grasp of native psychology," he said. "What happened out here this morning was exactly as you predicted. Whatever my recommendation's worth, you have it. Can you trust your native driver to take your car back to Bluelake alone?"

"Yes, of course."

"Then suppose you ride in with me in my car. We'll talk about it on the way in, and go see General Maith at once."

Bluelake was peaceful as they flew in over it, but it was an uneasy peace. They began running into military contragravity twenty miles beyond the open farmlands-they were the chlorophyll green of Terran vegetation-and the natives at work in the fields were being watched by more military and police vehicles. The carniculture plants, where Terran-type animal tissue was grown in nutrient-vats, were even more heavily guarded, and the native city was being patroled from above and the streets were empty, even of the hordes of native children who usually played in them.

The Terran city had no streets. Its dwellers moved about on contragravity, and tall buildings rose, singly or in clumps, among the landing-staged residences and the green transplanted trees. There was a triple wire fence around it, the inner one masked by vines and the middle one electrified, with warning lights on. Even a government dedicated to the betterment of the natives and unwilling to order military action against them was, it appeared, unwilling to take too many chances.

Major General Denis Maith, the Federation Army commander on Kwannon, was considerably more than willing to find a temporary home for his witch doctors, now numbering close to two hundred. He did insist that they be kept under military guard, and on assigning his aide, Captain Travis, to co-operate on the project. Beyond that, he gave Miles a free hand.

Miles and Travis got very little rest in the next ten hours. A half-company of engineer troops was also kept busy, as were a number of Kwannon Planetwide News technicians and some Terran and native mechanics borrowed from different private business concerns in the city. Even the most guarded hints of what he had in mind were enough to get this last co-operation; he had been running a news-service in Bluelake long enough to have the confidence of the business people.

He tried, as far as possible, to keep any intimation of what was going on from Government House. That, unfortunately, hadn't been far enough. He found that out when General Maith was on his screen, in the middle of the work on the fourth and fifth floors of the Suzikami Building.

"The governor general just screened me," Maith said. "He's in a tizzy about our shoonoon. Claims that keeping them in the Suzikami Building will endanger the whole Terran city."

"Is that the best he can do? Well, that's rubbish, and he knows it. There are less than two hundred of them, I have them on the fifth floor, twenty stories above the ground, and the floor's completely sealed off from the floor below. They can't get out, and I have tanks of sleep-gas all over the place which can be opened either individually or all together from a switch on the fourth floor, where your sepoys are quartered."

"I know, Mr. Gilbert; I screen-viewed the whole installation. I've seen regular maximum-security prisons that would be easier to get out of."

"Governor general Kovac is not objecting personally. He has been pressured into it by this Native Welfare government-within-the-Government. They don't know what I'm doing with those shoonoon, but whatever it is, they're afraid of it."

"Well, for the present," Maith said, "I think I'm holding them off. The Civil Government doesn't want the responsibility of keeping them in custody, I refused to assume responsibility for them if they were kept anywhere else, and Kovac simply won't consider releasing them, so that leaves things as they are. I did have to make one compromise, though." That didn't sound good. It sounded less so when Maith continued: "They insisted on having one of their people at the Suzikami Building as an observer. I had to grant that."

"That's going to mean trouble."

"Oh, I shouldn't think so. This observer will observe, and nothing else. She will take no part in anything you're doing, will voice no objections, and will not interrupt anything you are saying to the shoonoon. I was quite firm on that, and the governor general agreed completely."

"She?"

"Yes. A Miss Edith Shaw; do you know anything about her?"

"I've met her a few times; cocktail parties and so on." She was young enough, and new enough to Kwannon, not to have a completely indurated mind. On the other hand, she was EETA which was bad, and had a master's in sociography from Adelaide, which was worse. "When can I look for her?"

"Well, the governor general's going to screen me and find out when you'll have the shoonoon on hand."

Doesn't want to talk to me at all, Miles thought. Afraid he might say something and get quoted.

"For your information, they'll be here inside an hour. They will have to eat, and they're all tired and sleepy. I should say 'bout oh-eight-hundred. Oh, and will you tell the governor general to tell Miss Shaw to bring an overnight kit with her. She's going to need it."

He was up at 0400, just a little after Beta-rise. He might be a civilian big-wheel in an Army psychological warfare project, but he still had four newscasts a day to produce. He spent a couple of hours checking the 0600 'cast and briefing Harry Walsh for the indeterminate period in which he would be acting chief editor and producer. At 0700, Foxx Travis put in an appearance. They went down to the fourth floor, to the little room they had fitted out as command-post, control room and office for Operation Shoonoo.

There was a rectangular black traveling-case, initialed E. S., beside the open office door. Travis nodded at it, and they grinned at one another; she'd come early, possibly hoping to catch them hiding something they didn't want her to see. Entering the office quietly, they found her seated facing the big viewscreen, smoking and watching a couple of enlisted men of the First Kwannon Native Infantry at work in another room where the pickup was. There were close to a dozen lipstick-tinted cigarette butts in the ashtray beside her. Her private face wasn't particularly happy. Maybe she was being earnest and concerned about the betterment of the underpriviledged, or the satanic maneuvers of the selfish planters.

Then she realized that somebody had entered; with a slight start, she turned, then rose. She was about the height of Foxx Travis, a few inches shorter than Miles, and slender. Light blond; green suit costume. She ditched her private face and got on her public one, a pleasant and deferential smile, with a trace of uncertainty behind it. Miles introduced Travis, and they sat down again facing the screen.

It gave a view, from one of the long sides and near the ceiling, of a big room. In the center, a number of seats-the drum-shaped cushions the natives had adopted in place of the seats carved from sections of tree trunk that they had been using when the Terrans had come to Kwannon-were arranged in a semicircle, one in the middle slightly in advance of the others. Facing them were three armchairs, a remote-control box beside one and another Kwann cushion behind and between the other two. There was a large globe of Kwannon, and on the wall behind the chairs an array of viewscreens.

"There'll be an interpreter, a native Army sergeant, between you and Captain Travis," he said. "I don't know how good you are with native languages, Miss Shaw; the captain is not very fluent."

"Cushions for them, I see, and chairs for the lordly Terrans," she commented. "Never miss a chance to rub our superiority in, do you?"

"I never deliberately force them to adopt our ways," he replied. "Our chairs are as uncomfortable for them as their low seats are for us. Difference, you know, doesn't mean inferiority or superiority. It just means difference."

"Well, what are you trying to do, here?"

"I'm trying to find out a little more about the psychology back of these frenzies and swarmings."

"It hasn't occurred to you to look for them in the economic wrongs these people are suffering at the hands of the planters and traders, I suppose."

"So they're committing suicide, and that's all you can call these swarmings, and the fire-frenzies in the south, from economic motives," Travis said. "How does one better oneself economically by dying?"

She ignored the question, which was easier than trying to answer it.

"And why are you bothering to talk to these witch doctors? They aren't representative of the native people. They're a lot of cynical charlatans, with a vested interest in ignorance and superstition —"

"Miss Shaw, for the past eight centuries, earnest souls have been bewailing the fact that progress in the social sciences has always lagged behind progress in the physical sciences. I would suggest that the explanation might be in difference of approach. The physical scientist works *with* physical forces, even when he is trying, as in the case of contragravity, to nullify them. The social scientist works *against* social forces."

"And the result's usually a miserable failure, even on the physical-accomplishment level," Foxx Travis added. "This storm shelter project that was set up ten years ago and got nowhere, for instance. Ramón Gonzales set up a shelter project of his own seventy-five hours ago, and he's half through with it now."

"Yes, by forced labor!"

"Field surgery's brutal, too, especially when the anaesthetics run out. It's better than letting your wounded die, though."

"Well, we were talking about these shoonoon. They are a force among the natives; that can't be denied. So, since we want to influence the natives, why not use them?"

"Mr. Gilbert, these shoonoon are blocking everything we are trying to do for the natives. If you use them for propaganda work in the villages, you will only increase their prestige and make it that much harder for us to better the natives' condition, both economically and culturally —"

"That's it, Miles," Travis said. "She isn't interested in facts about specific humanoid people on Kwannon. She has a lot of high-order abstractions she got in a classroom at Adelaide on Terra."

"No. Her idea of bettering the natives' condition is to rope in a lot of young Kwanns, put them in Government schools, overload them with information they aren't prepared to digest, teach them to despise their own people, and then send them out to the villages, where they behave with such insufferable arrogance that the wonder is that so few of them stop an arrow or a charge of buckshot, instead of so many. And when that happens, as it does occasionally, Welfare says they're murdered at the instigation of the shoonoon."

"You know, Miss Shaw, this isn't just the roughneck's scorn for the egghead," Travis said. "Miles went to school on Terra, and majored in extraterrestrial sociography, and got a master's, just like you did. At Montevideo," he added. "And he spent two more years traveling on a Paula von Schlicten Fellowship."

Edith Shaw didn't say anything. She even tried desperately not to look impressed. It occurred to him that he'd never mentioned that fellowship to Travis. Army Intelligence must have a pretty good *dossier* on him. Before anybody could say anything further, a Terran captain and a native sergeant of the First K.N.I. came in. In the screen, the four sepoys who had been fussing around straightening things picked up auto-carbines and posted themselves two on either side of a door across from the pickup, taking positions that would permit them to fire into whatever came through without hitting each other.

What came through was one hundred and eighty-four shoonoon. Some wore robes of loose gauze strips, and some wore fire-dance cloaks of red and yellow and orange ribbons. Many were almost completely naked, but they were all amulet-ed to the teeth. There must have been a couple of miles of brass and bright-alloy wire among them, and half a ton of bright scrap-metal, and the skulls, bones, claws, teeth, tails and other components of most of the native fauna. They debouched into the big room, stopped, and stood looking around them. A native sergeant and a couple more sepoys followed. They got the shoonoon over to the semicircle of cushions, having to chase a couple of them away from the single seat at front and center, and induced them to sit down.

The native sergeant in the little room said something under his breath; the captain laughed. Edith Shaw gaped for an instant and said, "*Muggawsh!*" Travis simply remarked that he'd be damned.

"They do look kind of unusual, don't they?" Miles said. "I wouldn't doubt that this is the biggest assemblage of shoonoon in history. They aren't exactly a gregarious lot."

"Maybe this is the beginning of a new era. First meeting of the Kwannon Thaumaturgical Society."

A couple more K.N.I. privates came in with serving-tables on contragravity floats and began passing bowls of a frozen native-food delicacy of which all Kwanns had become passionately fond since its introduction by the Terrans. He let them finish, and then, after they had been relieved of the empty bowls, he nodded to the K.N.I. sergeant, who opened a door on the left. They all went through into the room they had been seeing in the screen. There was a stir when the shoonoon saw him, and he heard his name, in its usual native mispronunciation, repeated back and forth.

"You all know me," he said, after they were seated. "Have I ever been an enemy to you or to the People?"

"No," one of them said. "He speaks for us to the other Terrans. When we are wronged, he tries to get the wrongs righted. In times of famine he has spoken of our troubles, and gifts of food have come while the Government argued about what to do."

He wished he could see Edith Shaw's face.

"There was a sickness in our village, and my magic could not cure it," another said. "Mailsh Heelbare gave me oomphel to cure it, and told me how to use it. He did this privately, so that I would not be made to look small to the people of the village."

And that had infuriated EETA; it was a question whether unofficial help to the natives or support of the prestige of a shoonoo had angered them more.

"His father was a trader; he gave good oomphel, and did not cheat. Mailsh Heelbare grew up among us; he took the Manhood Test with the boys of the village," another oldster said. "He listened with respect to the grandfather-stories. No, Mailsh Heelbare is not our enemy. He is our friend."

"And so I will prove myself now," he told them. "The Government is angry with the People, but I will try to take their anger away, and in the meantime I am permitted to come here and talk with you. Here is a chief of soldiers, and one of the Government people, and your words will be heard by the oomphel machine that remembers and repeats, for the Governor and the Great Soldier Chief."

They all brightened. To make a voice recording was a wonderful honor. Then one of them said:

"But what good will that do now? The Last Hot Time is here. Let us be permitted to return to our villages, where our people need us."

"It is of that that I wish to speak. But first of all, I must hear your words, and know what is in your minds. Who is the eldest among you? Let him come forth and sit in the front, where I may speak with him."

Then he relaxed while they argued in respectfully subdued voices. Finally one decrepit oldster, wearing a cloak of yellow ribbons and carrying a highly obscene and ineffably sacred wooden image, was brought forward and installed on the front-and-center cushion. He'd come from some village to the west that hadn't gotten the word of the swarming; Gonzales' men had snagged him while he was making crop-fertility magic.

Miles showed him the respect due his advanced age and obviously great magical powers, displaying, as he did, an understanding of the regalia.

"I have indeed lived long," the old shoonoo replied. "I saw the Hot Time before; I was a child of so high." He measured about two and a half feet off the floor; that would make him ninety-five or thereabouts. "I remember it."

"Speak to us, then. Tell us of the Gone Ones, and of the Sky Fire, and of the Last Hot Time. Speak as though you alone knew these things, and as though you were teaching me."

Delighted, the oldster whooshed a couple of times to clear his outlets and began:

"In the long-ago time, there was only the Great Spirit. The Great Spirit made the World, and he made the People. In that time, there were no more People in the World than would be in one village, now. The Gone Ones dwelt among them, and spoke to them as I speak to you. Then, as more People were born, and died and went to join the Gone Ones, the Gone Ones became many, and they went away and build a place for themselves, and built the Sky Fire around it, and in the Place of the Gone Ones, at the middle of the Sky Fire, it is cool. From their place in the Sky Fire, the Gone Ones send wisdom to the people in dreams.

"The Sky Fire passes across the sky, from east to west, as the Always-Same does, but it is farther away than the Always-Same, because sometimes the Always Same passes in front of it, but the Sky Fire never passes in front of the Always-Same. None of the grandfather-stories, not even the oldest, tell of a time when this happened.

"Sometimes the Sky Fire is big and bright; that is when the Gone Ones feast and dance. Sometimes it is smaller and dimmer; then the Gone Ones rest and sleep. Sometimes it is close, and there is a Hot Time; sometimes it goes far away, and then there is a Cool Time.

"Now, the Last Hot Time has come. The Sky Fire will come closer and closer, and it will pass the Always-Same, and then it will burn up the World. Then will be a new World, and the Gone Ones will return, and the People will be given new bodies. When this happens, the Sky Fire will go out, and the Gone Ones will live in the World again with the People; the Gone Ones will make great magic and teach wisdom as I teach to you, and will no longer have to send dreams. In that time the crops will grow without planting or tending or the work of women; in that time, the game will come into the villages to be killed in the gathering-places. There will be no more hunger and no more hard work, and no more of the People will die or be slain. And that time is now here," he finished. "All the People know this."

"Tell me, Grandfather; how is this known? There have been many Hot Times before. Why should this one be the Last Hot Time?"

"The Terrans have come, and brought oomphel into the World," the old shoonoo said. "It is a sign."

"It was not prophesied beforetime. None of the People had prophesies of the coming of the Terrans. I ask you, who were the father of children and the grandfather of children's children when the Terrans came; was there any such prophesy?"

The old shoonoo was silent, turning his pornographic ikon in his hands and looked at it.

"No," he admitted, at length. "Before the Terrans came, there were no prophesies among the People of their coming. Afterward, of course, there were many such prophesies, but there were none before."

"That is strange. When a happening is a sign of something to come, it is prophesied beforetime." He left that seed of doubt alone to grow, and continued: "Now, Grandfather, speak to us about what the People believe concerning the Terrans."

"The Terrans came to the World when my eldest daughter bore her first child," the old shoonoo said. "They came in great round ships, such as come often now, but which had never before been seen. They said that they came from another world like the World of People, but so far away that even the Sky Fire could not be seen from it. They still say this, and many of the People believe it, but it is not real.

"At first, it was thought that the Terrans were great shoonoon who made powerful magic, but this is not real either. The Terrans have no magic and no wisdom of their own. All they have is the oomphel, and the oomphel works magic for them and teaches them their wisdom. Even in the schools which the Terrans have made for the People, it is the oomphel which teaches." He went on to describe, not too incorrectly, the reading-screens and viewscreens and audio-visual equipment. "Nor do the Terrans make the oomphel, as they say. The oomphel makes more oomphel for them."

"Then where did the Terrans get the first oomphel?"

"They stole it from the Gone Ones," the old shoonoo replied. "The Gone Ones make it in their place in the middle of the Sky Fire, for themselves and to give to the People when they return. The Terrans stole it from them. For this reason, there is much hatred of the Terrans among the People. The Terrans live in the Dark Place, under the World, where the Sky Fire and the Always-Same go when they are not in the sky. It is there that the Terrans get the oomphel from the Gone Ones, and now they have come to the World, and they are using oomphel to hold back the Sky-Fire and keep it beyond the Always-Same so that the Last Hot Time will not come and the Gone Ones will not return. For this reason, too, there is much hatred of the Terrans among the People."

"Grandfather, if this were real there would be good reason for such hatred, and I would be ashamed for what my people had done and were doing. But it is not real." He had to rise and hold up his hands to quell the indignant outcry "Have any of you known me to tell not-real things and try to make the People act as though they were real? Then trust me in this. I will show you real things, which you will all see, and I will give you great secrets, which it is now time for you to have and use for the good of the People. Even the greatest secret," he added.

There was a pause of a few seconds. Then they burst out, in a hundred and eighty-four —no, three hundred and sixty eight-voices:

"The Oomphel Secret, Mailsh Heelbare?"

He nodded slowly. "Yes. The Oomphel Secret will be given."

He leaned back and relaxed again while they were getting over the excitement. Foxx Travis looked at him apprehensively.

"Rushing things, aren't you? What are you going to tell them?"

"Oh, a big pack of lies, I suppose," Edith Shaw said scornfully.

Behind her and Travis, the native noncom interpreter was muttering something in his own language that translated roughly as: "This better be good!"

The shoonoon had quieted, now, and were waiting breathlessly.

"But if the Oomphel Secret is given, what will become of the shoonoon?" he asked. "You, yourselves, say that we Terrans have no need for magic, because the oomphel works magic for us. This is real. If the People get the Oomphel Secret, how much need will they have for you shoonoon?"

Evidently that hadn't occurred to them before. There was a brief flurry of whis-pered-whooshed, rather-conversation, and then they were silent again. The eldest shoonoo said:

"We trust you, Mailsh Heelbare. You will do what is best for the People, and you will not let us be thrown out like broken pots, either."

"No, I will not," he promised. "The Oomphel Secret will be given to you shoonoon." He thought for a moment of Foxx Travis' joking remark about the Kwannon Thaumaturgical Soci-ety. "You have been jealous of one another, each keeping his own secrets," he said. "This must be put away. You will all receive the Oomphel Secret equally, for the good of all the People. You must all swear brotherhood, one with another, and later if any other shoonoo comes to you for the secret, you must swear brotherhood with him and teach it to him. Do you agree to this?"

The eldest shoonoo rose to his feet, begged leave, and then led the others to the rear of the room, where they went into a huddle. They didn't stay huddled long; inside of ten minutes they came back and took their seats.

"We are agreed, Mailsh Heelbare," the spokesman said.

Edith Shaw was impressed, more than by anything else she had seen. "Well, that was a quick decision!" she whispered.

"You have done well, Grandfathers. You will not be thrown out by the People like broken pots; you will be greater among them than ever. I will show you how this will be.

"But first, I must speak around the Oomphel Secret." He groped briefly for a comprehensible analogy, and thought of a native vegetable, layered like an onion, with a hard kernel in the middle. "The Oomphel Secret is like a fooshkoot. There are many lesser secrets around it, each of which must be peeled off like the skins of a fooshkoot and eaten. Then you will find the nut in the middle."

"But the nut of the fooshkoot is bitter," somebody said.

He nodded, slowly and solemnly. "The nut of the fooshkoot is bitter," he agreed.

They looked at one another, disquieted by his words. Before anybody could comment, he was continuing:

"Before this secret is given, there are things to be learned. You would not understand it if I gave it to you now. You believe many not-real things which must be chased out of your minds, otherwise they would spoil your understanding."

That was verbatim what they told adolescents before giving them the Manhood Secret. Some of them huffed a little; most of them laughed. Then one called out: "Speak on, Grandfather of Grandfathers," and they all laughed. That was fine, it had been about time for teacher to crack his little joke. Now he became serious again.

"The first of these not-real things you must chase from your mind is this which you believe about the home of the Terrans. It is not real that they come from the Dark Place under the World. There is no Dark Place under the World."

Bedlam for a few seconds; that was a pretty stiff jolt. No Dark Place; who ever heard of such a thing? The eldest shoonoo rose, cradling his graven image in his arms, and the noise quieted.

"Mailsh Heelbare, if there is no Dark Place where do the Sky Fire and the Always-Same go when they are not in the sky?"

"They never leave the sky; the World is round, and there is sky everywhere around it."

They knew that, or had at least heard it, since the Terrans had come. They just couldn't believe it. It was against common sense. The oldest shoonoo said as much, and more:

"These young ones who have gone to the Terran schools have come to the villages with such tales, but who listens to them? They show disrespect for the chiefs and the elders, and even for the shoonoon. They mock at the Grandfather-stories. They say men should do women's work and women do no work at all. They break taboos, and cause trouble. They are fools."

"Am I a fool, Grandfather? Do I mock at the old stories, or show disrespect to elders and shoonoon? Yet I, Mailsh Heelbare, tell you this. The World is indeed round, and I will show you."

The shoonoo looked contemptuously at the globe. "I have seen those things," he said. "That is not the World; that is only a make-like." He held up his phallic wood-carving. "I could say that this is a make-like of the World, but that would not make it so."

"I will show you for real. We will all go in a ship." He looked at his watch. "The Sky Fire is about to set. We will follow it all around the world to the west, and come back here from the east, and the Sky Fire will still be setting when we return. If I show you that, will you believe me?"

"If you show us for real, and it is not a trick, we will have to believe you."

When they emerged from the escalators, Alpha was just touching the western horizon, and Beta was a little past zenith. The ship was moored on contragravity beside the landing stage, her gangplank run out. The shoonoon, who had gone up ahead, had all stopped short and were staring at her; then they began gabbling among themselves, overcome by the wonder of being about to board such a monster and ride on her. She was the biggest ship any of them had ever seen. Maybe a few of them had been on small freighters; many of them had never been off the ground. They didn't look or act like cynical charlatans or implacable enemies of progress and enlightenment. They were more like a lot of schoolboys whose teacher is taking them on a surprise outing.

"Bet this'll be the biggest day in their lives," Travis said.

"Oh, sure. This'll be a grandfather-story ten generations from now."

"I can't get over the way they made up their minds, down there," Edith Shaw was saying. "Why, they just went and talked for a few minutes and came back with a decision."

They hadn't any organization, or any place to maintain on an organizational pecking-order. Nobody was obliged to attack anybody else's proposition in order to keep up his own status. He thought of the Colonial Government taking ten years not to build those storm-shelters.

Foxx Travis was commenting on the ship, now:

"I never saw that ship before; didn't know there was anything like that on the planet. Why, you could lift a whole regiment, with supplies and equipment —"

"She's been laid up for the last five years, since the heat and the native troubles stopped the tourist business here. She's the old *Hesperus*. Excursion craft. This sun-chasing trip we're going to make used to be a must for tourists here."

"I thought she was something like that, with all the glassed observation deck forward. Who's the owner?"

"Kwannon Air Transport, Ltd. I told them what I needed her for, and they made her available and furnished officers and crew and provisions for the trip. They were working to put her in commission while we were fitting up the fourth and fifth floors, downstairs."

"You just asked for that ship, and they just let you have it?" Edith Shaw was incredulous and shocked. They wouldn't have done that for the Government.

"They want to see these native troubles stopped, too. Bad for business. You know; selfish profit-move. That's another social force it's a good idea to work with instead of against."

The shoonoon were getting aboard, now, shepherded by the K.N.I. officer and a couple of his men and some of the ship's crew. A couple of sepoys were lugging the big globe that had been brought up from below after them. Everybody assembled on the forward top observation deck, and Miles called for attention and, finally, got it. He pointed out the three viewscreens mounted below the bridge, amidships. One on the left, was tuned to a pickup on the top of the Air Terminal tower, where the Terran city, the military reservation and the spaceport met. It showed the view to the west, with Alpha on the horizon. The one on the right, from the same point, gave a view in the opposite direction, to the east. The middle screen presented a magnified view of the navigational globe on the bridge.

Viewscreens were no novelty to the shoonoon. They were a very familiar type of oomphel. He didn't even need to do more than tell them that the little spot of light on the globe would show the position of the ship. When he was sure that they understood that they could see what was happening in Bluelake while they were away, he called the bridge and ordered Up Ship, telling the officer on duty to hold her at five thousand feet.

The ship rose slowly, turning toward the setting M-giant. Somebody called attention that the views in the screens weren't changing. Somebody else said:

"Of course not. What we see for real changes because the ship is moving. What we see in the screens is what the oomphel on the big building sees, and it does not move. That is for real as the oomphel sees it."

"Nice going," Edith said. "Your class has just discovered relativity." Travis was looking at the eastward viewscreen. He stepped over beside Miles and lowered his voice.

"Trouble over there to the east of town. Big swarm of combat contragravity working on something on the ground. And something's on fire, too."

"I see it."

"That's where those evacuees are camped. Why in blazes they had to bring them here to Bluelake —"

That had been EETA, too. When the solar tides had gotten high enough to flood the coastal area, the natives who had been evacuated from the district had been brought here because the Native Education people wanted them exposed to urban influences. About half of the shoonoon who had been rounded up locally had come in from the tide-inundated area.

"Parked right in the middle of the Terran-type food production area," Travis was continuing.

That was worrying him. Maybe he wasn't used to planets where the biochemistry wasn't Terra-type and a Terran would be poisoned or, at best, starve to death, on the local food; maybe, as a soldier he knew how fragile even the best logistics system can be. It was something to worry about. Travis excused himself and went off in the direction of the bridge. Going to call HQ and find out what was happening.

Excitement among the shoonoon; they had spotted the ship on which they were riding in the westward screen. They watched it until it had vanished from "sight of the seeing-oomphel," and by then were over the upland forests from whence they had been brought to Bluelake. Now and then one of them would identify his own village, and that would start more excitement.

Three infantry troop-carriers and a squadron of air cavalry were rushing past the eastward pickup in the right hand screen; another fire had started in the trouble area.

The crowd that had gathered around the globe that had been brought aboard began calling for Mailsh Heelbare to show them how they would go around the world and what countries they would pass over. Edith accompanied him and listened while he talked to them. She was bubbling with happy excitement, now. It had just dawned on her that shoonoon were fun.

None of them had ever seen the mountains along the western side of the continent except from a great distance. Now they were passing over them; the ship had to gain altitude and even then make a detour around one snow-capped peak. The whole hundred and eighty-four rushed to the starboard side to watch it as they passed. The ocean, half an hour later, started a rush forward. The score or so of them from the Tidewater knew what an ocean was, but none of them had known that there was another one to the west. Miles' view of the education program of the EETA, never bright at best, became even dimmer. *The young men who have gone to the Terran schools … who listens to them? They are fools.*

There were a few islands off the coast; the shoonoon identified them on the screen globe, and on the one on deck. Some of them wanted to know why there wasn't a spot of light on this globe, too. It didn't have the oomphel inside to do that; that was a satisfactory explanation. Edith started to explain about the orbital beacon-stations off-planet and the radio beams, and then stopped.

"I'm sorry; I'm not supposed to say anything to them," she apologized.

"Oh, that's all right. I wouldn't go into all that, though. We don't want to overload them."

She asked permission, a little later, to explain why the triangle tip of the arctic continent, which had begun to edge into sight on the screen globe, couldn't be seen from the ship. When he told her to go ahead, she got a platinum half-sol piece from her purse, held it on the globe from the classroom and explained about the curvature and told them they could see nothing farther away than the circle the coin covered. It was beginning to look as though the psycho-logical-warfare experiment might show another, unexpected, success.

There was nothing, after the islands passed, but a lot of empty water. The shoonoon were getting hungry, but they refused to go below to eat. They were afraid they might miss something. So their dinner was brought up on deck for them. Miles and Travis and Edith went to the officers' dining room back of the bridge. Edith, by now, was even more excited than the shoonoon.

"They're so anxious to learn!" She was having trouble adjusting to that; that was dead against EETA doctrine. "But why wouldn't they listen to the teachers we sent to the villages?"

"You heard old Shatresh-the fellow with the pornographic sculpture and the yellow robe. These young twerps act like fools, and sensible people don't pay any attention to fools. What's more, they've been sent out indoctrinated with the idea that shoonoon are a lot of lying old fakes, and the shoonoon resent that. You know, they're not lying old fakes. Within their limitations, they are honest and ethical professional people."

"Oh, come, now! I know, I think they're sort of wonderful, but let's don't give them too much credit."

"I'm not. You're doing that."

"*Huh?*" She looked at him in amazement. "Me?"

"Yes, you. You know better than to believe in magic, so you expect them to know better, too. Well, they don't. You know that under the macroscopic world-of-the senses there exists a complex of biological, chemical and physical phenomena down to the subnucleonic level. They realize that there must be something beyond what they can see and handle, but they think it's magic. Well, as a race, so did we until only a few centuries pre-atomic. These people are still lower Neolithic, a hunting people who have just learned agriculture. Where we were twenty thousand years ago.

"You think any glib-talking Kwann can hang a lot of rags, bones and old iron onto himself, go through some impromptu mummery, and set up as shoonoo? Well, he can't. The shoonoon are a hereditary caste. A shoonoo father will begin teaching his son as soon as he can walk and talk, and he keeps on teaching him till he's the age-equivalent of a graduate M.D. or a science Ph. D."

"Well, what all is there to learn —?"

"The theoretical basis and practical applications of sympathetic magic. Action-at-a-distance by one object upon another. Homeopathic magic: the principle that things which resemble one another will interact. For instance, there's an animal the natives call a shynph. It has an excrescence of horn on its brow like an arrowhead, and it arches its back like a bow when it jumps. Therefore, a shynph is equal to a bow and arrow, and for that reason the Kwanns made their bowstrings out of shynph-gut. Now they use tensilon because it won't break as easily or get wet and stretch. So they have to turn the tensilon into shynph-gut. They used to do that by drawing a picture of a shynph on the spool, and then the traders began labeling the spools with pictures of shynph. I think my father was one of the first to do that.

"Then, there's contagious magic. Anything that's been part of anything else or come in contact with it will interact permanently with it. I wish I had a sol for every time I've seen a Kwann pull the wad out of a shot-shell, pick up a pinch of dirt from the footprint of some animal he's tracking, put it in among the buckshot, and then crimp the wad in again.

"Everything a Kwann does has some sort of magical implications. It's the shoonoo's business to know all this; to be able to tell just what magical influences have to be produced, and what influences must be avoided. And there are circumstances in which magic simply will not work, even in theory. The reason is that there is some powerful counter-influence at work. He has to know when he can't use magic, and he has to be able to explain why. And when he's theoretically able to do something by magic, he has to have a plausible explanation why it won't produce results-just as any highly civilized and ethical Terran M.D. has to be able to explain his failures to the satisfaction of his late patient's relatives. Only a shoonoo doesn't get sued for malpractice; he gets a spear stuck in him. Under those circumstances, a caste of hereditary magicians is literally bred for quick thinking. These old gaffers we have aboard are the intellectual top crust among the natives. Any of them can think rings around your Government school products. As for preying on the ignorance and credulity of the other natives, they're only infinitesimally less ignorant and credulous themselves. But they want to learn-from anybody who can gain their respect by respecting them."

Edith Shaw didn't say anything in reply. She was thoughtful during the rest of the meal, and when they were back on the observation deck he noticed that she seemed to be looking at the shoonoon with new eyes.

In the screen-views of Bluelake, Beta had already set, and the sky was fading; stars had begun to twinkle. There were more fires-one, close to the city in the east, a regular conflagration-and fighting had broken out in the native city itself. He was wishing now, that he hadn't thought it necessary to use those screens. The shoonoon were noticing what was going on in them, and talking among themselves. Travis, after one look at the situation, hurried back to the bridge to make a screen-call. After a while, he returned, almost crackling with suppressed excitement.

"Well, it's finally happened! Maith's forced Kovac to declare martial rule!" he said in an exultant undertone.

"Forced him?" Edith was puzzled. "The Army can't force the Civil Government —"

"He threatened to do it himself. Intervene and suspend civil rule."

"But I thought only the Navy could do that."

"Any planetary commander of Armed Forces can, in a state of extreme emergency. I think you'll both agree that this emergency is about as extreme as they come. Kovac knew that Maith was unwilling to do it-he'd have to stand court-martial to justify his action-but he also knew that a governor general who has his Colony taken away from him by the Armed Forces never gets it back; he's finished. So it was just a case of the weaker man in the weaker position yielding."

"Where does this put us?"

"We are a civilian scientific project. You are under orders of General Maith. I am under your orders. I don't know about Edith."

"Can I draft her, or do I have to get you to get General Maith to do it?"

"Listen, don't do that," Edith protested. "I still have to work for Government House, and this martial rule won't last forever. They'll all be prejudiced against me —"

"You can shove your Government job on the air lock," Miles told her. "You'll have a better one with Planetwide News, at half again as much pay. And after the shakeup at Government House, about a year from now, you may be going back as director of EETA. When they find out on Terra just how badly this Government has been mismanaging things there'll be a lot of vacancies."

The shoonoon had been watching the fighting in the viewscreens. Then somebody noticed that the spot of light on the navigational globe was approaching a coastline, and they all rushed forward for a look.

Travis and Edith slept for a while; when they returned to relieve him, Alpha was rising to the east of Bluelake, and the fighting in the city was still going on. The shoonoon were still wakeful and interested; Kwanns could go without sleep for much longer periods than Terrans. The lack of any fixed cycle of daylight and darkness on their planet had left them unconditioned to any regular sleeping-and-waking rhythm.

"I just called in," Travis said. "Things aren't good, at all. Most of the natives in the evacuee cantonments have gotten into the native city, now, and they've gotten hold of a lot of firearms somehow. And they're getting nasty in the west, beyond where Gonzales is occupying, and in the northeast, and we only have about half enough troops to cope with everything. The general wants to know how you're making out with the shoonoon."

"I'll call him before I get in the sack."

He went up on the bridge and made the call. General Maith looked as sleepy as he felt; they both yawned as they greeted each other. There wasn't much he could tell the general, and it sounded like the glib reassurances one gets from a hospital about a friend's condition.

"We'll check in with you as soon as we get back and get our shoonoon put away. We understand what's motivating these frenzies, now, and in about twenty-five to thirty hours we'll be able to start doing something about it."

The general, in the screen, grimaced.

"That's a long time, Mr. Gilbert. Longer than we can afford to take, I'm afraid. You're not cruising at full speed now, are you?"

"Oh, no, general. We're just trying to keep Alpha level on the horizon." He thought for a moment. "We don't need to keep down to that. It may make an even bigger impression if we speed up."

He went back to the observation deck, picked up the PA-phone, and called for attention.

"You have seen, now, that we can travel around the world, so fast that we keep up with the Sky Fire and it is not seen to set. Now we will travel even faster, and I will show you a new wonder. I will show you the Sky Fire rising in the west; it and the Always-Same will seem to go backward in the sky. This will not be for real; it will only be seen so because we will be traveling faster. Watch, now, and see." He called the bridge for full speed, and then told them to look at the Sky-Fire and then see in the screens where it stood over Bluelake.

That was even better; now they were racing with the Sky-Fire and catching up to it. After half an hour he left them still excited and whooping gleefully over the steady gain. Five hours later, when he came back after a nap and a hasty breakfast, they were still whooping. Edith Shaw was excited, too; the shoonoon were trying to estimate how soon they would be back to Bluelake by comparing the position of the Sky Fire with its position in the screen.

General Maith received them in his private office at Army HQ; Foxx Travis mixed drinks for the four of them while the general checked the microphones to make sure they had privacy.

"I blame myself for not having forced martial rule on them hundreds of hours ago," he said. "I have three brigades; the one General Gonzales had here originally, and the two I brought with me when I took over here. We have to keep at least half a brigade in the south, to keep the tribes there from starting any more forest fires. I can't hold Bluelake with anything less than half a brigade. Gonzales has his hands full in his area. He had a nasty business while you were off on that world cruise-natives in one village caught the men stationed there off guard and wiped them out, and then started another frenzy. It spread to two other villages before he got it stopped. And we need the Third Brigade in the northeast; there are three quarters of a million natives up there, inhabiting close to a million square miles. And if anything really breaks loose here, and what's been going on in the last few days is nothing even approaching what a real outbreak could be like, we'll have to pull in troops from everywhere. We must save the Terran-type crops and the carniculture plants. If we don't, we all starve."

Miles nodded. There wasn't anything he could think of saying to that.

"How soon can you begin to show results with those shoonoon, Mr. Gilbert?" the general asked. "You said from twenty-five to thirty hours. Can you cut that any? In twenty-five hours, all hell could be loose all over the continent."

Miles shook his head. "So far, I haven't accomplished anything positive," he said. "All I did with this trip around the world was convince them that I was telling the truth when I told them there was no Dark Place under the World, where Alpha and Beta go at night." He hastened, as the general began swearing, to add: "I know, that doesn't sound like much. But it was necessary. I have to convince them that there will be no Last Hot Time, and then —"

The shoonoon, on their drum-shaped cushions, stared at him in silence, aghast. All the happiness over the wonderful trip in the ship, when they had chased the Sky Fire around the World and caught it over Bluelake, and even their pleasure in the frozen delicacies they had just eaten, was gone.

"No-Last-Hot-Time?"

"Mailsh Heelbare, this is not real! It cannot be!"

"The Gone Ones—"

"The Always-Cool Time, when there will be no more hunger or hard work or death; it cannot be real that this will never come!"

He rose, holding up his hands; his action stopped the clamor.

"Why should the Gone Ones want to return to this poor world that they have gladly left?" he asked. "Have they not a better place in the middle of the Sky Fire, where it is always cool? And why should you want them to come back to this world? Will not each one of you pass, sooner or later, to the middle of the Sky Fire; will you not there be given new bodies and join the Gone Ones? There is the Always-Cool; there the crops grow without planting and without the work of women; there the game come into the villages to be killed in the gathering-places, without hunting. There you will talk with the other Gone Ones, your fathers and your fathers' fathers, as I talk with you. Why do you think this must come to the World of People? Can you not wait to join the Gone Ones in the Sky Fire?"

Then he sat down and folded his arms. They were looking at him in amazement; evidently they all saw the logic, but none of them had ever thought of it before. Now they would have to turn it over in their minds and accustom themselves to the new viewpoint. They began whooshing among themselves. At length, old Shatresh, who had seen the Hot Time before, spoke:

"Mailsh Heelbare, we trust you," he said. "You have told us of wonders, and you have shown us that they were real. But do you know this for real?"

"Do you tell me that you do not?" he demanded in surprise. "You have had fathers, and fathers' fathers. They have gone to join the Gone Ones. Why should you not, also? And why should the Gone Ones come back and destroy the World of People? Then your children will have no more children, and your children's children will never be. It is in the World of People that the People are born; it is in the World that they grow and gain wisdom to fit themselves to live in the Place of the Gone Ones when they are through with the bodies they use in the World. You should be happy that there will be no Last Hot Time, and that the line of your begettings will go on and not be cut short."

There were murmurs of agreement with this. Most of them were beginning to be relieved that there wouldn't be a Last Hot Time, after all. Then one of the class asked:

"Do the Terrans also go to the Place of the Gone Ones, or have they a place of their own?"

He was silent for a long time, looking down at the floor. Then he raised his head.

"I had hoped that I would not have to speak of this," he said. "But, since you have asked, it is right that I should tell you." He hesitated again, until the Kwanns in front of him had begun to fidget. Then he asked old Shatresh: "Speak of the beliefs of the People about how the World was made."

"The great Spirit made the world." He held up his carven obscenity. "He made the World out of himself. This is a make-like to show it."

"The Great Spirit made many worlds. The stars which you see in dark-time are all worlds, each with many smaller worlds around it. The Great Spirit made them all at one time, and made people on many of them. The Great Spirit made the World of People, and made the Always-Same and the Sky Fire, and inside the Sky Fire he made the Place of the Gone Ones. And when he made the Place of the Gone Ones, he put an Oomphel-Mother inside it, to bring forth oomphel."

This created a brief sensation. An Oomphel-Mother was something they had never thought of before, but now they were wondering why they hadn't. Of course there'd be an Oomphel-Mother; how else would there be oomphel?

"The World of the Terrans is far away from the World of People, as we have always told you. When the Great Spirit made it He gave it only an Always-Same, and no Sky Fire. Since there was no Sky Fire, there was no place to put a Place of the Gone Ones, so the Great Spirit made the

Terrans so that they would not die, but live forever in their own bodies. The Oomphel-Mother for the World of the Terrans the Great Spirit hid in a cave under a great mountain.

"The Terrans whom the Great Spirit made lived for a long time, and then, one day, a man and a woman found a crack in a rock, and went inside, and they found the cave of the Oomphel-Mother, and the Oomphel-Mother in it. So they called all the other Terrans, and they brought the Oomphel-Mother out, and the Oomphel-Mother began to bring forth Oomphel. The Oomphel-Mother brought forth metal, and cloth, and glass, and plastic; knives, and axes and guns and clothing—" He went on, cataloguing the products of human technology, the shoonoon staring more and more wide-eyed at him. "And oomphel to make oomphel, and oomphel to teach wisdom," he finished. "They became very wise and very rich.

"Then the Great Spirit saw what the Terrans had done, and became angry, for it was not meant for the Terrans to do this, and the Great Spirit cursed the Terrans with a curse of death. It was not death as you know it. Because the Terrans had sinned by laying hands on the Oomphel-Mother, not only their bodies must die, but their spirits also. A Terran has a short life in the body, after that no life."

"This, then, is the Oomphel Secret. The last skin of the fooshkoot has been peeled away; behold the bitter nut, upon which we Terrans have chewed for more time than anybody can count. Happy people! When you die or are slain, you go to the Place of the Gone Ones, to join your fathers and your fathers' fathers and to await your children and children's children. When we die or are slain, that is the end of us."

"But you have brought your oomphel into this world; have you not brought the curse with it?" somebody asked, frightened.

"No. The People did not sin against the Great Spirit; they have not laid hands on an Oomphel-Mother as we did. The oomphel we bring you will do no harm; do you think we would be so wicked as to bring the curse upon you? It will be good for you to learn about oomphel here; in your Place of the Gone Ones there is much oomphel."

"Why did your people come to this world, Mailsh Heelbare?" old Shatresh asked. "Was it to try to hide from the curse?"

"There is no hiding from the curse of the Great Spirit, but we Terrans are not a people who submit without strife to any fate. From the time of the Curse of Death on, we have been trying to make spirits for ourselves."

"But how can you do that?"

"We do not know. The oomphel will not teach us that, though it teaches everything else. We have only learned many ways in which it cannot be done. It cannot be done with oomphel, or with anything that is in our own world. But the Oomphel-Mother made us ships to go to other worlds, and we have gone to many of them, this one among them, seeking things from which we try to make spirits. We are trying to make spirits for ourselves from the crystals that grow in the klooba plants; we may fail with them, too. But I say this; I may die, and all the other Terrans now living may die, and be as though they had never been, but someday we will not fail. Someday our children, or our children's children, will make spirits for themselves and live forever, as you do."

"Why were we not told this before, Mailsh Heelbare?"

"We were ashamed to have you know it. We are ashamed to be people without spirits."

"Can we help you and your people? Maybe our magic might help."

"It well might. It would be worth trying. But first, you must help yourselves. You and your people are sinning against the Great Spirit as grievously as did the Terrans of old. Be warned in time, lest you answer it as grievously."

"What do you mean, Mailsh Heelbare?" Old Shatresh was frightened.

"You are making magic to bring the Sky Fire to the World. Do you know what will happen? The World of People will pass whole into the place of the Gone Ones, and both will be destroyed. The World of People is a world of death; everything that lives on it must die. The Place of the Gone Ones is a world of life; everything in it lives forever. The two will strive against each other, and will destroy one another, and there will be nothing in the Sky Fire or the World but fire. This is wisdom which our oomphel teaches us. We know this secret, and with it we make weapons of great destruction." He looked over the seated shoonoon, picking out those who wore the flame-colored cloaks of the fire-dance. "You-and you-and you," he said. "You have been making this dreadful magic, and leading your people in it. And which among the rest of you have not been guilty?"

"We did not know," one of them said. "Mailsh Heelbare, have we yet time to keep this from happening?"

"Yes. There is only a little time, but there is time. You have until the Always-Same passes across the face of the Sky-Fire." That would be seven hundred and fifty hours. "If this happens, all is safe. If the Sky Fire blots Out the Always Same, we are all lost together. You must go among your people and tell them what madness they are doing, and command them to stop. You must command them to lay down their arms and cease fighting. And you must tell them of the awful curse that was put upon the Terrans in the long-ago time, for a lesser sin than they are now committing."

"If we say that Mailsh Heelbare told us this, the people may not believe us. He is not known to all, and some would take no Terran's word, not even his."

"Would anybody tell a secret of this sort, about his own people, if it were not real?"

"We had better say nothing about Mailsh Heelbare. We will say that the Gone Ones told us in dreams."

"Let us say that the Great Spirit sent a dream of warning to each of us," another shoonoo said. "There has been too much talk about dreams from the Gone Ones already."

"But the Great Spirit has never sent a dream —"

"Nothing like this has ever happened before, either."

He rose, and they were silent. "Go to your living-place, now," he told them. "Talk of how best you may warn your people." He pointed to the clock. "You have an oomphel like that in your living-place; when the shorter spear has moved three places, I will speak with you again, and then you will be sent in air cars to your people to speak to them."

They went up the escalator and down the hall to Miles' office on the third floor without talking. Foxx Travis was singing softly, almost inaudibly:

> *"You will eeeeat … in the sweeeet … bye-and-bye,*
> *You'll get oooom … phel in the sky … when you die!"*

Inside, Edith Shaw slumped dispiritedly in a chair. Foxx Travis went to the coffee-maker and started it. Miles snapped on the communication screen and punched the combination of General Maith's headquarters. As soon as the uniformed girl who appeared in it saw him, her hands moved quickly; the screen flickered, and the general appeared in it.

"We have it made, general. They're sold; we're ready to start them out in three hours."

Maith's thin, weary face suddenly lighted. "You mean they are going to co-operate?"

He shook his head. "They think they're saving the world; they think we're co-operating with them."

The general laughed. "That's even better! How do you want them sent out?"

"The ones in the Bluelake area first. Better have some picked K.N.I. in native costume, with pistols, to go with them. They'll need protection, till they're able to get a hearing for themselves. After they're all out, the ones from Gonzales' area can be started." He thought for a moment. "I'll want four or five of them left here to help me when you start bringing more shoonoon in from other areas. How soon do you think you'll have another class for me?"

"Two or three days, if everything goes all right. We have the villages and plantations in the south under pretty tight control now; we can start gathering them up right away. As soon as we get things stabilized here, we can send reinforcements to the north. We'll have transport for you in three hours."

The general blanked out. He turned from the screen. Travis was laughing happily.

"Miles, did anybody ever tell you you were a genius?" he asked. "That last jolt you gave them was perfect. Why didn't you tell us about it in advance?"

"I didn't know about it in advance; I didn't think of it till I'd started talking to them. No cream or sugar for me."

"Cream," Edith said, lifelessly. "Why did you do it? Why didn't you just tell them the truth?"

Travis asked her to define the term. She started to say something bitter about Jesting Pilate. Miles interrupted.

"In spite of Lord Beacon, Pilate wasn't jesting," he said. "And he didn't stay for an answer because he knew he'd die of old age waiting for one. What kind of truth should I have told them?"

"Why, what you started to tell them. That Beta moves in a fixed orbit and can't get any closer to Alpha—"

"There's been some work done on the question since Pilate's time," Travis said. "My semantics prof at Command College had the start of an answer. He defined truth as a statement having a practical correspondence with reality on the physical levels of structure and observation and the verbal order of abstraction under consideration."

"He defined truth as a statement. A statement exists only in the mind of the person making it, and the mind of the person to whom it is made. If the person to whom it is made can't understand or accept it, it isn't the truth."

"They understood when you showed them that the planet is round, and they understood that tri-dimensional model of the system. Why didn't you let it go at that?"

"They accepted it intellectually. But when I told them that there wasn't any chance of Kwannon getting any closer to Alpha, they rebelled emotionally. It doesn't matter how conclusively you prove anything, if the person to whom you prove it can't accept your proof emotionally, it's still false. Not-real."

"They had all their emotional capital invested in this Always-Cool Time," Travis told her. "They couldn't let Miles wipe that out for them. So he shifted it from this world to the next, and convinced them that they were getting a better deal that way. You saw how quickly they picked it up. And he didn't have the sin of telling children there is no Easter Bunny on his conscience, either."

"But why did you tell them that story about the Oomphel Mother?" she insisted. "Now they'll go out and tell all the other natives, and they'll believe it."

"Would they have believed it if I'd told them about Terran scientific technology? Your people have been doing that for close to half a century. You see what impression it's made."

"But you told them-You told them that Terrans have no souls!"

"Can you prove that was a lie?" Travis asked. "Let's see yours. Draw—*soul*! Inspection—*soul*!"

Naturally. Foxx Travis would expect a soul to be carried in a holster.

"But they'll look down on us, now. They'll say we're just like animals," Edith almost wailed.

"Now it comes out," Travis said. "We won't be the lordly Terrans, any more, helping the poor benighted Kwanns out of the goodness of our hearts, scattering largess, bearing the Terran's Burden-new model, a give-away instead of a gun. Now *they'll* pity *us*; they'll think *we're* inferior beings."

"I don't think the natives are inferior beings!" She was almost in tears.

"If you don't, why did you come all the way to Kwannon to try to make them more like Terrans?"

"Knock it off, Foxx; stop heckling her." Travis looked faintly surprised. Maybe he hadn't realized, before, that a boss newsman learns to talk like a commanding officer. "You remember what Ramón Gonzales was saying, out at Sanders', about the inferior's hatred for the superior as superior? It's no wonder these Kwanns resent us. They have a right to; we've done them all an unforgivable injury. We've let them see us doing things they can't do. Of course they resent us. But now I've given them something to feel superior about. When they die, they'll go to the Place of the Gone Ones, and have oomphel in the sky, and they will live forever in new bodies, but when we die, we just die, period. So they'll pity us and politely try to hide their condescension toward us.

"And because they feel superior to us, they'll want to help us. They'll work hard on the plantations, so that we can have plenty of biocrystals, and their shoonoon will work magic for us, to help us poor benighted Terrans to grow souls for ourselves, so that we can almost be like them. Of course, they'll have a chance to exploit us, and get oomphel from us, too, but the important thing will be to help the poor Terrans. Maybe they'll even organize a Spiritual and Magical Assistance Agency."

THE END

A Slave is a Slave

By H. Beam Piper

> There has always been
> strong sympathy for the poor,
> meek, downtrodden slave —
> the kindly little man, oppressed
> by cruel and overbearing masters.
> Could it possibly have been misplaced...?

Jurgen, Prince Trevannion, accepted the coffee cup and lifted it to his lips, then lowered it. These Navy robots always poured coffee too hot; spacemen must have collapsium-lined throats. With the other hand, he punched a button on the robot's keyboard and received a lighted cigarette; turning, he placed the cup on the command-desk in front of him and looked about. The tension was relaxing in Battle-Control, the purposeful pandemonium of the last three hours dying rapidly. Officers of both sexes, in red and blue and yellow and green coveralls, were rising from seats, leaving their stations, gathering in groups. Laughter, a trifle loud; he realized, suddenly, that they had been worried, and wondered if he should not have been a little so himself. No. There would have been nothing he could have done about anything, so worry would not have been useful. He lifted the cup again and sipped cautiously.

"That's everything we can do now," the man beside him said. "Now we just sit and wait for the next move."

Like all the others, Line-Commodore Vann Shatrak wore shipboard battle-dress; his coveralls were black, splashed on breast and between shoulders with the gold insignia of his rank. His head was completely bald, and almost spherical; a beaklike nose carried down the curve of his brow, and the straight lines of mouth and chin chopped under it enhanced rather than spoiled the effect. He was getting coffee; he gulped it at once.

"It was very smart work, Commodore. I never saw a landing operation go so smoothly."

"Too smooth," Shatrak said. "I don't trust it." He looked suspiciously up at the row of viewscreens.

"It was absolutely unnecessary!"

That was young Obray, Count Erskyll, seated on the commodore's left. He was a generation younger than Prince Trevannion, as Shatrak was a generation older; they were both smooth-faced. It was odd, how beards went in and out of fashion with alternate generations. He had been worried, too, during the landing, but for a different reason from the others. Now he was reacting with anger.

"I told you, from the first, that it was unnecessary. You see? They weren't even able to defend themselves, let alone...."

His personal communication-screen buzzed; he set down the coffee and flicked the switch. It was Lanze Degbrend. On the books, Lanze was carried as Assistant to the Ministerial Secretary. In practice, Lanze was his chess-opponent, conversational foil, right hand, third eye and ear, and, sometimes, trigger-finger. Lanze was now wearing the combat coveralls of an officer of Navy Landing-Troops; he had a steel helmet with a transpex visor shoved up, and there was a carbine slung over his shoulder. He grinned and executed an exaggeratedly military salute. He chuckled.

"Well, look at you; aren't you the perfect picture of correct diplomatic dress?"

"You know, sir, I'm afraid I am, for this planet," Degbrend said. "Colonel Ravney insisted on it. He says the situation downstairs is still fluid, which I take to mean that everybody is shooting at everybody. He says he has the main telecast station, in the big building the locals call the Citadel."

"Oh, good. Get our announcement out as quickly as you can. Number Five. You and Colonel Ravney can decide what interpolations are needed to fit the situation."

"Number Five; the really tough one," Degbrend considered. "I take it that by interpolations you do not mean dilutions?"

"Oh, no; don't water the drink. Spike it."

Lanze Degbrend grinned at him. Then he snapped down the visor of his helmet, unslung his carbine, and presented it. He was still standing at present arms when Trevannion blanked the screen.

"That still doesn't excuse a wanton and unprovoked aggression!" Erskyll was telling Shatrak, his thin face flushed and his voice quivering with indignation. "We came here to help these people, not to murder them."

"We didn't come here to do either, Obray," he said, turning to face the younger man. "We came here to annex their planet to the Galactic Empire, whether they wish it annexed or not. Commodore Shatrak used the quickest and most effective method of doing that. It would have done no good to attempt to parley with them from off-planet. You heard those telecasts of theirs."

"Authoritarian," Shatrak said, then mimicked pompously: " 'Everybody is commanded to remain calm; the Mastership is taking action. The Convocation of the Lords-Master is in special session; they will decide how to deal with the invaders. The administrators are directed to reassure the supervisors; the overseers will keep the workers at their tasks. Any person disobeying the orders of the Mastership will be dealt with most severely.' "

"Static, too. No spaceships into this system for the last five hundred years; the Convocation-equals Parliament, I assume-hasn't been in special session for two hundred and fifty."

"Yes. I've taken over planets with that kind of government before," Shatrak said. "You can't argue with them. You just grab them by the center of authority, quick and hard."

Count Erskyll said nothing for a moment. He was opposed to the use of force. Force, he believed, was the last resort of incompetence; he had said so frequently enough since this operation had begun. Of course, he was absolutely right, though not in the way he meant. Only the incompetent wait until the last extremity to use force, and by then, it is usually too late to use anything, even prayer.

But, at the same time, he was opposed to authoritarianism, except, of course, when necessary for the real good of the people. And he did not like rulers who called themselves Lords-Master. Good democratic rulers called themselves Servants of the People. So he relapsed into silence and stared at the viewscreens.

One, from an outside pickup on the *Empress Eulalie* herself, showed the surface of the planet, a hundred miles down, the continent under them curving away to a distant sun-reflecting sea; beyond the curved horizon, the black sky was spangled with unwinking stars. Fifty miles down, the sun glinted from the three thousand foot globes of the two transport-cruisers, *Canopus* and *Mizar*.

Another screen, from *Mizar*, gave a clearer if more circumscribed view of the surface-green countryside, veined by rivers and wrinkled with mountains; little towns that were mere dots; a scatter of white clouds. Nothing that looked like roads. There had been no native sapient race on this planet, and in the thirteen centuries since it had been colonized the Terro-human population had never completely lost the use of contragravity vehicles. In that screen, farther down, the four destroyers, *Irma, Irene, Isobel* and *Iris*, were tiny twinkles.

From *Irene*, they had a magnified view of the city. On the maps, none later than eight hundred years old, it was called Zeggensburg; it had been built at the time of the first colonization under the old Terran Federation. Tall buildings, rising from wide interspaces of lawns and parks and gardens, and, at the very center, widely separated from anything else, the mass of the Citadel, a huge cylindrical tower rising from a cluster of smaller cylinders, with a broad circular landing stage above, topped by the newly raised flag of the Galactic Empire.

There was a second city, a thick crescent, to the south and east. The old maps placed the Zeggensburg spaceport there, but not a trace of that remained. In its place was what was evidently an industrial district, located where the prevailing winds would carry away the dust and smoke. There was quite a bit of both, but the surprising thing was the streets, long curved ones, and shorter ones crossing at regular intervals to form blocks. He had never seen a city with streets before, and he doubted if anybody else on the Empire ships had. Long boulevards to give unobstructed passage to low-level air-traffic, of course, and short winding walkways, but not things like these. Pictures, of course, of native cities on planets colonized at the time of the Federation, and even very ancient ones of cities on pre-Atomic Terra. But these people had contragravity; the towering, wide-spaced city beside this cross-gridded anachronism proved that.

They knew so little about this planet which they had come to bring under Imperial rule. It had been colonized thirteen centuries ago, during the last burst of expansion before the System States War and the disintegration of the Terran Federation, and it had been named Aditya, in the fashion of the times, for some forgotten deity of some obscure and ancient polytheism. A century or so later, it had seceded from or been abandoned by the Federation, then breaking up. That much they had gleaned from old Federation records still existing on Baldur. After that, darkness, lighted only by a brief flicker when more records had turned up on Morglay.

Morglay was one of the Sword-Worlds, settled by refugee rebels from the System States planets. Mostly they had been soldiers and spacemen; there had been many women with them, and many were skilled technicians, engineers, scientists. They had managed to carry off considerable equipment with them, and for three centuries they had lived in isolation, spreading over a dozen hitherto undiscovered planets. Excalibur, Tizona, Gram, Morglay, Durendal, Flamberge, Curtana, Quernbiter; the names were a roll-call of fabulous blades of Old Terran legend.

Then they had erupted, suddenly and calamitously, into what was left of the Terran Federation as the Space Vikings, carrying pillage and destruction, until the newborn Empire rose to vanquish them. In the sixth Century Pre-Empire, one of their fleets had come from Morglay to Aditya.

The Adityans of that time had been near-barbarians; the descendants of the original settlers had been serfs of other barbarians who had come as mercenaries in the service of one or another of the local chieftains and had remained to loot and rule. Subjugating them had been easy; the Space Vikings had taken Aditya and made it their home. For several centuries, there had been communication between them and their home planet. Then Morglay had become involved in one of the interplanetary dynastic wars that had begun the decadence of the Space Vikings, and again Aditya dropped out of history.

Until this morning, when history returned in the black ships of the Galactic Empire.

He stubbed out the cigarette and summoned the robot to give him another. Shatrak was speaking:

"You see, Count Erskyll, we really had to do it this way, for their own good." He wouldn't have credited the commodore with such guile; anything was justified, according to Obray of Erskyll, if done for somebody else's good. "What we did, we just landed suddenly, knocked out their army, seized the center of government, before anybody could do anything. If we'd landed the way you'd wanted us to, somebody would have resisted, and the next thing, we'd have had to kill about five or six thousand of them and blow down a couple of towns, and we'd have lost a lot of our own people doing it. You might say, we had to do it to save them from themselves."

Obray of Erskyll seemed to have doubts, but before he could articulate them, Shatrak's communication-screen was calling attention to itself. The commodore flicked the switch, and his executive officer, Captain Patrique Morvill, appeared in it.

"We've just gotten reports, sir, that some of Ravney's people have captured a half-dozen missile-launching sites around the city. His air-reconn tells him that that's the lot of them. I have an officer of one of the parties that participated. You ought to hear what he has to say, sir."

"Well, good!" Vann Shatrak whooshed out his breath. "I don't mind admitting, I was a little on edge about that."

"Wait till you hear what Lieutenant Carmath has to say." Morvill seemed to be strangling a laugh. "Ready for him, Commodore?"

Shatrak nodded; Morvill made a hand-signal and vanished in a flicker of rainbow colors; when the screen cleared, a young Landing-Troop lieutenant in battle-dress was looking out of it. He saluted and gave his name, rank and unit.

"This missile-launching site I'm occupying, sir; it's twenty miles north-west of the city. We took it thirty minutes ago; no resistance whatever. There are four hundred or so people here. Of them, twelve, one dozen, are soldiers. The rest are civilians. Ten enlisted men, a non-com of some sort, and something that appears to be an officer. The officer had a pistol, fully loaded. The non-com had a submachine gun, empty, with two loaded clips on his belt. The privates had rifles, empty, and no ammunition. The officer did not know where the rifle ammunition was stored."

Shatrak swore. The second lieutenant nodded. "Exactly my comment when he told me, sir. But this place is beautifully kept up. Lawns all mowed, trees neatly pruned, everything policed up like inspection morning. And there is a headquarters office building here adequate for an army division...."

"How about the armament, Lieutenant?" Shatrak asked with forced patience.

"Ah, yes; the armament, sir. There are eight big launching cradles for panplanetary or off-planet missiles. They are all polished up like the Crown Jewels. But none, repeat none, of them is operative. And there is not a single missile on the installation."

Shatrak's facial control didn't slip. It merely intensified, which amounted to the same thing.

"Lieutenant Carmath, I am morally certain I heard you correctly, but let's just check. You said...."

He repeated the lieutenant back, almost word for word. Carmath nodded.

"That was it, sir. The missile-crypts are stacked full of old photoprints and recording and microfilm spools. The sighting-and-guidance systems for all the launchers are completely missing. The letoff mechanisms all lack major parts. There is an elaborate set of detection equipment, which will detect absolutely nothing. I saw a few pairs of binoculars about; I suspect that that is what we were first observed with."

"This office, now; I suppose all the paperwork is up to the minute in quintulplicate, and initialed by everybody within sight or hearing?"

"I haven't checked on that yet, sir. If you're thinking of betting on it, please don't expect me to cover you, though."

"Well, thank you, Lieutenant Carmath. Stick around; I'm sending down a tech-intelligence crew to look at what's left of the place. While you're waiting, you might sort out whoever seems to be in charge and find out just what in Nifflheim he thinks that launching-station was maintained for."

"I think I can tell you that, now, Commodore," Prince Trevannion said as Shatrak blanked the screen. "We have a petrified authoritarianism. Quite likely some sort of an oligarchy; I'd guess that this Convocation thing they talk about consists of all the ruling class, everybody has equal voice, and nobody will take the responsibility for doing anything. And the actual work of government is probably handled by a corps of bureaucrats entrenched in their jobs, unwilling to exert any effort and afraid to invite any criticism, and living only to retire on their pensions. I've seen governments like that before." He named a few. "One thing; once a government like that has been bludgeoned into the Empire, it rarely makes any trouble later."

"Just to judge by this missileless non-launching station," Shatrak said, "they couldn't even decide on what kind of trouble to make, or how to start it. I think you're going to have a nice easy Proconsulate here, Count Erskyll."

Count Erskyll started to say something. No doubt he was about to tell Shatrak, cuttingly, that he didn't want an easy Proconsulate, but an opportunity to help these people. He was saved from this by the buzzing of Shatrak's communication-screen.

It was Colonel Pyairr Ravney, the Navy Landing-Troop commander. Like everybody else who had gone down to Zeggensburg, he was in battle-dress and armed; the transpex visor of his helmet was pushed up. Between Shatrak's generation and Count Erskyll's, he sported a pointed mustache and a spiky chin-beard, which, on his thin and dark-eyed face, looked distinctly Mephistophelean. He was grinning.

"Well, sir, I think we can call it a done job," he said. "There's a delegation here who want to talk to the Lords-Master of the ships on behalf of the Lords-Master of the Convocation. Two of them, with about a dozen portfolio-bearers and note-takers. I'm not too good in Lingua Terra, outside Basic, at best, and their brand is far from that. I gather that they're some kind of civil-servants, personal representatives of the top Lords-Master."

"Do we want to talk to them?" Shatrak asked.

"Well, we should only talk to the actual, titular, heads of the government-Mastership," Erskyll, suddenly protocol-conscious, objected. "We can't negotiate with subordinates."

"Oh, who's talking about negotiating; there isn't anything to negotiate. Aditya is now a part of the Galactic Empire. If this present regime assents to that, they can stay in power. If not, we will toss them out and install a new government. We will receive this delegation, inform them to that effect, and send them back to relay the information to their Lords-Master." He turned to the Commodore. "May I speak to Colonel Ravney?"

Shatrak assented. He asked Ravney where these Lords-Master were.

"Here in the Citadel, in what they call the Convocation Chamber. Close to a thousand of them, screaming recriminations at one another. Sounds like feeding time at the Imperial Zoo. I think they all want to surrender, but nobody dares propose it first. I've just put a cordon around it and placed it off limits to everybody. And everything outside off limits to the Convocation."

"Well thought of, Colonel. I suppose the Citadel teems with bureaucrats and such low life-forms?"

"Bulging with them. Literally thousands. Lanze Degbrend and Commander Douvrin and a few others are trying to get some sensible answers out of some of them."

"This delegation; how had you thought of sending them up?"

"Landing-craft to *Isobel*; *Isobel* will bring them the rest of the way."

He looked at his watch. "Well, don't be in too much of a rush to get them here, Colonel. We don't want them till after lunch. Delay them on *Isobel*; the skipper can see that they have their own lunch aboard. And entertain them with some educational films. Something to convince them that there is slightly more to the Empire than one ship-of-the-line, two cruisers and four destroyers."

Count Erskyll was dissatisfied about that, too. He wanted to see the delegation at once and make arrangements to talk to their superiors. Count Erskyll, among other things, was zealous, and of this he disapproved. Zealous statesmen perhaps did more mischief than anything in the Galaxy-with the possible exception of procrastinating soldiers. That could indicate the fundamental difference between statecraft and war. He'd have to play with that idea a little.

An Empire ship-of-the-line was almost a mile in diameter. It was more than a battle-craft; it also had political functions. The grand salon, on the outer zone where the curvature of the floors was less disconcerting, was as magnificent as any but a few of the rooms of the Imperial Palace at Asgard on Odin, the floor richly carpeted and the walls alternating mirrors and paintings. The movable furniture varied according to occasion; at present, it consisted of the bare desk at which they sat, the three chairs they occupied, and the three secretary-robots, their rectangular black casts blazened with the Sun and Cogwheel of the Empire. It faced the door, at the far end of the room; on either side, a rank of spacemen, in dress uniform and under arms, stood.

In principle, annexing a planet to the Empire was simplicity itself, but like so many things simple in principle, it was apt to be complicated in practice, and to this, he suspected, the present instance would be no exception.

In principle, one simply informed the planetary government that it was now subject to the sovereignty of his Imperial Majesty, the Galactic Emperor. This information was always conveyed by a Ministerial Secretary, directly under the Prime Minister and only one more step down from the Emperor, in the present instance Jurgen, Prince Trevannion. To make sure that the announcement carried conviction, the presumedly glad tidings were accompanied by the Imperial Space Navy, at present represented by Commodore Vann Shatrak and a seven ship battle-line unit, and two thousand Imperial Landing-Troops.

When the locals had been properly convinced-with as little bloodshed as necessary, but always beyond any dispute-an Imperial Proconsul, in this case Obray, Count Erskyll, would be installed. He would by no means govern the planet. The Imperial Constitution was definite on that point; every planetary government should be sovereign as to intraplanetary affairs. The Proconsul, within certain narrow and entirely inelastic limits, would merely govern the government.

Unfortunately, Obray, Count Erskyll, appeared not to understand this completely. It was his impression that he was a torch-bearer of Imperial civilization, or something equally picturesque and metaphorical. As he conceived it, it was the duty of the Empire, as represented by himself, to make over backward planets like Aditya in the image of Odin or Marduk or Osiris or Baldur or, preferably, his own home world of Aton.

This was Obray of Erskyll's first proconsular appointment, it was due to family influence, and it was a mistake. Mistakes, of course, were inevitable in anything as large and complex as the Galactic Empire, and any institution guided by men was subject to one kind of influence or another, family influence being no worse than any other kind. In this case, the ultra-conservative Erskylls of Aton, from old Errol, Duke of Yorvoy, down, had become alarmed at the political radicalism of young Obray, and had, on his graduation from the University of Nefertiti, persuaded the Prime Minister to appoint him to a Proconsulate as far from Aton as possible, where he would not embarrass them. Just at that time, more important matters having been gotten out of the way, Aditya had come up for annexation, and Obray of Erskyll had been named Proconsul.

That had been the mistake. He should have been sent to some planet which had been under Imperial rule for some time, where the Proconsulate ran itself in a well-worn groove, and where he could at leisure learn the procedures and unlearn some of the unrealisms absorbed at the University from professors too well insulated from the realities of politics.

There was a stir among the guards; helmet-visors were being snapped down; feet scuffed. They stiffened to attention, the great doors at the other end of the grand salon slid open, and the guards presented arms as the Adityan delegation was ushered in.

There were fourteen of them. They all wore ankle-length gowns, and they all had shaven heads. The one in the lead carried a staff and wore a pale green gown; he was apparently a herald. Behind him came two in white gowns, their empty hands folded on their breasts; one was a huge bulk of obesity with a bulging brow, protuberant eyes and a pursey little mouth, and the other was thin and cadaverous, with a skull-like, almost fleshless face. The ones behind, in dark green and pale blue, carried portfolios and slung sound-recorder cases. There was a metallic twinkle at each throat; as they approached, he could see that they all wore large silver gorgets. They came to a halt twenty feet from the desk. The herald raised his staff.

"I present the Admirable and Trusty Tchall Hozhet, personal chief-slave of the Lord-Master Olvir Nikkolon, Chairman of the Presidium of the Lords-Master's Convocation, and Khreggor Chmidd, chief-slave in office to the Lord-Master Rovard Javasan, Chief of Administration of Management of the Mastership," he said. Then he stopped, puzzled, looking from one to another of them. When his eyes fell on Vann Shatrak, he brightened.

"Are you," he asked, "the chief-slave of the chief Lord-Master of this ship?"

Shatrak's face turned pink; the pink darkened to red. He used a word; it was a completely unprintable word. So, except for a few scattered pronouns, conjunctions and prepositions, were the next fifty words he used. The herald stiffened. The two delegates behind him were aghast. The subordinate burden-bearers in the rear began looking around apprehensively.

"I," Shatrak finally managed, "am an officer of his Imperial Majesty's Space Navy. I am in command of this battle-line unit. I am *not*" —he reverted briefly to obscenity —"a slave."

"You mean, you are a Lord-Master, too?" That seemed to horrify the herald even more that the things Shatrak had been calling him. "Forgive me, Lord-Master. I did not think...."

"That's right; you didn't," Shatrak agreed. "And don't call me Lord-Master again, or I'll...."

"Just a moment, Commodore." He waved the herald aside and addressed the two in white gowns, shifting to Lingua Terra. "This is a ship of the Galactic Empire," he told them. "In the Empire, there are no slaves. Can you understand that?"

Evidently not. The huge one, Khreggor Chmidd, turned to the skull-faced Tchall Hozhet, saying: "Then they must all be Lords-Master." He saw the objection to that at once. "But how can one be a Lord-Master if there are no slaves?"

The horror was not all on the visitors' side of the desk, either. Obray of Erskyll was staring at the delegation and saying, "Slaves!" under his breath. Obray of Erskyll had never, in his not-too-long life, seen a slave before.

"They can't be," Tchall Hozhet replied. "A Lord-Master is one who owns slaves." He gave that a moment's consideration. "But if they aren't Lords-Master, they must be slaves, and...." No. That wouldn't do, either. "But a slave is one who belongs to a Lord-Master."

Rule of the Excluded Third; evidently Pre-Atomic formal logic had crept back to Aditya. Chmidd, looking around, saw the ranks of spacemen on either side, now at parade-rest.

"But aren't they slaves?" he asked.

"They are spacemen of the Imperial Navy," Shatrak roared. "Call one a slave to his face and you'll get a rifle-butt in yours. And I shan't lift a finger to stop it." He glared at Chmidd and Hozhet. "Who had the infernal impudence to send slaves to deal with the Empire? He needs to be taught a lesson."

"Why, I was sent by the Lord-Master Olvir Nikkolon, and...."

"Tchall!" Chmidd hissed at him. "We cannot speak to Lords-Master. We must speak to their chief-slaves."

"But they have no slaves," Hozhet objected. "Didn't you hear the ... the one with the small beard ... say so?"

"But that's ridiculous, Khreggor. Who does the work, and who tells them what to do? Who told these people to come here?"

"Our Emperor sent us. That is his picture, behind me. But we are not his slaves. He is merely the chief man among us. Do your Masters not have one among them who is chief?"

"That's right," Chmidd said to Hozhet. "In the Convocation, your Lord-Master is chief, and in the Mastership, my Lord-Master, Rovard Javasan, is chief."

"But they don't tell the other Lords-Master what to do. In Convocation, the other Lords-Master tell them...."

"That's what I meant about an oligarchy," he whispered, in Imperial, to Erskyll.

"Suppose we tell Ravney to herd these Lords-Master onto a couple of landing-craft and bring them up here?" Shatrak suggested. He made the suggestion in Lingua Terra Basic, and loudly.

"I think we can manage without that." He raised his voice, speaking in Lingua Terra Basic:

"It does not matter whether these slaves talk to us or not. This planet is now under the rule of his Imperial Majesty, Rodrik III. If this Mastership wants to govern the planet under the Emperor, they may do so. If not, we will make an end of them and set up a new government here."

He paused. Chmidd and Hozhet were looking at one another in shocked incredulity.

"Tchall, they mean it," Chmidd said. "They can do it, too."

"We have nothing more to say to you slaves," he continued. "Hereafter, we will speak directly to the Lords-Master."

"But....The Lords-Master never do business directly," Hozhet said. "It is un-Masterly. Such discussions are between chief-slaves."

"This thing they call the Convocation," Shatrak mentioned. "I wonder if the members have the business done entirely through their slaves."

"Oh, no!" That shocked Chmidd into direct address. "No slave is allowed in the Convocation Chamber."

He wondered how they kept the place swept out. Robots, no doubt. Or else, what happened when the Masters weren't there didn't count.

"Very well. Your people have recorders; are they on?"

Hozhet asked Chmidd; Chmidd asked the herald, who asked one of the menials in the rear, who asked somebody else. The reply came back through the same channels; they were.

"Very well. At this time tomorrow, we will speak to the Convocation of Lords-Master. Commodore Shatrak, see to it that Colonel Ravney has them in the Convocation Chamber, and that preparations in the room are made, so that we may address them in the dignity befitting representatives of his Imperial Majesty." He turned to the Adityan slaves. "That is all. You have permission to go."

They watched the delegation back out, with the honor-guard following. When the doors had closed behind them, Shatrak ran his hand over his bald head and laughed.

"Shaved heads, every one of them. That's probably why they thought I was your slave. Bet those gorgets are servile badges, too." He touched the Knight's Star of the Order of the Empire at his throat. "Probably thought that was what this was. We would have to draw something like this!"

"They simply can't imagine anybody not being either a slave or a slave-owner," Erskyll was saying. "That must mean that there is no free non-slave-holding class at all. Universal slavery! Well, we'll have to do something about that. Proclaim total emancipation, immediately."

"Oh, no; we can't do anything like that. The Constitution won't permit us to. Section Two, Article One: *Every Empire planet shall be self-governed as to its own affairs, in the manner of its own choice, and without interference.*"

"But slavery....Section Two, Article Six," Erskyll objected. "*There shall be no chattel slavery or serfdom anywhere in the Empire; no sapient being of any race whatsoever shall be the property of any being but himself.*"

"That's correct," he agreed. "If this Mastership intends to remain the planetary government under the Empire, they will be obliged to abolish slavery, but they will have to do it by their own act. We cannot do it for them."

"You know what I'd do, Prince Trevannion?" Shatrak said. "I'd just heave this Mastership thing out, and set up a nice tight military dictatorship. We have the planet under martial rule now; let's just keep it that way for about five years, till we can train a new government."

That suggestion seemed to pain Count Erskyll almost as much as the existing situation.

They dined late, in Commodore Shatrak's private dining room. Beside Shatrak, Erskyll and himself, there were Lanze Degbrend, and Count Erskyll's charge-d'affaires, Sharll Ernanday, and Patrique Morvill and Pyairr Ravney and the naval intelligence officer, Commander Andrey Douvrin. Ordinarily, he deplored serious discussion at meals, but under the circumstances it was unavoidable; nobody could think or talk of anything else. The discussion which he had hoped would follow the meal began before the soup-course.

"We have a total population of about twenty million," Lanze Degbrend reported. "A trifle over ten thousand Masters, all ages and both sexes. The remainder are all slaves."

"I find that incredible," Erskyll declared promptly. "Twenty million people, held in slavery by ten thousand! Why do they stand for it? Why don't they rebel?"

"Well, I can think of three good reasons," Douvrin said. "Three square meals a day."

"And no responsibilities; no need to make decisions," Degbrend added. "They've been slaves for seven and a half centuries. They don't even know the meaning of freedom, and it would frighten them if they did."

"Chain of command," Shatrak said. When that seemed not to convey any meaning to Erskyll, he elaborated: "We have a lot of dirty-necked working slaves. Over every dozen of them is an overseer with a big whip and a stungun. Over every couple of overseers there is a guard with a submachine gun. Over them is a supervisor, who doesn't need a gun because he can grab a handphone and call for troops. Over the supervisors, there are higher supervisors. Everybody has it just enough better than the level below him that he's afraid of losing his job and being busted back to fieldhand."

"That's it exactly, Commodore," Degbrend said. "The whole society is a slave hierarchy. Everybody curries favor with the echelon above, and keeps his eye on the echelon below to make sure he isn't being undercut. We have something not too unlike that, ourselves. Any organizational society is, in some ways, like a slave society. And everything is determined by established routine. The whole thing has simply been running on momentum for at least five centuries, and if we hadn't come smashing in with a situation none of the routines covered, it would have kept on running for another five, till everything wore out and stopped. I heard about those missile-stations, by the way. They're typical of everything here."

"That's another thing," Erskyll interrupted. "These Lords-Master are the descendants of the old Space-Vikings, and the slaves of the original inhabitants. The Space Vikings were a technologically advanced people; they had all the old Terran Federation science and technology, and a lot they developed for themselves on the Sword-Worlds."

"Well? They still had a lot of it, on the Sword-Worlds, two centuries ago when we took them over."

"But technology always drives out slavery; that's a fundamental law of socio-economics. Slavery is economically unsound; it cannot compete with power-industry, let alone cybernetics and robotics."

He was tempted to remind young Obray of Erskyll that there were no such things as fundamental laws of socio-economics; merely usually reliable generalized statements of what can more or less be depended upon to happen under most circumstances. He resisted the temptation. Count Erskyll had had enough shocks, today, without adding to them by gratuitous blasphemy.

"In this case, Obray, it worked in reverse. The Space Vikings enslaved the Adityans to hold them in subjugation. That was a politico-military necessity. Then, being committed to slavery, with a slave population who had to be made to earn their keep, they found cybernetics and robotics economically unsound."

"And almost at once, they began appointing slave overseers, and the technicians would begin training slave assistants. Then there would be slave supervisors to direct the overseers, slave administrators to direct them, slave secretaries and bookkeepers, slave technicians and engineers."

"How about the professions, Lanze?"

"All slave. Slave physicians, teachers, everything like that. All the Masters are taught by slaves; the slaves are educated by apprenticeship. The courts are in the hands of slaves; cases are heard by the chief slaves of judges who don't even know where their own courtrooms are; every Master has a team of slave lawyers. Most of the lawsuits are estate-inheritance cases; some of them have been in litigation for generations."

"What do the Lords-Master do?" Shatrak asked.

"Masterly things," Degbrend replied. "I was only down there since noon, but from what I could find out, that consists of feasting, making love to each other's wives, being entertained by slave performers, and feuding for social precedence like wealthy old ladies on Odin."

"You got this from the slaves? How did you get them to talk, Lanze?"

Degbrend and Ravney exchanged amused glances. Ravney said:

"Well, I detailed a sergeant and six privates to accompany Honorable Degbrend," Ravney said. "They....How would you put it, Lanze?"

"I asked a slave a question. If he refused to answer, somebody knocked him down with a rifle-butt," Degbrend replied. "I never had to do that more than once in any group, and I only had to do it three times in all. After that, when I asked questions, I was answered promptly and fully. It is surprising how rapidly news gets around the Citadel."

"You mean you had those poor slaves beaten?" Erskyll demanded.

"Oh, no. Beating implies repeated blows. We only gave one to a customer; that was enough."

"Well, how about the army, if that's what those people in the long red-brown coats were?" Shatrak changed the subject by asking Ravney.

"All slave, of course, officers and all. What will we do about them, sir? I have about three thousand, either confined to their barracks or penned up in the Citadel. I requisitioned food for them, paid for it in chits. There were a few isolated companies and platoons that gave us something of a fight; most of them just threw away their weapons and bawled for quarter. I've segregated the former; with your approval, I'll put them under Imperial officers and noncoms for a quickie training in our tactics, and then use them to train the rest."

"Do that, Pyairr. We only have two thousand men of our own, and that's not enough. Do you think you can make soldiers out of any of them?"

"Yes, I believe so, sir. They are trained, organized and armed for civil-order work, which is what we'll need them for ourselves. In the entire history of this army, all they have done has been to overawe unarmed slaves; I am sure they have never been in combat with regular troops. They have an elaborate set of training and field regulations for the sort of work for which they were intended. What they encountered today was entirely outside those regulations, which is why they behaved as they did."

"Did you have any trouble getting cooperation from the native officers?" Shatrak asked.

"Not in the least. They cooperated quite willingly, if not always too intelligently. I simply told them that they were now the personal property of his Imperial Majesty, Rodrik III. They were quite flattered by the change of ownership. If ordered to, I believe that they would fire on their former Lords-Master without hesitation."

"You told those slaves that they ...*belonged* ...to the *Emperor?*"

Count Erskyll was aghast. He stared at Ravney for an instant, then snatched up his brandy-glass —the meal had gotten to that point-and drained it at a gulp. The others watched solicitously while he coughed and spluttered over it.

"Commodore Shatrak," he said sternly. "I hope that you will take severe disciplinary action; this is the most outrageous...."

"I'll do nothing of the sort," Shatrak retorted. "The colonel is to be commended; did the best thing he could, under the circumstances. What are you going to do when slavery is abolished here, Colonel?"

"Oh, tell them that they have been given their freedom as a special reward for meritorious service, and then sign them up for a five year enlistment."

"That might work. Again, it might not."

"I think, Colonel, that before you do that, you had better disarm them again. You might possibly have some trouble, otherwise."

Ravney looked at him sharply. "They might not want to be free? I'd thought of that."

"Nonsense!" Erskyll declared. "Who ever heard of slaves rebelling against freedom?"

Freedom was a Good Thing. It was a Good Thing for everybody, everywhere and all the time. Count Erskyll knew it, because freedom was a Good Thing for him.

He thought, suddenly, of an old tomcat belonging to a lady of his acquaintance at Paris-on-Baldur, a most affectionate cat, who insisted on catching mice and bringing them as presents to all his human friends. To this cat's mind, it was inconceivable that anybody would not be most happy to receive a nice fresh-killed mouse.

"Too bad we have to set any of them free," Vann Shatrak said. "Too bad we can't just issue everybody new servile gorgets marked, *Personal Property of his Imperial Majesty* and let it go at that. But I guess we can't."

"Commodore Shatrak, you are joking," Erskyll began.

"I hope I am," Shatrak replied grimly.

The top landing-stage of the Citadel grew and filled the forward viewscreen of the ship's launch. It was only when he realized that the tiny specks were people, and the larger, birdseed-sized, specks vehicles, that the real size of the thing was apparent. Obray of Erskyll, beside him, had been silent. He had been looking at the crescent-shaped industrial city, like a servile gorget around Zeggensburg's neck.

"The way they've been crowded together!" he said. "And the buildings; no space between. And all that smoke! They must be using fossil-fuel!"

"It's probably too hard to process fissionables in large quantities, with what they have."

"You were right, last evening. These people have deliberately halted progress, even retrogressed, rather than give up slavery."

Halting progress, to say nothing of retrogression, was an unthinkable crime to him. Like freedom, progress was a Good Thing, anywhere, at all times, and without regard to direction.

Colonel Ravney met them when they left the launch. The top landing-stage was swarming with Imperial troops.

"Convocation Chamber's three stages down," he said. "About two thousand of them there now; been coming in all morning. We have everything set up." He laughed. "They tell me slaves are never permitted to enter it. Maybe, but they have the place bugged to the ceiling all around."

"Bugged? What with?" Shatrak asked, and Erskyll was wanting to know what he meant. No doubt he thought Ravney was talking about things crawling out of the woodwork.

"Screen pickups, radio pickups, wired microphones; you name it and it's there. I'll bet every slave in the Citadel knows everything that happens in there while it's happening."

Shatrak wanted to know if he had done anything about them. Ravney shook his head.

"If that's how they want to run a government, that's how they have a right to run it. Commander Douvrin put in a few of our own, a little better camouflaged than theirs."

There were more troops on the third stage down. They formed a procession down a long empty hallway, a few scared-looking slaves peeping from doorways at them. There were more troops where the corridor ended in great double doors, emblazoned with a straight broad-sword diagonally across an eight-pointed star. Emblematology of planets conquered by the Space Vikings always included swords and stars. An officer gave a signal; the doors started to slide apart, and within, from a screen-speaker, came a fanfare of trumpets.

At first, all he could see was the projection-screen, far ahead, and the tessellated aisle stretching toward it. The trumpets stopped, and they advanced, and then he saw the Lords-Master.

They were massed, standing among benches on either side, and if anything Pyairr Ravney had understated their numbers. They all wore black, trimmed with gold; he wondered if the coincidence that these were also the Imperial colors might be useful. Queer garments, tightly fitted tunics at the top which became flowing robes below the waist, deeply scalloped at the edges. The sleeves were exaggeratedly wide; a knife or a pistol, and not necessarily a small one, could be concealed in every one. He was sure that thought had entered Vann Shatrak's mind. They were armed, not with dress-daggers, but with swords; long, straight cross-hilted broadswords. They were the first actual swords he had ever seen, except in museums or on the stage.

There was a bench of gold and onyx at the front, where, normally the seven-man Presidium sat, and in front of it were thronelike seats for the Chiefs of Managements, equivalent to the Imperial Council of Ministers. Because of the projection screen that had been installed, they had all been moved to an improvised dais on the left. There was another dais on the right, under a canopy of black and gold velvet, emblazoned with the gold sun and superimposed black cogwheel of the Empire. There were three thrones, for himself, Shatrak, and Erskyll, and a number of lesser but still imposing chairs for their staffs.

They took their seats. He slipped the earplug of his memophone into his left ear and pressed the stud in the middle of his Grand Star of the Order of Odin. The memophone began giving him the names of the Presidium and of the Chiefs of Managements. He wondered how many upper-slaves had been gunbutted to produce them.

"Lords and Gentlemen," he said, after he had greeted them and introduced himself and the others, "I speak to you in the name of his Imperial Majesty, Rodrik III. His Majesty will now greet you in his own voice, by recording."

He pressed a button on the arm of his chair. The screen lighted, flickered, and steadied, and the trumpets blared again. When the fanfare ended, a voice thundered:

"The Emperor speaks!"

Rodrik III compromised on the beard question with a small mustache. He wore the stern but kindly expression the best theatrical directors in Asgard had taught him; Public Face Number Three. He inclined his head slightly and stiffly, as a man wearing a seven-pound crown must.

"We greet our subjects of Aditya to the fellowship of the Empire. We have long had good reports of you, and we are happy now to speak to you. Deserve well of us, and prosper under the Sun and Cogwheel."

Another fanfare, as the image vanished. Before any of the Lords-Master could find voice, he was speaking to them:

"Well, Lords and Gentlemen, you have been welcomed into the Empire by his Majesty. I know, there hasn't been a ship in or out of this system for five centuries, and I suppose you have a great many questions to ask about the Galactic Empire. Members of the Presidium and Chiefs of Managements may address me directly; others will please address the chairman."

Olvir Nikkolon, the owner of Tchall Hozhet, was on his feet at once. He had a loose-lipped mouth and a not entirely straight nose and pale eyes that were never entirely still.

"What I want to know is; why did you people have to come here to take our planet away from us? Isn't the rest of the Galaxy big enough for you?"

"No, Lord Nikkolon. The Galaxy is not big enough for any competition of sovereignty. There must be one and only one completely sovereign power. The Terran Federation was once such a power. It failed, and vanished; you know what followed. Darkness and anarchy. We are clawing our way up out of that darkness. We will not fail. We will create a peaceful and unified Galaxy."

He talked to them, about the collapse of the old Federation, about the interstellar wars, about the Neobarbarians, about the long night. He told them how the Empire had risen on a few planets five thousand light-years away, and how it had spread.

"We will not repeat the mistakes of the Terran Federation. We will not attempt to force every planetary government into a common pattern, or dictate the ways in which they govern themselves. We will foster in every way peaceful trade and communication. But we will not again permit the plague of competing sovereignties, the condition under which war is inevitable. The first attempt to set up such a sovereignty in competition with the Empire will be crushed mercilessly, and no planet inhabited by any sapient race will be permitted to remain outside the Empire.

"Lords and Gentlemen, permit me to show you a little of what we have already accomplished, in the past three hundred years."

He pressed another button. The screen flickered, and the show started. It lasted for almost two hours; he used a handphone to interject comments and explanations. He showed them planet after planet-Marduk, where the Empire had begun, Baldur, Vishnu, Belphegor, Morglay, whence their ancestors had come, Amaterasu, Irminsul, Fafnir, finally Odin, the Imperial Planet. He showed towering cities swarming with aircars; spaceports where the huge globes of interstellar ships landed and lifted out; farms and industries; vast crowds at public celebrations; troop-reviews and naval bases and fleet-maneuvers; historical views of the battles that had created Imperial power.

"That, Lords and Gentlemen, is what you have an opportunity to bring your planet into. If you accept, you will continue to rule Aditya under the Empire. If you refuse, you will only put us to the inconvenience of replacing you with a new planetary government, which will be annoying for us and, probably, fatal for you."

Nobody said anything for a few minutes. Then Rovard Javasan, the Chief of Administration and the owner of the mountainous Khreggor Chmidd, rose.

"Lords and Gentlemen, we cannot resist anything like this," he said. "We cannot even resist the force they have here; that was tried yesterday, and you all saw what happened. Now, Prince Trevannion; just to what extent will the Mastership retain its sovereignty under the Empire?"

"To practically the same extent as at present. You will, of course, acknowledge the Emperor as your supreme ruler, and will govern subject to the Imperial Constitution. Have you any colonies on any of the other planets of this system?"

"We had a shipyard and docks on the inner moon, and we had mines on the fourth planet of this system, but it is almost airless and the colony was limited to a couple of dome-cities. Both were abandoned years ago."

"Both will be reopened before long, I daresay. We'd better make the limits of your sovereignty the orbit of the outer planet of this system. You may have your own normal-space ships, but the Empire will control all hyperdrive craft, and all nuclear weapons. I take it you are the sole government on this planet? Then no other will be permitted to compete with you."

"Well, what are they taking away from us, then?" somebody in the rear asked.

"I assume that you are agreed to accept the sovereignty of his Imperial Majesty? Good. As a matter of form, Lord Nikkolon, will you take a vote? His Imperial Majesty would be most gratified if it were unanimous."

Somebody insisted that the question would have to be debated, which meant that everybody would have to make a speech, all two thousand of them. He informed them that there was nothing to debate; they were confronted with an accomplished fact which they must accept. So Nikkolon made a speech, telling them at what a great moment in Adityan history they stood, and concluded by saying:

"I take it that it is the unanimous will of this Convocation that the sovereignty of the Galactic Emperor be acknowledged, and that we, the 'Mastership of Aditya' do here proclaim our loyal allegiance to his Imperial Majesty, Rodrik the Third. Any dissent? Then it is ordered so recorded."

Then he had to make another speech, to inform the representatives of his new sovereign of the fact. Prince Trevannion, in the name of the Emperor, delivered the well-worn words of welcome, and Lanze Degbrend got the coronet out of the black velvet bag under his arm and the Imperial Proconsul, Obray, Count Erskyll, was crowned. Erskyll's charge-d'affaires, Sharll Ernanday, produced the scroll of the Imperial Constitution, and Erskyll began to read.

Section One: The universality of the Empire. The absolute powers of the Emperor. The rules of succession. The Emperor also to be Planetary King of Odin.

Section Two: Every planetary government to be sovereign in its own internal affairs.... Only one sovereign government upon any planet, or within normal-space travel distance.... All hyperspace ships, and all nuclear weapons.... No planetary government shall make war ... enter into any alliance ... tax, regulate or restrain interstellar trade or communication.... Every sapient being shall be equally protected....

Then he came to Article Six. He cleared his throat, raised his voice, and read:

"There shall be no chattel-slavery or serfdom anywhere in the Empire; no sapient being, of any race whatsoever, shall be the property of any being but himself."

The Convocation Chamber was silent, like a bomb with a defective fuse, for all of thirty seconds. Then it blew up with a roar. Out of the corner of his eye, he saw the doors slide apart and an airjeep, bristling with machine guns, float in and rise to the ceiling. The first inarticulate roar was followed by a babel of voices, like a tropical cloudburst on a prefab hut. Olvir Nikkolon's mouth was working as he shouted unheard.

He pressed another of the row of buttons on the arm of his chair. Out of the screen-speaker a voice, as loud, by actual sound-meter test, as an anti-vehicle gun, thundered:

"SILENCE!"

Into the shocked stillness which it produced, he spoke, like a schoolmaster who has returned to find his room in an uproar:

"Lord Nikkolon; what is this nonsense? You are Chairman of the Presidium; is this how you keep order here? What is this, a planetary parliament or a spaceport saloon?"

"You tricked us!" Nikkolon accused. "You didn't tell us about that article when we voted. Why, our whole society is based on slavery!"

Other voices joined in:

"That's all right for you people, you have robots...."

"Maybe you don't know it, but there are twenty million slaves on this planet...."

"Look, you can't free slaves! That's ridiculous. A slave's a *slave!*"

"Who'll do the work? And who would they belong to? They'd have to belong to somebody!"

"What I want to know," Rovard Javasan made himself heard, is, *"how* are you going to free them?"

There was an ancient word, originating in one of the lost languages of Pre-Atomic Terra — *sixtifor.* It meant, the basic, fundamental, question. Rovard Javasan, he suspected, had just asked the sixtifor. Of course, Obray, Count Erskyll, Planetary Proconsul of Aditya, didn't realize that. He didn't even know what Javasan meant. Just free them. Commodore Vann Shatrak couldn't see much of a problem, either. He would have answered, Just free them, and then shoot down the first two or three thousand who took it seriously. Jurgen, Prince Trevannion, had no intention whatever of attempting to answer the sixtifor.

"My dear Lord Javasan, that is the problem of the Adityan Mastership. They are your slaves; we have neither the intention nor the right to free them. But let me remind you that slavery is specifically prohibited by the Imperial Constitution; if you do not abolish it immediately, the Empire will be forced to intervene. I believe, toward the last of those audio-visuals, you saw some examples of Imperial intervention."

They had. A few looked apprehensively at the ceiling, as though expecting the hellburners and planet-busters and nega-matter-bombs at any moment. Then one of the members among the benches rose.

"We don't know how we are going to do it, Prince Trevannion," he said. "We will do it, since this is the Empire law, but you will have to tell us how."

"Well, the first thing will have to be an Act of Convocation, outlawing the ownership of one being by another. Set some definite date on which the slaves must all be freed; that need not be too immediate. Then, I would suggest that you set up some agency to handle all the details. And, as soon as you have enacted the abolition of slavery, which should be this afternoon, appoint a committee, say a dozen of you, to confer with Count Erskyll and myself. Say you have your committee aboard the *Empress Eulalie* in six hours. We'll have transportation arranged by then. And let me point out, I hope for the last time, that we discuss matters directly, without intermediaries. We don't want any more slaves, pardon, freedmen, coming aboard to talk for you, as happened yesterday."

Obray, Count Erskyll, was unhappy about it. He did not think that the Lords-Master were to be trusted to abolish slavery; he said so, on the launch, returning to the ship. Jurgen, Prince Trevannion was inclined to agree. He doubted if any of the Lords-Master he had seen were to be trusted, unassisted, to fix a broken mouse-trap.

Line-Commodore Vann Shatrak was also worried. He was wondering how long it would take for Pyairr Ravney to make useful troops out of the newly-surrendered slave soldiers, and where he was going to find contragravity to shift them expeditiously from trouble-spot to trouble-spot. Erskyll thought he was anticipating resistance on the part of the Masters, and for once he approved the use of force. Ordinarily, force was a Bad Thing, but this was a Good Cause, which justified any means.

They entertained the committee from the Convocation for dinner, that evening. They came aboard stiffly hostile-most understandably so, under the circumstances-and Prince Trevannion exerted all his copious charm to thaw them out, beginning with the pre-dinner cocktails and continuing through the meal. By the time they retired for coffee and brandy to the parlor where the conference was to be held, the Lords-ex-Masters were almost friendly.

"We've enacted the Emancipation Act," Olvir Nikkolon, who was ex officio chairman of the committee, reported. "Every slave on the planet must be free before the opening of the next Midyear Feasts."

"And when will that be?"

Aditya, he knew, had a three hundred and fifty-eight day year; even if the Midyear Feasts were just past, they were giving themselves very little time. In about a hundred and fifty days, Nikkolon said.

"Good heavens!" Erskyll began, indignantly.

"I should say so, myself," he put in, cutting off anything else the new Proconsul might have said. "You gentlemen are allowing yourselves dangerously little time. A hundred and fifty days will pass quite rapidly, and you have twenty million slaves to deal with. If you start at this moment and work continuously, you'll have a little under a second apiece for each slave."

The Lords-Master looked dismayed. So, he was happy to observe, did Count Erskyll.

"I assume you have some system of slave registration?" he continued.

That was safe. They had a bureaucracy, and bureaucracies tend to have registrations of practically everything.

"Oh, yes, of course," Rovard Javasan assured him. "That's your Management, isn't it, Sesar; Servile Affairs?"

"Yes, we have complete data on every slave on the planet," Sesar Martwynn, the Chief of Servile Management, said. "Of course, I'd have to ask Zhorzh about the details...."

Zhorzh was Zhorzh Khouzhik, Martwynn's chief-slave in office.

"At least, he was my chief-slave; now you people have taken him away from me. I don't know what I'm going to do without him. For that matter, I don't know what poor Zhorzh will do, either."

"Have you gentlemen informed your chief-slaves that they are free, yet?"

Nikkolon and Javasan looked at each other. Sesar Martwynn laughed.

"They know," Javasan said. "I must say they are much disturbed."

"Well, reassure them, as soon as you're back at the Citadel," he told them. "Tell them that while they are now free, they need not leave you unless they so desire; that you will provide for them as before."

"You mean, we can keep our chief-slaves?" somebody cried.

"Yes, of course-chief-freedmen, you'll have to call them, now. You'll have to pay them a salary...."

"You mean, give them money?" Ranal Valdry, the Lord Provost-Marshal demanded, incredulously. "Pay our own slaves?"

"You idiot," somebody told him, "they aren't our slaves any more. That's the whole point of this discussion."

"But ...but how can we pay slaves?" one of the committeemen-at-large asked. "Freedmen, I mean?"

"With money. You do have money, haven't you?"

"Of course we have. What do you think we are, savages?"

"What kind of money?"

Why, money; what did he think? The unit was the star-piece, the stelly. When he asked to see some of it, they were indignant. Nobody carried money; wasn't Masterly. A Master never even touched the stuff; that was what slaves were for. He wanted to know how it was secured, and they didn't know what he meant, and when he tried to explain their incomprehension deepened. It seemed that the Mastership issued money to finance itself, and individual Masters issued money on their personal credit, and it was handled through the Mastership Banks.

"That's Fedrig Daffysan's Management; he isn't here," Rovard Javasan said. "I can't explain it, myself."

And without his chief-slave, Fedrig Daffysan probably would not be able to, either.

"Yes, gentlemen. I understand. You have money. Now, the first thing you will have to do is furnish us with a complete list of all the slave-owners on the planet, and a list of all the slaves held by each. This will be sent back to Odin, and will be the basis for the compensation to be paid for the destruction of your property-rights in these slaves. How much is a slave worth, by the way?"

Nobody knew. Slaves were never sold; it wasn't Masterly to sell one's slaves. It wasn't even heard of.

"Well, we'll arrive at some valuation. Now, as soon as you get back to the Citadel, talk at once to your former chief-slaves, and their immediate subordinates, and explain the situation to them. This can be passed down through administrative freedmen to the workers; you must see to it that it is clearly understood, at all levels, that as long as the freedmen remain at their work they will be provided for and paid, but that if they quit your service they will receive nothing. Do you think you can do that?"

"You mean, give them everything we've been giving them now, and then pay them money?" Ranal Valdry almost howled.

"Oh, no. You pay them a fixed wage. You charge them for everything you give them, and deduct that from their wages. It will mean considerable extra bookkeeping, but outside of that I believe you'll find that things will go along much as they always did."

The Masters had begun to relax, and by the time he was finished all of them were smiling in relief. Count Erskyll, on the other hand, was almost writhing in his chair. It must be horrible to be a brilliant young Proconsul of liberal tendencies and to have to sit mute while a cynical old Ministerial Secretary, vastly one's superior in the Imperial Establishment and a distant cousin of the Emperor to boot, calmly bartered away the sacred liberties of twenty million people.

"But would that be legal, under the Imperial Constitution?" Olvir Nikkolon asked.

"I shouldn't have suggested it if it hadn't been. The Constitution only forbids physical ownership of one sapient being by another; it emphatically does not guarantee anyone an unearned livelihood."

The Convocation committee returned to Zeggensburg to start preparing the servile population for freedom, or reasonable facsimile. The chief-slaves would take care of that; each one seemed to have a list of other chief-slaves, and the word would spread from them on an each-one-call-five system. The public announcement would be postponed until the word could be passed out to the upper servile levels. A meeting with the chief-slaves in office of the various Managements was scheduled for the next afternoon.

Count Erskyll chatted with forced affability while the departing committeemen were being seen to the launch that would take them down. When the airlock closed behind them, he drew Prince Trevannion aside out of earshot of their subordinates.

"You know what you're doing?" he raged, in a hoarse whisper. "You're simply substituting peonage for outright slavery!"

"I'd call that something of a step." He motioned Erskyll into one of the small hall-cars, climbed in beside him, and lifted it, starting toward the living-area. "The Convocation has acknowledged the principle that sapient beings should not be property. That's a great deal, for one day."

"But the people will remain in servitude, you know that. The Masters will keep them in debt, and they'll be treated just as brutally...."

"Oh, there will be abuses; that's to be expected. This Freedmen's Management, nee Servile Management, will have to take care of that. Better make a memo to talk with this chief-freedman of Martwynn's, what's his name? Zhorzh Khouzhik; that's right, let Zhorzh do it. Employment Practices Code, investigation agency, enforcement. If he can't do the job, that's not our fault. The Empire does not guarantee every planet an honest, intelligent and efficient government; just a single one."

"But...."

"It will take two or three generations. At first, the freedmen will be exploited just as they always have been, but in time there will be protests, and disorders, and each time, there will be some small improvement. A society must evolve, Obray. Let these people earn their freedom. Then they will be worthy of it."

"They should have their freedom now."

"This present generation? What do you think freedom means to them? *We don't have to work, any more.* So down tools and let everything stop at once. *We can do anything we want to.* Let's kill the overseer. And: *Anything that belongs to the Masters belongs to us; we're Masters too, now.* No, I think it's better, for the present, to tell them that this freedom business is just a lot of Masterly funny-talk, and that things aren't really being changed at all. It will effect a considerable saving of his Imperial Majesty's ammunition, for one thing."

He dropped Erskyll at his apartment and sent the hall-car back from his own. Lanze Degbrend was waiting for him when he entered.

"Ravney's having trouble. That is the word he used," Degbrend said. In Pyairr Ravney's lexicon, trouble meant shooting. "The news of the Emancipation Act is leaking all over the place. Some of the troops in the north who haven't been disarmed yet are mutinying, and there are slave insurrections in a number of places."

"They think the Masters have forsaken them, and it's every slave for himself." He hadn't expected that to start so soon. "The announcement had better go out as quickly as possible. And I think we're going to have some trouble. You have information-taps into Count Erskyll's numerous staff? Use them as much as you can."

"You think he's going to try to sabotage this employment programme of yours, sir?"

"Oh, he won't think of it in those terms. He'll be preventing me from sabotaging the Emancipation. He doesn't want to wait three generations; he wants to free them at once. Everything has to be at once for six-month-old puppies, six-year-old children, and reformers of any age."

The announcement did not go out until nearly noon the next day. In terms comprehensible to any low-grade submoron, it was emphasized that all this meant was that slaves should henceforth be called freedmen, that they could have money just like Lords-Master, and that if they worked faithfully and obeyed orders they would be given everything they were now receiving. Ravney had been shuttling troops about, dealing with the sporadic outbreaks of disorder here and there: many of these had been put down, and the rest died out after the telecast explaining the situation.

In addition, some of Commander Douvrin's intelligence people had discovered that the only source of fissionables and radioactives for the planet was a complex of uranite mines, separation plants, refineries and reaction-plants on the smaller of Aditya's two continents, Austragonia. In spite of other urgent calls on his resources, Ravney landed troops to seize these, and a party of engineers followed them down from the *Empress Eulalie* to make an inspection.

At lunch, Count Erskyll was slightly less intransigent on the subject of the wage-employment proposals. No doubt some of his advisors had been telling him what would happen if any appreciable number of Aditya's labor-force stopped work suddenly, and the wave of uprisings that had broken out before any public announcement had been made puzzled him. He was also concerned about finding a suitable building for a proconsular palace; the business of the Empire on Aditya could not be conducted long from shipboard.

Going down to the Citadel that afternoon, they found the chief-freedmen of the non-functional Chiefs of Management assembled in a large room on the fifth level down. There was a cluster of big tables and communication-screens and wired telephones in the middle, with smaller tables around them, at which freedmen in variously colored gowns sat. The ones at the central tables, a dozen and a half, all wore chief-slaves' white gowns.

Trevannion and Erskyll and Patrique Morvill and Lanze Degbrend joined these; subordinates guided the rest of the party—a couple of Ravney's officers and Erskyll's numerous staff of advisors and specialists-to distribute themselves with their opposite numbers in the Mastership. Everybody on the Adityan side seemed uneasy with these strange hermaphrodite creatures who were neither slaves nor Lords-Master.

"Well, gentlemen," Count Erskyll began, "I suppose you have been informed by your former Lords-Master of how relations between them and you will be in the future?"

"Oh, yes, Lord Proconsul," Khreggor Chmidd replied happily. "Everything will be just as before, except that the Lords-Master will be called Lords-Employer, and the slaves will be called freedmen, and any time they want to starve to death, they can leave their Employers if they wish."

Count Erskyll frowned. That wasn't just exactly what he had hoped Emancipation would mean to these people.

"Nobody seems to understand about this money thing, though," Zhorzh Khouzhik, Sesar Martwynn's chief-freedman said. "My Lord-Master —" He slapped himself across the mouth and said, "Lord-Employer!" five times, rapidly. "My Lord-*Employer* tried to explain it to me, but I don't think he understands very clearly, himself."

"None of them do."

The speaker was a small man with pale eyes and a mouth like a rat-trap; Yakoop Zhannar, chief-freedman to Ranal Valdry, the Provost-Marshal.

"Its really your idea, Prince Trevannion," Erskyll said. "Perhaps you can explain it."

"Oh, it's very simple. You see...."

At least, it had seemed simple when he started. Labor was a commodity, which the worker sold and the employer purchased; a "fair wage" was one which enabled both to operate at a profit. Everybody knew that-except here on Aditya. On Aditya, a slave worked because he was a slave, and a Master provided for him because he was a Master, and that was all there was to it. But now, it seemed, there weren't any more Masters, and there weren't any more slaves.

"That's exactly it," he replied, when somebody said as much. "So now, if the slaves, I mean, freedmen, want to eat, they have to work to earn money to buy food, and if the Employers want work done, they have to pay people to do it."

"Then why go to all the trouble about the money?" That was an elderly chief-freedman, Mykhyl Eschkhaffar, whose Lord-Employer, Oraze Borztall, was Manager of Public Works. "Before your ships came, the slaves worked for the Masters, and the Masters took care of the slaves, and everybody was content. Why not leave it like that?"

"Because the Galactic Emperor, who is the Lord-Master of these people, says that there must be no more slaves. Don't ask me why," Tchall Hozhet snapped at him. "I don't know, either. But they are here with ships and guns and soldiers; what can we do?"

"That's very close to it," he admitted. "But there is one thing you haven't considered. A slave only gets what his master gives him. But a free worker for pay gets money which he can spend for whatever he wants, and he can save money, and if he finds that he can make more money working for somebody else, he can quit his employer and get a better job."

"We hadn't thought of that," Khreggor Chmidd said. "A slave, even a chief-slave, was never allowed to have money of his own, and if he got hold of any, he couldn't spend it. But now...." A glorious vista seemed to open in front of him. "And he can accumulate money. I don't suppose a common worker could, but an upper slave....Especially a chief-slave...." He slapped his mouth, and said, "Freedman!" five times.

"Yes, Khreggor." That was Ridgerd Schferts (Fedrig Daffysan; Fiscal Management). "I am sure we could all make quite a lot of money, now that we are freedmen."

Some of them were briefly puzzled; gradually, comprehension dawned. Obray, Count Erskyll, looked distressed; he seemed to be hoping, vainly, that they weren't thinking of what he suspected they were.

"How about the Mastership freedmen?" another asked. "We, here, will be paid by our Lords-Mas- ...Lords-Employer. But everybody from the green robes down were provided for by the Mastership. Who will pay them, now?"

"Why, the Mastership, of course," Ridgerd Schferts said. "My Management-my Lord-Employer's, I mean-will issue the money to pay them."

"You may need a new printing-press," Lanze Degbrend said. "And an awful lot of paper."

"This planet will need currency acceptable in interstellar trade," Erskyll said.

Everybody looked blankly at him. He changed the subject:

"Mr. Chmidd, could you or Mr. Hozhet tell me what kind of a constitution the Mastership has?"

"You mean, like the paper you read in the Convocation?" Hozhet asked. "Oh, there is nothing at all like that. The former Lords-Master simply ruled."

No. They reigned. This servile *tammanihal* —another ancient Terran word, of uncertain origin-ruled.

"Well, how is the Mastership organized, then?" Erskyll persisted. "How did the Lord Nikkolon get to be Chairman of the Presidium, and the Lord Javasan to be Chief of Administration?"

That was very simple. The Convocation, consisting of the heads of all the Masterly families, actually small clans, numbered about twenty-five hundred. They elected the seven members of the Presidium, who drew lots for the Chairmanship. They served for life. Vacancies were filled by election on nomination of the surviving members. The Presidium appointed the Chiefs of Managements, who also served for life.

At least, it had stability. It was self-perpetuating.

"Does the Convocation make the laws?" Erskyll asked.

Hozhet was perplexed. "*Make* laws, Lord Proconsul? Oh, no. We have laws."

There were planets, here and there through the Empire, where an attitude like that would have been distinctly beneficial; planets with elective parliaments, every member of which felt himself obligated to get as many laws enacted during his term of office as possible.

"But this is dreadful; you *must* have a constitution!" Obray of Erskyll was shocked. "We will have to get one drawn up and adopted."

"We don't know anything about that at all," Khreggor Chmidd admitted. "This is something new. You will have to help us."

"I certainly will, Mr. Chmidd. Suppose you form a committee-yourself, and Mr. Hozhet, and three or four others; select them among yourselves-and we can get together and talk over what will be needed. And another thing. We'll have to stop calling this the Mastership. There are no more Masters."

"The Employership?" Lanze Degbrend dead-panned.

Erskyll looked at him angrily. "This is something," he told the chief-freedmen, "that should not belong to the Employers alone. It should belong to everybody. Let us call it the Commonwealth. That means something everybody owns in common."

"Something everybody owns, nobody owns," Mykhyl Eschkhaffar objected.

"Oh, no, Mykhyl; it will belong to everybody," Khreggor Chmidd told him earnestly. "But somebody will have to take care of it for everybody. That," he added complacently, "will be you and me and the rest of us here."

"I believe," Yakoop Zhannar said, almost smiling, "that this freedom is going to be a wonderful thing. For us."

"I don't like it!" Mykhyl Eschkhaffar said stubbornly. "Too many new things, and too much changing names. We have to call slaves freedmen; we have to call Lords Master Lords-Employer; we have to call the Management of Servile Affairs the Management for Freedmen. Now we have to call the Mastership this new name, Commonwealth. And all these new things, for which we have no routine procedures and no directives. I wish these people had never heard of this planet."

"That makes at least two of us," Patrique Morvill said, *sotto voce.*

"Well, the planetary constitution can wait just a bit," Prince Trevannion suggested. "We have a great many items on the agenda which must be taken care of immediately. For instance, there's this thing about finding a proconsular palace...."

A surprising amount of work had been done at the small tables where Erskyll's staff of political and economic and technological experts had been conferring with the subordinate upper-freedmen. It began coming out during the pre-dinner cocktails aboard the *Empress Eulalie*, continued through the meal, and was fully detailed during the formal debriefing session afterward.

Finding a suitable building for the Proconsular Palace would present difficulties. Real estate was not sold on Aditya, any more than slaves were. It was not only un-Masterly but illegal; estates were all entailed and the inalienable property of Masterly families. What was wanted was one of the isolated residential towers in Zeggensburg, far enough from the Citadel to avoid an appearance of too close supervision. The last thing anybody wanted was to establish the Proconsul in the Citadel itself. The Management of Business of the Mastership, however, had promised to do something about it. That would mean, no doubt, that the *Empress Eulalie* would be hanging over Zeggensburg, serving as Proconsular Palace, for the next year or so.

The Servile Management, rechristened Freedmen's Management, would undertake to safeguard the rights of the newly emancipated slaves. There would be an Employment Code-Count Erskyll was invited to draw that up-and a force of investigators, and an enforcement agency, under Zhorzh Khouzhik.

One of Commander Douvrin's men, who had been at the Austragonia nuclear-industries establishment, was present and reported:

"Great Ghu, you ought to see that place! They've people working in places I wouldn't send an unshielded robot, and the hospital there is bulging with radiation-sickness cases. The equipment must have been brought here by the Space Vikings. What's left of it is the damnedest mess of goldbergery I ever saw. The whole thing ought to be shut down and completely rebuilt."

Erskyll wanted to know who owned it. The Mastership, he was told.

"That's right," one of his economics men agreed. "Management of Public Works." That would be Mykhyl Eschkhaffar, who had so bitterly objected to the new nomenclature. "If anybody needs fissionables for a power-reactor or radioactives for nuclear-electric conversion, his chief business slave gets what's needed. Furthermore, doesn't even have to sign for it."

"Don't they sell it for revenue?"

"Nifflheim, no! This government doesn't need revenue. This government supports itself by counterfeiting. When the Mastership needs money, they just have Ridgerd Schferts print up another batch. Like everybody else."

"Then the money simply isn't worth anything!" Erskyll was horrified, which was rapidly becoming his normal state.

"Who cares about money, Obray," he said. "Didn't you hear them, last evening? It's un-Masterly to bother about things like money. Of course, everybody owes everybody for everything, but it's all in the family."

"Well, something will have to be done about that!"

That was at least the tenth time he had said that, this evening.

It came practically as a thunderbolt when Khreggor Chmidd screened the ship the next afternoon to report that a Proconsular Palace had been found, and would be ready for occupancy in a day or so. The chief-freedmen of the Management of Business of the Mastership and of the Lord Chief Justiciar had found one, the Elegry Palace, which had been unoccupied except for what he described as a small caretaking staff for years, while two Masterly families disputed inheritance rights and slave lawyers quibbled endlessly before a slave judge. The chief freedman of the Lord Chief Justiciar had simply summoned judge and lawyers into his office and ordered them to settle the suit at once. The settlement had consisted of paying both litigants the full value of the building; this came to fifty million stellies apiece. Arbitrarily, the stelly was assigned a value in Imperial crowns of a hundred for one. A million crowns was about what the building would be worth, with contents, on Odin. It would be paid for with a draft on the Imperial Exchequer.

"Well, you have some hard currency on the planet, now," he told Count Erskyll, while they were having a pre-dinner drink together that evening. "I hope it doesn't touch off an inflation, if the term is permissible when applied to Adityan currency."

Erskyll snapped his fingers. "Yes! And there's the money we've been spending for supplies. And when we start compensation payments....Excuse me for a moment."

He dashed off, his drink in his hand. After a long interval, he was back, carrying a fresh one he had gotten from a bartending robot en route.

"Well, that's taken care of," he said. "My fiscal man's getting in touch with Ridgerd Schferts; the Elegry heirs will be paid in Adityan stellies, and the Imperial crowns will be held in the Commonwealth Bank, or, better, banked in Asgard, to give Aditya some off-planet credit. And we'll do the same with our other expenditures, and with the slave-compensation. This is going to be wonderful; this planet needs everything in the way of industrial equipment; this is how they're going to get it."

"But, Obray; the compensations are owing to the individual Masters. They should be paid in crowns. You know as well as I do that this hundred-for-one rate is purely a local fiction. On the interstellar exchange, these stellies have a crown value of precisely zero-point-zero."

"You know what would happen if these ci-devant Masters got hold of Imperial crowns," Erskyll said. "They'd only squander them back again for useless imported luxuries. This planet

needs a complete modernization, and this is the only way the money to pay for it can be gotten."
He was gesturing excitedly with the almost-full glass in his hand; Prince Trevannion stepped
back out of the way of the splash he anticipated. "I have no sympathy for these ci-devant
Masters. They own every stick and stone and pinch of dust on this planet, as it is. Is that fair?"

"Possibly not. But neither is what you're proposing to do."

Obray, Count Erskyll, couldn't see that. He was proposing to secure the Greatest Good for
the Greatest Number, and to Nifflheim with any minorities who happened to be in the way.

The Navy took over the Elegry Palace the next morning, ran up the Imperial Sun and Cogwheel flag, and began transmitting views of its interior up to the *Empress Eulalie*. It was considerably smaller than the Imperial Palace at Asgard on Odin, but room for room the furnishings
were rather more ornate and expensive. By the next afternoon, the counter-espionage team that
had gone down reported the Masterly living quarters clear of pickups, microphones, and other
apparatus of servile snooping, of which they had found many. The *Canopus* was recalled from
her station over the northern end of the continent and began sending down the proconsulate
furnishings stowed aboard, including several hundred domestic robots.

The skeleton caretaking staff Chmidd had mentioned proved to number five hundred.

"What are we going to do about them?" Erskyll wanted to know. "There's a limit to the
upkeep allowance for a proconsulate, and we can't pay five hundred useless servants. The chief-
freedman, and about a dozen assistants, and a few to operate the robots, when we train them,
but five hundred...!"

"Let Zhorzh do it," Prince Trevannion suggested. "Isn't that what this Freedmen's Management is for; to find employment for emancipated slaves? Just emancipate them and turn them
over to Khouzhik."

Khouzhik promptly placed all of them on the payroll of his Management. Khouzhik was
having his hands full. He had all his top mathematical experts, some of whom even understood
the use of the slide-rule, trying to work up a scale of wages. Erskyll loaned him a few of his
staff. None of the ideas any of them developed proved workable. Khouzhik had also organized
a corps of investigators, and he was beginning to annex the private guard-companies of the
Lords-ex-Master, whom he was organizing into a police force.

The nuclear works on Austragonia were closed down. Mykhyl Eschkhaffar ordered a programme of rationing and priorities to conserve the stock of plutonium and radioactive isotopes
on hand, and he decided that henceforth nuclear-energy materials would be sold instead of
furnished freely. He simply found out what the market quotations on Odin were, translated
that into stellies, and adopted it. This was just a base price; there would have to be bribes for
priority allocations, rakeoffs for the under-freedmen, and graft for the business-freedmen of
the Lords-ex-Masters who bought the stuff. The latter were completely unconcerned; none
of them even knew about it.

The Convocation adjourned until the next regular session, at the Midyear Feasts, an eight-day
intercalary period which permitted dividing the 358-day Adityan year into ten months of thirty-
five days each. Count Erskyll was satisfied to see them go. He was working on a constitution
for the Commonwealth of Aditya, and was making very little progress with it.

"It's one of these elaborate check-and-balance things," Lanze Degbrend reported. "To begin
with, it was the constitution of Aton, with an elective president substituted for a hereditary
king. Of course, there are a lot of added gadgets; Atonian Radical Democrat stuff. Chmidd
and Hozhet and the other chief-slaves don't like it, either."

"Slap your mouth and say, 'Freedmen,' five times."

"Nuts," his subordinate retorted insubordinately. "I know a slave when I see one. A slave is a slave, with or without a gorget; if he doesn't wear it around his neck, he has it tattooed on his soul. It takes at least three generations to rub it off."

"I could wish that Count Erskyll...." he began. "What else is our Proconsul doing?"

"Well, I'm afraid he's trying to set up some kind of a scheme for the complete nationalization of all farms, factories, transport facilities, and other means of production and distribution," Degbrend said.

"He's not going to try to do that himself, is he?" He was, he discovered, speaking sharply, and modified his tone. "He won't do it with Imperial authority, or with Imperial troops. Not as long as I'm here. And when we go back to Odin, I'll see to it that Vann Shatrak understands that."

"Oh, no. The Commonwealth of Aditya will do that," Degbrend said. "Chmidd and Hozhet and Yakoop Zhannar and Zhorzh Khouzhik and the rest of them, that is. He wants it done legitimately and legally. That means, he'll have to wait till the Midyear Feasts, when the Convocation assembles, and he can get his constitution enacted. If he can get it written by then."

Vann Shatrak sent two of the destroyers off to explore the moons of Aditya, of which there were two. The outer moon, Aditya-*Ba'*, was an irregular chunk of rock fifty miles in diameter, barely visible to the naked eye. The inner, Aditya-*Alif*, however, was an eight-hundred-mile sphere; it had once been the planetary ship-station and shipyard-base. It seemed to have been abandoned when the Adityan technology and economy had begun sagging under the weight of the slave system. Most of the installations remained, badly run down but repairable. Shatrak transferred as many of his technicians as he could spare to the *Mizar* and sent her to recondition the shipyard and render the underground city inhabitable again so that the satellite could be used as a base for his ships. He decided, then, to send the *Irma* back to Odin with reports of the annexation of Aditya, a proposal that Aditya-*Alif* be made a permanent Imperial naval-base, and a request for more troops.

Prince Trevannion taped up his own reports, describing the general situation on the newly annexed planet, and doing nothing to minimize the problems facing its Proconsul.

"Count Erskyll" he finished, "is doing the best possible under circumstances from which I myself would feel inclined to shrink. If not carried to excess, perhaps youthful idealism is not without value in Empire statecraft. I understand that Commodore Shatrak, who is also coping with some very trying problems, is requesting troop reenforcements. I believe this request amply justified, and would recommend that they be gotten here as speedily as possible.

"I understand that he is also recommending a permanent naval base on the larger of this planet's two satellites. This I also endorse unreservedly. It would have a most salutary effect on the local government. I would further recommend that Commodore Shatrak be placed in command of it, with suitable promotion, which he has long ago earned."

Erskyll was surprised that he was not himself returning to Odin on the destroyer, and evidently disturbed. He mentioned it during pre-dinner cocktails that evening.

"I know, my own work here is finished; was the moment the Convocation voted acknowledgment of Imperial rule." Prince Trevannion replied. "I would like to stay on for the Midyear Feasts, though. The Convocation will vote on your constitution, and I would like to be able to report their action to the Prime Minister. How is it progressing, by the way?"

"Well, we have a rough draft. I don't care much for it, myself, but Citizen Hozhet and Citizen Chmidd and Citizen Zhannar and the others are most enthusiastic, and, after all, they are the ones who will have to operate under it."

The Masterly estates would be the representative units; from each, the freedmen would elect representatives to regional elective councils, and these in turn would elect representatives to a central electoral council which would elect a Supreme People's Legislative Council. This would not only function as the legislative body, but would also elect a Manager-in-Chief, who would appoint the Chiefs of Management, who, in turn, would appoint their own subordinates.

"I don't like it, myself," Erskyll said. "It's not democratic enough. There should be a direct vote by the people. Well," he grudged, "I suppose it will take a little time for them to learn democracy." This was the first time he had come out and admitted that. "There is to be a Constituent Convention in five years, to draw up a new constitution."

"How about the Convocation? You don't expect them to vote themselves out of existence, do you?"

"Oh, we're keeping the Convocation, in the present constitution, but they won't have any power. Five years from now, we'll be rid of them entirely. Look here; you're not going to work against this, are you? You won't advise these ci-devant Lords-Master to vote against it, when it comes up?"

"Certainly not. I think your constitution-Khreggor Chmidd's and Tchall Hozhet's, to be exact-will be nothing short of a political disaster, but it will insure some political stability, which is all that matters from the Imperial point of view. An Empire statesman must always guard against sympathizing with local factions and interests, and I can think of no planet on which I could be safer from any such temptation. If these Lords-Master want to vote their throats cut, and the slaves want to re-enslave themselves, they may all do so with my complete blessing."

If he had been at all given to dramatic gestures he would then have sent for water and washed his hands.

Metaphorically, he did so at that moment; thereafter his interest in Adityan affairs was that of a spectator at a boring and stupid show, watching only because there is nothing else to watch, and wishing that it had been possible to have returned to Odin on the *Irma*. The Prime Minister, however, was entitled to a full and impartial report, which he would scarcely get from Count Erskyll, on this new jewel in the Imperial Crown. To be able to furnish that, he would have to remain until the Midyear Feasts, when the Convocation would act on the new constitution. Whether the constitution was adopted or rejected was, in itself, unimportant; in either case, Aditya would have a government recognizable as such by the Empire, which was already recognizing some fairly unlikely-looking governments. In either case, too, Aditya would make nobody on any other planet any trouble. It wouldn't have, at least for a long time, even if it had been left unannexed, but no planet inhabited by Terro-humans could be trusted to remain permanently peaceful and isolated. There is a spark of aggressive ambition in every Terro-human people, no matter how debased, which may smoulder for centuries or even millennia and then burst, fanned by some random wind, into flame. To shift the metaphor slightly, the Empire could afford to leave no unwatched pots around to boil over unexpectedly.

Occasionally, he did warn young Erskyll of the dangers of overwork and emotional over-involvement. Each time, the Proconsul would pour out some tale of bickering and rivalry among the chief-freedmen of the Managements. Citizen Khouzhik and Citizen Eschkhaffar-they were all calling each other Citizen, now-were contesting overlapping jurisdictions. Khouzhik wanted to change the name of his Management-he no longer bothered mentioning Sesar Martwynn-to Labor and Industry. To this, Mykhyl Eschkhaffar objected vehemently; any Industry that was going to be managed would be managed by his-Oraze Borztall was similarly left unmentioned-management of Public Works. And they were also feuding about the robotic and remote-controlled equipment that had been sent down from the *Empress Eulalie* to the Austragonia nuclear-power works.

Khouzhik was also in controversy with Yakoop Zhannar, who was already calling himself People's Provost-Marshal. Khouzhik had taken over all the private armed-guards on the Masterly farms and in the factories, and assimilated them into something he was calling the People's Labor Police, ostensibly to enforce the new Code of Employment Practice. Zhannar insisted that they should be under his Management; when Chmidd and Hozhet supported Khouzhik, he began clamoring for the return of the regular army to his control.

Commodore Shatrak was more than glad to get rid of the Adityan army, and so was Pyairr Ravney, who was in immediate command of them. The Adityans didn't care one way or the other. Zhannar was delighted, and so were Chmidd and Hozhet. So, oddly, was Zhorzh

Khouzhik. At the same time, the state of martial law proclaimed on the day of the landing was terminated.

The days slipped by. There were entertainments at the new Proconsular Palace for the Masterly residents of Zeggensburg, and Erskyll and his staff were entertained at Masterly palaces. The latter affairs pained Prince Trevannion excessively-hours on end of gorging uninspired cooking and guzzling too-sweet wine and watching ex-slave performers whose acts were either brutal or obscene and frequently both, and, more unforgivable, stupidly so. The Masterly conversation was simply stupid.

He borrowed a reconn-car from Ravney; he and Lanze Degbrend and, usually, one or another of Ravney's young officers, took long trips of exploration. They fished in mountain streams, and hunted the small deerlike game, and he found himself enjoying these excursions more than anything he had done in recent years; certainly anything since Aditya had come into the viewscreens of the *Empress Eulalie*. Once in a while, they claimed and received Masterly hospitality at some large farming estate. They were always greeted with fulsome cordiality, and there was always surprise that persons of their rank and consequence should travel unaccompanied by a retinue of servants.

He found things the same wherever he stopped. None of the farms were producing more than a quarter of the potential yield per acre, and all depleting the soil outrageously. Ten slaves-he didn't bother to think of them as freedmen-doing the work of one, and a hundred of them taking all day to do what one robot would have done before noon. White-gowned chief-slaves lording it over green and orange gowned supervisors and clerks; overseers still carrying and frequently using whips and knouts and sandbag flails.

Once or twice, when a Masterly back was turned, he caught a look of murderous hatred flickering into the eyes of some upper-slave. Once or twice, when a Master thought his was turned, he caught the same look in Masterly eyes, directed at him or at Lanze.

The Midyear Feasts approached; each time he returned to the city he found more excitement as preparations went on. Mykhyl Eschkhaffar's Management of Public Works was giving top priority to redecorating the Convocation Chamber and the lounges and dining-rooms around it in which the Masters would relax during recesses. More and more Masterly families flocked in from outlying estates, with contragravity-flotillas and retinues of attendants, to be entertained at the city palaces. There were more and gaudier banquets and balls and entertainments. By the time the Feasts began, every Masterly man, woman and child would be in the city.

There were long columns of military contragravity coming in, too; troop-carriers and combat-vehicles. Yakoop Zhannar was bringing in all his newly recovered army, and Zhorzh Khouzhik his newly organized People's Labor Police. Vann Shatrak, who was now commanding his battle-line unit by screen from the Proconsular Palace, began fretting.

"I wish I hadn't been in such a hurry to terminate martial rule," he said, once. "And I wish Pyairr hadn't been so confoundedly efficient in retraining those troops. That may cost us a few extra casualties, before we're through."

Count Erskyll laughed at his worries.

"It's just this rivalry between Citizen Khouzhik and Citizen Zhannar," he said, "They're like a couple of ci-devant Lords-Master competing to give more extravagant feasts. Zhannar's going to hold a review of his troops, and of course, Khouzhik intends to hold a review of his police. That's all there is to it."

"Well, just the same, I wish some reenforcements would get here from Odin," Shatrak said.

Erskyll was busy, in the days before the Midyear Feasts, either conferring at the Citadel with the ex-slaves who were the functional heads of the Managements or at the Proconsular Palace with Hozhet and Chmidd and the chief-freedmen of the influential Convocation leaders and Presidium members. Everybody was extremely optimistic about the constitution.

He couldn't quite understand the optimism, himself.

"If I were one of these Lords-Master, I wouldn't even consider the thing," he told Erskyll. "I know, they're stupid, but I can't believe they're stupid enough to commit suicide, and that's what this amounts to."

"Yes, it does," Erskyll agreed, cheerfully. "As soon as they enact it, they'll be of no more consequence than the Assemblage of Peers on Aton; they'll have no voice in the operation of the Commonwealth, and none in the new constitution that will be drawn up five years from now. And that will be the end of them. All the big estates, and the factories and mines and contragravity-ship lines will be nationalized."

"And they'll have nothing at all, except a hamper-full of repudiated paper stellies," he finished. "That's what I mean. What makes you think they'll be willing to vote for that?"

"They don't know they're voting for it. They'll think they're voting to keep control of the Mastership. People like Olvir Nikkolon and Rovard Javasan and Ranal Valdry and Sesar Martwynn think they still own their chief-freedmen; they think Hozhet and Chmidd and Zhannar and Khouzhik will do exactly what they tell them. And they believe anything the Hozhets and Chmidds and Zhannars tell them. And every chief-freedman is telling his Lord-Employer that the only way they can keep control is by adopting the constitution; that they can control the elections on their estates, and hand-pick the People's Legislative Council. I tell you, Prince Trevannion, the constitution is as good as enacted."

Two days before the opening of the Convocation, the *Irma* came into radio-range, five light-hours away, and began transmitting in taped matter at sixty-speed. Erskyll's report and his own acknowledged; a routine "well done" for the successful annexation. Commendation for Shatrak's handling of the landing operation. Orders to take over Aditya-*Alif* and begin construction of a permanent naval base. Notification of promotion to base-admiral, and blank commission as line-commodore; that would be Patrique Morvill. And advice that one transport-cruiser, *Algol*, with an Army contragravity brigade aboard, and two engineering ships, would leave Odin for Aditya in fifteen days. The last two words erased much of the new base-admiral's pleasure.

"Fifteen days, great Ghu! And those tubs won't make near the speed of *Irma*, getting here. We'll be lucky to see them in twenty. And Beelzebub only knows what'll be going on here then."

Four times, the big screen failed to respond. They were all crowded into one of the executive conference-rooms at the Proconsular Palace, the batteries of communication and recording equipment incongruously functional among the gold-encrusted luxury of the original Masterly furnishings. Shatrak swore.

"Andrey, I thought your people had planted those pickups where they couldn't be found," he said to Commander Douvrin.

"There is no such place, sir," the intelligence officer replied. "Just places where things are hard to find."

"Did you mention our pickups to Chmidd or Hozhet or any of the rest of the shaveheads?" Shatrak asked Erskyll.

"No. I didn't even know where they were. And it was the freedmen who found them," Erskyll said. "I don't know why they wouldn't want us looking in."

Lanze Degbrend, at the screen, twisted the dial again, and this time the screen flickered and cleared, and they were looking into the Convocation Chamber from the extreme rear, above the double doors. Far away, in front, Olvir Nikkolon was rising behind the gold and onyx bench, and from the speaker the call bell tolled slowly, and the buzz of over two thousand whispering voices diminished. Nikkolon began to speak:

"Seven and a half centuries ago, our fathers went forth from Morglay to plant upon this planet a new banner...."

It was evidently a set speech, one he had recited year after year, and every Lord Chairman of the Presidium before him. The splendid traditions. The glories of the Masterly race. The all-conquering Space Vikings. The proud heritage of the Sword-Worlds. Lanze was fiddling with the control knobs, stepping up magnification and focusing on the speaker's head and shoulders. Then everybody laughed; Nikkolon had a small plug in one ear, with a fine wire running down to vanish under his collar. Degbrend brought back the full view of the Convocation Chamber.

Nikkolon went on and on. Vann Shatrak summoned a robot to furnish him with a cold beer and another cigar. Erskyll was drumming an impatient devil's tattoo with his fingernails on the gold-encrusted table in front of him. Lanze Degbrend began interpolating sarcastic comments. And finally, Pyairr Ravney, who came from Lugaluru, reverted to the idiom of his planet's favorite sport:

"Come on, come on; turn out the bull! What's the matter, is the gate stuck?"

If so, it came quickly unstuck, and the bull emerged, pawing and snorting.

"This year, other conquerors have come to Aditya, here to plant another banner, the Sun and Cogwheel of the Galactic Empire, and I blush to say it, we are as helpless against these conquerors as were the miserable barbarians and their wretched serfs whom our fathers conquered seven hundred and sixty-two years ago, whose descendants, until this black day, had been our slaves."

He continued, his voice growing more impassioned and more belligerent. Count Erskyll fidgeted. This wasn't the way the Chmidd-Hozhet Constitution ought to be introduced.

"So, perforce, we accepted the sovereignty of this alien Empire. We are now the subjects of his Imperial Majesty, Rodrik III. We must govern Aditya subject to the Imperial Constitution." (Groans, boos; catcalls, if the Adityan equivalent of cats made noises like that.) "At one stroke, this Constitution has abolished our peculiar institution, upon which is based our entire social structure. This I know. But this same Imperial Constitution is a collapsium-strong shielding; let me call your attention to Article One, Section Two: *Every Empire planet shall be self-governed as to its own affairs, in the manner of its own choice and without interference.* Mark this well, for it is our guarantee that this government, of the Masters, by the Masters, and for the Masters, shall not perish from Aditya." (Prolonged cheering.)

"Now, these arrogant conquerors have overstepped their own supreme law. They have written for this Mastership a constitution, designed for the sole purpose of accomplishing the liquidation of the Masterly class and race. They have endeavored to force this planetary constitution upon us by threats of force, and by a shameful attempt to pervert the fidelity of our chief-slaves —I will not insult these loyal servitors with this disgusting new name, freedmen-so that we might, a second time, be tricked into voting assent to our own undoing. But in this, they have failed. Our chief-slaves have warned us of the trap concealed in this constitution written by the Proconsul, Count Erskyll. My faithful Tchall Hozhet has shown me all the pitfalls in this infamous document...."

Obray, Count Erskyll, was staring in dismay at the screen. Then he began cursing blasphemously, the first time he had ever been heard to do so, and, as he was at least nominally a Pantheist, this meant blaspheming the entire infinite universe.

"The rats! The dirty treacherous rats! We came here to help them, and look; they've betrayed us...!" He lost his voice in a wheezing sob, and then asked: "Why did they do it? Do they want to go on being slaves?"

Perhaps they did. It wasn't for love of their Lords-Master; he was sure of that. Even from the beginning, they had found it impossible to disguise their contempt....

Then he saw Olvir Nikkolon stop short and thrust out his arm, pointing directly below the pickup, and as he watched, something green-gray, a remote-control contragravity lorry, came floating into the field of the screen. One of the vehicles that had been sent down from the *Empress Eulalie* for use at the uranium mines. As it lifted and advanced toward the center of the room, the other Lords-Master were springing to their feet.

Vann Shatrak also sprang to his feet, reaching the controls of the screen and cutting the sound. He was just in time to save them from being, at least temporarily, deafened, for no sooner had he silenced the speaker than the lorry vanished in a flash that filled the entire room.

When the dazzle left their eyes, and the smoke and dust began to clear, they saw the Convocation Chamber in wreckage, showers of plaster and bits of plastiboard still falling from above. The gold and onyx bench was broken in a number of places; the Chiefs of Management in front of it, and the Presidium above, had vanished. Among the benches lay black-clad bodies, a few still moving. Smoke rose from burning clothing. Admiral Shatrak put on the sound again; from the screen came screams and cries of pain and fright.

Then the doors on the two long sides opened, and red-brown uniforms appeared. The soldiers advanced into the Chamber, unslinging rifles and submachine guns. Unheeding the still falling plaster, they moved forward, firing as they came. A few of them slung their firearms and picked up Masterly dress swords, using them to finish the wounded among the benches. The screams grew fewer, and then stopped.

Count Erskyll sat frozen, staring white-faced and horror-sick into the screen. Some of the others had begun to recover and were babbling excitedly. Vann Shatrak was at a communication-screen, talking to Commodore Patrique Morvill, aboard the *Empress Eulalie*:

"All the Landing-Troops, and all the crewmen you can spare and arm. And every vehicle you have. This is only the start of it; there'll be a general massacre of Masters next. I don't doubt it's started already."

At another screen, Pyairr Ravney was saying, to the officer of the day of the Palace Guard: "No, there's no telling what they'll do next. Whatever it is, be ready for it ten minutes ago."

He stubbed out his cigarette and rose, and as he did, Erskyll came out of his daze and onto his feet.

"Commodore Shatrak! I mean, Admiral," he corrected himself. "We must re-impose martial rule. I wish I'd never talked you into terminating it. Look at that!" He pointed at the screen; big dump-lorries were already coming in the doors under the pickup, with a mob of gowned civil-service people crowding in under them. They and the soldiers began dragging bodies out from among the seats to be loaded and hauled away. "There's the planetary government, murdered to the last man!"

"I'm afraid we can't do anything like that," he said. "This seems to be a simple transfer of power by *coup-d'etat*; rather more extreme than usual, but normal political practice on this sort of planet. The Empire has no right to interfere."

Erskyll turned on him indignantly. "But it's mass murder!"

"It's an accomplished fact. Whoever ordered this, Citizen Chmidd and Citizen Hozhet and Citizen Zhannar and the rest of your good democratic citizens, are now the planetary government of Aditya. As long as they don't attack us, or repudiate the sovereignty of the Emperor, you'll have to recognize them as such."

"A bloody-handed gang of murderers; recognize them?"

"All governments have a little blood here and there on their hands; you've seen this by screen instead of reading about it in a history book, but that shouldn't make any difference. And you've said, yourself, that the Masters would have to be eliminated. You've told Chmidd and Hozhet and the others that, repeatedly. Of course, you meant legally, by constitutional and democratic means, but that seemed just a bit too tedious to them. They had them all together in one room, where they could be eliminated easily, and ...Lanze; see if you can get anything on the Citadel telecast."

Degbrend put on another communication-screen and fiddled for a moment. What came on was a view, from another angle, of the Convocation Chamber. A voice was saying:

"...not one left alive. The People's Labor Police, acting on orders of People's Manager of Labor Zhorzh Khouzhik and People's Provost-Marshal Yakoop Zhannar, are now eliminating the rest of the ci-devant Masterly class, all of whom are here in Zeggensburg. The people are directed to cooperate; kill them all, men, women and children. We must allow none of these foul exploiters of the people live to see today's sun go down...."

"You mean, we sit here while those animals butcher women and children?" Shatrak demanded, looking from the Proconsul to the Ministerial Secretary. "Well, by Ghu, I won't! If I have to face a court for it, all well and good, but...."

"You won't, Admiral. I seem to recall, some years ago, a Commodore Hastings, who got a baronetcy for stopping a pogrom on Anath...."

"And broadcast an announcement that any of the Masterly class may find asylum here at the Proconsular Palace. They're political fugitives; scores of precedents for that," Erskyll added.

Shatrak was back at the screen to the *Empress Eulalie*.

"Patrique, get a jam-beam focussed on that telecast station at the Citadel; get it off the air. Then broadcast on the same wavelength; announce that anybody claiming sanctuary at the Proconsular Palace will be taken in and protected. And start getting troops down, and all the spacemen you can spare."

At the same time, Ravney was saying, into his own screen:

"Plan Four. Variation H-3; this is a rescue operation. This is not, repeat, underscore, *not* an intervention in planetary government. You are to protect members of the Masterly class in danger from mob violence. That's anybody with hair on his head. Stay away from the Citadel; the ones there are all dead. Start with the four buildings closest to us, and get them cleared out. If the shaveheads give you any trouble, don't argue with them, just shoot them...."

Erskyll, after his brief moment of decisiveness, was staring at the screen to the Convocation Chamber, where bodies were still being heaved into the lorries like black sacks of grain. Lanze Degbrend summoned a robot, had it pour a highball, and gave it to the Proconsul.

"Go ahead, Count Erskyll; drink it down. Medicinal," he was saying. "Believe me you certainly need it."

Erskyll gulped it down. "I think I could use another, if you please," he said, handing the glass back to Lanze. "And a cigarette." After he had tasted his second drink and puffed on the cigarette, he said: "I was so proud. I thought they were learning democracy."

"We don't, any of us, have too much to be proud about," Degbrend told him. "They must have been planning and preparing this for a couple of months, and we never caught a whisper of it."

That was correct. They had deluded Erskyll into thinking that they were going to let the Masters vote themselves out of power and set up a representative government. They had deluded the Masters into believing that they were in favor of the *status quo*, and opposed to Erkyll's democratization and socialization. There must be only a few of them in the conspiracy. Chmidd and Hozhet and Zhannar and Khouzhik and Schferts and the rest of the Citadel chief-slave clique. Among them, they controlled all the armed force. The bickering and rivalries must have been part of the camouflage. He supposed that a few of the upper army commanders had been in on it, too.

A communication-screen began making noises. Somebody flipped the switch, and Khreggor Chmidd appeared in it. Erskyll swore softly, and went to face the screen-image of the elephantine ex-slave of the ex-Lord Master, the late Rovard Javasan.

"Citizen Proconsul; why is our telecast station, which is vitally needed to give information to the people, jammed off the air, and why are you broadcasting, on our wavelength, advice to the criminals of the ci-devant Masterly class to take refuge in your Proconsular Palace from the just vengeance of the outraged victims of their century-long exploitation?" he began. "This is a flagrant violation of the Imperial Constitution; our Emperor will not be pleased at this unjustified intervention in the affairs, and this interference with the planetary authority, of the People's Commonwealth of Aditya!"

Obray of Erskyll must have realized, for the first time, that he was still holding a highball glass in one hand and a cigarette in the other. He flung both of them away.

"If the Imperial troops we are sending into the city to rescue women and children in danger from your hoodlums meet with the least resistance, you won't be in a position to find out what his Majesty thinks about it, because Admiral Shatrak will have you and your accomplices shot in the Convocation Chamber, where you massacred the legitimate government of this planet," he barked.

So the real Obray, Count Erskyll, had at last emerged. All the liberalism and socialism and egalitarianism, all the Helping-Hand, Torch-of-Democracy, idealism, was merely a surface stucco applied at the university during the last six years. For twenty-four years before that, from the day of his birth, he had been taught, by his parents, his nurse, his governess, his tutors, what it meant to be an Erskyll of Aton and a grandson of Errol, Duke of Yorvoy. As he watched Khreggor Chmidd in the screen, he grew angrier, if possible.

"Do you know what you blood-thirsty imbeciles have done?" he demanded. "You have just murdered, along with two thousand men, some five billion crowns, the money needed to finance all these fine modernization and industrialization plans. Or are you crazy enough to think that the Empire is going to indemnify you for being emancipated and pay that money over to you?"

"But, Citizen Proconsul...."

"And don't call me Citizen Proconsul! I am a noble of the Galactic Empire, and on this pig-pen of a planet I represent his Imperial Majesty. You will respect, and address, me accordingly."

Khreggor Chmidd no longer wore the gorget of servility, but, as Lanze Degbrend had once remarked, it was still tattooed on his soul. He gulped.

"Y-yes, Lord-Master Proconsul!"

They were together again in the big conference-room, which Vann Shatrak had been using, through the day, as an extemporised Battle-Control. They slumped wearily in chairs; they smoked and drank coffee; they anxiously looked from viewscreen to viewscreen, wondering when, and how soon, the trouble would break out again. It was dark, outside, now. Flood-lights threw a white dazzle from the top of the Proconsular Palace and from the tops of the four buildings around it that Imperial troops had cleared and occupied, and from contragrav-ity vehicles above. There was light and activity at the Citadel, and in the Servile City to the south-east; the rest of Zeggensburg was dark and quiet.

"I don't think we'll have any more trouble," Admiral Shatrak was saying. "They won't be fools enough to attack us here, and all the Masters are dead, except for the ones we're sheltering."

"How many did we save?" Count Erskyll asked.

Eight hundred odd, Shatrak told him. Erskyll caught his breath.

"So few! Why, there were almost twelve thousand of them in the city this morning."

"I'm surprised we saved so many," Lanze Degbrend said. He still wore combat coveralls, and a pistol-belt lay beside his chair. "Most of them were killed in the first hour."

And that had been before the landing-craft from the ships had gotten down, and there had only been seven hundred men and forty vehicles available. He had gone out with them, himself; it had been the first time he had worn battle-dress and helmet or carried a weapon except for sport in almost thirty years. It had been an ugly, bloody, business; one he wanted to forget as speedily as possible. There had been times, after seeing the mutilated bodies of Masterly women and children, when he had been forced to remind himself that he had come out to prevent, not to participate in, a massacre. Some of Ravney's men hadn't even tried. Atrocity has a horrible facility for begetting atrocity.

"What'll we do with them?" Erskyll asked. "We can't turn them loose; they'd all be murdered in a matter of hours, and in any case, they'd have nowhere to go. The Commonwealth," —he pronounced the name he had himself selected as though it were an obscenity —"has nationalized all the Masterly property."

That had been announced almost as soon as the Citadel telecast-station had been unjammed, and shortly thereafter they had begun encountering bodies of Yakoop Zhannar's soldiers and Zhorzh Khouzhik's police who had been sent out to stop looting and vandalism and occupy the Masterly palaces. There had been considerable shooting in the Servile City; evidently the ex-slaves had to be convinced that they must not pillage or destroy their places of employment.

"Evacuate them off-planet," Shatrak said. "As soon as *Algol* gets here, we'll load the lot of them onto *Mizar* or *Canopus* and haul them somewhere. Ghu only knows how they'll live, but...."

"Oh, they won't be paupers, or public charges, Admiral," he said. "You know, there's an estimated five billion crowns in slave-compensation, and when I return to Odin I shall represent most strongly that these survivors be paid the whole sum. But I shall emphatically not recommend that they be resettled on Odin. They won't be at all grateful to us for today's business, and on Odin they could easily stir up some very adverse public sentiment."

"My resignation will answer any criticism of the Establishment the public may make," Erskyll began.

"Oh, rubbish; don't talk about resigning, Obray. You made a few mistakes here, though I can't think of a better planet in the Galaxy on which you could have made them. But no matter what you did or did not do, this would have happened eventually."

"You really think so?" Obray, Count Erskyll, was desperately anxious to be assured of that. "Perhaps if I hadn't been so insistent on this constitution...."

"That wouldn't have made a particle of difference. We all made this inevitable simply by coming here. Before we came, it would have been impossible. No slave would have been able even to imagine a society without Lords-Master; you heard Chmidd and Hozhet, the first day, aboard the *Empress Eulalie*. A slave had to have a Master; he simply couldn't belong to nobody at all. And until you started talking socialization, nobody could have imagined property without a Masterly property-owning class. And a massacre like this would have been impossible to organize or execute. For one thing, it required an elaborate conspiratorial organization, and until we emancipated them, no slave would have dared trust any other slave; every one would have betrayed any other to curry favor with his Lord-Master. We taught them that they didn't need Lords-Master, or Masterly favor, any more. And we presented them with a situation their established routines didn't cover, and forced them into doing some original thinking, which must have hurt like Nifflheim at first. And we retrained the army and handed it over to Yakoop Zhannar, and inspired Zhorzh Khouzhik to organize the Labor Police, and fundamentally, no government is anything but armed force. Really, Obray, I can't see that you can be blamed for anything but speeding up an inevitable process slightly."

"You think they'll see it that way at Asgard?"

"You mean the Prime Minister and His Majesty? That will be the way I shall present it to them. That was another reason I wanted to stay on here. I anticipated that you might want a credible witness to what was going to happen," he said. "Now, you'll be here for not more than five years before you're promoted elsewhere. Nobody remains longer than that on a first Proconsular appointment. Just keep your eyes and ears and, especially, your mind, open while you are here. You will learn many things undreamed-of by the political-science faculty at the University of Nefertiti."

"You said I made mistakes," Erskyll mentioned, ready to start learning immediately.

"Yes. I pointed one of them out to you some time ago: emotional involvement with local groups. You began sympathizing with the servile class here almost immediately. I don't think either of us learned anything about them that the other didn't, yet I found them despicable, one and all. Why did you think them worthy of your sympathy?"

"Why, because...." For a moment, that was as far as he could get. His motivation had been thalamic rather than cortical and he was having trouble externalizing it verbally. "They were *slaves*. They were being exploited and oppressed...."

"And, of course, their exploiters were a lot of heartless villains, so that made the slaves good and virtuous innocents. That was your real, fundamental, mistake. You know, Obray, the down-trodden and long-suffering proletariat aren't at all good or innocent or virtuous. They are just incompetent; they lack the abilities necessary for overt villainy. You saw, this afternoon, what they were capable of doing when they were given an opportunity. You know, it's quite all right to give the underdog a hand, but only one hand. Keep the other hand on your pistol-or he'll try to eat the one you gave him! As you may have noticed, today, when underdogs get up, they tend to turn out to be wolves."

"What do you think this Commonwealth will develop into, under Chmidd and Hozhet and Khouzhik and the rest?" Lanze Degbrend asked, to keep the lecture going.

"Oh, a slave-state, of course; look who's running it, and whom it will govern. Not the kind of a slave-state we can do anything about," he hastened to add. "The Commonwealth will be very definite about recognizing that sapient beings cannot be property. But all the rest of the property will belong to the Commonwealth. Remember that remark of Chmidd's: 'It will belong to everybody, but somebody will have to take care of it for everybody. That will be you and me.'"

Erskyll frowned. "I remember that. I didn't like it, at the time. It sounded...."

Out of character, for a good and virtuous proletarian; almost Masterly, in fact. He continued:

"The Commonwealth will be sole employer as well as sole property-owner, and anybody who wants to eat will have to work for the Commonwealth on the Commonwealth's terms. Chmidd's and Hozhet's and Khouzhik's, that is. If that isn't substitution of peonage for chattel slavery, I don't know what the word peonage means. But you'll do nothing to interfere. You will see to it that Aditya stays in the empire and adheres to the Constitution and makes no trouble for anybody off-planet. I fancy you won't find that too difficult. They'll be good, as long as you deny them the means to be anything else. And make sure that they continue to call you Lord-Master Proconsul."

Lecturing, he found, was dry work. He summoned a bartending robot:

"Ho, slave! Attend your Lord-Master!"

Then he had to use his ultraviolet pencil-light to bring it to him, and dial for the brandy-and-soda he wanted. As long as that was necessary, there really wasn't anything to worry about. But some of these days, they'd build robots that would anticipate orders, and robots to operate robots, and robots to supervise them, and....

No. It wouldn't quite come to that. A slave is a slave, but a robot is only a robot. As long as they stuck to robots, they were reasonably safe.

Naudsonce

Bishop Berkeley's famous question
about the sound of a falling tree
may have no standing in Science.
But there is a highly interesting
question about "sound" that Science
needs to consider....

By H. Beam Piper

The sun warmed Mark Howell's back pleasantly. Underfoot, the mosslike stuff was soft and yielding, and there was a fragrance in the air unlike anything he had ever smelled. He was going to like this planet; he knew it. The question was, how would it, and its people, like him? He watched the little figures advancing across the fields from the mound, with the village out of sight on the other end of it and the combat-car circling lazily on contragravity above.

Major Luis Gofredo, the Marine officer, spoke without lowering his binoculars:

"They have a tubular thing about twelve feet long; six of them are carrying it on poles, three to a side, and a couple more are walking behind it. Mark, do you think it could be a cannon?"

So far, he didn't know enough to have an opinion, and said so, adding:

"What I saw of the village in the screen from the car, it looked pretty primitive. Of course, gunpowder's one of those things a primitive people could discover by accident, if the ingredients were available."

"We won't take any chances, then."

"You think they're hostile? I was hoping they were coming out to parley with us."

That was Paul Meillard. He had a right to be anxious; his whole future in the Colonial Office would be made or ruined by what was going to happen here.

The joint Space Navy-Colonial Office expedition was looking for new planets suitable for colonization; they had been out, now, for four years, which was close to maximum for an exploring expedition. They had entered eleven systems, and made landings on eight planets. Three had been reasonably close to Terra-type. There had been Fafnir; conditions there would correspond to Terra during the Cretaceous Period, but any Cretaceous dinosaur would have been cute and cuddly to the things on Fafnir. Then there had been Imhotep; in twenty or thirty thousand years, it would be a fine planet, but at present it was undergoing an extensive glaciation. And Irminsul, covered with forests of gigantic trees; it would have been fine except for the fauna, which was nasty, especially a race of subsapient near-humanoids who had just gotten as far as clubs and *coup-de-poing* axes. Contact with them had entailed heavy ammunition expenditure, with two men and a woman killed and a dozen injured. He'd had a limp, himself, for a while as a result.

As for the other five, one had been an all-out hell-planet, and the rest had been the sort that get colonized by irreconcilable minority-groups who want to get away from everybody else. The Colonial Office wouldn't even consider any of them.

Then they had found this one, third of a G0-star, eighty million miles from primary, less axial inclination than Terra, which would mean a more uniform year-round temperature, and about half land surface. On the evidence of a couple of sneak landings for specimens, the biochemistry was identical with Terra's and the organic matter was edible. It was the sort of planet every explorer dreams of finding, except for one thing.

It was inhabited by a sapient humanoid race, and some of them were civilized enough to put it in Class V, and Colonial Office doctrine on Class V planets was rigid. Friendly relations with the natives had to be established, and permission to settle had to be guaranteed in a treaty of some sort with somebody more or less authorized to make one.

If Paul Meillard could accomplish that, he had it made. He would stay on with forty or fifty of the ship's company to make preparations. In a year a couple of ships would come out from Terra, with a thousand colonists, and a battalion or so of Federation troops, to protect them from the natives and vice versa. Meillard would automatically be appointed governor-general.

But if he failed, he was through. Not out—just through. When he got back to Terra, he would be promoted to some home office position at slightly higher base pay but without the three hundred per cent extraterrestrial bonus, and he would vegetate there till he retired. Every time his name came up, somebody would say, "Oh, yes; he flubbed the contact on Whatzit."

It wouldn't do the rest of them any good, either. There would always be the suspicion that they had contributed to the failure.

The wavering sound hung for an instant in the air. A few seconds later, it was repeated, then repeated again.

"Our cannon's a horn," Gofredo said. "I can't see how they're blowing it, though."

There was a stir to right and left, among the Marines deployed in a crescent line on either side of the contact team; a metallic clatter as weapons were checked. A shadow fell in front of them as a combat-car moved into position above.

"What do you suppose it means?" Meillard wondered.

"Terrans, go home." He drew a frown from Meillard with the suggestion. "Maybe it's supposed to intimidate us."

"They're probably doing it to encourage themselves," Anna de Jong, the psychologist, said. "I'll bet they're really scared stiff."

"I see how they're blowing it," Gofredo said. "The man who's walking behind it has a hand-bellows." He raised his voice. "Fix bayonets! These people don't know anything about rifles, but they know what spears are. They have some of their own."

So they had. The six who walked in the lead were unarmed, unless the thing one of them carried was a spear. So, it seemed, were the horn-bearers. Behind them, however, in an open-order skirmish-line, came fifty-odd with weapons. Most of them had spears, the points glinting redly. Bronze, with a high copper content. A few had bows. They came slowly; details became more plainly visible.

The leader wore a long yellow robe; the thing in his hand was a bronze-headed staff. Three of his companions also wore robes; the other two were bare-legged in short tunics. The horn-bearers wore either robes or tunics; the spearmen and bowmen behind either wore tunics or were naked except for breechclouts. All wore sandals. They were red-brown in color, completely hairless; they had long necks, almost chinless lower jaws, and fleshy, beaklike noses that gave them an avian appearance which was heightened by red crests, like roosters' combs, on the tops of their heads.

"Well, aren't they something to see?" Lillian Ransby, the linguist asked.

"I wonder how we look to them," Paul Meillard said.

That was something to wonder about, too. The differences between one and another of the Terrans must puzzle them. Paul Meillard, as close to being a pure Negro as anybody in the Seventh Century of the Atomic Era was to being pure anything. Lillian Ransby, almost ash-blond. Major Gofredo, barely over the minimum Service height requirement; his name was Old Terran Spanish, but his ancestry must have been Polynesian, Amerind and Mongolian. Karl Dorver, the sociographer, six feet six, with red hair. Bennet Fayon, the biologist and physiologist, plump, pink-faced and balding. Willi Schallenmacher, with a bushy black beard....

They didn't have any ears, he noticed, and then he was taking stock of the things they wore and carried. Belts, with pouches, and knives with flat bronze blades and riveted handles. Three of the delegation had small flutes hung by cords around their necks, and a fourth had a reed

Pan-pipe. No shields, and no swords; that was good. Swords and shields mean organized warfare, possibly a warrior-caste. This crowd weren't warriors. The spearmen and bowmen weren't arrayed for battle, but for a drive-hunt, with the bows behind the spears to stop anything that broke through the line.

"All right; let's go meet them." The querulous, uncertain note was gone from Meillard's voice; he knew what to do and how to do it.

Gofredo called to the Marines to stand fast. Then they were advancing to meet the natives, and when they were twenty feet apart, both groups halted. The horn stopped blowing. The one in the yellow robe lifted his staff and said something that sounded like, *"Tweedle-eedle-oodly-eenk."*

The horn, he saw, was made of strips of leather, wound spirally and coated with some kind of varnish. Everything these people had was carefully and finely made. An old culture, but a static one. Probably tradition-bound as all get-out.

Meillard was raising his hands; solemnly he addressed the natives:

"'Twas brillig and the slithy toves were whooping it up in the Malemute Saloon, and the kid that handled the music box did gyre and gimble in the wabe, and back of the bar in a solo game all mimsy were the borogoves, and the mome raths outgabe the lady that's known as Lou."

That was supposed to show them that we, too, have a spoken language, to prove that their language and ours were mutually incomprehensible, and to demonstrate the need for devising a means of communication. At least that was what the book said. It demonstrated nothing of the sort to this crowd. It scared them. The dignitary with the staff twittered excitedly. One of his companions agreed with him at length. Another started to reach for his knife, then remembered his manners. The bellowsman pumped a few blasts on the horn.

"What do you think of the language?" he asked Lillian.

"They all sound that bad, when you first hear them. Give them a few seconds, and then we'll have Phase Two."

When the gibbering and skreeking began to fall off, she stepped forward. Lillian was, herself, a good test of how human aliens were; this gang weren't human enough to whistle at her. She touched herself on the breast. "Me," she said.

The natives seemed shocked. She repeated the gesture and the word, then turned and addressed Paul Meillard. "You."

"Me," Meillard said, pointing to himself. Then he said, "You," to Luis Gofredo. It went around the contact team; when it came to him, he returned it to point of origin.

"I don't think they get it at all," he added in a whisper.

"They ought to," Lillian said. "Every language has a word for self and a word for person-addressed."

"Well, look at them," Karl Dorver invited. "Six different opinions about what we mean, and now the band's starting an argument of their own."

"Phase Two-A," Lillian said firmly, stepping forward. She pointed to herself. "Me-Lillian Ransby. Lillian Ransby-me *name.* You —*name?*"

"Bwoooo!" the spokesman screamed in horror, clutching his staff as though to shield it from profanation. The others howled like a hound-pack at a full moon, except one of the short-tunic boys, who was slapping himself on the head with both hands and yodeling. The horn-crew hastily swung their piece around at the Terrans, pumping frantically.

"What do you suppose I said?" Lillian asked.

"Oh, something like, 'Curse your gods, death to your king, and spit in your mother's face,' I suppose."

"Let me try it," Gofredo said.

The little Marine major went through the same routine. At his first word, the uproar stopped; before he was through, the natives' faces were sagging and crumbling into expressions of utter and heartbroken grief.

"It's not as bad as all that, is it?" he said. "You try it, Mark."

"Me ... Mark ... Howell...." They looked bewildered.

"Let's try objects, and play-acting," Lillian suggested. "They're farmers; they ought to have a word for water."

They spent almost an hour at it. They poured out two gallons of water, pretended to be thirsty, gave each other drinks. The natives simply couldn't agree on the word, in their own language, for water. That or else they missed the point of the whole act. They tried fire, next. The efficiency of a steel hatchet was impressive, and so was the sudden flame of a pocket-lighter, but no word for fire emerged, either.

"Ah, to Niflheim with it!" Luis Gofredo cried in exasperation. "We're getting nowhere at five times light speed. Give them their presents and send them home, Paul."

"Sheath-knives; they'll have to be shown how sharp they are," he suggested. "Red bandannas. And costume jewelry."

"How about something to eat, Bennet?" Meillard asked Fayon.

"Extee Three, and C-H trade candy," Fayon said. Field Ration, Extraterrestrial Service, Type Three, could be eaten by anything with a carbon-hydrogen metabolism, and so could the trade candy. "Nothing else, though, till we have some idea what goes on inside them."

Dorver thought the six members of the delegation would be persons of special consequence, and should have something extra. That was probably so. Dorver was as quick to pick up clues to an alien social order as he was, himself, to deduce a culture pattern from a few artifacts. He and Lillian went back to the landing craft to collect the presents.

Everybody, horn-detail, armed guard and all, got one ten-inch bowie knife and sheath, a red bandanna neckcloth, and a piece of flashy junk jewelry. The (town council? prominent citizens? or what?) also received a colored table-spread apiece; these were draped over their shoulders and fastened with two-inch plastic pins advertising the candidacy of somebody for President of the Federation Member Republic of Venus a couple of elections ago. They all looked woebegone about it; that would be their expression of joy. Different type nerves and different facial musculature, Fayon thought. As soon as they sampled the Extee Three and candy, they looked crushed under all the sorrows of the galaxy.

By pantomime and pointing to the sun, Meillard managed to inform them that the next day, when the sun was in the same position, the Terrans would visit their village, bringing more gifts. The natives were quite agreeable, but Meillard was disgruntled that he had to use sign-talk. The natives started off toward the village on the mound, munching Extee Three and trying out their new knives. This time tomorrow, half of them would have bandaged thumbs.

The Marine riflemen and submachine-gunners were coming in, slinging their weapons and lighting cigarettes. A couple of Navy technicians were getting a snooper —a thing shaped like a short-tailed tadpole, six feet long by three at the widest, fitted with visible-light and infra-red screen pickups and crammed with detection instruments-ready to relieve the combat car over the village. The contact team crowded into the Number One landing craft, which had been fitted out as a temporary headquarters. Prefab-hut elements were already being unloaded from the other craft.

Everybody felt that a drink was in order, even if it was two hours short of cocktail time. They carried bottles and glasses and ice to the front of the landing craft and sat down in front of the battery of view and communication screens. The central screen was a two-way, tuned to one in the officers' lounge aboard the *Hubert Penrose*, two hundred miles above. In it, also provided with drinks, were Captain Guy Vindinho and two other Navy officers, and a Marine captain in shipboard blues. Like Gofredo, Vindinho must have gotten into the Service on tiptoe; he had a bald dome and a red beard, and he always looked as though he were gloating because nobody knew that his name was really Rumplestiltskin. He had been watching the contact by screen. He lifted his glass toward Meillard.

"Over the hump, Paul?"

Meillard raised his drink to Vindinho. "Over the first one. There's a whole string of them ahead. At least, we sent them away happy. I hope."

"You're going to make permanent camp where you are now?" one of the other officers asked. Lieutenant-Commander Dave Questell; ground engineering and construction officer. "What do you need?"

There were two viewscreens from pickups aboard the 2500-foot battle cruiser. One, at ten-power magnification, gave a maplike view of the broad valley and the uplands and mountain foothills to the south. It was only by tracing the course of the main river and its tributaries that they could find the tiny spot of the native village, and they couldn't see the landing craft at all. The other, at a hundred power, showed the oblong mound, with the village on its flat top, little dots around a circular central plaza. They could see the two turtle-shaped landing-craft, and the combat car, that had been circling over the mound, landing beside them, and, sometimes, a glint of sunlight from the snooper that had taken its place.

The snooper was also transmitting in, to another screen, from two hundred feet above the village. From the sound outlet came an incessant gibber of native voices. There were over a hundred houses, all small and square, with pyramidal roofs. On the end of the mound toward the Terran camp, animals of at least four different species were crowded, cattle that had been herded up from the meadows at the first alarm. The open circle in the middle of the village was crowded, and more natives lined the low palisade along the edge of the mound.

"Well, we're going to stay here till we learn the language," Meillard was saying. "This is the best place for it. It's completely isolated, forests on both sides, and seventy miles to the nearest other village. If we're careful, we can stay here as long as we want to and nobody'll find out about us. Then, after we can talk with these people, we'll go to the big town."

The big town was two hundred and fifty miles down the valley, at the forks of the main river, a veritable metropolis of almost three thousand people. That was where the treaty would have to be negotiated.

"You'll want more huts. You'll want a water tank, and a pipeline to that stream below you, and a pump," Questell said. "You think a month?"

Meillard looked at Lillian Ransby. "What do you think?"

"Poodly-doodly-oodly-foodle," she said. "You saw how far we didn't get this afternoon. All we found out was that none of the standard procedures work at all." She made a tossing gesture over her shoulder. "There goes the book; we have to do it off the cuff from here."

"Suppose we make another landing, back in the mountains, say two or three hundred miles south of you," Vindinho said. "It's not right to keep the rest aboard two hundred miles off planet, and you won't be wanting liberty parties coming down where you are."

"The country over there looks uninhabited," Meillard said. "No villages, anyhow. That wouldn't hurt, at all."

"Well, it'll suit me," Charley Loughran, the xeno-naturalist, said. "I want a chance to study the life-forms in a state of nature."

Vindinho nodded. "Luis, do you anticipate any trouble with this crowd here?" he asked.

"How about it, Mark? What do they look like to you? Warlike?"

"No." He stated the opinion he had formed. "I had a close look at their weapons when they came in for their presents. Hunting arms. Most of the spears have cross-guards, usually wooden, lashed on, to prevent a wounded animal from running up the spear-shaft at the hunter. They made boar-spears like that on Terra a thousand years ago. Maybe they have to fight raiding parties from the hills once in a while, but not often enough for them to develop special fighting weapons or techniques."

"Their village is fortified," Meillard mentioned.

"I question that," Gofredo differed. "There won't be more than a total of five hundred there; call that a fighting strength of two hundred, to defend a twenty-five-hundred-meter perimeter, with woodchoppers' axes and bows and spears. If you notice, there's no wall around the village itself. That palisade is just a fence."

"Why would they mound the village up?" Questell, in the screen wondered. "You don't think the river gets up that high, do you? Because if it does —"

Schallenmacher shook his head. "There just isn't enough watershed, and there's too much valley. I'll be very much surprised if that stream, there"—he nodded at the hundred-power screen—"ever gets more than six inches over the bank."

"I don't know what those houses are built of. This is all alluvial country; building stone would be almost unobtainable. I don't see anything like a brick kiln. I don't see any evidence of irrigation, either, so there must be plenty of rainfall. If they use adobe, or sun-dried brick, houses would start to crumble in a few years, and they would be pulled down and the rubble shoved aside to make room for a new house. The village has been rising on its own ruins, probably shifting back and forth from one end of that mound to the other."

"If that's it, they've been there a long time," Karl Dorver said. "And how far have they advanced?"

"Early bronze; I'll bet they still use a lot of stone implements. Pre-dynastic Egypt, or very early Tigris-Euphrates, in Terran terms. I can't see any evidence that they have the wheel. They have draft animals; when we were coming down, I saw a few of them pulling pole travoises. I'd say they've been farming for a long time. They have quite a diversity of crops, and I suspect that they have some idea of crop-rotation. I'm amazed at their musical instruments; they seem to have put more skill into making them than anything else. I'm going to take a jeep, while they're all in the village, and have a look around the fields, now."

Charley Loughran went along for specimens, and, for the ride, Lillian Ransby. Most of his guesses, he found, had been correct. He found a number of pole travoises, from which the animals had been unhitched in the first panic when the landing craft had been coming down. Some of them had big baskets permanently attached. There were drag-marks everywhere in the soft ground, but not a single wheel track. He found one plow, cunningly put together with wooden pegs and rawhide lashings; the point was stone, and it would only score a narrow groove, not a proper furrow. It was, however, fitted with a big bronze ring to which a draft animal could be hitched. Most of the cultivation seemed to have been done with spades and hoes. He found a couple of each, bronze, cast flat in an open-top mold. They hadn't learned to make composite molds.

There was an even wider variety of crops than he had expected: two cereals, a number of different root-plants, and a lot of different legumes, and things like tomatoes and pumpkins.

"Bet these people had a pretty good life, here-before the Terrans came," Charley observed.

"Don't say that in front of Paul," Lillian warned. "He has enough to worry about now, without starting him on whether we'll do these people more harm than good."

Two more landing craft had come down from the *Hubert Penrose*; they found Dave Questell superintending the unloading of more prefab-huts, and two were already up that had been brought down with the first landing.

A name for the planet had also arrived.

"Svantovit," Karl Dorver told him. "Principal god of the Baltic Slavs, about three thousand years ago. Guy Vindinho dug it out of the 'Encyclopedia of Mythology.' Svantovit was represented as holding a bow in one hand and a horn in the other."

"Well, that fits. What will we call the natives; Svantovitians, or Svantovese?"

"Well, Paul wanted to call them Svantovese, but Luis persuaded him to call them Svants. He said everybody'd call them that, anyhow, so we might as well make it official from the start."

"We can call the language Svantovese," Lillian decided. "After dinner, I am going to start playing back recordings and running off audiovisuals. I will be so happy to know that I have a name for what I'm studying. Probably be all I will know."

After dinner, he and Karl and Paul went into a huddle on what sort of gifts to give the natives, and the advisability of trading with them, and for what. Nothing too far in advance of their present culture level. Wheels; they could be made in the fabricating shop aboard the ship.

"You know, it's odd," Karl Dorver said. "These people here have never seen a wheel, and, except in documentary or historical-drama films, neither have a lot of Terrans."

That was true. As a means of transportation, the wheel had been completely obsolete since the development of contragravity, six centuries ago. Well, a lot of Terrans in the Year Zero had never seen a suit of armor, or an harquebus, or even a tinder box or a spinning wheel.

Wheelbarrows; now there was something they'd find useful. He screened Max Milzer, in charge of the fabricating and repair shops on the ship. Max had never even heard of a wheelbarrow.

"I can make them up, Mark; better send me some drawings, though. Did you just invent it?"

"As far as I know, a man named Leonardo da Vinci invented it, in the Sixth Century Pre-Atomic. How soon can you get me half a dozen of them?"

"Well, let's see. Welded sheet metal, and pipe for the frame and handles. I'll have some of them for you by noon tomorrow. Now, about hoes; how tall are these people, and how long are their arms, and how far can they stoop over?"

They were all up late, that night. So were the Svants; there was a fire burning in the middle of the village, and watch-fires along the edge of the mound. Luis Gofredo was just as distrustful of them as they were of the Terrans; he kept the camp lighted, a strong guard on the alert, and the area of darkness beyond infra red lighted and covered by photoelectric sentries on the ground and snoopers in the air. Like Paul Meillard, Luis Gofredo was a worrier and a pessimist. Everything happened for the worst in this worst of all possible galaxies, and if anything could conceivably go wrong, it infallibly would. That was probably why he was still alive and had never had a command massacred.

The wheelbarrows, four of them, came down from the ship by midmorning. With them came a grindstone, a couple of crosscut saws, and a lot of picks and shovels and axes, and cases of sheath knives and mess gear and miscellaneous trade goods, including a lot of the empty wine and whisky bottles that had been hoarded for the past four years.

At lunch, the talk was almost exclusively about the language problem. Lillian Ransby, who had not gotten to sleep before sunrise and had just gotten up, was discouraged.

"I don't know what we're going to do next," she admitted. "Glenn Orent and Anna and I were on it all night, and we're nowhere. We have about a hundred wordlike sounds isolated, and twenty or so are used repeatedly, and we can't assign a meaning to any of them. And none of the Svants ever reacted the same way twice to anything we said to them. There's just no one-to-one relationship anywhere."

"I'm beginning to doubt they have a language," the Navy intelligence officer said. "Sure, they make a lot of vocal noise. So do chipmunks."

"They have to have a language," Anna de Jong declared. "No sapient thought is possible without verbalization."

"Well, no society like that is possible without some means of communication," Karl Dorver supported her from the other flank. He seemed to have made that point before. "You know," he added, "I'm beginning to wonder if it mightn't be telepathy."

He evidently hadn't suggested that before. The others looked at him in surprise. Anna started to say, "Oh, I doubt if—" and then stopped.

"I know, the race of telepaths is an old gimmick that's been used in new-planet adventure stories for centuries, but maybe we've finally found one."

"I don't like it, Karl," Loughran said. "If they're telepaths, why don't they understand us? And if they're telepaths, why do they talk at all? And you can't convince me that this boodly-oodly-doodle of theirs isn't talking."

"Well, our neural structure and theirs won't be nearly alike," Fayon said. "I know, this analogy between telepathy and radio is full of holes, but it's good enough for this. Our wave length can't be picked up with their sets."

"The deuce it can't," Gofredo contradicted. "I've been bothered about that from the beginning. These people act as though they got meaning from us. Not the meaning we intend, but some meaning. When Paul made the gobbledygook speech, they all reacted in the same way-frightened, and then defensive. The you-me routine simply bewildered them, as we'd be at a set of semantically lucid but self-contradictory statements. When Lillian tried to introduce herself, they were shocked and horrified...."

"It looked to me like actual physical disgust," Anna interpolated.

"When I tried it, they acted like a lot of puppies being petted, and when Mark tried it, they were simply baffled. I watched Mark explaining that steel knives were dangerously sharp; they got the demonstration, but when he tried to tie words onto it, it threw them completely."

"ALL RIGHT. Pass that," Loughran conceded. "But if they have telepathy, why do they use spoken words?"

"Oh, I can answer that," Anna said. "Say they communicated by speech originally, and developed their telepathic faculty slowly and without realizing it. They'd go on using speech, and since the message would be received telepathically ahead of the spoken message, nobody would pay any attention to the words as such. Everybody would have a spoken language of his own; it would be sort of the instrumental accompaniment to the song."

"Some of them don't bother speaking," Karl nodded. "They just toot."

"I'll buy that, right away," Loughran agreed. "In mating, or in group-danger situations, telepathy would be a race-survival characteristic. It would be selected for genetically, and the non-gifted strains would tend to die out."

It wouldn't do. It wouldn't do at all. He said so.

"Look at their technology. We either have a young race, just emerged from savagery, or an old, stagnant race. All indications seem to favor the latter. A young race would not have time to develop telepathy as Anna suggests. An old race would have gone much farther than these people have. Progress is a matter of communication and pooling ideas and discoveries. Make a trend-graph of technological progress on Terra; every big jump comes after an improvement in communications. The printing press; railways and steamships; the telegraph; radio. Then think how telepathy would speed up progress."

The sun was barely past noon meridian before the Svants, who had ventured down into the fields at sunrise, were returning to the mound-village. In the snooper-screen, they could be seen coming up in tunics and breechclouts, entering houses, and emerging in long robes. There seemed to be no bows or spears in evidence, but the big horn sounded occasionally. Paul Meillard was pleased. Even if it had been by sign-talk, which he rated with worm-fishing for trout or shooting sitting rabbits, he had gotten something across to them.

When they went to the village, at 1500, they had trouble getting their lorry down. A couple of Marines in a jeep had to go in first to get the crowd out of the way. Several of the locals, including the one with the staff, joined with them; this quick co-operation delighted Meillard. When they had the lorry down and were all out of it, the dignitary with the staff, his scarlet tablecloth over his yellow robe, began an oration, apparently with every confidence that he was being understood. In spite of his objections at lunch, the telepathy theory was beginning to seem more persuasive.

"Give them the Shooting of Dan McJabberwock again," he told Meillard. "This is where we came in yesterday."

Something Meillard had noticed was exciting him. "Wait a moment. They're going to do something."

They were indeed. The one with the staff and three of his henchmen advanced. The staff bearer touched himself on the brow. *"Fwoonk,"* he said. Then he pointed to Meillard. *"Hoonkle,"* he said.

"They got it!" Lillian was hugging herself joyfully. "I knew they ought to!"

Meillard indicated himself and said, *"Fwoonk."*

That wasn't right. The village elder immediately corrected him. The word, it seemed, was, *"Fwoonk."*

His three companions agreed that that was the word for self, but that was as far as the agreement went. They rendered it, respectively, as *"Pwink," "Tweelt"* and *"Kroosh."*

Gofredo gave a barking laugh. He was right; anything that could go wrong would go wrong. Lillian used a word; it was not a ladylike word at all. The Svants looked at them as though wondering what could possibly be the matter. Then they went into a huddle, arguing vehemently. The argument spread, like a ripple in a pool; soon everybody was twittering vocally or blowing on flutes and Panpipes. Then the big horn started blaring. Immediately, Gofredo snatched the hand-phone of his belt radio and began speaking urgently into it.

"What are you doing, Luis?" Meillard asked anxiously.

"Calling the reserve in. I'm not taking chances on this." He spoke again into the phone, then called over his shoulder: "Rienet; three one-second bursts, in the air!"

A Marine pointed a submachine gun skyward and ripped off a string of shots, then another, and another. There was silence after the first burst. Then a frightful howling arose.

"Luis, you imbecile!" Meillard was shouting.

Gofredo jumped onto the top of an airjeep, where they could all see him; drawing his pistol, he fired twice into the air.

"Be quiet, all of you!" he shouted, as though that would do any good.

It did. Silence fell, bounced noisily, and then settled over the crowd. Gofredo went on talking to them: "Take it easy, now; easy." He might have been speaking to a frightened dog or a fractious horse. "Nobody's going to hurt you. This is nothing but the great noise-magic of the Terrans...."

"Get the presents unloaded," Meillard was saying. "Make a big show of it. The table first."

The horn, which had started, stopped blowing. As they were getting off the long table and piling it with trade goods, another lorry came in, disgorging twenty Marine riflemen. They had their bayonets fixed; the natives looked apprehensively at the bare steel, but went on listening to Gofredo. Meillard pulled the (Lord Mayor? Archbishop? Lord of the Manor?) aside, and began making sign-talk to him.

When quiet was restored, Howell put a pick and shovel into a wheelbarrow and pushed them out into the space that had been cleared in front of the table. He swung the pick for a while, then shoveled the barrow full of ground. After pushing it around for a while, he dumped it back in the hole and leveled it off. Two Marines brought out an eight-inch log and chopped a couple of billets off it with an ax, then cut off another with one of the saws, split them up, and filled the wheelbarrow with the firewood.

The knives, jewelry and other small items would be no problem; they had enough of them to go around. The other stuff would be harder to distribute, and Paul Meillard and Karl Dorver were arguing about how to handle it. If they weren't careful, a lot of new bowie knives would get bloodied.

"Have them form a queue," Anna suggested. "That will give them the idea of equal sharing, and we'll be able to learn something about their status levels and social hierarchy and agonistic relations."

The one with the staff took it as a matter of course that he would go first; his associates began falling in behind him, and the rest of the villagers behind them. Whether they'd gotten one the day before or not, everybody was given a knife and a bandanna and one piece of flashy junk-jewelry, also a stainless steel cup and mess plate, a bucket, and an empty bottle with a cork. The women didn't carry sheath knives, so they got Boy Scout knives on lanyards. They were all lavishly supplied with Extee Three and candy. Any of the children who looked big enough to be trusted with them got knives too, and plenty of candy.

Anna and Karl were standing where the queue was forming, watching how they fell into line; so was Lillian, with an audiovisual camera. Having seen that the Marine enlisted men were getting the presents handed out properly, Howell strolled over to them. Just as he came up, a couple approached hesitantly, a man in a breechclout under a leather apron, and a woman, much smaller, in a ragged and soiled tunic. As soon as they fell into line, another Svant, in a blue robe, pushed them aside and took their place.

"Here, you can't do that!" Lillian cried. "Karl, make him step back."

Karl was saying something about social status and precedence. The couple tried to get into line behind the man who had pushed them aside. Another villager tried to shove them out of his way. Howell advanced, his right fist closing. Then he remembered that he didn't know what he'd be punching; he might break the fellow's neck, or his own knuckles. He grabbed the blue-robed Svant by the wrist with both hands, kicked a foot out from under him, and jerked, sending him flying for six feet and then sliding in the dust for another couple of yards. He pushed the others back, and put the couple into place in the line.

"Mark, you shouldn't have done that," Dorver was expostulating. "We don't know...."

The Svant sat up, shaking his head groggily. Then he realized what had been done to him. With a snarl of rage, he was on his feet, his knife in his hand. It was a Terran bowie knife. Without conscious volition, Howell's pistol was out and he was thumbing the safety off.

The Svant stopped short, then dropped the knife, ducked his head, and threw his arms over it to shield his comb. He backed away a few steps, then turned and bolted into the nearest house. The others, including the woman in the ragged tunic, were twittering in alarm. Only the man in the leather apron was calm; he was saying, tonelessly, *"Ghrooogh-ghrooogh."*

Luis Gofredo was coming up on the double, followed by three of his riflemen.

"What happened, Mark? Trouble?"

"All over now." He told Gofredo what had happened. Dorver was still objecting:

"...Social precedence; the Svant may have been right, according to local customs."

"Local customs be damned!" Gofredo became angry. "This is a Terran Federation handout; we make the rules, and one of them is, no pushing people out of line. Teach the buggers that now and we won't have to work so hard at it later." He called back over his shoulder, "Situation under control; get the show going again."

The natives were all grimacing heartbrokenly with pleasure. Maybe the one who got thrown on his ear-no, he didn't have any-was not one of the more popular characters in the village.

"You just pulled your gun, and he dropped the knife and ran?" Gofredo asked. "And the others were scared, too?"

"That's right. They all saw you fire yours; the noise scared them."

Gofredo nodded. "We'll avoid promiscuous shooting, then. No use letting them find out the noise won't hurt them any sooner than we have to."

Paul Meillard had worked out a way to distribute the picks and shovels and axes. Considering each house as representing a family unit, which might or might not be the case, there were picks and shovels enough to go around, and an ax for every third house. They took them around in an airjeep and left them at the doors. The houses, he found, weren't adobe at all. They were built of logs, plastered with adobe on the outside. That demolished his theory that the houses were torn down periodically, and left the mound itself unexplained.

The wheelbarrows and the grindstone and the two crosscut saws were another matter. Nobody was quite sure that the (nobility? capitalist-class? politicians? prominent citizens?) wouldn't simply appropriate them for themselves. Paul Meillard was worried about that; everybody else was willing to let matters take their course. Before they were off the ground in their vehicles, a violent dispute had begun, with a bedlam of jabbering and shrieking. By the time they were landing at the camp, the big laminated leather horn had begun to bellow.

One of the huts had been fitted as contact-team headquarters, with all the view and communication screens installed, and one end partitioned off and soundproofed for Lillian to study recordings in. It was cocktail time when they returned; conversationally, it was a continuation from lunch. Karl Dorver was even more convinced than ever of his telepathic hypothesis, and he had completely converted Anna de Jong to it.

"Look at that." He pointed at the snooper screen, which gave a view of the plaza from directly above. "They're reaching an agreement already."

So they seemed to be, though upon what was less apparent. The horn had stopped, and the noise was diminishing. The odd thing was that peace was being restored, or was restoring itself, as the uproar had begun-outwardly from the center of the plaza to the periphery of the crowd. The same thing had happened when Gofredo had ordered the submachine gun fired, and, now that he recalled, when he had dealt with the line-crasher.

"Suppose a few of them, in the middle, are agreed," Anna said. "They are all thinking in unison, combining their telepathic powers. They dominate those nearest to them, who join and amplify their telepathic signal, and it spreads out through the whole group. A mental chain-reaction."

"That would explain the mechanism of community leadership, and I'd been wondering about that," Dorver said, becoming more excited. "It's a mental aristocracy; an especially gifted group of telepaths, in agreement and using their powers in concert, implanting their opinions in the minds of all the others. I'll bet the purpose of the horn is to distract the thoughts of the others, so that they can be more easily dominated. And the noise of the shots shocked them out of communication with each other; no wonder they were frightened."

Bennet Fayon was far from convinced. "So far, this telepathy theory is only an assumption. I find it a lot easier to assume some fundamental difference between the way they translate sound into sense-data and the way we do. We *think* those combs on top of their heads are their external hearing organs, but we have no idea what's back of them, or what kind of a neural hookup is connected to them. I wish I knew how these people dispose of their dead. I need a couple of fresh cadavers. Too bad they aren't warlike. Nothing like a good bloody battle to advance the science of anatomy, and what we don't know about Svant anatomy is practically the entire subject."

"I should imagine the animals hear in the same way," Meillard said. "When the wagon wheels and the hoes and the blacksmith tools come down from the ship, we'll trade for cattle."

"When they make the second landing in the mountains, I'm going to do a lot of hunting," Loughran added. "I'll get wild animals for you."

"Well, I'm going to assume that the vocal noises they make are meaningful speech," Lillian Ransby said. "So far, I've just been trying to analyze them for phonetic values. Now I'm going to analyze them for sound-wave patterns. No matter what goes on inside their private nervous systems, the sounds exist as waves in the public atmosphere. I'm going to assume that the Lord Mayor and his stooges were all trying to say the same thing when they were pointing to themselves, and I'm going to see if all four of those sounds have any common characteristic."

By the time dinner was over, they were all talking in circles, none of them hopefully. They all made recordings of the speech about the slithy toves in the Malemute Saloon; Lillian wanted to find out what was different about them. Luis Gofredo saw to it that the camp itself would be visible-lighted, and beyond the lights he set up more photoelectric robot sentries and put a couple of snoopers to circling on contragravity, with infra-red lights and receptors. He also insisted that all his own men and all Dave Questell's Navy construction engineers keep their weapons ready to hand. The natives in the village were equally distrustful. They didn't herd the cattle up from the meadows where they had been pastured, but they lighted watch-fires along the edge of the mound as soon as it became dark.

It was three hours after nightfall when something on the indicator-board for the robot sentries went off like a startled rattlesnake. Everybody, talking idly or concentrating on writing up the day's observations, stiffened. Luis Gofredo, dozing in a chair, was on his feet instantly and crossing the hut to the instruments. His second-in-command, who had been playing chess with Willi Schallenmacher, rose and snatched his belt from the back of his chair, putting it on.

"Take it easy," Gofredo said. "Probably just a cow or a horse-local equivalent-that's strayed over from the other side."

He sat down in front of one of the snooper screens and twisted knobs on the remote controls. The monochrome view, transformed from infra red, rotated as the snooper circled and changed course. The other screen showed the camp receding and the area around it widening as its snooper gained altitude.

"It's not a big party," Gofredo was saying. "I can't see-Oh, yes I can. Only two of them."

The humanoid figures, one larger than the other, were moving cautiously across the fields, crouching low. The snooper went down toward them, and then he recognized them. The man and woman whom the blue-robed villager had tried to shove out of the queue, that afternoon. Gofredo recognized them, too.

"Your friends, Mark. Harry," he told his subordinate, "go out and pass the word around. Only two, and we think they're friendly. Keep everybody out of sight; we don't want to scare them away."

The snooper followed closely behind them. The man was no longer wearing his apron; the woman's tunic was even more tattered and soiled. She was leading him by the hand. Now and then, she would stop and turn her head to the rear. The snooper over the mound showed nothing but half a dozen fire-watchers dozing by their fires. Then the pair were at the edge of the camp lights. As they advanced, they seemed to realize that they had passed a point-of-no-return. They straightened and came forward steadily, the woman seeming to be guiding her companion.

"What's happening, Mark?"

It was Lillian; she must have just come out of the soundproof speech-lab.

"You know them; the pair in the queue, this afternoon. I think we've annexed a couple of friendly natives."

They all went outside. The two natives, having come into the camp, had stopped. For a moment, the man in the breechclout seemed undecided whether he was more afraid to turn and run than advance. The woman, holding his hand, led him forward. They were both bruised, and both had minor cuts, and neither of them had any of the things that had been given to them that afternoon.

"Rest of the gang beat them up and robbed them," Gofredo began angrily.

"See what you did?" Dorver began. "According to their own customs, they had no right to be ahead of those others, and now you've gotten them punished for it."

"I'd have done more to that fellow then Mark did, if I'd been there when it happened." The Marine officer turned to Meillard. "Look, this is your show, Paul; how you run it is your job. But in your place, I'd take that pair back to the village and have them point out who beat them up, and teach the whole gang of them a lesson. If you're going to colonize this planet, you're going to have to establish Federation law, and Federation law says you mustn't gang up on people and beat and rob them. We don't have to speak Svantese to make them understand what we'll put up with and what we won't."

"Later, Luis. After we've gotten a treaty with somebody." Meillard broke off. "Watch this!"

The woman was making sign-talk. She pointed to the village on the mound. Then, with her hands, she shaped a bucket like the ones that had been given to them, and made a snatching gesture away from herself. She indicated the neckcloths, and the sheath knife and the other things, and snatched them away too. She made beating motions, and touched her bruises and the man's. All the time, she was talking excitedly, in a high, shrill voice. The man made the same *ghroogh-ghroogh* noises that he had that afternoon.

"No; we can't take any punitive action. Not now," Meillard said. "But we'll have to do something for them."

Vengeance, it seemed, wasn't what they wanted. The woman made vehement gestures of rejection toward the village, then bowed, placing her hands on her brow. The man imitated her obeisance, then they both straightened. The woman pointed to herself and to the man, and around the circle of huts and landing craft. She began scuttling about, picking up imaginary litter and sweeping with an imaginary broom. The man started pounding with an imaginary hammer, then chopping with an imaginary ax.

Lillian was clapping her hands softly. "Good; got it the first time. 'You let us stay; we work for you.' How about it, Paul?"

Meillard nodded. "Punitive action's unadvisable, but we will show our attitude by taking them in. You tell them, Luis; these people seem to like your voice."

Gofredo put a hand on each of their shoulders. "You ... stay ... with us." He pointed around the camp. "You ... stay ... this ... place."

Their faces broke into that funny just-before-tears expression that meant happiness with them. The man confined his vocal expressions to his odd *ghroogh-ghroogh*-ing; the woman twittered joyfully. Gofredo put a hand on the woman's shoulder, pointed to the man and from him back to her. "Unh?" he inquired.

The woman put a hand on the man's head, then brought it down to within a foot of the ground. She picked up the imaginary infant and rocked it in her arms, then set it down and grew it up until she had her hand on the top of the man's head again.

"That was good, Mom," Gofredo told her. "Now, you and Sonny come along; we'll issue you equipment and find you billets." He added, "What in blazes are we going to feed them; Extee Three?"

They gave them replacements for all the things that had been taken away from them. They gave the man a one-piece suit of Marine combat coveralls; Lillian gave the woman a lavender bathrobe, and Anna contributed a red scarf. They found them quarters in one end of a store shed, after making sure that there was nothing they could get at that would hurt them or that they could damage. They gave each of them a pair of blankets and a pneumatic mattress, which delighted them, although the cots puzzled them at first.

"What do you think about feeding them, Bennet?" Meillard asked, when the two Svants had gone to bed and they were back in the headquarters hut. "You said the food on this planet is safe for Terrans."

"So I did, and it is, but the rule's not reversible. Things we eat might kill them," Fayon said. "Meats will be especially dangerous. And no caffeine, and no alcohol."

"Alcohol won't hurt them," Schallenmacher said. "I saw big jars full of fermenting fruit-mash back of some of those houses; in about a year, it ought to be fairly good wine. C_2H_5OH is the same on any planet."

"Well, we'll get native foodstuffs tomorrow," Meillard said. "We'll have to do that by signs, too," he regretted.

"Get Mom to help you; she's pretty sharp," Lillian advised. "But I think Sonny's the village half-wit."

Anna de Jong agreed. "Even if we don't understand Svant psychology, that's evident; he's definitely subnormal. The way he clings to his mother for guidance is absolutely pathetic. He's a mature adult, but mentally he's still a little child."

"That may explain it!" Dorver cried. "A mental defective, in a community of telepaths, constantly invading the minds of others with irrational and disgusting thoughts; no wonder he is rejected and persecuted. And in a community on this culture level, the mother of an abnormal child is often regarded with superstitious detestation —"

"Yes, of course!" Anna de Jong instantly agreed, and began to go into the villagers' hostility to both mother and son; both of them were now taking the telepathy hypothesis for granted.

Well, maybe so. He turned to Lillian.

"What did you find out?"

"Well, there is a common characteristic in all four sounds. A little patch on the screen at seventeen-twenty cycles. The odd thing is that when I try to repeat the sound, it isn't there."

Odd indeed. If a Svant said something, he made sound waves; if she imitated the sound, she ought to imitate the wave pattern. He said so, and she agreed.

"But come back here and look at this," she invited.

She had been using a visibilizing analyzer; in it, a sound was broken by a set of filters into frequency-groups, translated into light from dull red to violet paling into pure white. It photographed the light-pattern on high-speed film, automatically developed it, and then made a print-copy and projected the film in slow motion on a screen. When she pressed a button, a recorded voice said, *"Fwoonk."* An instant later, a pattern of vertical lines in various colors and lengths was projected on the screen.

"Those green lines," she said. "That's it. Now, watch this."

She pressed another button, got the photoprint out of a slot, and propped it beside the screen. Then she picked up a hand-phone and said, *"Fwoonk,"* into it. It sounded like the first one, but the pattern that danced onto the screen was quite different. Where the green had been, there was a patch of pale-blue lines. She ran the other three Svants' voices, each saying, presumably, "Me." Some were mainly up in blue, others had a good deal of yellow and orange, but they all had the little patch of green lines.

"Well, that seems to be the information," he said. "The rest is just noise."

"Maybe one of them is saying, 'John Doe, *me*, son of Joe Blow,' and another is saying, 'Tough guy, *me*; lick anybody in town.'"

"All in one syllable?" Then he shrugged. How did he know what these people could pack into one syllable? He picked up the hand-phone and said, "Fwoonk," into it. The pattern, a little deeper in color and with longer lines, was recognizably like hers, and unlike any of the Svants'.

The others came in, singly and in pairs and threes. They watched the colors dance on the screen to picture the four Svant words which might or might not all mean *me*. They tried to duplicate them. Luis Gofredo and Willi Schallenmacher came closest of anybody. Bennet Fayon was still insisting that the Svants had a perfectly comprehensible language-to other Svants. Anna de Jong had started to veer a little away from the Dorver Hypothesis. There was a difference between event-level sound, which was a series of waves of alternately crowded and rarefied molecules of air, and object-level sound, which was an auditory sensation inside the nervous system, she admitted. That, Fayon crowed, was what he'd been saying all along; their auditory system was probably such that *fwoonk* and *pwink* and *tweelt* and *kroosh* all sounded alike to them.

By this time, *fwoonk* and *pwink* and *tweelt* and *kroosh* had become swear words among the joint Space Navy-Colonial Office contact team.

"Well, if I hear the two sounds alike, why doesn't the analyzer hear them alike?" Karl Dorver demanded.

"It has better ears than you do, Karl. Look how many different frequencies there are in that word, all crowding up behind each other," Lillian said. "But it isn't sensitive or selective enough. I'm going to see what Ayesha Keithley can do about building me a better one."

Ayesha was signals and detection officer on the *Hubert Penrose*. Dave Questell mentioned that she'd had a hard day, and was probably making sack-time, and she wouldn't welcome being called at 0130. Nobody seemed to have realized that it had gotten that late.

"Well, I'll call the ship and have a recording made for her for when she gets up. But till we get something that'll sort this mess out and make sense of it, I'm stopped."

"You're stopped, period, Lillian," Dorver told her. "What these people gibber at us doesn't even make as much sense as the Shooting of Dan McJabberwock. The real information is conveyed by telepathy."

Lieutenant j.g. Ayesha Keithley was on the screen the next morning while they were eating breakfast. She was a blonde, like Lillian.

"I got your message; you seem to have problems, don't you?"

"Speaking conservatively, yes. You see what we're up against?"

"You don't know what their vocal organs are like, do you?" the girl in naval uniform in the screen asked.

Lillian shook her head. "Bennet Fayon's hoping for a war, or an epidemic, or something to break out, so that he can get a few cadavers to dissect."

"Well, he'll find that they're pretty complex," Ayesha Keithley said. "I identified stick-and-slip sounds and percussion sounds, and plucked-string sounds, along with the ordinary hiss-and-buzz speech-sounds. Making a vocoder to reproduce that speech is going to be fun. Just what are you using, in the way of equipment?"

Lillian was still talking about that when the two landing craft from the ship were sighted, coming down. Charley Loughran and Willi Schallenmacher, who were returning to the *Hubert Penrose* to join the other landing party, began assembling their luggage. The others went outside, Howell among them.

Mom and Sonny were watching the two craft grow larger and closer above, keeping close to a group of spacemen; Sonny was looking around excitedly, while Mom clung to his arm, like a hen with an oversized chick. The reasoning was clear-these people knew all about big things that came down out of the sky and weren't afraid of them; stick close to them, and it would be perfectly safe. Sonny saw the contact team emerging from their hut and grabbed his mother's arm, pointing. They both beamed happily; that expression didn't look sad, at all, now that you knew what it meant. Sonny began ghroogh-ghrooghing hideously; Mom hushed him with a hand over his mouth, and they both made eating gestures, rubbed their abdomens comfortably, and pointed toward the mess hut. Bennet Fayon was frightened. He turned and started on the double toward the cook, who was standing in the doorway of the hut, calling out to him.

The cook spoke inaudibly. Fayon stopped short. "Unholy Saint Beelzebub, no!" he cried. The cook said something in reply, shrugging. Fayon came back, talking to himself.

"Terran carniculture pork," he said, when he returned. "Zarathustra pool-ball fruit. Potato-flour hotcakes, with Baldur honey and Odin flameberry jam. And two big cups of coffee apiece. It's a miracle they aren't dead now. If they're alive for lunch, we won't need to worry about feeding them anything we eat, but I'm glad somebody else has the moral responsibility for this."

Lillian Ransby came out of the headquarters hut. "Ayesha's coming down this afternoon, with a lot of equipment," she said. "We're not exactly going to count air molecules in the sound waves, but we'll do everything short of that. We'll need more lab space, soundproofed."

"Tell Dave Questell what you want," Meillard said. "Do you really think you can get anything?"

She shrugged. "If there's anything there to get. How long it'll take is another question."

The two sixty-foot collapsium-armored turtles settled to the ground and went off contragravity. The ports opened, and things began being floated off on lifter-skids: framework for the water tower, and curved titanium sheets for the tank. Anna de Jong said something about hot showers, and not having to take any more sponge-baths. Howell was watching the stuff come off the other landing craft. A dozen pairs of four-foot wagon wheels, with axles. Hoes, in bundles. Scythe blades. A hand forge, with a crank-driven fan blower, and a hundred and fifty pound anvil, and sledges and cutters and swages and tongs.

Everybody was busy, and Mom and Sonny were fidgeting, gesturing toward the work with their own empty hands. *Hey, boss; whatta we gonna do?* He patted them on the shoulders.

"Take it easy." He hoped his tone would convey nonurgency. "We'll find something for you to do."

He wasn't particularly happy about most of what was coming off. Giving these Svants tools was fine, but it was more important to give them technologies. The people on the ship hadn't thought of that. These wheels, now; machined steel hubs, steel rims, tubular steel spokes, drop-forged and machined axles. The Svants wouldn't be able to copy them in a thousand years. Well, in a hundred, if somebody showed them where and how to mine iron and how to smelt and work it. And how to build a steam engine.

He went over and pulled a hoe out of one of the bundles. Blades stamped out with a power press, welded to tubular steel handles. Well, wood for hoe handles was hard to come by on a spaceship, even a battle cruiser almost half a mile in diameter; he had to admit that. And they were about two thousand per cent more efficient than the bronze scrapers the Svants used. That wasn't the idea, though. Even supposing that the first wave of colonists came out in a year and a half, it would be close to twenty years before Terran-operated factories would be in mass production for the native trade. The idea was to teach these people to make better things for themselves; give them a leg up, so that the next generation would be ready for contragravity and nuclear and electric power.

Mom didn't know what to make of any of it. Sonny did, though; he was excited, grabbing Howell's arm, pointing, saying, *"Ghroogh! Ghroogh!"* He pointed at the wheels, and then made a stooping, lifting and pushing gesture. *Like wheelbarrow?*

"That's right." He nodded, wondering if Sonny recognized that as an affirmative sign. "Like big wheelbarrow."

One thing puzzled Sonny, though. Wheelbarrow wheels were small-his hands indicated the size-and single. These were big, and double.

"Let me show you this, Sonny."

He squatted, took a pad and pencil from his pocket, and drew two pairs of wheels, and then put a wagon on them, and drew a quadruped hitched to it, and a Svant with a stick walking beside it. Sonny looked at the picture-Svants seemed to have pictoral sense, for which make us thankful! —and then caught his mother's sleeve and showed it to her. Mom didn't get it. Sonny took the pencil and drew another animal, with a pole travois. He made gestures. A travois dragged; it went slow. A wagon had wheels that went around; it went fast.

So Lillian and Anna thought he was the village half-wit. Village genius, more likely; the other peasants didn't understand him, and resented his superiority. They went over for a closer look at the wheels, and pushed them. Sonny was almost beside himself. Mom was puzzled, but she thought they were pretty wonderful.

Then they looked at blacksmith tools. Tongs; Sonny had never seen anything like them. Howell wondered what the Svants used to handle hot metal; probably big tweezers made by tying two green sticks together. There was an old Arabian legend that Allah had made the first tongs and given them to the first smith, because nobody could make tongs without having a pair already.

Sonny didn't understand the fan-blower until it was taken apart. Then he made a great discovery. The wheels, and the fan, and the pivoted tongs, all embodied the same principle, one his people had evidently never discovered. A whole new world seemed to open before him; from then on, he was constantly finding things pierced and rotating on pivots.

By this time, Mom was fidgeting again. She ought to be doing something to justify her presence in the camp. He was wondering what sort of work he could invent for her when Karl Dorver called to him from the door of the headquarters hut.

"Mark, can you spare Mom for a while?" he asked. "We want her to look at pictures and show us which of the animals are meat-cattle, and which of the crops are ripe."

"Think you can get anything out of her?"

"Sign-talk, yes. We may get a few words from her, too."

At first, Mom was unwilling to leave Sonny. She finally decided that it would be safe, and trotted over to Dorver, entering the hut.

Dave Questell's construction crew began at once on the water tank, using a power shovel to dig the foundation. They had to haul water in a tank from the river a quarter-mile away to mix the concrete. Sonny watched that interestedly. So did a number of the villagers, who gathered safely out of bowshot. They noticed Sonny among the Terrans and pointed at him. Sonny noticed that. He unobtrusively picked up a double-bitted ax and kept it to hand.

He and Mom had lunch with the contact team. As they showed no ill effects from breakfast, Fayon decided that it was safe to let them have anything the Terrans ate or drank. They liked wine; they knew what it was, all right, but this seemed to have a delightfully different flavor. They each tried a cigarette, choked over the first few puffs, and decided that they didn't like smoking.

"Mom gave us a lot of information, as far as she could, on the crops and animals. The big things, the size of rhinoceroses, are draft animals and nothing else; they're not eaten," Dorver said. "I don't know whether the meat isn't good, or is taboo, or they are too valuable to eat. They eat all the other three species, and milk two of them. I have an idea they grind their grain in big stone mortars as needed."

That was right; he'd seen things like that.

"Willi, when you're over in the mountains, see if you can find something we can make millstones out of. We can shape them with sono-cutters; after they get the idea, they can do it themselves by hand. One of those big animals could be used to turn the mill. Did you get any words from her?"

Paul Meillard shook his head gloomily. "Nothing we can be sure of. It was the same thing as in the village, yesterday. She'd say something, I'd repeat it, and she'd tell us it was wrong and say the same thing over again. Lillian took recordings; she got the same results as last night. Ask her about it later."

"She has the same effect on Mom as on the others?"

"Yes. Mom was very polite and tried not to show it, but —"

Lillian took him aside, out of earshot of the two Svants, after lunch. She was almost distracted.

"Mark, I don't know what I'm going to do. She's like the others. Every time I open my mouth in front of her, she's simply horrified. It's as though my voice does something loathsome to her. And I'm the one who's supposed to learn to talk to them."

"Well, those who can do, and those who can't teach," he told her. "You can study recordings, and tell us what the words are and teach us how to recognize and pronounce them. You're the only linguist we have."

That seemed to comfort her a little. He hoped it would work out that way. If they could communicate with these people and did leave a party here to prepare for the first colonization, he'd stay on, to teach the natives Terran technologies and study theirs. He'd been expecting that Lillian would stay, too. She was the linguist; she'd have to stay. But now, if it turned out that she would be no help but a liability, she'd go back with the *Hubert Penrose*. Paul wouldn't keep a linguist who offended the natives' every sensibility with every word she spoke. He didn't want that to happen. Lillian and he had come to mean a little too much to each other to be parted now.

Paul Meillard and Karl Dorver had considerable difficulty with Mom, that afternoon. They wanted her to go with them and help trade for cattle. Mom didn't want to; she was afraid. They had to do a lot of play-acting, with half a dozen Marines pretending to guard her with fixed bayonets from some of Dave Questell's Navy construction men who had red bandannas on their heads to simulate combs before she got the idea. Then she was afraid to get into the contragravity lorry that was to carry the hoes and the wagon wheels. Sonny managed to reassure her, and insisted on going along, and he insisted on taking his ax with him. That meant doubling the guard, to make sure Sonny didn't lose his self-control when he saw his former persecutors within chopping distance.

It went off much better than either Paul Meillard or Luis Gofredo expected. After the first shock of being air-borne had worn off, Mom found that she liked contragravity-riding; Sonny was wildly delighted with it from the start. The natives showed neither of them any hostility. Mom's lavender bathrobe and Sonny's green coveralls and big ax seemed to be symbols of a new and exalted status; even the Lord Mayor was extremely polite to them.

The Lord Mayor and half a dozen others got a contragravity ride, too, to the meadows to pick out cattle. A dozen animals, including a pair of the two-ton draft beasts, were driven to the Terran camp. A couple of lorry-loads of assorted vegetables were brought in, too. Everybody seemed very happy about the deal, especially Bennet Fayon. He wanted to slaughter one of the sheep-sized meat-and-milk animals at once and get to work on it. Gofredo advised him to put it off till the next morning. He wanted a large native audience to see the animal being shot with a rifle.

The water tower was finished, and the big spherical tank hoisted on top of it and made fast. A pump, and a filter-system were installed. There was no water for hot showers that evening, though. They would have to run a pipeline to the river, and that would entail a ditch that would cut through several cultivated fields, which, in turn, would provoke an uproar. Paul Meillard didn't want that happening until he'd concluded the cattle-trade.

Charley Loughran and Willi Schallenmacher had gone up to the ship on one of the landing craft; they accompanied the landing party that went down into the mountains. Ayesha Keithley arrived late in the afternoon on another landing craft, with five or six tons of instruments and parts and equipment, and a male Navy warrant-officer helper.

They looked around the lab Lillian had been using at one end of the headquarters hut.

"This won't do," the girl Navy officer said. "We can't get a quarter of the apparatus we're going to need in here. We'll have to build something."

Dave Questell was drawn into the discussion. Yes, he could put up something big enough for everything the girls would need to install, and soundproof it. Concrete, he decided; they'd have to wait till he got the water line down and the pump going, though.

There was a crowd of natives in the fields, gaping at the Terran camp, the next morning, and Gofredo decided to kill the animal-until they learned the native name, they were calling it Domesticated Type C. It was herded out where everyone could watch, and a Marine stepped forward unslung his rifle took a kneeling position, and aimed at it. It was a hundred and fifty yards away. Mom had come out to see what was going on; Sonny and Howell, who had been consulting by signs over the construction of a wagon, were standing side by side. The Marine squeezed his trigger. The rifle banged, and the Domesticated-C bounded into the air, dropped, and kicked a few times and was still. The natives, however, missed that part of it; they were howling piteously and rubbing their heads. All but Sonny. He was just mildly surprised at what had happened to the Dom.-C.

Sonny, it would appear, was stone deaf.

As anticipated, there was another uproar later in the morning when the ditching machine started north across the meadow. A mob of Svants, seeing its relentless progress toward a field of something like turnips, gathered in front of it, twittering and brandishing implements of agriculture, many of them Terran-made.

Paul Meillard was ready for this. Two lorries went out; one loaded with Marines, who jumped off with their rifles ready. By this time, all the Svants knew what rifles would do beside make a noise. Meillard, Dorver, Gofredo and a few others got out of the other vehicle, and unloaded presents. Gofredo did all the talking. The Svants couldn't understand him, but they liked it. They also liked the presents, which included a dozen empty half-gallon rum demijohns, tarpaulins, and a lot of assorted knickknacks. The pipeline went through.

He and Sonny got the forge set up. There was no fuel for it. A party of Marines had gone out to the woods to the east to cut wood; when they got back, they'd burn some charcoal in the pit that had been dug beside the camp. Until then, he and Sonny were drawing plans for a wooden wheel with a metal tire when Lillian came out of the headquarters hut with a clipboard under her arm. She motioned to him.

"Come on over," he told her. "You can talk in front of Sonny; he won't mind. He can't hear."

"Can't hear?" she echoed. "You mean —?"

"That's right. Sonny's stone deaf. He didn't even hear that rifle going off. The only one of this gang that has brains enough to pour sand out of a boot with directions on the bottom of the heel, and he's a total linguistic loss."

"So he isn't a half-wit, after all."

"He's got an IQ close to genius level. Look at this; he never saw a wheel before yesterday; now he's designing one."

Lillian's eyes widened. "So that's why Mom's so sharp about sign-talk. She's been doing it all his life." Then she remembered what she had come out to show him, and held out the clipboard. "You know how that analyzer of mine works? Well, here's what Ayesha's going to do. After breaking a sound into frequency bands instead of being photographed and projected, each band goes to an analyzer of its own, and is projected on its own screen. There'll be forty of them, each for a band of a hundred cycles, from zero to four thousand. That seems to be the Svant vocal range."

The diagram passed from hand to hand during cocktail time, before dinner. Bennet Fayon had been working all day dissecting the animal they were all calling a *domsee*, a name which would stick even if and when they learned the native name. He glanced disinterestedly at the drawing, then looked again, more closely. Then he set down the drink he was holding in his other hand and studied it intently.

"You know what you have here?" he asked. "This is a very close analogy to the hearing organs of that animal I was working on. The comb, as we've assumed, is the external organ. It's covered with small flaps and fissures. Back of each fissure is a long, narrow membrane; they're paired, one on each side of the comb, and from them nerves lead to clusters of small round membranes. Nerves lead from them to a complex nerve-cable at the bottom of the comb and into the brain at the base of the skull. I couldn't understand how the system functioned, but now I see it. Each of the larger membranes on the outside responds to a sound-frequency band, and the small ones on the inside break the bands down to individual frequencies."

"How many of the little ones are there?" Ayesha asked.

"Thousands of them; the inner comb is simply packed with them. Wait; I'll show you."

He rose and went away, returning with a sheaf of photo-enlargements and a number of blocks of lucite in which specimens were mounted. Everybody examined them. Anna de Jong, as a practicing psychologist, had an M.D. and to get that she'd had to know a modicum of anatomy; she was puzzled.

"I can't understand how they hear with those things. I'll grant that the membranes will respond to sound, but I can't see how they transmit it."

"But they do hear," Meillard said. "Their musical instruments, their reactions to our voices, the way they are affected by sounds like gunfire —"

"They hear, but they don't hear in the same way we do," Fayon replied. "If you can't be convinced by anything else, look at these things, and compare them with the structure of the human ear, or the ear of any member of any other sapient race we're ever contacted. That's what I've been saying from the beginning."

"They have sound-perception to an extent that makes ours look almost like deafness," Ayesha Keithley said. "I wish I could design a sound-detector one-tenth as good as this must be."

Yes. The way the Lord Mayor said *fwoonk* and the way Paul Meillard said it sounded entirely different to them. Of course, *fwoonk* and *pwink* and *tweelt* and *kroosh* sounded alike to them, but let's don't be too picky about things.

There were no hot showers that evening; Dave Questell's gang had trouble with the pump and needed some new parts made up aboard the ship. They were still working on it the next morning. He had meant to start teaching Sonny blacksmithing, but during the evening Lillian and Anna had decided to try teaching Mom a nonphonetic, ideographic, alphabet, and in the morning they co-opted Sonny to help. Deprived of his disciple, he strolled over to watch the work on the pump. About twenty Svants had come in from the fields and were also watching, from the meadow.

After a while, the job was finished. The petty officer in charge of the work pushed in the switch, and the pump started, sucking dry with a harsh racket. The natives twittered in surprise. Then the water came, and the pump settled down to a steady *thugg-thugg, thugg-thugg.*

The Svants seemed to like the new sound; they grimaced in pleasure and moved closer; within forty or fifty feet, they all squatted on the ground and sat entranced. Others came in from the fields, drawn by the sound. They, too, came up and squatted, until there was a semicircle of them. The tank took a long time to fill; until it did, they all sat immobile and fascinated. Even after it stopped, many remained, hoping that it would start again. Paul Meillard began wondering, a trifle uneasily, if that would happen every time the pump went on.

"They get a positive pleasure from it. It affects them the same way Luis' voice does."

"Mean I have a voice like a pump?" Gofredo demanded.

"Well, I'm going to find out," Ayesha Keithley said. "The next time that starts, I'm going to make a recording, and compare it with your voice-recording. I'll give five to one there'll be a similarity."

Questell got the foundation for the sonics lab dug, and began pouring concrete. That took water, and the pump ran continuously that afternoon. Concrete-mixing took more water the next day, and by noon the whole village population, down to the smallest child, was massed at the pumphouse, enthralled. Mom was snared by the sound like any of the rest; only Sonny was unaffected. Lillian and Ayesha compared recordings of the voices of the team with the pump-sound; in Gofredo's they found an identical frequency-pattern.

"We'll need the new apparatus to be positive about it, but it's there, all right," Ayesha said. "That's why Luis' voice pleases them."

"That tags me; Old Pump-Mouth," Gofredo said. "It'll get all through the Corps, and they'll be calling me that when I'm a four-star general, if I live that long."

Meillard was really worried, now. So was Bennet Fayon. He said so that afternoon at cocktail time.

"It's an addiction," he declared. "Once they hear it, they have no will to resist; they just squat and listen. I don't know what it's doing to them, but I'm scared of it."

"I know one thing it's doing," Meillard said. "It's keeping them from their work in the fields. For all we know, it may cause them to lose a crop they need badly for subsistence."

The native they had come to call the Lord Mayor evidently thought so, too. He was with the others, the next morning, squatting with his staff across his knees, as bemused as any of them, but when the pump stopped he rose and approached a group of Terrans, launching into what could only be an impassioned tirade. He pointed with his staff to the pump house, and to the semicircle of still motionless villagers. He pointed to the fields, and back to the people, and to the pump house again, gesturing vehemently with his other hand.

You make the noise. My people will not work while they hear it. The fields lie untended. Stop the noise, and let my people work.

Couldn't possibly be any plainer.

Then the pump started again. The Lord Mayor's hands tightened on the staff; he was struggling tormentedly with himself, in vain. His face relaxed into the heartbroken expression of joy; he turned and shuffled over, dropping onto his haunches with the others.

"Shut down the pump, Dave!" Meillard called out. "Cut the power off."

The *thugg-thugg*-ing stopped. The Lord Mayor rose, made an odd salaamlike bow toward the Terrans, and then turned on the people, striking with his staff and shrieking at them. A few got to their feet and joined him, screaming, pushing, tugging. Others joined. In a little while, they were all on their feet, straggling away across the fields.

Dave Questell wanted to know what it meant; Meillard explained.

"Well, what are we going to do for water?" the Navy engineer asked.

"Soundproof the pump house. You can do that, can't you?"

"Sure. Mound it over with earth. We'll have that done in a few hours."

That started Gofredo worrying. "This happens every time we colonize an inhabited planet. We give the natives something new. Then we find out it's bad for them, and we try to take it away from them. And then the knives come out, and the shooting starts."

Luis Gofredo was also a specialist, speaking on his subject.

While they were at lunch, Charley Loughran screened in from the other camp and wanted to talk to Bennet Fayon.

"A funny thing, Bennet. I took a shot at a bird … no, a flying mammal … and dropped it. It was dead when it hit the ground, but there isn't a mark on it. I want you to do an autopsy, and find out how I can kill things by missing them."

"How far away was it?"

"Call it forty feet; no more."

"What were you using, Charley?" Ayesha Keithley called from the table.

"Eight-point-five Mars-Consolidated pistol," Loughran said. "I'd laid my shotgun down and walked away from it —"

"Twelve hundred foot-seconds," Ayesha said. "Bow-wave as well as muzzle-blast."

"You think the report was what did it?" Fayon asked.

"You want to bet it didn't?" she countered.

Nobody did.

Mom was sulky. She didn't like what Dave Questell's men were doing to the nice-noise-place. Ayesha and Lillian consoled her by taking her into the soundproofed room and playing the recording of the pump-noise for her. Sonny couldn't care less, one way or another; he spent the afternoon teaching Mark Howell what the marks on paper meant. It took a lot of signs and play-acting. He had learned about thirty ideographs; by combining them and drawing little pictures, he could express a number of simple ideas. There was, of course, a limit to how many of those things anybody could learn and remember-look how long it took an Old Terran Chinese scribe to learn his profession-but it was the beginning of a method of communication.

Questell got the pump house mounded over. Ayesha came out and tried a sound-meter, and also Mom, on it while the pump was running. Neither reacted.

A good many Svants were watching the work. They began to demonstrate angrily. A couple tried to interfere and were knocked down with rifle butts. The Lord Mayor and his Board of Aldermen came out with the big horn and harangued them at length, and finally got them to go back to the fields. As nearly as anybody could tell, he was friendly to and co-operative with the Terrans. The snooper over the village reported excitement in the plaza.

Bennet Fayon had taken an airjeep to the other camp immediately after lunch. He was back by 1500, accompanied by Loughran. They carried a cloth-wrapped package into Fayon's dissecting-room. At cocktail time, Paul Meillard had to go and get them.

"Sorry," Fayon said, joining the group. "Didn't notice how late it was getting. We're still doing a post on this svant-bat; that's what Charley's calling it, till we get the native name.

"The immediate cause of death was spasmodic contraction of every muscle in the thing's body; some of them were partly relaxed before we could get to work on it, but not completely. Every bone that isn't broken is dislocated; a good many both. There is not the slightest trace of external injury. Everything was done by its own muscles." He looked around. "I hope nobody covered Ayesha's bet, after I left. If they did, she collects. The large outer membranes in the comb seem to be unaffected, but there is considerable compression of the small round ones inside, in just one area, and more on the left side than on the right. Charley says it was flying across in front of him from left to right."

"The receptor-area responding to the frequencies of the report," Ayesha said.

Anna de Jong made a passing gesture toward Fayon. "The baby's yours, Bennet," she said. "This isn't psychological. I won't accept a case of psychosomatic compound fracture."

"Don't be too premature about it, Anna. I think that's more or less what you have, here."

Everybody looked at him, surprised. His subject was comparative technology. The bio- and psycho-sciences were completely outside his field.

"A lot of things have been bothering me, ever since the first contact. I'm beginning to think I'm on the edge of understanding them, now. Bennet, the higher life-forms here-the people, and that domsee, and Charley's svant-bat —are structurally identical with us. I don't mean gross structure, like ears and combs. I mean molecular and cellular and tissue structure. Is that right?"

Fayon nodded. "Biology on this planet is exactly Terra type. Yes. With adequate safeguards, I'd even say you could make a viable tissue-graft from a Svant to a Terran, or vice versa."

"Ayesha, would the sound waves from that pistol-shot in any conceivable way have the sort of physical effect we're considering?"

"Absolutely not," she said, and Luis Gofredo said: "I've been shot at and missed with pistols at closer range than that."

"Then it was the effect on the animal's nervous system."

Anna shrugged. "It's still Bennet's baby. I'm a psychologist, not a neurologist."

"What I've been saying, all along," Fayon reiterated complacently. "Their hearing is different from ours. This proves it."

"It proves that they don't hear at all."

He had expected an explosion; he wasn't disappointed. They all contradicted him, many derisively. Signal reactions. Only Paul Meillard made the semantically appropriate response:

"What do you mean, Mark?"

"They don't *hear* sound; they *feel* it. You all saw what they have inside their combs. Those things don't transmit sound like the ears of any sound-sensitive life-form we've ever seen. They transform sound waves into tactile sensations."

Fayon cursed, slowly and luridly. Anna de Jong looked at him wide-eyed. He finished his cocktail and poured another. In the snooper screen, what looked like an indignation meeting was making uproar in the village plaza. Gofredo cut the volume of the speaker even lower.

"That would explain a lot of things," Meillard said slowly. "How hard it was for them to realize that we didn't understand when they talked to us. A punch in the nose feels the same to anybody. They thought they were giving us bodily feelings. They didn't know we were insensible to them."

"But they do ... they do have a language," Lillian faltered. "They talk."

"Not the way we understand it. If they want to say, 'Me,' it's *tickle-pinch-rub*, even if it sounds like *fwoonk* to us, when it doesn't sound like *pwink* or *tweelt* or *kroosh*. The tactile sensations, to a Svant, feel no more different than a massage by four different hands. Analogous to a word pronounced by four different voices, to us. They'll have a code for expressing meanings in tactile sensation, just as we have a code for expressing meanings in audible sound."

"Except that when a Svant tells another, 'I am happy,' or 'I have a stomach-ache,' he makes the other one feel that way too," Anna said. "That would carry an awful lot more conviction. I don't imagine symptom-swapping is popular among Svants. Karl! You were nearly right, at that. This isn't telepathy, but it's a lot like it."

"So it is," Dorver, who had been mourning his departed telepathy theory, said brightly. "And look how it explains their society. Peaceful, everybody in quick agreement —" He looked at the screen and gulped. The Lord Mayor and his party had formed one clump, and the opposition was grouped at the other side of the plaza; they were screaming in unison at each other. "They make their decisions by endurance; the party that can resist the feelings of the other longest converts their opponents."

"Pure democracy," Gofredo declared. "Rule by the party that can make the most noise."

"And I'll bet that when they're sick, they go around chanting, 'I am well; I feel just fine!'" Anna said. "Autosuggestion would really work, here. Think of the feedback, too. One Svant has a feeling. He verbalizes it, and the sound of his own voice re-enforces it in him. It is induced in his hearers, and they verbalize it, re-enforcing it in themselves and in him. This could go on and on."

"Yes. It has. Look at their technology." He felt more comfortable, now he was on home ground again. "A friend of mine, speaking about a mutual acquaintance, once said, 'When they installed her circuits, they put in such big feeling circuits that there was no room left for any thinking circuits.' I think that's a perfect description of what I estimate Svant mentality to be. Take these bronze knives, and the musical instruments. Wonderful; the work of individuals trying to express feeling in metal or wood. But get an idea like the wheel, or even a pair of tongs? Poo! How would you state the First Law of Motion, or the Second Law of Thermodynamics, in tickle-pinch-rub terms? Sonny could grasp an idea like that. Sonny's handicap, if you call it that, cuts him off from feel-thinking; he can think logically instead of sensually."

He sipped his cocktail and continued: "I can understand why the village is mounded up, too. I realized that while I was watching Dave's gang bury the pump house. I'd been bothered by that, and by the absence of granaries for all the grain they raise, and by the number of people for so few and such small houses. I think the village is mostly underground, and the houses are just entrances, soundproofed, to shelter them from uncomfortable natural noises —thunderstorms, for instance."

The horn was braying in the snooper-screen speaker; somebody wondered what it was for. Gofredo laughed.

"I thought, at first, that it was a war-horn. It isn't. It's a peace-horn," he said. "Public tranquilizer. The first day, they brought it out and blew it at us to make us peaceable."

"Now I see why Sonny is rejected and persecuted," Anna was saying. "He must make all sorts of horrible noises that he can't hear ... that's not the word; we have none for it ... and nobody but his mother can stand being near him."

"Like me," Lillian said. "Now I understand. Just think of the most revolting thing that could be done to you physically; that's what I do to them every time I speak. And I always thought I had a nice voice," she added, pathetically.

"You have, for Terrans," Ayesha said. "For Svants, you'll just have to change it."

"But how —?"

"Use an analyzer; train it. That was why I took up sonics, in the first place. I had a voice like a crow with a sore throat, but by practicing with an analyzer, an hour a day, I gave myself an entirely different voice in a couple of months. Just try to get some pump-sound frequencies into it, like Luis'."

"But why? I'm no use here. I'm a linguist, and these people haven't any language that I could ever learn, and they couldn't even learn ours. They couldn't learn to make sounds, as sounds."

"You've been doing very good work with Mom on those ideographs," Meillard said. "Keep it up till you've taught her the Lingua Terra Basic vocabulary, and with her help we can train a few more. They can be our interpreters; we can write what we want them to say to the others. It'll be clumsy, but it will work, and it's about the only thing I can think of that will."

"And it will improve in time," Ayesha added. "And we can make vocoders and visibilizers. Paul, you have authority to requisition personnel from the ship's company. Draft me; I'll stay here and work on it."

The rumpus in the village plaza was getting worse. The Lord Mayor and his adherents were being out-shouted by the opposition.

"Better do something about that in a hurry, Paul, if you don't want a lot of Svants shot," Gofredo said. "Give that another half hour and we'll have visitors, with bows and spears."

"Ayesha, you have a recording of the pump," Meillard said. "Load a record-player onto a jeep and fly over the village and play it for them. Do it right away. Anna, get Mom in here. We want to get her to tell that gang that from now on, at noon and for a couple of hours after sunset, when the work's done, there will be free public pump-concerts, over the village plaza."

<hr>

Ayesha and her warrant-officer helper and a Marine lieutenant went out hastily. Everybody else faced the screen to watch. In fifteen minutes, an airjeep was coming in on the village. As it circled low, a new sound, the steady *thugg-thugg, thugg-thugg* of the pump, began.

The yelling and twittering and the blaring of the peace-horn died out almost at once. As the jeep circled down to housetop level, the two contending faction-clumps broke apart; their component individuals moved into the center of the plaza and squatted, staring up, letting the delicious waves of sound caress them.

"Do we have to send a detail in a jeep to do that twice a day?" Gofredo asked. "We keep a snooper over the village; fit it with a loud-speaker and a timer; it can give them their *thugg-thugg*, on schedule, automatically."

"We might give the Lord Mayor a recording and a player and let him decide when the people ought to listen-if that's the word-to it," Dorver said. "Then it would be something of their own."

"No!" He spoke so vehemently that the others started. "You know what would happen? Nobody would be able to turn it off; they'd all be hypnotized, or doped, or whatever it is. They'd just sit in a circle around it till they starved to death, and when the power-unit gave out, the record-player would be surrounded by a ring of skeletons. We'll just have to keep on playing it for them ourselves. Terrans' Burden."

"That'll give us a sanction over them," Gofredo observed. "Extra *thugg-thugg* if they're very good; shut it off on them if they act nasty. And find out what Lillian has in her voice that the rest of us don't have, and make a good loud recording of that, and stash it away along with the rest of the heavy-weapons ammunition. You know, you're not going to have any trouble at all, when we go down-country to talk to the king or whatever. This is better than fire-water ever was."

"We must never misuse our advantage, Luis," Meillard said seriously. "We must use it only for their good."

He really meant it. Only-You had to know some general history to study technological history, and it seemed to him that that pious assertion had been made a few times before. Some of the others who had made it had really meant it, too, but that had made little difference in the long run.

Fayon and Anna were talking enthusiastically about the work ahead of them.

"I don't know where your subject ends and mine begins," Anna was saying. "We'll just have to handle it between us. What are we going to call it? We certainly can't call it hearing."

"Nonauditory sonic sense is the only thing I can think of," Fayon said. "And that's such a clumsy term."

"Mark; you thought of it first," Anna said. "What do you think?"

"Nonauditory sonic sense. It isn't any worse than Domesticated Type C, and that got cut down to size. *Naudsonce.*"

Little Fuzzy

by

H. Beam Piper

I

Jack Holloway found himself squinting, the orange sun full in his eyes. He raised a hand to push his hat forward, then lowered it to the controls to alter the pulse rate of the contragravity-field generators and lift the manipulator another hundred feet. For a moment he sat, puffing on the short pipe that had yellowed the corners of his white mustache, and looked down at the red rag tied to a bush against the rock face of the gorge five hundred yards away. He was smiling in anticipation.

"This'll be a good one," he told himself aloud, in the manner of men who have long been their own and only company. "I want to see this one go up."

He always did. He could remember at least a thousand blast-shots he had fired back along the years and on more planets than he could name at the moment, including a few thermonuclears, but they were all different and they were always something to watch, even a little one like this. Flipping the switch, his thumb found the discharger button and sent out a radio impulse; the red rag vanished in an upsurge of smoke and dust that mounted out of the gorge and turned to copper when the sunlight touched it. The big manipulator, weightless on contragravity, rocked gently; falling debris pelted the trees and splashed in the little stream.

He waited till the machine stabilized, then glided it down to where he had ripped a gash in the cliff with the charge of cataclysmite. Good shot: brought down a lot of sandstone, cracked the vein of flint and hadn't thrown it around too much. A lot of big slabs were loose. Extending the forward claw-arms, he pulled and tugged, and then used the underside grapples to pick up a chunk and drop it on the flat ground between the cliff and the stream. He dropped another chunk on it, breaking both of them, and then another and another, until he had all he could work over the rest of the day. Then he set down, got the toolbox and the long-handled contragravity lifter, and climbed to the ground where he opened the box, put on gloves and an eyescreen and got out a microray scanner and a vibrohammer.

The first chunk he cracked off had nothing in it; the scanner gave the uninterrupted pattern of homogenous structure. Picking it up with the lifter, he swung it and threw it into the stream. On the fifteenth chunk, he got an interruption pattern that told him that a sunstone-or something, probably something-was inside.

Some fifty million years ago, when the planet that had been called Zarathustra (for the last twenty-five million) was young, there had existed a marine life form, something like a jellyfish. As these died, they had sunk into the sea-bottom ooze; sand had covered the ooze and pressed it tighter and tighter, until it had become glassy flint, and the entombed jellyfish little beans of dense stone. Some of them, by some ancient biochemical quirk, were intensely thermofluorescent; worn as gems, they glowed from the wearer's body heat.

On Terra or Baldur or Freya or Ishtar, a single cut of polished sunstone was worth a small fortune. Even here, they brought respectable prices from the Zarathustra Company's gem buyers. Keeping his point of expectation safely low, he got a smaller vibrohammer from the toolbox and began chipping cautiously around the foreign object, until the flint split open and revealed a smooth yellow ellipsoid, half an inch long.

"Worth a thousand sols-if it's worth anything," he commented. A deft tap here, another there, and the yellow bean came loose from the flint. Picking it up, he rubbed it between gloved palms. "I don't think it is." He rubbed harder, then held it against the hot bowl of his pipe. It still didn't respond. He dropped it. "Another jellyfish that didn't live right."

Behind him, something moved in the brush with a dry rustling. He dropped the loose glove from his right hand and turned, reaching toward his hip. Then he saw what had made the noise —a hard-shelled thing a foot in length, with twelve legs, long antennae and two pairs of clawed mandibles. He stopped and picked up a shard of flint, throwing it with an oath. Another damned infernal land-prawn.

He detested land-prawns. They were horrible things, which, of course, wasn't their fault. More to the point, they were destructive. They got into things at camp; they would try to eat anything. They crawled into machinery, possibly finding the lubrication tasty, and caused jams. They cut into electric insulation. And they got into his bedding, and bit, or rather pinched, painfully. Nobody loved a land-prawn, not even another land-prawn.

This one dodged the thrown flint, scuttled off a few feet and turned, waving its antennae in what looked like derision. Jack reached for his hip again, then checked the motion. Pistol cartridges cost like crazy; they weren't to be wasted in fits of childish pique. Then he reflected that no cartridge fired at a target is really wasted, and that he hadn't done any shooting recently. Stooping again, he picked up another stone and tossed it a foot short and to the left of the prawn. As soon as it was out of his fingers, his hand went for the butt of the long automatic. It was out and the safety off before the flint landed; as the prawn fled, he fired from the hip. The quasi-crustacean disintegrated. He nodded pleasantly.

"Ol' man Holloway's still hitting things he shoots at."

Was a time, not so long ago, when he took his abilities for granted. Now he was getting old enough to have to verify them. He thumbed on the safety and holstered the pistol, then picked up the glove and put it on again.

Never saw so blasted many land-prawns as this summer. They'd been bad last year, but nothing like this. Even the oldtimers who'd been on Zarathustra since the first colonization said so. There'd be some simple explanation, of course; something that would amaze him at his own obtuseness for not having seen it at once. Maybe the abnormally dry weather had something to do with it. Or increase of something they ate, or decrease of natural enemies.

He'd heard that land-prawns had no natural enemies; he questioned that. Something killed them. He'd seen crushed prawn shells, some of them close to his camp. Maybe stamped on by something with hoofs, and then picked clean by insects. He'd ask Ben Rainsford; Ben ought to know.

Half an hour later, the scanner gave him another interruption pattern. He laid it aside and took up the small vibrohammer. This time it was a large bean, light pink in color, He separated it from its matrix of flint and rubbed it, and instantly it began glowing.

"Ahhh! This is something like it, now!"

He rubbed harder; warmed further on his pipe bowl, it fairly blazed. Better than a thousand sols, he told himself. Good color, too. Getting his gloves off, he drew out the little leather bag from under his shirt, loosening the drawstrings by which it hung around his neck. There were a dozen and a half stones inside, all bright as live coals. He looked at them for a moment, and dropped the new sunstone in among them, chuckling happily.

Victor Grego, listening to his own recorded voice, rubbed the sunstone on his left finger with the heel of his right palm and watched it brighten. There was, he noticed, a boastful ring to his voice-not the suave, unemphatic tone considered proper on a message-tape. Well, if anybody wondered why, when they played that tape off six months from now in Johannesburg on Terra, they could look in the cargo holds of the ship that had brought it across five hundred light-years of space. Ingots of gold and platinum and gadolinium. Furs and biochemicals and brandy. Perfumes that defied synthetic imitation; hardwoods no plastic could copy. Spices. And the steel coffer full of sunstones. Almost all luxury goods, the only really dependable commodities in interstellar trade.

And he had spoken of other things. Veldbeest meat, up seven per cent from last month, twenty per cent from last year, still in demand on a dozen planets unable to produce Terran-type foodstuffs. Grain, leather, lumber. And he had added a dozen more items to the lengthening list of what Zarathustra could now produce in adequate quantities and no longer needed to import. Not fishhooks and boot buckles, either-blasting explosives and propellants, contra-gravity-field generator parts, power tools, pharmaceuticals, synthetic textiles. The Company didn't need to carry Zarathustra any more; Zarathustra could carry the Company, and itself.

Fifteen years ago, when the Zarathustra Company had sent him here, there had been a cluster of log and prefab huts beside an improvised landing field, almost exactly where this skyscraper now stood. Today, Mallorysport was a city of seventy thousand; in all, the planet had a population of nearly a million, and it was still growing. There were steel mills and chemical plants and reaction plants and machine works. They produced all their own fissionables, and had recently begun to export a little refined plutonium; they had even started producing collapsium shielding.

The recorded voice stopped. He ran back the spool, set for sixty-speed, and transmitted it to the radio office. In twenty minutes, a copy would be aboard the ship that would hyper out for Terra that night. While he was finishing, his communication screen buzzed.

"Dr. Kellogg's screening you, Mr. Grego," the girl in the outside office told him.

He nodded. Her hands moved, and she vanished in a polychromatic explosion; when it cleared, the chief of the Division of Scientific Study and Research was looking out of the screen instead. Looking slightly upward at the showback over his own screen, Victor was getting his warm, sympathetic, sincere and slightly too toothy smile on straight.

"Hello, Leonard. Everything going all right?"

It either was and Leonard Kellogg wanted more credit than he deserved or it wasn't and he was trying to get somebody else blamed for it before anybody could blame him.

"Good afternoon, Victor." Just the right shade of deference about using the first name-big wheel to bigger wheel. "Has Nick Emmert been talking to you about the Big Blackwater project today?"

Nick was the Federation's resident-general; on Zarathustra he was, to all intents and purposes, the Terran Federation Government. He was also a large stockholder in the chartered Zarathustra Company.

"No. Is he likely to?"

"Well, I wondered, Victor. He was on my screen just now. He says there's some adverse talk about the effect on the rainfall in the Piedmont area of Beta Continent. He was worried about it."

"Well, it would affect the rainfall. After all, we drained half a million square miles of swamp, and the prevailing winds are from the west. There'd be less atmospheric moisture to the east of it. Who's talking adversely about it, and what worries Nick?"

"Well, Nick's afraid of the effect on public opinion on Terra. You know how strong conservation sentiment is; everybody's very much opposed to any sort of destructive exploitation."

"Good Lord! The man doesn't call the creation of five hundred thousand square miles of new farmland destructive exploitation, does he?"

"Well, no, Nick doesn't call it that; of course not. But he's concerned about some garbled story getting to Terra about our upsetting the ecological balance and causing droughts. Fact is, I'm rather concerned myself."

He knew what was worrying both of them. Emmert was afraid the Federation Colonial Office would blame him for drawing fire on them from the conservationists. Kellogg was afraid he'd be blamed for not predicting the effects before his division endorsed the project. As a division chief, he had advanced as far as he would in the Company hierarchy; now he was on a Red Queen's racetrack, running like hell to stay in the same place.

"The rainfall's dropped ten per cent from last year, and fifteen per cent from the year before that," Kellogg was saying. "And some non-Company people have gotten hold of it, and so had Interworld News. Why, even some of my people are talking about ecological side-effects. You know what will happen when a story like that gets back to Terra. The conservation fanatics will get hold of it, and the Company'll be criticized."

That would hurt Leonard. He identified himself with the Company. It was something bigger and more powerful than he was, like God.

Victor Grego identified the Company with himself. It was something big and powerful, like a vehicle, and he was at the controls.

"Leonard, a little criticism won't hurt the Company," he said. "Not where it matters, on the dividends. I'm afraid you're too sensitive to criticism. Where did Emmert get this story anyhow? From your people?"

"No, absolutely not, Victor. That's what worries him. It was this man Rainsford who started it."

"Rainsford?"

"Dr. Bennett Rainsford, the naturalist. Institute of Zeno-Sciences. I never trusted any of those people; they always poke their noses into things, and the Institute always reports their findings to the Colonial Office."

"I know who you mean now; little fellow with red whiskers, always looks as though he'd been sleeping in his clothes. Why, of course the Zeno-Sciences people poke their noses into things, and of course they report their findings to the government." He was beginning to lose patience. "I don't see what all this is about, Leonard. This man Rainsford just made a routine observation of meteorological effects. I suggest you have your meteorologists check it, and if it's correct pass it on to the news services along with your other scientific findings."

"Nick Emmert thinks Rainsford is a Federation undercover agent."

That made him laugh. Of course there were undercover agents on Zarathustra, hundreds of them. The Company had people here checking on him; he knew and accepted that. So did the big stockholders, like Interstellar Explorations and the Banking Cartel and Terra Baldur-Marduk Spacelines. Nick Emmert had his corps of spies and stool pigeons, and the Terran Federation had people here watching both him and Emmert. Rainsford could be a Federation agent —a roving naturalist would have a wonderful cover occupation. But this Big Blackwater business was so utterly silly. Nick Emmert had too much graft on his conscience; it was too bad that overloaded consciences couldn't blow fuses.

"Suppose he is, Leonard. What could he report on us? We are a chartered company, and we have an excellent legal department, which keeps us safely inside our charter. It is a very liberal charter, too. This is a Class-III uninhabited planet; the Company owns the whole thing outright. We can do anything we want as long as we don't violate colonial law or the Federation Constitution. As long as we don't do that, Nick Emmert hasn't anything to worry about. Now forget this whole damned business, Leonard!" He was beginning to speak sharply, and Kellogg was looking hurt. "I know you were concerned about injurious reports getting back to Terra, and that was quite commendable, but...."

By the time he got through, Kellogg was happy again. Victor blanked the screen, leaned back in his chair and began laughing. In a moment, the screen buzzed again. When he snapped it on, his screen-girl said:

"Mr. Henry Stenson's on, Mr. Grego."

"Well, put him on." He caught himself just before adding that it would be a welcome change to talk to somebody with sense.

The face that appeared was elderly and thin; the mouth was tight, and there were squint-wrinkles at the corners of the eyes.

"Well, Mr. Stenson. Good of you to call. How are you?"

"Very well, thank you. And you?" When he also admitted to good health, the caller continued: "How is the globe running? Still in synchronization?"

Victor looked across the office at his most prized possession, the big globe of Zarathustra that Henry Stenson had built for him, supported six feet from the floor on its own contragravity unit, spotlighted in orange to represent the KO sun, its two satellites circling about it as it revolved slowly.

"The globe itself is keeping perfect time, and Darius is all right, Xerxes is a few seconds of longitude ahead of true position."

"That's dreadful, Mr. Grego!" Stenson was deeply shocked. "I must adjust that the first thing tomorrow. I should have called to check on it long ago, but you know how it is. So many things to do, and so little time."

"I find the same trouble myself, Mr. Stenson." They chatted for a while, and then Stenson apologized for taking up so much of Mr. Grego's valuable time. What he meant was that his own time, just as valuable to him, was wasting. After the screen blanked, Grego sat looking at it for a moment, wishing he had a hundred men like Henry Stenson in his own organization. Just men with Stenson's brains and character; wishing for a hundred instrument makers with Stenson's skills would have been unreasonable, even for wishing. There was only one Henry Stenson, just as there had been only one Antonio Stradivari. Why a man like that worked in a little shop on a frontier planet like Zarathustra....

Then he looked, pridefully, at the globe. Alpha Continent had moved slowly to the right, with the little speck that represented Mallorysport twinkling in the orange light. Darius, the inner moon, where the Terra-Baldur-Marduk Spacelines had their leased terminal, was almost directly over it, and the other moon, Xerxes, was edging into sight. Xerxes was the one thing about Zarathustra that the Company didn't own; the Terran Federation had retained that as a naval base. It was the one reminder that there was something bigger and more powerful than the Company.

Gerd van Riebeek saw Ruth Ortheris leave the escalator, step aside and stand looking around the cocktail lounge. He set his glass, with its inch of tepid highball, on the bar; when her eyes shifted in his direction, he waved to her, saw her brighten and wave back and then went to meet her. She gave him a quick kiss on the cheek, dodged when he reached for her and took his arm.

"Drink before we eat?" he asked.

"Oh, Lord, yes! I've just about had it for today."

He guided her toward one of the bartending machines, inserted his credit key, and put a four-portion jug under the spout, dialing the cocktail they always had when they drank together. As he did, he noticed what she was wearing: short black jacket, lavender neckerchief, light gray skirt. Not her usual vacation get-up.

"School department drag you back?" he asked as the jug filled.

"Juvenile court." She got a couple of glasses from the shelf under the machine as he picked up the jug. "A fifteen-year-old burglar."

They found a table at the rear of the room, out of the worst of the cocktail-hour uproar. As soon as he filled her glass, she drank half of it, then lit a cigarette.

"Junktown?" he asked.

She nodded. "Only twenty-five years since this planet was discovered, and we have slums already. I was over there most of the afternoon, with a pair of city police." She didn't seem to want to talk about it. "What were you doing today?"

"Ruth, you ought to ask Doc Mallin to drop in on Leonard Kellogg sometime, and give him an unobstusive going over."

"You haven't been having trouble with him again?" she asked anxiously.

He made a face, and then tasted his drink. "It's trouble just being around that character. Ruth, to use one of those expressions your profession deplores, Len Kellogg is just plain nuts!" He drank some more of his cocktail and helped himself to one of her cigarettes. "Here," he continued, after lighting it. "A couple of days ago, he told me he'd been getting inquiries about this plague of land-prawns they're having over on Beta. He wanted me to set up a research project to find out why and what to do about it."

"Well?"

"I did. I made two screen calls, and then I wrote a report and sent it up to him. That was where I jerked my trigger; I ought to have taken a couple of weeks and made a real production out of it."

"What did you tell him?"

"The facts. The limiting factor on land-prawn increase is the weather. The eggs hatch underground and the immature prawns dig their way out in the spring. If there's been a lot of rain, most of them drown in their holes or as soon as they emerge. According to growth rings on trees, last spring was the driest in the Beta Piedmont in centuries, so most of them survived, and as they're parthenogenetic females, they all laid eggs. This spring, it was even drier, so now they have land prawns all over central Beta. And I don't know that anything can be done about them."

"Well, did he think you were just guessing?"

He shook his head in exasperation. "I don't know what he thinks. You're the psychologist, you try to figure it. I sent him that report yesterday morning. He seemed quite satisfied with it at the time. Today, just after noon, he sent for me and told me it wouldn't do at all. Tried to insist that the rainfall on Beta had been normal. That was silly; I referred him to his meteorologists and climatologists, where I'd gotten my information. He complained that the news services were after him for an explanation. I told him I'd given him the only explanation there was. He said he simply couldn't use it. There had to be some other explanation."

"If you don't like the facts, you ignore them, and if you need facts, dream up some you do like," she said. "That's typical rejection of reality. Not psychotic, not even psychoneurotic. But certainly not sane." She had finished her first drink and was sipping slowly at her second. "You know, this is interesting. Does he have some theory that would disqualify yours?"

"Not that I know of. I got the impression that he just didn't want the subject of rainfall on Beta discussed at all."

"That is odd. Has anything else peculiar been happening over on Beta lately?"

"No. Not that I know of," he repeated. "Of course, that swamp-drainage project over there was what caused the dry weather, last year and this year, but I don't see...." His own glass was empty, and when he tilted the jug over it, a few drops trickled out. He looked at his watch. "Think we could have another cocktail before dinner?" he asked.

II

Jack Holloway landed the manipulator in front of the cluster of prefab huts. For a moment he sat still, realizing that he was tired, and then he climbed down from the control cabin and crossed the open grass to the door of the main living hut, opening it and reaching in to turn on the lights. Then he hesitated, looking up at Darius.

There was a wide ring around it, and he remembered noticing the wisps of cirrus clouds gathering overhead through the afternoon. Maybe it would rain tonight. This dry weather couldn't last forever. He'd been letting the manipulator stand out overnight lately. He decided to put it in the hangar. He went and opened the door of the vehicle shed, got back onto the machine and floated it inside. When he came back to the living hut, he saw that he had left the door wide open.

"Damn fool!" he rebuked himself. "Place could be crawling with prawns by now."

He looked quickly around the living room-under the big combination desk and library table, under the gunrack, under the chairs, back of the communication screen and the viewscreen, beyond the metal cabinet of the microfilm library-and saw nothing. Then he hung up his hat, took off his pistol and laid it on the table, and went back to the bathroom to wash his hands.

As soon as he put on the light, something inside the shower stall said, "*Yeeeek!*" in a startled voice.

He turned quickly to see two wide eyes staring up at him out of a ball of golden fur. Whatever it was, it had a round head and big ears and a vaguely humanoid face with a little snub nose. It was sitting on its haunches, and in that position it was about a foot high. It had two tiny hands with opposing thumbs. He squatted to have a better look at it.

"Hello there, little fellow," he greeted it. "I never saw anything like you before. What are you anyhow?"

The small creature looked at him seriously and said, "Yeek," in a timid voice.

"Why, sure; you're a Little Fuzzy, that's what you are."

He moved closer, careful to make no alarmingly sudden movements, and kept on talking to it.

"Bet you slipped in while I left the door open. Well, if a Little Fuzzy finds a door open, I'd like to know why he shouldn't come in and look around."

He touched it gently. It started to draw back, then reached out a little hand and felt the material of his shirt-sleeve. He stroked it, and told it that it had the softest, silkiest fur ever. Then he took it on his lap. It yeeked in pleasure, and stretched an arm up around his neck.

"Why, sure; we're going to be good friends, aren't we? Would you like something to eat? Well, suppose you and I go see what we can find."

He put one hand under it, to support it like a baby-at least, he seemed to recall having seen babies supported in that way; babies were things he didn't fool with if he could help it-and straightened. It weighed between fifteen and twenty pounds. At first, it struggled in panic, then quieted and seemed to enjoy being carried. In the living room he sat down in his favorite armchair, under a standing lamp, and examined his new acquaintance.

It was a mammal-there was a fairly large mammalian class on Zarathustra-but beyond that he was stumped. It wasn't a primate, in the Terran sense. It wasn't like anything Terran, or anything else on Zarathustra. Being a biped put it in a class by itself for this planet. It was just a Little Fuzzy, and that was the best he could do.

That sort of nomenclature was the best anybody could do on a Class-III planet. On a Class-IV planet, say Loki, or Shesha, or Thor, naming animals was a cinch. You pointed to something and asked a native, and he'd gargle a mouthful of syllables at you, which might only mean, "Whaddaya wanna know for?" and you took it down in phonetic alphabet and the whatzit had a name. But on Zarathustra, there were no natives to ask. So this was a Little Fuzzy.

"What would you like to eat, Little Fuzzy?" he asked. "Open your mouth, and let Pappy Jack see what you have to chew with."

Little Fuzzy's dental equipment, allowing for the fact that his jaw was rounder, was very much like his own.

"You're probably omnivorous. How would you like some nice Terran Federation Space Forces Emergency Ration, Extraterrestrial, Type Three?" he asked.

Little Fuzzy made what sounded like an expression of willingness to try it. It would be safe enough; Extee Three had been fed to a number of Zarathustran mammals without ill effects. He carried Little Fuzzy out into the kitchen and put him on the floor, then got out a tin of the field ration and opened it, breaking off a small piece and handing it down. Little Fuzzy took the piece of golden-brown cake, sniffed at it, gave a delighted yeek and crammed the whole piece in his mouth.

"You never had to live on that stuff and nothing else for a month, that's for sure!"

He broke the cake in half and broke one half into manageable pieces and put it down on a saucer. Maybe Little Fuzzy would want a drink, too. He started to fill a pan with water, as he would for a dog, then looked at his visitor sitting on his haunches eating with both hands and changed his mind. He rinsed a plastic cup cap from an empty whisky bottle and put it down beside a deep bowl of water. Little Fuzzy was thirsty, and he didn't have to be shown what the cup was for.

It was too late to get himself anything elaborate; he found some leftovers in the refrigerator and combined them into a stew. While it was heating, he sat down at the kitchen table and lit his pipe. The spurt of flame from the lighter opened Little Fuzzy's eyes, but what really awed him was Pappy Jack blowing smoke. He sat watching this phenomenon, until, a few minutes later, the stew was hot and the pipe was laid aside; then Little Fuzzy went back to nibbling Extee Three.

Suddenly he gave a yeek of petulance and scampered into the living room. In a moment, he was back with something elongated and metallic which he laid on the floor beside him.

"What have you got there, Little Fuzzy? Let Pappy Jack see?"

Then he recognized it as his own one-inch wood chisel. He remembered leaving it in the outside shed after doing some work about a week ago, and not being able to find it when he had gone to look for it. That had worried him; people who got absent-minded about equipment didn't last long in the wilderness. After he finished eating and took the dishes to the sink, he went over and squatted beside his new friend.

"Let Pappy Jack look at it, Little Fuzzy," he said. "Oh, I'm not going to take it away from you. I just want to see it."

The edge was dulled and nicked; it had been used for a lot of things wood chisels oughtn't to be used for. Digging, and prying, and most likely, it had been used as a weapon. It was a handy-sized, all-purpose tool for a Little Fuzzy. He laid it on the floor where he had gotten it and started washing the dishes.

Little Fuzzy watched him with interest for a while, and then he began investigating the kitchen. Some of the things he wanted to investigate had to be taken away from him; at first that angered him, but he soon learned that there were things he wasn't supposed to have. Eventually, the dishes got washed.

There were more things to investigate in the living room. One of them was the wastebasket. He found that it could be dumped, and promptly dumped it, pulling out everything that hadn't fallen out. He bit a corner off a sheet of paper, chewed on it and spat it out in disgust. Then he found that crumpled paper could be flattened out and so he flattened a few sheets, and then discovered that it could also be folded. Then he got himself gleefully tangled in a snarl of wornout recording tape. Finally he lost interest and started away. Jack caught him and brought him back.

"No, Little Fuzzy," he said. "You do not dump wastebaskets and then walk away from them. You put things back in." He touched the container and said, slowly and distinctly, "Waste… basket." Then he righted it, doing it as Little Fuzzy would have to, and picked up a piece of paper, tossing it in from Little Fuzzy's shoulder height. Then he handed Little Fuzzy a wad of paper and repeated, "Waste… basket."

Little Fuzzy looked at him and said something that sounded as though it might be: "What's the matter with you, Pappy; you crazy or something?" After a couple more tries, however, he got it, and began throwing things in. In a few minutes, he had everything back in except a brightly colored plastic cartridge box and a wide-mouthed bottle with a screw cap. He held these up and said, "Yeek?"

"Yes, you can have them. Here; let Pappy Jack show you something."

He showed Little Fuzzy how the box could be opened and shut. Then, holding it where Little Fuzzy could watch, he unscrewed the cap and then screwed it on again.

"There, now. You try it."

Little Fuzzy looked up inquiringly, then took the bottle, sitting down and holding it between his knees. Unfortunately, he tried twisting it the wrong way and only screwed the cap on tighter. He yeeked plaintively.

"No, go ahead. You can do it."

Little Fuzzy looked at the bottle again. Then he tried twisting the cap the other way, and it loosened. He gave a yeek that couldn't possibly be anything but "Eureka!" and promptly took it off, holding it up. After being commended, he examined both the bottle and the cap, feeling the threads, and then screwed the cap back on again.

"You know, you're a smart Little Fuzzy." It took a few seconds to realize just how smart. Little Fuzzy had wondered why you twisted the cap one way to take it off and the other way to put it on, and he had found out. For pure reasoning ability, that topped anything in the way of animal intelligence he'd ever seen. "I'm going to tell Ben Rainsford about you."

Going to the communication screen, he punched out the wave-length combination of the naturalist's camp, seventy miles down Snake River from the mouth of Cold Creek. Rainsford's screen must have been on automatic; it lit as soon as he was through punching. There was a card set up in front of it, lettered: AWAY ON TRIP, BACK THE FIFTEENTH. RECORDER ON.

"Ben, Jack Holloway," he said. "I just ran into something interesting." He explained briefly what it was. "I hope he stays around till you get back. He's totally unlike anything I've ever seen on this planet."

Little Fuzzy was disappointed when Jack turned off the screen; that had been interesting. He picked him up and carried him over to the armchair, taking him on his lap.

"Now," he said, reaching for the control panel of the viewscreen. "Watch this; we're going to see something nice."

When he put on the screen, at random, he got a view, from close up, of the great fires that were raging where the Company people were burning off the dead forests on what used to be Big Blackwater Swamp. Little Fuzzy cried out in alarm, flung his arms around Pappy Jack's neck and buried his face in the bosom of his shirt. Well, forest fires started from lightning sometimes, and they'd be bad things for a Little Fuzzy. He worked the selector and got another pickup, this time on the top of Company House in Mallorysport, three time zones west, with the city spread out below and the sunset blazing in the west. Little Fuzzy stared at it in wonder. It was pretty impressive for a little fellow who'd spent all his life in the big woods.

So was the spaceport, and a lot of other things he saw, though a view of the planet as a whole from Darius puzzled him considerably. Then, in the middle of a symphony orchestra concert from Mallorysport Opera House, he wriggled loose, dropped to the floor and caught up his wood chisel, swinging it back over his shoulder like a two-handed sword.

"What the devil? Oh-oh!"

A land-prawn, which must have gotten in while the door was open, was crossing the living room. Little Fuzzy ran after and past it, pivoted and brought the corner of the chisel edge down on the prawn's neck, neatly beheading it. He looked at his victim for a moment, then slid the chisel under it and flopped it over on its back, slapping it twice with the flat and cracking the undershell. The he began pulling the dead prawn apart, tearing out pieces of meat and eating them delicately. After disposing of the larger chunks, he used the chisel to chop off one of the prawn's mandibles to use as a pick to get at the less accessible morsels. When he had finished, he licked his fingers clean and started back to the armchair.

"No." Jack pointed at the prawn shell. "Wastebasket."

"Yeek?"

"Wastebasket."

Little Fuzzy gathered up the bits of shell, putting them where they belonged. Then he came back and climbed up on Pappy Jack's lap, and looked at things in the screen until he fell asleep.

Jack lifted him carefully and put him down on the warm chair seat without wakening him, then went to the kitchen, poured himself a drink and brought it in to the big table, where he lit his pipe and began writing up his diary for the day. After a while, Little Fuzzy woke, found that the lap he had gone to sleep on had vanished, and yeeked disconsolately.

A folded blanket in one corner of the bedroom made a satisfactory bed, once Little Fuzzy had assured himself that there were no bugs in it. He brought in his bottle and his plastic box and put them on the floor beside it. Then he ran to the front door in the living room and yeeked to be let out. Going about twenty feet from the house, he used the chisel to dig a small hole, and after it had served its purpose he filled it in carefully and came running back.

Well, maybe Fuzzies were naturally gregarious, and were homemakers-den-holes, or nests, or something like that. Nobody wants messes made in the house, and when the young ones did it, their parents would bang them around to teach them better manners. This was Little Fuzzy's home now; he knew how he ought to behave in it.

The next morning at daylight, he was up on the bed, trying to dig Pappy Jack out from under the blankets. Besides being a most efficient land-prawn eradicator, he made a first rate alarm clock. But best of all, he was Pappy Jack's Little Fuzzy. He wanted out; this time Jack took his movie camera and got the whole operation on film. One thing, there'd have to be a little door, with a spring to hold it shut, that little Fuzzy could operate himself. That was designed during breakfast. It only took a couple of hours to make and install it; Little Fuzzy got the idea as soon as he saw it, and figured out how to work it for himself.

Jack went back to the workshop, built a fire on the hand forge and forged a pointed and rather broad blade, four inches long, on the end of a foot of quarter-inch round tool-steel. It was too point-heavy when finished, so he welded a knob on the other end to balance it. Little Fuzzy knew what that was for right away; running outside, he dug a couple of practice holes with it, and then began casting about in the grass for land-prawns.

Jack followed him with the camera and got movies of a couple of prawn killings, accomplished with smooth, by-the-numbers precision. Little Fuzzy hadn't learned that chop-clap-clap routine in the week since he had found the wood chisel.

Going into the shed, he hunted for something without more than a general idea of what it would look like, and found it where Little Fuzzy had discarded it when he found the chisel. It was a stock of hardwood a foot long, rubbed down and polished smooth, apparently with sandstone. There was a paddle at one end, with enough of an edge to behead a prawn, and the other end had been worked to a point. He took it into the living hut and sat down at the desk to examine it with a magnifying glass. Bits of soil embedded in the sharp end-that had been used as a pick. The paddle end had been used as a shovel, beheader and shell-cracker. Little Fuzzy had known exactly what he wanted when he'd started making that thing, he'd kept on until it was as perfect as possible, and had stopped short of spoiling it by overrefinement.

Finally, Jack put it away in the top drawer of the desk. He was thinking about what to get for lunch when Little Fuzzy burst into the living room, clutching his new weapon and yeeking excitedly.

"What's the matter, kid? You got troubles?" He rose and went to the gunrack, picking down a rifle and checking the chamber. "Show Pappy Jack what it is."

Little Fuzzy followed him to the big door for human-type people, ready to bolt back inside if necessary.

The trouble was a harpy—a thing about the size and general design of a Terran Jurassic pterodactyl, big enough to take a Little Fuzzy at one mouthful. It must have made one swoop at him already, and was circling back for another. It ran into a 6-mm rifle bullet, went into a backward loop and dropped like a stone.

Little Fuzzy made a very surprised remark, looked at the dead harpy for a moment and then spotted the ejected empty cartridge. He grabbed it and held it up, asking if he could have it. When told that he could, he ran back to the bedroom with it. When he returned, Pappy Jack picked him up and carried him to the hangar and up into the control cabin of the manipulator.

The throbbing of the contragravity-field generator and the sense of rising worried him at first, but after they had picked up the harpy with the grapples and risen to five hundred feet he began to enjoy the ride. They dropped the harpy a couple of miles up what the latest maps were designating as Holloway's Run, and then made a wide circle back over the mountains. Little Fuzzy thought it was fun.

After lunch, Little Fuzzy had a nap on Pappy Jack's bed. Jack took the manipulator up to the diggings, put off a couple more shots, uncovered more flint and found another sunstone. It wasn't often that he found stones on two successive days. When he returned to the camp, Little Fuzzy was picking another land-prawn apart in front of the living hut.

After dinner-Little Fuzzy liked cooked food, too, if it wasn't too hot-they went into the living room. He remembered having seen a bolt and nut in the desk drawer when he had been putting the wooden prawn-killer away, and he got it out, showing it to Little Fuzzy. Little Fuzzy studied it for a moment, then ran into the bedroom and came back with his screw-top bottle. He took the top off, put it on again and then screwed the nut off the bolt, holding it up.

"See, Pappy?" Or yeeks to that effect. "Nothing to it."

Then he unscrewed the bottle top, dropped the bolt inside after replacing the nut and screwed the cap on again.

"Yeek," he said, with considerable self-satisfaction.

He had a right to be satisfied with himself. What he'd been doing had been generalizing. Bottle tops and nuts belonged to the general class of things-that-screwed-onto-things. To take them off, you turned left; to put them on again, you turned right, after making sure that the threads engaged. And since he could conceive of right- and left-handedness, that might mean that he could think of properties apart from objects, and that was forming abstract ideas. Maybe that was going a little far, but....

"You know, Pappy Jack's got himself a mighty smart Little Fuzzy. Are you a grown-up Little Fuzzy, or are you just a baby Little Fuzzy? Shucks, I'll bet you're Professor Doctor Fuzzy."

He wondered what to give the professor, if that was what he was, to work on next, and he doubted the wisdom of teaching him too much about taking things apart, just at present. Sometime he might come home and find something important taken apart, or, worse, taken apart and put together incorrectly. Finally, he went to a closet, rummaging in it until he found a tin canister. By the time he returned, Little Fuzzy had gotten up on the chair, found his pipe in the ashtray and was puffing on it and coughing.

"Hey, I don't think that's good for you!"

He recovered the pipe, wiped the stem on his shirt-sleeve and put it in his mouth, then placed the canister on the floor, and put Little Fuzzy on the floor beside it. There were about ten pounds of stones in it. When he had first settled here, he had made a collection of the local minerals, and, after learning what he'd wanted to, he had thrown them out, all but twenty or thirty of the prettiest specimens. He was glad, now, that he had kept these.

Little Fuzzy looked the can over, decided that the lid was a member of the class of things-that-screwed-onto-things and got it off. The inside of the lid was mirror-shiny, and it took him a little thought to discover that what he saw in it was only himself. He yeeked about that, and looked into the can. This, he decided, belonged to the class of things-that-can-be-dumped, like wastebaskets, so he dumped it on the floor. Then he began examining the stones and sorting them by color.

Except for an interest in colorful views on the screen, this was the first real evidence that Fuzzies possessed color perception. He proceeded to give further and more impressive proof, laying out the stones by shade, in correct spectral order, from a lump of amethystlike quartz to a dark red stone. Well, maybe he'd seen rainbows. Maybe he'd lived near a big misty waterfall, where there was always a rainbow when the sun was shining. Or maybe that was just his natural way of seeing colors.

Then, when he saw what he had to work with, he began making arrangements with them, laying them out in odd circular and spiral patterns. Each time he finished a pattern, he would yeek happily to call attention to it, sit and look at it for a while, and then take it apart and start a new one. Little Fuzzy was capable of artistic gratification too. He made useless things, just for the pleasure of making and looking at them.

Finally, he put the stones back into the tin, put the lid on and rolled it into the bedroom, righting it beside his bed along with his other treasures. The new weapon he laid on the blanket beside him when he went to bed.

The next morning, Jack broke up a whole cake of Extee Three and put it down, filled the bowl with water, and, after making sure he had left nothing lying around that Little Fuzzy could damage or on which he might hurt himself, took the manipulator up to the diggings. He worked all morning, cracking nearly a ton and a half of flint, and found nothing. Then he set off a string of shots, brought down an avalanche of sandstone and exposed more flint, and sat down under a pool-ball tree to eat his lunch.

Half an hour after he went back to work, he found the fossil of some jellyfish that hadn't eaten the right things in the right combinations, but a little later, he found four nodules, one after another, and two of them were sunstones; four or five chunks later, he found a third. Why, this must be the Dying Place of the Jellyfish! By late afternoon, when he had cleaned up all his loose flint, he had nine, including one deep red monster an inch in diameter. There must have been some convection current in the ancient ocean that had swirled them all into this one place. He considered setting off some more shots, decided that it was too late and returned to camp.

"Little Fuzzy!" he called, opening the living-room door. "Where are you, Little Fuzzy? Pappy Jack's rich; we're going to celebrate!"

Silence. He called again; still no reply or scamper of feet. Probably cleaned up all the prawns around the camp and went hunting farther out into the woods, thought Jack. Unbuckling his gun and dropping it onto the table, he went out to the kitchen. Most of the Extee Three was gone. In the bedroom, he found that Little Fuzzy had dumped the stones out of the biscuit tin and made an arrangement, and laid the wood chisel in a neat diagonal across the blanket.

After getting dinner assembled and in the oven, he went out and called for a while, then mixed a highball and took it into the living room, sitting down with it to go over his day's findings. Rather incredulously, he realized that he had cracked out at least seventy-five thousand sols' worth of stones today. He put them into the bag and sat sipping the highball and thinking pleasant thoughts until the bell on the stove warned him that dinner was ready.

He ate alone-after all the years he had been doing that contentedly, it had suddenly become intolerable-and in the evening he dialed through his micro-film library, finding only books he had read and reread a dozen times, or books he kept for reference. Several times he thought he heard the little door open, but each time he was mistaken. Finally he went to bed.

As soon as he woke, he looked across at the folded blanket, but the wood chisel was still lying athwart it. He put down more Extee Three and changed the water in the bowl before leaving for the diggings. That day he found three more sunstones, and put them in the bag mechanically and without pleasure. He quit work early and spent over an hour spiraling around the camp, but saw nothing. The Extee Three in the kitchen was untouched.

Maybe the little fellow ran into something too big for him, even with his fine new weapon —a hobthrush, or a bush-goblin, or another harpy. Or maybe he'd just gotten tired staying in one place, and had moved on.

No; he'd liked it here. He'd had fun, and been happy. He shook his head sadly. Once he, too, had lived in a pleasant place, where he'd had fun, and could have been happy if he hadn't thought there was something he'd had to do. So he had gone away, leaving grieved people behind him. Maybe that was how it was with Little Fuzzy. Maybe he didn't realize how much of a place he had made for himself here, or how empty he was leaving it.

He started for the kitchen to get a drink, and checked himself. Take a drink because you pity yourself, and then the drink pities you and has a drink, and then two good drinks get together and that calls for drinks all around. No; he'd have one drink, maybe a little bigger than usual, before he went to bed.

He started awake, rubbed his eyes and looked at the clock. Past twenty-two hundred; now it really was time for a drink, and then to bed. He rose stiffly and went out to the kitchen, pouring the whisky and bringing it in to the table desk, where he sat down and got out his diary. He was almost finished with the day's entry when the little door behind him opened and a small voice said, "Yeeek." He turned quickly.

"Little Fuzzy?"

The small sound was repeated, impatiently. Little Fuzzy was holding the door open, and there was an answer from outside. Then another Fuzzy came in, and another; four of them, one carrying a tiny, squirming ball of white fur in her arms. They all had prawn-killers like the one in the drawer, and they stopped just inside the room and gaped about them in bewilderment. Then, laying down his weapon, Little Fuzzy ran to him; stooping from the chair, he caught him and then sat down on the floor with him.

"So that's why you ran off and worried Pappy Jack? You wanted your family here, too!"

The others piled the things they were carrying with Little Fuzzy's steel weapon and approached hesitantly. He talked to them, and so did Little Fuzzy-at least it sounded like that-and finally one came over and fingered his shirt, and then reached up and pulled his mustache. Soon all of them were climbing onto him, even the female with the baby. It was small enough to sit on his palm, but in a minute it had climbed to his shoulder, and then it was sitting on his head.

"You people want dinner?" he asked.

Little Fuzzy yeeked emphatically; that was a word he recognized. He took them all into the kitchen and tried them on cold roast veldbeest and yummiyams and fried pool-ball fruit; while they were eating from a couple of big pans, he went back to the living room to examine the things they had brought with them. Two of the prawn-killers were wood, like the one Little Fuzzy had discarded in the shed. A third was of horn, beautifully polished, and the fourth looked as though it had been made from the shoulder bone of something like a zebralope. Then there was a small *coup de poing* ax, rather low paleolithic, and a chipped implement of flint the shape of a slice of orange and about five inches along the straight edge. For a hand the size of his own, he would have called it a scraper. He puzzled over it for a while, noticed that the edge was serrated, and decided that it was a saw. And there were three very good flake knives, and some shells, evidently drinking vessels.

Mamma Fuzzy came in while he was finishing the examination. She seemed suspicious, until she saw that none of the family property had been taken or damaged. Baby Fuzzy was clinging to her fur with one hand and holding a slice of pool-ball fruit, on which he was munching, with the other. He crammed what was left of the fruit into his mouth, climbed up on Jack and sat down on his head again. Have to do something to break him of that. One of these days, he'd be getting too big for it.

In a few minutes, the rest of the family came in, chasing and pummeling each other and yeeking happily. Mamma jumped off his lap and joined the free-for-all, and then Baby took off from his head and landed on Mamma's back. And he thought he'd lost his Little Fuzzy, and, gosh, here he had five Fuzzies and a Baby Fuzzy. When they were tired romping, he made beds for them in the living room, and brought out Little Fuzzy's bedding and his treasures. One Little Fuzzy in the bedroom was just fine; five and a Baby Fuzzy were a little too much of a good thing.

They were swarming over the bed, Baby and all, to waken him the next morning.

The next morning he made a steel chopper-digger for each of them, and half a dozen extras for replacements in case more Fuzzies showed up. He also made a miniature ax with a hardwood handle, a handsaw out of a piece of broken power-saw blade and half a dozen little knives forged in one piece from quarter-inch coil-spring material. He had less trouble trading the Fuzzies' own things away from them than he had expected. They had a very keen property sense, but they knew a good deal when one was offered. He put the wooden and horn and bone and stone artifacts away in the desk drawer. Start of the Holloway Collection of Zarathustran Fuzzy Weapons and Implements. Maybe he'd will it to the Federation Institute of Xeno-Sciences.

Of course, the family had to try out the new chopper-diggers on land-prawns, and he followed them around with the movie camera. They killed a dozen and a half that morning, and there was very little interest in lunch, though they did sit around nibbling, just to be doing what he was doing. As soon as they finished, they all went in for a nap on his bed. He spent the afternoon pottering about camp doing odd jobs that he had been postponing for months. The Fuzzies all emerged in the late afternoon for a romp in the grass outside.

He was in the kitchen, getting dinner, when they all came pelting in through the little door into the living room, making an excited outcry. Little Fuzzy and one of the other males came into the kitchen. Little Fuzzy squatted, put one hand on his lower jaw, with thumb and little finger extended, and the other on his forehead, first finger upright. Then he thrust out his right arm stiffly and made a barking noise of a sort he had never made before. He had to do it a second time before Jack got it.

There was a large and unpleasant carnivore, called a damnthing-another example of zoological nomenclature on uninhabited planets-which had a single horn on its forehead and one on either side of the lower jaw. It was something for Fuzzies, and even for human-type people, to get excited about. He laid down the paring knife and the yummiyam he had been peeling, wiped his hands and went into the living room, taking a quick nose count and satisfying himself that none of the family were missing as he crossed to the gunrack.

This time, instead of the 6-mm he had used on the harpy, he lifted down a big 12.7 double express, making sure that it was loaded and pocketing a few spare rounds. Little Fuzzy followed him outside, pointing around the living hut to the left. The rest of the family stayed indoors.

Stepping out about twenty feet, he started around counter-clockwise. There was no damnthing on the north side, and he was about to go around to the east side when Little Fuzzy came dashing past him, pointing to the rear. He whirled, to see the damnthing charging him from behind, head down, and middle horn lowered. He should have thought of that; damnthings would double and hunt their hunters.

He lined the sights instinctively and squeezed. The big rifle roared and banged his shoulder, and the bullet caught the damnthing and hurled all half-ton of it backward. The second shot caught it just below one of the fungoid-looking ears, and the beast gave a spasmodic all-over twitch and was still. He reloaded mechanically, but there was no need for a third shot. The damnthing was as dead as he would have been except for Little Fuzzy's warning.

He mentioned that to Little Fuzzy, who was calmly retrieving the empty cartridges. Then, rubbing his shoulder where the big rifle had pounded him, he went in and returned the weapon to the rack. He used the manipulator to carry the damnthing away from the camp and drop it into a treetop, where it would furnish a welcome if puzzling treat for the harpies.

There was another alarm in the evening after dinner. The family had come in from their sunset romp and were gathered in the living room, where Little Fuzzy was demonstrating the principle of things-that-screwed-onto-things with the wide-mouthed bottle and the bolt and nut, when something huge began hooting directly overhead. They all froze, looking up at the ceiling, and then ran over and got under the gunrack. This must be something far more serious than a damnthing, and what Pappy Jack would do about it would be nothing short of catastrophic. They were startled to see Pappy Jack merely go to the door, open it and step outside. After all, none of them had ever heard a Constabulary aircar klaxon before.

The car settled onto the grass in front of the camp, gave a slight lurch and went off contragravity. Two men in uniform got out, and in the moonlight he recognized both of them: Lieutenant George Lunt and his driver, Ahmed Khadra. He called a greeting to them.

"Anything wrong?" he asked.

"No; just thought we'd drop in and see how you were making out," Lunt told him. "We don't get up this way often. Haven't had any trouble lately, have you?"

"Not since the last time." The last time had been a couple of woods tramps, out-of-work veldbeest herders from the south, who had heard about the little bag he carried around his neck. All the Constabulary had needed to do was remove the bodies and write up a report. "Come on in and hang up your guns awhile. I have something I want to show you."

Little Fuzzy had come out and was pulling at his trouser leg; he stooped and picked him up, setting him on his shoulder. The rest of the family, deciding that it must be safe, had come to the door and were looking out.

"Hey! What the devil are those things?" Lunt asked, stopping short halfway from the car.

"Fuzzies. Mean to tell me you've never seen Fuzzies before?"

"No, I haven't. What are they?"

The two Constabulary men came closer, and Jack stepped back into the house, shooing the Fuzzies out of the way. Lunt and Khadra stopped inside the door.

"I just told you. They're Fuzzies. That's all the name I know for them."

A couple of Fuzzies came over and looked up at Lieutenant Lunt; one of them said, "Yeek?"

"They want to know what you are, so that makes it mutual."

Lunt hesitated for a moment, then took off his belt and holster and hung it on one of the pegs inside the door, putting his beret over it. Khadra followed his example promptly. That meant that they considered themselves temporarily off duty and would accept a drink if one were offered. A Fuzzy was pulling at Ahmed Khadra's trouser leg and asking to be noticed, and Mamma Fuzzy was holding Baby up to show to Lunt. Khadra, rather hesitantly, picked up the Fuzzy who was trying to attract his attention.

"Never saw anything like them before, Jack," he said. "Where did they come from?"

"Ahmed; you don't know anything about those things," Lunt reproved.

"They won't hurt me, Lieutenant; they haven't hurt Jack, have they?" He sat down on the floor, and a couple more came to him. "Why don't you get acquainted with them? They're cute."

George Lunt wouldn't let one of his men do anything he was afraid to do; he sat down on the floor, too, and Mamma brought her baby to him. Immediately, the baby jumped onto his shoulder and tried to get onto his head.

"Relax, George," Jack told him, "They're just Fuzzies; they want to make friends with you."

"I'm always worried about strange life forms," Lunt said. "You've been around enough to know some of the things that have happened —"

"They are not a strange life form; they are Zarathustran mammals. The same life form you've had for dinner every day since you came here. Their biochemistry's identical with ours. Think they'll give you the Polka-Dot Plague, or something?" He put Little Fuzzy down on the floor with the others. "We've been exploring this planet for twenty-five years, and nobody's found anything like that here."

"You said it yourself, Lieutenant," Khadra put in. "Jack's been around enough to know."

"Well.... They are cute little fellows." Lunt lifted Baby down off his head and gave him back to Mamma. Little Fuzzy had gotten hold of the chain of his whistle and was trying to find out what was on the other end. "Bet they're a lot of company for you."

"You just get acquainted with them. Make yourselves at home; I'll go rustle up some refreshments."

While he was in the kitchen, filling a soda siphon and getting ice out of the refrigerator, a police whistle began shrilling in the living room. He was opening a bottle of whisky when Little Fuzzy came dashing out, blowing on it, a couple more of the family pursuing him and trying to get it away from him. He opened a tin of Extee Three for the Fuzzies, as he did, another whistle in the living room began blowing.

"We have a whole shoebox full of them at the post," Lunt yelled to him above the din. "We'll just write these two off as expended in service."

"Well, that's real nice of you, George. I want to tell you that the Fuzzies appreciate that. Ahmed, suppose you do the bartending while I give the kids their candy."

By the time Khadra had the drinks mixed and he had distributed the Extee Three to the Fuzzies, Lunt had gotten into the easy chair, and the Fuzzies were sitting on the floor in front of him, still looking him over curiously. At least the Extee Three had taken their minds off the whistles for a while.

"What I want to know, Jack, is where they came from," Lunt said, taking his drink. "I've been up here for five years, and I never saw anything like them before."

"I've been here five years longer, and I never saw them before, either. I think they came down from the north, from the country between the Cordilleras and the West Coast Range. Outside of an air survey at ten thousand feet and a few spot landings here and there, none of that country has been explored. For all anybody knows, it could be full of Fuzzies."

He began with his first encounter with Little Fuzzy, and by the time he had gotten as far as the wood chisel and the killing of the land-prawn, Lunt and Khadra were looking at each other in amazement.

"That's it!" Khadra said. "I've found prawn-shells cracked open and the meat picked out, just the way you describe it. I always wondered what did that. But they don't all have wood chisels. What do you suppose they used ordinarily?"

"Ah!" He pulled the drawer open and began getting things out. "Here's the one Little Fuzzy discarded when he found my chisel. The rest of this stuff the others brought in when they came."

Lunt and Khadra rose and came over to look at the things. Lunt tried to argue that the Fuzzies couldn't have made that stuff. He wasn't even able to convince himself. Having finished their Extee Three, the Fuzzies were looking expectantly at the viewscreen, and it occurred to him that none of them except Little Fuzzy had ever seen it on. Then Little Fuzzy jumped up on the chair Lunt had vacated, reached over to the control-panel and switched it on. What he got was an empty stretch of moonlit plain to the south, from a pickup on one of the steel towers the veldbeest herders used. That wasn't very interesting; he twiddled the selector and finally got a night soccer game at Mallorysport. That was just fine; he jumped down and joined the others in front of the screen.

"I've seen Terran monkeys and Freyan Kholphs that liked to watch screens and could turn them on and work the selector," Lunt said. It sounded like the token last salvo before the surrender.

"Kholphs are smart," Khadra agreed. "They use tools."

"Do they make tools? Or tools to make tools with, like that saw?" There was no argument on that. "No. Nobody does that except people like us and the Fuzzies."

It was the first time he had come right out and said that; the first time he had even consciously thought it. He realized that he had been convinced of it all along, though. It startled the constabulary lieutenant and trooper.

"You mean you think —?" Lunt began.

"They don't talk, and they don't build fires," Ahmed Khadra said, as though that settled it.

"Ahmed, you know better than that. That talk-and-build-a-fire rule isn't any scientific test at all."

"It's a legal test." Lunt supported his subordinate.

"It's a rule-of-thumb that was set up so that settlers on new planets couldn't get away with murdering and enslaving the natives by claiming they thought they were only hunting and do-mesticating wild animals," he said. "Anything that talks and builds a fire is a sapient being, yes. That's the law. But that doesn't mean that anything that doesn't isn't. I haven't seen any of this gang building fires, and as I don't want to come home sometime and find myself burned out, I'm not going to teach them. But I'm sure they have means of communication among themselves."

"Has Ben Rainsford seen them yet?" Lunt asked.

"Ben's off on a trip somewhere. I called him as soon as Little Fuzzy, over there, showed up here. He won't be back till Friday."

"Yes, that's right; I did know that." Lunt was still looking dubiously at the Fuzzies. "I'd like to hear what he thinks about them."

If Ben said they were safe, Lunt would accept that. Ben was an expert, and Lunt respected expert testimony. Until then, he wasn't sure. He'd probably order a medical check-up for himself and Khadra the first thing tomorrow, to make sure they hadn't picked up some kind of bug.

IV

The Fuzzies took the manipulator quite calmly the next morning. That wasn't any horrible monster, that was just something Pappy Jack took rides in. He found one rather indifferent sunstone in the morning and two good ones in the afternoon. He came home early and found the family in the living room; they had dumped the wastebasket and were putting things back into it. Another land-prawn seemed to have gotten into the house; its picked shell was with the other rubbish in the basket. They had dinner early, and he loaded the lot of them into the airjeep and took them for a long ride to the south and west.

The following day, he located the flint vein on the other side of the gorge and spent most of the morning blasting away the sandstone above it. The next time he went into Mallorysport, he decided, he was going to shop around for a good power-shovel. He had to blast a channel to keep the little stream from damming up on him. He didn't get any flint cracked at all that day. There was another harpy circling around the camp when he got back; he chased it with the manipulator and shot it down with his pistol. Harpies probably found Fuzzies as tasty as Fuzzies found land-prawns. The family were all sitting under the gunrack when he entered the living room.

The next day he cracked flint, and found three more stones. It really looked as though he had found the Dying Place of the Jellyfish at that. He knocked off early that afternoon, and when he came in sight of the camp, he saw an airjeep grounded on the lawn and a small man with a red beard in a faded Khaki bush-jacket sitting on the bench by the kitchen door, surrounded by Fuzzies. There was a camera and some other equipment laid up where the Fuzzies couldn't get at it. Baby Fuzzy, of course, was sitting on his head. He looked up and waved, and then handed Baby to his mother and rose to his feet.

"Well, what do you think of them, Ben?" Jack called down, as he grounded the manipulator.

"My God, don't start me on that now!" Ben Rainsford replied, and then laughed. "I stopped at the constabulary post on the way home. I thought George Lunt had turned into the biggest liar in the known galaxy. Then I went home, and found your call on the recorder, so I came over here."

"Been waiting long?"

The Fuzzies had all abandoned Rainsford and come trooping over as soon as the manipulator was off contragravity. He climbed down among them, and they followed him across the grass, catching at his trouser legs and yeeking happily.

"Not so long." Rainsford looked at his watch. "Good Lord, three and half hours is all. Well, the time passed quickly. You know, your little fellows have good ears. They heard you coming a long time before I did."

"Did you see them killing any prawns?"

"I should say! I got a lot of movies of it." He shook his head slowly. "Jack, this is almost incredible."

"You're staying for dinner, of course?"

"You try and chase me away. I want to hear all about this. Want you to make a tape about them, if you're willing."

"Glad to. We'll do that after we eat." He sat down on the bench, and the Fuzzies began climbing upon and beside him. "This is the original, Little Fuzzy. He brought the rest in a couple of days later. Mamma Fuzzy, and Baby Fuzzy. And these are Mike and Mitzi. I call this one Ko-Ko, because of the ceremonious way he beheads land-prawns."

"George says you call them all Fuzzies. Want that for the official designation?"

"Sure. That's what they are, isn't it?"

"Well, let's call the order Hollowayans," Rainsford said. "Family, Fuzzies; genus, Fuzzy. Species, Holloway's Fuzzy —*Fuzzy fuzzy holloway.* How'll that be?"

That would be all right, he supposed. At least, they didn't try to Latinize things in extraterrestrial zoology any more.

"I suppose our bumper crop of land-prawns is what brought them into this section?"

"Yes, of course. George was telling me you thought they'd come down from the north; about the only place they could have come from. This is probably just the advance guard; we'll be having Fuzzies all over the place before long. I wonder how fast they breed."

"Not very fast. Three males and two females in this crowd, and only one young one." He set Mike and Mitzi off his lap and got to his feet. "I'll go start dinner now. While I'm doing that, you can look at the stuff they brought in with them."

When he had placed the dinner in the oven and taken a couple of highballs into the living room, Rainsford was still sitting at the desk, looking at the artifacts. He accepted his drink and sipped it absently, then raised his head.

"Jack, this stuff is absolutely amazing," he said.

"It's better than that. It's unique. Only collection of native weapons and implements on Zarathustra."

Ben Rainsford looked up sharply. "You mean what I think you mean?" he asked. "Yes; you do." He drank some of his highball, set down the glass and picked up the polished-horn prawn-killer. "Anything-pardon, anybody-who does this kind of work is good enough native for me." He hesitated briefly. "Why, Jack this tape you said you'd make. Can I transmit a copy to Juan Jimenez? He's chief mammalogist with the Company science division; we exchange information. And there's another Company man I'd like to have hear it. Gerd van Riebeek. He's a general xeno-naturalist, like me, but he's especially interested in animal evolution."

"Why not? The Fuzzies are a scientific discovery. Discoveries ought to be reported."

Little Fuzzy, Mike and Mitzi strolled in from the kitchen. Little Fuzzy jumped up on the armchair and switched on the viewscreen. Fiddling with the selector, he got the Big Blackwater woods-burning. Mike and Mitzi shrieked delightedly, like a couple of kids watching a horror show. They knew, by now, that nothing in the screen could get out and hurt them.

"Would you mind if they came out here and saw the Fuzzies?"

"Why, the Fuzzies would love that. They like company."

Mamma and Baby and Ko-Ko came in, seemed to approve what was on the screen and sat down to watch it. When the bell on the stove rang, they all got up, and Ko-Ko jumped onto the chair and snapped the screen off. Ben Rainsford looked at him for a moment.

"You know, I have married friends with children who have a hell of a time teaching eight-year-olds to turn off screens when they're through watching them," he commented.

It took an hour, after dinner, to get the whole story, from the first little yeek in the shower stall, on tape. When he had finished, Ben Rainsford made a few remarks and shut off the recorder, then looked at his watch.

"Twenty hundred; it'll be seventeen hundred in Mallorysport," he said. "I could catch Jimenez at Science Center if I called now. He usually works a little late."

"Go ahead. Want to show him some Fuzzies?" He moved his pistol and some other impedimenta off the table and set Little Fuzzy and Mamma Fuzzy and Baby upon it, then drew up a chair beside it, in range of the communication screen, and sat down with Mike and Mitzi and Ko-Ko. Rainsford punched out a wavelength combination. Then he picked up Baby Fuzzy and set him on his head.

In a moment, the screen flickered and cleared, and a young man looked out of it, with the momentary upward glance of one who wants to make sure his public face is on straight. It was a bland, tranquilized, life-adjusted, group-integrated sort of face-the face turned out in thousands of copies every year by the educational production lines on Terra.

"Why, Bennett, this is a pleasant surprise," he began. "I never expec —" Then he choked; at least, he emitted a sound of surprise. "What in the name of Dai-Butsu are those things on the table in front of you?" he demanded. "I never saw anything —*And what is that on your head?*"

"Family group of Fuzzies," Rainsford said. "Mature male, mature female, immature male." He lifted Baby Fuzzy down and put him in Mamma's arms. "Species *Fuzzy fuzzy holloway zarathustra*. The gentleman on my left is Jack Holloway, the sunstone operator, who is the original discoverer. Jack, Juan Jimenez."

They shook their own hands at one another in the ancient Terran-Chinese gesture that was used on communication screens, and assured each other-Jimenez rather absently-that it was a pleasure. He couldn't take his eyes off the Fuzzies.

"Where did they come from?" he wanted to know. "Are you sure they're indigenous?"

"They're not quite up to spaceships, yet, Dr. Jimenez. Fairly early Paleolithic, I'd say."

Jimenez thought he was joking, and laughed. The sort of a laugh that could be turned on and off, like a light. Rainsford assured him that the Fuzzies were really indigenous.

"We have everything that's known about them on tape," he said. "About an hour of it. Can you take sixty-speed?" He was making adjustments on the recorder as he spoke. "All right, set and we'll transmit to you. And can you get hold of Gerd van Riebeek? I'd like him to hear it too; it's as much up his alley as anybody's."

When Jimenez was ready, Rainsford pressed the play-off button, and for a minute the recorder gave a high, wavering squeak. The Fuzzies all looked startled. Then it ended.

"I think, when you hear this, that you and Gerd will both want to come out and see these little people. If you can, bring somebody who's a qualified psychologist, somebody capable of evaluating the Fuzzies' mentation. Jack wasn't kidding about early Paleolithic. If they're not sapient, they only miss it by about one atomic diameter."

Jimenez looked almost as startled as the Fuzzies had. "You surely don't mean that?" He looked from Rainsford to Jack Holloway and back. "Well, I'll call you back, when we've both heard the tape. You're three time zones west of us, aren't you? Then we'll try to make it before your midnight-that'll be twenty-one hundred."

He called back half an hour short of that. This time, it was from the living room of an apartment instead of an office. There was a portable record player in the foreground and a low table with snacks and drinks, and two other people were with him. One was a man of about Jimenez's age with a good-humored, non-life-adjusted, non-group-integrated and slightly weather-beaten face. The other was a woman with glossy black hair and a Mona Lisa-ish smile. The Fuzzies had gotten sleepy, and had been bribed with Extee Three to stay up a little longer. Immediately, they registered interest. This was more fun than the viewscreen.

Jimenez introduced his companions as Gerd van Riebeek and Ruth Ortheris. "Ruth is with Dr. Mallin's section; she's been working with the school department and the juvenile court. She can probably do as well with your Fuzzies as a regular xeno-psychologist."

"Well, I have worked with extraterrestrials," the woman said. "I've been on Loki and Thor and Shesha."

Jack nodded. "Been on the same planets myself. Are you people coming out here?"

"Oh, yes," van Riebeek said. "We'll be out by noon tomorrow. We may stay a couple of days, but that won't put you to any trouble; I have a boat that's big enough for the three of us to camp on. Now, how do we get to your place?"

Jack told him, and gave map coordinates. Van Riebeek noted them down.

"There's one thing, though, I'm going to have to get firm about. I don't want to have to speak about it again. These little people are to be treated with consideration, and not as laboratory animals. You will not hurt them, or annoy them, or force them to do anything they don't want to do."

"We understand that. We won't do anything with the Fuzzies without your approval. Is there anything you'd want us to bring out?"

"Yes. A few things for the camp that I'm short of; I'll pay you for them when you get here. And about three cases of Extee Three. And some toys. Dr. Ortheris, you heard the tape, didn't you? Well, just think what you'd like to have if you were a Fuzzy, and bring it."

V

Victor Grego crushed out his cigarette slowly and deliberately.

"Yes, Leonard," he said patiently. "It's very interesting, and doubtless an important discovery, but I can't see why you're making such a production of it. Are you afraid I'll blame you for letting non-Company people beat you to it? Or do you merely suspect that anything Bennett Rainsford's mixed up in is necessarily a diabolical plot against the Company and, by consequence, human civilization?"

Leonard Kellogg looked pained. "What I was about to say, Victor, is that both Rainsford and this man Holloway seem convinced that these things they call Fuzzies aren't animals at all. They believe them to be sapient beings."

"Well, that's —" He bit that off short as the significance of what Kellogg had just said hit him. "Good God, Leonard! I beg your pardon abjectly; I don't blame you for taking it seriously. Why, that would make Zarathustra a Class-IV inhabited planet."

"For which the Company holds a Class-III charter," Kellogg added. "For an uninhabited planet."

Automatically void if any race of sapient beings were discovered on Zarathustra.

"You know what will happen if this is true?"

"Well, I should imagine the charter would have to be renegotiated, and now that the Colonial Office knows what sort of a planet this is, they'll be anything but generous with the Company...."

"They won't renegotiate anything, Leonard. The Federation government will simply take the position that the Company has already made an adequate return on the original investments, and they'll award us what we can show as in our actual possession —I hope-and throw the rest into the public domain."

The vast plains on Beta and Delta continents, with their herds of veldbeest-all open range, and every 'beest that didn't carry a Company brand a maverick. And all the untapped mineral wealth, and the untilled arable land; it would take years of litigation even to make the Company's claim to Big Blackwater stick. And Terra-Baldur-Marduk Spacelines would lose their monopolistic franchise and get sticky about it in the courts, and in any case, the Company's import-export monopoly would go out the airlock. And the squatters rushing in and swamping everything —

"Why, we won't be any better off than the Yggdrasil Company, squatting on a guano heap on one continent!" he burst out. "Five years from now, they'll be making more money out of bat dung than we'll be making out of this whole world!"

And the Company's good friend and substantial stockholder, Nick Emmert, would be out, too, and a Colonial Governor General would move in, with regular army troops and a complicated bureaucracy. Elections, and a representative parliament, and every Tom, Dick and Harry with a grudge against the Company would be trying to get laws passed-And, of course, a Native Affairs Commission, with its nose in everything.

"But they couldn't just leave us without any kind of a charter," Kellogg insisted. Who was he trying to kid-besides himself? "It wouldn't be fair!" As though that clinched it. "It isn't our fault!"

He forced more patience into his voice. "Leonard, please try to realize that the Terran Federation government doesn't give one shrill soprano hoot on Nifflheim whether it's fair or not, or whose fault what is. The Federation government's been repenting that charter they gave the Company ever since they found out what they'd chartered away. Why, this planet is a better world than Terra ever was, even before the Atomic Wars. Now, if they have a chance to get it back, with improvements, you think they won't take it? And what will stop them? If those creatures over on Beta Continent are sapient beings, our charter isn't worth the parchment it's engrossed on, and that's an end of it." He was silent for a moment. "You heard that tape Rainsford transmitted to Jimenez. Did either he or Holloway actually claim, in so many words, that these things really are sapient beings?"

"Well, no; not in so many words. Holloway consistently alluded to them as people, but he's just an ignorant old prospector. Rainsford wouldn't come out and commit himself one way or another, but he left the door wide open for anybody else to."

"Accepting their account, could these Fuzzies be sapient?"

"Accepting the account, yes," Kellogg said, in distress. "They could be."

They probably were, if Leonard Kellogg couldn't wish the evidence out of existence.

"Then they'll look sapient to these people of yours who went over to Beta this morning, and they'll treat it purely as a scientific question and never consider the legal aspects. Leonard, you'll have to take charge of the investigation, before they make any reports everybody'll be sorry for."

Kellogg didn't seem to like that. It would mean having to exercise authority and getting tough with people, and he hated anything like that. He nodded very reluctantly.

"Yes. I suppose I will. Let me think about it for a moment, Victor."

One thing about Leonard; you handed him something he couldn't delegate or dodge and he'd go to work on it. Maybe not cheerfully, but conscientiously.

"I'll take Ernst Mallin along," he said at length. "This man Rainsford has no grounding whatever in any of the psychosciences. He may be able to impose on Ruth Ortheris, but not on Ernst Mallin. Not after I've talked to Mallin first." He thought some more. "We'll have to get these Fuzzies away from this man Holloway. Then we'll issue a report of discovery, being careful to give full credit to both Rainsford and Holloway-we'll even accept the designation they've coined for them-but we'll make it very clear that while highly intelligent, the Fuzzies are not a race of sapient beings. If Rainsford persists in making any such claim, we will brand it as a deliberate hoax."

"Do you think he's gotten any report off to the Institute of Xeno-Sciences yet?"

Kellogg shook his head. "I think he wants to trick some of our people into supporting his sapience claims; at least, corroborating his and Holloway's alleged observations. That's why I'll have to get over to Beta as soon as possible."

By now, Kellogg had managed to convince himself that going over to Beta had been his idea all along. Probably also convincing himself that Rainsford's report was nothing but a pack of lies. Well, if he could work better that way, that was his business.

"He will, before long, if he isn't stopped. And a year from now, there'll be a small army of investigators here from Terra. By that time, you should have both Rainsford and Holloway thoroughly discredited. Leonard, you get those Fuzzies away from Holloway and I'll personally guarantee they won't be available for investigation by then. Fuzzies," he said reflectively. "Fur-bearing animals, I take it?"

"Holloway spoke, on the tape, of their soft and silky fur."

"Good. Emphasize that in your report. As soon as it's published, the Company will offer two thousand sols apiece for Fuzzy pelts. By the time Rainsford's report brings anybody here from Terra, we may have them all trapped out."

Kellogg began to look worried.

"But, Victor, that's genocide!"

"Nonsense! Genocide is defined as the extermination of a race of sapient beings. These are fur-bearing animals. It's up to you and Ernst Mallin to prove that."

The Fuzzies, playing on the lawn in front of the camp, froze into immobility, their faces turned to the west. Then they all ran to the bench by the kitchen door and scrambled up onto it.

"Now what?" Jack Holloway wondered.

"They hear the airboat," Rainsford told him. "That's the way they acted yesterday when you were coming in with your machine." He looked at the picnic table they had been spreading under the featherleaf trees. "Everything ready?"

"Everything but lunch; that won't be cooked for an hour yet. I see them now."

"You have better eyes than I do, Jack. Oh, I see it. I hope the kids put on a good show for them," he said anxiously.

He'd been jittery ever since he arrived, shortly after breakfast. It wasn't that these people from Mallorysport were so important themselves; Ben had a bigger name in scientific circles than any of this Company crowd. He was just excited about the Fuzzies.

The airboat grew from a barely visible speck, and came spiraling down to land in the clearing. When it was grounded and off contragravity, they started across the grass toward it, and the Fuzzies all jumped down from the bench and ran along with them.

The three visitors climbed down. Ruth Ortheris wore slacks and a sweater, but the slacks were bloused over a pair of ankle boots. Gerd van Riebeek had evidently done a lot of field work: his boots were stout, and he wore old, faded khakis and a serviceable-looking sidearm that showed he knew what to expect up here in the Piedmont. Juan Jimenez was in the same sports casuals in which he had appeared on screen last evening. All of them carried photographic equipment. They shook hands all around and exchanged greetings, and then the Fuzzies began clamoring to be noticed. Finally all of them, Fuzzies and other people, drifted over to the table under the trees.

Ruth Ortheris sat down on the grass with Mamma and Baby. Immediately Baby became interested in a silver charm which she wore on a chain around her neck which tinkled fascinatingly. Then he tried to sit on her head. She spent some time gently but firmly discouraging this. Juan Jimenez was squatting between Mike and Mitzi, examining them alternately and talking into a miniature recorder phone on his breast, mostly in Latin. Gerd van Riebeek dropped himself into a folding chair and took Little Fuzzy on his lap.

"You know, this is kind of surprising," he said. "Not only finding something like this, after twenty-five years, but finding something as unique as this. Look, he doesn't have the least vestige of a tail, and there isn't another tailless mammal on the planet. Fact, there isn't another mammal on this planet that has the slightest kinship to him. Take ourselves; we belong to a pretty big family, about fifty-odd genera of primates. But this little fellow hasn't any relatives at all."

"Yeek?"

"And he couldn't care less, could he?" Van Riebeek pummeled Little Fuzzy gently. "One thing, you have the smallest humanoid known; that's one record you can claim. Oh-oh, what goes on?"

Ko-Ko, who had climbed upon Rainsford's lap, jumped suddenly to the ground, grabbed the chopper-digger he had left beside the chair and started across the grass. Everybody got to their feet, the visitors getting cameras out. The Fuzzies seemed perplexed by all the excitement. It was only another land-prawn, wasn't it?

Ko-Ko got in front of it, poked it on the nose to stop it and then struck a dramatic pose, flourishing his weapon and bringing it down on the prawn's neck. Then, after flopping it over, he looked at it almost in sorrow and hit it a couple of whacks with the flat. He began pulling it apart and eating it.

"I see why you call him Ko-Ko," Ruth said, aiming her camera, "Don't the others do it that way?"

"Well, Little Fuzzy runs along beside them and pivots and gives them a quick chop. Mike and Mitzi flop theirs over first and behead them on their backs. And Mamma takes a swipe at their legs first. But beheading and breaking the undershell, they all do that."

"Uh-huh; that's basic," she said. "Instinctive. The technique is either self-learned or copied. When Baby begins killing his own prawns, see if he doesn't do it the way Mamma does!"

"Hey, look!" Jimenez cried. "He's making a lobster pick for himself!"

Through lunch, they talked exclusively about Fuzzies. The subjects of the discussion nibbled things that were given to them, and yeeked among themselves. Gerd van Riebeek suggested that they were discussing the odd habits of human-type people. Juan Jimenez looked at him, slightly disturbed, as though wondering just how seriously he meant it.

"You know, what impressed me most in the taped account was the incident of the damnthing," said Ruth Ortheris. "Any animal associating with man will try to attract attention if something's wrong, but I never heard of one, not even a Freyan kholph or a Terran chimpanzee, that would use descriptive pantomime. Little Fuzzy was actually making a symbolic representation, by abstracting the distinguishing characteristic of the damnthing."

"Think that stiff-arm gesture and bark might have been intended to represent a rifle?" Gerd van Riebeek asked. "He'd seen you shooting before, hadn't he?"

"I don't think it was anything else. He was telling me, 'Big nasty damnthing outside; shoot it like you did the harpy.' And if he hadn't run past me and pointed back, that damnthing would have killed me."

Jimenez, hesitantly, said, "I know I'm speaking from ignorance. You're the Fuzzy expert. But isn't it possible that you're overanthropomorphizing? Endowing them with your own characteristics and mental traits?"

"Juan, I'm not going to answer that right now. I don't think I'll answer at all. You wait till you've been around these Fuzzies a little longer, and then ask it again, only ask yourself."

"So you see, Ernst, that's the problem."

Leonard Kellogg laid the words like a paperweight on the other words he had been saying, and waited. Ernst Mallin sat motionless, his elbows on the desk and his chin in his hands. A little pair of wrinkles, like parentheses, appeared at the corners of his mouth.

"Yes. I'm not a lawyer, of course, but...."

"It's not a legal question. It's a question for a psychologist."

That left it back with Ernst Mallin, and he knew it.

"I'd have to see them myself before I could express an opinion. You have that tape of Holloway's with you?" When Kellogg nodded, Mallin continued: "Did either of them make any actual, overt claim of sapience?"

He answered it as he had when Victor Grego had asked the same question, adding:

"The account consists almost entirely of Holloway's uncorroborated statements concerning things to which he claims to have been the sole witness."

"Ah." Mallin permitted himself a tight little smile. "And he's not a qualified observer. Neither, for that matter, is Rainsford. Regardless of his position as a xeno-naturalist, he is a complete layman in the psychosciences. He's just taken this other man's statements uncritically. As for what he claims to have observed for himself, how do we know he isn't including a lot of erroneous inferences with his descriptive statements?"

"How do we know he's not perpetrating a deliberate hoax?"

"But, Leonard, that's a pretty serious accusation."

"It's happened before. That fellow who carved a Late Upland Martian inscription in that cave in Kenya, for instance. Or Hellermann's claim to have cross-bred Terran mice with Thoran tilbras. Or the Piltdown Man, back in the first century Pre-Atomic?"

Mallin nodded. "None of us like to think of a thing like that, but, as you say, it's happened. You know, this man Rainsford is just the type to do something like that, too. Fundamentally an individualistic egoist; badly adjusted personality type. Say he wants to make some sensational discovery which will assure him the position in the scientific world to which he believes himself entitled. He finds this lonely old prospector, into whose isolated camp some little animals have strayed. The old man has made pets of them, taught them a few tricks, finally so projected his own personality onto them that he has convinced himself that they are people like himself. This is Rainsford's great opportunity; he will present himself as the discoverer of a new sapient race and bring the whole learned world to his feet." Mallin smiled again. "Yes, Leonard, it is altogether possible."

"Then it's our plain duty to stop this thing before it develops into another major scientific scandal like Hellermann's hybrids."

"First we must go over this tape recording and see what we have on our hands. Then we must make a thorough, unbiased study of these animals, and show Rainsford and his accomplice that they cannot hope to foist these ridiculous claims on the scientific world with impunity. If we can't convince them privately, there'll be nothing to do but expose them publicly."

"I've heard the tape already, but let's play if off now. We want to analyze these tricks this man Holloway has taught these animals, and see what they show."

"Yes, of course. We must do that at once," Mallin said. "Then we'll have to consider what sort of statement we must issue, and what sort of evidence we will need to support it."

After dinner was romptime for Fuzzies on the lawn, but when the dusk came creeping into the ravine, they all went inside and were given one of their new toys from Mallorysport —a big box of many-colored balls and short sticks of transparent plastic. They didn't know that it was a molecule-model kit, but they soon found that the sticks would go into holes in the balls, and that they could be built into three-dimensional designs.

This was much more fun than the colored stones. They made a few experimental shapes, then dismantled them and began on a single large design. Several times they tore it down, entirely or in part, and began over again, usually with considerable yeeking and gesticulation.

"They have artistic sense," Van Riebeek said. "I've seen lots of abstract sculpture that wasn't half as good as that job they're doing."

"Good engineering, too," Jack said. "They understand balance and center-of-gravity. They're bracing it well, and not making it top-heavy."

"Jack, I've been thinking about that question I was supposed to ask myself," Jimenez said. "You know, I came out here loaded with suspicion. Not that I doubted your honesty; I just thought you'd let your obvious affection for the Fuzzies lead you into giving them credit for more intelligence than they possess. Now I think you've consistently understated it. Short of actual sapience, I've never seen anything like them."

"Why short of it?" van Riebeek asked. "Ruth, you've been pretty quiet this evening. What do you think?"

Ruth Ortheris looked uncomfortable. "Gerd, it's too early to form opinions like that. I know the way they're working together looks like cooperation on an agreed-upon purpose, but I simply can't make speech out of that yeek-yeek-yeek."

"Let's keep the talk-and-build-a-fire rule out of it," van Riebeek said. "If they're working together on a common project, they must be communicating somehow."

"It isn't communication, it's symbolization. You simply can't think sapiently except in verbal symbols. Try it. Not something like changing the spools on a recorder or field-stripping a pistol; they're just learned tricks. I mean ideas."

"How about Helen Keller?" Rainsford asked. "Mean to say she only started thinking sapiently after Anna Sullivan taught her what words were?"

"No, of course not. She thought sapiently-And she only thought in sense-imagery limited to feeling." She looked at Rainsford reproachfully; he'd knocked a breach in one of her fundamental postulates. "Of course, she had inherited the cerebroneural equipment for sapient thinking." She let that trail off, before somebody asked her how she knew that the Fuzzies hadn't.

"I'll suggest, just to keep the argument going, that speech couldn't have been invented without pre-existing sapience," Jack said.

Ruth laughed. "Now you're taking me back to college. That used to be one of the burning questions in first-year psych students' bull sessions. By the time we got to be sophomores, we'd realized that it was only an egg-and-chicken argument and dropped it."

"That's a pity," Ben Rainsford said. "It's a good question."

"It would be if it could be answered."

"Maybe it can be," Gerd said. "There's a clue to it, right there. I'll say that those fellows are on the edge of sapience, and it's an even-money bet which side."

"I'll bet every sunstone in my bag they're over."

"Well, maybe they're just slightly sapient," Jimenez suggested.

Ruth Ortheris hooted at that. "That's like talking about being just slightly dead or just slightly pregnant," she said. "You either are or you aren't."

Gerd van Riebeek was talking at the same time. "This sapience question is just as important in my field as yours, Ruth. Sapience is the result of evolution by natural selection, just as much as a physical characteristic, and it's the most important step in the evolution of any species, our own included."

"Wait a minute, Gerd," Rainsford said. "Ruth, what do you mean by that? Aren't there degrees of sapience?"

"No. There are degrees of mentation-intelligence, if you prefer-just as there are degrees of temperature. When psychology becomes an exact science like physics, we'll be able to calibrate mentation like temperature. But sapience is qualitatively different from nonsapience. It's more than just a higher degree of mental temperature. You might call it a sort of mental boiling point."

"I think that's a damn good analogy," Rainsford said. "But what happens when the boiling point is reached?"

"That's what we have to find out," van Riebeek told him. "That's what I was talking about a moment ago. We don't know any more about how sapience appeared today than we did in the year zero, or in the year 654 Pre-Atomic for that matter."

"Wait a minute," Jack interrupted. "Before we go any deeper, let's agree on a definition of sapience."

Van Riebeek laughed. "Ever try to get a definition of life from a biologist?" he asked. "Or a definition of number from a mathematician?"

"That's about it." Ruth looked at the Fuzzies, who were looking at their colored-ball construction as though wondering if they could add anything more without spoiling the design. "I'd say: a level of mentation qualitatively different from nonsapience in that it includes ability to symbolize ideas and store and transmit them, ability to generalize and ability to form abstract ideas. There; I didn't say a word about talk-and-build-a-fire, did I?"

"Little Fuzzy symbolizes and generalizes," Jack said. "He symbolizes a damnthing by three horns, and he symbolizes a rifle by a long thing that points and makes noises. Rifles kill animals. Harpies and damnthings are both animals. If a rifle will kill a harpy, it'll kill a damnthing too."

Juan Jimenez had been frowning in thought; he looked up and asked, "What's the lowest known sapient race?"

"Yggdrasil Khooghras," Gerd van Riebeek said promptly. "Any of you ever been on Yggdrasil?"

"I saw a man shot once on Mimir, for calling another man a son of a Khooghra," Jack said. "The man who shot him had been on Yggdrasil and knew what he was being called."

"I spent a couple of years among them," Gerd said. "They do build fires; I'll give them that. They char points on sticks to make spears. And they talk. I learned their language, all eighty-two words of it. I taught a few of the intelligentsia how to use machetes without maiming themselves, and there was one mental giant I could trust to carry some of my equipment, if I kept an eye on him, but I never let him touch my rifle or my camera."

"Can they generalize?" Ruth asked.

"Honey, they can't do nothin' else but! Every word in their language is a high-order generalization. *Hroosha*, live-thing. *Noosha*, bad-thing. *Dhishta*, thing-to-eat. Want me to go on? There are only seventy-nine more of them."

Before anybody could stop him, the communication screen got itself into an uproar. The Fuzzies all ran over in front of it, and Jack switched it on. The caller was a man in gray semiformals; he had wavy gray hair and a face that looked like Juan Jimenez's twenty years from now.

"Good evening; Holloway here."

"Oh, Mr. Holloway, good evening." The caller shook hands with himself, turning on a dazzling smile. "I'm Leonard Kellogg, chief of the Company's science division. I just heard the tape you made about the-the Fuzzies?" He looked down at the floor. "Are these some of the animals?"

"These are the Fuzzies." He hoped it sounded like the correction it was intended to be. "Dr. Bennett Rainsford's here with me now, and so are Dr. Jimenez, Dr. van Riebeek and Dr. Ortheris." Out of the corner of his eye he could see Jimenez squirming as though afflicted with ants, van Riebeek getting his poker face battened down and Ben Rainsford suppressing a grin. "Some of us are out of screen range, and I'm sure you'll want to ask a lot of questions. Pardon us a moment, while we close in."

He ignored Kellogg's genial protest that that wouldn't be necessary until the chairs were placed facing the screen. As an afterthought, he handed Fuzzies around, giving Little Fuzzy to Ben, Ko-Ko to Gerd, Mitzi to Ruth, Mike to Jimenez and taking Mamma and Baby on his own lap.

Baby immediately started to climb up onto his head, as expected. It seemed to disconcert Kellogg, also as expected. He decided to teach Baby to thumb his nose when given some unobtrusive signal.

"Now, about that tape I recorded last evening," he began.

"Yes, Mr. Holloway." Kellogg's smile was getting more mechanical every minute. He was having trouble keeping his eyes off Baby. "I must say, I was simply astounded at the high order of intelligence claimed for these creatures."

"And you wanted to see how big a liar I was. I don't blame you; I had trouble believing it myself at first."

Kellogg gave a musically blithe laugh, showing even more dental equipment.

"Oh, no. Mr. Holloway; please don't misunderstand me. I never thought anything like that."

"I hope not," Ben Rainsford said, not too pleasantly. "I vouched for Mr. Holloway's statements, if you'll recall."

"Of course, Bennett; that goes without saying. Permit me to congratulate you upon a most remarkable scientific discovery. An entirely new order of mammals —"

"Which may be the ninth extrasolar sapient race," Rainsford added.

"Good heavens, Bennett!" Kellogg jettisoned his smile and slid on a look of shocked surprise. "You surely can't be serious?" He looked again at the Fuzzies, pulled the smile back on and gave a light laugh.

"I thought you'd heard that tape," Rainsford said.

"Of course, and the things reported were most remarkable. But sapiences! Just because they've been taught a few tricks, and use sticks and stones for weapons —" He got rid of the smile again, and quick-changed to seriousness. "Such an extreme claim must only be made after careful study."

"Well, I won't claim they're sapient," Ruth Ortheris told him. "Not till day after tomorrow, at the earliest. But they very easily could be. They have learning and reasoning capacity equal to that of any eight-year-old Terran Human child, and well above that of the adults of some recognizedly sapient races. And they have not been taught tricks; they have learned by observation and reasoning."

"Well, Dr. Kellogg, mentation levels isn't my subject," Jimenez took it up, "but they do have all the physical characteristics shared by other sapient races-lower limbs specialized for locomotion and upper limbs for manipulation, erect posture, stereoscopic vision, color perception, hand with opposing thumb-all the characteristics we consider as prerequisite to the development of sapience."

"I think they're sapient, myself," Gerd van Riebeek said, "but that's not as important as the fact that they're on the very threshold of sapience. This is the first race of this mental level anybody's ever seen. I believe that study of the Fuzzies will help us solve the problem of how sapience developed in any race."

Kellogg had been laboring to pump up a head of enthusiasm; now he was ready to valve it off.

"But this is amazing! This will make scientific history! Now, of course, you all realize how pricelessly valuable these Fuzzies are. They must be brought at once to Mallorysport, where they can be studied under laboratory conditions by qualified psychologists, and —"

"No."

Jack lifted Baby Fuzzy off his head and handed him to Mamma, and set Mamma on the floor. That was reflex; the thinking part of his brain knew he didn't need to clear for action when arguing with the electronic image of a man twenty-five hundred miles away.

"Just forget that part of it and start over," he advised.

Kellogg ignored him. "Gerd, you have your airboat; fix up some nice comfortable cages —"

"*Kellogg!*"

The man in the screen stopped talking and stared in amazed indignation. It was the first time in years he had been addressed by his naked patronymic, and possibly the first time in his life he had been shouted at.

"Didn't you hear me the first time Kellogg? Then stop gibbering about cages. These Fuzzies aren't being taken anywhere."

"But Mr. Holloway! Don't you realize that these little beings must be carefully studied? Don't you want them given their rightful place in the hierarchy of nature?"

"If you want to study them, come out here and do it. That's so long as you don't annoy them, or me. As far as study's concerned, they're being studied now. Dr. Rainsford's studying them, and so are three of your people, and when it comes to that, I'm studying them myself."

"And I'd like you to clarify that remark about qualified psychologists," Ruth Ortheris added, in a voice approaching zero-Kelvin. "You wouldn't be challenging my professional qualifications, would you?"

"Oh, Ruth, you know I didn't mean anything like that. Please don't misunderstand me," Kellogg begged. "But this is highly specialized work —"

"Yes; how many Fuzzy specialists have you at Science Center, Leonard?" Rainsford wanted to know. "The only one I can think of is Jack Holloway, here."

"Well, I'd thought of Dr. Mallin, the Company's head psychologist."

"He can come too, just as long as he understands that he'll have to have my permission for anything he wants to do with the Fuzzies," Jack said. "When can we expect you?"

Kellogg thought some time late the next afternoon. He didn't have to ask how to get to the camp. He made a few efforts to restore the conversation to its original note of cordiality, gave that up as a bad job and blanked out. There was a brief silence in the living room. Then Jimenez said reproachfully:

"You certainly weren't very gracious to Dr. Kellogg, Jack. Maybe you don't realize it, but he is a very important man."

"He isn't important to me, and I wasn't gracious to him at all. It doesn't pay to be gracious to people like that. If you are, they always try to take advantage of it."

"Why, I didn't know you knew Len," van Riebeek said.

"I never saw the individual before. The species is very common and widely distributed." He turned to Rainsford. "You think he and this Mallin will be out tomorrow?"

"Of course they will. This is a little too big for underlings and non-Company people to be allowed to monkey with. You know, we'll have to watch out or in a year we'll be hearing from Terra about the discovery of a sapient race on Zarathustra; *Fuzzy fuzzy Kellogg*. As Juan says, Dr. Kellogg is a very important man. That's how he got important."

VI

The recorded voice ceased; for a moment the record player hummed voicelessly. Loud in the silence, a photocell acted with a double click, opening one segment of the sun shielding and closing another at the opposite side of the dome. Space Commodore Alex Napier glanced up from his desk and out at the harshly angular landscape of Xerxes and the blackness of airless space beyond the disquietingly close horizon. Then he picked up his pipe and knocked the heel out into the ashtray. Nobody said anything. He began packing tobacco into the bowl.

"Well, gentlemen?" He invited comment.

"Pancho?" Captain Conrad Greibenfeld, the Exec., turned to Lieutenant Ybarra, the chief psychologist.

"How reliable is this stuff?" Ybarra asked.

"Well, I knew Jack Holloway thirty years ago, on Fenris, when I was just an ensign. He must be past seventy now," he parenthesized. "If he says he saw anything, I'll believe it. And Bennett Rainsford's absolutely reliable, of course."

"How about the agent?" Ybarra insisted.

He and Stephen Aelborg, the Intelligence officer, exchanged glances. He nodded, and Aelborg said:

"One of the best. One of our own, lieutenant j.g., Naval Reserve. You don't need to worry about credibility, Pancho."

"They sound sapient to me," Ybarra said. "You know, this is something I've always been half hoping and half afraid would happen."

"You mean an excuse to intervene in that mess down there?" Greibenfeld asked.

Ybarra looked blankly at him for a moment. "No. No, I meant a case of borderline sapience; something our sacred talk-and-build-a-fire rule won't cover. Just how did this come to our attention, Stephen?"

"Well, it was transmitted to us from Contact Center in Mallorysport late Friday night. There seem to be a number of copies of this tape around; our agent got hold of one of them and transmitted it to Contact Center, and it was relayed on to us, with the agent's comments," Aelborg said. "Contact Center ordered a routine surveillance inside Company House and, to play safe, at the Residency. At the time, there seemed no reason to give the thing any beat-to-quarters-and-man-guns treatment, but we got a report on Saturday afternoon-Mallorysport time, that is-that Leonard Kellogg had played off the copy of the tape that Juan Jimenez had made for file, and had alerted Victor Grego immediately.

"Of course, Grego saw the implications at once. He sent Kellogg and the chief Company psychologist, Ernst Mallin, out to Beta Continent with orders to brand Rainsford's and Holloway's claims as a deliberate hoax. Then the Company intends to encourage the trapping of Fuzzies for their fur, in hopes that the whole species will be exterminated before anybody can get out from Terra to check on Rainsford's story."

"I hadn't heard that last detail before."

"Well, we can prove it," Aelborg assured him.

It sounded like a Victor Grego idea. He lit his pipe slowly. Damnit, he didn't want to have to intervene. No Space Navy C.O. did. Justifying intervention on a Colonial planet was too much bother-always a board of inquiry, often a courtmartial. And supersession of civil authority was completely against Service Doctrine. Of course, there were other and more important tenets of Service Doctrine. The sovereignty of the Terran Federation for one, and the inviolability of the Federation Constitution. And the rights of extraterrestrials, too. Conrad Greibenfeld, too, seemed to have been thinking about that.

"If those Fuzzies are sapient beings, that whole setup down there is illegal. Company, Colonial administration and all," he said. "Zarathustra's a Class-IV planet, and that's all you can make out of it."

"We won't intervene unless we're forced to. Pancho, I think the decision will be largely up to you."

Pancho Ybarra was horrified.

"Good God, Alex! You can't mean that. Who am I? A nobody. All I have is an ordinary M.D., and a Psych.D. Why, the best psychological brains in the Federation —"

"Aren't on Zarathustra, Pancho. They're on Terra, five hundred light-years, six months' ship voyage each way. Intervention, of course, is my responsibility, but the sapience question is yours. I don't envy you, but I can't relieve you of it."

Gerd van Riebeek's suggestion that all three of the visitors sleep aboard the airboat hadn't been treated seriously at all. Gerd himself was accommodated in the spare room of the living hut. Juan Jimenez went with Ben Rainsford to his camp for the night. Ruth Ortheris had the cabin of the boat to herself. Rainsford was on the screen the next morning, while Jack and Gerd and Ruth and the Fuzzies were having breakfast; he and Jimenez had decided to take his airjeep and work down from the head of Cold Creek in the belief that there must be more Fuzzies around in the woods.

Both Gerd and Ruth decided to spend the morning at the camp and get acquainted with the Fuzzies on hand. The family had had enough breakfast to leave them neutral on the subject of land-prawns, and they were given another of the new toys, a big colored ball. They rolled it around in the grass for a while, decided to save it for their evening romp and took it into the house. Then they began playing aimlessly among some junk in the shed outside the workshop. Once in a while one of them would drift away to look for a prawn, more for sport than food.

Ruth and Gerd and Jack were sitting at the breakfast table on the grass, talking idly and trying to think of excuses for not washing the dishes. Mamma Fuzzy and Baby were poking about in the tall grass. Suddenly Mamma gave a shrill cry and started back for the shed, chasing Baby ahead of her and slapping him on the bottom with the flat of her chopper-digger to hurry him along.

Jack started for the house at a run. Gerd grabbed his camera and jumped up on the table. It was Ruth who saw the cause of the disturbance.

"Jack! Look, over there!" She pointed to the edge of the clearing. "Two strange Fuzzies!"

He kept on running, but instead of the rifle he had been going for, he collected his movie camera, two of the spare chopper-diggers and some Extee Three. When he emerged again, the two Fuzzies had come into the clearing and stood side by side, looking around. Both were females, and they both carried wooden prawn-killers.

"You have plenty of film?" he asked Gerd. "Here, Ruth; take this." He handed her his own camera. "Keep far enough away from me to get what I'm doing and what they're doing. I'm going to try to trade with them."

He went forward, the steel weapons in his hip pocket and the Extee Three in his hand, talking softly and soothingly to the newcomers. When he was as close to them as he could get without stampeding them, he stopped.

"Our gang's coming up behind you," Gerd told him. "Regular skirmish line; choppers at high port. Now they've stopped, about thirty feet behind you."

He broke off a piece of Extee Three, put it in his mouth and ate it. Then he broke off two more pieces and held them out. The two Fuzzies were tempted, but not to the point of rashness. He threw both pieces within a few feet of them. One darted forward, threw a piece to her companion and then snatched the other piece and ran back with it. They stood together, nibbling and making soft delighted noises.

His own family seemed to disapprove strenuously of this lavishing of delicacies upon outsiders. However, the two strangers decided that it would be safe to come closer, and soon he had them taking bits of field ration from his hand. Then he took the two steel chopper-diggers out of his pocket, and managed to convey the idea that he wanted to trade. The two strange Fuzzies were incredulously delighted. This was too much for his own tribe; they came up yeeking angrily.

The two strange females retreated a few steps, their new weapon ready. Everybody seemed to expect a fight, and nobody wanted one. From what he could remember of Old Terran history, this was a situation which could develop into serious trouble. Then Ko-Ko advanced, dragging his chopper-digger in an obviously pacific manner, and approached the two females, yeeking softly and touching first one and then the other. Then he laid his weapon down and put his foot on it. The two females began stroking and caressing him.

Immediately the crisis evaporated. The others of the family came forward, stuck their weapons in the ground and began fondling the strangers. Then they all sat in a circle, swaying their bodies rhythmically and making soft noises. Finally Ko-Ko and the two females rose, picked up their weapons and started for the woods.

"Jack, stop them," Ruth called out. "They're going away."

"If they want to go, I have no right to stop them."

When they were almost at the edge of the woods, Ko-Ko stopped, drove the point of his weapon into the ground and came running back to Pappy Jack, throwing his arms around the human knees and yeeking. Jack stooped and stroked him, but didn't try to pick him up. One of the two females pulled his chopper-digger out, and they both came back slowly. At the same time, Little Fuzzy, Mamma Fuzzy, Mike and Mitzi came running back. For a while, all the Fuzzies embraced one another, yeeking happily. Then they all trooped across the grass and went into the house.

"Get that all, Gerd?" he asked.

"On film, yes. That's the only way I did, though. What happened?"

"You have just made the first film of intertribal social and mating customs, Zarathustran Fuzzy. This is the family's home; they don't want any strange Fuzzies hanging around. They were going to run the girls off. Then Ko-Ko decided he liked their looks, and he decided he'd team up with them. That made everything different; the family sat down with them to tell them what a fine husband they were getting and to tell Ko-Ko good-bye. Then Ko-Ko remembered that he hadn't told me good-bye, and he came back. The family decided that two more Fuzzies wouldn't be in excess of the carrying capacity of this habitat, seeing what a good provider Pappy Jack is, so now I should imagine they're showing the girls the family treasures. You know, they married into a mighty well-to-do family."

The girls were named Goldilocks and Cinderella. When lunch was ready, they were all in the living room, with the viewscreen on; after lunch, the whole gang went into the bedroom for a nap on Pappy Jack's bed. He spent the afternoon developing movie film, while Gerd and Ruth wrote up the notes they had made the day before and collaborated on an account of the adoption. By late afternoon, when they were finished, the Fuzzies came out for a frolic and prawn hunt.

They all heard the aircar before any of the human people did, and they all ran over and climbed up on the bench beside the kitchen door. It was a constabulary cruise car; it landed, and a couple of troopers got out, saying that they'd stopped to see the Fuzzies. They wanted to know where the extras had come from, and when Jack told them, they looked at one another.

"Next gang that comes along, call us and keep them entertained till we can get here," one of them said. "We want some at the post, for prawns if nothing else."

"What's George's attitude?" he asked. "The other night, when he was here, he seemed half scared of them."

"Aah, he's got over that," one of the troopers said. "He called Ben Rainsford; Ben said they were perfectly safe. Hey, Ben says they're not animals; they're people."

He started to tell them about some of the things the Fuzzies did. He was still talking when the Fuzzies heard another aircar and called attention to it. This time, it was Ben Rainsford and Juan Jimenez. They piled out as soon as they were off contragravity, dragging cameras after them.

"Jack, there are Fuzzies all over the place up there," Rainsford began, while he was getting out. "All headed down this way; regular *Volkerwanderung*. We saw over fifty of them-four families, and individuals and pairs. I'm sure we missed ten for every one we saw."

"We better get up there with a car tomorrow," one of the troopers said. "Ben, just where were you?"

"I'll show you on the map." Then he saw Goldilocks and Cinderella. "Hey! Where'd you two girls come from? I never saw you around here before."

There was another clearing across the stream, with a log footbridge and a path to the camp. Jack guided the big airboat down onto it, and put his airjeep alongside with the canopy up. There were two men on the forward deck of the boat, Kellogg and another man who would be Ernst Mallin. A third man came out of the control cabin after the boat was off contragravity. Jack didn't like Mallin. He had a tight, secretive face, with arrogance and bigotry showing underneath. The third man was younger. His face didn't show anything much, but his coat showed a bulge under the left arm. After being introduced by Kellogg, Mallin introduced him as Kurt Borch, his assistant.

Mallin had to introduce Borch again at the camp, not only to Ben Rainsford but also to van Riebeek, to Jimenez and even to Ruth Ortheris, which seemed a little odd. Ruth seemed to think so, too, and Mallin hastened to tell her that Borch was with Personnel, giving some kind of tests. That appeared to puzzle her even more. None of the three seemed happy about the presence of the constabulary troopers, either; they were all relieved when the cruise car lifted out.

Kellogg became interested in the Fuzzies immediately, squatting to examine them. He said something to Mallin, who compressed his lips and shook his head, saying:

"We simply cannot assume sapience until we find something in their behavior which cannot be explained under any other hypothesis. We would be much safer to assume nonsapience and proceed to test that assumption."

That seemed to establish the keynote. Kellogg straightened, and he and Mallin started one of those "of course I agree, doctor, but don't you find, on the other hand, that you must agree" sort of arguments, about the difference between scientific evidence and scientific proof. Jimenez got into it to the extent of agreeing with everything Kellogg said, and differing politely with everything Mallin said that he thought Kellogg would differ with. Borch said nothing; he just stood and looked at the Fuzzies with ill-concealed hostility. Gerd and Ruth decided to help getting dinner.

They ate outside on the picnic table, with the Fuzzies watching them interestedly. Kellogg and Mallin carefully avoided discussing them. It wasn't until after dusk, when the Fuzzies brought their ball inside and everybody was in the living room, that Kellogg, adopting a presiding-officer manner, got the conversation onto the subject. For some time, without giving anyone else an opportunity to say anything, he gushed about what an important discovery the Fuzzies were. The Fuzzies themselves ignored him and began dismantling the stick-and-ball construction. For a while Goldilocks and Cinderella watched interestedly, and then they began assisting.

"Unfortunately," Kellogg continued, "so much of our data is in the form of uncorroborated statements by Mr. Holloway. Now, please don't misunderstand me. I don't, myself, doubt for a moment anything Mr. Holloway said on that tape, but you must realize that professional scientists are most reluctant to accept the unsubstantiated reports of what, if you'll pardon me, they think of as nonqualified observers."

"Oh, rubbish, Leonard!" Rainsford broke in impatiently. "I'm a professional scientist, of a good many more years' standing than you, and I accept Jack Holloway's statements. A frontiersman like Jack is a very careful and exact observer. People who aren't don't live long on frontier planets."

"Now, please don't misunderstand me," Kellogg reiterated. "I don't doubt Mr. Holloway's statements. I was just thinking of how they would be received on Terra."

"I shouldn't worry about that, Leonard. The Institute accepts my reports, and I'm vouching for Jack's reliability. I can substantiate most of what he told me from personal observation."

"Yes, and there's more than just verbal statements," Gerd van Riebeek chimed in. "A camera is not a nonqualified observer. We have quite a bit of film of the Fuzzies."

"Oh, yes; there was some mention of movies," Mallin said. "You don't have any of them developed yet, do you?"

"Quite a lot. Everything except what was taken out in the woods this afternoon. We can run them off right now."

He pulled down the screen in front of the gunrack, got the film and loaded his projector. The Fuzzies, who had begun on a new stick-and-ball construction, were irritated when the lights went out, then wildly excited when Little Fuzzy, digging a toilet pit with the wood chisel, appeared. Little Fuzzy in particular was excited about that; if he didn't recognize himself, he recognized the chisel. Then there were pictures of Little Fuzzy killing and eating land-prawns, Little Fuzzy taking the nut off the bolt and putting it on again, and pictures of the others, after they had come in, hunting and at play. Finally, there was the film of the adoption of Goldilocks and Cinderella.

"What Juan and I got this afternoon, up in the woods, isn't so good, I'm afraid," Rainsford said when the show was over and the lights were on again. "Mostly it's rear views disappearing into the brush. It was very hard to get close to them in the jeep. Their hearing is remarkably acute. But I'm sure the pictures we took this afternoon will show the things they were carrying-wooden prawn-killers like the two that were traded from the new ones in that last film."

Mallin and Kellogg looked at one another in what seemed oddly like consternation.

"You didn't tell us there were more of them around," Mallin said, as though it were an accusation of duplicity. He turned to Kellogg. "This alters the situation."

"Yes, indeed, Ernst," Kellogg burbled delightedly. "This is a wonderful opportunity. Mr. Holloway, I understand that all this country up here is your property, by landgrant purchase. That's right, isn't it? Well, would you allow us to camp on that clearing across the run, where our boat is now? We'll get prefab huts-Red Hill's the nearest town, isn't it? —and have a Company construction gang set them up for us, and we won't be any bother at all to you. We had only intended staying tonight on our boat, and returning to Mallorysport in the morning, but with all these Fuzzies swarming around in the woods, we can't think of leaving now. You don't have any objection, do you?"

He had lots of objections. The whole business was rapidly developing into an acute pain in the neck for him. But if he didn't let Kellogg camp across the run, the three of them could move seventy or eighty miles in any direction and be off his land. He knew what they'd do then. They'd live-trap or sleep-gas Fuzzies; they'd put them in cages, and torment them with maze and electric-shock experiments, and kill a few for dissection, or maybe not bother killing them first. On his own land, if they did anything like that, he could do something about it.

"Not at all. I'll have to remind you again, though, that you're to treat these little people with consideration."

"Oh, we won't do anything to your Fuzzies," Mallin said.

"You won't hurt any Fuzzies. Not more than once, anyhow."

The next morning, during breakfast, Kellogg and Kurt Borch put in an appearance, Borch wearing old clothes and field boots and carrying his pistol on his belt. They had a list of things they thought they would need for their camp. Neither of them seemed to have more than the foggiest notion of camp requirements. Jack made some suggestions which they accepted. There was a lot of scientific equipment on the list, including an X-ray machine. He promptly ran a pencil line through that.

"We don't know what these Fuzzies' level of radiation tolerance is. We're not going to find out by overdosing one of my Fuzzies."

Somewhat to his surprise, neither of them gave him any argument. Gerd and Ruth and Kellogg borrowed his airjeep and started north; he and Borch went across the run to make measurements after Rainsford and Jimenez arrived and picked up Mallin. Borch took off soon after with the boat for Red Hill. Left alone, he loafed around the camp, and developed the rest of the movie film, making three copies of everything. Toward noon, Borch brought the boat back, followed by a couple of scowlike farmboats. In a few hours, the Company construction men from Red Hill had the new camp set up. Among other things, they brought two more air jeeps.

The two jeeps returned late in the afternoon, everybody excited. Between them, the parties had seen almost a hundred Fuzzies, and had found three camps, two among rocks and one in a hollow pool-ball tree. All three had been spotted by belts of filled-in toilet pits around them; two had been abandoned and the third was still occupied. Kellogg insisted on playing host to Jack and Rainsford for dinner at the camp across the run. The meal, because everything had been brought ready-cooked and only needed warming, was excellent.

Returning to his own camp with Rainsford, Jack found the Fuzzies finished with their evening meal and in the living room, starting a new construction-he could think of no other name for it-with the molecule-model balls and sticks. Goldilocks left the others and came over to him with a couple of balls fastened together, holding them up with one hand while she pulled his trouser leg with the other.

"Yes, I see. It's very beautiful," he told her.

She tugged harder and pointed at the thing the others were making. Finally, he understood.

"She wants me to work on it, too," he said. "Ben, you know where the coffee is; fix us a pot. I'm going to be busy here."

He sat down on the floor, and was putting sticks and balls together when Ben brought in the coffee. This was more fun than he'd had in a couple of days. He said so while Ben was distributing Extee Three to the Fuzzies.

"Yes, I ought to let you kick me all around the camp for getting this started," Rainsford said, pouring the coffee. "I could make some excuses, but they'd all sound like 'I didn't know it was loaded.'"

"Hell, I didn't know it was loaded, either." He rose and took his coffee cup, blowing on it to cool it. "What do you think Kellogg's up to, anyhow? That whole act he's been putting on since he came here is phony as a nine-sol bill."

"What I told you, evening before last," Rainsford said. "He doesn't want non-Company people making discoveries on Zarathustra. You notice how hard he and Mallin are straining to talk me out of sending a report back to Terra before he can investigate the Fuzzies? He wants to get his own report in first. Well, the hell with him! You know what I'm going to do? I'm going home, and I'm going to sit up all night getting a report into shape. Tomorrow morning I'm going to give it to George Lunt and let him send it to Mallorysport in the constabulary mail pouch. It'll be on a ship for Terra before any of this gang knows it's been sent. Do you have any copies of those movies you can spare?"

"About a mile and a half. I made copies of everything, even the stuff the others took."

"Good. We'll send that, too. Let Kellogg read about it in the papers a year from now." He thought for a moment, then said: "Gerd and Ruth and Juan are bunking at the other camp now; suppose I move in here with you tomorrow. I assume you don't want to leave the Fuzzies alone while that gang's here. I can help you keep an eye on them."

"But, Ben, you don't want to drop whatever else you're doing —"

"What I'm doing, now, is learning to be a Fuzzyologist, and this is the only place I can do it. I'll see you tomorrow, after I stop at the constabulary post."

The people across the run-Kellogg, Mallin and Borch, and van Riebeek, Jimenez and Ruth Ortheris-were still up when Rainsford went out to his airjeep. After watching him lift out, Jack went back into the house, played with his family in the living room for a while and went to bed. The next morning he watched Kellogg, Ruth and Jimenez leave in one jeep and, shortly after, Mallin and van Riebeek in the other. Kellogg didn't seem to be willing to let the three who had come to the camp first wander around unchaperoned. He wondered about that.

Ben Rainsford's airjeep came over the mountains from the south in the late morning and settled onto the grass. Jack helped him inside with his luggage, and then they sat down under the big featherleaf trees to smoke their pipes and watch the Fuzzies playing in the grass. Occasionally they saw Kurt Borch pottering around outside the other camp.

"I sent the report off," Rainsford said, then looked at his watch. "It ought to be on the mail boat for Mallorysport by now; this time tomorrow it'll be in hyperspace for Terra. We won't say anything about it; just sit back and watch Len Kellogg and Ernst Mallin working up a sweat trying to talk us out of sending it." He chuckled. "I made a definite claim of sapience; by the time I got the report in shape to tape off, I couldn't see any other alternative."

"Damned if I can. You hear that, kids?" he asked Mike and Mitzi, who had come over in hope that there might be goodies for them. "Uncle Ben says you're sapient."

"Yeek?"

"They want to know if it's good to eat. What'll happen now?"

"Nothing, for about a year. Six months from now, when the ship gets in, the Institute will release it to the press, and then they'll send an investigation team here. So will any of the other universities or scientific institutes that may be interested. I suppose the government'll send somebody, too. After all, subcivilized natives on colonized planets are wards of the Terran Federation."

He didn't know that he liked that. The less he had to do with the government the better, and his Fuzzies were wards of Pappy Jack Holloway. He said as much.

Rainsford picked up Mitzi and stroked her. "Nice fur," he said. "Fur like that would bring good prices. It will, if we don't get these people recognized as sapient beings."

He looked across the run at the new camp and wondered. Maybe Leonard Kellogg saw that, too, and saw profits for the Company in Fuzzy fur.

The airjeeps returned in the middle of the afternoon, first Mallin's, and then Kellogg's. Everybody went inside. An hour later, a constabulary car landed in front of the Kellogg camp. George Lunt and Ahmed Khadra got out. Kellogg came outside, spoke with them and then took them into the main living hut. Half an hour later, the lieutenant and the trooper emerged, lifted their car across the run and set it down on the lawn. The Fuzzies ran to meet them, possibly expecting more whistles, and followed them into the living room. Lunt and Khadra took off their berets, but made no move to unbuckle their gun belts.

"We got your package off all right Ben," Lunt said. He sat down and took Goldilocks on his lap; immediately Cinderella jumped up, also. "Jack, what the hell's that gang over there up to anyhow?"

"You got that, too?"

"You can smell it on them for a mile, against the wind. In the first place, that Borch. I wish I could get his prints; I'll bet we have them on file. And the whole gang's trying to hide something, and what they're trying to hide is something they're scared of, like a body in a closet. When we were over there, Kellogg did all the talking; anybody else who tried to say anything got shut up fast. Kellogg doesn't like you, Jack and he doesn't like Ben, and he doesn't like the Fuzzies. Most of all he doesn't like the Fuzzies."

"Well, I told you what I thought this morning," Rainsford said. "They don't want outsiders discovering things on this planet. It wouldn't make them look good to the home office on Terra. Remember, it was some non-Company people who discovered the first sunstones, back in 'Forty-eight."

George Lunt looked thoughtful. On him, it was a scowl.

"I don't think that's it, Ben. When we were talking to him, he admitted very freely that you and Jack discovered the Fuzzies. The way he talked, he didn't seem to think they were worth discovering at all. And he asked a lot of funny questions about you, Jack. The kind of questions I'd ask if I was checking up on somebody's mental competence." The scowl became one of anger now. "By God, I wish I had an excuse to question him-with a veridicator!"

Kellogg didn't want the Fuzzies to be sapient beings. If they weren't they'd be...fur-bearing animals. Jack thought of some overfed society dowager on Terra or Baldur, wearing the skins of Little Fuzzy and Mamma Fuzzy and Mike and Mitzi and Ko-Ko and Cinderella and Goldilocks wrapped around her adipose carcass. It made him feel sick.

VII

Tuesday dawned hot and windless, a scarlet sun coming up in a hard, brassy sky. The Fuzzies, who were in to wake Pappy Jack with their whistles, didn't like it; they were edgy and restless. Maybe it would rain today after all. They had breakfast outside on the picnic table, and then Ben decided he'd go back to his camp and pick up a few things he hadn't brought and now decided he needed.

"My hunting rifle's one," he said, "and I think I'll circle down to the edge of the brush country and see if I can pick off a zebralope. We ought to have some more fresh meat."

So, after eating, Rainsford got into his jeep and lifted away. Across the run, Kellogg and Mallin were walking back and forth in front of the camp, talking earnestly. When Ruth Ortheris and Gerd van Riebeek came out, they stopped, broke off their conversation and spoke briefly with them. Then Gerd and Ruth crossed the footbridge and came up the path together.

The Fuzzies had scattered, by this time, to hunt prawns. Little Fuzzy and Ko-Ko and Goldilocks ran to meet them; Ruth picked Goldilocks up and carried her, and Ko-Ko and Little Fuzzy ran on ahead. They greeted Jack, declining coffee; Ruth sat down in a chair with Goldilocks, Little Fuzzy jumped up on the table and began looking for goodies, and when Gerd stretched out on his back on the grass Ko-Ko sat down on his chest.

"Goldilocks is my favorite Fuzzy," Ruth was saying. "She is the sweetest thing. Of course, they're all pretty nice. I can't get over how affectionate and trusting they are; the ones we saw out in the woods were so timid."

"Well, the ones out in the woods don't have any Pappy Jack to look after them" Gerd said. "I'd imagine they're very affectionate among themselves, but they have so many things to be afraid of. You know, there's another prerequisite for sapience. It develops in some small, relatively defenseless, animal surrounded by large and dangerous enemies he can't outrun or outfight. So, to survive, he has to learn to outthink them. Like our own remote ancestors, or like Little Fuzzy; he had his choice of getting sapient or getting exterminated."

Ruth seemed troubled. "Gerd, Dr. Mallin has found absolutely nothing about them that indicates true sapience."

"Oh, Mallin be bloodied; he doesn't know what sapience is any more than I do. And a good deal less than you do, I'd say. I think he's trying to prove that the Fuzzies aren't sapient."

Ruth looked startled. "What makes you say that?"

"It's been sticking out all over him ever since he came here. You're a psychologist; don't tell me you haven't seen it. Maybe if the Fuzzies were proven sapient it would invalidate some theory he's gotten out of a book, and he'd have to do some thinking for himself. He wouldn't like that. But you have to admit he's been fighting the idea, intellectually and emotionally, right from the start. Why, they could sit down with pencils and slide rules and start working differential calculus and it wouldn't convince him."

"Dr. Mallin's trying to —" she began angrily. Then she broke it off. "Jack, excuse us. We didn't really come over here to have a fight. We came to meet some Fuzzies. Didn't we, Goldilocks?"

Goldilocks was playing with the silver charm on the chain around her neck, holding it to her ear and shaking it to make it tinkle, making small delighted sounds. Finally she held it up and said, "Yeek?"

"Yes, sweetie-pie, you can have it." Ruth took the chain from around her neck and put it over Goldilocks' head; she had to loop it three times before it would fit. "There now; that's your very own."

"Oh, you mustn't give her things like that."

"Why not. It's just cheap trade-junk. You've been on Loki, Jack, you know what it is." He did; he'd traded stuff like that to the natives himself. "Some of the girls at the hospital there gave it to me for a joke. I only wear it because I have it. Goldilocks likes it a lot better than I do."

An airjeep rose from the other side and floated across. Juan Jimenez was piloting it; Ernst Mallin stuck his head out the window on the right, asked her if she were ready and told Gerd that Kellogg would pick him up in a few minutes. After she had gotten into the jeep and it had lifted out, Gerd put Ko-Ko off his chest and sat up, getting cigarettes from his shirt pocket.

"I don't know what the devil's gotten into her," he said, watching the jeep vanish. "Oh, yes, I do. She's gotten the Word from On High. Kellogg hath spoken. Fuzzies are just silly little animals," he said bitterly.

"You work for Kellogg, too, don't you?"

"Yes. He doesn't dictate my professional opinion, though. You know, I thought, in the evil hour when I took this job —" He rose to his feet, hitching his belt to balance the weight of the pistol on the right against the camera-binoculars on the left, and changed the subject abruptly. "Jack, has Ben Rainsford sent a report on the Fuzzies to the Institute yet?" he asked.

"Why?"

"If he hasn't, tell him to hurry up and get one in."

There wasn't time to go into that further. Kellogg's jeep was rising from the camp across the run and approaching.

He decided to let the breakfast dishes go till after lunch. Kurt Borch had stayed behind at the Kellogg camp, so he kept an eye on the Fuzzies and brought them back when they started to stray toward the footbridge. Ben Rainsford hadn't returned by lunchtime, but zebralope hunting took a little time, even from the air. While he was eating, outside, one of the rented airjeeps returned from the northeast in a hurry, disgorging Ernst Mallin, Juan Jimenez and Ruth Ortheris. Kurt Borch came hurrying out; they talked for a few minutes, and then they all went inside. A little later, the second jeep came in, even faster, and landed; Kellogg and van Riebeek hastened into the living hut. There wasn't anything more to see. He carried the dishes into the kitchen and washed them, and the Fuzzies went into the bedroom for their nap.

He was sitting at the table in the living room when Gerd van Riebeek knocked on the open door.

"Jack, can I talk to you for a minute?" he asked.

"Sure. Come in."

Van Riebeek entered, unbuckling his gun belt. He shifted a chair so that he could see the door from it, and laid the belt on the floor at his feet when he sat down. Then he began to curse Leonard Kellogg in four or five languages.

"Well, I agree, in principle; why in particular, though?"

"You know what that son of a Khooghra's doing?" Gerd asked. "He and that —" He used a couple of Sheshan words, viler than anything in Lingua Terra. " —that quack headshrinker,

Mallin, are preparing a report, accusing you and Ben Rainsford of perpetrating a deliberate scientific hoax. You taught the Fuzzies some tricks; you and Rainsford, between you, made those artifacts yourselves and the two of you are conspiring to foist the Fuzzies off as sapient beings. Jack, if it weren't so goddamn stinking contemptible, it would be the biggest joke of the century!"

"I take it they wanted you to sign this report, too?"

"Yes, and I told Kellogg he could —" What Kellogg could do, it seemed, was both appalling and physiologically impossible. He cursed again, and then lit a cigarette and got hold of himself. "Here's what happened. Kellogg and I went up that stream, about twenty miles down Cold Creek, the one you've been working on, and up onto the high flat to a spring and a stream that flows down in the opposite direction. Know where I mean? Well, we found where some Fuzzies had been camping, among a lot of fallen timber. And we found a little grave, where the Fuzzies had buried one of their people."

He should have expected something like that, and yet it startled him. "You mean, they bury their dead? What was the grave like?"

"A little stone cairn, about a foot and a half by three, a foot high. Kellogg said it was just a big toilet pit, but I was sure of what it was. I opened it. Stones under the cairn, and then filled-in earth, and then a dead Fuzzy wrapped in grass. A female; she'd been mangled by something, maybe a bush-goblin. And get this Jack; they'd buried her prawn-stick with her."

"They bury their dead! What was Kellogg doing, while you were opening the grave?"

"Dithering around having ants. I'd been taking snaps of the grave, and I was burbling away like an ass about how important this was and how it was positive proof of sapience, and he was insisting that we get back to camp at once. He called the other jeep and told Mallin to get to camp immediately, and Mallin and Ruth and Juan were there when we got in. As soon as Kellogg told them what we'd found, Mallin turned fish-belly white and wanted to know how we were going to suppress it. I asked him if he was nuts, and then Kellogg came out with it. They don't dare let the Fuzzies be proven sapient."

"Because the Company wants to sell Fuzzy furs?"

Van Riebeek looked at him in surprise. "I never thought of that. I doubt if they did, either. No. Because if the Fuzzies are sapient beings, the Company's charter is automatically void."

This time Jack cursed, not Kellogg but himself.

"I am a senile old dotard! Good Lord, I know colonial law; I've been skating on the edge of it on more planets than you're years old. And I never thought of that; why, of course it would. Where are you now, with the Company, by the way?"

"Out, but I couldn't care less. I have enough in the bank for the trip back to Terra, not counting what I can raise on my boat and some other things. Xeno-naturalists don't need to worry about finding jobs. There's Ben's outfit, for instance. And, brother, when I get back to Terra, what I'll spill about this deal!"

"If you get back. If you don't have an accident before you get on the ship." He thought for a moment. "Know anything about geology?"

"Why, some; I have to work with fossils. I'm as much a paleontologist as a zoologist. Why?"

"How'd you like to stay here with me and hunt fossil jellyfish for a while? We won't make twice as much, together, as I'm making now, but you can look one way while I'm looking the other, and we may both stay alive longer that way."

"You mean that, Jack?"

"I said it, didn't I?"

Van Riebeek rose and held out his hand; Jack came around the table and shook it. Then he reached back and picked up his belt, putting it on.

"Better put yours on, too, partner. Borch is probably the only one we'll need a gun for, but —"

Van Riebeek buckled on his belt, then drew his pistol and worked the slide to load the chamber. "What are we going to do?" he asked.

"Well, we're going to try to handle it legally. Fact is, I'm even going to call the cops."

He punched out a combination on the communication screen. It lighted and opened a window into the constabulary post. The sergeant who looked out of it recognized him and grinned.

"Hi, Jack. How's the family?" he asked. "I'm coming up, one of these evenings, to see them."

"You can see some now." Ko-Ko and Goldilocks and Cinderella were coming out of the hall from the bedroom; he gathered them up and put them on the table. The sergeant was fascinated. Then he must have noticed that both Jack and Gerd were wearing their guns in the house. His eyes narrowed slightly.

"You got problems, Jack?" he asked.

"Little ones; they may grow, though. I have some guests here who have outstayed their welcome. For the record, better make it that I have squatters I want evicted. If there were a couple of blue uniforms around, maybe it might save me the price of a few cartridges."

"I read you. George was mentioning that you might regret inviting that gang to camp on you." He picked up a handphone. "Calderon to Car Three," he said. "Do you read me, Three? Well, Jack Holloway's got a little squatter trouble. Yeah; that's it. He's ordering them off his grant, and he thinks they might try to give him an argument. Yeah, sure, Peace Lovin' Jack Holloway, that's him. Well, go chase his squatters for him, and if they give you anything about being Company big wheels, we don't care what kind of wheels they are, just so's they start rolling." He replaced the phone. "Look for them in about an hour, Jack."

"Why, thanks, Phil. Drop in some evening when you can hang up your gun and stay awhile."

He blanked the screen and began punching again. This time he got a girl, and then the Company construction boss at Red Hill.

"Oh, hello, Jack; is Dr. Kellogg comfortable?"

"Not very. He's moving out this afternoon. I wish you'd have your gang come up with those scows and get that stuff out of my back yard."

"Well, he told us he was staying for a couple of weeks."

"He got his mind changed for him. He's to be off my land by sunset."

The Company man looked troubled. "Jack, you haven't been having trouble with Dr. Kellogg, have you?" he asked. "He's a big man with the Company."

"That's what he tells me. You'll still have to come and get that stuff, though."

He blanked the screen. "You know," he said, "I think it would be no more than fair to let Kellogg in on this. What's his screen combination?"

Gerd supplied it, and he punched it out. One of those tricky special Company combinations. Kurt Borch appeared in the screen immediately.

"I want to talk to Kellogg."

"Doctor Kellogg is very busy, at present."

"He's going to be a damned sight busier; this is moving day. The whole gang of you have till eighteen hundred to get off my grant."

Borch was shoved aside, and Kellogg appeared. "What's this nonsense?" he demanded angrily.

"You're ordered to move. You want to know why? I can let Gerd van Riebeek talk to you; I think there are a few things he's forgotten to call you."

"You can't order us out like this. Why, you gave us permission —"

"Permission cancelled. I've called Mike Hennen in Red Hill; he's sending his scows back for the stuff he brought here. Lieutenant Lunt will have a couple of troopers here, too. I'll expect you to have your personal things aboard your airboat when they arrive."

He blanked the screen while Kellogg was trying to tell him that it was all a misunderstanding.

"I think that's everything. It's quite a while till sundown," he added, "but I move for suspension of rules while we pour a small libation to sprinkle our new partnership. Then we can go outside and observe the enemy."

There was no observable enemy action when they went out and sat down on the bench by the kitchen door. Kellogg would be screening Mike Hennen and the constabulary post for verification, and there would be a lot of gathering up and packing to do. Finally, Kurt Borch emerged with a contragravity lifter piled with boxes and luggage, and Jimenez walking beside to steady the load. Jimenez climbed up onto the airboat and Borch floated the load up to him and then went back into the huts. This was repeated several times. In the meantime, Kellogg and Mallin seemed to be having some sort of exchange of recriminations in front. Ruth Ortheris came out, carrying a briefcase, and sat down on the edge of a table under the awning.

Neither of them had been watching the Fuzzies, until they saw one of them start down the path toward the footbridge, a glint of silver at the throat identifying Goldilocks.

"Look at that fool kid; you stay put, Gerd, and I'll bring her back."

He started down the path; by the time he had reached the bridge, Goldilocks was across and had vanished behind one of the airjeeps parked in front of the Kellogg camp. When he was across and within twenty feet of the vehicle, he heard a sound across and within twenty feet of the vehicle, he heard a sound he had never heard before—a shrill, thin shriek, like a file on saw teeth. At the same time, Ruth's voice screamed.

"Don't! Leonard, stop that!"

As he ran around the jeep, the shrieking broke off suddenly. Goldilocks was on the ground, her fur reddened. Kellogg stood over her, one foot raised. He was wearing white shoes, and they were both spotted with blood. He stamped the foot down on the little bleeding body, and then Jack was within reach of him, and something crunched under the fist he drove into Kellogg's face. Kellogg staggered and tried to raise his hands; he made a strangled noise, and for an instant the idiotic thought crossed Jack's mind that he was trying to say, "Now, please don't misunderstand me." He caught Kellogg's shirt front in his left hand, and punched him again in the face, and again, and again. He didn't know how many times he punched Kellogg before he heard Ruth Ortheris' voice:

"Jack! Watch out! Behind you!"

He let go of Kellogg's shirt and jumped aside, turning and reaching for his gun. Kurt Borch, twenty feet away, had a pistol drawn and pointed at him.

His first shot went off as soon as the pistol was clear of the holster. He fired the second while it was still recoiling; there was a spot of red on Borch's shirt that gave him an aiming point for the third. Borch dropped the pistol he hadn't been able to fire, and started folding at the knees and then at the waist. He went down in a heap on his face.

Behind him, Gerd van Riebeek's voice was saying, "Hold it, all of you; get your hands up. You, too, Kellogg."

Kellogg, who had fallen, pushed himself erect. Blood was gushing from his nose, and he tried to stanch it on the sleeve of his jacket. As he stumbled toward his companions, he blundered into Ruth Ortheris, who pushed him angrily away from her. Then she went to the little crushed body, dropping to her knees beside it and touching it. The silver charm bell on the neck chain jingled faintly. Ruth began to cry.

Juan Jimenez had climbed down from the airboat; he was looking at the body of Kurt Borch in horror.

"You killed him!" he accused. A moment later, he changed that to "murdered." Then he started to run toward the living hut.

Gerd van Riebeek fired a bullet into the ground ahead of him, bringing him up short.

"You'll stop the next one, Juan," he said. "Go help Dr. Kellogg; he got himself hurt."

"Call the constabulary," Mallin was saying. "Ruth, you go; they won't shoot at you."

"Don't bother. I called them. Remember?"

Jimenez had gotten a wad of handkerchief tissue out of his pocket and was trying to stop his superior's nosebleed. Through it, Kellogg was trying to tell Mallin that he hadn't been able to help it.

"The little beast attacked me; it cut me with that spear it was carrying."

Ruth Ortheris looked up. The other Fuzzies were with her by the body of Goldilocks; they must have come as soon as they had heard the screaming.

"She came up to him and pulled at his trouser leg, the way they all do when they want to attract your attention," she said. "She wanted him to look at her new jingle." Her voice broke, and it was a moment before she could recover it. "And he kicked her, and then stamped her to death."

"Ruth, keep your mouth shut!" Mallin ordered. "The thing attacked Leonard; it might have given him a serious wound."

"It did!" Still holding the wad of tissue to his nose with one hand, Kellogg pulled up his trouser leg with the other and showed a scar on his shin. It looked like a briar scratch. "You saw it yourself."

"Yes, I saw it. I saw you kick her and jump on her. And all she wanted was to show you her new jingle."

Jack was beginning to regret that he hadn't shot Kellogg as soon as he saw what was going on. The other Fuzzies had been trying to get Goldilocks onto her feet. When they realized that it was no use, they let the body down again and crouched in a circle around it, making soft, lamenting sounds.

"Well, when the constabulary get here, you keep quiet," Mallin was saying. "Let me do the talking."

"Intimidating witnesses, Mallin?" Gerd inquired. "Don't you know everybody'll have to testify at the constabulary post under veridication? And you're drawing pay for being a psychologist, too." Then he saw some of the Fuzzies raise their heads and look toward the southeastern horizon. "Here come the cops, now."

However, it was Ben Rainsford's airjeep, with a zebralope carcass lashed along one side. It circled the Kellogg camp and then let down quickly; Rainsford jumped out as soon as it was grounded, his pistol drawn.

"What happened, Jack?" he asked, then glanced around, from Goldilocks to Kellogg to Borch to the pistol beside Borch's body. "I get it. Last time anybody pulled a gun on you, they called it suicide."

"That's what this was, more or less. You have a movie camera in your jeep? Well, get some shots of Borch, and some of Goldilocks. Then stand by, and if the Fuzzies start doing anything different, get it all. I don't think you'll be disappointed."

Rainsford looked puzzled, but he holstered his pistol and went back to his jeep, returning with a camera. Mallin began insisting that, as a licensed M.D., he had a right to treat Kellogg's injuries. Gerd van Riebeek followed him into the living hut for a first-aid kit. They were just emerging, van Riebeek's automatic in the small of Mallin's back, when a constabulary car grounded beside Rainsford's airjeep. It wasn't Car Three. George Lunt jumped out, unsnapping the flap of his holster, while Ahmed Khadra was talking into the radio.

"What's happened, Jack? Why didn't you wait till we got here?"

"This maniac assaulted me and murdered that man over there!" Kellogg began vociferating.

"Is your name Jack too?" Lunt demanded.

"My name's Leonard Kellogg, and I'm a chief of division with the Company —"

"Then keep quiet till I ask you something. Ahmed, call the post; get Knabber and Yorimitsu, with investigative equipment, and find out what's tying up Car Three."

Mallin had opened the first-aid kit by now; Gerd, on seeing the constabulary, had holstered his pistol. Kellogg, still holding the sodden tissues to his nose, was wanting to know what there was to investigate.

"There's the murderer; you have him red-handed. Why don't you arrest him?"

"Jack, let's get over where we can watch these people without having to listen to them," Lunt said. He glanced toward the body of Goldilocks. "That happen first?"

"Watch out, Lieutenant! He still has his pistol!" Mallin shouted warningly.

They went over and sat down on the contragravity-field generator housing of one of the rented airjeeps. Jack started with Gerd van Riebeek's visit immediately after noon.

"Yes, I thought of that angle myself," Lunt said disgustedly. "I didn't think of it till this morning, though, and I didn't think things would blow up as fast as this. Hell, I just didn't think! Well, go on."

He interrupted a little later to ask: "Kellogg was stamping on the Fuzzy when you hit him. You were trying to stop him?"

"That's right. You can veridicate me on that if you want to."

"I will; I'll veridicate this whole damn gang. And this guy Borch had his heater out when you turned around? Nothing to it, Jack. We'll have to have some kind of a hearing, but it's just plain self-defense. Think any of this gang will tell the truth here, without taking them in and putting them under veridication?"

"Ruth Ortheris will, I think."

"Send her over here, will you."

She was still with the Fuzzies, and Ben Rainsford was standing beside her, his camera ready. The Fuzzies were still swaying and yeeking plaintively. She nodded and rose without speaking, going over to where Lunt waited.

"Just what did happen, Jack?" Rainsford wanted to know. "And whose side is he on?" He nodded toward van Riebeek, standing guard over Kellogg and Mallin, his thumbs in his pistol belt.

"Ours. He's quit the Company."

Just as he was finishing, Car Three put in an appearance; he had to tell the same story over again. The area in front of the Kellogg camp was getting congested; he hoped Mike Hennen's labor gang would stay away for a while. Lunt talked to van Riebeek when he had finished with Ruth, and then with Jimenez and Mallin and Kellogg. Then he and one of the men from Car Three came over to where Jack and Rainsford were standing. Gerd van Riebeek joined them just as Lunt was saying:

"Jack, Kellogg's made a murder complaint against you. I told him it was self-defense, but he wouldn't listen. So, according to the book, I have to arrest you."

"All right." He unbuckled his gun and handed it over. "Now, George, I herewith make complaint and accusation against Leonard Kellogg, charging him with the unlawful and unjustified killing of a sapient being, to wit, an aboriginal native of the planet of Zarathustra commonly known as Goldilocks."

Lunt looked at the small battered body and the six mourners around it.

"But, Jack, they aren't legally sapient beings."

"There is no such thing. A sapient being is a being on the mental level of sapience, not a being that has been declared sapient."

"Fuzzies are sapient beings," Rainsford said. "That's the opinion of a qualified xeno-naturalist."

"Two of them," Gerd van Riebeek said. "That is the body of a sapient being. There's the man who killed her. Go ahead, Lieutenant, make your pinch."

"Hey! Wait a minute!"

The Fuzzies were rising, sliding their chopper-diggers under the body of Goldilocks and lifting it on the steel shafts. Ben Rainsford was aiming his camera as Cinderella picked up her sister's weapon and followed, carrying it; the others carried the body toward the far corner of the clearing, away from the camp. Rainsford kept just behind them, pausing to photograph and then hurrying to keep up with them.

They set the body down. Mike and Mitzi and Cinderella began digging; the others scattered to hunt for stones. Coming up behind them, George Lunt took off his beret and stood holding it in both hands; he bowed his head as the grass-wrapped body was placed in the little grave and covered.

Then, when the cairn was finished, he replaced it, drew his pistol and checked the chamber.

"That does it, Jack," he said. "I am now going to arrest Leonard Kellogg for the murder of a sapient being."

VIII

Jack Holloway had been out on bail before, but never for quite so much. It was almost worth it, though, to see Leslie Coombes's eyes widen and Mohammed Ali O'Brien's jaw drop when he dumped the bag of sunstones, blazing with the heat of the day and of his body, on George Lunt's magisterial bench and invited George to pick out twenty-five thousand sols' worth. Especially after the production Coombes had made of posting Kellogg's bail with one of those precertified Company checks.

He looked at the whisky bottle in his hand, and then reached into the cupboard for another one. One for Gus Brannhard, and one for the rest of them. There was a widespread belief that that was why Gustavus Adolphus Brannhard was practicing sporadic law out here in the boondocks of a boondock planet, defending gun fighters and veldbeest rustlers. It wasn't. Nobody on Zarathustra knew the reason, but it wasn't whisky. Whisky was only the weapon with which Gus Brannhard fought off the memory of the reason.

He was in the biggest chair in the living room, which was none too ample for him; a mountain of a man with tousled gray-brown hair, his broad face masked in a tangle of gray-brown beard. He wore a faded and grimy bush jacket with clips of rifle cartridges on the breast, no shirt and a torn undershirt over a shag of gray-brown chest hair. Between the bottoms of his shorts and the tops of his ragged hose and muddy boots, his legs were covered with hair. Baby Fuzzy was sitting on his head, and Mamma Fuzzy was on his lap. Mike and Mitzi sat one on either knee. The Fuzzies had taken instantly to Gus. Bet they thought he was a Big Fuzzy.

"Aaaah!" he rumbled, as the bottle and glass were placed beside him. "Been staying alive for hours hoping for this."

"Well, don't let any of the kids get at it. Little Fuzzy trying to smoke pipes is bad enough; I don't want any dipsos in the family, too."

Gus filled the glass. To be on the safe side, he promptly emptied it into himself.

"You got a nice family, Jack. Make a wonderful impression in court-as long as Baby doesn't try to sit on the judge's head. Any jury that sees them and hears that Ortheris girl's story will acquit you from the box, with a vote of censure for not shooting Kellogg, too."

"I'm not worried about that. What I want is Kellogg convicted."

"You better worry, Jack," Rainsford said. "You saw the combination against us at the hearing."

Leslie Coombes, the Company's top attorney, had come out from Mallorysport in a yacht rated at Mach 6, and he must have crowded it to the limit all the way. With him, almost on a leash, had come Mohammed Ali O'Brien, the Colonial Attorney General, who doubled as Chief Prosecutor. They had both tried to get the whole thing dismissed-self-defense for Holloway, and killing an unprotected wild animal for Kellogg. When that had failed, they had teamed in flagrant collusion to fight the inclusion of any evidence about the Fuzzies. After all it was only a complaint court; Lieutenant Lunt, as a police magistrate, had only the most limited powers.

"You saw how far they got, didn't you?"

"I hope we don't wish they'd succeeded," Rainsford said gloomily.

"What do you mean, Ben?" Brannhard asked. "What do you think they'll do?"

"I don't know. That's what worries me. We're threatening the Zarathustra Company, and the Company's too big to be threatened safely," Rainsford replied. "They'll try to frame something on Jack."

"With veridication? That's ridiculous, Ben."

"Don't you think we can prove sapience?" Gerd van Riebeek demanded.

"Who's going to define sapience? And how?" Rainsford asked. "Why, between them, Coombes and O'Brien can even agree to accept the talk-and-build-a-fire rule."

"Huh-uh!" Brannhard was positive. "Court ruling on that, about forty years ago, on Vishnu. Infanticide case, woman charged with murder in the death of her infant child. Her lawyer moved for dismissal on the grounds that murder is defined as the killing of a sapient being, a sapient being is defined as one that can talk and build a fire, and a newborn infant can do neither. Motion denied; the court ruled that while ability to speak and produce fire is positive proof of sapience, inability to do either or both does not constitute legal proof of nonsapience. If O'Brien doesn't know that, and I doubt if he does, Coombes will." Brannhard poured another drink and gulped it before the sapient beings around him could get at it. "You know what? I will make a small wager, and I will even give odds, that the first thing Ham O'Brien does when he gets back to Mallorysport will be to enter *nolle prosequi* on both charges. What I'd like would be for him to *nol. pros.* Kellogg and let the charge against Jack go to court. He would be dumb enough to do that himself, but Leslie Coombes wouldn't let him."

"But if he throws out the Kellogg case, that's it," Gerd van Riebeek said. "When Jack comes to trial, nobody'll say a mumblin' word about sapience."

"I will, and I will not mumble it. You all know colonial law on homicide. In the case of any person killed while in commission of a felony, no prosecution may be brought in any degree, against anybody. I'm going to contend that Leonard Kellogg was murdering a sapient being, that Jack Holloway acted lawfully in attempting to stop it and that when Kurt Borch attempted to come to Kellogg's assistance he, himself, was guilty of felony, and consequently any prosecution against Jack Holloway is illegal. And to make that contention stick, I shall have to say a great many words, and produce a great deal of testimony, about the sapience of Fuzzies."

"It'll have to be expert testimony," Rainsford said. "The testimony of psychologists. I suppose you know that the only psychologists on this planet are employed by the chartered Zarathustra Company." He drank what was left of his highball, looked at the bits of ice in the bottom of his glass and then rose to mix another one. "I'd have done the same as you did, Jack, but I still wish this hadn't happened."

"*Huh!*" Mamma Fuzzy looked up, startled by the exclamation. "What do you think Victor Grego's wishing, right now?"

Victor Grego replaced the hand-phone. "Leslie, on the yacht," he said. "They're coming in now. They'll stop at the hospital to drop Kellogg, and then they're coming here."

Nick Emmert nibbled a canape. He had reddish hair, pale eyes and a wide, bovine face.

"Holloway must have done him up pretty badly," he said.

"I wish Holloway'd killed him!" He blurted it angrily, and saw the Resident General's shocked expression.

"You don't really mean that, Victor?"

"The devil I don't!" He gestured at the recorder-player, which had just finished the tape of the hearing, transmitted from the yacht at sixty-speed. "That's only a teaser to what'll come out at the trial. You know what the Company's epitaph will be? *Kicked to death, along with a Fuzzy, by Leonard Kellogg.*"

Everything would have worked out perfectly if Kellogg had only kept his head and avoided collision with Holloway. Why, even the killing of the Fuzzy and the shooting of Borch, inexcusable as that had been, wouldn't have been so bad if it hadn't been for that asinine murder complaint. That was what had provoked Holloway's counter-complaint, which was what had done the damage.

And, now that he thought of it, it had been one of Kellogg's people, van Riebeek, who had touched off the explosion in the first place. He didn't know van Riebeek himself, but Kellogg should have, and he had handled him the wrong way. He should have known what van Riebeek would go along with and what he wouldn't.

"But, Victor, they won't convict Leonard of murder," Emmert was saying. "Not for killing one of those little things."

"'Murder shall consist of the deliberate and unjustified killing of any sapient being, of any race,'" he quoted. "That's the law. If they can prove in court that the Fuzzies are sapient beings...."

Then, some morning, a couple of deputy marshals would take Leonard Kellogg out in the jail yard and put a bullet through the back of his head, which, in itself, would be no loss. The trouble was, they would also be shooting an irreparable hole in the Zarathustra Company's charter. Maybe Kellogg could be kept out of court, at that. There wasn't a ship blasted off from Darius without a couple of drunken spacemen being hustled aboard at the last moment; with the job Holloway must have done, Kellogg should look just right as a drunken spaceman. The twenty-five thousand sols' bond could be written off; that was pennies to the Company. No, that would still leave them stuck with the Holloway trial.

"You want me out of here when the others come, Victor?" Emmert asked, popping another canape into his mouth.

"No, no; sit still. This will be the last chance we'll have to get everybody together; after this, we'll have to avoid anything that'll look like collusion."

"Well, anything I can do to help; you know that, Victor," Emmert said.

Yes, he knew that. If worst came to utter worst and the Company charter were invalidated, he could still hang on here, doing what he could to salvage something out of the wreckage-if not for the Company, then for Victor Grego. But if Zarathustra were reclassified, Nick would be finished. His title, his social position, his sinecure, his grafts and perquisites, his alias-shrouded Company expense account-all out the airlock. Nick would be counted upon to do anything he could-however much that would be.

He looked across the room at the levitated globe, revolving imperceptibly in the orange spotlight. It was full dark on Beta Continent now, where Leonard Kellogg had killed a Fuzzy named Goldilocks and Jack Holloway had killed a gunman named Kurt Borch. That angered him, too; hell of a gunman! Clear shot at the broad of a man's back, and still got himself killed. Borch hadn't been any better choice than Kellogg himself. What was the matter with him; couldn't he pick men for jobs any more? And Ham O'Brien! No, he didn't have to blame himself for O'Brien. O'Brien was one of Nick Emmert's boys. And he hadn't picked Nick, either.

The squawk-box on the desk made a premonitory noise, and a feminine voice advised him that Mr. Coombes and his party had arrived.

"All right; show them in."

Coombes entered first, tall suavely elegant, with a calm, untroubled face. Leslie Coombes would wear the same serene expression in the midst of a bombardment or an earthquake. He had chosen Coombes for chief attorney, and thinking of that made him feel better. Mohammed Ali O'Brien was neither tall, elegant nor calm. His skin was almost black-he'd been born on Agni, under a hot B3 sun. His bald head glistened, and a big nose peeped over the ambuscade of a bushy white mustache. What was it they said about him? Only man on Zarathustra who could strut sitting down. And behind them, the remnant of the expedition to Beta Continent-Ernst Mallin, Juan Jimenez and Ruth Ortheris. Mallin was saying that it was a pity Dr. Kellogg wasn't with them.

"I question that. Well, please be seated. We have a great deal to discuss, I'm afraid."

Mr. Chief Justice Frederic Pendarvis moved the ashtray a few inches to the right and the slender vase with the spray of starflowers a few inches to the left. He set the framed photograph of the gentle-faced, white-haired woman directly in front of him. Then he took a thin cigar from the silver box, carefully punctured the end and lit it. Then, unable to think of further delaying tactics, he drew the two bulky loose-leaf books toward him and opened the red one, the criminal-case docket.

Something would have to be done about this; he always told himself so at this hour. Shoveling all this stuff onto Central Courts had been all right when Mallorysport had had a population of less than five thousand and nothing else on the planet had had more than five hundred, but that time was ten years past. The Chief Justice of a planetary colony shouldn't have to wade through all this to see who had been accused of blotting the brand on a veldbeest calf or who'd taken a shot at whom in a barroom. Well, at least he'd managed to get a few misdemeanor and small-claims courts established; that was something.

The first case, of course, was a homicide. It usually was. From Beta, Constabulary Fifteen, Lieutenant George Lunt. Jack Holloway-so old Jack had cut another notch on his gun-Cold Creek Valley, Federation citizen, race Terran human; willful killing of a sapient being, to wit Kurt Borch, Mallorysport, Federation citizen, race Terran human. Complainant, Leonard Kellogg, the same. Attorney of record for the defendant, Gustavus Adolphus Brannhard. The last time Jack Holloway had killed anybody, it had been a couple of thugs who'd tried to steal his sunstones; it hadn't even gotten into complaint court. This time he might be in trouble. Kellogg was a Company executive. He decided he'd better try the case himself. The Company might try to exert pressure.

The next charge was also homicide, from Constabulary, Beta Fifteen. He read it and blinked. Leonard Kellogg, willful killing of a sapient being, to wit, Jane Doe alias Goldilocks, aborigine, race Zarathustran Fuzzy, complainant, Jack Holloway, defendant's attorney of record, Leslie Coombes. In spite of the outrageous frivolity of the charge, he began to laugh. It was obviously an attempt to ridicule Kellogg's own complaint out of court. Every judicial jurisdiction ought to have at least one Gus Brannhard to liven things up a little. Race Zarathustran Fuzzy!

Then he stopped laughing suddenly and became deadly serious, like an engineer who finds a cataclysmite cartridge lying around primed and connected to a discharger. He reached out to the screen panel and began punching a combination. A spectacled young man appeared and greeted him deferentially.

"Good morning, Mr. Wilkins," he replied. "A couple of homicides at the head of this morning's docket-Holloway and Kellogg, both from Beta Fifteen. What is known about them?"

The young man began to laugh. "Oh, your Honor, they're both a lot of nonsense. Dr. Kellogg killed some pet belonging to old Jack Holloway, the sunstone digger, and in the ensuing unpleasantness-Holloway can be very unpleasant, if he feels he has to-this man Borch, who seems to have been Kellogg's bodyguard, made the suicidal error of trying to draw a gun on Holloway. I'm surprised at Lieutenant Lunt for letting either of those charges get past hearing court. Mr. O'Brien has entered *nolle prosequi* on both of them, so the whole thing can be disregarded."

Mohammed O'Brien knew a charge of cataclysmite when he saw one, too. His impulse had been to pull the detonator. Well, maybe this charge ought to be shot, just to see what it would bring down.

"I haven't approved the *nolle prosequi* yet, Mr. Wilkins," he mentioned gently. "Would you please transmit to me the hearing tapes on these cases, at sixty-speed? I'll take them on the recorder of this screen. Thank you."

He reached out and made the necessary adjustments. Wilkins, the Clerk of the Courts, left the screen, and returned. There was a wavering scream for a minute and a half. Going to take more time than he had expected. Well....

There wasn't enough ice in the glass, and Leonard Kellogg put more in. Then there was too much, and he added more brandy. He shouldn't have started drinking this early, be drunk by dinnertime if he kept it up, but what else was there to do? He couldn't go out, not with his face like this. In any case, he wasn't sure he wanted to.

They were all down on him. Ernst Mallin, and Ruth Ortheris, and even Juan Jimenez. At the constabulary post, Coombes and O'Brien had treated him like an idiot child who has to be hushed in front of company and coming back to Mallorysport they had ignored him completely.

He drank quickly, and then there was too much ice in the glass again. Victor Grego had told him he'd better take a vacation till the trial was over, and put Mallin in charge of the division. Said he oughtn't to be in charge while the division was working on defense evidence. Well, maybe; it looked like the first step toward shoving him completely out of the Company.

He dropped into a chair and lit a cigarette. It tasted badly, and after a few puffs he crushed it out. Well, what else could he have done? After they'd found that little grave, he had to make Gerd understand what it would mean to the Company. Juan and Ruth had been all right, but Gerd-The things Gerd had called him; the things he'd said about the Company. And then that call from Holloway, and the humiliation of being ordered out like a tramp.

And then that disgusting little beast had come pulling at his clothes, and he had pushed it away-well, kicked it maybe-and it had struck at him with the little spear it was carrying. Nobody but a lunatic would give a thing like that to an animal anyhow. And he had kicked it again, and it had screamed....

The communication screen in the next room was buzzing. Maybe that was Victor. He gulped the brandy left in the glass and hurried to it.

It was Leslie Coombes, his face remotely expressionless.

"Oh, hello, Leslie."

"Good afternoon, Dr. Kellogg." The formality of address was studiously rebuking. "The Chief Prosecutor just called me; Judge Pendarvis has denied the *nolle prosequi* he entered in your case and in Mr. Holloway's, and ordered both cases to trial."

"You mean they're actually taking this seriously?"

"It is serious. If you're convicted, the Company's charter will be almost automatically voided. And, although this is important only to you personally, you might, very probably, be sentenced to be shot." He shrugged that off, and continued: "Now, I'll want to talk to you about your defense, for which I am responsible. Say ten-thirty tomorrow, at my office. I should, by that time, know what sort of evidence is going to be used against you. I will be expecting you, Dr. Kellogg."

He must have said more than that, but that was all that registered. Leonard wasn't really conscious of going back to the other room, until he realized that he was sitting in his relaxer chair, filling the glass with brandy. There was only a little ice in it, but he didn't care.

They were going to try him for murder for killing that little animal, and Ham O'Brien had said they wouldn't, he'd promised he'd keep the case from trial and he hadn't, they were going to try him anyhow and if they convicted him they would take him out and shoot him for just killing a silly little animal he had killed it he'd kicked it and jumped on it he could still hear it screaming and feel the horrible soft crunching under his feet....

He gulped what was left in the glass and poured and gulped more. Then he staggered to his feet and stumbled over to the couch and threw himself onto it, face down, among the cushions.

Leslie Coombes found Nick Emmert with Victor Grego in the latter's office when he entered. They both rose to greet him, and Grego said "You've heard?"

"Yes. O'Brien called me immediately. I called my client-my client of record, that is-and told him. I'm afraid it was rather a shock to him."

"It wasn't any shock to me," Grego said as they sat down. "When Ham O'Brien's as positive about anything as he was about that, I always expect the worst."

"Pendarvis is going to try the case himself," Emmert said. "I always thought he was a reasonable man, but what's he trying to do now? Cut the Company's throat?"

"He isn't anti-Company. He isn't pro-Company either. He's just pro-law. The law says that a planet with native sapient inhabitants is a Class-IV planet, and has to have a Class-IV colonial government. If Zarathustra is a Class-IV planet, he wants it established, and the proper laws applied. If it's a Class-IV planet, the Zarathustra Company is illegally chartered. It's his job to put a stop to illegality. Frederic Pendarvis' religion is the law, and he is its priest. You never get anywhere by arguing religion with a priest."

They were both silent for a while after he had finished. Grego was looking at the globe, and he realized, now, that while he was proud of it, his pride was the pride in a paste jewel that stands for a real one in a bank vault. Now he was afraid that the real jewel was going to be stolen from him. Nick Emmert was just afraid.

"You were right yesterday, Victor. I wish Holloway'd killed that son of a Khooghra. Maybe it's not too late —"

"Yes, it is, Nick. It's too late to do anything like that. It's too late to do anything but win the case in court." He turned to Grego. "What are your people doing?"

Grego took his eyes from the globe. "Ernest Mallin's studying all the filmed evidence we have and all the descriptions of Fuzzy behavior, and trying to prove that none of it is the result of sapient mentation. Ruth Ortheris is doing the same, only she's working on the line of instinct and conditioned reflexes and nonsapient, single-stage reasoning. She has a lot of rats, and some dogs and monkeys, and a lot of apparatus, and some technician from Henry Stenson's instrument shop helping her. Juan Jimenez is studying mentation of Terran dogs, cats and primates, and Freyan kholphs and Mimir black slinkers."

"He hasn't turned up any simian or canine parallels to that funeral, has he?"

Grego said nothing, merely shook his head. Emmert muttered something inaudible and probably indecent.

"I didn't think he had. I only hope those Fuzzies don't get up in court, build a bonfire and start making speeches in Lingua Terra."

Nick Emmert cried out in panic. "You believe they're sapient yourself!"

"Of course. Don't you?"

Grego laughed sourly. "Nick thinks you have to believe a thing to prove it. It helps but it isn't necessary. Say we're a debating team; we've been handed the negative of the question. *Resolved: that Fuzzies are Sapient Beings.* Personally, I think we have the short end of it, but that only means we'll have to work harder on it."

"You know, I was on a debating team at college," Emmert said brightly. When that was disregarded, he added: "If I remember, the first thing was definition of terms."

Grego looked up quickly. "Leslie, I think Nick has something. What is the legal definition of a sapient being?"

"As far as I know, there isn't any. Sapience is something that's just taken for granted."

"How about talk-and-build-a-fire?"

He shook his head. "*People of the Colony of Vishnu* versus *Emily Morrosh*, 612 A.E." He told them about the infanticide case. "I was looking up rulings on sapience; I passed the word on to Ham O'Brien. You know, what your people will have to do will be to produce a definition of sapience, acceptable to the court, that will include all known sapient races and at the same time exclude the Fuzzies. I don't envy them."

"We need some Fuzzies of our own to study," Grego said.

"Too bad we can't get hold of Holloway's," Emmert said. "Maybe we could, if he leaves them alone at his camp."

"No. We can't risk that." He thought for a moment. "Wait a moment. I think we might be able to do it at that. Legally."

IX

Jack Holloway saw Little Fuzzy eying the pipe he had laid in the ashtray, and picked it up, putting it in his mouth. Little Fuzzy looked reproachfully at him and started to get down onto the floor. Pappy Jack was mean; didn't he think a Fuzzy might want to smoke a pipe, too? Well, maybe it wouldn't hurt him. He picked Little Fuzzy up and set him back on his lap, offering the pipestem. Little Fuzzy took a puff. He didn't cough over it; evidently he had learned how to avoid inhaling.

"They scheduled the Kellogg trial first," Gus Brannhard was saying, "and there wasn't any way I could stop that. You see what the idea is? They'll try him first, with Leslie Coombes running both the prosecution and the defense, and if they can get him acquitted, it'll prejudice the sapience evidence we introduce in your trial."

Mamma Fuzzy made another try at intercepting the drink he was hoisting, but he frustrated that. Baby had stopped trying to sit on his head, and was playing peek-a-boo from behind his whiskers.

"First," he continued, "they'll exclude every bit of evidence about the Fuzzies that they can. That won't be much, but there'll be a fight to get any of it in. What they can't exclude, they'll attack. They'll attack credibility. Of course, with veridication, they can't claim anybody's lying, but they can claim self-deception. You make a statement you believe, true or false, and the veridicator'll back you up on it. They'll attack qualifications on expert testimony. They'll quibble about statements of fact and statements of opinion. And what they can't exclude or attack, they'll accept, and then deny that it's proof of sapience."

"What the hell do they want for proof of sapience?" Gerd demanded. "Nuclear energy and contragravity and hyperdrive?"

"They will have a nice, neat, pedantic definition of sapience, tailored especially to exclude the Fuzzies, and they will present it in court and try to get it accepted, and it's up to us to guess in advance what that will be, and have a refutation of it ready, and also a definition of our own."

"Their definition will have to include Khooghras. Gerd, do the Khooghras bury their dead?"

"Hell, no; they eat them. But you have to give them this, they cook them first."

"Look, we won't get anywhere arguing about what Fuzzies do and Khooghras don't do," Rainsford said. "We'll have to get a definition of sapience. Remember what Ruth said Saturday night?"

Gerd van Riebeek looked as though he didn't want to remember what Ruth had said, or even remember Ruth herself. Jack nodded, and repeated it. "I got the impression of non-sapient intelligence shading up to a sharp line, and then sapience shading up from there, maybe a different color, or wavy lines instead of straight ones."

"That's a good graphic representation," Gerd said. "You know, that line's so sharp I'd be tempted to think of sapience as a result of mutation, except that I can't quite buy the same mutation happening in the same way on so many different planets."

Ben Rainsford started to say something, then stopped short when a constabulary siren hooted over the camp. The Fuzzies looked up interestedly. They knew what that was. Pappy Jack's friends in the blue clothes. Jack went to the door and opened it, putting the outside light on.

The car was landing; George Lunt, two of his men and two men in civilian clothes were getting out. Both the latter were armed, and one of them carried a bundle under his arm.

"Hello, George; come on in."

"We want to talk to you, Jack." Lunt's voice was strained, empty of warmth or friendliness. "At least, these men do."

"Why, yes. Sure."

He backed into the room to permit them to enter. Something was wrong; something bad had come up. Khadra came in first, placing himself beside and a little behind him. Lunt followed, glancing quickly around and placing himself between Jack and the gunrack and also the holstered pistols on the table. The third trooper let the two strangers in ahead of him, and then closed the door and put his back against it. He wondered if the court might have cancelled his bond and ordered him into custody. The two strangers —a beefy man with a scrubby black mustache, and a smaller one with a thin, saturnine face-were looking expectantly at Lunt. Rainsford and van Riebeek were on their feet. Gus Brannhard leaned over to refill his glass, but did not rise.

"Let me have the papers," Lunt said to the beefy stranger.

The other took a folded document and handed it over.

"Jack, this isn't my idea," Lunt said. "I don't want to do it, but I have to. I wouldn't want to shoot you, either, but you make any resistance and I will. I'm no Kurt Borch; I know you, and I won't take any chances."

"If you're going to serve that paper, serve it," the bigger of the two strangers said. "Don't stand yakking all night."

"Jack," Lunt said uncomfortably, "this is a court order to impound your Fuzzies as evidence in the Kellogg case. These men are deputy marshals from Central Courts; they've been ordered to bring the Fuzzies into Mallorysport."

"Let me see the order, Jack," Brannhard said, still remaining seated.

Lunt handed it to Jack, and he handed it across to Brannhard. Gus had been drinking steadily all evening; maybe he was afraid he'd show it if he stood up. He looked at it briefly and nodded.

"Court order, all right, signed by the Chief Justice." He handed it back. "They have to take the Fuzzies, and that's all there is to it. Keep that order, though, and make them give you a signed and thumbprinted receipt. Type it up for them now, Jack."

Gus wanted to busy him with something, so he wouldn't have to watch what was going on. The smaller of the two deputies had dropped the bundle from under his arm. It was a number of canvas sacks. He sat down at the typewriter, closing his ears to the noises in the room, and wrote the receipt, naming the Fuzzies and describing them, and specifying that they were in good health and uninjured. One of them tried to climb to his lap, yeeking frantically; it clutched his shirt, but it was snatched away. He was finished with his work before the invaders were with theirs. They had three Fuzzies already in sacks. Khadra was catching Cinderella. Ko-Ko and Little Fuzzy had run for the little door in the outside wall, but Lunt was standing with his heels against it, holding it shut; when they saw that, both of them began burrowing in the bedding. The third trooper and the smaller of the two deputies dragged them out and stuffed them into sacks.

He got to his feet, still stunned and only half comprehending, and took the receipt out of the typewriter. There was an argument about it; Lunt told the deputies to sign it or get the hell out without the Fuzzies. They signed, inked their thumbs and printed after their signatures. Jack gave the paper to Gus, trying not to look at the six bulging, writhing sacks, or hear the frightened little sounds.

"George, you'll let them have some of their things, won't you?" he asked.

"Sure. What kind of things?"

"Their bedding. Some of their toys."

"You mean this junk?" The smaller of the two deputies kicked the ball-and-stick construction. "All we got orders to take is the Fuzzies."

"You heard the gentleman." Lunt made the word sound worse than son of a Khooghra. He turned to the two deputies. "Well, you have them; what are you waiting for?"

Jack watched from the door as they put the sacks into the aircar, climbed in after them and lifted out. Then he came back and sat down at the table.

"They don't know anything about court orders," he said. "They don't know why I didn't stop it. They think Pappy Jack let them down."

"Have they gone, Jack?" Brannhard asked. "Sure?" Then he rose, reaching behind him, and took up a little ball of white fur. Baby Fuzzy caught his beard with both tiny hands, yeeking happily.

"Baby! They didn't get him!"

Brannhard disengaged the little hands from his beard and handed him over.

"No, and they signed for him, too." Brannhard downed what was left of his drink, got a cigar out of his pocket and lit it. "Now, we're going to go to Mallorysport and get the rest of them back."

"But.... But the Chief Justice signed that order. He won't give them back just because we ask him to."

Brannhard made an impolite noise. "I'll bet everything I own Pendarvis never saw that order. They have stacks of those things, signed in blank, in the Chief of the Court's office. If they had to wait to get one of the judges to sign an order every time they wanted to subpoena a witness or impound physical evidence, they'd never get anything done. If Ham O'Brien didn't think this up for himself, Leslie Coombes thought it up for him."

"We'll use my airboat," Gerd said. "You coming along, Ben? Let's get started."

He couldn't understand. The Big Ones in the blue clothes had been friends; they had given the whistles, and shown sorrow when the killed one was put in the ground. And why had Pappy Jack not gotten the big gun and stopped them. It couldn't be that he was afraid; Pappy Jack was afraid of nothing.

The others were near, in bags like the one in which he had been put; he could hear them, and called to them. Then he felt the edge of the little knife Pappy Jack had made. He could cut his way out of this bag now and free the others, but that would be no use. They were in one of the things the Big Ones went up into the sky in, and if he got out now, there would be nowhere to go and they would be caught at once. Better to wait.

The one thing that really worried him was that he would not know where they were being taken. When they did get away, how would they ever find Pappy Jack again?

Gus Brannhard was nervous, showing it by being overtalkative, and that worried Jack. He'd stopped twice at mirrors along the hallway to make sure that his gold-threaded gray neckcloth was properly knotted and that his black jacket was zipped up far enough and not too far. Now, in front of the door marked THE CHIEF JUSTICE, he paused before pushing the button to fluff his newly shampooed beard.

There were two men in the Chief Justice's private chambers. Pendarvis he had seen once or twice, but their paths had never crossed. He had a good face, thin and ascetic, the face of a man at peace with himself. With him was Mohammed Ali O'Brien, who seemed surprised to see them enter, and then apprehensive. Nobody shook hands; the Chief Justice bowed slightly and invited them to be seated.

"Now," he continued, when they found chairs, "Miss Ugatori tells me that you are making complaint against an action by Mr. O'Brien here."

"We are indeed, your Honor." Brannhard opened his briefcase and produced two papers-the writ, and the receipt for the Fuzzies, handing them across the desk. "My client and I wish to know upon what basis of legality your Honor sanctioned this act, and by what right Mr. O'Brien sent his officers to Mr. Holloway's camp to snatch these little people from their friend and protector, Mr. Holloway."

The judge looked at the two papers. "As you know, Miss Ugatori took prints of them when you called to make this appointment. I've seen them. But believe me, Mr. Brannhard, this is the first time I have seen the original of this writ. You know how these things are signed in blank. It's a practice that has saved considerable time and effort, and until now they have only been used when there was no question that I or any other judge would approve. Such a question should certainly have existed in this case, because had I seen this writ I would never have signed it." He turned to the now fidgeting Chief Prosecutor. "Mr. O'Brien," he said, "one simply does not impound sapient beings as evidence, as, say, one impounds a veldbeest calf in a brand-alteration case. The fact that the sapience of these Fuzzies is still *sub judice* includes the presumption of its possibility. Now you know perfectly well that the courts may take no action in the face of the possibility that some innocent person may suffer wrong."

"And, your Honor," Brannhard leaped into the breach, "it cannot be denied that these Fuzzies have suffered a most outrageous wrong! Picture them-no, picture innocent and artless children, for that is what these Fuzzies are, happy trusting little children, who, until then, had known only kindness and affection-rudely kidnapped, stuffed into sacks by brutal and callous men —"

"Your Honor!" O'Brien's face turned even blacker than the hot sun of Agni had made it. "I cannot hear officers of the court so characterized without raising my voice in protest!"

"Mr. O'Brien seems to forget that he is speaking in the presence of two eye witnesses to this brutal abduction."

"If the officers of the court need defense, Mr. O'Brien, the court will defend them. I believe that you should presently consider a defense of your own actions."

"Your Honor, I insist that I only acted as I felt to be my duty," O'Brien said. "These Fuzzies are a key exhibit in the case of *People* versus *Kellogg*, since only by demonstration of their sapience can any prosecution against the defendant be maintained."

"Then why," Brannhard demanded, "did you endanger them in this criminally reckless manner?"

"Endanger them?" O'Brien was horrified. "Your Honor, I acted only to insure their safety and appearance in court."

"So you took them away from the only man on this planet who knows anything about their proper care, a man who loves them as he would his own human children, and you subjected them to abuse, which, for all you knew, might have been fatal to them."

Judge Pendarvis nodded. "I don't believe, Mr. Brannhard, that you have overstated the case. Mr. O'Brien, I take a very unfavorable view of your action in this matter. You had no right to have what are at least putatively sapient beings treated in this way, and even viewing them as mere physical evidence I must agree with Mr. Brannhard's characterization of your conduct as criminally reckless. Now, speaking judicially, I order you to produce those Fuzzies immediately and return them to the custody of Mr. Holloway."

"Well, of course, your Honor." O'Brien had been growing progressively distraught, and his face now had the gray-over-brown hue of a walnut gunstock that has been out in the rain all day. "It'll take an hour or so to send for them and have them brought here."

"You mean they're not in this building?" Pendarvis asked.

"Oh, no, your Honor, there are no facilities here. I had them taken to Science Center —"

"*What?*"

Jack had determined to keep his mouth shut and let Gus do the talking. The exclamation was literally forced out of him. Nobody noticed; it had also been forced out of both Gus Brannhard and Judge Pendarvis. Pendarvis leaned forward and spoke with dangerous mildness:

"Do you refer, Mr. O'Brien, to the establishment of the Division of Scientific Study and Research of the chartered Zarathustra Company?"

"Why, yes; they have facilities for keeping all kinds of live animals, and they do all the scientific work for —"

Pendarvis cursed blasphemously. Brannhard looked as startled as though his own briefcase had jumped at his throat and tried to bite him. He didn't look half as startled as Ham O'Brien did.

"So you think," Pendarvis said, recovering his composure with visible effort, "that the logical custodian of prosecution evidence in a murder trial is the defendant? Mr. O'Brien, you simply enlarge my view of the possible!"

"The Zarathustra Company isn't the defendant," O'Brien argued sullenly.

"Not of record, no," Brannhard agreed. "But isn't the Zarathustra Company's scientific division headed by one Leonard Kellogg?"

"Dr. Kellogg's been relieved of his duties, pending the outcome of the trial. The division is now headed by Dr. Ernst Mallin."

"Chief scientific witness for the defense; I fail to see any practical difference."

"Well, Mr. Emmert said it would be all right," O'Brien mumbled.

"Jack, did you hear that?" Brannhard asked. "Treasure it in your memory. You may have to testify to it in court sometime." He turned to the Chief Justice. "Your Honor, may I suggest the recovery of these Fuzzies be entrusted to Colonial Marshal Fane, and may I further suggest that Mr. O'Brien be kept away from any communication equipment until they are recovered."

"That sounds like a prudent suggestion, Mr. Brannhard. Now, I'll give you an order for the surrender of the Fuzzies, and a search warrant, just to be on the safe side. And, I think, an Orphans' Court form naming Mr. Holloway as guardian of these putatively sapient beings. What are their names? Oh, I have them here on this receipt." He smiled pleasantly. "See, Mr. O'Brien, we're saving you a lot of trouble."

O'Brien had little enough wit to protest. "But these are the defendant and his attorney in another murder case I'm prosecuting," he began.

Pendarvis stopped smiling. "Mr. O'Brien, I doubt if you'll be allowed to prosecute anything or anybody around here any more, and I am specifically relieving you of any connection with either the Kellogg or the Holloway trial, and if I hear any argument out of you about it, I will issue a bench warrant for your arrest on charges of malfeasance in office."

X

Colonial Marshal Max Fane was as heavy as Gus Brannhard and considerably shorter. Wedged between them on the back seat of the marshal's car, Jack Holloway contemplated the backs of the two uniformed deputies on the front seat and felt a happy smile spread through him. Going to get his Fuzzies back. Little Fuzzy, and Ko-Ko, and Mike, and Mamma Fuzzy, and Mitzi, and Cinderella; he named them over and imagined them crowding around him, happy to be back with Pappy Jack.

The car settled onto the top landing stage of the Company's Science Center, and immediately a Company cop came running up. Gus opened the door, and Jack climbed out after him.

"Hey, you can't land here!" the cop was shouting. "This is for Company executives only!"

Max Fane emerged behind them and stepped forward; the two deputies piled out from in front.

"The hell you say, now," Fane said. "A court order lands anywhere. Bring him along, boys; we wouldn't want him to go and bump himself on a communication screen anywhere."

The Company cop started to protest, then subsided and fell in between the deputies. Maybe it was beginning to dawn on him that the Federation courts were bigger than the chartered Zarathustra Company after all. Or maybe he just thought there'd been a revolution.

Leonard Kellogg's—temporarily Ernst Mallin's—office was on the first floor of the penthouse, counting down from the top landing stage. When they stepped from the escalator, the hall was crowded with office people, gabbling excitedly in groups; they all stopped talking as soon as they saw what was coming. In the division chief's outer office three or four girls jumped to their feet; one of them jumped into the bulk of Marshal Fane, which had interposed itself between her and the communication screen. They were all shooed out into the hall, and one of the deputies was dropped there with the prisoner. The middle office was empty. Fane took his badgeholder in his left hand as he pushed through the door to the inner office.

Kellogg's—temporarily Mallin's—secretary seemed to have preceded them by a few seconds; she was standing in front of the desk sputtering incoherently. Mallin, starting to rise from his chair, froze, hunched forward over the desk. Juan Jimenez, standing in the middle of the room, seemed to have seen them first; he was looking about wildly as though for some way of escape.

Fane pushed past the secretary and went up to the desk, showing Mallin his badge and then serving the papers. Mallin looked at him in bewilderment.

"But we're keeping those Fuzzies for Mr. O'Brien, the Chief Prosecutor," he said. "We can't turn them over without his authorization."

"This," Max Fane said gently, "is an order of the court, issued by Chief Justice Pendarvis. As for Mr. O'Brien, I doubt if he's Chief Prosecutor any more. In fact, I suspect that he's in jail. *And that*," he shouted, leaning forward as far as his waistline would permit and banging on the desk with his fist, "*is where I'm going to stuff you, if you don't get those Fuzzies in here and turn them over immediately!*"

If Fane had suddenly metamorphosed himself into a damnthing, it couldn't have shaken Mallin more. Involuntarily he cringed from the marshal, and that finished him.

"But I can't," he protested. "We don't know exactly where they are at the moment."

"You don't know." Fane's voice sank almost to a whisper. "You admit you're holding them here, but you…don't…know…where. *Now start over again; tell the truth this time!*"

At that moment, the communication screen began making a fuss. Ruth Ortheris, in a light blue tailored costume, appeared in it.

"Dr. Mallin, what *is* going on here?" she wanted to know. "I just came in from lunch, and a gang of men are tearing my office up. Haven't you found the Fuzzies yet?"

"What's that?" Jack yelled. At the same time, Mallin was almost screaming: "Ruth! Shut up! Blank out and get out of the building!"

With surprising speed for a man of his girth, Fane whirled and was in front of the screen, holding his badge out.

"I'm Colonel Marshal Fane. Now, young woman; I want you up here right away. Don't make me send anybody after you, because I won't like that and neither will you."

"Right away, Marshal." She blanked the screen.

Fane turned to Mallin. "Now." He wasn't bothering with vocal tricks any more. "Are you going to tell me the truth, or am I going to run you in and put a veridicator on you? Where are those Fuzzies?"

"But I don't know!" Mallin wailed. "Juan, you tell him; you took charge of them. I haven't seen them since they were brought here."

Jack managed to fight down the fright that was clutching at him and got control of his voice.

"If anything's happened to those Fuzzies, you two are going to envy Kurt Borch before I'm through with you," he said.

"All right, how about it?" Fane asked Jimenez. "Start with when you and Ham O'Brien picked up the Fuzzies at Central Courts Building last night.

"Well, we brought them here. I'd gotten some cages fixed up for them, and —"

Ruth Ortheris came in. She didn't try to avoid Jack's eyes, nor did she try to brazen it out with him. She merely nodded distantly, as though they'd met on a ship sometime, and sat down.

"What happened, Marshal?" she asked. "Why are you here with these gentlemen?"

"The court's ordered the Fuzzies returned to Mr. Holloway." Mallin was in a dither. "He has some kind a writ or something, and we don't know where they are."

"Oh, *no!*" Ruth's face, for an instant, was dismay itself. "Not when —" Then she froze shut.

"I came in about o-seven-hundred," Jimenez was saying, "to give them food and water, and they'd broken out of their cages. The netting was broken loose on one cage and the Fuzzy that had been in it had gotten out and let the others out. They got into my office-they made a perfect shambles of it-and got out the door into the hall, and now we don't know where they are. And I don't know how they did any of it."

Cages built for something with no hands and almost no brains. Ever since Kellogg and Mallin had come to the camp, Mallin had been hypnotizing himself into the just-silly-little-animals doctrine. He must have succeeded; last night he'd acted accordingly.

"We want to see the cages," Jack said.

"Yeah." Fane went to the outer door. "Miguel."

The deputy came in, herding the Company cop ahead of him.

"You heard what happened?" Fane asked.

"Yeah. Big Fuzzy jailbreak. What did they do, make little wooden pistols and bluff their way out?"

"By God, I wouldn't put it past them. Come along. Bring Chummy along with you; he knows the inside of this place better than we do. Piet, call in. We want six more men. Tell Chang to borrow from the constabulary if he has to."

"Wait a minute," Jack said. He turned to Ruth. "What do you know about this?"

"Well, not much. I was with Dr. Mallin here when Mr. Grego —I mean, Mr. O'Brien-called to tell us that the Fuzzies were going to be kept here till the trial. We were going to fix up a room for them, but till that could be done, Juan got some cages to put them in. That was all I knew about it till o-nine-thirty, when I came in and found everything in an uproar and was told that the Fuzzies had gotten loose during the night. I knew they couldn't get out of the building, so I went to my office and lab to start overhauling some equipment we were going to need with the Fuzzies. About ten-hundred, I found I couldn't do anything with it, and my assistant and I loaded it on a pickup truck and took it to Henry Stenson's instrument shop. By the time I was through there, I had lunch and then came back here."

He wondered briefly how a polyencephalographic veridicator would react to some of those statements; might be a good idea if Max Fane found out.

"I'll stay here," Gus Brannhard was saying, "and see if I can get some more truth out of these people."

"Why don't you screen the hotel and tell Gerd and Ben what's happened?" he asked. "Gerd used to work here; maybe he could help us hunt."

"Good idea. Piet, tell our re-enforcements to stop at the Mallory on the way and pick him up." Fane turned to Jimenez. "Come along; show us where you had these Fuzzies and how they got away."

"You say one of them broke out of his cage and then released the others," Jack said to Jimenez as they were going down on the escalator. "Do you know which one it was?"

Jimenez shook his head. "We just took them out of the bags and put them into the cages."

That would be Little Fuzzy; he'd always been the brains of the family. With his leadership, they might have a chance. The trouble was that this place was full of dangers Fuzzies knew nothing about-radiation and poisons and electric wiring and things like that. If they really had escaped. That was a possibility that began worrying Jack.

On each floor they passed going down, he could glimpse parties of Company employees in the halls, armed with nets and blankets and other catching equipment. When they got off Jimenez led them through a big room of glass cases-mounted specimens and articulated skeletons of Zarathustran mammals. More people were there, looking around and behind and even into the cases. He began to think that the escape was genuine, and not just a cover-up for the murder of the Fuzzies.

Jimenez took them down a narrow hall beyond to an open door at the end. Inside, the permanent night light made a blue-white glow; a swivel chair stood just inside the door. Jimenez pointed to it.

"They must have gotten up on that to work the latch and open the door," he said.

It was like the doors at the camp, spring latch, with a handle instead of a knob. They'd have learned how to work it from watching him. Fane was trying the latch.

"Not too stiff," he said. "Your little fellows strong enough to work it?"

He tried it and agreed. "Sure. And they'd be smart enough to do it, too. Even Baby Fuzzy, the one your men didn't get, would be able to figure that out."

"And look what they did to my office," Jimenez said, putting on the lights.

They'd made quite a mess of it. They hadn't delayed long to do it, just thrown things around. Everything was thrown off the top of the desk. They had dumped the wastebasket, and left it dumped. He saw that and chuckled. The escape had been genuine all right.

"Probably hunting for things they could use as weapons, and doing as much damage as they could in the process." There was evidently a pretty wide streak of vindictiveness in Fuzzy character. "I don't think they like you, Juan."

"Wouldn't blame them," Fane said. "Let's see what kind of a houdini they did on these cages now."

The cages were in a room-file room, storeroom, junk room-behind Jimenez's office. It had a spring lock, too, and the Fuzzies had dragged one of the cages over and stood on it to open the door. The cages themselves were about three feet wide and five feet long, with plywood bottoms, wooden frames and quarter-inch netting on the sides and tops. The tops were hinged, and fastened with hasps, and bolts slipped through the staples with nuts screwed on them. The nuts had been unscrewed from five and the bolts slipped out; the sixth cage had been broken open from the inside, the netting cut away from the frame at one corner and bent back in a triangle big enough for a Fuzzy to crawl through.

"I can't understand that," Jimenez was saying. "Why that wire looks as though it had been cut."

"It was cut. Marshal, I'd pull somebody's belt about this, if I were you. Your men aren't very careful about searching prisoners. One of the Fuzzies hid a knife out on them." He remembered how Little Fuzzy and Ko-Ko had burrowed into the bedding in apparently unreasoning panic, and explained about the little spring-steel knives he had made. "I suppose he palmed it and hugged himself into a ball, as though he was scared witless, when they put him in the bag."

"Waited till he was sure he wouldn't get caught before he used it, too," the marshal said. "That wire's soft enough to cut easily." He turned to Jimenez. "You people ought to be glad I'm ineligible for jury duty. Why don't you just throw it in and let Kellogg cop a plea?"

Gerd van Riebeek stopped for a moment in the doorway and looked into what had been Leonard Kellogg's office. The last time he'd been here, Kellogg had had him on the carpet about that land-prawn business. Now Ernst Mallin was sitting in Kellogg's chair, trying to look unconcerned and not making a very good job of it. Gus Brannhard sprawled in an armchair, smoking a cigar and looking at Mallin as he would look at a river pig when he doubted whether it was worth shooting it or not. A uniformed deputy turned quickly, then went back to studying an elaborate wall chart showing the interrelation of Zarathustran mammals-he'd made the original of that chart himself. And Ruth Ortheris sat apart from the desk and the three men, smoking. She looked up and then, when she saw that he was looking past and away from her, she lowered her eyes.

"You haven't found them?" he asked Brannhard.

The fluffy-bearded lawyer shook his head. "Jack has a gang down in the cellar, working up. Max is in the psychology lab, putting the Company cops who were on duty last night under veridication. They all claim, and the veridicator backs them up, that it was impossible for the Fuzzies to get out of the building."

"They don't know what's impossible, for a Fuzzy."

"That's what I told him. He didn't give me any argument, either. He's pretty impressed with how they got out of those cages."

Ruth spoke. "Gerd, we didn't hurt them. We weren't going to hurt them at all. Juan put them in cages because we didn't have any other place for them, but we were going to fix up a nice room, where they could play together...." Then she must have seen that he wasn't listening, and stopped, crushing out her cigarette and rising. "Dr. Mallin, if these people haven't any more questions to ask me, I have a lot of work to do."

"You want to ask her anything, Gerd?" Brannhard inquired.

Once he had had something very important he had wanted to ask her. He was glad, now, that he hadn't gotten around to it. Hell, she was so married to the Company it'd be bigamy if she married him too.

"No, I don't want to talk to her at all."

She started for the door, then hesitated. "Gerd, I...." she began. Then she went out. Gus Brannhard looked after her, and dropped the ash of his cigar on Leonard Kellogg's —now Ernst Mallin's —floor.

Gerd detested her, and she wouldn't have had any respect for him if he didn't. She ought to have known that something like this would happen. It always did, in the business. A smart girl, in the business, never got involved with any one man; she always got herself four or five boyfriends, on all possible sides, and played them off one against another.

She'd have to get out of the Science Center right away. Marshal Fane was questioning people under veridication; she didn't dare let him get around to her. She didn't dare go to her office; the veridicator was in the lab across the hall, and that's where he was working. And she didn't dare —

Yes, she could do that, by screen. She went into an office down the hall; a dozen people recognized her at once and began bombarding her with questions about the Fuzzies. She brushed them off and went to a screen, punching a combination. After a slight delay, an elderly man with a thin-lipped, bloodless face appeared. When he recognized her, there was a brief look of annoyance on the thin face.

"Mr. Stenson," she began, before he could say anything: "That apparatus I brought to your shop this morning-the sensory-response detector-we've made a simply frightful mistake. There's nothing wrong with it whatever, and if anything's done with it, it may cause serious damage."

"I don't think I understand, Dr. Ortheris."

"Well, it was a perfectly natural mistake. You see, we're all at our wits' end here. Mr. Holloway and his lawyer and the Colonial Marshal are here with an order from Judge Pendarvis for the return of those Fuzzies. None of us know what we're doing at all. Why the whole trouble with the apparatus was the fault of the operator. We'll have to have it back immediately, all of it."

"I see, Dr. Ortheris." The old instrument maker looked worried. "But I'm afraid the apparatus has already gone to the workroom. Mr. Stephenson has it now, and I can't get in touch with him at present. If the mistake can be corrected, what do you want done?"

"Just hold it; I'll call or send for it."

She blanked the screen. Old Johnson, the chief data synthesist, tried to detain her with some question.

"I'm sorry, Mr. Johnson. I can't stop now. I have to go over to Company House right away."

The suite at the Hotel Mallory was crowded when Jack Holloway returned with Gerd van Riebeek; it was noisy with voices, and the ventilators were laboring to get rid of the tobacco smoke. Gus Brannhard, Ben Rainsford and Baby Fuzzy were meeting the press.

"Oh, Mr. Holloway!" somebody shouted as he entered. "Have you found them yet?"

"No; we've been all over Science Center from top to bottom. We know they went down a few floors from where they'd been caged, but that's all. I don't think they could have gotten outside; the only exit on the ground level's through a vestibule where a Company policeman was on duty, and there's no way for them to have climbed down from any of the terraces or landing stages."

"Well, Mr. Holloway, I hate to suggest this," somebody else said, "but have you eliminated the possibility that they may have hidden in a trash bin and been dumped into the mass-energy converter?"

"We thought of that. The converter's underground, in a vault that can be entered only by one door, and that was locked. No trash was disposed of between the time they were brought there and the time the search started, and everything that's been sent to the converter since has been checked piece by piece."

"Well, I'm glad to hear that, Mr. Holloway, and I know that everybody hearing this will be glad, too. I take it you've not given up looking for them?"

"Are we on the air now? No, I have not; I'm staying here in Mallorysport until I either find them or am convinced that they aren't in the city. And I am offering a reward of two thousand sols apiece for their return to me. If you'll wait a moment, I'll have descriptions ready for you...."

Victor Grego unstoppered the refrigerated cocktail jug. "More?" he asked Leslie Coombes.

"Yes, thank you." Coombes held his glass until it was filled. "As you say, Victor, you made the decision, but you made it on my advice, and the advice was bad."

He couldn't disagree, even politely, with that. He hoped it hadn't been ruinously bad. One thing, Leslie wasn't trying to pass the buck, and considering how Ham O'Brien had mishandled his end of it, he could have done so quite plausibly.

"I used bad judgment," Coombes said dispassionately, as though discussing some mistake Hitler had made, or Napoleon. "I thought O'Brien wouldn't try to use one of those presigned writs, and I didn't think Pendarvis would admit, publicly, that he signed court orders in blank. He's been severely criticized by the press about that."

He hadn't thought Brannhard and Holloway would try to fight a court order either. That was one of the consequences of being too long in a seemingly irresistible position; you didn't expect resistance. Kellogg hadn't expected Jack Holloway to order him off his land grant. Kurt Borch had thought all he needed to do with a gun was pull it and wave it around. And Jimenez had expected the Fuzzies to just sit in their cages.

"I wonder where they got to," Coombes was saying. "I understand they couldn't be found at all in the building."

"Ruth Ortheris has an idea. She got away from Science Center before Fane could get hold of her and veridicate her. It seems she and an assistant took some apparatus out, about ten o'clock, in a truck. She thinks the Fuzzies hitched a ride with her. I know that sounds rather improbable, but hell, everything else sounds impossible. I'll have it followed up. Maybe we can find them before Holloway does. They're not inside Science Center, that's sure." His own glass was empty; he debated a refill and voted against it. "O'Brien's definitely out, I take it?"

"Completely. Pendarvis gave him his choice of resigning or facing malfeasance charges."

"They couldn't really convict him of malfeasance for that, could they? Misfeasance, maybe, but —"

"They could charge him. And then they could interrogate him under veridication about his whole conduct in office, and you know what they would bring out," Coombes said. "He almost broke an arm signing his resignation. He's still Attorney General of the Colony, of course; Nick issued a statement supporting him. That hasn't done Nick as much harm as O'Brien could do spilling what he knows about Residency affairs.

"Now Brannhard is talking about bringing suit against the Company, and he's furnishing copies of all the Fuzzy films Holloway has to the news services. Interworld News is going hog-wild with it, and even the services we control can't play it down too much. I don't know who's going to be prosecuting these cases; but whoever it is, he won't dare pull any punches. And the whole thing's made Pendarvis hostile to us. I know, the law and the evidence and nothing but the law and the evidence, but the evidence is going to filter into his conscious mind through this hostility. He's called a conference with Brannhard and myself for tomorrow afternoon; I don't know what that's going to be like."

XI

The two lawyers had risen hastily when Chief Justice Pendarvis entered; he responded to their greetings and seated himself at his desk, reaching for the silver cigar box and taking out a panatela. Gustavus Adolphus Brannhard picked up the cigar he had laid aside and began puffing on it; Leslie Coombes took a cigarette from his case. They both looked at him, waiting like two drawn weapons — a battle ax and a rapier.

"Well, gentlemen, as you know, we have a couple of homicide cases and nobody to prosecute them," he began.

"Why bother, your Honor?" Coombes asked. "Both charges are completely frivolous. One man killed a wild animal, and the other killed a man who was trying to kill him."

"Well, your Honor, I don't believe my client is guilty of anything, legally or morally," Brannhard said. "I want that established by an acquittal." He looked at Coombes. "I should think Mr. Coombes would be just as anxious to have his client cleared of any stigma of murder, too."

"I am quite agreed. People who have been charged with crimes ought to have public vindication if they are innocent. Now, in the first place, I planned to hold the Kellogg trial first, and then the Holloway trial. Are you both satisfied with that arrangement?"

"Absolutely not, your Honor," Brannhard said promptly. "The whole basis of the Holloway defense is that this man Borch was killed in commission of a felony. We're prepared to prove that, but we don't want our case prejudiced by an earlier trial."

Coombes laughed. "Mr. Brannhard wants to clear his client by preconvicting mine. We can't agree to anything like that."

"Yes, and he is making the same objection to trying your client first. Well, I'm going to remove both objections. I'm going to order the two cases combined, and both defendants tried together."

A momentary glow of unholy glee on Gus Brannhard's face; Coombes didn't like the idea at all.

"Your Honor, I trust that that suggestion was only made facetiously," he said.

"It wasn't, Mr. Coombes."

"Then if your Honor will not hold me in contempt for saying so, it is the most shockingly irregular —I won't go so far as to say improper-trial procedure I've ever heard of. This is not a case of accomplices charged with the same crime; this is a case of two men charged with different criminal acts, and the conviction of either would mean the almost automatic acquittal of the other. I don't know who's going to be named to take Mohammed O'Brien's place, but I pity him from the bottom of my heart. Why, Mr. Brannhard and I could go off somewhere and play poker while the prosecutor would smash the case to pieces."

"Well, we won't have just one prosecutor, Mr. Coombes, we will have two. I'll swear you and Mr. Brannhard in as special prosecutors, and you can prosecute Mr. Brannhard's client, and he yours. I think that would remove any further objections."

It was all he could do to keep his face judicially grave and unmirthful. Brannhard was almost purring, like a big tiger that had just gotten the better of a young goat; Leslie Coombes's suavity was beginning to crumble slightly at the edges.

"Your Honor, that is a most excellent suggestion," Brannhard declared. "I will prosecute Mr. Coombes's client with the greatest pleasure in the universe."

"Well, all I can say, your Honor, is that if the first proposal was the most irregular I had ever heard, the record didn't last long!"

"Why, Mr. Coombes, I went over the law and the rules of jurisprudence very carefully, and I couldn't find a word that could be construed as disallowing such a procedure."

"I'll bet you didn't find any precedent for it either!"

Leslie Coombes should have known better than that; in colonial law, you can find a precedent for almost anything.

"How much do you bet, Leslie?" Brannhard asked, a larcenous gleam in his eye.

"Don't let him take your money away from you. I found, inside an hour, sixteen precedents, from twelve different planetary jurisdictions."

"All right, your Honor," Coombes capitulated. "But I hope you know what you're doing. You're turning a couple of cases of the People of the Colony into a common civil lawsuit."

Gus Brannhard laughed. "What else is it?" he demanded. "*Friends of Little Fuzzy* versus *The chartered Zarathustra Company*; I'm bringing action as friend of incompetent aborigines for recognition of sapience, and Mr. Coombes, on behalf of the Zarathustra Company, is contesting to preserve the Company's charter, and that's all there is or ever was to this case."

That was impolite of Gus. Leslie Coombes had wanted to go on to the end pretending that the Company charter had absolutely nothing to do with it.

There was an unending stream of reports of Fuzzies seen here and there, often simultaneously in impossibly distant parts of the city. Some were from publicity seekers and pathological liars and crackpots; some were the result of honest mistakes or overimaginativeness. There was some reason to suspect that not a few had originated with the Company, to confuse the search. One thing did come to light which heartened Jack Holloway. An intensive if concealed search was being made by the Company police, and by the Mallorysport police department, which the Company controlled.

Max Fane was giving every available moment to the hunt. This wasn't because of ill will for the Company, though that was present, nor because the Chief Justice was riding him. The Colonial Marshal was pro-Fuzzy. So were the Colonial Constabulary, over whom Nick Emmert's administration seemed to have little if any authority. Colonel Ian Ferguson, the commandant, had his appointment direct from the Colonial Office on Terra. He had called by screen to offer his help, and George Lunt, over on Beta, screened daily to learn what progress was being made.

Living at the Hotel Mallory was expensive, and Jack had to sell some sunstones. The Company gem buyers were barely civil to him; he didn't try to be civil at all. There was also a noticeable coolness toward him at the bank. On the other hand, on several occasions, Space Navy officers and ratings down from Xerxes Base went out of their way to accost him, introduce themselves, shake hands with him and give him their best wishes.

Once, in one of the weather-domed business centers, an elderly man with white hair showing under his black beret greeted him.

"Mr. Holloway I want to tell you how grieved I am to learn about the disappearance of those little people of yours," he said. "I'm afraid there's nothing I can do to help you, but I hope they turn up safely."

"Why, thank you, Mr. Stenson." He shook hands with the old master instrument maker. "If you could make me a pocket veridicator, to use on some of these people who claim they saw them, it would be a big help."

"Well, I do make rather small portable veridicators for the constabulary, but I think what you need is an instrument for detection of psychopaths, and that's slightly beyond science at present. But if you're still prospecting for sunstones, I have an improved micro-ray scanner I just developed, and...."

He walked with Stenson to his shop, had a cup of tea and looked at the scanner. From Stenson's screen, he called Max Fane. Six more people had claimed to have seen the Fuzzies.

Within a week, the films taken at the camp had been shown so frequently on telecast as to wear out their interest value. Baby, however, was still available for new pictures, and in a few days a girl had to be hired to take care of his fan mail. Once, entering a bar, Jack thought he saw Baby sitting on a woman's head. A second look showed that it was only a life-sized doll, held on with an elastic band. Within a week, he was seeing Baby Fuzzy hats all over town, and shop windows were full of life-sized Fuzzy dolls.

In the late afternoon, two weeks after the Fuzzies had vanished, Marshal Fane dropped him at the hotel. They sat in the car for a moment, and Fane said:

"I think this is the end of it. We're all out of cranks and exhibitionists now."

He nodded. "That woman we were talking to. She's crazy as a bedbug."

"Yeah. In the past ten years she's confessed to every unsolved crime on the planet. It shows you how hard up we are that I waste your time and mine listening to her."

"Max, nobody's seen them. You think they just aren't, any more, don't you?"

The fat man looked troubled. "Well, Jack, it isn't so much that nobody's seen them. Nobody's seen any trace of them. There are land-prawns all around, but nobody's found a cracked shell. And six active, playful, inquisitive Fuzzies ought to be getting into things. They ought to be raiding food markets, and fruit stands, getting into places and ransacking. But there hasn't been a thing. The Company police have stopped looking for them now."

"Well, I won't. They must be around somewhere." He shook Fane's hand, and got out of the car. "You've been awfully helpful, Max. I want you to know how much I thank you."

He watched the car lift away, and then looked out over the city —a vista of treetop green, with roofs and the domes of shopping centers and business centers and amusement centers showing through, and the angular buttes of tall buildings rising above. The streetless contragravity city of a new planet that had never known ground traffic. The Fuzzies could be hiding anywhere among those trees-or they could all be dead in some man-made trap. He thought of all the deadly places into which they could have wandered. Machinery, dormant and quiet, until somebody threw a switch. Conduits, which could be flooded without warning, or filled with scalding steam or choking gas. Poor little Fuzzies, they'd think a city was as safe as the woods of home, where there was nothing worse than harpies and damnthings.

Gus Brannhard was out when he went down to the suite; Ben Rainsford was at a reading screen, studying a psychology text, and Gerd was working at a desk that had been brought in. Baby was playing on the floor with the bright new toys they had gotten for him. When Pappy Jack came in, he dropped them and ran to be picked up and held.

"George called," Gerd said. "They have a family of Fuzzies at the post now."

"Well, that's great." He tried to make it sound enthusiastic. "How many?"

"Five, three males and two females. They call them Dr. Crippen, Dillinger, Ned Kelly, Lizzie Borden and Calamity Jane."

Wouldn't it be just like a bunch of cops to hang names like that on innocent Fuzzies?

"Why don't you call the post and say hello to them?" Ben asked.

"Baby likes them; he'd think it was fun to talk to them again."

He let himself be urged into it, and punched out the combination. They were nice Fuzzies; almost, but of course not quite, as nice as his own.

"If your family doesn't turn up in time for the trial, have Gus subpoena ours," Lunt told him. "You ought to have some to produce in court. Two weeks from now, this mob of ours will be doing all kinds of things. You ought to see them now, and we only got them yesterday afternoon."

He said he hoped he'd have his own by then; he realized that he was saying it without much conviction.

They had a drink when Gus came in. He was delighted with the offer from Lunt. Another one who didn't expect to see Pappy Jack's Fuzzies alive again.

"I'm not doing a damn thing here," Rainsford said. "I'm going back to Beta till the trial. Maybe I can pick up some ideas from George Lunt's Fuzzies. I'm damned if I'm getting away from this crap!" He gestured at the reading screen. "All I have is a vocabulary, and I don't know what half the words mean." He snapped it off. "I'm beginning to wonder if maybe Jimenez mightn't have been right and Ruth Ortheris is wrong. Maybe you can be just a little bit sapient."

"Maybe it's possible to be sapient and not know it," Gus said. "Like the character in the old French play who didn't know he was talking prose."

"What do you mean, Gus?" Gerd asked.

"I'm not sure I know. It's just an idea that occurred to me today. Kick it around and see if you can get anything out of it."

"I believe the difference lies in the area of consciousness," Ernst Mallin was saying. "You all know, of course, the axiom that only one-tenth, never more than one-eighth, of our mental activity occurs above the level of consciousness. Now let us imagine a hypothetical race whose entire mentation is conscious."

"I hope they stay hypothetical," Victor Grego, in his office across the city, said out of the screen. "They wouldn't recognize us as sapient at all."

"We wouldn't be sapient, as they'd define the term," Leslie Coombes, in the same screen with Grego, said. "They'd have some equivalent of the talk-and-build-a-fire rule, based on abilities of which we can't even conceive."

Maybe, Ruth thought, they might recognize us as one-tenth to as much as one-eighth sapient. No, then we'd have to recognize, say, a chimpanzee as being one-one-hundredth sapient, and a flatworm as being sapient to the order of one-billionth.

"Wait a minute," she said. "If I understand, you mean that nonsapient beings think, but only subconsciously?"

"That's correct, Ruth. When confronted by some entirely novel situation, a nonsapient animal will think, but never consciously. Of course, familiar situations are dealt with by pure habit and memory-response."

"You know, I've just thought of something," Grego said. "I think we can explain that funeral that's been bothering all of us in nonsapient terms." He lit a cigarette, while they all looked at him expectantly. "Fuzzies," he continued, "bury their ordure: they do this to avoid an unpleasant sense-stimulus, a bad smell. Dead bodies quickly putrefy and smell badly; they are thus equated, subconsciously, with ordure and must be buried. All Fuzzies carry weapons. A Fuzzy's weapon is-still subconsciously-regarded as a part of the Fuzzy, hence it must also be buried."

Mallin frowned portentously. The idea seemed to appeal to him, but of course he simply couldn't agree too promptly with a mere layman, even the boss.

"Well, so far you're on fairly safe ground, Mr. Grego," he admitted. "Association of otherwise dissimilar things because of some apparent similarity is a recognized element of nonsapient animal behavior." He frowned again. "That *could* be an explanation. I'll have to think of it."

About this time tomorrow, it would be his own idea, with grudging recognition of a suggestion by Victor Grego. In time, that would be forgotten; it would be the Mallin Theory. Grego was apparently agreeable, as long as the job got done.

"Well, if you can make anything out of it, pass it on to Mr. Coombes as soon as possible, to be worked up for use in court," he said.

XII

Ben Rainsford went back to Beta Continent, and Gerd van Riebeek remained in Mallorysport. The constabulary at Post Fifteen had made steel chopper-diggers for their Fuzzies, and reported a gratifying abatement of the land-prawn nuisance. They also made a set of scaled-down carpenter tools, and their Fuzzies were building themselves a house out of scrap crates and boxes. A pair of Fuzzies showed up at Ben Rainsford's camp, and he adopted them, naming them Flora and Fauna.

Everybody had Fuzzies now, and Pappy Jack only had Baby. He was lying on the floor of the parlor, teaching Baby to tie knots in a piece of string. Gus Brannhard, who spent most of the day in the office in the Central Courts building which had been furnished to him as special prosecutor, was lolling in an armchair in red-and-blue pajamas, smoking a cigar, drinking coffee-his whisky consumption was down to a couple of drinks a day-and studying texts on two reading screens at once, making an occasional remark into a stenomemophone. Gerd was at the desk, spoiling notepaper in an effort to work something out by symbolic logic. Suddenly he crumpled a sheet and threw it across the room, cursing. Brannhard looked away from his screens.

"Trouble, Gerd?"

Gerd cursed again. "How the devil can I tell whether Fuzzies generalize?" he demanded. "How can I tell whether they form abstract ideas? How can I prove, even, that they have ideas at all? Hell's blazes, how can I even prove, to your satisfaction, that I think consciously?"

"Working on that idea I mentioned?" Brannhard asked.

"I was. It seemed like a good idea but...."

"Suppose we go back to specific instances of Fuzzy behavior, and present them as evidence of sapience?" Brannhard asked. "That funeral, for instance."

"They'll still insist that we define sapience."

The communication screen began buzzing. Baby Fuzzy looked up disinterestedly, and then went back to trying to untie a figure-eight knot he had tied. Jack shoved himself to his feet and put the screen on. It was Max Fane, and for the first time that he could remember, the Colonial Marshal was excited.

"Jack, have you had any news on the screen lately?"

"No. Something turn up?"

"God, yes! The cops are all over the city hunting the Fuzzies; they have orders to shoot on sight. Nick Emmert was just on the air with a reward offer-five hundred sols apiece, dead or alive."

It took a few seconds for that to register. Then he became frightened. Gus and Gerd were both on their feet and crowding to the screen behind him.

"They have some bum from that squatters' camp over on the East Side who claims the Fuzzies beat up his ten-year-old daughter," Fane was saying. "They have both of them at police head-quarters, and they've handed the story out to Zarathustra News, and Planetwide Coverage. Of course, they're Company-controlled; they're playing it for all it's worth."

"Have they been veridicated?" Brannhard demanded.

"No, and the city cops are keeping them under cover. The girl says she was playing outdoors and these Fuzzies jumped her and began beating her with sticks. Her injuries are listed as multiple bruises, fractured wrist and general shock."

"I don't believe it! They wouldn't attack a child."

"I want to talk to that girl and her father," Brannhard was saying. "And I'm going to demand that they make their statements under veridication. This thing's a frameup, Max; I'd bet my ears on it. Timing's just right; only a week till the trial."

Maybe the Fuzzies had wanted the child to play with them, and she'd gotten frightened and hurt one of them. A ten-year-old human child would look dangerously large to a Fuzzy, and if they thought they were menaced they would fight back savagely.

They were still alive and in the city. That was one thing. But they were in worse danger than they had ever been; that was another. Fane was asking Brannhard how soon he could be dressed.

"Five minutes? Good, I'll be along to pick you up," he said. "Be seeing you."

Jack hurried into the bedroom he and Brannhard shared; he kicked off his moccasins and began pulling on his boots. Brannhard, pulling his trousers up over his pajama pants, wanted to know where he thought he was going.

"With you. I've got to find them before some dumb son of a Khooghra shoots them."

"You stay here," Gus ordered. "Stay by the communication screen, and keep the viewscreen on for news. But don't stop putting your boots on; you may have to get out of here fast if I call you and tell you they've been located. I'll call you as soon as I get anything definite."

Gerd had the screen on for news, and was getting Planetwide, openly owned and operated by the Company. The newscaster was wrought up about the brutal attack on the innocent child, but he was having trouble focusing the blame. After all, who'd let the Fuzzies escape in the first place? And even a skilled semanticist had trouble in making anything called a Fuzzy sound menacing. At least he gave particulars, true or not.

The child, Lolita Lurkin, had been playing outside her home at about twenty-one hundred when she had suddenly been set upon by six Fuzzies, armed with clubs. Without provocation, they had dragged her down and beaten her severely. Her screams had brought her father, and he had driven the Fuzzies away. Police had brought both the girl and her father, Oscar Lurkin, to headquarters, where they had told their story. City police, Company police and constabu-lary troopers and parties of armed citizens were combing the eastern side of the city; Resident General Emmert had acted at once to offer a reward of five thousand sols apiece....

"The kid's lying, and if they ever get a veridicator on her, they'll prove it", he said. "Emmert, or Grego, or the two of them together, bribed those people to tell that story."

"Oh, I take that for granted," Gerd said. "I know that place. Junktown. Ruth does a lot of work there for juvenile court." He stopped briefly, pain in his eyes, and then continued: "You can hire anybody to do anything over there for a hundred sols, especially if the cops are fixed in advance."

He shifted to the Interworld News frequency; they were covering the Fuzzy hunt from an aircar. The shanties and parked airjalopies of Junktown were floodlighted from above; lines of men were beating the brush and poking among them. Once a car passed directly below the pickup, a man staring at the ground from it over a machine gun.

"Wooo! Am I glad I'm not in that mess!" Gerd exclaimed. "Anybody sees something he thinks is a Fuzzy and half that gang'll massacre each other in ten seconds."

"I hope they do!"

Interworld News was pro-Fuzzy; the commentator in the car was being extremely sarcastic about the whole thing. Into the middle of one view of a rifle-bristling line of beaters somebody in the studio cut a view of the Fuzzies, taken at the camp, looking up appealingly while waiting for breakfast. "These," a voice said, "are the terrible monsters against whom all these brave men are protecting us."

A few moments later, a rifle flash and a bang, and then a fusillade brought Jack's heart into his throat. The pickup car jetted toward it; by the time it reached the spot, the shooting had stopped, and a crowd was gathering around something white on the ground. He had to force himself to look, then gave a shuddering breath of relief. It was a zaragoat, a three-horned domesticated ungulate.

"Oh-Oh! Some squatter's milk supply finished." The commentator laughed. "Not the first one tonight either. Attorney General-former Chief Prosecutor —O'Brien's going to have quite a few suits against the administration to defend as a result of this business."

"He's going to have a goddamn thundering big one from Jack Holloway!"

The communication screen buzzed; Gerd snapped it on.

"I just talked to Judge Pendarvis," Gus Brannhard reported out of it. "He's issuing an order restraining Emmert from paying any reward except for Fuzzies turned over alive and uninjured to Marshal Fane. And he's issuing a warning that until the status of the Fuzzies is determined, anybody killing one will face charges of murder."

"That's fine, Gus! Have you seen the girl or her father yet?"

Brannhard snarled angrily. "The girl's in the Company hospital, in a private room. The doctors won't let anybody see her. I think Emmert's hiding the father in the Residency. And I haven't seen the two cops who brought them in, or the desk sergeant who booked the complaint, or the detective lieutenant who was on duty here. They've all lammed out. Max has a couple of men over in Junktown, trying to find out who called the cops in the first place. We may get something out of that."

The Chief Justice's action was announced a few minutes later; it got to the hunters a few minutes after that and the Fuzzy hunt began falling apart. The City and Company police dropped out immediately. Most of the civilians, hoping to grab five thousand sols' worth of live Fuzzy, stayed on for twenty minutes, and so, apparently to control them, did the constabulary. Then the reward was cancelled, the airborne floodlights went off and the whole thing broke up.

Gus Brannhard came in shortly afterward, starting to undress as soon as he heeled the door shut after him. When he had his jacket and neckcloth off, he dropped into a chair, filled a water tumbler with whisky, gulped half of it and then began pulling off his boots.

"If that drink has a kid sister, I'll take it," Gerd muttered. "What happened, Gus?"

Brannhard began to curse. "The whole thing's a fake; it stinks from here to Nifflheim. It would stink *on* Nifflheim." He picked up a cigar butt he had laid aside when Fane's call had come in and relighted it. "We found the woman who called the police. Neighbor; she says she saw Lurkin come home drunk, and a little later she heard the girl screaming. She says he beats her up every time he gets drunk, which is about five times a week, and she'd made up her mind to stop it the next chance she got. She denied having seen anything that even looked like a Fuzzy anywhere around."

The excitement of the night before had incubated a new brood of Fuzzy reports; Jack went to the marshal's office to interview the people making them. The first dozen were of a piece with the ones that had come in originally. Then he talked to a young man who had something of different quality.

"I saw them as plain as I'm seeing you, not more than fifty feet away," he said. "I had an autocarbine, and I pulled up on them, but gosh, I couldn't shoot them. They were just like little people, Mr. Holloway, and they looked so scared and helpless. So I held over their heads and let off a two-second burst to scare them away before anybody else saw them and shot them."

"Well, son, I'd like to shake your hand for that. You know, you thought you were throwing away a lot of money there. How many did you see?"

"Well, only four. I'd heard that there were six, but the other two could have been back in the brush where I didn't see them."

He pointed out on the map where it had happened. There were three other people who had actually seen Fuzzies; none were sure how many, but they were all positive about locations and times. Plotting the reports on the map, it was apparent that the Fuzzies were moving north and west across the outskirts of the city.

Brannhard showed up for lunch at the hotel, still swearing, but half amusedly.

"They've exhumed Ham O'Brien, and they've put him to work harassing us," he said. "Whole flock of civil suits and dangerous-nuisance complaints and that sort of thing; idea's to keep me amused with them while Leslie Coombes is working up his case for the trial. Even tried to get the manager here to evict Baby; I threatened him with a racial-discrimination suit, and that stopped that. And I just filed suit against the Company for seven million sols on behalf of the Fuzzies-million apiece for them and a million for their lawyer."

"This evening," Jack said, "I'm going out in a car with a couple of Max's deputies. We're going to take Baby, and we'll have a loud-speaker on the car." He unfolded the city map. "They seem to be traveling this way; they ought to be about here, and with Baby at the speaker, we ought to attract their attention."

They didn't see anything, though they kept at it till dusk. Baby had a wonderful time with the loud-speaker; when he yeeked into it, he produced an ear-splitting noise, until the three humans in the car flinched every time he opened his mouth. It affected dogs too; as the car moved back and forth, it was followed by a chorus of howling and baying on the ground.

The next day, there were some scattered reports, mostly of small thefts. A blanket spread on the grass behind a house had vanished. A couple of cushions had been taken from a porch couch. A frenzied mother reported having found her six-year-old son playing with some Fuzzies; when she had rushed to rescue him, the Fuzzies had scampered away and the child had begun weeping. Jack and Gerd rushed to the scene. The child's story, jumbled and imagination-colored, was definite on one point-the Fuzzies had been nice to him and hadn't hurt him. They got a recording of that on the air at once.

When they got back to the hotel, Gus Brannhard was there, bubbling with glee.

"The Chief Justice gave me another job of special prosecuting," he said. "I'm to conduct an investigation into the possibility that this thing, the other night, was a frame-up, and I'm to prepare complaints against anybody who's done anything prosecutable. I have authority to hold hearings, and subpoena witnesses, and interrogate them under veridication. Max Fane has specific orders to cooperate. We're going to start, tomorrow, with Chief of Police Dumont and work down. And maybe we can work up, too, as far as Nick Emmert and Victor Grego." He gave a rumbling laugh. "Maybe that'll give Leslie Coombes something to worry about."

Gerd brought the car down beside the rectangular excavation. It was fifty feet square and twenty feet deep, and still going deeper, with a power shovel in it and a couple of dump scows beside. Five or six men in coveralls and ankle boots advanced to meet them as they got out.

"Good morning, Mr. Holloway," one of them said. "It's right down over the edge of the hill. We haven't disturbed anything."

"Mind running over what you saw again? My partner here wasn't in when you called."

The foreman turned to Gerd. "We put off a couple of shots about an hour ago. Some of the men, who'd gone down over the edge of the hill, saw these Fuzzies run out from under that rock ledge down there, and up the hollow, that way." He pointed. "They called me, and I went down for a look, and saw where they'd been camping. The rock's pretty hard here, and we used pretty heavy charges. Shock waves in the ground was what scared them."

They started down a path through the flower-dappled tall grass toward the edge of the hill, and down past the gray outcropping of limestone that formed a miniature bluff twenty feet high and a hundred in length. Under an overhanging ledge, they found two cushions, a red-and-gray blanket, and some odds and ends of old garments that looked as though they had once been used for polishing rags. There was a broken kitchen spoon, and a cold chisel, and some other metal articles.

"That's it, all right. I talked to the people who lost the blanket and the cushions. They must have made camp last night, after your gang stopped work; the blasting chased them out. You say you saw them go up that way?" he asked, pointing up the little stream that came down from the mountains to the north.

The stream was deep and rapid, too much so for easy fording by Fuzzies; they'd follow it back into the foothills. He took everybody's names and thanked them. If he found the Fuzzies himself and had to pay off on an information-received basis, it would take a mathematical genius to decide how much reward to pay whom.

"Gerd, if you were a Fuzzy, where would you go up there?" he asked.

Gerd looked up the stream that came rushing down from among the wooded foothills.

"There are a couple more houses farther up," he said. "I'd get above them. Then I'd go up one of those side ravines, and get up among the rocks, where the damnthings couldn't get me. Of course, there are no damnthings this close to town, but they wouldn't know that."

"We'll need a few more cars. I'll call Colonel Ferguson and see what he can do for me. Max is going to have his hands full with this investigation Gus started."

Piet Dumont, the Mallorysport chief of police, might have been a good cop once, but for as long as Gus Brannhard had known him, he had been what he was now-an empty shell of unsupported arrogance, with a sagging waistline and a puffy face that tried to look tough and only succeeded in looking unpleasant. He was sitting in a seat that looked like an old fashioned electric chair, or like one of those instruments of torture to which beauty-shop customers submit themselves. There was a bright conical helmet on his head, and electrodes had been clamped to various portions of his anatomy. On the wall behind him was a circular screen which ought to have been a calm turquoise blue, but which was flickering from dark blue through violet to mauve. That was simple nervous tension and guilt and anger at the humiliation of being subjected to veridicated interrogation. Now and then there would be a stabbing flicker of bright red as he toyed mentally with some deliberate misstatement of fact.

"You know, yourself, that the Fuzzies didn't hurt that girl," Brannhard told him.

"I don't know anything of the kind," the police chief retorted. "All I know's what was reported to me."

That had started out a bright red; gradually it faded into purple. Evidently Piet Dumont was adopting a rules-of-evidence definition of truth.

"Who told you about it?"

"Luther Woller. Detective lieutenant on duty at the time."

The veridicator agreed that that was the truth and not much of anything but the truth.

"But you know that what really happened was that Lurkin beat the girl himself, and Woller persuaded them both to say the Fuzzies did it," Max Fane said.

"I don't know anything of the kind!" Dumont almost yelled. The screen blazed red. "All I know's what they told me; nobody said anything else." Red and blue, juggling in a typical quibbling pattern. "As far as I know, it was the Fuzzies done it."

"Now, Piet," Fane told him patiently. "You've used this same veridicator here often enough to know you can't get away with lying on it. Woller's making you the patsy for this, and you know that, too. Isn't it true, now, that to the best of your knowledge and belief those Fuzzies never touched that girl, and it wasn't till Woller talked to Lurkin and his daughter at headquarters that anybody even mentioned Fuzzies?"

The screen darkened to midnight blue, and then, slowly, it lightened.

"Yeah, that's true," Dumont admitted. He avoided their eyes, and his voice was surly. "I thought that was how it was, and I asked Woller. He just laughed at me and told me to forget it." The screen seethed momentarily with anger. "That son of a Khooghra thinks he's chief, not me. One word from me and he does just what he damn pleases!"

"Now you're being smart, Piet," Fane said. "Let's start all over...."

A constabulary corporal was at the controls of the car Jack had rented from the hotel: Gerd had taken his place in one of the two constabulary cars. The third car shuttled between them, and all three talked back and forth by radio.

"Mr. Holloway." It was the trooper in the car Gerd had been piloting. "Your partner's down on the ground; he just called me with his portable. He's found a cracked prawn-shell."

"Keep talking; give me direction," the corporal at the controls said, lifting up.

In a moment, they sighted the other car, hovering over a narrow ravine on the left bank of the stream. The third car was coming in from the north. Gerd was still squatting on the ground when they let down beside him. He looked up as they jumped out.

"This is it, Jack" he said. "Regular Fuzzy job."

So it was. Whatever they had used, it hadn't been anything sharp; the head was smashed instead of being cleanly severed. The shell, however, had been broken from underneath in the standard manner, and all four mandibles had been broken off for picks. They must have all eaten at the prawn, share alike. It had been done quite recently.

They sent the car up, and while all three of them circled about, they went up the ravine on foot, calling: "Little Fuzzy! Little Fuzzy!" They found a footprint, and then another, where seepage water had moistened the ground. Gerd was talking excitedly into the portable radio he carried slung on his chest.

"One of you, go ahead a quarter of a mile, and then circle back. They're in here somewhere."

"I see them! I see them!" a voice whooped out of the radio. "They're going up the slope on your right, among the rocks!"

"Keep them in sight; somebody come and pick us up, and we'll get above them and head them off."

The rental car dropped quickly, the corporal getting the door open. He didn't bother going off contragravity; as soon as they were in and had pulled the door shut behind them, he was lifting again. For a moment, the hill swung giddily as the car turned, and then Jack saw them, climbing the steep slope among the rocks. Only four of them, and one was helping another. He wondered which ones they were, what had happened to the other two and if the one that needed help had been badly hurt.

The car landed on the top, among the rocks, settling at an awkward angle. He, Gerd and the pilot piled out and started climbing and sliding down the declivity. Then he found himself within reach of a Fuzzy and grabbed. Two more dashed past him, up the steep hill. The one he snatched at had something in his hand, and aimed a vicious blow at his face with it; he had barely time to block it with his forearm. Then he was clutching the Fuzzy and disarming him; the weapon was a quarter-pound ballpeen hammer. He put it in his hip pocket and then picked up the struggling Fuzzy with both hands.

"You hit Pappy Jack!" he said reproachfully. "Don't you know Pappy any more? Poor scared little thing!"

The Fuzzy in his arms yeeked angrily. Then he looked, and it was no Fuzzy he had ever seen before-not Little Fuzzy, nor funny, pompous Ko-Ko, nor mischievous Mike. It was a stranger Fuzzy.

"Well, no wonder; of course you didn't know Pappy Jack. You aren't one of Pappy Jack's Fuzzies at all!"

At the top, the constabulary corporal was sitting on a rock, clutching two Fuzzies, one under each arm. They stopped struggling and yeeked piteously when they saw their companion also a captive.

"Your partner's down below, chasing the other one," the corporal said. "You better take these too; you know them and I don't."

"Hang onto them; they don't know me any better than they do you."

With one hand, he got a bit of Extee Three out of his coat and offered it; the Fuzzy gave a cry of surprised pleasure, snatched it and gobbled it. He must have eaten it before. When he gave some to the corporal, the other two, a male and a female, also seemed familiar with it. From below, Gerd was calling:

"I got one, It's a girl Fuzzy; I don't know if it's Mitzi or Cinderella. And, my God, wait till you see what she was carrying."

Gerd came into sight, the fourth Fuzzy struggling under one arm and a little kitten, black with a white face, peeping over the crook of his other elbow. He was too stunned with disappointment to look at it with more than vague curiosity.

"They aren't our Fuzzies, Gerd. I never saw any of them before."

"Jack, are you sure?"

"Of course I'm sure!" He was indignant. "Don't you think I know my own Fuzzies? Don't you think they'd know me?"

"Where'd the pussy come from?" the corporal wanted to know.

"God knows. They must have picked it up somewhere. She was carrying it in her arms, like a baby."

"They're somebody's Fuzzies. They've been fed Extee Three. We'll take them to the hotel. Whoever it is, I'll bet he misses them as much as I do mine."

His own Fuzzies, whom he would never see again. The full realization didn't hit him until he and Gerd were in the car again. There had been no trace of his Fuzzies from the time they had broken out of their cages at Science Center. This quartet had appeared the night the city police had manufactured the story of the attack on the Lurkin girl, and from the moment they had been seen by the youth who couldn't bring himself to fire on them, they had left a trail that he had been able to pick up at once and follow. Why hadn't his own Fuzzies attracted as much notice in the three weeks since they had vanished?

Because his own Fuzzies didn't exist any more. They had never gotten out of Science Center alive. Somebody Max Fane hadn't been able to question under veridication had murdered them. There was no use, any more, trying to convince himself differently.

"We'll stop at their camp and pick up the blanket and the cushions and the rest of the things. I'll send the people who lost them checks," he said. "The Fuzzies ought to have those things."

XIII

The management of the Hotel Mallory appeared to have undergone a change of heart, or of policy, toward Fuzzies. It might have been Gus Brannhard's threats of action for racial discrimination and the possibility that the Fuzzies might turn out to be a race instead of an animal species after all. The manager might have been shamed by the way the Lurkin story had crumbled into discredit, and influenced by the revived public sympathy for the Fuzzies. Or maybe he just decided that the chartered Zarathustra Company wasn't as omnipotent as he'd believed. At any rate, a large room, usually used for banquets, was made available for the Fuzzies

George Lunt and Ben Rainsford were bringing in for the trial, and the four strangers and their black-and-white kitten were installed there. There were a lot of toys of different sorts, courtesy of the management, and a big view screen. The four strange Fuzzies dashed for this immediately and turned it on, yeeking in delight as they watched landing craft coming down and lifting out at the municipal spaceport. They found it very interesting. It only bored the kitten.

With some misgivings, Jack brought Baby down and introduced him. They were delighted with Baby, and Baby thought the kitten was the most wonderful thing he had ever seen. When it was time to feed them, Jack had his own dinner brought in, and ate with them. Gus and Gerd came down and joined him later.

"We got the Lurkin kid and her father," Gus said, and then falsettoed: "'Naw, Pop gimme a beatin', and the cops told me to say it was the Fuzzies.'"

"She say that?"

"Under veridication, with the screen blue as a sapphire, in front of half a dozen witnesses and with audiovisuals on. Interworld's putting it on the air this evening. Her father admitted it, too; named Woller and the desk sergeant. We're still looking for them; till we get them, we aren't any closer to Emmert or Grego. We did pick up the two car cops, but they don't know anything on anybody but Woller."

That was good enough, as far as it went, Brannhard thought, but it didn't go far enough. There were those four strange Fuzzies showing up out of nowhere, right in the middle of Nick Emmert's drive-hunt. They'd been kept somewhere by somebody-that was how they'd learned to eat Extee Three and found out about viewscreens. Their appearance was too well synchronized to be accidental. The whole thing smelled to him of a booby trap.

One good thing had happened. Judge Pendarvis had decided that it would be next to impossible, in view of the widespread public interest in the case and the influence of the Zarathustra Company, to get an impartial jury, and had proposed a judicial trial by a panel of three judges, himself one of them. Even Leslie Coombes had felt forced to agree to that.

He told Jack about the decision. Jack listened with apparent attentiveness, and then said:

"You know, Gus, I'll always be glad I let Little Fuzzy smoke my pipe when he wanted to, that night out at camp."

The way he was feeling, he wouldn't have cared less if the case was going to be tried by a panel of three zaragoats.

Ben Rainsford, his two Fuzzies, and George Lunt, Ahmed Khadra and the other constabulary witnesses and their family, arrived shortly before noon on Saturday. The Fuzzies were quartered in the stripped-out banquet room, and quickly made friends with the four already there, and with Baby. Each family bedded down apart, but they ate together and played with each others' toys and sat in a clump to watch the viewscreen. At first, the Ferny Creek family showed jealousy when too much attention was paid to their kitten, until they decided that nobody was trying to steal it.

It would have been a lot of fun, eleven Fuzzies and a Baby Fuzzy and a black-and-white kitten, if Jack hadn't kept seeing his own family, six quiet little ghosts watching but unable to join the frolicking.

Max Fane brightened when he saw who was on his screen.

"Well, Colonel Ferguson, glad to see you."

"Marshal," Ferguson was smiling broadly. "You'll be even gladder in a minute. A couple of my men, from Post Eight, picked up Woller and that desk sergeant, Fuentes."

"Ha!" He started feeling warm inside, as though he had just downed a slug of Baldur honey-rum. "How?"

"Well, you know Nick Emmert has a hunting lodge down there. Post Eight keeps an eye on it for him. This afternoon, one of Lieutenant Obefemi's cars was passing over it, and they picked up some radiation and infrared on their detectors, as though the power was on inside. When they went down to investigate, they found Woller and Fuentes making themselves at home. They brought them in, and both of them admitted under veridication that Emmert had given them the keys and sent them down there to hide out till after the trial.

"They denied that Emmert had originated the frameup. That had been one of Woller's own flashes of genius, but Emmert knew what the score was and went right along with it. They're being brought up here the first thing tomorrow morning."

"Well, that's swell, Colonel! Has it gotten out to the news services yet?"

"No. We would like to have them both questioned here in Mallorysport, and their confessions recorded, before we let the story out. Otherwise, somebody might try to take steps to shut them up for good."

That had been what he had been thinking of. He said so, and Ferguson nodded. Then he hesitated for a moment, and said:

"Max, do you like the situation here in Mallorysport? Be damned if I do."

"What do you mean?"

"There are too many strangers in town," Ian Ferguson said. "All the same kind of strangers-husky-looking young men, twenty to thirty, going around in pairs and small groups. I've been noticing it since day before last, and there seem to be more of them every time I look around."

"Well, Ian, it's a young man's planet, and we can expect a big crowd in town for the trial...."

He didn't really believe that. He just wanted Ian Ferguson to put a name on it first. Ferguson shook his head.

"No, Max. This isn't a trial-day crowd. We both know what they're like; remember when they tried the Gawn brothers? No whooping it up in bars, no excitement, no big crap games; this crowd's just walking around, keeping quiet, as though they expected a word from somebody."

"Infiltration." Goddamit, he'd said it first, himself after all! "Victor Grego's worried about this."

"I know it, Max. And Victor Grego's like a veldbeest bull; he isn't dangerous till he's scared, and then watch out. And against the gang that's moving in here, the men you and I have together would last about as long as a pint of trade-gin at a Sheshan funeral."

"You thinking of pushing the panic-button?"

The constabulary commander frowned. "I don't want to. A dim view would be taken back on Terra if I did it without needing to. Dimmer view would be taken of needing to without doing it, though. I'll make another check, first."

Gerd van Riebeek sorted the papers on the desk into piles, lit a cigarette and then started to mix himself a highball.

"Fuzzies are members of a sapient race," he declared. "They reason logically, both deductively and inductively. They learn by experiment, analysis and association. They formulate general principles, and apply them to specific instances. They plan their activities in advance. They make designed artifacts, and artifacts to make artifacts. They are able to symbolize, and convey ideas in symbolic form, and form symbols by abstracting from objects.

"They have aesthetic sense and creativity," he continued. "They become bored in idleness, and they enjoy solving problems for the pleasure of solving them. They bury their dead ceremoniously, and bury artifacts with them."

He blew a smoke ring, and then tasted his drink. "They do all these things, and they also do carpenter work, blow police whistles, make eating tools to eat land-prawns with and put molecule-model balls together. Obviously they are sapient beings. But don't please don't ask me to define sapience, because God damn it to Nifflheim, I still can't!"

"I think you just did," Jack said.

"No, that won't do. I need a definition."

"Don't worry, Gerd," Gus Brannhard told him. "Leslie Coombes will bring a nice shiny new definition into court. We'll just use that."

XIV

They walked together, Frederic and Claudette Pendarvis, down through the roof garden toward the landing stage, and, as she always did, Claudette stopped and cut a flower and fastened it in his lapel.

"Will the Fuzzies be in court?" she asked.

"Oh, they'll have to be. I don't know about this morning; it'll be mostly formalities." He made a grimace that was half a frown and half a smile. "I really don't know whether to consider them as witnesses or as exhibits, and I hope I'm not called on to rule on that, at least at the start. Either way, Coombes or Brannhard would accuse me of showing prejudice."

"I want to see them. I've seen them on screen, but I want to see them for real."

"You haven't been in one of my courts for a long time, Claudette. If I find that they'll be brought in today, I'll call you. I'll even abuse my position to the extent of arranging for you to see them outside the courtroom. Would you like that?"

She'd love it. Claudette had a limitless capacity for delight in things like that. They kissed good-bye, and he went to where his driver was holding open the door of the aircar and got in. At a thousand feet he looked back; she was still standing at the edge of the roof garden, looking up.

He'd have to find out whether it would be safe for her to come in. Max Fane was worried about the possibility of trouble, and so was Ian Ferguson, and neither was given to timorous imaginings. As the car began to descend toward the Central Courts buildings, he saw that there were guards on the roof, and they weren't just carrying pistols-he caught the glint of rifle barrels, and the twinkle of steel helmets. Then, as he came in, he saw that their uniforms were a lighter shade of blue than the constabulary wore. Ankle boots and red-striped trousers; Space Marines in dress blues. So Ian Ferguson had pushed the button. It occurred to him that Claudette might be safer here than at home.

A sergeant and a couple of men came up as he got out; the sergeant touched the beak of his helmet in the nearest thing to a salute a Marine ever gave anybody in civilian clothes.

"Judge Pendarvis? Good morning, sir."

"Good morning, sergeant. Just why are Federation Marines guarding the court building?"

"Standing by, sir. Orders of Commodore Napier. You'll find that Marshal Fane's people are in charge below-decks, but Marine Captain Casagra and Navy Captain Greibenfeld are waiting to see you in your office."

As he started toward the elevators, a big Zarathustra Company car was coming in. The sergeant turned quickly, beckoned a couple of his men and went toward it on the double. He wondered what Leslie Coombes would think about those Marines.

The two officers in his private chambers were both wearing sidearms. So, also, was Marshal Fane, who was with them. They all rose to greet him, sitting down when he was at his desk. He asked the same question he had of the sergeant above.

"Well, Constabulary Colonel Ferguson called Commodore Napier last evening and requested armed assistance, your Honor," the officer in Space Navy black said. "He suspected, he said, that the city had been infiltrated. In that, your Honor, he was perfectly correct; beginning Wednesday afternoon, Marine Captain Casagra, here, on Commodore Napier's orders, began landing a Marine infiltration force, preparatory to taking over the Residency. That's been accomplished now; Commodore Napier is there, and both Resident General Emmert and Attorney General O'Brien are under arrest, on a variety of malfeasance and corrupt-practice charges, but that won't come into your Honor's court. They'll be sent back to Terra for trial."

"Then Commodore Napier's taken over the civil government?"

"Well, say he's assumed control of it, pending the outcome of this trial. We want to know whether the present administration's legal or not."

"Then you won't interfere with the trial itself?"

"That depends, your Honor. We are certainly going to participate." He looked at his watch. "You won't convene court for another hour? Then perhaps I'll have time to explain."

Max Fane met them at the courtroom door with a pleasant greeting. Then he saw Baby Fuzzy on Jack's shoulder and looked dubious.

"I don't know about him, Jack. I don't think he'll be allowed in the courtroom."

"Nonsense!" Gus Brannhard told him. "I admit, he is both a minor child and an incompetent aborigine, but he is the only surviving member of the family of the decedent Jane Doe alias Goldilocks, and as such has an indisputable right to be present."

"Well, just as long as you keep him from sitting on people's heads. Gus, you and Jack sit over there; Ben, you and Gerd find seats in the witness section."

It would be half an hour till court would convene, but already the spectators' seats were full, and so was the balcony. The jury box, on the left of the bench, was occupied by a number of officers in Navy black and Marine blue. Since there would be no jury, they had apparently appropriated it for themselves. The press box was jammed and bristling with equipment.

Baby was looking up interestedly at the big screen behind the judges' seats; while transmitting the court scene to the public, it also showed, like a nonreversing mirror, the same view to the spectators. Baby wasn't long in identifying himself in it, and waved his arms excitedly. At that moment, there was a bustle at the door by which they had entered, and Leslie Coombes came in, followed by Ernst Mallin and a couple of his assistants, Ruth Ortheris, Juan Jimenez-and Leonard Kellogg. The last time he had seen Kellogg had been at George Lunt's complaint court, his face bandaged and his feet in a pair of borrowed moccasins because his shoes, stained with the blood of Goldilocks, had been impounded as evidence.

Coombes glanced toward the table where he and Brannhard were sitting, caught sight of Baby waving to himself in the big screen and turned to Fane with an indignant protest. Fane shook his head. Coombes protested again, and drew another headshake. Finally he shrugged and led Kellogg to the table reserved for them, where they sat down.

Once Pendarvis and his two associates —a short, roundfaced man on his right, a tall, slender man with white hair and a black mustache on his left-were seated, the trial got underway briskly. The charges were read, and then Brannhard, as the Kellogg prosecutor, addressed the court — "being known as Goldilocks...sapient member of a sapient race...willful and deliberate act of the said Leonard Kellogg...brutal and unprovoked murder." He backed away, sat on the edge of the table and picked up Baby Fuzzy, fondling him while Leslie Coombes accused Jack Holloway of brutally assaulting the said Leonard Kellogg and ruthlessly shooting down Kurt Borch.

"Well, gentlemen, I believe we can now begin hearing the witnesses," the Chief Justice said. "Who will start prosecuting whom?"

Gus handed Baby to Jack and went forward: Coombes stepped up beside him.

"Your Honor, this entire trial hinges upon the question of whether a member of the species *Fuzzy fuzzy holloway zarathustra* is or is not a sapient being," Gus said. "However, before any attempt is made to determine this question, we should first establish, by testimony, just what happened at Holloway's Camp, in Cold Creek Valley, on the afternoon of June 19, Atomic Era Six Fifty-Four, and once this is established, we can then proceed to the question of whether or not the said Goldilocks was truly a sapient being."

"I agree," Coombes said equably. "Most of these witnesses will have to be recalled to the stand later, but in general I think Mr. Brannhard's suggestion will be economical of the court's time."

"Will Mr. Coombes agree to stipulate that any evidence tending to prove or disprove the sapience of Fuzzies in general be accepted as proving or disproving the sapience of the being referred to as Goldilocks?"

Coombes looked that over carefully, decided that it wasn't booby-trapped and agreed. A deputy marshal went over to the witness stand, made some adjustments and snapped on a switch at the back of the chair. Immediately the two-foot globe in a standard behind it lit, a clear blue. George Lunt's name was called; the lieutenant took his seat and the bright helmet was let down over his head and the electrodes attached.

The globe stayed a calm, untroubled blue while he stated his name and rank. Then he waited while Coombes and Brannhard conferred. Finally Brannhard took a silver half-sol piece from his pocket, shook it between cupped palms and slapped it onto his wrist. Coombes said, "Heads," and Brannhard uncovered it, bowed slightly and stepped back.

"Now, Lieutenant Lunt," Coombes began, "when you arrived at the temporary camp across the run from Holloway's camp, what did you find there?"

"Two dead people," Lunt said. "A Terran human, who had been shot three times through the chest, and a Fuzzy, who had been kicked or trampled to death."

"Your Honors!" Coombes expostulated, "I must ask that the witness be requested to rephrase his answer, and that the answer he has just made be stricken from the record. The witness, under the circumstances, has no right to refer to the Fuzzies as 'people.'"

"Your Honors," Brannhard caught it up, "Mr. Coombes's objection is no less prejudicial. He has no right, under the circumstances, to deny that the Fuzzies be referred to as 'people.' This is tantamount to insisting that the witness speak of them as nonsapient animals."

It went on like that for five minutes. Jack began doodling on a notepad. Baby picked up a pencil with both hands and began making doodles too. They looked rather like the knots he had been learning to tie. Finally, the court intervened and told Lunt to tell, in his own words, why he went to Holloway's camp, what he found there, what he was told and what he did. There was some argument between Coombes and Brannhard, at one point, about the difference between hearsay and *res gestae*. When he was through, Coombes said, "No questions."

"Lieutenant, you placed Leonard Kellogg under arrest on a complaint of homicide by Jack Holloway. I take it that you considered this complaint a valid one?"

"Yes, sir. I believed that Leonard Kellogg had killed a sapient being. Only sapient beings bury their dead."

Ahmed Khadra testified. The two troopers who had come in the other car, and the men who had brought the investigative equipment and done the photographing at the scene testified. Brannhard called Ruth Ortheris to the stand, and, after some futile objections by Coombes, she was allowed to tell her own story of the killing of Goldilocks, the beating of Kellogg and the shooting of Borch. When she had finished, the Chief Justice rapped with his gavel.

"I believe that this testimony is sufficient to establish the fact that the being referred to as Jane Doe alias Goldilocks was in fact kicked and trampled to death by the defendant Leonard Kellogg, and that the Terran human known as Kurt Borch was in fact shot to death by Jack Holloway. This being the case, we may now consider whether or not either or both of these killings constitute murder within the meaning of the law. It is now eleven forty. We will adjourn for lunch, and court will reconvene at fourteen hundred. There are a number of things, including some alterations to the courtroom, which must be done before the afternoon session.... Yes, Mr. Brannhard?"

"Your Honors, there is only one member of the species *Fuzzy fuzzy holloway zarathustra* at present in court, an immature and hence nonrepresentative individual." He picked up Baby and exhibited him. "If we are to take up the question of the sapience of this species, or race, would it not be well to send for the Fuzzies now staying at the Hotel Mallory and have them on hand?"

"Well, Mr. Brannhard," Pendarvis said, "we will certainly want Fuzzies in court, but let me suggest that we wait until after court reconvenes before sending for them. It may be that they will not be needed this afternoon. Anything else?" He tapped with his gavel. "Then court is adjourned until fourteen hundred."

Some alterations in the courtroom had been a conservative way of putting it. Four rows of spectators' seats had been abolished, and the dividing rail moved back. The witness chair, originally at the side of the bench, had been moved to the dividing rail and now faced the bench, and a large number of tables had been brought in and ranged in an arc with the witness chair in the middle of it. Everybody at the tables could face the judges, and also see everybody else by looking into the big screen. A witness on the chair could also see the veridicator in the same way.

Gus Brannhard looked around, when he entered with Jack, and swore softly.

"No wonder they gave us two hours for lunch. I wonder what the idea is." Then he gave a short laugh. "Look at Coombes; he doesn't like it a bit."

A deputy with a seating diagram came up to them.

"Mr. Brannhard, you and Mr. Holloway over here, at this table." He pointed to one a little apart from the others, at the extreme right facing the bench. "And Dr. van Riebeek, and Dr. Rainsford over here, please."

The court crier's loud-speaker, overhead, gave two sharp whistles and began:

"Now hear this! Now hear this! Court will convene in five minutes —"

Brannhard's head jerked around instantly, and Jack's eyes followed his. The court crier was a Space Navy petty officer.

"What the devil is this?" Brannhard demanded. "A Navy court-martial?"

"That's what I've been wondering, Mr. Brannhard," the deputy said. "They've taken over the whole planet, you know."

"Maybe we're in luck, Gus. I've always heard that if you're innocent you're better off before a court-martial and if you're guilty you're better off in a civil court."

He saw Leslie Coombes and Leonard Kellogg being seated at a similar table at the opposite side of the bench. Apparently Coombes had also heard that. The seating arrangements at the other tables seemed a little odd too. Gerd van Riebeek was next to Ruth Ortheris, and Ernst Mallin was next to Ben Rainsford, with Juan Jimenez on his other side. Gus was looking up at the balcony.

"I'll bet every lawyer on the planet's taking this in," he said. "Oh-oh! See the white-haired lady in the blue dress, Jack? That's the Chief Justice's wife. This is the first time she's been in court for years."

"Hear ye! Hear ye! Hear ye! Rise for the Honorable Court!"

Somebody must have given the petty officer a quick briefing on courtroom phraseology. He stood up, holding Baby Fuzzy, while the three judges filed in and took their seats. As soon as they sat down, the Chief Justice rapped briskly with his gavel.

"In order to forestall a spate of objections, I want to say that these present arrangements are temporary, and so will be the procedures which will be followed. We are not, at the moment, trying Jack Holloway or Leonard Kellogg. For the rest of this day, and, I fear, for a good many days to come, we will be concerned exclusively with determining the level of mentation of *Fuzzy fuzzy holloway zarathustra*.

"For this purpose, we are temporarily abandoning some of the traditional trial procedures. We will call witnesses; statements of purported fact will be made under veridication as usual. We will also have a general discussion, in which all of you at these tables will be free to participate. I and my associates will preside; as we can't have everybody shouting disputations at once, anyone wishing to speak will have to be recognized. At least, I hope we will be able to conduct the discussion in this manner.

"You will all have noticed the presence of a number of officers from Xerxes Naval Base, and I suppose you have all heard that Commodore Napier has assumed control of the civil government. Captain Greibenfeld, will you please rise and be seen? He is here participating as *amicus curiae*, and I have given him the right to question witnesses and to delegate that right to any of his officers he may deem proper. Mr. Coombes and Mr. Brannhard may also delegate that right as they see fit."

Coombes was on his feet at once. "Your Honors, if we are now to discuss the sapience question, I would suggest that the first item on our order of business be the presentation of some acceptable definition of sapience. I should, for my part, very much like to know what it is that the Kellogg prosecution and the Holloway defense mean when they use that term."

That's it. They want us to define it. Gerd van Riebeek was looking chagrined; Ernst Mallin was smirking. Gus Brannhard, however, was pleased.

"Jack, they haven't any more damn definition than we do," he whispered.

Captain Greibenfeld, who had seated himself after rising at the request of the court, was on his feet again.

"Your Honors, during the past month we at Xerxes Naval Base have been working on exactly that problem. We have a very considerable interest in having the classification of this planet established, and we also feel that this may not be the last time a question of disputable sapience may arise. I believe, your Honors, that we have approached such a definition. However, before we begin discussing it, I would like the court's permission to present a demonstration which may be of help in understanding the problems involved."

"Captain Greibenfeld has already discussed this demonstration with me, and it has my approval. Will you please proceed, Captain," the Chief Justice said.

Greibenfeld nodded, and a deputy marshal opened the door on the right of the bench. Two spacemen came in, carrying cartons. One went up to the bench; the other started around in front of the tables, distributing small battery-powered hearing aids.

"Please put them in your ears and turn them on," he said. "Thank you."

Baby Fuzzy tried to get Jack's. He put the plug in his ear and switched on the power. Instantly he began hearing a number of small sounds he had never heard before, and Baby was saying to him: "*He-inta sa-wa'aka; igga sa geeda?*"

"Muhgawd, Gus, he's talking!"

"Yes, I hear him; what do you suppose —?"

"Ultrasonic; God, why didn't we think of that long ago?"

He snapped off the hearing aid. Baby Fuzzy was saying, "Yeeek." When he turned it on again, Baby was saying, "*Kukk-ina za zeeva.*"

"No, Baby, Pappy Jack doesn't understand. We'll have to be awfully patient, and learn each other's language."

"*Pa-pee Jaaak!*" Baby cried. "*Ba-bee za-hinga; Pa-pee Jaak za zag ga he-izza!*"

"That yeeking is just the audible edge of their speech; bet we have a lot of transsonic tones in our voices, too."

"Well, he can hear what we say; he's picked up his name and yours."

"Mr. Brannhard, Mr. Holloway," Judge Pendarvis was saying, "may we please have your attention? Now, have you all your earplugs in and turned on? Very well; carry on, Captain."

This time, an ensign went out and came back with a crowd of enlisted men, who had six Fuzzies with them. They set them down in the open space between the bench and the arc of tables and backed away. The Fuzzies drew together into a clump and stared around them, and he stared, unbelievingly, at them. They couldn't be; they didn't exist any more. But they were- Little Fuzzy and Mamma Fuzzy and Mike and Mitzi and Ko-Ko and Cinderella. Baby whooped something and leaped from the table, and Mamma came stumbling to meet him, clasping him in her arms. Then they all saw him and began clamoring: "*Pa-pee Jaaak! Pa-pee Jaaak!*"

He wasn't aware of rising and leaving the table; the next thing he realized, he was sitting on the floor, his family mobbing him and hugging him, gabbling with joy. Dimly he heard the gavel hammering, and the voice of Chief Justice Pendarvis: "Court is recessed for ten minutes!" By that time, Gus was with him; gathering the family up, they carried them over to their table.

They stumbled and staggered when they moved, and that frightened him for a moment. Then he realized that they weren't sick or drugged. They'd just been in low-G for a while and hadn't become reaccustomed to normal weight. Now he knew why he hadn't been able to find any trace of them. He noticed that each of them was wearing a little shoulder bag —a Marine

Corps first-aid pouch-slung from a webbing strap. Why the devil hadn't he thought of making them something like that? He touched one and commented, trying to pitch his voice as nearly like theirs as he could. They all babbled in reply and began opening the little bags and showing him what they had in them-little knives and miniature tools and bits of bright or colored junk they had picked up. Little Fuzzy produced a tiny pipe with a hardwood bowl, and a little pouch of tobacco from which he filled it. Finally, he got out a small lighter.

"Your Honors!" Gus shouted, "I know court is recessed, but please observe what Little Fuzzy is doing."

While they watched, Little Fuzzy snapped the lighter and held the flame to the pipe bowl, puffing.

Across on the other side, Leslie Coombes swallowed once or twice and closed his eyes.

When Pendarvis rapped for attention and declared court reconvened, he said:

"Ladies and gentlemen, you have all seen and heard this demonstration of Captain Greibenfeld's. You have heard these Fuzzies uttering what certainly sounds like meaningful speech, and you have seen one of them light a pipe and smoke. Incidentally, while smoking in court is discountenanced, we are going to make an exception, during this trial, in favor of Fuzzies. Other people will please not feel themselves discriminated against."

That brought Coombes to his feet with a rush. He started around the table and then remembered that under the new rules he didn't have to.

"Your Honors, I objected strongly to the use of that term by a witness this morning; I must object even more emphatically to its employment from the bench. I have indeed heard these Fuzzies make sounds which might be mistaken for words, but I must deny that this is true speech. As to this trick of using a lighter, I will undertake, in not more than thirty days, to teach it to any Terran primate or Freyan kholph."

Greibenfeld rose immediately. "Your Honors, in the past thirty days, while these Fuzzies were at Xerxes Naval Base, we have compiled a vocabulary of a hundred-odd Fuzzy words, for all of which definite meanings have been established, and a great many more for which we have not as yet learned the meanings. We even have the beginning of a Fuzzy grammar. As for this so-called trick of using a lighter, Little Fuzzy-we didn't know his name then and referred to him as M2—learned that for himself, by observation. We didn't teach him to smoke a pipe either; he knew that before we had anything to do with him."

Jack rose while Greibenfeld was still speaking. As soon as the Space Navy captain had finished, he said:

"Captain Greibenfeld, I want to thank you and your people for taking care of the Fuzzies, and I'm very glad you learned how to hear what they're saying, and thank you for all the nice things you gave them, but why couldn't you have let me know they were safe? I haven't been very happy the last month, you know."

"I know that, Mr. Holloway, and if it's any comfort to you, we were all very sorry for you, but we could not take the risk of compromising our secret intelligence agent in the Company's Science Center, the one who smuggled the Fuzzies out the morning after their escape." He looked quickly across in front of the bench to the table at the other end of the arc. Kellogg was sitting with his face in his hands, oblivious to everything that was going on, but Leslie Coombes's well-disciplined face had broken, briefly, into a look of consternation. "By the time you and Mr. Brannhard and Marshal Fane arrived with an order of the court for the Fuzzies' recovery, they had already been taken from Science Center and were on a Navy landing craft for Xerxes. We couldn't do anything without exposing our agent. That, I am glad to say, is no longer a consideration."

"Well, Captain Greibenfeld," the Chief Justice said, "I assume you mean to introduce further testimony about the observations and studies made by your people on Xerxes. For the record, we'd like to have it established that they were actually taken there, and when, and how."

"Yes, your Honor. If you will call the fourth name on the list I gave you, and allow me to do the questioning, we can establish that."

The Chief Justice picked up a paper. "Lieutenant j.g. Ruth Ortheris, TFN Reserve," he called out.

This time, Jack Holloway looked up into the big screen, in which he could see everybody. Gerd van Riebeek, who had been trying to ignore the existence of the woman beside him, had turned to stare at her in amazement. Coombes's face was ghastly for an instant, then froze into corpselike immobility: Ernst Mallin was dithering in incredulous anger; beside him Ben Rainsford was grinning in just as incredulous delight. As Ruth came around in front of the bench, the Fuzzies gave her an ovation; they remembered and liked her. Gus Brannhard was gripping his arm and saying: "Oh, brother! This is it, Jack; it's all over but shooting the cripples!"

Lieutenant j.g. Ortheris, under a calmly blue globe, testified to coming to Zarathustra as a Federation Naval Reserve officer recalled to duty with Intelligence, and taking a position with the Company.

"As a regularly qualified doctor of psychology, I worked under Dr. Mallin in the scientific division, and also with the school department and the juvenile court. At the same time I was regularly transmitting reports to Commander Aelborg, the chief of Intelligence on Xerxes. The object of this surveillance was to make sure that the Zarathustra Company was not violating the provisions of their charter or Federation law. Until the middle of last month, I had nothing to report beyond some rather irregular financial transactions involving Resident General Emmert. Then, on the evening of June fifteen —"

That was when Ben had transmitted the tape to Juan Jimenez; she described how it had come to her attention.

"As soon as possible, I transmitted a copy of this tape to Commander Aelborg. The next night, I called Xerxes from the screen on Dr. van Riebeek's boat and reported what I'd learned about the Fuzzies. I was then informed that Leonard Kellogg had gotten hold of a copy of the Holloway-Rainsford tape and had alerted Victor Grego; that Kellogg and Ernst Mallin were being sent to Beta Continent with instructions to prevent publication of any report claiming sapience for the Fuzzies and to fabricate evidence to support an accusation that Dr. Rainsford and Mr. Holloway were perpetrating a deliberate scientific hoax."

"Here, I'll have to object to this, your Honor," Coombes said, rising. "This is nothing but hearsay."

"This is part of a Navy Intelligence situation estimate given to Lieutenant Ortheris, based on reports we had received from other agents," Captain Greibenfeld said. "She isn't the only one we have on Zarathustra, you know. Mr. Coombes, if I hear another word of objection to this officer's testimony from you, I am going to ask Mr. Brannhard to subpoena Victor Grego and question him under veridication about it."

"Mr. Brannhard will be more than happy to oblige, Commander," Gus said loudly and distinctly.

Coombes sat down hastily.

"Well, Lieutenant Ortheris, this is most interesting, but at the moment, what we're trying to establish is how these Fuzzies got to Xerxes Naval Base," the chubby associate justice, Ruiz, put in.

"I'll try to get them there as quickly as possible, your Honor," she said. "On the night of Friday the twenty-second, the Fuzzies were taken from Mr. Holloway and brought into Mallorysport; they were turned over by Mohammed O'Brien to Juan Jimenez, who took them to Science Center and put them in cages in a room back of his office. They immediately escaped. I found them, the next morning, and was able to get them out of the building, and to turn them over to Commander Aelborg, who had come down from Xerxes to take personal charge of the Fuzzy operation. I will not testify as to how I was able to do this. I am at present and was then an officer of the Terran Federation Armed Forces; the courts have no power to compel a Federation officer to give testimony involving breach of military security. I was informed, through my contact in Mallorysport, from time to time, of the progress of the work of measuring the Fuzzies' mental level there; I was able to pass on suggestions occasionally. Any time any of these suggestions was based on ideas originating with Dr. Mallin, I was careful to give him full credit."

Mallin looked singularly unappreciative.

Brannhard got up. "Before this witness is excused, I'd like to ask if she knows anything about four other Fuzzies, the ones found by Jack Holloway up Ferny Creek on Friday."

"Why, yes; they're my Fuzzies, and I was worried about them. Their names are Complex, Syndrome, Id and Superego."

"Your Fuzzies, Lieutenant?"

"Well, I took care of them and worked with them; Juan Jimenez and some Company hunters caught them over on Beta Continent. They were kept at a farm center about five hundred miles north of here, which had been vacated for the purpose. I spent all my time with them, and Dr. Mallin was with them most of the time. Then, on Monday night, Mr. Coombes came and got them."

"Mr. Coombes, did you say?" Gus Brannhard asked.

"Mr. Leslie Coombes, the Company attorney. He said they were needed in Mallorysport. It wasn't till the next day that I found out what they were needed for. They'd been turned loose in front of that Fuzzy hunt, in the hope that they would be killed."

She looked across at Coombes; if looks were bullets, he'd have been deader than Kurt Borch.

"Why would they sacrifice four Fuzzies merely to support a story that was bound to come apart anyhow?" Brannhard asked.

"That was no sacrifice. They had to get rid of those Fuzzies, and they were afraid to kill them themselves for fear they'd be charged with murder along with Leonard Kellogg. Everybody, from Ernst Mallin down, who had anything to do with them was convinced of their sapience. For one thing, we'd been using those hearing aids ourselves; I suggested it, after getting the idea from Xerxes. Ask Dr. Mallin about it, under veridication. Ask him about the multiordinal polyencephalograph experiments, too."

"Well, we have the Holloway Fuzzies placed on Xerxes," the Chief Justice said. "We can hear the testimony of the people who worked with them there at any time. Now, I want to hear from Dr. Ernst Mallin."

Coombes was on his feet again. "Your Honors, before any further testimony is heard, I would like to confer with my client privately."

"I fail to see any reason why we should interrupt proceedings for that purpose, Mr. Coombes. You can confer as much as you wish with your client after this session, and I can assure you that you will be called upon to do nothing on his behalf until then." He gave a light tap with his gavel and then said: "Dr. Ernst Mallin will please take the stand."

XV

Ernst Mallin shrank, as though trying to pull himself into himself, when he heard his name. He didn't want to testify. He had been dreading this moment for days. Now he would have to sit in that chair, and they would ask him questions, and he couldn't answer them truthfully and the globe over his head —

When the deputy marshal touched his shoulder and spoke to him, he didn't think, at first, that his legs would support him. It seemed miles, with all the staring faces on either side of him. Somehow, he reached the chair and sat down, and they fitted the helmet over his head and attached the electrodes. They used to make a witness take some kind of an oath to tell the truth. They didn't any more. They didn't need to.

As soon as the veridicator was on, he looked up at the big screen behind the three judges; the globe above his head was a glaring red. There was a titter of laughter. Nobody in the

Courtroom knew better than he what was happening. He had screens in his laboratory that broke it all down into individual patterns-the steady pulsing waves from the cortex, the alpha and beta waves; beta-aleph and beta-beth and beta-gimel and beta-daleth. The thalamic waves. He thought of all of them, and of the electromagnetic events which accompanied brain activity. As he did, the red faded and the globe became blue. He was no longer suppressing statements and substituting other statements he knew to be false. If he could keep it that way. But, sooner or later, he knew, he wouldn't be able to.

The globe stayed blue while he named himself and stated his professional background. There was a brief flicker of red while he was listing his publication-that paper, entirely the work of one of his students, which he had published under his own name. He had forgotten about that, but his conscience hadn't.

"Dr. Mallin," the oldest of the three judges, who sat in the middle, began, "what, in your professional opinion, is the difference between sapient and nonsapient mentation?"

"The ability to think consciously," he stated. The globe stayed blue.

"Do you mean that nonsapient animals aren't conscious, or do you mean they don't think?"

"Well, neither. Any life form with a central nervous system has some consciousness-awareness of existence and of its surroundings. And anything having a brain thinks, to use the term at its loosest. What I meant was that only the sapient mind thinks and knows that it is thinking."

He was perfectly safe so far. He talked about sensory stimuli and responses, and about conditioned reflexes. He went back to the first century Pre-Atomic, and Pavlov and Korzybski and Freud. The globe never flickered.

"The nonsapient animal is conscious only of what is immediately present to the senses and responds automatically. It will perceive something and make a single statement about it-this is good to eat, this sensation is unpleasant, this is a sex-gratification object, this is dangerous. The sapient mind, on the other hand, is conscious of thinking about these sense stimuli, and makes descriptive statements about them, and then makes statements about those statements, in a connected chain. I have a structural differential at my seat; if somebody will bring it to me —"

"Well, never mind now, Dr. Mallin. When you're off the stand and the discussion begins you can show what you mean. We just want your opinion in general terms, now."

"Well, the sapient mind can generalize. To the nonsapient animal, every experience is either totally novel or identical with some remembered experience. A rabbit will flee from one dog because to the rabbit mind it is identical with another dog that has chased it. A bird will be attracted to an apple, and each apple will be a unique red thing to peck at. The sapient being will say, 'These red objects are apples; as a class, they are edible and flavorsome.' He sets up a class under the general label of apples. This, in turn, leads to the formation of abstract ideas-redness, flavor, et cetera-conceived of apart from any specific physical object, and to the ordering of abstractions —'fruit' as distinguished from apples, 'food' as distinguished from fruit."

The globe was still placidly blue. The three judges waited, and he continued:

"Having formed these abstract ideas, it becomes necessary to symbolize them, in order to deal with them apart from the actual object. The sapient being is a symbolizer, and a symbol communicator; he is able to convey to other sapient beings his ideas in symbolic form."

"Like '*Pa-pee Jaak*'?" the judge on his right, with the black mustache, asked.

The globe flashed red at once.

"Your Honors, I cannot consider words picked up at random and learned by rote speech. The Fuzzies have merely learned to associate that sound with a specific human, and use it as a signal, not as a symbol."

The globe was still red. The Chief Justice, in the middle, rapped with his gavel.

"Dr. Mallin! Of all the people on this planet, you at least should know the impossibility of lying under veridication. Other people just know it can't be done; you know why. Now I'm going to rephrase Judge Janiver's question, and I'll expect you to answer truthfully. If you don't I'm going to hold you in contempt. When those Fuzzies cried out, 'Pappy Jack!' do you or do you not believe that they were using a verbal expression which stood, in their minds, for Mr. Holloway?"

He couldn't say it. This sapience was all a big fake; he had to believe that. The Fuzzies were only little mindless animals.

But he didn't believe it. He knew better. He gulped for a moment.

"Yes, your Honor. The term 'Pappy Jack' is, in their minds, a symbol standing for Mr. Jack Holloway."

He looked at the globe. The red had turned to mauve, the mauve was becoming violet, and then clear blue. He felt better than he had felt since the afternoon Leonard Kellogg had told him about the Fuzzies.

"Then Fuzzies do think consciously, Dr. Mallin?" That was Pendarvis.

"Oh, yes. The fact that they use verbal symbols indicates that, even without other evidence. And the instrumental evidence was most impressive. The mentation pictures we got by encephalography compare very favorably with those of any human child of ten or twelve years old, and so does their learning and puzzle-solving ability. On puzzles, they always think the problem out first, and then do the mechanical work with about the same mental effort, say, as a man washing his hands or tying his neckcloth."

The globe was perfectly blue. Mallin had given up trying to lie; he was simply gushing out everything he thought.

Leonard Kellogg slumped forward, his head buried in his elbows on the table, and misery washed over him in tides.

I am a murderer; I killed a person. Only a funny little person with fur, but she was a person, and I knew it when I killed her, I knew it when I saw that little grave out in the woods, and they'll put me in that chair and make me admit it to everybody, and then they'll take me out in the jail yard and somebody will shoot me through the head with a pistol, and —

And all the poor little thing wanted was to show me her new jingle!

"Does anybody want to ask the witness any questions?" the Chief Justice was asking.

"I don't," Captain Greibenfeld said. "Do you, Lieutenant?"

"No, I don't think so," Lieutenant Ybarra said. "Dr. Mallin's given us a very lucid statement of his opinions."

He had, at that, after he'd decided he couldn't beat the veridicator. Jack found himself sympathizing with Mallin. He'd disliked the man from the first, but he looked different now-sort of cleaned and washed out inside. Maybe everybody ought to be veridicated, now and then, to teach them that honesty begins with honesty to self.

"Mr. Coombes?" Mr. Coombes looked as though he never wanted to ask another witness another question as long as he lived. "Mr. Brannhard?"

Gus got up, holding a sapient member of a sapient race who was hanging onto his beard, and thanked Ernst Mallin fulsomely.

"In that case, we'll adjourn until o-nine-hundred tomorrow. Mr. Coombes, I have here a check on the chartered Zarathustra Company for twenty-five thousand sols. I am returning it to you and I am canceling Dr. Kellogg's bail," Judge Pendarvis said, as a couple of attendants began getting Mallin loose from the veridicator.

"Are you also canceling Jack Holloway's?"

"No, and I would advise you not to make an issue of it, Mr. Coombes. The only reason I haven't dismissed the charge against Mr. Holloway is that I don't want to handicap you by cutting off your foothold in the prosecution. I do not consider Mr. Holloway a bail risk. I do so consider your client, Dr. Kellogg."

"Frankly, your Honor, so do I," Coombes admitted. "My protest was merely an example of what Dr. Mallin would call conditioned reflex."

Then a crowd began pushing up around the table; Ben Rainsford, George Lunt and his troopers, Gerd and Ruth, shoving in among them, their arms around each other.

"We'll be at the hotel after a while, Jack," Gerd was saying. "Ruth and I are going out for a drink and something to eat; we'll be around later to pick up her Fuzzies."

Now his partner had his girl back, and his partner's girl had a Fuzzy family of her own. This was going to be real fun. What were their names now? Syndrome, Complex, Id and Superego. The things some people named Fuzzies!

XVI

They stopped whispering at the door, turned right, and ascended to the bench, bearing themselves like images in a procession, Ruiz first, then himself and then Janiver. They turned to the screen so that the public whom they served might see the faces of the judges, and then sat down. The court crier began his chant. They could almost feel the tension in the courtroom. Yves Janiver whispered to them:

"They all know about it."

As soon as the crier had stopped, Max Fane approached the bench, his face blankly expressionless.

"Your Honors, I am ashamed to have to report that the defendant, Leonard Kellogg, cannot be produced in court. He is dead; he committed suicide in his cell last night. While in my custody," he added bitterly.

The stir that went through the courtroom was not shocked surprise, it was a sigh of fulfilled expectation. They all knew about it.

"How did this happen, Marshal?" he asked, almost conversationally.

"The prisoner was put in a cell by himself; there was a pickup eye, and one of my deputies was keeping him under observation by screen." Fane spoke in a toneless, almost robotlike voice. "At twenty-two thirty, the prisoner went to bed, still wearing his shirt. He pulled the blankets up over his head. The deputy observing him thought nothing of that; many prisoners do that, on account of the light. He tossed about for a while, and then appeared to fall asleep.

"When a guard went in to rouse him this morning, the cot, under the blanket, was found saturated with blood. Kellogg had cut his throat, by sawing the zipper track of his shirt back and forth till he severed his jugular vein. He was dead."

"Good heavens, Marshal!" He was shocked. The way he'd heard it, Kellogg had hidden a penknife, and he was prepared to be severe with Fane about it. But a thing like this! He found himself fingering the toothed track of his own jacket zipper. "I don't believe you can be at all censured for not anticipating a thing like that. It isn't a thing anybody would expect."

Janiver and Ruiz spoke briefly in agreement. Marshal Fane bowed slightly and went off to one side.

Leslie Coombes, who seemed to be making a very considerable effort to look grieved and shocked, rose.

"Your Honors, I find myself here without a client," he said. "In fact, I find myself here without any business at all; the case against Mr. Holloway is absolutely insupportable. He shot a man who was trying to kill him, and that's all there is to it. I therefore pray your Honors to dismiss the case against him and discharge him from custody."

Captain Greibenfeld bounded to his feet.

"Your Honors, I fully realize that the defendant is now beyond the jurisdiction of this court, but let me point out that I and my associates are here participating in this case in the hope that the classification of this planet may be determined, and some adequate definition of sapience established. These are most serious questions, your Honors."

"But, your Honors," Coombes protested, "we can't go through the farce of trying a dead man."

"*People of the Colony of Baphomet* versus *Jamshar Singh, Deceased*, charge of arson and sabotage, A.E. 604," the Honorable Gustavus Adolphus Brannhard interrupted.

Yes, you could find a precedent in colonial law for almost anything.

Jack Holloway was on his feet, a Fuzzy cradled in the crook of his left arm, his white mustache bristling truculently.

"I am not a dead man, your Honors, and I am on trial here. The reason I'm not dead is why I am on trial. My defense is that I shot Kurt Borch while he was aiding and abetting in the killing of a Fuzzy. I want it established in this court that it is murder to kill a Fuzzy."

The judge nodded slowly. "I will not dismiss the charges against Mr. Holloway," he said. "Mr. Holloway had been arraigned on a charge of murder; if he is not guilty, he is entitled to the vindication of an acquittal. I am afraid, Mr. Coombes, that you will have to go on prosecuting him."

Another brief stir, like a breath of wind over a grain field, ran through the courtroom. The show was going on after all.

All the Fuzzies were in court this morning; Jack's six, and the five from the constabulary post, and Ben's Flora and Fauna, and the four Ruth Ortheris claimed. There was too much discussion going on for anybody to keep an eye on them. Finally one of the constabulary Fuzzies, either Dillinger or Dr. Crippen, and Ben Rainsford's Flora and Fauna, came sauntering out into the open space between the tables and the bench dragging the hose of a vacuum-duster. Ahmed Khadra ducked under a table and tried to get it away from them. This was wonderful; screaming in delight, they all laid hold of the other end, and Mike and Mitzi and Superego and Complex ran to help them. The seven of them dragged Khadra about ten feet before he gave up and let go. At the same time, an incipient fight broke out on the other side of the arc of tables between the head of the language department at Mallorysport Academy and a spinsterish amateur phoneticist. At this point, Judge Pendarvis, deciding that if you can't prevent it, relax and enjoy it, rapped a few times with his gavel, and announced that court was recessed.

"You will all please remain here; this is not an adjournment, and if any of the various groups who seem to be discussing different aspects of the problem reach any conclusion they feel should be presented in evidence, will they please notify the bench so that court can be reconvened. In any case, we will reconvene at eleven thirty."

Somebody wanted to know if smoking would be permitted during the recess. The Chief Justice said that it would. He got out a cigar and lit it. Mamma Fuzzy wanted a puff: she didn't like it. Out of the corner of his eye, he saw Mike and Mitzi, Flora and Fauna scampering around and up the steps behind the bench. When he looked again, they were all up on it, and Mitzi was showing the court what she had in her shoulder bag.

He got up, with Mamma and Baby, and crossed to where Leslie Coombes was sitting. By this time, somebody was bringing in a coffee urn from the cafeteria. Fuzzies ought to happen oftener in court.

The gavel tapped slowly. Little Fuzzy scrambled up onto Jack Holloway's lap. After five days in court, they had all learned that the gavel meant for Fuzzies and other people to be quiet. It might be a good idea, Jack thought, to make a little gavel, when he got home, and keep it on the table in the living room for when the family got too boisterous. Baby, who wasn't gavel-trained yet, started out onto the floor; Mamma dashed after him and brought him back under the table.

The place looked like a courtroom again. The tables were ranged in a neat row facing the bench, and the witness chair and the jury box were back where they belonged. The ashtrays and the coffee urn and the ice tubs for beer and soft drinks had vanished. It looked like the party was over. He was almost regretful; it had been fun. Especially for seventeen Fuzzies and a Baby Fuzzy and a little black-and-white kitten.

There was one unusual feature; there was now a fourth man on the bench, in gold-braided Navy black; sitting a little apart from the judges, trying to look as though he weren't there at all-Space Commodore Alex Napier.

Judge Pendarvis laid down his gavel. "Ladies and gentlemen, are you ready to present the opinions you have reached?" he asked.

Lieutenant Ybarra, the Navy psychologist, rose. There was a reading screen in front of him; he snapped it on.

"Your Honors," he began, "there still exists considerable difference of opinion on matters of detail but we are in agreement on all major points. This is quite a lengthy report, and it has already been incorporated into the permanent record. Have I the court's permission to summarize it?"

The court told him he had. Ybarra glanced down at the screen in front of him and continued:

"It is our opinion," he said, "that sapience may be defined as differing from nonsapience in that it is characterized by conscious thought, by ability to think in logical sequence and by ability to think in terms other than mere sense data. We-meaning every member of every sapient race-think consciously, and we know what we are thinking. This is not to say that all our mental activity is conscious. The science of psychology is based, to a large extent, upon our realization that only a small portion of our mental activity occurs above the level of consciousness, and for centuries we have been diagraming the mind as an iceberg, one-tenth exposed and nine-tenths submerged. The art of psychiatry consists largely in bringing into consciousness some of the content of this submerged nine-tenths, and as a practitioner I can testify to its difficulty and uncertainty.

"We are so habituated to conscious thought that when we reach some conclusion by any nonconscious process, we speak of it as a 'hunch,' or an 'intuition,' and question its validity. We are so habituated to acting upon consciously formed decisions that we must laboriously acquire, by systematic drill, those automatic responses upon which we depend for survival in combat or other emergencies. And we are by nature so unaware of this vast submerged mental area that it was not until the first century Pre-Atomic that its existence was more than vaguely suspected, and its nature is still the subject of acrimonious professional disputes."

There had been a few of those, off and on, during the past four days, too.

"If we depict sapient mentation as an iceberg, we might depict nonsapient mentation as the sunlight reflected from its surface. This is a considerably less exact analogy; while the non-sapient mind deals, consciously, with nothing but present sense data, there is a considerable absorption and re-emission of subconscious memories. Also, there are occasional flashes of what must be conscious mental activity, in dealing with some novel situation. Dr. van Riebeek, who is especially interested in the evolutionary aspect of the question, suggests that the intro-duction of novelty because of drastic environmental changes may have forced nonsapient beings into more or less sustained conscious thinking and so initiated mental habits which, in time, gave rise to true sapience.

"The sapient mind not only thinks consciously by habit, but it thinks in connected sequence. It associates one thing with another. It reasons logically, and forms conclusions, and uses those conclusions as premises from which to arrive at further conclusions. It groups associations together, and generalizes. Here we pass completely beyond any comparison with nonsapience. This is not merely more consciousness, or more thinking; it is thinking of a radically different kind. The nonsapient mind deals exclusively with crude sensory material. The sapient mind translates sense impressions into ideas, and then forms ideas of ideas, in ascending orders of abstraction, almost without limit.

"This, finally, brings us to one of the recognized overt manifestations of sapience. The sapient being is a symbol user. The nonsapient being cannot symbolize, because the nonsapient mind is incapable of concepts beyond mere sense images."

Ybarra drank some water, and twisted the dial of his reading screen with the other hand.

"The sapient being," he continued, "can do one other thing. It is a combination of the three abilities already enumerated, but combining them creates something much greater than the mere sum of the parts. The sapient being can imagine. He can conceive of something which has no existence whatever in the sense-available world of reality, and then he can work and plan toward making it a part of reality. He can not only imagine, but he can also create."

He paused for a moment. "This is our definition of sapience. When we encounter any being whose mentation includes these characteristics, we may know him for a sapient brother. It is the considered opinion of all of us that the beings called Fuzzies are such beings."

Jack hugged the small sapient one on his lap, and Little Fuzzy looked up and murmured, "*He-inta?*"

"You're in, kid," he whispered. "You just joined the people."

Ybarra was saying, "They think consciously and continuously. We know that by instrumental analysis of their electroencephalographic patterns, which compare closely to those of an intelligent human child of ten. They think in connected sequence; I invite consideration of all the different logical steps involved in the invention, designing and making of their prawn-killing weapons, and in the development of tools with which to make them. We have abundant evidence of their ability to think beyond present sense data, to associate, to generalize, to abstract and to symbolize.

"And above all, they can imagine, not only a new implement, but a new way of life. We see this in the first human contact with the race which, I submit, should be designated as *Fuzzy sapiens*. Little Fuzzy found a strange and wonderful place in the forest, a place unlike anything he had ever seen, in which lived a powerful being. He imagined himself living in this place, enjoying the friendship and protection of this mysterious being. So he slipped inside, made friends with Jack Holloway and lived with him. And then he imagined his family sharing this precious comfort and companionship with him, and he went and found them and brought them back with him. Like so many other sapient beings, Little Fuzzy had a beautiful dream; like a fortunate few, he made it real."

The Chief Justice allowed the applause to run on for a few minutes before using his gavel to silence it. There was a brief colloquy among the three judges, and then the Chief Justice rapped again. Little Fuzzy looked perplexed. Everybody had been quiet after he did it the first time, hadn't they?

"It is the unanimous decision of the court to accept the report already entered into the record and just summarized by Lieutenant Ybarra, TFN, and to thank him and all who have been associated with him.

"It is now the ruling of this court that the species known as *Fuzzy fuzzy holloway zarathustra* is in fact a race of sapient beings, entitled to the respect of all other sapient beings and to the full protection of the law of the Terran Federation." He rapped again, slowly, pounding the decision into the legal framework.

Space Commodore Napier leaned over and whispered; all three of the judges nodded emphatically. The naval officer rose.

"Lieutenant Ybarra, on behalf of the Service and of the Federation, I thank you and those associated with you for a lucid and excellent report, the culmination of work which reflects credit upon all who participated in it. I also wish to state that a suggestion made to me by Lieutenant Ybarra regarding possible instrumental detection of sapient mentation is being credited to him in my own report, with the recommendation that it be given important priority by the Bureau of Research and Development. Perhaps the next time we find people who speak beyond the range of human audition, who have fur and live in a mild climate, and who like their food raw, we'll know what they are from the beginning."

Bet Ybarra gets another stripe, and a good job out of this. Jack hoped so. Then Pendarvis was pounding again.

"I had almost forgotten; this is a criminal trial," he confessed. "It is the verdict of this court that the defendant, Jack Holloway, is not guilty as here charged. He is herewith discharged from custody. If he or his attorney will step up here, the bail bond will be refunded." He puzzled Little Fuzzy by hammering again with his gavel to adjourn court.

This time, instead of keeping quiet, everybody made all the noise they could, and Uncle Gus was holding him high over his head and shouting:

"The *winnah*! By unanimous decision!"

XVII

Ruth Ortheris sipped at the tart, cold cocktail. It was good; oh, it was good, all good! The music was soft, the lights were dim, the tables were far apart; just she and Gerd, and nobody was paying any attention to them. And she was clear out of the business, too. An agent who testified in court always was expended in service like a fired round. They'd want her back, a year from now, to testify when the board of inquiry came out from Terra, but she wouldn't be Lieutenant j.g. Ortheris then, she'd be Mrs. Gerd van Riebeek. She set down the glass and rubbed the sunstone on her finger. It was a lovely sunstone, and it meant such a lovely thing.

And we're getting married with a ready-made family, too. Four Fuzzies and a black-and-white kitten.

"You're sure you really want to go to Beta?" Gerd asked. "When Napier gets this new government organized, it'll be taking over Science Center. We could both get our old jobs back. Maybe something better."

"You don't want to go back?" He shook his head. "Neither do I. I want to go to Beta and be a sunstone digger's wife."

"And a Fuzzyologist."

"And a Fuzzyologist. I couldn't drop that now. Gerd, we're only beginning with them. We know next to nothing about their psychology."

He nodded seriously. "You know, they may turn out to be even wiser than we are."

She laughed. "Oh, Gerd! Let's don't get too excited about them. Why, they're like little children. All they think about is having fun."

"That's right. I said they were wiser than we are. They stick to important things." He smoked silently for a moment. "It's not just their psychology; we don't know anything much about their physiology, or biology either." He picked up his glass and drank. "Here; we had eighteen of them in all. Seventeen adults and one little one. Now what kind of ratio is that? And the ones we saw in the woods ran about the same. In all, we sighted about a hundred and fifty adults and only ten children."

"Maybe last year's crop have grown up," she began.

"You know any other sapient races with a one-year maturation period?" he asked. "I'll bet they take ten or fifteen years to mature. Jack's Baby Fuzzy hasn't gained a pound in the last month. And another puzzle; this craving for Extee Three. That's not a natural food; except for the cereal bulk matter, it's purely synthetic. I was talking to Ybarra; he was wondering if there mightn't be something in it that caused an addiction."

"Maybe it satisfies some kind of dietary deficiency."

"Well, we'll find out." He inverted the jug over his glass. "Think we could stand another cocktail before dinner?"

Space Commodore Napier sat at the desk that had been Nick Emmert's and looked at the little man with the red whiskers and the rumpled suit, who was looking back at him in consternation.

"Good Lord, Commodore; you can't be serious?"

"But I am. Quite serious, Dr. Rainsford."

"Then you're nuts!" Rainsford exploded. "I'm no more qualified to be Governor General than I'd be to command Xerxes Base. Why, I never held an administrative position in my life."

"That might be a recommendation. You're replacing a veteran administrator."

"And I have a job. The Institute of Zeno-Sciences —"

"I think they'll be glad to give you leave, under the circumstances. Doctor, you're the logical man for this job. You're an ecologist; you know how disastrous the effects of upsetting the balance of nature can be. The Zarathustra Company took care of this planet, when it was their property, but now nine-tenths of it is public domain, and people will be coming in from all over the Federation, scrambling to get rich overnight. You'll know how to control things."

"Yes, as Commissioner of Conservation, or something I'm qualified for."

"As Governor General. Your job will be to make policy. You can appoint the administrators."

"Well, who, for instance?"

"Well, you're going to need an Attorney General right away. Who will you appoint for that position?"

"Gus Brannhard," Rainsford said instantly.

"Good. And who-this question is purely rhetorical-will you appoint as Commissioner of Native Affairs?"

Jack Holloway was going back to Beta Continent on the constabulary airboat. Official passenger: Mr. Commissioner Jack Holloway. And his staff: Little Fuzzy, Mamma Fuzzy, Baby Fuzzy, Mike, Mitzi, Ko-Ko and Cinderella. Bet they didn't know they had official positions!

Somehow he wished he didn't have one himself.

"Want a good job, George?" he asked Lunt.

"I have a good job."

"This'll be a better one. Rank of major, eighteen thousand a year. Commandant, Native Protection Force. And you won't lose seniority in the constabulary; Colonel Ferguson'll give you indefinite leave."

"Well, cripes, Jack, I'd like to, but I don't want to leave the kids. And I can't take them away from the rest of the gang."

"Bring the rest of the gang along. I'm authorized to borrow twenty men from the constabulary as a training cadre, and you only have sixteen. Your sergeants'll get commissions, and all your men will be sergeants. I'm going to have a force of a hundred and fifty for a start."

"You must think the Fuzzies are going to need a lot of protection."

"They will. The whole country between the Cordilleras and the West Coast Range will be Fuzzy Reservation and that'll have to be policed. Then the Fuzzies outside that will have to be protected. You know what's going to happen. Everybody wants Fuzzies; why, even Judge Pendarvis approached me about getting a pair for his wife. There'll be gangs hunting them to sell, using stun-bombs and sleepgas and everything. I'm going to have to set up an adoption bureau; Ruth will be in charge of that. And that'll mean a lot of investigators —"

Oh, it was going to be one hell of a job! Fifty thousand a year would be chicken feed to what he'd lose by not working his diggings. But somebody would have to do it, and the Fuzzies were his responsibility.

Hadn't he gone to law to prove their sapience?

They were going home, home to the Wonderful Place. They had seen many wonderful places, since the night they had been put in the bags: the place where everything had been light and they had been able to jump so high and land so gently, and the place where they had met all the others of their people and had so much fun. But now they were going back to the old Wonderful Place in the woods, where it had all started.

And they had met so many Big Ones, too. Some Big Ones were bad, but only a few; most Big Ones were good. Even the one who had done the killing had felt sorry for what he had done; they were all sure of that. And the other Big Ones had taken him away, and they had never seen him again.

He had talked about that with the others-with Flora and Fauna, and Dr. Crippen, and Complex, and Superego, and Dillinger and Lizzie Borden. Now that they were all going to live with the Big Ones, they would have to use those funny names. Someday they would find out what they meant, and that would be fun, too. And they could; now the Big Ones could put things in their ears and hear what they were saying, and Pappy Jack was learning some of their words, and teaching them some of his.

And soon all the people would find Big Ones to live with, who would take care of them and have fun with them and love them, and give them the Wonderful Food. And with the Big Ones taking care of them, maybe more of their babies would live and not die so soon. And they would pay the Big Ones back. First they would give their love and make them happy. Later, when they learned how, they would give their help, too.

www.ingramcontent.com/pod-product-compliance
Lightning Source LLC
Chambersburg PA
CBHW070148310726
48976CB00001B/22